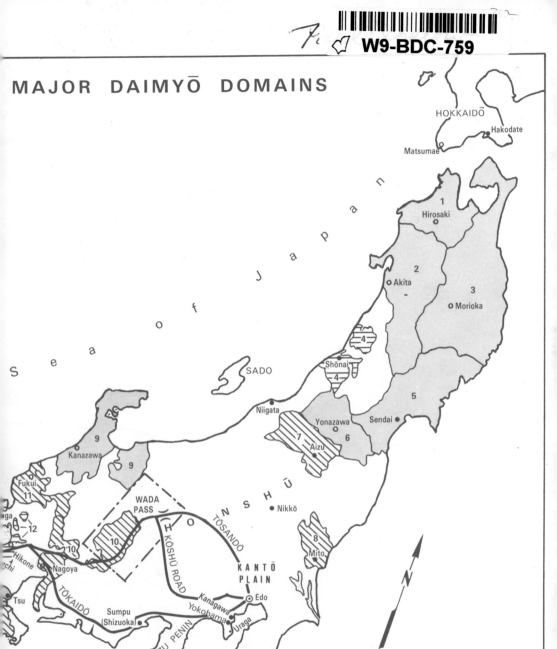

MAJOR DAIMYŌ DOMAINS

HOKKAIDŌ

Hakodate

Matsumae

1
Hirosaki

2
Akita

3
Morioka

4

Shōnai
4

SADO

Niigata

Yonazawa
6
Sendai

5

1
Aizu

9
Kanazawa

9

Fukui
11

12

Hikone
Nagoya

10

10

WADA
PASS

KŌSHŪ ROAD

TŌSANDŌ

Nikkō

H O N S H Ū

8
Mito

KANTŌ
PLAIN

Tsu

TOKAIDŌ

Sumpu
(Shizuoka)

Kanagawa
Yokohama
Uraga

Edo

IZU PENIN.

Shimoda

S e a   o f   J a p a n

S e a   o f

Scale is generalized

O C E A N

BEFORE
THE
DAWN

To one who was for
too short a time
a valued colleague
I hope we can
try again some time

W— E. N____

BEFORE
THE
DAWN

SHIMAZAKI TŌSON

Translated by
WILLIAM E. NAFF

University of Hawaii Press
Honolulu

Published with the support of the Kamigata Bunka Kenkyūkai at the University of Hawaii and by grants from Sumitomo Metal Industries, Ltd., Suntory Limited, Matsushita Electric Industrial Co., Ltd., Sumitomo Bank, Ltd., and Kansai Electric Power Co., Inc.

Endpapers: Adapted, by permission, from John K. Fairbank, Edwin O. Reischauer, and Albert M. Craig, *East Asia: Tradition and Transformation,* pp. 402–403. Copyright © 1973 by Houghton Mifflin Company.

Library of Congress Cataloging-in-Publication Data

Shimazaki, Tōson, 1872–1943.
  Before the dawn.

  Translation of: Yoakemae.
  Includes bibliographies.
  1. Naff, William E. II. Title.
PL816.H55Y613   1987   895.6'34   87–5046
ISBN 0–8248–0914–9

CONTENTS

MAPS

PREFACE

THIS TRANSLATION has grown out of research on the Meiji restoration done under Marius Jansen at the University of Washington many years ago. That research created an enduring interest in the disillusionment in the Meiji restoration which overtook many of its most enthusiastic early supporters. When I mentioned my interest to the late Professor Ōta Saburō of the Tokyo Institute of Technology, he recommended that I look at *Before the Dawn.* The resulting doctoral dissertation on Shimazaki Tōson was directed by Richard N. McKinnon of the University of Washington.

It is, as always, impossible to express fully my gratitude and indebtedness to others who have offered counsel and assistance. This is especially true of J. Thomas Rimer of the Library of Congress. It is also true of Warren Anderson, George Cuomo, Morris Golden, and Frederick Will of the University of Massachusetts, all of whom kindly read early samples from the translation and offered invaluable suggestions. Yasuko Fukumi, Japanese bibliographer at the University, has helped me in countless ways. Leonard Grzanka was of incalculable assistance in establishing the English voices of the narrator and the major characters in the first volume. John M. Maki, Professor Emeritus of Political Science at the University of Massachusetts, had a number of important and cogent suggestions to make at crucial points in the undertaking. Hiroshi Miyaji of Middlebury College checked the glossary entries for accuracy, and Sheryl Chappell of Amherst read the entire manuscript. The University of Massachusetts gave travel assistance.

The most demanding and long-term assistance came from two people. One was Hsieh Chih-hsien, who contributed not only typing but endless hours of assistance and advice with the text. The other was Stuart Kiang, my editor at the University of Hawaii Press, whose wisdom, care, and patience have contributed immeasurably to whatever virtues this translation may possess. The quality of the support and advice I have received only make it all the more obvious that I bear sole and inescapable responsibility for any shortcomings and infelicities that remain.

Japanese names are given in Japanese style, with surnames first. The transcription of Japanese terms follows the Hepburn system, but with some modifications. Macrons to indicate long vowels are shown in the front and back matter but not in the body of the text. Certain vowel sequences are broken up by apostrophes to remind readers that there are no true diphthongs in Japanese; for example, Sho'un, Ko'unsai. The apostrophe is also used to indicate the presence of the syllabic nasal between vowels, as in Man'en, which consists not of two syllables, as the English reader's instincts would suggest, but of four morae: ma/ n/ e/ n. The syllabic nasal is indicated by an 'm' before bilabials: Kimbei, Temmei, Mampukuji.

INTRODUCTION

SHIMAZAKI TŌSON's flight to Paris in 1913 made him the first established Japanese writer to take up residence abroad. The move was occasioned by the pregnancy of a niece who had come to help with the children after the death of his wife three years earlier. His initial success in keeping secret the real reason for going away only seemed to diminish further any likelihood that either his sense of himself as a man of probity and honor or the closely related public persona that was his prime asset as an autobiographical novelist could survive. He left Japan intending never to return, but family responsibilities and the outbreak of World War I brought him home after only three years. The process of healing the injury he had done to himself and others took much longer.

One step in that rehabilitation was the writing of a confessional novel about the affair with his niece. This novel, *New Life* (1919), continues to be a focal point of the controversy that almost any aspect of Tōson's life and career can still inspire. Akutagawa Ryūnosuke was perhaps the most eminent figure to be caught in the pitfalls it holds for the hasty reader when he dismissed it as cynical, self-serving, and hypocritical, failing to perceive that the egoism and deviousness of the author's alter ego in the novel do not in any way constitute an apology but are rather part of a merciless exposure of the shortcomings the author had discovered in himself. In spite of the extraliterary questions that are raised by *New Life*, it remains a successful work of art. A few years later Tōson would write another novel, this time telling the story of his father's life and of Japan in the middle of the nineteenth century. That novel was *Before the Dawn* and it proved to be his masterpiece.

Tōson's writings while he was in Paris reflected the expatriate's renewed sense of connection with his native country. The columns he wrote for the Tokyo *Asahi* newspaper tell about the challenge and hardship of coming to terms with a new culture and they include the obligatory sketches of Paris life, appreciations of the character and manner of living of French friends such as the Sanskrit scholar Sylvain Levy, and reviews of premiere performances of works by Debussy and Maeterlinck. But interspersed among these subjects were penetrating comments on the alienation from Japanese life and experience that Tōson observed in some members of the Japanese community in Paris, reinforced by expressions of dismay over the general ignorance of and indifference to recent Japanese history both in Japan and in the world at large.

One of those Paris columns offers a revealing glimpse into Tōson's thoughts in those years.

> If only someone in our country would write a study of the nineteenth century! With what pleasure I should read it! We usually divide the century up between the Tokugawa and the Meiji periods but if we try to look at it as a whole it takes on a different meaning. I want to read a study of those times, beginning from around the death of Motoori Norinaga. I want to read about how the studies of the *Man'yōshū,* the revival of the spirit of the old poetry, and the loving attention given to our language served as the basis for the sense of national identity that was just beginning to awaken around that time. . . . If, on the one hand, the scholarship of the Confucian academies displayed an infatuation with things Chinese in literature, in taste, and in morals, Dutch Learning on the other hand was showing great vigor. The old and the new were living together in the greatest intimacy during the early years of the nineteenth century. I want to read about this. It is only about forty-five years since the systematic importation of Western culture began and there are those who say that today's new Japan was created in that brief period of time, but I feel they are underrating us. . . .
>
> In our country the nineteenth century was a time when the old was being discarded even though the new things to replace them had not yet really been created. It was the time when that great class known as "samurai" passed into oblivion. How can we ever count up the tragedies that resulted? I want to read about them. I want to read about how the Japanese language was consolidated through the great labor of unifying the written and spoken languages inaugurated by Futabatei Shimei and Yamada Bimyō. It was also around the end of the nineteenth century that the new poetry made its first tentative appearance. . . .
>
> For better or worse, we must know our fathers. We must know their times. If only there were someone to write the kind of study I want to read! What a vast number of topics we might find treated in it! I would not stop with mere comparisons of literature and the fine arts in presenting the essence of the way the people of those times thought. It was Kitamura Tōgoku who tried to seek out in the humor and satire of the light fiction of such writers as Samba and Ikku the morality and the nihilistic tendencies present in the common people of that time. I want to read all about such things. (From "The Spirit of Inquiry into the Previous Century," republished in *Waiting for Spring.*)

These thoughts reflected a new state of mind not only for Tōson but for Japan as a whole. Just as the history of Tōson's family had long seemed too painful and embarrassing for him to face, much of the history of nineteenth-century Japan had also been too painful and too filled with ambiguity to be confronted systematically by the Japanese public. Now Tōson's need to recover the past was matched by his hunger for a more complete and satisfying approach to many of the still-burning questions about Japan in the nineteenth century than was then available in either the Japanese culture at large or in academic histories. Tōson was very much a man of his time and his personal needs were matched by a new public willingness to reconsider past times. Not only did that new public and private willingness make possible the writing of *Before the Dawn* but Tōson's version of the story of the Meiji restoration has played a major role in defining the form in which those great events of the middle third of the nineteenth century have entered the Japanese national consciousness.

The writing of this immense novel marked the apex of a career that had long since earned its author a secure place among the leading figures in modern Japanese literature and its appearance was the major literary event of its time. Yet in the early stages of its initial publication, as a serial appearing four times a year in the monthly journal *Chūō Kōron* between April 1929 and October 1935, many failed to grasp what Tōson was doing. He had never before attempted anything on this scale or anything that might be called historical fiction. Kume Masao spoke for many early readers when he complained that the work contained too much undigested history for a novel and too much fiction for history. However inadequate that response may have been, it was correct in at least one important respect. Critical responses to *Before the Dawn* would have to address historical as well as literary questions. The importance of the work and the response it continues to evoke have created a virtual industry of *Before the Dawn* scholarship. A 1983 volume of literary studies of Tōson contains a "selected bibliography" that lists one hundred thirty-four books, forty-seven special journal issues, and some seven hundred articles and essays, a large proportion of which are concerned with this one novel.

One of the earliest and most important efforts to come to grips with the salient qualities of the work took the form of a roundtable discussion in the November 1936 issue of *Literary World (Bungakkai)*. Discussants included the playwright Murayama Tomoyoshi, who created the stage adaptation of the novel, Hayashi Fusao, a onetime Marxist critic who had recently converted to the position of the nationalist and anti-modernist Japanese Romanticists, several leading novelists, and the distinguished critic Kobayashi Hideo, who contributed a thoughtful and cogent afterword. In the course of their discussion of the novel, they agreed that Tōson had in fact resolved most, if not all, of the inherent conflicts between the demands of historical scholarship and the needs of a successful work of literature and predicted that *Before the Dawn* would occupy a high place in the history of modern Japanese literature. That appraisal still stands.

The implications of what took place in nineteenth-century Japan are still unfolding in our own day. No nation or individual in the world remains untouched by them. Yet in spite of the immense body of Japanese scholarship and the large and growing body of studies in European languages, the scale and character of Japanese accomplishments during the past century and a half remain imperfectly noted by the rest of the world. Full recognition has been impeded by the persistence of a remarkably durable set of stereotypes which, for all their familiarity, have only the most tenuous relationship to what actually happened. What actually happened is far too complex ever to be fully grasped or completely reconstructed. It is also far richer in universal human significance than the stereotypes will allow for, and it is, above all, infinitely more interesting.

The historical anthropologist Haga Noboru argues that *Before the Dawn* is a greater achievement than even those austere and cerebral works by Mori Ōgai that are usually cited as the most distinguished achievements of Japanese historical fiction. Ōgai explored with extraordinary power and penetration some of the more distant premodern sources out of which modern Japan grew. But in *Before the Dawn* there appeared the first sustained and fully articulated vision of a Meiji restoration in which the driving force had come from the bottom up, and in which the primary cause of the disillusionment and tragedy that followed was to be found in the almost immediate reversal of that thrust by the new Meiji government once it had come to power.

A general consensus concerning the nature and origins of the Meiji restoration now prevails among historians in spite of often bitter disagreement about process, implications, and detail. Fifty years after its writing, the vision of nineteenth-century Japan presented in *Before the Dawn* not only is in agreement with most of the essentials of that consensus but helped to create it. Although Tōson was not writing as a historian, he made a twofold contribution to historical scholarship. First was a massive attack on the then widely held view of the Meiji restoration as an almost complete historical discontinuity—a leap in one step from medievalism to modernity or even from darkness and savagery to enlightenment and civilization. He launched this attack by dramatizing the richness and intellectual vigor of traditional Japanese culture and then by reminding his readers that for all its political bankruptcy the shogunate enjoyed the services of a number of men of exceptional vision, wisdom, and courage. He made clear as never before that although Meiji constituted perhaps the most brilliant and sustained national response to the challenges of the modern world that had yet been seen anywhere, there was nevertheless something to be said for those who protested that it had also betrayed many of its own brightest promises. Many Meiji leaders had initially gained national attention through their activities on behalf of the most obscurantist and reactionary aspects of the movement to "revere the emperor and expel the barbarians," and not all of them had greatly changed after coming to power. Far too many promptly fell into a cold-blooded pursuit of personal advantage and even the most enlightened often felt themselves forced by events to place the stark question of national survival ahead of their ideals.

The second of Tōson's contributions to a heightened awareness of the implications of mid-nineteenth-century Japanese experience follows from the first. He introduced a new point of view—that of the numerous and active class of rural intellectuals, of which Tōson's father had been a member. The vision and style of this previously neglected group are presented with a richness and conviction that reflect Tōson's personal involvement in the subject, and it is this impassioned quality, however deeply it may lay hidden beneath the outward coolness of the narrative style, that distinguishes this novel from conventional historical scholarship as sharply as does the inclusion of fictional elements. That sense of first-hand involvement also distinguishes *Before the*

Dawn from the general run of historical fiction. By virtue of its being in effect the testament of the Shimazaki family, the novel is an important historical document in its own right.

The line of historical scholarship that derives in significant part from Tōson's vision is represented by the work of Haga and Irokawa Daikichi, whose *Culture of the Meiji Era* has now been translated into English. Irokawa emphasizes the extraordinarily high level of sophistication with which rural intellectuals voiced their objections to the course set by the Meiji government. When it was found that those objections would invariably be either ignored or contemptuously rejected, verbal protest was replaced by direct action, culminating in the Chichibu uprisings of 1884. Their crushing defeat put an effective end to the intellectual engagement, the pride, the optimism, and the dreams of *yo-naoshi* or "putting the world to rights" that had marked Japanese village life during the preceding century. The official explanation of these uprisings—that they were the product of the blind conservatism of ignorant peasants—had long been accepted at face value by virtually the entire spectrum of Japanese intellectuals. This misapprehension is only now being corrected by historians of Irokawa's generation. Although the case presented by *Before the Dawn* is somewhat more ambiguous than the ones taken up by Irokawa, it made its point as powerfully as it could possibly be made at the time it was being written. The matter could be taken further only with the restoration of free inquiry after World War II, and even then it first had to wage a long and bitter struggle with an anti-rural prejudice that was often as strong among those who were otherwise in the habit of questioning the official line as it was among those who habitually accepted it.

In examining the historical and ethnological background of *Before the Dawn*, Haga joins other scholars in noting that Tōson's grasp of some aspects of National Learning was defective and that there are errors of detail in his description of the operating procedures of the post station system. Nevertheless he emphasizes that none of these shortcomings in any way negates the fundamental validity of Tōson's portrayal of the years from 1853 to 1886. He also points out the salutary influence of Tōson's close friend Yanagita Kunio, the charismatic founder of modern Japanese ethnological and folklore studies, in the depictions of rural life and beliefs. In an argument too complex and wide-ranging for ready summary, Haga further demonstrates that many present-day objections to Tōson's historical scholarship are themselves the result of studies carried out in direct or indirect response to this work.

For all the novelty of its point of view, early favorable responses to *Before the Dawn* ranged across the entire political spectrum to include the apolitical as well. The Marxist critic Aono Suekichi wrote extensive and perceptive appreciations of each of the two volumes shortly after their serial runs were completed. Murayama Tomoyoshi, whose stage adaptation of *Before the Dawn* was well received both in its original 1936 production and in subsequent revivals (the reception of the 1955 film version by the director Yoshimura Kimisaburō was somewhat more muted but it is still a powerful experience for viewers already familiar with the novel), was a prominent figure in avant garde and proletarian literary circles. Both Murayama's play and Aono's criticism reflect the fact that many among the first readers to appreciate the magnitude of Tōson's achievement were from the political left. They often saw Aoyama Hanzō as a prototype of their own most favored tragic heroes: progressive intellectuals and artists hopelessly ahead of their time in a Japan that was unprepared to hear them. Some may find this reading to be unhelpful or even misleading, but the value of their contributions in bringing the serious nature of *Before the Dawn* to the attention of a wider range of readers remains beyond question. Tōson was not hostile to the political left but he also had no particular interest in wooing it, and he responded to comments from that quarter on an individual rather than an ideological basis.

The political left was also the source of some of the harshest criticisms in the years following World War II. Those criticisms often centered around the objection that the points of view in the novel are for the most part limited to the very uppermost level of the agricultural classes. Taken by itself this observation is a truism rather than a criticism. It is true that the protagonist, Aoyama Hanzō, is sympathetically presented and that his ideas are not always what a twentieth-century reader might want them to be. It is, however, quite clear that this thinking is Hanzō's, not Tōson's; no one holding some of the opinions Hanzō expresses could ever have produced *Before the Dawn*. Tōson has not left us enough evidence concerning his political views to make discussion of the subject worthwhile, but his commitment to humane values is clear throughout the entire body of his work. The fact that other Marxist critics have given this novel some of its best readings demonstrates that what is at issue here is not really a question of ideology but of a willingness to read what is actually in the text.

The Meiji restoration is the second of the four attempts that major nations have made to reconstitute themselves during the past century and a half. In some cases the attempt has created a literary masterpiece to fit the event. The position of *Before the Dawn* in modern Japanese literature is comparable to that of Mikhail Sholokov's treatment of the much later but somewhat analogous stage of Russian experience in *The Quiet Don*. If Tōson's story is, for all the disappointment and tragedy it encompasses, more pleasing than Sholokov's, it is in part because the Japanese writer has a less painful story to tell. The Meiji restoration entailed its full share of gratuitous loss and suffering, betrayed ideals and missed opportunities, but it was less bloody in its inception and in its subsequent period of consolidation than was either the Russian or the Chinese revolution. It was also much less destructive of the best elements of the native cultural heritage and more successful in moving toward its goals.

The creation of modern Germany was the only one of these national reconstructions that preceded the Meiji restoration. The German experience was closest to Japan's not only in time but in the creation of a modern nation out of a multitude of feudal states, and it was on the German experience that Japan drew most heavily in developing its new institutions. Germany was the model for the top-down structure of modernization that the Meiji government chose to adopt, and on one level *Before the Dawn* may be read as an extended protest against that choice. Although Tōson firmly believed that any new Japanese order had first of all to be Japanese, he was also fully cognizant of Japan's long record of successfully adapting foreign ideas to strengthen and improve its own institutions. He found much more congenial the British and American models that had figured so prominently in his education at a Protestant mission school in Tokyo, although he was by no means prepared to accept them in their entirety; his paradoxical but urgent calls to resist at the same time that one borrows resound throughout the novel. It is one of the few points on which he is in firm agreement with his father's idol, Hirata Atsutane.

That protest seems to be supported by two and a half centuries of family experience. Hanzō knew that when the demands associated with carrying out his responsibilities along the highway became unbearable under the shogunate he could appeal on human terms to the old feudal bureaucracy. Even shogunal officials would sometimes, although not nearly often enough, hear those appeals and would sometimes even initiate meliorative steps, tardy and ludicrously inadequate though they might be. When appeals on other matters were addresssed to the officials of Owari *han,* a feudal domain notable for its grasp of the intimate relationship between the security of rulers and the welfare of the ruled, people at Hanzō's level could usually expect a response that would be, within the narrow and rigid limits imposed by the feudal order, prompt, rational, and humane. But when Hanzō collides with the Bismarkian bureaucracy of the new Meiji government he learns with a sudden and brutal finality that there is no room among its procedural obsessions for humane considerations, much less for the accumulated wisdom and practical experience of the old rural elite.

There have been certain parallels in the subsequent roles that Germany and Japan have played on the world stage and in the way they have been perceived by the world. If there is some truth in these perceived parallels they are also in fact much more apparent than real. In its depiction of Germany's transition to a modern social and political order, it is Thomas Mann's *Buddenbroooks,* a very different book about a very different world, that may be the closest German analogue to *Before the Dawn.*

We may leave to other venues the question of whether it is useful to argue about which of these four national reconstructions were or were not true revolutions. Nevertheless Japan, as Edwin O. Reischauer has pointed out, was free from the foreign ideological imperatives that helped to shape the later Russian and Chinese revolutions. It was, like Germany, able to retain much of its traditional lore and world view to draw upon in the new age. This continuity was a source of liabilities as well as assets for both countries; but while the negative aspects of the Meiji restoration place it heartbreakingly short of the humane ideals to which Aoyama Hanzō and his associates aspired and against which one might wish to measure all historical processes, its more positive aspects compare quite favorably with the far higher prices that have so often been paid in other places at other times for much smaller gains.

Tōson brings us back again and again to one of his main points of emphasis: the vigor, creativity, and sophistication of traditional Japanese culture. Japan was never so completely isolated as popular myth would have it. Behind the many distinguished names dropped in passing in the course of the narrative lies a Japan that possessed considerable knowledge about the rest of the world and could look back on nearly a millenium and a half of intensely literate high civilization of its own. European astronomy, as presented in Chinese books that were a product of the influence of Matteo Ricci and other Jesuits in the Ch'ing court, had been drawn upon in the early eighteenth century in the course of improving the local calendar. A growing interest in European medicine had begun in the latter decades of that century, but in certain circles there had been an ongoing awareness of European medicine and painting throughout the preceding three centuries and significant Japanese innovations had been made in both of those fields. From the late eighteenth century on there had been a steady growth in knowledge of a wide range of European sciences, with a tendency to concentrate on military science as the threat of European colonialism loomed larger.

The founding in 1855 of the shogunal Institute for the Study of Foreign Books was less a mark of the by-no-means-negligible awareness of the greater world to be found within the shogunate than an indication of one more way in which the shogunate was lagging behind the more advanced elements in the country; some of the *han* had long since begun the systematic import of foreign knowledge. When Perry exhibited his model telegraph and railway there were almost certainly people in his audience who had some understanding of the principles involved even though they had never seen the devices in operation before. Although he was in no way prepared even to suspect it, Perry was visiting one of the world's more advanced nations. Only a handful of others had any claims to cultural superiority as it was then defined and even those claims were far from all-inclusive.

In 1853 Japan was, as it had been for most of the preceding millenium, one of the world's most highly literate nations. It was during the Tokugawa period that literacy, often enriched by literary interest and even by literary accomplishment, came to be taken for granted in anyone holding any position of responsibility. That literacy had, of course, been employed to support the status quo but there was also a long tradition of viewing literacy as a way to effect personal and social improvement. That tradition possessed roots that went back past the beginnings of high civilization in Japan to the great Chinese thinkers of the fifth and fourth centuries before Christ. As we are constantly reminded by what Hanzō reads, writes, and does, East Asian culture sees man as inherently good and education as an instrument that enables both the individual and the society to benefit more fully from that goodness. In real life the model for Asami Keizō was eighteen years older than Shimazaki Masaki, the model for Aoyama Hanzō, and yet he and Masaki did in fact study National Learning side by side. Education was a lifelong process, the everyday concern of many who had no professional connection with learning.

The preoccupation with learning shown by many of the characters in *Before the Dawn* is remarkable but was not at all exceptional in mid-nineteenth-century Japan.

While learning was both a moral and a practical necessity throughout the nation, that view manifested itself with particular intensity in the Kiso. The region was just enough in contact with metropolitan developments for its people to be keenly aware of their isolation and at the same time sufficiently remote to have some degree of freedom from Tokugawa controls. Under these conditions the pursuit of learning often bordered on the obsessive. The landlocked modern Nagano prefecture, the old Shinano province in which Magome and the Kiso are located, is notable in contemporary Japan for the number of important figures in publishing, education, and the arts it continues to produce as traditional preoccupations remain vital down to the present day.

These beliefs in education and in the innate goodness of humanity operated in a context of harsh constraint under the Tokugawa shogunate, but throughout the two and a half centuries of Tokugawa rule those constraints were being slowly but inevitably eroded by the growth of a new social reality that rendered the Tokugawa order steadily less relevant to the real issues of life in Japan. By the beginning of the eighteenth century, Edo was already the world's largest city and Japan the most highly urbanized society in the world. Books were readily accessible and people in all the cities were reading not only the same classics but the same ephemera. It was commonplace for those in the most remote provinces to struggle, as we see Hanzō and his friends struggling, not to fall too far behind metropolitan culture. Advances in science, medicine, and the arts were concentrated in the four great urban centers of Kyoto, Osaka, Edo, and Nagoya, but significant contributions were being made in some of the most remote country towns. An example is the world's first documented use of a general anaesthetic in an operation for breast cancer, performed at the end of the eighteenth century, after more than twenty years of experimentation and research, by Hanaoka Seishū, a country doctor in Kii province whose background of classical and medical training in Kyoto was remarkably similar to that of Majima Seian, the model for Hanzō's mentor Miyagawa Kansai.

One of the stimulants of the rich intellectual ferment of the late Edo period came about as an unanticipated side effect of a shogunal policy of calculated oppressiveness. The institution of alternate attendance kept large numbers of people in constant circulation between the cities and the most remote provinces and those people, supplemented by traders, pilgrims, and private travelers, were important instruments of a constant interchange of ideas, techniques, and fashions. Irokawa comments on the remarkably wide distribution through the nation of birthplaces of major figures of the Meiji period, a consequence of the cultural diffusion that was one of the unforeseen results of the constant stirring of the cultural pot under the Tokugawa order, a quality that is noted in all studies of this time, regardless of specific focus, from the scholarly works of people like Haga Noboru and Hayashiya Tatsusaburō to the brilliant and thoughtful popularizations of historical novelists and essayists like Shiba Ryōtarō.

Even under the shogunate there was a deep-seated belief in the possibility of personal improvement, both moral and economic, and a restless drive to achieve that improvement through personal discipline and education. Popular best-sellers of Tokugawa times frequently promised worldly gain or told inspiring tales of poor people making good through prudence, diligence, and hard work in the manner of the first Sōemon of Magome. The relatively high level of education and the intellectual, social, and economic development it engendered had contributed to the hopeless obsolescence of the Tokugawa order as Japan moved into the nineteenth century. Factories complete with workers' dormitories had already begun to appear while Japanese agriculture had undergone a modest technological revolution and workers leaving Japanese farms for steam-powered silk mills or shipyards seem to have been able to make the transition with about the same degree of facility as did their contemporaries in Western Europe and the United States.

It may well be that nothing so became the Tokugawa shogunate as did its departure from the scene, but it left some important assets for its successors. Foremost among them was a long tradition of order and stability. It was the foreboding and anxiety caused by the rapid erosion of that order and stability, every bit as much as the growing resentment of the shogunate, that set the tone of the first volume of *Before the Dawn*. If the character of that order was in many respects arbitrary and obstructionist it approached the optimal in others. The negative qualities of the Tokugawa shogunate had been at least in part balanced by positive achievements. It had applied the finishing touches to the long process of creating a coherent national style but its power had not been sufficiently absolute to eradicate local styles and local loyalties. As a result, Japan came into the new age with not only a strong tradition of personal and social discipline but also a rich, often turbulent, mixture of human resources representing widely diverging points of view.

Of all the Tokugawa heritages it was, however, social discipline that gave Japan its greatest single advantage in meeting the modern world. The best and the worst often come from the same sources, and this discipline and the heavy emphasis on sharp division of social roles that accompanies it also underlie some of the saddest chapters in modern Japanese history. But in the selfless dedication to duty and the uncompromising sense of responsibility of such people as Kichizaemon and Kimbei and in the dream of a more humane and enlightened Japan held to with such passion and at such terrible cost by Hanzō and his friends, we can see some of the very finest qualities of that discipline.

Xenophobia and obscurantism had both played their roles in bringing about the relative isolation of Tokugawa Japan but it was the country's geographical remoteness that alone made the policy of seclusion not only thinkable but, for a long time, workable. There was also a strong tendency, ironically most pronounced among the National Scholars to whom "Chi-

nese-mindedness'' was anathema, to adapt the China-centered world view of
the Chinese scholarly tradition to support a Japan-centered outlook. Juheiji
repeatedly tries to bring this contradiction and its implications to Hanzō's
attention but Hanzō is never prepared to listen. He is too completely taken
up in the archaizing dreams of the National Scholars to realize that in their
attempts to find the answers to current Japanese problems in ancient Japanese
texts, they were, as is so often the case with those who claim to be the con-
servators of the national tradition, in fact proposing a radical departure from
Japanese traditional practice. What Tōson particularly wanted to convey to
his readers was that once Japan commenced full participation in the modern
world, she did undertake the kind of creative cultural borrowing that can be
carried out only by societies that are literate, sophisticated, vigorous, and self-
confident. These are the same qualities that characterized the European tradition itself during its great periods of growth and creativity, periods that were
themselves marked by massive cultural, technological, and intellectual borrowing.

Not even the most ambitious successors of *Before the Dawn* have made any
attempt to challenge it on its own ground. Its reception in the Kiso river district of Nagano prefecture where the main action is set suggests why. A late-
twentieth-century visitor soon notices that he is seldom out of sight of some
part of the text. He will most often be seeing the opening lines of the prologue, lines which draw some of their power and resonance from *A Guide to
Famous Scenes of the Kiso,* an eighteenth-century guidebook which itself car-
ries the echoes of a millenium of earlier writings about life and travel in this
rugged and beautiful country. Those lines appear on a monument in the garden of the museum of local history in the proud and attractive town of
Fukushima, on matchboxes and billboards, on plaques in the alcoves of guest
rooms of inns, and even on the packaging of souvenir bottles of sake sold on
the platforms of nearby railway stations. Such popularity and ubiquity are a
harsh test but Tōson's words retain their force in spite of the overexposure
just as Magome and the Kiso remain richly rewarding to visitors even when
there may seem to be more of them than the land will comfortably hold. The
fame that Tōson brought to Magome has made a major tourist attraction out
of a once remote and obscure village. It is flourishing as never before in its
history, its original character all but swamped by a flood of sightseers and literary pilgrims.

In spite of numerous twentieth-century touches, the village of Magome
still preserves much of its nineteenth-century configuration as it climbs eastward up the back of its steep ridge, a single row of buildings on either side of
a gentle S-curve in the old Tōsandō. The temple, called the Eishōji in real life,
stands guard over its graveyard among the cedar trees on high ground across
the swale to the northwest. Just above it on the same side road is the Yomo-
giya, a fine small inn founded by Tōson's son Kusuo. The main street leaves
the village to continue its winding climb up to the hamlet of Tōge, which
takes its name from the summit of Magome pass just beyond. From there the

old highway still invites the hiker to proceed on to the neighboring village of Tsumago, which is well preserved, having been fortunate with fires during this century. It enjoys, and fully deserves, a considerable tourist industry of its own as a model post station of the old Tōsandō.

Turning back to the west and heading downhill from the center of Magome, the visitor finds the view dominated by Mt. Ena towering over the village to the southeast while the fine overview of the Mino basin so often mentioned by Tōson lies directly ahead. The old highway winds from Magome itself down Stonemason slope, past the village shrine in Aramachi with its memorial tablet to Shimazaki Masaki, and then down a steeper pitch along mostly unsettled mountainside to Shinjaya, which stands on its shoulder of mountain just inside the prefectural boundary and just above the plunge down Jikkyoku pass to Ochiai, seven miles and hundreds of feet below. The isolated teahouse which gives Shinjaya its name is still in operation on the right side of the road directly across from the Bashō monument. Beyond the teahouse is another, newer monument on the former site of the milepost described in the novel. A large natural stone now stands there, inscribed, in Tōson's calligraphy, with the legend *Kore yori kita wa Kisoji,* "From here northward is the Kiso road."

In Magome itself the site of the old *honjin* is now occupied by the Tōson Memorial. Behind a black wooden fence pierced by a generous gateway is a new building covering much the same ground that the old *honjin* once covered. It and the retirement quarters, all that survives of the old *honjin* buildings, house an important collection of manuscripts, Tōson's personal library, paintings, and other memorabilia of the family and the region. In his book *Kiso Magome,* Kikuchi Saburō has told of the building of this memorial, conceived and planned by the villagers during the dark days immediately after World War II and built with volunteer labor and donated materials as a gesture of pride in the past and faith in the future. Not even the most sanguine of the workers in those days was likely to have dreamed of the scale of the response that the memorial would eventually call up. If they had, they might have experienced much the same ambivalence shared by many today as they watch the daily flood of taxis coming up from the railway station at Nakatsu-gawa, and the private cars and buses from all over that quickly overflow the huge parking lots that have been gouged out of the mountainside just below the village.

By the time Tōson began preparations for the writing of *Before the Dawn,* he was enjoying a personal and financial security that he had not known before. An important source of that security was an increase in royalties due to the highly successful introduction in the early 1920's of large, uniform editions of masterpieces of modern Japanese literature. Things were made still better by the fact that, at the same time that his income was increased, the families of his older siblings had at last ended their economic dependence on him. After the *New Life* affair had been settled and his personal life stabilized, Tōson's attention turned back to the country he had left behind him as a

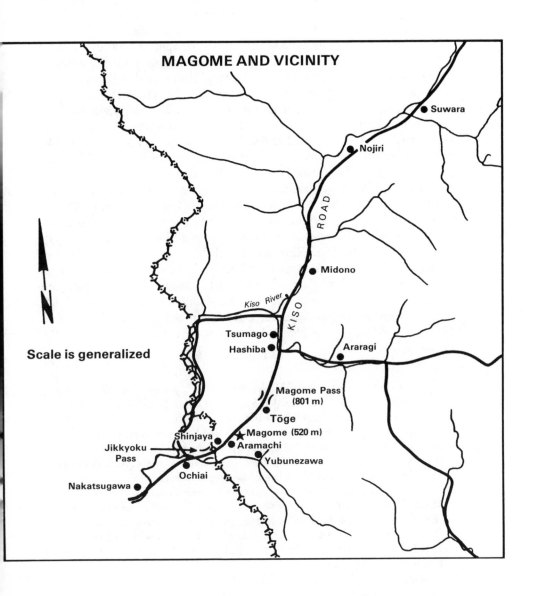

MAGOME AND VICINITY

Suwara

Nojiri

ROAD

Midono

Kiso River

KISO

Tsumago
Hashiba

Araragi

Magome Pass
(801 m)

Tōge

Magome (520 m)

Shinjaya

Jikkyoku
Pass

Aramachi

Yubunezawa

Nakatsugawa

Ochiai

N

Scale is generalized

child. His reawakened sense of that time and place was reinforced by his efforts to reestablish rapport with his children and he wrote a number of stories and memoirs about life in Magome and the Kiso region to make them aware of their heritage. Those efforts produced the collections *Home Country* in 1920 and *Tales of Childhood* in 1924, the year after he bought a house in Magome for his eldest son, Kusuo. The business of reestablishing a Shimazaki presence in the ancestral village, the repair and remodeling of the house, and the purchase of farmland and agricultural equipment took up much of Tōson's time during the two years immediately preceding the beginning of formal research for *Before the Dawn* and seem to have played an important role in renewing his sense of connection to Magome and its history.

In Magome Tōson found the most important single source upon which he drew when writing *Before the Dawn*. Insuperable obstacles seemed to have been placed in his way by the fire that had roared up the steep, chimney-like village street in 1895, destroying all the remaining records kept by seventeen generations of the Shimazaki family, but he found that the household next door had preserved its records intact. Ōwaki Nobuoki, the model for Satake Kimbei in the novel, had kept a record of life in Magome between 1826 and 1870 that reflected his scrupulous regard for fact and detail. Known as the Daikokuya Nikki after the name of the household (Fushimiya in the novel), these diaries constitute a fascinating and reliable record of life and times in Magome. Their availability convinced Tōson that he would be able to do an honest job of telling his father's story as he felt it should be told. Preparations began in earnest with a summer's study of Nobuoki's diaries. This was followed by several years of research, aided by an assistant, Tanaka Uichirō. Tōson later described this phase of the work in a short piece entitled "A Memorandum."

I still have not finished putting things in order after my long labors. In order to write *Before the Dawn* I had to read all kinds of old records that had some bearing on this type of work and there was no end of old diaries and accounts that I had borrowed from everywhere, some of which I have already returned but many of which remain in my hands. I keep thinking that I must return this or that I must take that back, but all I want to do these days is rest. Such things as the old records of the Matsuhara family, headmen in Ōtaki village, or of the Tsuchiya family, headmen at Oiwake station on the Nakasendō, or from the Yamazaki of Shinji village, Ueshina county, Shinano, as well as the historical records from the Kiso-Fukushima station, the tax records and *honjin* diaries from Tsumago, and the household records of the Yawataya belonging to the Hachiya family of Magome were of the greatest value in learning about the highway and other matters.

Many of these old records were difficult to read. Some were written on the backs of used papers; some were written in a running version of the calligraphic style used for official documents in the Tokugawa period. Some reduced me to despair. Yet it was only thanks to the people who had left such records that I was at last able to ascertain the conditions of life around the time of the Meiji restoration. By reading them I came to know that some were citing orders from the lords of Nagoya [Owari] *han* around the end of the eighteenth century and that people had collected old records going back to the time of Lord Kei [Tokugawa Yoshinao, 1600–1650, the first lord of Owari]. I also relied heavily on the holdings of the Hōsa archives of the present Owari house of Tokugawa.

Before the Dawn became the slightly fictionalized story of the Shimazaki family, a family of samurai origin. A Shimazaki had founded the village of Magome in 1558 and the next generation had rendered assistance to Tokugawa Ieyasu. Samurai status lapsed sometime during the seventeenth century. It was never revoked; it simply ceased to be relevant to the hereditary family roles. Modern Japanese historical scholarship places the Shimazaki family in the rather diffuse and unwieldy category of *gōnō*, or "wealthy farmers." Samurai status was nominally restored toward the end of the Tokugawa period when the failing shogunate was struggling to give as many people as possible a vested interest in the continuation of the system, and since samurai status was one of the few things it had left to pass out, these awards soon lost whatever value they might once have possessed.

What was more significant was that marriage relationships, as was the rule for the families of headmen, at least in this part of Japan, tended to be contracted not only with samurai families but with comparatively distinguished members of that often destitute class. Hanzō's stepgrandmother, Oman's mother, came from such a background and his daughter Okume marries into a substantial samurai family from Fukushima. Throughout its centuries-long history, the Shimazaki family had always known a measure of dignity and financial security; until the end of the Tokugawa period, it owned nearly sixty percent of the arable land of the village.

It was in part the very intensity with which the Shimazaki family had tried to live up to the best ideals of its traditional responsibilities that led to its destruction. There was a proud tradition of care for the traveler along the old highway. Tōson is alluding to Bashō early in Book One when he says that "all who traveled this highway were pilgrims," but he is describing quite literally the way in which the old *honjin* saw its duties. At the same time the Shimazaki family saw themselves, as headmen, standing between the otherwise helpless villagers and the arbitrary and unreasonable demands of the feudal authorities; they attempted to moderate those demands before passing them down and tried to look after the welfare of the villagers, expending their own wealth and influence in the process whenever necessary. Such expenditures had already weakened the family during Kichizaemon's time and Hanzō continues that tradition, opening the family storehouses to the villagers during a famine before calling on anyone else to do so. This paternalistic generosity prepares the way for the family bankruptcy that follows the liquidation of the feudal order as much as any failings in management, yet Hanzō's sense of himself is built on this proud tradition. He continues to honor the traditional family imperatives even after the family offices of headman, *honjin*, and *toiya* have been eliminated, never able to grasp the fact that his family might be a focus of resentment in the village. When it becomes possible after the restoration for the villagers to express those feelings he is both deeply hurt and utterly baffled. His paternalism has been too ingrained to enable him to perceive that from the villager's point of view the headman might appear to be simply the person who in the end relayed the relentless demands of the feudal authorities, demands which, however mitigated, nevertheless continued to cause often needless inconvenience and loss to the comparatively secure while making the poverty and hardship of the poor even more desperate.

In *Before the Dawn* Tōson was confronting a much broader range of personal problems than those he had faced in *New Life.* Shibusawa Gyō has pointed out that Tōson's first novel, *The Broken Commandment* (1905), had already focused upon the relationship between father and son as well as upon the natural human tendency to conceal awkwardnesses in personal and family life. The problem of Segawa Ushimatsu, the protagonist of that novel, is his outcast background which his father had brought him up to believe is a secret that must be kept at all costs, a belief that compels him to live a lie. Ushimatsu resolves his problem through a public confession which Tōson quite deliberately stages in the style of Dostoevski's Raskolnikov. But Tōson himself was another of the models for the secret-ridden protagonist of *The Broken Commandment.* For him the humiliation and deprivation that followed the collapse of the family fortunes, the circumstances of his father's death, and certain awkward facts about the personal lives of his father and mother made up a set of secrets much more complex and at least as burdensome as those of Ushimatsu, as did on another level the betrayal of so many popular hopes by the new Meiji government. *Before the Dawn* is even more of a confessional novel than was *The Broken Commandment.* As Tōson recalled the love his father had given him as a small child and his own later alienation during the deepening tragedy of his father's final years, he was forced to confront questions about the very sources of his personality that he had been trying to avoid since childhood.

As he entered middle age, Tōson had begun increasingly to identify with his father. In one well-known episode he tells of looking down at his hands as they rested on the rim of a brazier and recognizing his father's hands. If Tōson was ever to come fully to terms with himself he had first to come to terms with his father's life. Yet there were certain limits beyond which he could not go. He had not known his father well and he had to include much of himself in order to flesh out the portrait that appears in the novel, so much so that Hanzō has been described as "Tōson with an old-fashioned haircut." In its merciless probing of some of the author's most painful associations and memories *Before the Dawn* has much in common with *New Life* but what is confessed in it was even more threatening. As in the writing of *New Life,* the writing of *Before the Dawn* seems to have served as a catharsis and once it was written it is unlikely that Tōson ever again felt threatened by his family history.

Tōson's decision to come to grips with the history of his family in

Magome entailed an extensive investment of time, energy, and intellectual commitment. His perspective was as radically different from that of his father as was his experience. The final collapse of the family fortunes was already under way when he was born in 1872 and his father soon sent him off to Tokyo to be educated for life in that new world from which he himself was completely alienated. Tōson had grown up in the city, often in privation and insecurity, and separated from his family and home. The tragic futility of Hanzō's efforts to reach out to his beloved son on his last visit to Tokyo makes poignantly clear how, as a child and as a young man, Tōson had found his father's world as irretrievably alien as his father found the modernizing city of Tokyo to be. Tōson was at last able to find his way back into the mind and time of his father but only after overcoming a lifetime of external conditioning and personal choices that had almost all led in the opposite direction. His success in doing so constituted a personal triumph of character and intellect that is in its way even more impressive than the artistic success it produced.

Tōson's father, Shimazaki Masaki, the model for Aoyama Hanzō, had been a passionate believer in the Hirata school of National Learning. He died believing that his life had been pointless and futile, but in writing this fictionalized account of that life, Tōson has given it new meaning. In the process he has created a monument to his father such as few sons are ever able to do. Yet Hanzō is not so much the protagonist of the story as he is its unifying theme. As the story progresses, the reader is transported back and forth between the macrocosm of national and world politics and the microcosm of the Kiso district and the lives of the people who were formed by the special conditions and traditions of life in that mountainous region.

The tension between Tōson's very private personality and an intellectual commitment to confession that came in part from a late-adolescent reading of Rousseau is notable throughout his career, but there is a second polarity that was perhaps even more important in determining his handling of the confessional mode in *Before the Dawn*. This was the tension between his ideal of ruthless honesty and a strong predisposition toward the lyrical, the idealized, even the utopian. While these qualities are very much on the surface of his early poetry, they are more deeply integrated into his prose works. It is true for *Before the Dawn* as it is for *New Life* that, as his niece once put it in speaking of that work, "what is written there is true but there are many other things that are also true that were not written."

The tools that Tōson most often employed in attempting to resolve the tensions between what he wanted to say and what had to be said were idealization and very careful control of the point of view. Kichizaemon's neighbor and colleague Kimbei has qualities that can create problems and which might have made him an extremely difficult person to deal with in a society less effective in grinding off personal rough edges. In Tōson's portrayal those qualities are kept in soft focus; although the other side is still there we tend to see Kimbei only when he is at his best. The same is true of others among the foreground characters and it is true of the depiction of Tokugawa society itself. The negative aspects are there for the observant to see, but they are seldom in the center of the picture. Some of the most perceptive of Tōson's readers have described the work as "tactful" in tone, referring to that gift so necessary in village headmen who had constantly to emphasize the common interests and ideals and the shared experiences that linked the community together and to play down the conflicting interests and personal crotchets that constantly threatened to pull it apart. The narrative voice shares the same tactfulness that controlled the reflexes of Kichizaemon and Kimbei and it is that very quality that gives the work its power to convey both the flavor and the objective conditions of life in a time now lost. Even more than in most traditional discourse, what the narrative voice refrains from saying is often as significant, and sometimes more significant, than what it says. This narrator may be omniscient but he is also reticent and, like those of whom he writes, very careful not to insult the observer by spelling out for him things that the action has already made clear to anyone who is reasonably alert. The success of Tōson's narrative technique lies in the nearly perfect matching of the way in which things are said with what is being said.

Mention of the still-intact character of Magome, the rugged beauty of the surrounding countryside, and the associations they had for the author will prepare the reader for the pervasive lyricism that marks *Before the Dawn* as well as for its concern with hierarchy, formality, place, time, and character. All help to remind us that Tōson made his first appearance on the literary scene as one of the key figures in the development of modern Japanese poetry. He was the first important poet in the new Meiji style that blended European-style stance, choice of subject matter, and freedom of form with traditional diction and sensibility. He speaks of the "new poetry" in the *Asahi* column in a characteristically oblique reference to his own early achievements. The nineteenth-century generations of the Shimazaki family were linked together by an interest in poetry that at the same time dramatizes the distance between those generations. Kichizaemon's interest was in the Mino school of *haikai*, a rural outgrowth of the plebian *haikai* movements of the great cities of the Edo period. That interest reflects his complete and matter-of-fact identification with the world in which he lived. Hanzō's preference for the court poetry tradition speaks of alienation from the Tokugawa order and from his family's hereditary place in that order. The role that Tōson, the son of Hanzō's real-life counterpart, played in the creation of modern Japanese poetry is an extension of the family interest in poetry into yet another generation and it is also a measure of Tōson's alienation from the worlds of both his father and grandfather. It reminds us, perhaps more clearly than any other single fact about Tōson, what a very long distance he had to travel in order to place himself back in those worlds.

Tōson stopped writing poetry rather early in his career but he never stopped being a poet. He always chose his language with a care, both for wording and for pace, that is so downplayed that his style may strike some as naive, but the cool, understated quality of the narrative is fully controlled and that quality, far from being a liability, makes room for the prodigal richness of the narrative on other levels. The original language of *Before the Dawn* ranges from pure classical Chinese through various gradations of traditional mixed styles, the pure Japanese of classical and archaic poetry, and the studied archaisms of the eighteenth-century and nineteenth-century writers of the National Learning movement down to the deceptively matter-of-fact twentieth-century cadences of the narrative voice. It is idiomatic in its presentation of the minutiae of feudal offices, rules, procedures, and orders on both the national and local levels even though that linguistic realm had vanished more than half a century before the novel was written and before most of the scholarship that is now so indispensable to all who wish to understand those times had been done. The degree to which Tōson was able to reconstruct this linguistic realm constitutes a *tour de force* in itself. Much of the technical terminology of feudal administration and social structure was already only dimly comprehensible even to the novel's first readers. In most cases it would have served simply to enrich the period flavor; the referrents often remained unclear. Tōson himself speaks of at least one term that he had not fully understood until long after the novel had completed its serial run.

Elsewhere in the novel the language ranges from formal metropolitan usages to dialect and folksong. Dialect is played down; the original work already presents sufficient philological problems for both reader and writer without it. But the native richness of language is further enhanced with the unobtrusive Anglicisms and Gallicisms that reflect those very important parts of the author's cultural baggage. Tōson's usages tend to be somewhat elevated, even in expository passages, and his main characters speak with decorum and dignity. It is almost impossible for the translator to do more than hint at the vast range of written and spoken Japanese in the novel; much of the variation in language is along dimensions that have no exact English equivalent, and even where there may appear to be English equivalents they are likely to awaken inappropriate resonances. Not only do the richness of English and the richness of Japanese differ but both languages have become comparatively impoverished in some areas during the past half century. It is quite unlikely that a nonspecialist Japanese reader of today would readily concede that Tōson had kept the promise he made in the advance notice of *Before the Dawn* in the January 1929 issue of *Chūō Kōron*, that he would undertake the writing of "his fifth [sic] full-length novel in the simplest and easiest colloquial language possible," even though that promise was in fact remarkably well kept given the subject matter and the time of writing.

In the very fact of its being Japanese, Tōson's language reflects the hierarchy that pervaded every aspect of traditional Japanese life. Nothing could be said or done without in some way reflecting on the relative positions of the speakers or actors in that hierarchy. Formality in speech and action was in part generated by hierarchy but in traditional Japanese society it was also generated by strong feelings; structured formality provided a finely defined scale against which to measure every nuance of emotion and individuality. To attempt to carry over into a translation the emotional richness and precision of tone that result from the broad range of minute gradations of status-related usages in traditional Japanese is to make unreasonable demands on current English in one of its areas of greatest weakness.

If the linguistic ramifications of hierarchy and formality are all-pervasive, so too is a sense of place, particularly in the parts of the story that are set in Magome. The foreground characters of the novel are rooted in their homes in a way that is almost unimaginable to most people a hundred years or more later whether they live inside or outside Japan. Despite the often appalling strictures imposed by the Tokugawa order, everyday life tended to center on the human rather than the doctrinaire. Tōson emphasizes those aspects of the hierarchical order that did not dehumanize so much as it defined clearly the roles through which each individual experienced and expressed his humanity. Yet it is character that is the prime concern. The presentation of character is thorough and penetrating but, like almost everything else in *Before the Dawn*, low-keyed, so much so that it has been overlooked by many readers, who thereby also miss the fact that this is a novel of character. Even minor figures like Fumidayū, the garrulous headman of Oiwake, or Kōzō, the farmer dragooned into the service of the Mito *rōnin*, are vividly alive and present; the speeches and actions of even the most humble characters are given close attention. They are genuinely important to the parts of the story where they are on stage and they are never patronized or exploited for cheap comic effect. On the rare occasions when they are being funny they are being funny as full-fledged human beings. All this goes to make clear yet another of Tōson's concerns: to demonstrate that, within the limitations of its suffocatingly rigorous hierarchy and its often harsh and arbitrary discipline, the traditional society was also marked by a certain amount of warmth and mutual respect. The number of people who would really want the Tokugawa regime back seems to be small, but it is nevertheless capable of generating honest nostalgia. On balance and at a safe distance it can sometimes still appear today, as it did to Hanzō, to leave more space for human dignity than does the modern order which replaced it.

The concern with character also reflects a preoccupation with individuality, a quality that is of central importance in a culture oriented toward the specific. Each situation is unique, and unique individuals are, in each of the never-to-be-repeated moments of their lives, continually being confronted by unique configurations of events. Only constant observation of the most rigorous standards of discipline can maintain order in such a world. This concern with specificity is expressed throughout the novel in the emphasis on detail—in the way that people are trained, in the way they carry out their duties, and in the way that, for better or worse, they live under the scrutiny of those, both higher and lower in the social scale, around them. The same respectful attention to detail is to be found in the depiction of the physical conditions of life. In the Kiso physical labor of the most demanding kind was a large part of the lives of most people and its stages, processes, rhythms, and techniques are keenly and honestly observed.

Time is the context in which these unique configurations of events succeed one another. Rigorous attention to season, year, era, personal age, and the shape of a career and of a lifetime is necessary if life is not to sink into chaos. Even the most minor episodes in the novel are usually placed in their particular time of year by some image or reference in a manner reminiscent of traditional poetic usage. In isolation these time references may sometimes appear gratuitous but their cumulative effect is important. Traditional Japanese culture viewed time as nemesis, and that outlook is rendered still more poignant by the reader's awareness that for these people and their world the nemesis had prevailed long before Tōson wrote. This concern with time makes the change in the reckoning of years, months, and hours after the adoption of the international calendar and clock in 1873 one of the most powerful exemplars of the disorienting shifts that were taking place during the restoration.

Whether it be called tact or a tendency to idealize, Tōson's stance, however successful overall, created problems of its own, not all of which were completely resolved. Some of the most important questions about the relation of *Before the Dawn* to historical fact center around the treatment of National Learning. Critics have frequently remarked that the Hirata school that Tōson describes is in many ways more attractive than most twentieth-century readers might find the real article to be. Here too it is the more universally sympathetic aspects of Atsutane's teachings that are emphasized and the fanatical and obscurantist side that is usually only hinted at; present but not at center stage. The ironies that surround Miyagawa Kansai and Kitamura Zuiken as they try their first beef dinner in circumstances made perilous by the very same anti-foreign sentiment preached by the Hirata school that Miyagawa so steadfastly supports are not overlooked. Like the irony of Miyagawa's conduct itself, they are there for the reader to find but Tōson has too much respect for his readers to insist on them.

The National Learning movement is presented much more from the perspective of the breadth and generosity of spirit of Motoori Norinaga than from that of the much narrower and more dogmatic Hirata Atsutane. If Tōson's Norinaga also seems to have a bit more in common with Rousseau than did the original, that too makes him both more sympathetic and more accessible to his readers in Japan as well as in the rest of the world—yet another of the countless reminders in Japanese life that many parts of the European cultural tradition are at least as much alive in Japan as they are in the nations that claim to be its direct heirs.

All of Tōson's characters were drawn from life, although the names of the foreground characters were changed in recognition of the liberties that had to be taken with them if they were to function as characters in a novel. But they remain very close to their models. An example of the way Tōson adapted historical reality is to be seen in the depiction of Hanzō's brother-in-law Juheiji, whose real life counterpart was six years younger. By making him and Hanzō close in age, Tōson has made it possible for Juheiji to serve as a foil to Hanzō, his level-headedness and practical common sense serving both to balance and to highlight Hanzō's passionate dreaminess. The names of the background characters remained unchanged. They represent Tōson's best understanding of their actual personalities and historical roles, an understanding that draws on careful and far-ranging research as well as on years of reflection and the actual experience of the previous generation of his family and his own child-hood. It must, however, be noted that not only did Tōson fail to give us any fresh revelations about the major national personalities of the time but his perception of them often failed to make use of the insights afforded by the historical scholarship of his day.

Although *Before the Dawn* is about Japanese experience, its author drew inspiration from a broad range of world literature. The precise import of the title has been a subject of some uncertainty. One possible influence was *Vor Sonnen Aufgang* by Gerhardt Hauptmann, a playwright whose works were well known in Japan. Hauptmann tells of a provincial, *nouveau riche* family that is being destroyed by a congenital moral and physical squalor. Tōson tells of a fine old provincial family that goes into precipitious decline as the nega-tive aspects of its heritage collide with a new social and political order. He shares with Hauptmann the naturalist vision of a dark genetic legacy but for Tōson that vision stands in productive tension with compassion and respect for the lives his forebears had lived in traditional Japan, making the tone and social implications of the two works completely different.

While Hauptmann's play may in some ways be reflected in Tōson's novel, it does not seem to have been the inspiration for the title. In the first half of *Before the Dawn* the longed-for restoration of imperial prerogatives is fre-quently compared to the promise of the breaking dawn. There is even a fam-ily story that the title was inspired by Tōson's working habits. It is also pos-sible that the title alludes to the darkness that was gathering over Japanese life during the years in which the novel was being written, but the most impor-tant source is probably the term *reimeiki* or "period of dawning," which Japa-nese cultural historians often date from around 1887. It was then that the first desperate rush of almost indiscriminate foreign borrowing in the hope that at least some of it would help to ensure national survival was superceded by years still tense and perilous but marked by the emergence of a new gener-ation that had both the time and the training to think more critically about the problem of European influence. One of the rare points of total agreement between Hirata Atsutane and Hanzō on the one side and Tōson on the other is the repeated emphasis on the necessity for Japan to resist the West at the same time that it is borrowing from the West if it is to retain its identity. But the primary resonance in the title is with the life of the story's progatonist. Aoyama Hanzō represents all those who lived through the darkest times that Japan was to know until World War II, only to die just before first light. The ironies do not end there. The mid-1880's also marked the suppression of the popular rights movement and the death of many of the brightest hopes that ordinary people in Japan had held for their country during the years immedi-ately following the fall of the shogunate. By the end of Hanzō's life the once proud cultural and social institutions of the village were entering a precipi-tous decline from which they would not soon recover.

The parts of the narrative that deal with Magome, the Aoyama family, and

Hanzō are consistently successful in their interweaving of the historical and the fictional modes. Themes of national and international scale are not always quite so thoroughly assimilated. This is particularly notable around the beginning of Book Two, where extended quotations from historical sources may make some demands on the reader's patience for all their intrinsic interest and their eventual integration into the narrative. Yet even here the greatest weakness is a certain excess of earnestness that comes and goes for a time and then disappears altogether as Tōson returns to the Kiso and its people. Other historical set pieces such as the uprising of the Mito *rōnin*, the opening of the ports of Yokohama and Kobe, and the events leading up to Japan's first imperial audience for foreign emissaries are treated with great effectiveness.

The most severe test of Tōson's professional discipline came in describing Hanzō's final years. These years were painful for anyone connected with the family to contemplate; especially so for one who was at last confronting his own nature in the nature he discovers in his father. In his examination of the decline and death of the story's protagonist, the "headman's tact" that characterizes Tōson's narrative stance could be of only limited usefulness. The facts of the situation are so complex and so replete with ambiguity that it is unlikely that any final statement could have been made about them even at the time, much less forty years later. It is even difficult to know if such questions have any meaning in these circumstances.

Some have described Hanzō's story as one of unrequited love, expanding on Tōson's treatment of this theme. Hanzō loved his family but in the end his family rejected him. The exception was his beloved eldest child, Okume, but in the harrowing final years she is away from him most of the time, trapped in a hopeless marriage. He loved Magome, the Kiso region, and its people, but his neighbors came to see him as an embarrassment, to be kept out of sight and forgotten about whenever possible. He loved Japan so much that, once convinced that the best hopes for Japan's future were to be found in the teachings of the Hirata school, he did not hesitate to sacrifice his own interests and those of his family and home to the imperatives he found in those teachings. But the Hirata school quickly declined into political and intellectual impotence, leaving Hanzō to feel, far too late, that his faith and trust had been more than a little simple-minded. Above all else, he had loved the imperial institution, or his vision of it, but this love too brought him only disappointment, humiliation, and isolation. Of all the shocks he had to endure in the opening years of the restoration, the program of Europeanization, so quickly initiated by the new imperial government once it came to power, was hardest to bear. He had staked everything on his belief that once power was restored to the imperial court a restoration of Japanese culture in its pristine state would inevitably follow. Both the adoption of European styles of dress and protocol at court and the arguably sound reasons for doing so lay completely outside Hanzō's purview.

Tōson's success in making a work of art out of his father's life story is demonstrated by the way in which the fictional characters win out over their real-life models. What really happened at the end of Shimazaki Masaki's life is important only to the descendants of those directly involved, but the fate of Aoyama Hanzō has universal human meaning. It rewards the reader with a fresh, revitalized version of the familiar story of the romantic young rural idealist full of noble but naive dreams and the long course to the disillusionment of his final years. Whatever may have happened to Masaki, Hanzō proves fully capable of carrying the burden that is the inescapable lot of the protagonist of such a story. When he is gone there is no more story to tell. Many questions remain. Some will be resolved in later years. Some are probably never to be resolved but those questions are all parts of another story or of many other stories. In experiencing Hanzō's humanity the reader acquires a new perspective on his own.

Tōson had originally planned to carry the narrative of *Before the Dawn* as far as the nineteen-twenties. He suspended that plan because of physical exhaustion and the unmanageable size of such a work but he did not abandon it altogether. At the time of his death, in August 1943, he was writing the third installment of another piece of historical fiction that seems to have been planned as a sequel. It was called *The Gate to the East* after the title of a painting by Puvis de Chavannes that Tōson had seen in Marseilles. The story shares much of its setting and many of its characters with *Before the Dawn*. In the completed portion the priest Shō'un is the central figure. Hanzō's daughter Okume and his old friends Osumi and Takichi make appearances. *The Gate to the East* remains a frustrating but impressive fragment.

Although *Before the Dawn* is the story of the author's family and of the Meiji restoration, it is more than that; the aftermath of the events that form its context have fundamentally altered the nature of the world we live in. Its author was a man of sophistication and erudition even though he was not given to virtuoso displays of either quality. He created this novel out of his personal and artistic needs, and out of his sense of the need of Japan and the world community to know the story he tells in it. Japan has been richly served by the original. But Tōson had a worldwide as well as a Japanese audience in mind when he wrote *Before the Dawn*. This translation has been done in the hope of contributing to that undertaking.

Before the Dawn looks back on the adventure, turmoil, and tragedy of the mid-nineteenth century with a clear and unsentimental vision, but it speaks of those times in tones of tact, humility, and deference. It is a celebration of the humanity of its characters and the richness, complexity, and diversity of the lives they lived during the final years of the Tokugawa shogunate and the first two decades of the Meiji era. For all the weight of its historical concerns, it maintains its lyrical tone even when the subject is external threat, internal political turmoil, the grinding hardship of maintaining the old post system, or the bitter disappointments that the new age brought to so many of those who had worked hardest and sacrificed most to bring it into being. It has been followed not only by scholarly studies but also by an immense outpouring of historical fiction, family and local histories, and other publications drawing on the rich store of old diaries and official records preserved throughout the country. These later works often illuminate the period from points of view that were not accessible to any of Tōson's characters, but *Before the Dawn* remains the standard against which all others are measured.

BEFORE
THE
DAWN

PRINCIPAL CHARACTERS

In Magome

At the Honjin

Aoyama Hanzō. Seventeenth head of the Magome branch of the family; hereditary *honjin*, headman, and *toiya*.

Aoyama Kichizaemon. Father of Hanzō and his predecessor in the family offices.

Aoyama Masaki. Third child and second son of Hanzō and Otami; adopted by Juheiji and Osato.

Aoyama Morio. Fourth child and third son of Hanzō and Otami.

Aoyama Okisa. Daughter of Oman; stepsister to Hanzō.

Aoyama Okume. Eldest surviving child and only daughter of Hanzō and Otami.

Aoyama Oman. Second wife of Kichizaemon and stepmother of Hanzō.

Aoyama Osode. First wife of Kichizaemon and mother of Hanzō.

Aoyama Otami. Wife of Hanzō; sister of Juheiji.

Aoyama Sōta. Second child and eldest son of Hanzō and Otami.

Aoyama Wasuke. Fifth surviving child and fourth son of Hanzō and Otami.

Eikichi. Cousin to Hanzō and his assistant in the *toiya;* from the Kameya.

Seisuke. Relative and chief clerk in the *honjin* under Hanzō; from the Wadaya.

Ofuki. Former nurse of Hanzō.

Sakichi. Manservant in the Aoyama household.

Kenkichi. Tenant farmer of the Aoyama family.

Sōsaku. Tenant farmer of the Aoyama family.

3

At the Fushimiya

Satake Inosuke. Adopted heir of Satake Kimbei and Hanzō's close friend.

Satake Kimbei. Village elder and sake brewer, master of the Fushimiya, and Kichizaemon's closest friend.

Satake Otama. Wife of Kimbei.

Satake Otomi. Wife of Inosuke.

Satake Senjūrō. Nephew of Kimbei, master of the Upper Fushimiya, and first husband of Aoyama Okisa.

Satake Tsurumatsu. Son of Kimbei.

Other Villagers of Magome

Gisuke. Assistant *honjin* and village elder; master of the Masudaya.

Kozaemon. Son and heir of Gisuke.

Heibei. Assistant headman from Tōge hamlet.

Heisuke. Assistant headman.

Kyūdayū. Son and heir of Kyūrōbei.

Kyūrōbei. Second *toiya* of Magome, alternating in the post with Kichizaemon.

Shinshichi. Village elder; master of the Hōraiya.

Shinsuke. Son and heir of Shinshichi.

Shōbei. Assistant headman; master of the Sasaya.

Shōsuke. Son and heir of Shōbei.

Shōshichi. Master of the Kozasaya.

Shōnosuke. Son and heir of Shōshichi.

Gosuke. Son and heir of Yojiemon.

Yojiemon. Village elder; master of the Umeya.

Matsushita Chisato. Priest of the Suwa shrine in Aramachi hamlet, the Magome village Shinto shrine.

Shō'un. Priest of the Mampukuji, the Zen Buddhist temple in Magome.

In Tsumago

Aoyama Juheiji. Head of the Tsumago branch of the family; hereditary *honjin*, headman, and *toiya;* brother of Hanzō's wife, Otami, and foster father of their son Masaki.

Aoyama Osato. Wife of Juheiji.

Aoyama Kotoji. Daughter of Juheiji and Osato.

Tokuemon. Assistant *honjin* and colleague of Juheiji; master of the Ōgiya.

In Fukushima

Uematsu Shōsuke. Finance officer, hereditary instructor in firearms, and commander of the guards at the Fukushima barrier.

Uematsu Yumio. Son of Shōsuke and husband of Aoyama Okume.

In Ochiai

Hayashi Gijūrō. Village elder and sake brewer; master of the Inabaya.

Hayashi Katsushige. Son of Gijūrō; loyal disciple of Hanzō.

In Nakatsugawa

Asami Keizō. *Honjin* and headman; friend of Hanzō and fellow student of the Hirata school of National Learning.

Hachiya Kōzō. *Toiya* and village elder; friend of Hanzō and fellow student of the Hirata school of National Learning.

Miyagawa Kansai. Physician and member of the Hirata school; teacher of Hanzō and his friends.

In the Ina District

Matsuo Taseko. Leading woman activist of the Hirata school.

Kitahara Inao. Headman of Zakōji village and a prominent exponent of the Hirata school.

In Miura

Yamagami Shichirōzaemon. Head of the family from which the Aoyama had branched off before going to Shinano some three centuries earlier.

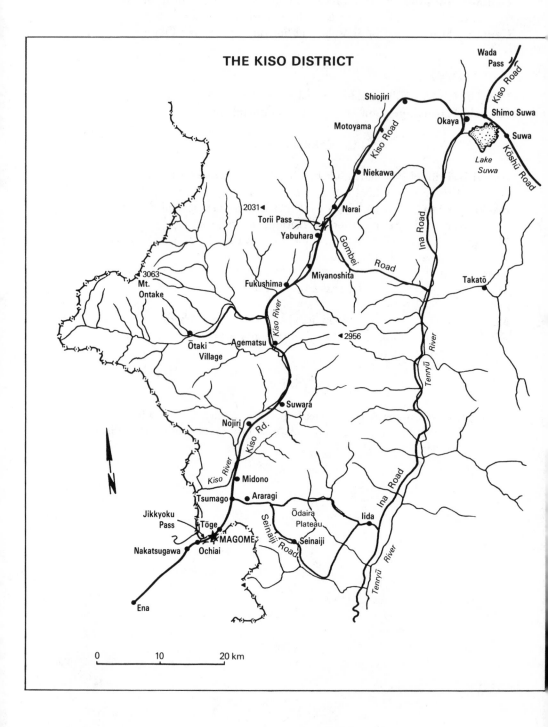

THE KISO DISTRICT

Wada Pass

Kiso Road

Shiojiri

Motoyama

Kiso Road

Okaya

Shimo Suwa

Suwa

Lake Suwa

Kōshū Road

Niekawa

Ina Road

2031◀

Torii Pass

Narai

Yabuhara

Gombei Road

Miyanoshita

Takatō

3063 Mt. Ontake

Fukushima

Kiso River

2956

Ōtaki Village

Agematsu

Tennyū River

Suwara

Nojiri

Kiso Rd.

Kiso River

Midono

Tsumago

Araragi

Ōdaira Plateau

Iida

Jikkyoku Pass

Tōge

Seinaiji Road

Seinaiji

Nakatsugawa

MAGOME

Ochiai

Ina Road

Tennyū River

N

Ena

0   10   20 km

PROLOGUE

1

THE KISO ROAD lies entirely in the mountains. In some places it cuts across the face of a precipice. In others it follows the banks of the Kiso river, far above the stream. Elsewhere it winds around a ridge and into another valley. All of it runs through dense forest.

The eleven Kiso post stations are scattered along the bottom of the Kiso valley from the town of Sakurazawa in the east to the Jikkyoku pass in the west, a distance of fifty miles. The road has shifted and the old routes have vanished into the mountainsides. Even the famous hanging bridge of ivy where the traveler once had to entrust himself to the swaying strands has disappeared. A solid bridge had replaced it in the later years of the Tokugawa era. As the road was relocated over and over again it gradually descended toward the bottom of the valley. Where necessary it was widened by laying logs side by side and binding them together with vines. Each change in the road eased passage through these mountains. Still, the flooding of the river after every heavy rain would create new obstacles for travelers who would often have to wait at the nearest inn until the road was reopened.

Centuries of feudalism and the extreme caution characteristic of such an order were reflected in these changes in the road which still left travel more difficult than it needed to be. The roads remained unsuitable for wheeled traffic as a matter of national policy and travelers were searched for guns or to see if there were any women among them. No place was so well suited for this purpose as this deep valley through which all inland travelers between eastern and western Japan had to pass. The barrier at Kiso-Fukushima was located in the deepest part of the valley.

This highway was part of the post road called the Tosando or sometimes, taking its name from its most famous section, the Sixty-nine Stations of the Kiso Highway. In the east it left Edo by way of Itabashi and it passed through the eleven Kiso post stations before turning away from the river toward Otsu and Kyoto in the west. Travelers who did not take the coastal route known as the Tokaido had no choice but to trudge over this road. In the old days there was a stone marker or an elm tree at regular intervals to mark one's progress. Travelers with their indispensable diaries tucked into the front of their kimono would walk in stages from one post station to the next.

Magome was one of the eleven Kiso post stations. It was located at the end of the long valley, at the western entrance of the Kiso road and near the boundary of Mino province. A traveler coming from Mino would ascend Jikkyoku pass and at the summit of this tortuous stretch of mountain road would catch his first glimpse of the post station. The homes of the residents were built on low stone walls along either side of the road. Shingled roofs weighted with stones against wind and snow lined both sides of a steep, narrow street. Clustered around the post station notice board were the honjin, the lodging for important official travelers, the name of which was also the title of the senior post official in charge, the toiya or transportation office, and the homes of the more important villagers. These included the village elders who assisted the honjin in his additional capacity as village headman, the keepers of the post horses, the porters, the landless laborers, and the couriers. In all there were about a hundred households in the main part of town. There were also about sixty other households that maintained some connection with the post station. They were located in other parts of the administrative area of the village, which included the hamlets of Aramachi, Hachiya, Yokote, Nakanochaya, Iwata, and Toge. On the edge of Magome was a shop which sold the patent medicine known as Kitsune Ointment, and a resting place advertising a local dish made of rice and chestnuts. Deep in the mountains though it was, a broad and open sky stretched as far as Mt. Ena with a sweeping view of the Mino basin. There was something of the feeling of western Japan in the air.

The honjin Kichizaemon and the village elder Kimbei had been born in this village. Kichizaemon was from the Aoyama family, Kimbei was a Satake; both were seasoned post officials. Kichizaemon was fifty-five, Kimbei fifty-seven. It was not at all unusual in those days for post officials to be still in service at those ages. Although people in other occupations often retired early, Kichizaemon's father, Hanroku, did not give up the position of honjin until he was sixty-six. Kichizaemon already had an heir in his only son, Hanzo, but he was not yet ready to retire. He had his commission from the officials in Fukushima and he intended to serve as long as he could. Kimbei was not willing to be outdone.

2

In mountain villages the spring comes late. Each year, in the third month of the old calendar, when the snow began to melt along the Ena range, people would suddenly start traveling in large numbers. Merchants from Nakatsugawa came through to check their accounts along the "inner line," by which was meant Midono, Agematsu, Fukushima, and the Kiso valley as far as

Narai. People from Iida would come over to rent costumes and properties for festivals in the Ina valley. Dai Kagura performers came through and bands of pilgrims bound for Ise, Tsushima, Kompira, and Zenkoji would bring the road back to life as they passed by.

Greater or lesser western daimyo bound for Edo on the required alternate attendance, imperial emissaries bringing annual offerings to the tombs of the Tokugawa at Nikko, the Osaka commissioners, the supernumerary guards for Edo castle—all would pass this way. Kichizaemon and Kimbei, formally dressed, without swords and with fans thrust in their sashes, would call together the other post officials and go out to the western edge of the village to greet important arrivals. The processions would be provided with porters and horses for their freight and baggage, and escorted as far as the old camp-site or to the top of the pass to the east. There were many things for the local officials to do in moving a party from one station to the next. They did not dare fail in any detail when handling large groups or in rendering services when some great personage rested for a moment at their station. Thus they might go out to meet a procession taking a precious tea caddy to Mito or to welcome the shogun's falconers.

These, however, were commonplace; matters which could be handled without involving in any way the village finances or the management of crop and forest lands. It was when they were meeting the Fukushima finance officer or the Owari timber officials who directly controlled the entire Kiso region that they could not get by with simply sending out a welcoming party and providing an escort through town.

Some very distressing scenes have taken place along this highway. In the twelfth month of the ninth year of Bunsei, 1826, some farmers from the village of Kurokawa were released from prison and exiled to a hopeless life beyond the borders of Mino province. Twenty-two of them riding in ordinary post litters arrived at Magome at the old fifth hour of the morning, eight o'clock. It was a wintry day at year's end. Kichizaemon and Kimbei dashed here and there in the snow, overseeing everything from the preparation of the noon meal at the village's two inns to escorting the prisoners to the border of the province. Four foot soldiers from Fukushima accompanied the prisoners, who were all bound hand and foot.

The most memorable procession in all of Kichizaemon's fifty-five years was the one that brought the body of the lord of Owari down this road. The lord had died in Edo in 1839 and his bier was carried back to Nagoya through this Kiso valley which was part of his domain. The Yamamura family, hereditary deputies at Fukushima, held administrative control over the people of the Kiso region at the pleasure of this great lord whose residence was in Nagoya. Kichizaemon and his colleagues thus had two masters. They distinguished between them by calling the lord of Nagoya castle "tono-sama" and his subordinate the Yamamura of Fukushima "danna-sama."

"That was in the tenth year of Tempo. It was absolutely unprecedented."

Each time Kimbei said this, humorous wrinkles would form on either side of Kichizaemon's large, imposing "honjin" nose. He would look at the face of his colleague, still fair and unlined in spite of his age, as if to say, "There goes Kimbei with his 'absolutely unprecedented' again!" But it had been completely unprecedented just as Kimbei said.

An escort of some one thousand six hundred and seventy men had overflowed the station. Kyudayu, the other toiya, and Gisuke, Shinshichi, and Yojiemon, the other elders; everyone from the assistant headman to the lowliest villager had been called out. The seven hundred porters regularly in service in the Kiso valley were insufficient and another thousand or so had to be brought in from the villages in the Ina district that were responsible for such emergency services. Two hundred twenty-four horses were gathered from all quarters. Kichizaemon's home, the honjin, the largest in the village, was filled to capacity and even Kimbei had to take care of two officials and more than eighty men as well as two horses.

There is so little arable land in the narrow Kiso valley that not enough rice was available for the needs of this procession. Packhorses laden with rice had plodded one after another down the Kiso road, the songs of their drivers harmonizing with the horse bells as they came in from the Gombei road out of the Ina region of the neighboring Tenryu river valley.

3

There were countless things to remind one of just how deep in the mountains Magome was. Deer lived in the village forest, and the timid animals would often come down to drink from the Orisaka river in the southeast corner of the village.

To the south one could look straight through the historic Misaka pass toward the mountains of the Ena range. The first Kiso road, which was opened early in the eighth century, was said to have gone by way of Misaka. Off on the lower slopes of the Ena range, several valleys away, could be seen the old pasture lands of the Kirigahara plateau.

This was mountain country. Once a ferocious wild boar had charged out onto a part of the road that was lined with houses. It came out of the place called Shiozawa, crossed the campsite at the edge of the village, passed before the shrine of the healing Buddha, and ran on toward the village stage. There was much shouting and people came running with guns and other weapons, but by the end of the day no one had found the animal. Once, however, when a deer had drifted down from the nearby mountains, it ran up Stonemason slope and tried to hide in the Nanamawari bamboo grove. A great crowd of people came out of the village and the deer was finally brought down with a single arrow. There was a protest from the neighboring village of Yubunezawa, which also claimed the deer, and a heated dispute followed.

"Quarrels are always more interesting than deer!" laughed Kichizaemon, glancing over at Kimbei. These two were usually brought into anything concerning the village but they would have nothing to do with this.

The five trees of the Kiso were the hinoki, sawara, asuhi, koya maki, and nezuko, all evergreens. The mountains around had been divided by the shogunate and by Owari into nesting forests where hawks for the use of the imperial court and the shogunate nested, closed forests, and open forests. The nesting forests and the closed forests were strictly forbidden to the villagers. Even in the open forests, the only ones that were freely accessible, it was forbidden to cut any of the five trees without special permission. This had been done to preserve the forests. The fine timber produced in this region was important to Owari, and the rules were rigorously enforced. Whenever anyone tried to get around them by cutting a slab of wood out of the side of a living tree, the headmen of all the thirty-three villages of the Kiso valley would be called up to the forestry offices at Agematsu. Kichizaemon's family had served for generations as headmen, honjin, and toiya, and at such times he would have to explain the conduct of those villagers who had violated the rigid prohibitions. Not a single hinoki was overlooked. It seemed as though to the officials at Agematsu trees were more precious than life itself. They repeatedly reminded everyone that "In the old days, when a tree fell in the Kiso, a head went with it."

Whenever it was rumored that the officials were coming to check on the villagers, there would be an uproar far surpassing that caused by boars or deer. Some people would panic and burn all their extra lumber. Others would move the hinoki boards that they had hidden away. Particularly upset were the villagers who had secretly taken large amounts of timber, cut it up into lumber, and sold it. An inquiry into such clandestine cutting was so grave a matter that it could lead to a house-by-house search for contraband or signs of illegal trade.

Yahei the informer had long lived in the village, working at that despicable trade that was so much a part of shogunal times. The day Yahei guided the officials from Fukushima into the village remained forever fresh in Kichizaemon's memory. He would never forget it. The trial was conducted in the courtyard of the honjin. Nothing in the entire history of the village had ever brought grief to so many. The senior official in charge, his assistants, and his scribes sat in a line on the highest step of the entrance hall while four foot soldiers stood guard. Everyone in the village was called before them. Those found guilty were handcuffed and tied together and put in the custody of the post station officials. As a special dispensation, those above the age of seventy were not bound and those who had already died were let off with a reprimand so that their families did not have to undergo punishment in their places as would otherwise have been the case.

Several people tried to watch the proceedings from the cover of a pear tree in the corner of the courtyard. Among them was Kichizaemon's son, Hanzo. The seventeen-year-old youth gazed in fascination at the actions of the officials and at the villagers in their bonds.

"Go away! Go away! You can't stand there!" scolded Kichizaemon as soon as he noticed the spectators.

Sixty-one people from the village were placed in the custody of the post officials. Ten of them were allotted to Kimbei. Although assistant headman and an official of the post station, Kimbei could not bear it. As soon as the officials disappeared in the direction of Yubunezawa, he made use of his discretionary powers to order that those under reprimand be pardoned and that an all-night religious vigil be held for the people of the village. An amulet from the vigil was given to each household.

About twenty days after this incident, all those under reprimand were at last permitted to have their manacles removed. Three officials came from Fukushima to make the announcement. One of the more impoverished whose bonds had just been cut walked out, kneeled before the officials, and said timidly,

"Although it may be out of place, I must speak. As you well know, the Kiso is in the mountains. It is a region with little farmland. I hesitate to speak before you officials, but I have to say that there is no way for us to live without using the forests in these mountains."

4

The rule of the Tokugawa had still been secure when a mound topped by a stone inscribed with a verse by Basho was set up beside the road in Shinjaya hamlet at the western edge of Magome.

To create a new attraction at the western entrance to the Kiso, to set up a memorial at the foot of a gentle slope near the stone marking the border between the provinces of Mino and Shinano in a spot where everyone would be sure to see it, to have stones from the mountains brought in and peonies and orchids planted to give the place a restful feeling—that such a delightful thought should have occurred to Kimbei came as a complete surprise to Kichizaemon. He had never known Kimbei to take an interest in haikai linked verse. Kichizaemon himself had a love of elegant and refined things, and in the intervals between his duties as honjin and headman he would at times lose himself in the writing of haikai, in the tradition of the Mino school.

Few things had ever given Kichizaemon such a strong sense of his life in a mountain village. Saying that the stonecutter was almost finished, Kimbei invited Kichizaemon to inspect the work on the mound. The two of them set out, dressed in the baggy trousers of mountain men.

"My father was fond of haikai. He always used to say that he intended to set up a Basho memorial during his lifetime. So I got the idea of doing it myself in remembrance of my father," said Kimbei as he took Kichizaemon up to the memorial. Kichizaemon looked closely at the finished stone. There was an inscription on it.

> After being seen
> Off, and seeing off:
> The Kiso autumn.

> Basho

"It's beautifully written."

"I'm not altogether pleased with the character for 'autumn,' " Kimbei remarked. "The left side is a cursive form of the grain radical and the right side is 'tortoise.' Right?"

"Well, some people do write it that way."

"But in cursive, the grain radical looks much like the insect radical and now everyone will read it as 'The Kiso houseflies.' "

It had already been a long time since that conversation in 1843, the fourteenth year of the Tempo era. That had been the time of the so-called Tempo reforms, when the Tokugawa shogunate made one last effort to bring itself out of economic chaos. There had been talk about remaking the world. All the ledgers and records of the village officials had been audited. The tax officer and the superintendent of public works came from their Fukushima offices. Everything in the village that contained silver, from tobacco cases and purses to women's hair ornaments, was collected and stamps were affixed. It was all weighed and placed in the care of the headman. Then came the commissioner of temples and shrines from Owari, and then the superintendent of timber. The superintendent even claimed that the hinoki for the torii at the village shrine in Aramachi had been cut illegally. He demanded a written account of the matter. When administration became this petty it might seem that no one would be setting up Basho memorials. But society still provided a bit of leeway in those days.

The Basho memorial was dedicated at the beginning of the fourth month of the year. Unfortunately, it was an overcast day and rain fell from midafternoon on. The invited guests were for the most part members of the haikai circle from Mino and they brought rustic gifts. Some brought fans and bean candy, others brought fresh oak mushrooms, and one even brought a box of the tiny rice crackers known as "hailstones," of which he said Kimbei's father had been particularly fond. When they had all gathered at Kimbei's place, the people and the accents of two provinces blended together. In the company was the haikai master and priest Susa, who came from Ochiai, the next post station down from the pass. Thanks to him, the Mino group was able to carry on linked-verse sessions in a setting appropriate to the school of Kagami Shiko, with actual samples of Shiko's calligraphy hung on the walls.

Since Kimbei was acting as host and could not participate directly in the composition of fifty or hundred line linked verse, he passed around lavish refreshments and plied his guests with sake.

Everyone had planned to gather at the foot of the newly constructed mound to conduct a memorial service and to chant verses. But since it took until dusk to complete the day's linked verse, the chanting was done at Kimbei's house. Only the memorial service was held at Shinjaya.

Kimbei, who scrupulously followed the old customs, later went all the way down to Ochiai to present a brown-striped, cotton-filled winter jacket to the haikai master Susa, to thank him for presiding over the day's poetry composition. Kimbei told Susa that it had once belonged to his father.

"You really are my best friend," Kichizaemon told Kimbei that day.

5

The hot summer came. Merchants from Nakatsugawa going to Ina to buy silkworm cocoons trudged by on a road radiating the heat of the sun of the old fifth month. Processions of daimyo going up to the capital or back down to the provinces passed by through hot days filled with the scent of growing things. The Fukushima horse fair, held annually at the end of the fifth month, drew near, inspiring renewed interest in colt judging in every village. Ii Kamon no Kami, the lord of Hikone and a great power in the shogunate, passed down the Kiso road on one of his rare visits home. He spent the night at Suwara, had his noon meal at Tsumago, and stopped at Magome for a brief rest.

In the sixth month there was a long stretch of fair weather. The sun grew stronger day by day. It became so hot that prayers for rain were undertaken in Aramachi.

A farmer came down the road from the pass, leading two horses. He appeared to be on the way home from the Fukushima horse fair and a spirited-looking colt followed along behind him together with a gray mare.

The impatient Kyudayu caught sight of him and called out.

"Hey! Where have you been?"

"Buying horses."

"Don't you know there's been a drought? The rice fields all dried up while you were gone. Around Aramachi they've started to climb Mt. Bonten to pray for rain. And look at the shrine of the tutelary deity! The Thousand Attendances have begun!"

"When you put it that way, I have nothing to say."

"If this weather keeps up, we're going to have to cut an Ise log for sure."

An Ise log was a consecrated log that was thrown into the Kiso river as an offering to the shrine at Ise, so that prayers for rain might be answered. It was a custom that had been observed in these mountains since ancient times. Such a log was offered in only the most exceptional of years.

On the sixth day of the sixth month, everyone in the village stayed out of the fields and gathered at the shrine in Aramachi. All the officials of the village were assembled to discuss the cutting of a white fir tree from the shrine grove.

"One Ise log will not be enough," said Kichizaemon.

It was Kimbei who responded. "Let me donate one. I have a fine fir tree in my grove."

The two logs were hung with straw ropes and the priest said a prayer before them. At the end of the day, the sacred logs, pure and clean, were at last brought out before the torii. The villagers divided into two groups, left and right, and began to shout as they tugged at the heavy ropes.

"Yoi-yo! Yoi-yo!"

The shouts of the villagers trying to outdo each other resounded from the edge of Aramachi as far as the notice board in the center of Magome. Kichizaemon had his duties to perform as headman, and Kimbei was responsible for the evening meal as part of his donation of the tree. When he went out later with a group of people from Magome to see how things were going, the Aramachi farmers had pulled the Ise logs as far as Shinjaya. When they tried to bring them back to the shrine, their prescribed stopping place for the night, pushing and shoving broke out on the paving stones. When the Ise logs were at last left in Aramachi and everyone had returned home exhausted, the first cocks were crowing.

"This year just isn't going right."

"Now that you mention it, strange things have been happening ever since the beginning of the year. I heard that on the third night of the year something shining flew out from behind the mountains to the east and went off toward the southwest. They say it frightened everyone who saw it. And it wasn't just Magome. They saw it in Tsumago and Yamaguchi and Nakatsugawa too."

Kimbei and Kichizaemon talked as they hurried to where the villagers had assembled to work with the Ise logs. People who lived in mountain villages were likely to interpret anything unusual as an omen.

The villagers finally cast the logs into the river at Ochiai after three days of hard work, but there was no sign of a response to their prayers. The people of Toge prayed to the great avatar of Kumano and those of Aramachi to that of Mt. Atago. Each group lit one hundred and eight torches as part of the ritual. In Magome itself the inhabitants divided into two groups to carry out nightlong ceremonies. They even sent two representatives to the great shrine at Suwa to pray for rain and to "borrow water." As an offering they would present ten ryo and each representative was given one bu two shu for expenses on the road. This cost each of the one hundred sixty households nineteen mon.

It was during these prayers that the first rumors reached the village of the sudden, frightening appearance of Black Ships off Kurihama at the station of Uraga on the eastern circuit.

Kyudayu first heard the news from a Hikone courier and he reported it to Kichizaemon and Kimbei. With the appearance of these Black Ships, the lord of Hikone had abruptly been ordered by the shogunate to take charge of the situation.

On the tenth day of the sixth month in the sixth year of Kaei, 1853, just as the two village representatives were rushing back from Suwa, a Hikone messenger had hurried westward past Magome through the desiccated night. It took several days for news from Edo to pass over the Kiso highway and reach Magome by even the fastest courier. Nothing was clearly known except that Black Ships, foreign vessels, had appeared ominously off the coast. There was no way for anyone in Magome to know that an American, Commodore Matthew Calbraith Perry, had arrived in Japan in command of a squadron of four ships.

"They must really be upset in Edo."

Kimbei whispered only that and no more to Kichizaemon.

BOOK
ONE

CHAPTER ONE

1

EARLY IN THE SEVENTH MONTH, Kichizaemon returned home from business in Fukushima. He had been obliged the previous year to raise one hundred ryo in Magome and by the end of the year the villagers had underwritten half of that sum. Sending the money on to Fukushima, Kichizaemon had applied the accrued interest to the payment as well. When the subscription was completed, he went to the finance office in Fukushima to report that the entire amount had been donated. The officials there made a formal acknowledgment.

Kimbei, who had awaited Kichizaemon's return with impatience, greeted his friend in his own large parlor. Built by sake brewers, Kimbei's house, the Fushimiya, was one of those places that could be found along a major highway; a large ball made of cedar boughs hung under the eaves as a signboard. Kichizaemon removed the items he had received in Fukushima from a carrying cloth and placed them before Kimbei.

"There, that's it."

There was a gratuity for each of the villagers who had taken part in the subscription and two muslin carrying cloths. The cloths had been sent to Kimbei and to Gisuke of the Masudaya in recognition of their especially large contributions.

This was not all that Kichizaemon had to report. At the very last he took out a document and showed it to Kimbei:

It has pleased us to impose this special levy and your rare cooperation in setting up the subscription, in informing the farmers, and in you yourself making a special contribution is noted. Therefore we grant you permission for one generation to bear a surname and to wear swords. Take note of this order.

The sixth month of the sixth year of Kaei.

> Mitsu Issaku
> Ishi Dannojo
> Ogi Jozaemon
> Shiro Shingozaemon

To: Aoyama Kichizaemon

"Why they've given you permission to use a surname and wear swords."

"Well, that's what it says here."

"It's for your generation only, Kichizaemon, but it's still an honor."

Kichizaemon made a wry face as Kimbei spoke.

"If only this had happened ten years earlier, right?"

Kichizaemon had carried out his duties but had come back with the feeling that he'd smelled something unpleasant among the officials at the finance office.

"Kimbei, surely you've noticed that I've come to think that a headman's duties are painful."

Such was Kichizaemon's reaction to his new honors.

Just then Senjuro of the Upper Fushimiya looked in, so they dropped the subject for the time being. Senjuro, who called Kimbei "uncle" and regarded Kichizaemon as a father, had established a branch of the Fushimiya known as the Upper Fushimiya. He was three years older than Hanzo and the kind of young man who showed his awareness of new fashions by wearing a silver tobacco case at his hip. He was helping Kimbei in his duties and had come to discuss a business matter.

"Senjuro! Won't you come in and have a drink with us?" said Kimbei. But in the presence of Kichizaemon Senjuro became very formal and would not take even a cup of tea. He seemed to be under some kind of constraint, unable to remain still, and he soon left.

"What kind of people are they becoming?" Kichizaemon remarked as he watched Senjuro leave. "Both Senjuro and Hanzo."

Kimbei was equally concerned about the younger generation. Just now there was the coming of the American, Perry, and the confusion it left in its wake, but there had long been things in the air that they wished to hide from the young. Murders, robberies, elopements, love suicides, rumors of corruption among the officials; these had all become commonplace along this highway.

Thirty years at the same station—Kichizaemon and Kimbei, bound together by memories of the post road, would have it that the severe supervision they had always received from their superiors was good for keeping the affairs of the highway in order. It maintained the feudal harmony. Yet it was precisely from those in high positions that threats came to this harmony. Gambling, for instance, was unthinkable. Yet each year at the Fukushima horse fair, it was the officials who permitted open gambling and counted it as a contribution to the prosperity of the region. Bribery was unthinkable. Yet it was the imperial emissaries going to make offerings at the Tokugawa shrine in Nikko who never passed through the Kiso without demanding substantial donations for drinks and "offerings." Murder was unthinkable. Yet at the side of the road on the long grade at Yazawa, it was a member of the Koike family from Ise who had argued with a Tosa retainer, killed him, and then cut off the thumb of a person who tried to intercede, thus setting the example for swordplay along this highway. Women could not pass through the barriers without special passports. Yet it was the lord of Hikone who always ordered a woman's palanquin whenever he traveled on the Kiso road, and anyone who cared to look could readily see that the woman accompanying him was not his wife.

Kichizaemon sighed. "It makes you wonder what the world is coming to. When the officials from the finance office came to ask me to initiate the subscription, sitting there in the place of honor in my living room and saying that it was on the orders of the lord of Owari, I could only think, 'Here we go again.' And after they left, Kimbei, I felt there was no end of difficult questions that needed to be asked . . .'"

Kichizaemon and Kimbei had paid little attention when the news of the Black Ships at Uraga first reached their ears. Even when Kimbei surmised that Edo must be really upset, they thought of it as something that would soon pass. It was still a time when those who lived in the mountains of the Kiso, two hundred fifty miles from Edo, continued the long sleep that had begun with the closing of the country. They had not even been aware that a place such as America existed.

Rumors came rolling down the highway gathering mass like a snowball. The Hikone courier had brought the first account on the tenth day of the sixth month and by the fourteenth there came the incredible report that there were eighty-six Black Ships off Uraga. Since 1633 all Japanese ships had been forbidden to leave the country and no ship of more than five hundred koku or ninety tons capacity could be built. All foreign vessels, except those of Holland, China, and Korea, were strictly forbidden entry into Japanese waters. Now there were people coming directly into Edo bay who chose to ignore this policy, who deliberately set out to violate it. The shogunate had recently moved its maritime checkpoint from Shimoda to Uraga and it was astonishing that these foreign ships had come knowing even this detail.

All kinds of rumors began to come in, one after another. As officials of the post station, Kichizaemon and his colleagues felt compelled to protect the villagers from them.

The advance party for a major procession came through, immediately followed by the retainers of the lord of Owari, on their way to service in Edo. Naruse Hayato-no-sho led this great procession in the place of Tokugawa Yoshikatsu, the lord of Owari. As soon as they had passed, a procession of retainers from Hikone came in on their heels. These retainers were given the same special treatment as a shogunal tea caddy. Ten great chests of equipment from Nagoya castle followed. The soldiers in the escort brought one hundred fifty porters and it was difficult to handle so many. Magome was able to get only twenty extra hands from Yamaguchi village.

Then, when it was heard that the Black Ships had already left, some who had been en route to Edo turned back for home. Chests of equipment that had been sent from Magome in the morning were stopped at Tsumago, and the next morning the same chests would reappear before the Magome post station. While the baggage could be left to the toiya in each village, the passage of men and horses had become so disorderly that an inspector had to come out to oversee the work.

This wild confusion had subsided just two weeks earlier. The foreign ships that had forced their way in at Uraga had disappeared, to the great relief of everyone. But still the rumors from Edo came in.

While Kichizaemon was talking with Kimbei in the parlor of the Fushimiya, the vanguard of a detachment of Owari soldiers came up the road from the west. Kichizaemon and Kimbei left their conversation unfinished and hurried out to join the other post station officials in meeting them. The Owari men were moving a huge cannon to Edo and they had paused to rest beside the post station. The area in front of the honjin and toiya was buried under broad conical hats and heavy walking sticks. Porters stripped to their loincloths were wiping the sweat that ran down their backs. Everyone expressed amazement that such a heavy object could be lifted and carried up Jikkyoku pass, and Kichizaemon and Kimbei and all the others praised them for their efforts. Then Kichizaemon, Kimbei, Kyudayu, and Gisuke of the Masudaya rushed back and forth through the crowd making preparations to transport the cannon to the next station at Tsumago.

The villagers had all come out onto the highway to look. Among them was Hanzo. He was tall like his father and his scalp shone blue where his forelock was shaven. He presented a manly appearance. Beside him stood Miyagawa Kansai, the physician from Nakatsugawa. Both were well back out of the way. Kansai had long been Hanzo's teacher and he was up for a summer visit. Hanzo said nothing. Kansai was also silent. There was only a slight movement of the fan held at the chest of this man with the look of a physician about him.

"Hanzo!"

Senjuro came and stood beside Hanzo, who seemed sunk in thought. The big cannon, weighing some 1,340 pounds, was being hauled by twenty-two porters. There were five smaller cannon, borne by seven to ten porters each. Presently the six cannon were carried past the eyes of the villagers. There had never been any moving of cannon from provincial domains to Edo residences before that day.

Soon the Owari retainers passed from view, but a strange silence remained. The silence came from the feeling, even here deep in the mountains, that something must be happening in Edo. The constant movement of the daimyo over the Kiso road since the sixth month had all been connected with the coming of the Black Ships. Some of the activity had been for the purpose of strengthening the coastal defenses around Edo bay, some for the protection of Edo castle and its immediate environs.

Kimbei touched Kichizaemon's sleeve.

"Ah, you're back already," he said. "It's been a big job, but we got through it. Thanks to you. It's nothing so grand as a recognition of your efforts, but I've asked Otama to prepare something tonight. I'd like it if you would come over, even though I won't be able to offer you any great feast."

* * * * * * *

Thinly sliced cucumbers seasoned with salt and green shiso were to be served with the sake. There were green soybeans boiled in the pod in salted water, small dried sardines in sheets of seaweed that had been sent as a gift, freshly pickled eggplants, and wild yam gruel. Otama had prepared the dishes herself so that Kimbei could invite Kichizaemon to dinner.

Saying that the parlor was too hot, Otama opened up the second floor to serve them there. The water had been heated in their mountain-style bath. Kichizaemon, the guest of honor, refreshed by a hot bath, climbed up the stairs at the corner of the spacious hearth room. The stair treads with their dark luster from generations of polishing bespoke the atmosphere of the Fushimiya. In the west room on the second floor an elegantly mounted sheet of illustrated autographs of haikai by poets of the Mino school hung on the wall, apparently in memory of Kimbei's father. Eight poets had collaborated in the linked verse and the sketches of eight scenes from around Magome. As he passed before this hanging scroll with its haikai themes, Kichizaemon was delighted.

Dinner was served. Otama brought the footed trays. It was an ordinary meal prepared from the things at hand but the fresh, green vegetables looked cool on the serving trays. Sake was served immediately.

"Kichizaemon! It's little enough to offer you but please eat what you like."

"Well, serve him a cup of sake!" Kimbei said to Otama.

"Kichizaemon, now you can use a surname and wear swords. You're no longer the same Kichizaemon as before. Congratulations!"

Kichizaemon rubbed his head. "Not at all! In these times when the right to use surnames and wear swords is being peddled so cheaply, it's not all that much to be thankful for."

"But it can't be that bad. Now you can put two swords in your sash and announce yourself as Aoyama Kichizaemon. You can cut a fine figure anywhere you go."

"Please don't talk about it! Why don't you just let me drink my sake instead?"

Kichizaemon was fond of sake. Sitting across from Kimbei, he drank cup after cup, served attentively and skillfully by Otama. This second floor was the place where everyone, including the haikai master Susa from Ochiai, had gathered for the linked verse session on the occasion of the dedication of the Basho memorial. It reminded them that many of their old friends were no longer in this world. One was the painter Rankei, born in Magome, who had specialized in ink paintings of landscapes and still lifes. Rankei had passed on too soon to know of the Black Ships.

"Forgive me for saying it, Otama, but when I drink like this I forget about everything. And I remember the old days. Kimbei, remember when we each ate thirty sparrows and three bowls of tea-over-rice?"

"Yes!" said Kimbei. "I was just going to mention it."

Thirty sparrows and three bowls of tea-over-rice. That was in 1849, the second year of Kaei, the year when vast numbers of small birds were taken in the mountains. In Odaira village it was said that an incredible three thousand had been netted in a single day, and many people came from Odaira to sell them. Even here in the Kiso mountains, where people boasted of living in a prime area for small birds, there had seldom been years like that one.

That was the time when a group of friends got together and decided to have a party. If anyone could eat thirty birds and three bowls of tea-over-rice, he would get another thirty birds as a reward. If, on the other hand, he failed to eat this much, he would have to contribute sixty birds. The place was the Horaiya. The eaters were Kichizaemon and Kimbei. The hosts were Shobei of the Sasaya and Shoshichi of the Kozasaya. It began at the old seventh hour, four o'clock. Someone had to supervise the bets. Shinshichi of the Horaiya agreed to serve as judge. So they ate. Kichizaemon and Kimbei both finished their thirty birds and three bowls of tea-over-rice, leaving nothing behind. Each received the reward of thirty birds. The sparrows were small and their bones were soft. It was quite different from eating something like thrushes, but it was still a very substantial meal. Yet neither of them was uncomfortable. They moved on to the parlor of the Horaiya and drank a great deal of tea. Nor should their ages at the time be overlooked. Kimbei had just turned fifty-three. Still they could display such splendid appetites.

"That was the best time we ever had."

"Right! We laughed so much! It was absolutely unprecedented."

"There it is again! Kimbei's 'absolutely unprecedented'!"

Such talk went pleasantly with the sake. Neighbors and fellow officials of the post station, they forgot all about the shortness of the summer night as they put aside the business of the highway for a time, talked steadily, and ate wild yam gruel.

It was not the Fushimiya but the Masudaya that first brewed sake in Magome. Soemon, the founder of the family, and his son had checked the density of the water and learned that the Orisaka river tested at 460, the well of the Masudaya at 480, and the well of the Fushimiya at 490. It was the father and son together who had first shown that good sake could be made with Magome water. Up to that time there had been no shop in Magome that made its own sake.

Soemon and his son were the first to raise themselves in this way from among the families of the village. They were also the ones, for better or worse, who opened the route to advancement for those like Kimbei coming up after. Long ago, in 1757, the seventh year of Horyaku, the founder of the Masudaya had built a new house two doors up the street from the Fushimiya. Soemon was sixty-five at the time and his son twenty-five. It had been still another forty years earlier when Soemon had separated from his original family, the Umeya, and begun to make his own way.

Magome was the kind of place where huge stones were to be found, even in the fields; a place where life had never been easy. Soemon had been born in this village and had succeeded his father at the age of eighteen, carrying out

the work of a farmer, content among the boulders. For generations his family
had been counted among the village elders, so Soemon, young as he was, also
fulfilled this role. It was at the age of twenty-eight or twenty-nine that this
young man began to think of building a lodging house to cater to the travelers along this highway. In the Magome of those days it was necessary to go
either to Tsumago or to Nakatsugawa to borrow even the smallest sum of
money. When debts fell due at year's end, the old man from the Bizen'ya in
Nakatsugawa would come to stay in Magome for ten days, loaning out small
amounts of cash. Magome was the kind of place where this money would
barely enable people to scrape past the new year.

The history of Soemon, the founder of the Masudaya, and of his wife and
four children is the history of people who fought fiercely to survive in this
impoverished village of Magome. As farmers, they would cut two loads of
grass every morning from the time it began to show green in early spring
until the killing frosts of late autumn. During the day he would work as a
regular post official. At night the needs and wishes of the travelers would
come first. In between he would sell a bit of rice. His wife also made bean
curd to sell while looking after four children. Late every night, she would
still be turning the stone mortar to grind the beans. When the construction
of the new inn was finished, this woman would kindle the leftover scraps of
wood and then use the fire to light the oil lamps before hanging the night
lantern out in front of the inn. And each morning, before dawn, it was she
who did the first sweeping and cleaning, using the same cloths to wipe down
the tracks for the sliding doors. This impoverished couple, determined not to
leave their children destitute, worked desperately with hardly ever an unin-
terrupted night's sleep.

At that time, Soemon's parents' house, the Umeya, served as a lodging for
the porters who came from the neighboring village of Yubunezawa. Using
this connection, the couple asked each of those porters who were on familiar
terms with them to secretly loan them a bushel and a half of rice in the
spring, which they would repay with two bushels in the fall. So they planted
their land, which they could not afford to let go to grass or garden, and with
this rice and the barley that they grew on the land immediately around the
inn, they managed to make a living.

Such were the origins of the founder Soemon, keeper of an inn and over-
worked farmer. Since there was no other good inn in Magome and since his
building was new, business was good and he gradually built up a regular
trade. He was able to employ maids and to raise the annual salary of his
workers from three bu to one ryo. He progressed from selling rice a few
pounds at a time to selling it by the bag, and finally to bringing it in by packhorse from Nakatsugawa. The master of the new Masudaya was no longer a
mere peasant. He was now a townsman who ran an inn and who was going
bit by bit into other lines of trade.

The second Soemon was born as the last child of this couple. It was the
custom among the peasants from whom they had sprung for the first son to
inherit the family property. Second and third sons had no such hope and from

the age of thirteen or fourteen they would be sent out to cut grass. At best they might end up as bathhouse attendants. Those were still the days when a last son was certain to rise no higher than herder of packhorses or litter bearer. In spite of this custom, Soemon did not send the child out to cut grass as soon as he was old enough to work and made a point of keeping him by his side. This second Soemon increased his patrimony by several fold.

As is well known, most of the rice that the daimyo exacted from the farmers in taxes was transported to Osaka and exchanged for money. Osaka was one great rice exchange. As the scope of his business affairs broadened, this second Soemon was not one to overlook the Osaka rice market. He eventually got to the point where he could easily accept subscription levies of one thousand ryo, and it was said that there was no one in the entire Kiso district who could match him for wealth. Throughout his life he continued to carry to extremes his father's struggle to escape poverty. He had no tradition of which to boast or any past of which to be ashamed. He moved nonchalantly ahead on his own.

The second Soemon turned fifty-three in 1786, the sixth year of Temmei. By then he was sitting in his huge sake brewery, directing his sons as they heated the new sake to stabilize it, and reflecting on the eighty years since his father had started the family on its upward course. He taught his children to look upon all the wealth and property that they would inherit from their ancestors as a trust from heaven. He taught them to think of money as the treasure of Japan. He taught them that if they should ever presume to use it for selfish purposes, as if it were their own property, there would surely come a time when heaven would hear of it. He died still worrying that his sons and grandsons would forget just where the first Soemon had started.

Kimbei of the Fushimiya was the successor to Soemon and his son. In his cheerful, light-hearted way, Kimbei was not just a brewer and sake shop keeper. He also ran a pawnshop on the side. He had horses and croplands and from time to time he dabbled in the rice market. He had even lent money to the great shogunal vassals in Kukuri in Mino province.

Miyagawa Kansai of Nakatsugawa often compared these two neighbors, Kichizaemon and Kimbei. According to this learned country physician, Magome was on the border; hence in Kimbei with his townsman's character, as well as in Soemon and his son, was mixed the blood of the Mino people, while Kichizaemon was a Shinano farmer.

The Aoyama family to which Kichizaemon belonged was old, like the forests it owned in the mountains behind Magome. The man who founded the settlement of Magome at the western extremity of the Kiso valley was the second son of Aoyama Kemmotsu, who had come from Miura in Sagami province. This second son established a temple in Magome and called it the Mampukuji. The founder of the Mampukuji, posthumous name Densho-oku Jokyu Zenjomon, known in the world as Aoyama Jirozaemon who took the religious name Dosai after his retirement, went to his repose in the graveyard of the temple he had built in a year now long past, 1583, the eleventh year of Tensho.

"Kimbei's family and our family are different."

Whenever Kichizaemon said this to his son he was referring to the long history of his family. When Kichizaemon had succeeded as the head of this house, he had become the sixteenth in a line that marked the Aoyama family as one of the oldest in the Kiso district.

There was no way to know the distant past of Magome. It was in the time of Kiso Yoshimasa that the Aoyama family had come to the Kiso, making them, no doubt, even older than the Yamamura of Fukushima. It seemed that thereafter, as country samurai, they had served as deputies in Magome and several other villages in the region. In the Keicho era, at the beginning of the seventeenth century, Ishida Mitsunari had called up the daimyo of western Japan and set out for Sekigahara in Mino while Tokugawa Hidetada, the eldest son of Ieyasu, was moving westward over the Kiso road, also headed for Sekigahara. Among his guides through the Kiso were Yamamura Jimbei, Baba Hanzaemon, and Chimura Hiuemon. Aoyama Shosaburo, also known as Shigenaga, in the second generation of the Magome family, joined the Tokugawa side and held off the Inuyama forces from his fortifications around Magome. The then lord of Inuyama castle, Ishikawa Bizen no Kami, had been on the point of initiating a drive into the Kiso but, upon learning that the country samurai of the region were all aligned with the Tokugawa, with-drew without heavy fighting. After that time, the Aoyama family reverted to agrarian rank but their status for generation after generation as honjin, headmen, and toiya had been part of their reward for their services in these wars.

The original Aoyama residence was located just below Stonemason slope. But everything that remained from the old days, even the weapons and horse fittings, had been burned in the great fire of the Kan'ei era, in the 1620's. Only two lances were saved, and in that spot only the place name "deputy's residence" remained. Then, in the cadastral survey of 1724, the spot became known as Stonemason slope out of deference to the Tokugawa of Owari. The new name apparently came from the fact that the site was strewn with boul-ders and there were great stone outcroppings nearby.

As a child Hanzo had often sat before his father to be told these stories. Sometimes, when he was in a good mood after drinking sake, Kichizaemon would lead Hanzo to stand under the two lances that hung over the beams in the main entry and tease him, saying, "Look! The ancestors are watching. Don't be naughty!"

It was his father's talk in the evenings around the footwarmer, heard from an early age, that deeply impressed the young Hanzo with this tradition which their neighbors of the Fushimiya did not share. Whenever he spoke to his son about their forebears, Kichizaemon's eyes would hold a special light.

" 'Deputy's land' is still a term that remains among the place names. Dur-ing the time when our ancestors were serving as deputies, paddy fields were built up by hand. They were called 'deputy's land.' Now we call them the town fields. In those days all the peasants in the village would be called out to plant the area, and on planting day our house would give out five gallons of

sake. If anyone fell drunk into the paddies, it was said that they could expect
a good harvest that year."

Such stories came up regularly.

Even in Kichizaemon's time there were thirteen farming families who
served the post station, most of them in a way that was close to serfdom. The
source of the feelings that led Kichizaemon, but not his neighbor Kimbei, to
look upon the farmers of the village almost as though they were his own sons
lay in this distant past.

2

"Black Ships again!"

On the twenty-sixth day of the seventh month, a messenger from the shogunate had come from Edo announcing the death of the twelfth shogun,
Ieyoshi. An order had been issued by the commissioners of transport forbidding all building and all ringing of bells and chimes or beating of drums. It
was the time of the annual festival along the highway in Nakatsugawa. The
plays were broken off in the midst of rehearsals and the committee showed its
respect by canceling all stage presentations. Just three days after that,
Kyudayu startled Kichizaemon and Kimbei with his "Black Ships again!"

"What day is it? Isn't it the twenty-ninth? It's only been three days since
the shogunate's messenger came through."

Kichizaemon and Kimbei looked at each other. According to the rumors,
the foreign ships that had arrived in Nagasaki were not from America but
from some other foreign country. But here in the mountains there was no
way to be certain. Most people thought they were the same ships that had
been at Uraga.

"They say things are very tense in Nagasaki," said Kimbei.

At that moment they were preparing to meet the Nagasaki commissioner,
whose lead porters were expected to appear imminently. The commissioner
was making a hurried trip and covering the distance in unusual stages; the
highway officials were hard pressed to get him through smoothly. This new
commissioner, Mizuno Chikugo no Kami, was one of the most outstanding
members of the shogunate. He arrived on the first day of the eighth month,
lances wrapped in dark brown leather borne before him.

Kichizaemon rushed home to change his jacket. His wife, Oman, brought
his swords and fittings.

"No! It's quite enough for me to be the Magome honjin."

Kichizaemon had made no move to indulge in his new privilege of thrusting the long and short swords through his sash. Wearing a familiar jacket,
swordless as always, he set off to meet the procession.

As was customary whenever an official passed through, Kichizaemon
approached the commissioner's palanquin to offer his respects. The Nagasaki

commissioner was in too great a hurry to get out of the palanquin. He merely stopped before the honjin to give his bearers a brief rest. Writing paper was brought on a ceremonial stand. Then Kichizaemon kneeled beside the palanquin and spoke simply.

"I am Kichizaemon, the honjin of this station. I have the honor to be in your presence."

"Ah, the Magome honjin, is it?" The commissioner's reply was relaxed and informal.

Although Mizuno Chikugo no Kami's official stipend was two thousand koku, on this special occasion he was traveling with an entourage appropriate to a daimyo with a revenue of one hundred thousand koku.

The day came to an end along the highway. Kimbei and the other officials who had gone out to meet the commissioner had returned to their homes. It was the time of day when the packhorsemen who had taken the commissioner's baggage to Ochiai, the next post station, were finally leading their horses back home.

Children had gathered in the highway to chase the bats that came out into the dusk in great numbers. Here in the mountains the nighthawks began their cries. At the gate of the Umeya, directly across the street from the honjin, the night lantern was already lit and hanging under the eaves.

Kichizaemon, finished with the day's work, stepped outside his house for a breath of mountain air. After a short time he returned to the hearth room, where Oman was working with the two serving girls.

"Hanzo?" he asked Oman.

"He was just here talking with Senjuro. The foreign ships have come again, haven't they? I don't know where Hanzo heard it, but he was saying that they were ships from Russia. Senjuro insisted they were from America. They were saying, 'Russia!' 'No, America!' After a while they went outside."

"We don't know a thing about what's happening in Nagasaki—anyway, I'm really tired today."

A country bath and a simple evening meal awaited Kichizaemon. It was the first day of the eighth month, his birthday. Everyone remembers things on such a day and Kichizaemon began to think about his long experience of the highway. Whether in wind or in rain, he would be responsible for this section of the highway, the traveler's safety always uppermost in his mind. His had been the burden of providing horses, oxen, and porters, of calling up reserves from neighboring villages whenever the demand exceeded Magome's resources, and of maintaining and improving the highway itself. The problems of this stretch of road were beyond description.

Kichizaemon celebrated his fifty-fifth year in the hearth room. Oman had heated a container of sake to go with his trout broiled in salt, a dish which had been sent in from outside Magome. He talked with Oman.

"I was quite impressed by the Nagasaki commissioner today. Mizuno Chikugo no Kami—they say his stipend is only two thousand koku but today he was traveling in the style of a daimyo with revenues of one hundred thousand. That is really extraordinary! I've never heard of a person moving up that far in rank in just one step. That alone makes me feel the rule of the Tokugawa must be changing. So long as things stay peaceful even the most helpless people can assume the airs of a samurai. But just think of what would happen in an emergency."

"Well, it's all because of the uproar over those foreign ships."

"That's the kind of world it has become."

The retiring room, as it was known, opened onto the hearth room on one end and onto a spacious central room on the other. It was this room that Kichizaemon treated as his own, night and day. He went into it now and looked around, repeating to himself, "Thank you for all your hard work! Thank you!"

"Who are you talking to?" asked Oman.

"Myself. There's no one to say to me, 'Thank you for all your hard work,' so I'm just saying it to myself."

Oman forced a smile. Kichizaemon went on.

"But isn't it a strange world? If you do some little favor for the lord of Owari, they give you permission to use a surname and wear swords. But although I've borne the responsibility for this part of the highway for thirty years, no one has ever said so much as thank you. Even though all the unnoticed things I've done for this highway have been a far greater burden."

Once he had gotten this far there was nothing more to say.

There was no way of knowing how many people he had met and sent on their way as honjin. It had all been dull labor, but Kichizaemon had managed to do it with a certain elegance. In his eyes all those who traveled this highway were pilgrims.

The subject of Hanzo's wedding began to come up frequently in the conversations of Kichizaemon and Oman. The younger sister of Aoyama Juheiji of Tsumago, the neighboring honjin, had been selected as Hanzo's future wife. Kichizaemon had great hopes for the marriage of his son. One hope was that it would lift Hanzo out of what Kichizaemon saw as the painful perplexities of youth. Another was that he might then be able to pass on his responsibilities to the next generation just as he had accepted them when his father, Hanroku, at the age of sixty-six, had served to the limit of his ability. Hanzo's marriage would also forge another link between the honjin of Magome and Tsumago. Not only did the two families bear the same surname, Aoyama, but it had been passed down in the traditions of both families that they were descended from Aoyama Kemmotsu, who had come from Miura in Sagami province to settle at Tsumago. His two sons had lived only five miles apart in the valley, the elder in Tsumago and the younger in Magome. This centuries-old relationship would be renewed by the marriage, and Hanzo and the strong, reliable Juheiji would become brothers-in-law.

From the beginning Kichizaemon had consulted with Kimbei about these marriage plans. After Kichizaemon and Hanzo had paid a call to the Tsumago honjin, they first reported the results of the journey to Kimbei.

One day as Kichizaemon and Kimbei discussed the construction of a stage that was to be ready in time for the autumn festival, their conversation turned to the young.

"Kichizaemon, how old is the daughter of the Tsumago honjin?"

"Sixteen."

Kimbei counted on his fingers. "Well then, that would make her just six years younger than Hanzo."

It was clear from the way Kimbei spoke that he was expressing his approval of the match. Neither Kichizaemon nor Kimbei thought of this marriage of a man of twenty-two and a woman of sixteen as being early in any way. Early marriages were viewed as the normal thing and even as a very fine custom. In those days there were marriages in the Kiso between fifteen-year-old grooms and fourteen-year-old brides and no one questioned them.

"Just the same, Kimbei, Hanzo's wedding has come very quickly. As a rule, I don't think much about it, but when something like this happens I realize I'm getting old."

"But it's a good thing for you, isn't it? A bride is coming into your family and a wedding is taking place between the two honjin."

"Hanzo! I hear that the daughter of the honjin at Tsumago is coming to your place as a bride. You've really grown up!"

Ofuki, who belonged to a family attached to the Aoyama household, came over just to say this. Ofuki had been Hanzo's wetnurse. It was she who had held the still tiny Hanzo in her arms and carried him around on her back. When Hanzo's wedding had been decided upon, this old woman was even more pleased than the other farmers attached to the Aoyama household.

Again, Ofuki came when Oman, the honjin's present "elder sister," was out and spoke to Hanzo in her cracked voice.

"Hanzo, you don't remember anything about it, but I remember your mother well. Osode—she was a beautiful woman. The travelers along the road would say that even in Edo there was no one to match her. It was only about twenty days after your birth when Osode fell ill and died. I picked you up and took you to her bedside. That was the last time. And she was just thirty-two and in her best years. And then right away you came down with jaundice. Everyone just about gave up on you. The master was really beside himself. If only your mother could be alive and in good health today to see your wedding—"

Hanzo had reached an age when he often tried to imagine his mother. He also tried to imagine his father struggling to carry out the roles of both parents. But whenever he saw Ofuki he recaptured his childhood. It was this old woman who remembered the things he had liked to eat and the things he had not liked when a child, and who had taught him of the fresh scent of Kiso-style parched rice and counted out for him his dumplings made of buckwheat flour and taro.

This mountain village of Magome was not only a place set among forests and boulders; insofar as the education of the village children was concerned, it was virgin territory. There was not even a temple school and it was widely believed that foxes and tanuki could place spells on people. Other superstitions were rampant as well. Born in this mountain village where many could not even write their names, Hanzo found himself to be fond of learning. When he was still only fifteen he began to think about educating the children of the village. In the busiest years some sixteen or seventeen children, such as Tsurumatsu from next door or the young son of the Masudaya, would come for lessons in reading and writing and using the abacus. They came from as far as Toge, Aramachi, and Nakanochaya, and sometimes even from the villages of Yubunezawa and Yamaguchi. Hanzo tried not just to educate himself but also to teach the children, who had no other opportunity for learning.

It was not easy for Hanzo to carry on his studies in this mountain village. The first difficulty was the lack of a good teacher. A physician from Ueda, one Kodama Masao, had lived in Magome for a time and he had begun Hanzo's instruction in the *Book of Odes*. But after one chapter Kodama had left the village and there was no one to continue the lessons. The Zen priest So'en in the Mampukuji did not have the patience to be a teacher. At the age of twelve, Hanzo read the *True Jewels of Ancient Writings*, an anthology of Chinese poetry and prose, with his father, Kichizaemon. At that age Hanzo had not yet acquired a strong interest in learning and he had done nothing more than sit beside his father and practice writing by copying passages from the book. Later he struggled by himself through an unpunctuated edition of the Four Books of the Chinese Classics, and by the time he was fourteen he had begun to be acquainted with the *Book of Changes* and the *Spring and Autumn Chronicles*. Since Kichizaemon had been instructed in Japanese mathematics by Ono Hoho of Onomura in Ina and had become quite accomplished, Hanzo learned mathematics from his father. Among the village youths, who for the most part spent their time fishing or playing go or chess, Hanzo alone paid no attention to such amusements. Scarcely ever talking to anyone, he devoted himself to studying. His struggle to teach himself, unmindful of heat or cold, continued until he was around sixteen. Fortunately, he then found a companion in his studies in Nakatsugawa. His name was Hachiya Kozo and it was he who encouraged Hanzo to continue his studies. After their friendship established itself, the more than seven miles between Magome and Nakatsugawa no longer seemed a great distance.

Miyagawa Kansai, who lived in Nakatsugawa, was the husband of Kozo's older sister and a physician proficient in Chinese learning. He also knew a great deal about National Learning. Hanzo of Magome and Kozo of Nakatsugawa—the "two Zo's"—urged each other on as they worked under Kansai's instruction.

"I am self-taught and as a result I am rigid and out of date. Of course I have seen and heard very little here in the mountains. I must learn more."

This became Hanzo's preoccupation. Born into the ancient Aoyama family, Hanzo turned his attention to National Learning under the guidance of this master. At twenty-two, he had become familiar with the joy of learning that he had discovered in the world of print, and he dreamed of leaving behind him great works like those of his predecessors, Kamo Mabuchi, Motoori Norinaga, and Hirata Atsutane.

This was the young Hanzo who first became aware of the Black Ships.

3

By the eleventh month of 1853 Hanzo's wedding plans had progressed to the point where presents had been sent to the honjin of Tsumago. Snow had already come to Mt. Ena.

One day Oman was setting out for the clay-walled storehouse that stood to the rear of the grounds. As was the custom in mountain households, all the dishes and utensils of value were kept in this storehouse. One of the duties of the mistress of the house was to move boxes labeled as containing so many sets of serving dishes or so many serving trays to and from the main house.

Just then a messenger came from Fukushima with a writ. It was addressed to the Magome honjin. Oman went to find her husband.

"The master . . . ?" she asked a serving girl.

"He went out to the storehouse."

Oman walked out through the back door of the main house, turned to one side, and approached the storehouse. Her husband's wooden clogs were there on the stone step. The door was unlocked. It appeared that he had had the same thought and had gone to check the dishes and utensils for the wedding ceremony. Hearing activity on the second floor, Oman climbed the ladder and found Kichizaemon.

"Here's a writ from Fukushima."

Kichizaemon was making use of a rare bit of free time to put the second floor of the storehouse in order. A great number of old bookcases were stacked against the wall. They held all of his books of haikai and works in Chinese and Japanese. He took the writ from Oman and moved to the window to read it.

The writ stated that the shogunate's outlay for coastal defenses had been immense and the time had come to repay one's debt to the nation. An order had therefore been issued from Edo establishing a special tax to be levied not only in the three principal cities but also in the domains of the emperor and the daimyo and even in all the country villages. It further stated that since the four American ships at Uraga and the four Russian ships at Nagasaki had been rebuffed, the coasts now had to be defended against them.

"They're ordering a special contribution to the nation. It's storming out there but here we're preparing for a celebration. It looks like I'm going to have to get busy."

As the day approached, it became clear that Hanzo's wedding ceremony would mark the beginning of many changes in the Aoyama household. Kichizaemon's aged mother fled from the uproar of the preparations to take up residence in the retirement quarters on the second floor of the building next to the storehouse. The tatami makers went to work in the parlor, which was to be the living room for the new couple. A manservant of long standing left and a new one named Sakichi took his place.

After Oman had gone back down the ladder, Kichizaemon returned to the window. The winter sun cast a soft light through the iron grill. All alone, he quietly reflected on the writ from Fukushima with its demand for a special tax. He recalled rumors that the shogunate's treasury was empty, rumors that had never before been heard since the Tokugawa came to power. The old-fashioned Kichizaemon thought of these things and felt disgust with those who talked about them freely before the young. He did not want the gentle and impressionable Hanzo to see the darker side of society just yet. He wanted Hanzo to prepare himself gradually until he reached an age when he would be able to bear hearing of the ugly secrets among men. Kichizaemon thought of how he would like to have his son continue to think of authority as sacred. No doubt Kimbei next door had the same feelings. He continued to worry about these matters as he descended the ladder.

The party of the Nagasaki commissioner whom they had been expecting was soon coming down the road with plans to spend the night in Nakatsugawa. The weather was fine although there had been a heavy snowfall. It was a great procession. Seven hundred fifty porters had been engaged at Nojiri to serve until Ochiai and their feet crunched the snow as they moved the procession toward Nagasaki. It took three days for the procession to pass through.

Then over the same highway came wooden chests from the Tsumago honjin, packed with new bedding to be taken to Kichizaemon's house.

The first day of the twelfth month, which had been chosen as an auspicious day, arrived at last. Early in the morning Kimbei went over to the honjin to assist Kichizaemon in receiving the guests. The laughing voices of Otama, Okisa, and Ofuki, who had come to help, rose from the hearth room, which served as both kitchen and reception room.

Senjuro also came, his face grave and serious. It was he who went back and forth between the retiring room and the parlor, taking care not to inconvenience Hanzo. In the midst of the confusion Kimbei found a moment to speak to Hanzo.

"Hanzo, is there anyone you'd like to invite?"

"As a guest? I'd like to send word to Miyagawa Kansai and Kozo from Nakatsugawa, and also Keizo."

Asami Keizo was the heir to the honjin at Nakatsugawa and a companion in studies to whom Hanzo had been introduced by Kozo. Like Hanzo, Keizo had first taken to Chinese studies and his turn to National Learning had also been due to Miyagawa Kansai's influence.

"Well, of course we'll invite the people from Nakatsugawa, Hanzo.

Besides, even if we didn't invite them they would come to offer their congratulations anyway. We've already sent a messenger to tell them to come tomorrow."

Senjuro joined the conversation, hoping to elicit a laugh. "Well now, me too, right? I'd like to offer my congratulations all over again."

It was an unusual winter for mountain households. There had only been the one snowfall of eight inches along the highway and it had all been washed away by heavy rains. After that came a stretch of warm weather which was unheard of even to people of Kimbei's age. Kichizaemon, who usually suffered from the cold, was using neither footwarmer nor braziers and was able to get by with just the live coals that were kept with the smoking set. The bright, sunny weather made the joyous occasion in the honjin all the more pleasurable.

In the afternoon, when Juheiji and his sister would already have left the Tsumago honjin, Kichizaemon found himself pacing about in the large, wood-floored section of the entrance hall. He was dressed in formal clothing and his broad-shouldered jacket was marked with the family crest. The man-servant Sakichi was going in and out of the front entrance as though unable to be still.

"Sakichi! Isn't this weather unusually warm? If it's this way here it must be warm in Tsumago, too."

"Must be. I thought I'd make a bonfire in front of the gate tonight. I brought some wood down from the mountain."

"If it's going to be this warm, we won't need a bonfire."

"But it wouldn't do just to hang lanterns out tonight."

At that point Kimbei came out and began to talk about travelers' reports from Tsumago.

"It was the evening of the day before yesterday. Gisuke of the Masudaya had been called to Fukushima at night on business. There wasn't a bit of snow on the road coming or going. He didn't even feel a chill when he sat down to rest at the open front of a tea shop. It seems as though it's warm everywhere. That's what Gisuke is saying."

"Kimbei, this winter is absolutely unprecedented, right?"

"Absolutely."

Around dusk, the people of the village began to gather before the honjin. They formed a solid crowd stretching from the wooden grill in front of the Umeya to the stone wall in front of the toiya. As was customary in this region, the litter bearing the new bride did not immediately enter the gate of the honjin.

Juheiji and the others in his party, guided by those who had gone to the top of the pass to meet them, stopped before the gate. Everyone gathered close. Then, in the light of paper lanterns, they began to sing the "Kiso-bushi." The baggage bearers from Tsumago formed a circle around the litter and danced to the rhythm of the song. One figure after another appeared, hands waving and hips moving. The ring of rustic dancers circled the bride's litter nine times.

That night, after the sake cups had been exchanged by the bride and groom, Hanzo and Otami passed through a time that seemed not at all like a winter's night. This was not the first time that Hanzo had seen Otami, for he had gone with his father to visit her home in Tsumago. But their marriage was not something they had decided for themselves. In those days even the relationship between parent and child was close to that between lord and vassal, and the marriage had been left up to parents and an older brother. The bride and groom had been obedient, but not passive. The first time they saw each other in Tsumago, everything had been instantly decided. It was not something that took a long time to settle; it had taken only a glance.

The parlor faced the east, and outside the door stood a pine tree of which Hanzo was fond. The fresh green matting of the room, wafting a clean scent that made one expect to hear birds singing, brought the blood rushing to the head of the completely inexperienced Hanzo. Feeling as though he were entering an unknown world, he discovered Otami beside him, trembling in youth and fear.

"Father, if it's just for me, I would have liked the celebration to be as simple as possible."

"You don't have to tell me. I'd prefer it simple, too. But for honjin there are honjin standards. We have to invite all the guests we can. I will see to everything."

This conversation took place on the morning of the third day of continuous festivities.

That morning the inspector general and a public works officer from Owari arrived unexpectedly in Magome. They announced it had been decided that in the coming third month the lord of Owari would make his progress to Edo by way of the Kiso road. They and their attendants were inspecting each of the honjin along the route during the winter.

At such times Kimbei and Kyudayu were indispensable. Knowing their jobs thoroughly, they had taken their cue from Kichizaemon's nonplused expression and taken the officials directly to the Umeya. Kimbei then returned alone to report to Kichizaemon.

"We were really lucky. A little further and they might have been pulled right into the middle of all this. I told them, 'There is a wedding at the honjin. It's frightfully rude to ask such a thing of you but would you mind if you were to take your rest at the Umeya?' They consented. I made arrangements for them to take their noon meal there."

The Umeya and the honjin faced each other across the street, in easy hailing distance. After lunch, the inspector general and his companion wearing rush slippers provided by the Umeya came across the dry roadway. The scent of their large topknots, the dignity of the swords they wore, the rustling of their trousers, and the officious way in which they announced themselves all combined to give the entrance hall of the honjin a severity that clashed with the tone of the wedding festivities. Guided by Kichizaemon, they proceeded directly to a room-by-room inspection of the honjin.

Kichizaemon spoke to the inspector general.

"I am hesitant to mention it, but I understand that the middle councillor may pass through here in the spring. What is it that may be expected of this station?"

"He may stop here for his noon meal, although I am not yet certain."

The wedding celebration lasted four days. On the last day the most humble people—the farmers attached to the honjin, the attendants from the town office, the women who had come to help with the festivities—were invited. The carpenters and the tatami makers came. Even Naoji the hairdresser, who usually called on Kichizaemon and Hanzo carrying his oil-stained box of equipment, was now sitting solemnly before his serving tray dressed in a formal jacket.

Kimbei sat before the farmers attached to the honjin. Senjuro sat before Naoji, and Kichizaemon was opposite Ofuki, who was weeping with joy that she had lived to see this day. After the guests were formally greeted Kichizaemon moved from his position before Ofuki to take a seat with the farmers.

"Come on! Drink up!" He took the flask of heated sake that had been placed beside him and offered it.

"For me? It's embarrassing to have you pour for me, sir."

Just then another farmer spoke.

"Sir—about that money we contributed. This was different from the other times so we talked among ourselves and decided to contribute our share."

"Oh, that special tax?"

"Yes, sir. That was something that not only the the land-owning farmers but even the bean curd maker and the masseur were required to contribute to, so we couldn't just stand by and watch. All the people in the village did what they could; two ryo two bu for eighteen people, three ryo two bu for fifty-six people. So we seven, we each contributed one shu—"

"Stop it!" Senjuro, who was pouring sake for the guests, cut in. "Talking about contributions at a time like this! Just wait and see what happens when a divine wind blows up from Ise. There's no telling where those foreign ships will be blown! So don't even think about it. Drink up instead!"

"You put it very well, sir," said the farmer as he accepted Senjuro's cup.

"Master of the Upper Fushimiya!" came a loud voice from a distant seat. "I agree with you completely! What do four or five foreign ships amount to against the might of the Tokugawa?"

As the sake took effect, conversation began to lose out to old-fashioned songs like "Grinding in the Quarry." The Kiso people are good drinkers. Everyone drinks. Even the young people are served freely and old women like Ofuki are not left in the corner. When Senjuro came to sit beside Hanzo he was already in high spirits. Hanzo, too, unable to refuse the endless congratulatory cups, was soon red in the face.

Senjuro began to sing the "Kisobushi," the traditional song about how the god of Mt. Ontake once intervened to prevent a disaster in the rafting of logs down the Kiso river. Okisa, Senjuro's wife and Hanzo's stepsister, was sitting beside Otami, across from Hanzo. Her eyes narrowed as she listened to her husband's high, clear voice. He was the best singer of all present.

"This is the first time you've heard me sing, Hanzo!"

Senjuro laughed as he once more began to clap his hands to the rhythm of the song. Everyone from the farmers down to Ofuki began to sway and clap along with him. The parched voice of Naoji picked up the next verse and the whole rustic chorus joined in.

For all its being the honjin, life in Kichizaemon's home was simple, with roasted potato dumplings and the like served for winter breakfasts.

By the morning of the sixth day, the rush of guests had stilled, the farmers had all gone home, and the full day's cleanup was finished. Oman roasted the potato dumplings at the hearth as a treat for the family.

Hanzo and Otami were sleeping in the parlor and neither had yet awakened.

"The young master always used to get up so early. These last two or three days have been different."

Oman could hear the voices of the two serving girls at work by the back door. She paid no attention to their talk, wanting to let Hanzo and Otami sleep as long as possible.

Ofuki dropped in to see how the newlyweds were getting along.

"Elder sister."

"Ah! Ofuki?"

Seeing that Oman was at the hearth, Ofuki remained at ground level in the entry as she spoke.

"Elder sister. This morning I got up early and went out to dig mountain yams. Both the master and Hanzo are fond of them so I've brought you some. I suppose they're not up yet in the parlor?"

The warmth of Ofuki's heart was evident even in the straw bundle in which she had wrapped the yams. Then she stepped up to the hearthside just as she had in the days when she was Hanzo's wetnurse.

"Ofuki, you've come at a good time. Today I want to roast some gohei mochi for the newlyweds and I have the walnuts all ready. Please help me."

"I won't just help! There's nothing doing for us farmers right now. You really picked a good time to think of gohei mochi."

"And then I wanted to invite young Tsurumatsu from next door to keep them company."

"Oh, I see. Then I'll just go over to the Fushimiya. I suppose they'll be up in the parlor by the time I get back."

The unusually warm weather was still holding and it was pleasant beside the hearth. The fire glowed red beneath the soot-blackened bamboo pole and the carved wooden fish of the adjustable pothook hanging from the ceiling. When Ofuki came back, Hanzo and Otami were up and were stoking the fire with pine sticks. The potato dumplings on the grill, in their white dusting of taro flour, had cooled. Ofuki rewarmed the dumplings, grated some radish to go with them, and served the young couple.

"Otami! Come here and let's fix your hair."

Oman called Otami to the small sitting room that faced the interior court. To have accepted this girl from the Tsumago honjin so completely was unlike Oman. Otami, who as yet had barely glimpsed the adult world, felt slightly embarrassed. But she brought the comb case that had been given to her by a friend in Tsumago when her hair had first been put up at sixteen over to Oman and showed it to her.

"What do you need?"

Oman had tied up her sleeves and she placed Otami before an old-fashioned mirror stand. She unbound her hair, treating her like a doll. Otami's thick hair, still young and girlish, overflowed in Oman's hands.

"What long hair! It reminds me how my own was. When the time comes to cut this off and to shave your eyebrows—the time of the first visit home— it really makes me long for the old days. That's when you leave your girl-hood behind. It's something all women go through."

Talking as she worked, Oman grasped the oiled hair near the roots with her left hand and with her right took up the Oroku comb, a famous product of the Kiso. As the comb pressed heavily from the forehead along toward the temple, Otami narrowed her eyes and gave herself up to the hands of the woman she would have to serve for many years as a daughter-in-law.

"Why, Kuma!"

Oman repeated the name of the black cat that had come to her side. Kuma belonged to the honjin and was enjoyed by everyone except Kichizaemon's aged mother, who despised it. It was said that she resented it because every-one else's affections were monopolized by this small animal. She would even go so far as to strike the cat when Oman and the maids were not looking. As Oman was putting up Otami's hair she told her even about this, adding, "I hadn't realized grandmother was getting that old."

Soon Otami's hair was done up as befitted the bride of a honjin. The bright ornaments decorating her hair since the ceremony had all been removed, and replaced by simple lacquer combs. With her lively, apple-red cheeks, she looked like a new person in the mirror.

"Your hair is finished. Now I'll show you through the house."

Otami followed Oman on a tour of every room in the house. Accustomed as she was to the honjin in which she had been born, Otami found much that was familiar as she went through this house that stood by the side of the same road. Even the way in which every room was given a name—inner room, middle room, connecting room, retiring room—was much like home. The floor of the room called the chamber of honor was raised above the others, and with its large ornamental alcove, its paper windows with wooden grills, and its Korean-style edging on the mats showing black clouds on a white ground, it resembled all the other rooms that daimyo and important sho-gunal officials lodged in as they passed over the Kiso road.

Kuma, his bell tinkling, followed Oman and Otami wherever they went.

If they went to the window facing westward from the middle room, he went there too. This black cat had no fear of newcomers and it played with the skirts of Otami, who was still half a guest.

"Otami, come look! You can see Mt. Ena today. What about in Tsumago? Can you hear the sound of the Kiso river?"

"Yes, some days you can hear it quite clearly. But our house isn't right on the river."

"I suppose Tsumago would be like that. The river can't be heard here, but we can sometimes hear the winds roaring around Mt. Ena. It seems so close you could touch it."

"What a fine view!"

"Well, Magome is at the top of a mountain pass. You can see clear over into the next province. For that matter, on fine days you can sometimes see as far as the Ibuki range."

Otami, accustomed to living not only deep in the forest but also deep in a valley, looked out onto an open sky to the west. Everything was new and wonderful to her. Even though Tsumago and Magome were only five miles apart, there were already slight differences to be found in the pronunciation of certain words. In this village she could taste such foods as the reddish pickle known as "zuiki," which was not made in the Tsumago honjin.

A new life had begun for Hanzo and Otami.

In the afternoon, Oman, carrying the key to the storehouse and saying that she would show her all the grounds and outbuildings, was about to lead Otami out of the main house. From the hearthside came the mountain household sound of walnuts being cracked as Ofuki and the two serving girls prepared the gohei mochi.

At that moment Kichizaemon's mother hunted up her walking stick beside the entry step and proposed to accompany Oman and Otami as far as the retirement quarters. Her health was better than it had been for some time and she was again taking her meals at the main house.

The Magome honjin was divided into two buildings called the main house and the new house. The new house was located alongside the main gate, facing the highway. There was a separate entrance on the highway for the village offices and the toiya that were located on the honjin grounds. In the rear, several rooms of various sizes had been added on. These rooms looked up at the Fushimiya next door, which stood high on its stone foundations. There were extra guest rooms here which were used when travel was especially heavy. Oman pointed out to Otami the small separate sitting room with the heavy shutters that were tightly closed. From long ago it had been the custom of this household that the women would separate themselves from the family, even cooking for themselves, whenever they suffered a woman's inconveniences.

"Otami! Come see!"

Oman opened up the storeroom under the retirement quarters. Tubs of bean paste, soy sauce, pickles and the like were inside. Oman then led Otami to the door of the storehouse, opened the heavy, metal-reinforced door, and showed her everything, even the dark second floor. There the old chests that Oman had brought when she was married were standing alongside the new chests belonging to Otami.

Below the stone stairway that ran alongside the storehouse, and in front of a deep well, stood the granary and woodshed. This was the world of Sakichi. With a proprietary air, he took them to the corner next to the Fushimiya and showed them the wooden back gate. Outside it was a quiet village street, paralleling the highway in front. He also opened the wooden gate over by the pond. The honjin's Inari shrine was hidden away there among oak and holly trees.

That evening everyone in the household, from the grandmother and Kichizaemon down to Sakichi, gathered by the hearth. Tsurumatsu had come over from next door and was sitting beside Hanzo. The aroma of the gohei mochi that Ofuki was roasting on the fire filled the room.

"Tsuru, this is our bride."

Oman introduced the son of the Fushimiya to Otami and then put a skewer of gohei mochi on his tray. The rich brown colors of the roasted dumplings looked delicious. Walnuts with soy sauce were put on the trays of the bride and groom. And with this simple, heartfelt mountain meal Kichizaemon and Oman expressed their best wishes for Hanzo and Otami.

CHAPTER TWO

1

A WELCOMING PARTY had assembled at Shinjaya at the top of Jikkyoku
pass. The new priest for the Mampukuji in Magome had at last gained the
approval of the home temple in Kyoto and, having changed his name from
Chigen to Sho'un, was coming to take charge of the temple. Shobei of the
Sasaya and several others waited to greet him.

It was the time of year when the rains of the old second month come to the
mountain villages. The year was 1854 and the era name had just been
changed to Ansei. Sho'un was to have spent the previous night at the Sogenji
in Tekano village in Mino, and one of the temple attendants had been sent
with two porters to meet him there. It was time for them to be returning.

"Thank you all for coming out today."

Hanzo, representing his father, greeted the welcoming party as he arrived
from the honjin.

Old customs had not yet deteriorated and there was minute attention
given in these welcoming parties to questions of who was to go just how far
in meeting the honored individual. The village officials, for example, would
go as far as Stonemason slope in Magome while those in the priest's retinue
would go as far as Shinjaya on the outskirts of town. Hanzo paid no attention to this kind of thing. In fact, he took special pleasure in coming down
here to sit and watch the travelers who had stopped to rest their feet, the
packhorsemen leading their horses by, or even the porters, still in their sandals, entering the hearth room of the teahouse to carry out the huge Kiso-
style splitwood baskets.

Shobei, representing the farmers of Magome as assistant headman, kept
going in and out of the teahouse watching for the appearance of the priest
and his party. But at last he stopped to sit with his companions. From the
eaves of the teahouse hung an ancient signboard bearing the legend REST
STATION. On it were many plaques commemorating pilgrimages, the
mossy green of the older ones contrasting with the weathered brown wood
of the newer ones. The Basho memorial could be seen beyond the eaves. The
stone monument was black in the falling rain.

Hanzo was soon joined by Tsurumatsu of the Fushimiya, representing his father, Kimbei. He wore a serious expression.

"Master!"

"Oh, have you come too?" said Hanzo. "Look how fine the Basho memorial is! Your father built that."

"I don't remember it at all."

As Hanzo talked with Tsurumatsu, Shobei joined in. "That's right. Tsuru-sama couldn't possibly remember."

A light shower of rain passed over. There was still no sign of Sho'un and his escort, so Hanzo invited Tsurumatsu to walk through Shinjaya with him.

At the side of the road the soil had been piled high and an elm tree planted at the top. This was what was known as a "one-league marker" in the days of the post roads. Here it was used to mark the boundary between Mino and Shinano provinces. It was where one entered the Kiso road when coming from the west.

Hanzo stood for a time at the top of the pass, letting his thoughts run out toward the Mino basin where his friends Kozo and Keizo lived. Even without counting Sekigahara, where eastern and western daimyo had settled their fates in a great battle, one had to recognize that from ancient times Mino had been the meeting place of eastern and western Japan. It was not surprising that this neighboring province should be so advanced in learning, religion, trade, and the arts. Hanzo could not help envying Sho'un, who had done his training as a priest and forged his spirit in the advanced climate of Mino. Everything here in this mountain village was behind the times when compared with the neighboring province. Even the spring that came into the Kiso valley from the west each year, bringing out the buds on the zelkova along the river banks, took a full month to penetrate the hinterlands. Everything was late in arriving here.

Hanzo glanced back at Tsurumatsu.

"Nakatsugawa is just this side of that mountain. Mino is really a fine province!"

He gazed off in the direction of Mino and Owari, an expression almost of longing on his face.

When Hanzo and Tsurumatsu returned to the teahouse, a servant from the Fushimiya had just arrived.

"The master is waiting at the temple. Hasn't the priest arrived yet?"

"We've been waiting for quite a while but he's not here yet."

"But we sent two porters out with lunch."

"They will have met up with him somewhere along the way."

Hanzo awaited this priest with much the same feelings he would have had waiting for the return of anyone from western Japan. The relationships between his family and the Mampukuji were deep. It was the founder of the Aoyama line in Magome who had built the temple and given it its name. As Hanzo thought about the new priest and imagined the religion in which this person believed, he could not avoid a certain premonition of things as yet unsuspected by those around him.

This is getting a bit ahead of the story, but Hanzo was the disciple of Miyagawa Kansai of Nakatsugawa, who followed the school of National Learning of Hirata Atsutane. Hanzo had learned from this master to reject the dark Japanese middle ages. He had learned that he should separate himself from the manners imposed by the bookish and legalistic standards of conduct mandated under the Chinese learning that had ruled morality ever since the middle ages, and that at the same time he should separate himself from the Buddhist outlook. He had learned that he should return to the state of mind of the people of antiquity prior to these influences and should look upon this world once again in an open and generous way. From the ideas of the founder, Kada no Azumamaro, and from Kamo Mabuchi, Motoori Norinaga, Hirata Atsutane, and all the other masters in the line, had developed a spirit of resistance. So far as Hanzo was concerned, the lofty path of these learned ones seemed remote. Yet if he were to follow that path, he would surely find himself in conflict with this priest for whom he was waiting and with this priest's faith.

Unaware that such an heir to the honjin was waiting for him, Sho'un and his escort came up the steep slope of Jikkyoku pass and arrived at the teahouse considerably later than had been expected.

To the surprise of those who had come out to meet him, Sho'un did not seem to be travel worn. Nor did he look like a man who had spent seven long years in pilgrimage, journeying as far as the home temple in Kyoto. Among the six or seven people accompanying him, in addition to the Magome porters who had been sent out to meet him, was the old priest of the Sosenji in Nakatsugawa.

"This is quite overwhelming. I am truly grateful to all of you."

As he spoke, Sho'un untied the cords of his conical traveler's hat and bowed before Hanzo and again before Shobei.

"Is this Tsuru-san? You have grown so much that I didn't recognize you."

He bowed once again before the heir of the Fushimiya. He had come all the way from Tekano through the rains and it was as a traveler that Hanzo first saw him, drenched from the top of his hat to his sandals.

"Is this the new priest of the Mampukuji?"

Hanzo could not suppress the thought. Sho'un, barely past thirty, was young to be a resident priest. He was no more than six or seven years older than Hanzo himself.

Deciding that he wanted to rest at the teahouse, Sho'un began to talk about his trips to Kyoto and other places. He had been in Kyoto on the seventeenth, in Nagoya on the sixth, and then, after three days on the Mino road, had spent one night at the Sogenji in Tekano—he spoke of all this in the tone peculiar to Zen priests. After spending nearly an hour with Sho'un, Hanzo found that he gave an impression of learning and discipline that could not be despised.

Then they set out from Shinjaya for the main station at Magome. On the way Sho'un remarked to Shobei, "The road is so much better that I hardly recognize it."

"The lord of Owari will be going to Edo this spring. Haven't you heard?"

"I did hear something about it."

"Road work is being done from Shinjaya up to the summit at Toge. The officials have already come out from Owari to assign lodgings. Everybody is busy with the roads."

Tokugawa Yoshikatsu, the lord of Owari, would be going to Edo at the beginning of the third month. The welcoming party continued to talk about the highway as they walked, and eventually they arrived at Stonemason slope, where they were met by the post station officials. The toiya Kyudayu, Gisuke of the Masudaya, Shinshichi of the Horaiya, and Yojiemon of the Umeya, all in formal dress and carrying umbrellas against the rain, greeted Sho'un and his party.

It was the custom then that when a new resident priest came to the village, he did not go immediately to the temple but went to the honjin first. As one who had renounced worldly things, Sho'un did not feel entirely comfortable with being accorded such a welcome, but he had decided to leave everything up to Hanzo's father. Thus it was in a room at the honjin that Sho'un received his final instructions from the old priest of Nakatsugawa and changed out of his traveling clothes. When he set out from Kichizaemon's house in a litter preceded by baggage chests and a ceremonial umbrella, the children of the village swarmed after the spectacle all the way to the temple path.

The Mampukuji was on a small hill. It looked down through the great cedars in the graveyard outside the temple gate toward the shingled roofs of the houses lined along the opposite slope. Sho'un's return to his temple began when he passed through the gate on his way to the priest's residence, where it concluded with an act of obeisance. After a light repast of boiled noodles, the temple staff from the neighboring villages, the Magome officials, and those who had helped in one way or another all withdrew to go their separate ways.

"Reverend sir . . ."

It was the temple servant of many years' standing who now came to Sho'un's side to report on what had happened during his master's absence.

"You may want to express your appreciation to Kimbei of the Fushimiya. He looked in frequently while you were gone and set up a big new drum in the main sanctuary. He also had the roofs rethatched. It took five hundred and twenty bundles.—Well, where should I begin? In the year of the big windstorm, the bell tower went down and again it was Kimbei who took care of the repairs . . ."

Sho'un nodded.

To his eyes, after his travels, the temple buildings seemed so small that he could hardly believe this was actually the Mampukuji of Magome. Although the retired priest from a neighboring village had come over to look after things during his long absence, the place still seemed run down. In the priest's quarters, to welcome him home, a portrait of Bodhidharma had been hung on the wall that his predecessor must have stared at for six long years.

"There are no greater or lesser temples, only greater or lesser priests."

Sho'un recited the proverb to lift his spirits. He looked around. There were any number of things calling for his attention. What was the condition of the family registers which were maintained by the temple? And the condition of the name tablets of the deceased in the memorial hall? When he began to count them up, there were so many things to do that it was difficult to know where to begin. Moreover, the approaching anniversary of the founding of the temple, with its collection of offerings, could not be forgotten. He thought it over. At any rate, nothing could be done until tomorrow. He considered measures to ensure that he would rise early every morning and decided that he himself would sound the eighteen strokes of the morning bell rather than leaving it to his two disciples or the temple servant.

It was still raining the next morning. Sho'un got out of bed as night was ending and washed his face with the cold pure water that ran down from the mountain. Leaving the morning drum and prayers for later, he set off for the bell tower. From there the peaks of the Ena range that seemed to command all the villages of the region could not yet be made out, but he could dimly hear the faint crowing of roosters from the distant side of the valley. The great holly tree loomed dark before the main sanctuary. At that moment the clear voice of the great bell sounded, shattering the calm of the morning air. It boomed as Sho'un swung the heavy log against it with all his strength. The peal sounded from valley to valley, hurtling over the fields and echoing off toward the still unstarted village waterwheel, and as far as the half-asleep stables.

2

One morning Hanzo awoke beside his wife to hear the sound of men and horses moving along the highway. He looked over toward Otami asleep beside him. Her face was still girlish, as if reluctant to awaken on this sweet and peaceful spring dawn. Taking care not to disturb her, Hanzo got up, opened the door of the parlor, and looked out.

Snow, rare at the beginning of the third month, was piled up outside the door. It had been warmer than usual since the beginning of the year, but now it had snowed. The wall of the forecourt faced directly onto the road and from beyond it came the sound of men and horses treading the snow. Listening carefully, Hanzo realized it was the vanguard of the lord of Owari's procession, for which they had been preparing.

"Here comes the advance baggage of Owari," he said to himself.

The money apportioned to each of the post stations to subsidize this progress had come to forty-one ryo for Magome alone. The money had been placed in Kimbei's care and from the size of the allotment it could easily be imagined that the progress to Edo would be carried out on a lavish scale. Hanzo had heard some of the details from his father and he found it impossible to stay in his room. He went to the kitchen to wash his face and looked out again through the falling snow. Then he went out.

At the meeting room he saw that the work of moving the procession had been going on since early morning. Kyudayu had been the first of the officials to leave his house and rush out into the snow. Beyond the wave after wave of porters still coming up the slope Hanzo could hear the approaching bells of the packhorses. It was still early and the breath came steaming white out of the horses' nostrils. From time to time one would whinny bravely.

The American ships that had menaced Edo bay in the sixth month of the previous year had been standing offshore again since the first month. It was rumored that the original force of four ships had grown to eight or nine, which were now demanding that the ports be opened. The Tokugawa government could not deal with the situation by military means. Daimyo from all over Japan were gathering in Edo castle to consider the momentous question of the opening of trade. Hanzo recalled that on the twenty-fifth day of the first month Owari had sent a great cannon and twenty-two chests of military supplies over this highway to Edo; there had also been twenty-one manloads of smaller equipment. Hanzo watched as this new procession of porters and packhorses passed before him.

When Hanzo returned to the house, Kichizaemon was relaxing before the fire with his morning tea.

"Was this morning's freight all from Owari, father?"

"That's right."

"How many days will it take for the freight to pass through?"

"Oh, about three days, I suppose. The last time the foreign ships came, everyone in Edo and the provinces got very upset. But there will be no fighting this time. It's just a great nuisance for the lord of Owari."

Both father and son felt close to the lord of Owari, and not only because he was master of the Kiso valley. During a trip to Nagoya Kichizaemon had been brought into the presence of the lord, and it brought joy to Hanzo's heart that this family had been lords of Owari ever since the time of Lord Minamoto Kei, the compiler of *A Treasury of Deities* and the *Classified Annals of Japan*. He thought of this work of Minamoto Kei in the same way as he did that of Tokugawa Mitsunari of Mito, who had initiated the vast *History of Great Japan* and enabled the priest Keichu to compile his *Commentaries on the Man'yoshu*. Contemplating them, Hanzo would find his thoughts returning to that pristine age before Confucianism had come to Japan. Hanzo's regard for his lord was similar to that of the young men of Mito for theirs.

"If I stay back in these mountains much longer, I'm going to go out of my mind. Everyone here talks about such petty things, but this is just not that kind of time."

Otami came in. Still in the spring of her eighteenth year, she had shaved her eyebrows since returning from her first visit to her former home. This had changed the shape of her face but she had only become more girlish.

"I've brewed some of the mimosa tea that you like. What are you so thoughtful about?"

"Me? I'm not thinking about anything at all. I've just been sitting here. It must be about a hundred days that you and I have been together. No, it's not just a hundred days, it's been four full months. I was trying to think of what I've done during that time. I cut some tobacco for father and I looked after mother when she was sick. That's about all."

Hanzo, unable to remain intoxicated with the joys of the newlywed, had to tell Otami of his grief over the neglect of his studies.

"I was just going to mention the date," said Otami, "but you were so buried in thought. Isn't it already the third month? But you can't do anything until the lord of Owari goes through, anyway, can you?"

The beginning of married life had been painful in some ways for Otami, barely out of girlhood as she was. But by the time marriage matured into a new pleasure, she had begun to spend most of her days in the parlor.

After a while Hanzo turned toward Otami. He sat with his legs extended in front of him and his hands flat on the tatami behind, and watched her as she told him about the dolls for the girl's festival that she had brought back from Tsumago. Her striped homespun kimono, worn long in the fashion of the day, was quite becoming. There was even something womanly in the faint blue of her shaved eyebrows. But it was Otami's hands that Hanzo found most pleasing; those girlish hands, white as snow. He took pleasure in gazing on those hands whenever they were alone together.

Suddenly she burst into tears.

"Oh, isn't that what you're always talking about? When you talk about scholarship with me, I don't understand a thing. And I can't do things the way your mother does. There was no one in Tsumago to teach me!"

Otami could not stop weeping. Hanzo was astonished. As he went to comfort her, she pleaded, "Teach me . . . !" and buried her face in his lap.

"Otami, please look in on grandmother," Hanzo said, sending her off to the old woman, who had just fallen ill, so that he could recover his own spirits.

It had long been his practice to take out the books by Hirata Atsutane that he always kept near and read them whenever he felt discouraged. *The Pillar of the Soul, The Jeweled Sleeve-Cords, The Essence of the Way of Antiquity*—he never tired of them no matter how often he read them. He felt a fondness for the books themselves, for their large, pale indigo covers sewn with old-fashioned purple thread. From collections of Atsutane's writings such as *The Tranquil Cave* and his attack on Chinese scholarship entitled *A Survey of Western Learning* to the long account of his life at Ibukinoya that went out of print after only three hundred copies, Hanzo's books were the embodiment of the passionate commitment with which he had sought them out. Atsutane had died in 1843, the fourteenth year of the Tempo era, and had never known of the Black Ships. If only he were alive now—young men like Hanzo had to hide their thoughts about what he might have done.

New forces were quickening. Movements completely different in character and in their implications were appearing almost simultaneously. Yoshida Shoin, a man from Hagi in Choshu, had tried to leave the country illegally and failed, and there was a rumor that Sakuma Shozan of Matsushiro in Shinano province had been jailed as a result. It was no longer unusual to hear of things like the young man of Ogaki in Mino province who had set out for distant Nagasaki determined to acquire Western learning.

"Black Ships!"

Repeating these words to himself, Hanzo stood near the shoji, illuminated by the light reflecting off the snow outside. He tried to imagine what it must be like in distant Edo bay with eight or nine ships standing offshore. He felt keenly how difficult it must be for the lord of Owari to be setting out for the capital at a time like this.

The great procession passed through Magome on the fourth day of the third month using seven hundred thirty porters from the Kiso and one thousand seven hundred seventy porters from the assisting districts in Ina—twenty-five hundred men in all. At the station, the packhorse contingent alone amounted to one hundred eighty men and one hundred eighty animals.

On that day, the priest Sho'un was still not fully settled in at the Mampu-kuji after his long absence. The fierce thunderstorm of the previous night had subsided and the sky had cleared after midnight. The passage of men and horses began at dawn.

When they heard that the lord of Owari was passing through Magome on his way to Edo, the assistant priest and the other members of the temple staff could not remain still. People in the neighborhood were rushing down the path that ran through the graveyard below the temple on the opposite hill-side so that they could watch the progress of this great lord.

"You might as well go out to greet the lord too," said Sho'un, dismissing his disciples and his servant.

During the time he had been away, Sho'un had occasionally succumbed to feelings of great discouragement. Once in his lodging in Kyoto he had sent a letter to Kimbei of the Fushimiya asking for more money; the letter had been very difficult to write. As a result he had come back from his travels with the feeling that, having returned safely, he would try to be of service to the people of the village. He wanted to educate the children of the poor farmers. But how uneasy the atmosphere was! He wondered how a priest could, in the midst of all this upheaval, give guidance to the poor and to the young of the village.

"Osho-sama."

It was the old woman who did the laundry for the temple. A mountain woman with a sickle stuck in her sash, straw sandals on her feet, and big, strong hands like a man's, she had come in through the back door looking for him.

"I thought you would be out."

"Of course you did."

"I was just out in the garden, but there isn't a bit of artemisia for the festival cakes. They say he'll be passing through at the fifth hour. He'll ride his horse up to the front of the Sasaya and then walk to the honjin. You should go out and see him too."

"Oh, I'll just stay and look after things here."

"But why should you stay in the temple on a day like this?"

"That's just the way it is with a priest. I don't even go to see my relatives unless I have business there. I look after the temple. That's enough."

The woman laughed. The customary black stain on her teeth had nearly faded away. She stood talking in the courtyard for a while and then left through the back door.

As the fifth hour approached, the sound of footsteps rushing past the front of the temple ceased. There was not a sound to be heard. All outcry was stilled.

The bright warm sun had swelled the buds of the flowers in the valley earlier than in most years. It was the season when the lord of Owari, having taken a fresh horse at Shinjaya, might well hope to find himself traveling among the blossoms of the mountain cherries along the Kiso road.

Without even leaving the temple, Sho'un could see quite clearly in his mind Kyudayu acting as the advance guide, the procession itself, and the local people whispering among themselves about what a splendid thing it is to be able to see their lord. He could see the honjin and his son reverentially greeting the lord of Owari in their own home.

The priest's residence was utterly quiet. It seemed altogether deserted. Sho'un, in solitude, continued to sit before the portrait of Bodhidharma that hung on the ancient wall.

3

Processions of daimyo and other high officials passed through Magome one after another like waves of cloud in a storm front. None was as huge as the progress of the lord of Owari, but from the west came the daimyo of Tosa, Izumo, and Sanuki, to name just a few. From the east came the procession of the Nagasaki deputy, Nagai Iwanojo. And around the middle of the fifth month, the steward of Higo, Nagaoka Kemmotsu, came up the highway accompanied by eight hundred men carrying muskets on their shoulders and field rations at their hips.

Then stories came in from Kyoto about a fire that had broken out in the Sendo palace and burned all the way to Nishijin. It was even worse than the great fire of the Temmei era in the 1780's.

Although the excitement had filled Hanzo and the other young people with curiosity, the village elders' only concern was to keep some degree of control over the situation. Since the arrival of the Black Ships the daimyo had passed back and forth at an alarming rate, requiring great numbers of porters to be brought in from the assisting districts in Ina. The undesirable consequences had become manifest in a great increase in drinking and gambling. Shortly before the Fukushima horse fair, Kichizaemon, with the support of the post station officials, announced a strict prohibition of gambling and had the word passed to each and every villager.

"Those were good times."

Whenever Kimbei and Kichizaemon got together, they were likely to talk about the past. For these neighbors with a shared experience of the highway, it was hard to forget the time when the Tokugawa regime had still been secure. They recalled those days with pleasure and longing—the days of the building of the Basho memorial in Shinjaya, the linked verse session afterwards, and the time they had each eaten thirty sparrows and three bowls of tea-over-rice in the inner room of the Horaiya. For these two, their homes no longer seemed really like home. The road brought endless and painful problems. Without being able to entertain at leisure the visitors who came over from Tsumago for the night, or to go off themselves to the festivals in Ochiai in Mino or to see the plays in Nakatsugawa, staying two or three days at the homes of friends and relatives—without these pastimes, things just did not feel right for these two.

In meetings at the honjin a consensus developed to make this year's festival plays in Magome something special. The assistant headman, Shobei, agreed. A new stage had been completed in the tenth month of the previous year, and from the collection of suitable trees to be donated for lumber for the new stage to the raising of the stage itself, even to the provision of refreshments at the ceremony marking its completion, everything had been due to the efforts of Kimbei. Constructed on the back hill near the Mampukuji, the stage was ready for the delights of the autumn festivals.

Festival plays had been part of the Kiso for a very long time, and the local people had a lively interest in Kabuki and other theatrical performances. The most highly developed places for theatre then were in southern Shinano and Mino, with Iida in the immediate vicinity and Nagoya in the distance. It was not at all unusual for Edo actors like Ichikawa Ebizo to appear on the Iida stage. The theatre lovers here in the mountains, whenever they heard of such an event, would set out with their entire households, including even the maids, to cross the Odaira pass and attend the theatre. Even for those in Hirose and Araragi who had to cross through the deep forests, Iida was not too far to go to see a good performance.

Kimbei was one such enthusiast. Unable to wait for the autumn festivals, he suddenly absented himself from the village in the intercalary seventh month. While Kichizaemon and Hanzo wondered about their whereabouts, Kimbei and his son made a quick tour through Toyokawa, Nagoya, Komaki, Ontake, and Oi. The stories they brought back aroused the envy of the local theatre lovers. At the Wakamiya Theatre in Nagoya, Ichikawa Danjuro VIII had just ended an engagement, and in the Tachibana district, Mimasu Daigoro, Seki Sanjuro, Otani Hirouemon, and their entire troupe, also from Edo, had been performing.

As the ninth month approached, the young people of the village began rehearsing for the plays. Eleven people came from Aramachi to build a road to the new stage. At last the time had come when there would be a use for the prop swords, both long and short, that Kimbei had long since provided for his beloved son. He had decided to put on the stage not only Tsurumatsu but Senjuro of the Upper Fushimiya as well, hoping that this might raise Senjuro's spirits. Kimbei was one who thought nothing of spending one bu two shu for a good wig for his son.

The program was set: *Shiki Sambaso. Goban Taiheiki. Shiraishibanashi* in the number three position as the most important play. *Kokura Shikishi.* And *Modori-kago* to end. Senjuro was given roles in *Shiki Sambaso* and *Kokura Shikishi* while Tsurumatsu took the role of Naniwa Jirosaku in *Modori-kago.* When Kimbei went to watch the rehearsals for the first time, enough actors had somehow been found among the young people of the village to put on this program.

That year's autumn festival brought unusual activity in other villages as well. They were all in virtual competition. If Magome was making a special effort, Yamaguchi and Yubunezawa were not going to be outdone. The festival performances in Nakatsugawa were held a month before the ones in Magome, and Kimbei rushed off with Senjuro, Kichizaemon, and Oman to see them. The frightful dustiness of the highway in this season went unnoticed in the joyous festival spirit.

Meanwhile, two packhorse loads of costumes that had been ordered arrived. The young people working hard at rehearsals so as not to be outshone by the other villages decided to ask Umezo from Iida for the dances, Jihei from Nagoya for the songs, and Nakamura Kagizo to play the samisen. The pleasures of the festival were not confined to the festival day itself but were to be found in each day of preparation. That the Joruri musicians and chanters were already in the village—or that the people in charge of makeup had to rush off to Nagoya—just to exchange such news brought joy to the village girls.

Of course, Kimbei could not remain still in the midst of all this. He spent every day at the stage, even setting up the grandstands. At the Fushimiya, Otama was completely taken up with preparations for Tsurumatsu's first stage appearance. A relative from Nakatsugawa even came to help make the costumes.

"It's a fine day."

From the front of his shop, Kimbei gazed at the sky above the highway as he greeted the twenty-fourth day of the ninth month. Every year this day marked the beginning of the festival plays. Early in the morning Kimbei called in Naoji the hairdresser and had his hair dressed in a style appropriate to his age. The oldest of the village officials, having served as village elder long enough to reach his fifty-eighth year, Kimbei felt quite jubilant as his hair was drawn up tight with a white cord to form the base of his topknot. His jaw was tinged with blue after an immaculate shave and he seemed much younger than usual.

"Tsuru, perform well for me!"

"Yes, father, you don't have to worry."

Just then Senjuro appeared. Kimbei looked at his nephew and said, "Do well, Senjuro. I'm counting on it. You'll be making the first appearance of the day in *Shiki Sambaso*."

Senjuro had come up to Magome from the family seat in Mino to establish the Upper Fushimiya. On festival days like this he was lively and cheerful, as if he were a different person. He seemed far too handsome to be living in a mountain village and his pleasure-loving nature did not fit very well the role of assistant to a brewer and retailer of sake.

"Yes. Well, today I'm going to give it all I've got. I'm going to dance right through the stage floor."

That was the way Senjuro talked.

Before the performance began, Kimbei inspected the grandstands and then went to the dressing room. He watched his nephew don a tall, striped hat and take up a cluster of bells to complete the splendid Sambaso costume. When his son came out in *Modori-kago*, dressed as a palanquin bearer and carrying a staff, a cry of "Fushimiya!" went up from the stands. Kimbei was deeply moved.

"Really, that's the kind of fool I am."

Kimbei said this to himself as he rushed in and out the gate of the Fushimiya that was marked as the entrance to a sake shop by its large ball made of cedar boughs.

The three days of performance were well received. Even though the finance office in Fukushima had refused to grant a short-term loan to cover the plays' expenses, the official they sent to guard against any possible "perversion of customs" went home satisfied after toasting the success of the performances.

The plays dominated fireside conversations for some time. After all, the festival came only once a year. All the villagers could talk about was the splendor in every respect of Senjuro's Sambaso: his looks, his movements, his costume. And how moving had been the twelve-year-old Tsurumatsu's appearance as Naniwa Jirosaku! Even as the time for the radish harvest drew near, the talk still had not died out.

The fourth day of the eleventh month was the day following the winter solstice. This eventful year had proceeded without a pause through the Ebisu rituals for prosperity up to the time for celebrating the winter solstice. Then there was an earthquake. A mere forty days after everyone in the village, young and old, had decorated their houses and celebrated the season, the earth began to tremble. It went on and on until it seemed it would never stop.

At Kichizaemon's house, everyone rushed out to the bamboo grove in the back. Oman and Otami, one barefoot, the other in stocking feet, had to be assisted by Hanzo until they could reach the others behind the woodshed. By that time the grandmother was no longer with them. She had lived seventy-five years and now, without seeing Otami tie on the maternal sash in the fifth month of her pregnancy, or seeing a son born to Otami, or seeing it die almost immediately, without seeing this joy and sorrow that had come almost together, she lay in the graveyard of the Mampukuji since the fourth month.

"Don't wander away! Everyone please stay together!"

Oman was worrying about Kichizaemon as she spoke. Otami, very pale, stood at her side; barely thirty days had elapsed since she had given birth. Each time the shocks started again, everyone down to Sakichi and the two maids would exchange terrified looks.

The grove was firmly laced together by the tough roots of the green bamboo. Once there Hanzo was able to pull himself together. When he and Kichizaemon set out to check the neighborhood they found that almost everyone had fled the buildings in the immediate vicinity of the honjin. They were particularly concerned about their neighbors in the Fushimiya, but Otama and Tsurumatsu had already withdrawn to the hay barn below the village stage. Kimbei, however, self-possessed even in the midst of the tumult, had remained behind with a manservant to pay off a courier who had come from Kyoto. He was recording the transaction in his account books.

"It's just been too warm this year right from the start. I kept thinking something was strange."

As Kichizaemon spoke, Kimbei nodded in agreement.

"That's right. Starting the year's work in straw sandals just doesn't happen in the Kiso. And then, when the camelias on the other side of the temple road were coming into bloom and it was time to make the third-day cakes, the artemesia was already in full leaf. All that must have been telling us an earthquake was coming. Anyway, Kichizaemon, we had just finished Senjuro's initiation and, thanks to you, he's become an assistant headman. I can now face my ancestors. I was putting away the things from the celebration when the earthquake hit."

"They say the earthquake at Zenkoji in the year of the monkey was big, but I don't think it was anything like this. Not even the earthquake in the sixth month of the year of the tiger was this bad."

"No, this earthquake is unprecedented. Absolutely."

Kichizaemon and Kimbei next began urgent consultations on how to gather all the old people and women and children in one place and how to guard the village against fire and looting. The village officials decided that the gathering point would be in front of the toiya and the Fushimiya. Then they arranged for a subscription to be taken up in the village. The mountain people, alarmed by upheavals in heaven and earth, added up the coming of the American ships to Edo and Uraga since spring, the Russian ships that had appeared from time to time along the coast from Nagasaki to Osaka, the fire in the Sendo palace, and now this earthquake, and saw them all as portents of still greater change to come. No one slept much that night. Hanzo, concerned about Otami's condition and thinking about the people spending the night in the bamboo groves or out in the fields, waited for the sun to rise.

The next day was cloudy and the aftershocks showed no sign of stopping. Groups of young people were continually forming and dispersing in front of the toiya and the Fushimiya. There were rumors that the earthquake had been even worse in Oi and Nakatsugawa in Mino and that things were about the same in Tsumago as here. No one seemed to know where these reports came from but everyone seemed to have a story to contribute. It was the young people who reported that there had been great landslides on the far slopes of Mt. Ena, Mt. Kaore, and Mt. Kamazawa and that they could be seen from Nenoue. The joy and excitement of the recent festival, the talk about the performances, all were now swept away in the turmoil of the earthquake.

The aftershocks went on day after day for another six days. Nightwatchmen were on duty at the post station, eighteen at a time, to guard the highway and the back streets. A representative of the village was dispatched to Nagoya to offer prayers at the Atsuta shrine. In the meantime, reports drifting in made it clear that the earthquake had been particularly severe in the Kansai. A tidal wave had hit near Okazaki on the Tokaido and the guard station at Arai had been washed away.

By the time a courier reached the village with a report from the man who went to Atsuta, even the strange threatening clouds had cleared from the sky and things were once again fairly quiet. Kichizaemon ordered the attendants at the meeting room to distribute the prayer cards from the Atsuta shrine to every household in the village.

Kimbei came to the honjin to say, "It looks as though we're going to be all right from now on, Kichizaemon. Tomorrow is the tenth day of the eleventh month. I thought I would hold Buddhist services and serve tea. I would like for you to attend if you have the time."

"You have thought of just the right thing. Buddhist services would certainly be deeply felt and effective at a time like this."

Kimbei then took out a letter and showed it to Kichizaemon. It was an informal note from the priest Sho'un, who was ill. It began with an apology for having to send a disciple in his place to preside over the services in the Fushimiya and then went on to say that he hoped even such a person as he might render some service to the village in these extraordinary times. Returning from his long pilgrimage with that thought uppermost in his mind, he therefore especially regretted being unable to serve on this occasion. The walls had come down in the library and elsewhere and severe cracking had occurred in the storehouse; fortunately, no one had been injured. He sent his regards to the master of the honjin.

"He's really conscientious, that priest. Really conscientious."

"Well, anyway, he's just back from six years of pilgrimage. He's probably worn out from all that traveling," replied Kichizaemon.

"How is your family?"

"Everyone is still out back in the bamboo grove. Please come with me and talk to Oman."

Kichizaemon led Kimbei past the badly damaged storehouse. Beyond the woodshed, they came to the bamboo grove, dense and dark. A temporary hut with shutters for walls had been erected there to protect the most valuable things that had been removed from the house.

"I feel so sorry for Otami," said Kimbei as he greeted Oman. "To experience a big earthquake like this just a year after coming over as a bride from Tsumago is just too much."

"Is everyone all right at your place?" replied Oman.

"Why, yes, thank you. We've just got one peculiar one. I guess you couldn't say he's all right. It's our servant, Genkichi. In all this uproar he keeps disappearing somewhere. I don't like it. It's too much like the Americans."

"Like the Americans!" Kichizaemon laughed. "That's a good one. Leave it to Kimbei to find the right word!"

While they were talking, Okisa of the Upper Fushimiya came to see her parents and Ofuki, the old nurse, came to look in on Hanzo and Otami, each coming from her own place of refuge. Everyone there, including the lowliest servants, without distinctions of status, shared the same food and worried about the adequacy of each other's clothes. It was a scene that could only take place at the time of a disaster in this feudal age with its rigorous distinctions between superior and subordinate.

On the thirteenth day of the eleventh month, the people of the village at last returned to their homes. It was the tenth day after the first tremors. Throughout that time, Hanzo had worked the night watches, made inspections, and delivered assistance to the destitute in the villages. He had borrowed woodblock illustrations of the Osaka earthquake from the Fushimiya and showed them to Kichizaemon, but the truth of the earthquake was far worse than the rumors. The center had been between Yamada in Ise province and Toba in Shima. Along the Tokaido, the number of fires and devastated buildings was beyond counting. From Miya to Yoshiwara only two stations had escaped serious damage.

Then the first cold of the year came to the mountains and a great snow began to fall on the evening of the sixteenth, plunging everything into silence. The next day a wind came up and the weather improved a bit, but there was another heavy snowfall that night. In all about two and a half feet of snow fell. The shingled roofs of the mountain houses were buried under the desolate snow.

"I just don't think the year is going right, Kyudayu."

"Well, how about this? Let's have a festival in Magome to start the year over again."

"That's a good idea."

"I've been hearing about villages all along the highway that are planning to have another celebration, and some of them already have their pine trees up."

"Let's get the elders and the assistant headmen together to discuss it."

This conversation between the honjin Kichizaemon and the toiya Kyudayu took place in the spring following the earthquake. It was the beginning of the third month in the second year of Ansei, 1855.

Rumors. Only rumors. Yet it was true that this third month of the year was inauspicious and that throughout the land there were frightful epidemics, windstorms, cloudbursts, and famine. If the year could be started anew by means of a special festival, it might be possible to escape further disasters. Such were the stories that came drifting up the highway and Kyudayu had spoken out because of them.

The results of the meeting of the post station officials were presently made known to the villagers. On the third day of the third month, the year would begin again in a special observance. On that day and the preceding one, all work in the fields would be suspended. The effect of the rumors had been widespread; the sound of glutenous rice being pounded for the cakes for this untimely New Year's celebration could be heard throughout the village. Pines began to appear before all the doorways. The largest pines, heavily decorated, were placed before the honjin, and the tenant farmers attached to it now approached with a special air in their daily comings and goings. One of them came up to Kichizaemon, wringing his gnarled hands.

"Sir, I want to ask you something. If we have a second New Year this year, will we all be two years older? Everyone in the village has been asking about this and they are all upset. At our place, you see, we have a daughter who was born at the end of last year. She is two years old now. Is she going to be three after this festival?"

"Wait a minute."

If one counted the way this farmer suggested, Kichizaemon would become fifty-eight and Kimbei would be sixty at a single leap.

"No, you've got it all wrong. Isn't it just a simple redoing of New Year's?" Kichizaemon replied with the utmost seriousness.

So in the end they celebrated the new year twice in one year. It seemed completely unreal. The more enthusiastic immediately starting talking about preparing New Year's dishes and drinking the New Year's wine, and by the day before the festival they had already achieved a New Year's mood. On the appointed day, everyone in the village made a visit to the tutelary deity at the Suwa shrine and then assembled before the honjin gate. Kichizaemon, smiling, in his formal dress of hemp, with his big nose and his quiet mouth, looked every inch the master of Magome station as he received everyone's greetings that morning.

"Odanna! Happy New Year!"

"And to you, too!"

All this provided only a temporary respite.

On the seventh day of the tenth month of that year, the second year of Ansei, came the great earthquake in Edo. Here in the mountains they learned of it from a courier bound for Hikone. He reported that seventy percent of the heart of Edo had been smashed. Great fires had broken out, burning nearly everything. The people in the provinces were moved by these reports, coming as they did less than a year after they themselves had suffered an earthquake. Even in distant Magome a considerable shock had been felt. It was so severe at first that everyone had rushed outside. Now they understood that the weak aftershocks they had felt night and day for some time afterward had been coming over two hundred miles from Edo.

After a time the effects of the Edo earthquake could be seen in the refugees appearing on the highway. Some in the village gave various things to those who had been burned out in Edo; others only watched them pass by. Toward the end of the month, Kichizaemon called his household together and spread out the mass-produced illustrations of the Edo disaster that had been sent to him. Frightful scenes from the brushes of ukiyo-e artists like Ichiosai Kunichika and Yoshitsuna revealed a living hell. In a view of the main thoroughfare in Shitaya, looking toward the pagoda of Kinryusan, smoke and flames could be seen rising over the streets in six places. Crowds of fleeing people formed a solid mass from Shihogura in Kyobashi to Takebashi. A scene of the Fukagawa district showed the homes of samurai and townsmen all aflame. There was a fire watch tower wreathed in smoke that was particularly horrifying. They could scarcely bear to look at it.

Men like Fujita Toko and Toda Hoken of Mito had perished in the Edo earthquake. To the young men of the time, there was probably no place that was as exciting as Mito. They were inspired by the work being done in ethics and history at the Mito research institute and by the scholarship of the Mito academy. The ruling family, moreover, had produced in succession Mitsukuni, Harutoshi, and Nariaki, each of whom had demonstrated that while theirs was one of the three great houses of the Tokugawa, the Mito line had firmly maintained its righteousness and propriety. Fujita Toko, the author of *Hitachi Sash* and *Poems That Changed the World,* had always seemed to Hanzo to be one of the seminal figures in Mito. Hanzo still cherished the feelings he had had when reciting Toko's *Song of the Righteous Mind.* Now Fujita Toko had fallen just when the unrest in Mito was beginning to have serious implications; the curtain was rising on a confrontation between those who would drive the barbarians out and those who would open the ports.

"If only Master Toko had not died," Hanzo thought. He viewed the death of Fujita Toko has a great loss to Mito.

At last the time for the Koshin festival with its all-night vigil came to the village. Looking up at the clear wintery sky, Hanzo felt that his twenty-fifth year had also passed emptily, spent in standing alongside an isolated stretch of the highway.

4

The third year of Ansei, 1856, was the year Sho'un opened the temple school at the Mampukuji.

As the year following the great Edo earthquake began, the tales of disaster died out and the refugees disappeared from the highway. It felt somehow as if a great storm had passed on. The earthquake that had struck Edo, the heart of Japan at the time, had transformed the atmosphere of feudal society. It seemed as though all of the uneasiness that had been in the air since the arrival of the Black Ships in the sixth year of Kaei, 1853, had been submerged in the shock of the earthquake.

It was true that the effect of the lord of Owari's journey to Edo remained unclear. Already there were rumors that the port of Shimoda would be opened and that the roju or shogunal council was sitting with folded arms throughout the dispute over the beginning of trade. In the Kiso, however, the upheavals had subsided, order had gradually been restored along the highway, and the price of rice had even come down.

When three officials from Fukushima came to announce a survey of all the villages, everything still showed the effects of the recent earthquake. The local people, after preparing miso for the new year, were looking forward to a good harvest and had even begun discussing the planting of cedar saplings.

Hanzo now reached a turning point in his life. In the third month of the year, he found himself holding a baby girl, with Otami at his side. Okume was the child's name and in her tiny movements, all so new to him, and in her pleading cries, her innocent yawns, her unselfconscious smiles, he discovered the deep satisfactions of fatherhood. This new experience turned him away from his preoccupation with distant things and opened his eyes to what was near at hand.

"I just can't go on this way."

Thinking this whenever he was brought up short by his loneliness and lack of freedom in these remote mountains, Hanzo would stare helplessly at his surroundings.

"Say, you ox drovers from Toge! Nothing has come up from Nakatsugawa. What's the matter?"

Kyudayu stood squarely in the middle of the road as he accosted one of the drovers.

"We seem to be taking a holiday."

"Don't try to be funny!"

"Well, what do I know about it? Just recently I got word not to move any freight for Kadoju. I don't know why, but since it's an order I have to follow it. I can't do anything else."

"What a mess! If you fellows don't bring the freight up, how are you going to eat? Ask the head drover about that the next time you see him!"

From Shinjaya in the west to Sakurazawa in the east, freight was carried over the Kiso road not only by horses but by oxen too. At first Hanzo did not understand what the problem was. He knew that the drovers had organized and were boycotting Kadoju, the toiya in Nakatsugawa who had handled the freight up to now. He also knew that the master of Kadoju, Kadoya Jubei, had come up from Nakatsugawa to ask Kichizaemon to intercede and that Kimbei had gone back and forth between Jubei and the head of the ox drovers as a mediator. As a result of these discussions, Kimbei had decided that the horses and oxen should move as before and that the sources of both parties' dissatisfaction should be investigated and corrected.

Tampering with the bills of lading and holding out on freight payments— malfeasance on the part of the toiya of the old post roads was usually concealed in these areas. Kadoju's had been an extreme case. During the eighth month of the year, beginning on the day of the opening of the autumn pastures, Kimbei had tried for three solid days to mediate the dispute but with little success. Representatives of Kadoju had come up from Nakatsugawa, and Risaburo, the head drover, had come from Toge. The ox drovers from twelve other villages were allied with him. Heisuke, the assistant headman from Toge, could not stand by and watch so he plunged into the quarrel also, but to no avail.

Hanzo emerged from the gate of the honjin and began to walk toward Toge. There was a flume full of fresh pure water running along the bank beside the road. Hanzo was fond of this back road because of the fine shade trees along the way. Here he met Risaburo coming from Toge.

"You fellows have really started something, haven't you."

"Master Hanzo. So you've heard about it, too."

"Heisuke has been saying you ox drovers are giving him a lot of trouble."

"Now you're making fun of me."

Hanzo recalled what he had heard from the assistant headman from Toge. Heisuke had told him of Kimbei's position—that since people had come all the way from Nakatsugawa to deal with the situation, they should discuss it in good faith, draw up an agreement, and handle things from here on so that there would be no further abuses or injustice.

"No, please sit down. I might want to speak to my father about this."

The ox drover squatted on his heels, yielding an old stump at the foot of a cedar tree to Hanzo, and tore at the grass along the roadside as he talked.

"This trouble didn't start just yesterday or the day before. It's been at least four or five years since the toiya down on the coast and at the transfer point in Imado, and even the shippers too, agreed that they wanted to stop using toiya like Kadoju and rely more on the others. Since then Kadoju's way of doing things has become completely untrustworthy and both of the head drovers in Toge got angry. That's how it all happened. The master of the Fushimiya seems to have decided that if he intercedes everything will work out, but it's not going to be that easy. It's not just the ox drovers in Toge. It's also Yajiemon and Yakichi in Miyanokoshi and the drovers in Minagami and Yamada. And there are others, too, even some of the senior packhorsemen. The ox drovers are going to hold fast. Kadoju is just too greedy. That's what started it all."

Hanzo did his best to understand the problem. He obtained a copy of the "Articles of the Ox Drovers," which read as follows:

Item: In the matter of freighting charges, up to now the bill of lading has always been kept out of sight and the freight charges written up in separate papers, while new bills of lading have been prepared and sent on to the shippers. This has been a constant source of grievance. If, in the future, the ox drovers may be accorded the kindness of being apprised of the true situation and shown the bills of lading, they will all be reassured.

Item: Among the ox drovers, Kadoju is pleasant to those with whom he feels at ease and favors them in his freight charges, but he will not deal with those whom he does not like, particularly those associated with the Maru-kameya, nor will he promptly turn over to them the freight he has on hand unless he has specific orders to do so from a superior. He should treat everyone the same way as he does his favored drovers and turn the freight over promptly. (Of course, when there is no freight brought in, nothing can be done, but the ox drovers would like to have plans made for such eventualities.)

Item: In the case of the soy bean trade, the toiya's profit should be fixed at 450 mon per packload and the remainder should be given to the ox drovers.

Item: Charges for freight originating at Nakatsugawa should be fixed at one bu per packload and the remainder without exception should be given to the ox drovers. The strictest attention should be given to this in the future.

Item: Freight in transit should be charged half the rate from Nagoya to Fukushima and the remainder should be given to the ox drovers without holding any back.

Item: In dispatching freight, it should be given to the first drover to come, whether or not he is favored by the shop, just as the toiya in Imado operates without playing favorites or giving special consideration.

Item: It is a source of great difficulty and unpleasantness to the ox drovers when freight is retained for long periods of time by the toiya, so that the shipper has to intervene. They request that freight be forwarded as expeditiously as possible.

Item: All agreements made upon this occasion must be honored rigorously by both sides. If there should be misconduct on the part of the toiya, it must be possible for the ox drovers to work with a different toiya without suffering in any way. Provisions for this must be made at this stage.

This document was written from the point of view of the mediator, and the head drovers from Toge would not say if it had the full support of all the drovers. In the end strong opposition came from Minagami village. As a result of the talks held on the tenth day of the eighth month, when representatives of the ox drovers came to the Fushimiya to have the document read to them, it was decided that there were several points they could not accept.

The drovers requested that a new document be drawn up and the first document be turned over to the two head drovers. Negotiations seemed once again to be stalled.

The Nakatsugawa physician Miyagawa Kansai, Hanzo's teacher, happened to come to Magome to attend a sick person at the Masudaya. From Kansai Hanzo was able to learn the sources of the ox drovers' problems. There had been manifest favoritism in Kadoju's conduct, and in his rewriting of freight charges there was much that was unforgivable. It did not seem likely that the two parties could reach an agreement. Now, after the consultation among the drovers, there was a consensus that they should so inform the Fushimiya. The ox drovers were polite and proper, but unyielding.

The quarrel had begun on the sixth day of the eighth month and it had continued for twenty-five days. The longer it lasted, the greater was the advantage enjoyed by the ox drovers. Six or seven shippers from the lower stretches of the highway came to see Kadoju. They said nothing like what the ox drovers had been saying. They simply expressed their appreciation for the services that had been rendered to date, said that they would be using the services of a new toiya in the future, bowed, and took their leave. It was reported that Kadoya Jubei was stunned. On the next day six porcelain traders came to Nakatsugawa and entered into consultations to set up a new toiya under new regulations.

To Hanzo, the Izumiya in Nakatsugawa was the home of his close friend and fellow student Hachiya Kozo. That the Izumiya was to replace Kadoju as toiya seemed to Hanzo a remarkable turn of fate. He also took note of the fact that after all the stress and dislocation, the quarrel had ended in a victory for the ox drovers. All the toiya were going to have to give this incident a great deal of thought. Indeed, it was shifting the very ground under their feet. Only those others, the nameless ordinary people, were still not fully aware of this fact.

Longing for his mother had given Hanzo a melancholy character. That feeling of longing was what drew him close to his friends and his teacher and made him feel a deep sympathy for the orphan children of the village. When he was still only seventeen, sixty-one people from the village had been convicted of violating the restrictions on access to the Kiso forests and of stealing large amounts of trees and timber. Those villagers had been summoned into the courtyard of the honjin to be interrogated by the officials from Fukushima. Hanzo, hidden in the shade of the pear tree in the corner of the courtyard, had observed the unfortunate villagers who were bound hand and foot. That was when he had first become aware of the sufferings of the poor. Although he had been born into the ancient house of the Magome honjin, his eyes had not turned upward toward the officials and the powerful samurai but always toward the nameless farmers, toward those who were obedient and long-suffering, again in part because of the deep sense of loss hidden within him. Never completely satisfied, he passed through a childhood of caution and restraint before his stepmother. It was with these eyes that he began to understand the actions of the ox drovers who moved freight over this highway, members of the lowest level of society.

5

"May I come in?"

A visitor and his companion stood in the entry of the Magome honjin.

"The guests from Tsumago are here."

When she heard the maid's announcement, Otami rushed to the hearth room. It was her brother, Juheiji.

"Brother! I'm so glad you've come!"

Otami ran back to tell Oman, who was at the rear of the house, and to bring Hanzo, who was in the front room.

The spacious hearth room of the honjin, which served as both kitchen and dining room, also became the reception room when friends and relatives called. Under its high, soot-stained roof, beside the darkly lustrous old wooden pillars, hosts and guests exchanged greetings.

"Please don't sit over there on the edge. Take off your sandals and come on up!"

Oman spoke in her best "elder lady of the honjin" manner to Juheiji's companion. It was customary in the Kiso to have someone to walk with over the mountain roads even when paying a call at the next village, only five miles away. The season for chestnuts, which are so plentiful in these mountains, had just begun and Juheiji's companion said what a pleasant trip it had been.

Otami, quickly setting the middle room in order, prepared seats for the guests where they could look out to the west at the broad autumn sky. Consultations between the honjin of Magome and Tsumago were frequent, and Hanzo would call at Juheiji's house whenever he made a trip to Fukushima. But on this day he was receiving Juheiji for a rare, unhurried visit in his own home.

"First, let me tell you a good one."

Otami returned from the hearth room, carrying the tea utensils and refreshments. When she was ready, Juheiji continued.

"Well, now, it was the day of my last visit here. On my way back, I came out onto the upper road to Tozo's house, over toward Shiono. There were all sorts of little paths and I began to think I'd gotten turned around. I wandered along a road through the middle of the woods and eventually came out in front of Heizo's house in Orisaka. When I finally got back to Tsumago, I was completely befuddled. A tanuki couldn't have done it better. It was already the eighth hour!"

Hanzo and Otami burst out laughing.

Juheiji was Otami's only brother and she his only sister. During the previous new year, he had passed through the rituals for his twenty-fifth year, a dangerous time by the old reckoning. Their father had died while on business in Fukushima, leaving Juheiji in charge of the Tsumago honjin at an early age. Consequently he looked somewhat older than his years, and his way of speaking was usually grave and mature. Although Juheiji's stature was short, it was compensated for by the breadth of his shoulders. When he was with Hanzo, one year his senior, people never guessed which of them was the elder. As they were about the same age, they enjoyed talking with each other.

"This time, Hanzo, I brought a good story with me," said Juheiji, his eyes sparkling.

"That was certainly no ordinary story."

"Now you're bragging," said Otami, laughing again.

"Otami, please call father and mother."

"Should I call Okisa, too? She is separated from Senjuro and living here now."

"Please do. I want everyone to hear this story."

"Oh, that's funny! Very funny!"

Kichizaemon had come in from outside to hear Juheiji's story from Hanzo.

"Father, Juheiji says he started from Shiono and came out in Orisaka. Whose woods was he wandering around in?"

"That would surely have been the Umeya's forest. Juheiji taken in by a tanuki? That's a good one!"

"That's a real mountain story," said Otami as she went into the next room. She returned with the baby that had just started to cry.

"Here, just look at Kume. She's gotten so big."

"Ah, that's a fine girl."

"Look, Juheiji, she can laugh already," said Oman, leaning over to pat the face of the granddaughter in Otami's arms. "Girls become aware very early."

The report that Juheiji brought that day had to do with a man who had taken lodging in Tsumago while traveling the Kiso road with his servant. Seeing the crest of the Tsumago honjin, this man had called the master of the house to point out that the crest was the same as his own, a bird's nest pattern. He spoke of the very strange feeling that this coincidence in family crests had given him. Then he asked if Juheiji also had an alternate crest. Three bars in a circle was the reply. Now the man was even more amazed. He asked if the ancestor of the house might have come from Miura in Sagami province. Yes. He asked if that ancestor's name might not have been Aoyama Kemmotsu. Indeed it was. The man slapped his knee, saying there really were wondrous things in this world.

He then introduced himself as Yamagami Shichirozaemon of Miura county in Sagami province. He had heard that one of his ancestors was named Aoyama Kemmotsu and that this Aoyama had left Miura and moved to the Kiso to form a branch house. They were relatives.

Juheiji was astonished. He and Yamagami exchanged drinks to honor the relation that had been reestablished by this chance night's lodging. Comparing genealogies, Juheiji suddenly found that he had ancestors going back far beyond Aoyama Kemmotsu, ancestors about whom the Aoyama family had never known before. The next morning he and his guest parted with promises to meet again.

"I was really amazed. I had heard that our ancestors came from Miura in Sagami but I had no idea that the family would still be there and getting along so splendidly."

Kichizaemon gave a loud grunt in response.

"Did you tell your guest about our family too, Juheiji?"

"Of course I did. I told him that Aoyama Kemmotsu had two sons and that the elder became the deputy at Tsumago and the younger at Magome."

So the centuries-old Aoyama house had still more distant ancestors, a still more ancient history. And the original line was still thriving! Oman, Otami, and Okisa all gazed at Juheiji in amazement.

"What kind of person was this?" asked Oman.

"He was really a splendid person. It was clear from the way he spoke that he comes from an old family. As soon as he got back to Sagami he sent me a letter and a genealogy. He also urged me to visit him some time."

"Otami, please bring me brush and paper from my desk in the front room," said Hanzo. Then he turned back to Juheiji. "Please give me Yamagami's address. I want to write it down so I won't forget it."

Hanzo spread out the paper and in a youthful but beautiful hand took down the address as Juheiji gave it:

Yamagami Shichirozaemon
Kugo Village, Yokosuka
Miura County, Sagami Province

"Juheiji," Hanzo began, "are you going to—"

"Certainly. I was thinking about the two of us going down there for a visit."

"A visit? This gets more and more interesting."

Everyone fell silent for a time.

"I wish you had brought Yamagami's genealogy along so we could see it."

"I'll send it over. It shows how the Aoyama line branched off from the Yamagami family and how they came from the Miura. So it would appear that our distant ancestor was a direct descendant of the Miura who were so famous in the Kamakura period."

"That is clear from the 'Miura of Sagami,' " put in Kichizaemon.

"If you're planning to go to Sagami, Juheiji, when would you do it?"

"How about the end of the tenth month?"

"I am completely in favor of that," said Kichizaemon. "Hanzo should make up his mind to go along with you. You should see Edo too—and you ought to make a pilgrimage to Nikko while you're at it."

Juheiji's companion went back to Tsumago but Oman insisted that Juheiji spend the night. Hanzo invited him into the front room and they talked by the light of an old-fashioned lamp until it grew late. They brought out the genealogy that had been kept at the Magome honjin for generations and spread it out on the floor. In it was written the name Aoyama Dosai, founder of Magome, and the name of the retired head of the Tsumago family who had come over to look after things at a time when the Magome line had all been women. Hanzo's was the seventeenth generation since Dosai. Hanzo and Juheiji laid out their bedding side by side that night, but Hanzo was too filled with thoughts of the trip for which his father had given approval to get much sleep.

Thus it was that by the sheerest accident Hanzo gained an opportunity to visit Edo and Sagami. The next day, while it was still early, Otami invited Hanzo and Juheiji to walk out to the family graves at the Mampukuji. Juheiji said that he would like very much to visit the graves since he had not done so in a long time. Otami, who had helped her husband nurse his grandmother, also wished to visit that old woman who had already lain there for some time.

Hanzo and Juheiji set out slightly ahead of Otami. They went through the wooden back gate, passed alongside the sake warehouse of the Fushimiya, and came out next to the dense bamboo grove. There they picked up the quiet back road that led to the temple and waited for Otami to catch up. Otami, carrying smoking incense sticks, was accompanied by a servant who had Okume on her back. Together they crossed a small stream and followed the road through the rice fields.

The Mampukuji stood on a small hill, separated from the village by a shallow valley. The graveyard was beside the stream, on a steep slope that looked up toward the temple gate. They found the graveyard clean and well cared for, a great change from its condition under the previous priest. Sho'un had started a small school for the village children, and now the daughter of the hairdresser and the son of the carpenter and the other children who no longer came to the honjin for their schooling appeared at the temple every day, copybooks in their arms. Sho'un's quiet, unassuming diligence had even extended to putting the graveyard in order. Hanzo took up the bamboo broom that was provided and started to sweep the area before the family graves, but the job was only a matter of clearing away a few leaves that had recently fallen. Even the weeds had been pulled up and removed. Everything was clean and pure.

Juheiji and Otami joined Hanzo before his grandmother's grave.

"See, brother, grandmother's name was carved alongside grandfather's while she was still alive, only then it was painted red," said Otami. Then she turned to the child on the servant's back.

"Look, it's grandma!" she said.

The ancient, moss-grown gravestone of the founder stood tall in the central portion of the plot. On the face of this stone, beaten by centuries of wind and rain, could be read the characters MAMPUKUJI DENSHO-OKU JOKYU ZENJO-

MON. Aoyama Dosai slept there. It was as though he were tirelessly watching over the fortunes of the highway and the mountain village he had founded.

Juheiji turned to Hanzo.

"It seems just right for the grave of a person of long ago."

"His religious title must be in commemoration of his founding of the Mampukuji. They say that he also founded our Hall of the Healing Buddha because he thought it would be unfitting for the village elders not to have another place to meet."

The two never ran out of things to talk about.

There was a rear view of the village to be seen through the trees in front of the graveyard. Hanzo and Juheiji stood there for a time, gazing at the view, the scent of the cedar trees fresh in their nostrils. Hanzo was already beginning to see things differently, his thoughts filled with the prospect of the coming journey. He felt a slight distance from familiar scenes as he pointed out to Juheiji a certain persimmon twig here or a white wall there. The view of this village nestling at the foot of Mt. Ena was one of which Juheiji too, coming as he did from Tsumago, never tired.

"Juheiji, do we need to get together one more time before we begin our trip?"

"No, we can make all the arrangements by letter."

After this conversation, Juheiji returned to Tsumago.

The poverty of his experience and the narrowness of his knowledge had always been a source of regret for Hanzo. Now he had an opportunity to get out and see things. It was just a year after the great earthquake in Edo and the rebuilding there was in full swing. Edo, moreover, was where the National Scholar Hirata Kanetane, the successor to Atsutane, lived.

Hanzo was determined to be accepted as a posthumous disciple of Hirata Atsutane and this was at last a precious opportunity. He would also be going to Kugo village on the Yokosuka coastline, near the point where the Black Ships had actually landed. His heart pounded.

CHAPTER THREE

1

DEAR HACHIYA:

Quite soon I will be setting out for Edo and for Miura in Sagami province. I am going with my brother-in-law, Juheiji, the honjin of Tsumago. We intend to visit the descendants of our distant ancestors in Kugo village in Yokosuka, but I want to see Edo too. After being shut away in these mountains for so long, I am actually going on a trip for the first time.

Hanzo's letter was addressed to his close friend Hachiya Kozo of Nakatsu-gawa.

There is one joy I wish to share with you. While on this trip I will be able to join the Hirata school as I have so long wanted to do. Recently I acquired a book by the great agrarian scholar Sato Nobuhiro, and in it I learned that he comes from the same region as our master, Hirata, and that he was deeply influenced by the master. There is nothing so commonly misunderstood as the National Learning of Motoori and Hirata. Are we never again to see in this world that simple and direct turn of mind that we perceive in the people of antiquity? Somehow or other I want to return to that starting point and then look at the world with new eyes.

Hanzo's plan to visit Edo was soon known to everyone in Magome. His old nurse, Ofuki, who had known Hanzo since his infancy, gave thought to his coming journey and came to talk to him.

"It's good to be a man, Hanzo. A man can go anywhere. But think of us women. How can we do anything like that? Here I am in the mountains without even a hope of going to Edo. Do you realize there are women here in the country whose greatest dream is just to see Nagoya before they die?"

Hanzo hoped to obtain his father's permission to join the Hirata school before setting out for Edo. It was his intention to be accepted as a posthumous disciple, since the master was already deceased. He felt this would make his own position clear as well as offer the advantages of association with his fellow disciples.

68

Kichizaemon was not unconcerned that this son over whom he had watched for so long, this Hanzo who would sooner or later succeed to the Magome honjin, was becoming ever more deeply preoccupied with the teachings of the Hirata school. But Kichizaemon was himself fond of learning and painfully aware of his own lack of scholarship. He only looked into Hanzo's eyes, saying, "So your love of scholarship has come to this?" and granted Hanzo's wish.

Atsutane's work had been entrusted to eight principal disciples, one of whom was Kanetane, who had succeeded as head of the Hirata family. There were said to be several hundred disciples of the Hirata school throughout the country and many of them were to be found in the region of southern Shinano and eastern Mino. As Hanzo's initiation was being sponsored by Miyagawa Kansai, he had received permission to call upon Kanetane and be received into the school whenever he came to Edo.

"I am most grateful that you have given your consent, father. It seems as though I have been waiting for this day for a very long time."

Hanzo's respect for his elders showed plainly in his face as he told Kichizaemon how happy for him his friends in Nakatsugawa would be, since they too hoped to follow the same path.

"Well, we'll see how it turns out," Kichizaemon replied, furrows showing above his "honjin" nose. Kichizaemon had merely listened to Hanzo telling him about the procedure for the initiation and said nothing about getting in too deep.

It was eighty-three leagues—over two hundred miles—from the western extremity of the Kiso valley to Edo. The travelers would have to cross four mountain passes and go through two internal customs barriers. Although Kichizaemon was as uninformed about matters in eastern Japan as he was knowledgeable about the western part of the country, he had been called to Edo several times by the commissioners of transport and he had seen a bit of the city on these occasions. So he gave his son advice for the journey.

Juheiji would be an ideal companion, but since anything could happen to two young men all alone, Kichizaemon recommended that they take along at least one person to Edo and Yokosuka. The travelers of that time, hiring horses and porters, welcomed each person they could add to their parties. Kichizaemon pointed out that they would not take the trouble to do so if there were not good reasons for it.

"Those who travel alone won't even be accepted at inns," he cautioned.

After consulting with Juheiji, the departure date was moved up to the first part of the tenth month. The day was fast approaching. Oman sewed an amulet bag of blue cotton for Hanzo while Otami prepared such things as muslin underclothing. As he looked at them, Hanzo felt a certain trepidation about the road before him. People who traveled long distances in those days simply had to reach the lodging they had planned for each day, even if it meant passing through the fiercest storms. Only flooded rivers could be permitted to delay one's passage. The trip would be no simple outing.

* * * * * * *

"Sakichi! Are you going with Hanzo?"

"Yes! Hanzo said so, and the master gave his permission."

When Ofuki came, earlier than anyone else to see Hanzo off, she found Sakichi in the hearth room, preparing for travel. Sakichi had not been with the family very long and he was as young as Hanzo. He was delighted at being chosen to go along to Edo, and he had brought in a supply of pine wood from the mountains and stacked it in the woodshed to last the household hearth while he was gone.

The day of departure came at last. Hanzo put on a cape of blue Kawachi cotton, wrapped on his leggings, and transformed himself into a traveler. He wrapped in a calico bag the hilt of the dagger he would carry and thrust it into his sash.

"Now, here you are. If you have this, you will be permitted to pass any barrier."

Kichizaemon handed Hanzo a certificate of identity, which was to serve as his passport for the internal customs barriers. It was dated the tenth month of the third year of Ansei, 1856, and it bore the signatures of the post station officials and the seal of the Magome station.

"It looks as though it will be frosty again tomorrow. That's not good for Hanzo," said Oman.

Then she and Otami, who held Okume with one arm as she handed Hanzo his broad conical traveler's hat, said their farewells. Hanzo made his brave departure.

Ofuki's eyes filled with tears as she stood at the gate with the other women of the honjin as they saw him off.

Kichizaemon and Shobei, the assistant headman, walked with Hanzo as far as the top of the pass. They were accompanied by Tsurumatsu and some of the other children Hanzo had taught. Heisuke, another assistant headman, lived in Toge, where the teahouse whose signboard advertised the famous rice with chestnuts was located. In the custom of the time, they all exchanged cups of sake at the teahouse before parting and those who were remaining behind gave their last minute advice to the travelers. Shobei cautioned Hanzo that people were inclined to be careless about their feet at the beginning of a journey; it was most important to be careful of one's feet and legs at first. Heisuke advised that it was best to take ten days for a nine days' journey. Hanzo was touched that Sho'un of the Mampukuji, clad in the somber robes of a Zen priest, had come all this distance to see him off.

"Be careful about traveling after dark. Try to get started as early as you can and get to your next stop while there is still light."

After receiving this parting advice from Kichizaemon, Hanzo and Sakichi set off from the top of the pass. In these mountains there are insects delicate as fireflies known as "trail blazers" and their red and blue backs flying up ahead seemed to guide them along the road.

"I've asked Sakichi to come along with us, Juheiji. That's why he's here. He wants to see Edo and he can help with your baggage too."

Juheiji was pleased to hear this. He had been waiting at the honjin in Tsu-mago, where they were to spend the first night of the journey. Whenever he saw Juheiji, Hanzo was amazed that one so young could carry out the duties of the three offices of honjin, toiya, and headman. In Juheiji's room there was a record book that had been handed down from previous generations and in it were recorded the most minute details of each occasion when daimyo had stayed at the honjin: the number of men in the party, the charges for lodging, the number of baths taken, the number of braziers for heating, the number of candles used. The daimyo would bring their own bedding and utensils, pay-ing the honjin only for rooms and services. Juheiji, in his turn, had not neglected the troublesome task of recording every last fact for future genera-tions. Hanzo gazed upon this record with deep feeling.

The next morning Sakichi got up before anyone else. By the time Hanzo and Juheiji were awake, he had set out a new pair of straw sandals for each of them. He had his own traveler's hat and carrying pole ready, and he waited quietly beside the hearth for his masters to complete their preparations.

Juheiji left the affairs of the honjin in the hands of Tokuemon of the neighboring Ogiya, his assistant. Like Hanzo, he had provided himself with a passport for the barriers, and now he put on a persimmon-colored woolen cape with a black twill collar.

His grandmother, who had always looked after him but now was very old, joined the other members of the house at the gate. She was the one who had made Otami known to Hanzo and had welcomed Juheiji's bride, Osato, to the honjin. She also made it a point to mention from time to time Osato's continuing childlessness.

"If only you were a little taller," she said to Juheiji, bringing a rueful smile to his lips. She seemed to be not only comparing him with the taller Hanzo but reminding him not to bring any shame to their family while in Edo.

Hanzo and Juheiji put on their hats. Sakichi picked up the baggage and fol-lowed them as all three stepped out lightly in their straw sandals.

2

The eleven post stations of the Kiso are generally divided into three groups. Magome, Tsumago, Midono, and Nojiri are called the lower four stations while Suwara, Agematsu, and Fukushima form the middle three. The upper four stations are Miyanokoshi, Yabuhara, Narai, and Niekawa. The road over which Hanzo and his companions were walking was still in the district of the lower four stations. Even so, to be out together in this way was something special and all three shared the excitement and fascination of the road unfold-ing before them. Hinoki berries might be drying in front of that shed there, while over here was a mountain country dog, brown and stocky with sharply pointed ears. They laughed often as they walked along discussing these things. If one of them broke a string on his sandals, the other two would wait until the damage was repaired.

Scenes of deep forest surrounded them. Juheiji was familiar with the road from Tsumago to Fukushima and Hanzo, too, having taken his father's place when the Magome honjin was summoned to Fukushima, had traveled this road many times. Since Hanzo had grown up observing this road he could tell the condition of the way ahead from the perspiration of the packhorse-men, the porters, and the litter bearers they passed on the way. Flies left over from the previous month swarmed around men and horses alike, another part of the discomfort of travel on the Kiso road.

"How are you doing, Sakichi?"

"My legs are in fine shape. How about you?"

"No trouble at all."

Hanzo, walking beside Juheiji, would occasionally look back at Sakichi to say something and then move on.

Autumn was coming to an end and the valley floor was covered with brightly colored leaves. Those passing along this road in the appropriate season would see logs being readied for rafting. It was a bit late for bringing the logs in on the tributary streams but still early for rafting them down the Kiso. There was no sign of the day laborers who would soon be building dams and weirs in the stream beds. The work of those who would start the logs on their way and of those who would tend them en route had not yet begun. Nor had the officials arrived. They would come to the banks of the river, sometimes armed with guns, to ensure that no logs were lost or stolen.

The first rains of winter had already passed over the highway, but there was nothing urgent in the movement of the three travelers. They would often pause to rest by the river, setting their hats down on the grass alongside the road. Before them were pine-shaded islands in midstream and mountains falling sheer to the opposite bank. Dense forests of hinoki and sawara covered the bluffs, and the sharp, triangular boughs overlapping each other gave a sense of great depth. The waters of the Kiso river, a brilliant blue, sparkled as they tumbled down from upstream, endlessly wetting the boulders of the riverbed.

This year was said to mark the first good harvest since the earthquakes. Even such poor land as that above Toge had reported a yield of about one hundred fifty bales, about sixty koku more than usual. But beyond Magome and Tsumago, there were few fields to receive this bounty of nature. The valley became very narrow around the middle three stations and the only bits of land that could be cultivated were on the slopes of the riverbanks or just above. To these travelers, raised in the mountains and seeing the trees of these mountains almost as their friends, it was easy to spot the hanging, beanlike pods of the soap-acacia growing along the riverbanks, or the fine-branched jujube trees on the higher ground. The local monuments that had been set up alongside the road also provided diversion. On this side would be a flower-bed; over there, an altar dedicated to the horse-headed Kannon.

Living deep in the valleys, it was not at all strange that the people of the

Kiso should draw their strength from the mountains and forests. At that time the entire region was controlled by Owari and the forests had been divided into three categories, only one of which could be entered and used freely. Even there, the five trees could not be cut without special permission. Hanzo was well aware that the inspectors from Nagoya concentrated their attention on these forests. From the Shiragi watch station in Ichikokutochi to the garrison at Agematsu, not a day passed without the officials checking the forests. However, even with the nesting forests and the closed forests, there was only a small area into which the people of the Kiso could not enter. The open forests made up by far the greater part of the Kiso mountains. So long as the prohibition against cutting the five trees was not violated, the people could enter the open forests whenever they wished, to cut the less valuable trees or to make charcoal.

The people of the Kiso relied on the wood in these forests for many things in their everyday life—hats, Oroku combs, splitwood baskets, various kinds of lacquerware. There was little arable land and agriculture was difficult. Because of this there were certain villages that were hard put to find materials for the lacquerware industries that sustained them. Some of these villages were given permission to cut a thousand packhorse loads of hinoki each year —this was called "approved hinoki"—while others, in lieu of the six thousand packhorse loads they had been permitted to cut ever since the Keicho era of the early seventeenth century, were now given cash payments called the "substitute cut." All of this came from Owari's determination to preserve the Kiso forests, to which it was linked by history. This was a region that could not survive without the products of mountain and forest. The road that Hanzo and Juheiji walked over passed directly through this great forest region.

When they reached Nezame, they met a long line of oxen loaded with freight from Agematsu.

"Master Hanzo! Where are you going?" one of the ox drovers called out. It was Risaburo, the chief drover from Toge. He had taken charge of a consignment of freight in Fukushima and was on his way to Imado in Mino province.

When Juheiji looked inquiringly at Hanzo, Sakichi explained jovially, "He's one of the drovers from Toge."

"You probably heard about it too, Juheiji. He was one of the main parties in the ox drovers' incident."

They turned to watch as Risaburo, dressed in a rough cape with horizontal stripes, moved his animals down the road.

The feudal authorities had long maintained themselves by pursuing a policy of not awakening the farmers and lower classes. But Hanzo was unable to shake the feeling he got from the ox drovers' incident, this completely new phenomenon on the highway. He reflected that when he unexpectedly met this man in the course of his travels he was unable to laugh at the sight of ox drovers silently at work. It was all because of that incident.

They were gradually approaching the Fukushima barrier. Treading on the ceaselessly falling leaves, the three moved ever deeper into the mountains. Just when it seemed that they had reached the end of the valley, another valley would appear beyond, with blue smoke rising above the shingled roof of the teahouse hidden there. When they crossed the hanging bridge and the ford where the Kiso is joined by a major tributary, the river began to show the characteristics of its upper reaches. The road gradually descended into the bottom of the valley. After crossing another bridge, they came to the place where the road to Mt. Ontake branched off. Ahead was the castle town of Fukushima.

"Is this where the barrier is?" Sakichi called from the rear, his face solemn.

The Fukushima barrier was also known as the Kiso barrier. It was located on the outskirts of town, just across the river from the great gate of the Yamamura estate. Here, in the days of watching for "departing women and entering guns," travelers from the west were searched to see if they were carrying firearms, and travelers from the east to see if there were women among them. The prohibition of travel by women was particularly strict; not only those with long hair but nuns, young girls, bald persons, and even priests with shaven heads would be checked, to their breasts if necessary, and categorized. This spoke at once of the system of alternate attendance centering on Edo and of the position of women at that time. For ordinary travelers whose papers were in order, there was nothing to be concerned about. Still, whenever a traveler approached the Fukushima barrier, he would automatically remove his hat or head cloth and straighten his collar.

In his house overlooking the Fukushima barrier, they called on Uematsu Shosuke to whom Hanzo had a letter of introduction from his father. Shosuke, who had taken a second wife from the prominent Miyatani family of Nagoya, was entrusted with the maintenance of the barrier. He was also an instructor in firearms and one of the leading samurai of Fukushima. Still, he had occasionally gone all the way to the Fushimiya in Magome to try to raise money. It had become a trying time even for samurai.

Happening to be off duty that day, Shosuke received Hanzo and his companions familiarly.

"Well, have a good trip! By the way, you both have your passports, don't you? This barrier is famous for its strictness. Not even daimyo's maids can pass through if they don't have their papers. Anyway, I'll escort you through."

As a parting gift, Shosuke gave them some medicine made according to a secret formula passed down from his ancestors. Then, wearing broad trousers, a formal jacket with crests, and two swords in his sash, he led them to the barrier.

On one side of the checkpoint was the abrupt slope of the mountain; on the other, the precipitous banks of the Kiso river. A commissioner representing Yamamura Jimbei and three guard commanders were at their posts, each attended by two foot soldiers. Two more guards to the east and one to the west ensured that the mighty gates were kept under firm control. Hanzo and his companions walked across the fine sand covering the ground inside the gates and waited until the travelers ahead of them were cleared.

Among those travelers was a woman who appeared to be of distinguished family; her palanquin had been stopped so that she could be checked without emerging from it. Hanzo heard a voice from beside the palanquin announce, "One woman!" Then, once she had given a gratuity to the guard for his wife, the woman who had arrived in the palanquin passed on without difficulty.

Hanzo and his companions' turn was next. They could see hanging on the wall of the inspection station the menacing tools used to take reluctant individuals into custody: the catching pole, the sleeve tangler, and the crescent-shaped pinning wedge. They passed down a stairway, presented their passports to the officials, and then were free to proceed.

Shosuke took his leave. As Hanzo looked back once more at the barrier, he sensed how completely a matter of form it had all been.

The Torii pass led from this barrier to the two stations of Miyanokoshi and Yabuhara. Although the sun shone brilliantly, the wind was cold. Here on this high pass, with its altar for worshipping Mt. Ontake at a distance, they were made more aware of the length of their journey than when they were laboring over the steep, crooked roads during the first part of the trip. Now they were separated for a time from the Kiso river.

"How far did you say it was from Edo to Yokosuka, Juheiji?"

"Forty miles. I checked it in a guide book."

"When you add the distance to Edo, that makes two hundred forty miles."

"I suppose it will work out to just about that."

"There are still two Kiso stations ahead of us," Sakichi put in. "Edo is a long way off yet."

Talking as they went, rushing against the end of daylight, the three at last came down from the pass.

"Please stop here!"

"This is the place to stay in Narai!"

"Here is where the Naniwa chanters lodge!"

The relentless cries of the women pouring out of the guesthouses lining the street to solicit lodgers sounded almost like a battle scene. Hanzo, Juheiji, and Sakichi had entered Narai, at the foot of the Torii pass, at the time of day when travelers were beginning to think about taking lodgings.

Hanzo had decided to stay at the house of the headman, who was a close friend of his father, and he led Juheiji and Sakichi there. The architecture, so characteristic of the great highways, was the same as in Magome and Tsumago. A front hallway ran along the second floor of each of the houses and they seemed to thrust themselves out into the street.

"I picked up some blisters today, Hanzo!"

Juheiji laughed as he plunged his feet, badly chafed by the straw sandals, into a pail of hot water. Hanzo washed his feet too. Then they were conducted through a spacious hearth room to a sitting room overlooking the back garden. It was an unpretentious household, the sort of place where mushrooms, beans, peppers, and herbs could be found drying on the veranda.

"It's peaceful here."

Juheiji laid his dagger in the alcove as he said this. Such stillness was not to be found in a place like Fukushima where the sound of the river was always in one's ears.

The master of the house said that he had often met Hanzo's father in Fukushima and that he had put up Kichizaemon in this very room. Because of this connection, he took special pleasure in entertaining these young travelers on their way to Edo. And, as it was the peak season for small birds, he offered to serve some for dinner.

The thrushes of the Torii pass were famous, but one could also hear robins and mountain cuckoos as well as the broad-billed roller, known hereabouts from its song as the "bupposo" or "Buddhist priest." Those who lived in Narai could hear the birds singing from across the street when in the front of the house and their singing in the garden when in the back. This was the kind of thing the master of the house told them.

Although he was still on the Kiso road, Hanzo had come to its easternmost station. Once he had crossed the Torii pass, the western Kiso where his parents, his wife, and his child were, would be far away. But here on the peaceful lower slope of the mountain, Hanzo felt renewed as he removed his cape and leggings and washed away the perspiration of the mountain paths in a country bath.

"They hold only the office of headman in this family. The honjin and toiya are separate."

"So I understand."

Hanzo and Juheiji, refreshed after their baths, sat in the back room of the house and compared their impressions. A quilt-covered brazier had been set up in the room, as the mornings and evenings were chilly, and a maid had just brought a lamp. Juheiji reached for the lamp and pulled it closer. Then he took out his travel diary and writing set and proceeded to record in great detail how much he had paid for straw sandals in Yabuwara and how much for refreshments at the teahouse in the pass.

"I really admire you for that, Juheiji."

"For what?"

"I looked at the account book on your desk in Tsumago. You're so rigorous and precise."

Hanzo spoke out of a keen awareness that the duties of honjin, toiya, and headman lay ahead of him. Both he and Juheiji had begun their apprenticeships at the age of eighteen by going to Fukushima on business and by learning to receive daimyo and send them off. There was no part of the training they had received from childhood that had not been directed to this end. The only difference was that Juheiji was already a headman while Hanzo had not yet become head of his family.

Hanzo sighed.

"I know what my father is thinking. He'd rather have me be a suitable successor to the honjin than see me burying my head in books so much that I neglect family affairs. After all, he is getting old."

"Aren't you heaving a few too many sighs, Hanzo?"

"Maybe, but you're lucky. You're really suited for the job."

"That's just because you always make things seem so difficult. To be a headman is to speak for the people, and to be a honjin or toiya is to take part in the work of the highway. Just try thinking of it that way. At any rate, it's worthwhile work."

The aroma of small birds roasting on the hearth presently reached their room. The maid put the wooden frame of the brazier in order and set it up as a table. On it were placed a small bottle of heated sake for each of them and serving dishes heaped with thrushes roasted on skewers, tokens of the hospitality of the master of a house accustomed to serving guests. Hanzo called to Sakichi, who had been placed in the next room.

"Sakichi! Why don't you bring your dinner in here? This is a trip. Let's drink tonight!"

Hanzo's invitation made Sakichi smile. Although he was younger, his capacity for sake was greater than Hanzo's.

"I'll have mine out by the hearth. It's more convenient that way," he replied.

"Juheiji, somehow it seems strange that I should be able to go on a trip like this. We really seem to have gotten away from everything."

"Why don't you just relax? Here, drink up!"

So the two young men drank, forgetting the fatigue of the journey.

The master of the house joined them in eating the thrushes. Chewing and crunching the bones of the birds was part of the pleasure.

"But you do talk a lot more now, Hanzo. You used to be awfully quiet."

"I've noticed that myself. I have permission to become a disciple of the Hirata school on this trip. That's the way my father is. He was happy for me. If only I had a younger brother, I'd let him succeed in the family. I'd like to get out on my own more than is possible now."

"You're already talking like somebody who's getting ready to retire. Hanzo—you seem like the kind of person who might take up religion. At least it seems that way to me."

"I hadn't really thought about it."

"But aren't the teachings of the Hirata school a religion?"

"I suppose you could say that. But even though what the master teaches is a religion, its spirit is completely different from other religions."

"I'm glad to hear that."

They sat across from each other over the covered brazier, talking far into the night. Over the upper reaches of the Narai river, over the silent mountains behind, the eastern Kiso winter had come. The mountain air was sharp, threatening frost for the morning.

By the time they reached Oiwake, they began to hear news direct from Edo. They had passed through Shiojiri and Shimo-Suwa, then over the Wada pass and across the Chikuma river, finally emerging onto the plateau at the juncture of the Kiso road and the Zenkoji road. The headman in Oiwake, a man named Fumidayu, was a village elder who had been on close terms with Juheiji's father and he could not bear to let the young men pass through his village without stopping.

In his quasi-military dress and sword harness, Fumidayu was in charge of the hayfields of eleven villages, some of them in the holdings of the local daimyo and some in land belonging to the Tokugawa. He was also the person who kept track of dead and dying trees in the mountains, recording windfalls, snow and ice damage, and fallen limbs. Detained at his home to sample the soup made of miso from Saku and the pickles made from crisp local radishes, the travelers learned how different the forests of the Asama range were from those of their home valleys. Their host explained that red pine and larch predominated here, and then he proceeded to give a lengthy discourse on the broad open fields, the lava, the sand, and the general conditions of the land.

That was not all, however. This otherwise pointless stay in Oiwake enabled the travelers to receive some unexpected news. That night Fumidayu brought out a document to show to Hanzo and Juheiji and said it was one that he had copied from a samurai from Matsushiro. It was dated the eleventh day of the sixth month of the sixth year of Kaei, 1853, and it was an account of the alarm in Edo that had attended the arrival of the Black Ships.

> All Edo is tense because of the Black Ships. Urgent messages follow one another along the Tokaido and defense assignments have been given to all the daimyo. When the shogunal council learned that foreign ships had appeared off the shore of Kanagawa, they rushed to the castle in the middle of the night and issued orders that posts be taken up as follows:
>
> *Item:* Matsudaira Echizen no Kami, Lord of Fukui in Echizen, will guard Goten-yama in Shinagawa.
> *Item:* Hosokawa Etchu no Kami, Lord of Kumamoto in Higo, will guard the village of Omori.
> *Item:* Matsudaira Taizendayu, Lord of Choshu, will guard the coastal batteries and Tsukuda island in Edo harbor.
> *Item:* Matsudaira Awa no Kami, Lord of Tokushima in Awa, will guard the Seaside palace.
> *Item:* Sakai Uta no Kami, Lord of Himeji in Harima, will guard all of Fukagawa.
> *Item:* Tachibana Sakon Shoken will guard Oshima island off Izu. Matsudaira Shimosa no Kami will guard the two provinces of Awa and Kazusa. All

other daimyo, from Matsudaira Yamato no Kami, Lord of Kawagoe castle, on down have been given various defense assignments.

The shogunal inspectors, Togawa Nakatsukasa Shoyu and Matsudaira Jurobei, are to visit the encampments and also Uraga on the night of the sixth so that they may report on the movements of the ships.

Now, inquiries were made into the nationality of these foreign ships. They proved to be from North America. There are four large ships. A gun is fired from the ships each morning and evening. The townspeople and the people of the district have been pressed into corvee service, and the greater part of the dwellings along the seacoast have been razed so that fortifications might be constructed. Some of the people displaced have fled with their wives and children. The price of rice rises so much each day that people cannot keep up with it. It is like wartime.

At dawn on the eighth came the following dispatch:

Item: If the foreign vessels should come into the bay and an urgent alarm be raised, the fire stations along the Yashirozu waterfront will sound their bells more rapidly than the usual fire alarm.

Item: If the fire bells are rung as described above, you will set fires as you see fit to close the roads to Edo castle and other crucial routes.

Item: Since there may be places on the outskirts of Edo where these fire bells cannot be heard, all establishments with a revenue of more than ten thousand koku will commence a rapid sounding of their half-bells.

All of the above constitutes the orders of the shogunal council. We have hurriedly informed you of conditions here.

The uncertainties that had been troubling Hanzo were immediately dispelled. These details had never reached the limited world of the Kiso, where news only arrived as vague rumors. Hanzo was at last able to perceive a certain pattern in the report of disturbances in Edo that had been brought by the Hikone courier, in the wild rushing up and down the highway since then, and in the changes that had come to the highway.

"What do you think of this letter, Juheiji?"

"I hadn't realized there was that much to it."

Hanzo and Juheiji could not hide their feelings of excitement and concern from each other.

3

On the eleventh day of the journey, the three travelers approached Itabashi. As they crossed the river on the Todagawa ferry, they left the Kiso road behind. Edo was now near.

Leaving Itabashi early in the morning of the twelfth day, their pace was quickened by the knowledge that it was only five miles to Edo. Up to this point they had relied on a guide book, but from here on they would need the Edo street map. The great crowds of people from the samurai residences who had taken refuge from the earthquake of the previous year had already returned to the city, leaving behind temporary huts and still-twisted buildings with newly repaired walls. Looking to the left and right as they went, the travelers followed the road past the Kanda shrine, turned into the Sujikai outer gate, and entered a city under reconstruction.

"So this is Edo."

After more than two hundred miles of highway, Hanzo and his companions found themselves before the notice board in Sujikai square, next to the gate. From there they could see the residence of a daimyo fronting on the square and several fire towers. Officials were coming and going through the city on horseback, accompanied by retainers on foot. Some of them carried spears. A new Institute for Military Science had recently opened, and crowds of people from bannermen and retainers to arrière vassals and ronin were enrolling for instruction amid much pomp and display.

The lodging they were bound for was the Juichiya near Ryogoku. Although travelers from the provinces usually stayed in the central districts of Koami-cho, Bakuro-cho, and Nihombashi Yashiki-cho, they had chosen to stay in the less convenient Ryogoku because the Juichiya inn was run by a man from their own province. On hearing that they could go by river from the Shohei bridge to Ryogoku, they boarded a boat and rode downstream between banks lined with willow trees. As they passed the famous Asakusa bridge, they saw a square resembling the one they had passed through at Sujikai. From the riverbank at Ryogoku they walked to the end of a crowded commercial street and found their inn. The sober signboard showed it to be a respectable place. Workers carrying huge cloth-wrapped bundles and apprentices dangling account books hurried up and down the street. It was still morning.

"You're all from the Kiso? Please come in."

Greeted by the young lady of the house, Hanzo and Juheiji untied their straw sandals. Sakichi set the baggage down and all three washed their weary feet.

"At last! At last!" Hanzo and Juheiji exclaimed once they had been shown to their rooms on the second floor. Both were still wearing their leggings.

"Everyone is wearing lined clothing, even the maids in this inn," said Juheiji. "When you come this far from home, things are certainly different."

With that, he began to pace excitedly about the room.

At the time of Hanzo's visit to Edo, it was virtually unheard of for a young man from the Kiso to study in the city. The only exception Hanzo knew of was Takei Setsuzo from Fukushima. It was said that Setsuzo had

studied under the Chinese scholar Koga Doan and that he had been mentioned to Shionoya Toin and Matsuzaki Kodo, and had become acquainted
with Yasui Sokken. He had also enrolled for a time in the shogunal academy
at Ochanomizu. However, as his family was poor and his father ailing, he
had returned home some years ago.

Hanzo was still young. In his quest for the proper way to live, he felt
drawn to Edo. What aroused his interest the most was the news that an
Institute for the Study of Foreign Books had recently been established. A
group had formed around the Dutch scholars Mitsukuri Gempo and Sugita
Seikei and they had begun the translation of foreign books.

Now that he was actually in Edo, Hanzo found the impact of the foreign
countries increasing daily; it was far greater than he had imagined. He
learned that three British ships had come to Nagasaki in the eighth month of
the year. He also learned that there was great concern with naval preparedness and that coastal batteries were being installed off Shinagawa. With successive waves of officials assigned to deal with the foreigners, and with
rumors coming out of Edo castle of an imminent trade agreement, in this
year following the earthquake the people of Edo seemed to expect some new
development every day.

On the day after their arrival in Ryogoku, Hanzo and Juheiji were resting
in their room on the second floor of the Juichiya and listening to the distant
sound of artillery practice echoing through the city streets. Sakichi was resting in another room downstairs. The retired master of the Juichiya, having
heard that they were from the Kiso, came up to talk with them. This garrulous old gentleman told them of his struggles from the time he had left the
Kiso to the establishment of the inn.

"You want me to tell you about Edo, but I don't really know all that
much."

He said that what he found most unforgettable of all was the sixth year of
Kaei when he learned of the passing of the twelfth shogun.

Although his knowledge was all by hearsay, it was quite complete. On the
very next day after Perry first appeared at Uraga, the shogun took to his bed.
The heat was terrible and he grew weaker day by day in spite of the attentions of numerous physicians. Knowing that he would not recover, he summoned his council and told them that he saw the present events as the most
extraordinary since the beginning of heaven and earth. He was greatly concerned, but unfortunately, as he was stricken with illness, he could do nothing. After his death the council should consult with Nariaki, the retired lord
of Mito, who had long been concerned about affairs overseas and was well
informed. That night the American ships moved into Edo bay.

Hearing from his attendants that Ise, the councillor Abe, and Bingo, the
councillor Makino, had entered the castle, the shogun ordered that they be
brought to him immediately. He called for his audience robes but by then he
was exhausted. In great pain, he started to lose consciousness. Nevertheless,
he insisted that his attendants dress him and help him to his usual formal sit-

ting position. He was about to have the councillors called in, but since they had just learned that the American ships had suddenly put out to sea again the councillors reported this and withdrew without receiving audience. The next day the shogun passed away in his retiring room.

The master of the Juichiya had his information from one of the shogun's physicians, Kitamura Zuiken, who was a frequent lodger at the inn. He resumed his story.

"Tears come to my eyes whenever I recall that story about the shogun. After all, that was when all of Edo was in an uproar over the foreign ships entering the bay for the first time. Daimyo were rushing to the castle in fire-fighting gear or fortifying the positions they had been assigned. Special fire warnings were sent out. Armor, swords, and guns were selling for twice their usual prices. People who lived along the shore fled, carrying their possessions with them. I've seen a lot in this business, but the world is different now since all of that happened."

After the old man left, Hanzo and Juheiji sensed that here in the intense atmosphere of Edo they were obtaining the true fruits of their travel. They were amazed at how different everything was from the way they had imagined it.

"Hanzo, I think I'll write a letter home today."

"I think I'll send one to Magome, too."

"Take Sakichi with you and go over to Master Hirata's tomorrow."

After agreeing on this, Hanzo and Juheiji decided to rest for the remainder of the day. They had only limited time and could not stay for long in Edo. The trips to Nikko and Yokosuka still lay ahead.

Juheiji clapped his hands to summon the lady of the house. She told them that if they had arrived just a bit earlier, they would have been in time to see the Ebisu performances as well as the annual pickle fair in Otemma-cho. When they asked about the theatre, she replied that the new playbills had just been posted at the Ichimura, the Nakamura, and the Morita theatres. She offered the opinion that even if they did go to see the decorations at the tea-houses, the lanterns, the paper lamps, and the gifts, they should definitely wait until the first of the month for the new plays. Then they would see something contemporary and by the most popular playwright, performed by Shodanji.

"On the first of the month the companies will start their introductions at the seventh hour of the morning. Even to see the chanters doing *Sambaso* you have to get up while it's still dark to make it."

"I see. Theatre going in Edo takes the whole day!"

Such conversations gave Hanzo and Juheiji the sense of being on a great journey.

After dinner, Hanzo took from his bags a piece of paper he had carefully packed before leaving Magome.

"Would you like to see this, Juheiji? This is the oath I will be taking tomorrow." He placed the paper in front of Juheiji.

Oath

It is my earnest wish at this time to be approved and accepted as one of the disciples of this school.

I will believe in and support the Way of this Imperial Nation. I will not be lax in my reverence for the gods, and I will never, so long as I live, forget the obligations between master and disciple.

I will not violate the laws of the State. In all things I will base my conduct on the Learning of Antiquity, and I will do nothing at variance with the customs of the world. I will refrain from that which might disturb those who hear or see me, and I will never lie or distort the truth before my masters.

In accordance with tradition, I will firmly guard all secrets with which I am entrusted and will never speak of them. I will not commit base or contemptible acts that would soil the name of the Learning of Antiquity.

I will always be obedient and friendly to my fellow disciples. I will work with them to realize the ideals of the Learning of Antiquity, without ever putting forward my own opinions.

I will rigorously keep all of these vows. If I should ever betray them, let it be known to all the eight hundred myriads of gods of heaven and earth.

> To the Master, Hirata Kanetane
> Third year of Ansei, Tenth Month
> Magome Village, Kiso, Shinano Province
> Aoyama Hanzo

"This looks very serious."

"In addition to that, I will be entered into the register. My age as of the current year, my father's name and position, and even the name of the person sponsoring me will be written there."

Hanzo stepped to the door to check prospects for tomorrow's weather. When he returned, Juheiji gazed at him thoughtfully and said, "In your oath the term Learning of Antiquity is used often. Do the National Scholars really guide themselves by old times?"

"That's right."

"Does the past have all that much meaning? I wonder."

"The past you speak of is the dead past, but the past that Master Atsutane speaks of is the living past. Everyone is always talking about tomorrow, tomorrow. But no matter how long you wait, that tomorrow will never come. Today, you see, passes in the twinkling of an eye. Isn't the past all that is genuine and real?"

"That much I can follow."

"But the National Scholars do not guide themselves by the past alone. They do think that things have gone muddy since the middle ages."

"Wait a minute. I'm not all that well informed but I can't help thinking that the learning of the Hirata school is one-sided. What good is the Learning of Antiquity in a situation like the one we're in now?"

"That's just where it's most useful. The more the foreign countries provoke us, the more we'll look back to our own past. I'm not the only one who thinks so. Keizo and Kozo in Nakatsugawa think the same way."

The weather remained unsettled. A winter rain, dreary but not yet really cold, could be heard falling outside.

Edo was so huge that on this first visit Hanzo and Juheiji could form no clear impression of its true extent. There are no precise figures on the population of that time, but it must have been around two million.

It was in the direction of the rather thinly populated quarter where the houses of the samurai were most numerous that Hanzo, accompanied by Sakichi, would first venture out into that city. He had already been struck by the vastness of the city when he came to Ryogoku, but that was only one small district in the northeastern part of Edo.

Within a few days of arriving in Edo, Hanzo called at the Hirata residence in Yamashita-cho. He presented his oath together with offerings of sake, some seafood, and a fan. He was well received. Requesting that his name be recorded in the register of the Hirata house, he placed his offerings before Atsutane's shrine. Kanetane, whom he had faithfully followed for so long, told him to maintain his sense of purpose and to do his best in his studies. Then Hanzo returned to the inn.

Juheiji had gone to the theatre in Saruwaka-cho.

After that day Hanzo and Juheiji extended their walks into the city and gradually developed a better sense of its scale. Edo, as the popular saying had it, was made up of eight hundred and eight neighborhoods.

For gifts to take home, such as hair cords, oil, and toothpicks, the master of the Juichiya recommended going to Oyajibashi. From the foot of the bridge there, Hanzo and Juheiji looked out toward the Yoroi ferry. Countless town houses as far as the eye could see, the long lines of eaves, the tall fire towers, the long shop curtains, and the shadows cast by the godowns across the river created the harmony of black-and-white that was part of the atmosphere of Edo.

Yet that world was still in the feudal age. There were some fifteen or sixteen bastions serving as checkpoints at the entrances to Edo castle along the inner moat, and to reach them it was necessary to pass through one of the ten gates along the outer moat. Moreover, the residences of the greater and lesser daimyo were distributed in strategic locations, making it possible to judge the size of the establishment, the area of the grounds, the extent of the gardens, and even the number of trees. In the careful distribution of sites to the vassal lords and to the allied lords could be seen a scale model of the entire nation. It could even be said that all Edo was one vast internal customs barrier. There were wooden gates at every intersection and beside each gate was a guard post. As they had observed at the Kiso-Fukushima barrier, the officials not only inspected everyone who went through but also kept each other under surveillance. Even the magistrate could not escape being watched by his subordinates. Magnify all this many thousands of times, and that was Edo.

Their time in the city passed quickly and the last day soon arrived. Hanzo had not bought one-tenth of the books he had planned to get, nor had he called upon his fellow disciples as he had hoped. He had not even been able to visit the site of the former residence of Kamo Mabuchi. But he had gone to the Hirata house and been cordially received as a disciple, and he had made the acquaintance of Kanetane and his son Nobutane. He felt a deep sense of satisfaction as he began packing his bags at the Juichiya.

When he finally stepped out into the corridor, it was already near evening.

"Hanzo! I went out shopping by myself today and I saw some fine girls!"

This was Juheiji's report as he came in carrying gifts for the people back home.

"Sometimes it seems as though that's all you ever look for."

As he replied, Hanzo found himself blushing. Then, leaning against the bannister in the upper corridor of the inn, the two talked for a while about their journey and the things they had seen. They agreed that the cool refinement of the young women with casually elegant hair styles and tie-dyed sashes was something that could only be seen in a great city. And while the girls of the Kiso would blow on dried onion stalks in their play, the girls here blew on the fruits of lantern plants. Then there was the artlessness of the little Edo girls on their way to their lessons, carrying their sober, dull orange indoor slippers under their arms, and there was the intense sexuality of the women wearing kimono with black beaded collars standing with pensive expressions just inside the curtains of the teahouses. The fully matured Edo taste and refinement, they agreed, seemed to have gone as far as it could possibly go.

Presently, Hanzo called Sakichi and asked him to assemble the baggage for the next morning's departure. Sakichi still listened carefully whenever the street sellers came along crying their wares, whether it be sardines or crabs. Now he began telling Juheiji about the day he and Hanzo had gone to the Hirata residence. On their way back, around noon, they had stepped into a shop that served light refreshments. Sakichi had been startled by the loud welcome given them by the footwear attendant.

"Hey! Come on in!"

Sakichi tried in his quiet voice to mimic the tone.

"That 'Hey! Come on in!' really scared me. I stopped dead in my tracks," he said, laughing again.

"Sakichi, we're leaving Edo. Let's have dinner together tonight."

They gathered in the kitchen of the inn and the trays of food were served. Sakichi sat quietly, as if he were back at the hearthside in Magome tending the fire as he ate with the family. Although the food at the Juichiya was usually austere, the departing guests were treated to sashimi in honor of the occasion. In the Kiso, people ate birds from the forest or the flesh of bears, deer, and wild boar; for a special treat, they might serve the larvae of ground wasps. When it came to fish, there was salted mackerel or sardines, or for the New Year's festivities, larger salted fish. Instead, Hanzo and Juheiji were now served with the rich raw meat of the tuna, accompanied by delicate garnishes of thin green seaweed known as "sea hair" and green shiso seeds on their slender stalks. There were also yellow chrysanthemums and, beside the grated white radish, a small mound of fierce, green Japanese horseradish.

"In a place like this, we're just savages from the mountains." Juheiji was speaking to the waitress who sat before them in a kimono, red inner collar fashionably showing.

"There's a story about that," said Sakichi, rising to his knees. "They say that when Yamamura of Fukushima came to Edo, everyone called him Yama-zaru, or 'mountain monkey,' and he just couldn't stand it. One day he decided to invite the people who had been saying this to come to the residence of the lord of Owari. When they arrived they found Yamamura roasting chestnuts in a hibachi and stirring them with the point of an arrow. 'These are the famous Kiso chestnuts,' he said."

"Showing them what a real wild man looks like, eh?" Juheiji burst out laughing, but Hanzo cut him off.

"Juheiji, Edo is too sophisticated. It's too much for us. We're better off as mountain monkeys."

After dinner they again compared their impressions of the journey. Juheiji was most taken with the roadside tea shops and the attractive waitresses, while Hanzo remembered the sound of books being read aloud by students in the daimyo residences.

That night they lay side by side but did not sleep well. Disturbed by the sound of the nightwatchman's clappers, Hanzo checked the dagger that he had placed beside the dim night-light. Reassured, he pulled the quilts over his head and thought about the day he had called at the Hirata residence. He had come away encouraged by Kanetane to persevere in promoting the Learning of Antiquity. The world was soiled. Edo had reached a dead end. Yet in spite of all the shouting and confusion, Hanzo felt certain that the dreams of the National Scholars could be realized in this land.

"Fools like me get along somehow."

His thoughts carried him that far.

The next morning, they were determined to get the earliest possible start. Hanzo had put on his blue cape, and Juheiji his persimmon one. Sakichi had already tied the strings of his straw sandals. They were ready to go.

The master of the Juichiya came in.

"I thank you. We have not been able to do as well by you as we might have wished, but please come again soon," he said, wringing his hands as he spoke.

His young wife, born in Edo and knowing nothing of the Kiso, came to his side and joined in the farewells.

"It makes us feel homesick when we see people from the Kiso."

It was not far from the Juichiya to the Ryogoku bridge and Hanzo suggested that they have one more look at the Sumida river as a farewell to Edo.

In a few minutes they came to the wharves at the riverside. It was still early and the great city of Edo was not yet awake. A riverboat was passing downstream under the bridge, riding the swirling waters of the Sumida. Among the swarms of moored small boats, still half-wrapped in dream, the first sounds of life on the water were the shouts of the crewmen on the riverboat. Hanzo knew from the stories he had heard at the Juichiya that this was the mail boat rushing from Kawagoe in Saitama province to the shore at Ise-cho.

"It's sunrise!"

All three spoke in unison. Stamping their feet in the cold, they turned around to see the sun rising in the early winter sky, off in the direction of Honjo. It was reddish, but not blindingly brilliant. In the remote mountains of the Kiso, they were accustomed to watching the sky grow gradually brighter above the valleys; they had never before seen the sun rising from their own level in this way. They set out quickly in the direction of Senju, quietly leaving the bridge behind.

4

From Senju to Nikko was a round trip of two hundred twenty miles, plus another eighty miles to Yokosuka and back. Add the distance between Edo and the Kiso and the total journey came to something like seven hundred miles.

By the time they had completed their trip to Nikko and returned to Senju, it was already the tenth day of the eleventh month. They went straight from Senju to Takanawa, passing through the great wooden gate at Fudagatsuji, and by the guard station, and emerged onto the shore at Sodegaura. According to the rumors, construction work had already been completed on the coastal batteries, and they could see five gun emplacements pointing at the horizon. As they walked along the shore to Omori, Hanzo suddenly stopped short. There, just offshore, was the first steamship he had ever seen. It was the Kanko Maru, a sidewheeler that had been bought from the Dutch.

Their travels had at last brought them in sight of the deep blue of the ocean. They went from Kanagawa to Kanazawa in order to catch the boat to Yokosuka, and when they arrived at the harbor the ship lay just offshore waiting for freight and passengers.

"It really feels as though we've come a long way. I wonder how things are at home."

"Yes, I wonder too."

"By the time we get back, there will probably be snow on the ground."

"I suppose so. Anyway, back home they'll have made breakfast as usual and right now they're probably talking about us."

During this conversation the boat left the Kanazawa shore. The sea leaped under the moving ship. Hanzo and Juheiji were discussing the people they would see in Kugo village in Yokosuka. The Yamagami house had a history of more than five hundred years and the founder of the Aoyama line, a direct descendant of the Miura, had formed a branch of that house. As they talked, they imagined the seas their ancestor must have crossed and the roads he must have traveled before reaching the remote western end of the Kiso valley.

At that time Yokosuka was still a fishing village. Hanzo and his companions, viewing a shoreline from a ship for the first time in their lives, had no basis for comparison but they could easily imagine what it would have been like had they continued their journey among the many large and small islands that lay off the shores of the Miura peninsula. The harbor of Yokosuka was hidden in a place that seemed to lie in the embrace of mountains stretching down to the shore.

Kugo village was only a stone's throw from the fishing hamlet where they landed. When they went into Yokosuka to ask for directions to the Yamagami residence they learned that it was an ancient mansion well known to all the fishermen. The village was very different from what they had anticipated during their long journey from the Kiso. Far more tranquil, it seemed like an enchanted village where the distant crowing of roosters could be heard and where the smoke rose above the dwellings of fisher folk.

"To the honjin of Tsumago, Aoyama Juheiji, one short sword. The sword is old but unsigned."

"To the Magome honjin, Aoyama Hanzo, one hanging scroll of the Islands of the Immortals, painted by Korin."

Shichirozaemon, the present head of the Yamagami house, had long since chosen these gifts for his guests and he had been eagerly awaiting their arrival.

"They ought to be here by now. Have someone go out and see."

Once Shichirozaemon had heard that Hanzo and Juheiji were going to walk more than two hundred fifty miles to visit him, he could hardly keep still. Moving quietly from the twenty-mat main room of the mansion, past pillars thick enough for a man to hide behind, he made his way to the fifteen-mat and the ten-mat sitting rooms, where he had planned to receive his guests. The two gifts he had so carefully selected were waiting on ceremonial stands in the alcove, and on the walls, for his guests' enjoyment, hung scroll paintings that had been passed down in his family for generations.

Many things had been kept for centuries in Shichirozaemon's house, from the finely detailed genealogy showing the descent of the Yamagami from the Miura, and the Aoyama from the Yamagami, to various pieces of ancient battle dress, armaments, paintings, and ceramics. In his chests, too, was a bottomless supply of old books that he wanted to show to his guests. Running through the preparations in his mind, he gazed out at the ancient garden where trees had been arranged to blend into the pattern of the pine-covered mountains behind, in the style favored by gardeners of long ago. Azaleas and maples were planted among harsh boulders, and the miniature mountain was covered with moss. There was a calm, solid stone lantern in the ancient style and near it were clusters of large-leaved low plants. Here, the times of distant ancestors seemed to be manifest, alive and breathing before the eyes of their descendants.

"When they arrive, I'll bring them to see this garden. I've enjoyed it since I was a child. It has scarcely changed in that time."

While Shichirozaemon was sunk in these thoughts, Hanzo and his companions arrived. Summoning his servants, Shichirozaemon changed into formal dress and then went to the entrance hall to greet his guests. On the walls of the entrance hall hung many ancient lances and spears.

"I am delighted! I am delighted!"

Shichirozaemon's voice was so full of joy that he sounded as if he might be in shock.

"These are the members of the house. Please take off your sandals and come in."

His wife stepped forward to add her greetings and then they followed the master of the house inside; Juheiji had a grave expression on his face and Hanzo, one of lively interest. Sakichi tied up the strings of the straw sandals.

In the sitting room, Shichirozaemon formally observed his reunion with Juheiji and his first meeting with Hanzo. This person was introduced as a son, this as his younger brother, these are the sons' brides, and even after all these there were still the younger children coming in one after another, round-eyed, to make their bows. The two lost count of all the retainers and relatives that their host brought in to pay their respects, each in turn.

"So here we are, Aoyama; three couples in all."

These words of Shichirozaemon made a deep impression on Hanzo and Juheiji.

Refreshments were quickly provided, and served in the style of a family that placed great value in the old ways of doing things. After the white-haired grandmother had brought in the dishes on ceremonial trays and made her greetings, a sixteen or seventeen-year-old granddaughter brought in a long-necked jug of sake.

"Ah, ah, such fine young men!" The old woman bowed before Hanzo and again before Juheiji.

"Please do not hesitate to accept this," she said as she placed before each of them a set of three earthenware dishes on a ceremonial stand of unfinished white wood. Then she offered them unheated sake.

"Once again I drink with my relatives!"

Hearing Shichirozaemon's joyful toast, Juheiji accepted his cup. Then Hanzo, too, drained his.

"Isn't it a marvelous connection that brings us together this way," said Shichirozaemon to his mother. "When I enjoyed a night's hospitality at the Aoyama house in Tsumago, I noticed that we had the same crests and realized there must be an ancient connection. They have the circle with three bars, and the bird's nest. If it hadn't been for that, I would have passed through without knowing, and we couldn't have enjoyed this rare and wonderful privilege of having them come all this distance to visit us. It seems like a dream for us to be here exchanging cups this way!"

"It was surely our ancestors who brought you together." The old woman spoke as old women do.

To Hanzo, coming to Kugo village on the Miura peninsula in Sagami province meant coming close to Uraga, where the Black Ships had landed.

Now, settled comfortably in this old mansion in Kugo village, he at last was able to sort out the impressions he had gained from the letter Fumidayu had shown them in Oiwake, and from his conversations with the old man at the Juichiya. The highway lined with pine trees that ran between here and Edo was the same one over which couriers had shuttled back and forth when the American, Perry, had first come three years ago, in the sixth month. The forces from Owari and then from Hikone and other han had rushed to take up positions along this seacoast, or had gone directly to Uraga.

Hanzo was deeply grateful to Juheiji for having invited him along on the journey. If it had not been for Juheiji, there would have been little likelihood of his ever having had such an opportunity to travel. He was also grateful to Sakichi for accompanying them. Sakichi had followed them through wind and rain over the long road, staying with his masters like a shadow, and taking care of their needs all the way. Thanks to his companions, Hanzo had realized his desire to be accepted as a disciple of the Hirata school, and he had seen Edo. He had seen Nikko, too, and finally, his perspectives broadened by travel, he had been able to come to Miura to talk with such a person as Shichirozaemon.

One of Shichirozaemon's duties was to report every unusual occurrence to the officials at Uraga. He was a person of such importance in the area that in effect every ship that entered Edo bay did so only with his permission.

When the traditional exchange of sake cups had been completed, Shichirozaemon's wife brought in some confections.

"Why don't you take them out to the teahouse?"

"Very well. But I wonder if I should."

"Wouldn't it be better there? It's quieter and more comfortable."

"Well," he said to Hanzo and Juheiji, "there are all kinds of things I want to talk with you about. But right now, I would like you to see the genealogy that has been kept in this house. Then I'll take you to the teahouse."

Shichirozaemon removed a scroll from a cupboard. It looked as though it might be ten or twenty feet long when fully unrolled. He laid it out between Hanzo and Juheiji.

The names of distant ancestors from the time when the Yamagami forebears still bore the name Miura were written in it. There was the garrison commander Miura Tadamichi, and also Miura Heidayu, who built Kinugasa castle and established his domain in the Miura peninsula. Then they found the name of Miura Osuke Yoshiaki, who killed himself in Kinugasa castle in the eighth month of the fourth year of Jisho, 1181, at the age of eighty-nine. There, too, was the name of Miura Wakasa no Kami Yasumura, who committed suicide with his family in the Hokkedo in the sixth month of the first year of Hoji, 1247, when his plot to restore the former shogun Yoritsune had been frustrated.

"Look, Hanzo, here's the name of Miura Hyoenojo. He held the junior lower fifth court rank. In the second month of the second year of Genko, he joined with Nitta Yoshisada in the attack on Kamakura, destroying the entire Hojo family to avenge his ancestors."

"All of them were people who took part in the wars."

Hanzo and Juheiji gazed at the wonderfully detailed genealogy, burning with curiosity.

"As you can see, the house of Miura was nearly destroyed by Hojo So'un, and then it rose again," said Shichirozaemon. "One branch received a grant of seventy-five hundred acres of land and it took the name of Yamagami. They say that long ago the country hereabouts used to be called Kugo no Ura or Otazu. There is a place here on the Miura peninsula called Aburatsubo. The graves of Miura Dosun and his son are there."

Presently, Shichirozaemon led Hanzo and Juheiji along the path through the garden to the teahouse. They went past the Inari shrine that stood at the foot of the slope, walked through a rock garden, and came to a spot behind the miniature mountain.

Juheiji looked back at Hanzo.

"I'm really amazed. The second head of this family was adopted from the house of Kusonoki. Every year, at New Year's, they place a portrait of Kusonoki Masashige in the alcove and place offerings of cake and sake before it."

"We thought our family was old but this one is far older."

The teahouse looked out over the ocean from its site among pine trees on the mountainside. When his guests had taken their seats, Shichirozaemon finally began to describe his tour of guard duty at Uraga. In great detail he told them all about the time the American warships had entered the harbor at Uraga with two thousand sailors aboard.

Shichirozaemon himself had seen Commodore Perry's three-masted flagship, the *Mississippi*. When the Uraga commissioner learned of the Americans' arrival, he immediately gave orders to reinforce all strategic positions and declared that Uraga was not the proper place to meet with foreigners. If they wished to present their letter from the president of the United States, they should go to Nagasaki. But the Americans' determination to open relations with Japan was no sudden whim; they were persistent and unshakable. If the letter could not be delivered at Uraga, they would go to Edo. If that still did not achieve their purpose, they would unleash their warships. They placed the local garrisons under tremendous pressure. Not only did Perry send out a survey party to take soundings of Uraga harbor, but the fleet also entered Uraga bay, passing beyond Kannon cape at the entrance and proceeding as far as Hashirimizu. The meeting at Kurihama between Perry and the commissioner took place after that. The elaborate curtains of a field headquarters were set up on the beach and five thousand warriors armed with bows and arrows and firearms stood guard. Two thousand marines came ashore and took up formations. The sound of the great guns on the warships reverberated among the mountains as they fired their salutes.

In conformity with his previous position, the commissioner spoke not a single word. He simply accepted the letter and then the meeting was over. It lasted only about an hour from start to finish.

Thereafter, Perry continued to make a great show of military strength, pressing the Japanese as if determined to bring their noses down out of the air a bit. The entire fleet advanced from Koshiba to the waters off Haneda, from where the streets of Edo could be seen in the distance. Then they withdrew, leaving word that if their letter could not be delivered they would have to resort to extreme measures. The demands did not stop there. If Japan should remain unbending in her refusal to open the country, the Americans would correct that attitude, with military force if necessary. The Japanese were entitled to fight back in accordance with their laws, but the Americans were certain to win. They sent two white flags ashore, instructing the Japanese that when they acknowledged their defeat and wished to sue for peace, they should display the flags. Then the bombardment would stop.

"I saw the American ships. I saw the nine ships that came the second time, too. You know that the second time they came, they remained offshore for three months. I tell you, they anchored there as if to say they would not move until they got the answer they wanted from us, no matter what we might think about it. They just sat there, solid and threatening as boulders."

Shichirozaemon's story made Hanzo and Juheiji aware of the difficulty their country had faced. It also made them feel, as young men of the time, that such uneasiness was to be expected. At the same time, they were moved to contemplate how these dark new currents of world affairs had not hesitated to roll up even to the shores of this idyllic fishing village on the Miura peninsula.

"Well, that's the story up to now. I am rather clumsy at serving tea, but since you have come all this way, I should like to offer you some."

Shichirozaemon wiped the lid of the tea container with a silk cloth. He put some of the fragrant powdered tea into a tea bowl. With the power of his intimacy with water and the heating of water, he filled the tea bowl with the emptiness of rank, high or low, of wealth or poverty, with astringency, with sweetness, with richness, with delicacy. The froth and the brew seemed to melt into each other in the powerful scent of the tea. Hanzo and Juheiji forgot for the moment just how far from home they were.

A servant came from the house to inform them that the bath was ready. Shichirozaemon glanced from the servant to Juheiji.

"Aoyama of Tsumago has no doubt forgotten you."

"I accompanied the master on his journey and you gave me a night's lodging at your home in the Kiso," the servant explained.

The evening sun flowed into the clearings in the pine forest. The sea glistened.

"With such a brilliant sunset, tomorrow should be clear. Let's go to the seashore and I'll show you how to cast a net. I hope you'll give your feet a good long rest here in Miura."

In Shichirozaemon's words they could hear the accents of a person of their ancestral homeland. From here had come the Aoyama, who had founded mountain villages in the Kiso. Below the cliffs, the surf dashed against the shore in a steady rhythm, like the beating of the great pulse of all the life of the planet. Hanzo and Juheiji were reluctant to leave, and they gazed back at the sea repeatedly as they returned through the pine forest.

5

Foreigners—both Americans and Russians; in the broadest sense, Europeans. Foreigners who were neither Chinese nor Korean nor Indian. The first impression they left with the people of this country was by no means as pleasing as later generations might imagine.

If only the Black Ships had not come with the kind of men who would leave white flags on the coasts of this country. If only the Black Ships had not come with people who would demand the opening of the country, by force if necessary. If only they had brought emissaries of peace and friendship instead, then those who lived here might not have looked upon the visitors with such revulsion. We might even have had a history that included a warm welcome for them.

I don't know about China or India, but if these visitors had come prepared to teach us about the true mutual responsibilities of nations, I am certain our people would have welcomed them. And we might very well have managed to avoid the shock and deceit and confusion that took place within our nation. Unfortunately, the Europeans came to the people of this island nation in the guise of world conquerors. "To realize the mighty goal of the total conquest of all primitive conditions of nature through the invincible manifestation of the organized will of mankind"—this was what the Black Ships signified.

At that time we did have the words *komo*, meaning "red-hairs," and *keto-jin*, meaning "hairy foreigners"—literally, "hairy Chinamen." But the meaning of the words stopped with the relatively trivial reference to the different hair coloring of the foreigners. They were used in a half-joking sense. They did not in any way imply that we were uncivilized savages as the foreigners on board the Black Ships came so perversely to imagine.

In fact, it must not be forgotten that long before the 1850's, for more than two hundred fifty years, we had carried on relations with Europeans. The earlier Europeans included Portuguese among them but for the most part they were Dutch. And they weren't limited to notables such as Siebold, the great figure in the introduction of Dutch medicine to Japan by way of Nagasaki. The profits that the Dutch realized in trade with Japan were said to have averaged more than one hundred fifty thousand ryo each year. They imported all kinds of woolen cloths and calico, exquisite glassware and cut glass, and other rare artifacts and products from Europe, Siam, and the East Indies. They did not lose a single opportunity to profit by their association with us. They even put up with being treated by our officials more as slaves than as free men, and would meekly accept any affront, even from the prostitutes in the ports. It was those traders who set the precedents and gave the Japanese officials their ideas about foreigners.

So it was the Dutch who first made Japan known to the world, and indeed, it was the Dutch who introduced Europe to this country, acting as interpreters for their fellow Europeans as well as fierce competitors. Our first negotiations with foreigners were conducted for the most part in Dutch, and everything passed through a Dutch interpreter. Even the letters presented by Perry were accompanied by Dutch translations. We had no direct conversations with the Americans at all.

In addition to lacking a common language, East and West had different moral standards and expectations. When we could not even understand what they were saying, how could we distinguish between Americans and Russians, between the British and the Dutch? How could we have known that the new foreigners coming in waves to Nagasaki, to Uraga, to Shimoda would so violently reject the posture the Dutch had always taken up to that time? How could we have known that ambassadors from foreign countries would insist on being treated on the basis of that absolute equality which alone would not injure the dignity of representatives of sovereign nations? We lost our first opportunity to observe Europe quietly and peacefully. Pressing in upon us was a complete unknown, whose true scale we had no way of measuring. And what they wanted from us was not the culture that Japan had built up over the centuries, but sulfur, camphor, silk, and the gold and silver produced in these islands.

On the twelfth day of the eleventh month, Hanzo and Juheiji left Kugo village after a two-day visit. They carefully packed the short sword and the Korin scroll that Shichirozaemon had given them, took their leave of the Yamagami house, and set off toward their own mountains. On the road home, they would be seeing the second full moon of their journey.

For Hanzo the elation of the journey was mixed with eager and apprehensive thoughts about the future. Shichirozaemon had walked with them to a place on the highway where they could see the ocean and, at the moment of parting, had pointed out the direction in which Shimoda lay. The foreigners were no longer the distant creatures of cheap woodblock prints. Across Sagami bay in the harbor of Shimoda, Townsend Harris, the first American consul, and Heusken, his secretary, had already come ashore and taken up temporary residence in the Chosenji, where a red, white, and blue flag had been raised high.

CHAPTER FOUR

1

IN 1859, the sixth year of Ansei, the Nakatsugawa merchant Yorozuya Yasubei, accompanied by his head clerk, Kakichi, and by Yamatoya Risuke, set out from Mino for the newly opened port of Yokohama with a load of raw silk to sell to the foreigners there. Miyagawa Kansai, the Nakatsugawa physician who had been Hanzo's teacher, went with them. It was, of course, no mere sight-seeing trip for Kansai; he was hoping to make a little money as Yasubei's secretary.

Leaving Nakatsugawa in the tenth month, they crossed over the Magome pass and followed the Kiso road to Edo, where they took temporary lodgings at the Juichiya in Ryogoku. They planned to remain there until they got their bearings and then go on to Yokohama. They knew that the retired master of the Juichiya was a Kiso man who enjoyed looking after people; the sort of person who would give them some assistance even if they were from Mino. Since Hanzo had stayed with him earlier and now he was entertaining Miyagawa Kansai, the old man of the inn said that the appearance first of disciple and then of master seemed to signify some special connection among them.

"I don't think there are any inns in Yokohama yet, so you'll probably have to stay in Kanagawa. The Botan'ya in Kanagawa has been in business a long time. They will take good care of you."

After hearing the old man's opinions, the four travelers set off down the Tokaido to Yokohama.

Yokohama was dreary. Set under cliffs steeper than those at Kanazawa, it had all the qualities of a newly opened port. Foreign trading vessels frequently called, but their crews would invariably return to their own ships to sleep or else go on to Kanagawa.

The British, American, French, and Dutch consulates that had been moved from Shimoda to come up to Kanagawa had found this lively town on the Tokaido far preferable to the desolate Yokohama, and they showed no signs of leaving their temporary quarters in the Hongakuji and the other temples in the area. Once they had seen all this for themselves, the four traders decided to follow the advice of the retired master of the Juichiya and take up lodging at the Botan'ya in Kanagawa.

For them it was a considerable adventure to have come all this way from Mino in the hope of making money. For one thing, transporting the raw silk on horseback over the more than two hundred miles of roadway from Naka-tsugawa to Kanagawa had been no easy matter, and besides that the people with whom they planned to trade were foreigners about whom they knew nothing.

In those days all sorts of tales about foreigners were still going around. It was said, for instance, that on an earlier occasion a foreigner had come to Japan and, seeing a woman of this country, had become enamored of her. But his declarations were to no avail. He then said if that was how it was to be, would they please give him just three hairs from her head. Since there seemed to be no good reason to refuse, he was given the three hairs. The woman, however, was put under a spell by the foreigner's magic and in the end went off to the foreign country. When the next foreigner came and asked for three hairs from a woman's head, three hairs were pulled out of a mesh sifter and given to him. Everyone was astonished when the sifter soon rose into the air and flew off to the foreign country. All agreed that the foreigner must have been a Christian. It was said that everyone was terrified.

The ignorance of foreign countries was so profound that there were even stories about the empty bottles that had drifted ashore from the Black Ships. The crews of Perry's ships had thrown many bottles into the sea. When there was no wind some of these bottles would float with just their necks out of the water and the waves would carry them in to shore. The people who picked them up and took them home without reporting them were punished. Each bottle that was found had to be reported. According to the officials, they must surely contain poison; they must surely be intended to harm the Japanese people. A single place had been designated for their disposal and a strict order was put out that anyone who failed to report a bottle would be severely punished. So the bottles were duly reported: five bottles from this village, three from that village. The officials collected the bottles each day and piled them up in an empty house rented for this purpose. They locked all the doors and windows. They never suspected that the bottles had contained nothing more than the liquor that the Americans drank every day.

That was the way everything was. If a rattan chair swept off deck by the wind happened to wash ashore, it would be treated as a great mystery. A reg-ular deck chair would be still another great mystery. Among the gifts that Perry had left behind for the shogun were goods in bottles, boxes, and cans. The day after he left, these gifts were all burned on the jetty at Uraga after due consultation with Edo. It was feared that they might be carrying a curse. When Miyagawa Kansai arrived in Kanagawa, the people there had still not shaken off their terror of the Black Ships.

This was just after the great purge of the Ansei era. There is now no way of knowing just how much hidden struggle there was during the time that Ii

Kamon no Kami Naosuke, lord of Hikone, held the title of tairo, or great councillor. There was contention between Hikone and Mito, between Kii and Hitotsubashi, and among officials within the shogunate over whether the Treaty of Kanagawa was to be signed and who would succeed to the then vacant office of shogun. But this was only the prelude to an even greater struggle. Ii's purpose may have been to realize a unified national policy, but he made his appearance on the national stage as a rare specimen of divisiveness. Not only did he order the reprimand and house arrest of Nariaki, the retired lord of Mito and head of the opposition, and of all the daimyo and officials supporting Nariaki, but he also cast a fearful blight over the seedbeds of the new forces that were just beginning to sprout in distant Kyoto. He pressured the heads of the three noble houses of Takatsukasa, Konoe, and Sanjo into taking religious orders, and all other court nobles suspected of hostility toward the shogunate were ordered to be silent. Some of them were transported to Edo, traveling under the category of "old women," to be kept in detention. The arrests and punishments of activists, ronin, farmers, and townsmen continued relentlessly. One was ordered to commit suicide, another was sent to prison, five were executed, seven were exiled, nine were placed under house arrest, three were banished, seven were absolved, and three were severely reprimanded. Six other people, including Umeda Umbin of Wakasa, who had been singled out as the firebrand of the extremist "Revere the Emperor, Expel the Barbarians" movement, died in prison. Ajima Tatewaki of Mito, Hashimoto Sanai of Echizen, Rai Ogai of Kyoto, Yoshida Shoin of Choshu—all fell victim to Ii's anger.

The Nakatsugawa traders found that they had thrown themselves among foreigners in whom no one was yet able to place any confidence. But the Treaty of Kanagawa had been signed and foreign trade was being carried on openly. There was nothing for the traders to fear in the selling of raw silk. The prohibition of the building of ships of more than five hundred-koku capacity, which had been in force since 1633, the tenth year of Kan'ei, had been lifted and the seas were truly opened. Although the country had remained closed for more than two hundred years, the dreams of the navigators of old were now being revived.

Kansai was nearly sixty when he made this trip to Yokohama. He had cared for many patients with the Chinese medicine that he practiced, enjoying particular success in the treatment of eye disorders. Most of his practice had been in the immediate vicinity of Nakatsugawa, but he had often been summoned to Magome at the top of the pass and would go as far as Midono, Araragi, Hirose, and even Seinaiji. Whenever he had a bit of leisure he would read his books and teach students. In this way he had come to be known as a learned eccentric and his practice in Nakatsugawa had begun to fail. Recently he had been considering the idea of retiring to Iida in Shinano province. The master of the Yorozuya, who had brought him to Yokohama, had been a patient of his and Kansai had come on the trip with the promise that if he gave as much assistance as he could, he would be given a share of the large profits which the merchants expected to gain from the sale of the raw silk. Kansai was getting old and he was feeling apprehensive. He had no other wish than to be able to spend the rest of his life in some "hidden retreat."

Kansai's responsibility was to help Yasubei and the others feel out the conditions of the market in Yokohama. The newly arrived Westerners had understood that in order to cultivate prospective suppliers they would have to waste some money at the outset on things they did not particularly want, and so they were prepared to buy anything. This opportunity brought out the hand-to-mouth types among the Edo traders, those who had never been able to accumulate anything but who now decided to have another try in the new port of Yokohama. They found that the Westerners prized even the simple toys that they could put together with the two or three mon of capital they had brought with them. They learned, too, that they could sell even dubious treasures such as a reworked candleholder from a Buddhist altar for as much as two ryo so long as they claimed that it had once belonged to a daimyo. No other traders of raw silk had as yet come from the hinterlands and Yorozuya Yasubei and Yamatoya Risuke felt that they could not let this opportunity slip by.

They began gradually to understand some things. They learned that there were now, from the consuls to the secretaries, about forty foreigners in all. They learned that they had only to introduce themselves to make a sale. They even found someone who could serve as a rudimentary but useful interpreter.

Kansai was taken along when Yasubei at last went to meet a foreigner. At this time the twenty or so dwellings that made up the beginnings of the foreign quarter were situated in an area separated from the rest of the town on the Kanagawa bluff. An Englishman with a name something like "Keusukii" was living temporarily in Kanagawa until his new shop was completed on the Yokohama waterfront. This was the first foreigner that Kansai had ever seen. He was dressed in matching woolen jacket and trousers, and his jacket was fastened with buttons instead of being tied with cord. He also followed the foreign practice of keeping all the small articles he carried about in pockets in his clothing. He kept his handkerchief in a pocket in his jacket, and his purse in a pocket in his trousers; his watch was in a pocket in his waistcoat, with a chain running from it up to a buttonhole. And he was strangely shod—in Japan shoes made of leather were used only as substitutes for straw snow boots. He was impressed, however, by the sample of raw silk the merchants brought to him. He seemed to say that he would buy any amount of such splendid goods, but he twittered away as rapidly as a sparrow and their interpreter could not make much out of it.

Gazing upon Yasubei's neatly dressed topknot and Miyagawa's shaven head as though he were observing some rare specimens, the foreigner brought out tobacco, offered it to his guests, and then began to smoke with great relish. Kansai found that this Westerner, the first he had observed at close range, had hair and eyes of a different color but was in no way the terrifying apparition associated with the Black Ships. He was neither a ghost nor a demon. He was, after all, simply another flesh and blood human being.

"He says that he will pay one ryo for thirteen ounces."

Yasubei and his companions were greatly encouraged by these words. One ryo for thirteen ounces was an unheard of price.

Having learned the methods of trade and the price of silk, Yasubei and Risuke now agreed that they should leave Kanagawa as quickly as possible and buy up as much silk as they could by the following spring. They even sold all the silk brought as samples left in the care of the master of the Botan'ya and that alone had brought in one hundred thirty ryo.

"Master Miyagawa. We would like you to remain behind in Kanagawa," said Yasubei.

Kansai had no choice but to agree.

"You'll be all alone. Don't let the rats drag you off!"

The head clerk, Kakichi, spoke in his usual manner as he asked Kansai to look after things in Yokohama* while they were gone. All communication between Kanagawa and Nakatsugawa was left in Kansai's hands.

2

In the beginning of the eleventh month, Kansai found himself alone in his room at the rear of the second floor of the Botan'ya.

"I feel like an exile."

Whenever the loneliness became unbearable, he would climb to the high ground in Kanagawa where he could see the ocean. The top of a steep road led directly out to a corner of the Kanagawa bluff. A dismal Yokohama sprawled below. The new location of the transplanted half-farming, half-fishing village that had originally occupied the site was in one area; in another were the crude huts, little more than walls and roofs hung on posts set in the ground, that marked the new district, with the customs office at its center. In still another area the rice fields had just begun to be filled in and were being laid out in building lots. Off beyond the Benten forest there was only a thin scattering of lone trees for the eye to seize upon. It was all wet ground and there was still nothing about it that looked like the new harbor it was supposed to be.

Unable to bear looking at the ocean for long, Kansai would rush back to the inn as if pursued. Outside his second-floor window the cawing of the crows was a reminder that he was near a seaport. The cries would draw his thoughts back to his home, to his wife, to his children and his former disciples.

There had been an old paulownia wood desk in his study. There had been books on it. His disciples would gather—the son of the Magome honjin, the son of the Izumiya in Nakatsugawa, the son of the Nakatsugawa honjin. More than ten years had passed since the time they had regularly gathered beside his desk . . . Aoyama Hanzo of Magome, Hachiya Kozo and Asami

Keizo from his home town of Nakatsugawa. These had been the disciples in whom he had placed the highest hopes out of all those who had come to read books with him. He had taken pleasure in calling them the "three Zo's." As Kansai reflected on what kind of men they had become, it was Hanzo's determination and concentration that made him stand out as the most remarkable. Once he had decided upon a course of action, Hanzo was absolutely incapable of altering it.

As he continued his thoughts, Kansai reflected on a certain ambiguity that he sensed in his present position, an ambiguity that he would have felt called upon to explain if his three disciples had been standing before him at that moment.

"But it is certain that all three of them are dubious about this venture of mine."

"To say that one does not want money is the kind of falsehood characteristic of people afflicted with Chinese-mindedness."

These words from the twelfth chapter of the *The Jeweled Basket,* by that great forerunner Motoori Norinaga, now proved to be a powerful ally for Miyagawa Kansai. They helped him understand that to say one did not want money when in fact one really did was no better than the usual hypocrisy of Chinese-minded scholars.

"There is no one who does not want money."

That was why Kansai had accompanied the Nakatsugawa merchants to Yokohama. He understood that there is a great openness and magnanimity of spirit in people like the master Motoori. All things are forgiven before such a person, and yet those who are vigorous and direct as this great master was would not readily forgive an impoverished old age.

In absorbing the teachings of Motoori and Hirata, Kansai had long since come to share their dream of restoring antiquity. These aspirations inevitably brought him into contact with the movements in support of the imperial house that were beginning to rise up in Kyoto. That all three of his disciples were inclined to sympathize with the pro-imperial party was in fact the harvest of seeds he had sown. This had brought them into danger; all the victims of the purge of Ansei, six women among them, had been caught up in this maelstrom. Kansai could readily imagine how this would arouse the sensitive Hanzo back in Magome.

A considerable gulf had by now opened between the old master and his former students. It appeared to Kansai that Hanzo's learning was leading him closer and closer to direct action. He knew his disciples very well. He could understand their feeling that the time had come for an upwelling of that "manly spirit" observed in the ancient Japanese; their feeling that without it Japan could not pass through this greatest crisis of her long history.

Five European powers were joined in applying pressure to Japan. The question whether these pressures would liberate the country or place it in subjugation was still a source of painful uncertainty. The overwhelming first impression made by the Black Ships was not quickly forgotten. Ii Naosuke

had unilaterally opened the three ports of Yokohama, Nagasaki, and Hakodate without waiting for the emperor's approval, and it was said that Kyoto
had been greatly disturbed. Reports came in that the august mind of the
emperor himself had been discomfited. Open the ports? Expel the barbarians?
No two slogans could be more completely in contradiction. Nor could any
words more fully express the agony of the people of that time. From the
point of view of those who held to the former position, the idea of expelling
the barbarians arose out of blind obstinacy; for those who took the latter
position, the opening of the ports amounted to capitulation. All who
attempted to nurture and realize the best within themselves suffered these
contradictions and shared in the agony of the times.

There was a great oak in back of the Botan'ya whose limbs thrust out
almost to the roof of the second-floor corridor. Kansai stepped into the quiet
hallway and, all alone, wrung his hands.

"As a disciple of the Hirata school, I cannot remain unmoved by this terrible purge. But as far as I am concerned personally, I am resigned to it."

"You must be terribly bored."

The aged master of the Botan'ya would say this often as he looked in on
Kansai. This lodging on the Tokaido in Kanagawa was an old establishment,
the kind of place where guests would be offered an old-style smoking stand
with a handle on the top, and a chopstick case shaped like a folded fan would
be put out beside the great pastry box. Yet it was completely lacking in pre-
tension and guests were treated kindly.

Kansai could see the oak every time he passed along the hall outside his
room. It inspired him to practice his calligraphy. After gazing at the wintry
branches of the tree, he would begin writing with great intensity. This is
how the master of the inn found him one day when he went to his room.

"I have noticed that you scarcely ever go out except on business. Now you
are practicing calligraphy?"

"You know what they say about writing practice at sixty."

The master of the inn spoke without any trace of conscious social skill. He
told Kansai about the great camphor tree near the shore in Yokohama and
about the uncertainties that had been caused by the Treaty of Kanagawa. He
related that in a place known thereabouts as the forest of the sea god of
Komagata, there was a white crow that made its nest in a camphor tree. Each
year, with the coming of winter, it vanished to unknown regions. He also
told Kansai that they had chosen a good time to begin the selling of raw silk
or of anything else for that matter, because most trade was now completely
free. Only commerce in items bearing crests, in registers of court and military families, in books on warfare, and in swords and armor was still strictly
prohibited.

There came a cold day in the twelfth month. A scattering of snow sifted
down from the skies over the harbor. As before, Kansai kneeled facing his
desk, practicing calligraphy in an effort to comfort himself in the midst of
thoughts rushing in from afar. The aged mistress of the inn brought him two

letters, saying that they had come from the Juichiya in Ryogoku. Concerned for her guest, she had a maid bring up a bowl of noodles from downstairs. They were Kansai's favorite kind.

"You're treating me to noodles? Thank you very much."

"I boil them in water and then reheat them in soup stock and season with salt. I think that gives them the purest and lightest flavor. Please try some."

"These are very fine noodles. But what's really good on a cold day like this is sake. That helps a lot."

"I had hoped you would like them. We often make them for our older guests."

That was how the Botan'ya looked after all its guests.

One of the letters had come from the Kiso by way of Edo. It was a rare letter from Kimbei of the Fushimiya in Magome. It reported the death of Kimbei's only son, Tsurumatsu. He had been a sickly child. As a physician who had been repeatedly summoned to the Fushimiya, packing his medicine box and going by litter up the Jikkyoku pass on the border between Mino and Shinano, Kansai was well aware of this. Kimbei wrote at great length and with great feeling, beginning with his thanks for the services that Kansai had rendered to Tsurumatsu during his short life and then explaining how they had tried every possible prayer and ritual of intercession in the desperate hope that he might somehow be saved. A representative was sent all the way to the great shrine at Taga to pray for a complete recovery; a barrel of ceremonial sake was thrown from the bridge at Ochiai as an offering to the great avatar of Kumano. In Kansai's absence, they had called in a physician from Ogaki and an official physician from Wakasa who happened to be passing through the Kiso. They had even managed to get the physician attached to the retinue of the daughter of the lord of Mito to examine him. Kimbei's regret that all the efforts to save his son's life had been fruitless were reflected in every despairing word of the letter.

Kansai was deeply moved. That the simple and kindly Kimbei should have received such a shock at the age of sixty-three . . .

The other letter was from an old acquaintance. Here were written, in short phrases and in a weak and shaky hand, the most distressing complaints about the writer's debility and old age. He was only just barely alive. The letter spoke of his longing for old acquaintances and asked if there was not some possibility of one more meeting. "I am pleased that you are still among the living," it added.

" 'Pleased that you are still among the living.' How awful," thought Kansai as he bowed his head, not really knowing if he was laughing or crying.

Kansai's old acquaintances were dying off one by one. Those who were still working and in good health could be counted on one's fingers. There was Kimbei, preceded in death by his sixteen-year-old son; there was Hanzo's father, Kichizaemon—the count could not be taken much beyond this.

While Kansai was wishing that the winds of impermanence might blow him back to Mino, reports came from Yokohama of attacks by masterless samurai on foreigners and suspected foreign sympathizers.

3

Kansai greeted the new year in the inn at Kanagawa. He would go out to the
harbor district every day to check on market conditions and dispatch a report
to Nakatsugawa. Each time there would be a reply from the Yorozuya but he
still had no idea when Yasubei would be coming back to Kanagawa.

As the first year of Man'en, 1860, began, the number of people moving to
Yokohama increased day by day. Now, when Kansai went up to the Kanagawa bluff to look out over the ocean, the bustle appropriate to a harbor city
was at last apparent. The filling in of the swampy land over toward Benten
had been completed and long row houses of rental apartments had been built.
It was reported that the number of foreigners who had applied to lease land
had risen to twenty or thirty. The rebuilding of Yoshida bridge had begun
and ferry boats were beginning to shuttle between Kanagawa and Yokohama. One day, as Kansai walked up to the top of the Kanagawa bluff on
business, he saw that Mt. Noge was dimly misted while across the bay the
distant cliffs of Kazusa glistened in the sun. He realized that it would not be
long before spring came to this dreary new port.

A vessel moved dreamlike into Kansai's field of vision, catching the distant
ocean breezes in its sails. It was the *Kanrin Maru,* passing by Kanagawa as it
headed out to America with Japan's first foreign mission on board. This small
warship, purchased from the Dutch by the Tokugawa shogunate, was sailing
from Shinagawa with a Japanese crew. Its captain was Kimura Settsu no
Kami and Katsu Rintaro was the officer in charge. Every crew member, from
the navigators and the deck crew to the stokers in the boiler room, was Japanese. Not a single foreign crewman had been recruited for this epoch-making
voyage. That his countrymen should have the audacity to set out across the
Pacific ocean after only five years of instruction in the art of steam navigation
from the Dutch astounded Kansai. It had been reported that crewmen from
an American vessel wrecked off the shores of Satsuma and placed under the
Tokugawa government's protection were being sent home on this voyage.
The vessel was so small that it used its steam engines only when leaving or
entering port and depended entirely on the winds once it was at sea. There
was something slightly unsatisfactory in the appearance it presented as it
moved past Kanagawa with no smoke issuing from its funnel. But it had
created a great stir and the top of the Kanagawa bluff was packed solid with
people. Later reports had it that there was active discussion of the number of
straw sandals the mission had provided itself with for its travels in unknown
lands. It was also reported that Fukuzawa Yukichi, then twenty-six years of
age, was on board the ship as companion to Lord Kimura.

Early in the second month, Kansai received an unexpected communication
from the retired master of the Juichiya in Ryogoku. He said that he would be
coming to Yokohama for some sightseeing in the company of one of the
Tokugawa court physicians. He asked for Kansai's assistance.

*   *   *   *   *   *   *

The guest that Kansai, himself a traveler, awaited was Kitamura Zuiken, who had held the high rank of official pharmacist among the Tokugawa court physicians. At the time a crew was being recruited for the test sailing of the *Kanko Maru,* he had tried to join but had only succeeded in incurring the disfavor of the then chief physician. He had been reprimanded and then banished to the still wild reaches of Hokkaido. He had moved his family to Hokkaido two years earlier and he was now supervising the development of the port of Hakodate. He had come briefly down to Edo on business and he wanted to see the new port of Yokohama on this trip. All this was in the letter from the Juichiya.

On the evening of a fine day, Zuiken, accompanied by a single servant and guided by the retired master of the Juichiya, arrived at the Botan'ya. Kansai was impressed that Zuiken should choose to stay at an old inn like the Botan'ya rather than stay with any of the magistrates and commissioners who resided in Kanagawa. Upon meeting him, Kansai found Zuiken younger than he had expected. He looked to be no more than thirty-one or thirty-two.

"Our guest seems very young to be so famous," said the master of the Botan'ya, pulling at Kansai's sleeve as he spoke.

The next day Kansai and the master of the Botan'ya guided their three guests from Edo up to the Kanagawa bluff. There they passed through the great wooden gate and set out on the road to Yokohama. From the guard station the way led around the cliffs along the shore of the bay, where it eventually joined the road from Hodogaya. The residences of the commissioner and the Echizen garrison were here in Noge. From there they crossed the Noge bridge, went along the embankment road, and, after crossing the temporary span of the Yoshida bridge, entered the reservation.

"Yokohama is certainly a dreary place!"

"It was far worse when I first arrived."

Chatting together as they walked, Zuiken and Kansai strolled past the notice board near the customs office and then through the abandoned rice fields that had once given Ota Shinden, or "new fields," its name.

In distant Hokkaido there were hurried plans to search for medicinal plants and to establish hospitals, drainage systems, and silkworm plantations. Zuiken had many questions for Kansai and the master of the Botan'ya as he compared Yokohama with Hakodate. At that time the Yokohama reservation was shaped something like a butterfly. The two wharves jutting out from the shore corresponded to the antennae while the neighborhoods surrounding the customs office were the two wings. The part at the extreme left, which took in the forests around the Benten shrine, constituted the single spot of beauty on the butterfly's wings. But the greater part of the wings was still rice paddies and ponds.

As though to emphasize Yokohama's obligation to set a splendid example for the newly opened ports, construction was proceeding on a vast and luxurious brothel quarter. The master of the Botan'ya explained that since the streets were not yet organized in Yokohama, a headman had been appointed for every block or so and an elder placed over all the headmen. All this was coordinated from the town hall, which was next to the customs office.

Presently they came to a point on the waterfront near the wharves, where a scene of bustle and confusion met their eyes. Everything from single-masted and two-masted ships built along Western lines to ships from each of the five great powers, to all kinds of freight and courier vessels, fishing boats, and rowboats, some at anchor and some under way, became visible through air dense with seagulls and smoke. The two wharves, the piloting services, and the diplomatic and tariff functions carried on at the harbor offices had all been created just for the new harbor. A foreign ship entering the harbor upset the balance of the scene.

From their vantage point on the wharf, the master of the Botan'ya pointed out the site over toward Yamashita where the ninety households of the original fishing village of Yokohama had been forced to relocate. He made clear to Kansai and Zuiken what it had meant when so many people, both foreign and local, had begun to pour into Yokohama and to lease land in the newly developed areas. He told them about a new drainage channel being dug some three-quarters of a mile from south of the Ooka river to the edge of the Zotokuin. The sea wind felt different out here on the wharves. Zuiken stood motionless for a time, gazing at the foreign ship that had just entered the harbor. Then he turned back to Kansai.

"It's really well built. Even though they are all steamships, there is something different about the foreign ones."

"I'm not sure I like being out with you, Kitamura," put in the old man from the Juichiya.

"Why?"

"Because all you do is look at the ships."

"But, Juichiya, don't you want us to build fine ships like those in our country as soon as possible? Right now, even Satsuma, Tosa, and Echizen have only two or three steamships among them. And they were all bought from other countries. You've heard of the *Shohei Maru,* haven't you? It was built in the summer of the second year of Ansei by the lord of Satsuma, who presented it to the shogunate. That was the first three-masted sailing vessel the shogunate had ever owned. But listen to this! When they were building the *Shohei Maru* they still didn't know about screws, and they used nothing but plain, straight, ordinary nails in building it. So in the year of the big storm it simply came all to pieces off Shinagawa."

"You certainly know a great deal about these things."

"Even in Hakodate we still have only two-masters. One is the *Hakodate Maru.* The other is the *Kameda Maru.* It was built by a shipwright named Toyoharu who had been commissioned by Takadaya Kahei."

"Do you have to concern yourself with even the ships at Hakodate?"

"It amounts to that. But everybody there says it's too much for a quack doctor like me."

The words "quack doctor" brought a groan from Kansai.

A crowd which included several foreigners apparently out to meet the arriving ship had by now gathered around Kansai and the others. An old woman had set out her stock of tangerines to sell. Beside her another woman had unslung the child from her back and was sitting down to rest. A man wearing a dagger in his sash and straw sandals on his feet was walking around looking for some line of business requiring no capital. Waiting impatiently for the ship to come in was a Chinese moneychanger wearing a curious round hat and carrying a money bag on his back.

As they watched, a small boat flying a crested ensign that had put the harbor officials on board the ship was being rowed back to shore. Behind it came two or three lighters, tossing in the waves. They landed disgorging an unhesitating, utterly miscellaneous assortment of humanity that included people from the home countries and from the colonies as well as nondescript adventurers. Not a single woman was to be seen among them; they were all hard-bitten Western men. Some of them glanced back at their companions as they strove to be the first to set foot on Japanese soil. A pair who appeared to be uncle and nephew greeted each other effusively, embracing each other even though they were men. Right before Kansai and Zuiken's eyes, they passionately rubbed their cheeks together.

Zuiken playfully confessed that he had really come not to see Yokohama but to try eating beef. It appeared that this request was going to be rather troublesome for his hosts. Kansai himself wanted only to get back to Kanagawa while there was still daylight, because the sight of the setting sun inevitably turned his thoughts toward the skies of Mino.

The section of Yokohama that lay along the shore had been plotted in neat lines, streets were in, and there was a gate at each intersection. For the return, Kansai took the first street off Motomachi that led to the shore. They came out at a landing place for ferry boats. The ferries went to Miyashita in Kanagawa, and it would be possible to return without making the bothersome detour around Mt. Noge. The master of the Botan'ya bought the meat that Zuiken had ordered in Yokohama and carried it on the ferry ride back to Kanagawa.

"There are certainly a lot of crows in Yokohama."

"In Hokkaido we have what we call 'gome.' They're a kind of seagull. The sound of their cries really gives you a feeling of the North. By the way, didn't I hear that foreign missionaries are coming here to Yokohama?"

"What does the Treaty of Kanagawa say about Christianity, anyway?"

"Of course, it's still prohibited for Japanese. Apparently they are only allowed to preach to the foreigners who have come here."

"An American physician has also come to Kanagawa."

"All kinds of things are beginning to happen."

This desultory conversation continued throughout the ferry ride.

After they returned to the Botan'ya, Kansai had a little time to rest by himself. From the front hallway of the second floor of the inn, a part of the town of Kanagawa could be seen. There was still a vast distance separating his present situation from the rich Ina valley in Shinano where he hoped to spend his last years. He would have a very lonely road to tread before he reached his final "hidden dwelling."

The foreboding atmosphere that persisted after the great purge of Ansei also made him uneasy. He did not know what to make of the increasing strictness with which all the towns were being controlled, or of the menacing silence of the activists and the masterless samurai. There were already some who called for immediate action. One night in the seventh month of the previous year, two Russian naval officers had been killed in the Motomachi district of Yokohama. And in the eleventh month an employee of the French consulate had been stabbed near Kozakimachi. Most recently two Dutchmen, one a sailor and the other a merchant, had been killed in Motomachi. The streets of Yokohama were that frightful. No one who had not experienced it could appreciate the darkness that seemed to have crawled up from the sea into this newly opened port. Kansai congratulated himself on having had the privilege to serve as guide to such a person as Zuiken and to have returned to the Botan'ya while it was still light.

"Dinner is served."

Kansai went downstairs, following the maid who had come to make the announcement, to a large room facing the garden. He had not been in it before, but Zuiken and the retired master of the Juichiya were already there.

It was Juichiya who spoke first.

"I don't like to mention this before Kitamura and Miyakawa but I was astonished by the brothels in Yokohama."

"As soon as the place began to flourish, the first things that were built were sake shops and brothels," responded the master of the Botan'ya, who had come to look in on their evening meal.

The beef was cooked in the garden. The maids brought out a brazier and set it up on a stepping stone to prepare the dish. The old grandmother at the Botan'ya would not permit it to be cooked inside. Her voice could be heard from the interior as she cried out, "What a stench! What a stench!"

"It looks as though there are anti-Westerners here, too!" said Zuiken with a laugh, and the master, wringing his hands, replied, "No, I don't think so, but my mother is quite upset. She keeps saying that we'll be in for it if the smell of beef should linger. I'm telling you, there are old people here in Kanagawa who would cross the street to avoid walking in front of the butcher shop."

As he began on his sake, Kansai quietly observed Zuiken. In the way he repeatedly filled his sake cup and brought it up to pursed lips, the guest of honor too seemed not at all casual about his drinking. Kansai thought to himself that this was a man he could talk with. He spoke up impulsively.

"There's something I want to tell you. I think it was around the seventh month of the year before last. The British ambassador, Lord Elgin, had come up from Shimoda to Shinagawa in a warship, saying that he wanted to present the shogunate with a steamship. The people of Shinagawa must have felt they had a rare opportunity to entertain an ambassador, for the next day they sent a number of prostitutes out to the warship. Apparently the

Englishmen were outraged and what they said later was really good. 'What is this? Is this how the people of Japan regard their women?' Now isn't that just what Englishmen would say?''

"Why, I heard that kind of story too." Juichiya leaned forward. "They say that Westerners find the shaved eyebrows and blackened teeth of our women quite repulsive. Is that really so? After all, from our point of view it seems a very refined custom."

"Both sides seem to be repelled. Those who don't know what is going on keep saying all kinds of evil things: 'The high officials of the shogunate are conspiring with the foreigners! What's going to happen?' and so on. What about those who keep saying 'Close the ports and expel the barbarians'? If you ask me, it wasn't so much that the shogunate didn't know enough to close the ports and expel the foreigners, but that they did it far too early. Reading Western books was forbidden and it was impossible to work closely with Western scholars. Nor did they stop there. They even 'closed up and expelled' talented men within the country. Just look! They expelled Takahashi Sakuzaemon. They expelled Habu Genseki. And after that they drove out Watanabe Kazan and Takano Choei. In consequence, Japan became narrow and backward. It even became shameful to think about foreign countries—"

"The beef is ready," said Juichiya, cutting off Zuiken's speech.

A maid laid a sheet of white paper before each guest, on which they were to lay the chopsticks that had touched the meat. The beef dish was brought from the garden to the veranda. From within the house, a voice could be heard ordering the people of the Botan'ya to open all the sliding doors and air out the rooms.

Hearing this, Juichiya said, "Waitress, just tell them that the time will come when the grandmother and the lady of the house will come running when they smell this aroma."

"Well, should I prescribe a dose for myself?"

Kansai savored the smell of the cooking meat as he spoke. With his beloved sake before him, he could forget everything for a while. As a drinking companion he had a guest who was far heartier than he had imagined anyone in the shogunate could possibly be, and there was also the beef that he was tasting for the first time.

4

The decision to open the ports of Yokohama and Hakodate at a time when voices critical of the shogunate were being raised throughout the nation proved to be disastrous. With differences in race, morals, and customs generally being explained by East and West as marks of ignorance and savagery on the part of the other, these rapacious Westerners could not so easily be permitted to tread the soil of this nation. There were those who ground their teeth as they maintained that the opening of the ports not only violated the will of Tokugawa Ieyasu, now enshrined in the Toshogu, but constituted an act of *lèse majesté* against the imperial court itself.

But, according to Zuiken, nothing in this world had been more seriously misrepresented than the shogunate. If one wished to know of the circumstances surrounding the Treaty of Kanagawa, then one had to consider Iwase Higo no Kami, the man who had actually drafted the treaty. It was also necessary to know that he had previously been a censor for the shogunate.

What did it mean to be a censor? The emoluments of the office were not great nor was the rank particularly high, but there was no office with which it was not connected. Neither the most important of the commissioners nor even the senior council could make a decision without the approval of the censors. If anyone should try to act on his own in spite of the objections of the censors, nothing could prevent them from going to the council or to the shogun himself. No body of men was more concerned about the promotions or advances of others. The censorate could even be seen as determining the success or failure of an age by the quality of the men who occupied it. With the coming of the American ships to Japan in the Kaei era, a great shock was transmitted throughout the entire shogunate. That shock led to an extraordinary shuffling of offices as the government realized it had to obtain the services of the best men. Previously, positions had been passed from father to son, and, even if the son was outstanding, he could not be permitted to surpass his father. This policy was now corrected and three new men were appointed to the censorate. One of them was Iwase Higo no Kami.

Iwase's given name was Tadanari, and his alternate name was Hyakuri. His residence was in the damp and low-lying Tsukiji district, so he used the pen name Senshu, or "Toadland." All the best people supported him and considered him the most able man in the shogunate. When the Dutch presented the shogunate with a steamship, it was Iwase who took Yatabori Keizo and Katsu Rintaro from minor posts in the Bureau of Public Works and put them to studying navigation. He also assigned Shimosone Kensaburo and Egawa Tarozaemon to the task of learning about Western artillery, and placed Mitsukuri Gempo and Sugita Gentan in charge of the Institute for the Study of Foreign Books. The list could be extended indefinitely. Among men like Matsudaira Kawachi no Kami, Kawaji Saemon, Okubo Ukon, and Mizuno Chikugo no Kami, there was not one who had the best interests of the country at heart who was not also on close terms with Iwase. It was in fact Iwase who played the key role in leading the major figures in the han administrations toward actions appropriate to the times.

Zuiken went on to explain that in a time when virtually all the high officials were still lumping together English, Americans, Russians, French, and Dutch into the single category of "hairy Chinamen," the effort and anguish involved in exerting one's influence to lead the shogunate in a slightly more enlightened direction were beyond imagination. When Harris, the first American consul, came to Japan and attempted to open negotiations for a treaty of trade and friendship, all of the appropriate shogunal officials hung back, unwilling to accept responsibility. They all folded their arms and left things up to Iwase. Although he had no illusions about the fact that he was making a sacrificial victim of himself, Iwase shuttled back and forth between Edo and Shimoda. A draft treaty was at last produced after several months of effort.

When it was ready the daimyo were called to Edo castle. On that occasion, Ii Naosuke, the tairo, stepped forward and explained that the treaty of trade and friendship was inevitable. He then asked Iwase to speak on the matter. After Iwase had been given a careful hearing, Ii asked the daimyo to express their opinions. Ii withdrew and Iwase met with the daimyo in his place. Iwase then presented his closely reasoned arguments in a strong, firm voice; no one expressed disagreement. They all left in good spirits, feeling that his plan fit the needs of the time. Yet some days later, when it came time for the daimyo to submit their formal recommendations, many reneged on their word and tried to destroy every point in Iwase's argument. This was the work of subordinate officials, for the most part. Although they called themselves daimyo, the feudal lords could not control these people. Iwase thereupon met with Tokugawa Nariaki of Mito, Tokugawa Yoshikatsu of Owari, and with Matsudaira Shungaku, Nabeshima Kanso, and Yamauchi Yodo, asking their cooperation. It was from this time forward that the name of Iwase Higo no Kami began to be heard everywhere.

Still, one should not forget that the attitude of the Europeans with whom the negotiations were being carried on began gradually to change. Among the men who came, not all had the same attitude as Perry. The American consul Harris, his secretary Heusken, the British envoy Elgin and his secretary Oliphant—these men came to know Japan and to understand the state of affairs in Japan. And there were others who said that their first impression upon coming to Japan was of an unexpectedly high level of civilization. Very little of this came to be known, however, except to people like Iwase who were directly involved with them.

Many stories have been told about Iwase. The British were astonished by his quickness and intelligence. It was said that he noted down on his fan some of the things that the Englishmen said to him, and on their next meeting made use of those same English phrases with good pronunciation. The British were impressed, too, with the Japanese fan, finding that it could be used as a notebook, as an instrument to create a cool breeze, and as a solace in times of boredom.

Now Nariaki, the retired lord of Mito, was not all that obstinate a person. In the beginning, to be sure, he had been so unbending in his attitude toward all things foreign that the famous slogan of the time, "Revere the Emperor, Expel the Barbarians," was created by him as a motto for the Kodokan. But, as he listened to Iwase, he came to understand much that he had not understood before. He was by nature of a quick and open intelligence and he readily understood Iwase's explanation that today's "barbarians" were not the savages one read about in the old books. He became convinced that a mindless war could only do great damage to Japan. The retired lord told Iwase a story on that occasion. There was a beautiful girl. There was a man who wanted to marry her. He had been rejected two or three times without seeming to make any progress in his suit. But when he was at last granted the girl's hand in marriage, the love that developed between them was all the richer—in fact, far superior to that which obtains when an impulsive lover is immediately accepted. It was clear from this story that the retired lord of Mito had in effect given his consent to the treaty. He had accepted the fact that foreign relations were to be carried on, and he even urged his views on other daimyo, both vassal and allied. As a result, Fujita Toko and Toda Hoken, two shogunal officials from Mito who had hitherto supported Nariaki in advocating the closing of the nation and expulsion of the barbarians, both modified their own positions.

Then came the great earthquake of Ansei, in which these Mito leaders were crushed to death. The old lord had lost both his wings, but his own position grew more and more enlightened. In his long life the period in which he came to know Iwase became very special to him, and it was during that time that he began to change his opinions concerning foreign countries.

Iwase, however, met with a misfortune that was to ruin him. Iesada, the thirteenth shogun, was by nature weak and sickly and given to long silences. It was absolutely necessary that a strong successor be found for him, since busy days had to be passed in calming the han and responding to foreign pressures.

Only Hitotsubashi Yoshinobu among all the eligible Tokugawa was suitable. Furthermore, his father was Nariaki, retired lord of Mito, the most influential man of his age. So the officials concerned met and decided to recommend Yoshinobu as heir. Iwase was the main supporter of this move. It was taken for granted that Mito would encounter no opposition from the imperial court in Kyoto, but an opposing point of view emerged closer to home. Some began to claim that it would be truer to the spirit of a strict tradition of hereditary succession if the more closely related Yoshitomi of Kii were declared the heir. Support for his candidacy came from the women's quarters in Edo castle and from certain high officials of the other han who deeply distrusted the house of Mito.

When Iwase was informed of this, he brushed aside the argument of blood relationship and insisted that the crucial issue was to assure a capable and mature successor to the shogunate. The majority of the high officials in the shogunate supported his position. When the news leaked out to the country at large, the best elements among the general populace expressed their approval and pleasure. They eagerly awaited the succession, telling each other that the sun would soon begin to shine. But, after only five years in office, the young Iesada was suddenly stricken with beri-beri and died. Once again the advocates of Yoshitomi's candidacy gained strength and the tairo Ii Naosuke himself stated that it was in accord with the late shogun's will.

Ii's decision ended Iwase's political career. Virtually everyone who had supported Iwase, from Nariaki to the lords of Owari, Echizen, and Tosa, gathered at Edo castle and disputed violently with Ii. But the tairo was immovable. This marked the end of the prelude to the great purge of Ansei. Iwase was severely reprimanded for his advocacy and was forced to withdraw from public life. He was restricted in his movements and forbidden to see anyone without permission. Ii maintained that Iwase and his party, although low in rank, had tried to bypass him, the most important officer of the shogunate, in order to decide the succession on their own. Their offense therefore amounted to the most despicable kind of disloyalty and immorality. Ii further stated that the only reason he was not condemning these men to death was that Iwase too had had the peace and security of Japan at heart, to such an extent that his great labors could not be overlooked. Ii was therefore moved to spare him in what he called an extraordinary act of leniency.

Zuiken said that when he looked around Edo now, he found that everyone who had disagreed with Ii Naosuke, from Nariaki on down, had been dismissed. All the key officials had been changed. The high offices of the shogunate were filled with what amounted to little more than a clique of the tairo's followers. Before the overwhelming power of the tairo the shogunal officials could only stand aside, transfixed by terror. It was reported that Iwase was under house arrest in Mukojima, where, having changed his pen name to Osho, or "Gullsite," he was finding some consolation in his days of grief through his lifelong love of painting.

The master of the Juichiya left for Edo ahead of Zuiken, who remained behind in Kanagawa for two or three days while Kansai treated him for an upset stomach.

"Well, I'm going back to Hokkaido to sleep my days away again," said Zuiken when he gave his farewells to Kansai and the master of the Botan'ya. Then he set off, accompanied by the manservant who had come with him from Hokkaido.

Once his guests had departed, Kansai found himself facing days that were even more lonely than before. There was nothing to talk about, only trivialities such as the possible evil portent in the flashing of the meteors that were appearing in the skies almost every night. There were constant rumors, however, including one that another secret emissary had been sent from the imperial court to Mito and that, to throw off the ever-present Tokugawa spies, he had traveled down the Tokkaido in the guise of a priest on pilgrimage. People would come by and speak about all this with great animation, as though they had witnessed it themselves. There were also ceaseless rumors that masterless samurai were plotting an attack on Yokohama to expel the foreigners.

Several warm rains came and went. The white crow that had gone away somewhere during the winter returned to the great camphor tree near the Yokohama shore. The third month of the old calendar approached. Kansai found himself waiting with growing impatience for news of the Nakatsugawa merchants. His most recent inquiries into the market had shown a steady rise in prices, leading to talk of a price as high as one ryo for six or seven ounces of raw silk. He also learned that silk merchants from Omi and

Kai provinces and from around Iida in Shinano were coming into Yokohama one after another, making it necessary to be cautious. People were saying that foreigners such as the English merchant they had met saw a great future for Yokohama and wanted to build wooden stores and warehouses as soon as possible.

"Yorozuya is certainly taking his time, isn't he," said the master of the Botan'ya as he came up to Kansai's room for a visit.

On the morning of the third day of the third month, there was an unseasonal, heavy snowfall. When Kansai stepped into the corridor to enjoy the sight, he saw the leaves of the oak tree weighted down with snow until the branches seemed almost ready to break. But despite the snow, the maids were bustling about preparing white sake and boiling beans for the first girl's festival to be celebrated by the tiny granddaughter of the Botan'ya. Even the lonely Kansai would find the festive bent-wood box and the special sake and side dishes for the occasion on his serving tray that evening.

Kansai passed that entire day listening to the sound of melting snow dropping heavily from the branches of the oak. At last, when the leaves, all the brighter for having been wet with snow, began again to glisten in the newly emerged sun, a traveler from Edo brought news of an incident at Sakurada gate.

Some seventeen assassins had tossed a petition into the Mito compound during the snowstorm, thereby observing the formality of removing their names from the han rolls. They were now, technically speaking, masterless samurai. Nevertheless, they were still from Mito and they had lain in wait for Ii Naosuke and had taken his head. The news of this incident was transmitted from mouth to mouth almost as if the speakers were trying to hide it. Each of the assassins was reported to have carried a statement on his person to the effect that in killing the tairo he was carrying out the removal of a traitor, and spelling out clearly the reasons.

"I wonder how Kitamura Zuiken felt when he heard about this up in Edo," said Kansai, and his eyes met those of the master of the Botan'ya.

An uneasy quiet pervaded the atmosphere, as though the very act of trying to keep the tairo's death a secret gave some hint of the changes to come. Few had anything good to say about Ii, the late tairo, but there were some who noted that only when such a thoroughly hated person was dead could his greatness be finally recognized. Even though people still had evil things to say about him, the tairo had possessed one unique quality. In carrying out foreign policy, he had been neither intimidated by the prestige of the imperial court nor moved by the opinions of the daimyo and their retainers. Not only had he undertaken the signing of the treaty on his own authority but he had then attempted to extort the consent of the imperial court after the fact. There were many who felt that this constituted a grave offense, but what would have happened to Japan without such decisiveness? It might very well have suffered the loss not only of Hokkaido, whose importance was still not fully appreciated, but of Iki and Tsushima as well. Concessions would have been established on the main islands and heavy reparations demanded by the foreigners, so that Japan, like China around 1850 at the end of the Tao-kuang era, would have found it impossible to maintain her independence. The way in which the tairo had faced these great dangers and difficulties had to be recognized as a singular service to the nation. Such were the arguments advanced. At any rate, with the death of the tairo came the collapse of the strict position on the consanguinity of the shogunal successor. Kansai could readily imagine the rage with which the samurai of the tairo's han of Hikone would receive this news. With this threat of open hostilities between Hikone and Mito, it was impossible to know what lay ahead.

In the area that included Kanagawa and Yokohama, police surveillance became even stricter than before. Huge square pillars of cedar were set up at the approaches to Tsurumi bridge and a great beam passed among them, creating a new customs barrier. When night fell the two barriers in Kanagawa were closed completely, and a watchman, wearing a jacket with crests and in formal trousers, accompanied by three porters, kept strict watch on the temples occupied by the various consulates and foreign residents in Kanagawa. Few people were out on the streets at night; there was only the forbidding sound of the great watch drums.

5

In the intercalary third month of that year, cases of raw silk bearing Yorozuya's Kakuman trademark began to arrive at last at Kansai's inn. Kansai took care of each one in turn. As he examined the cases that had passed down all the stations of the Kiso road to Edo before reaching him, he knew that the Nakatsugawa traders would soon be coming to join him. He felt a certain amazement that these shipments of raw silk had actually arrived in good order in such disturbed times.

In the latter part of the same month, Yorozuya Yasubei set out from Mino accompanied by his head clerk, Kakichi. The two took the same route as before, staying in the Juichiya in Ryogoku and then going down to the Botan'ya in Kanagawa at the beginning of the fourth month.

Things suddenly became very lively around Kansai. Yasubei had arrived; his travel dagger was lying in the alcove. In a corner of the room sat Kakichi, untying his leggings. Both of them brought news of people back home whom Kansai was anxious to hear about—his wife and children, his friends, former disciples, and an endless list of others. But even more, they seemed to bring the very atmosphere of the east Mino basin to Kansai.

Kakichi came up beside the eager Kansai and spoke in his capacity as head clerk. "We have really kept you waiting a long time, Miyagawa sensei. But there was nothing we could do until the spring silkworm crop was ready."

Yasubei also expressed his appreciation.

"You have been most patient. I had intended, if it took this long, for you to go home and come back again . . ." A merchant such as Yasubei, prepared to carry on a trade in raw silk over more than two hundred fifty miles of highway, was certain to have such concerns. "But if we didn't have someone here, we would not have known the conditions in Yokohama and we couldn't leave it to strangers—it was a great comfort to know that you were the one staying here."

Presently it came time to light the lamps, and the three ate their first meal together in a long time.

They could hear the sound of the watch drum approaching. The death of Ii Naosuke, concealed until the beginning of the month, had now been made public but there was no slackening of the state of alert in Kanagawa. Kakichi went to the front hallway to have a look. A watchman passed by, helmeted and wearing two swords, and before him walked two attendants, each carrying a paper lantern on a bowed stick. A third attendant carried the drum. Kakichi returned to Kansai's room, his eyes sparkling.

"When it comes to that, I think Miyagawa has begun to take on a little bit of Yokohama himself," he began to tease.

"Don't be silly."

But in Kakichi's eyes was the question of how Kansai had passed seven long months without seeing any familiar face, without talking with anyone close.

"Well, shall I show you?"

Kansai laughed and brought out into the light of the lamp the wastepaper from his daily writing practice. The past seven months, with no companion other than the oak tree that stood in back of the inn, had seemed like two or three years to Kansai. Gradual but quite noticeable changes had appeared in his calligraphy as he had gazed at that oak day after day.

Kansai addressed both Yasubei and Kakichi.

"Since the tenth month of last year, Yokohama has changed so much you wouldn't recognize it."

The silk was readily sold at a price of one ryo in gold for nine ounces. This transaction was carried out in the English merchant's temporary quarters in the foreign quarter on the Kanagawa bluff, where the Japanese merchants and their interpreter had first met him. Yasubei and Kakichi sat side by side while Kansai took care of the necessary documents.

The Englishman was one who seldom smiled, but now there was good humor in his blue eyes as he spoke through his interpreter.

"I will soon be building a two-story shop on the waterfront in Yokohama. Here in Kanagawa there are also the Englishmen Barber and Hall. But I want to be the first to complete my building, so that I can say 'First English Merchant' on my signboard."

He shook hands with Yasubei and Kakichi to indicate that the business was settled. He then went to Kansai and put out his huge hand. His grip was very firm.

"The transaction is finished. We can now hand over the silk."

Yasubei spoke in a tone of relief as they left the foreigner's residence. Kakichi, walking alongside, reminded him, "Master, there are still things to be done. We still have to get the cash safely back home."

"That will be a big job."

Kansai followed them out to the port of Kanagawa, where there was a view of the bay. As far as the eye could see, the harbor was in the midst of development. Noge-cho and Tobe-cho had already been filled in, and there was no way of knowing just how many people had moved into this former village that had once held only a hundred households. The second day of the coming sixth month would mark one full year since the opening of the ports. There were plans to hold a Benten festival in observance of the anniversary. According to the master of the Botan'ya, there would not only be portable shrines and floats but Tekomai dancers and Kumo no hyoshi dancers would take part as well. Every effort would be made to have the biggest possible celebration. However much some may have objected to the opening of the ports, once they were open the currents of the world began to flow in, heedless of all protest. Calico, taffeta, cloth-of-gold, medicines, wines and such things came in, and raw silk, lacquer wares, tea, vegetable oils, and copper would go out. It was apparent that, for better or for worse, the intercourse between East and West had begun.

Kansai began to think again about his wife and children, waiting for him at home. His thoughts went out, too, to Kozo of Nakatsugawa and Hanzo of Magome, and he wondered how those two high-spirited men would come through such difficult times.

The transport of the twenty-four hundred ryo that had been realized from the sale of the raw silk was entrusted to Kansai. Yasubei and Kakichi planned to remain in Kanagawa until the sixth month. There were all kinds of stories about the difficulty of transporting large amounts of gold and silver in those days. One man had wrapped his money in dried squid to make the whole thing look like a shipment of seafood. Another merchant, from Kawagoe in Musashi, had been rushing back home by litter one night when he was robbed by his bearers. It was said that if a passenger was carrying more than fifty ryo the bearers could sense the added weight. Such were the times in which Kansai had to move twenty-four hundred ryo. It was more money than he had ever seen in his whole life.

Kansai was in his room at the Botan'ya. Yasubei came and sat before him, taking a pipe full of tobacco from the smoking stand.

"I am relieved to know that you are taking care of this. It is almost as though this was really what I had you come to Kanagawa for," he confessed.

But there was no need for Yasubei to say this; Kansai had been aware of it all the while.

Kansai was feeling apprehensive about the two hundred fifty miles that lay ahead of him. Half his body was already affected by old age. He was almost deaf in his right ear and his right eye was weak. But he gathered his declining powers for this final adventure that would bring him to his "hidden dwelling."

Yasubei brought a transport master to him.

"This man will go with you."

He appeared to be a sturdy enough fellow to guard the shipment. Kakichi came to help with the packing of the money chests.

Around the tenth of the fourth month, Kansai found himself getting up early, making his preparations, thrusting his dagger into his sash, and putting an end to his seven months of lonely life at the inn. The master of the Botan'ya had the parting cup brought in. Yasubei sat before Kansai. Draining the cup at one draught, he set it before Kansai. Their parting cups of water were exchanged with the deepest feelings.

"Hey! We're ready, we're ready!" came a voice from outside. Three pieces of baggage were carried out past the maids standing in the hall and taken downstairs. Each of the chests was so heavy that Kakichi and a manservant from the inn could barely lift it.

The master of the inn approached Kansai for the final courtesies.

"Oh, are you ready to go? I suppose you will be staying in Ryogoku when you reach Edo. Please give my regards to the old gentleman at the Juichiya."

There was one full packhorse load. Kansai and the transport master left the Botan'ya with it. Yasubei and Kakichi, accompanying the travelers to the edge of town, crossed the bridge at Takinohashi, passed before the Choenji, where a high-flying flag marked the residence of the Dutch consul, and came to the high ground at the edge of town.

Now thoughts of his old disciples came vividly to Kansai. He was about to step out onto the busy Tokaido. With a feeling like that of the aged songbird recalling the world, he listened to the dull sound of the packhorse's straw-shod hooves as he began the long journey up to Edo, out through Itabashi, and along the Kiso road.

CHAPTER FIVE

1

IN MINO it was already known that Miyagawa Kansai was on his way home, leaving the master and the head clerk of the Yorozuya in Kanagawa. Since Nakatsugawa was a small place, this soon came to the ears of his former disciples Keizo and Kozo. Hanzo, too, seven miles away in Magome, learned that Kansai had left Itabashi and was on his way up the Kiso road.

By now the effect of the opening of the ports was beginning to make itself felt along the major highways. In the Magome honjin Hanzo had already heard the cries of passing coin dealers buying up copper or silver coins. Even in the provinces the buying up of old coins such as the two shu gold pieces and the eighteenth-century gold pieces known as *koban* had begun. Rumors of this came to him every day. One day he would hear that a coin buyer from Omi coming to the Masudaya in Magome to buy *koban* was offering one ryo three bu for the coin's face value of one ryo, and then the next day at the Yamatoya in Nakatsugawa someone would sell one hundred of the old *koban* for two hundred twenty-five ryo in the new *koban*. That amounted to two ryo one bu for each ryo of face value. People were beginning to offer two ryo two bu or even three ryo.

The old-fashioned Kimbei of the Fushimiya next door was astonished. He would sometimes speak wryly of this world of surprises in which his generation could reap profits their grandfathers had never dreamed of. At other times he spoke in a way that betrayed his concern over the possible consequences of all this buying and selling.

Surrounded by such uncertainties, Hanzo eagerly awaited the return of his old master from the trading venture in Yokohama.

Kindness and generosity in entertaining travelers was a tradition deeply rooted among the people who lived along the old highways. Not only did their songs immortalize the plight of travelers of long ago who had eaten their rice from oak leaves, but the travel gods whose statues stood alongside the roadways reminded them all their lives of a spirit of concern and compassion for travelers.

These feelings were especially strong in the people of the Kiso, where the mountains stood range on range in all directions and where the rivers flooded so frequently. It was these people who most thoroughly understood the hardships of travel in those times. Hanzo was keenly aware of the nature of the journey through the densely forested Kiso region where the road lay in deep shadows even at noon, and of what it would mean for his teacher. The man who had sponsored his membership in the Hirata school was now setting out on the two hundred and fifty miles of highway between his home and Kanagawa.

Hanzo went out to the road almost every day in hope of hearing some news of his old master. This was already the third year since he and Juheiji had returned from their journey to Edo and Yokosuka. The village was rebuilding after the great fire of the year following that trip. Although the honjin and the Fushimiya had escaped the fire, all the opposite side of the village had burned. The recently completed house of Kyudayu looked very new.

This money-making venture of their former master had raised some doubts among his disciples. Just when Hanzo and a few of the others had begun to think of some way to ensure a secure old age for Kansai, they began to hear rumors that he might go to Yokohama. The subject came up frequently from that time on. Even though Kansai had said that there was no need for him to make a special trip to gain their consent, the consensus among his disciples was that there were still things that would need to be talked about when he returned. Hanzo thought that at the very least Kansai should stop by the honjin and tell his old disciple what he was doing.

On the twenty-second day of the fourth month, Kansai and his packhorse, escorted by the transport master, came down from Toge along the steep street with new buildings on one side. Kansai stopped his horse before the Fushimiya and went in to express his condolences to Kimbei and his family. He told Kimbei of how he had brought back two thousand four hundred ryo from the trading venture in Yokohama and that Yasubei would probably return in the sixth month. The trade in raw silk was evidently quite profitable, and one could now sell *koban* for three ryo two bu each in the port cities. He then went directly on to Nakatsugawa without calling on Hanzo, who had been so eager to see him.

Hanzo learned of the visit from his neighbors, but only after it was over. He was crushed. His disillusionment in his master was now as great as his faith in him had once been.

2

"It's amazing the way the *koban* are being bought up. I heard about it again just now on my way here."

Kozo of Nakatsugawa had come up to Magome by way of Jikkyoku pass with more such stories to tell.

Although Hanzo had not yet become the head of his household, Kozo was already the toiya in Nakatsugawa. He looked like a man in his prime. Keizo was the oldest of the three friends, Kozo was next, and Hanzo the youngest, and Hanzo was already thirty. As they sat talking in the parlor of the honjin, which had become Hanzo's room, Kozo playfully observed that Kansai was now one of the newly rich.

What had most disturbed Hanzo and his friends was the way the Yokohama trade had led to a sudden sharp increase in prices, because of the buying up of money. The quality of the old coins was so far in excess of their current nominal values that even the American consul Harris had warned the shogunate about it. Those who exported the coins made scandalous profits. As an emergency measure the shogunate had minted new gold coins of a debased quality but this had only been a further invitation to monetary disaster. The shogunate lacked both the power and the public trust to enable it to call in all the old coins and remint them. The local merchants, unable to pass up the opportunity, began a wild selling rush and high quality gold coinage poured out of the country. Although there were a few American dollars coming in, most of the replacement was low quality silver.

"What do you think of these coin sellers, Hanzo?" asked Kozo. "They are saying nine hundred thousand ryo in *koban* have already left the country. And that is the most conservative estimate. Isn't it incredible? There's really no reason to think that the officials of the shogunate were actually acting under foreign orders, but they did go ahead and open the ports without proper preparation and the result has been this terrible rise in prices. That might have made some people in Yokohama a lot of money but most have suffered terribly."

The first anniversary of the opening of the port of Yokohama was coming up on the second day of the sixth month. Since it was seen by many as an anniversary of shame, a hot wave of xenophobia began to sweep over the country. To Hanzo and his friends, who could see so much suffering before their own eyes, this did not sound at all like prejudice and obstinacy.

"I'm not going to say anything more about Miyagawa sensei," Hanzo began, "but I really do wish he might have continued to accept a dignified poverty as he always had before."

"Now, I ask you," replied Kozo, "don't National Scholars have a certain position to maintain as National Scholars? They can't throw all that away and set out just to make money, can they?"

"If only sensei had come to consult with us before going off to Yokohama. I can see no reason why he should have avoided us this way."

"It must mean that he did not want us to involve ourselves in the matter."

A sudden shower came up and the conversation was cut off. Hanzo closed the shutters in the parlor, leaving one slightly ajar to let in light. The two friends sat for a time watching the rain pour into the rear garden. Soon the rain began to blow into the room. It was impossible to leave any opening.

"Otami!"

It had grown too dark to carry on a conversation without a light. Hanzo's wife was now twenty-four, the young mother of two children, and as she came in from another room carrying a lamp, one of them followed her to look in at the guest in the parlor.

By the light of an untimely lamp the two friends continued to talk about their master as they sat listening to the storm outside. The more they talked, the more complex their feelings became. Neither Hanzo nor Kozo could ever forget the personal warmth of Kansai, the teacher who had introduced them to the Learning of Antiquity. Since he was growing old, neither of them could find it in his heart to reproach him. Hanzo said that if Kansai wanted to retire to Iida, he would not want to spoil his happiness. It was finally Kozo who, even though he was a relative, proposed that they separate themselves from their master.

The legacy of that great elder in National Learning, Motoori Norinaga, had come to seem all the more brilliant in Hanzo's eyes. Above all, his strength lay in his possession of the key to language. He had spent thirty-five years in study of the *Kojiki* and that was the beginning of his discovery of the true and complete national character in the records of ancient times. The morality of North China, which had come to Japan in the form of Confucianism, and the religions of South China, which had come in the forms of Zen and Taoism—it was this master who had cast out all these borrowings from other countries. From his point of view, all of the so-called Ways were foreign inventions; it was the people of China who had regarded as "sages" those who invented such difficult terms as "benevolence," "justice," "propriety," "humility," "filial piety," "obedience," "loyalty," and "trustworthiness," and then used them to bind helpless human beings. So he had cast out all "Chinese-mindedness" and taught that we must return to the ancient Age of the Gods, an age free from empty verbalizations.

What the master had discovered from his study of antiquity was "the soul restored." Put into words, what he taught was a "return to the spontaneous." Everything started there—his revelation of a brighter world, his dream of a return to antiquity, the rejection of the middle ages, the liberation of man, his view of romantic love, his teachings of *mono no aware*. It seemed astonishing to Hanzo that such a man, a native of Iidaka county in the province of Ise, should have come into being during the Temmei and Kansei eras of the late eighteenth century. This great master, who seemed to have been born to announce the coming dawn, had passed away in the autumn of the first year of Jowa, 1801, just as a new century was beginning, leaving those who came after him to grope their way through this dark world. To Hanzo and his friends, it was this venerable master of the Suzunoya who was truly the father of the new age.

"Now I begin to understand. Miyagawa Kansai has come to be recognized as the leader in National Scholarship in the Nakatsugawa area, but the older he gets the more he seems to revert to Chinese learning. In some ways he never completely freed himself from Chinese-mindedness."

"When I hear you talk that way, Kozo, I don't know what to say. When people start their studies with the Four Books and the Five Classics, the marks of Confucianism just don't wash out all that easily."

Not only did the heavy rain not let up but thunder rolled among the clouds and a strong wind blew without respite until evening. It was so bad that a traveler from Nagoya on his way to Fukushima was forced to ask for early lodging at the honjin.

Kozo, too, could not return to Nakatsugawa that night. The next morning the wind had subsided but the weather had not improved greatly. There had been extensive damage to the roads and bridges farther up the valley and reports came in that the horse fair in Fukushima had been postponed.

This was a time when Hanzo's father had been called to Nagoya on business for Owari. Hanzo left Kozo beside the hearth and went out to check the village offices. No one was passing along the highway. He met his manservant Sakichi, still wearing a rain hat and straw raincoat, who had just returned from checking the rice field dikes. From him Hanzo heard the report that the bridge at Nakatsugawa had been washed out.

"Kozo! They say that the big bridge is out. Why don't you wait here until we know a little more?"

"What can you do in all this rain?" added Oman, who had joined them at the fireside. "Anyway, people will soon be coming up from Nakatsugawa, so why don't you just wait here and see what happens. Please."

Hoping to divert his friend now that he was detained by the rain, Hanzo led him away from the hearth through an inner room to another room facing the inner court. Opening one of the shutters slightly, Kozo saw that they were in the room reserved for high-ranking guests. Watery daylight shone in on the tatami with their Korean edgings of black cloud designs on white fabric. This was where the daimyo passing over the Kiso road would stay. Over the three years since his journey to Yokosuka, Hanzo could count such important guests as Ii Naosuke from Hikone, the elder Manabe Shimosa no Kami, the lord rector Hayashi, and the censor Iwase Higo no Kami. All these officials of the shogunate—some now dead at the hands of assassins, others still living, one going down to Edo to assume the office of tairo, others rushing off to Kyoto to present the Treaty of Kanagawa to the imperial court— could be sensed as passing presences in this room. As he showed this remote room to his friend, Hanzo was moved to look back on the chaotic passage of time.

Standing beside the sliding doors, Hanzo waited for an opportunity to draw Kozo's attention to the alcove. Hidden away on that dark wall was the scroll by Ogata Korin that had been given to him by Yamagami Shichiro-zaemon in far-off Kugo village in Yokosuka, Sagami province.

"Kozo, that's the gift I brought back from Yokosuka."

"You really talk about Yokosuka a lot. I understand the person who gave you that is head of the main line of your family."

"They gave an unsigned sword to the Aoyama of Tsumago and this scroll to us. I will never forget that trip. When I got back I was a completely different person—at least in my intentions. I was starting life again under a new order."

To Hanzo, thankful for the opportunity to prolong his friend's visit by even half a day, the continued rain and storm came as a blessing. Returning down the hallway past the middle room which had become his stepmother's work room, he seated Kozo once again in the parlor.

"Well, Kozo, how about it? Shall I show you one of my bad poems?"

Hanzo placed a draft of a poem on current affairs before his friend. The handwriting was still tentative and he had put it away where no one could see it.

> Who is it who says an American dollar
>   is the equal of Japanese silver?
> Who is it who would have bad dollars and good silver
>   stand even in the balance,
> Without considering how cheap we are when
>   we sell our nation dear?
> Will it make us rich if we sell ourselves
>   at a good price,
> Heaping up dollars like mountains of dirt?
> How cruel it is to convert into dollars
>   the labors of this people of the gods!
> We must question the power of the dollar
>   throughout this great land of eight islands.
> This age of fools!
> We know these dollars are inferior
>   and we do not heed what we know.
> If the nation's treasures be exhausted,
> Though we've heaped up dollars like mountains:
>   What will we buy?

The dollars mentioned in this poem were actually the inferior Mexican or Hong Kong dollars that the foreign merchants were bringing in. Most of them were not in general circulation but were going directly to the shogunate, which was reminting them into one bu coins.

"I don't usually write such poems," said Hanzo.

"But among all of Miyagawa sensei's old students, you were the best at poetry," replied Kozo.

"That's right, and it was after the Yokosuka trip that even I began to think something worthwhile might come of it. That trip certainly brought out the poems. When I look at some of them, I myself begin to think that perhaps I can write.

"All the same, Kozo, there is a great difference between the way my father enjoys haikai and my interest in classical verse. I base my efforts on Motoori sensei's poems, to try to recover the purity and simplicity of heart of the people of antiquity by writing classical verse myself. I suppose it is a measure of how much people living in this age are out of touch with their own true natures. What do you think?"

Hanzo tried to look at everything in this manner. Not only did he take the teachings bequeathed by Motoori Norinaga as the teachings of the elders but it was the extreme positions advanced by the indomitable spirit of Hirata Atsutane, so revered by Hanzo and his circle, that had opened the way to action for him. According to Hanzo, there was in Norinaga, the venerable master of the Suzunoya, the breadth of vision of the Temmei and Jowa eras. Atsutane, the master of the Ibukinoya, was narrow by contrast, but in his endlessly painstaking thoroughness he was in tune with the people of his time. This was the source of much misunderstanding about the scholarship of Hirata Atsutane, and he had suffered greatly at the hands of the shogunate. During the time when he was writing his *Reflections on the Nation of Japan* and *The Eternal Calendar of the Imperial Court,* not only was publication banned but he was even forbidden to write any more and was forced to retire to his home province of Akita. But to the end of his sixty-eight years of life, the master never broke under the pressure. As he looked over his own times, Hanzo felt there was no scholar whose total dedication could be compared with that of Hirata Atsutane.

Since it was now past the tenth day of the fifth month, the memorial services for those who had died in the great purge of Ansei were fast approaching. Memories of such people as Umeda Umbin, Yoshida Shoin, and Rai Ogai, also known as Mikisaburo, returned with the new spring leaves. Hanzo and Kozo held firmly to what they had learned from these great predecessors among the disciples of Hirata Atsutane. Together they were determined to plunge into the swirling waters of revolution.

The prolonged rains of the fifth month did not simply delay the departure of Hanzo's guest; it brought the two of them closer together. Kozo was pleased to learn that Hanzo had acquired a new disciple who was now making his residence in the honjin. He was the son of the Inabaya in the neighboring station of Ochiai, and the boy's name was Hayashi Katsushige. Hanzo told Kozo that among all the boys who came to the Magome honjin for the sake of learning, none seemed so promising as Katsushige. From time to time Katsushige would leave his study and come down to where the two friends were talking to ask Hanzo something. His youthful appearance in his short trousers, with a pale yellow underrobe showing at the collar as he gazed at them from under a shaven forehead, reminded Hanzo and his guest of their own youth.

"Yes, indeed. We must have been like that once. I was just Katsushige's age when I began to go to Miyagawa sensei's house every day," said Hanzo.

After a while, Kozo began to be concerned about his family in Nakatsu-gawa. From further reports about the effects of the storm, they learned that some houses in Aramachi had been blown down by the wind, a house in Toge was severely damaged, and a horse had been killed by a falling beam. All the barley, too, had been blown down in the fields, a rare occurrence even in Magome where the winds were often severe.

Oman came to the parlor.

"Kozo, we know you are worrying about your family, but if you leave today we will be worried. I've had Sakichi fire up the bath, so please stay one more day. Please listen to your elders."

When his stepmother came in, Hanzo quickly assumed a formal sitting position. It had become almost a reflex for him to do so in Oman's presence.

"May we come in?" said Otami, helping a small child over the threshold of the room. Their daughter Okume was now five but since the arrival of her little brother, Sota, she had begun to act very grown up. Assisted by her mother, she brought tea to the guest. Her manner was appealingly childlike as she concentrated all her attention on the guest, walking very carefully so as not to spill the tea.

"Well, look here, Kozo!" said Oman. "Okume has brought you some tea."

"I told her I would carry it, but she wouldn't listen," added Otami, laughing.

Even the children of the family had come to entertain the guest who had been delayed by the rains.

Kozo spent two nights at Magome. Before he left on the third day, he promised Hanzo that he would make contact with all the Hirata disciples from eastern Mino to the Ina valley and that he would aid their fellows in Nagoya and Kyoto when the occasion called for it.

After Kozo's departure, Hanzo passed some especially dismal rainy days in his mountain home. The rain continued through the fourth day and there was still a bit of wind when the call went out for one person from each household to assist in repairs to the bridges and to the roof of the stage.

With no break in the rain and the clouds remaining as threatening as ever, everyone feared further damage. Some of the clay-walled storehouses in the village began to crumble in the long downpour. The rain went into a fifth day, and the road washed out along the stretch in Shiozawa where it had been built across the face of a precipice. There were excited reports that three houses had been washed away in the vicinity of the great bridge near Kozo's home in Nakatsugawa. The waters of the Kiso river rose day by day and no one crossed over the remaining bridges. Traffic along the highway came to a halt.

Around the seventeenth of the fifth month, travelers at last began to move again. The finance commissioner, the head of the public works office, and the commissioner of the town of Nishikori came up to the forest region to look for materials for a construction project in the inner section of Edo castle. The Nagasaki commissioner came through, behind schedule due to the rains.

"We've had all we need of the Black Ships for a while," thought Hanzo as he watched the Nagasaki commissioner pass through town. This procession had required the calling up of one hundred porters from the Kiso and two hundred more from Ina. There were reports that a German ship was riding at anchor in the distant port of Nagasaki, demanding trading rights like those granted the other European powers.

3

At the beginning of the seventh month, Kansai turned his Nakatsugawa house over to his adopted son-in-law and left the familiar Mino basin for the Ina valley in Shinano, where he had long planned to retire. From his home in Magome Hanzo noted the departure with deep regret.

Reflecting that this seemed to be the final parting with his master, Hanzo leaned against the doorway of the parlor in the honjin and let his thoughts run to the valley where Kansai had settled. The senior disciple Hara Nobuyoshi lived in Seinaiji, halfway between Tsumago and the Ina valley. To disciples like Hanzo, he was the most important one of all. In the Ina valley, separated from Magome by the Misaka and Kazekoshi passes of the Ena range, were great numbers of ardent disciples of Hirata Atsutane, particularly in the town of Iida and in the villages of Okawara, Yamabuki, and Zakoji. Among them were such men as Kitahara Inao of Zakoji, who was preparing to print Atsutane's greatest work, the thirty-volume *Commentaries on Ancient History*, which had remained unpublished up to this time. There were also people like Katagiri Shun'ichi of Yamabuki, who had initiated group readings of the master's works.

In Hanzo's part of the country the teachings of Hirata Atsutane had spread with startling speed among the people of the Ina district. There was Matsuo Taseko, for instance, in the village of Tomono near Iida. She had become a posthumous disciple of Atsutane after passing the age of fifty and, though a woman, had committed herself totally to the emperor's cause. There was also a splendid successor to Atsutane in the person of Kanetane in Edo, who did not neglect to give guidance to disciples in the provinces. All those who entered the movement were accepted as posthumous disciples of Atsutane; they were not claimed by Kanetane as his own. Hanzo perceived himself as occupying a crucial position linking these people of Ina with their counterparts in eastern Mino. If the teachings were considered to be an undying flame of scholarship passed from Kamo Mabuchi to Motoori Norinaga, and from Norinaga to Hirata Atsutane, then from his home in the mountains of the Kiso Hanzo could look out in one direction on the lights burning in the Ina valley, and in another direction at those that burned here and there in Mino—in Nakatsugawa where his friends lived, in Ochiai, in Tsukechi, in Naegi, in Oi, in Iwamura.

The headmen were at that time beginning to become more aware of their positions among the people. For the moment, Hanzo too, thinking of the day when he would succeed his father, found need to prepare himself mentally. Kichizaemon and Kimbei had both sent requests to Fukushima that they be relieved of their offices at the beginning of that year, 1860, the first year of Man'en.

When Kichizaemon decided to retire, he had for many years operated what might be thought of as a unit of local government, filling the three posts of honjin, toiya, and headman, and had at the same time looked after all the needs of his stretch of the highway. He was already sixty-one and Kimbei was sixty-three, but Hanzo did not yet know if their resignations had been accepted.

Stepping out to look around the village, Hanzo met his father and Kimbei out for a walk. Kichizaemon was now an old man, leaning on a stick. He was on his way to look in on the new dwelling of Hanzo's stepsister, Okisa, who had remarried. Kimbei was spending much of his time going to and from the temple, his rosary in his sleeve, now setting up a memorial, now offering a wooden gong. He seemed unable to forget his dead son Tsuru-matsu, whom Hanzo had once taught. Hanzo also met Kyudayu at the toiya.

"Kyudayu is getting old, too," he thought.

In Kimbei's home there was an adopted son named Inosuke who had come from Oi in Mino. In Kyudayu's home his successor Kyurobei was now in charge.

"Otami, this year or next you will become the lady of the honjin."

"I know."

"Do you think you can manage it?"

"I think so."

His father had succeeded his predecessor, Hanroku, at the age of forty-one; Hanzo was twelve years younger. All the same, there was already Sota, reaching childish hands into Otami's kimono to find her breast, and there was Okume, now old enough to enjoy the balls of salted rice wrapped in *ho* leaves that Otami gave her.

"Just think of it, Otami! Father has been in office twenty-one years. If you count his apprenticeship, it comes to thirty-seven or thirty-eight years. Grandfather was so reluctant to pass on the responsibilities of the honjin that he held on as long as he could. We have to be that careful, too. Now, I have been in apprenticeship since I was sixteen. But I am not good at business like your brother, Juheiji. I am not the kind of person who will record every candle and every last bit of room rent collected when a daimyo passes through—I guess I'm pretty worthless."

"Why should you say a thing like that?"

"Because I have to warn you of what lies ahead. Your brother put it correctly. He said we must think about the fact that as headmen we represent the will of the people and that as honjin and toiya we take part in the transportation along the great highways. But I am the son of a headman myself. I am also a disciple of Hirata Atsutane. I'll do the best I can."

"Hanzo! A summons has come from Fukushima. It looks as though we will have to ask you to go and represent us." One of the villagers had come to the honjin bringing this report.

It was about a quarrel over grasslands. Because the area was almost all forest with very little grassland, such disputes were forever occurring. These quarrels over grasslands were so incessant in the Kiso that they even had their own name of "mountain dispute."

With the rise in coin prices and the buying of silver that had accompanied the Yokohama trade, there were now the newly rich who had taken full advantage of the changes in financial practice. The sufferings of the poor were severe. Rice was expensive—one ryo would buy about nine bushels. Soybeans cost two ryo three bu per packhorse load; a half-gallon of sake cost two hundred thirty mon; tofu cost forty-two mon per block. Everything was like this. There was no reason to expect that the people could remain calm in the midst of mounting instability. Even the mountain disputes had grown more open and ugly.

There was nothing that so depressed Hanzo as these utterly ruthless quarrels among the farmers. The present quarrel had gone so far as to lead to a summons from Fukushima. The plaintiffs were the villagers of neighboring Yubunezawa; the defendants were the farmers of Toge. It had come out into the open just the previous summer when the Toge farmers had fifteen sickles taken away from them. The officials in Magome had interceded and the quarrel seemed to have been settled out of court. It had lasted from the two hundred twentieth day of the year until the twentieth of the ninth month, about two months in all. At that time everyone from Ogiya Tokuemon, the assistant honjin at Tsumago, to the assistant headman of Yamaguchi had come to serve as witnesses. Everyone had packed a lunch and climbed up the mountain to verify the boundaries of the grasslands. But there had been dissatisfaction with that settlement among the villagers of Yubunezawa, and now the case had gone up to Fukushima.

Two representatives of the farmers, one from Toge and one from Magome itself, were called to Fukushima. When the two arrived in Fukushima they were immediately sent to the prison at Yazawa. Another summons then came from Fukushima ordering the headman of Magome and representatives from his village elders to appear in Fukushima. Hanzo could not delay an instant.

"Otami! I am going to Fukushima in father's place," he said as he began to get out his formal clothing. Then he dressed himself, tying his sash firmly and evenly.

"The people are not in a good mood."

Kichizaemon was speaking to Hanzo while they awaited the completion of preparations for the trip to Fukushima.

In a manner that bespoke his approaching retirement, Kichizaemon went into the room adjoining the hearth room and took out an old map of Magome and Yubunezawa.

"You may use these as references, Hanzo," he said as he placed them before his son.

"It's difficult to say just how the claims of the two villages add up. There have been many mountain disputes before now but they were usually settled out of court," Kichizaemon added casually, but his concern that the two unfortunate prisoners should be freed as soon as possible showed clearly.

The assistant headman and seven other farmers from Yubunezawa were called to Fukushima. The village elders Gisuke and Yojiemon from Magome and the assistant headman Heisuke from Toge also went. Inosuke, the adopted son of the Fushimiya, would go later in place of Kimbei. Since the quarrel over the grasslands was being fought out in public as a formal legal proceeding, the elders had selected these representatives to accompany Hanzo.

"I have already asked to be relieved of my duties, so I will not show my face this time," said Kichizaemon when Heisuke arrived back from Fukushima to accompany Hanzo. Encouraged by the prospect of Heisuke's company, Hanzo looked vigorous and ready as he donned his leg wrappings and straw sandals and tucked up the skirts of his kimono.

Peasant uprisings were beginning to break out in all the provinces in spite of strict prohibitions against them. Unlike many of the older men in the village, Hanzo could not look upon these uprisings as mere insubordination among the farmers. The lightest punishments for participation in a peasant uprising were whipping, tattooing, or banishment, and harsh sentences ran to life imprisonment or beheading. Such a spirit of self-sacrifice in the face of heavy punishment, such needs driving the farmers in all sincerity to seek actively for martyrdom were to be found in no other society. In the current crisis the lower classes were not being taught; it was rather they who were doing the teaching.

"We really have nothing to tell the farmers. Now they are preoccupied with internal quarrels like these mountain disputes, but soon the time will come when their eyes are fully opened."

Such were Hanzo's thoughts as he set out in his father's place for the Fukushima offices. Once on the road he had to say to himself what he wanted so much to say to the others.

"Stop fighting each other! This is not the time for that sort of thing!"

4

The business in Fukushima was completed thirteen days later and the villages of Toge and Yubunezawa were once again at peace.

Those released from the prison at Yazawa and those who had stayed in Fukushima as guarantors were all hurrying back to their homes. On the fourteenth day Hanzo, his neighbor Inosuke, and Heisuke from Toge walked westward along the hot Kiso road. They spent one night at Suwara. When Hanzo reached his gate bearing news of the peaceful settlement of the mountain dispute, Kichizaemon was hard at work cleaning up the garden.

"Hanzo is back!"

Oman caught sight of him before anyone else and she went out to tell Kichizaemon, who was sweeping up around the tree peony in front of the living room.

"Father, I am back."

Hanzo propped his hat against the trunk of the pear tree in the front garden and wiped the perspiration from his face and arms. He reported briefly to his father how the two villages had been persuaded to come to terms. He also reported all the conditions that had been attached at Fukushima: that the boundaries between the grasslands of the two villages were now fixed; that new earthen boundary markers were to be heaped up; and that only those farmers living nearest the boundaries would be permitted to cut grass there.

"Oh, that's good to hear," said Kichizaemon, broom still in hand. "You were gone so long I was beginning to worry."

Autumn came. As the people living around Magome complained of the brutal heat, the crickets began to sing in the stone walls. Hanzo, who had been constantly on the run on village business, spent that year's Bon festival in Fukushima.

Presently it was time to build the boundary markers in the mountain grasslands that had occasioned the recent quarrel. In the company of the village officials, the farmers, and the lesser families, Hanzo walked through the mountains, lush with summer grass. All the farmers, the headman, and four assistant headmen came from Yubunezawa. A total of about two hundred people from the two villages gathered at the deep swamp that had been designated as the beginning of the boundary.

"We can't go on doing stupid things like that!"

"Come on, pile that dirt up!"

All around him Hanzo could hear the voices of the farmers at work.

Four mounds of earth were to be built along the boundary. Their locations were fixed by sighting on the opening of a cave or on a certain pine or the like. As each site was dug up, the smell of freshly turned earth struck Hanzo's nostrils. Construction had begun. The farmers of the two villages were hard at work around the mounds, ignoring the swarms of mosquitoes.

Someone came up behind Hanzo and lightly tapped him on the shoulder. It was Juheiji, who had come in his capacity as headman of the neighboring village. He stood there, laughing.

"Why don't you stay at our place tonight, Juheiji?"

"No, I have people with me today, so I'll go back home. I can't leave them to cover five miles of roadway alone in the dark."

As Hanzo and Juheiji talked, the sun set behind the mountains. It soon became so dark that they had to sight with torches to locate the fourth boundary marker, and they put off until the next day the construction of the embankment that was to run from the tree at the center of the boundary to a certain boulder.

It rained the next day, so it was on the following day that the farmers of the two villages again gathered at the same place. After glaring at each other for more than a year, they were at last satisfied and the long dispute was over.

The day was once more coming to an end. Hanzo invited Juheiji to accompany him as he set out for home. The two had kept in close touch since the trip to Yokosuka. Not only were they brothers-in-law but now they were both headmen.

"Hanzo," said Juheiji as they walked down the stony mountain path, "things are getting to be more blatant, aren't they."

"They are," replied Hanzo.

"Just look at this mountain dispute, Hanzo. And it's not only this quarrel over grasslands. Everything you hear or see these days is bald and brutal. The other day a ronin from Mito came by our place. After talking about all kinds of things, he said that he wanted to write something and asked me to bring paper and a brush. He inscribed two fans and for that he tried to hold me up for twenty ounces of sake, one hundred mon in money, and even a pair of straw sandals. I ran him out. He was dead drunk and went straight over to the Ogiya; they say he finally spent the night at Tokuemon's place. Just look at what is happening along this highway! Take the day that the inspector from Nagasaki came through on his way to Edo. One of his retainers, by the name of Nagai or something, got into a quarrel with the toiya of my village, complaining that the porters were late, and five of them beat up the toiya. They broke a practice sword on him and he had five wounds on his head. Everything is getting blatant and ugly. Now when you and I went to Miura —it wasn't that way at all."

"Master!"

A lantern from the village approached in the darkness, accompanied by the voice of a youth calling out. The people at home, worrying about the lateness of Hanzo's return, had sent his disciple Katsushige and his manservant Sakichi to meet him.

When Hanzo and the others reached the Magome honjin, the lamps of the post station were shining along both sides of the highway. Otami had prepared the bath and was waiting for her husband and her brother. That evening Juheiji washed off the perspiration of the day's work in the mountains and came to Hanzo's room to relax.

"There are lots of flies in the Kiso, but it is pleasant to be able to get by without mosquito netting. It must be because the water is so pure and cold."

Otami was delighted to hear her brother's familiar voice.

"Otami, don't tell mother about it, but warm me up a bottle of sake tonight," said Hanzo. Even at his age, he avoided drinking in the presence of his stepmother. From his earliest youth he had always been so circumspect in all things concerning her that it had become second nature to him. He was far more afraid of his shrewd stepmother than he was of his much more experienced father.

With their sake Hanzo and Juheiji had chilled tofu with spices, ground fresh ginger, and green shiso. There were also sliced cucumbers and freshly pickled eggplant. They sat near the open side of the parlor while they ate and drank.

"Now that I am here, I remember. This is the room I stayed in when I came over to ask you to go along on the trip to Yokosuka."

"Edo seems to have changed a lot since we saw it then."

"Tremendously. Just recently a courier came to my place with a gift from

Edo and, according to what he had to say, the idea of driving out the foreigners has a lot of support. The ronin are running wild, foreigners are being killed, all the students of Western learning are being threatened. Stores in Edo that sell foreign goods are being smashed up, and everyone is frightened. That's what he said."

"I suppose that's the way it appears if you only look at the surface."

"But Hanzo, everyone under the sun is mouthing this slogan about expelling the foreigners—I ask you, is that really good enough?"

Hanzo had had enough sake to forget his fatigue. He got up and went over to gaze for a moment out past the overhanging roof at the sky above the highway. Lightning, reminding them that it was the season for weeding the rice fields, flashed before his eyes.

"Hanzo, this 'expel the barbarian' stuff is the very Chinese-mindedness that you are always talking about. To look upon all foreign nations as barbarous and to exclude them, isn't that something we learned from China?"

"You just said something very interesting."

"And you know very well that the foreign countries today are different from the barbarians of the old days. In trade or in communication, there is no stopping world trends. I would like to see us think these things through a little bit better and open the country up."

Hanzo returned to sit facing Juheiji.

"This is really crazy," continued Juheiji, bursting into laughter. "No matter what they are talking about, they haul out 'expel the barbarians.' What do your friends have to say about our current 'expel the barbarians' fad?"

"They don't look upon it lightly as you do. Even you are suffering from the dislocations in this society, aren't you? Good coins are disappearing, prices are rising, life is becoming more difficult—once you realize that this is the result of opening the ports, then all the anti-foreign feelings are not so hard to understand."

It grew late as the two talked on, forgetting the time. The sake cooled and the tofu crumbled in the bowls of once chilly water.

5

This was the time when disciples of Hirata Atsutane began to consider direct action. Some people from Ina had proposed taking up residence in a house in the Shirakawa district of Kyoto to proselytize among the court nobles. Some were already in Kyoto. There were even reports that Hirata disciples in Edo were becoming active.

The roju Ando Tsushima no Kami had now become the central figure following the assassination of Ii Naosuke. All sorts of vague rumors were making their rounds. It was said that in the bureau which verified the ancient status of court offices, a certain Hanawa Jiro, acting on the orders of Ando

Tsushima no Kami, was investigating the old proposal by the Hojo family to do away with the emperor. It was even said that the shogunate had decided to go so far as to assassinate the present emperor in order to uproot the entire movement to "revere the emperor and expel the barbarians." It was the kind of time when the most preposterous rumors were going about. Then came the shocking news of the suicide of the commissioner for foreign affairs, Hori Oribe no Kami. That news gave rise to another rumor. It was said that Ando Tsushima was secretly in complicity with the foreigners and had even presented Alcock, the British chargé d'affaires, with a favorite concubine. Hori Oribe had objected but his counsel was not accepted until he turned his own sword on himself. This rumor was even supported by a widely circulated but obviously fraudulent letter of remonstrance written in Chinese. Great numbers of people mourned the death of Hori Oribe and incense never ceased to burn before his grave in those days.

Everyone doubted these rumors and yet at the same time believed them. Cries that the power of the Tokugawa had already lost its foundation and the allegiance of the people had turned away from the shogunate, so that the time had come for a restoration of imperial power—all this could not fail to excite the younger people.

In the eighth month of that year Hanzo learned of the death of the retired lord of Mito. Among all the daimyo whose movements had been restricted by the Ansei purge—beginning with Tokugawa Yoshikatsu, indirectly the lord of Kichizaemon and Hanzo, and including Hitotsubashi Yoshinobu, Matsudaira Shungaku, Yamauchi Yodo, and others—only the retired lord of Mito had not been released from house arrest. His eventful life ended in his villa in the Komagome district of Edo. He was sixty years of age when he followed his old enemy Ii Naosuke into death. His departure was like the setting of the sun on an era.

Hanzo's friend Kozo from Nakatsugawa was a relative of Kitahara Inao, a Hirata disciple in Ina, and he was also connected with Matsuo Taseko, another disciple. Kozo came to talk with Hanzo about his wish to go with them to Kyoto for a while and to make some contribution to national affairs as a disciple of Hirata Atsutane. Even Kozo, who had always been so unassuming and so little desirous of fame, had come to feel this way. Hanzo could no longer remain tranquil. His father was old and he was busy with the highway. The duties of honjin, toiya, and headman had fallen on his shoulders whether he liked it or not.

On the nineteenth of the tenth month of that year, sixteen buildings burned in Magome. Among them was the old house in which Hanzo had been born; it was reduced to ashes in a single night. The Fushimiya, the new addition to the honjin, everything was gone. Even for the village of Magome with its strong winds, this second major conflagration within three years came as a great shock.

The following year, 1861, was the first year of Bunkyu. Hanzo and Otami were living in the rear storehouse, which had escaped the fire. A rough lean-to had been added to the front of the storehouse and enclosed with boards. Here the maids cooked on a hastily improvised stove. Kichizaemon, his wife, and their grandchildren were living temporarily on the second floor of the miso shed, which had also escaped damage. There were two rooms here and this was where Hanzo's grandfather, Hanroku, had spent his retirement. From here on down the stone stairway leading toward the well, past the woodshed and the granary where Sakichi worked, there had been no fire.

It was the second month by the old calendar and snow was still on the ground. Hanzo stepped out of the improvised toilet and walked toward the ruins, where workmen were sifting the ashes for nails and other metal objects. There was no trace of the chamber of honor where the daimyo had been lodged, or of the inner room, the central room, the passageway, the retiring room, the parlor, or the great, wood-floored room by the entrance hall. Only a bit of the wall that had faced the highway remained.

What was most sorely missed in this post station was the meeting room where the post officials could get together. Fortunately, Kyudayu's house had not been burned and the meeting place was temporarily moved there. The duties of toiya had hitherto been exchanged between Kichizaemon and Kyudayu every half month, but now they were temporarily transferred to Kyudayu. Everything was temporary, dreary, unsettled. Kichizaemon tried to encourage Hanzo as they began to prepare for rebuilding, asking him to call a carpenter and to draw up plans.

While the village was still cleaning up after the fire, a letter arrived announcing that the emperor's younger sister, the princess Kazu, would be passing through on her way to Edo to become the bride of the shogun Iemochi.

All the post station officials and assistant headmen had to meet to discuss the official notice from the Fukushima offices. Even Kimbei, who had been staying indoors most of the time with a chronic cough, was brought out for these meetings.

Kichizaemon came from the second floor of the miso shed and Kimbei arrived from his temporary quarters at the Upper Fushimiya. When Kichizaemon saw his old friend he said, "Kimbei, they say that even Magome has been ordered to prepare illustrations of the route."

The duties of honjin, toiya, and headman now weighed heavily on Hanzo's shoulders. He had to put all his own interests aside and help his aged father to deal with the passage of Princess Kazu over the Kiso road.

CHAPTER SIX

1

WHEN THE WEDDING PLANS for Princess Kazu became known they aroused strong feelings along the route she was to take to Edo. This was not the first time there had been talk of an alliance by marriage between the shogunal and the imperial houses, but always before circumstances had prevented anything from coming of it. The present proposal to Princess Kazu seemed likely to be successful. Not only was the wedding itself unprecedented but it was also without precedent that the princess should travel to Edo for her wedding. It was a very great honor for the stations and villages along her route to be able to witness such an occasion.

It did not, however, end with mere honors for the four lower Kiso stations and their officials. They were both frightened and perplexed. Years of experience had taught them the number of horses that could be brought into service along this highway. They also had a good idea of the number of porters that could be called up in the Kiso valley. It was simply impossible for them to avoid calling for great numbers of men and horses from the Ina villages.

The sixty-nine stations of the Kiso highway were no longer what they had been at the coming of Perry. They were still less what they had been when Kichizaemon and Kimbei had known them in the Tempo era of the 1830's. It was now very doubtful just how long the farmers from Ina would continue to accept the orders of the commissioners of transport to supply such a large number of men and horses.

One horse in every four was called up, one man in every five. Only the very strongest of men and horses were chosen. Old men, very young men, or weak horses were not to be used.

This was the contract that had been drawn up between the representatives of the Ina villages and the officials of the lower four post stations of the Kiso some fifty years earlier. The "one horse in four" and "one man in five" were calculated on the basis of local revenues and the various villages were assigned a share of the total responsibility on the basis of the sources of the revenue. Of course the distribution had undergone considerable readjustment since the original agreement but the plan remained generally the same.

To understand the post stations, one must know about this harsh system.

It had been established to supplement the men and horses at the immediate disposal of each post station in order to expedite traffic. The system was known as the "assisting districts." According to Tokugawa policy, all districts and villages in the general area of a post station had a duty to render assistance when needed. The "assisting districts" edict was therefore to be strictly obeyed. A commissioner would come to the Kiso from time to time to see that the rule was being followed. The total revenues of the villages subject to the "assisting districts" rule were calculated at 10,200 koku of rice, and this was divided among the villages. For example, the largest village was assigned a revenue value of 1,614 koku and the smallest 600. In thirty-one villages along the Tenryu river, later sixty-five villages, the farmers would have to put down their hoes, leave their fields, cross the mountain passes from the Ina valley to the Kiso valley, and carry out this compulsory labor whenever the call came.

It must also not be forgotten that even though this was an age when travel was difficult, the travels of the daimyo on alternate attendance in Edo or the officials on government business were carried out on an extremely lavish scale. Whenever the call for labor came the villagers of the assisting districts would be divided into an upper and a lower band; the upper band would go to Nojiri and Midono in the Kiso, and the lower band to Tsumago and Magome, where they would be further divided into morning and afternoon shifts. If there was difficulty for the villagers who lived close to the left bank, because of floods on the Tenryu river or the like, then there was an inflexible rule that all able-bodied persons in the accessible villages would be called out.

As final proof of just how much emphasis the Tokugawa placed on this system of post stations, one had only to note that its administration was placed directly under the commissioners of transport. The commissioners required one person from each of the assisting districts to act as a guarantor, and further, to assure a plentiful supply of men and horses for public service, the commissioners prepared letters reflecting their full authority and had a seal made up which they sent to each of the post stations along the road. If anyone seemed to be resisting service, the authority of the seal was to be used to ensure his participation. Now from the point of view of the farmers, the season when travel was heaviest along the highways was also the season when they were busiest in the fields. They had been obedient and they had borne up well. But there had been cases of extreme hardship, villages that had pleaded the extenuating circumstances of landslides, washouts, or floods in order to avoid service.

This was the situation into which the entourage of Princess Kazu would be coming. Such a procession would normally travel over the Tokaido but it was decided that this one should go over the Kiso road instead, because the Tokaido was in great disorder. A plan had been reported among the activists and ronin to close the highway to the princess's party. Consequently, the commissioners sent out strict orders to each of the post stations that they must provide themselves with men and horses regardless of the costs and be fully prepared for the day that would arrive for each in turn.

*   *   *   *   *   *   *

In the Tsumago honjin Juheiji was awaiting the return of Ogiya Tokuemon, who had gone to check the mood of the sixty-five villages making up
the assisting districts of Ina. Hanzo's wife, Otami, arrived from Magome on
her first visit home in half a year. Happy to be home, she went out the
kitchen door of the main house and crossed the back garden to where her
brother was.

"You're here," Juheiji said simply.

They were in the corner of a garden that extended into the mountain
behind. Juheiji had set up a twenty-yard archery range with a crude shelter
where he practiced whenever he had a spare moment. Otami was surprised to
find her brother in the formal trousers befitting his rank, one shoulder bare,
the leather cords of the hand guard wrapped around his right hand.

Otami spoke with her usual high spirits. "You really have it easy! So now
you've taken up archery?"

"No matter how busy I get, I always try to practice with the bow a bit."

As his sister watched, Juheiji nocked an arrow to the string. Against the
backstop an eight-inch target glistened in the sun that had just emerged after
a shower.

"Is Hanzo well?" asked Juheiji as he took aim. He released the arrow, and
it missed. He tried another and it too buried itself in the sand of the backstop.

Juheiji went over to recover the arrows. Then he returned to where Otami
was waiting.

"How did Kichizaemon and Kimbei's applications for retirement turn
out?"

"We haven't heard anything about them yet."

"Oh, they're reluctant to grant permission, eh? Well, I'm not surprised."

Juheiji nodded, thinking of the busy highway.

"Otami, you get a good rest. Stay here at Tsumago for two or three
days."

"That's all very well for you to say."

As brother and sister were talking, Tokuemon, just back from Ina, came
walking casually into the garden. Tokuemon was not merely the kind of person who could be sent on missions to the powerful representatives of the
assisting districts of Shimada and Yamaura; he had assisted Juheiji as the assistant honjin of Tsumago and as a village elder ever since Juheiji's father's early
death. Tokuemon's family were sake brewers and in this too they resembled
the Fushimiya of Magome.

Juheiji signaled with his eyes that Otami was to leave, and he watched her
walk around the garden back to the house. There was a spot on the wall of
the shelter where bows could be hung. Juheiji unlaced his hand guard and in
this quiet, secluded place conferred with a worried Tokuemon.

Tokuemon's report was just as Juheiji had feared. This was not the first
time that the assisting districts of the Kiso had sent appeals either directly to
the commissioners or through the post officials of the lower four Kiso post
stations. It was such an appeal that had already led to sixty-five villages being

assigned the duties of assisting districts instead of the original thirty-one. According to the precedents set long ago, villages would serve as assisting districts for a term of five years and be responsible each year for seventeen men, which amounted to two bu three rin three mo for each hundred koku of annual revenue. But this had been long ago, in the Tempo era of the 1830's, and since then the duties of the assisting districts had been expanded.

Since the coming of the Black Ships in the Kaei era, the travels of the daimyo and the officials had greatly increased. It was only natural that each time people were called up for work along the precipitous Kiso road, men and horses would tire, people would fall ill or die, and villages would begin to resist the duty. After all, to serve one day on the highway, porters of the assisting districts had to leave their villages the day before, cross the mountains, and reach the post station that night so that they could work the following day. Once they had moved freight to a still more distant station, they would be unable to return to their homes the same night. One day's duty thus required an absence from home of three or even four days. Moreover, food and lodging were expensive and with other expenses on the road coming and going, there would be nothing left of the pay they received for the day's work when they got back home. The hardships were particularly severe for the most distant villages and they were permitted, after conferring with the toiya, to make cash contributions in lieu of men and horses. But these charges had also become extremely high. The suffering of the villagers was no trifling matter. Since the regularly assigned horses and porters attached to the post stations were completely inadequate for such heavy use, great numbers of men and horses were supplied by the assisting districts; they simply could not continue to perform their duties indefinitely. Prices would rise, the farmers would fall behind in their work, and the fields, left to women and the aged, would deteriorate. How could the farmers manage their own work under such conditions? The representatives of the assisting districts reported that they would be unable to respond effectively to the general discontent unless the officials of the post stations were able to think of some way to make it possible for the villagers to make their livings. In the assisting districts people were saying that this of all times was one in which they could not put out work orders.

"They really made a fuss," continued Tokuemon. "I talked with them, telling them they had to get people to go along with this somehow. I told them they wouldn't have to do it all by themselves. We'll appeal to the commissioners' office to have the number of assisting villages increased. And then we can be sure that Owari will not just stand by and watch all this. They will surely give us something. Finally, I pointed out that a procession on this scale would not occur again, and at that point they began to yield, saying that they would consult with everyone. I left them and came back with that promise."

"You've had a bad time of it. We'll have to prepare an appeal to the commissioners' office right away. Let's put it out in the names of the headmen of Nojiri, Midono, Tsumago, and Magome. I think Hanzo will agree."

"That would be best. I could really feel it on this trip to Ina. It's gotten so that the farmers will not listen anymore to arguments based on the prestige of the Tokugawa."

"It's too late for that, Tokuemon. It seems to me that the daimyo could do with a little bit less traveling. That would help the assisting districts. There are those who say that alternate attendance is already outdated."

"That's because there are now headmen going around saying such things."

Saying "One more round," Juheiji took up the bow hanging on the wall of the shed and began putting rosin on the string. Tokuemon watched him for a moment.

"There's a tremendous fad for that in Ina too. The samurai are pawning their swords and the headmen are taking up archery, eh? Things are really changing."

"You could put it that way. I want to get myself in better condition. In a time of upheaval like this, we need to toughen up."

Juheiji arched his chest, raised his arms high, faced the target, and took a deep breath. The effort of pushing with his bow arm and pulling with the string arm brought a flush to his face and the muscles in his arms rose up and quivered. He was short, but he was just thirty and in the prime of life. Both he and Hanzo were of an age when they looked like real Kiso "mountain monkeys." Beside him, responding to everything he said, stood Tokuemon, who seemed like an uncle.

Twang!

"That just won't do."

Juheiji set directly to work on the draft of the appeal. First, they requested that for the time being additional assisting districts be assigned in Ina so that the burdens of the farmers might be reduced. Next, since an extraordinary burden would be placed on the facilities of the post stations in the coming progress of the imperial princess, each station should be given a special loan of one hundred ryo. This debt would be retired in ten years. At present there was a shortage of rice, leading to great hardship on the part of those serving the post stations. Therefore the above mentioned money would be used to buy rice, millet, and soybeans for distribution among the men and horses serving the procession. Fifty packhorse loads of rice and fifty of millet would be needed for each station. These were the essential points of the appeal.

The draft was completed. Then the officials of the lower four stations gathered at the Tsumago honjin. Inosuke came from Magome representing his foster father, Kimbei. Juheiji, Tokuemon, and Tokuemon's adopted son, Jitsuzo, sat down with them.

"It seems to me that an addition to the assisting districts is just what is needed, but what if it should set a precedent?"

"But there just isn't going to be another procession like this one."

Various opinions were aired among the post officials. Tokuemon informed them about the mood of the assisting districts in Ina, maintaining that they had no choice but to send out such an appeal. He reassured them that there was nothing in it to give cause for worry in the future.

"How about it? Shall we accept the draft as it stands?" said Inosuke, and the headmen were asked to affix their seals.

2

Hidden away in the archery range at the back of the garden, bow in hand, Juheiji was going over in his mind the letter he had recently received from the Fukushima offices. It had nothing to do with the progress of Princess Kazu but rather dealt with the question of Shinto burial rites about which so much was being said these days. The letter asked whether he accepted the principle or not.

Juheiji could not deal casually with this question. His brother-in-law Hanzo was a disciple of Hirata Atsutane and this matter of Shinto burial seemed to be part of the effort to restore antiquity that had been initiated by the Hirata school of National Learning.

"I really don't know what to make of the National Learning movement. There's no telling what those people will do," Juheiji thought to himself as he continued to pace back and forth between the shed and the target twenty yards away on the heaped up sand of the backstop.

Juheiji was no less dissatisfied with the tone of the times than was Hanzo. But to remove the funeral rituals so deeply rooted in belief and custom from the temples, and to reform them in every aspect, was too much for him to assimilate. This had all grown out of the anti-Buddhist movement in Mito and it amounted to a religious revolution. Juheiji simply could not understand how the National Scholars, with their dreams of a return to antiquity, could have generated so much passion. He muttered to himself as he thought about it.

"I really have my doubts about Shinto funeral ceremonies. I doubt that a return to antiquity can be carried out in these times. There's a contradiction in what the Hirata people are trying to do."

Otami was still visiting at Tsumago, so Juheiji put away his bow and arrows, picked up the target, and carried it off to join his wife, Osato, and his sister. Reaching the main house, he heard the sound of a handloom.

Juheiji's home was old as Mt. Oshiro behind Tsumago was old. According to tradition, it had been the Aoyama household where in olden times the village fair had been held on the eighth, eighteenth, and twenty-eighth of each month. One of the things that was appropriate to this ancient house was the old work-stained loom which was said to have been there since before the time when Juheiji and Otami's grandmother came as a bride. Now, in these times when womanliness was still measured by the seclusion in which one lived, Otami and Osato had come to the loom to talk about the coming procession and about what a beautiful person Princess Kazu must be on the eve of her journey down to Edo to become the bride of Iemochi, the fourteenth Tokugawa shogun.

The world of these women, who took pleasure in light handiwork whenever there was a bit of leisure from the business of the highway, was pleasing to Juheiji. Osato was seated at the loom. Otami, beside her, was watching her sister-in-law, who was the same age as she, at work. Nearby was the little girl Okume, who had come from Magome with her mother, playing with her ball. The grandmother, unable to be still for a moment, was bringing one after another of her tasty creations for Otami to sample, showing the great pleasure that she took in her granddaughter's visit home.

Otami spoke to her brother.

"Grandmother just said that you are spending all your time at archery."

"That wasn't grandmother. I'm quite sure you two were the ones who have been saying that. Something seems to be wrong with me though. I couldn't hit anything today. But hasn't Hanzo taken up archery too?"

"If my husband has any time he reads books or teaches his disciples. Men come in all varieties. You help us pick out our sashes, but my husband never even knows what I am wearing."

"That's the way Hanzo would be."

Osato, who was not usually very talkative, sat at her loom ordering the threads for the country-style striped cloth she was weaving while she listened to the conversation between brother and sister. Otami seemed suddenly to remember her presence.

"Anyway, Osato, please let me weave a little. Whenever I see this loom I remember my girlhood."

"But is it all right for you to do this kind of work?"

Otami flushed when Osato said this. In contrast to the sickly and childless Osato, Otami was a plump and fully fleshed young matron.

"I suppose you know, Juheiji," said Otami, her face still colored. "I may be in a condition that will not let me come to Tsumago again for a long time."

"You people are doing well. It shows that your married life is going well. Look at us. I don't know whether it is my fault or Osato's, but we have been married six years and we still have no children. I envy you."

The grandmother came back in. She told them that someone had left a rare gift from Yokohama and she showed it to Otami.

"Here it is. They say it is something you use in washing, but the man who gave it to me wasn't sure just how you use it. He said that he saw it in the foreign settlement in Yokohama and it was so pretty he bought it. It was a merchant from Iida who gave it to us."

At that time no one knew the word for soap. Neither the old woman nor the Iida merchant had ever heard the word *shabon,* by which it soon came to be known. When she opened the wrapper and showed its contents to Otami, one could see that it was in the shape of some foreign flower and there were white ones and pale pink ones.

"Just see! It has such a fine scent!" said the grandmother, and Otami partly closed her eyes and smelled. She was amazed by the perfume.

"Okume! Smell this!"

Otami held one of the white cakes to the girl's nose. Okume snatched it and tried to put it in her mouth.

"That's not to be eaten!" cried Otami, snatching it back. "She thought it was candy!"

This new foreign scent was to make a deeper impression on Juheiji than on anyone else. The beautiful flower shapes, the crisp lettering running horizontally across it—it had a kind of beauty that one did not see in standard Edo souvenirs in the pure Japanese style, such as block prints or sandals. This purely accidental influence cured Juheiji of his dislike of Western things. He had always liked to collect old coins but now he began to collect Western silver coins and to enjoy them in secret. With the Western coins mixed in among his old Japanese and Chinese coins, he could begin to imagine a bit about the West. But he let no one know about this.

"I wonder how you use it," the grandmother was saying to Otami. "Somebody said you dissolve it in water, so I tried boiling one in a pot. I'm telling you, it just spun round and round in the pot and dissolved right away. When I stirred the pot with a stick, it got all foamy. Somehow I didn't like the look of it so I buried it, pot and all. It doesn't look to me as though it was for washing after all."

"But I've never seen anything like it. Please give me one. I'd like to take it to show the people in Magome," said Otami.

"You'd better forget about that," said Juheiji, speaking in his elder brother tone.

It was the beginning of the sixth month in the first year of Bunkyu, 1861, and a wave of the most virulent anti-foreign sentiment was sweeping the whole country. There were reports that in the previous month ronin from Mito had attacked the British legation in the Tozenji temple in the Takanawa section of Edo. It was said that three Mito men were killed in the fighting, one had been captured, and three had killed themselves at Shinagawa. Fourteen of the soldiers guarding the Tozenji were said to have been killed or wounded, and a secretary and the Nagasaki consul were wounded. The movement to expel the barbarians had now reached this pitch. One did not dare carry even this innocent gift from an Iida merchant out of the house.

When it came time for Otami to return to Magome, Juheiji accompanied her, saying that he had business with Hanzo's father. He had to ask Kichizaemon to affix his seal to the petition about the Ina assisting districts. He already had the seal impressions from Nojiri and Midono and he needed only that of Magome.

Sakichi came over from Magome to assist Otami. He put Okume on his back, taking charge of the tiny child and protecting her with his arms. Otami was ready, and they set out.

"Master Juheiji, this reminds me of Yokosuka."

That trip of nearly four years ago was still fresh in Sakichi's mind.

Juheiji's village was located on the river and near the Shizumo and Araragi forests in one of the most beautiful valleys in all the Kiso. In going to Magome, one's back was turned to the entrance of this valley and the highway led five miles over the pass. It was a great pleasure for Otami, who seldom left the house, to walk over this mountain road in the company of her brother. The summer forest stood along both sides of the road, and beyond rose mountain after mountain. Between Tsumago and Magome was the Shiragi guard station, set up to watch for illegal cutting as part of the forest conservation policy of Owari han.

As the cool shadows of evening began to fall, Juheiji's party entered Magome, which was once again in the process of rebuilding. In all directions the devastation of the fire could still be seen along with the reconstruction that was just getting under way. Here were piles of lumber; from there could be heard the sound of logs being dragged in. They went directly to the burnt-out honjin, where they found Hanzo and Kichizaemon at work in a little construction shed amid the scent of fresh lumber.

Hanzo welcomed his wife, his child, and his brother-in-law. He told Juheiji that the meeting room had been restored, pointing out a tile-roofed building in one corner of the honjin site, in the same location alongside the highway as its predecessor. This building and the toiya were the first buildings that had to be restored in a post station.

Juheiji stood before Hanzo and surveyed the scene.

"I'm really amazed at the progress you've made."

"That's because everyone has worked very hard. We can thank them all for having gotten us this far."

Kichizaemon took up the conversation. "For most villages, it would really be too much to have two major fires in three years. We started rebuilding our place on the third of last month, but it won't be finished until around the two hundred tenth day of the year. It can't possibly be ready for the progress of Princess Kazu."

Juheiji then said that he had come to get Kichizaemon's seal impression on the petition about the assisting districts. Hanzo replied, "Well, sit there," and joined him on a pile of lumber in the construction site. Otami walked past them to the temporary lodging at the rear of the lot, to join her mother-in-law, Oman.

"You've done a good piece of work, Juheiji. We heard about the assisting districts from Inosuke next door. Of course, father agrees," Hanzo said.

"Well, I wonder what's going to happen in the assisting districts from now on," said Juheiji with a thoughtful expression. "That's the big question. When the Osaka censor came down the road on the twenty-second of last month, it required two hundred men from the assisting districts in Ina. And then, think about the time when the Nikko emissary came through.

That was on the sixth of the fourth month. Even though we called for four hundred porters, not a single one came over from Ina."

"At any rate, we can't continue under the present arrangements for the assisting districts," Hanzo added. "Extra business is no boon to a station. We simply have to think about how the farmers along the highway are going to make a living."

"We have done our best at Magome with that method. But they say they are having the same problems along the Tokaido. It's not easy there, either," said Kichizaemon.

"It all comes down to the fact," continued Juheiji, "that it just isn't reasonable to have to call out two hundred or four hundred men every time someone decides to take a trip."

"So the daimyo and the officials are going to have to travel more simply," put in Hanzo.

"We're gradually coming to such times," said Kichizaemon with deep feeling. "I think something is going to happen to alternate attendance quite soon. In the first place, the finances of the han won't stand for such frequent travel."

But what about the consequences? Kichizaemon, for all his sixty-two years and his long, successful experience as a headman, could say nothing about what might lie ahead. He looked a bit tired from the work of rebuilding.

"I'll put my seal to the document, Juheiji, and I want to hear what you have to say, so come up to our quarters. Oman will want to see you, too."

In the more private areas of the enclosure, the family could be seen at work. Oman was out in front of the miso shed, her sleeves tied up and a kerchief on her head, working with the maids at pickling fresh, cool-looking eggplant. Beside her stood Otami, holding her second child, Sota. Cutting the stem ends off the eggplants on a board placed on top of a pickle tub, Oman gave two to Okume, who immediately grasped them between her toes and ran around the area making "horse tracks." From the direction of the woodshed came Sakichi, who had pickled some ripe plums to give to the children.

"Father, I understand that your application for retirement has not yet been accepted."

"That's right. It seems hard to get it through."

Juheiji was in the habit of addressing Kichizaemon as "father." This conversation took place after dinner that night, at a time when Hanzo had gone out saying that he was going to look in at the new meeting room.

"Juheiji," said Kichizaemon with a smile, "an official came all the way over here to see about that. He called Kimbei and me before him and talked to us. He said that he wanted both of us to try to stay with our duties another two or three years. Kimbei and I both agreed and left his presence. It seems that people heard about that later."

They were talking on the second floor of the miso shed, where Kichizaemon and Oman had been living with their grandchildren since the fire.

Juheiji felt called upon to go up to the Upper Fushimiya, where Kimbei too was in temporary quarters, to take lodging for the night.

"It doesn't look as though I am ever going to reach the payoff," said Kichizaemon as he came to the bottom of the stairs with Juheiji. Then he noticed a blazing star in the evening sky and pointed it out as though he saw some kind of portent in it.

"A comet! It's just like the one that showed up in the northern sky during the year of the horse. It doesn't look like a good year."

Juheiji made no reply as he walked away from the miso shed, out onto the street, and up the steep stone path. The moon was not yet out, but the stars were cool. He was about to pass by the new meeting room when he noticed the wooden porch at the front of the building and the open entry. Juheiji stopped for a moment, startled.

"That not only Hanzo but you too, Inosuke, have gone along with this is completely unexpected."

"But when you know that the consequences of a thing are evil, it is necessary to correct it."

He could hear the voices quite distinctly. Light was pouring out of the room and a meeting was in progress.

"There isn't sufficient reason to change the rituals as they were passed down to us from our ancestors."

"But if we are going to change people's minds, I don't think we will get anywhere unless we change them at the source."

"That's an empty argument."

"When sixty-nine renegade priests were found frequenting the brothel quarters of Yoshiwara, Fukagawa, Shinjuku, and Shinagawa, rosaries in hand, not only were they subjected to exposure at Nihombashi but one resident priest of a temple was exiled and the others were punished according to the rules of their temples."

They were arguing about the question of restoring Shinto funeral ceremonies. It seemed that Hanzo and Inosuke were in favor of them and were being opposed by Kyudayu.

"Since you mention the temples, people are used to thinking uncritically of them as good places and for a long time have been donating large amounts of land, entrusting them with the tablets of their ancestors, and paying no heed whatsoever to the consequences," came Hanzo's voice.

There was a certain amount of reason on Hanzo's side. According to him, ever since Shotoku Taishi first promoted Buddhism in this country the emperors had all revered the priests, had constructed vast temples and monasteries for them, and had used up the nation's treasure in expressing their faith, while the priests had done nothing in return for the great favors bestowed on them by the nation. Not only that, but mountain priests from the seven temples of Mt. Hiei had come bearing portable shrines into Kyoto, creating disturbances and intimidating both court and populace. Great temples had warred with each other, killing innumerable people, setting innumerable fires. From Heian times onward, great numbers of persons from the imperial household and the noble court families had taken orders and had seen nothing but grief in this world. Therefore the hearts of helpless ordinary people had gradually withdrawn from the imperial household and everyone began to bow down before the new might of the military.

In this land there are many Buddhist temples and monasteries, and the tax-free estates given them by the daimyo are vast in extent. The priests, nuns, acolytes, catamites and low-ranking officials who live in them cultivate no land but eat the best rice; they neither spin nor weave but wear the finest of silks. No matter how impoverished the people of the country may be, no priest proposes that the temple revenues be reduced to ease their lot. Instead they try to take advantage of the bad years to enrich the temples still further. Although farmers can starve to death, no one ever hears of priests starving to death. Of course long-established customs have great power, and it has come to be accepted that there should be millions of people throughout the country who eat without toil in these temples. This has come from making far too many concessions. To help awaken the people, it would be only proper to take away the funeral services from the temples and return them to the customs of antiquity.

"There have been few times when religion has become as soiled as it is today," Hanzo's voice continued. "Just look at the temples and shrines throughout the country. When they talk of 'assimilation' they claim that the gods of this land are simply local manifestations of Mahavairocana or Amitabha. As a result the gods and the Buddhas have become totally confounded in the minds of the people."

"You're still young," came Kyudayu's voice. "There are avatars and there is the bodhisattva of the northern constellation, and there is Kompira and any number of others. No one can say for sure if they are gods or Buddhas. Isn't it quite enough to know of their miraculous power?"

"We don't think so. We think it is proof of a terrible degeneracy. This theory that the Japanese gods are no more than local manifestations of Buddhist figures is really outrageous. Doesn't it imply that the gods can get by only by clinging to the Buddhas? That is nothing but blasphemy against the gods. How can you stand for it?—I'm changing the subject for the moment, but I was just twenty-two when the Black Ships first came here. But it is a mistake to think that those were the first Black Ships. If you think about it, you will realize that there is no way to count all the Black Ships that have come to this country since the beginning. The way we look at it, Dengyo and Kukai and all the other founders of Buddhist sects were Black Ships."

"How can someone who expects to succeed to the honjin say such things? If that is the case, I am going to have to check with the Upper Fushimiya. Kimbei is on my side. He has done a lot for the temple. And one more thing you shouldn't forget—the Mampukuji here in Magome is your family temple, founded by your ancestor, Aoyama Dosai!"

Now Kyudayu was fiercely proud that he was one of only two people in the eleven post stations to have a name with the elegant ending "-dayu." He was fond of talking about "Kyudayu of Magome and Gondayu of Niekawa."

Moreover, although it was Kichizaemon's residence that had been designated a rest stop for the progress of Princess Kazu, the honjin was still being rebuilt and the place for the rest stop had been changed to Kyudayu's residence. He had become quite puffed up about it.

Quite unexpectedly, in overhearing their argument Juheiji had learned that the return to Shinto funeral ceremonies was a reform proposed by the Hirata school. He paced back and forth before the meeting room, unable to go away.

That evening, Otami waited in their temporary quarters in the storehouse for Hanzo to return. It was a hot stuffy evening such as rarely occurred in the mountains; the rain shutters were still open on the second floor of the miso shed where Hanzo's parents were living.

"Aren't you awfully late?" said Otami, seeing Hanzo at the entrance as he came listlessly back from the meeting room. Since the fire, their older child, Okume, had been sleeping with her grandparents over the miso shed and only Sota was with them. An old-fashioned lamp stood by the child's bedside. Otami poured the hot water she had prepared into the mimosa tea and offered it to her husband.

Hanzo went to look at the sleeping child and then came back to sip the tea. "I had a little quarrel with Kyudayu over Shinto funeral ceremonies. I know very well that if you beat on a wall your fist is going to hurt, but Kyudayu is so obstinate. He became very angry. He said he was going to go up to Fukushima to report the matter and all kinds of other things as he headed off to see Kimbei. I was really thankful to have Inosuke there with me, on my side. You can really count on him."

It was the time of year when nights were shortest. Otami's pregnancy was not yet noticeable, but she had already begun to feel a bit sluggish and she went to bed beside Sota while her husband stayed up. Hanzo had tried not to let Otami know just how upset he had been that evening but now he could not calm down. He sat near the door of the storehouse, enjoying the night breeze blowing up the stone stairway from the direction of the persimmon tree. After a while Otami, also unable to sleep, came to join him in her night clothes.

"You should take better care of yourself."

"Let me tell you what the people in Tsumago were saying."

"What were they saying in Tsumago?"

"They were saying that Kichizaemon and Hanzo over in Magome are a fine father and son."

"Is that right?"

"That's because my brother and I lost our parents early."

"Did they say anything about the Shinto funeral question?"

"If they did, I didn't hear it. My brother did say one thing—he said, 'Hanzo is a dreamer.' "

"It seems to me that I don't dream enough. It seems to me that there is nothing so dismal as the life of a person without dreams."

"But what I hear you say to Kozo is different from what I hear you say to my brother."

"That's because Kozo and I are the same kind of person. But it's your brother who is always pointing out things in me that I hadn't recognized myself. Whenever I see your brother I want to say things."

"Don't you like my brother?"

"Why should you ask that? Juheiji and I were both born into this old Aoyama family and while we may not always see eye to eye, brothers are brothers."

Concerned about Otami's condition, Hanzo made her go back to bed. He tried to lie down and rest by her side, but he still could not sleep. Getting up again he went over to the entry and opened the door. To the southeast the dark night sky carried a low-lying band of faint yellow light that was very slowly brightening, making the night seem all the deeper.

In the temple where the memorial tablets and the graves of the Aoyama family had been entrusted for centuries was the priest Sho'un, whose presence was becoming increasingly problematic for Hanzo. He remembered the day he had gone down to Shinjaya to welcome the new priest. It had been raining and when Sho'un, coming up from the west at the end of six years of pilgrimage and religious discipline, had at last reached the top of the pass, his cap and leggings were soaked. Hanzo had been young then, but he had already committed himself to the Hirata school of National Learning and he had made up his mind to reject both the Buddhist world view and the Chinese learning that had held moral supremacy since the middle ages. He remembered that even then, in thinking about the new priest and the religion in which that priest believed, he had felt a premonition that they would sooner or later find themselves at odds. That time had come. Of course, the question of Shinto funeral ceremonies had as yet progressed only to the point of eliciting a letter of inquiry from the Fukushima offices.

At some time the dark sky had filled with summer light. It shone dimly on the cool stone stairway in front of the storehouse. It shone across his legs as he lay there, the only one awake. And, bit by bit, the moon also began to rise.

If people recognize their evil, it will be corrected though it has persisted eight
　　hundred thousand years.
If perceived in true sincerity, then gods of righteousness will set it straight.
If that which is before one's eyes be only righteous, then no one will ever stray.
Comrade: When you enter on the way of righteousness, then the praise and
　　blame of ordinary men will not matter.

Such were Hanzo's feelings.

3

When the ninth month of the old calendar came around, it was time for small birds to appear on Magome pass. Already the advance parties of the escort sent out from Edo to bring Princess Kazu back were passing through almost every day, and from that time on the regular contingent of porters was no longer able to handle the traffic. Ogasawara Mino no Kami had been dispatched by the transport commissioners' office to inspect the post stations.

At the beginning of the tenth month, Hanzo noticed a still further increase in the number of people traveling along the highway to prepare for the coming procession. Officials from Owari rushed up from Mino. The headman of Agematsu proceeded to Fukushima. There were even people arriving in Magome by fast litter in the dead of night. Then it was reported that a thousand porters dispatched from the Owari domains had arrived at their temporary post in the neighboring station of Ochiai in the midst of a fierce rain and wind storm.

"Hanzo! It just doesn't look as though there is going to be enough men and horses. I'm going to go down and talk with the people in Nakatsugawa and then go on to Kyoto from there."

"Do you think you should?"

As father and son exchanged these words, Hanzo was amazed to learn that although a company of porters matching the perquisites of one having a revenue level of 660,000 koku had been called up, a close figuring of needs showed that number of men still to be inadequate.

"They say that in Mino some people have been given permission to draw porters from the Ise road and that they have already set out to make arrangements. From Unuma in Mino to Motoyama in Shinano, there is nothing to do but pass the porters along from station to station. I am going to go after the commissioner, who is now in Kyoto, and ask that this be done. I expect this to be my final duty."

This display of concern and determination on the part of his aged father worried Hanzo deeply, but he could not possibly take Kichizaemon's place. A vast amount of work awaited him here on this stretch of road. Just then Oman came over to Kichizaemon, a worried expression on her face.

"This is a terrible strain on you. Everything is getting out of hand."

Kichizaemon was in excellent health. For all his sixty-two years, he was still forceful and capable of bawling out orders for a palanquin in a voice that would make those around him leap when the occasion called for it.

The road was jammed for nine consecutive days with the vast escort that was being sent to Kyoto to meet the princess. Farmers from Ina, apparently satisfied that their demands had been met, began coming into Magome to be divided into working bands of twenty-five men each. Hanzo was touched as he met these men coming in for the morning and afternoon shifts so soon after that difficult negotiation on the matter of the additional assisting districts. But even with this huge influx of assistance, there were still not enough men to deal with the westward passage of the escort. A great uproar took place as the Owari porters who were staying in Ochiai began to help with the movement of freight. On one occasion Hanzo stood in the disorderly crowd and watched four litters come down from Midono. Some carpenters from Owari were being sent home after being injured when a hut had collapsed at the construction office in Midono, which had been designated as a lodging for the princess on an overnight stop. By now the question of Shinto funerals had been completely overshadowed by the turmoil along the highway. No one spoke of anything but the coming procession.

The princess's formal title was Chikako Naishinno. She was the younger half-sister of the present emperor. She had many brothers and sisters, being the eighth daughter born to the previous emperor. Most of them had died and the princess was the last surviving younger sister of the emperor. He naturally felt especially close to her. From early childhood she had been betrothed to a member of the Arisugawa family and it had been solely on the initiative of the shogunate that she was to be married to Iemochi instead.

Of course, the idea of a union between court and shogunate was not something that had just been introduced by the roju Ando Tsushima no Kami. Tenshoin, the shogun's mother, was a widow but the Shimazu of Satsuma who had sent her as a bride to the Tokugawa supported such a union, and there were many among the high shogunal officials and the daimyo who were sympathetic. One might call it an expression of harmony that emerged as the nation was entering a time when difficulties pressed in from many directions. The roju decided that the most suitable way of effecting this union was to arrange a marriage between the shogun and the imperial princess, and they sent a petition to that effect through the Kyoto commander and the regent to the emperor himself. The emperor noted that she had already been promised to the Arisugawa family and added that he would be concerned in any case about sending the young princess into the turbulent atmosphere of Edo. He refused the proposal.

The princess herself also refused to consider the match. However, there was a powerful faction in Kyoto made up of Iwakura Tomomi, Kuga Tatemichi, Chigusa Tatebumi, Tominokoji Hironao, and others who favored the union of court and shogunate. They worked through Horikawa no Tenji. Horikawa no Tenji was the emperor's favorite concubine and the emperor was inclined to listen to her. Although the princess had at first shown no sign of relenting in her adamant refusal to accept the match, she finally began to listen to the entreaties of her nurse Ejima, who was also friendly to the union faction. Soon the young princess underwent a change of heart and began actively to pursue the match and the fearful role it entailed.

The princess sent an unusual present to her betrothed, the fourteenth shogun, Iemochi. This was the imperial exhortation to promise that he would defend the nation against the barbarians. From the standpoint of the shogunate the time was not yet opportune for resorting to military force, so it responded that in seven or eight years, ten years at most, military preparedness would have been achieved and at that time it would set the imperial mind at ease, either by abrogating the treaties or by carrying out a direct attack on the foreigners.

At the same time, this unlikely marriage aroused the opposition of many. According to these people, the shogunate had no will to resist the foreigners. They maintained that in the absence of this will, to continue to swear to oppose the foreigners, and to take up a position demanded by everyone else in the country, was to deceive both the people and themselves. The marriage of the shogun and the imperial princess would not lead to the union of court and shogunate but would instead be a marriage of political expediency. When the shogunate sent delicacies to the emperor and gifts of money to influential court officials to demonstrate its commitment to the union of court and shogunate, it only further inflamed the feelings of its opponents.

"Fraud! Fraud!"

There was no way of knowing where the cries began. After all, from Otsu in the west to Itabashi in the east, twelve han would be guarding the passage of the princess and twenty-nine others would be responsible for the security of the route itself—an incredible network of protection was laid down for her. Owari was responsible for the stretch of highway between the stations of Unuma in Mino and Motoyama in Shinano. The area between Motoyama and Shimo-Suwa was the responsibility of Matsudaira Tamba no Kami, and the forces of Suwa Inaba no Kami were stationed between Shimo-Suwa and Wada.

Around the tenth of the tenth month, Takekoshi Yamashiro no Kami set out from Edo castle to inspect all the bridges along the Kiso from Motoyama westward and to inspect all the honjin that would be used either for rest stops or overnight lodgings. This was while Kichizaemon was away on his trip to Kyoto, so Hanzo met the group in his father's place. Accompanied by Kimbei, Hanzo escorted them to Kyudayu's house. A thin, late autumn rain was falling on the pass. Hanzo, who could not help letting his private feelings intrude as he remembered the night when he and Kyudayu had quarreled, regretted his father's absence.

"Inosuke, forty-eight bales of rice for special supplies are coming in from Owari. I'd like your father, Kimbei, to take care of it."

When Hanzo went back out to the highway with Inosuke, the rice had arrived. These shipments from Owari to each of the post stations along the route where the princess would be staying involved a huge number of people, who had to come up to the inner road to handle it. As the freight came in from the west, there would sometimes be nine hundred porters staying at Midono and another eight hundred at Tsumago.

"Juheiji must be having a time of it over in Tsumago."

Hanzo's thoughts then turned to his friend Kozo, who was working in Nakatsugawa, and Keizo, who had just returned from Kyoto. He often spoke to Inosuke about them.

In Magome they were even beginning to borrow the brood mares from

Toge in order to move the vast quantity of freight that was coming in every day. Risaburo of Toge, the head of the ox drovers, was indispensable at such times. Of course Kimbei, who was fond of taking charge, was hard at work and virtually everyone in the village was fully engaged, from the toiya Kyudayu and Gisuke, the village elders Shinshichi and Yojiemon and the others, all the way down to the assistant headman Shobei, who represented all the farmers. It was apparent that most of the work was being done by the younger generation: Kyudayu's son Kyurobei, Shobei's son Shosuke, and so on.

On the twelfth day of the tenth month, Princess Kazu set out from Kyoto. Kichizaemon had not yet returned. Hanzo passed the days with his family, worrying about his father. Around dawn of the twenty-second, when the procession had reached Kusatsu in Omi, Kichizaemon returned home, having ridden through the night in a litter.

As Kichizaemon described how he had come by way of Nagoya, Hanzo could picture the vast number of people at work along the way. It was said that on the day of the princess's departure, the emperor secretly left the Katsura palace and went out to see her in her travel clothes.

"How did the freight hauling go?"

As Kichizaemon, safely home at last, asked his questions, Hanzo reported that the huge amount of freight coming up from Owari had already been passing over the highway for eleven days. Extra porters had been called up from Otaki and Nishino in the Kiso, from the remote villages along the Sue river, and from Tsukechi village in Mukai county, and they had managed to get the work done.

Road repairs were begun the next day. Hanzo had been ordered by the inspectors to move back a two-foot stone wall that ran along the front of the honjin and to repair another wall. The road was supposed to be twelve feet wide and they had to see to it that the entire road met these requirements. The stone walls in front of all the houses were torn down. After this confusion attention was shifted to the food preparations for the actual day of the procession. Hanzo's household was still very busy with rebuilding but even so they took on a large part of the burden. The Upper Fushimiya was one of several that undertook to supply meals for a hundred people.

At last, after spending the previous night in Nakatsugawa, the commissioner of transport arrived. His stern expression as he made sure all the preparations were complete made everyone aware that the time was drawing near. According to the planned itinerary, the princess would have her noon meal on the twenty-seventh at Unuma and spend that night at Ochiai. People began to come into Magome from Yamaguchi and Iida to view the procession, and all now awaited the passage of the princess.

First came the vanguard. They had left Kyoto on the twentieth. On their eighth day on the road they came over Jikkyoku pass from Ochiai to Magome. One hundred twenty men from the party went to the Mampukuji to rest. In the morning, at half past five by the old clock, the vanguard passed on. More than a thousand porters from Owari followed them past the watching crowd.

There were many among the assembled porters from Ina who massaged their arms and said that they wanted to bear the princess's palanquin. Everyone was enjoying the show. Hanzo and his father wore wide-shouldered, sleeveless jackets and formal trousers over their kimono, and both were rushing here and there.

"If it was the princess's palanquin, I would like to help carry it too!" cried the voice of an enthusiastic onlooker.

The princess was due to spend the following night in Ochiai. It rained that day and from the middle of the night the rainfall became extremely heavy. But the guards from Owari came pouring into Magome right through the driving rain. Hanzo and Kichizaemon spent a sleepless night.

At last the day arrived when the princess would be passing through Magome. When Oman woke up beside her grandchild in the temporary quarters that morning, she saw that Hanzo and Kichizaemon had been busy through the night and had scarcely been near the living quarters. When she looked in on Otami, she found her breathing heavily, wrapped in shapeless garments to hide her swollen body.

Oman decided to have Sakichi carry Okume on his back and take her out to the edge of the village to meet the princess's party. She gave Sota to her daughter Okisa, Hanzo's stepsister, and sent them along with the maids.

"Okume, come here," said Sakichi, and he took the little girl on his back. Facing her toward Oman, he said, "Do you suppose Okume will remember what she sees today when she has grown up?"

"What do you mean? She's five already!"

"So she will remember."

"Not only that," said Okisa, joining in the conversation, "she will probably remember things even earlier than this, as though they had been dreams. Even I can dimly remember things that happened when I was four years old."

"It's certainly too bad it had to rain today," said Oman. "I wanted to see this procession more than anything, but I can't go with Otami this way. We'll have to stay home."

They went out to Stonemason slope, Sakichi carrying Okume and Okisa carrying Sota. There they joined the crowd that had gathered to watch the approaching procession.

It was such a huge procession that Sakichi and the others caught no glimpse of Kichizaemon or Hanzo at work. Moreover, the precautions that had been taken were so rigorous that along the entire route, whether in shogunal or private domains, no other travelers were permitted to move within three days' journey either way of the station in which the princess would be lodging that night.

At nine and a half hours by the old clock, the palanquin in which the princess was riding, guarded ahead and behind as though on campaign, passed over the rain-soaked road. The forbidding guns, the elaborate guidons and trappings of the guards—everything looked just like wartime. The escort of court nobles followed behind, wearing black helmets shaped like tortoise shells and carrying field rations at their hips. Each was accompanied by a manservant. Among them could be seen the grand councillor Nakayama, the middle councillor Kikutei, the commanders Chigusa Arifumi and Iwakura Tomomi, and the female attendants Saisho no Tenji and Myobu Noto. The Kyoto city commissioner Seki Izumo no Kami was on guard immediately before the princess's palanquin. She herself was attended by a group from Edo that included the junior councillor Kano Totomi no Kami and the chief female officer of the shogunal palace's women's quarters. It was already growing dark by the time the princess's party had departed from the village, but people did not stop moving along the highway until nightfall.

"You have all worked hard and well. Very hard."

Kichizaemon was in the village meeting room to finish up various details on the day after the procession. He had accompanied Takekoshi Yamashiro no Kami as far as the next major stop at Midono, and he seemed to be talking to himself at the same time he was expressing his appreciation to the others who were there. He kept repeating, "You've worked very hard."

As if the extreme fatigue of the past several days were not enough, it had rained hard again from that morning on. Everyone was so tired that no one was sitting up properly. Kimbei was there too, recalling his long service on the road.

"Kichizaemon, you know about this too, but in my memory there have been three great processions along this highway. One was when the lord of Mito's daughter came through on her way to her wedding. The second was when the late lord of Owari passed away in Edo and his body was brought back up this highway. The third was when the Black Ships came and the present lord of Owari went down to Edo in the midst of the arguments over whether to begin trade and diplomatic relations. On the occasion when the late lord's body was being brought back, the seven hundred thirty porters from the Kiso valley were not nearly enough and a thousand more came from Ina. We managed to get two hundred twenty horses together from all sorts of places—"

"Kimbei really has a good memory," said one of the clerks, who was lying on the tatami with his chin propped on his hands.

"Now, just listen! When the present lord went down to Edo, there were seven hundred thirty porters from the Kiso and one thousand seven hundred seventy porters from Ina, a total of two thousand five hundred. I think there were one hundred eighty horses at Magome that time. But even that was nothing like this progress of Princess Kazu. I have never heard even the oldest people speak of anything like it."

"How about it, Kimbei, this is certainly 'absolutely unprecedented,'" said another voice.

Kimbei shook his head. "Absolutely unprecedented is not the word for it. There has never been a procession like this since the beginning of the world."

Everyone laughed.

Kichizaemon began to snore. He was lying in a corner of the room, stretched out as though dead.

Scarcely a single post station along the way was in sound condition. Some of the meeting rooms were damaged. Some had been smashed up. These depredations had been witnessed by the officials under the commissioners of transport and by the officials from Owari. Many people had been killed or injured in Nakatsugawa and Midono, and corpses of porters who had collapsed under their burdens were discovered along the highway.

On the second day after passing through Magome, Princess Kazu's retinue passed through Fukushima and Yabuhara, went over the Torii pass, had a short rest at Narai, and took its noon meal at Niekawa. Hanzo and Inosuke came back together from Midono on that day. Inosuke was overseer of the Ina porters and Hanzo had been seeing to various remaining details on the road in his father's place. Kichizaemon was visiting with Kimbei at the Upper Fushimiya and they were deep in conversation over their servings of green tea-over-rice when Hanzo and Inosuke found them there.

Now it came out. Lowering his voice, Inosuke told them how he had been forced to offer up a gratuity of two hundred twenty ryo from the lower four stations of the Kiso to the Kyoto officials. This gratuity in name only had been such an outrage that even the officials at Fukushima had bitten their lips. He further told them that those greedy Kyoto officials might not have gone so far if they had only seen the tremendous effort and intense concern with which the people of the post stations had prepared for the procession, beginning with the negotiations over the assisting districts in Ina and the procuring of porters from as far away as the provinces of Echizen and Etchu.

"To extort such a gratuity from us under cover of the confusion of the progress—there are no words to describe it," he said, looking at Kichizaemon and Kimbei.

Kimbei, no less than Kichizaemon, was concerned about the young. At the time of the Black Ships and even long before then, whenever they had felt most strongly the injustice and degeneracy of the feudal order, these two had tried their best to conceal it from the eyes and ears of the young. As headman and as village elder these two fathers had wanted throughout their lives to preserve the traditions of the Tokugawa order; they had wanted more than anything to show its power and its prestige to their children as something sacred, and to pass it unchanged to their heirs. According to what Inosuke had said, there was no difference at all between the corruption of the Kyoto officials and that of the Edo officials. The two fathers could no longer hide what they had tried to hide for so long.

On the sixth day following the passage, when the princess and her party would have reached Wada station, the Owari men who had served as guards as far as Motoyama began to come back through. Porters who had worked as far as the inner portion of the road also came straggling back. On the seventh day the first snow of the season fell on the highway.

*   *   *   *   *   *   *

It was extraordinary that the wedding of one person could have the power to move people's feelings as strongly as it did when such a young and delicate woman as the princess, brought up with such care and refinement in the imperial palace, came down to the Kanto where customs were so different, to be the bride in a military household. Awaiting her in distant Edo was Tenshoin, her future mother-in-law. On the fifteenth of the eleventh month, the princess would have arrived in Edo. She would then have had her first meeting with Tenshoin, that strong-willed woman from Satsuma. There were those who felt the keenest appreciation of the womanly self-sacrifice the princess was making. This long journey of twenty-five days over the Kiso road, although planned by the roju Ando Tsushima no Kami to further the interests of the Tokugawa, succeeded instead in focusing attention on the imperial court.

The imperial court had suffered a long decline under the oppression of the military, but it had never been completely eclipsed and now it was beginning to recover. The location of this island nation, on the edge of Asia where it had seldom been threatened from abroad however torn it might be with internal strife, may have helped to preserve the continuity of the court. When it comes to the past poverty of the imperial court, one may understand something of it by reflecting on how it had inspired such people as Gamo Kumpei, who was moved to espouse the imperial cause by his travels to the desolate tombs of the early emperors, and Takayama Hikokuro, who wept as he looked upon the dismal quarters in which the emperor then had to live. After the Onin wars of the 1460's, Kyoto was even more run-down than before and life became difficult for the court nobles. Although perhaps an exaggeration, it was said that in those days the palace was so meanly built that one could see the lamps in the imperial quarters all the way from the great bridge on Sanjo street. That this imperial court should once again be moving toward recovery seemed to Hanzo to be filled with the deepest meaning.

Times became chaotic. Once Hikone and Mito had inflicted severe damage on one another, impulsive han such as Satsuma began to assume leading roles. There was no reason to expect Choshu to look on quietly either, suffering as it had been from severe restraints ever since Sekigahara. But even these great han could not hope to gain popular support unless they rallied around the emperor in Kyoto. Not even Ii Naosuke, with the might of the shogunate as a shield, had found it possible to carry out his own policies without regard for the prestige of the court or for the opinions of the han. He had tried after the fact to gain the support of the court. It had been necessary even for him. The activists of Satsuma and Choshu struggled to get to Kyoto, either to present secret letters from their lords or to pledge their swords to the service of the imperial court.

To Hanzo, the son of a headman, this was not without reason. The seeds sown in the *History of Great Japan* of Mito or the *Classified Annals of Japan* of Owari, or in the *Unofficial History of Japan* by Rai San'yo, had taken root

deeply in the hearts of people who wished to reform political life in this country. The "retrospection" of the Southern court, the "longing for antiquity"
of the Yoshino court, the worshipfulness of Kusunoki Masashige—there was
nothing he could mention that did not indicate the direction of the thoughts
of the people. Due to the powerful cumulative effect of the feelings of the
people that resulted from the work of such forerunners as Motoori Norinaga
and with the rejection of the middle ages by the National Scholars of the
Hirata school, there was a steady increase in demands for direct rule by the
emperor and yet . . .

By the beginning of 1862, the second year of Bunkyu, Hanzo had already
moved into the newly rebuilt honjin. Kichizaemon came down from the second floor of the miso shed and Otami came in from the dismal storehouse.
Everyone was together now in this one building fragrant with new wood.
Hanzo's disciple Katsushige, who had temporarily gone home to Ochiai after
the fire, also returned. Everything in the new honjin, from its impressive
gate to the arrangement of the rooms, was just the same as it had been before
the fire. The honjin even incorporated the village meeting room once again.
Although the old pine in the corner of the garden that had survived the fire
had finally died, the newly rebuilt parlor that faced the spot where the pine
had been still received the southern sun.

Looking toward Misaka pass from the southern veranda of the new building, Hanzo could see the peaks along the Mino border, Mt. Ena the highest
among them. He had loved these mountains since childhood. Even though
the sound of their mighty avalanches could not be heard from this veranda,
he could see the snow that buried them from the highest precipices to the
deepest valleys. Sometimes Hanzo would also gaze up at the beautiful, glowing winter clouds that formed in the sky above Mt. Ena, trying to imagine
something with which to compare the great sun, setting each night only to
blaze forth in renewed splendor each dawn. Nothing, however, but the
emperor himself was anything like that mighty morning sun soaring above
all else throughout the ages.

Shortly after the beginning of the year Hanzo was called to Fukushima in
his father's place to receive, along with the other headmen of the eleven Kiso
stations, a distribution of funds amounting to one hundred ryo each. This
money was in compensation for the extraordinary expenses recently incurred
by these stations.

The household had just held a belated New Year's celebration on the twentieth of the first month. At the same time they had prepared the special rice
and red beans for the boy who had been born at the end of the year. With
Okume, Sota, and this new child who was named Masaki, Kichizaemon and
Oman were now grandparents three times over. Otami was still recuperating
in bed when Hanzo returned from Fukushima. He reported to his father that
the special money which was supposed to have come to them before the
progress of Princess Kazu had at last come down from Owari.

"The assisting districts are going to be a problem from now on. The farmers are not going to put up with that kind of service any longer," Kichizaemon said as he warmed his hands over the brazier.

That day Hanzo drew upon Kichizaemon's knowledge to pay off various obligations outstanding since the princess's progress. But just as the last remaining bits of that job were being disposed of, rumors began to circulate concerning an incident at the Sakashita gate in Edo.

On the fifteenth of the month—the day when New Year's decorations are burned in mountain households—six assassins had hidden among the willow trees on the banks of the moat of Edo castle waiting for the roju Ando Tsushima no Kami to return to the castle. They first fired guns at his palanquin. When this proved ineffective one of the assassins then rushed upon the palanquin with drawn sword and thrust it through. Although he was painfully wounded, Ando had managed to get out of the palanquin and take cover inside the Sakashita gate, barely escaping with his life. Some of the people were talking about the attack as though they had seen it themselves.

"Again?"

Kichizaemon's comment indicated to Hanzo that he too had not forgotten the Sakurada gate incident in which Ii Naosuke had been killed.

It was said that the assassins each carried a paper describing their determination to kill a traitor. Although the shogunate tried to keep the incident a secret, it became known when a seventh conspirator rushed into the Choshu mansion in Edo and disemboweled himself. The text began with the statement that the perpetrators felt in no way differently toward the shogunate than those who had killed Ii Naosuke in the year of the monkey. This made their attitude very clear. As they saw it, Ii Tairo had, out of fear of the barbarians, scorned the position of wrathful righteousness assumed by the loyalists. He had flaunted his power by entering into treasonous plots, behaving like a criminal in this land of the gods and showing disrespect for the imperial court. By striking down this minister they expected that they would bring the shogunate to repent, and it would henceforth treat the emperor with reverence and the barbarians with hatred, thus responding to the nation's danger and the feelings of the people.

Although everyone who had participated in that attack had given his life in the effort, no sign of repentance had come from the shogunate. It had continued to grow ever more high-handed and violent, and although this was a crime of which all the shogunal officials were equally guilty, Ando Tsushima no Kami was the foremost among them.

Such was the main import of the paper carried by the assassins. It listed as one of Ando's crimes the wedding of Princess Kazu. Although on the surface the wedding was made to appear as a step initiated by the imperial court under the banner of uniting the court and the military, they claimed that it had in fact been an evil plot by Ando, who had virtually arranged for her abduction. It was a ruse whereby an imperial princess could be held hostage while trade and diplomatic relations were developed with the foreigners. It further stated that there were plans to have the emperor deposed if he did not accede to the plans of the shogunate. This was truly a disgraceful act and the Tokugawa shogunate would be recalled in infamy for myriads of generations. It was an even greater outrage than the actions of the Hojo and the Ashikaga —mere words could not serve to express the wrath it engendered.

It was also reported that the paper had raised the question of the way the barbarians had been handled. It stated that Ando had done everything the barbarians had demanded; he had permitted them to take soundings off the Japanese coast, he had informed them of conditions in the country, he had yielded to them all of Mt. Goten in Shinagawa, the most strategic spot in Edo, and moreover, he was displaying the greatest kindness to the foreigners while at the same time looking upon righteous and ardent loyalists within his own country as his personal enemies. For these reasons he could only be regarded as the worst kind of bandit.

The paper did not stop there. It spoke a great deal about concern for "tomorrow." If the present evil ways of the government should go unchecked, the daimyo and even the lesser authorities in the country would turn away from the shogunate and begin to think only of securing their own provinces and districts. What then could be done if our hands were already full in dealing with the barbarians? If a single daimyo should start to raise the banner of expelling the barbarians, then the most dangerous time of all would come. The shogunate must not forget the established practices of this imperial nation; it must not fail to recognize the proprieties that exist between ruler and ruled, between high and low. The paper also stated that if the shogunate should ever for one moment turn its back on the emperor, then no official or samurai of true loyalty would ever again be willing to give his life for it.

It became known that most of the assailants were from Mito. It also was revealed that most of them were around thirty but that one youth of nineteen had joined in the attack. By extraordinary luck Ando's wounds proved to be relatively light, but the sympathy of most people went not to Ando, who had barely escaped with his life, but to the young men who had fallen in the attack. Still, after there had been time to reflect upon the incident, there were those who regretted it, saying that this tragedy had been a product of all the groundless rumors and misunderstandings that were currently going about. If Ando had been lost, there was no one else who showed the least possibility of being able to take his place in the diplomatic negotiations. Most informed people said that there was no one among the roju who could equal him in dealing with the foreign ambassadors. Whether he was with the American Harris or the Englishman Alcock, he became neither too familiar nor too submissive. He deflected the excessive demands of the ambassadors and maintained a commanding presence.

Now there was no one left in the shogunate to be feared; there was no reality left to be feared. Ii Naosuke was dead, Iwase Higo had died of a pulmonary hemorrhage, and Ando was wounded. Contempt poured in from all sides, the Confucians attacking from the point of view of the classics, the samurai assassins from the standpoint of the way of the warrior. Physicians,

Shinto priests, National Scholars, Buddhist priests—all began to say whatever they pleased. The shogunate was unable to do anything about it. Then came the report that a Russian naval force had landed at Osaki bay on Tsushima island and had taken up positions there. A great storm of anti-foreign sentiment rose throughout the nation, demanding that the ports be closed and the foreigners be driven out.

4

A traveler from Kyoto came hurrying into Nakatsugawa.

The traveler was a samurai in the prime of life who until recently had served with the Yubikan, the medical academy that Choshu had set up at its Sakurada residence in Edo. This man, deciding that he wanted to achieve a rapprochement between Mito and Choshu, had eluded the suspicious shogunal officials by meeting on board the *Heishin Maru* with a Mito activist and the captain of the Choshu warship as it lay at anchor off Shinagawa. He also had certain connections with the Sakashita gate incident, since the Mito activists had brought him into the planning for the attack on Ando, but he had had misgivings about such a violent course of action and had finally withdrawn from it.

Hanzo's friend Keizo was away from the Nakatsugawa honjin at the time. He had gone to Kyoto as a follower of Hirata Atsutane, to seek an active role in national affairs. The traveler was pleased by the town of Nakatsugawa with its view of Mt. Ena to the east, and he thought the honjin would be a good place to remain inconspicuous while he waited for the lord of Choshu, Mori Yoshichika, to come through on his way from his Edo residence in Azabu to Kyoto. The traveler was acting on secret orders from the Mori heir apparent, Sadahiro, to inform the lord of Choshu of the violent changes taking place in Kyoto and to warn him that both the union of court and military and free navigation, the established policies up to then, no longer had any possibility of realization. The traveler was to recommend a major shift in policy and the taking up of a strong position in favor of abrogating the treaties and expelling the foreigners. The rallying of the great allied han, so long awaited by the Choshu activists, had now brought them to full readiness for action.

The lord of Choshu, who had been traveling, did not know of the great changes in Kyoto. Nor did he know that this traveler, under secret orders from his heir, would be awaiting him in Nakatsugawa. As a consequence of his memorial to the shogunate, he had already come to be relied on by the shogunate for his good offices in negotiations between the court and the military, and he had set out on this journey with the purpose of formally instituting such a role. This daimyo was aware that Shimazu Hisamitsu of Satsuma, the younger half-brother of his old rival, Lord Nariakira, had already begun to move his forces into Kyoto. As he entered Suwa in the middle of the sixth month, he was thinking of the vigorous activity by Satsuma which had led to the dispatching of Ohara Shigenori, commander of the Left Imperial Guards, to Edo. All this was taking place in the midst of a severe epidemic of measles. The daimyo and his retinue stayed at Suwa for three days. Then, leaving some four hundred of his retainers behind, he spent a night at Midono and proceeded along the Kiso road. When he arrived before the Magome honjin, he saw the formal announcement of his passage posted on the wall before the gate.

REST STOP FOR MATSUDAIRA DAIZEN DAIYU

Matsudaira Daizen Daiyu was his courtesy title. It meant that he was lord of Choshu, the province of Nagato, with a revenue of 360,900 koku of rice.

Hanzo came out of the honjin and greeted the commander of the escort.

"I am the son of Kichizaemon. He has been stricken with paralysis since the middle of the fourth month and is still in and out of bed. We have prepared your noon meal. If you should have any other need of us, we await your orders."

"Your father is ill? He must take care. How far is it to Nakatsugawa?"

"It is said to be seven miles. It is all downhill from this pass so the going will not be difficult."

Upon hearing Hanzo's words, the commander turned to the men guarding the gate of the honjin, both within and without, and shouted, "They say it is seven miles to Nakatsugawa! We'll have our noon meal here."

Only ten days earlier the new lord of Hikone, Ii Naosuke's successor, had passed through on his way to Edo. This sixteen-year-old lord was accompanied by his chamberlain and his stewards, and his retinue had been immense, his train impressive. Yet there was nothing of the feeling that had prevailed whenever his father, Ii Kamon no Kami, had passed over this road as lord of Hikone. The Choshu retinue, with its crest design of Chinese coins of the Yung-lo era and its lance handles wrapped in wisteria bark topped with black plumes, moved in with a force and vigor that presented a marked contrast to the Hikone men.

Hanzo, acting in place of his father, went with his neighbor Inosuke and the toiya Kyurobei to accompany the Choshu party to Stonemason slope at the edge of the village. Then he returned to the house and looked into his father's room.

Kichizaemon was sitting up in bed. He seemed fatigued by the heat of the sixth month. Hanzo, still hoping for his father's recovery, had massaged his chest from time to time and had told him as little as possible about anything that might cause him worry. In fact Hanzo had received reports from his friend Keizo, who was still in Kyoto, of the tensions there. He had heard about the incident at the Teradaya inn in Fushimi, when eight warriors dedicated to the restoration of imperial rule and the overthrow of the shogunate had lost their lives. It was reported that all of Kyoto had come under martial law when the lord of Satsuma, taking upon himself the responsibility of promoting good relations between the court and the military, led more than a thousand of his warriors into the city. Hanzo said nothing of this to his father.

In the evening he passed along the southern hallway on his way to the toilet. It was dark off toward Nakatsugawa where the daimyo of Choshu was said to be staying that night, and he could see a distant reflection of the setting sun on the vast slope of Mt. Ena. Kichizaemon was still not strong enough to go up to the second floor of the miso shed to recuperate. His feet were too unsteady to manage the stairs to those quarters where his father, Hanroku, had passed his retirement. So he had remained, since falling ill in the fourth month, in the retiring room, close to the bath, where it was easy for the people of the house to take him to be bathed. The other side of the room opened onto the hearth room and the kitchen entrance, making it especially convenient for the others to look after him. Hanzo, on the other hand, was not happy to see his father's sickbed set up for so long in that room, since people calling on business were passing through it all day. Whenever he saw his father, forever wanting to have his head cooled or his feet warmed, he felt saddened. In the loneliness and boredom of his illness, Kichizaemon was constantly asking for explanations of things that had come to his ear. It seemed that he was unable to accept being stricken with this completely unexpected paralysis at the age of sixty-three. It also seemed as though he could not bear to leave everything to Hanzo, since his own request to be permitted to resign had not yet been acted upon and he was therefore still the senior official of the Magome station. Hanzo for his part was receiving various reports from the Hirata people in Edo and Kyoto, and at these times it seemed to him that he could not bear to remain here in the mountains. But each time he mastered the feeling and worked on as honjin, toiya, and headman in his father's place.

The conference at Nakatsugawa was concluded and the lord of Choshu began to make a complete change in the orientation of his policy. After his entry into the capital, he and his party openly favored abrogating the treaties and expelling the barbarians, reversing the policy of free navigation that they had advocated ever since the time of Yoshida Shoin. Between the twentieth of the sixth month and the beginning of the seventh month, the lord of Choshu called upon the court nobles and sounded out the feelings of the imperial party. Since an imperial messenger had been dispatched to Edo, he announced that he would act in concert with Satsuma to carry out the imperial commands by every means in his power. As for the personal protection of the emperor, again to be undertaken in cooperation with Satsuma, the Choshu heir Sadahiro, who was living in their Kyoto residence, had already given the order.

Satsuma and Choshu had now drawn the attention of the other han. Some of them began to have misgivings. Others were greatly encouraged. It was, of course, the shogunate that was most concerned about Satsuma and Choshu's intervention in Kyoto. It had always been the shogunate's practice

to intervene in Kyoto whenever and however it wished. For an imperial messenger to come down to Edo and demand that the shogunate undertake the
expulsion of the foreigners which it had solemnly promised at the time of
Princess Kazu's wedding, and further demand, in view of recent "political
changes," that the shogun come to Kyoto marked a complete reversal of
roles. Intervention was in fact now issuing from Kyoto. And behind this
intervention stood Shimazu Hisamitsu, at the head of his fierce Satsuma warriors. All this proved a severe shock to everyone in the shogunate, both high
and low. The shock moved them to try to eliminate the favoritism and abuses
of many years standing. It taught them that politics had become more
enlightened.

The times began to change rapidly and with a frightful decisiveness. Hitotsubashi Yoshinobu, on whose behalf Iwase Higo had destroyed his political
career in a quarrel with Ii Naosuke, came to act as the power behind the
scenes in the shogunate. Matsudaira Shungaku, lord of Echizen, took charge
of all political affairs. Ando Tsushima no Kami, about whom there had been
some discontent within the shogunate, was left with no choice but to resign,
along with his ally Kuse Yamato no Kami. As an apology to the imperial
court for past discourtesies, not only were Ando and Kuse banished to
obscure places and put under house arrest, but even Ii Naosuke, who had carried out the great purge of Ansei, was posthumously punished. For the most
part, those officials who had come to hold shogunal office during the Ansei
and Man'en eras as the creatures of Ii Tairo now began to leave office. Some
of the higher officials had their stipend lands reduced by a value of as much as
ten thousand koku, and among the lower officials stipends were reduced by
as much as two thousand koku. Others were forced into complete retirement
from public life, placed under temporary or permanent house arrest, or
banished.

It was in such an atmosphere that Hanzo prayed for his father's recovery
and awaited further change along the highways. Since his illness Kichizaemon had given up his beloved sake and had cut down on his smoking. He
now amused himself only by looking at books on haikai and chess. One day,
while Hanzo was trying to think of some way to comfort his father, a large,
four-man litter accompanied by a freight agent came up to the door of the
honjin.

The freight agent addressed Hanzo: "Master, these are textile goats that
are being sent as a gift from the shogun to the lord of Echizen. They are rare
beasts. We are on our way to deliver them and would like permission to rest
in your courtyard for a while."

They had brought three sheep all the way from Edo. This was the first
time the animals had ever been seen in the Kiso. Hanzo immediately called
Otami and had her prepare cushions so that Kichizaemon could come out and
sit in the entry hall.

"Come here, all of you!" Oman called to her grandchildren.

"A gift to Echizen, is it?" said Kichizaemon as he came out and sat down
quietly. "Speaking of Echizen, didn't the lord pass over this road on the

eleventh of the fifth month? I was in bed and didn't see him, but that daimyo's the one who has now taken full charge of political affairs."

Kichizaemon tried to read in the movements of the daimyo over this highway all their actions and vicissitudes.

"You should forget about that now," said Oman. "You said yourself that when you are being sick it is best to make a full-time job of it, so don't think about such things. Look at what gentle eyes the creatures have!"

The measles epidemic had just passed over the highway, leaving dead and afflicted in its wake, and people were only beginning to catch their breath. Calm and quiet days had come in which they could discuss the prospects for the sour persimmon crop; it seemed impossible that fierce struggles could be going on in Edo and Kyoto. Okume and Sota, both fond of animals, were delighted when they saw the three sheep standing in the litter with their heads together, twitching their noses. Even Kimbei, whose chronic cough had been keeping him close to home, came down from the Upper Fushimiya to have a look. Soon a crowd had gathered around the gates of the honjin.

"Kimbei, when you see that such strange beasts have come to Japan, you know that times have changed. I have never seen such a creature in all my life," said Kichizaemon, gazing thoughtfully up at the faintly autumnal sky.

"Just look, Hanzo. See how my leg is now," said Kichizaemon, stretching out his left leg, wasted by illness, in front of Hanzo. He was much improved. Dinner had been finished early that evening and the season for the autumn festivals had arrived in the neighboring villages.

"It's more than three and a half months since you fell ill, father."

Hanzo stretched out his hand and touched the leg his father extended before him. He could not imagine what had happened to the muscles that had propelled his father up and down this road in good health. Kichizaemon was suffering most from the effects of being bedfast for fifty days following his first major illness. His once firm and powerful calf was small and soft as a child's.

"Isn't it awful?" said Kichizaemon as he drew his leg back under the covers. "When people have a stroke you always ask if it was the left side or the right side. Well, I got it on the right. Even my right ear is deaf now." He laughed and changed his tone. "But today is really a beautiful day. I think I'll go up to have a bath at Kimbei's."

Hanzo was almost overcome with happiness to see his father feeling so well.

"I'll go with you, father!" he said, rising to his feet.

A recent report from the office of the commissioners of transport in Edo weighed on the minds of both father and son. The long-rumored changes in the alternate attendance system were becoming a reality. Although it was said that many of the shogunal officials opposed it, the intelligent and open-minded Hitotsubashi Yoshinobu and his main councillor, Matsudaira Shungaku, had embarked on this bold new plan without hesitation. Alternate

attendance was of course a policy of major importance in the assertion of shogunal control over the han. It would not have been changed had the times
not demanded it. Such a great change had in fact been long under consideration by the more perceptive of the high officials, but when viewed from
below by people like Hanzo and Kichizaemon it was the weakness of the shogunate, leaving it with no alternative to these reforms, that was most obvious. So long as the daimyo continued to ignore the voices of the people along
their routes of travel, failing to moderate their demands for service, it was
clear that most of the farmers would no longer come out to serve them
merely because of the authority of the Tokugawa.

As they went out through the gate of the honjin, Kichizaemon asked
Hanzo about this.

"Have you read this notice that just came in? It doesn't mean that alternate attendance is to be completely abolished."

"No, it won't be completely abolished, father. The ordinary daimyo are
still supposed to go to Edo once every three years, and the three cadet houses
of the Tokugawa, Owari, Kii, and Mito, as well as those in direct service to
the shogun are to spend one month out of each year in Edo. But since wives
and children of the daimyo are now permitted to return to the provinces,
there doesn't seem to be any teeth left in the system."

Kichizaemon tended to get very tired by evening and usually retired early.
This was the first time since his illness that he had proposed to do so much as
walk up to the Upper Fushimiya in the evening. He stepped out into the
street with the air of someone leaving his house for the first time in a long
while and stood silently before the gate, gazing out at the highway where it
was not yet fully dark.

"Hanzo, what's to become of this highway?"

"You mean after alternate attendance is ended?"

"Well, even if alternate attendance is ended, I don't think the highway
will completely cease to function. Let's go see what Kimbei has to say
about it."

Assisted by a solicitous Hanzo, Kichizaemon walked very slowly up the
steep Magome street. The houses lined both sides of the street. On the right
was the toiya and the Horaiya, and on the left was the newly reconstructed
Fushimiya. As they climbed the street, they met a tenant farmer standing
beside a stone wall. When the farmer saw Kichizaemon he quickly pulled off
his kerchief and came running up.

"Master! Where are you going? And Hanzo is with you! This must be the
first time that you have been able to walk around the village since you
fell ill."

"Yes, thank you. I'm getting better day by day."

"You have no idea how worried I was. You were so sick that it didn't
seem any use to try to cool your head with well-water. I went all the way up
to Mt. Ena to get snow for you."

In Kichizaemon's eyes these small farmers were all his children.

So they approached the Upper Fushimiya. Kimbei had just returned that evening from spending two days watching the festival plays in Yamaguchi village.

"Why, Kichizaemon! This is a rare treat!"

Kimbei and Otama greeted them joyously.

Kichizaemon and Kimbei both knew that the day of their retirement was very near. Kimbei had left the newly rebuilt Fushimiya to his adopted son Inosuke and had remained at the Upper Fushimiya after the fire, spending all his time in preparation for his retirement. Since turning sixty-five, he had had four hundred evergreen seedlings planted in Naka no Shinden and one hundred in Aono.

"Otama, see if the bath is ready," said Kimbei.

Hanzo led his father to the dark bath room. Since his illness Kichizaemon was unable to take long baths. Hanzo undressed himself and quickly washed his father's back, then his paralyzed arm and leg.

"You mustn't take a chill, father. We can't have a relapse." Hanzo concerned himself over every detail of his father's convalescence.

Soon the host and guests gathered in the parlor of the Upper Fushimiya and relaxed with conversation by lamp light.

"I'm lucky to be alive, Kimbei," said Kichizaemon. "For a while I didn't expect to make it through each day. I was in bed a long time."

"You have never been quite right since Princess Kazu's party went through," said Kimbei as he offered them tea and refreshments. "Oman was saying at the time that we would be lucky if your health was not affected."

"I'm all right now. Except that I can't hold a broom and I can't use a writing brush—that is what's most depressing."

"Your garden sweeping is famous," said Kimbei with a laugh.

Just then Inosuke came up from the new house. Everyone began to talk about the coming reform of the alternate attendance system and its profound implications for the future of the post station.

"I just don't know what to do about the assisting districts," said Kimbei. "The progress of the princess was a special case, but even so the times will no longer permit such a thing. Now that we have established a precedent for additional assisting districts, we'll never be able to go back to doing things the way we did before."

"It was bound to happen," said Kichizaemon.

"That's right," Inosuke joined in. "It was the eighth of the fourth month when that group of court nobles came through. They stayed here in large numbers and ordered me to provide six hundred porters from the assisting districts. No one came until I gave them wages in cash."

"It was foolish for court nobles even to ask for six hundred porters," said Hanzo.

"That's right," continued Kimbei. "Didn't the village lose four ryo two bu three shu in excess expenses when they went through?"

"Anyway, I would like to see them travel more simply," said Hanzo. "These reforms must have resulted from suggestions made to the commissioners of transport. I don't have any idea either about what's going to happen to the highways, but whether you're looking at it from above or below, there is no way that these ceremonial processions for alternate attendance can be continued forever. We need to do away with all the frills and red tape and put the money to better use. The burdens of the people must be lightened—isn't that the real meaning of the reforms?"

"Kimbei, what do you think about this change?" asked Kichizaemon. "They say that the wives and children of the daimyo who have been held hostage in Edo are going to be permitted to return to their provinces."

His old friend only shook his head.

"Well, I just don't know—except that I am surprised."

By this time a certain pathetic determination was beginning to manifest itself in the reforms being announced from Edo. Not only did the shogunate ungrudgingly abandon the policy of alternate attendance that had been of such importance to it, but it also declared a general amnesty, it had the imperial tombs repaired, and it went on yielding to Kyoto as it discarded one long-established practice after another. It even withdrew the guard that the shogunal officials had long maintained at the nine gates of the imperial enclosure.

Those things which the shogunate still had the power to dispose were being carried out by a new cabinet formed around Matsudaira Shungaku, with Yamauchi Yodo serving as consultant.

The modernization of things left over from the feudal age had begun without waiting for a new government. Matsudaira Shungaku and Yamauchi Yodo, in spite of the very different conditions of their respective domains, had in common a recognition of the course of events and an early advocacy of reforms in the shogunate. They also had in common a sympathy with and an understanding of the shogunate from the time they were installed in office. Together with the retired lord of Mito, the lord of Higo, Nabeshima Kanzo, and the lord of Satsuma, Shimazu Hisamitsu, they had learned much from Iwase Higo no Kami while he was still living. It was not surprising that the policy of opening the nation advocated by Iwase Higo, now dead before reaching his fortieth birthday, should have begun to grow in influence after his death. The Institute for the Study of Foreign Books changed its name to the Institute for the Study of Western Books; this was the institution that later became the Kaiseisho, which was in turn a forerunner of Tokyo Imperial University. At the military academy drills in archery and dog shooting were abandoned, and the three divisions of infantry, artillery, and cavalry were established. Talented men who had been driven out of public life during the time of Ii Naosuke were brought back from their places of refuge. Lord Matsudaira Katamori of Aizu, prominent both in his relation to the Tokugawa house and in military power, was given the important responsibility of guarding Kyoto and he had set out to take up his new duties.

It was then that Hanzo learned of the students being sent for schooling in Holland. It sounded like something out of a dream. Rumors had it that the copper coins minted during the tenure of Ii Naosuke by the roju Mizuno Echizen no Kami for the reconstruction of Edo castle, which had burned down a second time, were being used to send the students. It was also rumored that this had exhausted the last of the shogunal treasury. Hanzo was amazed to learn that in such unstable times the cabinet was still determined to send people to Holland to seek after new knowledge.

At the time, Kichizaemon was still in the retiring room, continuing with his preparations for giving up his official and family duties. His father, Hanroku, had borne his responsibilities as head of the house until he was sixty-six before passing them on, but Kichizaemon was to retire at the age of sixty-three. After looking in briefly on his father, Hanzo went out to walk along the long southern veranda. Reflecting on the students being sent to Holland, he muttered to himself.

"It looks as though we are just going to keep on getting more and more Black Ships."

The day came when Hanzo was called before his father to receive the old books and effects that had been passed down in the Aoyama household. It was only a matter of time until his father retired.

Ledgers containing the essential records for the performance of the three offices of honjin, toiya, and headman—surveys of croplands and building lots, crop tax for the lord, the crop tax for the landowner, and so on—were each brought out before Hanzo. Kichizaemon asked Hanzo to untie the old leather cords that bound one of the boxes. In it he found the official, seal-bearing letters from the imperial office of provincial administration in Kyoto, from the commissioners of transport in Edo, and from all the han certifying their authority in this post station. Kichizaemon then had Hanzo untie another box. Here were all the tax records, going back to the beginning of the seventeenth century. Since the records were certain to have become damaged or disordered over the centuries, there was also a scroll made up of the successive summaries left by each of their ancestors.

Kichizaemon would not listen to anything that Hanzo tried to say. That which the father passed on the son was to receive. He had decided this for himself and he had taken out several dozen ledgers and documents. For the village there was the record of the religious affiliations of the various households of the village. This served as a population register in those days. There were the land surveys, the annual taxes, the removals of families from the village, the marriage contracts, divorces, and records of law suits.

"This is also a very important old record."

Kichizaemon pushed another ledger over to Hanzo with his left hand. It was a record of all the timber that had been sent through Magome as authorized freight from the Kiso forests. It was clearly recorded here that even among the five trees that were so rigorously protected, the village of Magome was permitted two hundred packhorse loads each of hinoki and sawara per year.

"Somehow it feels to me as though I have come a long way," said Kichizaemon. "Kimbei has been with me during the whole time and we have come this far without quarreling. In all those dozens of years I have scarcely had even an argument with him. Just twice—that's right, just two times. Once was over the baby that was born to Okisa and Senjuro of the Upper Fushimiya. The other time was about the old lands. You probably remember that. Kimbei got very angry about that land question and he said that it had all come about because of the greed of the Aoyama family. He said that he had hoped we could always remain on good terms but now that this kind of problem had arisen he was going to have to concern himself about the welfare of his descendants. I heard that from someone else afterward. At any rate, that was when Kimbei came rushing over here to show me old documents and the like. That may very well have been caused by a mistaken memory on my part, but Kimbei really didn't have to say all those things. However close we've been as friends, he and I are different. When I look back now, I am really amazed that we have been able to get along this far together. Now I am as I am but when it comes to Kimbei, he's really tightfisted. He puts paper bags over the pears on the pear tree out in front of his storehouse and he will tell you that of the three pears that fell in the last windstorm, the largest one weighed eighteen ounces and the smallest seven ounces."

The greater part of the books and papers of the Magome honjin had been lost in the fire of the previous year. Only those things which they had managed to carry out and put in the storehouse remained. The hanging scroll painted by Korin and the two lances that had hung in the entrance hall were all that was left to remind them of their distant ancestors. Kichizaemon laid out the Aoyama family genealogy before Hanzo.

"As you know, Hanzo, there are thirteen farming families attached to our household. Among them are some who accompanied the person who came to this family as a bride from Mino. Those who come at New Year's to put up the decorations at the doors or to pound rice for rice cakes have been with us since the time of our ancestors. Keep an eye on those farmers. And there is just one more thing I want to say. When the time comes and I am retired, you do everything as you see fit. I will not say anything at all."

That was the way Kichizaemon spoke. It was as though Hanzo had now accepted full responsibility for all village affairs and for all duties along the highway.

After he left his father's room, Hanzo went back to the parlor. He had long been anticipating this day. He was not unhappy about succeeding as head of the Aoyama household with its long history and being able to direct it in its future undertakings. But he was not at all certain that this was the path he should take. While most of his comrades in the National Learning movement, and particularly his friend Keizo, were forgetting about food and rest as they took part in national affairs, he was all alone, his father was ill, and he had no real brothers or sisters. Although there was Shujiro, the newly adopted husband of his stepsister Okisa, they lived in their own new home and the two men seldom had an opportunity to talk.

Autumnlike days had come. In the parlor a katydid that seemed to have flown in from the bamboo grove out back was slowly crawling across the shoji, flexing its long, slender legs. Hanzo absently followed its movement for a time, attracted by the cool appearance of its green wings.

Otami came into the parlor.

"Aren't you a little pale?"

"That's life."

Otami did not pursue the matter. Then Oman came in, bringing a man with her.

"Hanzo, Seisuke will be coming over every day to help us out from now on."

This was Seisuke of the Wadaya, who was a distant relative of Hanzo's family. He was the kind of person who could be called upon to take care of errands and petty matters connected with the offices of honjin, toiya, and headman. As one might expect of a person selected by Kichizaemon, he had already begun preparations for the celebration for Hanzo even though there was still no word from Fukushima on the resignations. He kept rubbing his clean-shaven blue jaw as he worked. The guests would be post officials and the assistant headmen. Everyone else would be given a serving of cheap sake on that day. It was Seisuke who made all these arrangements, in consultation with Oman.

Very soon afterward the documents came from Fukushima granting the permission that had been so long awaited in both the Aoyama and the Satake households. The sons of Aoyama Kichizaemon and Satake Kimbei were ordered to the Fukushima offices. They were to be accompanied by two men and two representatives of the post station. Since Kichizaemon and Kimbei's long-standing request to retire had at last been honored, everyone could easily read the import of these documents even though they did not specifically name the two sons as successors.

Hanzo was now committed. He and Inosuke set out for Fukushima.

Around the time when the late autumn rains began to fall among the chestnut forests along the Kiso, they were on their way back in the company of Kozaemon of the Masudaya, representatives of the other post station offices who had come with them from Magome, and Hanzo's servant Sakichi. When Hanzo and his party came out of the inner road and reached Tsumago, they met Juheiji, who was waiting to accompany Hanzo the rest of the way home.

"Juheiji, I have at last entered your company."

"Everyone has been saying that it was about time Hanzo was made headman. Your father must be delighted," said Juheiji, laughing and offering his congratulations.

Before setting out once more along the highway in the company of his fellows, Hanzo spent one more night at the Tsumago honjin. He had been disturbed to learn that Iwakura, Chigusa, and Tominokoji, the three court officials who had supported the union of court and military at the time of the wedding of Princess Kazu, had been ordered to withdraw from public life, placed under house arrest, and finally stripped of their honors in the great changes that were sweeping Kyoto. Out of consideration for those who were waiting for him, Hanzo had sent news ahead of his return from the Tsumago honjin.

"Is there any other late news, Juheiji? From Edo?"

"The only really startling thing I've heard of recently is the Namamugi incident."

"We've already heard about that. We must have gone through there on our way to Yokosuka."

Namamugi was in Musashi province, near Yokohama. It was reported from Edo that an Englishman had been killed when trying to ride his horse across the road through the retinue of Shimazu Hisamitsu as that lord was rushing homeward escorting an imperial messenger. These reports were so fresh in Hanzo's mind that he still found it troubling to think about them as he walked through the deep, swampy valley of Otaru.

"Juheiji, I am more concerned about why the Satsuma people were headed home in such a rush. So much so that I wonder if the Namamugi incident itself has not been used to draw attention away from that. How are things in Kyoto? The wind is really beginning to blow from there, isn't it?"

"Could be."

"Juheiji, have you heard that Iwakura is under house arrest?"

"This is the first time I've heard anything about it."

"When you add it all up, it seems that something must have happened in Kyoto."

"Have your friends told you anything? There must be a lot of Hirata people in Kyoto."

"I haven't heard from Keizo for some time now."

"There's really a lot happening these days. The next three years as headmen might very well prove to be as much as twenty years were in our fathers' times."

The two talked on as they walked along the road.

When they reached Ichikokutochi, near the border between Tsumago and Magome, Hanzo and Juheiji had fallen off in their pace and they were overtaken by Inosuke and Kozaemon.

"Congratulations, master!"

At the top of the pass, Hanzo heard the voices of the assistant headman from Toge and two or three other people who had been waiting for him there.

At Shimizu, they were met by the heads of each of the village mutual responsibility groups. They all continued as far as the campground. Here sixteen or seventeen people were waiting, including Kyurobei from the toiya, Shosuke, the assistant headman of Magome representing the farmers, Shujiro from the new honjin residence, Hanzo's disciple Katsushige, and several other children he was teaching. There was even someone who had come up from Aramachi. When Hanzo reached Kamimachi, the toiya Kyudayu and the masters of the Masudaya, the Horaiya, and the Umeya, were awaiting with grave expressions the arrival of the new master of the Magome post station.

5

"Are you a supporter of the emperor?"

"What do you mean, 'supporter of the emperor'?"

"Someone who takes his side, so they say."

"Why are you asking me this, Otami?"

Hanzo was in the chamber of honor in the back of the honjin. This was the room reserved for daimyo, and family members seldom entered it. Otami had come from the middle room to see her husband, who had been putting it in order.

"No particular reason," said Otami, "but mother has been saying that."

Hanzo looked at his wife sharply. "I hardly ever speak of 'supporting the emperor.' Nowadays when I see the face of a person who calls himself a 'supporter of the emperor,' I want to throw up. Such people are trading on that expression. Look! Anyone who really supports the emperor is not going to be speaking of it so casually!"

"I was only asking. Just because mother said it."

"That's all the more reason for you not to talk about it!"

Otami looked about. The room faced north and from the alcove to the black-and-white Korean-style bindings on the tatami it had the peaceful austerity of the teahouse about it. The thick walls blocked out the noise from the highway. Winter had come to the tiny garden outside the room, a winter warmer than those of Tsumago on the other side of the mountains.

"Well, then. This is a change of subject, but when my brother was here he told me that the shogunate was watching Hirata sensei's followers and for me to be careful."

"What? Juheiji said that?"

Hitotsubashi was to go ahead and make advance preparations for the shogun's trip to Kyoto. Notice had been given that he would leave Edo on the eighth day of the tenth month and would be coming over the Kiso road. The officials who inspect bridges and assign lodgings had already been to Magome many times. Hanzo, anticipating the time when he would entertain Lord Hitotsubashi in this mountain house, was pacing about the chamber of honor.

"Well, I've got to go hang the radishes up to dry."

Otami went out. This was the season for pickling radishes and they had to be dried first. Everyone was getting ready for winter. In Hanzo's home the gathering and preserving of vegetables and the pickling of turnips and radishes were like annual festivals. After Otami left, Hanzo thought about what she had said. He thought about Oman as well. She had lived her entire life apart from the world. Now, at the age of fifty-three, she was always saying, "I'm just an old woman now." Yet she always knew exactly what he was thinking. It made him all the more afraid of her.

A few days later, Hanzo received a notice from the commissioners of transport in Edo that Hitotsubashi Yoshinobu's projected route to Kyoto had suddenly been shifted to the Tokaido. Although the lord's plans to use the Kiso road had gone as far as specifying the repairs to be made on the highway, something had caused him to change his mind. Later that winter, all unofficial travelers were ordered to use the Kiso road after the ninth day of the twelfth month, because so many of the shogun's party would be using the Tokaido.

"The road is going to be crowded next year," observed Seisuke.

"I know," answered Hanzo.

This was all that Seisuke and Hanzo said about it.

The year ended. The new year was Bunkyu 3, 1863. Now the feet of the travelers, which up to this time had been flowing eastward, suddenly reversed their course. It appeared that the center had already left Edo and was shifting to Kyoto. Hanzo could read the signs in the activities along the highway. Since his assumption of new responsibilities he had begun to observe the movements of the travelers more carefully.

Sixty-three mon for a regular packhorse. Forty mon for a saddle horse. Forty-two mon for a porter. These were the rates to Ochiai as Hanzo heard them recited every day around the station. In the second month of the new year, shortly before the shogun was to leave for Kyoto, Hanzo watched the Shinsengumi, the specially selected ronin that the shogunate had hired as counter terrorists, passing through on their way to Kyoto. Seven companies came up the snowy road to Magome in disciplined formations. They were swordsmen who had all been recruited in Edo. They had sworn to serve the nation with absolute loyalty, and now were being sent out against the activists and ronin in Kyoto who advocated expelling the barbarians. The arms borne by two hundred forty men resounded before the toiya in Magome—men who were everything from instructors in the military arts to nameless samurai to thugs and drifters.

As the second month drew to a close, a visitor came to Hanzo. It was already well into the night, not an hour in which a lost traveler was likely to come asking for lodging. The highway had long been utterly still.

"Master, a man by the name of Ogusa Senzo has come."

Sakichi, who had been making straw sandals beside the hearth, came to Hanzo with this message.

"Ogusa Senzo?"

"He said you would understand if you saw him. He's out by the entry to the hearth room."

Puzzled, Hanzo went to see. There, standing in the earthen-floored entrance, wearing snow boots and a long kimono but without trousers or jacket, stood a Hirata disciple about whose activities in Kyoto Hanzo had heard. Ogusa Senzo was an assumed name; he was really Kureta Masaka, a senior disciple to Hanzo.

"I have come to ask a favor of you, Aoyama," he said, but would say no more without knowing who might be listening. He sat down on the edge of the raised floor as though exhausted from walking. He first made sure that there was no one in the hearth room. Then he looked around the entry, even gazing up at the bird cage built high on the wall. At last he spoke.

"Actually, I have just come from Nakatsugawa. Your friend Asami Keizo was away, but they let me stay there last night. I know I have inconvenienced you, Aoyama, coming in so late like this, but could you please give me lodging for the night? You probably don't know anything about what has happened to me."

"I haven't heard from Asami for a long time."

"I think I'm going into hiding over in Ina."

His visitor said little. Hanzo did not understand the situation but since it was something that had called for arriving late at night under an assumed name, it was obviously no minor affair.

"This man probably has the shogun's spies after him." The thought flashed through Hanzo's mind.

"Kureta, come over here. Please wait just a moment. I'll ask about the details later."

Hanzo slipped down into a pair of sandals in the entry and opened the door between the kitchen and the rear of the house. He hid Kureta just outside.

This was a serious problem from any point of view. There were informers in the village. It was a small place and people talked a lot. Hanzo tried to think of how he could protect his comrade and get him safely into the Ina valley. He wondered whom he could call on for help. Since the beginning of the new year, his father had been sleeping in the rooms above the miso shed. Otami was inside, putting the children to bed. Seisuke had already gone home. Katsushige was still very young and Sakichi and the maids would be of no use.

"I'm going to have to talk to mother."

This decision made, Hanzo sought out Oman to tell her exactly what was happening and to ask her where to hide the visitor.

"A disciple of Hirata sensei? If it's just for one night, the storehouse should be all right," replied Oman, quickly taking charge.

Kureta was originally from the same province as Hanzo, but he had gone to Edo to study at the academy of Fujita Toko of Mito. After Toko's death, he had parted with the Mito school and had become involved in the Hirata school's study of antiquity. It was this same Kureta who had persuaded Kurasawa Yoshiyuki of the village of Ono in north Ina county, Shinano, to hear the lectures of Hirata Kanetane. Since Yoshiyuki later became the founder of the Hirata movement in north Ina county, there was no one among the many disciples of Hirata in southern Shinano who did not know Masaka's name.

Oman set out, lantern in hand, to lead the visitor to the storehouse out back. Hanzo followed, carrying cushions and matting.

"Watch your step. We have to go down some stone stairs here," said Oman. Then she went out, as though she herself had business in the storehouse, took up a huge key, and unlocked the door. Inside were the quarters where Hanzo and Otami had lived for a time after the fire. Once the matting was spread it became a presentable place to lodge a guest.

"Your visitor must be hungry," said Oman to Hanzo, speaking quite matter-of-factly, and Masaka at last began to speak in a more relaxed tone.

"Thank you, but no. I had something along the way. The main thing is that when I left Kyoto I walked for two days and nights without stopping. My legs were completely numb. Since then I have been sleeping in the daytime and walking at night."

Oman hung the lantern in the corner and left the two in the storehouse.

"I'll bring bedding for our guest a little later, Hanzo," she said as she went out.

"We did it, Aoyama!"

When they were alone Masaka began to talk freely. His voice sounded at once casual and impatient to Hanzo, impulsive and determined.

On the night of the twenty-third, nine comrades, most of whom were either disciples or associates of the Hirata school, had gone to the Tojiin, struck the heads off the wooden statues of Ashikaga Takauji and another shogun, and exposed them on the riverbed at the intersection of Sanjo and Kawaramachi. With the heads they had posted a notice saying that in the present generation there were those whose evil was greater even than that of the Ashikaga and that if those evils were not promptly corrected and loyalty and virtue encouraged, the nation's men of spirit would certainly act. However, among the people who had planned the exploit there proved to be an Aizu man who was a police spy, and he had taken some of them into custody. Masaka had escaped only by walking for two days and nights without stopping.

Masaka said that the shogun would soon be coming to the capital. The display on the riverbed was a protest against this and an expression of loyalty to the emperor. He added that while it might seem a childish prank to expose the heads of long-dead shoguns, its moral effect had been great and that was what they had intended.

Hanzo was shocked by the boldness of this elder disciple. Forced to recognize that what he had always thought of as a study group was now moving toward direct action, he also had to reflect that however much this elder disciple was a member of the Hirata school, there was still much of the Mito school remaining in him.

"Someone is calling you."

Masaka put his hand to his ear as though following the movements of the person approaching the door. It was Otami. She and Sakichi had brought the bedding.

"You seem terribly tired, Kureta, so I will leave you now. We'll talk tomorrow. Good night."

Hanzo left Masaka and went back to the main house. He did not sleep that night, thinking of how people in Kyoto were beginning to move and of his friend Keizo.

After noon the next day, Hanzo slipped out quietly to see Masaka. Amid the storehouse shelves, with their labels of serving trays for so many, plates for so many, and so on, he was sitting forlornly on a cushion on the matting. Masaka was different from the unapproachable person of the night before; Hanzo now found him a sensitive and straightforward National Scholar.

Hanzo held out the gourd he had carried with him. He put a wooden cup before Masaka, offering sake to comfort the guest who had come to him so exhausted.

"Ah!" Masaka's eyes grew round. "You have brought a real treat."

"This is Magome sake. Right now the Fushimiya and the Masudaya are making it. Try a little of our mountain sake."

"It really sounds different being poured out of the little opening in a gourd! Pop, pop, pop! This is the best possible thing after a long trip!"

He was like a child. It seemed incredible that this person now expressing his delight by imitating the sound of sake pouring out of a gourd was the same warrior who last night had told of the happenings at the Tojiin with fists clenched and fingers taut, demonstrating how he had taken the head of the wooden statue as though grabbing someone from behind by the ears.

Nor was that all. Masaka mentioned a name that all the National Scholars in the Nakatsugawa and Ina regions knew well, that of the brave and loyal owner of the dye shop Isekyu in the Fuyamachi district in Kyoto. He spoke of other places in Kyoto—the corner of Nijo and Koromonotana, where there was a spirited band of Hirata disciples that included Miwata Koichiro and Morooka Masatane. He spoke of Nishikikoji, where Hirata Kanetane had taken up residence as armorer for Akita. All these people had visited Kanetane, accompanied by the Hirata men Nojiri Hirosuke, Umemura Shin'ichiro, and Masaka himself.

He also spoke warmly of the woman Matsuo Taseko, who had come out of Ina to serve as liaison between the activists and the court nobles. She was to draw near the imperial court itself, and to do everything she could to aid the National Learning movement. He told of how she dressed soberly in a dark kimono, the hilt of her dagger showing above her black nankeen sash, and her severe hairstyle relieved only by a single long hairpin. Masaka did not simply bring the news about Kanetane and his disciples for which Hanzo had been longing; he brought the very atmosphere of Kyoto itself.

"Well now, Aoyama," said Masaka, putting down his cup and assuming a formal sitting position. "What do you think about things in Kyoto since Princess Kazu's wedding? Satsuma has come, and Choshu, and Tosa too.

Now Aizu is there. It's a mistake to think that the times have changed because the daimyo have started to act. It is precisely because the times have changed that daimyo like the lord of Satsuma have come to keep order. The lord of Choshu has completely changed his policy and come in too. You see, it was Princess Kazu's marriage that taught the people down in Edo that times were changing. But they just wouldn't wake up. Now that an imperial messenger has gone down and very clearly ordered Yoshinobu to take control of the shogunate behind the scenes, and for the lord of Echizen to assume full charge of political affairs, they may have opened their eyes a bit. But isn't this an amazing world? No matter how much the lords of Satsuma, Echizen, or Tosa may meddle in this, they can't really do anything about it, however great their reputations. Just look—during the time when the lord of Satsuma was sent to escort the imperial messenger to Edo, things changed completely in Kyoto.

"On the twenty-first of the first month of this year, someone murdered a famous physician attached to the shogunate and threw one of his ears into the residence of the grand councillor Nakayama. On the twenty-eighth, someone killed a Chigusa retainer and threw his right arm into the Chigusa residence, and the left into the Iwakura residence. It was said to be an "Expel the Barbarians Blood Festival," but it was really just a little palpitation. Hasn't Iwakura been frightened into hiding? Just go to Kyoto and see for yourself. Everyone is going wild. That's because a lot of them don't even think about Edo any more. Just recently someone said that if you came from a place like Edo and saw all this, you'd think that Kyoto was a nest of savages. But it is also quite lively. A new group of activist court nobles calling itself the People Committed to Government Service has been formed, and anyone from the most remote part of the country can grasp what is happening just by going over to the Imperial Academy. Just look—there's everything in Kyoto now. Everything from Union of Court and Military supporters to Abrogate the Treaties people to Expelling the Barbarians. They are all stirring things up. But this 'union of court and military' is something we mustn't let ourselves be taken in by. That's the whole point. We wanted to raise the imperial banner high. We wanted to point out the proper direction for the nation to move in. The idea of exposing the head of Ashikaga Takauji's statue came from that."

Hanzo interrupted his companion's long speech. "What does Kanetane think of all this, Kureta?"

"About what we just did? Well, I'll tell you. If we had consulted Kanetane on this matter, he would have surely laughed at us. So we did it without consulting him. Miwata Genko was the chief planner but he was not with us that night."

After that there was silence.

Hanzo could not keep his guest in the storehouse for long. He told Masaka that he would have to leave Magome before dark, or at the very least during the night, and be shown the road to Seinaiji. Their fellow disciple Hara

Nobuyoshi lived there, and if he reached the town of Seinaiji he would be on the road to Ina.

Hanzo put a direct question to Masaka.

"Kureta, is this your first time on the Kiso road?"

"I've gone over the Gombei road to Ina but this is my first time here."

"In that case you had better do this. If you go from here toward Tsumago, there is a place called Hashiba. When you cross the bridge there, the road divides into two. The right fork is the Ina road. I have consulted with mother and we have decided to have our manservant accompany you as far as the bridge."

"That is very kind of you."

"From there on it is all pretty deep forest, although there are occasional villages, but it is passable to horses. The freight between Nakatsugawa and Iida is shipped that way. If you just pick up the Araragi river and follow it on to the southeast, you will be all right."

Oman brought out leggings and other furnishings for the guest who had come to them so ill-equipped for travel. She even offered him a cape, apologizing for its condition. Sakichi was ready and there was a new pair of straw sandals outside the storehouse door.

Masaka was a mercurial personality and he easily and artlessly accepted the cape. Expressing his thanks, he immediately put on the sandals and began walking around the persimmon tree before the storehouse.

"I'll go along with you for a little way, Kureta," said Hanzo as he led the guest out, not through the front gate but down past the woodshed. Beyond the wooden back gate was the Inari shrine belonging to the honjin, and a small path that led through the family bamboo grove. They followed the path to where it cut across the highway.

Once there, Masaka breathed a sigh of relief. He turned to Hanzo as the three of them walked along. "Aoyama, I hear that Atsutane sensei's *Commentaries on Ancient History* is being published by the people in Ina. Do you have anything to do with that?"

"Yes, I do. We finally got out the first part in the eighth month of last year."

"That is an immense undertaking for publishers in the provinces. When Kanetane learned that this work was being done in Iida when it had not yet even been planned for in Atsutane's home province of Akita, he was happy to support it. They are really active over in Ina, aren't they? According to the master, the disciples there are increasing in number every year."

"In some of the villages one could almost say that everyone is a disciple— even though when the merchant Matsuzawa Yoshiaki first passed through there, selling notions and telling them about the Way, they say no one had ever heard of the Learning of Antiquity."

"The times keep changing. People today cannot hold themselves aloof from the question of where they stand on the teachings of Motoori and Hirata."

Hanzo walked to the top of the pass with his guest. As they parted, he asked, "Kureta, do you know a physician by the name of Miyagawa Kansai?"

"A National Scholar from Mino? I have often heard his name but I have never met him."

"Keizo and Kozo of Nakatsugawa and I are three of his former disciples. It was Miyagawa who gave me my introduction to Kanetane sensei. He is now in Ina. I wonder how he is getting along."

"I understand that you met Kanetane sensei only once. But to Kanetane, disciples whom he has only seen once and others who have been at his side for ten years are exactly the same. He often speaks of you."

Hanzo could never forget the words that his guest left with him.

The warm rains had already begun to fall. Leaving Kyoto at the end of the second month, Masaka could not have known that the lords of the great Owari and Sendai han were coming to Kyoto at the command of the emperor. At the same time that he was fleeing Kyoto through the night, the retinues of these great lords were passing over the Kiso. Three thousand five hundred porters came up from Owari to meet them at Magome. All the two hundred forty available horses had to be pressed into service. Although the lord of Sendai, who was said to be making his first journey over the Kiso road, had reduced his retinue because of the new conditions on the highway, sixteen hundred men still accompanied him as he passed through Magome on his way to Kyoto. The people at the station had no choice but to try to deal with their incomprehensible northeastern dialect.

"Hanzo, I wonder if your visitor made it safely to Ono village in Ina?"

When Oman said this, the peach trees were already in bloom. Hitotsubashi Yoshinobu's bold plan to alter the system of alternate attendance had begun to have startling consequences along the highway.

Until now, the women and children of the daimyo households, although permitted to take part in such diversions as the women's festival in spring, trips to see a No performance, or pilgrimages to the ancestral tombs, had been kept strictly confined as virtual hostages in Edo. Now, when the weather improved during the old third month, parties of these people began to come down the highway one after the other on their way to their own provinces, exactly like prisoners released from their chains.

The women of Echizen. The young heir to the house of Owari and his mother—an endless stream of parties made up of women and children were stopping their palanquins for a rest at the Magome honjin. The women of the household of the Owari retainer Naruse Hayato-no-sho, the women of the house of Shimabara in Hizen, the women of the household of the lord of Inaba—all came through in an endless stream. Some showed interest in finding themselves actually at the Magome pass. Others seemed impelled to speak of their feelings in at last being able to breathe freely of the mountain air. Some of the women, once they had taken lodgings at Hanzo's house, went off in groups of five or six to see the lotus pond at the convent or to wash their underclothes in the stream.

Kimbei of the Upper Fushimiya was, like Hanzo's father, now retired, but it was not in his nature to sit quietly through all of this. Yesterday the women of the household of Matsudaira Oki no Kami, a branch house of Inaba, had passed through. Today it was the wife and children of the house of Iwamura. When he heard about them, Kimbei invited his old friend over.

"Even though you are still convalescing, Kichizaemon, you don't have to stay shut away the way you've been doing. Try coming out a bit. I don't know whether to say that they are beautiful or that they are magnificent, but as I watched them, tears came to my eyes."

Parties of women seemed to be coming through every day. It did not seem all that magnificent to Hanzo and Inosuke. An extra five hundred porters had been assigned to the lower four Kiso stations in order to handle this mass homecoming. Special high wages had been authorized and a hundred farmers from Ina were billeted at Magome. Edo, said to be made up of four parts townsmen and six parts samurai, was being abandoned by these people from the samurai residences who gave no thought to the terrible economic crisis their departure was causing in the city they had lived in for so long.

"Homeward! Homeward!"

In these voices—in these shouts of exultation from the members of the liberated daimyo families—it seemed that one could almost hear the sound of the mighty institution that Tokugawa Ieyasu had established three hundred years earlier beginning to crumble away from within. That was why there could now be the unbelievable spectacle of parties of women walking directly through Magome, passing nonchalantly by the crowds of villagers and ordinary travelers.

At about the time the short Kiso spring was racing from peach blossoms toward wild cherries, the retired lord of Satsuma, then the women of his household, and finally the party of his consort followed one another through in rapid succession.

CHAPTER SEVEN

1

EIGHTEEN SIXTY-THREE, Bunkyu 3, was the year when anti-foreign sentiment reached its peak. The long-rumored visit of the shogun Iemochi to the
imperial court took place in the midst of the outcry.

The shogun left Edo on the thirteenth day of the second month. It had
been announced that the procession would be as simple as possible, in keeping
with the temper of the times, yet it was so vast and so strictly guarded that
all other travel along the Tokaido came to a temporary halt. The party arrived
in Kyoto on the fourth day of the third month and took up residence in Nijo
castle, where the shogun was guarded by three thousand soldiers. This visit
to Kyoto not only revived the ceremony of attendance at court which had
been faithfully observed up to the time of Iemitsu, the third Tokugawa shogun; it also furnished proof that the shogunate itself had come to reflect on
the matter of the rectification of society, about which it had been hearing
from all quarters. Yet, while the visit constituted something of an apology
for the hitherto frequent breaches of etiquette on the part of the shogunate, it
provided an opportunity to present the case for the union of court and military and for leaving all political action in the hands of the Kanto, just as it had
been. Princess Kazu was now married to the shogun, so he and the emperor
were brothers-in-law. It was no wonder that the Kanto people should have
come with high hopes, feeling that if this visit helped to strengthen the bonds
between court and shogunate, circumventing the danger that each might
pursue its own political course, then it would be well worth the immense
cost of carrying it out. They also felt that it would aid in calming the growing restlessness of the great feudal lords.

When the Tokugawa shoguns had come to Kyoto back in the Kan'ei era in
the second quarter of the seventeenth century, they were said to have been
overbearing toward the emperor, even forcing him to come to call on them at
Nijo castle. When it came time for the shogun to attend court, vast numbers
of court nobles were required to stand along the way in full ceremonial dress,
to serve as guides. Since then, the more than two centuries that had passed
had not simply changed the position of the shogun; they had transformed the
very context in which he operated. It could be said that Kyoto, with all the

talk about the display in the riverbed at Sanjo, the activists and ronin loitering on the streets, the various declarations of deadly enmity to the shogunate, and the machinations of the court nobles, was now enveloped in a dark and forbidding atmosphere far worse than could have been imagined by the Kanto people who had come to the capital. The lord of Mito entered Kyoto at about the same time and yet the shogun's entry into the capital was far more circumspect; few people turned out to watch his retinue pass along its route. Nor was that all. His close retainers were worried about his physical safety. They watched over his movements with terror and anxiety, ready to take whatever measures might be necessary to protect him.

The shogun was not yet twenty years of age. It was reported that these retainers, being samurai and therefore ineligible to accompany him into the palace, had provided him with a good dagger to conceal in his robe. Iemochi was not willing to carry such a thing into court. When it was presented to him, his expression clouded over and he threw it down on the table, saying there was no reason for anyone to do harm to a person coming to pay his sincere respects to the imperial court. To carry a dagger into the palace, furthermore, would be tantamount to harboring evil suspicions against the imperial court itself, the greatest possible discourtesy. According to reports, the roju Itakura Iga no Kami, unable to reply, picked up the dagger and left the shogun's presence. The shogun was in court dress. They were ready to proceed. Fifty samurai in wide-shouldered white hempen jackets and trousers cleared the way for him. With an air of the most solemn reverence, they set out from Nijo castle on the morning of the seventh day of the third month. The unsettled nature of the times could be read in the face of this youthful shogun, said to resemble the second Tokugawa shogun, Hidetada, as he proceeded to the lesser imperial palace and quietly and circumspectly took up his position.

The shogun's attendance at court had first been proposed by the lord of Choshu. But there were others in Kyoto ready to take advantage of this occasion to put pressure on the Kanto people. Already in the Koka and Ansei eras in the 1840's and 1850's, a group of activists with Maki Izumi no Kami at their head had claimed that a major change in the nation was at hand and the restoration of imperial rule was not far distant. The Teradaya incident was a manifestation of this movement, which gradually came to include those court nobles who were determined to bring about the revival of imperial power. Resenting the weakness of the court and raging against the arbitrary exercise of power by the shogunate, the movement took shape under the leadership of Choshu, a han historically at odds with the shogunate. The slogan "Revere the Emperor, Expel the Barbarians" was its rallying cry. Its sources ran completely pure. In its plans, the expulsion of the foreigners and the overthrow of the shogunate went hand-in-hand, for it aimed to bring about the collapse of the shogunate under the guise of expelling the barbarians. This slogan, "Revere the Emperor, Expel the Barbarians," first voiced by the Mito samurai Fujita Toko and Toda Hoken, had passed through many vicissitudes before at last reaching this point.

*　　*　　*　　*　　*　　*　　*

The cries of opposition to all things foreign grew still louder. Of course the shogunal officials who had embarked on the policy of opening the ports had not completely neglected the problem of coastal defenses. One of the reasons the key policy of alternate attendance had been so readily abandoned was so that the daimyo, relieved of the needless expense of traveling back and forth to Edo, might instead bring their armed forces up to strength and achieve complete military preparedness. But unfortunately the Tokugawa shogunate enjoyed neither the trust nor the power needed to unify the daimyo to resist the might of Europe effectively. Even so, it had given its solemn assent to the requests made by the emperor at the time of Princess Kazu's wedding. It had said that it would defend the nation against the barbarians. It would abrogate the treaties made with the foreign powers. It would chastise those who had unlawfully intruded upon the country. But this temporary palliative had not satisfied Kyoto. The situation no longer permitted vague posturings. Now even Hitotsubashi Yoshinobu, who had gone ahead to Kyoto to make preparations for the shogunal visit, was met by a group of court nobles including Sanjo Sanetomi and Ano Kimmi, acting in their official capacities, accompanied by Shigenoi Saneari, Ogimachi Kintada, and Anenokoji Kintomo, acting privately. These men informed him that the barbarians should already have been expelled before the shogun came to Kyoto. With the shogunal visit under way, it would be impossible for the shogun to leave after the scheduled ten days unless there was a clear resolution to this difficult issue. This was true even though the emperor felt a deep personal sympathy for the shogun and in spite of the strenuous and wide-ranging exertions of Yoshinobu.

Yet it would not do to overlook the fact that a fleet of eleven British warships was at anchor in the distant harbor of Yokohama. Nor would it do to overlook the fact that these ships appeared ready to go into action at the slightest provocation. We must therefore know more about the Namamugi incident.

By the fifth year following the opening of the port of Yokohama, not only had an anti-foreign attack on Yokohama by masterless samurai been rumored any number of times, but the British legation at the Tozenji in Takanawa had in fact been attacked and there had been any number of attacks on individual foreigners. Heusken, secretary to the American mission since it was first set up in Shimoda, had been one of the victims. He had been with Harris from the beginning, and although he was said to have had a deep understanding and sympathy for Japan, he was nevertheless struck down near the Mita-Furukawa bridge in Edo. So severe had the anti-foreign feeling become that the shogunate had been forced to set up a special office and assign some three hundred guards to the protection of foreigners. Then came the Namamugi incident.

What was the Namamugi incident? It was an occurrence on the Tokaido that proved to have unexpectedly disastrous effects on foreign relations. The time had been the twenty-first day of the eighth month of the previous year, and the place the village of Namamugi, not far from the Kawasaki post station. Richardson, an English merchant resident in Hong Kong, the wife of another merchant from Hong Kong, and two English traders named Marshall and Clark who were living in Yokohama had made up a party of four to ride on horseback from Yokohama to Kawasaki. They happened to meet with the retinue of Shimazu Hisamitsu, then on his way back to Kyoto. The imperial envoy Ohara Saemon no Kami was with him and their party was very large. It must have jammed all the roads in the vicinity.

The Kanagawa commissioner, concerned that an incident might arise involving foreigners who did not understand local ways, had sent out an order to all the foreign consulates advising that no one venture out on the main road in Kanagawa that day. He had asked them to inform all the foreigners living in Yokohama, but it seems that the meaning of this order was not clearly understood.

The mounted Englishmen did not attempt to ride into the column. But, either because they did not know the language or because they were unfamiliar with customs, they did not seem to understand the meaning of the warnings shouted at them by the Satsuma vanguard. They simply continued on their way as though there could be no possible objection to the free use of a public highway.

That was a fatal error. As Hisamitsu's palanquin, guarded by an escort of some five or six hundred men, drew near, the swords of two warriors suddenly flashed out beside the Englishmen. Startled, two of the party began to gallop back toward Yokohama; another momentarily reigned in his horse and then fled from the scene. The remaining person, Richardson, fell from his horse, which then ran away riderless. The Satsuma warriors, seeing that he was mortally wounded, took him by the hands and threw him into a field. Among those who fled, one was wounded in the shoulder, another was slashed in the head, and even the woman, who had escaped most lightly, made her way back to the foreign concession with her hat and part of her hair cut away.

British and French soldiers went to the scene immediately upon hearing the report. After a confrontation with the Kanagawa commissioner, they placed Richardson's body on a stretcher and brought it back to the foreign concession. The next day all the foreign shops in Yokohama were closed. A solemn funeral was held. Furthermore, the foreigners met together and decided to take a strong stand. Through the Kanagawa magistrate, they lodged a demand that Hisamitsu be stopped from going any further westward until the two assailants were taken into custody. But the Satsuma column had long since proceeded on to the west as though nothing had happened.

In the month prior to this incident, two officers attached to the French legation had been seriously wounded in Kozaki-cho in Yokohama, and one section of the foreign legation district which the shogunate was building on Mt. Goten in Shinagawa had been burned by Choshu samurai. The anti-foreign forces stopped at virtually nothing. Neale, the British chargé d'affaires, seemed to feel that the Japanese attitude must be changed. In his capacity as the representative of the foreigners living in Yokohama, he pressed inquiries about the Namamugi incident upon the shogunate with unshakable determination. The result was that a rear admiral in command of a fleet of eleven vessels steamed to Yokohama under direct orders from the home government.

All this became known in Kyoto while the shogun Iemochi was there. The position of the British was adamant. Either the Japanese government was remiss in its plain duty in dealing with this brutal act in which an innocent British citizen had been killed, or else its unwillingness to have the lord of Satsuma deliver up his two guilty retainers was a direct insult to the British government. There must be an immediate apology for this crime and it must be accompanied by an indemnity of one hundred thousand pounds. If a satisfactory answer was not received, the commander of the British naval forces would take whatever action might prove necessary to achieve the desired results. If the Japanese government should find it impossible to arrest the guilty retainers now in the Satsuma domains, England would negotiate directly with the lord of Satsuma. The fleet would proceed directly to Satsuma, take the guilty retainers into custody, and have them beheaded before witnessing British naval officers. The British further demanded that an indemnity of twenty-five thousand pounds be paid to the wounded victims and to the family of the deceased.

These demands came as a great shock. It was made even worse by the fact that when the activists from various han gathered at the Imperial Academy to discuss the demands, they had at hand only the most garbled version of the British statement. They were told that England had asked for a response to the following three demands:

1. Shimazu Hisamitsu, lord of Satsuma, must be handed over to the British.
2. An indemnity of 100,000 pounds must be paid.
3. A punitive campaign must be launched against Satsuma.

Conditions pertaining to defense against the British fleet having reached a point of utmost gravity in the Kanto region, it is only natural to discuss the return of the shogun to Edo. It goes without saying that the military forces in Kyoto and along the nearby seacoasts will place themselves under the shogun's command. At the time of the ultimate battle to expel the barbarians, it will be absolutely necessary that there be complete harmony between the emperor and his ministers. If, when the shogun has returned to Edo castle, there should be a rift between the imperial court and the shogunate, then the emperor and his ministers would be at cross-purposes, they would become alienated from each other, and it would be impossible to save the nation. Since it would not set the mind of the emperor at ease if the shogun were to return at this point, he will remain in Kyoto and will consult closely with the emperor on defense policies. The British will be asked to bring their fleet to Osaka, where a final disposition will be made. If it should become necessary to resort to military force, then the shogun himself will go into the field and take personal command. That being the case, it will provide a great opportunity for the nation to recover its pride. You are commanded to select the best people and take appropriate measures for the protection of the Kanto.

This was the letter that the lord regent presented to Hitotsubashi Yoshinobu in the lesser palace. All of the activists who had gathered at the Imperial Academy had their own copies of this document. The shogunate sent notice to all the han that first priority must be given to coastal defense, and the British were requested to extend their ultimatum. In the strained Kyoto atmosphere in which the regent's message was being read, the Kyoto deputy waited for the reaction. Some said that the British demands had already been rejected; others said that the French emissary had offered to intercede. Still others said that the other side would surely attack. None of the theories about the situation seemed adequate and it was difficult to know what was coming.

The Namamugi incident, involving the killing or wounding of four foreigners, had led to a grave diplomatic crisis. The long-raging fever of xenophobia had invited such a result. However, the anti-foreign faction did not bother to reflect on this. Most of the activists who were trying to overthrow the shogunate saw only an opportunity that must not be missed. Matsudaira Shungaku, who was in Kyoto at the time, apparently feeling that there was now little hope for a union of court and military, resigned his position as de facto head of government and returned home. Shimazu Hisamitsu rushed up to Kyoto as soon as he heard of the emergency, but found himself in an untenable position. He returned home within a few days, explaining that he had to look to the defense of the shores of his own province. Konoe Takahiro went into hiding, as did Nakagawa no Miya.

2

Kozo in the toiya at Nakatsugawa and Hanzo in the Magome honjin passed their days beside the Kiso road in deep concern over events in Kyoto. Keizo, also a posthumous disciple of Hirata Atsutane, was engaged in political activities in Kyoto and the two frequently received letters from him. Many things were reported in these letters. The emperor had gone to offer prayers at the Kamo shrines and all the officials under Iemochi and Hitotsubashi Yoshinobu, as well as samurai from various han who were in Kyoto, had escorted the imperial carriages. Again, the emperor was reported to have expressed a wish to make a progress to Iwashimizu where, before the altar of the Otokoyama shrine to Hachiman the war god, he would present a sword to the shogun as a parting gift for the coming campaign to expel the barbarians. These were reported to be actions taken in accord with the memorials

presented by the activists advocating expulsion of the barbarians. In spite of
that, Keizo wrote that there were some who were hoping that the emperor
himself would take personal command. Reading each of these letters, Hanzo
and Kozo sensed keenly the difficulty of the times.

In the beginning of the fourth month, Kozo followed Keizo to Kyoto.
Now only Hanzo remained behind at his post in the Magome honjin.

"How can I bear it," he would say to himself.

Hanzo envied the way Kozo could leave the affairs of the Nakatsugawa
toiya to his family and go off to Kyoto. He reflected that the day his friend
entered Kyoto would be the day Kozo's actions would be joined with those
of Hirata Kanetane, whose guidance Hanzo craved. The master's enterprise
was the true restoration of antiquity and it was already under way. Hanzo
thought of his own certainty that Kanetane would be following the will of
his predecessor, Hirata Atsutane, not straying because of confusion over
praise or blame, unmoved by the interests of the feudal domains, always
keeping the main purpose in sight as he moved forward.

Kichizaemon could be seen favoring his illness-shattered body as he went
up and down the stairs leading to his rooms above the miso shed. That he had
not said a single word about the affairs of the highway since turning over to
Hanzo the three offices of honjin, toiya, and headman was just as one would
expect of him. When Kichizaemon was first stricken he had been unable to
speak, stand, or move his hands. Everything possible had been done to aid his
recovery and at last half his body was more or less sound. Kichizaemon had
always liked everything clean and orderly, often sweeping out the garden and
grounds of the honjin himself, but since his illness his arm had withered and
it was difficult for him to hold a broom. He had been a gifted calligrapher,
writing beautifully formed characters in his own distinctive style, but since
his illness he could not even write small characters. His handwriting had
become like that of a child of six or seven. He spoke only of how fortunate he
was that his treatment had been effective enough to restore movement to half
his body, so that he could now feed himself and go to the toilet without bur-
dening others, but in fact he was very sad about not being able to handle
broom or writing brush. Whenever he heard his father's sighs, Hanzo was
pierced to the heart. He could not bring himself to cast aside family responsibilities to go to Kyoto as his friend Kozo had done.

The second floor of the miso shed with its eight-mat room and its three-
mat room was Kichizaemon's retirement quarters. Here Hanzo's father
spread out his beloved books on the Mino school of haikai and the Ninagawa
style of chess and, with these books as his daylong companions, found such
solace as he could. As is always the case with those suffering from a stroke,
there was no speedy method of treatment. His recovery was so slow as to
arouse impatience in outsiders.

"Otami, I'm going up to Otaki. I've told Seisuke to look after things,"
said Hanzo to his wife.

Otaki village was at the foot of Mt. Ontake, where the main shrine for the

Kiso district was located. Hanzo had decided to make a pilgrimage there to pray for his father's recovery. Some time had passed since the uproar following the reform of the alternate attendance system, and the flight of the daimyo households out of Edo had halted for the time being. Taking advantage of this respite, Hanzo planned to take a few days off so that he might pray before the god of Mt. Ontake, famous as a healer. Exciting as his friend Kozo's departure for Kyoto was, Hanzo found himself moving in the opposite direction to pass a quiet time deep in the mountains.

Hanzo wrote a long poem to present to the god at Otaki. Although he usually wrote the short, thirty-one syllable classical poems, he had occasionally composed long poems and now he tried his hand at one on the subject of petition and prayer.

"Are you about ready to leave, Hanzo?" asked Oman as she came to his side.

Oman was an indispensable person to the Magome honjin, caring for Kichizaemon and even helping with the housework as she went back and forth between the second floor of the miso shed and the main house. She was well educated, as befitted a person who came from the prominent Sakamoto family in Takato, and it was she who had been directing the seven-year-old Okume in reading poems from the great tenth-century *Collection of Ancient and Modern Verse.*

"Mother, please look after things while I'm away," said Hanzo. "I don't expect to be gone long. I'll come right back as soon as I have spent the three days at the shrine."

"It's good that you can go once you've made up your mind to do so. Your father seems to be pleased, too."

After having been granted leave for seven days, Hanzo was ready to set out for Otaki. Although Sakichi wanted to go with him, he had decided to take his disciple Katsushige instead because the boy, just passing from childhood into adolescence, had pleaded so often to be included. Hanzo was traveling lightly, taking with him only rice for the offering before the deity, two volumes of *The Tranquil Cave,* and clean white robes to wear at the shrine. Katsushige, delighted to be accompanying his master, was excited by the prospect of this venture into the mountains. At the hearthside of the honjin, Hanzo and his family gathered to drink tea together as was the custom in those times. A completely unexpected visitor found them there.

"Hanzo! Are you going somewhere?"

The man who spoke as he came in from the entry to the familiar hearth room was none other than the physician who three years previously had moved from Nakatsugawa to Ina. It was Miyagawa Kansai.

Disappointed in the Ina valley to which he had moved at such great cost and finding the Hirata disciples there uncongenial, Kansai had given up his "hidden dwelling" in Ina to return to Nakatsugawa. It brought back memories for him to be traveling again on this part of the same highway on which he had returned with twenty-four hundred ryo of profits from the Yokohama venture and a guard to protect him. His wife had been with him when he went to Ina but she had passed away. Now, coming back through Magome all alone, he found his old acquaintances changed. Kimbei of the Fushimiya was retired and Hanzo's father had been stricken by illness. Kansai himself had aged greatly.

"Sensei! You're too far away over there by the entrance! Please come up here!" said Hanzo, leading his old master from the edge of the raised floor over to the hearth. When Kansai heard that Hanzo was on the point of leaving for Otaki he said that he would keep on going, but they had been out of touch for so long that there was much for them to talk about.

"No, these three years in Ina were a disaster," said Kansai, scratching his head. "I confess it now. That Yokohama trip was accursed. It set people against me everywhere I went. I just couldn't stand it. It was a terrible mistake not to consult with all of you about it before I went. But please let's not talk about Yokohama any more."

"I'm glad to hear you say it. To tell the truth, I've been waiting for the day when you would come."

"I can tell you this, Hanzo. I lost everything I had by going to Ina. On top of that, there were no patients over there and no students came to me. About all I have to show for those three years is that I helped a little in the publication of the *Commentaries on Ancient History*. All the Hirata people in Ina—Maejima Masasuke, Iwasaki Nagayo, Kitahara Inao, Katagiri Shun'ichi —are working very hard on it and the publication is attracting a good deal of favorable attention. In Ina they are encouraged when they receive letters from places like Tsuwano and so on . . .

"That reminds me. I understand that you helped Kureta Masaka when he was escaping from Kyoto."

"Yes, that's right. I was really surprised when he showed up here, dressed in a plain kimono and snow boots."

"That was quite a thing he did. To cut off the head of the statue of Ashikaga Takauji! Morooka Masatane was also involved in that affair and they say that people went to Kyoto from as far away as Ina to try to rescue their comrades. Kureta Masaka has to live in hiding now. But even so, he can't keep quiet and he's always wanting people in Ina to make some kind of gesture of unity with their comrades in Kyoto. Ina is quite different now from what it was when I first went there. There's a lot going on in that valley."

While relating all this, Kansai would start to get up repeatedly, tucking his tobacco case into his sash, and then he would settle down and take it out again. Otami came in to offer tea.

"Why don't you take sensei into the parlor? Mother is saying that she wants to see him too."

"No, you mustn't do that!" said Kansai. "Hanzo is just leaving. I had no intention of putting everyone to so much trouble. What I came by about today is that I have been thinking of a subscription. I have just been to the Upper Fushimiya and I have already talked to Kimbei. I would like you to work on this too, Hanzo."

"I'll be very happy to. Of course, it will have to wait until I get back from Otaki."

"I know I'm not the only one. Unfortunately, Kozo is now in Kyoto too, so you're the only one I can count on. Old men are not pleasant things to have around and I don't want to become a burden on my son-in-law. I still haven't decided whether or not I will settle in Nakatsugawa. I'm making one last spurt. I may even go on to Ise."

After asking Hanzo to take part in the subscription, Kansai at last left the Magome honjin. Afterward, Hanzo stood at the edge of the raised floor, stock-still, gazing at the faces of Otami and the baby boy she was holding.

"What a pity. What a strange life," he said to his wife. "It was that man who first opened my eyes to National Learning. Just look at him now, at his age and separated from his wife by her death."

"Wasn't his wife the older sister of Kozo in Nakatsugawa? There must have been a great difference in her age and Kozo's."

"Sensei has only one daughter. She is brilliant, known throughout the Nakatsugawa area for her intelligence. They adopted a husband for her and he is the Miyagawa who is now practicing medicine there."

"I didn't know that."

"But isn't it a strange world, Otami? I never really believed that Miyagawa sensei had turned his back on his disciples. I always thought that he would come back to us some day. That day has come."

3

With his mind still on Kyoto, Hanzo set out for Otaki accompanied by his disciple Katsushige. They planned to spend that night in Suwara, but they looked in briefly on Juheiji at the Tsumago honjin since it was on the way. Juheiji, after all, was not only Otami's elder brother but one of the headmen on this same stretch of highway. Hanzo could share the worries of his post with him.

"I'll walk with you, Hanzo," called Juheiji as he stepped into his sandals and came running after Hanzo.

They were just coming into the beginning of the fourth month, the best season for traveling, and there were great numbers of religious travelers on the road. Bands of pilgrims were heading for Ise, for Kompira, or for Zenkoji, and there were merchants on their way to the hinterlands. It was the time of year when the loaded packhorses had new blankets, red leather bridles, and hemp fly-whisks that moved every time the horses shook their heads. They brought a feeling of liveliness to the highway.

"That's quite a trip, Ontake," said Juheiji as they walked along together. "There's still a lot of snow in the mountains. I don't see how you'll be able to climb it."

"Yes, it's going to be hard to get even as far as the third station. I'm just going to go to Otaki and spend two or three days there."

"Your father's condition is still that bad? It must be hard for you. By the way, I suppose you've heard the news from Edo."

"Yes. I was afraid it might come to this."

"They say there was a real commotion in Edo when the British warships came. Isn't the eighth of next month the time limit set on the reply? I suppose they'll have to pay the indemnities. It's all these people with their talk about 'expelling the barbarians.' That's what brought this all on. I suppose that even they must be motivated by concern for the nation, but I just can't understand them. How can we let internal politics and foreign relations get so completely mixed up with each other?"

"That's a good question."

"Hanzo, if I hadn't been born into a headman's family, I might very well be in Kyoto myself right now, going on about closing the ports and expelling the barbarians. If you and I didn't have to concern ourselves with what might happen on the highways, and with how everyone is going to suffer, then we wouldn't have to worry about a thing."

After parting from Juheiji at the edge of Tsumago, Hanzo and Katsushige followed the highway toward the interior. They left Suwara early the next morning and pressed on, reaching the hanging bridge about noon. Thrushes were singing. The mountain road leading up to Otaki was on the opposite bank. People intending to climb Mt. Ontake would take this road which passed through the villages of Koshitachi, Shimojo, and Kuroda before finally reaching the vicinity of the Tokiwa ford.

Hanzo and Katsushige left the highway and turned off into a deep, heavily forested valley. The leaf buds on the deciduous trees were just beginning to open. Life was returning to the forest all around them as they moved on. When they reached the Sawahodo pass, marking the first league of the climb, they found a spot set aside for distant worship and from it they could see Mt. Ontake all the way from Marishiten to the inner temple.

"Katsushige! There's Mt. Ontake! It's still covered with snow," exclaimed Hanzo.

The mountains stood in rank upon rank of superimposed triangular forms, each with its own steepness of pitch and with Tsurugigamine, the "sword peak," soaring up at the apex of the awesome mass. In the hidden fastness were solitude and calm. Here people could gaze up at the form of a great mountain that would prevail amidst the endless changes of the human world. It was said that the bones of early climbers such as the twelfth-century priest Kakumyo Gyoja were buried at the edge of the precipice at its summit.

"Let's hurry, master!" said Katsushige, but he was not the only eager one. Hanzo too was struck by the solemn dignity of the mountains and he could not linger here. He was impatient to press on to Otaki.

*   *   *   *   *   *   *

An old priest's house leaning against the steep slope high above the Otaki river awaited Hanzo and Katsushige. The building served as both local shrine and lodging for people preparing to undertake austerities on the mountain. There was no bridge over the river. Logs had been cut from the mountain and bound together for a raft to serve the needs of residents and visitors. Hanzo crossed the river at a place called Misawa and arrived at this house late in the day.

"You're from Magome? I am happy that you have come. I have often heard of the honjin in Magome," said the priest, whose name was Miyashita. "The cherry blossoms are already finished there, aren't they?"

"About a third of the wild cherries are left," replied Hanzo.

"I thought so. There is a tremendous range of climates here in the Kiso, isn't there? A full month passes between the time we hear reports of cherry blossoms in the south and our first sight of them here. It will still be a long time before there are any cherry blossoms in Otaki."

"We saw lots of lavender azaleas along the road as we came up, didn't we, master?" Katsushige put in, gazing around with youthful eyes.

Hanzo and Katsushige were conducted to a room which looked out on a deep valley filled with the light of the setting sun. A river phoebe came to their window. In the alcove there was a hanging scroll inscribed with the legend THE GREAT DIAMOND WORLD AVATAR OF ONTAKE, and on the wall was a straw rope of the kind used in Shinto to mark consecrated areas.

"Come and see this, Katsushige. This is what they mean by Dual Shinto," said Hanzo as he stood before the scroll. The complete confounding of Buddhist and Shinto practices reflected in this scroll was disturbing to him. Yet the lodging was in no way remiss in its treatment of guests. The family that lived here was both kind and generous in its reception of the tired travelers and pilgrims that came to it. It was an old family; the present priest was the seventeenth or eighteenth in his line. There were white-haired old men and women about and there was no way of telling just how many of them were living in the house.

Miyashita, the master of the house, came to look in on Hanzo and to invite him and his companion to enjoy a bath and a mountain meal. He told them that organized bands of pilgrims would not be coming in until the mountain was opened for the summer, at the beginning of the seventh month. But even during the coldest part of the winter, between the fifteenth of the first month and the fifteenth of the second month, there were always a few people making pilgrimages in the intense cold, so the yearly round of visitors never completely ceased. The old priest added that he wished he could show them the bustle in this valley in the summer when bands of pilgrims led by priests from all the provinces would come pouring in, to the accompaniment of blaring conch shells.

After the evening meal, Miyashita came again to see Hanzo.

"You are beginning your vigil tomorrow morning? Now, some give up salt while they are here, others give up cereals. There are many kinds of abstentions. There are some who undertake the discipline of uncooked food, using no fire at all and living on buckwheat flour soaked in water with a bit of fruit. But if you take just one meal a day, keep yourself in a state of purification, and avoid stray thoughts, everything should be all right."

At last! Hanzo found himself in this mountain village among mountain villages where even his distracted mind might be able to find repose. The nights seemed especially deep in Otaki. The dimly lighted houses along the bottom of the dark valley, the night mists boiling up along the river—everything seemed utterly still. Hanzo was pleased to be among these quiet forests when the misty moon of the fourth month was in the sky.

It had already been three years since Katsushige had come to Hanzo's house as a disciple from the Inabaya in Ochiai. The Katsushige who had worn short trousers, shaved his forelock, and read his books so intently had suddenly become a young man, handsome in his kimono with the pale yellow collar of his underrobe showing beneath. He was a meticulous, scholarly person who took little interest in his appearance, but everyone in the Magome station was aware of his natural good looks. The young girls came in relays to peep in on him and Hanzo was powerless to stop it.

"Go ahead and lie down if you're tired, Katsushige."

"I think I will, master. I was really amazed at how fast you go. The walk over the mountains from Suwara to Otaki today was quite a trip."

Katsushige was soon snoring loudly. Hanzo sat up for a long time by the desk, gazing at the flame of the lamp. On the desk were the two volumes of *The Tranquil Cave* which he had put into his carrying cloth when he left Magome, thinking that it would be good to look into them at Otaki. These were lectures by Hirata Atsutane that had been written down by his disciples, and Hanzo loved these books right down to the light blue covers bound with purple cord in the old style.

The lonely sound of the river led Hanzo's thoughts toward that great master who had for so long given him intellectual guidance. If Atsutane had lived to meet the swift tides of this third year of Bunkyu, what course might he have steered past the shoals of the age?

How would he have responded to the bloodthirsty cries of "expel the barbarians," cries which did not subside even at the prospect of war? Collecting his thoughts in solitude in this still, hidden valley, Hanzo could hear Atsutane's voice more clearly than when he was under the press of business in Magome. When he saw his two friends Keizo and Kozo depart for Kyoto, he had not been able to calm himself. He had had to cool his fevered mind, suppress his racing heart, and hide his feelings as a disciple of the Hirata school. Hanzo had come to realize then that among the supporters of the imperial cause there were two great currents. One of them flowed from the Mito activist Fujita Toko while the other found its source in the teachings of Motoori and Hirata. The two were not the same. As was written on the famous plaque in the buildings of the Kodokan, it was the aim of the Mito school to respect the Ways of this land of the gods but at the same time to revere the teachings of the Confucian masters. From the point of view of the National Scholars, this position was tinged with Chinese-mindedness. The men who held to this doctrine were dedicated to repaying their boundless obligation to their country by attempting to realize the warrior's dream that had been pursued in vain by Kusunoki and his son—they had created, under the banner of expelling the barbarians, a movement to overthrow the shogunate. Of course their position was extreme. But however deplorable their extremism might be, Maki Izumi no Kami and his band of activists had demonstrated an implacable spirit. There was no longer any room to doubt that they would take their cause as far as possible.

What was to become of the country tomorrow? The day after tomorrow? As his thoughts revolved around this problem, Hanzo felt an even greater reverence for the teachings bequeathed by his master Motoori. To be sure, many in previous times had turned to the past out of dissatisfaction with their own age. Nevertheless, Hanzo felt a special gratitude for the National Scholar epitomized in Motoori. He had fixed his eyes on the most distant past, had found there the newest way, and had pointed it out for those who came after him.

"Don't catch cold, Katsushige! You had better go to bed and get some real sleep."

Hanzo woke the youth who was dozing in the lamplight, got him into bed, and then returned to *The Tranquil Cave*. These lectures recorded by the master's disciples were written in clear and simple language in order to reach the widest possible audience. Here Hanzo found the master speaking about foreign countries. Atsutane had died in 1843, the fourteenth year of Tempo, so he was without knowledge of the uproar ten years later when American ships came to Uraga in Sagami province. Still less could he have known about the upheavals that were culminating with a fleet of eleven British warships coming to Yokohama harbor. Yet Hanzo found in the the master's vision of Europe, in his way of looking at it and thinking about it, rare and precious lessons which brought him joy. It said in *The Tranquil Cave*:

> And again, there has recently come from the land of Holland in the extreme
> west a school of learning which is called Dutch learning. In that land it seems
> that they have always been gifted in understanding the principles of things, and
> they claim to have made not a few discoveries. Without touching on what we
> know about their astronomy and geography, we can say that their success with
> machinery has startled observers and that they are particularly knowledgeable
> about the refining and alloying of metals. It would therefore seem that it might
> be in accord with the will of the gods that their books should come in one after
> another and begin to circulate widely in our land. Yet, among their medicines
> we find those of the most powerful effectiveness, and in the metals they forge,
> those of the most frightful kind. If one uses a good medicine to treat the symp-
> toms for which it is appropriate, one will obtain outstanding results. But if one

does not understand the character of the medicine or if, even though under-standing the character of the medicine, one does not know when to use it, or if one should attempt to use it to treat symptoms for which it is not appropriate, then great harm will result which may even lead to the loss of human life. It is the same as giving a keen sword to an ape or letting a madman fire a musket— it is truly most dangerous. Now, although their great knowledge of science is by no means an evil thing, these red-haired barbarians have no knowledge of the true gods of this world. In applying limited human knowledge to the limit-less problems of the universe, they have come up with an extremely large num-ber of theories, and because they are by nature an impertinent people, they occupy themselves with the details before them while remaining all the more unshakably unaware of the will of the mysterious gods. For that reason, their teachings are extremely narrow and there is much in them that is in conflict with our way of antiquity. And yet, when we consider the present state of the world, it seems that because of our love of the novel and exotic, these teachings are beginning to spread like the flourishing of Confucian studies before them. Nevertheless, although there are among them a great many things which might benefit the country and the people, I believe that those things which may be harmful are also by no means few. It is precisely by remaining aware that their evil things must follow after their good things that we can arrive at a proper appreciation of them. Therefore, we must think carefully about the august will of the emperor, who, being open and generous in all things, would be inclined to accept everything that comes from the foreign countries to our august land without discriminating between those that are good and those that are evil. And, though it is frightening to say it, we must think of the rule handed down by our many great gods that we must select carefully those things which we are to adopt from among all that comes from the foreign countries.

Hanzo breathed a deep sigh. It was one of despair over his own shallow-ness of learning, his narrowness and rigidity, his honest naiveté. Atsutane was generally thought to have despised everything that came from foreign countries as being heterodox and evil, but when one opened *The Tranquil Cave* and looked inside, one saw him taking the broad view in which the gathering of things from other countries—from Korea, China, and India nearby, and even from places such as Holland—was fully in accord with the will of the gods. Although the master had taught that we should cast off for-eign borrowings and return to what was essential in Japan, he never said that we should carry this to irresponsible extremes.

In *The Tranquil Cave* Atsutane even took up the ancient word *ebisu*, the term now being used in the sense of "barbarian," and showed that it referred only to things different from that which was customarily seen or heard. A serving tray presented backwards, for example, was called an "ebisu tray." Paper that was supposed to be rectangular and was not was called "ebisu paper," and the herbaceous peony, usually used as an external medicine but also effective if taken internally, was called in such cases "ebisu medicine" when the name was read in Japanese. So these people were called "ebisu" simply because their hair, which one would expect to be black, was reddish, and their eyes, which one would expect to be brown, were blue.

"How great is the master," Hanzo said to himself.

The Hirata Atsutane he visualized was not the big handsome man he pictured Motoori Norinaga to be. He had once seen a portrait of Atsutane, who had a broad, square forehead, large ears, and eyes that seemed to gaze into the distance. The impression that Hanzo received from this portrait was of a rather long-faced, bony, somehow angular man. The portrait showed Atsutane apparently in his late forties. His hair, which was knotted high on the crown of his head in the style of the Tempo era, was still black and he looked vigorous. His reading stand was at his side. There was a sense of the man in the crests on his jacket and the folds of his clothing, and the way he rested his left hand on his thigh while holding a fan in his lap with his right was especially striking. Hanzo remembered gazing into that portrait. On the reading stand was a manuscript volume of the *Commentaries on Ancient History*, Atsutane's masterpiece. It seemed to Hanzo as though the master had moved forward out of that portrait and was saying to him, "All things are as the gods would have them."

4

As dawn of the morning he was to enter the shrine drew near, Hanzo found himself unable to sleep any longer. He took care not to awaken Katsushige, and taking advantage of the moonlight, got up, went outside, and brought in the ablution basin. When he had completed his purification he felt warm and fresh. Just changing into the ritual dress of white kimono and trousers gave him a sense of austere commitment.

Two or three people were leaving the mountain early in the lingering darkness. It was as though having brought their prayers from distant provinces, they were now treading the moonlight as they departed for home. They were a striking sight in their traveler's hats, their staffs, their white clothing and white carrying cloths.

In that dawn Hanzo followed the priest on morning duty up the road a few hundred yards to the village shrine. Two or three persons who seemed to have been undergoing austerities for several days were already waiting for the coming of full light as they listened to the priest's great drum resound through the nearby forests. On this occasion, Hanzo stayed only for the dawn service and then returned to his lodging to look after Katsushige and to make preparations for his vigil.

"Master!" called Katsushige, also dressed in white, and waiting for Hanzo to descend from the mountain.

"I have something to tell you, Katsushige. When I was leaving Magome,

Seisuke stopped me. He asked me if I was taking a young person like you along on a vigil. I said it was because you wanted to go. He said, 'Look here! These vigils are often too much even for the priests.' "

"Why?"

"Why? Because when you go to the shrine, there is nothing but prayer. Other than that there is complete silence. It's a place where people go who have mastered hunger and cold. Moreover, it is something that I have to do now that I am here. Our cases are different."

"If that's so, then you should pray for your father and I will pray for you."

"I give up. If that's the way you feel, I'll leave it up to you. When you get sleepy, come back here and rest. Here the laws of the mountain apply and it's different from what you might have imagined it to be back home. All right? Don't overdo it!"

Katsushige nodded.

Hanzo and Katsushige walked to the village shrine, carrying a head of unthreshed rice, some cooked rice to offer to the gods, and a change of fresh, white ceremonial robes.

Between the priest's lodging, surrounded by plum trees in blossom, and the shrine lay a steep, narrow road running from the entrance at Otaki up to the Ontake road. Just walking up this narrow road helped to purify the hearts of the pilgrims. In the mountain morning, the clouds in the sky gradually turned white, fresh, and pure. As they climbed the road, the mist-shrouded valley spread out below them.

"I hear a pheasant, master!"

"I wonder how this looked when the adepts Kakumyo and Fukan were climbing up here. I had always thought that those two were the first to climb this mountain but when I talked to the priest I found that this was not so. But they were the ones who first brought bands of pilgrims here."

The two continued to talk as they climbed. When they arrived before the new stone torii that the lord of Owari had contributed the previous year, they met a worshipper coming down the road. He was a wild-looking sight with a rosary wrapped around his neck and a staff in hand. He appeared to have undergone the most extreme austerities, as though he had come out of some deep cave or had dropped down out of the snow-covered mass of the mountain. Hanzo was amazed to find that such persons lived in these mountains.

Soon Hanzo began to climb the two-hundred-yard-long stone stairway. It was made of a series of flights of sixteen to twenty steps each. The shrine was built at the top of the stairway with the vast, high wall of the mountain directly behind it. It was to this spot, enfolded by a sloping black valley with patches of snow remaining here and there among dark groves of cedar and hinoki, that Hanzo had come to pray for his father's health. It was a place that reminded him of the title of a book by the late master. It was truly a "still stone house."

*   *   *   *   *   *   *

At last Hanzo could kneel before the reliquary at the back of the main hall and present the poem of entreaty he had prepared. He would find a place in the corner of the hall among the other worshippers where he could kneel on a crude, round straw mat.

All was quiet. Nothing could be heard but the sound of the pure water flowing down from the high boulders behind the wall. Two huge *tengu* masks hanging on the wall could easily be seen from where Hanzo sat. All around him, deepening the religious atmosphere, were tablets bearing the names of shrines or of individual believers that had been presented as far back as the Kaei era or, in some cases, even far earlier. Among these tablets was one in memory of the great man of the Kiso, Yamamura Somon, who had had the hall rebuilt in its present form. But it was the two *tengu* masks that particularly caught Hanzo's attention. Their great mouths, open nearly to the ears and exposing long fangs, were like those of wild beasts, while their glittering golden eyes were like those of the gods. They were creatures that combined the wildness of the mountains, the freedom of the winged birds, and the mystical nature of the gods. The makers of the masks had provided them with both masculine and feminine qualities and had endowed them with the feeling of the mountains. Their long hair hung down like cryptomeria leaves and their beards were like the rankest, most overgrown grass. They seemed to shimmer before Hanzo's eyes as if the dark middle ages still remained in this place.

Then his gaze shifted to the tablets. This was a holy place completely taken over by Dual Shinto. It was the "world of discipline" with a mountain peak as its training ground, a place ruled by a mystical religion that confounded the gods and the Buddhas. This dual teaching had enthralled the minds of the people from the middle ages on. Hanzo, who had come here to pray for his father's health, wanted not these gods of a religion that had passed beyond this world, but the more human Onamuchi and Sukunabikona, the Shinto deities of this mountain.

With a pungent scent of smoldering sumac bark, the Buddhist *goma* ceremony spread its austere influence over the consecrated site. An image of the Buddha Mahavairocana appeared to be enshrined in the altar at the back of the hall. The pilgrims came rattling their rosaries, one after another, to kneel before it. From behind the screens came the sound of sutra reading.

"Is this the dwelling of the gods?" Hanzo wondered.

Most of what he saw and most of what he heard interfered with his prayers for his father. His mind strayed to the inquiry about Shinto funeral ceremonies that had come down just before the passage of Princess Kazu and to the problem of respect for the gods that was being debated among the National Scholars. But at the same time he felt only the deepest reverence for Buddhists such as Kakumyo, Fukan, Isshin, and Issen, who had led their disciples into these mountains, clearing precipices, opening roads, forming groups of the faithful, gathering believers from every province, and pouring out their heart's blood for these mountains.

*   *   *   *   *   *   *

Hanzo sat motionless all day.

After a time his mind turned back to the Magome honjin that he had been so eager to get away from. The village notice board was there. There were the two toiya. He could see the faces of Inosuke from the Fushimiya, Kyurobei from the toiya, and the other village officials. It was becoming more difficult to move men and goods over the highway. That had been made clear just before he left Magome by the passage of the lord of Sendai on his way from Kyoto to Edo. His retinue had spent the night at Nakatsugawa with two hundred eighty porters and one hundred eighty horses of its own. The confusion and the pressures on the post officials had been beyond description. By the eighth hour in the afternoon forty-five packhorse loads of freight remained unaccounted for. It was finally moved by the porters and oxen.

As he reflected on this, he noted that the increased difficulty of transport on the highways and the return of the lord of Sendai seemed not at all unrelated to the increased tensions between Kyoto and Edo. An untimely sounding of the bell in the Mampukuji in Magome boomed out over the highway. It marked a prayer for the leading of men's minds into righteousness, for peace in the nation, and for the shogun's safe return from Kyoto. A solemn reading of the *Maha Prajna Paramita Sutra* was held. The priests of the Shogenji temple in Tekano village, the Kotokuji in Tsumago, the Tentokuji in Yubunezawa, the Togakuji in Midono, and the priests from the temples in Yamaguchi and Tadachi, six priests in all, came to the ceremony.

As he recalled that solemn event Hanzo found himself thinking about a recent tragedy. Risaburo, the head of the ox drovers, was an unforgettable figure. He was the one who had led the struggle of the ox drovers against Kadoya Jubei, the former toiya of Nakatsugawa. It was not surprising that such a firm, unyielding man, working silently and in obscurity, should have clashed with the *kumosuke,* the drifters and thugs who banded together to perform services such as carrying litters or bearing people across river fords when they were not busy as petty criminals and extortionists. Risaburo had been attacked just below Shimizu valley as he was moving freight for Owari. Three *kumosuke* had beaten him with bamboo clubs and he was left bleeding profusely from two or three blows to the head. It was enough to leave even an ox drover more dead than alive. The people of the village rushed to the scene as soon as they heard of the attack. When it was reported to the post station, two officials set off in the company of the informer Yahei, but Risaburo was already dead when they arrived. This was no isolated incident. It only symbolized what had been happening since the reform of the alternate attendance system.

"What terrible sacrifices the highways have claimed," thought Hanzo. From the ronin above down to the *kumosuke* below, all the changes in manners that were appearing in this time of transition made Hanzo aware that fundamental social changes were on the way. As headman he had to protect those below in all sorts of ways . . .

Hanzo came back to himself with the peaceful sound of sutra reading in his ears. Suddenly, the brilliant light of the sun broke through the grove of cedar outside and filled the hall. As he observed the other worshippers, everything forgotten in their absorption in simple faith, Hanzo was ashamed of his own straying mind. That evening a priest came and left a single ball of salted rice beside him.

By the fourth day, Hanzo had fulfilled his vow. He was offering his final prayer before the gods. He prayed that he might exchange a year of his own life in return for his father's health. If that was not enough, he would not begrudge two or even three years.

When he left the hall, he found that it was raining. Katsushige had come up from the priest's lodging to wait for him with an umbrella. The rain that was filling out the parched grass seemed to bring Hanzo back to life after his austerities.

"What did you do, Katsushige?"

Hanzo spoke as they stood beneath the high stone cliffs outside the hall. He was conscious of breaking three days of silence.

"Are you tired, master? I just stayed there one day and after that I came up regularly to look in on you. Yesterday I walked around the shrine alone. I found all kinds of rare herbs—grampa-and-gramma, elves' breeches, and lady camphor."

"I'm glad you came along. Even when I was alone up there, it really helped to know that you were nearby."

There were stone lanterns and stone lion dogs along their return route. There were shrines where deities like Sampokojin with his three faces and six buttocks, dancing on the back of the boar, displayed baldly their foreign lineage. The Twelve Avatars, the Spirit of the Sacred Mountain, the Deity of the Diamond Way and the like, their names inscribed on the stone tablets beside the road, stood together with the bronze statue of Fudo, representing Maha Vairocana in his enraged phase, driving evil from the world. The stupas memorializing the thirty-three annual services carried out for some deceased person under the rules of Pure Land Buddhism also spoke of the nature of Dual Shinto. Some of the tablets bore the names of pilgrim bands from Hida, some from Musashi, some from Kazusa, some from Echigo. This was the principal Shinto shrine of the Kiso in name only. In fact, it was the Buddhist temple of the avatar of Ontake. Hanzo was troubled by all he encountered as he walked along, wondering how one could possibly think of this as the dwelling of the two Shinto deities.

As they came down the mountain road nearly to the priest's house, they met a boy wearing the baggy trousers of the mountain country. This was the priest's son. He had taken up an umbrella and had come out that far to meet them. Soon they were among villagers in broad hats and straw capes who moved along unhindered by the rain. Accustomed to bearing heavy burdens on their backs or working nonchalantly on the steep slopes, they presented a scene that could be repeated anywhere in the Kiso.

"Ah, you have returned! You must be very tired!" said the wife of the priest when she caught sight of Hanzo. She was well versed in caring for those who went up the mountain and she supplied him with many small comforts.

"After a vigil, you have to be careful about food. In a mountain house like this we don't have anything proper to offer you, but how would you like some parsley gruel? I made it with unstrained bean paste, since I thought that would be lightest and easiest to digest. Please try some."

She set the gruel fragrant with wild parsley before him.

The warm, quiet rain continued to fall. Hanzo was delighted to accept the priest's invitation to remain in Otaki that day to rest and bathe.

"It's the hairdresser. Do you have need of me?"

The village hairdresser had been called by the people of the lodging and he came to Hanzo's room carrying his oil-stained workbox with him. After sleeping soundly for half the day, Hanzo had his hair set straight again. With his hair in order, his mind felt stronger. His feelings became clearer. This quiet priest's lodging proved to be just the place to talk with Katsushige about their hopes and fears for the future.

"You won't be able to stay with me all that much longer, Katsushige. Sometime around next year you'll have to go back to Ochiai. I am sure your family has marriage plans for you."

"I want to study more. They spoke to me about marrying, but I refused. I told them it was too early."

Katsushige was at the age when he still blushed in speaking of such things. Just then the priest came in to visit with Hanzo. He now felt on sufficiently close terms to address him as Aoyama. He had brought with him an amulet memorializing Hanzo's vigil at the shrine, white rice for an offering to the gods, and other small gifts, all of which he placed in the alcove.

"Please take these back to Magome with you," said the priest. "I have one other thing to ask of you. I saw the fine poem you offered to the gods. Here in the backwoods I don't have the proper kind of paper for it, but would you please leave us something to remember you by?"

The priest clapped his hands to call a servant. He had his son brought to the room.

"He's just eight, Aoyama. An eight-year-old who came to us late, but he is fond of calligraphy and books. As you can well imagine, we have been unable to find a proper teacher for him here in the mountains. I hope that we can establish some relationship through him before you leave these mountains. Please teach this child his books."

That was the way the priest spoke to Hanzo.

"They say that it is twelve miles from here to Fukushima but it is really only eleven. You are often in Fukushima on business, I suppose. If you walk from the Gyonin bridge there up the Ontake road until you come to the Tokiwa ford, you will be on the same road you came up on this time. Please come for a visit the next time on your way back from Fukushima."

"Yes, I really like Otaki. I had never imagined that there was such an enchanted land here in the Kiso. I will drop in on you the next time I have a chance. But I am busy and you know how things are right now, so who knows when I will be able to come again? I'll have a good listen to the sound of the Otaki river to take home with me."

Hanzo had Katsushige prepare ink for him. Then he autographed a poem sheet as the priest had asked.

> Plum blossoms:
> Without their scent
> The falling rain-
> Drenched traveler's road
> Would be impassable.
>
>   Hanzo

Hanzo was beginning to feel concern about things in Magome. He thought about how, in contrast to Otaki where the season was a full month behind, the day when he would be able to delight his father with stories of Mt. Ontake would be one of fresh green foliage. He wondered about the letters that would be waiting for him from Kozo in Kyoto, where the shogun now was. He regretted the fruitless passage of his own springtime in the midst of this universal unease.

"Well, I shall do my best right down here where I am. A headman must be a headman," he corrected himself. With his new experience of the mountain vigil, in which he had disciplined himself by pouring cold water over his body, by extreme fasting, and at times by standing under an icy waterfall, he now set out to apply himself once more to the duties of the head of the Magome post station.

As Hanzo prepared to leave Mt. Ontake, he reflected on his surroundings and found that the influence of the Black Ships had poured deeply even into this remote Kiso valley. Each time they received a new stimulus from Europe, some of those who had been sleeping would awaken and old values would begin to be overthrown. Old weapons were going out of date very rapidly. Old systems were collapsing before one's very eyes. Not only the lower classes and the peasants but even the emperor himself, in spite of his extraordinary powers of discrimination, had come to think no longer of living in peace and order. Although the husk of foreign customs that had confined the nation since the middle ages had not yet been fully shed, it was now necessary to fight against a new incursion of Black Ships. Hanzo reread the words of the master in *The Tranquil Cave* and once more felt awe before the will of the gods.

CHAPTER EIGHT

1

"IT'S ABOUT TIME Hanzo was getting back from Otaki."

Retired though he might be, Kichizaemon was concerned about his son's absence and he would come down from the second floor of the miso shed every morning as soon as he finished breakfast. It was his custom to wear simple, semi-formal trousers even when he was just going out to have a look around, and he leaned on a staff as he moved about in his straw sandals. The right side of his body was still not fully recovered.

It was now more than half a year since Kichizaemon had yielded his responsibilities to Hanzo and retired from the three offices of honjin, toiya, and headman. In the previous year, Bunkyu 2, he had been bedfast from summer into fall and unable to meet the lord of Choshu's retinue when it passed over the Kiso road on its way from Edo to Kyoto. That passage had been delayed for three days at Suwa, during a virulent outbreak of measles that had spread through Edo, Kyoto, Osaka, and the entire nation. Its victims, even after apparent recovery, fell easy prey to other illnesses and the number of dead in all quarters had risen to frightful levels. Since everyone feels a certain sense of relief with the celebration of the new year, Kimbei was not one to remain silent when he learned that there was no other way to ward off the god of illness and disasters. Even though it was the middle of the eighth month, he had the pine and bamboo New Year decorations set up at the gates of each household, celebrating the new year twice in a single year in a ceremony called "correcting the year." This was at the very end of Kichizaemon's long career on the highway. On the twenty-ninth day of that same eighth month he and Kimbei received permission to retire. Since that time Kichizaemon had lived very much to himself. It was now very unusual for him to be concerned about conditions at the post station or to take notice of the news along the highway, or to go around to the toiya in his son's absence.

The shogun Iemochi was still in Kyoto and no one knew when he planned to return to Edo. The fleet of eleven British warships in Yokohama harbor showed no signs of going away. It was a time of many rumors. Kichizaemon's footsteps turned toward the main building of the honjin where his grandchildren were.

*   *   *   *   *   *   *

"Oh! So you're the Nikko emissary!"

Sakichi was playing with the children by the hearth and Oman had come down from the second floor of the miso shed to join Otami. Some members of the household had already finished an early breakfast; others were still eating when Kichizaemon came in.

"No, Masaki, you are not the Nikko emissary," Oman said to her grandson.

"No. You are quiet and you clean your rice bowl so you can't be the Nikko emissary," repeated Sakichi. It was his habit to sit at the edge of the hearth room floor, one leg curled under him, keeping his straw sandals on even while he was eating.

"I am not the Nikko emissary, Sakichi," said Sota, the elder son, and everyone at the hearthside laughed.

Kichizaemon's grandchildren were growing up. Okume was seven, Sota was five, Masaki was two. If it seems puzzling that such young children should be talking about the Nikko emissary, it was because, along this highway, "Nikko emissary" had become a name for troublesome people. The retinue of this emissary came down from Kyoto once each year to harass the porters, wring money out of every lodging house, and bring all kinds of suffering to the people along their route. The farmers along the way compared this personal representative of the emperor to the fearful storms that often struck around the two hundred tenth day of the year. This year's retinue had numbered five hundred, including court nobles and major ecclesiastics, and they had come into Magome behind their gold tassels of state, extorting an "offering" of twenty ryo, while Hanzo was away at Otaki.

Kichizaemon moved from the spacious hearth room to the retiring room. This was where Hanzo, with Seisuke's assistance, carried on the business of the honjin.

"I will leave everything to Hanzo's judgment. I won't say a word about anything."

These had been Kichizaemon's words when he retired and his feelings had not changed since. Nor did he have the slightest intention of intruding now. He was satisfied merely to look around Hanzo's work room.

He looked into the parlor. A pine tree of interesting shape had been brought down from the mountains to replace the one that had burned in the fire, and from the ashes in the garden the tree peony had once again sprouted, displaying its huge white buds. Hanzo was fond of these plants and he had even called his own book of poetry *Pine Boughs* after the tree in the yard. But it was not the garden so much as it was the books piled up in the alcove of the parlor that caught Kichizaemon's eyes—all sorts of things relating to the Motoori and Hirata schools of learning. There were also books by Sato Nobuhiro, from the same province as Hirata Atsutane, who had written on the development of agriculture.

"Look at those books!" Kichizaemon said to himself. "It seems that's where Hanzo's mind really is."

It was still early in the morning. Seisuke, who came over every day to help, had not yet appeared. Kichizaemon went out the front door of the main house, walked through the front garden, and looked out from the main gate. Aside from a few travelers leaving Magome early to go up or down the road, there was hardly anyone on the highway. It was the kind of day when the work of the post station could begin with a clear roadway.

Ever since the shogun had gone to Kyoto, the guarding of the officials and daimyo who passed along this road had become far more vigilant. The Nikko emissary this year was a court noble with only one hundred fifty koku of revenue but he had been guarded by eight musketeers and two mounted warriors. It was even said that he had taken advantage of a heavy rainstorm to leave Kyoto in relative safety. The rumors also had it that one of the mounted warriors was from Mito and the other from the shogunate, but afterward it became known that both had been provided by Owari. This emissary, whose function was to strengthen the bond between the Tokugawa shogunate and the imperial court, was more than a mere failure in the service of court and military; he was a great liability. It was now necessary for the hated Nikko emissary to have the protection of eight musketeers and two mounted warriors when he passed over this highway.

The duties of toiya, which were performed at Hanzo's house during the first half of each month and at Kyudayu's during the second half, were just now the responsibility of Hanzo's household. Kichizaemon went over to the toiya office. Here Kameya Eikichi, who had been newly engaged as a clerk, had come to work early and was putting things in order with the help of the errand boy. Eikichi had succeeded to the household into which Kichizaemon had originally been born. He was a nephew to Kichizaemon and a cousin to Hanzo and he had been engaged by Kichizaemon to assist Hanzo in the duties of the toiya.

"Why, uncle! Aren't you up and about early?"

"I was thinking that it's about time Hanzo should be coming back, and I was just having a look around. You seem to have quite a bit of freight on hand."

"Do you think so? That freight is for Fukushima. The oxen aren't down from Toge yet this morning."

A raised area of the room served as the supervisor's office and Eikichi came over and kneeled, resting his hands on the edge, while Kichizaemon stood in the general freight area and leaned against it from below. They continued their conversation. Kichizaemon, not wanting to have it said that the Aoyama were remiss in their duties, wished he could have a look at the books of the toiya since his retirement, so that he could form some impression of the way Hanzo was performing his duties, but he could not bring himself to ask for them. Instead he listened intently to whatever Eikichi had to say about the business of the toiya.

"Master, why don't you come up here and have some tea. Nobody is here yet," said the caretaker.

Kichizaemon took advantage of the invitation to pass through the gravel-floored main room and sit at the edge of the meeting room. It was called the meeting room because the four elders—the heads of the Fushimiya, the Masudaya, the Horaiya, and the Umeya—would all gather here along with Kyurobei to consult with one another whenever there were problems. Kichizaemon put his stick down at the edge of the floor and sat down to drink his tea. Then he called out to his nephew.

"Eikichi! Could you let me have a look at the ledgers? I want to check something."

Eikichi brought out the ledgers where important things such as the labor from the assisting districts were recorded. Kichizaemon was retired and he was not going to say anything about the operations of the highway. He was satisfied merely to turn the pages of the ledgers and see what Hanzo had written.

"Things are getting bad along the highway, uncle," said Eikichi. "Everyone seems to be relying on brute force. The other day a samurai came to Kyudayu's house and went on a rampage in the toiya because the porters had been delayed. There really are some terrible people in this world. The samurai jumped up onto the floor of the toiya office in his muddy sandals. Now Kyurobei was there and he wouldn't stand for it. They say he shoved the samurai right back down. Of course, that made the samurai even madder and he put his hand to his sword, but big old Kyurobei jumped right down there with him and told him to go ahead and cut away if he thought he was man enough. A daimyo's palanquin happened to be passing by outside and he heard the row. He called the samurai out and calmed him down. It just goes to show, you've really got to be careful these days."

"Now that you mention it, I heard that prominent samurai from various han are being recruited by Kyoto and being promised a stipend of ten thousand koku of rice apiece. Is that true?"

"I've heard that, too."

"It's all because of this reform in alternate attendance. There's just no telling how far that's going to go."

At the end of this conversation, Kichizaemon got to his feet as though he had stayed longer than he had intended. He went out of the toiya through the open shoji to the shaded porch. He gazed thoughtfully at the highway that lay there under the sun of the fourth month. Then he turned back to Eikichi.

"Up to now the daimyo were all heading for Edo on alternate attendance. Now they are going to Kyoto instead. The world has changed."

Kichizaemon was worried over the possibility that Hanzo might go off to Kyoto to join his two friends there. What would they do if the day ever came when Hanzo followed Keizo and Kozo? The ailing Kichizaemon returned to his retirement quarters in a pensive mood. Once he was back, Oman came over from the main house to look in on him.

"This morning the toiya was very quiet. Only Eikichi was there. None of the other officials had come in yet."

Kichizaemon removed his trousers. Then, dressed in his kimono, he continued to pace back and forth in front of the sliding panels that dated from the time of his father's retirement. Only these rooms had survived the fire of a few years earlier, and Kichizaemon took comfort in the firm calligraphy of the large characters that someone had written on the panels.

"It's about time Hanzo was coming home," he said to his wife. "The highway is getting to be quite disorderly. Even Eikichi is worried. It seems that people around town are starting to talk."

"About Hanzo?" said Oman, looking closely into her husband's face.

"I wonder if he is keeping up the honjin records."

"Well, I can tell you about that. The honjin records were lying on the desk here the other day and I just glanced at them without really thinking about it. Right after he took over, Hanzo kept the records in great detail just as you used to, but as time went on there were days when he would only record the weather. 'Clear. Cloudy. Clear. Cloudy.' Sometimes there would be seven or eight days like that."

"I was afraid of that. Well, if he is not good at these things, that's just his nature and nothing can be done about it. But I do wish he had just a bit more business sense."

Placing the old smoking stand between them, this companionable couple sat and talked about their concern for their son's future. Oman puffed on her long bamboo-stemmed pipe with its tiny bowl.

"I've been wanting to say something for quite a while. I just can't stand to hear what they are saying about Hanzo. Even Kimbei seems to be wondering if Hanzo can handle the business of honjin and toiya for Magome."

"Well, I had my doubts about that, too. That's why I brought in Seisuke and Eikichi. Seisuke can help with the duties of honjin and headman and Eikichi can help out with the toiya business. With those two helping, even Hanzo could handle things if these were ordinary times."

"Yes, that's right. Because the foundations are already there for him."

"If you look at his friends, you will see what's on his mind. The son of the Nakatsugawa honjin and the son of the new toiya, the Izumiya—both of them have thrown over their duties and gone off to Kyoto."

"Hanzo is pretty worked up over that. I know that very well. With his two friends off in Kyoto, Hanzo might just leave us one day if he reaches the point where he can't bear it any longer."

"That's just it. Kimbei says that I made a bad mistake in encouraging Hanzo's studies. He says that scholarship is really a terrible thing. But I have always regretted my own lack of learning. I couldn't see anything evil in letting Hanzo study and in letting the Aoyama produce at least one learned headman. That's why I did it. Then he got interested in Hirata sensei. But I let him try it out. When he wanted to join the Hirata school, I didn't say a thing. If he is going to waste his life on scholarship, that's just the way he is and there is nothing I can do about it. The way I see it, the work of a human being is limited to his own generation. We say that we would like to pass on the parent's experience to the child, but no child has ever accepted that experience. I have given this highway my very best, but Hanzo is Hanzo and this is all a new crop in a new field. When you think about it, he was born into a difficult time."

"Well, it does no good to just go on worrying like this. Why don't we call Seisuke and talk it over with him?"

"Let's do that. If only he hasn't run off to Kyoto—that's all I ask. His friends are probably telling him that this is no time to be concerned about family affairs."

From below came the sound of footsteps. Hearing them, Oman looked out.

"Sakichi? Please tell Seisuke that we have made some tea here and we would like him to come up for a talk."

While they waited for Seisuke, Kichizaemon lay down for a rest. Since his illness he had formed the habit of lying down at every opportunity.

"Pillow!" said Kichizaemon.

Scarcely had the alert Oman placed the old-fashioned wooden pillow beneath her husband's head when Seisuke came up the stairs, dressed in Kiso-style work trousers. Once he saw Seisuke, so conscientious in his discharge of honjin duties, Kichizaemon immediately sat up, recovering the strength to begin talking about Hanzo.

"Seisuke, the master and I have just been talking about Hanzo. The master is worried," said Oman.

"Is that it? I was wondering on the way over because the master usually only wants me for a chess partner, but it's too early for that."

Seisuke was in high spirits and he laughed as he rubbed his clean-shaven jaw with its heavy blue shading of beard. While Oman was preparing tea, Kichizaemon turned to Seisuke.

"Please have a cushion."

"No, that's all right. Well, I suppose that every honjin has its people who want to say how the work should be done. I very much appreciate the way you have looked on in silence, but Kimbei is always butting in."

"Is he saying that Hanzo is not doing things right?"

"Let me say this. No one has had anything bad to say about the teacher's household. Virtually everyone in this village who can read and write owes it to Hanzo. But when it comes to the business of the toiya, Kimbei really gets after us. For example, he is always saying that the pack oxen that come into the toiya used to be better cared for, that you used to have the first oxen to come in unloaded first, that you used to entrust the freight payments to those whom you especially trusted, and that we really ought to take better care of the oxen."

"This is the first time I have heard about it."

"And then he is always saying that the post horse keepers of the station should be treated differently than the porters from the assisting districts who lodge here. He says that Hanzo should let the post horse keepers have more in the way of special privileges. I know very well how Hanzo feels about it but I wondered just what Kimbei meant by 'these people who want more privileges,' so I asked him. He's not a bit grateful to the others who come all the way over here from Ina to help at the cost of such effort. Even though many of them make straw articles or practice their arithmetic or their reading during the evenings while they are here, the character of the men coming over from the assisting districts has gotten worse lately, according to Kimbei. They gamble and drink up the wages paid them by the honjin and then make up complaints when they get back home—they say that we work them like horses or oxen and then don't pay them anything, or something like that. All big stories. Kimbei says that Hanzo just doesn't understand this sort of thing. Every time he comes by, he talks about nothing but how much better it was in your time."

"Wait a moment. Does he make it sound as though I played favorites when I was in charge?"

"Please listen to me, master. Hanzo often says that alternate attendance is out of date. He says that when the people of the village hear this, they wonder how they are going to eat if the post station should be abandoned."

"Exactly. Even Hanzo is concerned about that. Who isn't worried about the decline of this highway? But if the travels of the officials were to become more frequent again, then the work would also become very difficult again and men and horses would be exhausted. For better or worse, these are the times that have come. Therefore, I suppose Hanzo feels that things like alternate attendance that are carried on for pure show cannot be expected to continue forever. I think Juheiji in Tsumago agrees with him on that. When you think about it a bit, it's better on any highway the more travel you have. More money will come to the post stations, so the more great processions you have the better. But we're different here than the way they are on the Tokaido. In a place like the Kiso, where you have to conscript so many men and horses, the duties of the toiya become impossible. Most people probably don't know this, but there are precedents for the headmen of the eleven Kiso stations meeting together and sending a petition to the commissioners of transportation to route as many of the great processions as possible over the Tokaido. I'm an old timer and I would like to see alternate attendance continue, but I think there is something to be said for the position of Hanzo and Juheiji."

"You are quite right. But what I see is that Kyudayu and the others are looking toward Edo while Hanzo is looking toward Kyoto. Kyudayu and Hanzo have taken completely opposing positions. None of the older people of the post station think that it would be appropriate for the daimyo to go to Kyoto for their attendance."

"I've gradually begun to realize something while I've been listening to you. Our family has never thought of the office of toiya as a business. It has been the nature of our house, passed down through the generations, to think of the villagers and the farmers here as our children. I am sure that even Hanzo thinks of the offices of honjin and toiya as no more than honorary positions. If you just think of the history of our family, you will understand that. In these mountain post stations, the attitudes of townsmen and farmers are jumbled together. It makes them very difficult to administer in some ways."

"It sounds as though you're really getting worked up," said Oman, laughing softly as she brought in the tea utensils. She placed the tea, perfectly brewed as always even here in the retirement quarters, before Kichizaemon and Seisuke, took a sip of her own tea, and joined in the conversation.

"Well, now," said Oman with a studied casualness. "Didn't Hanzo and Kyudayu have a big set-to over this Shinto burial question? I heard that they haven't had very much good to say about him at Kyudayu's place ever since then."

"That's not true," said Seisuke. "I don't know about Kyudayu, but that's not at all true of Kyurobei. And then, no matter what anyone says, no one but Hanzo would have gone to the mountains to undertake a vigil to pray for his father's recovery."

"Yes, I appreciate that in him. But even that is because there is still something thoroughly childlike in Hanzo. If he doesn't pay a bit more attention to details I really doubt if he can handle this station."

"But master, there just isn't the kind of attention to detail in Hanzo that there is in Kimbei. Every time Kimbei sees the sun shining on the highway, he comes running out with a parasol."

"But isn't Kimbei right? To put Hanzo in charge of the toiya is like putting someone who doesn't know the price of rice in charge of the granary. Kimbei is really sharp."

"Well, Eikichi is here now so you needn't worry about it. Just watch, Hanzo can handle it."

"Seisuke," Kichizaemon interrupted, "as we talk an example has come to me from chess. We're both fond of chess. Now, some pieces advance only one square at a time. Some advance by leaps. Some pieces can leap but they cannot advance by single squares. Others can advance by single squares but leaping is beyond their powers. That's true even of the people who are born along this highway. You hardly ever see anyone who can both leap and move ahead one square at a time.

"Speaking in terms of chess, Kimbei is a pawn that has made it to the back row. A pawn to which that happens is called *narikin*. When that word is used to refer to a human being, it means "newly rich."

"And the 'kin' of *narikin* is the same as the 'kin' of Kimbei? That's good."

Oman laughed too. Then she took up the conversation. "Well, right now Hanzo is sure to be sneezing away somewhere. Hanzo and Otami. Both of them are young yet. Recently I've come to feel that the best thing about being young is that the young do not see ahead."

"That shows you're getting old, too," laughed Kichizaemon.

"That may be," said Oman. Then she changed her tone. "But haven't you left the most important thing for last? Weren't you just saying that what we are really worried about is that Hanzo might follow his friends to Kyoto, and that you wanted Seisuke to watch out for any signs of restlessness?''

"That's right," said Kichizaemon. "I was just going to mention it."

Seisuke nodded.

2

Hanzo, concerned about what might have happened in his absence, hastened back from Otaki with the amulet and the offering rice that he and Katsushige had been given at the priest's lodging. Kichizaemon was delighted to receive them.

On Hanzo's desk in the retiring room was a letter that had come from Kozo during his absence. He had been waiting for this letter and so he opened and read it before anything else. He was not greatly surprised to find that Kozo reported the atmosphere of the capital to be dark, foreboding, and at variance with the expectations with which his friend had left Nakatsu-gawa. Hanzo learned several things from the letter. Kozo was staying with the dyer Isekyu in Fuyamachi, whom Kureta had described as a Hirata disciple and a public-spirited merchant. Kozo had also established, immediately upon arriving in the capital, a close relationship with Shirakawa Sukekuni, a high-ranking Shinto priest who served as a liaison between the court nobles and the activists. Through this connection, Kozo had begun to meet the most ardent activists from Choshu, Higo, Shimabara, and other han. And there was more. Hanzo learned that Morooka Masatane and the other Hirata disciples who had been taken into custody following the exposure of the head of the statue of Ashikaga Takauji in the riverbed at Sanjo had all escaped the death penalty and had been given prison sentences of six years each. Masaka had been placed in the custody of Ueda han. Hanzo also learned that Kozo had been profoundly moved by the deaths of the two Hirata disciples who had fallen when Masatane was resisting arrest at his home in Nijo-Koromo no Tana.

No one else was in the honjin parlor. Hanzo carried Kozo's letter from Kyoto over to the windows and reread it.

"Here's a letter from Keizo," said Otami, handing another envelope to him. Letters from Kyoto were reaching Hanzo in all kinds of ways.

"Otami, who brought this letter?"

"It was sent up from the Yorozuya in Nakatsugawa. They said that Yasu-bei picked it up while he was on business in Kyoto."

Otami gazed at her husband, amazed that he did not seem more exhausted by his vigil on Mt. Ontake. She looked intently at his face. His high, fleshy "honjin" nose and the deep laugh lines and quiet mouth seemed to resemble his father's more and more each day. Then she moved away in her usual busy manner.

"You must be tired, master," said Katsushige, coming to look in on Hanzo.

"Not particularly. How about you?"

"I'm fine. When you think of the trip up, coming back was really easy. I'm going out to help broil some fish. Everybody's out around the hearth getting it ready for you."

"Mountain pepper buds should be ready by now. And it was still plum blossom time at Otaki!"

Katsushige went away, and Hanzo opened the letter that Otami had brought.

Keizo, who had been in Kyoto for some time participating in national affairs and proselytizing for the Hirata school, seemed to Hanzo like an elder brother. In contrast to the letters he received from Kozo, who was about his own age, Keizo's letters were quite businesslike. In this letter he mentioned his pleasure in welcoming Kozo to Kyoto and reported the events of the day of the imperial progress to Iwashimizu, about which there had been many rumors.

Keizo's letter was extremely detailed. There had been a great deal of talk about this progress. According to the rumors, Nakayama Tadamitsu, who had been serving on the board of foreign affairs, had resigned his rank and fled to Choshu, where he had taken up the name of Mori Shinsai and gathered together a band of activists who planned to abduct the emperor during the progress. It was said that the Aizu people who were responsible for security in the capital had been much troubled by this rumor. They had posted a large notice at the approach to the Sanjo bridge saying that while it was impossible to insure against some unfortunate incident occurring during the visit to the Hachiman shrine, just in case there should be some truth to the rumors everyone in Kyoto, samurai and townsman alike, should take special concern for the emperor's safety. It was said that the charred remains of this notice were soon deposited before their offices. Iwashimizu was about eight miles from the center of Kyoto. The emperor himself had reportedly been reluctant to venture out on the day of the journey, but under the encouragement of the court nobles and the lord of Choshu, and because of his deep concern about the future of the nation, he had left Kyoto to offer his prayers. The shogun was ill, and Matsudaira Katamori, the constable of Kyoto, was unable to attend, as he was in mourning, so Yokoyama Tsunenori took his place at the head of the guards that day. According to Keizo, the so-called verbatim transcript that had been widely distributed by couriers from the Urokogataya had not by any means been an accurate account of the happenings of that day. Those notes had told this story:

On the eleventh day of the fourth month, on the occasion of the imperial progress to Iwashimizu, the shogun was ill. When Hitotsubashi Yoshinobu, who was representing the shogun, was presented with a "barbarian expelling" sword, he fled the scene.

It seems that "fled the scene" was a bit of an exaggeration. Keizo wrote that he preferred to believe that Hitotsubashi, too, was suddenly stricken by some kind of illness. Whatever the case, it seemed likely that something would happen that day. This uneasy anticipation of an incident was shared not only by the Kanto people but by those from Kyoto as well, Keizo added. The progress to Iwashimizu was the emperor's first trip outside Kyoto. Since he had never before had an opportunity to observe great mountains and rivers closely, he first stopped to view the flow of the Yodo river. While there he reflected on the situation. Taking personal command of the campaign against the barbarians would be difficult to carry out, he realized. Moreover, the imperial judgment was that the interests of the nation dictated that he not expose the imperial person to unnecessary danger. Keizo's letter even gave an account of the emperor's fatigue on his return journey, and how he stopped for a drink of water at the carriage gate of the Shishinden, the imperial audience hall.

Even though based on hearsay, this report from Hanzo's older friend was well informed. Keizo's close relative in Kyoto was Matsuo Taseko, the Iida woman who was a disciple of Hirata Atsutane. She had drawn close to palace circles through her interest in traditional verse and was well acquainted with many of the female officials. Hanzo assumed that she must be the source of much of Keizo's information. At any rate, to let Hanzo know just what kind of atmosphere prevailed in Kyoto, Keizo included in his letter a copy of the notice that had attracted so much attention when it was posted at the Sanjo bridge just after the imperial progress to Iwashimizu.

TOKUGAWA IEMOCHI:

Although the above-named person has had the opportunity since coming to Kyoto to hear the imperial will directly, he has consistently given only a false, superficial appearance of respect for the imperial command. He has twisted his words in innumerable ways and has gone so far as to deceive the emperor on matters such as the time limit set for driving out the foreigners. Not only has he thought to return to Edo, but on the occasion of the imperial progress to Iwashimizu, he even feigned illness and sent the middle councillor Hitotsubashi in his place, thereby displaying the most extreme contempt for the august person of the emperor. In addition, great numbers of traitorous officials still surround him, including Itakura Suo no Kami and Okabe Suruga no Kami. They, continuing the policies of Ii Kamon no Kami and Ando Tsushima no Kami, are offering bribes and carrying out all kinds of treacherous plots. There are really no words to describe the extent of their insolence. All this is a matter for which the nation would be united in imposing the death penalty. But since Iemochi is still young and since it is said that he has begun to extricate himself from the counsels of these traitorous officials, we will be extraordinarily indulgent and excuse these traitors for the time being. However, the shogun must quickly recognize the nature of their offenses and administer severe punishments to his disloyal retainers. If he should delay, all will suffer the punishment of heaven within ten days.

> 4th month, 17th day, year of the boar
> The righteous samurai of the realm

This astonishing notice—which clearly had been written in the most deadly earnest—had had, so Keizo wrote, the effect of causing the shogun to make public the date on which the foreigners were to be expelled. Keizo now felt that war with England was unavoidable. He himself had always been firmly opposed to the foreigners, and now that things had come to this point he believed that their expulsion was certain to be carried out. "Expulsion of the foreigners" was no longer empty rhetoric. Yet, he also reported that many among those in Kyoto who called themselves "the righteous samurai of the realm" or "the loyal retainers of the empire" or "the loyal and righteous samurai" were beginning to grow weary. At the end of his letter, Keizo added that now that he had experienced life in Kyoto for a while, he had less confidence in speaking of Kyoto affairs.

Even Keizo, who had always tended to understate his own virtues and do nothing to undermine the harmony of the group, had reached this point. Hanzo's imagination raced as he reread Keizo's letter from Kyoto. He saw his friend, even though touched by this impurity, nevertheless advancing, holding high the banner of reverence for the emperor.

"So how about it, Aoyama? We need every last supporter of the imperial cause. Don't you want to leave home now and come join us?"

Hanzo seemed to hear Keizo's voice deep within his ears.

It was very soon after this that regular couriers brought, even into this remote stretch of the highway, an announcement in the form of a verbatim transcript under the name of Iemochi that the foreigners would be expelled as of the tenth day of the coming fifth month.

Hanzo was hard pressed by his duties. One of them involved the petition the regular assisting districts had lodged as a consequence of the reform of the alternate attendance system. Its substance was that, in addition to the twenty-five men and twenty-five horses regularly assigned to each of the post stations, there should be an officially prescribed number of supplementary men and horses. Under this scheme, the regular assisting districts would be called upon when the usual numbers of men and horses could not handle the traffic. In the case of great retinues which even these augmented forces could not handle, the additional assisting districts would be called in. This system had not yet been fully defined along the Kiso road.

From the eleven Kiso post stations—the upper four, the middle three, and the lower four—some four or five representatives had been chosen to go to Edo and explain fully to the officials of the transport commission the conditions in the district since the reforms. They were to make the appeal that those who served from the assisting districts be relieved of all direct taxes, whether in money, in rice, or in labor, and that the conditions under which the farmers were to respond to a call for service should be made clear. Above all, disorder along the highway must be prevented. On these matters the opinions from the eleven post stations were unanimous. They were to state further that since there was little likelihood that anyone other than the regular twenty-five men and twenty-five horses would turn out to move the freight if this petition were not granted, they wished to be given permission to hold over until the next day any freight that could not be moved promptly. The elder Shinshichi of the Horaiya was one of the representatives. Kichizaemon and Kimbei had already retired, Kyudayu was retired, Inosuke was at the Fushimiya, and Kyurobei was at the toiya. Among the other post station officials, the elder Kozaemon had replaced his father Gisuke at the Masudaya, and Gosuke had replaced his father Yojiemon at the Umeya. The only one of the old group still in service was Shinshichi of the Horaiya. He completed his preparations for the trip to Edo and came to Hanzo to obtain his seal.

On the seventh day of the fifth month, the post station officials gathered in the meeting room to discuss the difficulties caused by the long-standing failure to establish a clear-cut category of assisting districts. The problem had become urgent with the recent notice that the lord of Owari, currently entrusted with the defense of Edo, was about to pass over the Kiso road on his way to Kyoto.

"Why is he going to Kyoto?" Hanzo wondered, anticipating the thirteenth of that month when Magome would have to deal with this great entourage. The shogunate had promised to make its response to the British ultimatum concerning the Namamugi incident on the eighth, and the tenth had been announced by Edo and the han as the day on which they would expel the barbarians. As he had seen in the letters from his friends in Kyoto, a clash with England seemed unavoidable.

"Hanzo, what should I tell the people in the other villages?" asked his cousin Eikichi, who had come over from the toiya. "Two thousand porters will be coming from Owari to wait for the lord at Fukushima and Nojiri, so it looks as though there will be no difficulty in moving the freight," he added.

"Well then, we can do it if we call out everyone in the villages."

"I suppose I should tell them to get their work in the fields well in hand before the lord comes through."

"Please do that."

Seisuke, who had joined them, counted off the days before the lord of the Kiso district passed through.

"If it is to be the thirteenth, then we have only six more days."

They had just celebrated the spring festivals and were now harvesting the silkworm cocoons and observing the iris festival. Presently the assistant headman Shosuke and the other representatives from the village had divided up the region among themselves and had rushed off to the nearby valleys and the isolated villages deep in the mountains to tell everyone about the thirteenth.

Rice transplanting was just beginning. When they heard that the lord of Owari was coming through, both men and women went out to the rice fields to try to speed up the work.

The lord of Owari whose passage the people of the Kiso district awaited was named Mochinori. He had succeeded the retired lord, Yoshikatsu, to rule over a domain with a revenue of 619,500 koku. Not only were the Yama-mura of Fukushima under his command, but he also watched over the great forests of the entire Kiso valley.

Since the shogun and his most important advisors, Hitotsubashi Yoshinobu and Matsudaira Katamori, were all in Kyoto, it had been necessary for some-one to remain in Edo. The British had said that they would use the power of the fleet now at anchor in Yokohama harbor to carry out whatever action was necessary if they did not receive a satisfactory answer by the promised date, so the duties assigned to Owari in Edo were grave. The lord of Owari and his older brother, Yoshikatsu of Mito, were responsible for the defense of the city.

But even this description cannot give an adequate understanding of the position of Owari. In Kyoto, Echizen had withdrawn, Satsuma was quiet, and everything seemed to be left to Choshu. Yet there was a complex interac-tion of forces taking place. It would not do to forget that among these powers Aizu, which saw itself as the protector of Kyoto, was on close terms with the court and was beginning to take its place as a rival of Choshu. Even though there was no difference in their commitment to the imperial cause, one had turned its back on the shogunate from an early stage while the other had been especially trusted by the shogunate. Moreover, the two han were allied with different factions of court nobles, the forces at their disposal were different, and the character and outlook of their home regions were different. It was Owari that found itself caught between these two powers, one to the east and one to the west, that seemed to represent opposite extremes in every-thing. There was of course no lack of capable people in Owari. Long before the shogun went to Kyoto, the prominent retainer Naruse Masamitsu had been assisting the retired lord of Owari, who had taken up residence in Kyoto, in carrying out the imperial commands. It was also Owari that was responsible for the security of the Ise and Atsuta shrines and for the shores of Settsu province. One could even say that the retired lord of Owari repre-sented all the han of central Japan in Kyoto.

Unfortunately, the clash between the opinions of the retired lord and those of the present daimyo reflected the clash between Edo and Kyoto. Lord Mochinori did not know that his father's trusted retainer received a special stipend of eight hundred koku. It was also kept secret from him that well-known supporters of the imperial cause such as Tamiya Jo'un were being lavishly supported. The retired lord had opposed Ii Tairo during the Ansei purge and had been placed under house arrest. He had embraced the program of Minamoto Kei, editor of the works known as the *Treasury of Sacred Texts* and the *Classified Chronicles of Japan,* and he was an early supporter of the emperor. Even though his house was one of the three cadet branches of the Tokugawa, the retired lord had not accepted the foreign policy of the shogunate. Around him were men who took a firm anti-foreign position but to the men around his son, the present lord, the idea of "expelling the barbarians" was a mistake. The Kintetsugumi or "league of steel" so prominent in Owari was a group that advocated rejection of the unlawful demands of the British. The lord of Owari, who had been left in charge of Edo and thereby placed in the position of de facto executor of foreign relations, was absolutely opposed to this position. He saw that an ill-advised war might threaten not only the future of the house of Tokugawa but, if it should end badly for Japan, could disgrace the nation before all the countries of the world. He maintained that the welfare of the nation and the people had to be given first consideration.

The reparations demanded for the killing of Richardson were immense. At last, on the advice of the roju Ogasawara Zusho no Kami, and after consulting with Mito Yoshikatsu, who shared responsibility for Edo in the shogun's absence, the lord of Owari paid an indemnity of one hundred thousand pounds to the British, even though it nearly stripped the already depleted shogunal treasury. The lord of Owari then left Edo on the third day of the fifth month to report the settlement to the imperial court. He passed through Itabashi and headed up the Kiso road, planning to reach Kyoto after twenty days of travel. When he reached Sakurazawa at the eastern extremity of the Kiso, he was entering his own domains. The times required that he be heavily guarded, and with escorting warriors, foot soldiers, and immediate attendants his retinue consisted of two thousand men. As the letter of notice had promised, they reached the outskirts of Magome on the thirteenth day of the month.

The rain had let up for the day. As master of the post station, Hanzo went out to meet the procession in the company of Inosuke, Kyurobei, Kozaemon, Gosuke, and the other post station officials, all dressed in hempen jackets and trousers, just as his father had done in his day. Ceremonial heaps of clean sand were in place by the entrance to the honjin. To guard against fire, casks made of basketry lined with heavy paper had been filled with water and placed outside the honjin gate. Before the entrance hall two layers of curtains had been stretched. The steep street of Magome took on a borrowed opulence as lacquered boxes, chests, long-handled parasols, guns and other implements marked with gold hollyhock crests filled the scene. The black tufts of the plumes decorating the eighteen-foot lances and the gleaming metal at their tips all expressed the might of a great han, and lesser officials, dressed in black jackets, rushed to and fro among the company. For a normal passage, a daimyo of over two hundred thousand koku revenue would call for fifteen to twenty horses and around twenty to thirty porters. The common porters who had come to meet this procession numbered two thousand, and they overflowed the station.

The location of the eleven stations of the Kiso was almost exactly half way between Edo and Kyoto. To be precise, the halfway point was near Torii pass and Magome was some thirty-six miles to the west. It may be said that the eleven Kiso stations together made up the middle portion of the road. However, in order to pass out onto the Kanto plain in the east, one had to negotiate four passes: the Torii, the Shiojiri, the Wada, and the Usui, while the Mino plain stretched out before the eye from the western edge of Magome. It goes without saying that news from Kyoto reached Magome several days sooner than news from Edo, and again that news from Edo was known in Magome several days before it reached Kyoto. It was not surprising, then, that people generally wanted to know about conditions further west once they had come to the top of this pass.

The lord of Owari was to stay in Nakatsugawa that day and he passed through Magome with only a brief rest stop.

"Bow down! Bow down!"

The voices clearing the road could be heard resounding from a distance as the procession moved westward from Stonemason slope toward Aramachi. The vast crowd of men and women who had come to see the sight kneeled along the sides of the road.

Hanzo had a very busy time of it. After seeing the lord's retinue to the western edge of town, he worked his way back through the crowd to the honjin. There, from a word let slip by one of the officials seeing to left-over business, Hanzo at last learned the significance of the lord of Owari's trip to Kyoto.

The official had come to report the activities of the daimyo during the rest stop, pay the charges for the special horses and porters, and ask if there had been any inconvenience. Then he left. Hanzo stood for a while, gazing at the disorder around him as the household began cleaning up. He could imagine how Kyoto would be when it heard that the daimyo was coming there. He could well believe that the lord of Owari would meet with fierce opposition from within his own domain, and even as he passed through his own castle city of Nagoya. That he would be able to enter Kyoto, where the opposition would be even more severe, seemed very doubtful. Still less would he be able to obtain his father's endorsement of his action.

The reparations had already been paid to the British. Hanzo sought out Kichizaemon to let him know before anyone else. As always at such times, the farm men and women attached to the household had come to help. Hanzo made his way through them and asked Otami where his father was as soon as he saw her. He asked Seisuke the same question when he saw him.

"Where is father?"

The relationship between father and son at the Magome honjin and the lord of Owari was deep-rooted. Kichizaemon in particular had worked very hard to help the hard-pressed han to raise funds, and he had been given special recognition by the daimyo on three occasions. At first he had been given permission to bear a surname and to wear two swords during his own generation. The second time, this right had been made hereditary in his family. On the third occasion, he had been given the right of audience with the lord of Owari. Therefore, even though he was in retirement, Kichizaemon had put on formal dress to welcome this daimyo to his home. When Hanzo found his father in an inner room of the honjin, Kichizaemon was still in his formal clothing.

"Well, well. Are we going to get by without a war after all?" was Kichizaemon's response when he heard what the official had said.

"But, father, what's going to happen when they find out about this in Kyoto? Some are certain to ask him why he paid the indemnity."

3

"Your jacket collar is straight now. Shouldn't you call in the hairdresser and get everything right on a day like this?"

"It's all right."

"Just a little while ago, someone came over from the Miuraya. He said that six chanters from the Edo puppet theatre were staying at their place and that you ought to come over. He said they are not at all like ordinary traveling performers, as you will realize as soon as you hear them. They will be doing the *Taiheiki* or something of the sort."

"Well, I don't much care one way or the other."

"Did something happen today?"

"I just can't stop thinking. I came in by the hearth to try sitting here a while."

When this conversation between Hanzo and his wife took place, it had been raining continuously for nine days following the lord of Owari's passage and it was still raining. Even before the lord's arrival, the frogs could be heard in the green, newly planted rice fields. For Hanzo, born in the fifth month of Tempo 2, and with no memory of his mother, the mood of these monsoon rains was especially gloomy.

"Otami, it's now thirty-three years since my mother died," he said. As he listened to the dismal sound of the rain, the depression that Hanzo had suffered repeatedly during his youth returned to him.

Otami watched her husband's slightly pallid face.

"You're heaving one sigh after another."

"That's because I'm trying to understand why I was born into such a family."

Hanzo remained by the hearth even after Otami had gone to the other room to look after the children. All alone, he gazed around him. Now that he had taken up the family responsibilities that had been passed down from his distant ancestors, it seemed amazing to him that his father Kichizaemon and his grandfather Hanroku had been able to carry out such difficult and painful duties. What did the honjin have to do? The construction and layout of the buildings and grounds convey the origins of the honjin better than anything else. If one were to say that it was a lodging house for civil and military officials, that would be essentially correct—and so it had to have a broad gate through which palanquins might be borne. It had to have a place where long lances could be racked, and a stable to care for the travelers' horses. It had to have tubs of water for fire fighting and lanterns hung on high poles for the guards at night. And it had to have a rear gate through which the occupants might flee in case of attack. The very name "honjin" signified a military encampment. Although more than two centuries of peace had brought many changes to the military households and to the country as a whole, the forms and the facilities of these establishments that served them on their travels remained much the same. The daimyo processions, carrying with them everything from eating utensils to bedding, continued the customs of the military households of old. Whenever one of them arrived at a post station, curtains would be set up before the entrance hall of the honjin just as if it were a military command post.

Other than daimyo, only court nobles, public officials, and samurai of rank could stay here or stop here to rest. The responsibility of the Aoyama family in its capacity as honjin was to maintain the establishment in readiness for such persons and to rent them rooms, which entailed heavy demands. Before the visitors themselves came, the advance party had to be dealt with. The members of the honjin would put up the notice stating the name of the personage who would be staying there, and they would take charge of the licenses to transport baggage through the barriers. Then, while awaiting the arrival of the high-ranking personages, they would renew the rush covers of the tatami, repaper the sliding screens, and sometimes even repaint the walls. They did not dare forget to supply the appropriate number of folding screens and candles, lamps, braziers, smoking sets, straw sandals, and meals for the dozens of persons in attendance on the official travelers. It was not a calling that could be followed successfully by one who did not genuinely wish to provide thoughtful care for travelers.

What were the duties of the toiya? The toiya that was attached to Hanzo's house was clearly of the same origin as the honjin. For the most part, it had been established to oversee the transport of grain, foodstuffs, weapons, and other items that the military needed. Although the times had changed, it was still necessary to give the closest attention to the forwarding of official baggage and freight being shipped by the various han. Everything had to be entered in the toiya records, not just the baggage that accompanied daimyo and high officials on their travels but the men and horses from the post station, the men and horses from the assisting districts, horses being returned to and from other post stations, horses among those at hand that were for hire to the general public, and the number of horses carrying commercial freight. In addition, every year or so they had to total up the number of men and horses used during that period and this "muster of men and horses" had to pass the inspection of the commissioners of transport. They knew nothing about the toiya on the other highways, nor even for that matter about Kyudayu's family in the same village, but in Hanzo's family where such duties were carried out as part of a hereditary trust, this too was seen as a part of their civic obligations.

In fact, all the duties of the family, except that in which they served as a unit of local self-government as village headmen, consisted of service to the military households. Nevertheless Hanzo, who in his capacity as headman could not involve himself in politics, was determined to ally himself with the imperial party, even though he remained in obscurity. Each time he reflected on his situation, he found it painful and burdensome to be associated with the other honjin and toiya.

From another room came the sound of Katsushige's voice, reciting his Chinese lessons. From time to time there was the laughter of children.

"It's really raining!"
The caretaker from the meeting room came in, closing up his umbrella.

His reverie suddenly ended, Hanzo got up to see what the man's business was. The Osaka guards would soon be passing through and it was necessary for everyone in the post station to begin preparing the necessary men and horses. The caretaker had come to inform him that there was to be a meeting of all the post station officials.

Passing along the highway before the front gate of the honjin were farmers and horse traders leading their Kiso horses back from the Fukushima horse fair. Hanzo, who had just received a retainer of the lord of Sendai, contemplated the relationship between Kyoto and Osaka on the one hand and Edo on the other. This matter was of constant concern to him in his capacity as honjin and toiya. The lord of Sendai's retainer, who had set out on something like the twelfth day of the month, had arrived drenched from the long rains. Possibly in return for the tea and brandy with which Hanzo and his family had entertained him, he had passed the dull, rainy day by talking about Edo during the shogun's absence.

There was a story making the rounds in Edo that the roju Ogasawara Zusho no Kami, who was then in charge of foreign relations, would soon set sail from Yokohama to land in Osaka with a force of some fifteen or sixteen hundred men. It was said that this was for the purpose of defending before the imperial court his decision to pay the indemnity in the Namamugi incident. From the way this Sendai retainer talked, Hanzo sensed that the shogun would be returning to Edo before long. He could imagine that the passage of the Osaka guards which he now awaited was not unrelated to these matters. He also could not avoid the feeling that the confusion and disorder of the Kanto people in Kyoto would soon be manifested in some form along this highway.

At this time there had been no clear reports on what had happened after the lord of Owari had proceeded to Kyoto on his grave mission. It was nine days since they had passed through Magome. According to the schedule, they should just now be entering Kyoto. Hanzo knew that the lord of Owari had reached Nagoya safely, but the reports that the couriers had brought from beyond that point were extremely vague. They said no more than that the present journey to the capital should result in an exchange of views. The Namamugi indemnity had been paid, but there was no indication that the ultimatum demanding that the foreigners leave by the tenth of the fifth month, an ultimatum that was tantamount to a declaration of war, had been either withdrawn or extended. And then there was Ogasawara Zusho no Kami, who opposed the expulsion of the barbarians and seemed about to raise a force to rescue the shogun from Kyoto. The uninformative reports coming out of Nagoya brought uneasiness to Hanzo and to Inosuke, his companion in his labors along the highway.

4

Reports had come in from Shimonoseki in the west of the firing upon an American merchant vessel by Choshu batteries as part of the campaign to expel the barbarians.

REPORT FROM KOKURA

From an Oral Report

On the tenth day of this month a foreign vessel came from the direction of Kyoto and dropped anchor off Cape Kori at Tanoura in Buzen province. A boat sent out to make inquiries learned that it was an American ship on its way from Edo to Nagasaki and that because of extremely bad weather it had come to this anchorage, from which it planned to sail again the next morning. Guard ships were posted around it. However, around the fourth hour of the night, the lord of Choshu dispatched a warship which fired two or three rounds from its cannon at the American ship as it lay at anchor; at the same time four or five rounds seemed to have been fired from the shore batteries in the vicinity. The foreign ship then fired two or three rounds and quickly set sail, proceeding back in the direction of Kyoto. Since the incident occurred at night, we are unable to give details, but we report this as it was observed on the scene.

> In the Service of Ogasawara Sakyo Dayu
> Seki Jurobei

A copy of this report, which had been circulated in Kyoto, was sent to Hanzo by Kozo. The following report was in the same envelope.

Fifth month, eleventh day

A COPY OF THE REPORT FROM SHIMONOSEKI

On the tenth day last a foreign ship dropped anchor at Tanoura. There was instantly great confusion and disorder. Throughout the city, goods were packed and old people, children, and courtesans fled to the countryside while all able-bodied men were called into service. It was reported that several dozen samurai and ronin had boarded the ship but were driven away. From the hour of the rat, several hundred rounds were fired from cannon at the foreign ship, which fired some scores of shots back, but none reached shore. This ship had been on its way down from the direction of Kyoto but when it could not pass through the straits, it turned back on its course and once again headed toward Kyoto. On the scene, some scores of warriors in full armor, with bare spears and wearing battle jackets, were joined by several hundred mounted men who hung lanterns on the eaves of every house in town. It was a scene of great confusion. Then two steamships belonging to Choshu came up firing their cannon. Two rounds were said to have struck. It is not known where the foreign ship fled after that. Calm was at last restored this morning. However, there are rumors that five or six other foreign ships are headed this way. If they try to force the straits, we will turn them back. We will report afterward in greater detail.

This bold action on the part of Choshu, ignoring as it did the stated policies of the shogunate, signified the opening not only of the campaign to expel the foreigners but of a campaign to overthrow the shogunate as well. As the report from Shimonoseki made clear, ronin had taken part in the bombardment of the foreign ship. After Hanzo had read these reports, he took them over to let his neighbor Inosuke read them. To most people the foreign countries were as yet an unknown quantity, but it looked as though the situation was moving toward still greater difficulty.

That was when the Osaka guards came through. It was now close to the end of the fifth month. As soon as Hanzo finished his breakfast, he put on the formal trousers befitting his rank and went to the toiya. There he divided the hundred or so Ina porters who had come over the previous day into two groups and had one group wait in front of Kyurobei's house and the other in front of his own.

"Upper Seinaiji! Lower Senaiji!"

As the name of each village was called, a group of porters would assemble before the gate of the toiya. There Eikichi had the population lists of the villages of the assisting districts spread out before him and he would call out the names of each of the farmers.

"You're from Seinaiji? Isn't there anyone here from Zakoji?" asked Hanzo.

"Master, I am from Zakoji," responded a voice from the crowd.

Seinaiji was where the senior Hirata disciple Hara Nobuyoshi lived. Zakoji was the home of Kitahara Inao, who had assumed principal responsibility for the printing of the thirty-two volumes of Hirata Atsutane's great posthumous work, *Commentaries on Ancient History*. The senior disciples in Ina would certainly know of these farmers who were reporting for work in response to the summons. For this reason Hanzo felt a certain familiarity with them.

"I am very sorry but we are forced to ask you to work as far as Suwara today."

Such was the business of the toiya. In Hanzo's house the toiya was usually closed after the middle of the month, but on days like this it was necessary to open up the office and assist Kyurobei.

It took three days for the Osaka guards to pass through. Around the third day, all the post stations began to run short of men and horses. They were forced to seek out every last man and to press even the brood mares into service to carry out their commitments. After that, the guards of Edo castle passed through in a two-day procession requiring the services of six hundred men at the post stations. On some days the men and horses from the assisting districts reported for work; on other days they did not. When that happened, the cost of hiring men and horses to take their places was frightful. At such a time Hanzo would have to run through the late monsoon downpour to the neighboring Fushimiya.

"Inosuke, please take out two days' worth of expenses for us. We are going to have to pay forty-five ryo in wages."

Hanzo and Inosuke continued to work furiously. After the guards of Edo castle, they had to deal with Matsudaira Hyobushoyu, commander of the Osaka guards, and the lord of Hirado in Hizen on the same day. They had just sent Shinshichi of the Horaiya to Edo with the petition for regularization of the assisting districts, but as yet there had not been time to begin to resolve the confusion and crowding that had come upon the highways after the reform of alternate attendance. When Hanzo heard that the procession of the commander of the Osaka guards, preceded by four musketeers and followed by four more musketeers with fixed bayonets, had arrived before the honjin gate, he rushed back from the toiya to his room. Otami got out his hempen formal wear and helped him into it. Then, as Kichizaemon had done in his time, he went out to the commander's palanquin to offer formal greetings. Just as his father had done, Hanzo took up the slack in the sides of his trousers and, kneeling beside the palanquin, called out his greetings.

"I am Hanzo of this station. Please deign to look upon me."

As soon as he had finished meeting this palanquin, Hanzo had to concern himself with preparations for the lord of Hirado. Thirty of the accompanying soldiers who would be staying the night in Magome had to be sent over to the Mampukuji.

From the tenth day of the sixth month it became necessary to deal with the Kanto people who were beginning to come back from Kyoto. The highway became still busier. It was said that the shogun Iemochi, having already had his audience of leave-taking, during which he had been questioned about the payment of the indemnity and ordered once again to expel the foreigners, had now left from Osaka on board a warship bound for Edo. But at this post station, during the desperate rush to get the radish crop planted, some ten horses presented to the shogun by the emperor arrived in Magome escorted by attendant officials. There were three grooms assigned to each horse.

"Hanzo."

Inosuke pulled on Hanzo's sleeve at dusk on a day of pouring rain. The imperial gift horses and their attendants had just been seen off after extorting one ryo two bu from the post station.

"They all make a lot of trouble but I have never seen such an unpleasant group as that one."

When Hanzo said this, Inosuke replied in a lowered voice, "Hanzo, what do you suppose the groom who came to the Masudaya to rest said? He said, 'What do you mean calling them shogunal horses?' That made Kozaemon shake all over and he asked, 'If it is wrong to call them shogunal horses, what should we call them?' The groom's reply was good. He said, 'Don't call them shogunal horses. Because once you say that, each of these horses is going to need a half-gallon of rice brandy to drink.' "

Hanzo and Inosuke looked at each other.

"Now if that had been all there was to it, it would have been all right. But Kozaemon was slow to respond, and so they led the shogunal horses right up onto the floor of the Masudaya, dirty feet, dirty hooves and all. Isn't that something? They trampled and kicked everything."

"It's an outrage to have the enemies of Kyoto coming to this station and beating up on us," said Hanzo with a sigh.

When fifty chests of the returning shogun's goods began to come down the Kiso road, the station was in even greater difficulty over the transport of freight. The horses that had come through on the tenth had been no more than the first trickle of the great flood of men and goods that was now pouring down the road in an unbroken stream. Hanzo consulted with Eikichi and the elders and then requested permission of Katakura Kojuro, the steward of Sendai on his way back to Edo, to hold up some of his baggage. Three chests and five horseloads of goods were placed by Hanzo into the keeping of the post officials.

The retired Kichizaemon had sunk into silence, but Inosuke's adoptive father Kimbei was not one to remain shut up in retirement at the Upper Fushimiya. With his inborn love of being in the thick of the action, Kimbei came out of the Upper Fushimiya, leaning on his stick, shrugging his shoulders, and casting his eyes about as though he could not bear to witness such confusion.

"You young people have poor memories," he said as he caught Hanzo and Inosuke in front of the toiya. "There's an office in Fukushima. We've called on them to send officials out to help any number of times now. Aren't they there for just such times as these?"

"Shosuke of the Sasaya has already gone to see about it. He went to Fukushima to ask about that and to take care of the rice loan."

This was Hanzo's reply. Shosuke and Inosuke, the one as head of the farmers and the other a village elder, were people on whose strength Hanzo could draw at these times.

Presently an official from Fukushima and his subordinates arrived at the post station. Accompanying them were the post officials from Nojiri and

Midono, who were making preparations to supply men and horses for the returning Kanto officials. In the frightful confusion, the men of the assisting districts in Ina were in no hurry to come out. It was not Magome alone that was finding it difficult to expedite the traffic of freight and men. It was exactly the same in Oi and Nakatsugawa in Mino. Hanzo could think of no better measure than to appeal to the Fukushima officials to permit them to close the station for a time. Every house in this small station at the top of the pass had been taken over as official lodgings and there were no proper places for the Fukushima officials to stay. They were given a night's lodging at Kimbei's retirement quarters.

"Master!"

On the sixth day of constant crisis after they had sent the shogun's chests through, Katsushige came running up to Hanzo. The Fukushima officials had stayed on, setting assignments for the various villages and sending people out to expedite the appearance of the required men and horses, but the Ina districts had still not responded. Baggage bound for Edo together with the men accompanying it had been left stranded in the village. When Hanzo at last heard that about one-third of the delayed freight had been sent on, he breathed a sigh of relief.

"Have you been reviewing your lessons, Katsushige? Of course you can't read your books in all this confusion. It's been a while, I know, since I've been able to give you any attention but such days will not continue much longer."

"No, that's not it. I'm no help at all. But master, I've just seen something very interesting in front of the toiya. Just imagine Eikichi telling a man from one of the parties that no matter how many times they tell him to move freight that can't be moved, it still can't be moved. Then the man stretches out his sleeve and demands something. Finally Eikichi has to drop a Tempo coin into his sleeve."

With an air of having peered in at the shocking world of adults, Katsushige flushed slightly and then continued.

"But, he didn't stop with Eikichi. He went over to Kyurobei's place after that. And Kyurobei had to put a Tempo coin in his sleeve, too. And then what does this man do but draw himself up and say, 'All right, all right. Now I'll overlook your affronts.' I was really amazed."

Around this time there were all kinds of stories told about extortion and forced tipping along the highways. The expression "true hospitality" came out of these times. To be "truly hospitable" meant to be obliging, and whenever the master of an inn or lodging had these words directed to him it always meant that he was required to give a gratuity. Nor did it stop with the townsmen and the farmers along the highways; even the palanquin bearers carrying their samurai customers might be asked to be "truly hospitable," at which time they would have to resign themselves to giving up one bu or one bu two hundred mon. It had reached the point where impoverished samurai or corrupt court nobles could expect to obtain at least a thousand ryo in the course of one round trip between Edo and Kyoto, enough to keep them going for two or three years. Stories of samurai extorting a Tempo coin were no longer in any way unusual.

There was also bribery on top of the forced tipping. In one sense it was not at all surprising that bribery should now be conducted out in the open. Up to now there had been fixed loads for the freight handled by the toiya. Pack-horses carried one hundred sixty-five pounds. A saddle horse doubling as a packhorse carried forty-two pounds, the same weight carried by a porter. An additional load of accessories such as purses, lanterns, raincoats, and bags for rain gear, to the extent of one packhorse load per consignment, was also permitted. To check for violations of these limits, load inspection offices had been established at the three stations of Itabashi, Oiwake, and Seba, manned by shogunal officials or on occasion by the local toiya. These had always been places where it was possible for the officials to get ahead in the world to a certain degree through bribery. But now it was even possible for them to rise to become direct vassals of the Tokugawa. Allotments of freight belonging to the feudal domains that exceeded the weight limits were coming through the Magome toiya in great numbers.

On the twenty-ninth day of the sixth month, the remainder of the shogun's goods passed through and quiet at last returned. The palanquins and litters bearing the hollyhock crests coming up from Kyoto had each been accompanied by forty retainers, and these overnight guests, pouring in ceaselessly from the west so that the lower-ranking samurai had even overflowed the Mampukuji, had all departed for Edo with their guns and chests. The processions of the lesser personages connected with the shogun's movements had come to an end. Now, after seeing how the Kanto people had breathed sighs of relief once they had arrived at the top of Magome pass, one hundred twenty-five miles from Otsu, the people of the post station could begin to appreciate fully the realization that the shogunal party, which had entered the capital confident that it would need to be there only about ten days, had been sorely tried during its long stay. Before going on his way, the steward of Sendai, traveling with his son and heir but hesitant to move until then, had thanked the post station officials for looking after his baggage and had given Hanzo and Inosuke a long account of events in Kyoto.

Even after the beginning of the seventh month, Hanzo could not overcome the fatigue brought on by so many days of overexertion. The two days of summer rain that came just when people were ready to begin picking tea made everyone all the more tired. Going to look in at the hearth room, Hanzo found Eikichi, Seisuke, Katsushige, and even Sakichi gathered there, all looking worn out. The old woman from the nearby stable keeper's house was there too, talking with them. The talk had still not died out about the way the shogunal horses and their attendants had ravaged so freely through the station.

"I was really surprised when those shogunal horses drank a half-gallon of rice brandy each."

"If you called them shogunal horses, they got mad. You had to call them 'august' shogunal horses."

"Anyway, the groom who was doing the talking must have meant 'let us drink it.' "

"There seems to be nothing but unpleasant stories these days. The highway just doesn't amount to much anymore. When you come down to it, there's absolutely nothing we can do about unreasonable samurai. Right away their hands are on their swords and they start pushing you around."

"That's the way I've begun to feel after all this, too. No matter how great the lord in question might be, people are just not going to put up with such behavior from the grooms traveling with the horses. It's unfortunate and all that, but aren't they just losing the trust of the people?"

"The time of the Tokugawa is coming to an end."

This shapeless, desultory conversation reflected the mood of the hearth room. Some, exhausted by the rain, were lying down. The rest were sitting with their legs stretched out in front of them. Hanzo's two sons, Sota and Masaki, were crawling about and walking among them in high spirits.

"Hanzo, I've got some business to talk about. As soon as you get something taken care of and begin to feel good, another post station problem crops up."

Hanzo had gone into the retiring room with his neighbor Inosuke to discuss the plan to ask the head of the Osaka guards to stop travel along the highway until the problem of the shortage of porters from the assisting districts could be solved.

"They say that someone has gone from Suwara representing the eleven Kiso post stations. He's already set off for Osaka."

"Well then, let's send someone from Magome too."

Hanzo called in Eikichi and Seisuke and the four of them set about selecting their messenger.

By now, the resolution of the problems with the assisting districts that had arisen following the reform in alternate attendance had come to be the most urgent business of this post station. The daimyo families, freed from generations of detention in Edo, had all returned home and this made it appear that the control established by Ieyasu was beginning to crumble from within. The failure of the porters from Ina to come during the long session of moving freight the previous month had proved that. Nor would it end there. Hanzo was counting heavily on the results of Horaiya Shinshichi's mission to Edo.

"Now we have a situation where not only are the daimyo in attendance at court but the shogun himself as well," Hanzo thought. "There's no telling these days how much longer the ritual of alternate attendance can be continued, but that is a separate problem from getting the roads back in working order."

In the very hottest part of the seventh month, Hanzo went to the Fukushima offices to see about the assisting districts problem and other village affairs. On his way back from Fukushima he heard a report coming in from the west. In addition to the one hundred thousand pound indemnity for the Namamugi incident, the payment of which had aroused such great resentment throughout the land, the British still demanded that twenty-five thousand pounds be paid to the injured and to the family of the deceased. This was a matter of great concern. The British had taken an unyielding posture and had gone so far as to try to negotiate directly with Satsuma, which had refused to respond. The courier that Hanzo met was carrying the report of the breakdown of these negotiations. He said that nine British warships were now in the harbor at Kagoshima. There had already been a fierce naval and land engagement.

5

DEAR AOYAMA:

I suppose you already know what happened here from the verbatim transcripts compiled by the Urokogataya and the other reports carried by the couriers. The imperial progress into Yamato was first discussed on the thirteenth day of the eighth month of last year. Its purpose was to pray for the expulsion of the barbarians at the tomb of the emperor Jimmu at Kasuga. After a time, with all the talk of a campaign against the foreigners to be led personally by the emperor, it was decided to go on to Ise. I first learned that this was being discussed in the capital when I got hold of the report being put out from Yanagi no Baba, down on Maruta street. That was only seven days ago.

On the night before last, the seventeenth, at the hour of the ox, I heard five or six cannon shots as I lay in bed. I also heard the sound of the muster drum coming from the east. I got up and went to the window, wondering what could be happening. Some Aizu people seemed to be heading for the palace. As I reached the street a detachment of men in fire-fighting gear with rain capes and hats passed directly before me. I did not understand anything at first. Then, from around the seventh hour, activists in the town began to put out sacred lanterns. After that everyone in town began to get up, and while the lanterns were still being hung out, day broke. Yesterday, all the gates to the imperial palace were shut tight. Choshu had taken control of the guard post at Sakai gate and court nobles with the ranks of councillor to the emperor, consultant to the emperor, imperial military counsel, and interior counsel have been prevented from entering the palace. I have learned that among those who went to the palace on the night of the seventeenth were Nakagawa no Miya, Lord Konoe and Lord Nijo, Matsudaira Katamori, the Kyoto constable, and many of the important personages of Satsuma and Aizu. All the daimyo then in Kyoto plus the stewards of Mito, Higo, Kagawa, and Sendai responded to the call and came to the palace in full martial dress. It was a scene beyond description. All movement before the nine gates has been forbidden.

. . . all of Kyoto is now held under virtual martial law by the soldiers of Aizu and Satsuma. The seven court nobles who had been placed under constraint—Sanjo, Nishi-Sanjo, Higashikuse, Mibu, Shijo, Nishikikoji, and Sawa—have all taken shelter in the Hokoji. It is said that tomorrow they will withdraw toward Yamaguchi escorted by more than seven hundred Choshu soldiers.

These events were described in the most recent letter from Kozo in Kyoto.

*   *   *   *   *   *   *

If it should be said that this had now become a naked struggle for power among the ruling classes, that would be true as far as it goes. But many things had led up to this situation in which the Choshu forces and the court nobles supporting an imperial restoration were forced to flee the capital. The anti-shogunal movement to "revere the emperor and expel the barbarians," led by Maki Izumi no Kami, had been given a severe setback. The shogunate had been particularly outraged when Anenokoji Kintomo, consultant to the emperor and one of the most brilliant of all the court nobles, was murdered outside the Sakuhei gate of the imperial palace, having been suspected of secretly counseling the emperor that expulsion of the barbarians could perhaps not be carried out all that readily. The rumor once again began to circulate, as on the occasion of the imperial progress to Iwashimizu, that a band of dissidents led by the former court official Nakayama Tadamitsu was planning to abduct the imperial palanquin on its way to Yamato. Moreover, this rumor appeared after the bloody anti-foreign disturbances had taken the lives of the Gojo steward in Yamato, Suzuki Gennai, and others.

The lord of Echizen, who had long since committed himself to the union of court and military and had even gone so far as to resign his office as chief of politics, could not watch these events in silence. There was also Shimazu Hisamitsu of Satsuma, one of the strongest supporters of a union of court and military. He too had been silent for some time. A fierce engagement with the British fleet had taken place in his home province. Even though the enemy's retreat may have been due to bad weather, the engagement had nevertheless been a standoff. Satsuma had lost a ship and its shore batteries had been destroyed, but at the very least it had made the Europeans realize that the people of this island nation were not to be so easily conquered. At the same time, having done what none of the other han had been able to do, Hisamitsu now found that he and Matsudaira Shungaku, lord of Echizen, had been presented with an opportunity to recoup their political strength. The anti-shogunal forces had retreated from Kyoto and were being replaced by those favoring the union of court and military. Plans for the progress to Yamato were abandoned and an imperial proclamation that the time for expelling the barbarians had not yet come was issued. Intense conflict departed from the political stage, to be replaced by harmony and forbearance.

But it would have been premature to think that the Kyoto situation had been restored to complete calm. In the ninth month, an emissary came rushing over the Kiso road.

"Another special courier!"

Seisuke and Eikichi put their work aside and went outside to see what was happening. The loud cries of the approaching courier could be heard by the people of the post station.

At last, as though it could wait no longer for the coming of the new age, the first signal fire had blazed up in the Yamato area. It took the form of an uprising of the League of Heavenly Chastisement, numbering more than one thousand men. The combined power of Kii, Tsu, Koriyama, and Hikone required more than half a month to suppress it. Even then this incident, flashing like lightning across a dark sky, had left a deep, unnamable foreboding in the hearts of the people. Although there had previously been movements that implicitly advocated the overthrow of the shogunate, there had never before been one that had shown such strength or had publicly taken a position of such direct defiance. To reach the distant pass of Magome, this report had been carried from Osaka to Kyoto by special messenger, a retainer of Naegi han in Mino. In Kyoto a copy was made by Yorozuya Yasubei, who happened to be there on business, and this copy was sent to Inosuke of the Fushimiya. The uprising was called the "Revolt of the Palace Peasants." It was led by the former court official Nakayama Tadamitsu and it marched under a banner bearing a solar disk with clouds on a red field. There were also flags for the various detachments, numbered from one to one hundred. Rumors put the strength of the uprising at more than one thousand at the beginning, and it drew large numbers of new recruits, including samurai from Choshu, Higo, and Arima, according to the reports. An encampment of the shogun's troops had been smashed and Yamato and Kawachi provinces had been thrown into disorder. It was said that the rebels would soon move on Kii province. There were even rumors that Osaka would be attacked. Yet this particular movement to overthrow the shogunate ended in failure, suffering a decisive defeat at a place called Tennokawa. Fujimoto Tesseki was killed in battle and the remnants of the League of Heavenly Chastisement were scattered in all directions.

On the twenty-seventh of the ninth month, officials of the Kiso post station were called to the Yamamura residence in Fukushima. In the guard room, in the company of the elders, the lieutenants, and the clerks, a written statement from the Yamamura was handed down and it was read to them by the secretary. Inosuke of the Fushimiya and Kyurobei of the toiya brought their copy back to Magome.

We hear repeated reports making it apparent that the uprising in the capital region is serious. Since stragglers have fled in various directions, we have been ordered by the roju to be particularly watchful for these people at the barriers. Now, concerning the heir of the Nakayama middle councillor, Tadamitsu has attacked a shogunal camp with several dozen warriors and has done great damage. All provinces are ordered to take him into custody. Moreover, Satsuma and Choshu have attacked the foreign ships and it seems the time is approaching for the expulsion of the foreigners. This is a difficult time with both internal disorder and external enemies. Although the Kiso is a remote district, vigilance cannot be permitted to lapse even for an hour. Since a major highway passes through the Kiso, we solemnly remind the post officials of the present danger. It goes without saying that the honjin, the toiya, the headmen, the elders and the like come for the most part from very old families in the Kiso and they are expected to carry out their duties in time of emergency. In addition, all are permitted to wear swords, and those from old households are ordered to give close attention to the martial arts . . .

Taking this proclamation from Inosuke, Hanzo noted that the supervision of the post stations by the shogunate was becoming more and more strict. At the same time he realized that Hirata disciples must surely be among the stragglers from the uprising.

By this time the followers of Hirata Atsutane had reached more than a thousand in number throughout the country, and among them were more than a few who were unwilling to content themselves with studying ancient history and recruiting new members. These disciples had thrown themselves into the anti-shogunal movements, as witness the demonstration in the river-bed at Sanjo from which Kureta Masaka had come fleeing out of Kyoto. Hanzo could not be certain that there were not others among the people passing through Magome who were stragglers from Yamato disguised in one way or another as they went on to Ina.

"But wait. There must have been Hirata people involved in this uprising," Hanzo thought to himself. "Whether they were wrong or not is not for me to say, but I am moved by the way they were destroyed while trying to stand up for the emperor."

Hanzo tried to hide these thoughts from everyone. Even those few around him who were acquainted with the Motoori and Hirata studies of antiquity still tended to see the disturbance in Yamato and Gojo as nothing more than the "uprising of vagrants" that the Yamamura of Fukushima had described.

The Yamamura, deputies for the Kiso region, had not stopped with a mere warning of present danger in their admonition to the post stations. A grain shortage had now been added to threats of armed conflict. Some villages had enough rice to last out the year but the upper Kiso stations from Agematsu on had to face the prospect of hunger. Each of the stations and each of the villages was ordered to store up rice against further emergencies. Everyone from the ages of sixteen to sixty had to be listed, noting those who were ill or disabled, and specifying their occupations: carpenter, logger, sawyer, and so on. This list was to be forwarded promptly to Fukushima. Supervision had become so strict that the people of the Kiso were even required to list the number of guns held in each of the villages along with the weight of the shot thrown by each gun.

6

The commissioners of transport in Edo had not taken kindly to the petition to regularize the system of assisting districts that the representatives of the eleven Kiso post stations had brought. To show their displeasure, they detained the Magome representative, Shinshichi of the Horaiya, while an official from the commissioners' office was sent out to inspect the freight-handling facilities in every station along the Kiso road.

The autumn rains had already come and gone many times when Juheiji and his assistant Tokuemon came to Magome with this official from Edo. Inosuke was in Fukushima on business, so only Hanzo and Kyurobei went out to meet them. They joined Juheiji and Tokuemon to escort the official on to Ochiai, the next station to the west.

On the way back from Ochiai, Juheiji and Hanzo walked together while Tokuemon and Kyurobei went on ahead. Sakichi, who had come with Hanzo, followed behind. Since they were returning from accompanying a shogunal official, the Magome and Tsumago officials were lightly dressed, having added only trousers and leather-soled sandals to their kimono. Hanzo had taken off his jacket and Sakichi was carrying it on his back, wrapped in a carrying cloth.

"So that makes two of your friends who are in Kyoto, Hanzo?"

"That's right."

"I wonder how they can stay away so long."

"I've been thinking about that, too."

"These are unsettled times we live in. But the people who know how to make money will go on making money."

Hanzo and Juheiji caught up with Tokuemon and Kyurobei just below Stonemason slope. "You know all about this, Kyurobei," said Juheiji. "Aren't the Hida tradesmen coming in and buying up all the four mon coins?"

"Oh, that? Well, the current exchange rate is one ryo for six kan four hundred mon, and they are offering one ryo for four kan four hundred mon. I heard that Kimbei sold six strings of four mon coins."

Kyurobei gestured with his whole body as he spoke. Tokuemon tapped the shoulder of his companion from Tsumago.

"Just think how much six strings of four mon coins comes to, Juheiji. That's more than twenty-seven ryo."

"I was just saying to Hanzo that some people can make money in spite of times like these."

"No, you're wrong. They're making money because of the times."

Everyone was laughing as they climbed Stonemason slope and came into the lower part of town.

Hanzo invited the two men from Tsumago into his house. He wanted to discuss the future of the post stations and highways and to ask how the freight handling was going in Tsumago. As for Juheiji, he had come with the intention of asking that the third child of his sister Otami be brought up in Tsumago. The childless Juheiji was finding life at the Tsumago honjin rather lonely, and Hanzo knew after one glance at his brother-in-law's face what he had in mind.

"Why, Tokuemon! Please come in."

Otami rushed out to the edge of the entry. It was a rare pleasure for her to welcome both her brother and Tokuemon, whom she had known so well in Tsumago.

"Well, now. Father hasn't seen you for a while. Would you like to come up to his room?"

Saying this, Hanzo guided his two guests from Tsumago straight to the rear of the compound. They soon found themselves in the retirement quarters, being asked to "get out of those uncomfortable trousers."

"How has your health been since I last saw you, father?"

"Good, thank you. I keep on getting better and better, so much so that I surprise myself. I'm beginning to feel that it's a waste to be retired like this."

By now it had become apparent that the consequences of the shogunate's abandonment of alternate attendance had not ended with the strengthening of the divisive forces in the various han. Kichizaemon did not put it in so many words, but it was impossible to foretell the ultimate effects of this change in the feudal system. Here on the Kiso road, a major artery of communications, they became more grave and more profound each day.

Presently the conversation turned to the inspection by the Edo official. Compared to Kichizaemon, who had already retired from service, and Tokuemon, who was thinking of doing the same, Hanzo and Juheiji had only slight experience of the highway.

"I had always thought so, but the assisting districts are a big problem," Kichizaemon began. "Now the way an old timer like me looks at it, the relationship between the post stations and the assisting districts was not originally based on money. No one put out contracts for porters and the like. The people from the assisting districts came out of a sense of duty. But what happens now that alternate attendance has ended and the wives and children of the daimyo are free to go home? That has an effect on the people below. They are bound to feel less of a desire to serve."

Although he had ceased to speak out since his retirement, Kichizaemon's deep private concern with the fate of the highway had not diminished. Tokuemon picked up the conversation.

"What you say is, of course, perfectly right, Kichizaemon, and yet it was because they were paid fairly good wages when the daimyo families were going home that they began to be hard to deal with later."

"That is the problem!" said Juheiji.

"Wait a moment! When the people from the assisting districts came to see the toiya, they had their grievances, too. Why couldn't the lodging allowance be divided among everyone? There are two sides to the problem," said Kichizaemon.

"But Kichizaemon," said Tokuemon. "Prices have gone up with each party that comes through. Now even the post horse keepers have begun to ask us for additional money. It gets to be more than the toiya can handle. Then the people from the assisting districts begin to think that the post horse keepers live on the highways and feed their wives and children doing that work while those who come to help are in no way dependent on the work for their livelihoods. And then, if you permit one village to have a rest because of excess work calls and don't do it for another village, they begin to say you are playing favorites. There is a difference, too, between the old and the new assisting districts in the way they feel about their duty to come out. You can talk about the general problem of assisting district porters not appearing for duty, but when you dig into it all kinds of things come up, depending on the village. Just look, even for toiya, there is no way of knowing just how much they differ from one place to the next."

At this point, Hanzo asked Oman to call Seisuke over from the main house to bring the petition he had received from the villagers. He laid it out before everyone. It said that prices were rising steadily and life was becoming difficult for those who worked as porters or supplied horses. They therefore requested that the wages to be paid to the post horse keepers, the porters, and the couriers all be raised. The petition asked that the rates be fixed at six ryo for a post horse, one ryo two bu for a porter. For a courier the summer rates would be one ryo two bu, and winter rates one ryo three bu.

"That's just how the trouble starts," said Tokuemon. "If the post horse keepers here in the villages ask for increases, the assisting districts will not look on quietly."

"What do you think, Hanzo?" asked Juheiji.

"Well," replied Hanzo, "I do want to see regular assisting districts established. It would have to be better than it is now. But to me, it seems that the real hope lies elsewhere."

"Tell us about it."

"You'll all just laugh at me for being a dreamer."

"No, we won't."

"Well, I will say that I would like to see a change in the system which requires the post horse keepers of the post stations to move all men and freight of the emissaries with shogunal tea caddies, or Nikko emissaries, or other special cases with papers stamped with the red seal. It's not being forced to carry out such duties that makes them so difficult to deal with. It's that they start to move the things that they want to handle and push the rest off on the assisting districts. My idea would be to abolish the distinction between the post horse keepers and the assisting districts. I want everyone to be considered 'from the assisting districts.' "

"All the people would be from the assisting districts, eh? Well, that's something that is still a very long way off."

"But Juheiji, think of what will happen if we go on this way."

"If you put it that way, I suppose I have to agree. I don't know about the old days but there was a major change in the assisting districts after the retinue of Princess Kazu went through and another major change after the reform of alternate attendance."

Tokuemon returned to Tsumago ahead of Juheiji to await word of the results of the petition sent to Edo by the eleven Kiso stations.

"I'm happy to have been able to see Kichizaemon today. At Tsumago the harvest is over and everyone is taking a breather," he said to Otami when he left.

Hanzo saw Tokuemon out and then set out cushions in the parlor of the main house. There he waited for Juheiji to come down from Kichizaemon's quarters.

"It looks as though Juheiji is being held up. When father gets hold of someone, he doesn't let go."

As Hanzo was saying this to Otami, Okume came back with her youngest brother, Masaki. They had been gathering chestnuts around the Inari shrine at the rear of the compound. Masaki was still very young and he did not know that he was to be adopted by the Tsumago honjin.

"Hey! Are you going to be a Tsumago kid?" asked Sota, rushing in and beginning to tease his little brother.

"Sota! That is not what a big brother should be saying," Otami scolded. "After all, isn't Tsumago where your mother was born?"

A scuffle between older and younger brother began. Masaki was just learning to talk but he was very stubborn and would not let his older brother get the better of him even in childish play.

"Well, tonight let's give Masaki and his brother a big feed of fresh buckwheat noodles to enjoy. And then hadn't we better send some along with him, as mother says?"

"You mean as a gift to the people at Tsumago? Wouldn't a fan and some dried bonito do?"

The two continued to talk while watching their children laugh and play together. Otami had no thought of refusing the request from Tsumago, but all the same she found it difficult to part with the young one.

"Master, please come here!"

The frightened call came from the front entrance and Katsushige, a look of terror on his young face, came running into the parlor. Realizing that it was another of the quarrels that were happening so frequently along the road, Hanzo called for his trousers and donned them, hurriedly tying the cords.

"Stop it, I say!"

He emerged from the honjin shouting. Over where the baggage was stacked before the toiya, a traveler, apparently a retainer of some daimyo or other, had hold of Eikichi and was pouring abuse on him. Hanzo quickly saw what was happening. He ran over and stood before the samurai, who was brandishing a wooden sword. The reek of sake from the samurai's breath filled Hanzo's nostrils.

"Hey there! You're too damned slow with the porters!" the samurai shouted, glowering over at Eikichi out of the corner of his eye. He then turned back to Eikichi, threatening to beat him with the wooden practice sword. Hanzo threw himself into the confrontation, sheltering his cousin with his own body.

"I am the toiya of this station. I am the one to beat if you have a problem."

Hearing the disturbance, Seisuke came running from the back of the honjin and Kyurobei rushed down the street from his house. When he caught sight of the huge frame of that same Kyurobei who had once thrown an unruly samurai down from the floor of the toiya, the traveler quietly put his sword down.

"Hanzo, you've got guests at the honjin. Leave this to me. Please."

Hanzo left Kyurobei in charge and went back to the honjin, but the stench of the stale sake that the drunken samurai had breathed on him seemed to cling to his clothing and body. He stood for a while by the camellia tree in the corner of the garden just inside the gate.

Returning to the parlor, Hanzo looked in and discovered Juheiji reading one of the books that had been lying on his desk.

"Hanzo! Was something wrong?"

"No, nothing important."

"Wasn't someone being pretty rough out at the toiya?"

"Oh, he was saying that the porters were too slow. These samurai who won't listen to explanations are enough to make a toiya weep."

"Everybody seems to be trying to muscle his way through these days. It seems that we have come into a time when everything is settled by force."

"Juheiji, what do you think Katsushige said the other day? He said, 'The time of the Tokugawa is coming to an end.' I was really startled to hear that! Really—that young fellow said that!"

Their conversation broke off as the children came in.

"Well, Masaki," said Juheiji, calling the child to his side, "are you going to Tsumago with uncle?"

"I'll go."

"I'm glad you're going," said Hanzo with a laugh.

"How about it, shall I give you a hug?"

As Juheiji embraced Masaki, Sota ran over to be hugged too.

"Me too, uncle!" cried Okume and she would not leave his side until she had received the same treatment.

"Oh, you're heavy!" said Juheiji in a strained voice as he picked up the little girl from behind and laid her down on the matting.

"Okume looks as though she is going to be a fine girl," Juheiji said to Hanzo. "She resembles her grandmother but she's a little different somehow. You two are really lucky to have a daughter like this. Our family is just not blessed."

Hanzo turned to the children.

"All of you go to your grandmother! They're making buckwheat noodles in the kitchen, so go and watch!"

The sunlight gradually dimmed on the shoji of the parlor, which faced to the southeast. Oman had planned a simple send-off for the child who was to go to Tsumago the next day, and she had invited Kichizaemon's old friend Kimbei to join them for some fresh buckwheat noodles. There was still a little time before the evening meal. In the stillness, Hanzo and Juheiji sat facing each other. Their earlier conversation with Kichizaemon in his quarters came up again.

"I've got something to show you, Juheiji."

Hanzo took four books out of the closet and brought them over.

"These are one of my accomplishments," he said as he set them before Juheiji. They were the second volume of the *Commentaries on Ancient History*.

The books were new, just back from Edo where the blocks had been cut, the pages printed, and the books made up.

"Oh, they've turned out to be fine looking books," said Juheiji, taking them up and inspecting them closely. "Everybody's name is here on the title page. Maejima Shosuke. Katagiri Shun'ichi. Iwasaki Nagayo. Kitahara Nobutada. Hara Nobuyoshi—oh? It says that Miyagawa Kansai of Nakatsugawa is one of the sponsors."

"What do you think? Aren't the blocks clean-cut and easy to read?"

"They really look like something special."

"The first volume was put out at the expense of the Ina disciples and the next one was sponsored by the disciples from Kai province. I have consulted with my father and I will be helping with the expenses for printing each of them."

"Hanzo, aren't Hirata sensei's works being very widely read these days? It's good for you to be doing this. The only thing that worries me is that you believe in people too much. You believe in everything too much."

"I understand what you mean. But still, isn't strong faith the best thing about the Hirata school?"

" 'To put faith above all else,' you mean?"

"If you take that spirit out of context that way, you are misunderstanding the study of antiquity as practiced by the Motoori and Hirata schools."

"That may be, but—how should I put it? You seem to believe too much—in your master and in your friends."

". . ."

"You've got to be careful about that."

". . ."

"By the way, Hanzo, how are Kozo and Keizo doing down in Kyoto? I'm amazed that they can leave their families in Nakatsugawa for so long."

"I've been wondering, too."

"I think you have been wanting to go to Kyoto to see for yourself."

"Well, these days I often have dreams about my friends in Kyoto. When I think of those dreams I suppose I am already halfway in Kyoto."

"Your father is worried about that. When I was alone with him just now, he talked about it a lot. Now I don't keep quiet about things the way your father does. I came down from his room thinking that I could at least say this much just between the two of us."

"If it weren't for father, I would already have left home—"

The maid came to announce the evening meal, so the two dropped this topic of conversation. When Hanzo conducted Juheiji into the retiring room, he found that Kichizaemon had come down from his quarters and Kimbei had come over.

"Just look, Juheiji, Kimbei is sixty-six this year! He's two years older than I am and see how healthy he is!"

"For that matter, Kichizaemon, isn't it you who talks about nothing but food whenever I see you these days?"

Surrounded by happy laughter, Hanzo sat down at a dinner tray next to

Juheiji. The sake had been sent over from the Fushimiya. The mountain-style handmade noodles were seasoned with green onions and red pepper. There were plates of small birds, mushrooms with grated radish, pickled vegetables, red radishes, and Oman's specialty, dried sweet potato vines dressed in plum-flavored vinegar.

The next morning, after spending the night at Magome, Juheiji asked, "What should I do about formally adopting Masaki?"

"Wouldn't it be best to leave that until later?" replied Hanzo. "For now, why don't you just take him along and see how it works out without saying anything at the temple?"

Oman and Otami came in and Oman said to Juheiji, "Masaki will eat anything now. He is so fond of things like pickled turnip greens that we don't know what to do. I'm sure your mother over in Tsumago knows this, but you mustn't dress him too warmly. As the old saying goes, 'A child is to be brought up in cold and hunger.' "

"Brother, Masaki doesn't know anybody over there, so I am sending Otake along with him for the time being."

Otake was the woman who had looked after Masaki. After the custom of this family, Okume and Sota too had each had a person in charge of their care.

A manservant came over from Tsumago. The day had come for the departure of the young boy from the hearthside at Magome. Otami said that she would accompany them along the back roads to the top of the pass and she began getting Okume and Sota ready to go out. On a day like this, Seisuke was, of course, not one to remain a silent observer.

"Now, Masaki, come here!" he said. He was so short that the child easily climbed up on his back.

Kichizaemon, Oman, Eikichi, and Katsushige, as well as Sakichi and the two maids, gathered outside the gate with Hanzo. It was a small village and everyone in the neighborhood already knew of the imminent departure of the child. From the Umeya across the road, from the toiya above it, from the Fushimiya across from the toiya, people had come out to see the party off.

Hanzo stood before his father and stepmother and said, "It will be good to know that he is being brought up at Juheiji's house. Masaki is fortunate."

Presently Juheiji and his party set out for Tsumago. Hanzo did not go directly back in to the house. He went straight down the road, around the corner of Stonemason slope, and followed a further series of slopes down to Aramachi. The village Shinto shrine, a branch of the Suwa shrine, was located there but after completing his call at the shrine of the tutelary deity, Hanzo still did not feel like returning home. Here at the lower edge of the station was where Kitsune Ointment and such things were sold. Huge black boulders lay alongside the road and a view of the Mino basin opened out below. Snow had already come once to the Ena range and melted away again. As he came to a place where he could look up at those vast slopes, Hanzo felt the urge to cry out at the top of his lungs.

What Juheiji had said before he left would not leave Hanzo's mind. Unlike

Juheiji, who treated most outside concerns as nonsense and went on with his solitary archery practice, Hanzo was unable to crave the security of everyday life. The night of the *koshin* vigil was fast approaching. After that would come five long cold months of the mountain winter with winds that would tear at the shingles on the roofs even though they were weighted down with stones—the feeling that winter was coming to let people sleep, mingled with his feelings of helplessness about his life, his need to get away, and the impossibility of doing so, seemed to cover him over and bear him down.

However, the farther he walked the more he felt like a happy child. He went on down the highway to Shinjaya at the edge of the village. There was the Basho tablet that Kimbei had put up alongside the road for Kiso travelers in memory of his late father. In the end Hanzo walked as far as the peaceful elm tree at the milestone marking the boundary between Shinano and Mino. He stood there, gazing out over the evergreen forests.

CHAPTER NINE

1

IT WAS 1864. The sixth month of Genji 1 had come to the teeming neighborhoods of Edo. From Itabashi, the entrance to Edo when traveling by way of the Kiso road, past the palanquin station in Sugamo, through the post station in Hongo, and finally to Ryogoku, three village headmen came from the Kiso, to remove their straw sandals at the Juichiya. Hanzo was one of them.

They had been summoned by the transport commission in Edo to represent the eleven post stations of the Kiso. The headman of Niekawa had come for the upper four Kiso stations, the headman of Fukushima for the middle three, and Hanzo of Magome represented the lower four stations.

Hanzo had set out from home in the middle of the fifth month; he had not expected to have an opportunity to see Edo a second time. He was already familiar with the Juichiya in Ryogoku and the other headmen, Kohei from Fukushima and Heisuke from Niekawa, found it convenient to stay at the same inn. The retired master of the Juichiya, a Kiso man who was fond of looking after people, was still there.

"Time has passed quickly. It must be nearly ten years."

The old man came to Hanzo and greeted him after the manner of an innkeeper. He had not forgotten the guests from the Kiso who had stayed at his inn almost a decade earlier. He even remembered that on the previous occasion Hanzo had been on his way to Yokosuka and had been traveling with Juheiji, the honjin of Tsumago.

"Juichiya, when we came before, the port of Yokohama had not been opened yet."

"That's right, that's right!" the old man recalled. "And after that, Miyagawa Kansai stayed here. Yes, and with him were Yorozuya from Nakatsugawa and one of his people. That was the year that the Yokohama trade began. I introduced them to the Botan'ya in Kanagawa. I'm grateful that you continue to favor us each time you come to Edo."

The old man had visibly aged but he was still in the same vigorous health as before. Although his wife was young, one soon realized one's mistake if one regarded them as father and daughter. Still, there seemed to be too great a difference in their ages for them to be husband and wife. That had been

Hanzo's earlier impression, but now he found the young wife carrying the child of the old man in her arms.

Everything Hanzo saw and heard brought back memories of his previous trip. It had been in the third year of Ansei, 1856, that Hanzo had decided to become a disciple of Hirata Atsutane. He had come to Edo and met Hirata Kanetane and his son, Nobutane, for the first time. That was when the first talk of the opening of foreign trade was being heard in Edo castle, and the news that the first British ship had entered Nagasaki harbor had brought a thrill of excitement to Hanzo. No matter what happened, it seemed, the power of the Tokugawa shogunate still held the entire nation firmly under its sway.

How had nearly ten years changed Hanzo's surroundings? How had it changed the highway down which he had just walked? When Hanzo set out this time, responding to the summons of the commissioners of transport, he found that once past the Kiso barrier, which controlled travel in the Kiso, there was great confusion. Perhaps because the shogunate had been alarmed by frequent reports of violence, the control of the post stations had become extremely severe. Notices had been sent from the officials to all the post stations that solitary travelers as a matter of course, but suspicious ronin as well were not to be given lodging, and unnecessary travel by haikai masters or masters of flower arranging would not be tolerated. Hanzo had been ordered to report immediately every suspicious person he saw along the highway. But that was only the beginning. Anyone creating a disturbance was to be detained in the village. If that person should prove difficult to handle, no official action would be forthcoming if he were cut down or shot.

On the way to Edo, Hanzo had stopped with his two companions to visit the hospitable Fumidayu in Oiwake. In his district an overseers' function had been established and watches of seven villagers at a time guarded the Mikage camp. Things were so disorderly that people were taking their own measures to protect themselves from armed robbers and brawlers. At the camp there was a new stockade with a perimeter of some seven hundred feet. Hanzo and his companions were told that bells, drums, and sounding boards had been issued as alarm signals in each village and that guns, bamboo lances, clothing tanglers, clubs, and torches were being kept close at hand. Anyone in the village who took to wearing a long sword or secretly harbored undesirables was severely dealt with. They were also told that on the fifth day of each month, the people of the surrounding villages were mustered in the stockade. Seventy-four villages in northern and southern Saku counties had joined in this arrangement, giving them an idea of how far people had been tried by the difficulty of the times. Some men had become drifters, wearing swords like ronin and terrorizing this stretch of the highway. Oiwake and Karuizawa were especially disorderly and it was there that one was most likely to meet up with people carrying long swords. At least the Kiso had not yet been driven to the extremity of forming local self-defense groups. They had not yet reached the point where the farmers could not work safely in their fields without such protection. Even Hanzo's companions, headmen who had frequently gone to Edo, said that this was the first time they had seen the road so dangerous. It had become two hundred miles of highway over which one could not pass without taking the greatest care, or without traveling companions for mutual protection.

The immediate business that had brought the three headmen to Edo was to report as representatives of the eleven Kiso stations at the official residence of Tsuzuki Suruga no Kami, one of the current commissioners of transport, and to present the ledgers of each of the eleven stations showing all the transactions involving men and horses.

These ledgers showed the total sums paid out for the hire of men and horses during the previous year. On the first day that Hanzo and his companions went to the commissioner's residence, a police inspector came out to receive them. After informing them that he would report to the commissioner all that passed between them, he told them the reason the commissioner had summoned them at this particular time. The present shogunal council intended to restore alternate attendance. According to the police inspector, the commissioner would summon them again and would take measures at that time to correct the current problem regarding men and horses in transport in the Kiso. Then they were dismissed. Kohei and Heisuke were both far senior to Hanzo, headmen with deep experience of the highway, but when they returned to the Juichiya the three talked freely with each other about the changes they had witnessed along the highway and future courses of action.

The change in the alternate attendance system had had a profound effect in Edo. After the departure of the families of the greater and lesser lords, certain neighborhoods in this city popularly said to be made up of six parts military and four parts townsmen were like shores from which the tide had retreated.

Looking around Edo for the second time, Hanzo found that there was no longer an Edo castle. The main keep and western enclosure had been destroyed in the great fire of the fifteenth day of the eleventh month of the previous year, and the shogun's family was said to be living in the adjoining Tayasu palace. Only the western enclosure was being rebuilt, and even that was straining the shogunal treasury to the limit. The shogunate was collecting donations of one hundred ryo here and two hundred ryo there from townspeople and farmers throughout the country. Yet, as Hanzo knew all too well from the orders that were coming into even such remote places as the Kiso, tiny contributions of one or two shu were entered into the shogunate's calculations. Just the restoration of the western enclosure had reduced it to these measures. Prospects for the restoration of the main keep were therefore extremely doubtful. The mighty castle that had towered in the morning and evening sunlight over the "eight hundred and eight neighborhoods" of Edo, dominating them completely with its peculiar windows and its high, white walls rising above groves of pine trees, had now lost the greater part of its beauty. Edo was in fact a great castle town, with the dwellings of the greater and lesser military families, the first, second, and third class com-

pounds, the minor compounds, and the barracks of the castle guards all centered on the great castle. The recent change in alternate attendance, however,
had reduced this feudal city to a state of something like suspended animation.
When the daimyo were permitted to return to their provinces, most of their
families left their Edo compounds. The condition of the Edo financial world
after this sudden exodus of consumers was beyond description.

The elimination of alternate attendance was a consequence of the reforms
that had been carried out in the Bunkyu era. It had earlier been considered by
the daimyo and their officials who had noted the trend of the times and had
decided to adopt a position favoring shogunal reforms. When their voice
became the majority, asserting that it was essential to bring some enlightenment into political life and to let fresh air into the politics of the nation, many
of the shogunal functions that properly belonged to Kyoto were eliminated,
including the posting of the guards at the nine gates of the imperial palace.
As the most important of these measures to curtail empty display, the shogunate unhesitatingly sacrificed alternate attendance. Matsudaira Shungaku of
Echizen had been the first to propose abandoning the policy that was so crucial to Tokugawa rule, and many had opposed him. But Hitotsubashi
Yoshinobu accepted the lord of Echizen's position and, sweeping aside the
opposition, had embarked on this broad plan of reform. To attempt the restoration of alternate attendance now would amount to a direct affront to
Yoshinobu, who was serving in Kyoto in the important posts of lord protector of Kyoto and commander of naval defenses. The bitter struggle between
the houses of Kii and Hitotsubashi that had flared up long before over the
shogunal succession was making itself felt once more.

Moreover, the center of political life had left Edo and was shifting to
Kyoto. Even to those like Hanzo who viewed these events from below, it
seemed unlikely that shogunal officials who still clung to the past glories of
Edo would be able to revive a policy once discarded and reverse the deteriora-
tion of the shogunate. It was even more doubtful that the daimyo, now
residing in their own domains to reduce unnecessary expenditures, build up
their military strength, and protect the nation's coasts, would obey an order
from the shogunate to come to Edo once again.

The families of the daimyo had been set free from their Edo compounds
shortly after Hanzo had taken over from Kichizaemon as head of the post station. He could not forget how hard pressed the Magome station had been to
meet the women of Echizen and send them off again, or the young heir and
wife of the lord of Owari, and the wife of the lord of Kii and her ladies-in-
waiting. Groups of women and children were coming down the highway
almost every day. One day the daughter of the lord of Akita arrived at the top
of the pass; the next day the ladies of Shimabara han in Hizen came through.
These people, until recently virtual hostages in their Edo compounds, passed
through with cries of joy, like prisoners freed from their chains. It was very
unlikely indeed that any of these retired elders or women, children,
and ladies-in-waiting would be willing to go back and try to restore life
to Edo.

Hanzo and his fellow headmen waited for several days for their summons to appear before the commissioners. In the meantime they went out each day to walk around the city, each in his own direction. Then they would return to the Juichiya to tell each other about what they had seen and heard. Kohei reported that he had called at the Edo residence of the Yamamura family of Fukushima, located in Higashi Katamachi, and had found it nearly deserted. Heisuke had made a duty call at the residence of the lord of Owari, master of the Kiso, and he reported seeing "For Rent" signs everywhere he went. Hanzo told them that at the approaches to the bridge in Yoshicho, then reputed to be the liveliest spot in Edo, the sake shop famous for its potato stew had been extremely crowded and that several hundred men looking for jobs were standing around in front of the big employment agency just across the street.

Each time the old man at the Juichiya welcomed Hanzo and the others back to his inn, he would give them the same advice.

"When you go out into the town, please be sure to get back here before dark. It's best to be out as little as possible at night."

At last the day came that the notice from the transport commissioners had named as the one on which the three headmen were to appear. On the second floor of the Juichiya, they changed out of their travel clothes into the formal clothing they had brought with them.

"Well, now we go before the commissioners," said Heisuke of Niekawa as he pulled at Hanzo's sleeve, a concerned look on his face. "We have to be careful what we say today. You are still young and I am afraid you might say something."

"Me? You know I'm not naturally very talkative and I won't be saying anything uncalled for today."

Then Kohei of Fukushima spoke half in jest as he tied up his formal headman's clothing.

"They say that you're a Hirata disciple, Hanzo, so you might be in for some special attention."

"No," said Hanzo, "everybody back home said things like that to me when I left. But they're not going to call in someone as a representative of the eleven Kiso post stations and then arrest him and throw him in prison."

Kohei and Heisuke both laughed. All three were ready. They left immediately.

The offices of Tsuzuki Suruga no Kami, commissioner of transport, were just on the outer side of the Kanda bridge. They were met there by the same police inspector as before and presently they were brought into a large chamber consisting of two contiguous rooms. It was early summer and all the sliding panels between the rooms and along the outside edges of the building had been taken away. Directly before them were seated the commissioners, and to the side were the subordinate transport officials. Police inspectors were coming and going among them. Then Jimbo Sado no Kami, newly appointed to the transport commission, entered and took his seat.

From the Owari Domains:

The station of Niekawa on the Tosando, representing the outer eleven stations.

In charge of the associated stations, to wit:

The headman of Niekawa station
  Toyama Heisuke

The headman of Fukushima station
  Tsutsumi Kohei

The headman, honjin, and toiya of Magome station
  Aoyama Hanzo.

The police inspector formally read out their names and titles to the commissioners. First Heisuke, then Kohei, and then Hanzo each kneeled in turn, laid his fan before him, and as his name was read, placed both hands on the floor and bowed.

Tsuzuki Suruga no Kami had formerly been a commissioner of finance while Jimbo Sado no Kami had been a censor before coming to his present post. They did not flaunt their rank as their subordinates did. Insofar as it did not threaten their dignity as commissioners they spoke informally, even laughing from time to time. As the three headmen had perhaps already heard from the police inspector, there was a desire in the shogunate to restore alternate attendance, which had now been suspended for two years. The commissioners had heard that the post stations had suffered grievously on the occasion of the shogun's visit to Kyoto. Since they had also heard that the daimyo found it particularly difficult to pass through the Kiso, they had called the headmen in for consultation. They asked them to relate the facts concerning transport in the Kiso without holding anything back.

The police inspector had ordered Heisuke not to dwell too much on detail in that day's meeting, but he nevertheless spoke of the effect of the greatly increased use of the highways by the daimyo after the coming of the Black Ships.

Heisuke described how the calls for men and horses had increased since the progress of Princess Kazu to Edo and the return to their provinces of the families of the daimyo. He explained exactly how the physical exhaustion of the post station personnel, the difficulties in augmenting the regularly assigned numbers of men and horses, and the failure of the assisting districts and reserve villages to send additional men and horses had all resulted from the excessive demands made on the available men and horses in the area.

"I speak with the greatest hesitation. From the third month through the seventh month of last year, the shogun's visit to Kyoto gave rise to a great flood of daimyo and officials passing through on the Kiso highway. There were delays in transport occurring almost daily. We were deeply concerned and we sent a petition from the eleven Kiso post stations to your office asking for the establishment of additional assisting districts. We sent four headmen and one elder—five people in all as representatives. They did not receive permission to establish fixed assisting districts. They returned to their villages with an order to make do with the present assisting districts between the second month and the eighth month of this year. Now there is little time remaining in that period and if your excellencies do not see fit to give particular attention to our area, it will be very unlikely that transport can be restored to its former state."

"We had expected you to say something like this and so we have the matter under consideration at this moment," said Tsuzuki Suruga.

Then Kohei presented the argument that the time had come for a reform in the organization of the assisting districts in the Kiso. He stated that in addition to the business of the shogunate and of the han which had hitherto made up the service of the post station, there had been a great increase in the number of people serving those who were traveling on unofficial or personal business. These included the commercial packhorsemen of Ina and the ox drovers and packhorsemen of the Kiso. Of course even on the Kiso there were some who made use of means other than the oxen which had hitherto been the sole transport for unofficial travelers and freight, but the commercial packhorsemen of Ina had begun to be a very important part of land transport and they were traveling regularly over the Mikawa and Owari highways and even on the Koshu highway. Some of them were starting to come over to take commissions along the Kiso. There were some one hundred sixty villages taking part in this trade and the largest village had one hundred forty-six horses engaged, while the smallest had ten horses. If, at this time, there were no clearly defined assisting districts established, no way to make use of these commercial carriers, and no way to make more clear and specific the claims against the farmers who were liable for transport duty, then the post stations would be overwhelmed by the more profitable commercial transport trade and the number of villages that failed to respond to calls for assistance would increase. The Fukushima headman requested that the officials give careful attention to the peculiar conditions of the Kiso district if they had any thought of restoring alternate attendance.

"You have asked for many things," said Tsuzuki Suruga. "The shogun has decided to go by warship when he visits Kyoto the next time. This shows the compassion he has felt for the long years of exertion on the part of the people. And, even if we should call the daimyo back to Edo—even if we do restore the old style of alternate attendance, we have decided to supply warships for those who wish to make use of them. You have every right to be concerned, but such excessive demands on the post stations will not occur again."

"The representative of the lower four Kiso post stations is also present," the police inspector cried out as soon as the commissioner had finished speaking. "It seems that the elder, Shinshichi, who came here last year was from the same station as Hanzo who is here now."

"The three of you have been very good to favor us with your time even though you are so busy. Well, Hanzo? May we hear your opinion too?"

The eyes of Tsuzuki Suruga and of Jimbo Sado, who, being new on the commission, had been tending to stare off vacantly, turned toward Hanzo. He had been sitting quietly beside the other two headmen, but now it was time for him to speak.

"Yes, sir," replied Hanzo. "In recent years, the lords have become more demanding and they now make use of their power in every situation. As you are well aware, the lower four Kiso stations are all small and their regular work force consists of only twenty-five men and twenty-five horses each. We get some assistance from Ochiai in Mino, but we cannot move large numbers of people at one time. When there are large numbers of people, we send out all of our men and horses and we have to ask those travelers who are left over to wait for their return. In some cases, we have to ask them to spend the night at our station. That was the situation in normal times, but in recent years the official travelers will not listen to these requests from the people of the stations. They insist that we move them on in any way we can and so we are forced to hire men and horses from the neighboring villages. Therefore our costs for labor rise year by year. It would seem that the cause of the difficulties of the stations is the increased tendency of official travelers to presume on their rank nowadays. If only it weren't for that, the work of the highway could be carried out much more easily."

"I am sure it is just as you say, " said Tsuzuki Suruga. Then turning to Jimbo Sado, he said, "What does my colleague think? I would like to have them write this up for us in detail, but . . . ?"

"I agree," replied Jimbo Sado, fanning himself about the chest as he spoke.

The lower-ranking transport officials were making free use of their fans as the police inspector, following the wishes of the commissioners, inspected the transport ledgers offered by the three headmen and told them that they would be hearing from the commission later. They were to forward immediately from their homes the account books that showed how much they had been paid by the retinues of the shogunate and its officials when they were on their way to Kyoto between the third and seventh months of the previous year, the year of the boar.

To send a written account later, giving all the details. This was the order with which Hanzo and the others left the offices of the commissioners at the outer end of Kanda bridge. As they walked through that part of town, they could not help but notice the shaven-headed tea stewards and others who seemed to be waiting for the day when the reconstruction of the western enclosure of Edo castle would be completed. That even these tea stewards who served as waiters in the palace should have stopped wearing the jackets of fine fabric which they had been so proud to receive from the various daimyo and were now wearing long swords instead of short daggers showed how completely military dress had prevailed in these times. The masters of swordsmanship who had been called up by the shogunate and who were cutting such fine figures had become immensely popular. The current fashion among the direct Tokugawa retainers and bannermen was yellowish-white hempen jackets with lacquered crests; this emphatically military costume, which Ieyasu had worn so long ago at Sekigahara and which Nariaki, the late retired lord of Mito, had favored as his everyday wear, was once again popular in Edo.

On the way back to Ryogoku, Heisuke looked back at his companions.

"Hanzo! You keep stopping and staring."

"Look! There's a little Miyamoto Musashi and Araki Mataemon having their duel."

"You're right. Even the children are in military training in Edo. I wonder if everyone feels this way."

Heisuke walked very slowly as he spoke.

It was a windy day. By the time they reached the Yanagiwara embankment they had been engulfed by clouds of dust several times. The wind had been behind them when they set out that morning and it was bearable, but now that they were walking into the wind it had become extremely unpleasant. On the embankment, everything was covered with sand, from the second-hand clothing in the stalls among the willows to the fortune tellers' booths. They could scarcely keep their eyes open, but still the dust swirled up around them. They closed their mouths, averted their faces, and waited for the gusts to pass. The sky over the city had turned yellow from the dry dust blown up from the streets.

Once they got back to their inn in Ryogoku they removed their wide-shouldered formal vests and trousers, set the seal cases they had worn at their hips in the alcove, and began to discuss the day's experience.

"At any rate, we should tell the people back home how things went today."

"I'll send word to Fukushima immediately."

"I'll send a letter to Magome, too, to tell them to send the account books right away."

Like most of the inns in Edo at that time, the Juichiya had no bathing facilities. Hanzo and the others went off to the neighborhood bathhouse to wash away the perspiration of the day. When they returned, washcloths over their shoulders, the wind had finally subsided and the streets were being wet down in front of every house. Once more they felt themselves in the midst of a great city neighborhood. In the kitchen of the Juichiya, where the guests usually ate together, dinner was ready.

While the three were relaxing in their room upstairs after dinner, the retired master of the Juichiya, still fond of talk and drawn to the guests from his former home, came up to join them. The old-fashioned lamp that the maid had placed in the corner of the room helped to create the atmosphere of an honest inn.

"No matter what you say, Edo is Edo," Heisuke began. "Today I heard the mosquito netting peddlers over in the samurai district."

"Ah yes! They have fine voices," said the old man. " 'Mosquito nettings? Mosquito nettings!' You can hear them coming a block away. They say that they are from Echigo but they are a famous Edo institution. Whenever I hear them, I am reminded of the time when I first came here from the Kiso."

Kohei pulled the smoking set over by its handle, took a puff of tobacco, and continued the conversation. "Edo seems to be having hard times, Juichiya."

"Times are really bad," replied the old man. "Even over in the samurai quarters. The old man from the panel-maker's shop came by yesterday and he was saying that orders are just not coming from the samurai residences any more. His son has been out of work since the end of last year. He was really downcast. Then he asked me what my son was doing. I had to admit that he has nothing at all to do and nowadays he just practices fencing like everyone else. We are even beginning to hear people say that if only there was a good fire in Edo, it would come back to life and there would be work. If you look at it the way these tradesmen do, that may be the truth."

"Things will come back to life if there's a fire? Edo's a big place!" said Heisuke, chuckling.

"No, he was serious. Fires are the flowers of Edo—I wonder who first said that. But all the same, no one could be more afraid of fire than Edo people. Recently we've been having fires even in the summer and so everyone has been very careful. And how about these rumors of arson. When times get bad people do things like that. They say that the worst ones even turn the bamboo rain gutters around so that they link up with the neighboring houses to ensure that the fire will run well."

"Things are in bad shape here in the shogun's city," said Hanzo. "I really feel that when I see Edo this time. Now that I have been looking around for several days, I can understand why they are talking about restoring alternate attendance."

Kohei and Hanzo were quite different in the way they assumed their roles of headmen, but traveling together had been wonderfully effective in making them forget their differences in age and point of view. Hanzo, feeling like a traveler in the crisp starchiness of the summer kimono supplied by the mistress of the inn, was content for the most part to listen quietly to the conversation.

"No one can afford to make any mistakes nowadays. Even the biggest stores are closing one after another. In the daytime you have to fear extortionists, and armed robbers at night. You cannot imagine how much Yoshinobu is hated for having sponsored the reform which allowed the retired lords and all the heirs, wives, and families of the daimyo to return to their home provinces. Even those who don't know anything at all are calling him 'Porky' half in fun, just because it was reported that he had tried eating pork. No, the people don't have anything good to say about Yoshinobu."

There was no end of things to talk about in Edo.

That night Hanzo stayed up late, writing a letter by lamplight to Inosuke back in Magome. In all the neighborhoods it was forbidden to walk out without a lantern at night, and the wooden gates at each intersection were tightly closed. The *rasotsu,* an early type of police that had been established in Edo in the fourth month of that year, made their rounds out from their barracks, crests at their shoulders. Even their patrols were irritating to the old man of the Juichiya.

2

The Edo inns catered either to official or to commercial trade, and there were almost no really luxurious inns like those in the Kyoto-Osaka area that charged three or four *momme* in silver for a night's lodging. Since they existed only to cater to the official or commercial travelers who came to Edo, the inns were very simple; there were no bathing facilities and meals were served in the kitchen. But there was a difference in the charges from the time when Hanzo had been here almost a decade earlier. It was no longer possible to have breakfast, dinner, and lodging for two hundred fifty mon.

After the audience with the transport commission, Hanzo decided to leave the Juichiya. A physician from Honjo who was a fellow Hirata disciple had repeatedly offered to obtain lodgings for him on the second floor of the home of a family he knew, so Hanzo moved to Aioi-cho in Honjo away from the other two with whom he had been traveling.

The house in Aioi-cho, just east of the Ekoin temple on the other side of the bridge, was not very far from the Juichiya. A very pleasant couple with one small child lived there. The man, Takichi, was a bookkeeper for a rice wholesaler in Fukagawa, and Aioi-cho was the kind of neighborhood where it was not surprising to find a famous sumo wrestler living nearby. Shortly after the move, Heisuke came over from the Juichiya, crossing the Ryogoku bridge to visit Hanzo.

"You've found a nice place."

Heisuke delivered this opinion after coming up to the second floor and looking around. Although second floor rooms were usually hot in the summer, Hanzo's room was unusually well ventilated. There was a window facing to the west. The two talked about these things for a while.

"Well, Hanzo," began Heisuke, "it certainly takes a long time to get any official business done. It was the end of the fourth month when our representatives came down from the Kiso last year. That took until the beginning of this year. It looks to me as though this is going to be another long one."

"The transport commissioners are being changed so frequently nowadays," Hanzo replied. "After a year or two, just when they are beginning to understand the conditions out in the provinces, they are forced to resign. No wonder nothing ever gets done."

"By the way, Hanzo, there is quite a story going around here in Edo. I just heard from the people over at the Yamamura residence that the captain for the Kamakura commissioner has been arrested. Now that's a story that just can't be ignored. Since he is the captain for the Kamakura commissioner, he is a person of fairly high rank. His family is in Choshu, and he just wrote them a letter. It was an ordinary letter to relatives, but they say it somehow got into the hands of a police spy. It said something to the effect that these were unsettled times, that we are all concerned about each other, and that he wished some able leader would appear to set things right. When the shogunal officials saw this, they said that it constituted disrespect to the shogun to say that conditions were unsettled and that to wish that some able leader other than the shogun would appear to set things right constituted an act of rebellion. The captain was immediately arrested and brought to the castle. Isn't that something? And then they say that his house was searched and he was promptly sent on to the Temmacho jail. Once there, he was given a very superficial questioning and then ordered to disembowel himself. When this story turned up at the compound in Higashi Katamachi, everyone was horrified. One of the people there knows a minor police official who had to witness the death of the captain. That official later described the appalling scene to him. After hearing that story I am afraid to stay in Edo any longer. Besides, it just doesn't seem right to go on living and eating at the inn at the expense of the people back home."

Like Heisuke, Hanzo was unhappy to be away from home for so long. But the headmen were not to be permitted to finish their business by simply presenting their ledgers and answering questions about conditions in their region. Neither Heisuke nor Hanzo could return home until they had carried out the will of the eleven Kiso stations by once again presenting their petition for the regularization of the assisting districts system.

Why was it that the transport commission had not accepted the petition brought in by the five Kiso representatives the previous year? Because it would have been very difficult to assign regular assisting districts without a thorough investigation of each of the villages concerned. However, since the petition presented by the Kiso representatives seemed to be concerned with an urgent problem, the commissioners had given permission for the creation of provisional assisting districts for a period of six months beginning with the second month of Genji 1. The lower four Kiso stations were assigned one hundred nineteen villages in Ina, the middle three stations were assigned ninety-nine villages in Ina, and the upper four had eighty-nine villages in Chikuma county and one hundred forty-four villages in Azumi county. When the more distant villages found it difficult to send men and horses and appealed for permission to make alternate arrangements, they were promised that their assessment would never exceed five ryo for each one hundred koku of their rice revenues.

After trying out this arrangement for nearly six months, Hanzo and the other headmen had found that the result of the startling increase in the number of assigned villages was an even greater rate of failures to send men and horses. This could only be corrected, they felt, by following the example of the Tokaido and assigning regular assisting districts. If the commissioners of transport were really sincere, it was to be hoped that they would determine the capabilities of the villages, correct the deficiencies of the present assisting district system, and prevent further disorder on the highways. If their petition was not honored, the post stations hoped to be permitted to delay the extra freight until the next day, since their regularly assigned twenty-five men and twenty-five horses could not be expected to fill the need. Heisuke and Hanzo talked about this.

Such were the times. In the west there was an uprising at Gojo in Yamato, followed by an uprising at the Ikuno silver mines. When that seemed to be subsiding, there was a third outburst in the east, around Mt. Tsukuba. People seemed unable to wait for the new age. A faction of Mito activists, under a banner reading "Revere the Emperor, Expel the Barbarians," had established connections with Choshu and had been taking part in this uprising since the fourth month. The struggle was still unresolved.

Hanzo left the house in Aioi-cho to accompany Heisuke back to the Juichiya. He was concerned about having his mail from home forwarded to him and he had gone along with the intention of asking the old man at the Juichiya to see to this.

"You can see Mt. Tsukuba from here, Heisuke," said Hanzo as they were walking over the long Ryogoku bridge.

"Oh, is that Mt. Tsukuba?"

Heisuke said only that, then lapsed back into silence. In his old-fashioned manner, he would speak of nothing beyond the concerns of the journey, and so he made no reference to the disorder in Mito or to the feelings that must be experienced by the retainers of the various han who were still in Edo or the relatives of the Tokugawa when they crossed this bridge. Just then Hanzo and Heisuke met two girls crossing the bridge from the opposite side. One of them was the daughter of the family Hanzo was staying with in Aioi-cho. They seemed to be returning from their Kiyomoto lessons since both of them were walking along carrying their music books under their arms. They were just of the age to remind Hanzo of Okume back home in Magome.

"Hanzo, is that the child in the place at Aioi-cho?"

As Heisuke spoke, one of the children came up to them, bowed, and walked on. She was delightful to watch as she walked away. With her hair cut in boyish style, her crisp summer kimono tied with a narrow calico sash, and pale yellow cords hanging down behind, she almost did not look like a girl. This odd way of dressing only made her all the more childishly captivating.

"Why, was that a girl? I was sure it was a boy!" laughed Heisuke.

"I thought you would be. They say that her parents are dressing her like a boy as part of some vow."

Hanzo continued to look after the two little girls. The other one had her hair done up in the worldly yet juvenile "tobacco dish" style and her summer kimono was dyed in a whirlpool design with a narrow, tie-dyed sash around her waist, reflecting her parents' refined taste. Even the purse she carried was childishly smart.

"Children brought up in the city are different," said Hanzo as he and Heisuke watched them walk away.

The old man at the Juichiya was in the front room of the inn, sitting behind the clerk's grill, changing the paper on some of the inn's hanging lanterns. When he discovered that Hanzo had come on business, he would not let it pass at that. He spoke of the river-opening festival that took place each year on the twenty-eighth of the fifth month, and said that this year neither he nor his son had received their usual invitation to see the fireworks with a retired gentleman from one of the great samurai residences. He wondered what was going to become of the pleasure boats moored in Yanagibashi that used to go as far as Suijin or at least to the nearby Kubio pine seeking out the coolness of the river. Without going so far as to mention the elaborate water entertainments the military houses used to put on in good times, when such fine boats as the *Kawaichi Maru*, the *Kanto Maru*, or the *Juikken Maru* would come drifting by, lances upright at their bows, he did describe how all the lanterns afloat along the river had lent their brilliance to the scene. That was in the days when there were still many daimyo and bannermen who would close off both sides of their houseboats with shoji as they came floating down the river at Asakusa to escape the heat.

"Hanzo, why don't you stay here and talk a while?" said Heisuke as he settled down in the front room to enjoy a round of traveler's tales. Then the old man spoke again in a tone of reminiscence.

"Aoyama, what has happened to Miyagawa sensei since I saw him? He must have made good money out of the Yokohama trade. I remember him setting out from here with a packhorse load of money and a guard on his way back to Nakatsugawa."

Hanzo could not answer. He did not want to speak casually of his beloved teacher's fortunes, so he simply said that his old master had recently left Nakatsugawa to spend his final years in Ina.

"When it comes to the Yokohama trade, that was really a curse to some people," said Heisuke. "Weren't there stories about some people from around Nakatsugawa who were called into the Ota offices and ordered by Owari to close their businesses? That's what comes of making too much money."

"And how is Yorozuya doing?" asked the old man.

"Well," replied Hanzo, "he hasn't been wasting any time. As soon as the price of raw silk seemed to be going down on the Yokohama market, he dropped out and now he has his sights set on Kyoto. I suppose he is sending a lot of raw silk to Kyoto these days."

"These Mino merchants are too much for me," said Heisuke. "There are really some go-getters around Nakatsugawa."

"Speaking of Miyagawa just reminded me," said the old man. "I saw him once at the Botan'ya in Kanagawa when I went down there with a person named Kitamura Zuiken. You probably haven't heard about him yet, Aoyama, but he has been through some big changes in his life. He started out as a house physician to the shogunate, but after the opening of the ports he went to Hakodate and served there a long time. While he was in Hakodate, he was given samurai status and soon afterwards he became the captain for the Hakodate commissioner. Now he is back in Edo and he has just been promoted from being head of the Shoheiko, the Tokugawa academy, to the office of censor. He is serving in the foreign relations division and if he keeps it up this way, he will soon be the commissioner for foreign relations. Now I've spent my life watching people come and go in this inn business, but I've never seen anyone get ahead like that."

"I guess you can't say that the Tokugawa shogunate lacks able men."

The old man broke into laughter at Heisuke's playful response. Hanzo could only wonder at the fortunes and disasters that had come to people as a consequence of the beginning of foreign trade and the opening of the ports.

From that day on, Hanzo fell into the habit of gazing at Mt. Tsukuba as he went back and forth from the Juichiya. With the skies of the Kanto plain becoming obscured by the dust of battle, he feared that the attention of the officials had been distracted, slowing down business in the offices and further prolonging their stay in Edo. Sometimes he leaned on the wooden railing of the six-hundred-foot-long bridge and gazed off to the northeast, toward that distant, green mountain. No matter how hot and unpleasant the day, there was always a breeze there. He could not think of the fate of Edo apart from this Sumida river flowing before his eyes. From the locations of the warehouses holding no one knew how much rice to nurture no one knew how many retainers and bannermen, it was apparent that almost all the remaining land on both sides of the river was occupied by the residences of the great military families. The vast number of pilings sunk along this part of the river banks was no doubt part of the plan to control the flooding of the river, but the waters of the Sumida flowing down from the direction of the Okawa bridge, now the Azuma bridge, seemed to run with a special swiftness as they boiled past these pilings and flowed on under the Ryogoku bridge, as if telling of more than two centuries of Edo history.

There was good reason for the three headmen to have chosen to bring a petition along with them on this trip to Edo. The abandonment of alternate attendance had been been forced by the circumstances not just of those in power but also of those below. Although the restoration of alternate attendance was being considered as a measure to reverse the decline in the power of the shogunate, and to rescue Edo from its profound depression, it would be the people in the provinces who would suffer if the old burdens of official display were restored.

The commissioners of transport, however, remained forever in consultation and the petition of the headmen was not acted upon. They waited through the Sanno festival, and they continued to wait after the end of the month when the shogun, his mother, Tenshoin, and his wife, Princess Kazu, moved into the newly reconstructed western enclosure of Edo castle.

When they had waited until around the twentieth day of the seventh month, another event took place which was to make their mission more difficult still.

"Choshu has rebelled."

This rumor began to pass from mouth to mouth. Special fast litters rushed through the streets one after another all day long. It was reported that things were very bad in Kyoto; there was even a report that fires set by cannon around noon on the nineteenth had burned most of the buildings in the city. On the twenty-third Hanzo went over to join Kohei and Heisuke at the Juichiya. Together they walked through the ugly mood of the city streets from the bastion at Asakusa bridge to the Sujikai bastion. There a large, excited crowd surrounded the notice board where a declaration of punitive action against Choshu had already been posted.

The twenty-ninth of the seventh month was the eve of the two hundred tenth day of the year, a time when typhoons are particularly feared. Hanzo and the two headmen, wanting to know more about the situation in Kyoto, had called on the retainers at the Higashi Katamachi residence of the Yamamura family of Fukushima. There they learned most of the essentials of the battles in Kyoto and that a special messenger had just been dispatched from the residence the previous evening to make direct reports of the uprising. From an authoritative report that had arrived from Nagoya they also learned that Choshu had been defeated.

It appeared that, in addition to the punitive action against Choshu, Matsudaira Daizen Dayu, the lord of Choshu, and his son had both been relieved of their court ranks and the right to use the surname Matsudaira, as well as forfeiting a certain character in their posthumous names the use of which had been granted by the shogunate. Along the highways all movement of goods to the two provinces of Nagato and Suwo was strictly prohibited.

One morning around the seventh hour, Hanzo was awakened in the house in Aioi-cho by the sound of alarm bells. He got up thinking that there must be a fire but when he opened the rain shutters of his room, he could see nothing that looked like smoke. Takichi, the master of the house, came upstairs in his nightclothes.

"I wonder where the fire is?" he said to Hanzo. Together they climbed from the second floor up to the clothes-drying stand on the roof. There they could look out across the rooftops. All the firetowers in the neighborhood were crowded with people trying to spot the fire.

"Aoyama! There's something going on out front!" called Takichi's wife from downstairs. As soon as they heard her, Hanzo and Takichi went back down to see.

People were running toward Ryogoku bridge. Hanzo and Takichi followed after them and when they reached the foot of the bridge, they found large numbers of firemen, all wearing thick, heavily stitched jackets and hoods and carrying pickaxes, rushing by. After this company came another carrying fire ladders. Still others, in leather hoods and coats, passed directly before Hanzo and Takichi.

The razing of the Choshu compound, ordered by the shogunate as a retaliation against the rebels, had begun. All the firemen in Edo were assigned the task of tearing down the Mori residence in Hibiya. Perhaps in anticipation of just such an eventuality, or because they were already turning their backs on Edo, Choshu had razed all the main buildings in the Hibiya mansion at the time that the daimyo and their families had been permitted to return to the provinces, so only the outbuildings remained to be brought down now. The secondary compound at Ryudocho in Azabu, popularly known as Choshu's "Hinoki mansion," still had twenty clay storehouses and other large buildings standing, and the wrecking was begun there. The thick wooden pillars were cut through with saws and axes, ropes were tied around them, and the buildings pulled down. The furnishings and books were burned at Etchujima and everything bearing the Mori crest was trampled.

At last an eagerly awaited letter arrived from Keizo in Kyoto, addressed to Hanzo at the Juichiya, Yonezawa-cho, Ryogoku. Hanzo had been concerned about the safety of his friend. He picked up the letter at the Juichiya and brought it back to his room in Aioi-cho, where he began to read it.

He first skimmed it quickly, learning that Keizo was safe, that the master Hirata Kanetane was safe, and that the Hirata disciples living in the Shimo-gyo district were also unharmed in spite of being burned out of their quarters. Then he reread the letter more carefully.

As always, Keizo's letter went into great detail. He wrote that the incidents occurring around the nineteenth of the seventh month had come as no surprise after the coup of the eighth month of the previous year. That was when the court nobles advocating an imperial restoration had been forced to leave the capital along with the Choshu retainers who were the main support of the pro-imperial, anti-foreign faction.

The incident at the Ikedaya had taken place at dawn on the fifth day of the sixth month. The constable of Kyoto and the shogun's Kyoto deputy, supported by irregulars from the Shinsengumi, had arrested more than twenty activists from various han who had gathered with plans to bolster the strength of the anti-foreign party in Kyoto. Their intention to thwart the efforts of the faction supported by Aizu and Satsuma favoring the union of court and military and to coordinate their actions with the Mito samurai now encamped at Mt. Tsukuba became known at this time through the capture of a man from Omi province. After this incident, Choshu decided it could wait no longer and it began to move its already assembled forces toward the capital. The shogunate, learning of this, began to strengthen its positions around Fushima and Otsu. With the sudden appearance at the palace of the constable Matsudaira Katamori and the closing of all nine gates to the imperial enclosure, disorder spread throughout Kyoto. On the eighteenth day of the seventh month, reports reached the capital that Choshu forces were advancing along three roads. When the nineteenth dawned, Keizo heard the sound of heavy firing at the Hamaguri and Nakadachiuri gates to the west and soon found himself surrounded by the fires which had started around Muromachi and were now spreading throughout the capital.

One fact that could not be overlooked by anyone following developments in Kyoto was the existence of several han that were in sympathy with Choshu. Another was the role of court nobles such as Prince Arisugawa, Ogimachi, Hino, and Ishiyama who were opposed to the shogunate and to the very idea of uniting the court and military. Keizo pointed out that concerned people in Kyoto had been aware of the existence of a plan to set fire to the imperial enclosure during a high wind, to attack Nakagawa and Matsudaira Katamori on their way to the palace, and to abduct the emperor to Mt. Hiei in the confusion. He wrote that stray shots had frequently struck the inner wall of the imperial enclosure, and he related how an enclosed palanquin had been brought into the imperial gardens so that the emperor could be taken away in it when Hitotsubashi Yoshinobu put a stop to the scheme. The Hamaguri gate was the scene of the fiercest struggle because Aizu and Kuwana were guarding that sector. On the west side of the imperial palace, there was a great camphor tree. With the palace walls being used for cover and the buildings being used as fortifications, the fighting was especially desperate around this tree. Here Choshu found itself in direct confrontation with Aizu. Although the Satsuma forces on the other side of the enclosure rendered great service to the shogunate, they were not so directly engaged as Aizu. The Aizu warriors, feeling responsible for the security of Kyoto, came out to meet the Choshu forces and made a splendid display of the bravery of warriors from the northeast. They repeatedly opened the Hamaguri gates and, ignoring the guns that were firing at them, sallied forth to close with the Choshu forces with lance and sword.

This street battle lasted until mid-afternoon. The Choshu forces had been shattered at the Nakadachiuri and Hamaguri gates and they fled, leaving around two hundred dead behind. Fires had broken out at mid-morning and the winds created by them became stronger and stronger. Flames began to mount up in all quarters as burning debris fell from the air. Between the Takase river on the east and the Hori river on the west, and as far south as the ninth avenue, almost all of the Shimo-gyo district was immersed in flames. Keizo wrote that men and women all around him had been helping the old to escape and carrying the young on their backs.

Keizo's letter went further, reporting the death of Maki Izumi no Kami, the man who had begun an anti-foreign, pro-imperial movement back in the 1840's and 1850's and who had been a guiding spirit of the age. This inspiration of the pro-imperial faction, through his plans with the court nobles and his discussions with the Choshu activists, had been responsible for the appearance of most of the troops that day. Now he had fallen in the tragic outcome of the struggle he had initiated. He had tried to carry on the struggle, but on the twenty-first the Choshu forces that had retreated with him to Yamazaki were scattered. After the death of Kusaka, Terajima, Irie, and the other brave men who had fought with him, he fled to Tenno mountain where he died by his own sword.

Keizo wrote of his feelings about the death of Maki Izumi, saying that the movement which had aimed to unify anti-foreign and pro-imperial sentiment ever since the 1850's had lost its most notable personage. He added that we disciples of Hirata Atsutane—particularly those of us who had come late to the scene—needed to reflect on the life of Maki Izumi no Kami and plot our future courses accordingly.

In that letter Hanzo learned that his friend Kozo was no longer in Kyoto. Keizo, too, was going to put an end to his long stay in Kyoto and return to Nakatsugawa permanently.

This news of the death of Maki Izumi no Kami brought many things into Hanzo's mind. It made him think of the meaning of the loss of this most unyielding of the unyielding in matters of foreign relations. The activists who had poured their strength into attacks on the pusillanimous policies of the shogunate had found nothing genuine in its offer to close the port of Yokohama or to send missions abroad. They had viewed the shogunate's proclamation of the expulsion of the foreigners as empty rhetoric. But with this battle in Kyoto, they had been removed from the political stage.

Moreover, Choshu had now turned to direct action in its effort to expel the foreigners, beginning with the bombardment of the American merchant ship at Tanoura in Buzen and continuing with the attacks on French and Italian warships passing through the straits of Shimonoseki. The result had been an attack on Choshu by a combined fleet of eighteen ships from England, America, France, and the Netherlands. Most of the Choshu batteries had been destroyed and Choshu was decisively beaten. It had even suffered the occupation of Shimonoseki itself, only to have the peace negotiations somehow shifted from Shimonoseki to Edo. These stories were the dominant topics of conversation at that time. Should the country be opened or should the foreigners be expelled? That had been the question ever since the four Black Ships had appeared off Kurihama in Uraga. It was a question that had aroused incalculably complex reactions, spreading panic and disorder among high and low throughout the nation. And it had claimed innumerable victims as voices denouncing the anti-foreign elements as obstinate and perverse arose on one side, while others in turn attacked the advocates of the opening of the country as traitors. Until the bitter experience of engaging four foreign nations in hostilities at Shimonoseki, there had been many in the country who still believed that it was possible to expel the foreigners. When, for better or for worse, the actual attempt had been made, the people of Choshu were not alone in recognizing the significance of the failure. It seemed to Hanzo that this anti-foreign frenzy which had raged over the country for so many years had now reached a dead end.

3

Late in the ninth month, Hanzo and the other headmen were still waiting to receive the decision of the commissioners of transport. They had presented the ledgers which the commissioners had requested and their petition as representatives of the eleven Kiso stations. They went time after time to the offices outside the Kanda bridge, but each time they were only told to "wait a bit, wait a bit." At the Juichiya, Kohei and Heisuke were worn out with waiting. They had even begun to talk in riddles about how it might be possible to get their business taken care of more quickly by going through the officials in charge of the Owari residence and using a little money. Such irresponsible talk made Hanzo feel all the more lonely.

"You must be getting pretty bored."

The master of the house in Aioi-cho would frequently go to Hanzo's room before he set out for his rice warehouse in the mornings. Having stayed in the house for almost four months, Hanzo had become sufficiently familiar with them to call the master of the house Takichi-san and the little girl who was taking Kiyomoto lessons Omiwa-san.

"My husband has to spend most of his time at work, Aoyama, but occasionally he gets some time off and then he likes to go to haikai gatherings more than anything else. Just look! There's not a white fan left in the house! By the end of the summer, he had written all over every last one of them."

Takichi was the kind of person who would laugh when his wife, Osumi, told such stories to Hanzo and then he would go off to his job in Fukagawa, careful not to forget to take his portable writing set along.

Even in these times, when the dust of battle had been raised in the skies over the Kanto plain by the uprising at Mt. Tsukuba, there were still people like Takichi, who ignored all the fighting and enjoyed himself with haikai. He had been born in Kawagoe, just upriver from Edo, and it was said that at one time he had been the owner of a large sake and rice wholesale establishment and had frequently traveled between Edo and Kawagoe by riverboat. When his innate generosity and his lack of business sense had led to the forced closing of his venerable house, there had been a time when his wife had gone out wearing straw sandals, and with her skirts tucked up, to sell her "Osumi dumplings." She was a strong woman who had worked side by side with her husband to make a new life in the city after their move to Edo.

Osumi was about the same age as Hanzo's wife, Otami. Whenever Hanzo saw her, he was reminded of Otami back home in the honjin, and whenever he saw the city-bred Omiwa, he thought of Okume waiting for him at her mother's side. The Tokugawa age had already reached the end of the first year of Genji. In the atmosphere of Edo, where the whole society seemed to be donning military array, just what did these matrons of townsman families, helpless to resist the times, draw on for spiritual support? From where did they draw the strength to live? When Hanzo looked at Osumi in this light, he saw her teaching her daughter always to speak the truth, telling her that if only one did that, then there was nothing in this world to fear. It was thanks to honesty that she herself had been protected from error. Her whole heart was given over to providing her daughter with proper guidance.

"I don't like to say this to you, Aoyama, but I have read two or three of those old blue-covered books on Chinese learning and I didn't get anything out of them at all."

"You're too much for me, madam."

Takichi's friends and fellow haikai enthusiasts came to the house and the sumo wrestler who lived nearby also dropped in now and then. There would occasionally be geisha, taking a breather between parties and drawing strength from Osumi. There was even a teacher of samisen who frequently came calling and who was Osumi's best friend even though, going about from one man to the next, she was of precisely the opposite temperament. She was nevertheless appealing in her big-city refinement and sophistication.

Osumi would say, "They talk about nothing but hard times, but the theatre still makes good money. Every troupe was sold out for the spring performances. How about it, shouldn't we take Aoyama to see a program in Saruwaka-cho?"

That was the tone of life at Aioi-cho.

Hanzo was increasingly concerned about the expenses that were being incurred as they waited through a fourth futile month for a response from the commissioners. There was a large number of retainers at the Higashi Katamachi residence but they were altogether different from the country samurai in Fukushima. Every last one was at ease in society. They would frequently come by to invite Hanzo out and it was impossible for him to excuse himself from going with them, first to a music hall on Hirokoji street in Ueno to hear readings of heroic tales and then to visit a sake shop afterward. When Hanzo, Kohei, and Heisuke were invited to a mansion, led into a splendid room, served tea or sake, and even favored with the company of women far more beautiful and accomplished than one might expect to find in the company of caretakers of an Edo mansion, they were obligated to offer a gift of at least three bu in value.

Even though Takichi's was not the sort of place that required great expenditures, the money that Hanzo had brought with him had nearly run out. His hosts treated him with the same kindness that they would show to a member of their own family. Although the food was simple and plain, they always served red beans and rice on the first and the fifteenth of the month, and Osumi took care of all his personal needs, ready to help whenever the occasion arose. As Hanzo continued his long stay in Edo, his purse reaching bottom, the rumor came that an army drawn from thirty-five han for a punitive expedition against Choshu under the command of the retired lord of Owari was ready to advance on the city of Yamaguchi.

What brought Hanzo some comfort during the long wait in Edo was being able to search the bookstores for items that he wanted to take home with him, or calling on fellow Hirata disciples with whom he was acquainted. Occasionally he would call at the Hirata residence itself to pay his respects to the family of Kanetane, who was then still in Kyoto. But what pleased him still more in Edo was Takichi and Osumi, and particularly to have discovered a person whose eyes were as bright as Osumi's.

Edo was no longer the Edo of the Ansei era. Still less was it the Edo of Bunka or Bunsei. While there were still the same handicrafts in paper, fabrics, ivory, jade, or precious metals as he had seen ten years earlier, there was not a single great master of whom this Genji era could boast. Hanzo often visited the dealers in illustrated books in various parts of town, but when he examined the love stories, the vendetta tales, or the tales of wonder that were being sold there, the books were noticeably smaller than before, the paper poorer in quality, the illustrations cruder, and everything grown flimsier. Even in the still flourishing Edo theatre, the weird elements had become still more weird and the subtle and delicate things still more subtle and delicate. Over-refined sensibilities and a tired, late-blooming facileness were tinged with a coloring of obscenity and decadence.

At the beginning of his stay in Edo, Hanzo had often thought how depressing it would be to see presented on the stage this flashiness for the sake of flashiness which he saw all around him. To see a favorite actor mount the stage dressed in a most unbecoming fashion, in a blue-dotted, lined robe, a checkered overrobe, and carrying a tie-dyed handkerchief—wouldn't he be simply catering to the devotees of the grotesque? After he had spent four months in Edo and associated with all kinds of Edo people, Hanzo found that this feeling had only come to the surface more strongly.

Now that he had observed Edo life more closely, he found that it was by no means true that all the people were living in decadence and disharmony, merely looking for that day's stimulation and without a thought for tomorrow. A person like Osumi, even though she was the obscure wife of a townsman and had little education, saw the changes in the world reflected on the stage and would confess that when she suddenly sensed the tone of the times in some scene or experience, she would weep helplessly at things that no one else was weeping about. She said that she could no longer casually go to the theatre with her friends.

In this feudal society where those who were not samurai were not recognized as human beings, Hanzo did not have to look very far to find townspeople who were obedient but far from servile. Here right at hand were people who were not awed by authority. There was this story about the mistress of the house in Aioi-cho, tall, fair in coloring, and bright of eye, but never using cosmetics, always hard at work in the kitchen. It had happened while her husband was still in Kawagoe, the young master of a large business establishment. At that time, the domain of Kawagoe had just been placed under a new daimyo brought in from another region. A strict order had come down to the merchant households of the han forbidding them to sell sake to samurai. Now the new samurai of the han were extremely overbearing toward the commoners, and one day one of these, a long sword thrust in his sash, came secretly at nightfall to Takichi's shop. Takichi was sitting in the storefront at the time, playing chess with his chief clerk. Suddenly set upon by this samurai with drawn sword demanding that they sell him sake, both Takichi and the chief clerk rushed into the back of the store, terrified. Osumi was only eighteen then, but she came out before the samurai and, unperturbed by his threats, curtly refused him service. He was enraged. With his sword he cut in two the lamp the apprentice had brought and slashed the tatami in the front of the shop. Then he asked if they were still going to refuse him sake. When Osumi replied that she could not disobey the orders of the daimyo no matter what he said to her, the samurai glared. Finally he said, "What kind of girl are you?" and left.

"What's going to happen to Edo?"

Hanzo said this when he went to visit Heisuke on the second floor of the Juichiya. Heisuke, who was in bed with a slight indisposition, looked at Hanzo's face and asked him to read one of the children's readers that was lying by his bed. By his side lay Kohei, hairy legs thrust out, exhausted by the long stay away from home.

At last, late in the tenth month, the three received a summons from the commissioners of transport. At the offices of Tsuzuki Suruga, the same police inspector received them, and after they were kept waiting in another room for a time, they were called before the commissioners.

"Suruga no Kami is just now in attendance on the shogun, so I will read this in his place."

One of the commission officials then read a document to the representatives of the eleven Kiso stations. It was to the effect that the request for the establishment of regular assisting districts seemed most reasonable, but that a decision could not be made until the original records of all the villages concerned had been thoroughly examined. It said that the meaning of regularly established assisting districts had always included the assignment of actual men and horses from the nearest villages to supplement the normal strength of the post stations and that therefore, unless the distances to the various post stations were thoroughly verified, there was no meaning to the concept of regular assisting districts. However, since the petition presented by the three representatives seemed to require it, a special grant of three hundred ryo would be made to each of the stations. This money was to be invested and the income used to supplement the station deficits each year. They each received a copy of the statement from the official with an order to provide a written receipt in return. On the documents was written the sum of money to be given as special assistance to the eleven stations and they bore the seals of Suruga and Sado.

The request to complete the organization of the assisting districts along the Kiso had been refused. The three headmen had to content themselves with a grant of money instead. They were given back the ledgers recording the use of men and horses and the financial records of the post stations and then they left the building.

"With only this little dab of salve, we're in trouble from now on," said Hanzo, unable to hide his despair, after they had returned to the Juichiya.

"You're still young, Hanzo," said Kohei. "If the officials had not taken a sincere interest in our problems we wouldn't have gotten anything."

"Well, we might as well go on back home now. There's no use staying around any longer," said Heisuke, speaking as he always did.

They had at least carried out their mission to Edo, even if it had been only to speak directly to the commissioners about the conditions in their district. They had been given written acknowledgments of their audiences. Now it was time to return home. Hanzo and the others had received a loan to cover the expenses of their stay in Edo, allowing them to pay off all the debts they had contracted. However, they heard from the people in Higashi Katamachi that there were many who wanted to give them a drink to celebrate the completion of their mission in Edo. These samurai stationed in Edo knew all about the good little restaurants that most people would not find and how to order sake and call in geisha. When Hanzo had taken his seat at the party and was offered cups of sake by his socially skilled hosts, he could not very well refuse them, but as one who had come on post station business, he did not drink it down easily. During the party that day, there came such a rain as one might expect at the end of the tenth month. Although the six in the room were all in good spirits, there were some who said that they had not yet drunk enough. These were the big drinkers who would go on to two or three other places before returning safely to their residences.

It was Hanzo's last night in his room in Aioi-cho. He had promised to return to the Juichiya and spend the following night there before departure with the other headmen. That evening his feelings about the stay in Edo all came together. He felt that he had incurred a great deal of unnecessary expense and that he really did not have the satisfaction of having been one of the representatives of the Kiso stations that he would have liked. He could not sleep. It seemed that Takichi and Osumi were also staying up late downstairs and he could dimly hear the sound of their voices as they talked. As he lay there, his thoughts turned to the highway back in Magome. He remembered that in the fourth year of Tempo, 1833 by the Western calendar, and again in the seventh year, there had been crop failures and many of the villagers had died or fled, so that the tiny post station on a hilltop had found it impossible to fulfill even its regular assignment of twenty-five men without assistance from the neighboring villages of Yamaguchi and Yubunezawa. He thought about the topography of the land for which he was responsible, from Jikkyoku pass to Magome pass. Whenever there was a heavy rain, the roadway became like a river and since the soil was heavy with clay, it was extremely taxing for men and horses to move over the steep grades. He remembered how difficult it was to move goods on the snowy or frozen roads of winter and spring, when the pain and hardship suffered by the post officials, the packhorses, the porters, and the couriers were beyond description. He recalled that sick or exhausted horses were not at all uncommon. Although one could feel the conflict of interest between the post station officials and the assisting districts when one was actually in the country, when he viewed it from here in distant Edo it seemed as though all had sweated alike in the service of the highway. He thought about the highway back home and how it would be to return once more to that station with his outlook colored by his experience in Edo. He was determined to bear up under the service to the military along with the rest of the people who labored there.

The restoration of the alternate attendance system that was to rescue Edo from economic disaster was announced even before Hanzo left Edo.

> *Item:* Having permitted, two years ago, in the year of the dog, an extension of the time between attendances in Edo for those having revenues of ten thousand koku of rice or more, we are, after careful thought, announcing that alternate attendance will once again be carried out according to the previously existing schedule.
>
> *Item:* Since the permission granted two years ago for the wives and sons of those possessing revenues of ten thousand koku of rice or more to return to the provinces together with those of their retinue, every one of these persons has done so. While we are on campaign, we are, after the most careful consideration, announcing a return to the former practice, so that all are ordered to call these people back to Edo.

The phrase "on campaign" in this document referred to the shogun's forthcoming move to Osaka castle; that is to say, it referred to the punitive expedition against Choshu under the command of the retired lord of Owari.

This announcement made all the more clear to the three headmen the reason they had been summoned to Edo and questioned on the actual conditions in the Kiso, a difficult place for the passage of the daimyo. It also explained the very temporary nature of the solution that had been presented to them.

There was no longer anything to hold them in Edo.

"It's useless to stay any longer."

This thought was not limited to the cautious Heisuke.

But it was not only because their stay in Edo had lasted from the sixth month through the tenth month that they became still more impatient to set out for home. On the day before they left, they learned that the people at the Yamamura residence had received reliable reports about the movements of the Mito ronin at Mt. Tsukuba.

Hanzo was already at the Juichiya with the other headmen but he could not bear to leave Edo that way. He slipped out early in the morning to make his farewells to Takichi and Osumi. There had been a frost and his straw sandals left footprints on the nearly deserted Ryogoku bridge as he hurried toward the house in Aioi-cho. When little Omiwa saw him appear at the gate dressed for travel in a blue Kawachi cotton cape and leggings, she called for Takichi and Osumi.

"Oh, so you're leaving now. I see you are all prepared," said Osumi.

Takichi came dashing out to speak with Hanzo. He asked Osumi to bring two pairs of straw sandals that had been interwoven with indigo cotton. Saying that this was a token of their parting, he wrapped them in a carrying cloth and placed them before Hanzo.

"This is what I needed more than anything else. I am very grateful. Thank you."

"They'll probably just be something more for you to carry, but maybe you can wear them on the way. We had them specially made for you."

"I might have expected such thoughtfulness from you."

Rushed as he was, Hanzo talked a while with the people in the house in Aioi-cho.

He had already completed his farewells and turned away when Takichi, his kimono tucked up into his sash, came running along after him. Takichi was reluctant to let Hanzo go and he volunteered to see him at least as far at the Juichiya.

"How about your baggage, Aoyama?"

"My baggage? We called for a packhorse yesterday."

"But you're leaving so early. In fact, we were hoping that you would be leaving from our place. I had talked about it with Osumi. But since you are with other people, we couldn't do anything about it. The next time you come to Edo, please come and see us. We'll put you up any time."

"I wonder if I will ever be able to come again."

At the Juichiya, Kohei and Heisuke were in their straw sandals, waiting for Hanzo. The horse they had called for was ready. There were reports that a tea caddy or something of the sort would be moving along the road today, so it was necessary to start as early as possible. Hanzo gathered his baggage together; one of the pieces was wrapped in a Ryukyu-style straw mat. Then, with the other headmen, he walked beside the packhorse toward Itabashi and the Kiso road.

4

In the latter part of the ninth month, the activists of the imperialist faction of Mito that had been gathered at Mt. Tsukuba since the fourth month moved to Nakaminato on the coast. There they joined with a friendly force and fought an engagement against the pro-Tokugawa Mito faction, which had been reinforced by troops from the shogunate. This battle at the harbor settled the fate of the Mito imperialists. Many were exhausted and surrendered to the shogunal forces. The Tsukuba force, which had held Nakaminato until the twenty-third, then joined with supporters assembled at Tateyama. They broke out of their encirclement by cutting a path to the west. The direction in which they were moving was clearly through the province of Kozuke toward Shinano. It was just when the reports of the fighting in Mito were coming in to Edo that the three headmen hurriedly left their inn in Ryogoku.

The beacon of rebellion that blazed forth in the skies over Mt. Tsukuba had not been without its connections to the western activists. The Tsukuba uprising had occurred about the same time that the Choshu forces were encircling Kyoto. Coordination between Mito and Choshu had in fact been planned several times, and even before the attack on the roju Ando Tsushima no Kami some of the activists of the two han had begun to exchange visits. The linked uprisings in the east and in the west had ended with the defeat of Choshu in the west and with the bitter struggle of the Mito band in the east.

After they broke out of Nakaminato, the Mito ronin passed through the village of Ishigami and began to move toward the village of Daigo in Kushi county. The opposing forces were unable to stop them there. They fought another engagement at Tsukiori pass, took billets in the Ungenji in Nasu, and headed up the Kozuke road.

Rather than that this group represented a certain faction, it might better be said that it constituted the last of the Mito activists, for it was made up entirely of outstanding people and its nucleus was formed by men who had studied in the han schools. The system of schools that had been set up by Nariaki in communities throughout Mito to educate both commoner and samurai children in the literate and martial arts somewhat resembled the later private schools of Kagoshima. In order to follow the fate of the Mito ronin, it is necessary to know something of their character.

Here is a temple. Nearby there is a playground for children. In the temple, there is a statue of Emma, the terrifying lord of the nether regions and judge of the dead. The eyes of Emma glitter and there is one child who thinks that they must be of fine crystal. He wants them so badly that at last he decides to steal them. He creeps into the ancient temple, deserted even at midday. When he approaches the statue, he finds that the eyes are beyond the reach of a child. He climbs up on the lap of the statue and digs the eyes out with his short sword. Then he leaves with them, thinking he has gained a great plunder. When he later learns that they are glass, he throws the eyes of King Emma away. This is a child of eight in the Mito of that time.

Here is a forest. There is the torii of a Shinto shrine. There are the grounds of the shrine, dark even at midday. One day, a youth casually starts to pass by these grounds when a voice calls out to him. "Wait a moment, boy!" When he looks up, he sees a tall man standing there whom the youth had jeered at as a vagrant ronin at the time of the festival at this shrine. Being at the height of mischievousness, he had gathered a crowd of other children and together they had showered the unfortunate man with abuse. The ronin, a lonely outsider, had pretended to ignore the taunts during the festival, but he had not forgiven the youth's behavior.

"You had a lot of terrible, humiliating things to say to me on the day of the festival," he says. "Now we will settle it man to man. Prepare yourself."

He grasps the hilt of his sword, but the youth is not alarmed. This is a youth who has been taught by his father that one cannot win a duel unless one kills the opponent with the first stroke, attacking with the same motion that brings the sword out of the sheath. It is already too late when both swords are drawn. He has been fully trained in this art, known as *iai,* and he merely says, "Very well." He removes the binding from his sword and uses it to tie up his sleeves; then he hitches up his trousers. When he glances at his opponent's feet he finds the stance to be that of a complete novice. He charges with a fierce cry and cuts at the man's forearm. He is still a mere child, however, and his sword is a child's sword only a foot and a half long. Before he can see whether he has cut his opponent or not, the ronin takes to his heels and disappears. The youth, badly shaken, runs home without looking behind him. This is a Mito youth of about fifteen.

It is upstairs. There is a sitting room. Sake is served. Beyond the railing of this second-floor sitting room in a wine shop, scores of unsheathed spears have been thrust up from below, forming a veritable palisade. Two samurai are surrounded here because they have been suspected by the town commissioner of plotting with other insubordinate samurai. When one of the samurai asks the person coming to take him into custody what this is all about since he has no recollection of having committed any crime, the reply is that the officer does not know himself, he is only following orders. "Well, then, first you will have to escort me," the samurai replies, and guarded by several men, he goes to the toilet where he throws all the papers from the breast of his kimono into the wastepot. Drawing his sword he thrusts the papers deep into the filth. Then, free of incriminating evidence, he lets himself be led away.

He is taken to the offices of the town commissioner in one of the net litters used for transporting criminals. There he is severely interrogated. There is no proof of the charges but he is nevertheless turned over to the wardens. This is at the time when the pro-shogunal forces in Mito have attained their greatest influence under the leadership of Ichikawa Sanzaemon and are just setting out to attack the imperialist faction at Mt. Tsukuba. There is confusion and disorder within the compound and the two samurai are guarded by only two soldiers.

Evening comes. One of the captive samurai whispers to his companion.

"The other side has been out to get me for a long time, and if I stay here I'm sure to be executed. Rather than being killed at their pleasure, it would be better to take care of these two guards and see how far we can get. What do you say?"

The other samurai is not under serious suspicion but he feels that it would violate the warrior's code not to help a fellow prisoner. And so he promises to join in a break that night before the moon rises.

"But the guards are not guilty of anything. It would be wrong to kill them," he argues. Then he calls the guards into the room. "It sounds as though Mito has fallen into terrible disorder. This is an autumn of great danger to the nation and a warrior cannot sit idly by. Therefore, we are leaving. If you let us go, nothing will happen to you, but if you feel that your duty compels you to try to hold us, we will be forced to try the edge of our swords on you. All right?"

As he speaks, he loosens his sword in its scabbard and displays its keen blade. The two guards give a single exclamation of assent, prostrate themselves on the ground, and do not look up.

"Well then, please excuse us. Look after things for us."

With these casual words the two samurai leave the room, climb over the wall of the compound, and disappear into the night.

Such were the members of the Tengu or imperialist band in Mito at that time. This fierce aggressiveness was shown to all who appeared to these Mito warriors as enemies, even the foreigners living in Yokohama and great shogunal officials such as Ii Tairo and the roju Ando. If such people, willing to stake their lives in an attack on any enemy, were to be found at the side of the Mito daimyo in Edo who opposed them or in Mito castle itself . . .

No han experienced such bitter struggles as Mito. There was an irreconcilable schism in han politics. Yet even now, when everyone was wavering, uncertain about which way to turn as the new age approached, there were still those in the han who continued in the old ways. The han had suffered no political unrest during the preceding two centuries and more. It was Mito that was carrying out the immense project of compiling the *History of Great Japan,* and it was Mito that called for the rectification of society in this age of the Tokugawa when some had even gone so far as to twist scholarship to the ends of flattery. The historical research of the Shokokan and the scholarship of the Kodokan had set such an example for the other han that there was scarcely a youth of the time who had not been influenced to some degree by Mito. Now Mito was caught in a terrible conflict between loyalty to the emperor and loyalty to the shogunate, a conflict personified in the turbulent life of Nariaki, the late retired lord. He had been heir to a tradition of deep reverence for the imperial family that dated back to Tokugawa Mitsukuni in the seventeenth century, and yet he was also, together with the lords of Kii and Owari, subject to a special responsibility to support the shogunate.

The torments of Mito had given rise to an imperialist faction that called itself the "Righteous party" and a pro-shogunal faction which it called the "Traitorous party." The han split in two and went to war with itself. Of course, there were factional clashes in other han during these times but none displayed the extreme ferocity of the struggle in Mito. The Righteous party fully believed the members of the Traitorous party to be completely evil. The members of the Traitorous party looked upon those of the Righteous party as disloyal retainers unconcerned about the needs of their own lord and indifferent to the interests of the senior branch of their lord's family, the shogunal house itself. This factional struggle in Mito took on the coloring of religious warfare, and many claimed that the issues went beyond victory or defeat, advantage or disadvantage. The Righteous party also called themselves the Tengu or "goblin band" while the Traitorous party called itself the Shoseito or "scholar's faction."

In the Mito of this time, all samurai of ability who were not Righteous were Traitorous and all who were not Traitorous were Righteous; the two were completely irreconcilable and fought each other bitterly. Those few who tried to stand between them were called "Willows," from the way they bent with every wind. When Ichikawa Sanzaemon, leader of the scholar's faction, came to hold decisive power in the han government, the goblin band took refuge on Mt. Tsukuba. They placed Tamaru Inaemon in command, offered up prayers to the spirit of Nariaki, and set out to realize their imperialist aims. The shogunate had long resented the imperialist faction in Mito. They suspected that Takeda Ko'unsai, one of the leaders of the goblin band, was in communication with the soldiers on Mt. Tsukuba and they placed him under house arrest. Then they ordered the eleven daimyo of the Kanto region to assist Ichikawa Sanzaemon, leader of the scholar's faction, in crushing the insurrection on Mt. Tsukuba. Sanzaemon left Edo at the head of a body of troops. Upon his arrival in Mito he promptly reported to the mother of the present lord and to the heir apparent, firmly establishing his authority. When Ko'unsai heard of this, he felt that the continued existence of the han was at stake. Breaking his house arrest, he fled from Mito. He denounced the lord of Mito, who was then in Edo, and began planning for the expulsion of the Traitorous warriors. With the han thus divided and in turmoil, Matsudaira Oinokami, also known as Baron Shishido, arrived in Yoshida in Mito on the twentieth of the eighth month to represent the daimyo. But Sanzaemon, already in Mito, saw that most of the warriors who accompanied this emissary of peace were opposed to him personally and that there were imperialists and supporters of Yoshimaru, the Mito heir apparent, in the group. He refused to admit them to the castle. This resulted in what was known as "the battle of the allies."

The confused struggle dragged on. Oinokami, Ko'unsai, and Inaemon each had his own ideas, but they were in firm agreement about support of the imperial cause. They also agreed that Sanzaemon, now based in Mito castle, was their common enemy. When Oinokami surrendered to Tanuma Gembanokami at the battle of Nakaminato, many officers and commoner soldiers also surrendered. The army of the Righteous faction broke apart and set fire to the encampments of its own allies. The number of men who surrendered to Tanuma Gembanokami rose to more than a thousand. Inaemon, who was leading the remnants of the Tsukuba group, had to withdraw from the Nakaminato battlefield, join forces with Ko'unsai at nearby Tateyama, and retreat with him to the west. The opposing forces in Nakaminato had been reinforced by troops from the shogunate and by large numbers of local men who saw their side as the winning one. Furthermore, Tanaka Genzo, a rather well known leader of the imperialist forces, had alienated the local people by looting them under the pretext of collecting military funds. But it was the defeat of the Choshu forces, who could otherwise have supplied them with all the money they needed, that was the heaviest blow.

The Mito band now began to move westward, surrounded by a cloud of rumors. Some said they were headed for Kyoto but most thought that they must be planning to go as far as Choshu.

It must not be forgotten, however, that these men were inspired by the example of the late lord Nariaki. They were rallying under his banner and attempting to carry out his will. The Tsukuba group, which constituted the nucleus of the Mito band, made up about three hundred of the total of more than nine hundred. The remaining six hundred were farmers from Hitachi and Shimotsuke. There were also some activists who had come down from Kyoto to help and even a few women. There were two physicians. Besides this well-organized group which possessed fighting ability, there were supply troops, cooks, service troops, and porters who swelled the numbers to well over a thousand. There were one hundred fifty war horses and many pack-horses. There was a signal drum and one hundred thirty-four battle flags. This was no rabble. Its actions were a manifestation of imperialist aims. That was what threw the shogunate into confusion.

Among the warriors was Fujita Koshiro. Eleven years had passed since Fujita Toko, who had inspired the late lord to take up the imperial cause, had left this world. His place had been taken by his son. It was Koshiro who had taken the initiative, speaking to the children in the han schools and winning over his immediate senior, Inaemon. At the very beginning he had taken refuge in Ohirayama in Shimotsuke province under the pretext of making a pilgrimage to Nikko. As one whose father had been steward of Mito, he did not fail to take his place as one of the four principal leaders of the group.

After winning a battle at Takazaki, the Mito warriors met almost no resistance as they advanced toward the village of Shimonita in Kozuke. The defenders of Takazaki had destroyed the bridge there and a force of some fifty men fired on the Mito ronin from a distance. The Kabura river flows through rich farmlands, but from its valley to Uchiyama pass the terrain is very rough. Even experienced packhorse drovers who set out from Shimonita early in the morning could not reach the top of the pass and get back before mid-afternoon. This was on the border between Kozuke and Shinano, a very difficult stretch, five miles up and four miles back down the other side. Here the Mito ronin found the road narrow and the bridges all down. The opposing forces appeared to be in full retreat before them. The roadside was littered with discarded weapons and supplies. The Mito warriors cut down trees, built rafts, loaded their clothing and equipment on them, and led their men and horses across the river. They took everything from cannon, ammunition cases, and chests of formal wear to palanquins over the steep pass and at last emerged onto the plateau region of Saku county in Shinano.

On the eighteenth day of the eleventh month, they crossed the Chikuma river and moved as far as Mochizuki. Reports came in that Matsumoto han had sent agents in disguise to spy on them. They redoubled their vigilance and strictly forbade their allies to engage in looting. On the nineteenth, the banners of the imperialist forces waved in the mountain air as they moved toward their evening billet at Wada.

CHAPTER TEN

1

A SCOUTING FORCE from Suwa han lay in wait at the top of Wada pass. Suganuma On'emon and Kurita Ichibei were there, each with five subordinates to assist them in keeping the castle informed. They were backed by three police inspectors, a scribe, three infantry scouts, each with his own porter, and a detachment of nineteen foot soldiers led by a lieutenant and a village headman. Two samurai equipped with the very latest rifles had also been sent to the scene.

The master of Takashima castle was serving in the shogun's council in Edo. Determined not to let the Mito men pass unscathed through his domain, he had sent a fast messenger to Takashima with orders for everyone to prepare the defenses. The portion of the Kiso road between the Wada stations was declared a war zone and the villagers living in Higashi Mochiya and Nishi Mochiya at the top of the pass were ordered to evacuate.

Even before events had reached this point the steward of Takashima castle had received a message by fast courier from the lord's residence in Edo. It was a special communication from the shogun to Suwa, reporting the westward movement of the Mito force and ordering that men be sent to Wada pass and the other passes immediately. Noting that a detour led from Wada pass toward Matsumoto, it ordered them to consult with Matsumoto han about assistance and to take every possible precaution. It further informed them that there might very well be additional assistance from Kofu in Kai province. They were to place their troops appropriately and to make sure that no opening was left either in the direction of Kai pass or up the Kiso road.

The day after this message reached Suwa, a general order went out from Edo to all the han in the region. It included as a matter of course all the daimyo with lands in the provinces of Musashi, Kozuke, Shimotsuke, Kai, and Shinano as well as daimyo in Sagami, Totomi, and Suruga provinces. Grave in tone and stern in content, it informed the daimyo that a large number of men from the rebel forces formerly encamped at Mt. Tsukuba were moving in the direction of Kai and the Kiso, and it ordered them to take all appropriate measures to capture the rebels, permitting none to escape. This order was accompanied by the statement that if the rebels did escape, assistance would be forthcoming from still other han and if such an escape was found to be due to negligence, appropriate punishment would follow. At the same time, the shogunate sent out an order to the daimyo in the provinces of Mikawa, Owari, Ise, Omi, Wakasa, Hida, Iga, and Echigo, alerting them that a band of the Tsukuba rebels was on the move and causing disorders in other areas. These daimyo were ordered to make preparations not only in their own domains but also in the adjacent areas and to take all suspicious persons into custody. Since the battle at Nakaminato, the rebels had been pursued by a force led by Tanuma Gembanokami, who had earlier led the shogunal troops to the assistance of the scholar's faction. Thus, as it was carrying out its campaign against Choshu, the shogunate also laid out a net across the country in an attempt to exterminate the Mito rebels.

At the time they received the order, the people in Suwa were hearing of almost unbelievable events some two hundred miles away. There was not a single person in Takashima castle who believed that they would ever see the Mito ronin. Even when they heard that the rebels had entered Kozuke, they were uncertain of the truth of the accounts and it was still many miles distant. There was utter complacency in Suwa. Then messengers began arriving with reports that the ronin had entered Shinano province, then that they had entered Saku county. The people in the castle quickly evaluated their position. Some blanched at the thought of confronting the resolute Mito men, saying that it was readily understandable why they were not being attacked along their route, since Suwa itself would not be able to withstand a force of more than one thousand men either. These people suggested that it would be best simply to defend the castle and wait until the Mito force had passed them by. If they then fired on them from behind, they would have fulfilled their duty to the shogunate. Others protested that since the lord of Suwa was in Edo in the high office of roju, his han could not permit the Mito ronin to do as they pleased, and still others insisted that the prowess of the Mito men had been exaggerated. There were also some who suggested that they should try to get by with a minimal response.

Then an emissary, an important elder retainer of the han, came rushing out from the Edo residence to the castle, bearing strict orders from the shogunate. When they received reports that the Mito ronin had reached Mochizuki and that they had with them fifteen cannon, one hundred fifty mounted warriors, seven hundred foot soldiers, everything in fact from banners to a supply train, the faces of all those in the castle went pale. Shiohara Hikoshichi, one of the senior retainers, stepped forward to say that the Mito ronin would surely be crossing Wada pass. There, in the place known as Toihashi, with the river on one side and the steep face of the mountain on the other, was the ancient battlefield made famous by Suwa Yorishige. It was only about eight miles from the castle.

"If we go there," insisted Shiohara, "and take advantage of the difficult terrain to fortify the strategic positions, we can capture the enemy."

Fortunately, it had been confirmed that Tanuma Gembanokami, the shogunal commander, was in pursuit of the Mito ronin with a large force. The steward and most of the other Suwa retainers were counting on Tanuma's support. Greatly encouraged by the idea of driving the Mito ronin into Wada pass, to be attacked from one direction by the Takashima force and from the other by the force under Tanuma, the han established its positions. That was the situation when the scouts were dispatched to Wada pass.

It was the nineteenth day of the eleventh month of Genji 1, 1864. A heavy rain had been falling in the pass since morning.

Presently, scouts who had gone off toward Wada returned to the pass. When the report came that the Mito ronin would be camped that night at the two stations of Nagakubo and Wada, Yajima Denzaemon, the field commander of the Suwa force, went out with an advance guard of nine men to the boundary marker in Wada pass. Accompanied by a group of unarmed youths, commoners armed with lances, sandal bearers, porters carrying armor, and flag bearers, they made a bold and impressive spectacle. The field commander's horse was led by two grooms.

"We must assume the enemy is near."

One of the guards was sent back to the castle to deliver this message. Without dismounting, he also relayed the field commander's order to move the remainder of the troops up to the frontier. Yajima was moving quickly about on his own horse making final arrangements. At the summit of the pass rain-drenched men and horses rushed back and forth through a downpour that obscured all but the nearest mountainsides.

Yajima chose a place in the pass called Shimekake to prepare so that it could at least be defended against the first attack. He ordered laborers to be sent in from the nearby villages to begin construction of the fortifications while he went out with subordinate officers to look for other defensible positions. Great logs were set up to form a stockade at Shimekake, guns were brought in, and men were placed in readiness. From Ohira to Umamichishita the steep mountain road was rendered impassable by blocking it with trees and boulders. At Shimekake preparations were made to bring the enemy troops under musket fire immediately and to roll logs and stones down upon them as they approached. It was felt that the Suwa right wing could hold against any force that might come through. In the meantime they were expecting to receive heavy reinforcements. Detachments of men were assigned their positions and given their orders. The field commander was rushing back and forth through the driving rain to make sure of everything. By the time all had been done, it was already noon. When Yajima came back down as far as Toihashi to take lunch, a large force of laborers was assembling there.

The guard Yajima had dispatched earlier to Takashima castle returned about that time to report that the rest of their forces would soon be arriving. While he was reporting, twenty-eight samurai, nineteen artillerymen, twenty-nine musketeers, and two guns firing one and a half pound balls, two three-quarter pound guns, and a Western-style field piece arrived from Suwa. The samurai now coming out from the castle relayed to Yajima the decision that had been reached to make the main stand at a place called Tozawaguchi, just above Toihashi. Discussion ensued about the danger of Higashi Mochiya and Nishi Mochiya providing shelter for the enemy, and it was decided that both villages would have to be burned out under orders from the local deputy. The suspension bridges would be taken down and the regular bridges destroyed. A detachment of soldiers and laborers was sent up toward the pass to see to it.

Three hundred fifty men sent out by Matsudaira Tamba no Kami, lord of Matsumoto han, had withdrawn from their camp at Nagakubo and were gathered at Higashi Mochiya. Tamba no Kami had sent the soldiers out in obedience to the orders of Tanuma Gembanokami, commander of the pursuing forces. They had gone to Nagakubo to hold the road there, but when they learned that neither Ueda, nor Matsushiro, nor Komoro was sending troops, they saw that it would be impossible for them to stand against the Mito ronin by themselves. They had now come with their leaders to request permission to join in the defense of Toihashi—a completely unexpected reinforcement for the Suwa men. Yajima immediately welcomed them and dispatched a message to the Matsumoto official that, though they were not properly prepared to make use of the men, they would accept his troops as a vanguard. The Matsumoto force hurriedly set fire to Higashi Mochiya and the Suwa force burned Nishi Mochiya to the ground while waiting for the Matsumoto troops to complete their passage.

Yajima was at Toihashi where he was expediting the efforts of some five or six hundred laborers to carry out the building of the defensive works in a continuing downpour. The Matsumoto force began coming in from the pass and Yajima loaned them the three houses at Toihashi for billets. He supplied them with three bales of polished rice, two kegs of miso, a keg of pickled vegetables, and a keg of sake, which he calculated would suffice for their noon meal. The Matsumoto force had brought two one-and-a-half pounders and fifty muskets.

The defense of the positions around Toihashi had for the most part been planned by Yajima with the strategic advice of the commander of the Suwa musketeers, Shiohara Hikoshichi. Throughout the daylong downpour, sounds of great trees being felled by hundreds of laborers dressed in rain caps and capes reverberated through the mountains. Here, a log footing was laid for a gun emplacement. There, sandbags were stacked up make a breastwork. When it was learned that the provisions sent out from Shimo-Suwa would not arrive in time, the command post was set up at Toihashi and the cooking of locally requisitioned supplies was begun. As night fell, the work was continued by torchlight illuminating the entire valley. The bridge at Taruki-iwa was broken up and the Ochiai bridge was also destroyed. In the Murakami forest flares were lighted alongside the highway and a rotating guard of four or five men at a time was posted.

The report of the westward movement of the Mito ronin brought chaos to the lives of the common people living along the route. It was the intention of

Suwa to stop the ronin at the positions above Toihashi, but their opponents were men who were veterans of a score or more of victories in other battles. What would happen if they were victorious here as well? The thought brought terror to the people along the route. Rumors were being passed on by everyone. It was said that if the Suwa forces were defeated at Wada pass they would surely burn Toihashi, or they would retreat to Shimo-Suwa and burn the station there, or they would make a stand at Shimo-Suwa and try to prevent a single enemy from entering Takashima. If the worst should happen, some said, Suwa would burn Shimohara village and possibly the neighboring villages of Kubo and Takei, while in the most extreme case even Takagi and Yamato would be burned to deny shelter to the enemy.

The people along the lines of march were in panic. Some put not only their valuables but even the doors and shoji from their houses into their fireproof storehouses. Those who did not have such storehouses stored their valuables in someone else's storehouse. Some even carried their possessions to nearby villages.

Again and again there came reports that everything in the path of the ronin was to be destroyed, even the storehouses. Those who heard this were even more alarmed and the valuables that they had already placed in their storehouses were taken out again. Some dug holes and buried their possessions in the ground and others carried their valuables out into the fields. Others took care to wear as many of their clothes as possible, saying that they would not otherwise last through this rainy weather. The people found themselves thrown together in this swirl of disorder and could read the turbulence of the time in each other's eyes. Everyone in the vicinity—young and old, men and women—vanished into the hills that night except for the few who hid out in the fields.

The Mito ronin left Wada before daybreak under the command of Takeda Ko'unsai Iga no Kami, with the former commissioner of the town of Mito, Tamaru Inaemon, as second-in-command and the former commander of guards, Yamakuni Hyobu, famous even in other han for his brilliance in military tactics, in charge of planning. They advanced along the highway at a rate of ten to twelve miles per day. This was a deliberate policy to avoid overtiring the foot soldiers, but on that day they had some eight miles to go just to reach the summit of the pass.

The weather was fine. There was not a single cloud in the morning sky. Presently the ronin were in the pass. Behind eight red and white banners, divided into three columns, the long black line of men and horses climbed up the hill. Both Mochiya were burned out and not a single Suwa soldier was seen. As the vanguard reached Incense Burner rock, the mounted troops heard four shots fired at them from the forest. None of the balls hit anyone— they flew off into the trees or struck the ground—but they betrayed the presence of enemy soldiers. A Suwa signal flag could be seen waving on the top of the mountain to the left.

There were fallen trees barricading the mountain road ahead. Those who tried to ride over the barriers, those who tried to remove them, and those who went to repair the suspension bridge beyond all used up a great deal of time in opening the way for the main force. Some of the ronin worked their way up the mountain beyond Incense Burner rock, where they waved a blue and white pennon. Then others went up the facing mountain and set up three red flags at a position from which they could look down upon the Suwa and Matsumoto forces.

As the Mito ronin approached, the Suwa force was still counting on assistance from the shogunal forces. But there was no sign in Wada pass of the constantly rumored force under Tanuma. There was nothing for the Suwa force to do now but join with the Matsumoto force in meeting a frontal attack. Soon the Mito troops had worked their way down from the summit of the pass to Hoshigusayama. Now they were only four or five hundred yards away from the Suwa force on the other side of the valley. The collision between the two forces began with the opening of fire from the Mito side. The sound of guns boiled up among the mountains and through the valleys.

The Suwa troops fought stubbornly. Gradually the Mito ronin, advancing with loud battle cries, pushed them down from Tozawaguchi toward Toihashi, but were thrown back by fire from the Suwa breastworks. The Suwa and Matsumoto forces were divided into five columns. The right wing was deployed in the usual order with the artillery in front and the lancers in the rear, but the left wing had the lancers in front and they would counterattack each time the ronin attempted to break through. Three times the ronin attacked and three times they failed; they could advance no further.

The battle began shortly after noon and continued until near sunset without anything being decided by the exchanges of cannon and musket fire. When the blazing evening sun began to shine directly into their eyes the Mito ronin found themselves at a disadvantage, unable to aim their muskets. Yamakuni Hyobu noted the difficulty and looked for a way out. Drawing on what he had learned about the terrain from his guides, he had a three-quarter pounder moved to the top of the mountain on the right to divert the attention of the Suwa forces, and then he sent a band of some fifty or sixty men across the river on their left to climb around the peak of Mt. Fukazawa where they took up a position on the mountainside from which they could fire down on the flank of the Matsumoto force. The move caught both the Matsumoto and the Suwa forces by surprise. The sun had set behind the mountains and the Matsumoto troops were exhausted. Then the Matsumoto commander was killed by a musket ball fired by a ronin from up on the mountainside. The Matsumoto men fell into disorder. Taking advantage of the confusion, the ronin charged down the mountainside, firing as they went.

Ko'unsai advanced to Tozawaguchi and set up his command post there. He struck the war drum himself to order the final charge. It was already dark. Some of the Suwa troops were beginning to waver while others worried about their path of retreat. The Suwa units in the positions at Toihashi were still holding firm and some detachments were determined to make a stand but they could do nothing once the entire order of battle began to crumble. It

now appeared that the Matsumoto force was in complete disorder and consequently more and more Suwa men were beginning to break away from the
battlefield.

In the end, Tanuma Gembanokami never appeared. The battle ended in
defeat for the Suwa and Matsumoto forces. Flames suddenly rose in the night
sky as the three houses at Toihashi were fired to deny shelter to the enemy. In
the light of the flames there were some who wanted once again to hold their
ground. One man even went back to the original position and fired two
more rounds from a cannon. There were scattered small skirmishes. Then the
fires began to burn down and in the skies of the twentieth day of the lunar
month there was no moon to take their place. A total darkness, in which no
one could distinguish friend from enemy, descended upon the fleeing Suwa
and Matsumoto forces.

In this battle at Tozawaguchi, seventeen ronin fell and more than a hundred were wounded. Their leader, Ko'unsai, was tired but still able to call all
his troops into Toihashi. The wife of the grand councillor, who had been
with the force ever since the battle of Nakaminato, was safe; Yamakuni and
his son were safe, as were Inaemon and Koshiro of the Tsukuba force. They
all spread out and surveyed the Suwa positions by torchlight. In these
emplacements and around the remains of the earthworks, among the discarded helmets, muskets, and swords and the abandoned camp stools and
jackets of the officers, lay the grisly sight of the dead, both friend and foe.
The stench of fresh blood rose on the night air and struck into their nostrils.

Ko'unsai, using a bare lance as a walking stick, strode among the soldiers
in the company of Inaemon, Hyobu, and Koshiro. They could not be sure
that there would be no counterattack, so they quickly reformed and firmed
up their positions. Then Ko'unsai ordered one of his commanders to examine
the bodies of the enemy dead, cut off their heads, and bury them deep in the
earth in appropriate places. There were ten men who were seriously
wounded. Foot soldiers were ordered to place these men on improvised
stretchers and to give them first aid. Now the two physicians accompanying
the force were needed. There was also an old woman who had come with the
force from Mito, and she worked intently with the physicians, a sword
thrust into her sash.

It was almost midnight. The ronin took care of the bodies of their own
dead. They carried the more important ones into a grass hut, which was then
burned. The others were partially burned where they were found and then
buried in the ground. The makeshift funeral ceremony was over. There were
abandoned lunches and other supplies around the Toihashi camp and all made
a meager repast of these. They were terribly hungry, terribly thirsty. Only
the station of Shimo-Suwa promised relief. They formed into companies of
twenty-five men each and prepared to leave Toihashi, the sound of the conch
shells resounding in the night skies.

There were two villages between Toihashi and Shimo-Suwa. The long line
of Mito ronin moved down the dark highway, scouts deployed ahead, show-

ing no lights for fear of enemy ambush. They passed Ochiai. They passed lower Hara village. There was not a single enemy soldier left in either place.

It was late at night when the advance force of the ronin entered Shimo-Suwa to the accompaniment of shots in the air and the sound of the battle drum. The retreating Suwa and Matsumoto forces had already passed through on their way to Takashima castle, and there were no enemy soldiers here either. The town was empty. The ronin entered house after house to find rice that had been abandoned while being washed for the evening meal. Ko'unsai went to the toiya, and Inaemon to the Raigo temple. Flares were lit at each intersection, before the torii of the Aki shrine, and at the meeting house beside the bathhouse and at various other places. Groups of four or five men patrolled in relays on guard against fires or a possible night attack by the enemy.

The rear guard of some three hundred men had difficulty in reaching Shimo-Suwa. They had been the reserve in that day's battle and now they were carrying the wounded. They could not help falling behind.

In the meantime the leaders in the field headquarters had made their plans for the next day. They had never intended to attack Takashima castle; it was only to open their route to the west that they had gone so far as to wage this bitter engagement with the Suwa forces. In that night's staff conference, the question was how to proceed from here. There were two roads open to them. Should they go over Shiojiri pass, through Kikyo meadow, past Seba Motoyama to Niekawa, and from there straight up the Kiso road? Or should they turn off through Okano and Tatsuya and proceed toward the Ina road? Their concern was not with evading the barrier at Fukushima. Rather, they knew that the entire fifty-odd miles through the Kiso mountains and forests, with its numerous steep grades, would prove difficult to maneuver in. They decided instead to go toward the Ina district with its broad valley and its numerous alternate routes.

Since their arrival in Shimo-Suwa they had passed the night virtually without sleep or rest. By the time the rear guard had reached the town and caught its breath, the main body was preparing to move on through the night. No one wanted to stay any longer in this pleasant hot-spring resort. Among the ronin preparing to leave, most had not even taken the time to sample the waters.

"Watch out for looters!"

The cry arose from both the staff and the more alert soldiers. In the confusion, some fifteen or sixteen storehouses had been broken into and looted by unknown parties. It had gone on unnoticed during the turmoil of preparations for departure in the unpoliced darkness.

By the sixth hour of the morning, all the ronin had left Shimo-Suwa. They were to have a brief rest at Hiraide station and their noon meal at Okaya. Among those hurrying down the road, some pushing munitions carts wore magnificent campaign jackets that betrayed their high rank. Others rode horses although they had no armor. Still others carried the wounded on stretchers. There was a heavy frost. The air was cold.

2

Of course, the ronin could not turn back. Reports continued to reach them that the punitive force under Tanuma was still in pursuit. The long column of more than a thousand men moved on into Ina on guard against dangers both ahead and behind.

The people along the way, having heard the rumors that the men from Tsukuba were no more than a band of marauders, were amazed that when the ronin passed through they paid the standard inn charge of two hundred fifty mon per man for lodging, meals, and a lunch to carry along. Others were equally startled to see the money boxes bearing the hollyhock crest of the Tokugawa, the long-handled parasols of state, the clothing chests with their crests, and the great palanquins that accompanied the procession, making the passage look exactly like that of a daimyo possessing revenues of thirty to forty thousand koku.

This was no accident. The crested money chests, the parasols, the clothing trunks, and the palanquins were all marked in memory of Nariaki, the late lord of Mito. Even though the lord himself was not with them, the column, as it moved along under a banner with the inscription "Grand Councillor of the Twelfth Rank," was exactly the same as one escorting a living person. The lord had died in his villa in Komagome in Edo without ever learning that he had been released from permanent house arrest or ever during his lifetime meeting an imperial emissary from Kyoto. This retinue, now moving instead toward Kyoto under banners inscribed with the slogan "Service to the Emperor," was made up of the Mito people and their allies, whom the late lord had loved as his own children and grandchildren. These people, called rebels by the shogunate and disloyal retainers by their opponents in Mito, holding fast to memory of the departed lord by making his goals their own, were moving with each step farther and farther away from their homes in distant Hitachi province.

The ronin were not able to relax their guard even when they reached the banks of the Tenryu river in the Ina valley. Everyone still wore full armor or tall black ceremonial caps and campaign jackets. Their red and white banner displayed on high and the guidons marking the separate divisions shone amidst the bare lances carried by the mounted warriors, making them seem a host vast beyond counting.

The squadrons were organized into six troops. Each was provided with two cannon, inscribed with copies of the late lord's calligraphy: "Totally Loyal in Service. Written by Minamoto Nariaki." This slogan was a point of special pride to the ronin. The banner with the inscription SONJO held so proudly aloft at the center of the column, together with the war drum, had been with them since Mt. Tsukuba. The staff officers were in the second troop. Mounted warriors constantly guarded the front, rear, and flanks of the column, their movement controlled by the sound of wooden clappers according to a system developed by the staff. Behind a banner inscribed "Service to the Emperor" came Ko'unsai with a hundred mounted warriors, preceded by a triple diamond guidon. They were followed by two hundred foot soldiers. Koshiro, a former personal attendant of the lord of Mito and now one of the commanders, his golden guidon flying before his mounted warriors, firmed up the central division, guarded by a hundred musketeers. Inaemon, accompanied by some fifty lancers, with a guidon in the shape of a paper mulberry leaf, brought up the rear with the authority appropriate to the second-in-command. There were, of course, other fathers and sons besides the Yamakuni in the force. The slogans inscribed on the banners of each detachment spoke of their pride in being the Mito force of righteousness. One of the banners read "First of the Hundred Flowers," expressing their sense of being early forerunners just beginning to break out of the hard shell of the middle ages and to raise their heads a bit.

In Ina, Takato han awaited them. The news of the battle of Wada pass had already reached that far. The report of the death in battle of Mizuno Shinzaemon, the steward of Matsumoto, and of many others, along with the capture by the Mito force of war drums, lances, armor, cannon, and assorted weaponry, brought a deep silence to Takato. Yet they could not reject the firm orders of the shogunate, and soldiers were sent out along both banks of the Tenryu river. But when it was heard that the ronin were coming, the Takato commander withdrew from his encampment at Hiraide toward a place called Tenjinyama. After that the ronin were free to continue their advance all the more bravely, gathered into a single, well-disciplined band.

No detachment got too far ahead; none fell behind. The voices of men chanting poetry could be heard among the ranks. Others sang from on horseback. Some passed out candy to the children along the roadside. There were youths fifteen or sixteen years old among them who would loiter along the way, fall behind, and then gallop wildly to catch up again.

They advanced still deeper into the valley. On the twenty-second, the ronin reached Kamiho and learned that Hori Iwami no Kami, lord of Iida, had built defensive works and placed several cannon at Yumiyazawa, near Ichida village. After overcoming one obstacle, the ronin were faced with still another.

"We are in complete sympathy with Mito. We have followed you, aware of your position and that of Iida, with the thought that we might offer our services. All three of us are disciples of Hirata Atsutane."

It was a completely unexpected group that appeared before the commanders of the Mito force to make this statement. Among them was Imamura Toyosaburo, one of the ardent band of National Scholars from Zakoji village in Ina. Another was Kureta Masaka, one of the men who had exposed the head of the wooden statue of Ashikaga Takauji in the riverbed in Kyoto and who had been living in hiding in Ina ever since.

On the alert for spies, the ronin were not prepared to place confidence in these three men. Tamura Unosuke, a transport officer present at this interview, said with a casual abruptness, "I have heard that the disciples of Hirata

Atsutane in Ina have set out to publish his *Commentaries on Ancient History.*
How many volumes are out now?''

"Oh that? Well, we have just finished the fourth case. Since there are
four volumes to a case, we have now put out sixteen volumes. I don't
know if you have heard, but the person who decided to publish this
work was Kitahara Inao of Zakoji. Imamura Toyosaburo here is his younger
brother.''

This reply disarmed the suspicions of the Mito commanders. The proposal
that the three came forward with was that, unqualified by rank though they
might be, they wished to serve as mediators with Iida, urging that the ronin
be permitted to pass through without a fight. Masaka and Toyosaburo then
attempted to ascertain the attitude of the ronin. Of course the Mito men did
not enjoy fighting either. No one could object to this plan to get them past
Iida without harm to the local people or to themselves, so there was no dissent. Upon hearing this, the three men left quickly in order to report back to
Kitahara Inao, who was waiting in Zakoji village, and to confer with the
officials of Iida.

On the twenty-third, the Mito force advanced to Katagiri. Along the valley floor from here to Iida there were several scores of villages scattered on
both sides of the Tenryu river. It was an area where the Hirata school was
firmly rooted, through the efforts of disciples such as Iwasaki Nagayo, Kitahara Inao, Katagiri Shun'ichi, and their associates. Ardent supporters of the
Hirata cause could also be found in Iida, in Yamakuni, in Tomono, in Ajima,
in Ichida, and in still other villages along the way. This was the Ina valley. It
was not surprising that such people as the Kitahara brothers should now
come forward, unable to remain silent onlookers any longer.

It was not far from Katagiri to Iida. There the castle of Hori Iwami no
Kami awaited the approach of the ronin, wrapped in a forbidding silence.
This outward calm, however, hid an unimaginable amount of confusion—of
staff conferences, preparations for sudden siege, hurried measures for the protection of key positions. If the castle should decide to withstand a siege, the
town would quickly be burned out. The terrible fires and dislocations of war
would sweep over all the people who lived there.

That night, Toyosaburo and his older brother, Kitahara Inao, came hurrying from Iida by fast litter, headed for the command post of Takeda Ko'unsai,
now located at the Katagiri toiya. Yokota Toshiro and Fujita Koshiro came
out to meet them. Warning that it was essential, because of the orders of the
shogunate, not to make public the permission for free passage through Iida
by a secondary road, the Kitahara brothers brought out the documents that
had resulted from their meeting with the Iida officials. The following three
concessions were written out.

1. Iida will withdraw from its defensive positions at Yumiyazawa.
2. Repairs will be made to the secondary road.
3. The town of Iida will contribute three thousand ryo for military expenses.

*   *   *   *   *   *   *

"Are you a farmer from these parts? We're short on porters, so we'd like you to carry a lance for us."

"No, I am a traveler. Please excuse me from accompanying you."

"Now don't try to give us that. If you just come along with us as far as Katagiri, we'll let you go then."

After this exchange a farmer from Sawado village had been forced to go as far as Katagiri with the last of the Mito column.

Presently it was morning. Under the agreement that the Kitahara brothers had worked out, the ronin were ready to leave Katagiri and press on through a side road. Some of the lancers of the vanguard were already in Komaba.

The ronin of the rear guard were not letting go of the farmer whom they had forced to accompany them. The farmer was twenty-five or twenty-six years of age, at the height of his strength, and a good hand for moving freight.

"Where are you from?" asked one of the ronin.

"Me? I was born in Iijima in Suwa and my name is Kozo. I have accompanied you to Katagiri as you asked. I will now take my leave."

"What! Suwa?"

The ronin quickly bound Kozo with his own sash before speaking again.

"I am taking you to justice, so resign yourself to it."

The ronin took the farmer to the nearby river, his hands tied behind his back. When Kozo inquired what he meant by justice, the ronin said it meant that he was going to cut off his head. The unfortunate farmer trembled.

"Samurai, I am not a criminal or an enemy. I had business in Ina and on the way I was overtaken by your column. I'll go with you as far as you want if only you'll spare me."

"Oh, will you? Well then, since I am with the combat troops, I'll turn you over to the supply people."

Such were the lengths to which the Mito ronin were forced to go just to recruit a single porter.

Soon the various troops were beginning to move one after another along the secondary road. This road bore away from the town of Iida and, turning to the right at Kami-Kuroda, went on from Nosokoyama by way of Kami-Iida toward Imamiya. When they reached Imamiya, it was time for the noon meal. When Kozo, the farmer from Suwa, had laid down the chest of armor that he had been carrying from Katagiri and was having a rest, he was given a numbered tag and a sword. One of the grooms from the supply troops then began to tease him, saying that if he wanted to send a message to his family, they would dispatch a courier. The groom told him that if he was tired of carrying the baggage they would let the others do that, so would he please stay with them all the way to Kyoto. Well aware that the farmer might flee, the groom had not forgotten to have a guard assigned to him.

When he heard Kyoto mentioned, the farmer said, "I have two old parents at home. Please forgive me, but I must leave now."

"If you talk that way, we'll take you to justice," was the groom's reply.

The ronin marched along the side road as far as Kireishi, where they came out again on the main Ina road. The Mikawa road continued on from there. Kitahara Inao went ahead to guide them as far as Osegi. On that day he was accompanied by one of the elders of the Hirata school in the Ina district, Kurasawa Yoshiyuki, who had worked inconspicuously but very hard to help get the Mito ronin past Iida without a fight. When they parted, the Mito ronin, grateful for Inao's work, tried to present him with a fine campaign jacket, but he would not accept it for fear of arousing the shogunate's suspicions. At Komaba, where the ronin were billeted for that night, disciples of the Hirata school were gathered: Kureta Masaka and Matsuo Makoto, eldest son of Matsuo Taseko, from Tomono. Masuda Heihachiro and Namiai Sagenta from Namiai. The Komaba physician, Yamada Bun'iku. At the house in Komaba which was serving as the command post, these men who knew the countryside instructed the Mito commanders about the back roads through the mountains that would be most free from pointless collisions with small han and their officials. The two men from Namiai told them that if they continued from that point onto the Mikawa road, they might have to fight the great han of Owari, or at the very least face very grave dangers along the way. The men from Tomono told them that along the Kiso road as far as Nakatsugawa, Hara Nobuyoshi of Seinaiji, Aoyama Hanzo of Magome, and Asami Keizo and Hachiya Kozo of Nakatsugawa could be counted upon to be sympathetic to the Mito ronin.

They decided to change their route and go through Seinaiji and on to Magome and Nakatsugawa.

"Gentlemen—go back to the north about two and a half miles from here. Turn left at a place called Yamamoto and go on toward Seinaiji."

The transport officers went around to each of the divisions with this order.

The route from the Ina valley to the western edge of the Kiso, whether they went by way of the Odaira pass or the Nashino pass, would be over a backwoods road. This was the road that caused so much hardship to the villagers of the one hundred nineteen Ina communities who were assigned to assist the lower four Kiso stations in times of heavy travel. Mountain leeches dropped from the trees, horseflies plagued the traveler, the wind howled over the bamboo grass. More than ten long miles of valley so densely forested that it was dark even at noon lay ahead of them before they could be rid of these discomforts. Travelers through this valley would discover a land inhabited only by charcoal makers, where it was too cold for even the most marginal farming. The Mito ronin had to transport the wounded from the battle of Wada pass and some dozen cannon through these mountains.

3

Hanzo was at the Magome honjin waiting for the arrival of the Mito ronin. Late in the tenth month, just as the first reports came in to Edo that the Mito ronin were moving to the west, he had hurriedly set out for home along the backroads in the company of the headmen of Niekawa and Fukushima. Already at that time his concern had been to protect the people of the village from the coming disorder along the road.

The attention of the country had been focused on the actions of the Mito men who had risen under the imperialist banner and on the events following the raising of troops at Mt. Tsukuba. There was also the question of how the shogunate would control the force of some twelve hundred men under Sakakibara Sazaemon who had surrendered, and the more than nine hundred men under Takeda Ko'unsai who had escaped after the battle of Nakaminato. Over the nearly thirty days that had passed since that battle, Hanzo had been able to learn a great deal about the fate of Baron Shishido, who had been captured by the Tokugawa forces. Tanuma Gembanokami, commander of the shogunate's punitive force, was said to have claimed that Takeda Ko'unsai had conspired with the traitor Ichikawa Sanzaemon, and so he had ordered the death of Baron Shishido. It was also reported that the death toll had reached forty-three, including twenty-eight of Shishido's followers who were put to death along with him, twelve Mito samurai also condemned, and several of Shishido's personal retainers who had disemboweled themselves when they heard of his death. The effect on the Mito ronin of the tragic end of Baron Shishido was immense. It could be said that these men, already accused of treason, first turned their feet westward upon hearing this news. These men who had set out with the conviction that "after all, Mito cannot go on toadying to the shogunate forever" were now irreconcilably estranged from the shogunate. Their only road was the one that lay ahead of them.

Hanzo found the terror that the coming of these men inspired in the people along the way difficult to understand. Why had this force, which had no interest in Takashima castle, been so feared in Suwa? Why had these men who did not want to fight been so feared in Takato and Iida? It was because the deadly determination with which these Mito samurai marched had made clear by contrast just how far the general loss of martial spirit had progressed during more than two centuries of peace, and it had shown to what a limited degree the loyalty of those below could be relied upon in a time of difficulty.

Even so, Hanzo had never imagined that the events around that Mt. Tsukuba which he had glimpsed so far off to the northeast from Ryogoku bridge in Edo would reach the Ina valley within a single month. He had been attracted to Mito scholarship since childhood and he could not forget even now the feelings with which he had once chanted Fujita Toko's "Song of Righteousness." But Hanzo had never expected that Fujita Toko's son would one day be in the nearby mountains or that he would be receiving him in his own home. Still less had he ever imagined that he, as a Hirata disciple, would be coming before these last members of the Mito school in this way.

It turned out that there were old friends of his among those who had committed themselves to the Mito cause. Recently he had learned that his fellow disciple Kameyama Yoshiharu had joined the supply troops of the Mito ronin on the fourteenth of the eighth month and had been with them ever since. At the time that the ronin changed their route, appearing to head down the Mikawa highway toward the Tokaido but in reality heading through Seinaiji toward Magome and Nakatsugawa, Hanzo had received along with the notice that they planned to take lodgings in Magome, a letter from his friend in the ronin camp. In that letter, Kameyama said that he had committed himself to this force as soon as he learned that the Mito samurai had risen in support of the imperialist cause, but that so far he had not distinguished himself in any way. He further said that he had pledged his life to Takeda and Fujita in support of this cause. Kameyama added that when he recently passed through Iijima in lower Ina county he had unexpectedly met their comrade Kureta Masaka. Kureta had expressed his gratitude for the lodging he had been given on that long-ago night and spoke of his desire to talk with Aoyama once again after so many years.

"What is this all about, Hanzo?" asked Juheiji, who had come over from Tsumago.

By that time, the Yamamura deputies in Fukushima had already sent out troops to close both ends of the Kiso valley in accordance with the orders of the shogunate. These guards were placed at Sakurazawa near Niekawa in the east and at Tsumago in the west. Of course, the fifty or sixty troops who had come to Tsumago under Uematsu Shosuke, the Fukushima master of artillery, had gone on to close off the Ina road. At night they had stretched a net with bells attached to its edges across the road, and placed guards in hiding, maintaining their vigil in the strictest silence. Juheiji had come over with this news from Tsumago and to find out how things were in Magome.

"Have you received any reports from Fukushima, Juheiji?"

"About the ronin? Nothing has come to the honjin or the toiya."

"It looks as though they have something in mind, but they have said nothing to me either. Usually, I would have expected to receive orders to refuse them lodging."

"Well, Hanzo, it seems as though the Yamamura want the ronin to go through with as little trouble as possible."

"They'll probably come from Seinaiji over towards Araragi and then turn out at the bridge. After that they will be coming here. If they reach Magome, I plan to receive them as travelers."

"I am relieved to hear that. Just let them get safely from Magome down to Nakatsugawa. That's what the Yamamura back at Fukushima really want, too."

"There's nothing to worry about at Tsumago. I have a request to make of you, Juheiji. I think it's going to be pretty busy around here tomorrow. If things at Tsumago will permit it, could you come over? This has all come up so suddenly. We haven't had time to make preparations. I had everyone to a meeting at the meeting room this morning and I put everyone in the village to work on it. I'm just taking a breather now."

"By the way, they have a lot to thank the Hirata people for in Iida. You people really get things done."

"So, it seems that even you are beginning to recognize the value of the Hirata people."

Soon the post station officials who had been assigned various parts of the village began to come back and report in. Inosuke was returning from Ara-machi, Kyurobei from Toge. Most of the houses within the village would be used to lodge the troops and even the Mampukuji would take as many as it could. Of course, the honjin, Inosuke's place, and Kimbei's retirement quar-ters at the Upper Fushimiya would lodge the twenty-one high-ranking guests.

"I'll be leaving now, Hanzo, but I'll be back tomorrow if I possibly can."

Juheiji left as inconspicuously as he had arrived.

Suddenly the appearance of the post station changed. When it became known that more than a thousand Mito ronin were ascending the Nashino pass, some of the villagers fled into the countryside. Others locked up their valuables in their storehouses. Still others packed their important records and their swords into chests and took them as far as Aono.

It was the end of the eleventh month by the old calendar. Early in the morning of the twenty-sixth, a wintry rain began to fall. By afternoon of that day there were few women and children remaining in their homes in Magome. Everyone had packed balls of cold rice flavored with dried bonito shavings and had fled into the surrounding mountains. Even in Hanzo's home, Otami had withdrawn with the children and maids to the retirement quarters on the second floor of the miso shed. Around the hearth only Eikichi and Seisuke, one of the tenant farmers, and Sakichi remained to help Oman.

"Madam."

An old woman from the neighborhood came from the kitchen entrance into the earthen-floored room as she spoke. She continued, looking around the room.

"Oh, you're all alone. Then do you plan to remain here? I have been wor-ried and I thought that if you were going to go I would go with you to hide in the honjin woods. I just came to see. It looks as though everyone is going to spend the night in the mountains. And then there's this awful rain on top of everything else."

Even this lonely old woman was preparing to flee.

Hanzo was having a busy time both inside and outside the honjin. When the preparations for receiving the Mito ronin in this remote station on the top of the pass had at last been completed, he went into the spacious hearth room. There he found his father, who had come down from the retirement quarters to have a look.

"Well, this has turned into a big stir," said Kichizaemon, a concerned expression on his face. "This is the most difficult thing since Princess Kazu came through in the tenth month of the first year of Bunkyu. A station like this can't put up a party of more than a thousand men."

"If that should be the case, father, the people at Ochiai say that they will take some."

"I hear that there are many old people among tonight's guests."

"That's what they say. I understand that Yamakuni Hyobu is more than seventy. And Takeda Ko'unsai and Tamaru Inaemon are both said to be over sixty."

"I heard that too. Just think—when a person gets to be sixty or seventy, he doesn't have much margin left. Even though this is a matter of life and death, it's still amazing."

"Toko sensei's son will be with them tonight. This Fujita Koshiro is still young. Isn't it remarkable that he should be one of the commanders at the age of twenty-two or twenty-three?"

"He sounds quite precocious."

"Well, father, it seems to me that if the ronin had all been young men they would never have tried to go to Kyoto. I think they would have died fighting around Mito castle."

"But then, Hanzo, if they had all been old men they never would have gone up to Mt. Tsukuba in the first place."

Father and son exchanged gazes.

Out of deference to the shogunate, Hanzo did not place a placard outside his gate reading "LODGING OF TAKEDA IGA NO KAMI" as he would have done in normal times, but he nevertheless had curtains put up before the entrance hall. He also refrained from making a show of receiving the guests, merely going out with Inosuke and Shosuke to meet them at the edge of the village.

"I'm leaving everything in your hands, mother," he said as he left the honjin.

Oman looked about in all directions, firmly retied her sash, and thrust a dagger into it.

They could hear the drums. Then, with a vanguard of six mounted warriors carrying naked spears, accompanied by twenty foot soldiers, the whole force began to come down from the east in good order.

In the retinue was an Iida merchant who had been taken hostage by the ronin and who was being led along on a rope. The ronin had heard that this merchant, Wan'ya Bunshichi, had made more than ten thousand ryo from the Yokohama trade and they had brought him along under guard, hoping to make him cough up at least two or three hundred ryo. This much was permitted to the ronin although looting was strictly forbidden under pain of expulsion from the group. Among the xenophobic Mito ronin were many who felt that while the question of whether or not the country should be opened to European contacts was an unresolved matter that would take many years to settle, to engage in the meantime in trade that was permitted by the shogunate but not authorized by the imperial court amounted to treason.

CHAPTER ELEVEN

1

Aoyama—There is to be a meeting of Hirata disciples in Iida, sponsored by the Iida people. This seems to us like a splendid opportunity. We want to invite you to go with us, and we will be coming to Magome with that in mind. Will it be possible for you? At least we will be calling on you.

At Nakatsugawa
Keizo
Kozo

IT WAS some seventeen days after the Mito ronin passed through that Hanzo received this letter from his two friends.

According to the reports received in Nakatsugawa, the pursuing force under Tanuma Gembanokami had arrived in Ina several days after the Mito men only to learn that they had changed their course and gone through Seinaiji, Magome, and Nakatsugawa. Outraged by the failure of Iida han to resist the passage of the ronin, the commander quickly nullified the work of the Kitahara brothers and the other Hirata disciples whose good offices had enabled the ronin to pass through on a secondary road. The steward of Iida han, accepting responsibility, disemboweled himself and the samurai in charge of the barrier at Seinaiji also performed seppuku at the same time. The visit that Keizo and Kozo now proposed to the town of Iida, which was just beginning to recover from the shock, came at a time when the two had not yet had an opportunity to discuss the passage of the Mito ronin with Hanzo, although everyone agreed that this had been the greatest event on the Kiso road since Princess Kazu passed through.

"How about it? Let's go if you're ready."

Kozo, having emerged from the toiya in Nakatsugawa, called in to Keizo's home from the gate. This was the honjin that had afforded shelter and lodging to so many of the activists—Naito Raizo, Isoyama Shinsuke, Hasegawa Tetsunoshin, Ito Yusuke, Futara Shiro, and Toda Kozo. It was also the site of the conference in the previous summer when the lord of Choshu, then on his

289

way from Kyoto to Edo, had made the great shift in policy from supporting
the union of court and military and free navigation to advocating abrogation
of the treaties and expulsion of the barbarians.

"What do you think, Kozo? Will there be snow on Odaira pass?"

"Well, I came prepared for it."

In spite of the difference in their ages, the two friends were fellow disciples
of the Hirata school who had been in Kyoto together, experiencing several
major political developments at first hand. Since Keizo was ready, Kozo proposed that they leave immediately and catch Hanzo by surprise. For this trip
they brought no servant along, feeling that if they had hats and sandals, that
would suffice. They wrapped themselves in their capes and set out into the
afternoon. The carrying cloths slung across their backs were packed with formal wear for the meetings in Iida and, of course, they had not forgotten
presents to take to Magome.

It was not far from Nakatsugawa to the western edge of the Kiso. Only
Ochiai station lay between. Travelers coming from Mino went through
Ochiai and ascended the Jikkyoku pass, from which they would emerge at
the border of Shinano province. Looking back, the two friends could remember when the regular charge had been fifty-five mon between stations for a
regular horse, thirty-six mon for a light horse, and twenty-eight mon for a
porter. By year's end, however, the cost of transport between the stations had
increased six and a half times.

The Mito ronin had spent the night at Magome and Ochiai and had eaten
their noon meal at Nakatsugawa before proceeding on to the west on the
twenty-seventh. From the time that the Kitahara brothers had managed to
secure their passage through the back roads of Iida, all the sympathy and
assistance that they had enjoyed on the road had come from the Hirata people
in the offices of honjin, toiya, and the like. The Hirata disciples, however,
had been placed under great stress, being concerned about shogunal reaction
on the one hand and the welfare of the local people on the other. Still, the disciples in the Kiso and in eastern Mino had been greatly stirred by the incident.

The Mito ronin left all kinds of stories in their wake. Keizo and Kozo had
vivid memories of being called out to the Inabaya in Ochiai, where one of the
ronin, a man named Yokota Toshiro, had presented them with a head
wrapped in oiled paper and asked them to give it a proper burial. He had been
carrying it ever since the battle of Wada pass, and all he said was, "This is the
head of my second son, Tosaburo, seventeen years of age at the time of his
death." Keizo, after consulting with Kozo, buried it secretly at night in his
family's graveyard. This Yokota Toshiro had been, along with Yamakuni
Hyobu of the planning staff and Kameyama of the supply train, one of the
few Hirata disciples among the Mito ronin.

This is another of the stories that was told after the ronin passed through.
It was the evening following the battle of Wada pass and the Shimo-Suwa
region was still in extreme disorder. Among the farmers of Shimohara vil-

lage, there was one who had waited too long to flee because of his aged mother, who had long been bedfast with back trouble. While he was carrying her on his back, searching desperately for a hiding place in the mountains, his mother suddenly complained of pain in her stomach. She said, "No one will harm an old woman like me, but you are young. There is no telling what they might do to you. You must hide quickly." The farmer, wondering how he could bear to abandon his mother, took out a mat and was obediently wrapping her in it when they were discovered by two of the ronin. "You must be from around here. If there is a temple nearby, show us the way to it. We want to bury the head of our master." The farmer replied, "I have my mother with me and she is very ill. Please excuse me from serving you." But when one of the ronin told him that he would assign his companion to watch over her, he could no longer refuse. He led the ronin to the Raigoji, less than a quarter of a mile away. The ronin carefully chose a spot, opened his fan, and set the head upon it. Then, addressing the head respectfully, exactly as if it were a living person, he brought his own face to the dark earth as he spoke: "I never thought that your fortunes as a warrior would run out in a place such as this. I feel the most profound regret that you did not live to see your aims accomplished. Please reconcile yourself to the uncertainties of battle." Then he dug a hole with his short sword and buried the head deep in the earth. When they returned to the original spot he offered the farmer who had guided him a short sword in payment. Military weapons had long been strictly forbidden to farmers and the man refused it, whereupon the samurai said, "Well, anyway, buy your mother some medicine," tossed him a one shu silver coin, and set off toward Shimo-Suwa with his companion.

Everyone who heard this story was struck by the attitude of the Mito ronin. Although their approach and passage had occasioned such terror, there were more than a few who came afterward to feel sympathy for them.

When Keizo and Kozo reached Ochiai, they encountered a young man on a street corner. It was Katsushige, the son of the Inabaya, who this spring had become old enough to return to his home in Ochiai to begin learning the business of a village elder.

"Katsushige has become a fine young man."

Gazing at his forehead and the still unshaven forelock, Keizo and Kozo asked him a great many questions and were amazed at his maturity. At Katsushige's invitation they decided to spend a few hours in Ochiai. They intended to spend the night in Magome, so there was no hurry. Since the Mito ronin had passed through, they had not had the opportunity to talk things over with Katsushige's father, Gijuro, the grand old man of the village.

When they arrived at the Inabaya, they found that there was no end of stories about the ronin there too. Keizo and Kozo said it must have come as quite a shock at the Inabaya when they were entrusted with the head of Yokota Toshiro's son. The old man then said that wasn't all that happened and went on to tell them that the next morning a person who appeared to be an important member of the staff had come down from Magome to Ochiai and called the Nakatsugawa merchants Yorozuya Yasubei and Yamatoya Risuke to the Inabaya to ask them for a contribution of two hundred ryo.

"I heard that story too," said Keizo, laughing.

"Well, the world is really turning around," said Kozo. "Yasubei, who made such big money in the Yokohama trade, being called out before the Mito ronin!"

"And then that Yasubei," continued Gijuro in his old-fashioned tone, "he replied that he couldn't give an immediate answer but that he would consult with his people. Then he went back to Nakatsugawa. And then, I tell you, he called everyone together who had had anything to do with the raw silk trade, talked them out of two hundred ryo, and brought it back here."

"I would have loved to see Yasubei with the Mito ronin," said Kozo.

Gijuro then told them about how unimaginably strict the discipline had been among the Mito ronin. One ronin from Tosa had evaded the vigilance of his commanders and looted a house. When he was discovered he was expelled from the band and executed at a nearby place called Sangozawa. Furthermore, the owners of the farmhouse he had broken into were given one ryo in compensation.

"But just the same, when that band came down from Magome with their bare lances and drawn swords, they were a fearful sight," said Gijuro. His son took up the conversation.

"Fujita Koshiro left a sample of his writing with us. When he laid down his big sword and said, 'I'm going to write something, so get some paper out,' my hand trembled as I handed it to him."

"Katsushige, bring it in and let Asami and Hachiya see it."

The ronin had left many mementoes behind. At Keizo's place, Tamaru Inaemon, the second-in-command, saying that he was deeply indebted, had left one sleeve of a suit of black-laced armor that had long been in his family. He had placed the gift in a bag of heavy cotton lined with white hemp, and with it he left a letter of appreciation in his thick, heavy handwriting.

"I heard that they left something at the Magome honjin, too," said Gijuro.

"Well, I guess they don't expect to be coming back from this trip," replied Keizo.

Then Katsushige, his youthful eyes flashing, brought Koshiro's memento from the other room. To the eyes of Keizo and the others, the fierce spirit of the Mito men seemed to leap from the page. It was written in a mature and dignified hand and it was difficult to believe that it had been done by a youth of twenty-two or twenty-three:

THE CHAMPION MUST SOAR BOLDLY:
HOW COULD HE HIDE CRAVENLY?

Fujita Shin

"I wonder where the ronin went after they left here?"

Such was the drift of the conversation between the travelers and the father and son of the Inabaya. They knew that the ronin had passed through Mino and entered Echizen, but they had had no definite news after that. According to the reports brought to Nakatsugawa and Ochiai by the couriers, the ronin, after leaving Nakatsugawa on the twenty-seventh day of the eleventh month, had avoided clashes with Kano and Ogaki. Then, learning that Hikone had sent soldiers to guard the strategic points around Akasaka and Tarui on the Kiso, they had turned their course toward the northwest and had apparently crossed the Nagara river. On the fourth or fifth of the twelfth month they were said to be crossing the Haeboshi pass on the border between Mino and Echizen.

"Just before that Haeboshi pass, there's a place called the 'Pitch-dark pass,' " said Gijuro. "It's a terrible place. For about eight miles it's just like groping in the dark. I've heard that there is already deep snow in those parts, so they must be having a bad time of it."

"It's a brutal trip," said Katsushige.

Soon thereafter Keizo and Kozo left the Inabaya and Ochiai station. Once they passed the shrine to Yakushi in Nakayama and negotiated Jikkyoku pass, coming out in Shinjaya, they were already in the next province. The road that until now had been spotted with snow gradually became pure white. The jagged boulders alongside the road were wet with snow, giving the two the feeling that they had indeed entered the Kiso road.

The first snow had fallen in Nakatsugawa and Ochiai on the fifth day of the twelfth month. Above Magome pass that night there had been a heavy snow and everyone was closed in for the winter from that time on. There amid the mountain-style shingled roofs weighted down with stones, the snow melting on the southern exposures but still frozen on the northern side, the two friends from Nakatsugawa joined the eagerly waiting Hanzo and his family.

Hanzo was delighted to make this trip to Ina. It was not simply that he felt he had come to the end of a phase in his work on the highway with the events of the past year, culminating as they did in the passage of the Mito ronin, but that he could not recover his equanimity after the excitement of that passage. The Hirata disciples in Ina had been galvanized by their contact with the Mito men and Hanzo could not miss this opportunity to visit them in the company of his two older friends, even if it did mean having to fight his way through the snows of Odaira pass.

In the parlor of the Magome honjin, around the covered brazier, the three friends brought each other up to date and looked forward eagerly to the next morning's departure. Kichizaemon, wearing a brown, sleeveless jacket over his regular clothing, came in to greet the guests and he immediately began talking about the Mito ronin.

"How was it at Nakatsugawa?"

"Yes, Kozo," added Hanzo, "it was different here at Magome than down your way. We were cut off from Tsumago. There were troops from Fukushima holding the entrance to Odaira pass. They really stirred things up."

"The Fukushima retainers were really disorganized," said Kichizaemon.

"When they opened up their supplies and checked them, they found that they had brought nothing but shot to the entrance to Sakurazawa and nothing but powder to the entrance to Odaira pass. We're not the only ones who are thankful that the Mito ronin got through here without a fight. And then there was another big stir when Tanuma Gembanokami was supposed to come through after the ronin. He had more than a thousand men, all in battle order, each one equipped with a musket and bayonet, and they were to arrive here from Hirose village in Ina the day after the ronin left. As you know, we gave the ronin lodging and so we didn't know what might happen. We were very worried. Well, two days later their advance baggage came through, but in the end Tanuma and his men did not show up. I really breathed a sigh of relief then. According to what we've heard, the steward of Iida performed seppuku, right? And then, the samurai at the Seinaiji barrier . . ."

Kichizaemon folded his aged hands in his lap and sighed.

After his father left, Hanzo brought out the gifts that the Mito leaders had left to express their gratitude. There were album leaves inscribed with poems in the hands of Takeda, Tamaru, Yamakuni, and Fujita, the sleeve of a suit of armor with pale pink lacings, and finally a poem by Kameyama Yoshiharu. It expressed the feelings of this Hirata disciple who had joined the Mito ronin about events at Iida and Magome.

> Though we passed through a storm of arrows and bullets
>> we could not move beyond the foot of Mt. Koma,
> We who had viewed the maple leaves of the mountain fastness
>> brilliant as the Yamato brocades of Shikishima.
> Among the rich and flourishing fields of Iida
>> we found a way to the emperor's service.
> How good it must be to dwell deep in these mountains,
>> untouched by the random and painful world.
> We who have no home in this world
>> must make our traveler's bed with the wild boar.
> If only warriors more numerous than the very gods might serve
>> as shield to our great lord!
> We who came striding over the endless peaks of the Kiso mountains
>> will become grass-covered corpses beside our lord.

"Kameyama left us the kind of poem that you would expect of him. It's the creation of a person who is truly committed."

When Keizo said this, Hanzo placed his hands on the covered brazier and replied.

"I talked to Kameyama all evening, right through all the noise. Of course, the guards were out in rotation and keeping flares lit, and the village people were moving about on constant fire watch. It was not a time for sleeping. I was excited too, and I stayed up alone the next night, rewriting some of my old poems and other things."

Just then Inosuke came in on business and Hanzo went to talk with him in the hearth room. He wanted to tell him about the Ina trip and to ask him to look after things. When Hanzo returned to the parlor, he found that his friends had taken Otami's suggestion and gone to warm themselves up in the bath.

"Hanzo, this is nothing special but serve some to your guests. And look, as soon as you say there are guests, the children are beside themselves. They're happy with anything that brings excitement," said Oman.

The shoji in the parlor were already dark. A maid came in with a lamp. Soon Hanzo was ready to offer his friends the mountain sake, served in mountain style, with the cover of the brazier serving in place of a table.

"This is splendid! Just splendid!" said Kozo to Otami when she brought in the food that had been so carefully prepared. "If you'll forgive me, madam, we three very seldom have a chance to get together this way. When Hanzo and I were together, Keizo was in Kyoto and when Keizo and I were together, Hanzo was in Edo. Today, for the first time in a long time, I feel the way we used to feel when we had our desks side by side at Miyagawa Kansai's house."

"There's a lot to talk about. This has been quite a year. Things have been taken care of one after another in this one year."

Keizo began speaking in this tone after dinner. Maki Izumi no Kami's death by his own sword at Tennoji, Sakuma Shozan's untimely death in Kyoto—the most famous opponent of the opening of the country and its most famous proponent had both died in the same year. The conversation turned to the Mito ronin.

"Revere the Emperor, Expel the Barbarians" was the slogan of the Mito men. According to Keizo, Maki Izumi had been the first to tie reverence for the emperor to an anti-foreign stance, forging a new movement out of these two firm resolves. It was clear that this linkage had grown out of rage at the high-handedness of the shogunate and the arrogance of the foreign emissaries, on the one hand, and grief over the decline in the prestige of the court, on the other. But gradually, more perceptive people were beginning to doubt that tying the one to the other would provide the best means for bringing about the restoration of imperial power. This was because the two issues were entirely separate. Reverence for the emperor was a long-term ideal. Expulsion of the foreigners was an immediate problem of foreign policy. Yet Maki Izumi had been sincere in linking the two, and it was his ardor that had given guidance to activists throughout the land long before anyone else. Now he was gone. The pro-imperial, anti-foreign movement had lost its central figure. Maki Izumi had been born into the family of a shrine official at the Suitengu in Chikugo. He had become a scholar in the Imperial Academy in Kyoto and had risen to become one of the most distinguished ministers in the imperial court. But even if he were still alive, what then? Would he have applied the same intense will to this cause that had shaken an age over the question of the imperial progress to Yamato? Would his pro-imperial, anti-foreign stance get the country past the crisis represented by the combined fleet of eighteen warships from England, America, Holland, and France?

Hadn't the time come to consider loyalty to the emperor and expulsion of the foreigners separately? Such was Keizo's opinion.

Hanzo then said, "I wonder. Perhaps the Mito people will be the last to pursue a program of reverence for the emperor and expulsion of the foreigners."

"But Keizo," said Kozo, picking up the argument that his older friend had developed. "Kameyama Yoshiharu and the others don't think that way."

"Well, Kameyama is Kameyama and we are who we are," said Keizo.

"Your opinion seems to grow out of your experience in Kyoto. That's how it looks to me."

"Well then, just look. In Choshu they're sending people like Ito Hirobumi and Inoue Kaoru to England. That was already settled last year. It is tremendously significant that such people are slipping out of the country. They are from the same Choshu that everyone saw as the core of the anti-foreign movement."

"The world is changing."

"It looks to me as though Mito is the only party that is really coming out in favor of an anti-foreign policy now. You have to give them credit for honesty and consistency."

It was already past the season for chestnuts in the Kiso mountains. It was late for roasted new rice. Hanzo had been warming his hands on the brazier cover and listening to his friends talk, but now he brought out some small, Shinano persimmons that had been left on the branch until snowfall to be ripened by the frost. Settling down once again around the covered brazier, the three friends began a long winter night's talk by lamplight.

For Hanzo, as for many of his contemporaries, the question of whether to accept European civilization was a painful one, so much so that he felt that even the master Hirata Atsutane, had he lived to this time, would surely have found it painful also. It was no longer possible to be concerned only about Holland, as they had been in Atsutane's day. Moreover, the shogunate must have had good reason to go ahead with the opening of the country in spite of the strenuous objections of the court. Yet it was hard to believe that the officials of the shogunate were all that farsighted. Of course, there had been ministers like Iwase Higo back in the Ansei and Man'en eras, but he was a very rare type. The great majority of the shogunal officials were said to be far more virulent haters of the West than were the anti-foreign elements in Kyoto. These were the people who had opened the ports. Could one say that this was only because they had been forced to do so by the bullying of the foreign emissaries? Hanzo took up the discussion of the policies of Mito to bring this mystery before his friends.

"There is this theory," said Keizo. "The shogunate wanted to keep all the profits from foreign trade for itself and that's why there has been so much anti-foreign talk. If they had just calculated each year's income and then given so much to the court, so much to the court nobles, and so much to the han great and small; if they had just made public the amount involved and then distributed it openly, everyone from the emperor himself down to the lowest minister in the smallest han might have been happy and there would not have been all this discontent. That's what they are beginning to say now."

"Well, there's no law that says that the government has to get all the profits from foreign trade," said Kozo, chuckling.

"But, isn't it interesting how they say that Alcock, the British chargé d'affaires, tried to warn the Tokugawa officials," said Keizo.

"Well, when you say that," said Hanzo, "it brings all kinds of things to mind."

"There is even a huge brothel specially for foreigners in Yokohama," added Kozo.

"You will understand it better if you just consider the indemnities paid after the Namamugi incident," said Keizo. "Look here. Where do you think a sum as big as one hundred thousand pounds could have come from? Wasn't it because the shogunal officials had been able to force the opening of the ports?"

All were silent for a while.

"Hanzo, just when did the anti-foreign policy begin to become such a big thing? Wasn't it just about then that they were saying that a great shogunal official had acted in collusion with the foreign traders and had given his favorite concubine to the British emissary?"

"This would mean that desire for profit has played a part even in the great controversy over reverence for the emperor and expulsion of the barbarians, because ever since the opening of Yokohama everyone has been thinking about the consequences. But all the same, wasn't the whole pro-imperial, anti-foreign cause more like a religious movement and didn't it rise out of feelings other than success or failure, profit or loss?"

"It may have been up to now, but what about from here on?"

"Just look at Kyoto. Both the court nobles and the samurai are surprisingly realistic. They aren't trapped in problems of principle like the Mito people."

"Since you two came back from Kyoto, you even talk differently."

That night, Hanzo had bedding put out for his guests in the parlor and he joined them there, the conversation continuing as they lay in the dark. They talked of their old master Miyagawa Kansai, so deeply linked to National Learning, now spending his final years in Ise. They talked of Hirata Kanetane, who was thinking of giving up his house in Edo and moving permanently to Kyoto. Their talk never ran out. Hanzo spoke of his experiences in Edo, Keizo and Kozo told of theirs in Kyoto, and they forgot the passage of time completely, until presently the first cock crowed.

2

"Sakichi says he will go with you to Iida," said Otami, coming to where Hanzo was sitting. He was hunched over on the edge of the raised floor, tying on a new pair of straw sandals. Keizo and Kozo were ready for the trip to Ina.

"Are the packhorses for Iida getting through?" asked Hanzo as he tied the cords on his sandals.

"They've already come through this morning."

"Well, if the horses are getting through, we'll be all right."

"The road sounds awfully bad," said Otami, handing Hanzo his hat.

Sakichi had packed the potato dumplings he had cooked at the hearth that morning along with the rest of the baggage. Everyone was ready. They set out.

The snow had not melted at the top of the frozen Magome pass. All the children, down to the little girls of the village, had gone out to the road to play on the hard-packed snow in this most pleasant season of the year. In their miniature work trousers, carrying ice-picks under their arms, they had been sliding on the ice on the steep road since early morning. Among them was Sota from the honjin.

Gazing up at the Ena range where the whiteness, the cold, and the depth of the snow increased day by day, the three left Magome pass. At Ichikoku-tochi they passed the dwelling of the Owari forest watchmen, known as the Shiragi guard station, where the smoke rose above the snow-covered roof of the bleak building deep in the swamps. Now they could see the mountains behind Magome pass, rising at last to Mt. Otaru at the gateway to the Kiso valley. Here in this constricted land the Araragi river, a tributary of the Kiso, raced down the steep valley and over the frozen stones with the force of an avalanche. There near Tsumago was the bridge and from there the highway led into Ina.

The early history of the valley of the Araragi river is not well known, but one can readily imagine that people had been coming over the roads from Owari and Mino, through Magome pass, and on toward Ina and Suwa since the earliest times. It was a vast swampy area among virgin forests ruled by a primordial silence. Squeezed in between the mountains and the banks of the river lies the village of Araragi. The forests were the main source of income for the village and the secrets of the famous Kiso handicrafts had been perfected and passed down there from generation to generation. The smell of the woven wooden traveler's hats being made, the pure, warm water trickling among the wintry rocks, the voices of the cocks and the dogs, audible over the snow from great distances, were all part of the valley. Hanzo and his companions rested for a time at one of these places, a mountain house among mountain houses.

From here it was not far to Seinaiji where the Mito troops had passed. The Seinaiji barrier was a gate guarded by samurai from Iida. Even those who were not samurai of this han could see why the men guarding this gate should have thought that there was nothing wrong in letting the more than one thousand Mito ronin pass through when they had already been given free passage by Iida. Hanzo and the others could keenly sense here the tragedy of the seppuku of the guard commander and that of the steward.

Beyond Araragi the road branches. The road on the right goes on to Seinaiji and the one on the left goes to Hirose and Odaira. They took the left fork. The road led sometimes through dark stands of fir, hinoki, and cedar, and sometimes through stands of bare deciduous trees. Eventually they came out on the summit of the great Kiso pass, where they could look back over a view stretching from the Araragi river all the way to Hirose. From time to time the snow piled on the boughs of the evergreens would slide off alongside the road, making a startling sound. A long slope of black trees and white snow—wherever the eyes of the traveler turned, nothing could be seen but the wintry pelt of the mountains.

Shortly after noon they reached a hamlet at the top of Odaira pass. The teahouse there was where all the travelers as well as the packhorse men hauling freight between Iida and Nakatsugawa stopped. Keizo was the first to strip off his hat and sit down to rest his feet at the fire. Hanzo and Kozo crowded in beside him, still wearing their sandals, warming the toes of their snow-soaked tabi.

"Shall I get out some potato dumplings?" asked Sakichi, digging into the pack he had carried from Magome. "When you eat them in the mountains, they're especially good roasted dark brown."

The dry branches in the hearth flared up warmly. Sakichi lined up several potato dumplings on a grill that had been placed close to the fire, and for a time everyone stared into the roaring flames while the cakes began to turn a rich brown. When the dumplings were broken open they gave out the aroma of buckwheat flour and showed the fresh whiteness of taro flour. They were best eaten with grated radish, so Sakichi ordered some from the old woman at the teahouse, put a bit on each dumpling, and passed them around to Hanzo and the others before serving himself.

Just then a hunter, gun on his shoulder, head covered with a piece of straw matting, stepped into the earthen-floored entry and stood there.

"Come on in and have a rest," called out the old woman as she washed dishes by the kitchen door. Hanzo, still sitting by the fire, also called out to him.

"Are you from around here?"

"Me? I'm from Seinaiji."

As he answered the hunter laid down his gun and a single bird.

When he heard the man say he was from Seinaiji, Hanzo left the fireside and went over to him, noticing that he was accompanied by a sharp-eared, curly-tailed hunting dog that immediately smelled the dumplings roasting by the fire.

"This may seem a strange thing to ask, but do you know just what happened at the barrier?"

"What should I know?" replied the hunter, pulling off his headdress.

"You must have heard something about the guards at the barrier there."

"Oh, that," said the hunter. "Well, I don't know any of the details. They say that when the Mito ronin came in there was one samurai with twenty or thirty foot soldiers at the barrier. What could they have done with a little force like that? They say the samurai just stood back and watched them go by."

Then he changed his tone. "I'm out in the mountains with my gun hunting every day, so I didn't hear about the death of the guard captain until later. I'm sure the old woman here would know more about that. I don't have anybody but my dog to talk to, but she has her customers."

Hanzo and his companions entered Iida around dusk. They had come to the place where the Mito ronin had made their decision to bypass the town, and the scene of the still greater upheaval when the townsmen had then to confront the pursuing shogunal army under Tanuma.

It was not for headmen or toiya from Nakatsugawa and Magome to know the details of the death by seppuku of the steward of Iida. Yet once they had settled down in an inn in this town so important to the people of the Kiso region, they found it possible to imagine something of the nature of that tragedy. When a person is directly confronted by a violent end, he has no choice but to yield to that fate. But why had the steward, the official most responsible for the han, been subjected to such a violent, pointless death? Why had the shogunal council brought its power to bear on this allied domain of less than twenty thousand koku revenue? To Hanzo and the others, it appeared that it was because Iida had gone too far in actually repairing the back roads, and had gone still further out of its way to contribute three thousand ryo to the Mito ronin for military expenses. Yet the order for the steward to disembowel himself had been given by a shogunal commander who had not come near Wada pass on the day of the desperate struggle by the Matsumoto and Suwa forces at Tozawa, and who had always been careful to maintain a distance of at least fifty miles between himself and the rebel army.

The death of the steward of Iida was a blow to the Hirata disciples who had had such influence in the Ina area. In the beginning, Iida had not tried to avoid a fight. Its officials had decided in a staff conference to prepare the castle for a siege, and to burn the town to the ground if the ronin entered it. There had been an unparalleled state of disorder in the town as a result. At this juncture, unable to stand by and watch this happen, the Kitahara brothers had offered their services. In the memorandum that Inao sent out to the district officials, he pointed out that the ronin had already passed through the domains of Suwa and Takato, so there would be no special stigma if they also passed through Iida. It was said that his younger brother Toyosaburo had taken this message to the castle just at the time when the staff was conferring. He had been taken to another room where the county commissioner had promised that he would do everything in his power to see to it that the ronin were permitted to pass through on a back road. Toyosaburo then met immediately with the town officials in Iida. He told them there could be no greater good for the town than to escape the burning of the town and the fighting of a battle there. After conferring among themselves, the townsmen decided that if the Kitahara brothers should be successful in preventing this, they would take up a subscription throughout all thirteen districts of the town, serve the ronin with their noon meal, and contribute three thousand ryo. Now of course all this money could not be delivered at once, and there were some who proposed to send the ronin along with only one thousand ryo in cash, so it was doubtful if the entire sum promised could in fact be delivered to the ronin.

"It was nothing but cruelty to punish them for that."

The Hirata disciples raised this cry throughout the Ina area. Great numbers came forward to mourn the steward and the commander of the guard, who had shown themselves to understand their responsibilities as samurai far better than did those who questioned them from above. Offerings of flowers and incense were constantly brought to their new graves. It was in the midst of this outpouring of sentiment that Hanzo, Keizo, and Kozo made their visit to the Ina valley.

The efforts of the Kitahara brothers to save the town of Iida from its unprecedented danger had by no means been in vain. Strictly speaking, there had up to now been only thirty-six Hirata disciples in Iida and its environs, but they had gained so much respect and sympathy that at year's end twenty-three people at one time had applied to become disciples.

The studies of Atsutane then being carried out by Katagiri Shun'ichi and others associated with the Yamabuki shrine suddenly began to take on a new life. The printing and distribution of the *Commentaries on Ancient History,* which men like Kitahara Inao had undertaken in the hope that they might thereby repay at least some small fraction of their obligation to the nation, now began to move much more quickly with the increased cooperation of the other disciples. There were many who saw religious reform as the first step in negating the middle ages, but it was Kurasawa Yoshiyuki of Ono and Hara Mayomi of Seinaiji who had actually set off for Kyoto to attack the confounding of Buddhism and Shinto and worked for the revival of early Shinto.

The Ina disciples, taking advantage of this turn in their fortunes, and seeing the possibility of having their dreams take concrete form, were planning some kind of memorial to honor their predecessors in National Learning. On the second day after Hanzo and his friends entered Iida, they attended a gathering at the home of an activist disciple in the town for preliminary consultations.

It is necessary here to make clear the position of the Hirata disciples. There were few among the samurai who were sympathetic to the teachings of Atsutane. The great majority of his followers were headmen, toiya, honjin, physi-

cians, farmers, or merchants. It was no mere coincidence that Miyagawa
Kansai, the former master of Hanzo's group, had been a physician from
Nakatsugawa.

It could be said that the disciples in the region from eastern Mino into Ina
were best represented by headmen, toiya, and honjin. But it must not be forgotten that at that time the people in these offices had the deepest relationship with the districts in which they lived. For example, the district where
Keizo and Kozo had been born was in the Owari domains. The Kiso river
separated that district from the Naegi domains on the one side, and on the
other side a range of hills shut it off from the Iwamura domains. The Naruse,
hereditary stewards of Owari, were at Inuyama, the Takekoshi were at Imao,
and the Ishikawa at Komazuka; in addition, the Mori family of Yagami and
some other early supporters of Tokugawa Ieyasu in the Kiso, who were
known collectively as the "Kukuri nine," were all dwelling in Mino province
and had their revenue lands there. The Nakatsugawa headman had to send
the annual rice tax to the Yamamura in Fukushima, but in all other respects
he was under the direct rule of Owari, the strongest of the three cadet houses
of the Tokugawa. The power of the shogunate in Edo did not directly touch
this district. The conditions of tenure in eastern Mino were different from
those in southern Mino, but the positions of the headmen, toiya, and honjin
were similar. In Ina, some places were the domains of an ordinary arrière vassal of Owari, while others belonged to the special class of arrière vassals that
had been required to go on alternate attendance like regular daimyo, such as
the great Owari bannermen, the Yamabuki. It was no coincidence that this
region should have become the seedbed of the Hirata movement. Only in the
Ina valley could a person like Kureta Masaka hide out indefinitely even
though he was wanted by the shogunate, staying first with the Kurasawa of
Ono, then being passed from the Maezawa of Tajima to the Matsuo of
Tomono, then to the Kitahara of Zakoji, next to the Sakurai of Iida, and then
to the Katagiri of Yamabuki. And it was surely only in this valley that activists such as Hasegawa Tetsunoshin, Gonda Naosuke, or Ochiai Naoki could
come to the Kurasawa home in Ono, sure of finding shelter.

The appointed time had come for the gathering of Hirata disciples. Hanzo
and his friends had their hair dressed by an Iida hairdresser and left their inn
together, feeling fresh and clean, their hair done up with new, pure white
cords. It was just at the end of the very eventful first year of Genji, and they
felt that there would be few such opportunities to walk with their friends
and to perform some small service for the great masters whom they had so
long revered. Among the three, it was Keizo who was the eldest and who
seemed to cut the gravest, most substantial figure. Kozo would raise his right
shoulder high when he spoke, and when he was just walking he would tense
it, or draw it in. Hanzo was the youngest, the heaviest of frame, and the
broadest of shoulder. As they passed through the town, they were observed
from deep within the lattices by more than a few ladies who found their
young manhood good to look upon, but the three paid no attention. On

their way to this day's meeting, they walked with a gravity and seriousness that went far beyond their usual demeanor.

A new shrine was to be built. The spirits of the four great masters, Kada no Azumamaro, Kamo Mabuchi, Motoori Norinaga, and Hirata Atsutane, were to be enshrined in it. They chose as the site a hill called Jozan, popularly known as Koedayama, which commanded a view of the entire Ina valley. They had been given about nine acres of land by the owner of the mountain and they sited their shrine in the midst of a stand of shapely trees.

Hanzo was more pleased than anyone by this delightful idea that had been brought forward by the Yamabuki shrine through the offices of the Hirata disciple Katagiri Shun'ichi. The wooden structure was to be built on the top of a lonely mountain. There would be a new reliquary where the four great masters who had shown the way to a brighter world, and had taught them that a sound and healthy national character could be found in antiquity, were to be enshrined. The memorial was one which the Hirata people could leave to their posterity in the region as a symbol of the restoration and renaissance for which they so devoutly longed.

The most important people from the Yamabuki shrine came to the house in Iida on that day to ask for the approval of the disciples gathered there. There was little likelihood that anyone would have any objections, much less people like Keizo, Kozo, and Hanzo, who were there more or less as guests. According to the explanations of the disciples from Yamabuki, the idea had originated with Katagiri Shun'ichi and the selection of the site, the acquisition of the land, and the supervision of the construction would all be handled by the Yamabuki shrine. It was not yet decided whether to call it the Koedayama Jinja, the Jozan Reisha, or the Kokugaku Reisha. They wanted Hirata Kanetane to choose the name. All the remaining personal effects of the four great masters should be transported from the Hirata residence to the shrine on the occasion of the enshrinement. Katagiri Shun'ichi was so intensely involved in the building of this shrine that he was close to tears throughout the discussion.

Hanzo and his friends were fascinated by the faces of the people at the gathering. Although they had long known all the names, they had never before had the opportunity to see the Iida colleagues who were gathered here —people like the physician Yamada Bun'iku from Komaba, and Masuda Heihachiro and Namiai Sagenta from Namiai. Matsuo Makoto, the son of Matsuo Taseko and a relative of Keizo, had come all the way from Tomono. Though they had all become disciples after the late master's death, they were bound together by the great work that still remained undone after the deaths of the four great masters.

Suddenly someone who had come into the gathering from another room tapped Hanzo on the shoulder.

"Aoyama!"

It was Kureta Masaka. That Masaka, who had been hiding out in various places ever since coming to the Ina valley, should appear at a meeting like this was just what one might expect of him. Absorbing the lessons about Hirata Atsutane sponsored by Kurasawa Yoshiyuki and others, he had even made himself something of an elder statesman by sowing the seeds of National Learning in northern Ina.

"The world has taken an interesting turn!"

Without anyone saying so in so many words, this new joy could be read on every face in the meeting. The notes that the people from the Yamabuki shrine brought with them constituted only an outline, a rough sketch, but if their plan to build a shrine on Koedayama were to become known to the other disciples throughout the country, what joy and elation would greet it. How pleased Master Kanetane in Kyoto would be when he heard of it! With discussion of this matter, the day's meeting was ended.

"Why don't you come with us as far as our inn, Kureta?"

It was Hanzo who asked Masaka to join him and his two friends. Parting from Matsuo Makoto, who said that he would be staying with relatives in Iida that night, the four set out together for the inn.

"I am staying with the Matsuo family now. You were very helpful when I came up from Kyoto. When I got to Nakatsugawa I had been walking for two days and two nights and I felt more dead than alive. I'll never forget being taken in by Asami's family in his absence and by Aoyama."

Tomono was where Hanzo's old teacher Miyagawa Kansai had gone to retire after ending his role in the Yokohama trade, and it was a strange coincidence to hear now that Kureta was staying with the Matsuo family in the same town. From what Hanzo had learned in his conversations since coming to Iida, it was apparent that the aged Kansai had had nothing but misfortune during the two or three years he spent in Tomono. Not only had he seemingly been placed under a curse by his association with the Yokohama trade, but stories still remained about his frequent quarrels with the younger Matsuo, a result of his tendency to speak too freely when he had been drinking.

"I would like to tell Miyagawa sensei over in Ise about this."

"If that old gentleman should hear about a shrine being built in honor of Hirata and the others, he would surely weep."

"For joy? People may say all kinds of things about him, but I have never seen a man weep as much as Miyagawa sensei."

The three friends often found themselves talking about their old master.

Once back at the inn, the three passed the evening in talk with their special guest. With Masaka present, they became even more lively, swapping yarns as the sake cups were passed around, and all kinds of stories came up, one after another. Masaka started.

"Well, should I tell a bad one? I think I will. When I was in the Magome honjin, I spent the night in their storehouse. Aoyama brought in a gourd of sake. I've never tasted such delicious sake before or since."

"Don't say that until you have tasted Iida sake," said Hanzo.

"Forgive me, Kureta, but I wonder what the Western scholars are doing now?" asked Kozo.

"There goes Kozo over the edge again," said Keizo, laughing. "When you pop off that way, sometimes you catch me completely by surprise. You're always thinking about the same thing."

"But I couldn't help thinking about the Black Ships," said Kozo.

There was nothing strange in that. The subject that his two older friends spoke of was also on Hanzo's mind. He could not, he just could not laugh at Kozo's one-track mind.

"Well, even Sakuma Shozan, whom they cut down in Kyoto this summer, was a Western scholar in some ways," said Masaka. "He went to Kyoto by way of the Kiso road. He must have stopped off for the night or for a rest at Aoyama's place."

"Yes, that was while I was away," replied Hanzo. "It was in the third month, just as the wild cherry blossoms were beginning to fall. I learned about it after I came back from a trip to Fukushima."

"How about Hachiya?"

"That was when I was in Kyoto with Keizo. Shozan was an arrière vassal of Matsushiro, but he really attracted a lot of attention when he came down to Kyoto from Matsushiro, supposedly on orders from the shogunate, with an escort of fifteen or sixteen men and with a European-style saddle on his horse."

"I'll bet he did. But since it was Shozan, he probably felt all would be well if he went, and came with great expectations. But isn't he the same person who spent nine years under house arrest after the Yoshida Shoin affair? How can you know what's going on without leaving your house? No matter how learned and brilliant a man may be, you can count on his being out of touch with things in Kyoto if he hasn't left his house for nine years. And so, less than three months after he comes to Kyoto, he is cut down. Kyoto is a frightful place nowadays. I don't know how many times I have seen things change completely there."

"Well, there was also this about it," said Keizo, taking up Masaka's lead. "Wasn't it just after the Ikedaya incident that Shozan was killed? Right, Kozo? I'm sure it was."

"Right, right. Everybody was all stirred up then."

"I think that must have been just before the Choshu forces surrounded Kyoto, when there was that plan to abduct the emperor to Mt. Hiei. And into all that comes Shozan from Matsushiro, with a rating of six hundred koku. According to the rumors, he went to see Prince Yamashina. He also met with Hitotsubashi Yoshinobu, and he planned to move the shogunal party out of town to Hikone. It looks as though he got in the way of some group of activists and they got rid of him."

"If he had been all so brilliant as he was supposed to have been, I should think he would have made himself a little bit less conspicuous," added Masaka. "That's one thing all the Western scholars have in common these days—they all seem to be saying, 'Hey! look at me!' That's what causes the problems. But it took a man like Shozan to produce an insight like 'Eastern Morality, Western Technology.' He seems to have had a lot of the East remaining in him. Now Western scholars like Shozan are quite sound, but it makes me uneasy just to watch some of these Western scholars who can't seem to see anything else at all."

"Look here! It's all these Western scholars nowadays who so casually say things like 'We must overthrow this oppressive Tokugawa government!' What makes me uneasy is that when you look around to see who is saying these things, they're scholars who are employed by the shogunate as interpreters and translators and the like, and they get everything they eat and everything they wear from the shogunate. These people who eat Tokugawa food and wear Tokugawa clothing and say 'Smash the Tokugawa!' Now I don't care what kind of arguments they might come up with, they're not employed by the Tokugawa because they are outstanding people. They're just there because they can read horizontal writing. It's the same as being put to work repairing sandals because you're a leather worker. These Western scholars are just like sandal makers. The lords can't be expected to touch ritually unclean work, but fortunately there's a leather worker around, so they have him take care of it. There's no difference at all. Who needs any high-powered arguments to explain all this? 'Smash them, but don't suggest that we take the initiative in doing it'—I tell you, that's the way many very learned Western scholars are talking right now. 'Well, of course the shogunate has to be overthrown very soon, but unfortunately the right men are not around so it looks as though there's nothing to be done.' That's what they are saying. When I think of all these Western scholars nowadays saying all these irresponsible things, I really get upset. They don't care what happens to anyone else. As long as they themselves are all right the farmers and the townsmen can get along any old way. How can you expect an ardent and disciplined spirit of reform to come out of such teachings?"

Before his juniors, this sensitive and honest elder disciple pulled the faded collar of his kimono together. It was as if he had experienced an intense perception of his own straitened circumstances.

"Anyway, come with me to Tomono, Hanzo. Matsuo insisted that I ask you and Kozo to visit him. He left this morning, along with Kureta Masaka."

"With all the people they have there, they still won't mind if we push in on them?"

"Of course not. It's not the kind of household that is going to be put to any trouble by another three or four guests."

"Well, I had been thinking that since I am already in Iida I would like to go over and attend the lectures at the Yamabuki shrine. I'd like to hear what they are teaching about Hirata Atsutane there. We don't get such good chances very often."

"Well then, let's do this. Let's go to Yamabuki from Tomono."

This decision was made by Keizo and Hanzo the next morning.

The day that Hanzo spent at Tomono as a result of this invitation from his friend was one that he was not likely to forget. At the Matsuo household, he found himself in a position to make calls upon all the nearby Hirata disciples, and to enjoy himself with Japanese verse, of which he was fond, in the company of new men and women friends. He also found extraordinarily interesting the letters that Matsuo Taseko sent to her son. She had made the acquaintance of Prince Iwakura, now living in lonely exile outside Kyoto, and she visited him almost daily.

On a day when the skies over the Ina valley were once again dropping snow, Hanzo separated from Keizo and Kozo, who were going back to Nakatsugawa. He had quietly kept Sakichi with them until this day so that he could send him back with his friends. He remained behind, alone in Ina to take advantage of the opportunity to listen in to meetings of the Giyushu, a group which might properly be called a society for the study of Atsutane. Since there were many people in Ina whom he wanted to see and since Odaira pass was virtually closed by a snowfall of four feet in a single night, Hanzo found himself greeting the new year in Iida.

This short trip served to open Hanzo's eyes to many aspects of the Hirata school.

"How moving! The hearts of the people of high antiquity were utterly direct!"

Just what did their predecessors mean by "high antiquity"? Now at last Hanzo realized that "high antiquity" was not what he had thought it to be. Above all, it was not what people generally called "ancient times." One might say that it was the high antiquity that had been discovered by the great masters Motoori and Hirata. Though born into a time of military domination going back to the middle ages, though finding themselves in an atmosphere where people were trapped by this or that foreign religion or doctrine, inventing such difficult and overbearing names as "humaneness," "righteousness," "propriety," "obedience," "filial piety," "deference to elders," "loyalty," and "trustworthiness," such masters as Motoori and Hirata had nevertheless managed to grope their way toward the true high antiquity. It was the great accomplishment of these masters to teach us to return not to the ordinary past as it has always been known but to a new past.

Once he had reached that point, Hanzo was able to begin thinking of this new past in relation to the recent past in which human knowledge was growing so rapidly. This new past could be gained only by breaking out of the shell of unrestrained authoritarianism left over from the middle ages. Only then would it be possible to go back to the time when there was nothing but the emperor and the people and set out once again, now firmly committed to the proper course, from that starting point. According to the understanding which he worked out, to return to the past was to return to the spontaneous order of things, and to return to the spontaneous order was to discover the new antiquity. The middle ages must be rejected. The new times must be faced. Somehow we have to overturn present-day life from its very roots and begin living by completely new rules. It was on this short journey to Ina that

Hanzo's thinking began to acquire a new focus and coherence. By the time he was ready to go back over Odaira pass, some Hirata disciples were already crying out for the abolition of the doctrine of assimilation and of Dual Shinto itself and were setting to work to reform the old burial rites. Here and there people were beginning to discard and burn the images of a dubious Buddhism in which the gods and Buddhas had become almost inextricably confused.

3

It was now the third month of Genji 2, 1865. The snows were melting in the valleys of Mt. Ena and at its foot the post station of Magome began to return to life. Pilgrims set out for Ise. The merchants from Nakatsugawa came through. For the people of the villages and the post stations the season marked the beginning of visits between the communities and of many consultations—on subscriptions, on the registration of sales of forest lands, on the observation of the fiftieth anniversary of the death of the priest Jozan, the restorer of the Mampukuji, and the fifteenth anniversary of the priest Sozan. As in every year, the activities of the highway which had almost come to a halt in the winter began again after the equinoctial observances. And from that time they began to see travelers from every province.

The spring in which alternate attendance was to be restored was awaited with high hopes by the shogunate. On the twenty-fifth of the first month, under the name of the roju Mizuno Izumi no Kami, it sent out to every han of more than ten thousand koku revenue the order attempting to place the three hundred daimyo once again under its absolute control.

The great inflation of prices was making travel very difficult for the daimyo. The costs along the highway were rising by ten percent at a time and from the third month of Genji 2 they rose by a total of fifty percent. There would be a further rise of fifty percent in the next three years, making a cumulative increase of one hundred percent. It remained to be seen whether the families of the daimyo would venture to make such a difficult and costly journey simply out of obedience to the shogunal order.

During this uncertainty, Hanzo received as a guest a fellow disciple for whom he had held warm feelings since his trip to Ina. This was Kurasawa Yoshiyuki of Ono village, to whom he had been introduced by Kureta Masaka. Yoshiyuki was on his way back from his first journey away from home, a very profitable trip of about fifty days that had included visits to Kyoto and Osaka.

Yoshiyuki's trip to Kyoto had been long awaited and the other disciples were expecting important results from it.

Yoshiyuki had gone from Ise and Yamato to Izumi, where he had visited Miyawada Tanekage, who was in hiding there. In Osaka he met with Iwasaki

Nagayo and his old friends in Takayama and Kawaguchi. From there he went to Kyoto, directly to the Shirakawa palace to have an audience with Sukenori, the minister of shrines, and was made a provincial retainer of that official's household. While in Kyoto he saw Fukuba Yoshikiyo, Ikemura Kuninori, Ogawa Kazutoshi, Makindo Gendo, Sunouchi Shikibu, and others. He said that he had discussed national affairs with these activists and had made certain plans with them. He had also quite by chance one day met with his old friend Kondo Munekuni, and had been taken by him to the Chorakuji in Higashiyama to see Shinagawa Yajiro, who had taken refuge there. From Shinagawa he had learned of the ways in which Choshu was serving as the vanguard of the anti-shogunal movements. However, becoming aware that all these visits to activists would be noted by the shogunate and feeling himself in danger, he had hurriedly left the capital, going to Yawata in Omi, where he called upon Nishikawa Zenroku, who gave him news of the other people who had been involved in the Ashikaga statue incident. From Omi he had taken a roundabout road to evade the shogun's police and now, having been on the road for about fifty days, was at last able to head for home.

There were several things in Yoshiyuki's account that caught Hanzo's attention. First was the strengthening of the relationship between the noble house of Shirakawa, traditionally in charge of Shinto affairs and with connections to the uppermost levels of court society, and the Hirata disciples who were coming up to the capital. Hara Mayomi of Seinaiji had been taken into its service as a preceptor, and they had assigned Yoshiyuki himself certain responsibilities to be carried out on their behalf in his home district. The second point was that contacts were being established with people in the west of Japan who were interested in the study of antiquity. A third point was that Iwasaki Nagayo, a man never to be forgotten by his fellow Hirata disciples after his twelve-year residence in Iida, was now in Osaka. But what made the greatest impression on Hanzo was learning that Mayomi had met regularly with the activists working for the overthrow of the shogunate, and that he had joined them in their planning.

Mayomi had started out in the Mito school, but after meeting Kureta Masaka he had turned away from the Confucianizing teachings of the Yoshikawa school of Shinto and from Confucianism itself, becoming an ardent practitioner of the purest study of antiquity. But Mayomi had also read Atsutane's treatise on military science, and recognizing the importance of the martial arts, had taken up the Itto school of swordsmanship. He counted among his predecessors men such as Matsuzawa Yoshiaki, who had come into the Ina district when the study of antiquity was not yet known there and had been active both as teacher and as merchant, and Iwasaki Nagayo, born in Kofu, who had drawn upon a special strength in classical Japanese verse and the No theatre in his efforts to broaden the impact of the study of antiquity in the area. Among the four senior disciples currently in Ina, if Katagiri Shun'ichi, Kitahara Inao, and Hara Mayomi represented the south, then it was Kurasawa Yoshiyuki who represented the northern part of the district.

"I never had a trip like this before, Aoyama. I had to be careful every minute."

Along with these words, Yoshiyuki left behind a vivid impression of side whiskers.

Hanzo reflected on Yoshiyuki's story of his travels. It had been very revealing. Defeated at the first uprising in Gojo in Yamato, defeated at the Ikino silver mines, smashed in the attempt to encircle Kyoto, then unsuccessful in the uprising at Mt. Tsukuba, and now cowering before the Choshu punitive expedition under the command of the retired lord of Owari—this could not be viewed as a very convincing anti-shogunal movement. Just where was it all leading?

Brought up short, Hanzo retreated a step and started his thinking over again. Up to now the farmers had been regarded as creatures without a thought for the morrow, as being of no consequence as human beings. The policy of the samurai toward them could be stated as "Let them live, don't kill them," yet this did not prevent the samurai from interfering with their lives even to the petty details of food, clothing, and shelter. At the very least, Hanzo realized, he was himself a country person who dealt with these farmers every day. Even if a hero, another Kusunoki Masashige, should arise in these final days of the Tokugawa to strike them down, just as the Ashikaga were once struck down, if this person were a samurai given to overestimating his own strength, wouldn't it all end up as simply another Tokugawa era under a different name? To those like Hanzo who viewed the situation from below, the speculation was unavoidable. Any hero would invariably promise to honor the will of the people when he first took power, but there had never been a case where the will of the people had actually been honored once the grasp on power had been firmly established. It was no wonder that Hanzo had been brought to this way of thinking, for it was precisely people in his situation and the farmers who had suffered most under the arrogant rule of the military. This was not quite the way Juheiji would have put it, but it was nevertheless true that so long as one did not have to worry about what was to become of the farmers, what was to become of the people, then there was nothing to worry about at all . . .

As his thoughts continued, Hanzo reflected on the way in which the old influence of Mito still worked on in Yoshiyuki, his elder from an earlier generation. This was because Mito learning was essentially samurai learning, and samurai learning had a certain amount of Chinese-mindedness to it. For example, among the Mito people there were those who had heroic notions of seizing power in Kyoto through sheer force—the emperor would be placed under their control and they would command the nation. Even if these were words wrung out of them by their outrage at the present state of the world, the idea of putting the emperor under their power was samurai thinking. From the point of view of the followers of Hirata, there was no question but that this was Chinese-mindedness.

The time of a society centered on the samurai was passing away. The elder disciple Yoshiyuki had formulated plans in company with the activists of the west, but if those plans did not involve a total change in his own way of life, if they stopped at simply finding a replacement for the Tokugawa family, then Yoshiyuki was straying far from the rejection of the middle ages that he had long ago learned in the writings of Motoori and Hirata. These thoughts brought an unspeakable grief to Hanzo.

The Suwa farmer who had been pressed into service as a porter by the Mito ronin now came plodding homeward over the Kiso road.

The farmer stopped by the Magome honjin and took an official letter out of his kimono, saying that he had been asked to give it to the master here. The letter was from the officials of the town of Tsuruga and was addressed to all the toiya along the highway. It began with the name and place of origin of the man, "Kozo, presently without residence, from Iijima village, Suwa county, Shinano province," and explained that this was a person who had been brought to Echizen by the Mito ronin and he had been examined and found to be without guilt. He was therefore permitted to return to his home. It added that he had been given one bu in gold for expenses on the road and that if he should run out of money along the way, the toiya were requested to help him.

Hanzo immediately grasped the significance of the arrival of this farmer. He had already received some word of the punishment of the Mito ronin, from Takeda Ko'unsai on down, and the appearance at his door of this farmer with this letter brought to his mind the unbelievable number of executions among the ronin.

"Master, I passed before your house carrying a lance on the twenty-seventh of the eleventh month of last year."

This was Kozo's greeting.

The farmer was in the main entrance of the honjin, kneeling down in a corner near the spacious, wood-floored section. Hanzo had just finished his noon meal.

Learning that the man had not yet eaten, he clapped his hands in the entry, calling someone from the kitchen to prepare a simple meal for him.

"I will honor this letter," said Hanzo, looking at Kozo. "There are many things I want to ask you, but we can't talk here in the entry. Please come around to the kitchen door. It's not much, but we'll give you some rice and tea."

Kozo, wringing his hands, walked around from the entrance hall to the edge of the hearth room and sat on the edge of the raised floor, still in his straw sandals.

"I hear that the Mito people really came to a horrible end."

Once Hanzo said this, the story of the final days of the Mito ronin came pouring out of the Suwa farmer. On the first and second days of the second month, there had been an interrogation of the leaders at the Honshoji in Tsuruga, and on the fourth, twenty-four men, beginning with Takeda Iga no Kami, were condemned to death. From the fifth, the others in the band were called forth one by one, and in the end even those like Kozo who had come as porters were interrogated. Kozo had been held in storehouse number 6 and he was brought before the officials where everyone in the entire force was examined in turn. Among the ronin, one hundred thirty-four men were beheaded on the fifteenth and one hundred three on the sixteenth. Then they came to the seventeenth of the second month, which was the anniversary of the death of Tokugawa Ieyasu. It was decided to draw lots at the shrine to determine whether to spare the lower-ranking members of the band. The lots favored sparing them. Kozo and the others were called to the Honshoji, where their leg-irons were struck off before the gate. Then all were required to leave the presence of the officials and go once again to the front of the gate where their hair was dressed. They were called back and their final pardon read to them. Each was required to apply his thumbprint to the document that had been read to the group. Finally everyone was released. Kozo reported that seventy-six men had been released with him.

"That's right," said Kozo, counting off just those who were from the same province as he. "Of the ones like me, there was a man from Shimo-Suwa, a homeless *kumosuke* from Saku county, one person from Wada, one from Matsumoto, and fourteen or fifteen from Matsushima in Ina. Yes, and then there was one man from Miyashiro in Takato han. Anyway, sir, I had been traveling hard since I left Ina in the eleventh month of last year and I was in pretty bad shape, so I stayed at the temple in Tsuruga for a while before I came back. I'm really lucky to be alive."

The maid brought in the rice container and a serving tray and set it at the edge of the raised floor as she had been instructed by Otami.

"I wonder what happened to Kameyama."

As Otami said this to Hanzo, Kozo did not hesitate. He pulled the rice container over and began shoveling down the cold rice and the young bracken sprouts then in season. Gazing on the huge hands of this farmer who had carried a lance, Hanzo asked him, "You didn't happen to hear anything of Kameyama Yoshiharu of the supply train, did you? He's an old friend of mine . . ."

"Well, I was in the supply section of the main force, so I don't know, but it doesn't seem that any of the important people got through it alive. As I just told you, I was sick at the time we were pardoned and I stayed on in Tsuruga a while. So I know a little bit about what happened after the seventeenth. On the nineteenth, seventy-six men were beheaded and another sixteen on the twenty-third."

"It looks as though Kameyama must have died with Takeda Ko'unsai and Fujita Koshiro," said Hanzo, exchanging glances with Otami.

Everyone in the household from Oman to Seisuke and the manservant Sakichi gathered around the farmer from Suwa to hear about the Mito ronin. They seemed to be reliving the fears of that rainy night of the eleventh month of the previous year.

According to the jumbled story that Kozo told, of all the bad spots through which the ronin had passed on their way through Mino and on to Echigo, the Haeboshi pass on the border of those two provinces had been the worst. Snow had fallen every day and they lost most of their horses there. The ronin had carried their supplies on their own backs. Kozo himself had been given a case of musket balls to carry and had suffered terribly under its weight. In the worst places they worked their way through the pass by grasping at the branches of trees and threading their way among the boulders. The five villages in the area had been burned and no houses remained. They were forced to camp in the burned-out ruins at night, suffering from inadequate provisions and the cold. Many of Kozo's fellow porters died there. After that the snow again fell every day and the passes came one after another until they lost track of the days. When they at last arrived at Imajo, they found that all the storehouses had been sealed with clay around the doors and windows and everyone was gone. There were only a few provisions set outside the houses for them. Papers asking them to be careful with fire were hung up here and there. When they left Imajo to start across the last pass before the Japan sea coast, they were all floundering in deep snow. By the time they reached the village of Shimpo, a place with some forty houses, all the members of the band were virtually walking corpses. By then the ronin were already encircled by a vast army made up of the troops of the great Kaga han of Kanazawa backed by those of other neighboring han.

Kozo saw with his own eyes a member of the Mito staff going to the camp of the Kaga forces with three or four companions, all unarmed. Men came out from the Kaga camp, also unarmed, and heard their passionate pleas to be permitted to proceed to Kyoto. From that time, supplies were sent from the Kaga camp every day. There was more rice, vegetables, beans, and the like than they could eat. Suddenly freed from their regular duties, Kozo and the others were set to building fires, washing rice for cooking, and delivering soy sauce to the various troops. On the tenth it was decided that they would surrender their weapons to the Kaga men. The second-in-command, Tamaru Inaemon, and the chief of planning, Yamakuni Hyobu, were among those who protested to Takeda Ko'unsai, saying they would not consider giving up their arms. They proposed that they attempt to break out of the encirclement in the eighth hour of that night. Kozo and the others were roused out at midnight to begin preparing breakfast, but in the end the weapons were handed over as Ko'unsai had ordered. On the twenty-fifth and the twenty-sixth, the Mito ronin, still encircled by Kaga troops, were moved to the coastal city of Tsuruga. There the entire band was lodged in three temple compounds. Kaga sent them fish to accompany their morning and evening meals and pickled vegetables to go with their noon meal, along with a daily bottle of sake for each man. They were well provided with such necessities as washcloths and tabi, and medicine was given to the sick. Physicians even came to administer expensive and elaborate treatments. Yet many of the ronin died in those temples.

On the twenty-seventh day of the first month of the year the ronin were transferred from the custody of Kaga to Tanuma Gembanokami, the commander of the shogunal army. On that day Kaga sent special refreshments, and Nagahara Jinshichiro, the steward of Kaga, came to say that he had hoped to be able to mediate and had done everything possible to gain the concurrence of the shogunal forces, but to no avail. He was therefore forced to withdraw. The shock that this statement brought to the Mito officers was beyond description. Others, realizing there was no hope left and that no one could help them now, composed their death verses in Chinese and Japanese. They were all transported in litters, even such insignificant people as Kozo, and put into one or another of sixteen dark storehouses. Every last scrap of spare clothing and personal effects was taken from them. Shackles for the hands and feet awaited Kozo and his companions there . . .

Seisuke looked over at the Suwa farmer.

"Why did you accompany them that way, clear over to Tsuruga in Echizen?"

"You have no idea how often I thought of trying to escape and go home. But whenever I talked of leaving them, they threatened to execute me. And then, it's strange, but as I carried a lance every day, or hauled baggage, and listened to what my commander had to say, I finally began to want to go with them to the end."

"Didn't you hear about Wada pass? They must have talked about that battle."

"Yes, they did. They said that it had been a terribly hard fight, and they came close to being defeated. From what I heard, it was a desperate battle. They just barely won because of Yamakuni Hyobu's idea to send troops around to the flank."

The people along the highway waited until the end of the month, thinking, "Well, maybe in the fourth month . . ." But so far hardly any of the western daimyo had left their domains. The women and children of the daimyo houses of Echizen, Owari, and Kii, and others on down to the wife of the lord of Satsuma—of these, none was considering going back up that road to Edo in order to restore life to the suffering city. Only the women of the very minor han of Naegi, who passed through on their way to Edo on the twenty-seventh of the fourth month, and the procession of the daimyo of the distant northern han of Hirosaki, which had stopped the previous night in Nakatsugawa, were seen.

This is not to say that all was quiet in the Magome honjin. While few daimyo took to the road once again in alternate attendance, there was a great crush of court officials and court nobles from the twenty-second of the third month through the seventh of the fourth month, and this kept Hanzo and his neighbor Inosuke very busy. The shogunate was sponsoring a great memorial service at Nikko on the seventeenth of the fourth month to commemorate the two hundred fiftieth anniversary of the death of Tokugawa Ieyasu. Priests of the imperial family and other high-ranking priests came down from Kyoto, while from Edo the shogunal council, of course, as well as the temple commissioner, a censor, the commissioner of the treasury, and officials all the way down to the master of the shogun's personal treasury were required to attend. Priests of the Tendai sect were assembled to perform ten thousand readings of the sutras and to display them before the crowds. In its determination to celebrate the two hundred fiftieth anniversary of Ieyasu's death on a grand scale, the shogunate had even changed the name of the era— the second year of Genji now became the first year of Keio. One can imagine the great undertaking this involved for the highway officials simply by considering that a group came from Mito carrying an offering of fifteen hundred ryo, and on some days there would be as many as a thousand porters in service. Almost every day great numbers of porters came up over Magome pass on their way to their station at Narai. A day on which five hundred porters had been called from the assisting districts was followed by one on which the imperial messenger required five thousand porters to get him past Suwara.

As this confusion began to subside, the details of the end of the Mito ronin gradually became clear. There was no chance that all news of an affair that had brought such excitement to the people along its long route could be suppressed. The tragic fate of the Mito ronin, which had been foreshadowed by the tragedy of Baron Shishido, was now known to everyone.

Many of these highly significant and moving events came to Hanzo's attention. When reports reached Kyoto that the forces of Takeda Ko'unsai were moving along the Kiso road in full battle gear, fighting pitched battles and pressing on toward Kyoto, it was Hitotsubashi Yoshinobu, lord protector of Kyoto, who said that this matter was of personal concern and proposed to lead a force out toward Omi to suppress the rebels in person. The court gave its consent. On the third day of the twelfth month of the previous year, the middle councillor Hitotsubashi, to use his court title, left Kyoto to establish his headquarters in Otsu. Soldiers from Kanazawa in the Kaga domains and from Odawara, Aizu, and Kuwana followed him there. In the meantime, the Mito ronin had reached Imajo. Spies from the various han were coming and going constantly, and it was an extraordinary scene. On the tenth day of the twelfth month, more than two thousand samurai and commoner soldiers under the command of Hitotsubashi arrived at the port of Tsuruga. They were followed by more than seven hundred men from Mito. In addition to these, Fukui, Ono, Hikone, and Maruyama sent troops out to hold all the strategic spots along the side roads, the seacoasts, and the mountains. It seems that the Kaga men under the personal command of the steward, Nagahara Jinshichiro, were in the van of these forces. Hanzo could picture the Mito ronin surrounded by this huge army, the fields and mountains around them almost covered with hostile troops.

When Takeda Ko'unsai heard that Kaga troops had encamped only a little more than a mile away from his position in Shimpo village, he immediately sent a letter to the Kaga camp, asking free passage to the west and saying that he felt no enmity toward the troops assembled against him there. He begged them to open the way for everyone's sake. The reply from the Kaga side was as follows:

> We have read your letter. We believe your statement that you only want free passage through and that you have not the slightest desire to engage us in hos-

tilities. However, since the Kaga middle councillor and those who are with him here are under strict orders from the middle councillor Hitotsubashi, we have no alternative but to oppose you. We will commence battle within the next two hours. We hereby give you notice.

Twelfth month, eleventh day, year of the rat

For the Kaga middle councillor
Nagahara Jinshichiro

To Takeda Iga no Kami
Ando Hikonoshin

There was more than ten feet of snow on the ground, the ronin were out of food, and their strength was at an end. Realizing this, the Kaga men felt no desire to open battle with opponents who were already suffering from cold and hunger. They immediately sent two hundred bales of white rice, ninety gallons of sake, ten kegs of pickled vegetables, and two thousand dried squid to Takeda's camp. They also sent along a letter saying that they would attack at dawn on the seventeenth. However, Ko'unsai, Fujita Koshiro, and three others went to the Kaga encampment to request an interview with Nagahara Jinshichiro. Nagahara was moved by the sincerity of these men, who had even discarded their swords. He sent them back with word that he would meet with their commander. He added that, since Ko'unsai had come alone and unarmed to his camp, this time he would go to the camp of the Mito men, but he required Ko'unsai to return to his own camp first. Then Jinshichiro set out. Takeda's command post in the village of Shimpo was surrounded by a wooden palisade and cannon were in place. The three hundred musketeers doused their matches and admitted Nagahara. Ko'unsai, wearing his sword, was clothed in a white woolen campaign jacket and shod in straw sandals when he met Nagahara. Stopping his own escort outside the command post, Nagahara permitted Takeda to escort him alone into the interior of the camp. He was met by some twenty-five officers, all without swords. This was the crucial moment. Nagahara, impressed by the attitude of the ronin and amazed at the good order of their camp, gradually changed his plan to offer battle. He agreed to relay their request for free passage to Hitotsubashi, and giving his promise to Ko'unsai, he left the ronin command post with a copy of their petition addressed to Hitotsubashi and a letter of explanation. The next day, Jinshichiro left his own camp before dawn and galloped back to Umezu in Omi province, the site of the main command post, to present the two letters to Hitotsubashi. The petition explained how, ever since the raising of troops at Mt. Tsukuba, the ronin had been slandered by people like Ichikawa Sanzaemon and had therefore suffered the unearned distrust of the shogunate. It said that they had found it impossible as loyal retainers to tolerate the efforts to destroy all that the late lord Nariaki had bequeathed to them, and for this reason as well as to correct the untruths that had been spoken about Baron Shishido, they had left their province and set out for Kyoto. They further insisted that their purpose in going to Kyoto was none other than to serve the emperor and to assist in the expulsion of the foreigners.

The story that Kozo, the Suwa farmer, had told Hanzo enabled him to piece together much of what had happened. He realized that by that time there were two factions in the ronin force. At first it was reported that when Nagahara Jinshichiro of Kaga had said in his letter of reply that he was going to commence battle, Takeda Ko'unsai had called a council. This was just when they had received a secret message inviting them to come to Choshu by way of Wakasa, Tango, and Iwami provinces. Yamakuni Hyobu, the oldest of the ronin and one of the most spirited, argued passionately for going to Choshu. He reportedly said that if they took the side roads to Choshu, they would no longer find it so difficult to carry out their great mission of service to the emperor and expulsion of the barbarians. It was therefore regrettable that they should be pleading now with the Kaga people. He advocated a decisive battle. Ko'unsai did not want to meet the Kaga warriors, forced as they were to act under the constraint of Hitotsubashi's orders, as enemies. Now for the first time, a difference appeared in the positions of Takeda and of Tamaru and Fujita, who had been with him since Tateyama. In fact, the position of people like Fujita, which had arisen from the feeling "How much longer can Mito go on toadying to the shogunate?" and that of Takeda, who placed service to the emperor and expelling the barbarians before all else, who was willing to entrust everything to an impartial judgment by Hitotsubashi Yoshinobu, and who felt that he could not rest without clearing the name of Baron Shishido from the slanders that had besmirched it, had never been the same from the beginning.

However that might be, Hanzo's feelings about the fate to which the Mito ronin had driven themselves were inspired not simply by the fact that it had claimed the lives of the Hirata disciples Yamakuni Hyobu, Yokota Toshiro, and Kameyama Yoshiharu. The shogunate had nearly exterminated all the activists in Mito who opposed its policies as well as most of the promising young people who had been coming up through the schools in the countryside, making it almost certain that Mito would no longer be a significant force in shogunal politics. Mito had been too far ahead of its time. They were early to proclaim the rectification of society which later engaged imaginations in other han, and they were early to leave the scene as the result of their violent internal struggles.

Hanzo learned many things from this uprising of the Mito ronin. There had been nothing like it for making clear the attitudes of all the han from the Kanto through western Honshu. He was also startled at the intensity of the shogunate's resentment of Hitotsubashi Yoshinobu. Through the uprising of the Mito ronin, he had unexpectedly gained an insight into just what it was that lay behind those dark and confused struggles between the high officials and the women's quarters in Edo castle, on the one hand, and the security forces and samurai of various han in Kyoto, on the other.

From the very beginning, Hitotsubashi Yoshinobu, who had wanted the office of shogun to be filled by Iemochi of Kii, was not a person beloved by the present shogunal authorities. During the time of Ii Tairo, it was Yoshinobu who had stood as competitor to the present shogun in the succession dispute. At the time when Satsuma and Choshu were intervening in Kyoto and had dispatched an imperial messenger to Edo, it was Yoshinobu who had accepted Kyoto's requests and had begun to act as the power behind the shogun. Moreover, it was Yoshinobu who had accepted the suggestion of Matsudaira Shungaku of Echizen to eliminate the alternate attendance system. This Yoshinobu, now in the crucial position of lord protector of Kyoto, dedicated to harmonious relations between court and military, was a man who possessed the vision to understand the nature of the times, and in no respect was he sufficiently misguided to place Edo first. In this beginning of the Keio era, when Matsudaira Shungaku had already withdrawn from public affairs, when Hisamitsu of Satsuma was also disaffected, and when harmony between court and military seemed out of the question, Yoshinobu's ardor and steadfastness were recognized by the court as being utterly sincere. And behind him stood the power of Aizu. In the end, it was Yoshinobu's popularity that protected the shogun. There was no question but that the shogunate in Edo found all this unbearable. Ultimately, the character of the shogunate's resentment was made manifest in its treatment of the Mito ronin.

Yoshinobu refused to pardon the Mito ronin. Therefore, Takeda Ko'unsai was left with no choice but to surrender all his forces to Kaga. But at the same time Yoshinobu, whose father was Nariaki of Mito, was secretly doing everything he could to have the ronin spared. Three of Nariaki's other natural sons, the barons Hamada, Kitsuregawa, and Shimabara, had sent petitions both to the court and to the shogunate, while the lords of Inaba and Bizen petitioned the emperor for lenient treatment of the ronin. Tanuma Gembanokami now arrived from Edo. Determined to obtain imperial recognition of his control over the final disposition of the uprising, an authority that he had held in fact ever since Mt. Tsukuba, Tanuma came to the eastern gate of Kyoto in the first month of the year. The court refused permission for him to enter Kyoto. Naturally, he was furious. He made a great thing of the insult which the court had thus inflicted upon the shogunate, and he reiterated his position that both political and military power lay with the shogunate. Apparently certain that Hitotsubashi Yoshinobu had had a hand in this rebuff, he immediately turned around and headed for Tsuruga. On the twenty-sixth day of the first month, Tanuma presented the shogunate's orders to the officials of Kaga, took custody of all the captured equipment, and announced that he would assume custody of Takeda and all his followers as of the twenty-eighth of the month. Taking his counsel from Ichikawa Sanzaemon, and hearing that Yoshinobu was at that very moment doing his utmost to obtain assurance from the court that Takeda and his followers would not be put to death, he rushed to stage his trials of the ronin.

Why could not Kaga, the richest of all the han, have saved the lives of the ronin? Various explanations were offered. Hanzo heard that some were saying that the Mito ronin had been taken in, that they had been deceived by

Kaga. It was reported that Kureta Masaka in Ina was one who took this position. Hanzo believed, however, that the account he had heard from the priest
of the Raigakuji in Suwa, who had come back from a trip to Hoki by way of
Tsuruga, proved this to be an overly suspicious theory. He preferred to
believe that an old-fashioned, honest warrior, Nagahara Jinshichiro, went to
call on Takeda and his officers at the Honshoji in Tsuruga, and that he had
been moved with genuine emotion after the surrender of men and arms had
been completed.

Popular criticism of Tanuma was heard from all quarters. It was reported
that even the personal councillor of the lord of Suwa, who had fought against
the Mito ronin and been wounded, had said something like this: "This person may serve on the junior council of the shogunate but he does not understand the values of the warrior; it has been too long since he himself strayed
from the way of the warrior." The councillor had further criticized Tanuma,
noting the abject cowardice, starting in terror at the "voice of the wind and
the cry of the cranes," that had led him to remain always at least fifty miles
behind the ronin as long as they had been strong. But once the ronin had surrendered to Kaga and been disarmed, he had assumed the ferocity of the tiger
in meting out arbitrary punishments. Others, however, maintained that
Tanuma himself was not the kind of person to behave in that way. He was
tall, heavy, and placid of personality, the kind of young aristocrat who, at the
beginning of the campaign against the Mito ronin, passed out candy to his
staff to help them ward off drowsiness when it was necessary to stand all-
night watches. These people maintained that he must have been goaded into
carrying out these cruel measures by his underlings.

Although the Mito force was usually described as consisting of more than a
thousand men, with their losses in battle, their wounded, and those who had
died along the way, no more than eight hundred and twenty or thirty men
reached Tsuruga. Of that number, three hundred fifty-three were executed in
the space of five days at the Matsubara village execution grounds in Tsuruga.
The heads of Takeda Ko'unsai and the other major commanders were placed
in head tubs and salted down, but the bodies of the rest were buried in five
great pits, each measuring eighteen feet on a side. Of the remainder, two
hundred fifty were exiled and one hundred eighty foot soldiers, porters, and
women were declared innocent and expelled from the province.

One day as Hanzo was walking along the hall from the parlor of the honjin, he looked in on the middle room where the women of the house were
gathered. Oman was talking with Otami about the great memorial services
at Nikko and about the Mito ronin as they wound yarn. Oman had the ball
of yarn in her hand, and Otami was holding the skein of freshly dyed, yellowish-white yarn in both hands. As Oman wound the yarn bit by bit, it
unwound evenly from around Otami's arms. The sunlight shone in under the
deep eaves and between the shoji, bringing out the subtle yellow in the yarn.

"Have you heard the news, mother?" asked Hanzo. "They say that the
heads of Ko'unsai and the others have been returned to Mito from Edo. They
are in the castle town now."

"That's an awful story," Oman replied, continuing to draw the yarn from around Otami's arms. "Your father was saying so, too. He said that he had never heard of such a thing as three hundred fifty men being executed."

Then Hanzo took out a memorandum that had been sent to him from Edo and showed it to his stepmother and his wife. The names of those who had been punished because they were relatives of the chief offenders were recorded in it. The name of Toki, Takeda Ko'unsai's forty-eight-year-old wife led the list. The names of his eight-year-old son Momomaru and his three-year-old son Kaneyoshi were written there. The names of Takeda Hikoemon's twelve-year-old son Saburo, his ten-year-old second son Kinshiro, and his eight-year-old third son Kumagoro were also written there. All six had been condemned to death and the heads of Momomaru and Saburo were to be exposed.

"Ichikawa and his people have been as cruel as they could be. Did they really think that these women and children would have pursued a vendetta against them if they had been allowed to live? And it is particularly horrible to impose death sentences on innocent children."

"Just look, mother, it says right here, 'Son of Takeda Iga, Momomaru, eight years of age.' That's the same age as our Sota," said Otami.

"And then it says here that when the rest of their families had been put in prison, the officials brought the heads of Ko'unsai and the others to the prison and showed them to the prisoners from outside, saying, 'It's flower-viewing time! Have a look at these flowers!' "

"What did they think they were doing, saying a thing like that?" said Oman, looking back and forth at the faces of Hanzo and Otami. "Did they think they were permitting the survivors a final parting with the dead, or did they simply intend to subject them to further humiliation?"

"Absolutely everyone agrees that this was utterly disgusting and completely lacking in feeling."

The sons of Takeda, Yamakuni, Tamaru, and the other leaders were all condemned to death. Their wives and daughters were condemned to life imprisonment, and those names were written out in the memorandum.

> Daughter of Takeda Iga
>   Yoshi, eleven years of age
> Concubine of the same
>   Mume, eighteen years of age
> Wife of Takeda Hikoemon
>   Iku, forty-three years of age
> Wife of Yamakuni Hyobu
>   Natsu, forty-three years of age
> Daughter of the same
>   Chii, thirty years of age
> Daughter of Yamakuni Jun'ichiro
>   Miyo, eleven years of age
> Daughter of the same
>   Yuki, seven years of age

Daughter of the same
　　Kuni, five years of age
Daughter of Tamaru Inaemon
　　Matsu, nineteen years of age
Daughter of the same
　　Mume, ten years of age

Oman spoke first. "What will your father say when he sees this, Hanzo? Nowadays, whenever I tell him anything back there in our room he just says, 'Ah, I have lived to the age of sixty-six and I have seen the end of this world.'"

4

The attempt to revive the alternate attendance system ended in a complete betrayal of the hopes of the Tokugawa, making it clear that sentiment in the han had already turned away from the shogunate. Anyone paying the least attention to the trend of the times could see that the han had begun to work out their own independent policies. The sudden expansion of sea transport, the increases in shipping tonnage, the sending of students abroad for study— all stemmed from this, and in all other affairs, whether it be military organization or industrial production, everyone who thought carefully about the future had begun to expand his activities on the han level.

Owari, the great han of central Honshu and one of the three cadet branches of the Tokugawa, was no exception. This was manifest even in the Kiso area, which formed a part of the Owari domains. Still greater attention was now given to the protection of the forests and the transport of prime timber. Salt supplies were being bought up and the han began to look upon the medicinal herbs that grew around Mt. Ontake as another source of income. The cultivation of ginseng was strongly encouraged in the Kiso and the Ina and Matsumoto areas, as well as in Iwamurata in Saku county, Ueda in Chiisagata county, and Iiyama in Minochi county. The ginseng was bought up exclusively by Owari. The Owari medical consignments coming down past Magome from the inner reaches of the Kiso, with hanging lanterns inscribed "Official Owari Business" and each with its banner inscribed "Official Business of the Owari Medicinal Plantation," were a sight the like of which was not to be seen on the other great highways.

At the beginning of the fifth month, Hanzo completed the business for which he had been called to the offices in Fukushima and returned to Magome with the other post officials who had accompanied him. The business had to do with a contribution of money that Owari had ordered in the last month of the previous year, and they had just now concluded it by taking the funds to Fukushima. There was no surprise in what the funds were to be used for. They were to support the punitive expedition against Choshu under the command of the retired lord of Owari.

The expedition against Choshu had first come up when Hanzo was in Edo as the representative of the lower four Kiso stations. At that time a request went out to all the headmen of the thirty-three villages of the Kiso valley in the form of a letter from the retired lord himself. The letter began with the statement that, due to the recent behavior of Choshu, he had received a special order which had required him to go to Edo in spite of illness. It was now necessary for him to take the field in western Japan. The letter went on to say that this difficult assignment had proved to be even more burdensome than anticipated and almost all sources of money that could be borrowed had disappeared. There was no course open but to ask the people in the Owari domains to share the expenses. This was not to be taken as meaning that the people of the Kiso would be asked to bear the burden alone. The letter recognized that this was only the latest of many such requests and expressed regrets that this should be so, but in these disorderly times it asked the headmen to have the people of their respective villages get the money together promptly.

Together with this letter from the retired lord was circulated another from the elders of the han. This also had to do with the request for money and it said that the elders were concerned about the costs of this emergency campaign which the retired lord had described in his letter. Only through the united efforts of high and low would they be able to respond effectively. The people of the han were urged to show utter sincerity in their desire to serve the nation. The letter closed by noting that they had repeatedly made such requests in the past and it was most distressing to have to do so again, but they had been left with no choice and they asked all to heed the request for the sake of the nation.

Summoned to Fukushima by Yamamura, the deputy, the headmen were called into the lance room. There, in the presence of the rice tax officials, the two letters from Nagoya were shown to the headmen and an announcement was read that the deputy himself had written to clarify the content of the letters. It requested that each of the headmen find out what he would be able to contribute and report in writing by the fifteenth of the first month.

The twenty-two country villages had raised a sum of more than three hundred fourteen ryo and the eleven post stations presented three hundred ryo, making a total contribution of over six hundred fourteen ryo from the Kiso valley. Now Hanzo was returning to the Magome meeting room feeling that at last the officials of the Magome station as well as those of the nearby villages of Yamaguchi and Yubunezawa would be relieved of this heavy burden.

"They say there is going to be another campaign against Choshu," Inosuke whispered to Hanzo. "The shogun himself is supposed to command this one."

"Yes, I heard that too. It looks as though it is true, doesn't it? The people are not even going to have a chance to catch their breaths," said Hanzo with a sigh.

It was a busy time on the highway. The processions of high-ranking officials went through one after another like rushing clouds. One day three express palanquins hurried down from the direction of Kyoto. They were followed from dusk until the fifth hour of the night by chests bound for Edo.

Soon after that the proclamation of a second campaign against Choshu was posted on the notice board in the center of Magome. From Edo came an order for each of the stations along the route to the west to provide eight hundred fifty pounds of fodder, one hundred koku of rice bran, and twelve koku of soy beans. The commissioner of construction and the inspector of police for commoners ordered everyone to the duties of moving men and horses for the new expedition against Choshu, calling in special porters from as far away as the western Japan sea coast.

Objections to the shogunate's plan for the expedition came in from one han after another. Even the houses of Echizen and Bizen, unable to look on in silence, sent memorials to the shogunate that amounted to letters of protest. In sum, their objections were as follows. As a result of the first Choshu expedition, led by the retired lord of Owari in retaliation for the siege of Kyoto, Choshu had already admitted its guilt, had punished the responsible officials and retainers, and had manifested proper contrition. Since appropriate action had been taken against the lord of Choshu and his son, the proclamation of a second punitive expedition could only lead to shock and confusion among the people of the nation. Fortunately, the first expedition had ended without actual fighting and everyone within and without the shogunate was just now beginning to feel a return to peace and security. Raising a great army at this time could not but result in difficulties for the daimyo and resentment among the people. Furthermore, there was no telling what kind of consequences that action might entail. It was necessary to refrain from undertaking such grave ventures so lightly; it was necessary to fear the creation of disorder in the nation. In high circles it was being said that serious consequences would arise if the expedition were carried out without reference to the feelings of the house of Mori, or if their punishment should be excessive. In the extreme, if father and son were forced to a stubborn defense, the situation would become intolerable. These were times when the hearts of the people were growing turbulent, and if any venture should be undertaken without consulting the imperial will, there was simply no telling what might happen, either at court or in the pacification of Choshu's home provinces of Suo and Nagato. The request was therefore made that this expedition be postponed and that the opinions of all the daimyo great and small be heard. If disorder should break out in the nation because of the single han of Choshu, then what seemed like a noble undertaking at the moment might prove to be a source of grief and suffering in later days.

The shogunate did not heed these memorials. Instead it found it intolerable that even traditionally loyal daimyo among the great han such as the Hosokawa of Kumamoto should have spoken out against the resumption of alternate attendance. The high officials of the shogunate were now determined to restore Tokugawa prestige and hegemony at whatever cost, and to cut down all who opposed them. They displayed their power, as in the spectacular ceremonies just conducted at Nikko and by executing more than three hundred fifty Mito samurai, and they even went so far as to change the era name to Keio on the occasion of the two hundred fiftieth anniversary of the death of Tokugawa Ieyasu. All this was done in order to assert their control over the processes of change.

In fact, the Tokugawa at that very time were preparing for the construction of two great warships, to be called the *Kaiten,* or "epoch maker," and the *Kaiyo,* or "sun raiser." Nothing spoke so clearly of the mood of the shogunate at this time as the names of these two ships. To wish to see the radiance of the sun once more was to wish to see once again the power of Tokugawa Ieyasu, whose posthumous name was "prince of the eastern light." The second Choshu expedition was thus born out of the obstinacy of shogunal officials unable to forget the grand old days of the Tokugawa. Although it was called the Choshu expedition, it was planned with several objectives in mind. One aim was to encourage the Shikoku forces favoring foreign contacts. Another was to demoralize those traditionally hostile han that were trying to ally themselves with the court. Some even said that the true purpose of the plan was the expulsion of Hitotsubashi Yoshinobu and the Aizu forces from positions of influence.

On the sixteenth day of the intercalary fifth month, the shogun at last launched the second Choshu punitive expedition. The guidon in the form of a golden fan, said to have been used by Ieyasu at the battle of Sekigahara, was once more raised on high. In the retinue were the traditionally loyal daimyo then in residence in Edo, the commissioner of land forces, the commissioner of infantry, the chief of cavalry, the masters of swordsmanship, lancemanship, and artillery, the censors, and the commissioner of naval forces. Those who witnessed this spectacle said that it actually gave the impression that the power of the Tokugawa was still intact. The shogunate budgeted one hundred seventy-four thousand two hundred ryo for each month of the expedition. Twenty Edo merchants had been required to supply from ten thousand to thirty thousand ryo each, and even the shrines and temples throughout the country were persuaded to make contributions for the sake of the nation. At the time, the shogunate had two treasuries; the one in Fujimi was called the private treasury and the other at Hasuike was called the outer treasury. The fact that the shogunate drew one million ryo out of the private treasury for this campaign shows just how great its scale was.

By the twenty-third of that month, the shogun was in Kyoto and on the twenty-fifth he entered Osaka castle. According to all reports, the expedition of the previous year, which had gone as far as the province of Aki under the leadership of the retired lord of Owari, had had every intention of fighting, whereas this expedition had not the slightest intention of doing so. However powerful a han Choshu might be, it could not expect to stand against the entire nation. Last year it had even gone to the camp of the retired lord of Owari and hung its head in admission of guilt. It was the shogun himself, now in Osaka, to whom the Mori, both father and son, would have to go to ask forgiveness for their wrongdoing and to await disposition of their case. Surely it would be no different than when Mori Terumoto had come before Ieyasu after the battle of Sekigahara. This was said to be the expectation of everyone on the shogunal side from the cabinet on down to the common foot soldiers. However, this second expedition forced Choshu into exactly the kind of corner that such daimyo as those of Bizen and Echizen had feared.

The shogunate had never had any intention of seeing this expedition engage in actual warfare. However brilliantly the golden fan guidon might glisten from on high, it made no move to advance beyond Osaka. The place where the great shogunal army was to pass its empty days and months was that very Osaka that had been so staunchly loyal to the heir of Hideyoshi, championing him against Ieyasu. According to the words of one observer, the wood thrush sang as it passed by the castle keep, the breezes of the fifth month ruffled the martial robes on the shores of Chinu bay, and the remaining martial spirits were steamed out in the brutal heat.

Into this uneasy atmosphere there burst a crisis in foreign relations even worse than the Namamugi incident.

It was now the eighth year since the signing of the treaties in Edo. According to those treaties, the three ports of Kanagawa, Nagasaki, and Hakodate were opened. Niigata was also opened, and after four years Edo, Osaka, and Hyogo were to be opened. Four years later, however, at the beginning of the Bunkyu era in 1861, the anti-foreign movement had reached fever pitch and it was impossible to open the strategic ports of Edo, Osaka, and Hyogo. Ando Tsushima, a roju at the time, asked for a five-year postponement of the opening of Niigata, Edo, Osaka, and Hyogo, offering a reduction of tariffs in return.

The ensuing four years had been a turbulent time of fierce debates over whether such a totally unprecedented number of windows should be opened to European influence. Choshu's bombardment of foreign vessels at Shimonoseki took place around then and it was solely because of the anti-foreign fever that the shogunate had been forced to pay the crippling indemnity of three million ryo.

The foreign envoys from four nations had at first demanded that this indemnity be paid by Choshu. Choshu, however, maintained that since the firing had been carried out in accordance with the orders of the court and the shogunate, those two bodies should pay the indemnity. Recognizing the difficulty of wringing this indemnity out of Choshu, the envoys of the four Western powers shifted their protest to the ground that the shogunate had been guilty of malfeasance and misfeasance in its duty of guiding and restraining the daimyo. The envoys further recognized that the indemnity was excessive, and they even went so far as to suggest in their communications at the time that if only the ports were opened they would not insist on the indemnity. The emissaries took advantage of every opportunity to try to force the shogunate to fulfill the obligations of the treaty. Four years had passed and it was now the first year of Keio, but the shogunate still showed no signs of preparing to open the ports. At this point, Parkes, the new British envoy, appeared. He argued that the Western powers should press the shogunate to open the port of Hyogo in return for a remission of two-thirds of the indemnity. It was mandatory that the shogunate request imperial permission to carry out the provisions of the treaty, as the alternative would be the dangerous one of failing to live up to treaty obligations. If the shogunate should prove unable to gain this permission, then the foreign envoys would no longer deal with the shogunate but would instead address their demands directly to the court. On the sixteenth day of the ninth month of Keio 1, 1865, a combined fleet of nine ships—four from Britain, three from France, and one each from Holland and the United States—sailed from Yokohama and entered the port of Hyogo. On the seventeenth, three of these ships took up positions off Mt. Tempo in Osaka and delivered letters from the ambassadors, saying that they had to have an answer within seven days. The great force that the shogunate had moved down from Edo at such fearful expense now had to face an even more powerful enemy. The punishment of Choshu, one of the most powerful han in the nation, was no longer the main issue. When the Western combined fleet had attacked Choshu, not only had Choshu been unable to stand against it but its shore batteries had been destroyed, its cities burned, and for a short time it had even suffered the occupation of some of its territory. This was the lesson of the battle of Shimonoseki.

When the departure of the combined fleet was reported to Edo, the tairo and the roju left in charge there realized that this was not something they could simply overlook. They rushed two special officials to Osaka to deal with the matter, having them travel day and night. One of these men was Yamaguchi Suruga no Kami.

Yamaguchi Suruga no Kami, the senior commissioner for foreign relations, used the pen name Sensho. He was on very close terms with Kitamura Zuiken, who had advanced from Hakodate commissioner to chief censor. When he arrived in Osaka and relayed the opinions of the roju back in Edo, the officials in audience with the shogun found themselves at a loss. No one had any reply when he asked what should be done now that the shogun had moved to the west, the country was in great difficulty, and additional foreign pressures were being brought to bear. Yamaguchi Suruga was given the status of censor as well as that of commissioner of foreign affairs and was ordered to go quickly to the foreign ships and negotiate. On the twenty-third, he boarded the *Shokaku Maru* in the company of the roju Abe Bungo no Kami to meet with the four foreign emissaries in Hyogo. The roju Abe, seemingly unimpressed with the situation, took full responsibility for the opening of the ports and came back from that meeting with a promise from the emissaries that they would extend their deadline until the twenty-sixth. At that time, the Aizu warriors guarding Kyoto were coming down to Osaka in a steady stream apparently concerned about the pressures on that city. They met with

Suruga and other officials, protesting that for the emissaries of the foreign countries to bring warships when requesting the opening of the ports amounted to negotiation by force with us in our own capital and was an intolerable insult. They added that if these foreigners should become still more importunate and try to go directly to Kyoto, the soldiers of Aizu, prepared to resist to the death, would see that they got not one step beyond Toba. They requested that they be taken into complete confidence on developments in the region.

A memorial to the shogun then came from Okubo Toshimichi of Satsuma, saying that as there was concern that great harm might follow from this incident, he hoped to hear an announcement to all the daimyo that the shogunate was not going to accept any of the proposals of the foreign emissaries. The memorial further stated that if the other side should initiate some kind of military action in the coming days, then although there were presently few people in the Satsuma residence in Kyoto, they all had their orders from Hisamitsu and would place themselves in the vanguard of the forces also prepared to resist to the death.

At the beginning of the tenth month, a report suddenly came from Kyoto that the two roju Abe Bungo no Kami and Matsumae Izu no Kami had been dismissed from office. The letter from the Kyoto spokesman for the court reported that they had been stripped of all their offices and ranks by imperial order and had been told to return to their homes. The order was endorsed by the imperial regent. The officials in Osaka castle were taken completely by surprise. They had no idea what the emperor's purpose might be and so they did not know how to respond. The shogun Iemochi himself was astonished. He called the lords of Owari and Kii, the roju, the junior council, the censors, and the commissioners of finance to his chambers and asked them to confer in the shogunal presence. It had been a precipitous decision. Just what did it mean for the court, in the midst of a major foreign policy crisis, to relieve the two officials in charge of negotiations of both their duties and their court ranks and to order them to return home? The court had strongly admonished the shogunate for carrying on these negotiations without proper consultation, but for the court to dismiss such high-ranking shogunal officials was altogether without precedent. Various arguments were advanced and the conference was a turbulent one.

Yamaguchi Suruga and another censor, Mukoyama Eigoro, then came forward together. They stated their belief that the advancement or the retirement, the rewarding or the penalization of the shogun's retainers was entirely in the shogun's hands and that the present order of the court was tantamount to a usurpation of shogunal authority. If the powers of the shogunate were once stolen away, the nation could not be governed. To interfere in this time of crisis and to remove the two people in charge of negotiations was to make it impossible for the shogun to carry out his responsibilities. This would bring disgrace to the emperor on high, betray the hopes of the people below, and render us unable to face our ancestors. They stated that the shogun should promptly give up his office, return to the Kanto, and show no regrets. No one accepted this. A storm of protest broke out among the members of the council. Then Iemochi responded, saying that both men had spoken well and that their opinion was very close to his own. He had succeeded to his office at a tender age and at a time when there was a multitude of problems, both foreign and domestic. It was a time when disorder could not be settled nor the people ruled. Now his most important ministers were being forced to resign. This he saw as a reflection of his lack of ability, and he said that any hopes of peace being maintained through his efforts were forlorn indeed. He proposed to give up the office with good grace, put Hitotsubashi Yoshinobu in his place, and follow the orders of the imperial court. Therefore, he told them, it was best to keep Bungo and Izu from entering the castle. As the shogun finished his speech and left the room, the sound of weeping could be heard from among his ministers.

The fortunes of the house of Tokugawa changed with stunning rapidity from that point on. The official resignation of the shogun came very shortly thereafter. The draft of the appeal to be relieved of his office was written by Mukoyama Eigoro. The youthful shogun had just reached the age of twenty. He copied out Mukoyama's draft in his own hand, signed it, and entrusted it to Tokugawa Shigenori, the lord of Owari. After consultation among the high shogunal officials, a second letter accompanied this one, explaining that it was impossible to prevent the opening of the ports and making clear that they were prepared to contest the imperial orders even at the risk of the office of shogun itself.

By this time no perceptive member of the shogunate could laugh any longer at Mito's factional quarrels. The roju and other high officials tried to escape from the daily pressures exerted on them by the foreigners while Yoshinobu did everything possible to maintain harmony between court and military, insisting that imperial orders must be strictly followed and displaying a clear intention to downplay the position of the shogunate. But the bitter behind-the-scenes struggles, as fierce as any caused by the purge of Ansei —these deep-rooted struggles over whether or not the Treaty of Kanagawa should have been signed or who the shogunal successor should have been still went on. The roju who now suspected Yoshinobu's ambitions were no different from those who had been suspicious of Mito's ambitions and had supported Yoshitomo of Kii in the Ansei period. As shogunal officials, the roju took particular offense from Yoshinobu's attitude. Never had the long-standing voices of opposition to Yoshinobu been raised in such grave and serious tones. Not only did the roju express their opposition to dismissing colleagues from office, but they led off their attack by noting that Yoshinobu had been "long at court, carrying out his duties." In response to the shogun Iemochi's request that Yoshinobu be his successor, they stated that they wanted to follow the same procedure now that had been followed in the case of the appointment of Iemochi himself, and they asked the court to so inform Yoshinobu.

The shogun had already moved to Fushimi. On the day he left Osaka, his followers, hearing now for the first time that their orders were to accompany the shogun back to the east, were all astonished. They went pale, glancing uneasily at each other without speaking. The captains of the musketeers and the commanders of the swordsmen and lancers, all products of the Kobusho, the shogunal military academy, conferred among themselves and spoke to their troops. The captains of the musketeers ordered their men to serve as a vanguard while the swordsmen and lancers were to guard the personal safety of the shogun. The musketeers accepted their orders immediately but the swordsmen and lancers protested. Everyone had a different opinion and extreme confusion followed. Nevertheless, it was said that there were some among them who remained quiet from beginning to end, swallowed their tears, and listened to the orders.

Upon hearing of the shogun's decision to resign, Hitotsubashi Yoshinobu conferred with the lord of Owari. Then, accompanied by the lords of Aizu and Kuwana, he rushed to the commissioner's residence in Fushimi. There he met with the shogun and tried to persuade him to change his mind. He spoke forcefully and insistently, pointing out that simply to withdraw after submitting his petition was not proper. Since the shogun and the emperor were brothers-in-law, it would be disrespectful to leave without going to Kyōto and speaking to the emperor on frank and familiar terms. Above all, the shogun should delay his plans for a while since this was no time for precipitous action. Moreover, his proposal to resign in favor of Yoshinobu was not at all pleasing to the rōju. At last the shogun returned to Kyōto, entered Nijō castle, and had Yoshinobu represent him at court.

Mukoyama Eigorō, having aroused the resentment of the court by drafting the letter of resignation, was quietly excluded from attendance at court. In less than three days he was relieved of office and placed under house arrest. When the news of these actions reached Edo castle there was further astonishment. It was reported that the women of the castle, from Tenshoin and Princess Kazu on down, were deeply grieved. Some of them wept aloud while others tried to cast themselves into wells or to kill themselves in other ways.

The fifth day of the tenth month of Keiō 1 is an important date in the history of this nation. This was the day when Hitotsubashi Yoshinobu, Ogasawara Iki no Kami, Matsudaira Etchū no Kami, and Matsudaira Higo no Kami jointly signed a petition to the emperor urging acceptance of the foreign treaties. High-ranking personages from the han had been called to the palace on the previous night for consultation. A council made up of thirty-six men from fifteen han was selected. There were three from Satsuma, three from Higo, three from Bizen, four from Tosa, two from Kurume, one from Inaba, one from Fukuoka, one from Kanazawa, one from Yanagawa, two from Tsu, one from Fukui, one from Saga, one from Hiroshima, five from Kuwana, and seven from Aizu. That the problems of the shogunal succession and the signing of the foreign treaties should have been decided not by the daimyo but by their retainers reflected the unsettled times. These treaties, which had been opposed by the court since the time of

Ii Tairo in spite of numerous appeals by the shogunate, were at last sanctioned when the court found itself facing a fleet representing the combined might of four nations, and when the shogunate had risked the office of shogun itself. The end of the nation's long isolation was approaching.

Yamaguchi Suruga was in Osaka. The shogun had left Osaka castle and the only other high officials remaining behind were the roju Matsudaira Hoki no Kami and the steward Makino Etchu no Kami. Other than these there was only the town commissioner and the captain of the guards. Yamaguchi had been left there in order to receive the foreign emissaries, but there was no one with whom he could consult and he spent his time in futile journeys back and forth between Osaka and Hyogo, trying to calm the foreigners. He had not yet had any clear response from Edo and he did not even know who was in charge of foreign affairs after the removal of Abe.

It was the sixth day of the tenth month. Yamaguchi was worried. After consultation with the censor Akamatsu Sakyo, he went to Kyoto to try to find out what was happening.

He left Osaka at dawn and went up the Yodo river as far as Yodo station. The teahouses were not yet open. He had one household aroused to heat sake and make rice gruel for him while he warmed himself for a while. Then he met a mounted detachment that came rushing down the riverside from Kyoto. An inspector named Matsura was carrying an imperial message. There Yamaguchi learned for the first time that there had been a great council in the palace on the previous night and that imperial sanction had been bestowed upon the foreign treaties. Many of the court nobles who had only recently been advocating the closing of the ports and the expulsion of the foreigners had gradually come to agree on this new course. The message stated that foreign treaties were now authorized and that appropriate actions should therefore be taken, but it also noted that there were problems with the existing treaty drafts and that these should be corrected in accordance with the decision of the council of representatives from the han. Among the details was the order that Matsudaira Hoki was to negotiate with the foreign emissaries. It was also written that "the port of Hyogo will remain closed." Exasperated, Suruga stared at the messenger, Matsura. This imperial message would surely not satisfy the foreign emissaries and they would be certain to force their way up to Kyoto to achieve their objectives. The affair was particularly unlikely to go well if Matsudaira Hoki was to be in charge of it. There were others far more conversant with foreign affairs. As Yamaguchi Suruga spoke of his difficulty in accepting the scheme, Matsura became upset, saying that he was only the messenger and that he "had not come to hear your arguments." Yamaguchi Suruga burst out laughing. He then parted from Matsura with the promise that he would return to Osaka and, if time permitted, he would try to go to Hyogo. Even though he probably could not get an extension of the ultimatum, he would do everything he could, and he would transfer the responsibility for the negotiations to Ogasawara Iki. He immediately borrowed a horse from the detachment so that he could get back to Osaka as quickly as possible.

On the afternoon of that day, Yamaguchi and the censor Akamatsu Sakyo went on board the *Jundo Maru,* which was riding at anchor off Mt. Tempo. He ordered the captain to sail immediately for Hyogo and to have the boilers stoked vigorously. Then he caught sight of a red riverboat flying a banner, coming from the direction of Kawaguchi. From the color of the boat, he knew that it carried a high official. When it drew near he found that it was not Ogasawara Iki, whom he had been hoping to see, but Matsudaira Hoki. Matsudaira was a warm and openhearted person but he was simply not the kind to take effective charge of foreign negotiations.

The red riverboat was rowed up to a nonplused Yamaguchi. Shortly afterward Matsudaira Hoki came aboard. His greetings were light and casual, to the effect that, having received a sudden order from Kyoto, he had come to carry out the intent of the imperial decree and wished to consult with Yamaguchi. His gaze was calm, as if there were no serious problems.

A huge foreign ship lay offshore. A boat was put down from it and rowed over, bearing a single foreigner. It bobbed on the waves as it approached. The British secretary, Alexander Seabolt, had come from Hyogo with a message demanding action. He announced that the ultimatum had expired, that they were awaiting the arrival of the Japanese plenipotentiary, and that the ships of the foreign fleet all had steam up and were ready to sail.

As the *Jundo Maru* approached Hyogo, the French secretary, Mermet de Cachon, was also waiting impatiently for the arrival of the Japanese plenipotentiary.

The discussions were begun on board a British ship. Since this was their first meeting with the British, Yamaguchi gave the names and ranks of the members of his party. The British emissary, Parkes, found this odd. He spoke to Matsudaira Hoki.

"This is the day you promised to make your reply. Why is Abe Bungo not here?"

"Abe Bungo? He was relieved of his position the other day."

"And Ogasawara Iki?"

"He is ill."

"Matsudaira Suo?"

"Oh, Matsudaira Suo is very much pressed by his duties and he found it impossible to attend this meeting."

When Parkes heard this he smiled coldly and said that he was most displeased that on this final conference none of the regular participants had come and it had all been left to newcomers. Matsudaira Hoki took no notice of this as he raised the imperial message in his right hand high above his head and read it out before Parkes.

Seabolt, the secretary, sat beside Yamaguchi and asked him about every character and phrase in the imperial message and then explained them one by one to the ambassador. Parkes' face instantly turned red as fire. He clenched his fist and pounded on the table; he got up from his chair and paced about the room with long strides. When he spoke spittle flew from his lips.

"What do you mean by saying that 'imperial sanction has now been given' for the treaties? Don't you know that the British empire and Japan signed treaties years ago? To keep the port of Hyogo closed is a violation of the treaty. Since the imperial message is given such weight, this shows that there is another authority more powerful than the Tokugawa shogunate. Therefore, I will consult directly with this more powerful authority. I have no further need to talk with such as you. Conduct me immediately to where the real authority in this nation lies. Furthermore, if this is really a message from the emperor, it should have his seal. How can we foreigners have faith in a mere scrap of paper that does not even bear an official seal? You have come here to deceive us. I am giving the captain of this ship orders to sail for Kyoto immediately. You gentlemen will be so good as to accompany me."

Matsudaira, calmly forcing a smile no matter what was said to him, sat face to face with Parkes. They could not speak directly to each other. The arrogant Parkes, determined to be deceived no further by the shogunate's diplomatic methods, was about to tear up the imperial message when Yamaguchi hurriedly stopped him, explained the internal circumstances that made it impossible to open the port of Hyogo at this moment, and said that the imperial message was originally addressed to the shogun and had not been intended for Parkes' eyes. He further noted that it was near the end of the day, the French ambassador was surely waiting, and after they met with him they would return to this ship. Parkes slowly softened. Thereupon the two men left the British ambassador and went to the French ship.

The French ambassador Roches was well acquainted with Yamaguchi, having met him often in Edo. Roches had already been helpful to the shogunate in many ways, from the administration of the shipyards in Yokosuka and the training of the army to the establishment of a French language school and the transporting of students abroad. Moreover, the French secretary, Mermet de Cachon, had, through the introduction of the Hakodate commissioner, studied Japanese with Yamaguchi's friend Kitamura Zuiken while both of them were in Hakodate. With these ties, Yamaguchi felt at ease with the French legation. The ambassador and secretary were not, of course, the least bit surprised to learn of the British attitude. They merely spread their arms and shrugged their shoulders in a gesture that appeared to be characteristic of the French.

Roches, aware of the meaning of the pains to which the shogunate had gone in bringing an imperial message, even went so far as to advise Matsudaira on the best course of action in this situation. He also asked to be shown the letter signed by the roju. He had already heard its general import from Yamaguchi by way of de Cachon's translation. He then asked them to draft a letter for him which would say that, due to the press of affairs within the country, it was impossible to carry out the agreement as it related to Hyogo. The opening of Hyogo had the approval of the shogunate and everything from this point on was the responsibility of Mizuno Izumi no Kami. They should therefore go directly to Edo to consult with him and the disposition of the matter could then be relayed to the court. Roches said that he would then take that note with him as proof of good faith and go around to consult with the other ambassadors that very evening to obtain their consent to set sail early the following morning. That would get them past the immediate crisis. Such was the thinking of the French ambassador.

"Well now, what should we do? If it only depended on me, I could draft such a letter immediately, but if it is to have the signatures of all the other roju then we will have to confer with them. That will lead to serious trouble."

This was said by Matsudaira Hoki after they had returned to the *Jundo Maru*.

It was already the eighth hour of the night, two o'clock. If they went to Kyoto for consultations, they could not possibly get back in time the next day. Yet it seemed to them an opportunity they dared not let pass. If on the following day the foreign ships were to sail to Osaka, enter the Yodo river, and steam up to Kyoto, it would be a shocking disgrace. Yamaguchi told Matsudaira they could not waste a single hour. If they were now to fritter away the goodwill of the French ambassador, they could never make up for it though they chewed their very navels out. If the other roju did not approve of what they had done, they would just have to accept the consequences but they simply could not await their pleasure now. Matsudaira could think of nothing else to do but to tell Yamaguchi to go ahead and do as he saw fit. If his colleagues disapproved, it would not be Matsudaira's fault. Yamaguchi quickly accepted the responsibility. A secretary drew up the letter. It bore the names of the roju Matsudaira Hoki no Kami, Matsudaira Suo no Kami, and Ogasawara Iki no Kami. Signatures were affixed for all three of them.

It was very late at night by the time this letter had been distributed through the hands of the French ambassador to the British and American ships. Yamaguchi went alone to the French ship to await the response. After a time Roches joined him, saying, *"Très bien! Très bien!"*

The meaning was that everything had gone as they had hoped. As the two stood on the deck of the French warship gazing out over the night sea, Roches told Yamaguchi that their ships would be leaving Hyogo in the evening of the following day and that they would sail out past Shikoku, along the coastline of Kyushu, and then back up to Yokohama. He added that they would now require the very best efforts of Mizuno back in Edo. On parting he shook Yamaguchi's hand warmly.

Matsudaira Hoki was waiting aboard the *Jundo Maru* for Yamaguchi's long-delayed return. When Yamaguchi brought the decision back, Matsudaira was still dubious.

"Is it certain they will leave tomorrow?"

"You need not concern yourself on that account. Roches has guaranteed it. You may rest assured."

"Well then, you stay here for the time being. Go up to Kyoto after all the ships have actually sailed. You should report to both the roju and the shogun."

After seeing Matsudaira off that same night for Osaka and Kyoto, Yamaguchi landed once again and passed an uneasy time in the company of the censor Akamatsu. The next morning, as the two were still waiting impatiently for the departure of the foreign ships, samurai from various han began to come to their inn. They asked about the reasons behind this promised withdrawal of the foreign fleet and the nature of the negotiations carried on by Matsudaira Hoki. They seemed to have no faith at all in these negotiations.

The time promised for the sailing of the foreign fleet had passed. Then it was the full morning of the ninth and whistles signaling impending departure were sounded on all the ships. The blasts resounded among the hills as if in promise of the early opening of the port of Hyogo.

It was already near dusk when Yamaguchi and Akamatsu reached Nijo castle in Kyoto with their report of the departure of the foreign ships. When they had once again entered the audience chamber and were about to make their report to the roju, Yamaguchi found that there was yet another surprise awaiting him.

"Well, Yamaguchi. Just a little more and you would have been ordered to perform seppuku."

It was Yoshinobu, a wry smile on his lips, who extended this greeting from the seat of honor.

Yamaguchi Suruga was stunned. As he started to ask why, the roju Ogasawara Iki no Kami called him into another room and explained that on the previous day there had been a rumor current in Kyoto that he had deliberately altered the imperial message and had been handling affairs according to his own whims. Because of that, the story went, the foreign emissaries had consented to leave, but there were some who were saying that his actions amounted to high treason and he should be required to perform seppuku immediately. The court had been on the point of agreeing to issue the order. However, the shogun and Yoshinobu had both cautioned against hasty action and Ogasawara had himself insisted that without hearing what the accused had to say, as well as Matsudaira Hoki's own story, they could not properly convict anyone. They had just now received Matsudaira Hoki's account and had realized that no serious accusation should be lodged.

"But my making use of our colleagues' names when I sent the letter was in no way an arbitrary action. I am most grateful to you."

Yamaguchi placed his hands on the tatami and bowed low. Then he spoke of the circumstances that had forced him to improvise.

"Yes, it was an extreme emergency. It was entirely proper for you to have made the decisions that you did."

Ogasawara spoke in sympathetic tones. Then he lowered his voice and told Yamaguchi that it would be extremely dangerous for him to remain in Kyoto. He had best leave this evening, go directly back to Edo, and once there remain quietly in his home. Ogasawara promised that he would do what he could for him here.

Somewhat reassured by Ogasawara's words, Yamaguchi slipped out. He suddenly thought of the censor Mukoyama Eigoro. Thinking that he would at least like to see Mukoyama and discuss with him the possible consequences of this situation, he asked one of the attendants where he was. The reply was that Mukoyama had been accused of a crime some days ago and was now confined to his inn.

Darkness was falling. The hallways of the castle were dim. Someone with disheveled hair was rushing down the hall toward him. That person was the friend who had come hurriedly from Edo as commissioner of naval forces and consultant on foreign affairs. It was the chief censor, Kitamura Zuiken. Yamaguchi called him into the shadows but there was no time to speak in detail. He could only tell him that he was forced by circumstances to leave and he asked Zuiken to make his best efforts in his place.

"I will leave everything in your hands."

After this brief word with Zuiken, he quickly left Nijo castle. He could not even take the time to look in on his colleagues from Osaka castle, who had now been moved to the palace.

5

A traveler returning from Kyoto stopped his horse in front of the Magome honjin. He was accompanied by two retainers wrapped in cloaks and by a manservant who set down his baggage.

From the time this traveler had left Edo in the middle of the ninth month, traveling day and night, until the time near the middle of the tenth month when he once again reached the western edge of the Kiso road, he had been on the move almost constantly and at work almost constantly, with no time to catch his breath. Looking back on a Kyoto sunk in its dark and forbidding atmosphere, he had at last cleared the danger zone and when he reached Magome pass, some one hundred and twenty miles from Otsu, he felt that he could once again breathe freely of the mountain air. The traveler was Yamaguchi Suruga no Kami.

When he heard that they had a guest for the night, Seisuke came out to the entry hall to greet him. The exhausted traveler came in. By the way he moved as he took off his hat and unlaced his sandals, Seisuke immediately recognized that he was an important person traveling incognito.

"We happen to have a very good room open. The master of the house is in Fukushima on business but he should be back very soon. Here in the mountains we can't really entertain you properly but please stay as long as you might wish."

As Seisuke spoke, he led his guest toward the chamber of honor at the very back of the main house. The two retainers he placed in the adjoining inner room and the manservant was lodged in a room near the front entry.

A certain small wren called *toya* was in season and there were many varieties of mushrooms. It was the best season for entertaining guests in the Kiso. Seisuke went back and forth between the inner rooms and the hearthside, continuing to check on everything from preparations for the bath to the menu for the evening meal, even though he had already consulted with Otami, who was working with the two maids. On the flat plates there would be fresh yams with yellow citron and in the bowls would be marsh mushrooms and bean curd cooked in soup stock. In spite of their remote location, they were even able to offer fresh octopus served with eggs. In addition to this part of the meal that Seisuke had planned, there was to be a plate containing two of the famous Kiso thrushes.

The two children always enjoyed the arrival of an important visitor because this meant that Otami would dress them in their best kimono. Okume, the elder, was already ten years old and it was she who listened for the voices of the guests in the inner rooms and relayed the word to Seisuke or the maids whenever they were summoned.

"They just clapped!"

Such was the tone of the honjin.

That evening Hanzo returned to Magome after completing the business for which he had been summoned to Fukushima and spending the previous night at Nojiri. It was only then that he learned that there were guests in the house and that the guest in the chamber of honor now drinking the sake of this mountain household and passing his time as a traveler was a censor and commissioner for foreign affairs traveling in disguise.

The next morning the travelers remained in bed. A rain that had begun at dawn had brought out their fatigue. At last, around noon, there was the sound of the shutters being opened in the chamber of honor. Although the retainers looked somewhat impatient, there was no sign that they were prepared to brave the rain and set out for the next station on schedule. When Hanzo went to pay his respects, Yamaguchi had come out from the chamber of honor into the rush-carpeted hallway and was leaning against a pillar, gazing out at the rain falling into the interior garden. Although one could not see such characteristic Kiso sights as the stone-weighted, shingled roofs or the boughs of the persimmon trees that still retained a few colorful leaves, there was a stillness both within and without this hallway that lent itself to the recovery of peace of mind.

"You rested very late. Is it your pleasure to spend the day here also?"

"With your permission, I think we will just rest today. We were in a great hurry to reach Edo, but once we got this far we realized how tired we are. I just can't bring myself to set out again in this weather. But it's not at all bad, once you're in the Kiso, to be rained in."

"It has been a very rainy year. It has rained almost every day since the intercalary fifth month. Not even the oldest people here can remember such heavy rains as we have had this year. It was worrying us quite a bit for a while. It is not at all unusual in these parts for travelers to have to stay over because the fords are closed."

Hanzo went to see his guests again that afternoon. The pale, watery daylight streamed in on the tatami with their Korean-style edgings of black clouds on a white ground. This was the room where Ii Tairo had always rested on his journeys between Hikone and Edo and where the censor Iwase Higo had spent the night on his way to Kyoto to ask for imperial sanction for the Treaty of Kanagawa. Hanzo's stories awakened the interest of Yamaguchi, who had himself been deeply involved in the drafting of the treaty.

"You probably have not yet heard, but the treaty has at last gained imperial sanction. That brings an end to one stage of the long battle over the treaty. The efforts of Ii Tairo and Iwase Higo have not been in vain after all. It is a great comfort to me to think of that. The terrible difficulty over expulsion of the foreigners should come to an end now. It won't be too long before this nation is opened."

As Yamaguchi told Hanzo about these events, he paced quietly around the room, almost as though he were addressing the walls and the pillars.

The words of this man who held the offices of censor and commissioner of foreign affairs made a deep impression on Hanzo. He had no way of knowing about the shogun's intention of resigning or that the person who had advocated such a course was standing before him. Still less did he dream that this person was hurrying to Edo to place himself under house arrest. He was only impressed that now, at the end of the Tokugawa era, such splendid personalities were still to be found among the shogunal officials, doing whatever they could to arrest the decline of shogunal power.

The endless autumnal rains showed no sign of letting up. The retainers who had accompanied Yamaguchi, apparently exhausted, each lay in a corner of their room, snoring loudly. Hanzo and Seisuke took care of the village business and then Hanzo returned to look in on his guest. He was concerned about the situation in Kyoto and Osaka and he wanted to ask for further details. He was completely unprepared to find his guest weeping violently but quietly.

CHAPTER TWELVE

1

"FATHER?"

As he stripped off his trousers at the end of the day's work, Hanzo asked Otami about Kichizaemon.

"Otami, I've been thinking that I might go down to Nagoya. If I do, please keep an eye on things while I'm away. I'll speak to father and mother too. I'm concerned about what is happening in the west." Hanzo gazed up at his wife's face. Their fourth child, a girl named Onatsu, had died after living for only sixty days. Otami was still pale.

The seventh month of Keio 2 was coming to the Magome station. It was 1866 by the Western calendar. Even though it was just before the Bon festival, a time when travel by the daimyo usually reached a peak, there were few travelers this year. The only retinue passing through Magome had been that of Makino Omi no Kami, lord of Komoro, who had spent nights at Nojiri and Ochiai on his way to Kyoto. The prevailing quiet did not seem to be limited to the Kiso road; pilgrims returning from the Toyokawa Inari and Mt. Akiba reported that travel was also light on the Tokaido. The normal movement of men and horses was not to be seen. The roads looked deserted.

"Whatever happened to the second Choshu expedition, Hanzo?"

This was Kichizaemon's first question when Hanzo went up to visit him after dinner. The unsettled character of the times allowed no peace of mind for either of them.

In the back rooms where Hanzo's parents lived, the sliding panels between the rooms had been taken away to let the air circulate as freely as possible in the oppressive late summer heat, but they had not put up a temporary awning as had been done before the parlor in the main house. Oman, who had been working all day in the main house, now returned to her husband's side. Hanzo's father was sitting in the very same room where his predecessor had lived out the last years of his life. Oman was there to massage his shoulders for him as he reflected on the sixty-seven years he had spent on this highway.

"What is happening in the west, I wonder," said Oman, seated behind Kichizaemon.

"I wonder," Hanzo replied. "It's just not possible to find out here in the mountains. I know there was a battle somewhere near Kokura but I haven't

338

seen any reliable reports since then. All I hear are vague rumors that the shogunate has certainly won or that there will soon be a great victory."

"Ah. Well, I am retired anyway," said Kichizaemon. "Today I went over
with Sakichi and cleaned the graves in the family plot. After all, it's getting
close to Bon."

Kichizaemon and Oman were more concerned about Otami, who had so
recently lost a child, than they were about Hanzo. They busied themselves
with typical old people's projects, going to Onatsu's new grave to make an
offering of cucumbers that had been sent from Nakatsugawa or to take
peaches they had received as a gift from some people who had gone to a place
called Motoya to buy horses. Looking at his father, tired from his day's work
at the Mampukuji, Hanzo was unable to speak directly of his plan to go to
Nagoya.

"How about it, mother—shall I take your place?" Hanzo got up and
started to move behind his father.

"Oh, are you going to be my masseur, Hanzo? My shoulders are all right.
Please rub my legs."

Kichizaemon extended his crippled right leg out before Hanzo, bringing
to view the effects of the stroke he had suffered. The calf that had borne him
easily over hundreds of miles of highway during the years when he was head
of the Magome post station now lay changed beyond recognition in Hanzo's
hands. There was nothing to see of the powerful muscle that had once been
there. The bones showed clearly from knee to foot.

"Are your feet always this cold, father?"

Hanzo kneaded his father's leg until the warmth returned to it. Kichizaemon was a little stronger than he had been the previous year when Hanzo
had gone to Mt. Ontake to pray for his health, but he had also aged quite
noticeably since then. It appeared that he did not have much longer to live.
Hanzo could sense this through his hands and it made him sad.

"Hanzo, there is someone calling from the highway," said Kichizaemon,
cocking an ear as he spoke. "Even an old man like me can hear if he thinks it
might be another courier."

With a trace of impatience, Hanzo left his father's side and went out to the
veranda of the second-floor room to look out over the highway. Pale moonlight shone on the walls of the storehouse where Kureta Masaka had once hid
while fleeing from Kyoto. The branches of the persimmon tree were dark in
the garden. The clouds rushing through the skies above the pass somehow
made him feel uneasy.

At first the shogunate had ordered that the obligations for military service,
which had been established around 1650 in the Keian era, be reduced by half,
but still the forces that accompanied the shogun when he set out in the fifth
month of the previous year had been vast. All samurai with stipends of more
than five hundred koku were permitted to make use of men and horses hired
by the post stations, and the people along the route had suffered greatly. Even
without that. cries of hardship and exhaustion had been rising throughout

the nation. The end of alternate attendance had already caused an economic depression in Edo, but the provisioning of the second Choshu expedition had further inflated prices there so that one ryo in gold would now buy only a bushel and a half of rice. Unprecedented rioting, greatly surpassing the riots during the famine of Temmei 7, 1787, broke out among the desperate populace, beginning on the twenty-eighth day of the fifth month in Shinagawa, Shibata-machi, and Yotsuya. It swept through the Shitamachi and Honjo sections, smashing up the establishments of merchants engaged in the Yokohama trade, rice dealers, and other wealthy houses, and continued for seven or eight days. The scarcity of foodstuffs, the hoarding of rice, and the rapid increase in prices that accompanied the departure of the Choshu expedition had driven the poor of Edo to such extremities.

The uprisings of the fifth month were not confined to Edo. On the fourteenth of that month, there were riots in Osaka with mobs moving from Naniwa to Nishi Yokobori-Kamimachi, from the east side to the west side of Temman, smashing up rice dealers, wineshops, and pawnshops. Several hundred people were arrested. The price of rice continued to rise sharply in the sixth month, and in the counties of Koma, Iruma, Hanzawa, and Chichibu in Musashi province, just outside Edo, there were uprisings that the military forces were barely able to suppress.

More than a year had passed since the shogunate had taken its great army from Edo to Osaka in this climate of social unrest. The shogun's proposal that he resign had pleased very few of his subordinates and he had consequently acquiesced to the imperial order refusing him permission to resign. He was still in office while the power of the shogunal family was draining quickly away. The shogunal armies, once they had come as far as Osaka castle, found themselves unable to advance or to retreat. They became playthings for Choshu, and at last they were forced to go into battle. The long battle line stretched across the island of Honshu from the coast of the sea of Japan to the Inland sea and down to Kyushu. An atmosphere of uncertainty prevailed. In Magome they heard that the troops of Ii and Sakakibara had retreated from the frontier of Aki province and were now back in Hiroshima. Then they heard that the *kiheitai*, special commoner troops of Choshu, had appeared at Hamada on the Iwami frontier. Hanzo could do nothing more than join the other people of his village in their anxiety over the outcome of the conflict.

The reports from the battlefront grew still more vague. In the most recent reports that Hanzo had received there was no solid information at all about the war zone. This made Hanzo extremely uneasy. He stood out on the veranda of the rear quarters and then turned back to his parents.

"These days the reports that the couriers give us are of no use. I can't concentrate on my work. I have been thinking that I would like to go to Nagoya so that I can find out what is really happening in the west. What do you think, father? Mother? May I ask you to look after things while I am away for a little while?"

*   *   *   *   *   *   *

"Well, just wait a moment. Hadn't we better lie down and talk about this?" said Kichizaemon. "Hanzo, you stretch your legs out over there. Oman, why don't you lie down too? This is the kind of thing we have to talk about while lying down."

It was an evening in the seventh month. Oman took the lamp into the next room and then came back to recline at Kichizaemon's side. There were no outsiders, only parents and child. When all three had made themselves comfortable, they could begin to talk in the dark. It was a situation of the greatest intimacy.

"Hanzo," Kichizaemon resumed, his head propped up on his hands, "you know very well that we have to be careful about what people say. If there should come to be talk that we at the honjin are neglecting our duties, we would have no excuse to offer before our ancestors. Really, for these past two or three years, I have been worried that you might leave us. I know very well that your friends say that these are not the times to concern yourself with family matters. But just think, if you should leave, who is going to take care of this part of the highway? I'm an old man. I do nothing but worry about your leaving home. But tonight is the first time I have been able to speak of it. That's because I am not so worried any longer. It makes me very happy that you have not left in silence but are consulting with us instead."

"Well, since your father feels this way, if you have really made up your mind it's best that you go and have a look for yourself. We'll look after things while you're gone," said Oman decisively.

It was not merely because he was getting old that Kichizaemon was worried. People were already beginning to talk about the way Hanzo had received the Mito ronin the previous year, and the way he and his friends were hiding people whom the shogunate was trying to find. According to Kichizaemon, Nakatsugawa and Magome were different even though they were both in the same Owari domains. It would not do to forget that in the thirty-three villages of the Kiso the surveillance of the Fukushima officials never ceased. Nor should one forget that for all that Yamamura was nominally an Owari official, he had in fact been directly entrusted by the shogunate with the maintenance of the strategic Fukushima barrier and was by no means certain to follow the dictates of the house of Owari in every eventuality. That he thought of himself as a direct bannerman of the Tokugawa was evident from just a look at the history of the house of Yamamura, which had rendered outstanding service to the Tokugawa at the time of the battle of Sekigahara by acting as guides over the Kiso road. It was perfectly clear without any need to spell it out just what Yamamura would think about a posthumous disciple of Hirata Atsutane. Because of the nature of these relationships, Hanzo as headman of Magome could not hope to have the kind of freedom enjoyed by Keizo and Kozo in Nakatsugawa. There was no telling what guise government spies might be taking to spy on the Hirata disciples here. After all, this was the highway.

"It's a world where even the walls have ears. I want you to be very careful, Hanzo," said Kichizaemon.

"Well then, this is what we had better do," said Oman. "I have relatives in Iwamura. If anyone comes around asking about you while you are away, we'll just say that you are visiting relatives in Mino. We won't say anything about your going to Nagoya."

"Well, mother, if you'll just do that and look after things while I'm gone, I can go with peace of mind," replied Hanzo. "I would never leave home without telling you beforehand. I feel that a headman has his duties laid out for him. You don't have to worry about me running out on them."

In Nagoya Hanzo had many connections through which he might find out what was happening in Kyoto and Osaka. Because the Kiso was in the Owari domains, there was frequent contact between the han and the Aoyama house in its capacity as honjin and toiya. And because his father had carried out the special service of collecting money for the lord of Owari for many years, he and his heirs had been granted permission to use a surname, to wear swords, and to have audience with the lord. In addition to this advantage, the han commissioners of finance, construction, and timber were accustomed to stopping at the honjin for a rest or for lodging whenever they passed over the Kiso road. There were in fact many Hirata sympathizers among the Owari retainers. Since the reform of the rules of the Meirindo, the Owari academy, extensive use was made of such works as the *Seiken Igen,* which vigorously supported the imperialist position. This leading branch of the house of Tokugawa had become a conduit through which reports of such trends of the times could reach even into the mountainous portions of its domain.

Now Mochinori, the lord of Owari, had opposed the second Choshu expedition from the outset, even before all had grown dark in the far west of the country. When the retired lord, Owari Yoshikatsu, had led the first expedition, Choshu had yielded to his skillful manipulations, presenting him with the heads of Masuda, Kunishi, and Fukuhara, the three responsible parties in the attack on Kyoto, while the plotters under Shishido Samanosuke were executed in Hagi castle. Mori and his son had gone into seclusion at the Tenjuin, their family temple. At that time the retired lord of Owari had argued that any further action against Choshu would serve only to invite calamity by enraging the people of Choshu. However, the officials then in power in the shogunate felt that such a disposal of the matter would be excessively lenient, and they paid no heed to the retired lord's petitions. Maintaining that there was still doubt concerning Choshu's contrition for its offenses, they were unrelenting in their demands that the Mori, father and son, and the five court nobles whom they were sheltering, including Sanjo Sanetomi, be brought to Edo. The consequence of this decision was the rise of the Choshu war party, determined to resist to the death.

Even from Hanzo's restricted perspective, it was clear that Owari's position had been extremely important at that time. This was manifest in the simple fact that the lord of Owari had been secretly informed in advance of the decision to undertake the second expedition. The lord of Owari, how-ever, had already changed his name from Mochinori to the religious name Gendo and had yielded his position to Inuchiyo, the son of the elder retired lord, thus becoming a retired lord himself. He had stepped aside because his attitudes toward court and shogunate were fundamentally different from those of the elder retired lord and it was bad for the two to be so much at odds with each other. Moreover, ever since his failure in the matter of the indemnity for the Namamugi incident, he had realized that the currents of the time were running against him. Mochinori had not accepted command of the first Choshu punitive expedition and there was no possibility that he would now accept command of the second expedition in the face of his father's opposition to the venture. The offer was passed on to the lord of Kii, Tokugawa Mochitsugu. Now each was refusing in favor of the other. In a let-ter to the lord of Kii, the lord of Owari outlined his position. He said that he was retired and therefore could not undertake further obligations to the nation. There were also internal han matters that made it impossible for him to accept the command. His sole reason for going up to Kyoto at this junc-ture was that he could not bear to be a mere bystander while the shogun's campaign was being launched. But, while his intentions were none other than to exhaust himself in loyal service, he could not accept the actual com-mand even if he were ordered to do so. He was most sorry and he hoped that Mochitsugu would not think ill of him. Mochitsugu, for his part, maintained that Kii was already exhausted from its long defense of Osaka and that in the twelfth month of the previous year it had made a contribution of one hun-dred thousand ryo to the shogunate and had evacuated its forces from Waka-noura by warship. It was obvious that he was also hesitant to accept the com-mand.

This is how it was even among the collateral houses of the Tokugawa. Mito was the first to be suspected, Hitotsubashi had been excluded, and even Owari had withdrawn. It seemed as though once the great power that had been passed down through fourteen generations had begun to decline, rela-tives in what was supposedly the senior branch of the family were treated as an embarrassment and were being deserted by one after another of the lesser branches. Organized in sixteen troops from vanguard to reserves, this sho-gunal army had supposedly been raised for the purpose of pressing its way on to Aki regardless of the cost, and of crushing all who opposed the shogunate, beginning with Choshu, but now it was difficult to see what lay before it. Along the Kiso road, nothing could be heard but empty claims that the vic-tory of the shogunate was assured or that a great victory would soon be announced.

On the morning that Hanzo was to leave for Nagoya, everyone from Otami to the manservant Sakichi rose before dawn and set to work in the hearth room and the kitchen. They wanted to get the head of the house off on his journey early, before neighbors were up and around.

"It's early, master!" Even Sakichi's greeting intensified the feeling of this day of early departure.

When Oman and Kichizaemon came from their quarters to see Hanzo off, it was still quite dark.

"What should we do this time, Hanzo?" asked Kichizaemon as he looked around him. "Should we send Sakichi with you as far as Nakatsugawa?"

"Yes, I'll go with you," said Sakichi eagerly. "I've been wanting to do that. I even have my sandals ready."

"I might be going to Nagoya with Kozo. I'll see what happens when I get to Nakatsugawa. I'm hoping to get a chance to meet the people in Mino this time," said Hanzo.

"Well, how does the weather look off toward the west?" said Kichizaemon. "If we have another big storm like the one the other day on top of all these war rumors, that would be just too much. At any rate, there is nothing but disorder around. You had better be careful on your trip, Hanzo."

Inosuke had just come back from a trip to the Tokaido to consult a physician. Outside his family, Hanzo had told only Inosuke of his plans and had asked him to look after matters on the highway. Seisuke and Eikichi would still be there to assist with the work of the honjin and the toiya.

"Please look after things for me, mother."

With those last words, Hanzo set out through the wooden door at the back of the house, accompanied by Sakichi. Even the children who always got up so early were still in bed and they did not know when Hanzo left the house and went out along the narrow path through the bamboo grove.

2

Hanzo returned at the end of the month by way of Toki and Oi, down the last fifty miles of road leading back to his home. Night fell while he was in Nakatsugawa and he walked the remaining eight miles to the edge of Magome in the dark.

There were no travelers on the highway and all was dark along Stonemason slope from Aramachi to the edge of Magome. The doors of the houses along both sides of the street were closed and only a bit of light leaked out from the paper panels of the lanterns with the names of the houses marked on them that stood by each gate. It was that late when Hanzo at last arrived safely back at the honjin.

"The children?"

That was the first thing he asked Otami, being the kind of person who did not worry about the household when he was leaving but was greatly concerned on his return.

"Father and mother have been staying here in the main house to look after things ever since you left. Father was up until just a little while ago. He went into the other room to rest but he told me to get him up if you came back," said Otami.

As Hanzo unwrapped his leggings in the retiring room, he began to tell Otami what a good thing his decision to go to Nagoya had turned out to be. Oman came in to listen to his story. He was telling them that he had gone to Nagoya with Kozo and that they had been able to meet with many of their acquaintances in Mino and Owari when Kichizaemon emerged from the back room carrying a smoking set.

"How did it go, Hanzo? Did you learn something about things in Kyoto and Osaka?"

According to the information that Hanzo brought back, it appeared that the idea of having the shogun lead the army in person had been a disaster. Now that it had gone to such extremes to raise this army and then to send it to a distant place without any intention of fighting, expending ruinous amounts of money in the process, what was to become of the shogunate? That was what many of the officials who had been left behind at Nagoya castle were saying. It looked as though the shogunate was finished. The officials had added that it would be best to turn the whole Choshu venture over to Hitotsubashi Yoshinobu, since he was already taking care of everything else, and bring the shogun back to the Kanto as quickly as possible. After that it would be best just to watch developments for a while. The shogunate, they suggested, would be wise to make use of the warships that were anchored off Kokura to bring the forces back to Edo. This was a time when the mood of the nation was like that of someone treading thin ice, and there was no telling what kind of disorders might result if the shogunate tried to bring the army back by land. That was not only the opinion of the shogunal officials, who had the best interest of their lord in mind, but also the course advocated by the French ambassador, Roches. Hanzo told his father how such judgments had dominated opinion in Nagoya.

"But how has the fighting been going?"

"Like this," replied Hanzo with an empty gesture. "It appears that none of the han set out with any intention of actually fighting—not a single one wanted to fight it out face to face with Choshu! They just went through the motions of raising troops out of a sense of obligation to the shogunate."

"But it has been three months since this campaign started, Hanzo. I have heard that there have been six or seven battles."

"That's right, father. There were battles on the Aki frontier, around Oshima, and around Shimonoseki. But those were all defensive measures against Choshu attacks. After that, it has been nothing but retreat, retreat. It seemed very odd to me. If the army had really intended to fight, they wouldn't have kept retreating like that just because they lost a few men. According to what the shogun's people are saying, the Sakakibara forces, for all their pride in being led by a descendant of Sakakibara Koheita, are worthless and Hikone is worthless too. They would shame the memory of Ii Naomasa, the ancestor of the present lord of Hikone who once made the name of the 'red demon' resound throughout the land. That is what even their friends are saying about them. But the people around Owari are not saying that. Instead, they are pointing out that all this trouble has come from making no distinction between external and internal powers and thinking only of the past glories of the Tokugawa. I'm getting ahead of myself, but people willing to die for the shogunate in Edo are becoming hard to find. In each of the han, the concern is to prevent harm to their own soldiers—they are not thinking about the Tokugawa government but only of their own han."

"For that matter, not even the farmers in the villages of the assisting districts are willing to move freight anymore merely because of the might of the Tokugawa."

"It really has the officials left in charge in Nagoya wondering how things are going to turn out if they keep going on this way. Owari was opposed to this adventure from the beginning. If only they had listened to the warnings of the retired lord, they would never have found themselves in this position. There is no one who is not indignant about this. And there are rumors that Hamada castle on the Iwami frontier has fallen. There are even rumors that the shogun himself is ill."

Kichizaemon heaved a deep sigh.

This trip to Nagoya had served to open Hanzo's eyes. Even though he had not gone on to Kyoto to see Hirata Kanetane, who was now urging on his followers throughout the nation, he had at least gone to Nagoya where currents from the west flowed in freely. He had met people like Tanaka Torasaburo and Tamba Juntaro and he had learned that vigorous and promising samurai such as these were beginning to make preparations for the time that was surely coming. That was the meaning of the trip for Hanzo.

"It's already late tonight. You should both get some rest."

Saying this, Hanzo moved into the parlor, still thinking about what he had learned in Nagoya. He could not get to sleep.

Although he had not mentioned it to his father, the situation in the Kansai would not let him sleep. It wasn't just what he had heard directly from such Owari retainers as Tamiya Jo'un, who had drawn close to the imperialists, but the fact that now even Satsuma, hitherto, along with Aizu, the main support of the shogunate, was turning from advocacy of the union of court and military to an anti-shogunal position. Consultation and collusion between Satsuma and Choshu had become an open secret and there were rumors that England was backing them. The voices speaking out for restoration of direct imperial rule were no longer speaking of the future. From the latter part of Keio 1, at about the time the facts concerning the attempted resignation of the shogun became known, these voices had begun echoing in every province. Even the people of Owari, with its close relationship to the shogunate, were beginning to consider the idea.

"Are you still up?"

Awaking in the middle of the night, Otami turned to her husband and found him sitting upright on the bedding, alone except for a huge shadow cast on the wall by the dim night-light beside the bed.

* * * * * * *

Heavy rains fell on Magome pass in the eighth month. The rain began on the sixth day and that night it changed into a thunderstorm. Strong winds came up and there were two days of severe weather. During the second night, the rain began to fall still harder from around the fifth hour and the direction of the wind began to change. An unheard of southwest gale set in and blew throughout the night. Finally, around dawn of the third day of the storm, when both wind and rain had subsided, Hanzo and Otami found themselves sitting in the parlor with water dripping from the ceiling above them. All the stone walls along the roadway from the honjin down to the next side street were washed out.

"Oh my!"

That was the voice of Otami, stunned by the night's ravages.

Hanzo quickly slipped into work trousers and went out to look around. Inosuke came running over from the Fushimiya to report that more than a hundred roof tiles that they had laid up temporarily had been blown away. Kyurobei, joining them, was of the opinion that while he had not yet seen the fields, such a storm must have done considerable damage to the rice crop. People were standing dumbly in the middle of the road looking at the damage left by the storm. Others were looking in on each other to see how they had come through. Some who had already been all around the village reported that it was the Mampukuji that had been most severely damaged. The roof of the main sanctuary was nearly gone and twelve great trees in all, six cedars and six hinoki, were uprooted and lying across the path to the cemetery. In the new fields over toward Aonohara, more than twenty pine trees were down. There was as yet no way of fully assessing the damage to the forests around Shinjaya and Oya.

Messages came in to Hanzo throughout the day, reporting damage to village properties from Aramachi all the way to Toge. It was rumored that damage had been light in the stations to the east from Tsumago on to Midono, and that Nakatsugawa had also escaped. Ochiai, however, had suffered much more than Magome. Some fourteen houses had been blown down and there had even been deaths. Such a storm was almost unheard of in this region. But frequent heavy rains had not been limited to that year; the unusual weather was continuing from the previous year and there had been more rain than anyone could remember. At Hanzo's home there had been worry over whether the rice crop would survive ever since the censor Yamaguchi Suruga had stayed with them.

The poor harvest of the year before had cut deeply into everyone's reserves and most of the late rice still remaining in the fields had not yet ripened. Now the villagers were beginning to talk about a crop failure.

"This is going to be the worst famine since Temmei 7, isn't it?"

These voices predicting the worst famine in nearly a hundred years filled Hanzo with alarm. Society was on a wartime footing, reports of internal difficulties and foreign threats were coming in from all quarters, and now there was a natural disaster to contend with.

*   *   *   *   *   *   *

The meeting room for the village officials was also heavily damaged. Seven chestnut boards for rebuilding the roof had been brought to the front of the toiya when Juheiji came over from Tsumago to look in after the storm.

Hanzo, now forced to concern himself with the shortage of food in the village, caught Juheiji alone and spoke to him about it.

"Juheiji, how is your village? Don't you have a little extra rice?"

Hanzo himself understood very well that this request was unreasonable. In Tsumago, most income came from forest products such as fir, hemlock, sawara, zelkova, chestnut, and hinoki, and there was little hope that there would be rice to share. There was even less land under cultivation from Tsumago eastward. Around Magome, there were bamboo groves on many of the southwest slopes exposed to the sun, but in the inner Kiso valley there were places where not even bamboo would grow.

None of the village officials could sit idly by in these times. Kyurobei, the elders Masudaya Kozaemon, Horaiya Shinshichi's son Shinsuke, and Umeya Gosuke, and the assistant headman Sasaya Shosuke were rushing desperately about their duties. Hanzo was standing with Juheiji in front of the meeting room when Inosuke and the retired Kimbei came back from a survey of the forests.

"Hanzo, today I have come out for the first time and I have been surveying the effects of the storm with Inosuke."

As always, Kimbei's report was in great detail. The number of fallen trees that he had observed in the forests of Shinjaya between the summit of the Ochiai frontier to Kazamichi road amounted to more than five hundred pines alone. There were also thirty-six cedars. Forty-five fir trees large and small. About six hundred chestnuts. In addition, there were fifteen pines down below Oya and another fifteen at Bikunidera and thirteen along the bank at Aonohara, making a total loss of about seven hundred thirty large and small trees. This report alone was enough to convey the frightful power of the storm.

"Well, I'll soon be seventy, but I don't remember any such windstorm as this. I'm sure Hanzo's father would agree. It is absolutely unprecedented," said Kimbei, taking a new grip on his stick. "The priest from the Mampukuji came to call on me last night. He mentioned the trees that are down in the graveyard and said that he would like to use the lumber to build the hall for the ancestral tablets that he had already discussed with everyone, and he asked me what I thought of that. I replied that it seemed to be a very good idea. It seems to me that what he suggested is exactly what he should have suggested."

"What are we going to do now about rice, Hanzo?" asked Inosuke.

"I was hoping that we might be able to get a loan from Tsumago. I was just this moment asking Juheiji about it. If there is no rice to spare in Tsumago, how about Yamaguchi?"

"Yamaguchi is out," said Inosuke. "I sent someone to see about that yesterday. It doesn't seem that they have any rice to share with Magome, so they turned us down. The person I sent came back empty-handed."

"If only I could help you," said Juheiji, looking around him.

Juheiji left soon afterward, and Kimbei went back to the Upper Fushimiya. All the post stations had suffered a serious crop failure and there was no rice on the market. In Magome they could not wait for things to get better. The situation was already so bad that even at Kimbei's place, where they dealt in rice, there was panic because they were short three bales of rice for their household needs for that month. Kimbei, who was fond of building, had started additions at both the main house and at his present residence and there were a great many workmen around.

In the circumstances there was nothing left for Magome to do but to buy rice in the more spacious and productive Mino basin. Messengers were sent almost every day to the Nakatsugawa merchants, particularly Yorozuya Yasubei, on this account. When they heard that there was rice in Iwamura, they had to buy it no matter how high the price to get through the immediate emergency, so the Iwamura rice was bought at a price of six bushels for ten ryo.

Hanzo went out to Setoda almost every day to look at the crops. At times he would go in the company of the village officials and the tenant farmers to inspect the fields laid waste by the storm. Unlike Hanzo's father, Kichizaemon, Kimbei could not stay quietly in his retirement quarters. Still vigorous, even at sixty-nine years of age, this retired gentleman would insist on going out with the younger ones, accompanying his adopted son Inosuke and Hanzo wherever they went. When they set out to inspect the harvest all the way from the fields in Toge in the east to Shiozawa, Iwata, and Oe, Kimbei went along. And two days later, when Hanzo and the others started at Setoda, came out below Noe along the road through Kutenoshiri, went around to Aonohara, checking Naka-Shinden, Bikunidera, Iri, and finally Machida on the way, Kimbei went along that time too. Everyone was hoping for some reason to reevaluate the rice crop; no one wanted to pronounce this year's crop a failure.

Again and again, concern about the crops in the valleys from the west to the east took Hanzo and the others out of Magome over every one of the back roads toward Hashizume and Aramachi. They looked at every field from Nakanokaya to Shinjaya and the Mino border. After the middle of the eighth month, people would come rushing to Hanzo to tell him that the crop prospects were somewhat improved. Unfortunately, the village officials had already spent all of their money and the rice being brought in from Mino was expensive. The hard-pressed tenant farmers came to request the convening of a meeting of the full population of the village and the officials agreed. In the end, even the carpenters and plasterers put down their work and all the tenants gathered in the Amida hall at the Mampukuji to discuss a petition to be relieved of their rice taxes for the year. Feelings became more and more uneasy each day.

When Kimbei next saw Hanzo, he spoke to him about this.

"We are really in a frightful position, Hanzo. Just now three of our tenant farmers came in together to ask that we relieve them of their established annual tax."

As he spoke, his expression betrayed the fact that it was extremely uncomfortable for him that his house and the Masudaya should have drawn special attention from the tenant farmers because they were two of the most wealthy households in the Kiso. It also betrayed the fact that he found it still more unpleasant that the shortage of rice forced him to reconsider his building plans, send home the carpenters he had hired from Fukushima, and lay off the other craftsmen. Then on top of that, people were still saying things about him.

"Kimbei," said Hanzo, "it is simply not true that a person like you who has built more than he can use has nothing to spare in these times."

"No, that is why I gave four bushels to Kenkichi, a bushel and a half to Michinosuke, and eleven bushels to Hanshiro—nineteen bushels in all to those three."

Hanzo could not stand to listen to him. As headman he felt that he had to save the tenant farmers at all costs. He was at the point of asking the crop survey officer from Fukushima to come out, or even to trouble the Owari deputy, Yamamura Jimbei, to speak to Nagoya about the crop failure in the Kiso and to ask him at the very least to cut the year's rice tax by half.

Unfortunately the rains came again, beginning during the morning with a heavy downpour that seemed quite uncalled for, and the wind direction changed from the north to the west. Water came through the floor in the inner room of the honjin and rain seeped into the closets. Hanzo was more concerned about the villagers than he was about his own household and he began making preparations to go out and look around the village once more. Hurriedly tying the waistband of his work trousers, he came out from the retiring room to the hearth room and called for Sakichi.

Hanzo first went out toward Machida. The rain-soaked rice heads seemed to be half-grown or a little more. Some were as much as four-fifths grown. Now that he knew for sure that the reports of the farmers that the rice crop could be saved were true, he breathed a sigh of relief.

It was in the midst of these concerns over a possible crop failure that the news came from Osaka of the death of Iemochi, the fourteenth shogun.

3

People were clustered around the notice board in the center of Magome, eager to read what was posted there. Merchants passing through stopped off to see what it was, and travelers got off their horses. They all stood before a notice that had been relayed through Owari:

The shogun, on his unprecedented venture, unable to give himself proper care, passed away at the hour of the hare of the twentieth past, at Osaka castle. As has already been announced, Hitotsubashi Yoshinobu is to succeed him, and should be regarded as having been shogun since the twentieth past. This we announce from Osaka.

Kichizaemon, who had recently been staying indoors most of the time, left his quarters on the second floor of the miso shed to read the notice. He stood beside his old friend Kimbei, who had come down from the Upper Fushimiya, and the two found it difficult to leave the vicinity of the notice board. It was as if by standing there on the highway they might be able to bid a proper farewell to this shogun who had died in his twenty-first year. The ringing of all bells and chimes was now forbidden. Just as on the occasion of the death of the previous shogun, all activity, even building, was suspended and everything was quiet and restrained.

At the beginning of the ninth month, the crop survey officer from Fukushima came on the annual visit that was always awaited with trepidation by everyone in the village. This time he brought the report that Yamamura, the deputy in Fukushima, would be going to Nagoya castle to plead the difficulty of paying the annual rice tax in the Kiso this year. When they heard this, the tenant farmers all felt a bit more at ease. The reports of the circumstances of the death of the shogun were beginning to filter into Magome both from Nagoya and from Fukushima. It was reported that the death had been announced on the twentieth of the eighth month in order to establish the succession and prepare the funeral ceremony, but in fact the shogun had died of heart failure due to beri-beri on the nineteenth day of the seventh month. Until the announcement the death had been kept secret and everyone had continued to act as though the shogun was still in Osaka directing the second Choshu expedition. But it had become known that the roju Ogasawara had left the battle zone. That meant that when Hanzo was on his trip to Nagoya, the shogun was already seriously ill. Now Hanzo finally understood the peculiar atmosphere of Nagoya castle.

Once they heard of the shogun's death, the soldiers from the various han began to withdraw from the battle front. An imperial order came down ending hostilities. There were also reports that the shogunate, which had been wishing for a pretext on which to base an armistice, issued with apparent relief an announcement of the resignation of his command by the lord of Kii, and an order for the withdrawal of all troops engaged in the expedition. It was said that the remains of the shogun, now in Osaka castle, were to be transported to Edo on the *Jundo Maru,* under the guard of the roju Inaba Mino no Kami. Hearing this report, Hanzo realized that the time would soon come when people would be returning eastward over this road. He could imagine his station crowded with soldiers who had experienced defeat in war.

Rumors of all kinds came through. Some said that the shogun's illness had been caused by the need to stand in constant opposition to Yoshinobu, who had been drawing close to Satsuma and Choshu, and that therefore Yoshinobu had caused the shogun's death. The bad ones said that those who hoped for later favors from Yoshinobu had neglected their duties in nursing the shogun in his illness, speeding his departure from this world. The very worst rumors said that Iemochi had died from poison concealed in his writing brush, and some people repeated this hideous charge as though it were already proven. But there were also some who said that the shogunate had found itself trapped in Osaka castle. They maintained that the unfortunate Iemochi had been a victim of circumstance, and they reviewed his life, marked by one crisis after another, his gentle and forbearing character, and his agonies over the Choshu expedition.

"So dark! So dark!"

Speaking to himself, Hanzo reflected on the atmosphere of this feudal society that could no longer get by without great changes. As he continued this line of thinking, he could almost hear the cries for a restoration of imperial power resounding through the land like the cries of a cock.

"Does service to the military really have to go this far?"

Hanzo said this as he sat in the meeting room with Inosuke, looking into his friend's face. Even he, a headman, had come to feel that little life remained for the shogunate in Edo. He had sensed this in the attitude of Owari. Yet at the same time, however much the power of the shogunate might be crumbling, he could not let up for a single day in his service to the highway. Still he had to protect the station from the hardship and exhaustion that resulted.

It was virtually impossible to administer the Magome station under such conditions. Hanzo conferred with Inosuke and the others and decided to appeal to Owari for aid to the post stations.

"No, there's nothing to be done now but to go hat in hand. I'll draw up the petition. Inosuke, you get the account books ready. When I was in Nagoya I heard one of the Owari people say, 'It's best to send a petition to the commissioners. The han won't be able to do anything about it either, but precisely because they can do nothing themselves they may be able to get action at a higher level.' "

They would ordinarily have sent this petition directly to the commissioners of transport in Edo. That they were now to send it to Owari and have it relayed by them to the commissioners showed how the times had changed. With all the confusion over the death of the shogun nothing would come of this petition even if they were to carry it all the way to Edo themselves, and the shogunal retinue itself would very soon be coming back over this highway toward Edo. Hanzo hurried to prepare the appeal as quickly as possible.

When the draft was finished he took it over to the Fushimiya, a well-lighted, two-story house on the next level up the hill. There he went over the draft with Inosuke.

PETITION FOR ASSISTANCE TO THE POST STATIONS

This do we most humbly petition:

We of this station constitute an unusually small establishment and the twenty-five men we have on regular duty as porters are maintained through the assistance of the neighboring villages of Yamaguchi and Yubunezawa. It is therefore natural that we should experience difficulties in carrying out our duty to offer lodging and assist movement up and down the highway. This was particularly true in the famines of the fourth and seventh years of Tempo when many died or fled. Though it is difficult for us to carry out our duties, we will do everything possible since we have long been in close relationship with you, and somehow, by your grace, we will discharge our responsibilities. This has always been a steep and barren country with only a few fields among the mountains. We have to buy food from nearby villages. Not only do salt, cotton, and oil have to be bought from elsewhere, but everything else as well, right down to firewood and charcoal. We get very little assistance, our debts mount year after year, and life is hard.

On the matter of the return to the Kanto, the officials, the post horse drovers, the porters, and the couriers have been at work every day on the most demanding roadways, laboring with great difficulty in the snowy or icy roads of winter and spring. The freight must be sorted out before it can be moved. Horses fall ill or are exhausted and replacements must be found for them before our duties can be carried out. Because of these conditions we have been receiving grants of rice and additional assistance money each year, and by your grace we have been able to fulfill our commitments. But in recent years, horses have been bought up by outsiders at excessive prices, so that we have been unable to buy replacement animals with our limited funds. Moreover, since foot gear is worn out rapidly on the difficult roads, the established wages are no longer sufficient, and it is not possible for the freight to be moved. Quite apart from questions of immediate profit, the difficulties are beyond the powers of language to express.

—In the matter of agricultural production, we have little arable land and must buy food elsewhere each year and pay for the cost of bringing it to Magome. Moreover, we have to rent grass lands, or else cross four or five miles of country so difficult that horses cannot be used, cut bamboo grass, and carry it in on our backs in order to fertilize our fields, with the result that our farmers are much worse off than in neighboring villages . . .

Hanzo gave a deep sigh as he read.

"Inosuke, when I first took over the three offices of honjin, toiya, and headman from my father, it was amazing to me that my forefathers had been able to serve in such a difficult position. And then in my time, the station had to go out and run up still bigger debts. Now if it had been my father, he might have been able to do better, but I am just not good at business."

Everything had been included in the petition, beginning with the sharp rise in prices that had accompanied the opening of foreign trade in 1858 and the two great fires of the eleventh month of that year and the tenth month of

Man'en 1. The progress to Edo of Princess Kazu in Bunkyu 1 and the progress of the lord of Owari two years later, followed by the return of the families of the daimyo to their home provinces, the return home of Lord Motochiyo and his family, the passage of the officials on the occasion of the return from Kyoto of the fourteenth shogun, and the journey of the retired lord of Owari to the capital and back, had all contributed to an unprecedented flow of traffic over the highway. Then, to add to the difficulties, there had been the great observances at Nikko, lasting for several days. The assisting districts had finally pleaded exhaustion and had refused to send a single additional man or horse. This had led to inexpressible hardships on the part of the post horse keepers and the small farmers. Because of all this, immense outlays for hiring men and horses had been incurred and it had become doubtful whether the stations would be able to continue to move men and freight. Therefore the eleven post stations of the Kiso had appealed for the establishment of permanently assigned assisting districts and several of the village officials had gone to Edo many times, but at this date they were still unable to obtain the understanding of the transport commissioners. Over a period of sixteen or seventeen years immense expenses had been incurred in going to Edo with these petitions. Therefore, to try to pay off the debts of the post station, a subscription had been carried out in the third year of Ansei and the amount added to the one hundred ryo that had been similarly raised earlier. But in recent years the expenses for hiring men and horses and for paying the interest on debts had continued to mount while the post station's income had not increased markedly, so that a situation of the greatest hardship now prevailed.

Hanzo began reading again:

—Thus this station has at last reached a desperate state. Even though we have husbanded our resources and have appealed for an extension of the time limits on the loans you have deigned to make to us, these will not cover any further rise in costs. It is no longer possible to institute a subscription. Since every expense in the operation of a post station is increasing and there are great numbers of other urgent demands on us, it is not possible to find additional sources of assistance. We are all at our wit's end in trying to see how we can continue to operate the post station.

—It is our humble desire that you should deign to consider carefully what we have written and that you should see fit to extend to us a loan of two thousand ryo, to be returned in the form of our taxes for the next twenty years. We would all be most extremely grateful.

Second year of Keio, year of the tiger, ninth month

To the office of the commissioners

Magome Station

Headman, Toiya

Hanzo and Inosuke exchanged their views on the petition. Inosuke did not have the sharpness of his adoptive father Kimbei, but he made up for it with his meticulous attention to detail and his restraint, making him a good person for Hanzo to consult. Inosuke fetched the account books and spread them out before Hanzo. The entire pattern of the income and expenses of the station was there, with no concealments or evasions. For the income of the station there was recorded the amount of the commissions taken in by the station on the wages paid each year for the hire of men and horses, and the amount gathered each year in the annual produce tax. They also had to calculate how much was left to the station out of the interest accumulated on the savings on commission funds that had traditionally been permitted in the Kiso valley after the assisting villages and the keepers of post horses and the other officials had been paid their share out of the tax equalization fund, which had such a long history in the Kiso.

In the debits were the expenses incurred in hiring men and horses for the passage of daimyo and other officials, the deficits incurred by the inn services in providing rest and lodging for official travelers during the year, the salaries of the bookkeeper in the toiya and the foremen of the packhorse drovers, the wages of the porters, the cost of palanquins, the payments to the assisting districts for men and horses, the costs of repairs and improvements to the notice board and the roadway, and miscellaneous expenses attendant upon the operation of the toiya. Over the past seven years, the average income had been two hundred thirty-six ryo three bu in gold and six kan three hundred eighty-one mon in copper coins. Expenses had averaged four hundred thirty-one ryo three bu in gold and nine kan six hundred thirty-three mon in copper. The average deficit was therefore one hundred ninety-five ryo in gold and three kan two hundred fifty-two mon in copper. Not only had that deficit mounted from year to year, but the indebtedness incurred by the post station to cover the deficit had increased sixteenfold since the Ansei and Man'en periods, and it was necessary to pay a sum of two hundred forty-four ryo one bu two shu each year just to cover the interest. The money had been borrowed from the officials, from offerings to the sun goddess, and from offerings to be made in the memory of the dead, as well as from merchants in Nakatsugawa and the chartered merchants in Iwamura. The list of creditors even included the Masudaya and the Upper Fushimiya in Magome. Without such expedients, the station might very well have gone bankrupt. The account books showed the situation they wanted the commission to take cognizance of, and that it would have to render assistance if the post station was to continue to function.

Even though Magome was a small station, it had incurred enormous expenses in the operation of the Kiso road. The question of whether or not the station would get through these difficult times rested on the shoulders of the station officials. It had not been easy for Kichizaemon. It was still less so for Hanzo. He and Inosuke looked at each other, humiliated by their helplessness.

*   *   *   *   *   *   *

Wind damage, poor crops in the Kiso valley, unheard of rice prices, difficulties in maintaining the post station; through all these trials Magome came at last into the tenth month.

Cold rains were beginning to fall on the pass. Through the dreary autumnal days, detachments of shogunal officials and troops began to send advance parties down the Kiso road on their way home. It became clear that there would be a great procession whose passing would require thirteen days, from the thirteenth through the twenty-fifth of the tenth month.

Seisuke, Hanzo's assistant at the honjin, came to him.

"How have they assigned the lodgings, Hanzo?"

"For the procession this time? They will probably spend the night in Midono and have their noon meal in Magome."

"The road is going to be jammed full again."

Both Seisuke and Eikichi in the toiya had been stunned when they heard that the procession would take thirteen days to pass.

Soon afterward officials had come down from Fukushima to assign lodgings and rest stops for the various troops. Hanzo's house, the honjin, was of course included, as were Inosuke's house next door and even the Upper Fushimiya where Kimbei lived in retirement. Inosuke, worried about the men and horses from the assisting districts, often came over to consult with Hanzo during this time.

One day Inosuke said, "But I wonder what they'll be like, these people coming back from losing a war."

In this spirit Hanzo and the other officials awaited the arrival of the shogunal forces that had now set out from Osaka.

It was, after all, a general retreat for the forlorn shogunate. On the fifteenth, somewhat later than scheduled, the detachments began to pass through the station one after another. By the seventeenth, the porters and horses were overtaxed and the post officials extremely hard pressed. One day the porters from Yamaguchi and Yubunezawa would not come, and in Magome they had to hunt out even the mares used for hauling grass and press them into service. Some of the officials from Fukushima who were staying in the village were so worried about the confusion in the post stations that they even set out from Magome in the middle of the night to check them.

It was now the twenty-third of the month and the great procession was still passing through. Detachment after detachment of soldiers went by. The warriors reached the top of Magome pass, spent the lunch hour there, then went on, saying virtually nothing about the war. Nor did they speak of the battlegrounds. They spoke only of the day when they would once again see Edo.

Hanzo was standing before the meeting room one morning. There he met Juheiji, who had come over from Tsumago to consult with him on business.

"Juheiji! Let's go inside. We can't talk here. It looks as though everyone is exhausted. No one has come out yet today."

He led Juheiji into the meeting room and the conversation began with mutual consolations on their extreme fatigue before passing on to the troops that were going by day after day.

"If you think of the time when the Mito ronin went through," said Hanzo, "it seems like a different age. You don't see helmets or armor or tall court hats anymore."

"We've come to a time when everything is changing," said Juheiji, "weapons and soldiers' dress among them."

"I suppose you could say that the Choshu expedition speeded all that up."

"But, Hanzo, I heard that the muskets and cannon of the shogun's forces were so old-fashioned they were useless. Didn't they say that the Choshu armies, right down to the conscripts, were all equipped with modern Western weapons and that they smashed the opposition? Those Minier rifles are supposed to have been given to Choshu by the British. If you have any doubt about the way things have been done in this country, you can investigate this all you want but you'll never hear of a case where arms were received directly from foreign countries. So now there's Choshu coming out so big with Satsuma and England backing them and sending in arms in a steady stream. That's just it! Look! Surely you remember just which han took the initiative in calling for the expulsion of the foreigners. Is it really acceptable for people to change their positions as easily as they might turn their hands over? If that's so, then just what was all this 'expel the foreigners' business about?"

"Hey, you really came over from Tsumago with a lot on your mind today!"

"But look here! Just when it seems everyone is advocating the abrogation of the treaties and the expulsion of the foreigners, they are suddenly giving up on free navigation of the seas, and then when imperial approval of the treaties comes out, they immediately link up with foreign countries. I am really amazed at how quickly the foreign countries took advantage of the opportunity. Now they may get away with it if they say this thing one time and that thing another time, but the honest man is going to get pretty confused. And then there are rumors that even the shogunate is trying to make use of French strength. They say that the French have really sold the shogunate a fine bill of goods maintaining that while England is waiting for this country to fall apart, France at least is not. But while people say that it is disgraceful for the shogunate to use foreign power to suppress the allied han, no one says anything about using foreign power to try to destroy the shogunate."

"But—what you're saying—you can't do anything about it by chewing on me!"

Juheiji burst out laughing. Then Hanzo took up the thread.

"But you can't say that even the Choshu people are blindly trusting an England that is betting on the fragmentation of this country. Aren't such perfectly respectable people as Takasugi Shinsaku to be found there? They are very well aware that the foreign powers will use them if they permit it."

"Well, that's true, too. I suppose if you're from Choshu you'll say that in extraordinary times you have to use extraordinary measures. They must feel that accepting arms from the British is a necessary means to an important end. That's because we're both headmen. If you look at it from below, it's sure to appear that way."

"Anyway, Juheiji, the West has come in. It's a time when we have to keep thinking."

After Juheiji had completed his business and headed back for Tsumago, Hanzo went from the meeting room around to the front gate of the honjin. Entering the house, he began to pace back and forth in the spacious, wood-floored entrance hall. It seemed that even though the great procession that had taken lunches here on each of the thirteen days it had required to pass had ended at last, the atmosphere of instability accompanying the total with-drawal of the shogun's forces remained behind.

Otami looked in for a moment.

"What were you and Juheiji talking about? The children looked in at the meeting room and came back saying you were quarreling. They were all upset."

"What? Is that what they said? Today Juheiji really got into a rare line of talk for him. I don't think I've ever seen him so excited."

"Was it that bad?"

"What do you mean? Nobody was quarreling. What Juheiji was saying wasn't directed at anyone in particular. Things are just changing too fast and he was questioning it all."

"That's because my brother won't accept anything without questioning it first."

"Just look around. When times get as disorderly as these, all kinds of char-acters come flying out. There are people who despair of the world, there are people who go mad. And there are people like that refined gentleman from Takazaki who come here to observe the Kiso autumn."

"You frighten me when you talk that way."

"Oh, but we won't go astray brilliantly," said Hanzo, in a playful mood. "We'll just go straight on stupidly."

The dream of the military houses that they would once again be able to spread their wings widely and bravely on the two hundred and fiftieth anni-versary of the death of Ieyasu proved to be empty. In that same Edo from which the shogun's forces had departed with Ieyasu's golden fan guidon borne so bravely on high before them, it was a city in mourning for Iemochi that now awaited their return. The grief was particularly great in the women's quarters, but that was not all. The disturbances now taking place were far more serious than those at the time of the departure of the shogun's army. Desperate with hunger, old and young, men and women gathered in the streets before the stores of the wealthy merchants and kneeled under ban-ners inscribed with the names of their neighborhoods to complain that the price not just of rice but of all commodities made it difficult to sustain life. They were pleading for help, and it was said that their appearance was more than one could bear to see. The wealthy distributed rice by the peck or the bushel along with lesser grains and yams, miso, and soy sauce. As soon as the starving people received these allotments, they immediately cooked up the food and ate. They had camped in the open grounds of the shrines and temples and it was an appalling sight. One after the other, all the han from the house of Kii on down had reduced the stipends of their samurai, arranged to have their local paper currencies accepted in general circulation, and obtained permission to mint one hundred sen coins. Things had degenerated to the point where counterfeit money was beginning to appear.

Revolution was near. The thought gave Hanzo no rest. The shogunate had exposed its powerlessness while the mounting strength of the han was reminiscent of the long age of disorder that had preceded the Tokugawa. In such times all that a headman could do with his minuscule power was to expend his strength in his own han to encourage it through words and deeds to join the imperialist cause. The situation of Owari, the great han of central Japan, caught between Aizu on one side and Satsuma and Choshu on the other, was beginning to make Hanzo and his colleagues uneasy. There were samurai who supported Mochinori, the younger retired lord, and there were others who supported Inuchiyo, the present lord. Han policies wavered between support of the shogun and support of the imperialists. It was no longer necessary to go to Kyoto—a narrow field of action was opening up in Owari for Hanzo and his associates. Hanzo, Kozo, and Keizo began to get in touch with other disciples throughout southern Shinano and eastern Mino in order to explore every possible course of action.

4

The third month of Keio 3, 1867, was a memorable time for the posthumous disciples of Hirata Atsutane. The new shrine being built in the Ina valley was at last ready. All construction was finished and the new building stood complete on the twenty-first day of the month. Enshrined mementoes of Kada no Azumamaro, Kamo Mabuchi, Motoori Norinaga, and Hirata Atsutane, the four great leaders of the movement, would be dedicated in a public ceremony at Koedayama in Yamabuki village.

The honored originator of the plans for the new shrine, the Hirata disciple Yamabuki Shun'ichi, had passed away in the ninth month of the previous year without living to see the completion of his plans. His death had brought work temporarily to a halt, but Shun'ichi's successor, Katagiri Emon, the head of a branch house, had gained the support of the other Hirata disciples and completed the project. The mementoes of the four great masters that were to be enshrined were objects they had owned which had been presented by their surviving families through the efforts of the people of the Yamabuki shrine. From the Motoori household in Matsuzaka there was a small bronze bell. From the Kamo house in Hamamatsu there was an unsigned dagger with a blade just under six inches long in a white sheath. From the Kada household there was a round mirror of yellow bronze. And from the Hirata family there was a sphere of crystal and a set of ancient lapis lazuli beads on a purple cord. There was also, through the special good offices of the Yamabuki parishioners, a stone phallus which had once belonged to Atsutane and which had been presented specially to the Yamabuki shrine.

When word reached Magome, Hanzo told his parents and his wife that he wished, no matter what, to attend the ceremony set for the twenty-fourth day of the month. But good works are always beset by demons and Hanzo was afflicted with an upset stomach two days before his scheduled departure. He was in bed when Kozo and Keizo came up from Nakatsugawa to join him for the trip.

"It looks as though Hanzo won't be able to go."

"That's really too bad. We made an agreement to go together back around the first of the year and I was looking forward to it."

When his two friends set out for Yamabuki village in Ina, Hanzo slipped on some everyday clothes over his nightclothes and went out to see them off. Afterward he returned to the parlor, opened the shoji on the south side of the room, and looked out. Although the mountain spring was at its height, his surroundings seemed desolate to him.

It was the third month of the year and of national mourning for the death of the emperor. The swelling buds of the peony in the yard reminded Hanzo that the news of the emperor's death had reached Magome on the tenth day of the first month, but the death had actually occurred on the twenty-ninth day of the twelfth month. The emperor had been ill since the beginning of that month and the illness was diagnosed as smallpox around the middle of the month. Soon afterward, the emperor, to whom the people looked up as a father in peace, ended his difficult life of thirty-seven years.

The court was divided between the people under Prince Iwakura, working to speed the restoration of imperial rule and the reform of the nation, and the people under the lord of Aizu, who had received a secret commission from the late emperor. Some were saying that the emperor's illness had been aggravated by his desire for a union of court and military. Hanzo could not imagine these "affairs above the clouds." Needless to say, the rumors that reached to the grass roots here in the remote hinterlands amounted to nothing at all. He was grieved, however, by the atmosphere that seemed to emanate from court society. Surely those who despaired of this world, upon hearing the unspeakable rumors of an age when even the emperor himself could not have things as he wished them, would feel still more inclined to turn their backs on this life.

Beside Hanzo's bed lay Motoori's *The Soul Restored* and he opened it. He had long since thought that those in the military houses who shared his commitment to the cause of imperial restoration had a different role to play than those who followed, as he did, the way of his late master, but that in the end what they sought was the same restoration of antiquity. Yet, as he reflected on the various rumors surrounding the death of the emperor, he found that the times no longer permitted such easy and safe rationalizations. In this spirit he read the writings of Motoori again and again, bringing himself into the presence of the masters who had long since been his primary support.

These were the words of Motoori Norinaga:

In the great age of antiquity, there was no such expression as "the Way."

Again:

To make rules about the way things ought to be, to teach complex things, and to speak of this as the Way is characteristic of the style of foreign countries. Because foreign countries do not know Amaterasu Omikami, the sun goddess, they have no lord to rule them—their places of worship are defiled, their things are crude and unformed. Moreover, the hearts of the people are evil and their customs are licentious. In the affairs of their nations the meanest slave may instantly be made sovereign, so that those on high take measures to ensure that their perquisites will not be stolen from them while those below plot to take advantage of any laxity on the part of those above, hoping to steal their perquisites from them. Each side sees the other as the enemy and looks after its own interests; thus it is impossible to rule the nation. Among them, there may arrive a personality of force and wisdom who attracts followers, who is skilled in planning the theft of a nation, or the prevention of a theft, and who rules the nation wisely for a while, establishing laws for a later time. In China, such a person is called a sage. Now such persons, while planning the theft of a nation, respond to all details, discipline themselves to accomplish as much good as possible, and attract followers. Therefore, these sages acquire a reputation for goodness and the Ways they invent are applied to all things and seen as beneficial. However, since they themselves turn their backs on their own laws, overthrow their own lords, and steal their countries from them, these so-called Ways are all lies and, far from being good people, they are in truth the most evil of the evil, since their Ways were from their very inception things created out of the foulness of their minds in order to deceive people. Although the people of later generations seem on the surface to follow these Ways, there is in fact not a single one who keeps to them, and they do not aid the state; only their names are spread abroad, nothing is actually followed through. The Way of the sage is nothing more than a trifle for Confucian scholars of later generations to sing about as they continue to insult the people.

Innumerable examples of the expediencies of power, of the stealing of nations, of plots and subterfuges, of coups, and of systems and masks of virtue are all exposed to laughter in the *The Soul Restored.* The military families from the Hojo and the Ashikaga down to the Oda, the Toyotomi, and the Tokugawa are not mentioned directly, but surely no one who reads with any attention can fail to be reminded of the history of our country. Again in *The Soul Restored* there is the deepest grief that politics and the system of rule in the nation had tended toward Chinese-mindedness ever since the beginning of the middle ages and that this trend was now to be found even in the minds of the ordinary people. It was written in *The Soul Restored* that the "failure to take the will of the emperor as the source of true feeling but instead to take each and every rebellious impulse as righteousness" was something learned from foreign countries. In this there was a hint about the time before the age of domination by military houses—to be precise, about the pre-military time before any confrontation between the Kusunoki and the Ashikaga. It taught that the rule of the emperors down through the ages was ultimately the rule of the gods and that it was therefore of itself the Way of the gods. It taught that the "Way of the gods" lay in that naturalness in which there was no talk of a "Way."

It was the master Motoori Norinaga's *The Soul Restored* that pointed the way for those who came after, commanding a "return to naturalness." It was the master's *Commentaries on the Kojiki,* which had occupied more than thirty years of his life, that reported in detail on the discovery of this antiquity from the standpoint of etymology. Their tone was: "Know this joy." In the title of *The Soul Restored* is the word "naobi," an ancient word meaning "spontaneous action." Here it signified being good in spirit, being good in body, being good in destruction, being good in rebuilding. The National Learning movement had its beginnings there. The restoration of antiquity of which the master spoke was a rebirth, a restoration. It was above all that which the master pointed out as the true way to revolution. It seemed that he had been born in order to make, sixty or seventy years ago, this early announcement of the coming dawn.

Gathering strength from these thoughts, Hanzo sat up in bed, hands in his lap, and said to himself, "This is not what Juheiji meant, but it is precisely we who look up from below who can think in this way."

On the day of the dedication ceremonies of the new shrine, Hanzo took up the bedding that had been spread for him in the parlor. His diarrhea had stopped but he was still very pale. Nevertheless, he had Otami assist him in cleaning the room and in setting the alcove in order.

Presently, as a gesture of distant respect, he placed papers bearing the posthumous names of the four great masters in the alcove: Kada no Sukune Hakura no Ushi. Kamo no Agatanushi Okabe no Ushi. Akitsu-Hiko Mizusakurane no Ushi. Tama no Mihashira no Ushi. It felt as though the four great masters had come calling at this remote mountain home to gladly accept the sacred wine and the consecrated rice that Hanzo and Otami offered them.

Seisuke was indispensable at such times. He was much better with his hands and so he arranged burdock root and carrots into a colorful display, added dried persimmons, and placed them on a stand to make the alcove seem more festive.

Hanzo and Otami's children were growing. Okume was eleven and her brother Sota was nine. They came into the parlor, led by Oman, bringing a huge bergamot and apple blossoms from the Fushimiya. Inosuke had heard about the dedication ceremonies and he had sent these things over to the honjin so that they could be placed in the alcove as offerings.

The children were excited over the unexpected holiday. Oman watched her granddaughter, now at her most appealing age, as she ran out of the room.

"But hasn't it been fast, Otami? It's not so noticeable with Sota yet, but Okume is beginning to pay attention to adult conversations. She just pricks up her ears and listens with all her might."

"Yes, I really have to watch what I say around her these days," said Otami, laughing.

It was said that the ceremony in Yamabuki village would be carried out at the pre-dawn hour of the ox. From the Ina valley all the way to Nakatsugawa, virtually all the Hirata disciples would be attending along with the ardent believers who, although publicly recognized, had not yet entered formally into the Hirata school. Hanzo thought of his being the only one not present. In a state of mind befitting his formal dress, he pictured how the relics of the four great masters would be brought from their temporary housing at Yamabuki village junction to be taken to the Koedayama shrine. He could easily imagine who would be playing what roles in the ceremony.

The preceding year had been one of bad harvests; now it was followed by a year of national mourning. Everyone in the post station had agreed to a year of restraint. Even the household prayers held every year in the first month had been observed in the honjin with a simple meal of buckwheat noodles, with only the members of the household present. On the day of the dedication of the shrine, Hanzo called Seisuke and Eikichi to the parlor and gave them each a small serving of wine with a bit of roasted dried squid. At about the time the lamp was being lit in the alcove, Inosuke put in an appearance and Hanzo joined him in an exchange of poems before the spirits of the four great masters. Inosuke had become a companion in poetry to Hanzo; in his leisure moments between his duties on the highway as village elder and his family enterprise of sake brewing, he would compose simple and straightforward poems that won Hanzo's admiration.

It grew late. Inosuke went home. When it got to be the time for the procession to begin in Yamabuki village, a solemn mood filled Hanzo's breast. He imagined the glare of torches moving through the deep night, the sacred branches and the banners, the sacred tassels, the bows, the spears. In his mind's eye he could see in the procession senior disciples such as Kureta Masaka and his friends Keizo and Kozo as clearly as if he were there himself. Then his thoughts turned to the relics of the four great masters which his colleagues were now going to consecrate and dedicate to the shrine.

Otami, too, did not sleep that night. She stayed up with her husband and took her turn going to the parlor door to look out at the sky in the southwest. It was in the old third month and from the darkness outside came the scent of flowers.

Two days later Keizo and Kozo came back over the Odaira pass to Magome to report that one hundred sixty people had taken part in the ceremonies, counting direct disciples as well as people otherwise associated with the Hirata school.

"Well, Aoyama, I'm finally able to get out under blue skies and broad day-light again," said Kureta Masaka, who had come with them from Ina.

Masaka had been included in the general amnesty accompanying the year of mourning and now he was ending his long years of life as a fugitive and head-ing back to Kyoto.

Hanzo was delighted to find himself entertaining not only his two friends but also this senior disciple. Inviting them into his home, he opened wide the shoji in the middle room so that they could enjoy the fine view to the west. He seated his guests. But before anything else was said, he asked about the ceremonies at the Koedayama shrine.

"Everything went very well," Keizo replied. "After the ceremonies, there were sword dances and Gagaku orchestral music to calm the spirits. It was really a rare ceremony for the Ina valley. There were green curtains contrib-uted by Kanetane's Gojo residence in Kyoto and several packhorse loads of printing blocks for Atsutane's books. Everyone in Ina asked after you. They all send their regards."

"At the least, I wish you could have seen the procession that night, Hanzo," said Kozo. "Matsuo's mother, Taseko, came all the way from Kyoto and there were four other women in the procession. Each of them car-ried a short sword in her sash and all eyes were on them as they made their offerings."

Then Masaka took out a small cask of consecrated sake and some dry pas-tries.

"Well, here you are," he said, giving Hanzo a share of the mementoes from the ceremony.

"Oh, how splendid! My father will be delighted with this gift!" Hanzo clapped his hands to call Otami.

When Otami came in, Masaka became more formal.

"Madam, I have only exchanged a few words with you and I have not yet had an opportunity to express my gratitude. I am Kureta, whom you were so kind as to hide in your storehouse."

Everyone burst out laughing.

When it came time for Hanzo to hear about the stone phallus which the Hirata family had donated to the Koedayama shrine as a relic of Atsutane, the laughter never ceased. This phallus was said to have been left by Atsutane with specific orders that it serve to symbolize him in the ancestral rites, but the Hirata family had kept this an absolute secret from outsiders. Eventually, however, it became known, the curious took an interest in it, and it was widely discussed. The people of Yamabuki shrine were determined that it should become part of the holdings of the shrine. It seemed that the Hirata family was extremely reluctant to consent. They said incredible things—for instance, that a member of the imperial court had asked them for it, so they were not at liberty to give it to the shrine. Earlier, they had said that there was no such thing, and even if there were, it was not something that would be appropriate to give to the shrine. But the people of Yamabuki, hearing that it was a genuine relic of the master, uncovered documentary proof of its existence and continued to press their request. The Hirata family at last yielded to their persistence and agreed to send the stone phallus. There were conditions attached. They made clear that they wanted it kept where it would not be seen by everyone, since it was an object offensive to good taste. They did not care how small or humble the place where it was to be kept might be—a portable shrine or a shelf shrine would do very well—they only wanted it kept by itself, apart from the other objects; perhaps in the open ground behind the main shrine and within a fence. They also wanted it to be kept fast by heavy chains, since it was quite possible that some curiosity seeker might try to steal it.

"But it was something that Hirata sensei himself had deliberately left behind as a memento."

"That's where he was different from Motoori sensei. Motoori sensei spoke a lot about the love between men and women and of the sadness of the experience of beauty. Hirata sensei was more direct in these matters. His thoughts were utterly naked: give birth—propagate—all you can!"

Masaka did not stay long at Hanzo's house that day. He merely reported the successful completion of the ceremonies before setting out once more with Keizo and Kozo. Hanzo's entire family was still trying to persuade them to stay the night as they stepped down into the garden and began tieing their sandals.

"Kureta is going to Kyoto. He can't stay," said Hanzo to Otami as he joined them in the garden. Then he invited his guests to leave by the rear gate instead of the front one.

"I'll show you the way, Kureta. There's a nice quiet road back here."

Kichizaemon, coming out from between his retirement quarters and the storehouse, was descending the stairs toward the well as Hanzo set out to guide them. They passed the woodshed and the rice granary and then went out through the rear gate. Now they could see the back road alongside the bamboo grove belonging to the honjin. The road ran parallel to the main highway.

"I wonder what Morooka Masatane is doing. I'll bet he has already gone back to Kyoto ahead of me. He must also feel that this amnesty has come in the nick of time."

Kureta continued to talk about his old friend as he strode along over the exposed green roots of the bamboo. The day of freedom had at last come even for this group of activists that had taken the head of the wooden statue of Ashikaga Takauji and exposed it to public view. Masaka told Hanzo what had been heard of Morooka Masatane since he had taken refuge in Ueda and reflected on the joy he must be feeling on this day.

On the far side of the swale stood the grove of cedar trees surrounding the Mampukuji. When they came to cultivated ground, Hanzo and Masaka stopped to wait for Keizo and Kozo, who had fallen behind. Here and there spring plants, forcing their way up through the hard soil, had come into bloom. Masaka, who seemed to be wondering what kind of spring would be waiting for him in Kyoto, stepped over to a persimmon tree that stood at the edge of the field.

"Well, what's all this going to lead to? It's too bad that this great struggle between the imperialists and the supporters of the shogun should have to deteriorate into a private quarrel. It won't do for one or two of the han to try to get even for Sekigahara. This has got to be a reconstruction that will make the nation strong."

"Yes, well anyway, Kanetane will be waiting for you in Kyoto."

"I expect to get a good scolding from him when I get there. But all the same, Aoyama, I did manage to learn a little bit in the course of all this drifting around."

The disciples suddenly began to stir. As Masaka had said, eight or nine men including Morooka Masatane, all of whom had been involved in the incident on the riverbed at Sanjo, had been included in the current amnesty and they were returning once again to gather around the master Kanetane. Masaka himself was going up to Kyoto to stay with the Sawa family while his fellow disciples Hara Nobuyoshi and Kurasawa Yoshiyuki, who had been made a provincial agent of the Shirakawa family, were awaiting the opportunity to join him there. It was certain that such an active woman as Matsuo Taseko, who had become known as the "dowager agent of the Iwakura family," would not be wasting her time now that she was back home. She had given her relative Keizo the idea of going back to Kyoto once more, and he too would soon be leaving.

That day Hanzo accompanied his guests to the edge of the village and then returned home by the same road. The consecrated sake and the dry pastries that his friends had brought as mementoes of the ceremonies in Yamabuki remained behind. Hanzo placed them on the shrine that sat on a high shelf in his room as his wife joined him.

"Let's all drink this sake together, Otami. And we'll divide the pastries."

"Father will surely be delighted."

"I'm looking forward to having some of this and then getting a good night's sleep. I have had so many things on my mind that I can't sleep at all anymore. You just have no idea how much exciting news is coming our way."

"You often have trouble sleeping these days, don't you?"

"Just think, Keizo will soon be off to Kyoto. It seems that he just cannot wait around."

"Please stay here with us. Stay by your father. Something could happen to him at any time."

"I know that very well—I'll have some of the sake from Koedayama shrine and sleep well tonight. In times like these no one pays any attention to the backwoods at all. Even behind-the-scenes workers like me—I think I might be called a behind-the-scenes worker, don't you? It does no good, I'm telling you, to talk about the demands of the work at the post station."

They went on talking to each other in this way.

The best season for travelers was coming on, and as with every year they were awaiting the arrival of the Nikko emissary. Reports of his imminent arrival would come as the fourth month began.

There was nothing that spoke more clearly of one aspect of the social conditions of the time than the passage of the Nikko emissary, so often compared in his depredations with the typhoons that came around the two hundred tenth day of the year. This annual visit amounted to nothing more than coercion and extortion. Even with the present high prices, the emissary would wring thirty or forty ryo out of the Magome station, enough to pay for eighteen to twenty-four bushels of rice from Mino.

In fact, the farmers in this district called the third and fourth months the "end of the eating." Moreover, this year it was an "end of the eating" following a year of bad harvests. With the price of rice high everywhere, there were frequent thefts and posters were put up in the middle of the night on the great gates of the two large sake brewers in the town, the Fushimiya and the Masudaya, demanding that their rice be sold at a low price. In the Upper Fushimiya, Kimbei distributed eight bushels of rice in the village under the pretext of celebrating his seventieth year but this did not begin to make up the shortage. By now, people were beginning to talk about the necessity of distributing rice to the most desperately impoverished in Magome, Aramachi, and Toge.

Into all this came the Nikko emissary with its crowd of court nobles and high-ranking ecclesiastics bent on wringing money out of every lodging house along the way, even forcing porters to work for nothing. Like a great storm, in formation around the high, gold-tasseled guidon marking the special character of the party, the emissary came into Magome on the sixth day of the fourth month after spending the previous night in Ochiai. There was no possibility that the hardship of the village would engage the sympathies of these violent men who counted on being able to live for at least a year on what they took in on this one round trip between Kyoto and Edo. The people of the region had always been submissive and obedient, but they could bear no more from this frightful emissary.

"Run! Hide!" The cry rose among the post officials and among the porters and packhorse drovers waiting before the toiya. Inosuke, who had been manning the meeting room came rushing to Hanzo in distraction and confusion.

"Hanzo, everyone from the meeting room has run away. There are people going around with drawn swords, chasing after porters, shouting 'He went this way,' or 'He went that way.' Come with me, please! Let's get out of here!"

Hanzo could not reply. He did not join Inosuke, but he did quietly slip out the back gate and into the honjin woods.

"This is terrible, terrible!"

With this cry, Kimbei ran out of the Upper Fushimiya. Kichizaemon came out of his quarters to look around. They met on the highway as though they had arranged it beforehand, and after amazed looks at each other, they inspected the town. The retinue of the Nikko emissary had already passed through on the way to Tsumago.

"Ha ha ha ha!" Not even Kichizaemon himself knew whether he was laughing or crying.

Hanzo was thirty-six years old and no longer so quick to take offense or to pass judgment as he had been in his younger years. He could now speak freely to any of the Fukushima officials about the conditions in the villages for which he was responsible, and he felt certain that he could bring them through a year no worse than this one. Around the time that the wisteria began to blossom along the Kiso road, he found himself traveling back and forth between Magome and Fukushima to encourage the Yamamura to take their case to Nagoya castle. There was, of course, no reason to expect that Owari would stand idly by in the face of such hardship among the people in their domain and such exhaustion in the post stations. Owari had always taken good care of the Kiso. In the winter of the previous year it had loaned the three stations of Miyanokoshi, Agematsu, and Magome six hundred ryo in assistance money, and on the first month of this year it had distributed a grant of five thousand ryo among the villages of the Kiso valley. In addition, it had relieved the villagers of Magome of half their annual taxes for the year in response to their petition, and as a special case, it had sent in rice and the money to buy rice on three separate occasions in the third month, to a total of three hundred bushels.

Unfortunately, the relief measures instituted by Owari could not bring concrete results immediately, and the people of the village found themselves starving while helping hands were extended before their very eyes. Hanzo called a meeting with Inosuke and the other officials in the meeting room and began the distribution of the donated rice, to be completed in the next fifteen days. The ration was to be one *go,* a little less than a third of a pint each for all able-bodied adults in Magome, Aramachi, and Toge, while children and old people would receive half that amount.

This went on for ten days. Some were holding off starvation by mixing pine bark with their rice and by digging wild yams. When he heard about it, Hanzo felt that he could not simply ignore it and he decided to call all the substantial people of the town together to arrange a suitable program of relief. But first of all, he opened his own storehouses to the starving people.

There came a morning when the smoke rose up from a fire of dry pine needles in the cooking oven that had been built beside the service entry to the honjin. A huge old cauldron normally used for cooking the glutinous rice for New Year's cakes was set up there, and some of the tenant farmers were carrying rice from the granary to the areas around the service entrance. Oman and Otami joined the others, their hair tied up in cloths and their sleeves bound up with cords, as they cooked gruel for those in the most desperate straits.

Hanzo called to Sakichi.

"Go around the village and tell everyone that we are giving out rice gruel for breakfast. Anyone who wants some should come with a container. Make sure everyone hears."

Seisuke came up beside him.

"Hanzo! Let's make out tickets showing how many people there are in each family. Then let's make the gruel, using one part of rice to eight parts of water, and allow three *go* for each person."

When this became known to the villagers, everyone down to the humblest day laborers called out to each other to join in the throng that gathered before the gates of the honjin. That morning Kichizaemon, a worried look on his face, came down from his retirement quarters to the main house, leaning on his stick.

"It's still nothing like the great famine of Temmei. There are records of that in our old ledgers. They were cooking rations at the Masudaya, the Fushimiya, and the Umeya too. They say that they fed from a hundred to a hundred twenty persons every morning."

Kichizaemon was speaking from his memories again.

As they came into the fifth month, the people of Magome found that their difficulties were becoming less extreme. Relief funds from Owari had been distributed and rice was coming in from Oi. Everyone gained strength after the barley harvest, and they set to with a will on their busy rounds of gathering brushwood and preparing the rice seedlings. Here and there people began to prepare the rice fields for planting. Kimbei noted that the weather was very good, unlike the windstorms and repeated heavy rains of the previous year. He decided to take a course of treatments from a physician in Asai in Mino province as a final adventure now that he was in his seventy-first year.

Hanzo began to receive letters from Keizo, who had gone to Kyoto at about the same time as Kureta Masaka. He read in these letters that the forty court nobles including Prince Arisugawa who had received an official reprimand from the emperor a few years earlier had been released from house arrest and the long-awaited permission for Iwakura Tomomi to reenter Kyoto had at last been granted. The faction in the palace that had held control until now had begun to withdraw and the center of power was shifting. Keizo reported that it was difficult to calculate just how far-reaching the effects of the late emperor's death had been. The new emperor was scarcely out of childhood. On one side was Satsuma, which had allied itself with Iwakura and was rallying the anti-shogunal forces, while on the other side Kuwana and Aizu were backing the new shogun, who maintained an ominous silence. Standing between them in a very delicate position were Owari, Tosa, Echizen and Aki. The letters reported that the points at issue were the opening of the port of Hyogo and the punishment of Choshu. People scarcely knew where to turn these days; there was nothing but division and factional strife among the han. No one but the emperor could unify the people. Surely there had been conflict ever since the age of the gods, but wasn't the unification of the people the great and divine mission of the imperial house?

5

"A retail shop with its own warehouse."

Those were the words that issued from the mouth of Oguri Kozuke, the person who might be said to have been playing the role of chief clerk in the desperate efforts to ward off the collapse of the Tokugawa fortunes. And what did he mean by "a retail shop with its own warehouse"? The Tokugawa shogunate had been hard put to maintain the ships it had received from foreign countries, and from the first year of Genji, 1864, Oguri, working with his close friend Kitamura Zuiken, had planned a new shipyard in Yokosuka. It was this shipyard, completed two years later in the first year of Keio, that he was referring to. Why should a shipyard be called a retail shop? And why should this shipyard, even though Oguri had had a special flag designed for it, with a folded paper motif dyed to serve as a banner, be ascribed the honor of having its own attached warehouse? This was no mere passing jest on the part of Oguri Kozuke. Its inner meaning was that, in these times when it already seemed too late to save the situation, these brave words might still come from the mouth of a man determined to carry out his duty for so long as the shogunate might continue to exist. There really were such people in the shogunate after all. And there were also people in the shogunate like Kitamura Zuiken, who said that those who understood it would understand it, though he found the import of the saying pitiful. But to come to the point, a new shipyard complex was being opened by the shogunate in Yokosuka, not far from the Yamagami family residence in Kugo. It was modeled on the French port of Toulon, although slightly reduced in scale, and it included steel plants, shipyards, docks, warehouses, and so on, such as had never before been seen in East Asia. So, while the shogunate's steady progress toward oblivion was indeed all too plain even to those within the shogunate, these modern appurtenances were being prepared in this obscure corner of the country in anticipation of the time that was to come.

Yoshinobu, the fifteenth shogun, seemed like one who had appeared in the final years of the shogunate for the sole purpose of viewing this signboard for the "retail shop with its own warehouse." This same Yoshinobu had come into the office of shogun from the house of Hitotsubashi; now everyone in the nation was required to look up to him regardless of their feelings about the man. It would not do to forget, however, that this new shogun, though he came from an exalted background, had worked with internal and foreign affairs for many years, was widely experienced, and was by no means the usual sort of aristocrat.

Yoshinobu commenced his new life by making preparations for extensive reforms. This was in conformity with his own desires ever since the reforms of the Bunkyu period, but it was also encouraged by the disillusionment that had resulted from the disastrous Choshu campaign. When the shogunate blindly marched its great army off to the west, it chose not to heed the objections raised by the retired lord of Owari and the lord of Echizen. It had now opened its eyes, but it was too late. Still it was better that the shogunate should have opened its eyes too late than not at all. The Choshu campaign had in fact convinced both the shogunate and the han to overhaul their military systems. Formerly, whenever a daimyo ventured out he would be accompanied by anywhere from several dozen to a hundred or more of his subordinate officials and retainers. This was now reduced to the point where a daimyo would be accompanied by only five men and those below that rank by a single samurai and a single sandal bearer. Two hundred and more years of empty official display had been eliminated with startling suddenness, and high and low competed to take up the simplicity of the Western style. During the rule of Yoshinobu, it came for the first time to be viewed as no hardship for even a high-ranking official to ride out or walk out all alone. Moreover, an army office under French guidance was set up while the office overseeing practice in Western navigation was transformed into the navy office, and English and French language academies were set up in Yokohama, all as part of this trend. Under Yoshinobu's reforms, six categories of guards and petty officials were abolished. Overlapping functions and old-fashioned sinecures were eliminated and plans were developed to reorganize the troops under the bannermen along Western lines. The bannermen themselves had returned to the ways of the late sixteenth century, rejecting ostentatious display and moving about their business alone, without retinue. All of the "eighty thousand warriors" under the bannermen, who were far fewer in reality, were to be formed into a Western-style army, and these new warriors were placed under French instructors. Those who had always kneeled formally, wearing their swords with traditional Japanese dress, were now clad in Western-style trousers or breeches, given imported firearms, and set to patrolling the environs of Edo castle. This alone indicated the degree to which the new shogun's rule had begun by attempting to reform the old systems.

These changes even reached into the provinces, where a reform of the old post horse system was being undertaken. The policy of supplying horses free to officials, a policy that had brought so much suffering to the people along the post roads, was discontinued and the number of men and horses that could be requisitioned during a daimyo's movements was decreased. There was also a decrease in the rate of the commissions that were taken out of the wages of the people in the assisting districts, which had become a source of hardship to them, and the system of lodgings along the highway was simplified. One of the unforgettable results of these reforms was that women were at last permitted to pass freely through the barriers without special passports. The women of the feudal age were breaking out of their long confinement and taking their first steps toward freedom.

Yoshinobu had not taken up the office of shogun on his own initiative. After the death of Iemochi, he had been unwilling to accept the office even after the lords of Kii and Owari had urged it. When pressures around him at last required him to undertake the leadership of the house of Tokugawa, he

accepted the office of shogun as well, as a purely hereditary obligation and
with no eagerness whatsoever. It had, after all, been his intention from the
time he assumed the office to discard it without hesitation at the proper
moment to facilitate a reconciliation of court and military, and he gave no
heed to Matsudaira Shungaku's protest that this would lead to the destruction of the Tokugawa.

It is rare for a man to be as universally misunderstood as was this fifteenth
shogun. While the anti-shogunal parties in the west of Japan, including the
court nobles and Satsuma, continued to threaten his emergence as shogun on
the political stage, there was also a substantial faction in the shogunate itself
that blamed Yoshinobu for the death of the previous shogun and could see
him only as an enemy. When Yoshinobu had accepted the leadership of the
Tokugawa while simultaneously protesting that he wished to refuse the office
of shogun, it was Iwakura Tomomi who had lent no credence to the story,
appraising Yoshinobu as an "infinitely resourceful liar." Okubo Toshimichi,
who felt there was little chance that the wise policies of the lord of Satsuma
would gain their proper acceptance, carried on a ceaseless behind-the-scenes
struggle with Yoshinobu's personal retainer Hara Ichinoshin, the distinguished Mito scholar widely known as "Yoshinobu's concealed weapon."
Only Kido Koin of Choshu saw Yoshinobu as a possible second Ieyasu and he
kept a close watch on his reforms of the army.

However, Yoshinobu was also a son of the late Nariaki of Mito. In his
veins ran the blood of that lord who had written "Revere the Emperor" on a
tablet at the Kodokan, the Mito academy. Yoshinobu was thus able to recognize the justice in the prevailing sense among the activists that only an end to
the division between court and shogunate on policy matters and the appearance of a new government under the emperor would make it possible for the
nation to resist the pressures from the foreign powers and maintain its independence. Consequently, this new shogun debated with himself the questions
of simply resigning the office and joining the other feudal lords in a system
where all power was centralized in the person of the emperor, all property
owned by him, and all benefits dispensed by him, or of attempting a reform
in the manner of the German states and creating a federation. Such plans had
taken root in the mind of this new shogun. Whichever course might be chosen, however, they both assumed above all else a harmony between court and
military. Yoshinobu had never experienced such a shock as the one he had had
when the late emperor died, bringing such passionate imperialists as Iwakura
Tomomi into action. Among all those who had held the late emperor in high
regard, there was none so grieved as Yoshinobu, misunderstood as he was in
word and deed. Surely he must already have begun, shortly after accepting
the office of shogun, to develop the resolve not to put off the restoration of
imperial rule until later but to resign straightaway and go off alone into the
frosty night.

The third year of Keio corresponded to 1867 in the Western calendar; the
nineteenth century was well into its second half. In France Napoleon III
reigned and in England, Queen Victoria. From the beginning of this new

Tokugawa regime, so keen to gather in new knowledge, Yoshinobu had made use of advice from Roches, the French ambassador. He had reorganized his cabinet, making way for men of merit to rise in the government, and he had imposed the first taxes ever to be placed on commerce and industry. The opening of mines and the development of transportation facilities were still further plans that had been made for the benefit of this "shop with its own warehouse." He even saw the day arriving when his younger brother Matsudaira Mimbudayu and the commissioner for foreign affairs Kitamura Zuiken would be going to France. But the more deeply involved with France the shogunate became, the more deeply Satsuma and Choshu became involved with England. An open competition was under way in Japan between the two great powers of Europe. Permission to open the port of Hyogo was soon granted, and Mori of Choshu and his son were pardoned. The effort to adopt the oldest and newest simultaneously grew day by day with the increasing rush of events, driving everyone into disorder and confusion.

In the ninth month of that year, the various forces making an imperial restoration inevitable became manifest before Yoshinobu's eyes. Tosa's support for a parliamentary system had by now begun to seem halfhearted, and it was forming an alliance with Choshu and Aki to settle all matters by force of arms. Their intent was to drive Yoshinobu and the Aizu and Kuwana forces out of Kyoto altogether; then by joining forces with Iwakura Tomomi, they would realize a complete restoration of imperial rule. It was not surprising that the vigorous young men in the domains of Matsudaira Shuridayu, as the lord of Choshu was known, who had been forced to withdraw into the western corner of Japan ever since the battle of Sekigahara, should now begin to gather their courage to throw off the effects of three centuries of Tokugawa repression. Moreover, while they had formed the vanguard of the anti-shogunal forces, pledging themselves to fight to the death, their opponents now had behind them the bitter experience of the failed Choshu expedition. Pushing them on was the fierce competition between Parkes and Roches. Satsuma had decided to raise soldiers and go up to Kyoto. They were due to arrive at the port of Mitajiri after coming up from Kyushu by sea, and Choshu, which was making preparations to send its own forces along with them, awaited their arrival. A mutual assistance alliance had been established between Satsuma, Choshu, and Aki. Yamauchi Yodo, lord of Tosa, found this disposition unsatisfactory and memorialized Yoshinobu, urging a complete restoration of imperial rule. He maintained that there was no profit in arguing the rights and wrongs of the past; instead, eyes must be opened wide and a new basis for the nation established, so that it need not feel any shame before the world. This would require a return to righteousness and justice among all the people of the nation and a change in the national polity of the past several hundred years. The perfect opportunity for the restoration of imperial rule had now arrived.

Thus it came about that Yoshinobu was at last able to return his powers to the emperor as he had so long hoped to do. The shogun, who understood that the Tokugawa era was coming to an end, had nevertheless not realized that the powers that would destroy the shogunate had already developed to this point. Now that the time was fully ripe for disaster, he decided to bow his head, not before the enemies who were advancing upon him, but to a higher authority. On the twelfth day of the tenth month, he called his high-ranking officials to Nijo castle in order to announce the return of his powers to the emperor. They were stunned, even though Yoshinobu pointed out that by this time they should not have expected anything else. The destruction in a single day of the power that had been handed down in the Tokugawa line since the days of Ieyasu was a terrifying responsibility to take before their ancestors. When Yoshinobu argued that his action continued the traditions set down by Ieyasu, who had restored order in the nation and had set the august mind at rest, the numerous officials disagreed and did not readily give up their views. Still Yoshinobu persisted. If the shogunal powers should now be returned to the imperial court without any reservations whatsoever, establishing a single center of power, and if the house of Tokugawa, as long as it should exist, should work with the other lords of the nation to assist the emperor, they would surely be able to ward off the insults of the foreign powers and thus the objectives of the nation would be realized. But even while Yoshinobu was speaking, whispers of dissent continued among the assembled officials. Yoshinobu argued his point, saying that they should think about the reason they had been in Kyoto all this time. Surely they all knew that it was to put down the disorders that were rising around the person of the emperor and to set the august mind at ease. If he were not to concede that it was his own unworthiness to be in Kyoto that had been at the root of the trouble, but should instead bring the implements of war into play to attack those who opposed him, he would not only add to the grief of the emperor but multiply the sufferings of the people as well. This would accord neither with righteousness nor with his aim to act always in true loyalty. Far better that he should reflect on his own role, recognize his own faults, give up selfish considerations, and correct the unrighteous rule that had hitherto prevailed. Together with the rest of the nation, they should assist the emperor in total fidelity and patriotism. There was nothing else to do. This would also surely accord with the will of Ieyasu, who had assumed political power in order to bring tranquility to the nation. Ieyasu had not assumed power for selfish reasons. Yoshinobu would be putting an end to the political power of the Tokugawa for the same purpose. Though it was his great ancestor who had assumed those same powers that he would be relinquishing, their acts would be the same in spirit insofar as the national well-being and loyal service to the court were concerned. Although some feared a fragmentation of political interests into purely local configurations once power had been returned to the throne, wasn't that precisely what had already happened?

The orders of the shogunate were not being carried out. Even though it called upon the daimyo, it could not control them. This was true not only of the shogunate but of the court as well. It might very well have been that at this juncture nothing could be done for Japan without first supporting imperial rule, then accepting the emperor's orders together with the other daimyo in order to apply all available strength to the common defense against the foreigners.

Yoshinobu was adamant. On the thirteenth day of the tenth month, the return of the shogunal powers to the imperial court was communicated to the han and on the fourteenth day it was reported to the emperor. In this return of political powers to the emperor and the subsequent resignation of the office of shogun was made manifest the true spirit of harmony between court and military. It was as though a bird, knowing well how to soar high in the sky and knowing also how to meet the wind with its wings, gave itself up to the power of the winds that naturally bore it up.

6

> Ain't it all right, ain't it all right?
> You yank it once, I'll yank it twice
> Yank it and yank it 'til it needs a splice.
> Ain't it all right, ain't it all right?
>
> Ain't it all right, ain't it all right?
> The mortar's so light, my partner's so right
> I won't change partners, even tomorrow night.
> Ain't it all right, ain't it all right?

At Magome station the voices of the villagers could be heard as they danced happily and playfully to the rhythm of this song almost every day along the highway.

The news that the shogun had surrendered his powers to the court brought a flood of rumors in its wake. One was the story that mysterious talismans had begun to fall from the sky in various places. At the same time there appeared the fad, beginning no one knew where, of sandwiching endless verses and nonsense words between repetitions of the refrain "ain't it all right."

> Ain't it all right, ain't it all right?
> It's for sure whose mortar will polish the rice
> Put on the pot, granny, add plenty of spice!
> Ain't it all right, ain't it all right?

Everyone thought the song trivial and yet everyone enjoyed it. It tended toward indecency but it was appealing in its cheerful silliness. It had a certain savage power to disorder the civilized breast.

Even the old people and the women and children of the village took up the song in high spirits. And then there were the talismans. It began with the falling of talismans that had originated in the Suwa shrine within the precincts of the tutelary deity in Aramachi; these were followed by talismans from the Ise shrine which fell on the roof of a shed behind the honjin and in an interior courtyard of the Masudaya. A cry came to celebrate the event and there was a great uproar as many of the young people of the village went out to dance wildly, dressed only in their underrobes. The households where the talismans had fallen were considered fortunate and in each a keg of sake was opened and rice cakes made to be distributed to all callers, in celebration of the miraculous event.

Everyone both believed in and at the same time doubted these mysterious events. There were those who claimed actually to have seen the talismans falling down out of a clear blue sky, while others suggested that it must be some kind of message from the great shrine at Ise. Still others saw it as the promise of a rich harvest that year. The "ain't it all right" craze was not limited to the Kiso valley. According to those who had just come down from Kyoto and Osaka, small Shinto shrines had been set up in every household and the talismans that had been gathered up were placed before them. In many places old and young, men and women, all dressed in bright costumes, danced about through the streets to the accompaniment of flutes and drums. The mysterious talismans and the mad "ain't it all right"—the town took on a rare festive appearance. Who could have imagined that such a thing would come to the people of Magome, these people who had been faced with famine as recently as the third and fourth months? It spread through all the provinces as a great effort to bury all the sadnesses of the past. It intoxicated the senses of vast numbers of people.

Talismans from the great shrine of Atsuta in Nagoya fell on the branches of the camellia in the garden of the Horaiya. They also fell inside the outer gates of the Fushimiya and on the high wall around the garden before the inner sitting room of the Umeya. In addition, talismans from the Hachiman shrine fell in two other places. In every case they were received with wonder and joy. The retired gentleman of the Upper Fushimiya, twice as energetic and twice as superstitious as most people, could not remain a mere passive onlooker to these events. Still less could he remain silent when he heard that the reluctance of some of the wealthiest houses to part with quantities of cakes and sake in these celebrations was being greeted with the chant "pauper! pauper!" set to the tune of another popular ditty of the time. If the Masudaya made up eight bushels of rice cakes, then Kimbei was determined to pass out sixteen bushels. He called on everyone, even the womenfolk among his relatives, to make cakes for the villagers. They tossed them out, time and time again. Sixteen bushels of cakes hurtled through the air to be stuffed into the sleeves and breasts of the robes of the villagers gathered in front of the Fushimiya. They also opened the bungs on sixteen-gallon sake kegs and served both clear and sweet sake, as much as anyone could drink.

There were even some shameless ones who cried out, "Hey! Free drinks! Free treats!"

The rebuilding of the village shrine was nearing completion, and the people of the village decided to organize a theatrical entertainment. The most eager among them had even begun rehearsals. This festive atmosphere, temporary as it was, helped them to forget the shock brought on by the collapse of the shogunal house to which they had so long been bound in service. It helped them to forget that the once mighty personage was now reported to have gone into retirement and to have arranged a marriage for his adopted son. It enabled them to forget the loss of their masters of over three hundred years, masters in whom they had believed so completely that they had felt safe from robbery or possession by foxes and tanuki when walking at night on the most remote mountain paths if only they could carry a lantern marked with the Tokugawa hollyhock crest.

There was no telling when the "ain't it all right" was going to stop. It had begun during the radish harvest in the village and it continued even as preparations for the plays celebrating the rededication of the village shrine were being completed. On this occasion a procession in masquerade came over from Tsumago to celebrate the falling of the talismans. The participants were made up to recall the passage of the Mito ronin four years earlier; there was an abundance of armor, helmets, bows, and spears, and everyone, even down to the children, rode on horses led by grooms.

At the honjin, everyone came out before the gate to watch—everyone from Sota, a lively child just beginning to learn his letters, to Kichizaemon, who now stayed in his rooms most of the time.

"Okume, come see! Hurry and come out!"

As Otami called, Okume, just recovering from a slight illness and somehow looking all the more girlish for her thinness, appeared beside her mother and grandmother. It was a rare occurrence for the entire family of the honjin to appear before their gate this way. The villagers were delighted to see that Kichizaemon, who had served them for so many years, was still in good health. Both sides of the street were lined with people watching the parade. Two girls, said to be daughters of the Onoya in Tsumago, came riding quietly on horseback, both dressed in tall court caps and fine campaign jackets.

"Here's a gift for you!"

The man accompanying the girls from the Onoya gave Okume and Sota each one of the cakes made for the celebration.

"Ain't it all right, ain't it all right!"

Even Sota was playfully imitating the popular chant in his childish voice.

"That's good, Sota! That's really good!"

The man from the Onoya clapped his hands with pleasure. Just then Juheiji cut through the parade to inquire after Okume's health and to see Hanzo. He stood for a moment with the rest of the family before the honjin gate; then, spotting Hanzo, he went over to speak to him.

"Hanzo, what's all this excitement about?"

"Isn't that what I should be asking?"

"We had a guest from Fukushima yesterday. He said that the talismans are falling all over there now."

"I'm glad to hear that."

"There are those who say quite matter of factly that when the world is changing as fast as it is now, it is good to have such auspicious omens. But I still feel a little as though we all have been taken in by a fox."

"Just the same, Juheiji, the farmers here around Magome haven't had anything to celebrate for the last ten years or more. If everyone wants to celebrate, let them celebrate. That's the way I look at it."

For all the surface gaiety along the highway, there was beneath it an unpleasant calm as though presaging a great storm. Certainly the news that was coming to Hanzo from Nagoya had nothing of "ain't it all right" about it. It had early been known at Nagoya that it was the real intent of Satsuma and Choshu to execute Yoshinobu as well as Matsudaira Katamori of Aizu and Matsudaira Sadanori of Kuwana. The retired lord of Owari was much concerned about this turn of events and in spite of his illness he had already gone up to Kyoto at the end of the tenth month to recommend that Aizu and Kuwana withdraw from the city. He could do this because the lord of Owari was in fact the elder brother of the lords of Aizu and Kuwana.

All the daimyo were assembling in Kyoto in response to the imperial summons. Those who hoped to determine the future course of the nation by mobilizing public opinion began to stir, centering their activities in Kyoto. By the end of the eleventh month, the atmosphere was full of the grave portents raised by the Shimazu of Satsuma, the Mori of Choshu, the lord of Aki, the heir of Tokuyama, and the steward of the house of Yoshikawa, each of whom was leading anywhere from three or four hundred to two or three thousand soldiers. Some had already entered the capital while others were still arriving on the seacoast at Settsu or at Nishi no Miya, waiting for orders to proceed up to the capital. The traffic between Kyoto and Nagoya became heavy, with the soldiers of the Kintetsugumi advancing to join the forces of Satsuma, Choshu, Hizen, and Tosa in the Kyoto district while the high-ranking members of the shogunal party were retreating. Hanzo got very clear reports of the way in which imperialists such as Naruse Masamitsu, Tamiya Jo'un, and Arakawa Jinsaku were urging action on the retired lord of Owari and doing everything possible to realize their goals. The restoration of imperial rule was now only a matter of time.

In the midst of all this, a completely unexpected new voice came to Hanzo's ears. It came from his friends in Kyoto, from the activists in Nagoya, and from the committed disciples around Iida.

"To restore imperial rule to the state of antiquity, it will not do to go back to the style of the abortive restoration of the fourteenth century; we must go back all the way to the style of Jimmu, the first emperor."

Hanzo had been longing to hear such a voice. Not only was the restoration of antiquity for which so many National Scholars had dreamed soon to be realized, but forces were beginning to move that would take this restoration back to the times before military dominance, just as Motoori had advocated in his works. This feeling seemed to him to be present to a surprising degree even among the Choshu activists who had served on the front line in over-throwing the shogunate.

In a manuscript that he borrowed from his friend Kozo, Hanzo found a discussion of the matter. When he saw it, he realized that there were self-sacrificing people, hidden away and unknown to the world, who could contrive to say what everyone wanted to say but had been unable to reduce to words. What the manuscript said was that the abortive fourteenth-century restoration had come from those above, not from the hearts of the people. Therefore, with the first faltering of imperial rule, the age immediately became a military one. However, the restoration of antiquity which we now await, unlike that earlier one, has risen from the grass roots. This is what it said. The restoration was rising from the very grass roots. From masterless samurai to samurai in the han, from samurai in the han to ministers of the han, and from ministers of the han to the lords of the han—as it gradually grew in potency, it naturally would call forth the restoration of antiquity. Therefore even if those above should change their minds, so long as the minds of the people did not change, they would never fall back into an age of domination by military houses. The manuscript went on. There are those who speak of a restoration of antiquity but who really are plotting the usurpation of power by the feudal lords—their calculations are utterly mistaken. That is because the roots of the restoration are among the people themselves, so that no matter what the lords might plan, they will never have that kind of latitude. It would be well for them to reflect upon just how this movement has risen up from the grass roots. That is to say, the proper ordering of society can be seen more clearly if one looks up from the bottom of society. This is why Ii Naosuke was assassinated at the Sakurada gate, and why the incidents at Gojo in Yamato and at Mt. Tsukuba occurred. And this is why there was Choshu and why Choshu has now been joined by Satsuma. No matter how harsh the measures taken by the shogunate, the few dozen Mito ronin it killed after the incident at the Sakurada gate soon became several hundred, and when the several hundred from the Tsukuba force were killed, they became several thousand. And when the shogunate was finally confronted by tens of thousands of men from Choshu, it could not control them. If the forces of western Japan should prove inadequate to bring about the restoration of antiquity, then they will rise in the east, or in the south, or in the north. Even if a new shogunate should appear and flaunt its might, it would not last more than a few years before the certain arrival of the restoration of antiquity. This is what was written in the manuscript.

As Hanzo read, he reflected that the rise of the movement to restore antiquity was no accident and that this ardent new voice being heard had emanated from the very grass roots that the author of the manuscript spoke of.

Snow had already fallen several times on Mt. Ena. The range of peaks which Hanzo often gazed at from the hallway along the west side of the house was gleaming white. Now that the "ain't it all right" fad, which had lasted for more than a month, had at last subsided, it was clear that a change

without precedent in this nation's history was approaching. More than six
hundred years of military domination was coming to an end. There were few
travelers on the highway and the mountain households were being shut up
for the winter. There was only the sound of the wooden clappers of the fire
watch echoing over the station.

One morning Hanzo was awakened by the sound of the bell at the Mampukuji. As he listened to it from his pillow in the parlor, Hanzo's thoughts
turned to the priest Sho'un, who never shirked his early morning duties. It
was the priest himself who had climbed up into the bell tower to greet the
day with these sounds. More than thirteen years had passed since he had
returned to the village as the new priest after long years of rigorous preparation all over Japan. According to the custom of the time, he had removed the
straw sandals marking him as a traveler in the entrance hall of the honjin and
had changed into his priest's robes before passing through the gate of the
temple. He had now sat before the portrait of Bodhidharma in the priest's
quarters for more than thirteen years.

Lying beside his wife, who was still fast asleep, Hanzo listened to the
sound of the bell. It resounded from valley to valley, leapt from field to field,
and its reverberations carried a clear and clean sound that still had the same
tranquility, the same relaxed quality, that it had had so long ago when, in the
first year of Ansei, the priest had changed his name from Chigen to Sho'un
and had assumed the responsibility for this temple.

One peal. Another. The meaning of the bell sounded in Hanzo's ears. In
contrast to the liveliness of the vulgar and silly "ain't it all right," this was a
sound from a distant world, from a realm of peace and calm. It made manifest
the discipline of a person who, throughout all these violent changes, was
moved no more than he was by the changing forms of the clouds or the succession of sun and moon. Hanzo was amazed at the calm of this religion
which had long since grown alien to him. And he was still more amazed to
think that such a person as this priest could be living in these difficult times
when great numbers of dedicated men were risking their lives to resist the
shogunate and to serve the nation.

"Otami."

Hanzo gently shook his wife awake. Then he got up quickly. He had
decided to visit his friend Kozo in Nakatsugawa to try to find out what was
happening in Kyoto.

"Here in the mountains I just don't know what's happening. Maybe the
restoration of imperial power has already taken place . . ."

His mind made up, he had Otami get the maids up to start the fire in the
hearth and to prepare an early breakfast for him before he left for Nakatsugawa.

It was the twelfth month of the third year of Keio and the roads were
white with snow. As soon as he finished eating, Hanzo put on the formal

trousers that went with his rank of headman and tied on his straw sandals. He walked down as far as the village shrine in Aramachi, his feet crunching in the snow. There he took the road leading to the boundary of the province and walked on to Shinjaya at the edge of the station. The Basho memorial beside the road was wet with snow. He stopped at the teahouse, and as he was resting there, he unexpectedly met Kozo coming up from Nakatsugawa, past the first milestone on the border, heading for Magome. Kozo was accompanied by Katsushige from Ochiai.

"Master!"

Hanzo heard Katsushige's familiar voice for the first time in some while. It was unchanged from the old days.

"Well, Hanzo, now you don't have to go down to Nakatsugawa and we don't have to go on up to Magome. We can talk here," Kozo suggested.

Thus it was that Hanzo learned of the restoration of imperial rule. The conference held by Prince Iwakura at the lesser imperial palace had included not only the han of Satsuma, Aki, Tosa, and Echizen but Owari as well. At this conference the court ranks of the Mori of Choshu had been restored and they had been given permission to enter the capital. The five court nobles, including Sanjo Sanetomi, who had been in Dazaifu near Fukuoka also had their court ranks restored and they were permitted to reenter Kyoto. A complete change had taken place. Yoshinobu and the representatives of Aizu and Kuwana had been excluded, and both Aizu and Kuwana were relieved of guard duty at the imperial palace. The offices of regent and civil dictator were eliminated. From that point on the shogunate was completely finished. The news had come from Kyoto in one of Keizo's letters, addressed to Hanzo as well as to Kozo. Kozo was bringing the letter to Hanzo.

"In an earlier letter from Kyoto, I learned something else. At almost the same time that Yoshinobu submitted his resignation to the emperor, reliable sources reported that a secret envoy from the emperor had been sent down to Satsuma and Choshu, ordering the overthrow of the shogunate. What do you think about that? They say that the envoy was quickly called back, but I wonder about that, too. I thought it was all very strange and I was just putting the letter away without showing it to anyone when this news of the restoration of antiquity came."

"Look here!" responded Hanzo. "In this letter it says that Owari was guarding the palace gates that day. It says that the men guarding the outside of the palace were the lord of Owari's bodyguard under Ose Shintaro and that their comrades were guarding the interior."

"Well, this may be a bit premature, but it looks as though the coup of the eighteenth of the eighth month of last year has been reversed. I was in Kyoto then and I saw that incident, so I can pretty well imagine what this one must have been like. At any rate something must have happened to bring things this far. This is certainly the final stage."

The two exchanged glances, then their conversation moved to the master Kanetane in Kyoto. Katsushige brought in some pine firewood, broke it up, and fed the fire in the hearth. The master of the teahouse, saying that he would serve his guests something warm, began to roast some fish on skewers.

"Well, Hanzo," said Kozo in an altered tone of voice, "I really didn't have all that much hope that this restoration would be different from the one that failed in the fourteenth century. It will go all the way back to Jimmu. Things have worked out well—I had thought we would have to wait ten years to get this far."

"After all, it was just a matter of someone's pointing out what was needed in these times."

"Yes, but it is best not to ask who it was that whispered such an idea into the ears of the people around Iwakura. Now in that manuscript I loaned you —isn't that just what the person who wrote it said? 'Arising from the grass roots.' That was enough."

"When it comes to that, Kozo, I've been wondering if Kanetane sensei has really been as quiet as he seems. When you look back at it now, he must surely have been doing something. And Kureta Masaka and the others said that they were going to Kyoto to put in a word. We'll never know just how many people worked behind the scenes to bring us to this day."

"It would be a great mistake to think that this restoration of antiquity could have been brought about by only two or three people."

"So then it's possible to see Motoori's *Commentaries on the Kojiki* as having been written to open the way for this day."

They were soon distracted by the aroma of the skewered fish cooking in the pot which the owner of the teahouse had put over the fire. The heated sake that Hanzo had ordered was brought. It was still a bit early in the day when the exchange of sake cups accompanied by miso and vegetables began beside the hearth at the teahouse.

"Sir," said the owner of the teahouse as he came over, "the merchants who pass through often bring salted squid with them. They have left some here. How would that go?"

Hearing the name of one of his favorite delicacies, Hanzo replied, "That would be excellent."

"There is nothing better than salted squid with grated horseradish," said Kozo, echoing the sentiment.

"Some beancurd soup will soon be ready. Please take all the time you wish," said the teahouse owner.

"Have a drink, Katsushige!" said Kozo.

"My father says I mustn't drink until I have my coming of age ceremony," said Katsushige, blushing slightly.

"Now, you don't have to say that. Today is special. But how about it, Katsushige? Did you think the shogunate would fall?"

"I didn't really think so. Although I did think that the time of the Tokugawa was going to end sooner or later."

"I suppose not. Because nobody ever dreamed that Yoshinobu would resign his office. Katsushige, you know the sound of bamboo breaking under a heavy snowfall. That's just how it sounded. I thought of bamboo breaking when I heard that Yoshinobu had resigned. When you think about it, it is amazing that this restoration of antiquity was achieved without terrible bloodshed. You have to give Yoshinobu credit for that."

"But, Kozo," Hanzo interjected, "what you were just saying—that we achieved the restoration without wholesale bloodshed. Doesn't that show our character as a nation? I don't think that could happen in other countries."

"That's right too," said Kozo.

"I just went to bed one night and when I woke up the next morning, the restoration of imperial rule had come," said Katsushige, addressing both Hanzo and Kozo.

"At last, at last!"

Saying this, Hanzo exchanged cups of mountain sake with his friend. Their drinks were accompanied by the skewered fish, the salted squid with grated radish, and the sliced radish and turnip pickles of which the master of the teahouse was so proud.

The winter sun poured into the teahouse, flooding everything with its light. After their meal, Hanzo and his companions went outside and walked across the road to the Basho memorial. The toes of their sandals glistened in the melting snow, and the more they walked the greater was the joy they felt. All the real changes were yet to come, but for now, back to the founder, the emperor Jimmu! To the starting point in distant antiquity! Just to think that the day of reconstruction had come caused a bold and great vision to rise before Hanzo's eyes.

And to Hanzo's mind came the words of the late master Atsutane, which he had found in *The Tranquil Cave:*

"All things are as the gods would have them."

BOOK
TWO

CHAPTER ONE

1

THE SHIPS of the "southern barbarians," as we used to call the Dutch, painted by Maruyama Okyo in the eighteenth century appear to have been three-masted sailing vessels that crossed the vast oceans under wind power. They were clumsy, old-fashioned trading vessels that had to be towed in and out of port. Nevertheless, whenever such vessels appeared off Nagasaki, signal fires would blaze up on the headlands, the guard stations would stir to life, and officers would hurtle off like arrows in all directions, some to the office of the commissioner and others to the magistrates' offices.

Try to imagine a trading vessel of eighteen sails. It would be one hundred sixty to one hundred seventy feet in length, have a beam of about fifty feet, and its hull would be some thirty to forty feet deep from rail to keel. It would carry about twenty cannon for protection against pirates and privateers. This would be a "southern barbarian" ship of the kind that came here as late as the 1840's. Okyo's picture of one of these ships shows the white banners of the Dutch factory of Dejima flying in the foreground and a great thunderhead in the skies over the harbor in the background. In the scene captured by the painter's brush, the ship has two lines fixed to its bow and it is being towed by a dozen or so Japanese boats. All sails are drawing on both the ship and the towboats.

The Black Ships that came from the mid-1850's on were no longer of that old-fashioned kind. They were steamships, sidewheelers. So much were the old times and the new intermingled that most of them were still dependent on the winds when navigating the open seas, even though they no longer had to be towed in and out of port.

Not only had the three outlying ports of Yokohama, Nagasaki, and Hakodate been opened by the power of these Black Ships, but those of Hyogo and Osaka as well, giving access to the commercial heartland of the nation. In fact, the opening of the port of Hyogo had been one of the original aims of the American Perry, and it had become an issue so bitterly fought between court and shogunate that the shogun himself had threatened to resign. Just what kind of people were coming to Japan on these Black Ships? At this point we had best go back and have a look at them.

2

Not all of the people whom we then called "redhairs" or "hairy Chinamen" were completely ignorant about this island nation of Japan. Those who had taken the trouble to look at the works of Engelbert Kaempfer knew that already in the late seventeenth century a Dutchman with a knowledge of science and medicine had come to this country. He had carefully observed Japanese society and the physical environment. This Dutchman lived in Japan for two years and traveled from Nagasaki to Edo and back in the party of the Dutch factor. He saw not only Edo but Kokura, Hyogo, Osaka, and Kyoto as well, leaving for those who came after him records of the hinterlands which were largely unknown to Europeans of that time. In these records he described the port of Hyogo. According to his account, Hyogo was in the province of Settsu, some ten or eleven miles from Akashi, and its harbor was enclosed on the south by a substantial barrier that jutted eastward into the sea from the foot of the Suma mountains. He reported that this was not a natural formation but that it had been built in the twelfth century by the Taira family as part of efforts to improve the harbor. An immense amount of labor must have been required to complete it. It had been twice destroyed by storms before a hero of the Taira at last cast himself into the ocean to calm the waves. Kaempfer also reported that Hyogo was the best port between Shimonoseki and Osaka and that when his party landed there, they found more than three hundred ships at anchor in the harbor. Although there was no castle at Hyogo, the town appeared to be about the same size as Nagasaki. The dwellings along the shore were rude buildings with thatched roofs but there were said to be large homes inland.

People like this had already scouted the way. The travel accounts of the Dutchman Kaempfer afford the best possible proof of how intensively foreigners had sought to comprehend the politics, religion, customs, mores, and products of this country. The image of the Japanese that registered in Kaempfer's eyes was one of uprightness and integrity. Nor did the Japanese slight the deities that had hitherto been unknown to them; once they declared their faith, their pride would never permit them to alter their vows. Aside from this pride and their weakness for quarrels, they were gentle and quick of mind and possessed of a curiosity beyond that of all other peoples. In their hearts the Japanese hoped for commercial relations with foreign nations and they longed to master the learning and technology of Europe. But at the same time they looked upon the Europeans themselves as mere traders and therefore of the lowest class of people. Kaempfer felt that this attitude was probably grounded in jealousy and mistrust and that it would be well if now, when they wished to establish friendly relations and to learn from others, they gave more attention to this problem. The most important thing was to get the people of this country to deal with financial matters without feeling ashamed, for them to calm their fears and to establish friendly relations with other nations. With these goals in mind, Kaempfer instructed all the Japanese who came into contact with him in pharmacology and astrology, gave them Western drinks, and, after finally winning their trust, went with extraordinary freedom wherever he wanted to go. In this way he came to know thoroughly this nation that had so long been closed away in secret from the world.

Kaempfer left many stories concerning the travels of the first Dutchmen to journey to the Far East. On the occasion when their party had just arrived in Edo for the first time, they were conducted to the great castle in which the fifth shogun, Tokugawa Tsunayoshi, was then living. They first came to a place called the "hundred man guard," a huge barracks for the guards of Edo castle. There they were ordered to wait, and were told that they would be received in audience by the shogun as soon as a conference of high officials was completed. Two samurai entertained these unusual guests graciously with tea and tobacco, and presently other officials came in to greet the party. They waited about thirty minutes, during which time the shogun's council and the other great ministers arrived, either on foot or in palanquins, to assemble within the palace. Then they were led through two gates and around a great open square into the palace, ascending several stairways. The space between the inner gate and the entrance hall of the palace was only about six feet wide and quite confined, but a considerable number of guards and other officials were assembled there. The party then ascended two more stairways and entered a spacious chamber. From this chamber they were conducted to another room on their right. This was the place where anyone wishing audience with the shogun or the council had to wait until permission to proceed was granted. The room was very large and with all the surrounding panels closed, it was quite dark. Only a little light came in from the next room through the decorative fretwork above the panels. Even so they were struck by the beauty and richness of the decorations which had been carried out with the greatest care on both walls and ceilings. They waited here for more than an hour before the shogun entered the audience hall. The factor was conducted alone into the shogunal presence and a loud voice called out.

"Oranda Kapitan!"

This was the signal for the factor to perform his obeisance as he approached the shogun. The shogun's attitude, even when giving audience to the mightiest lords of the country, was always extremely haughty. Daimyo called into the presence of the shogun would creep up to him on their hands and knees, pressing their foreheads against the matting as they performed their obeisances. At the conclusion of the audience, they would crawl backwards in the same attitude. In exactly the same way, the factor placed the gifts he was offering to the shogun before him, kneeled, touched his forehead to the matting, and, without uttering a single word, crawled backward like a crab as he left the presence.

Thus did the Dutchmen humble themselves before this mighty lord. This self-abasement was not, of course, merely in observation of protocol; they submitted to it because they sought trade with this country. When Kaempfer was at last permitted to enter the audience chamber, he noted that all the mats on the floor were the same size and quickly counted their number at one hundred, indicating an area of approximately eighteen hundred square feet. He closely inspected the sliding panels separating the rooms, and the windows and decorations. There was a small garden at one side and the area on the opposite side was divided by sliding panels into two other rooms. All the panels were open so that all three rooms commanded a view of the garden. The shogun was seated in the smaller of the two side rooms. Kaempfer tried to get a glimpse of the shogun's face but it was extremely difficult to do because not much light reached in as far as the shogun's position, the audience was very brief, and the faces of those participating in the audience were bowed so low that they had no opportunity to look at the shogun. Moreover, the shogun's councillors and other high officials were sitting in rows facing them and the scene was so overwhelming that guests tended to lose their presence of mind.

The self-abasement of the party of the Dutch factor did not, however, end with this. In earlier times the only thing required of the factor was to appear in audience, but at some time during the intervening years a strange custom had come to be established. The factor's party was no longer permitted to leave the palace upon the conclusion of the audience. They were instead led into another part of the palace so that the occupants of the women's quarters could also have a look at the foreigners. As a practitioner of Dutch medicine, Kaempfer was one of three members of the party that were called out. They followed the factor far into the depths of the palace. Several rooms opened up on each other to form an immense chamber. One of the rooms was laid out with fifteen of the three-by-six-foot tatami mats and another with eighteen. The mats were on slightly different levels in accord with the rank of the persons who were to sit on them. In the central area there was no matting; it was part of a hallway and therefore had a floor of lacquered wood. There the Dutchmen were ordered to kneel. The shogun and the ladies of highest rank were behind screens on their right. After obeisances were repeated, the solemn palace suddenly became a scene of farce. The Dutch party became the target of all kinds of silly and absurd questions, such as the latest European techniques for prolonging life. At first, the shogun was seated among the ladies at some distance from the Dutchmen, but he gradually drew nearer, getting as close to them as possible. When he was sitting directly behind the screen, they were ordered by the attendant officials to remove the capes that were part of their formal attire and to stand up so that he could see all of them. Then they were asked to walk, to stop, to bow, to dance, to behave as though drunk, to speak Japanese, to speak Dutch, and to sing. When asked to dance, Kaempfer accompanied himself with a love song in High German.

The party of the Dutch factor thus lowered itself to providing light entertainment. Kaempfer, however, did not forget to observe the details of the women's quarters of Edo castle as he performed his dance. Twice he was able to make out the elevated seat of the shogun's consort behind the screens. He noted that she had lovely dark eyes; a brown-skinned beauty with a discon-

certingly large and elaborate coiffure. She seemed exceptionally tall and must
have been thirty-five or thirty-six years of age. The screens were made of
woven rush backed with beautiful silk gauze. Various designs were painted
on them both for ornamental effect and to conceal the people sitting behind
them. The shogun himself occupied a very dark area of the room; if it had
not been for the sound of his low voice, Kaempfer would not have suspected
that anyone was there. They were separated from these men and women of
high rank only by the screens. Kaempfer noticed that at many points thickly
folded bits of paper were thrust into the screens to hold the rushes apart and
improve the view. He surreptitiously counted them and, finding that there
were thirty in all, assumed that there must have been at least that many people behind the screens.

The Dutchmen performed in this way for two hours, executing every
imaginable trick to amuse the shogun and his companions. Only the factor
did not participate. He was a man of great presence and unshakable dignity,
and Kaempfer noted that even to the Japanese it apparently seemed too
demeaning to insist that this representative of his nation make a fool of himself.

The next year was the fifth of Genroku in Japan and 1692 by the Western
calendar. The factor was again required to journey to Edo. Kaempfer was
once again a member of the party and on this trip he was able to revisit the
hinterlands. They left Dejima in Nagasaki at the beginning of the third
month and traveled by ship to Hyogo. After landing they called on the Osaka
commissioner and the Kyoto constable. This second journey through the
country proved a boon to Kaempfer far beyond the opportunity it provided
to observe Japanese society and the countryside. At the residence of the
Osaka commissioner Kaempfer learned from that official himself that a member of his household had suffered from a chronic complaint for more than ten
years and was still not recovered. He was asked if he could treat the complaint. When he said that he would have to make an examination, the commissioner refused, saying that the complaint involved a very secret part of the
body and that he should therefore hear of the symptoms in detail, make his
judgment on that basis, and prescribe treatment. Kaempfer did as he was
asked. The Osaka commissioner was in turn fascinated by the customs and
artifacts of Kaempfer's country. He took up Kaempfer's hat, turned it over,
and examined the inside. He then went further, asking members of the party
to remove their jackets, to write in the horizontal writing of Europe, to
draw a picture, to sing a song, to dance, and to perform all kinds of other
actions peculiar to Europeans, but Kaempfer's party refused to perform.
When they called on the high constable of Kyoto, a Japanese man brought
out a barometer and questioned them on its construction and use. The
barometer proved to have been a gift from a Dutchman who had been
through more than thirty years earlier.

Late in the fourth month the party at last finished their long journey, finding themselves once more before Edo castle. Unfortunately, being a rainy

time of the year, it was difficult to go out but again they dressed themselves with care, left the civilian district of the city, passed through the gates of Edo castle, and entered the third enclosure to await the audience with the shogun. While they were waiting they exchanged their rain-soaked shoes and stockings for fresh footwear. Then they were led into the audience chamber, where they were received by a tall, long-faced old gentleman whose cast of countenance somehow made him appear German. His movements were languid and he gave an impression of great culture. He was the upright and austere Makino Bingo, the most powerful of the shogun's councillors, a man whom the Dutch had already met the previous year. It was Makino's duty to pass the Dutch gifts on to the shogun and to relay the shogun's words back to them. After the audience ceremony was concluded, the party was given a brief rest. They were permitted, through the good will of the Nagasaki commissioner, to examine thoroughly the room in which they found themselves. The shoji facing the garden were wide open, perhaps to afford plenty of light for the foreign guests, and they walked up and down the corridor to relieve themselves of the agony brought on by the formal Japanese kneeling posture. As they did so, several high-ranking persons greeted them and asked questions about foreign lands.

Presently they were called once again into the women's quarters. The people of the palace were gathered in the dimness behind the screens. The shogun and two women were behind a screen to the right of the party when Makino Bingo came and sat before them. When the obeisances had been satisfactorily performed, Makino greeted the party in the name of the shogun. Then he asked them to perform various acts. The Dutch received their instructions through their aged interpreter: Sit up straight. Take off your jacket. Tell your name and age. Stand. Walk. Spin around. Dance. Sing. Bow to each other. Behave as though angry. Demonstrate how you would invite a guest to dinner. Converse among yourselves. Behave as parent and child. Greet each other as close friends. As husband and wife. Demonstrate how you take leave of one another. Show how you play with a baby. Hold a baby in your arms. Do all kinds of other things.

As before, they were also the targets of numerous questions, both serious and frivolous. What kinds of houses do Dutchmen live in? How do their customs differ from those of the Japanese? Where do they bury their dead and on what days do they hold funerals? Do they pray and carry idols in the same way that the Portuguese do? In Holland and other foreign countries do they have earthquakes, thunder and lightning, and conflagrations just the same as in Japan? Are people killed by lightning in other countries?

In this austere palace, Kaempfer soon found himself and his companions transformed into buffoons. They were ordered to put on their hats, to walk around the room talking together, and to take off and display the seventeenth-century style wigs that they were wearing. In the course of these antics, Kaempfer reported that he had several opportunities to observe the shogun's consort. From the fact that they heard the shogun say, in Japanese, that the Dutchmen were giving very close attention to the room they were in, he inferred that the shogun had left his original position and had come down to the front to sit among the ladies. Next the visitors were asked to remove their wigs once more, for all of them to leap into the air together, to dance, to act as though drunk. The commands came in an unbroken stream. The Japanese asked the factor and Kaempfer to guess the age of Makino. The factor guessed fifty, Kaempfer guessed forty-five. They were then informed that this great minister, the most important of the shogun's councillors, had already reached the advanced age of seventy, and everyone laughed that they should have thought him so young. Next they were asked by the Japanese to kiss like husband and wife and the ladies of the palace observed this with laughter and pronounced themselves greatly pleased. They were then asked to perform polite gestures in the European style—toward those of inferior rank, toward those of superior rank, to ladies of high station, to noblemen and toward the king. Next Kaempfer was singled out to perform a song, which he did. At last the farce was ended. They put on their jackets and each in turn was conducted before the screen where they took their leave in the same way that they would have done of their own king. Kaempfer reported that their comic performances in the palace had lasted for more than two hours.

Before leaving Edo, Kaempfer and his party went once more to the shogun's palace to take their leave. After again being kept waiting for thirty minutes at the guard station, they were called before the council, who, as always, had their subordinates read an admonition to the Dutchmen. They were not to inflict any damage on ships from China or the Ryukyus and the Dutch must never bring a Portuguese person or a Christian priest to Japan on their ships. Free trade would be continued only if these conditions were met. When the reading was completed, three ceremonial footed trays were set before the factor. On each of the trays there were ten suits of Japanese formal clothing appropriate to a samurai of middle rank. These were gifts from the shogun to the factor. The factor accepted them with great correctness, lifting one of the garments, which was indigo dyed and marked with five crests, high above his head and humbly expressing his gratitude. Everyone was then led into another room where they were informed that they were to be given their noon meal at the order of the shogun. Small footed serving trays in the Japanese style were placed before each of the guests. Kaempfer reports that they found the repast to be far too simple to be in keeping with the power and the pride of that great lord.

That did not complete the leave-taking. It was reported that the ladies of the palace also wished to see them once again. A priest about thirty years of age, dressed in green and white robes, came to guide them. He gravely asked their names and ages and then conducted them to the women's quarters, to the same set of rooms with their screens of state. They were first required to make their obeisances in the Japanese manner and then to come close to the screen and repeat them in the European style. They were then requested to sing. Kaempfer selected a song which he addressed to one of the ladies whom he had particularly admired. He sang of her beauty and her virtue and that she was more precious than all the treasures of this world. When the shogun ordered a translation of the song, Kaempfer replied that he had selected it as nothing other than the most appropriate for a foreign dignitary who wished to pray for the health, happiness, and prosperity of the shogun, the emperor, and the entire Japanese court. As in the previous audiences, the Dutchmen were made to remove their jackets and walk around the room and the factor joined them this time. Then they were asked to demonstrate how they met with and parted from friends, parents, and wives, how they would go about insulting one another, how friends might dispute and how they might then be reconciled. When that ended, a shaven-headed priest approached Kaempfer, requesting his opinion on a matter of health. Kaempfer took his pulse and realized that he was in good health, but noting from the appearance of his face and his red nose that the man was fond of drinking, he warned him not to overindulge. When the shogun and the others heard this, they all laughed without restraint.

All this and more is described in great detail in the travel accounts that Kaempfer left us. It was a time when the shogunate was at the height of its power and prestige. The Dutch seem to have thought that they were expressing their gratitude for trading privileges before the emperor himself. They believed that they had had the privilege of entering the living quarters of the emperor when they were conducted into the women's quarter of Edo castle and that the priest who asked their names and ages must have been either a physician or a retainer in personal attendance upon the emperor. They also believed that the councillor Makino Bingo, who had greeted them, was the emperor's mentor and advisor, one in his complete confidence.

3

Commodore Perry, the American who came some one hundred and sixty years later, did not share the attitudes of the Dutch. He was in no way prepared to act the buffoon in order to gain the trading privileges hitherto denied the Americans. Acting on a basis of absolute equality, he stripped away the masks that the Dutch had worn, to carry out an important mission for his country.

Yet it must not be forgotten that the Dutch, who had come early to the Far East, left valuable guidance to those who came after them. If it be assumed that starting in 1633, when Japanese were forbidden to voyage overseas and the construction of vessels of more than five hundred koku capacity was forbidden, the people of this nation were altogether uninformed about conditions overseas and those in other countries were totally lacking in knowledge of Japan, that would be an overly hasty conclusion. The route that Perry took was said to have led from the east coast of the United States to Madeira, around the Cape of Good Hope to Mauritius, Ceylon, and Singapore, and from there into the China Sea, but in fact Perry had undergone a long preparation for the voyage before he left Annapolis. He had sought out everything that had been written about Japan. He had read the invaluable works of the great Siebold and he had asked the United States government to buy other books. He was said to have persuaded the government to spend $30,000 to obtain the charts that the Dutch had prepared. Although Japan was so distant from America and unknown in American literature, it was reported that there were no people of East Asia about whom there was more information in the libraries of Europe. Still, the thing that Perry particularly wanted to learn but failed to learn was the current political situation in Japan and the true relationship between the emperor and the "taikun," or shogun.

After sending two steamships ahead to the Cape of Good Hope and Mauritius, Perry set out on his long voyage in command of four warships. From American scientists and other scholars had come a request that a representative of their number be sent along on the voyage. This in itself shows what an utterly unprecedented venture this was. Before he came to pound on the door of the closed nation of Japan, Perry first gained a detailed knowledge of the seas around the Ryukyus and the Japanese seacoast. Then at last he set out to drive full tilt straight into Edo bay, ignoring all Japanese objections. Before Perry reached the Japanese mainland, he stopped off in the Ryukyus, where he had an interview with the king and his ministers, and then he went to the Ogasawara islands, where he left with the white men who were living there cattle, sheep, seeds, and other necessities, along with an American flag. He was not coming with small plans. When he landed at Kurihama in Uraga it was just at the middle of the nineteenth century, a time when European powers were advancing into the Far East. America, which was already selling raw cotton on the Chinese market, was fully aware of the potential importance of the Far Eastern trade, having followed Britain in signing a commercial treaty with China. Now it was America's turn to come into the Japanese mainland and onto the Korean peninsula. Determined to carry out his orders, Perry had firmly resolved that he would not repeat the performance of Commodore Biddle, who had sailed into Edo bay to demand the opening of the ports in the 1840's. In his character Perry was said to have combined "the charm of the Jesuits with the simplicity and straightforwardness of the stoics," and in his lack of any hesitation in making use of the fears of the Japanese, he was the personification of the self-assertive American. At any rate, it was through force that he realized his aim. Then he sailed away, leaving behind a telegraph, a locomotive, a lifeboat, a wall clock, agricultural implements, weights and measures, maps, navigational charts, and other gifts rare to the Japan of that time. However, just as the Dutch before him, he entrusted the letter from his government to the emperor of Japan to the shogunate without recognizing the crucial fact that it could not be transmitted to Kyoto through those channels.

All the people who came in the Black Ships from that time on struggled to determine just where sovereignty actually resided in this country. This was true of Harris, the first American consul, and Elgin, the British envoy. The steamboat that the British envoy presented was intended as a gift to the emperor of Japan, but the Edo officials accepted it as a gift to the shogun and made no effort to send it on to Kyoto. It seemed to make no difference whether Kyoto existed or not. The military leaders who had usurped sovereignty controlled all military forces and they held all political power firmly in their grip.

The resident foreigners became aware of this distinction only gradually. People like the British ambassador Parkes appeared. The shogunate attempted to deceive Parkes into believing that the shogun was the supreme lord and held imperial power. When Parkes tried to force the opening of the port of Hyogo and the markets of Osaka, he was surprised to find that only then did the imperial assent come down for the treaty of commerce which had been signed years earlier. This enabled him at last to isolate the true locus of sovereignty. Considering all these circumstances, it is not at all strange that there should have been such violent arguments between the French ambassador Roches, who sympathized with the shogunate and supported the established policy for the opening of the ports, and the British ambassador Parkes, who understood that a revolution was taking place in this country and was encouraging the great western han of Japan.

4

What we have to say today is of the greatest importance. It is considered as such by the president of the United States. What we have to say will be spoken out of feelings of the deepest friendship and it is our hope that it will be heard in that spirit.

I want to quote briefly from the transcript of the oral statement by Townsend Harris, the first American consul. I want to let him speak for himself as the representative of America, as one who had come to open the markets of the Far East. Here is the core of the statement that Harris made at the official residence of Hotta Bichu no Kami in 1857, the fourth year of Ansei, after he had been granted an audience with the shogun.

. . . permit me to say exactly what is on our president's mind now that I have once again carefully examined the letters to your great lord the shogun from the president of the United States. It has proven difficult to make clear the extremely high regard in which our president holds the Japanese government, but in the following, out of the most sincere feelings of good will, he has chosen to speak directly without holding anything in reserve. Since the treaty which you have deigned to conclude with the United States is the first treaty that your honored nation has ever concluded with a foreign power, our president feels differently about your honored nation than he does about other countries, and he has the warmest feelings of friendship for Japan. The way in which the United States conducts its business is different from the way other nations conduct theirs, and we have no desire to acquire any new territorial holdings in the Far East. It is forbidden to the United States government to acquire new territories outside our own continental area. From time to time we have received requests from other countries that they might be made a part of the United States, but in every case where they have been distant from us this request has been refused. Just three years ago the Sandwich Islands requested to be made a part of the United States but they were refused. Although the United States has formed alliances with other countries, this has never been through force of arms, but only through treaty. I have told you this so that you may understand the customs of the United States.

. . . during the past fifty years there have been many changes in the West. Since the invention of the steamship even your esteemed nation, remote from us as it is, now seems very close. Since the invention of the telegraph, distant events may be quickly known. With steamships we can reach Japan from California in only eighteen days. With steamships trade has gradually grown more active in all quarters. That is why the wealth of the Western nations has increased. It is the hope of the nations of the West that through the use of the steamship all the world may become one. Those nations that stand in opposition to this vision and refuse external trade stand in the way of the unification of the world, and that opposition must be eliminated. No government has the right to stand in the way of this unification.

. . . We have two requests to make concerning this unification. The first is that we be permitted to station a person of ambassadorial rank in your capital. The second is that trade with all nations be made completely free. This is the desire not only of the United States but of all nations.

. . . Japan is in great danger. That danger comes from the other European powers. Britain is looking forward to a war with Japan. Let me tell you why. Britain is very much concerned about its East Indian holdings. Both Britain and France are likely to go to war with Russia because of Russia's habit of continually annexing territory. Russia holds Sakhalin and it is quite clear to Britain that from there they intend to take over Manchuria and China. If Manchuria and China were to fall under the domination of the Russians, they would then be powerful enough to take over British East India; and if that should be threatened there would surely be a war between Britain and Russia. If such a war should come about, Britain, in order to protect its right flank, which would be seriously menaced, would want to take control of Sakhalin, Hokkaido, and the port of Hakodate. Those places would be of great utility in resisting Russia. Britain is far more interested in Hokkaido than in Manchuria, which is directly contiguous to Russia.

Foreign countries were as yet an unknown quantity for most Japanese. As a result of the long policy of exclusion, Japan was no longer very clear even about affairs in East Asia, much less the world as a whole, and we were instructed in a great many prejudices by this first American consul. What did Harris say had changed the West in the previous fifty years? He said that it had been the invention of such communication facilities as the steamship and the telegraph. He said that it had been only since the invention of the steamship that the desire to unite the world through trade had come into being.

He further maintained that China and Japan had been left to their own resources because they did not maintain trade relationships like the Western nations. Eighteen years earlier China had fought a war with Britain. If there had been a British emissary resident in the Chinese capital, that would never have happened. He spoke of the attitude of the Chinese government, saying that it had been a serious miscalculation to think that everything could be handled by the commissioner in Canton, that the refusal of the government to deal directly with the foreigners had led to a breakdown in communications, that the Canton commissioner had falsified his reports and told the government only what he wanted them to hear while at the same time being extremely arrogant in his treatment of the British. That had been the cause of the war. A million Chinese had lost their lives in that war and not only had China's ports been taken over by the British but the capital city of Nanking itself had been conquered. China had been required to pay Britain an indemnity amounting to five million large gold coins. He said that China had originally been wealthy but because of conflicts like this it had grown weak. Just last year they had lost still more strength in their war with the Tartars. Moreover, with the British and the French joining to wage war against China it was difficult to see where it all would end. Under present conditions, China had no choice but to do Britain's bidding. If they did not, all of China was likely to end up as British territory. It appeared that France wished to occupy Korea and Britain to occupy Taiwan. It was important for Japan to take careful note of this. Harris swore before heaven that if there had been a diplomatic agent in Peking, this war would never have taken place. When the American president received requests from France and Britain to join in the war against China, he had refused. Of course, America was also displeased with the way the Chinese were handling their affairs. Twice Chinese fortresses had fired without provocation on American warships. The American admiral, Armstrong, was angered and he destroyed four of the batteries at the entrance to the harbor at Canton. Yet America had never joined the British in fighting against the Chinese. In counting the origins of the conflict in China, one was certainly opium. Opium was produced in British East India. Although opium was doing great harm in China, Britain made no effort to stop the trade, because it was so profitable. Instead they armed the ships that carried opium and continued the trade in secret. It is the opinion of the president of the United States that for Japan opium is still more dangerous than war. The president urged that special attention be given to the opium trade in Japan. If by any chance opium should be brought in by Americans, American authorities trust that the Japanese officials will seize and destroy it or take any other measures that seem appropriate. Nor would they have the slightest objection if fines were also to be imposed in addition to the confiscation.

Harris's oral statement continues:

. . . the president of the United States swears to you that considerations of national security demand that Japan should open her ports, commence trade, and accept embassies just as other countries do.

. . . Japan has had the good fortune to experience war only through historical texts; she has not seen it on her own soil. This is a great blessing. It is due entirely to your nation's being located in the distant East. If your country had been in close proximity to Britain and France, or to even just one of them, there would have been a war long before now. At the end of that war there would have been no way to avoid concluding a treaty. It is the hope of our president that treaty relationships may be established in mutual respect without having to go to war. A famous Western general has said, "It is better to win victories peacefully and unspectacularly than to win through battle."

. . . that which my president now has me saying to you is motivated by feelings of good will, and without any reservations. It is different in that respect from what is being said to you by other heads of state. Please reflect carefully on what I have said. On the current issue of the opening of the ports, it would clearly be in your best interests to look upon it not as a mere temporary concession but as a permanent disposition. My president reminds you that there will be no such consideration given you when you conclude a treaty with the British. Although many other countries are sending envoys to request the conclusion of treaty relationships, none of them will tell you the kinds of things that the United States, greatest of nations in the world, has just told you even though you might ask them. The president of the United States will make no unreasonable demands and he asks only that you give your consent on a basis of absolute equality with the people of the United States of America.

. . . the manners and customs of the foreign nations are very different now from what they were when you expelled the Spanish and the Portuguese some two hundred years ago. At that time, they wanted to convert everyone. In America religion is left to the wishes of each individual; none is prohibited, none imposed. People believe as they see fit. Now in Europe, this basis of belief is beginning to be recognized. Although there are many different sects, they all make men better. In America, Christian churches and Buddhist temples may stand side by side where both can be seen with the same glance, and it is understood that religions do not lead men into evil ways but that each in its own way enables us to pass our days in peace. When the Spanish and the Portuguese came to Japan they followed their own will, not that of your government. At that time they tried to carry on trade, to spread their religion, and furthermore to take possession of Japan through warfare. Such people as these were not straightforward and open but carried with them the intention of raising rebellions, and they were judged for doing so. Fortunately there are none like them among those who come at present.

. . . present customs are based on a sincere and friendly desire to unify the world, to transport wealth from one place to another, and to bring about equality. If, for example, Britain should have a shortage of food due to a series of crop failures, nations with abundant food would pause in their trading and send foodstuffs. Now, while trade relationships may seem to be limited to material commodities, yet another aspect of trade lies in the fact that new inventions soon become known to everyone, increasing the wealth of all nations. When nations trade freely with one another, the people of each nation may come to know the entire world. Agricultural production is of course most important, but not everyone in a nation engages in agricultural production. There are also craftsmen and entrepreneurs and they all complement one another. Depending on the country, it may be that in one place handicrafts can be beautifully executed for a good price. Those handicrafts that are produced in excess of the needs of the country of origin may be sent to another country, making available there products that are not produced locally. Therefore, through trade, great numbers of products can be made and one can enjoy access to foreign goods. Things which a country does not itself produce are readily available; that is the essence of trade. Since trade is truly convenient and is carried out in a spirit of benevolence, people naturally come to avoid wars. Of course, whenever commodities are brought into a nation from abroad, a tariff is paid on them. In America, internal expenses are paid out of these tariffs and the remainder is stored away year by year in the national treasury. We have various other kinds of tax laws, too, as it is not sufficient to rely solely on the income from taxes levied on imported goods.

. . . although at present the entire East India region has become British territory, it was originally divided into several countries that refused to conclude treaties with the West. The region was therefore unified by Britain. From this you can see that countries that try to stand alone may suffer grievous loss. It is most important that Japan and China give careful thought to the precedent of East India. Consider that if Japan chooses to open trade relations, then the flag of your nation will be seen in the harbors of the world. If a person with particularly good eyesight were to climb to the top of a tall mountain, he would see hundreds of American whaling vessels gathered in Japanese waters to carry on whaling. Thus Japan would, with ludicrous ease, attain from another country the benefits of a difficult enterprise in which she does not herself engage.

. . . according to those with privileged information, the present war being conducted by France and Britain against China is not likely to continue for long. That being the case, British and French envoys will soon be coming to this country. I hesitate to presume to give advice to such distinguished gentlemen, but I believe it to be of the greatest importance that you decide now how you are going to deal with them. It is my belief that there is no other course open to you than to conclude treaties with them. If I were to send notice under my own name to the high officials of France and Britain, informing them that Japan was prepared to conclude a treaty of commerce with us and to deal with other countries as well, then the fifty steamships that would otherwise be coming here would become one or at the most two or three. Today I have informed you of the intentions of the American president and of the thoughts of the British government.

. . . I count this day as the happiest day in my life. If what I have said today should be acted upon, so that Japan finds itself in a secure position, nothing would make me happier. What I have said reflects the present state of the world without prettifying of any kind.

That is what I have to say.

Such was Harris's long speech.

What this early arriving American taught us began, for better or worse, to have its effects upon the people of Japan. Unlike Commodore Perry, Harris was not trying to open the nation through force. He knew a great deal about Japan. He recognized the state of affairs in Japan and foreigner though he was, here was a man whom we could trust. What Harris taught us, at a time when the opening of the country was still controversial, settled into the breasts of the Japanese to become guiding assumptions. It had all the more influence on those who heard it at a young and impressionable age.

CHAPTER TWO

1

A DOZEN OR SO merchant ships and several warships rode at anchor in the harbor at Hyogo. They had come from Yokohama, from Nagasaki, from Hakodate, and from Shanghai. Half the foreign ships were British and the next most numerous were French; comparatively few were American. In all there were hundreds of ships and boats in the harbor—everything from sailing vessels of one and two masts to the great ocean-going ships of the foreign powers down to scows, barges, and rowboats. Some were under way, some were at anchor. The skies over the harbor and far out to sea resounded to a twenty-one gun salute from the foreign vessels offshore.

This was the seventh day of the twelfth month of Keio 3, 1867, and shore preparations were not yet complete for the opening of the port of Hyogo. Britain, America, France, and the other great powers, suspecting that the port of Hyogo was not going to be opened on the day specified in the treaties, had decided to make a show of force while checking on the progress of preparations for the opening. When the agreed-upon day arrived, the housing for the foreigners was not finished. However, a new customs house built in a mixture of Western and Japanese architecture now stood on the lonely seashore to the east of the village of Kobe. The local people delighted in it, calling it the "glass house." Three piers had been built and three warehouses completed. Things were not yet quite in readiness for the foreign and local tradesmen to commence business but the scene was clearly one of intense activity. The consuls of the foreign powers had raised their national flags before their temporary residences.

By the first month of the following year, when the day for the ending of the long age of isolation had come, all forms of confrontation between old and new came pouring in over this country like a flood. There were reports that in Edo a group of ronin led by Sagara Sozo of Satsuma was planning a series of break-ins, to set fires and commit robberies and do whatever else they could to create panic and confusion. Their militant attitude gave rise to rumors that a direct confrontation between the great han of western Japan and the shogunate itself had taken place not far away, on the banks of the Yodo river. It was said that a fierce engagement lasting four days had ended with the retreat of the Aizu forces. This soon came to be known among the foreigners resident in Hyogo and Kobe. One foreign ship sailed to carry the alarm to Yokohama and others set out for Nagasaki and Hakodate.

Such were the times that had come to this land upon which the foreigners now gazed from the once-protective sea. The battles between imperialist forces and those loyal to the Tokugawa had already been fought at Toba and Fushimi. There was literally a rumor to cover every imaginable situation. Some said that war had broken out between the "mikado," or emperor, and the "taikun," or shogun. Others said that it was a war of the new Kyoto government against the old Edo government and still others said that it was a war between the great provincial lords of the north and the south. The commerce which had gotten off to such a lively start was brought to a stop and only trade in guns and ammunition continued. There were serious doubts about the future of Japanese foreign relations.

Mermet de Cachon, the secretary attached to the French mission, was concerned about the disturbed state of affairs. He came down to Hyogo in a courier vessel from Yokohama to see for himself. In Hyogo, the French consul was renting a house pending the completion of his official residence. De Cachon joined his compatriot, reporting to him that almost all the foreigners living in the Edo area were now gathered in Yokohama. A detachment of marines from the British, American, French, and other warships was guarding the foreign residential areas. He reported that something of the same sort seemed to have been happening in Nagasaki also. It was not a time when Hyogo and Kobe would be able to do any differently. A man came to see the French consul. His name was Ikushima Shirodayu and he was the headman of the village of Kobe. He had only just been placed in charge of this district and he had come to point out that there were a great many warriors passing through on their way to the capital. Since the greater part of them knew absolutely nothing about foreign ways there were bound to be clashes. He requested that for the time being foreigners not walk out on the highways in the vicinity of Kobe.

"Where is the Hyogo commissioner?"

De Cachon relayed this question from the consul to the headman. Although he was no interpreter, de Cachon could speak Japanese.

"The commissioner?" asked the headman. "The commissioner is no longer in Hyogo."

Through de Cachon the consul made several protests. This amounted to utter anarchy. You are asking that foreigners not walk out but the terms of the treaty accord them the right to move about freely within a radius of twenty-five miles of Kobe. Hadn't the people of Hyogo and Kobe opened this new port in the hope of improving general conditions? De Cachon could not translate such details but he did succeed in getting his meaning across to the headman.

"Nevertheless," the Kobe headman replied, "it is going to be dangerous for you to go out for any great distance."

The Hyogo commissioner had already fled and the troops dispatched to guard the new port area were also gone. The few people who dared to be out on the streets were forming themselves into small groups for mutual protection. There was, aside from these measures, only the detachment of troops put ashore from the foreign warships to protect the foreign residents. The warriors of the western han were coming up to the capital because of their commitment to the imperial cause, and others were bringing reports of conditions back to the residences maintained by their han in Kyoto and Osaka. They were moving through Kobe and Hyogo night and day.

2

Thus was the new age unveiled. The port of Hyogo-Kobe was at center stage in the opening of the nation, and there it was acted out. To understand what happened it is necessary to know something of the difficult state of foreign relations at this time.

Alcock was the British emissary who had come to Japan before Parkes, and in Alcock's words, the foreign countries did not like war. Nor did they covet other nations' lands. There were only three conditions that could lead to the opening of hostilities. These were when treaties were concluded but not lived up to; when foreigners were killed for no reason; or when trade relationships were hindered out of groundless suspicion of foreigners.

Unfortunately, the same kind of incident that had occurred some years earlier in the village of Namamugi near Yokohama now took place at Sannomiya in Kobe very shortly after the restoration of imperial power. It occurred, moreover, in the context of the unrest and disorder that had come about when the new government in Kyoto ordered the punishment of Tokugawa Yoshinobu, set up a field headquarters for the campaign, and placed the imperial prince Taruhito in command, ordering him to proceed to Kyoto at the head of the troops of the loyalist han.

It was the eleventh day of the first month of Keio 4, 1868. An Englishman living in Hyogo was killed by a retainer of Bizen who was on his way to Kyoto. Another person was wounded while a third who fled the scene ran to the shore to report the incident to the warships at anchor there. British, French, and American warships had been in the harbor ever since the opening of the port. The British commander who received this report interpreted it as meaning that the Hyogo-Kobe area was in a state of complete anarchy and that it was necessary to protect the foreign residents. He hurriedly consulted with the French and Americans and then put troops ashore. A detachment of British troops advanced to where the Bizen troops were encamped at Ikuta and challenged them. Three squads of British troops then put up palisades within the town and prepared to fight. They occupied both gates of the Osaka road, stopping all samurai and other armed persons from passing, and placed the area under strict guard. Not only that, but the foreign warships in the harbor prevented the seventeen Western-style military transports belonging to various han from moving, and for a time the British took over the port facilities of Kobe.

The landing of the British marines led to panic among the residents of Hyogo and Kobe. They were terrified by the sudden preparations by the British for actual fighting. The sound of occasional small arms fire could be heard coming from Ikuta, and there was a rumor that the outnumbered Bizen forces, unable to resist the British, had fled in disorder toward Mt. Maya. These totally unexpected incidents caused panic among most of the people who lived along the roads.

When evening came, it was reported that the body of the Englishman had been carried away from the scene on a stretcher. The incident had begun when men of the Bizen retainer Heki Tatewaki, on their way to Kyoto, were just starting to eat their noon meal at Sannomiya in Kobe. Three Englishmen had tried to cut through the procession. Although the foreigners had been warned about being out on the highways by the Kobe headman Ikushima Shirodayu, his warning did not seem to have been fully understood. The Englishmen did not know about local customs that made cutting through such a procession a grave offense. It all came down to a failure to be understood. When one of the Bizen vanguard, thinking to correct the situation, made a threatening gesture with his lance, one of the Englishmen took a knife out of his pocket and assumed a posture of defiance. That could not be tolerated. The Bizen warrior became enraged, killing one of the men and wounding another. As a consequence of that killing the foreign troops were landed. These were the British who had taken such a firm attitude ever since the Namamugi incident. There was now no commissioner resident in Hyogo such as would normally mediate such a dispute. The Hyogo commissioner, Shibata Yoshinaka, was a shogunal official who had sensed the danger he would be in once a change of government took place and he had long since vanished. When he fled, he threw himself into a common litter wrapped in straw matting so that it would look like a consignment of merchandise being taken from one of the merchants to a ship. He had himself carried down to the shore, where he got on board a ship and sailed away. Dusk was beginning to fall on the scene in Kobe. Most of the local people were gathering their furniture and possessions together. Some of them were transporting things in secret to nearby villages. Others were directing the children and old people to take refuge in out of the way farmhouses.

By chance a Choshu ship from Osaka with three hundred Choshu soldiers on board arrived that night in Hyogo. It seems that they had been sent with orders to protect the port of Hyogo and the revenue it was bringing in now that the Kyoto-Osaka area had been pacified. The British knew nothing about this, and mistakenly assuming that a great force of Bizen men was coming into the port, they were on the point of opening fire. Even though the Choshu men denied that they were connected with Bizen, the foreigners did not believe them. Some of the Choshu soldiers became angry and demanded a reprisal against what they considered the cavalier attitude of the foreigners. At that point, cries were raised that the village was in danger of being set afire by the soldiers, further adding to the fears of the local people. The commander of the Choshu detachment had established himself at the residence of the honjin Takazaki Yagobei. Lanterns bearing the Choshu crest were hanging on either side of the gate, signifying that those within were Choshu soldiers, while within Yagobei's residence conferences were being held with British officers. By that time even the foreigners understood that these were not Bizen soldiers, but they refused to relinquish control of the area to them. The Choshu forces had no choice but to withdraw to the Zenshoji temple in the village of Okuhirano. Setting up their headquarters there, they moved out into the night to provide security to Hyogo and the surrounding area and to warn everyone of the emergency.

With the arrival of the Choshu troops, the residents of Hyogo and Kobe were at last able to get a good night's sleep. Having known no peace of mind for the previous two weeks, they now came in an endless stream to the Choshu troops in control to tell them of the terror of the preceding days and nights. Since the fall of the shogunate, not only had the sudden changes led to the flight of the Hyogo commissioner but many of the troops formerly attached to him had lost all restraint due to uncertainty about their positions and the failure to receive their wages. Together with self-proclaimed ronin they had run wild in the town, extorting loans that were really nothing more than armed robbery. The worst would smash in doors in broad daylight and terrorize the residents, taking whatever they pleased. The landing of the foreign troops had taken place while this was happening and each resident had taken measures to protect himself while awaiting in desperate anxiety the arrival of new representatives of authority.

Now, with the Choshu troops present, the townsmen could at last see smiles on each other's faces. They trusted the Choshu men to precisely the same degree that they had hated the shogunal authorities. Some came in to report that han officials who had been placed in charge of road construction by the Osaka magistrate had absconded with those funds. All kinds of errors of omission and commission were exposed. The resentment which the local people had long held against the shogunal officials came bursting out into the open. Without anyone seeming actually to suggest it and without anyone in particular seeming to start it, the chant of "ain't it all right" began to resound through the streets.

The chanting of "ain't it all right" still had not subsided by the fourteenth of the month. The voices of the crowds could be heard even by those in the new customs house on the shore at Kobe.

This was the so-called glass house, the first building to combine Japanese and Western architecture, built to commemorate the opening of the port at a time when buildings with glass windows had not yet been seen in Kobe. The foreign emissaries who had come down to Hyogo from their temporary residences in Osaka each brought along a secretary who was also a skilled interpreter. All in formal attire, they began to assemble in the large conference

room on the second floor of the building: Parkes, the British minister plenipotentiary, Roches, the French plenipotentiary, de la Tour, the Italian plenipotentiary sent over especially for the occasion, the Prussian von Brandt, the
Dutch van Polesbroek, and the American resident minister Van Valkenburgh.
It was the fourteenth and they had gathered in the Kobe customs house to
meet with the ministers of the new government in Kyoto.

The windows provided views of the district that had been set aside for foreign residences. While they were awaiting the arrival of the Japanese ministers, most of the diplomats went at one time or another to have a look. Kobe
sat under high bluffs and although its location made it already possible to
imagine something of its future prosperity, it was for now inescapably just
another newly opened port. The site for the future Dutch consulate was on
the edge of this little farming and fishing village and elsewhere construction
had already begun on what was to be the grounds of the British consulate. To
the south the sea glistened a bright blue. Five British ships, three French
ships, and one American ship could be seen riding at anchor in the harbor but
it was still not credible as a new seaport.

The sound of this silly, playful song came to the customs house. The voices
arose first in the direction of Sannomiya and gradually drew nearer. It had
been sung for more than a month and a half around the time of the resignation of the shogun in the previous winter and now it was being heard again.
This time the crowd gathered first in front of the shrine in Sannomiya and
then poured into the new port district around the customs house.

Wildly singing and dancing, they set up a tremendous noise. It was a festive mood such as was hard to connect with the people of this district who,
up to a few days earlier, had shown almost no signs of life. All the ministers
went to the window to look out at the excited crowd. Men with hand
towels wrapped around their foreheads were shoulder to shoulder with
others wearing pouches for flint and steel at their hips. There were women in
single dull gold or pale yellow underrobes, and men who had their hair done
up in topknots and headbands tied around their foreheads. It was a bold,
good-natured, and ridiculous procession. The foreigners at the windows
exchanged guesses about what might be taking place. Some asked what that
refrain meant but no one could answer. One of them, Mermet de Cachon,
opened one of the windows and shouted out "Bravo! Bravo!" to display his
approval of things Japanese. This young Frenchman was perhaps reminded of
the carnival season in his own country by this passing parade of young and
old, men and women, whose voices poured in like a great torrent.

In the meantime, the party of representatives of the new government came
in. It was headed by the councillor and minister in charge of foreign affairs,
Higashikuse Michitomi, and it included Terajima Munenori, Ito Hirobumi,
and Nakajima Sakutaro. This was the day of the new emperor's coming of
age ceremonies in Kyoto and the minister of the new government and his
attendants were solemn as they came into the room. Since this was the first
meeting, each official introduced himself in turn, giving name and title. All
the foreign dignitaries turned toward the head of the Japanese delegation.

Higashikuse Michitomi was wearing a tall black court headdress tied with purple cords and semi-formal robes. He carried a single sword at his hip in the fashion of a court noble. Ito Hirobumi, in formal Japanese jacket and trousers, was bustling about among the ministers. Ito had some years previously gone to England with Inoue Kaoru. Only Ito among all the members of the Japanese delegation had gotten rid of his samurai topknot and was wearing his hair short in the Western style. The entire group gave the impression of men newly appointed to their positions. Building and all, everything was a mixture of Japanese and Western styles. The furnishings were not yet complete and cheap chairs had been lined up to serve the needs of the occasion.

Presently Higashikuse took up the document bearing his official charge and holding it aloft in his right hand, read it aloud.

> The emperor of Japan addresses the kings and emperors of foreign lands and their ministers. The former shogun, Tokugawa Yoshinobu, has returned his political powers to me and I have taken full personal charge of all internal and external affairs. I therefore say to you that previously negotiated treaties, although concluded in the name of the shogun, shall henceforward be considered to be in the emperor's name and that all relations with foreign countries shall hereafter be carried out by me. May the ambassadors and representatives of all nations understand this.
>
> (In the imperial name)
>
> Tenth day, first month, Keio 4

This was the beginning of personal conduct of foreign affairs by the emperor.

In the afternoon, Parkes opened discussions with Higashikuse on the matter of the killing and wounding of the Englishmen at Sannomiya. Parkes was fully aware of the extremely disturbed state of affairs in the country at the time and he did not attempt to make a major issue of the matter. He agreed to relinquish Kobe that very day and immediately to withdraw the landing party. He named the single condition that the Japanese government see to it that the offender was severely punished.

Thus was the troublesome Sannomiya incident in the end quickly and easily resolved. As he spoke, Parkes stroked the curly whiskers growing in a patch on each of his plump cheeks with a certain elation.

"I have disposed of this matter with great forbearance as a token of good will toward the new government in Kyoto. This comes solely out of my esteem for your great nation; there is no other motivation. It will be very different when you open relations with other countries. This could never have had such a happy ending if the victims had been citizens of another foreign country."

His words were relayed through Mitford, his interpreter. Then, as though to confirm that what he had said was clearly understood, he extended his huge Englishman's hand for Higashikuse to shake.

* * * * * * *

It was a most gratifying period for Parkes. There was considerable reason why this British minister, the successor to Alcock, had assumed a stance in which he shook the hands of the warriors of Satsuma and Choshu with whom his country had previously fought as enemies, and had not hesitated to supply them with arms and ammunition. According to him, the entire world was now open and there was no nation that was not in contact with others. When nation was in contact with nation, the feelings of the various peoples could not help being in contact. The same would apply to commodity prices. Although there was a price to be paid for opening trading relationships, if, out of reluctance to pay that price, a nation interfered with free trade, it would certainly bring the greatest difficulties upon itself. The Europeans already knew this from long experience. The usual Eastern country had been concerned for centuries only with the rigid maintenance of custom. Trade was limited, foreign residents were restricted to certain areas, outside relationships were blocked altogether. We hoped to open things up, they hoped only to close them. As quarrels grew up about these matters, both sides grew unyielding, unwilling to consider giving up a single inch, and the matter had inevitably to be resolved with sword and gun. Therefore it has become necessary for both sides to arrive at a better understanding of each other. This has to be based on true information. Now why have the foreigners come to Japan? For no other reason than that they want to be on close terms with the government and with the Japanese people. Since the beginning of foreign trade no nation has ever been impoverished by this. If, by some unlikely chance, trade should result in a loss for one side, it would certainly be halted. If it was mutually profitable, it would surely continue to be carried on, and it was certain to produce wealth. If you trade, prices rise. If prices rise, imports decline. If too much is imported, trade becomes impossible. Therefore, the trade automatically regulates itself in the absence of conscious controls and trade can never fall into disorder.

Nor can the people of a nation ever be forced to face shortages.

In short, when human relations are arranged in such a clear and straightforward manner, with no twists and turns whatever, why should the Japanese look with such suspicion upon foreign nations? Is it that the residence of foreigners in Japan as provided for in the treaties will not be good for Japan? Will it do harm to the Japanese political order? Wouldn't everyone in Japan already be profiting from trade and be pleased thereat if only the spirit of the treaties had been followed? Certainly they would not be mistrustful, or see foreigners as enemies as they do today. This anti-foreign feeling arises solely out of the evil of the shogunate and the immense expenditures that the han have made since the beginning of foreign contacts. Its elimination must await the application of the power of the enlightened lords of Japan. Truly those who share the vision of the men of Satsuma and Choshu are most deeply concerned about this nation.

This was Parkes' position as he urged the adoption of the policy that the British had advocated ever since Alcock's time, rejecting the shogunate out of hand. Now he stood in the senior position among the foreign emissaries, flashing his arrogant smile across the table at the French, who were still committed to the shogunate.

Such a man was Parkes. As he had promised Higashikuse, he left the security of Kobe and Hyogo completely in the hands of the Choshu guards, immediately had the stockades taken down at both entrances to the highway, had the landing parties sent back to their ships, and gave permission to sail to all the ships belonging to the various han now in the harbor. Furthermore, he took up residence in temporary quarters in Hyogo, acting both as resident minister and consul, and watched the gradual emergence of a new order out of the anarchy that had prevailed in the region. The nature of the times was such that the Hyogo offices were first opened temporarily in the toiya meeting hall and then moved into the guard quarters formerly attendant upon the Osaka commissioner. When the day came for rebuilding the nation, all business had to be reconstituted under new rules and it seemed for a time almost unmanageable.

However, even among the emissaries, the attitude of the American representative toward the new government was a bit different. America had been the first foreign power to arrive in this country. The treaty that Japan had concluded with the United States was the first that it had ever concluded with a foreign country. The attitude of the British emissary in so peremptorily brushing aside priority of arrival was not pleasing to Van Valkenburgh, who thought of himself as the inheritor of a special friendship with Japan dating from the days of Townsend Harris.

Rumors came in that the imperial army charged with crushing the shogunate would soon set out along the Tokaido, the Tosando, and the Hokurikudo, the three great highways leading eastward. Prince Arisugawa, the commander-in-chief, had brought his brocade banner and sword of imperial command as far as Osaka. The persistent rumors that the nation now had an army of its own and was therefore no longer at the mercy of the shogunate had come to have some basis in fact. On the twenty-first, emissaries of six nations received a communication from Higashikuse informing them that the commander of the eastern expedition had initiated action. In this was read a warning not to bring in arms to assist Tokugawa Yoshinobu and his retainers. On the following day, the twenty-second, a garrison and court of law were set up in Hyogo and Higashikuse was placed in command.

This was the present atmosphere, but as recently as the third day of the last month of the previous year, Tokugawa Yoshinobu had called together all the foreign ambassadors in Osaka and announced to them that no matter what kind of political change might occur, he expected to continue to shoulder the responsibility for foreign relations. The emissaries now found it impossible to reverse their positions so suddenly and view the shogunate as a rebel party. When he saw this situation, Van Valkenburgh began to advocate a position of absolute neutrality for all the foreign powers. Thus he made clear the position of the United States as against the British, who were secretly supplying arms to the new government, and the French, who were supplying them to the shogunate.

Van Valkenburgh's proclamation was so correct that no one could directly oppose it. He stated that war had broken out between the mikado and the taikun and that the American people would maintain a posture of the strictest neutrality. The selling of warships or transport ships should be strictly forbidden. Not only the sending of troops but also the selling or lending of weapons, ammunition, supplies, or any other commodities relating to military needs should be strictly forbidden. If these rules were ignored by any party, that would be seen as a breach of the principle of absolute neutrality as defined under international law and would of course be viewed as a hostile act. If the perpetrators of such violations were taken under martial law, they should understand that neither the owner of the goods nor his accomplices would be able to escape misfortune. Under the terms of the treaty between the United States and Japan, it would be impossible for the Americans to protect even their own nationals if they should violate these strictures. An announcement to this effect was issued in Van Valkenburgh's name from the American mission in Kobe. None of the emissaries from the other nations having treaties with Japan made any open objection to the American statement. All of them followed the American lead, each country in the same language; only the name of the emissary was different. However, in the ports themselves, filled as they were with the most desperate kinds of adventurers, all was not so enlightened. The gunboat *Eugenie* was sold to Hizen for one hundred thousand dollars and the *Hinda* was sold for one hundred ten thousand dollars to Choshu. There were several other foreign vessels sold in the country, although the original owners and prices paid were not known in these cases. That the *Aterine,* which slipped into the port of Hyogo under cover of darkness, was for sale was immediately known to those interested in such matters.

3

At the beginning of the second month the emissaries at Hyogo all began making preparations to attend a conference in Osaka. This conference had been initiated by a statement signed by daimyo supporting the imperial cause including Shimazu of Satsuma, Mori of Choshu, Hosokawa of Kumamoto, Asano of Aki, Matsudaira Shungaku of Kaga, and Yamauchi Yodo of Tosa, saying that the business at hand could not be properly managed until procedures in foreign relations were clarified. They had now reached the stage of actually discussing the unprecedented step of receiving foreign ambassadors at court once the new government was recognized.

Nevertheless, the confidence of the foreign powers in the new government was still slight. It was after all a new government formed in that same Kyoto which had been known as a center of xenophobia. Even though they heard that the new government had given priority to carrying out reforms and opening the country, the foreign emissaries took conflicting positions and their doubts had not yet been resolved. The Sannomiya incident was seen as a sort of touchstone to test the sincerity and real power of the new government. On the ninth day of the second month, a letter of apology addressed to each of the emissaries arrived from Kyoto. It had been brought down by Mutsu Munemitsu and it was delivered to Parkes and the others by Terajima Munenori. It expressed the apologies of the new government at court for its negligence in the recent matter. It stated that in order to assure that relations hereafter could be carried on in an atmosphere of mutual trust, such a blind, impulsive act would not again be permitted to happen. It reported that the Bizen retainer Heki Tatewaki had been reprimanded and his subordinate Taki Zenzaburo ordered to disembowel himself; this letter was in accordance with an imperial command that the foreign emissaries be so notified. The letter bore the seal of Date Muneki, the Uwajima commander.

Learning that the punishment of the prime offender was to be carried out in the Eifukuji in Hyogo on that very day, Parkes decided to send two of his secretaries as witnesses. Ito Hirobumi and one other person served as witnesses for the Japanese side. On that occasion, Parkes said, "I have heard that seppuku is an honor for a Japanese warrior. This should not be an honorable death. After this, such people must be punished in such a way as to serve as a warning." Parkes himself made a show of attending.

By that time much was being said about the punishment of the killer of the foreigners. There were those who maintained that if the times were not so much out of joint, the man would be viewed simply as a warrior who had cut down some ill-mannered foreigners, for which he deserved to be praised. There were some who noted that he had shown no sign of weakness, that he had not flinched even in the face of death, and that he had written a death verse before the end. Others said that he had hoped to be spared right up to the very last moment, and that when one of his comrades from Bizen whispered something in his ear he suddenly blanched and began trembling. Some even said that he died very poorly and reluctantly.

Four days later the foreign emissaries and their secretaries set off for Osaka. They left the protection of the foreign settlement in the hands of the commander of the Choshu troops, and general business in the hands of the resident consular officials. The road from Hyogo through Nishinomiya to Osaka was carrying an extremely heavy load of traffic from eastern and western Japan and from Kyushu and the Japan sea coast. There was great congestion in the post stations. Every day two or three village officials would be brought in from points along the highway to receive orders from the toiya for porters and horses. The standard complement of twenty-five porters and twenty-five horses for each station had long since been in service and every last additional man and horse that could be found was also at work. It had even been announced that wages would be raised by sixty percent from the fourteenth of the month. The foreigners decided to take a warship as far as the landing at the foot of Mt. Tempo on the Osaka waterfront to avoid the congestion on the land route. At Parkes' insistence they also took a detachment of marines with them. Unlike previous occasions, the emissaries were now presenting themselves specifically as the representatives of their own nations.

In the middle of the second month the sea was calm. As they set out early in the morning from Hyogo, the Dutch chargé van Polesbroek began to say that things were going well. Roches observed that this was the same route over which Yamaguchi Suruga, the shogun's commissioner of foreign affairs, and Matsudaira Hoki had come so hurriedly by steamship just a year earlier. The American Van Valkenburgh was concerned about how they were to get beyond Osaka even if they were given permission to present their credentials in Kyoto.

The Japanese dignitaries had gathered at the Nishi Honganji temple in Osaka to await the arrival of the foreigners. Among them were Daigo Tadaosa, governor of Osaka and chief justice, and the assistant chief justice Date Muneki.

Gradually the ranks of those in charge of foreign relations were being filled out. Higashikuse Michitomi was chief justice in Hyogo, assisted by Ito Hirobumi. Into the room where these dignitaries awaited the arrival of the representatives of the han, there came, one by one, each escorted by a priest of the temple, the stewards of the han.

It was the fourteenth of the month and so it was the Satsuma troops who were providing the guard; they set out in a steam launch to meet the emissaries at the mouth of the Aji river. Higashikuse Michitomi played the leading role that day but he was by no means well versed in diplomacy. His duty at this, the first international conference in Osaka, was to report the formation of the new government and to seek the recognition of the foreign powers. It had been felt best that someone from among the court nobles should perform this function, but there was no one among the court nobles who had ever met with a foreign ambassador. There was no one who had even met a foreigner of any kind. Everyone insisted that Higashikuse take the assignment because he was the only one who had ever seen a foreigner. It was hoped that he would therefore be better able to deal with their high-handed ways.

Higashikuse had gone to Chikuzen during the winter of the previous year and while there he had been both encouraged by others and impelled by his own curiosity to inspect the newly opened port. He had asked Prince Sanjo Sanetomi to go to Nagasaki with him, but since Sanjo had then held the rank of general among the anti-foreign forces, he had felt uneasy about making such a journey, even in secret. So Higashikuse went alone. With the help of Oyama Kakunosuke he disguised himself as a Satsuma man and spent about three weeks in Nagasaki under an assumed name. He was able to meet with Dutch and British merchants with the help of the influential Satsuma merchant Godai Tomoatsu. He also met the American missionary Guido Verbeck and had occasion to see foreign warships as well as to hear languages spoken in the West.

It was well known that Higashikuse Michitomi was one of the seven court nobles who had fled to Choshu after the attempt in 1863 to get the emperor to take personal command of an expedition against the foreigners. He might be said to have been the outstanding man among the leaders of the anti-foreign movement. It was an extraordinary twist of fate that brought a person with his background into the position of host in ceremonies welcoming the coming of foreigners. Europe is far from Japan, and aside from those in Dutch there were few books from Europe in our libraries. Neither Higashikuse nor any of the others had any significant knowledge of the West. Yet Tokugawa Yoshinobu himself had set the precedent when, in the previous year, he had invited the foreign emissaries to this very same Osaka and met with them in person. It was now absolutely essential that those who wished to ensure the stability of the new government should, whatever their misgivings, gain the recognition of the Western powers for their new foreign office; they had to show that the new government was not simply a band of diehard xenophobes.

"International law," a term borrowed from the Chinese was a new word now current among those in government service. People determined to cast out the old and grasp the new took their bearings from this concept and set out to receive the foreigners in the spirit of "international law."

In the meantime, a messenger came up to report that the foreigners had landed. Led by a detachment of Satsuma soldiers, the marines set out from the foreign settlement with banners flying and rifles with fixed bayonets on their shoulders. The messenger also reported that an unanticipated number of men and women had come out to try to see the litters in which the foreigners were riding and that they formed a solid mass all the way from the front of the customs office through the foreign settlement and as far as Shin-Ohashi.

The party arrived safely at the Nishi Honganji. Since each minister was accompanied by a secretary, there were twelve foreigners in the party. In order to accord them a brief rest, the priest who received them led them into a room where acolytes in black served them refreshments on footed trays.

The great chamber of the temple was in readiness to serve as a meeting hall. The foreigners were conducted in to take their seats on the chairs lined up on the tatami matting. The stewards of the various han came in and took their seats. Higashikuse Michitomi opened the occasion by making a gesture of welcome. He informed them that the Japanese political establishment had carried out a restoration of antiquity, that the emperor himself had assumed direct political power and, as they had previously been informed while in Hyogo, the court was now responsible for all international relations. An office of foreign affairs had been established which would take charge of all matters pertaining to trade relationships. Today, together with representatives of those han that had supported the imperial cause, he was meeting with the ministers of the foreign powers to reaffirm the existing treaties. His statement was well received. The foreign emissaries replied that the search on the part of the emperor and the lords of the han for the broadest possible trust and friendship as a context in which the Japanese people might be able to carry out proper foreign relations was something which the foreign countries also earnestly desired. From now on, they would look on the imperial court as the center of government in Japan and entrust every matter to it.

Higashikuse then spoke again in a more formal tone, saying that it was the intention of the emperor, once the treaties had all been reviewed, to meet with the representatives of the foreign powers to pledge his commitment in person. He reported that it was the emperor's wish that the foreigners should come up to Kyoto at an early date. The foreigners expressed their gratitude and, after a short discussion among themselves, announced that their reply would be forthcoming on the day after tomorrow. Then Parkes stated that since the punitive expedition against Tokugawa Yoshinobu had already set out from Kyoto, there was concern about conditions in the Kanto. If the emissaries could not speedily receive audience with the emperor, they wished to leave the Osaka area in order to apply themselves to the protection of the foreign settlement in Yokohama. After Parkes spoke, the American minister glanced at the Italian and Prussian ministers seated on either side of him and then stated that it was their wish to leave for Yokohama on the following day, the fifteenth of the month.

Van Valkenburgh wrung his hands and explained over and over that he was concerned about the safety of the Yokohama foreign settlement. Higashikuse, seeing that he was very much in earnest, then spoke.

"Well then, what if we were to do it this way? I will get word tomorrow from Kyoto concerning the date of the audience. Could you please stay here until then before returning to Yokohama? It would be best if you did meet with the emperor now."

Among the foreign representatives at Osaka were those who were eager to have a date set for audience with the emperor, so that they could clarify what his commitment was to mean. Others were most reluctant to go to Kyoto. When these most recent reports came in to Kyoto, special couriers were dispatched back to Higashikuse to inform him that, because of objections from imperial household officials, it would be extremely difficult to have foreigners come to court and it was unthinkable that representatives of foreign countries should have audience with the emperor. They must not, therefore, enter Kyoto. The message was accompanied by a note from Sanjo and Iwakura stating their dismay at this turn of events and asking Higashikuse to try to provide them with arguments to advance to the imperial household.

Higashikuse was shocked but he immediately dispatched a messenger to Kyoto to tell the imperial household officials that this was no time for worrying about precedents. If Kyoto itself could not make a demonstration of trust and friendship, the country was likely to find itself confronted with incalculable difficulties arising out of a complete change of attitude on the part of the foreign powers. Just as the han have their resident ministers in Edo, so the foreign powers have their resident ministers with whom we cannot refuse to deal if we are to have relations with foreign countries. It is necessary that they be met. The Western powers associate with each other on terms of the greatest intimacy; they do not remain apart as Japan does. It is best, Higashikuse stated, to think of these ministers as though they were resident representatives of the han.

Conditions in the outside world no longer permitted Japan to stand alone. When the time came, this new government, now setting out to attack the Kanto as a feeble foreign policy gesture, found that it had to face the same agonies as the responsible officials in the shogunate had formerly had to do. Just as Iwase Higo had labored to lead the nation in a slightly more enlightened direction at a time when almost all the officials of the shogunate were still lumping Britain, France, America, and Russia together as "hairy Chinamen," now the turn of the officials of the new government had come to grapple with the same problems. Even though there were those who shared the goal of which Townsend Harris had spoken, "to unify the world through trade and diplomacy" and to force this Far Eastern nation as yet weak in industry and many other areas to advance without a backward look —even so everyone in the nation was going to have to make great concessions.

After the armies left Osaka for the pacification of the east, the city seemed drained and empty. All that was left were the caretakers from the various han and the people of the city, concerned over the fate of the departed soldiers. There were incessant rumors that Tokugawa Yoshinobu had already sent repeated messages of apology and conciliation through the retired lord of Owari and through Matsudaira Shungaku, or that Yoshinobu had entered the Tokugawa family temple in Edo, the Kan'eiji, as a gesture of submission.

It was the day following the meeting in the Osaka Nishi Honganji. From the French mission in Nakaderamachi came an invitation to dinner for the foreign ministers and the leading members of the Japanese delegation. Even Roches, known to be sympathetic to the shogunate, was satisfied with the previous day's meeting and the invitation was an expression of his good will.

An escort arrived from the French ministry. Daigo Tadaosa, Date Muneki, and Higashikuse Michitomi were to represent the Japanese, and they left with their escort.

Higashikuse brought along an important gift for his hosts. He could now inform them that the date for their audience in Kyoto had been set for the eighteenth of that month. His messenger had just brought this crucial word back from Kyoto. The imperial palace officials had seen fit to accept his proposal that the ministers be received in audience as though they were resident representatives of the han.

Roches and the others were awaiting Higashikuse's arrival at the French mission in Nakaderamachi. Mermet de Cachon, who spoke like a Japanese, was present, so there was no lack of informal interpreters.

When de Cachon relayed Higashikuse's message to Roches and the other ministers, he started his remarks in Japanese, saying, *"Saa, kore desu,"* before switching to French.

"Bon."

Roches' reply was brief.

The one short word that had come unbidden to his lips was then translated to the effect that "everything had gone very well." The Englishman Parkes, the American Van Valkenburgh, the Italian de la Tour, the Prussian von Brandt, the Dutchman van Polesbroek—the faces of all the ministers were cheerful and the conversation was full of anticipation of the coming audience on the eighteenth. Some said that they had never hoped to see Kyoto so soon. Others said that they had waited a very long time for this day.

De Cachon, announcing that the tables were prepared, came to conduct the Japanese guests to their seats. Date Muneki pulled at Higashikuse's sleeve.

"I have never attended this kind of banquet. I want to leave it all up to you and just stay here."

"But that would put me in a terribly difficult position. If we just do as everyone else does things should go well enough."

A Western-style meal, set out on a single huge table instead of on the individual, footed trays normally used in Japan, appeared before Higashikuse and his companions. Seating was not arranged according to rank but it was nevertheless apparent that great pains had been taken to seat people in an appropriate fashion. De Cachon conducted Higashikuse to a seat that seemed to have been reserved for the guest of honor. Parkes was seated next to Daigo Tadaosa, while Date Muneki was seated across from Van Valkenburgh. Instead of their accustomed chopsticks that functioned like a bird's beak, they were supplied with forks like the claws of beasts. There was also a large spoon and several beautifully polished knives at each place. The white napkins folded neatly before each guest added to the exotic appearance of the scene. The serving of the food was also quite different from what they were accustomed to. The bread that was brought in before the soup course would correspond in a Japanese meal to the rice balls that are eaten in informal lunches.

"Please begin! Does French food suit your taste?" inquired De Cachon, showing genuine concern for his guests.

When the waiters brought huge platters heaped with food and stood behind each guest inviting him to take what he liked, Higashikuse did as the Westerners did. If Parkes served himself with chicken, Higashikuse took chicken. If Van Valkenburgh took vegetables, Higashikuse took vegetables. He glanced from time to time at his companions while he was eating. Both Daigo and Date seemed to feel badly out of place and they only sniffed at the French cheese that their host urged upon them. They did not even seem able to enjoy the fine old wine that was being served.

For all this, the dinner was going along quite pleasantly when the foreigners began to leave the table one or two at a time. Higashikuse soon realized that something was wrong. He noticed a concerned expression on the faces of Daigo and Date. As they began to discuss among themselves what could be happening they looked around and saw that only they were left at the table. It had been in the middle of dinner that news reached Osaka of the violence at the Asahi teahouse in the neighboring city of Sakai. It seemed that there had been a considerable battle, with sailors from the French ship *Dupleix* being attacked by Tosa troops. The crew members had put down a boat and were rowing about the harbor when they were fired upon by Tosa troops, but the reports that had come in from the Asahi teahouse were quite confused. It was difficult to grasp just what had happened. The only thing that seemed certain was that four crew members had been instantly killed, seven wounded, and another seven were missing. It was also known that the seven who were missing had leaped into the water in an attempt to escape the fire from shore.

Higashikuse called promptly at the American mission on the next morning, the seventeenth. When he consulted with Van Valkenburgh about what he should do, he learned from him that the French warships were about to return to Yokohama. It was absolutely necessary that this be prevented. Higashikuse requested that the American ambassador take appropriate measures.

The French protest came in shortly thereafter. It was addressed to "General Higashikuse and Date Iyo no Kami of the Foreign Office of the Imperial Government" and it carried the following message:

> . . . Such incidents are unheard of. They must be likened to the acts of wild beasts. The minister wishes first to make known that the warship *Ouest* will be standing by and we wish to have the missing persons, dead or alive, brought to it. We expect this to be done by eight o'clock tomorrow morning and the authorities currently in charge of Osaka should be apprised of this fact. If this should not be done, then no matter what apologies might be made, there will exist a violation of the laws of civilized nations and a breach of the treaties we have just concluded. Again, we ask that, since these acts were perpetrated by the retainers of daimyo who are carrying positions of major responsibility in the imperial government, suitable and appropriate steps be taken by them. Thus we beg to inform you.
>
> Respectfully,
> Léon Roches
> French Minister Plenipotentiary in Japan
>
> Osaka, February, 1868

Through the efforts of Godai, Iwashita, and others, the deadline was extended from eight A.M. on the seventeenth to noon. They promised that the missing men would be returned by then and requested in exchange that the warships not go back to Yokohama. Higashikuse was stunned. He had been given absolute orders to find and return men of whose whereabouts he knew absolutely nothing.

On the afternoon of the sixteenth, Higashikuse set out for the Asahi teahouse in Sakai in a party that included Godai and Nakai. They learned nothing. The Tosa men pretended ignorance of the affair. If the seven bodies were not found by that evening, then Higashikuse, who had asked for the intercession of the American minister, would find himself in an impossible position. He promised thirty ryo in gold for the recovery of each body and the fishermen of the area all gathered, lighting torches and letting down grapples. One by one, the bodies of the seven foreigners were brought up out of the dark sea. All of them were naked. Higashikuse called to have them wrapped in blankets and later had them dressed in the uniforms that had been prepared for the new Tosa guards. The first cocks were crowing when Nakai Kozo brought the coffins back to Osaka.

It was a rainy, stormy day. It took Higashikuse some time to get the bodies to the *Ouest*. Komatsu Tatewaki of Satsuma was with him that day. Everyone was complaining of the rain. Yet if they did not show sufficient spirit to brave the squall the French would be unlikely to accept the bodies in good grace. It was already after the promised time. By turning their watches back to noon, they finally fulfilled their promise and prevented the warships from going back to Yokohama.

The waves were high. The French, commenting on the danger from the wind, put down a steam launch to send Higashikuse back to shore. The bodies had been delivered to the French. Now to the settlement of this difficult matter. Higashikuse continued to worry as he looked back from the launch toward the *Ouest*. The Black Ship maintained a menacing silence as it moved through the rain toward Kawaguchi.

Anti-foreign incidents were not uncommon. But this incident at the Asahi teahouse had come on the second day after the conference at the Osaka Nishi Honganji in which a policy of trust and friendship toward foreign countries had been promised. The movements of the storm clouds that covered the skies in those days were threatening and difficult to predict. In the midst of the confusion the new government rushed to proclaim the establishment of full diplomatic relations with the outside world. This proclamation, issued in the names of three of the major officials of the council of state, began by saying that the treaties which had hitherto been contracted with the shogunate were binding upon the government of Japan; although minor adjustments might be called for due to the passage of time, their overall ramifications were not to be tampered with. It called upon everyone to recognize that if these treaties were unilaterally altered by the imperial court, the result would be a loss of confidence by the foreign powers and the creation of immense difficulties. It further called for recognition of the fact that an accommodation of the unique political institutions of the nation with the requirements of international law was absolutely essential. To this end, the stage had been reached where, in acceptance of the memorial presented by Matsudaira Shungaku and his subordinates, after consultation with all responsible officials in the government and the han, the balance between the favorable and the unfavorable precedents was such that the ministers from the foreign nations were granted permission to enter the capital. Of course, everyone should recognize that punishment and reward would not be forgotten, for even if peace and friendship are proclaimed, right and wrong must be clearly distinguished. Although it goes without saying that the nation must be protected, the ports had already been opened under the previous reign and friendly relationships between the Japanese empire and foreign nations established from that time on. Now that imperial rule has been restored and all orders emanate from the court it is to be taken for granted that relations with foreign nations shall be conducted directly by the court. This decision had been reached at the very beginning of direct rule by the emperor, when we found ourselves in difficult times. With the deepest concern and the most earnest thought, all, in consultation with the responsible people of the nation, must cooperate to serve the imperial interest in improving foreign relations. Eyes must be opened to the urgent business at hand and the evils that have existed hitherto must be expunged.

This could be looked upon as a proclamation of the opening of the nation but in that statement was clearly lodged the implication that those who aspired to greatness must also humble themselves greatly. Move out into the world! When the situation calls for it, bow your heads to the foreigners. Take up their strong points to supplement our weak points and establish a basis for well-being through the ages. All, both high and low, must exert themselves. Such was the temper of the statement made on this occasion.

On the nineteenth day of the second month a five article proclamation came from the French minister. It requested a clear response within three days. By that time the facts of the Asahi teahouse incident were clear. Tosa troops had become suspicious of the activities of the French sailors and they had opened fire from shore without warning. It was known that one French sailor had swum to safety uninjured. The French asked the meaning of the killing of foreigners suspected of taking soundings in a nonmilitary harbor. If they wished to forbid such action all that they had needed to do was to admonish the sailors and tell them to leave. If the sailors had refused they could have been taken into custody and handed over to the French consul. It was pointed out that the number of Europeans and Americans who had been killed for no reason had already reached thirty.

"I report that on the day after tomorrow, the twenty-third, in the Myoko-kuji in Sakai, the Tosa troops guilty of violence will be ordered to perform seppuku. Now among the French, four people were killed, seven were wounded, and seven are missing, so it was suggested that about twenty among the Tosa men should be a satisfactory number. Twenty of those connected with the incident have therefore been ordered to perform seppuku."

"It's a terrible thing, but it can't be helped. They have insisted that the responsible persons be punished."

This was the conversation that took place between Higashikuse and his steward.

"Tell Godai Tomoatsu and Uno Keisuke to be in attendance on that day," Higashikuse added.

On the evening of the day set for the punishment of the Tosa troops at the Myokokuji, the steward again came to Higashikuse.

"Fukao Yasuomi, the acting steward of Tosa, stepped forward to announce that he would be officiating. Those to perform seppuku were called out by lot, and they say that they were magnificent—each recited a death verse. However, when it was time for the eleventh man to perform seppuku one of the French officers requested that he be spared. They could not bear to watch any longer and they asked that the seppuku be stopped. But all those present were men determined to uphold the honor of the nation and even though the French begged for mercy, they paid no attention but went ahead with disemboweling themselves. Then Godai Tomoatsu also decided that it was time to stop and gave a formal order to that effect."

Higashikuse did not know whether to laugh or cry over the phrasing "formal order to that effect."

The warm rains of the end of the old second month had come. There was an appeal for clemency from the French and the sentences of nine of the Tosa men were commuted to exile in Higo and Aki in the Asahi teahouse incident. Prince Yamashina had paid a call to a British warship, met with the French plenipotentiary Roches, and delivered to him one article of the soon to be promulgated Five Article Oath. Greatly disturbed by the affair, Yamauchi Yodo had left his sickbed to come up to Osaka from his domain and days were spent in negotiation with the French to have the indemnity of one hundred fifty thousand ryo divided into three payments instead of being paid all at once, and to send compensation from Tosa to the families of the eleven deceased and to the seven wounded.

4

As recently announced, the French, Dutch, and British ministers, representing all the powers, will leave Osaka on the twenty-seventh, travel by land and water, spend the night at Fushimi, and enter Kyoto on the twenty-eighth. Concerning the above, as has been previously proclaimed, everything is being carried out by the emperor in the spirit of international law. All must take care that there be no mistake and the various han must also take the strictest measures to maintain control.

When this proclamation was issued, the American, Italian, and Prussian ministers were no longer in Osaka. As soon as the funeral ceremony for the

French sailors had taken place in Kobe, they had all stated their concern over the situation in the Kanto and had returned to Yokohama. Behind them remained the French, Dutch, and British ministers, busy with preparations to go to Kyoto.

To Kyoto, the city forbidden to foreigners. This was more than merely pleasing to Parkes; he was secretly very proud to be going. He recalled that it was his predecessor Alcock who had seen that the advance of the European powers into the Far East had doomed the Japanese feudal system, and it was Parkes himself who had aided the western han in order to assist in the creation of the new society, thereby bringing about the actual restoration. A heady sense of self-importance on this account never left Parkes for a moment. With the attitude that the people of the new Japanese government, which included so many very young people, were all his students, Parkes set out for Kyoto on the twenty-seventh, accompanied by his secretary Mitford and a detachment of red-coated troops.

The French minister Roches and the Dutch chargé van Polesbroek left the next day. This was at the wish of the Japanese, who were concerned about the dangers en route and wished to avoid the congestion that would be created by a single party. It was still very early in the life of the new government but these men had already been through the shocking experiences of the Sannomiya incident and the Asahi teahouse incident. The council of state discontinued its policy of strict secrecy and made public the date on which the ministers would be leaving Osaka, noting that their coming to Kyoto for audience reflected the considered policy of the emperor himself and ordering that not only the town officials but each individual household be called upon to assure that no untoward incident occur. It reminded everyone that it would be most regrettable if anything should happen that would lead the country into still greater difficulties.

This was the time when the first newspapers were beginning to circulate in Edo. The circumstances of the departure of the forces for pacification of the Kanto had already been published by the foreigners in the *Times* and the *Herald,* the two English-language papers in Yokohama. In the Kyoto-Osaka region there was no news organ as yet other than the daily journal of the council of state. Even so, the daimyo of Aizu, Matsuyama, Takamatsu, and Otaki were regarded in Kyoto as enemies and reports that their lands and their dwellings were to be confiscated surfaced regularly. No one outside the officials directly concerned knew anything about the funds that had been appropriated for the Kanto expedition, but the stories of the Osaka merchants who had responded to calls for money, or of those who had become excited and had voluntarily contributed for patriotic reasons, were widely circulated among those townspeople who were knowledgeable about money matters.

Roches and his secretary de Cachon went to the waterfront at Ajikawa to board a launch. Two French captains were to accompany them to Kyoto at the head of a detachment of troops. When they met with the Dutch chargé van Polesbroek and his secretary, the chief members of the ministers' party came to a total of six. One boat was to carry the ministers and their party and the Japanese officials and French troops assigned to guard them. The other would carry guards from Satsuma. The plan was to spend the night in Fushimi after going up the Yodo river by water and land. A detachment of troops assigned to guard them by land had already set out up the Fushimi road. Hearing that foreigners were to have audience with the emperor, a vast crowd had turned out on the riverbank to see how the foreigners were dressed for the occasion. Nakai Kozo had gone up to Kyoto several days earlier, leaving Komatsu Tatewaki and Ito Hirobumi to depart from Osaka with the ministers. A personal representative of Higashikuse also came to the riverbank to see them off and to present Higashikuse's prayers for a safe journey.

Even after the steamboats began to move, the eyes of the Japanese members of the party, worried that something might happen, never left their guests with the strangely colored hair. At this season the willows that lined the stream as far as the eye could see delighted the travelers; spring had come to the huge triangular island at the mouth of the Yodo river. But Roches never took up the binoculars that hung from his shoulder.

"We don't need all this! Why do foreigners have to be watched so closely?"

When the Dutch chargé d'affaires, extremely irritated, had his interpreter ask this question, the senior Japanese official accompanying them simply shook his head.

"We must protect you gentlemen."

The rules for travel were galling. Instructions for the party once arrived in Kyoto were laid out in a maddeningly detailed document of many articles. They were free to go wherever they wished in Kyoto and its environs, to go shopping or sightseeing in even the most impoverished neighborhoods, but they were not permitted to enter teahouses or wineshops. They were forbidden to go out at night; when they met the parties of members of the imperial family they were to withdraw to the sides of the streets; when they met the entourages of court nobles or daimyo they were to pass them by, yielding half the road to them. There was even an appendix to this document saying that if they met with the party of a member of the imperial family and were so informed by their guides, they should make some appropriate gesture of courtesy if they knew of one.

Out of all the members of the party, only de Cachon was capable of reading this document with full comprehension. He translated it for Roches and van Polesbroek. A red carpet had been laid out in the cabin of the steamboat and crude chairs were lined up on it. Tea and other refreshments were being served. In order to have an unobstructed view, de Cachon left the cabin as soon as they were beyond Osaka and went out to the gallery along the side of the ship. French soldiers were standing guard. As he took out his smoking materials in a sheltered corner, a Japanese official came up to him, greeted him, and began to ask questions about foreign countries.

Although de Cachon was French, he was so accustomed to the Japanese way that he carried a Japanese smoking set in an inner pocket of his suit. The Japanese official who had joined him was startled to see it.

"Oh, do you smoke Japanese tobacco?" he asked with an air of amazement.

De Cachon shrugged his shoulders in the French manner. Then he took a Japanese flint and steel set out of another pocket. Not only did he proceed to enjoy a smoke while looking out over the scenery of the Kawachi plain but he sniffed at the scent of his deerskin tobacco pouch and filled up idle moments by fondling his thick-stemmed Japanese pipe, showing great satisfaction in these products of another culture. He put the pipe in his mouth and puffed on the finely cut leaf with evident enjoyment. His motions as he struck fire and brought the tinder to his pipe were fully practiced. The Japanese official watched this performance as though surprised that there could be such people among the foreigners.

"You really speak very well."

"Thank you."

"We Japanese could never do anything like that."

"Now you are surely joking with me."

"Who taught you such fine Japanese?"

"Well, it was while I was in Hokkaido. There was a person named Kitamura Zuiken who was serving under the Hakodate commissioner. I learned from him. You see, I was working in the consulate in Hakodate then. That's right. Kitamura was my teacher. He was a most interesting person to talk with. He knew the Chinese classics very well, and since he was originally a physician, he knew a great deal about medicine and medicinal herbs. I taught him French and he taught me Japanese. Kitamura was young then, and I too . . ."

"I have heard of Kitamura Zuiken. Isn't he in France now on a mission for the shogunate?"

"That's right. It's that Kitamura."

When he heard this, the official's expression suddenly turned sour and he stopped talking. De Cachon went on speaking, half to himself, as though there could be no possible objection to a neutral foreigner's reminiscences about an old teacher.

"He is sure to be amazed now. When he hears what has happened in Japan he will want to hurry home to see it all."

A well-tilled plain lay before them. None of the members of the party could conceal their pleasure in being free to travel in an area which had hitherto been forbidden. They were enjoying the opportunity to follow in the steps of the first Europeans to come this way.

Among the earlier Europeans to reach the Far East, there were a few who had received permission to enter the hinterlands. Some of these, having observed Japanese society at first hand, had rendered quite severe judgments on it. In their eyes the primary distinction between European and Oriental culture was that whereas the West rejected all falsehood, the East accepted all falsehood. The Japanese and the Chinese were not embarrassed to tell the most obvious lies and it was extremely difficult to understand how basic human relations could be maintained in a society in which there could be so little mutual trust. The morality of the Japanese and the philosophy that lies at the basis of their lives were completely different from that of Europeans. Some pointed out that Japanese women can in a single day go from the defilement of prostitution to a pure married life, raising the question of whether or not there is a clear line of demarcation between the moral and the immoral in that nation. Others, at the very beginning of their travels, remarked on the contrast between the richness of the land and the impoverished condition of the people who lived there. Not only in the villages but even in the towns where there was a considerable number of large houses, nothing looked lively and prosperous. The travelers could not readily explain to themselves whether this appearance of poverty was purely superficial or whether it reflected actual conditions—that is, whether the return from the land was really that poor. They also reported that it was very difficult to acquire knowledge of Japanese political life, or of its statistics, or of matters of learning. Others complained that the Japanese paid no attention at all to anything that did not have a direct relationship to them and their lives.

Yet there was no lack of Europeans who were ready to see Japan as the bearer of a high destiny. If the Japanese were ever to possess a full measure of scientific knowledge and their technology and industry were to become advanced, they would be able to compete with the people of Europe. Japan was a country as yet unknown in its literary and philosophical culture, but the houses were clean and beautiful, the clothing was practical, the keenness of the weapons beyond belief, and the originality and beauty of the arts and crafts were immensely rich. Of course, travelers' responses vary from person to person, but there were those who maintained that there was nothing elsewhere to compare with the singular and original culture that these people had created over the past three hundred years in spite of being cut off from contact with the outside world.

"We're finally going to get a look at the Japanese hinterland."

When de Cachon, having rejoined Roches, said this, Roches responded in a reproachful tone.

"De Cachon, no matter how you try to enter into Japanese life through its language, you will never reach the things that lie behind the words. We Europeans can never enter into the spirit of Orientals . . ."

The party was now moving out of the broad plains of the lower Yodo river into the hilly Kinai region, but there was unfortunately a low overcast and they could not see the distant mountains. The two small steamboats moved on up the center of the Yodo past villages and shrine groves. The mountains remained hidden in the clouds. If the weather had been good the party could have sated at least part of their curiosity with the mountains. They took a great deal of satisfaction from just hearing that there was now high ground all around them and that among these tall ranges there were several particularly high peaks in Yamashiro and Tamba provinces. De Cachon, who was the youngest among them, listened most intently to these explanations. However coldly most Europeans may have looked upon the Orient, de Cachon, as he gazed out upon early spring on the banks of the Yodo river, sensed deeply how blessed by nature this island nation was.

As it was announced that they were drawing near the landing at Yodo station, a light rain drifted over the river like smoke. Some among the Europeans were exhausted by the uncertainties of the journey and wanted to see Fushimi as soon as possible. Others were beginning to concern themselves about what might be waiting for them in Fushimi and Kyoto. Still others leaned on the railing of the steamboat and gazed with traveler's eyes on the warm but dispiriting rain.

For one so fond of Japan as de Cachon, even this smokelike rain provided the opportunity to see things that he had not yet had a chance to see. He tried to take in everything. Entranced by the riverboats plying the river between Dotombori in Osaka and Yodo, by the picturesque heavy thatch that covered the roofs of the cabins, and by the pilots standing by their helms in rain-drenched straw hats and capes, he forgot all about his secretarial duties for a while. Thinking to have a look at the other bank, he walked around the cabin to the other side of the boat where he found Roches in conversation with the Dutch chargé d'affaires. As he gazed out through the rain, he could not help overhearing their conversation.

"What will happen to Yokohama if Edo is attacked?"

"It will be in danger of course. No help can get to it from anywhere. I am afraid that the new Japanese government would find itself unable to protect the foreign concessions," replied van Polesbroek.

They were discussing the general attack on Edo that was now imminent. By this time the lower-ranking foreigners were all deeply fatigued from constant watchfulness and the heads of the mission were talking freely without trying to conceal the vulnerability of their position.

"But isn't Tokugawa Yoshinobu protesting his loyalty and submission over and over? Doesn't he say that he does not want to fight?" Van Polesbroek was speaking now.

"That's just it. Everyone recognizes that. Even the British ambassador is fully aware of the facts. How can justice and humanity permit an attack on those who so ardently declare their loyalty?" This was the voice of Roches.

"It is just as you say."

"Isn't there some way that the attack on Edo can be stopped? I simply cannot stand by and watch this horrible civil war any longer."

The Dutch chargé d'affaires was quite concerned about the situation in the Kanto. He saw putting an end to civil strife as the most urgent business now before the Japanese. They had best put an end to it if they wanted Japan to remain in Japanese hands. And they had best not make a display of internal weakness and disorder to foreign countries.

officials but who nevertheless permitted a pack of outlanders to enter the imperial presence were guilty of soiling the national polity. They called for the execution of both the responsible officials and the ambassadors themselves. Some tied their sleeves up and ground their teeth in helpless rage as they rushed here and there through crowds afire with curiosity. Both sides of the street in Sakaimachi where it cut across Nijo and Sanjo avenues were so crowded with people awaiting the passage of the ambassadors that there was not enough room left to stand a gimlet.

Kureta Masaka was a member of that crowd. He was staying at the Sawa residence and was back at work under the name of Tachibana Tozo, but now he too was standing at the corner of Sakai and Maruta streets amid a vast gathering of men and women waiting to see the ambassadors. He had, of course, not come out alone. With him was a man named Tatematsu Hosuke, a fellow disciple in the capital on business from Nanjo village in Ina, Shinano province.

Before them were the streets, beginning to dry out from the equinoctial rains. Many around them were stretching their necks out to look off toward the south. Although the French ambassador's route from the Sokokuji did not lead this way, the British ambassador coming from the Chion-in and the Dutch chargé d'affaire coming from Nanzenji were to pass along this very street. Neither Masaka nor Hosuke had ever seen a Westerner before. Yesterday's "red savages" were today's guests of state. Consciousness of this fact mingled curiously in their breasts with the ardor with which they had labored to help create the new government.

Soon behind the plum blossom banners of Kaga a detachment of soldiers carrying muskets with fixed bayonets on their shoulders came marching up Sakaimachi from the direction of Sanjo. They were the guards of the ambassadorial party. Shortly afterward litters bearing the Dutch chargé van Polesbroek and his secretary passed before Masaka and his companion.

People whom they had never thought of but as creatures of a distant world were now carried before the very eyes of the two Hirata disciples. They did their best to obtain a clear impression of the appearance of the Westerners, but this was not easy. The foreigners were in litters, the time was short, and they were in motion. At first Kureta and Tatematsu could see very little. The difficulty was compounded by officials dressed in Western style, carrying powder and shot pouches, and wearing swords at their sides who walked alongside the litters and kept a close watch on their surroundings.

The curtains in the litters were, however, rolled up. From time to time the four litter bearers would stop briefly to shift their burden to the opposite shoulder, and Kureta was able to get a clear glimpse of the ambassador deep within the litter's woolen sunshade. The elegant litter was floored with matting and had black lacquered sides. The determination of the new government to do away with all old standards was manifest in this use of such a conveyance for a foreign ambassador. These first Westerners that Masaka saw were by no means despicable people, and the Dutch chargé in particular wore a stern and impressive expression. The foreigners, different in hair color, in the color of their eyes, in the color of their skins, in everything from their customs to their speech, passed by Masaka's gaze looking as if they were about to say, "Oh, so this is the Kyoto that we have heard so much about."

The crowd, having observed the passage of the Dutch chargé, was now waiting for the appearance of the British ambassador. It was reported that this group would be accompanied by red-coated soldiers and would make a much better show. But no matter how long they waited the party of the British ambassador did not appear, although it should long since have left the Chion-in. Finally Masaka and his companion gave them up and left the more patient members of the crowd, who were still waiting.

"I feel as though this were all a dream," said Tatematsu as they walked away.

With the departure of the army for the Kanto, the activities of the men of the various han, the changes in the political and social systems, and the utterly unprecedented audience for the foreign ambassadors, Kyoto was still experiencing violent change.

"I'm glad you're here, Hosuke. Have a good look at Kyoto under the restoration."

He didn't say this out loud, but Masaka's eye made his meaning clear as they left Sakai street and started up Maruta street. They were close to Fuyamachi where the shop of the dyer Isekyu, so well known to all Hirata disciples, was located. It was also not far from Masaka's lodgings in Koromonotana.

Tatematsu Hosuke used the pen name of Chitari. He and Masaka were acquainted from the latter's days in Ina, and he was in the capital not only for his own business. The many posthumous disciples of Hirata Atsutane in Ina had heard that since Tokugawa Yoshinobu's resignation as shogun at the end of the previous year, things had been unsettled in the east, and now that fighting was about to break out in Edo, they began to worry about the manuscripts by Hirata Atsutane that were being kept there. Kitahara Inao of Zakoji village wanted to see these manuscripts moved to a safe place like the Ina valley, so he sent an appropriate person to Edo to talk with the Hirata family about the matter. Tatematsu Hosuke had been chosen. Hosuke had carried out his mission, moving all the manuscripts from Edo and bringing them safely to Zakoji at the end of the year. Master Kanetane, now resident in Kyoto, had been informed by letter of the successful completion of the project; Hosuke hoped to take advantage of this trip to Kyoto to report in person.

Masaka, wanting to share the good news with the master of the Isekyu, intended to introduce Hosuke to this most admirable person and to let him hear from Hosuke's own lips of the safe disposal of Atsutane's manuscripts. Dyer though he was, Iseya Kyubei had frequently been mentioned to Hosuke as a townsman with keen perceptions and a deep sense of justice.

"How about it, Hosuke? Let's drop in on Isekyu since we are in the neighborhood."

FOR ALL YOUR DYEING NEEDS

The Fuyamachi district where the blue shop curtains of the Iseya could be seen was utterly quiet. When Kureta and his visitor opened the shoji with their deep wooden panels at the bottom and entered the shop, they discovered the owner all by himself in the office enclosure at the left of the shop. Everyone in the family and all the employees had gone out to see the foreigners.

"Well, well!"

Kyubei was delighted to see Masaka and Hosuke.

"Please have a seat," said Kyubei as he brought cushions out from the living quarters and placed them by the accountant's enclosure where the ledgers were kept.

Kyubei was also a Hirata disciple. Though a townsman, he had early come to hope for an imperial restoration, and he was skillful in the composition of traditional verse. Many activists on the imperialist side had come to him during the final years of the shogunate and he had warmly entertained them all, arranging important introductions for many of them. Matsuo Taseko, who had come up to Kyoto in the Bunkyu era of the early 1860's, and Asami Keizo of Nakatsugawa, who had followed her a little later, had both taken lodgings at Isekyu for a time after their arrival. Indeed, there was no one from southern Shinano or eastern Mino who went to Kyoto to serve the imperial cause during those years who was not indebted to Kyubei.

"A great many people have come in from Ina since the beginning of the year."

Kyubei recited for Hosuke the names of the people who had rushed up to Kyoto as soon as they heard of the restoration of imperial power, in hope of serving the new government in some way. There were Kurasawa Yoshiyuki and Hara Nobuyoshi, who had been so active in promoting the restoration of Shinto burial rites as part of the unification of religion and government. There were Hara Yusai, who had taken up residence in the Iwakura mansion under the name Sakaki Shizue, Gonda Naosuke, who had once again become active after hiding out for so long in Ina, and his disciple Inoue Yorikuni. Then there was Matsuo Taseko herself, who had gone back to the capital and who had taken charge of the entertainment of guests, the direction of maids, and the education of the children at the Seyakuin residence of the Iwakura family. The number of Hirata people who had come to Kyoto from Ina alone was more than Kyubei could count on the fingers of both hands. The master Hirata Kanetane had brought his entire family to live with him in Kyoto and he was serving in the important capacity of special consultant to the new government.

"Well, let's have some tea first. Then I want to hear your story. It's too bad everyone has gone out."

Kyubei went into the family quarters and they could hear him bringing out tea utensils from behind the Osaka-style shoji with their delicate grill work. Masaka resumed his seat in the front of the store and began talking with Hosuke.

"Kyubei is an interesting person. He sells books by Master Atsutane at this shop. He has everything he wrote. In addition to dyeing, he also takes orders for formal dress for court officials. You could say that at the same time he does business he also makes known the Way."

"Really? What a splendid shop!"

Sitting in the front of the shop, the master would direct the work of the dyers from behind his grill. Masaka showed Hosuke the work area beyond the passageway extending back from the entrance to the drying area in the rear. It was spacious but all the grilled panels were closed around it and it was quite dark. The grills themselves, set on solid panels some three feet high, showed care and solidity in the weight of the bars and the sturdiness of the construction. Masaka also pointed out the dye pots set in groups of four. Dim beams of light came in through the grills and made them visible in the apparently deliberate dimness of the room. The dyes in the numerous groups of pots seemed to have been recently heated; they could catch the scent of the simmering liquids.

Kyubei brewed the tea himself and brought it into the front of the store. He set large teacups of the sort one might find in a merchant household before Masaka and Hosuke and poured them fragrant, perfectly brewed tea. As he sipped his own tea, he continued the conversation.

"Have you called on Kanetane at Nishinokoji, Tatematsu?"

But just as he was speaking there came the sound of the shoji at the entrance being opened and his family bustled in, back from viewing the foreigners. Someone reported that the British ambassador had failed to appear. Another speculated on what an outlandish stench would surely have been found to accompany the Dutch chargé if only one could have slipped up close enough to sniff it. "Disgusting! Disgusting!" came the voice of a young girl.

Kyubei listened to the account of how the manuscripts of the master had been moved to Ina as one who had long worked inconspicuously to support his fellow disciples.

"Master Kanetane must be relieved."

"After all, you moved those papers more than a hundred and fifty miles right through all the turmoil," added Masaka.

"That is really amazing," said Kyubei.

"No, you see," Hosuke took up the story, "when I got to Edo, the Hirata family was having a debate. Since Edo was so unsettled I called on them right away, and they were delighted when I offered to take charge of the materials. They were concerned about conditions along the road so they borrowed seals from the Shirakawa family. These were affixed to the containers and I assumed responsibility for them. I had this tremendous lot of papers loaded onto horses. I reached Zakoji on the eighteenth of the twelfth month last year and Kitahara Inao wrung my hands in gratitude. Maezawa Banri and Imamura Toyosaburo of Tajima had been worried too, and they came out and met me on the road."

There was no end to such stories.

Hosuke spent that day and the next calling on acquaintances and visiting the doll shops on Shijo avenue, trying to make time to drop in on Masaka once more before he left for home. Although he did not have the opportunity to experience fully the ambience of Kyoto under the restoration as Masaka had wished, he was well satisfied to call on Kanetane at his home, renew his old acquaintance with Masaka, and spend some time at the shop of Isekyu.

As Hosuke paid his respects and prepared to leave, Kyubei called him back.

"What, are you going back already? I haven't done a thing for you."

Then Kyubei began to speak as a dyer. In the third month of the previous year, during the national mourning for the death of the emperor, among those who had come to the capital once again, joining Kureta in many and varied activities, had been the honjin of Nakatsugawa, Asami Keizo. But when Keizo learned soon afterward that the procession of the commander of the pacification forces would pass through Mino, he promptly closed down his temporary residence in Kyoto and returned home. He had left an order for some dye work with Kyubei and it had not been easy to send the order to him in all the confusion and disorder. Kyubei then asked Hosuke if, since his return route would take him through Nakatsugawa, he would consent to the inconvenience of carrying Keizo's order with him.

"Please ask him too, Kureta," said Kyubei. "I know it is not right to request this of a person I have just met for the first time."

"What do you mean? This is the age of international law!"

"Well, I guess that's what everyone is saying these days." Kyubei gave a short laugh.

"Hosuke, you just take care of this in that spirit."

"There goes Kureta again," said Hosuke as he burst out laughing too. "When I came to Kyoto this time I couldn't get over how everyone was talking about international law. Well, this is what I'll do. I will be calling on Kureta once more. I'll stop by here too at that time."

The new government had taken special precautions for the visit to the capital by the British ambassador Parkes. When he left Osaka he was accompanied by Komatsu Tatewaki and Ito Hirobumi, and they were joined at Fushimi Inari by Nakai Kozo and Goto Shojiro for the entry into Kyoto.

The ambassador's party included a detachment of red-coated British guards and all arrived safely at the quarters prepared for them at the Chion-in. The next day, they were setting out by horseback or in litters to the audience when, just as they left the street before the temple and turned onto Nawade street, two anti-foreign extremists leaped out of the crowd. The new government had feared just such an incident, and they had had each han contribute at least twenty men to keep the ambassadors' routes under strict control. They had also set up encampments near each of the ambassadorial lodgings and a rigorous guard was maintained day and night, but they still had apparently not succeeded in convincing the anti-foreign elements of the value of sound international relations. When they saw the attackers, the soldiers in the vanguard opened fire. Panic struck the crowd and it began to scatter. The attack came on through the first line of guards. Nakai Kozo and Goto Shojiro were in direct attendance upon the ambassador, and when Goto saw the two attackers cutting their way through the redcoats, he drew his sword and cut one down. As he turned to the second attacker, the blade of his sword came loose from the handle and flew away. Nakai also met the attack but his parry was unsuccessful and he fell with a head wound. The second attacker was taken alive by the soldiers and the uproar was gradually quieted, but some eight or nine members of the British guard were wounded. Parkes, who had been on horseback in the middle of the procession, was fortunately untouched, but with this incident his attendance at the audience had to be reconsidered. That is why the British ambassador and his party had failed to appear.

The audience was held in the Shishinden with Parkes absent and only the other two ambassadors present. The new emperor, dressed in ceremonial trousers and a white robe, met with Roches and van Polesbroek. After the ceremony they were taken to the Crane Room, where they were served refreshments. Until now, when the Tokugawa shoguns had on rare occasions accorded audience to foreign representatives, the shogun had always assumed a very high posture. The emperor, on the other hand, had even omitted the ceremony of obeisance, and he had met with the foreigners on familiar terms, face to face. This one fact alone impressed upon Roches and van Polesbroek the almost unbelievable changes that had occurred. The two did not, however, remain unaware of what had happened on Nawade street. When the ceremony ended, Ito Hirobumi, who was serving as interpreter as well as escort, joined the ambassadors and handed them a letter from Parkes. It was addressed to the French ambassador and had been brought by a mounted British guard. Roches blanched when he read the letter, and shouting "There has been an attack," he took his leave and rode alone on horseback to the Chion-in. There he met Parkes and it was said that he proposed that they immediately withdraw to Hyogo, board the warships, and return to Yokohama. Parkes shook his head and refused to agree to the French ambassador's proposals.

Masaka brought the news with him when he went to visit Kyubei on the following afternoon. Hosuke, who had dropped by Koromonotana to take his leave, was with him and the two took their seats in the storefront of Isekyu.

"What a shock!"

Kyubei came rushing out. Those sitting in the front of the store and those working with customers around a brazier all stared at each other.

"Yesterday Iwakura went to call on him and Matsudaira went too. They say that things are really lively around the Chion-in," continued Kyubei. "Everyone was really worried last night."

"But isn't Parkes the one, though?" asked Masaka. " 'My guards have taken heavy casualties but I and my officers are safe, thanks to the bravery of Goto and Nakai. If I were to return now without having audience, it would be an act of disrespect to the emperor . . .' That's what they say he said!"

"Well, but how is all this going to be settled? Rumors are that they will want at least sixty or seventy thousand ryo in reparations."

It was soon announced that the imperial audience would be carried out two days later than originally scheduled and surveillance of the entire city was raised to an even higher pitch. Kyubei went behind the accountant's grill and brought out a notice that had just been distributed by town officials. He showed it to Masaka and Hosuke.

> On the day that the British ambassador is to go to the palace, all traffic will be stopped along Nawade street, and along Sanjo avenue to Sakai street, from the hour of the serpent. The gates will be closed on all the side streets. No one will be permitted to remain on the streets except for the merchants who reside there and their servants.

"Hey!" Hosuke's eyes opened wide. "It says that not only public but even private passage will be forbidden without special permission. If I wait around too long I won't be able to start for home."

"Kyoto is too unsettled now. All the people from the han have come in. There are those who would secretly like to see this new government over-turned—they've got to be careful."

Kyubei placed emphasis on each word as he spoke to Hosuke.

Just then Kyubei's adopted son put his head in from the rear of the shop. Unlike Kyubei, who was full of the townsman's spirit and who would have enjoyed bringing all the posthumous disciples of Atsutane together in the front of his shop, the adopted son was a dyer pure and simple. His hands and arms were deeply stained with indigo. Kyubei had him bring a paper package from a cupboard beside the ledger stand. On it was written "To your order, Isekyu." He placed it before Hosuke.

"Well, I would be most obliged if you could give this to Asami Keizo in Nakatsugawa. I realize that it will be an additional burden for you on your journey." Kyubei glanced back at his adopted son. "Shall we show them?"

"The colors came out quite well," the younger man said as he unwrapped the package.

"That's a splendid black," said Masaka.

"Only Kyoto water will bring out that shade. They talk about Edo purple because Edo water brings out the purple well, and Kyoto water is best for scarlet. You could very well speak of Kyoto scarlet. The black ground of this jacket was first dyed scarlet."

Kyubei went on about the lore of his trade.

"You can count on me," said Hosuke.

Then he went out under the indigo curtains with the shop name Isekyu dyed in white.

"Hosuke, I'll go along with you for a way," said Masaka as he followed him out.

So long as the foreigners were in residence, all callers were being extended the unprecedented indulgence of being permitted to pass through the nine gates of the imperial palace enclosure without dismounting from their horses or getting out of their carriages. It symbolized the way things were. A turbulent atmosphere in which all standards were being overthrown had come pouring into the mountain basin that contained Kyoto, bringing with it a sense of renewed life.

"Anyway, now we are in times when we must deal with the entire world."

For Hosuke, in from the remote countryside of Nanjo village in Ina, these feelings came readily, but for Masaka it was not easy to accept the fact that the day imperial rule was restored was also the day international relations were opened.

Hosuke turned to Masaka as they came out of Fuyamachi heading toward Sanjo avenue.

"Kureta, this is the way I look at it, coming in to see Kyoto right now. More than anything else, it is the han that are at the center of things. Those who have the support of the han can do what they think right. But we Hirata disciples are only physicians or headmen or honjin, or else we are farmers."

"When you come down to it, that's right. For most of the Hirata people, anyway."

"Right. We're all behind-the-scenes workers. We're doing all we can to support the new government. It hurts to think about it."

"But, Hosuke, you're saying that only the Hirata people are getting trampled underfoot. But there are still some of us of samurai rank."

"I suppose so."

"Look here. The other day I saw an old register of disciples from the Tempo period thirty years ago. At that time there were five hundred forty-nine disciples and among them were seventy-three samurai. Some seventeen different han throughout the nation, including Kagoshima, Tsuwano, Kochi, Nagoya, Kanazawa, Akita, and Sendai, produced those people. The best-represented han had fourteen, the least so had one. Now when you count them up, the number of samurai disciples in service in the han has actually increased. There's Yamabuki, and Naegi of course, but the seventeen han of that time have become thirty-five. That's the point. In every han, now that they are up against big problems, everyone is vacillating. They are thinking, 'Should we support the imperial cause or the shogunate?' At such times just think what the Hirata disciples can accomplish. I think Nakane Sekko of Echizen is a good example. He stood between the people of the han and his lord, Matsudaira Shungaku, and advocated the imperial cause. And then remember that there was also the poet Tachibana Akemi in Echizen—of course I really don't know whether he was samurai or not."

"Certainly the rate at which the number of disciples has increased is amazing, Kureta. I don't know about other districts, but at the time you came to hide out in Ina the increases in membership there must have been around twenty per year. For the number of new members to increase from eight or nine to twenty each year in just that little valley made us feel that things were really moving. But how does that look when you compare it with the fact that just from last winter into this spring we had a hundred new members?"

"At that rate there must be more than three thousand disciples throughout the country. And we don't stop with just samurai. There are at least thirty disciples among the higher levels of the court nobility. And why are so many people coming to seek membership in the Hirata school? Atsutane spoke of the 'pillar of the soul'—that's it, the soul's pillar. Isn't it because that is precisely what everyone has lost? What is this age looking for if not the chance simply to be alive once again?"

The two walked in silence for a time down Teramachi street. Then Hosuke started to speak, hesitated a moment, and then started over.

"You really don't need to come any further than this, Kureta. I'll be setting out early tomorrow morning. I'll go out through Otsu toward the Kiso road. Let's say good-bye here."

"No, let's go on together just a little further."

"How about it, Kureta? Have you heard about the report that came in to the Sawa household? Hasn't the commander of the pacifying forces found it hard going down the Kiso?"

"It certainly seems so."

"That's because there are so many han in Mino. And some of them are still supporting the Tokugawa."

"If you are going to go down the Kiso road, you should catch up with the commander's forces around Ogaki, shouldn't you?"

"Could be."

"Please give my best wishes to Asami in Nakatsugawa. And, if you go over Magome pass, I would like for you to look in on Aoyama Hanzo there."

Masaka walked along Teramachi street as far as Sanjo street with Hosuke. Then he accompanied him as far as the great Sanjo bridge. Masaka still felt a chill come over him whenever he looked into the riverbed there. Back in 1863, the third year of Bunkyu, he and eight other Hirata men had gone to the Jitoin, taken the heads from the wooden statues of Ashikaga Takauji and another shogun, and left them exposed in the riverbed to taunt the Tokugawa. Now in this very same place stood notice boards announcing imperial orders for a punitive expedition against Tokugawa Yoshinobu. Although the waters of the Kamo river remained unchanged, Kyoto was no longer the Kyoto of yesterday. The martial song "Miya sama, Miya sama," recently written to raise the spirits of the populace, had simple words and a catchy tune, and even the little girls who played by the bridge, with younger brothers and sisters on their backs and kerchiefs on their heads, were singing it.

CHAPTER THREE

1

IT WAS ALREADY well known in eastern Mino and southern Shinano that the expeditions against the shogunal loyalists were moving simultaneously through the Tokaido, the Tosando, and the Hokurikudo. When Asami Keizo received early notice of them in Kyoto he returned home immediately. Many of the other headmen, honjin, and toiya of the Tosando were also becoming conversant with events up to the proclamation of the order for the chastisement of Tokugawa Yoshinobu.

The vanguard moving over the Tosando toward the Kanto was carrying out its orders to pacify the provinces along the way. Originally, it had been intended that Prince Iwakura should personally lead this expedition but when the prince, who was now the key man in the new government, found it impossible to leave Kyoto, the two brothers Iwakura no Shosho Tomosada and Iwakura no Yachimaru Tomotsune were called upon to act in their father's name as commander-in-chief and deputy, respectively. They were accompanied by such people as Kagawa Keizo, Ijichi Masaharu, Itagaki Taisuke, and Akamatsu Gonosuke, serving as councillors or inspectors. The soldiers under their command were from Satsuma, Choshu, Tosa, and Inaba. Two representatives from each of these han were also taking part in the military councils. Asami Keizo relayed this information to his friends Hachiya Kozo and Aoyama Hanzo, and the three prepared to meet the Tosando army in their various capacities as honjin, toiya, and headmen.

Although many areas had fallen into lawlessness and disorder in the sudden changes accompanying the abolition of the shogunate, eastern Mino where Keizo and Kozo lived was still under the very effective control of Owari. But even this did not entirely spare them of uneasiness. It was the threat of disorder in the region that had occasioned Keizo's sudden return home.

Aoyama Hanzo in Magome and his two friends in Nakatsugawa waited for the arrival of the Tosando army. There had been good and ample reason why, in the excitement over the reestablishment of imperial rule that was bringing people racing into Kyoto from every part of the country, Keizo had closed his house there, had taken his leave of Master Kanetane, and had come rushing back to his home in Mino. Hanzo had learned much since Keizo's return. This Iwakura no Shosho who was on his first campaign as commander-in-chief of the Tosando army was a princeling just entering adolescence. If this was the age of the elder brother, one could easily estimate the maturity of his deputy, the younger brother. However important the role of their father in the new government, however much he might enjoy the confidence of the new emperor, these two sons of his were still very young. And what did the han along the way think of them? However awesome the array of heroes among the guards that accompanied these two young commanders, they seemed to possess little knowledge about conditions in the countryside through which they were marching. That Keizo had felt such serious concern and had come rushing home told very clearly what was happening.

Nor was this all. Since his return, Keizo was working with Kozo to alert all the Hirata disciples in eastern Mino to the opportunity to serve as guides for the approaching army. Hanzo's heart leaped when he learned of it. He would have wanted to work with his two friends if it had been possible, but it was very doubtful that the headman of Magome, being under the command of the Yamamura of Fukushima, would be permitted that much freedom.

Already in the first month a proclamation had been issued in the name of the steward of the commander of the Tosando army, reassuring the people along the route and asking for their support. Hanzo had read many similar announcements from the offices in Fukushima. These announcements were not without a certain bitter undertone, as though they had been written in obedience to firm orders from Owari but against the will of the local officials. The documents reflected a fundamental conflict between Owari and its subordinates in the Kiso. Nevertheless, in anticipation of a large number of official travelers, Hanzo began to concern himself with everything from the procurement of additional laborers to repairs on the highway. He had in hand a circular requesting that bedding for guests in each station be promptly inventoried and reports sent up. An immense number of torches had to be prepared for the passage of the imperial army. Since the Kiso valley was a forest region, a notice came out informing each village of how many torches it would have to provide.

Hanzo read this notice in the company of Seisuke before leaving the honjin to go to the meeting room where Inosuke and the other post station officials were waiting. Each village was required to provide between three thousand and three thousand five hundred torches. This requirement was not confined to the Magome area. Agematsu, Suwara, Nojiri, Midono, and Tsumago were included, and Kakisore village near Midono, being in a particularly heavily forested area, was required to provide seven thousand torches all by itself.

"Look here, Hanzo. It says that we are to count the places where hinoki branches are to be cut and the number of trees from which they are to be cut and report in writing immediately. Since the Kiso is in the Owari domains, this means that the wood for the torches is to be contributed by the han.

They're really after us for every last detail. They even tell the officials in charge of the cutting to make sure that the branches are cut in a way that will not injure the trees. It also says that the timber officials are going to be out taking control of things. They are going to collect the torches at places where the army is expected to camp and pass them out as needed. Everyone must be careful to ensure that there are no slipups."

The burden placed on the Kiso people by this order was not a light one. Magome was responsible for three thousand torches and Yamaguchi and Yubunezawa for three thousand five hundred each, so that just the small area for which Hanzo was responsible had to supply ten thousand torches. Hanzo did everything in his power to encourage the villagers to carry out this order.

Hanzo was looking forward to welcoming the imperial commanders. Although they had endured great hardships, he and the people who worked in the Magome station did not doubt their ability to cope with this new spring season. In this mood, even though he could not join his friends from Nakatsugawa, he set about eagerly, in his capacity as headman, to assist the approaching Tosando army. The earlier anti-shogunal movements—of Yamato Gojo, Ikuno, Mt. Tsukuba, Choshu, and Suwa—had seemed unable to wait for the coming of the new age. Yet events had now advanced to the point where a great army was moving eastward under the supreme command of the Imperial Prince Taruhito.

The proclamations issued to the people of the region by the steward of the commander of the army did not end by merely asking for their support. As no social order can exist without the consent of the people, the new government first had to appeal for wholehearted acceptance. Support for the new government was still quite shallow. The steward of the army therefore issued numerous statements promising to respect the will of the people. The conditions under which the army was now setting out under orders from the emperor were as previously announced but those living in the hinterlands should go about their affairs in confidence and peace. All who have hitherto suffered under cruel and oppressive administration, not only in Tokugawa domains but in all the han domains, or who have other matters to report should approach the army without hesitation. As the commander advances, he will give solace and succor to those along his route who are more than eighty years of age, are impoverished widows, or are alone or destitute. It is his intent to reward those who have been conspicuous for their loyalty, filial piety, honor, or chastity; therefore all officials in each province should review thoroughly all the people in their charge and submit appropriate documentation to the army. The steward further proclaimed that one of the aims of this army marching under imperial orders was to learn of conditions in the provinces and to rescue the people from hardship.

One reason for the new government's evident concern with gaining the support of the people in the hinterlands was that it could not be sure of the attitudes of the han through which its army would be passing. At first, when the fighting around Toba and Fushimi had ended with the flight of the Aizu forces, many of the han throughout the Tosando connected this with the uprising of the eighteenth day of the eighth month of the preceding year and saw it as simply a reversal of that coup. Of course there were all kinds of han along the way. The conditions of their domains were different and their relations with the former shoguns had been different. Among them were han such as Ogaki, which had joined directly in the fighting at Toba and Fushimi in an effort to support Aizu and Kuwana. Each han, however, was now taking a wait-and-see attitude toward events in Kyoto. When Yoshinobu had given up the office of shogun and withdrawn from Nijo castle, no one had expected this event to have nationwide repercussions. Even when they heard that Yoshinobu had boarded a warship and sailed for Edo, the retainers of the various han remained unperturbed. But when they learned that yesterday's shogun was now declared to be today's rebel, the shock they received was sudden and severe, resulting in an extraordinary breakdown of consensus among the han. Even those that had been allied for generations with the shogunate now had to appeal to the generosity of those who had devoted themselves wholeheartedly to the interests of the nation. If at this time they failed to follow the will of the new government, they would be guilty of high treason and could expect to be punished as enemies of the court. When they read this proclamation from the Tosando army, the retainers of the han at last understood that the old order could no longer be maintained. As might be expected, there were many who could not forget the old days of the warrior class. There were also many who went so far in trying to steal another moment of tranquility for their lord that they were ridiculed for their temporizing and vacillation. Still others tried to have things both ways. Emperor or shogun—the army was now moving to ascertain the attitudes in the han.

As for Yoshinobu, when he had called his officials together in Nijo castle on the twelfth day of the tenth month of the previous year and had announced his determination to resign his office, some of them had expressed the fear that there would be daimyo who would try to preserve their old status even after the return of shogunal powers to the emperor. Yoshinobu had replied by asking if that was not already happening, and had then resigned still deeply concerned about what might happen in the han after his resignation. Just how the ancient power of the shogunate was to be extirpated and how the problem of Yoshinobu was to be resolved were questions causing severe differences of opinion among the representatives of the han serving in Kyoto. The idea that it would be best to achieve the establishment of the new state through a public debate and according to the dictates of public opinion was put forward forcefully at this stage. But this position, for the most part supported by people from Tosa, aroused such strong opposition that it could not be realized. Men like Saigo Takamori were reported to be saying that matters should be settled by the sword alone. The time for discussion had passed and the time for action had come.

Among the activists watching this situation were some who set out on their own initiative to clear the way for the armies as they came east. At the beginning of the old second month, the vanguard of the Tosando army came down the road from Kyoto, something over one hundred and twenty men moving ahead of the main body and supported by two cannon. They brought with them promises of a fifty percent reduction in taxes.

2

While the Kyoto area was still in an uproar over the unprecedented imperial audience for the foreign ambassadors, some one hundred twenty men representing the court nobles Shigenoi and Ayanokoji came from the stations of Nakatsugawa and Ochiai to the west, entered the Kiso road, and advanced through Magome pass. They were met by chamberlains and commissioners from the han in some places, and by the local honjin and toiya in others.

"The vanguard is already here!"

All along the road those whose duty it was to receive the commander of the army responded. As they observed the cannon and the martial fittings of this corps, they could imagine the strength of the main force, and it seemed, with the promise of a reduction of taxes by half, that reforms beyond all belief must be coming. Soon the vanguard passed through the barrier at Fukushima and arrived at Shimo-Suwa. One detachment went from there over Wada pass, crossing the Chikuma river to reach the station of Oiwake.

That the Tosando army had managed to pass through the strategic areas of the provinces of Omi, Mino, and Shinano without encountering any trace of resistance had to be credited to skillful scouting. From Otsu in the west to Oiwake in the east, all the lands of the han through which the highway passed were administered either by daimyo traditionally loyal to the Tokugawa or by magistrates who had the same qualification, testifying to the care and cunning with which the old shogunate had controlled every strategic point. The Ii of Hikone, the Toda of Ogaki, the Matsudaira of Iwamura, the Toyama of Naegi, the Yamamura of Fukushima, the Suwa of Takashima— when one counted them all up, it became obvious that without their silent assent one hundred twenty men and two cannon could never have passed so freely over this road. The vanguard was led by Sagara Sozo and the detachment that went to Oiwake was commanded by his comrade Kanahara Chuzo. When Saigo Takamori had raised troops in the Kanto a year earlier, it was this same Sagara Sozo who had responded. Before there had been any open talk of the overthrow of the shogunate, Sagara Sozo and his comrades had gone on the offensive, using every means to sow disorder and confusion in Edo, and had clashed directly with the retainers of Shonai han then in charge of the security of Edo. The burning of the Satsuma residence in Mita was not the only consequence; these outbreaks were of such importance that they could be called the fuse which set off the battles of Toba and Fushimi in the west.

Incredibly, a memorandum issued by the steward of the commander-in-chief of the Tosando army was now being circulated among the officials of the han along the way. It was severely critical of the actions of the vanguard. It said that although the court nobles Shigenoi and Ayanokoji were reported to have assembled men for an expedition to the east, this was unfounded rumor. In fact, these men were not acting under imperial orders at all. They were simply adventurers who had deceived some young and inexperienced court officials. Ayanokoji and Shigenoi had already returned to the capital. While those claiming to be their retainers were still pressing on to the east, they were not the vanguard of the Tosando army. The memorandum further stated that although they would be trying to raise rations and travel expenses along the way and making use of porters and horses without pay under the pretext that they were part of the official army, this claim was without basis in fact. All han were advised to give the strictest attention to this matter in order not to be defrauded by these imposters. It added that still others might come through claiming to be retainers of Iwakura; if so they were without exception to be detained and their disposal determined upon the arrival of the army itself. If they offered resistance no questions would be asked about their deaths.

As the memorandum was recopied and sent on, it was inevitably distorted. It remained clear, however, that the staff of the army did not recognize this group which called itself the advance guard.

"Imposters!"

The outcry rose from Oiwake to nearby Komoro han. It had surprising effect. Even those who had hitherto planned to assist these troops were taken in by this ridiculous charge that they were imposters. Those who had given funds to Sagara Sozo and his men were subjected to severe interrogation not only in Oiwake but in Karuizawa and from Kutsukake to Iwamurata. Nor did it stop there. The effects were felt as far back as the Kiso and even in Mino. It was in connection with this matter that Aoyama Hanzo, the headman of Magome, was called to Fukushima.

The Fukushima district offices were located along the upper reaches of the Kiso river where it flowed through a deep valley surrounded by mountains covered with dark and gloomy woods sweeping down to the famous barrier. They were set in a neighborhood where some thirty or forty samurai residences clustered around the three tall, shingle-roofed buildings of the residence of the Yamamura deputy.

The offices themselves were spacious. All details of the management of the Kiso district were handled in these offices, and there was a waiting room set aside for those who had come on business. Hanzo, called up from Magome, was kept waiting there for some time. He had long since lost count of the number of trips he had made here on business, passing through the main gate and across the inner bridge in his capacity as one of the honjin of the eleven

Kiso stations or as one of the headmen of the thirty-three villages of the Kiso valley. Those trips, however, had been made in normal times, when there was no call for such an intimidating summons to be issued. This time was different.

Presently the bored voice of a man who seemed to be a foot soldier could be heard.

"The Magome honjin is here."

Hanzo was called before the officials and their subordinates. Among them was a chamberlain who had created a considerable stir with his impassioned support of the shogunal cause. He was to be the chief interrogator.

The day's business was to bring the highway under still more rigorous control in order to deal with the false army that had occasioned so much talk among the han. But the official in charge pursued the matter further. Striking his fan against his thigh, he looked toward Hanzo and began to ask questions about the party of Sagara Sozo.

"I have heard that when the men of Makino Totomi no Kami took them in custody in Oiwake, one of the packhorsemen picked up a package containing about three hundred ryo. He immediately reported it to the post officials and they, after conferring among themselves, checked the package once more and discovered that it had been dropped by the rebels in their flight. They reported this to the commander of the Tosando army. Now why should anyone in Sagara Sozo's party have been carrying such a large sum of money? What do you think about that, Hanzo?"

A personal attendant of the Yamamura family was present at the meeting and he added his interjections of agreement to the questions of the interrogator. Hanzo kneeled with both hands flat on the tatami as he told exactly what had happened when Sagara and his men passed through Magome. He described how their passage through the Owari domains had been orderly but that a contribution of twenty ryo in gold had been made to them in response to a request by one of Sagara's men, one Date Tetsunosuke.

"We knew nothing to suggest that they were not a genuine part of the army. I am now appalled that we gave money to them."

"Wait!" responded the interrogator. "Listen to me! All sorts of strange ideas are going around these days and a person just doesn't know what to expect. Everything bad is blamed on the Tokugawa. That's the kind of time it has become. But you should have thought about what Sagara Sozo and his people did the last time they were in Edo. Heaven sees everything. And look at what they have done, coming down this highway and creating all that trouble around Oiwake. You can't get away with anything you like simply by saying that you're part of the imperial army!"

"That's right!" It was Yamamura's personal attendant, warming his hands at the hibachi, who interrupted. "You put it very well. In fact, I was just about to say the very same thing myself."

"All the same," continued the interrogator, "even to you, my colleague, I will have to say that I just cannot stomach what has been going on ever since the imperial proclamation of chastisement was issued. I can't help thinking that if the previous emperor were still living, Yoshinobu and Aizu and Kuwana would not be subjected to this kind of treatment . . ."

Having received orders to appear before the officials once more on the following morning to hear their decision, Hanzo emerged from the gate of the official enclosure. Awaiting him was the assistant headman from Toge, Heisuke's successor Heibei.

"Hanzo!"

"Oh! Have you been waiting for me?"

"Yes, I've been terribly worried and I stayed right here from the time you went in."

The two men talked as they walked along the snow-covered road, over the bridge, and toward the part of town where their inn was located.

Kiso-Fukushima was no longer the Kiso-Fukushima of thirty years ago or even of five years ago. It was no longer the peaceful town that had once taken pride in the Seigakan Academy, founded by Watanabe Hoko, which later boasted Takei Yosetsu as headmaster. Nor was it any longer the town where each year during the horse fair swordsmen would come from near and far to observe the martial prowess of the master swordsman Endo Goheita. Still less was it the quiet castle town from which the national elder statesman Yamamura Somon had emerged to direct the affairs of Owari for more than ten years.

Surveillance had become very strict in all parts of town and no suspicious persons were permitted to stay overnight. As Hanzo and Heibei walked back to their inn, they were passed by one of the fast litters that now rushed incessantly day and night over the Kiso road. The bearers kicked up the snow as they went by.

Rumors were being rigorously suppressed. Notices from the commissioners' office had come down even to the inns in this post station town, saying that in these times it would have an adverse effect on the morale of the han if people persisted in offering criticism of current affairs; therefore such talk was strictly prohibited. The order applied not only to arguments among drinkers but even to the gossip of women and children. No rumors were to be repeated.

Hanzo returned to his inn and walked in through the earthen-floored entry with its hanging plaques announcing the names of various pilgrim groups that had come from all over the nation to the shrines of Mt. Ontake. When he reached the raised inner entry, he smelled the pungent smoke of pine wood burning in the open, flueless hearth. Two other travelers were in conversation at the fireside. Hanzo warmed himself for a time at the fire, drinking the hot mimosa tea that the lady of the house brought him. The conversation of his companions reminded him once again how impossible it was to put a stop to loose talk.

"Whenever I see the Tokugawa crest tears comes to my eyes."

"This is hardly the time for such sentiments!"

They were in heated argument. One man, his face tinted scarlet by the firelight, was furiously haranguing the other, who kept rearranging the ashes with a handmade bamboo scoop, both completely oblivious to the strictures against such talk contained in the memorandum from the commissioners' office.

"What do you mean? Isn't this new government likely to collapse at any moment?"

"Just whose side are you on, anyway?"

"Well—I'm both an imperialist and a supporter of the shogunate."

The agonies of the time lay behind the words of these men hidden away in a corner of this crowded hearth room.

With the regional officials picking at his every word, Hanzo could not relax until he heard the decision that was to be made the following morning. He passed the evening in the light of an inn lamp. At such a time he was grateful that Heibei was the kind of person who never caused any awkwardness or inconvenience.

The sun rose much later here in the valley than it did in Magome on its hilltop. Even though it was lively enough in the daytime, at night a depressing roar seemed to fill Hanzo's ears. He knew that it was made by the shallow water of the Kiso river flowing rapidly over the stones in the riverbed, but it sounded like a relentless, nightlong downpour. Somehow it called to mind the men in control of the Kiso valley and the unfathomable fate with which they were now confronted.

The placing of the barrier here at this most strategic spot between Edo and Kyoto had the same original significance as the placing of the great house of Ii in a domain of three hundred fifty thousand koku revenue in Hikone to watch over Kyoto from just beyond Otsu and Fushimi. The development of the feudal order over the centuries clearly reflected its profound cautiousness. The Yamamura family that was in charge of this barrier had been placed here as deputies of the shogunate because they had distinguished themselves, back in 1600, by guiding the Tokugawa forces through the mountains on their way to the battlefield at Sekigahara. Later, when the Kiso district came under the control of Nagoya, the Yamamura became deputies of Owari. Yet there were many samurai in Fukushima whose pride in once having been direct retainers of the Tokugawa, combined with their mountain men's exclusivity, did not allow them to mix any more than was absolutely necessary with the officials from Owari who came up to assert the power of their great lord in every matter. This silent opposition had not grown up in a single day.

Now the Tosando army was approaching. Each han had no choice but to make its position clear. Owari han, it appeared, had cast aside all previous customs and associations and was trying to come through this dark time by favoring those who had always been in the imperial party. It was making clear its commitment to the imperial cause. All the han officials in Nagoya who had hitherto been conspicuous in their support of the shogunate had been relieved of office. But here in Fukushima the retainers of the Yamamura continued to boast of their long martial tradition and obstinately refused to abandon their old commitments. Not only were voices raised in protest of the attitude of Owari, but some even publicly advocated seceding from Owari and setting themselves up as an independent Tokugawa domain. Others went so far as to insist that there was no course consistent with proper feelings other than to commit themselves to live or die with the house of Tokugawa —those who were unrighteous, disloyal, or careless of their obligations to their ancestors should be locked up.

"What's going to happen in Fukushima?"

Hanzo could think of nothing else. He had Heibei put out his bedding beside his own and they slept that night with their pillows aligned, the daggers they had carried on the road near to hand under their mattresses.

The next morning arrived and soon it was time to go back to the district offices. Hanzo had Heibei wait just inside the gate. After some time in the waiting room, he was again called to the next room. There, before the elders and personal attendants of the Yamamura assembled on the raised portion of the floor, he was given a severe reprimand. He was told that his conduct in receiving the party of Sagara Sozo which had posed as the advance guard of the imperial army, and in raising twenty ryo for Sagara's follower Date Tetsunosuke, had been improper. If these were normal times he might have received a more severe punishment; as it was, he would not be put into bonds but would merely be given a formal reprimand. This was in recognition of the many years of service rendered by Hanzo and his family and their scrupulous performance in raising subscriptions, a record of performance that could not be overlooked. He was, therefore, being favored by this special lenience.

"Yes! I understand."

With a shout of assent Hanzo lowered his face to the floor. He had no difficulty in accepting the scolding since he regarded it as just another aspect of service to the military households. Then he left the building.

"Aoyama!"

Someone came running up behind Hanzo, calling out his name. He and Heibei, having just set out on the way home, were approaching the signboard in a place called Yazawa on the western edge of Fukushima that informed travelers of the way to Mt. Ontake.

"Aoyama! Are you on your way back to Magome?"

The person who called out was wearing Kiso-style work trousers and he had a hunting gun on his shoulder. His name was Noguchi Shusaku and he lived outside the official limits of Fukushima. He had once studied with Owaki Jisho. Although Hanzo was not well acquainted with him, he had a way of speaking very familiarly to Hanzo whenever they met. He was always dropping the names of certain loyalist samurai from Nagoya such as Tanaka Torasaburo and Niwa Juntaro.

"Well, just let me go along with you for a little while," he said as he walked beside Hanzo. "Aoyama, this morning everyone knew that you had come to town and were being called before the officials. Yes, indeed. These things really get around fast. It's such a narrow little valley. I'm telling you, you even have to be careful how you clear your throat around here. That's the kind of place Fukushima is. Really—this valley's awful that way. I hate to say this, but the Hirata school just doesn't have any future around here. Everybody is all taken up with the Chinese classics instead. It's just not like it is over in Ina and Mino. We're terribly behind the times here. All the same, Aoyama, you just keep your eyes open. We're not without men of integrity even here in Fukushima."

He did not say it in so many words but it was clear from his behavior that Noguchi, for all that he looked like just another person going out after pheasant, was trying to line himself up on the imperial side against the coming of the new day.

After this unexpected companion left them, Hanzo and Heibei walked on over the crackling snow as far as a place called Aobuchi. Here the road turned sharply around the foot of a ridge and entered a side valley. Travelers coming from the west would catch their first glimpse of Fukushima from this steep slope. Hanzo was going the other way but when he reached this point he automatically turned back to look at the view and breathed a deep sigh.

3

It is often said that Nezame in the Kiso is a noontime place. Whether coming from Fukushima like Hanzo and Heibei or coming from the west, everyone who passed over the Kiso road would have the same experience of hurrying to a noon meal at Nezame. The place was famous for its buckwheat noodles.

Although it was supposed to be spring, the snow that still covered the stone-weighted roofs, the wooden clogs hung up along the roadside, and the smoke leaking through the walls all made the area around the noodle shop look as though it had not yet completely come out of hibernation. Hanzo and Heibei had been late in setting out from Fukushima that morning and they arrived just as a group of pilgrims bound for Ise was finishing its meal and getting ready to set out again. There was another guest in a short black cape sitting with a companion toward the back of the room. It was Keizo.

Hanzo thus found himself in the company of this friend who was on his way down the road in the opposite direction. Keizo was going to Fukushima. In response to questioning, he said that he had also received a summons from the district offices at Fukushima. He had been called out in exactly the same way that Hanzo had.

"What's this all about, Hanzo?"

That was the first thing that Keizo said. The two men looked at each other, trying to fathom the intent of the officials in Fukushima.

"Now look," began Keizo, "until that notice came out from the steward of the commander-in-chief of the Tosando army, no one said a thing about any false troops. Weren't they even let through the Fukushima barrier without question? What kind of thing is it for them to have sent all their own top officials out to greet Sagara and then to turn around and reprimand us?''

"That's just what I think. Because anyway, Sagara Sozo and his crowd ran pretty wild up in Edo last year. They couldn't help knowing about that and it had its consequences in Fukushima, Suwa, and Komoro. Then came that letter from the steward of the commander of the Tosando. They decided to catch their enemy on the wing.''

"We're still in a dark time."

Hanzo spoke with a sigh. For that reason alone, he wanted to see the Tosando army come through as soon as possible.

"Well, let's go on talking while we eat our noodles."

Hanzo sat down facing his friend and continued the conversation.

"Go ahead and eat. Don't mind me. When I get to talking about this not even good buckwheat noodles can stop me. But it was really a bit of luck meeting you here today."

"And it was a good thing for me, too. Now, thanks to you, I know what's up in Fukushima."

Keizo finished his noodles, poured the remainder of the broth from the pitcher into the dipping bowl, and drank it. As he was wiping his mouth, a little girl emerged with Hanzo's order from the kitchen near the entry and threaded her way among the long benches on the earthen floor.

"Sorry to have kept you waiting."

Along this old highway travelers would not be satisfied with anything less than a famous noodle shop or a famous dish. The little box of seasonings, the pitcher for the broth, the dipping bowl, and the disposable chopsticks of bright, fresh wood all spoke of Nezame's location in the mountains. The handmade buckwheat noodles were heaped up on a woven bamboo basket on a red lacquered base and served on a footed tray. Hanzo divided the noodles with Heibei and took up his chopsticks. Then he looked up at his friend as though something had suddenly come to mind.

"Keizo, that copy of the memorandum from the steward of the commander of the Tosando addressed to the high officials of Owari. Did it come to your place, too?''

"Yes, it did."

"What did you make of it?"

"Well—"

"Wasn't that something? It says that the high command did not recognize Sagara Sozo and his men as an advance guard."

"It speaks of them as an utter rabble."

"But if they were really as bad as all that, it would have been better to have kept them from going out as a vanguard in the beginning."

"That's just it. It looks as though Sagara Sozo and his men should never have been permitted to set out. I only realized that for the first time when I read that memorandum. It even made clear that although they set out in the name of Ayanokoji, they were never under official orders. And to think that

Sagara and his men were first brought together under Saigo Takamori! They should really be regarded as being under the command of Satsuma. The memorandum came out from the high command in Kyoto and from the staff of the Tosando army as well. But it looks as though the staff could not maintain military discipline with that crowd running free down the roads ahead of them and calling itself an advance guard.''

"And what about their promise to cut the taxes in half?''

"Well now, that's really a problem for the Tosando army. When they are asked by the han along the way if the new government has really promised to cut taxes in half, what are they going to say? Anyway, it's a good thing that Ayanokoji left them and went back. There are things going on that we know nothing about. But at least it looks as though it is now impossible for Sagara and his people to count on the Tosando army for financial support any longer.''

"Now you're coming to the real problem.''

"Well, there were more than a hundred and twenty of them and every last one was full of fight. Could we have done anything else?''

"But they were quite well behaved when they came through our station.''

"But not compared to the Mito ronin when they went through. A ronin from Tosa looted a farmhouse. When the commanders learned of it, they executed him at Sangosawa. The Mito ronin were strict about discipline and that's the way they handled things.''

"No, Sagara Sozo's men don't come off too well in comparison. They burned eleven houses over in Oiwake.''

"They were not an easy lot to handle. 'The wind howled and the waters of the river Yi were cold.' Isn't that the way the Chinese histories put it? That bunch was not about to quit until it got to where it was going. They were a brave lot but they were just a bit too wild.''

"Is something on your mind, Keizo?''

"What do you mean?''

"Nothing except that I get the feeling I'm being scolded.''

Keizo laughed.

"Well, when you put it that way, Hanzo, I was telling Kozo a few days ago that we're all too much taken up with what is going on right in front of our eyes and that this was a serious shortcoming. His reply was good. 'To be human is to be worried.' But when you look around, it is frightening. Now that the restoration of antiquity and imperial rule have come, how can there continue to be pro-imperial or pro-shogunal factions? Look here! The wind is blowing our way. With all these tremendous changes going on it would be a mistake not to keep a sharp watch as we move ahead.''

"But be careful, Keizo. It looks as though the officials are calling out every one of the activists from the districts where Sagara seemed to have sympathizers and questioning them all—that's what they are up to.''

Hanzo took leave of his friend who was preparing to depart from Nezame in the opposite direction.

"Well, I'll just go down to Fukushima and collect my reprimand.''

Those were Keizo's parting words. Hanzo turned to his companion.

"I suppose we might as well get going too, Heibei."

The two set out once again for Magome.

The stretch from Fukushima to Suwara is called the middle three stations of the Kiso valley. They spent that night at Nojiri and on the next morning headed for the lower four stations. Here and there, where the road was narrow, the snow had been cleared away and logs laid side by side and bound together with vines to widen it. They saw places where repairs to the bridges had already been completed. There were also places where torches cut in the deep forests had been hauled out and heaped in great stacks along the road. They heard that the supervisor of the guard post at Agematsu and the timber commissioner from Owari were out on this job. Everything spoke of the forthcoming passage of the Tosando army.

From time to time Hanzo and Heibei would overtake women traveling on pilgrimage to Ise. The women, who only recently could not have passed through the barriers without special permission, were now coming out of their seclusion and undertaking long journeys in the company of male relatives. Their appearance along the roads conveyed the strongest sense that this was indeed the first spring of the restoration. They wore coverings on the backs of their hands to ward off sunburn but were otherwise dressed exactly like male pilgrims, and they appeared to be ready to shout for joy at their release as they made their way down the road.

Hanzo and Heibei moved slowly along a road running with melted snow. The farther they walked the brighter the skies above the valley somehow seemed to become. It was the time of year when the early spring coming up the Kiso valley from the west seemed to be hesitating among the fields of young winter barley, as yet making no new growth in the still frozen soil. But when they reached Midono, they noticed that the buds on the plum trees, which in Fukushima had still been small and hard, were beginning to swell.

In the afternoon they reached the station of Tsumago, where there had recently been a major fire. Juheiji, honjin at Tsumago, his wife Osato, his aged grandmother, and the young Masaki whom they had adopted from Hanzo's family were all safe. They had barely escaped being burned out; the fire had come as far as the gate of the honjin meeting room in the home of the assistant honjin, Tokuemon. In this desolation Hanzo reported to Juheiji exactly how he had been reprimanded at the regional offices.

Of course Hanzo had visited Juheiji's family on his way to Fukushima but just in the few days since then, board fences had been put where there were none before and scaffoldings were to be seen where there had been no scaffoldings before. The construction of temporary huts had begun and the area overflowed with valiant efforts to get the place looking once more like a post station by the time the commander of the Tosando army arrived.

"I'm really at the end of my rope this time, Hanzo," said Juheiji. "It's not quite so bad at your place. You'll get by with furnishing provisions for the noon rest stop, but look at Tsumago. The commander-in-chief is going to be spending the night here, and we, we just had this fire."

"So Magome will take some of the overnight guests off your hands. The advance party will be coming through soon, so they'll know what to expect. Please send Tokuemon over to Magome to coordinate our plans."

"And as if all that wasn't enough, Tsumago has to supply three thousand torches. I'll tell you, the people here are doing a lot of grumbling."

"Well, we aren't going to be all that busy at Magome. Let us take over part of your share of the torches, too."

Hanzo felt that he could only be in the way here. He spoke briefly to little Masaki, who was flourishing under Juheiji's care, and started on toward home.

"Are you going home already?" called Juheiji, still dressed in his rough work clothes as he came hurrying out after Hanzo.

"I'm really amazed that you have been able to get so far with the rebuilding after such a bad fire," said Hanzo.

"Everyone has been doing his best. It seems that the fire broke out below the notice board and burned as far as Nishida to the west. On the east side we stopped it at the Yamamotoya. This was the worst fire I can remember. But the villagers are really determined."

Juheiji fell silent for a moment as he walked alongside Hanzo. The vigorous sound of wood being cut and planed could be heard everywhere. Presently he spoke again.

"The world is changing, Hanzo. I have no idea what might happen next."

"Things will probably get better once unification is achieved," said Hanzo, and Juheiji nodded. Then the two parted.

By the time Hanzo and Heibei reached the outskirts of Magome it was close to sundown. There they met Sakichi, who had brought Sota out as far as the campground, worried about the lateness of his master's return. They also encountered villagers with pack frames on their backs, bringing loads of torches down from the mountains where they had been cut. When they saw Hanzo every one of them removed the kerchief from his head and bowed to him.

"You are all working very hard," Hanzo called out to the villagers, his tone of voice sounding exactly like that of Kichizaemon.

After rejoining his wife and children for the evening meal at the fireside in the main house, Hanzo went to see his father in the retirement quarters after dinner. He climbed up the stairs to the rooms behind the Magome honjin to report on his trip to Fukushima.

"I'm back."

Both Kichizaemon, waiting for him huddled over the brazier, and Oman, bringing out her tea implements, were delighted to hear his voice.

"How was Fukushima, Hanzo?"

As Kichizaemon spoke, Oman came in from the next room.

"Keizo was called up too, the day before yesterday. He stopped in here for a moment."

"Did he? I met him at Nezame. I got by with a reprimand at the district office. They seem to suspect me of all kinds of ridiculous things. But then you knew what this summons was about, didn't you, father?"

"I knew only too well. I was worried. And you were late getting back, too."

The conversation had begun to lag when Seisuke, who had been in the main house, came up the stairs. He seemed relieved to see that Hanzo had returned safely.

"While you were away, Hanzo, there was a lot of talk about the headman in Oiwake. That's another worry," said Kichizaemon.

"It's this," interjected Seisuke. "They are saying that both the headman and his son were thrown in jail or that they were banished or exiled. All kinds of stories are going around. Really! That's what they're saying. Of course, we don't pay any attention to the rumors that are always drifting down the road but there are a lot of people here who love to gossip, and they keep trying to say all kinds of things like 'The master of the honjin won't get back safely this time'!"

Kichizaemon began to laugh. Then he asked Hanzo if he knew anything about the headman of Oiwake that would account for such stories, and spoke of how unlikely it was that a village headman would be shackled and bound and sent off to the custody of Matsushiro han. It was obvious at such times that Kichizaemon was still very much interested in the affairs of the station.

"On that matter, father," said Hanzo, "I heard that it put Sagara Sozo's people in the mood for a fight when people came up from Komoro to take them into custody. They burned down eleven houses in Oiwake. After that, when Komoro han sent sixteen bales of rice as relief for the people who had been burned out, the headman would not turn it over to them. He had been ordered to render assistance to the poor people but they say that he wouldn't even give them the sixteen bales of rice that had been taken from Sagara's men. They also say that he was then sent off to Matsushiro, but I wonder if that's really true. According to what I've heard, there are people who don't like the headman and they have been slandering him—he's accused of terrible things."

"That can happen," said Kichizaemon thoughtfully. "With all this confusion, you just can't divide rice and money to suit everyone. It's too bad for the headman at Oiwake. The people who tried to hand over the rice and money were asking too much."

"That's right. I agree completely," Seisuke replied. "Trying to relieve all the people immediately was the source of Sagara Sozo's downfall. Such things have to be handled with much greater care. They can't be carried out by any little advance detachment that happens to be passing through."

"Anyway," Hanzo continued, "that bunch wasn't working with the Tosando army. That's why they were accused of being imposters. And then some people took advantage of that. All the same, Sagara Sozo meant well. He came in a spirit befitting the vanguard of the imperial forces. That's why all the local activists worked so hard to raise funds for him. But I couldn't say that to the officials in Fukushima; I'll tell you because you are my father and mother, but the officials said some pretty harsh things the second time I went in. They said that since our family has served so well for so many years and has been so scrupulous in carrying out our responsibilities in the way of fund raising, we would be let off with a reprimand and they would excuse me from being shackled and bound. When they said all that, I just decided that taking such abuse was a part of my job."

Just then they heard the lively voices of the children, Okume and Sota, following their mother Otami up the stairs. Hanzo dropped the subject. The family gathering on the second floor of the back building soon turned to talk about the young sons of Prince Iwakura, that is to say, of the Tosando army.

"Okume, do you remember the procession of Princess Kazu," asked Seisuke.

"Not very well," Okume replied shamefacedly.

"Like a dream?"

"M-hm."

"I suppose so. You wouldn't be able to remember that far back."

"Try asking about the Mito ronin!" said Sota, cutting in.

"Asking who?"

"Me! Just try asking me!"

"Oh, you?"

"When it comes to the Mito ronin, even I know all about them."

"But just how is this passage going to go?" said Oman, turning toward her grandchildren. "This time it won't be such a frightening thing. There will be nothing to be afraid of. This time it will be the brocade banners of the emperor coming."

Hanzo's children were growing. In that spring of 1868, Okume was twelve years old and her brother Sota was ten. Otami learned that her husband had looked in on her old home in Tsumago both coming and going.

"Masaki must be growing too. He will be seven years old now."

"Yes, he's really growing. And by now he looks just like a native of Tsumago. When I called him, he came out wearing his little boy's trousers and bowed to me. But he looked a little bit awkward about it—as though he were lost in that big house."

Oman and Kichizaemon listened very closely to the talk about their grandson in Tsumago. Then Kichizaemon asked, "By the way, Hanzo, the army will be coming through in another twelve or thirteen days. Are there enough porters?"

"This time the old Tokugawa domains are also being called upon to supply supplemental porters. The chief of staff is pointing out that this is not limited to the Tokugawa holdings and he is calling on everyone right down to the tenant farmers in the villages to assist. I think that the whole system of assisting districts is going to change again with this passage."

"You mustn't do that, dear." Oman turned to Kichizaemon. "You've got to leave the porters and that sort of thing up to Hanzo. You're retired now and you shouldn't get yourself all worked up like that."

"I get nothing but scoldings from Oman these days," said Kichizaemon with a laugh.

But the long conversation had exhausted the enfeebled Kichizaemon. When he became aware of it, Hanzo called upon his wife, children, and Seisuke to follow him down the stairs. At the main house they found Shosuke, the assistant headman of Magome, sitting with his lantern neatly folded at the edge of the raised floor. He had come by both to see Hanzo and to have a bath. Shosuke too had been worried about the tardiness of Hanzo's return from Fukushima. That night, Hanzo warmed himself in the bath that had been heated by Sakichi and then, leaving the reception of guests to Otami, went straight in to the parlor. There he stretched himself out on the tatami in his own room. His fresh new paulownia wood desk, the red felt on it, and even the old inkstone all seemed to have been waiting for his return.

The children came to look in. Sota, who usually went to sleep early, could not get to sleep that night and he was with his sister. In contrast to Sota, whose face remained childish in spite of his increased height, Okume had suddenly become very much the elder sister. She was like a plum bud, still tightly folded against the bark of the branch, but beginning to show the first faint flush of pink.

"Ah, your father is very tired tonight. Sota, come here and tread my muscles!"

As Hanzo said this, he assumed a face down position on the tatami. Sota was delighted. Child though he was, Sota's body was heavy enough to drive the intense fatigue of the last several days out of Hanzo's legs. At the same time Hanzo experienced the special warmth and intimacy that came from contact with his own child.

"Come on, let me do it too," said Okume, and brother and sister took turns treading the backs of Hanzo's massive legs.

4

"Hanzo."

"Are you talking to me?"

"Oman has been worrying about you. She wants to know what is wrong."

"What indeed?"

"But won't your friends be coming along with the army?"

The conversation between Hanzo and his wife went on in that vein.

Warm showers had already come several times to Magome pass this spring. Then a heavy rain came unexpectedly in the middle of the night, washing away most of the snow from the valleys. Now only a few patches of snow shaped like arrowheads lay in the high valleys off toward Mt. Ena on the Mino border. The Tosando army had come as far as Mino, and reports came that they had set up their headquarters in Ogaki and were carrying on negotiations with the han along their projected route. They were going to have to spend some days there in order to recruit soldiers and horses and raise funds. There were numerous "men of spirit" in the district who, wishing to be counted among the imperial forces, asked permission to accompany the army.

"I just don't feel that I can go on this way."

When Hanzo said this, Otami turned and looked at her husband's face closely.

"That's just what's worrying mother."

"I'm not going anywhere, Otami. You may tell mother that if you wish. If I were going to go along, I would have to get permission from Yamamura in Fukushima. I'm in a different situation from my friends in Nakatsugawa. That outfit is still supporting the shogunate and it is not going to give me permission to go anywhere."

". . ."

"Listen! Keizo and Kozo are not simply going along with Iwakura. They have been given the position of official guides for the army. There will be some fourteen or fifteen men under them, all acting as guides. And every one of them is a Hirata disciple! I can't help envying them."

The honjin now acquired a new responsibility. An announcement came out from the chief of staff of the Tosando army stating that everyone who had suffered from cruel administration not only in Tokugawa domains but in the han domains as well were to report this without hesitation. The place where they were to make their report was the honjin. It was to the honjin, too, where all the reports on the condition of the poor which the local officials of each province had been ordered to produce were to be sent. Up to now the honjin had been no more than a kind of lodging house for court and military officials, a place where daimyo, court nobles, public officials, and samurai could spend the night or stop for a rest. But this order designated all the honjin as the places where the lords and the high officials of the various han were to demonstrate their submission to the commander of the army in his capacity as a representative of imperial power.

Hanzo had at hand a communication in the name of the chief of staff of the Tosando army, addressed to the toiya and post station officials from Ogaki all the way to Shimo-Suwa. According to it, four hundred Satsuma men and eighteen hundred Ogaki men would be coming through in the advance guard. Eight hundred men from Inaba would be traveling one station ahead of the main body, while eight hundred eighty-six men from Tosa and just over three hundred men from Choshu would set out on the same day as the main body, serving it as front and rear guards, respectively. In addition, there would be two hundred men on the command staff and one hundred fifty men from Hikone, traditionally the most loyal of all han to the shogunate, as well as one hundred men from Takasu, whose daimyo had formerly boasted of their close kinship to the Tokugawa. The orders directed the post stations to see to it that that number of men could pass through with no problems either for lodging and provisions or for porters, horses, and the like. However, the numbers given in this communication were obviously quite inaccurate. Hanzo, aware that it was most unlikely that such a huge body of troops would be coming from a place like Ogaki, grew uneasy. The attitudes of the han and the Tokugawa bannermen permitted no optimism.

In the meantime a steady stream of callers began to come in to announce the submission of various han from Mino all the way to Hida. They heard that Toyama Yuroku, lord of Naegi, had gone to Ogaki and also that Hase Ichiemon, a high official of Iwamura han, had gone there in the place of his lord to meet with the commander and to beg forgiveness for their error in having previously supported Tokugawa Yoshinobu. Kano, Gunjo, Takatomi —all were said to be doing the same thing. Rumors like these reached Hanzo every day. Even Hikone, which had always remained true to the memory of that bastion of the shogunate, the tairo Ii Naosuke, had now joined the punitive expedition, and Ogaki, an ally of Aizu at the battles of Toba and Fushimi, was joining Satsuma to make up the advance party that was coming down this highway.

It is necessary to keep in mind how influential was the position taken by Owari, the dominant han in central Honshu. Owari, with all its prestige as one of the three cadet houses of the Tokugawa, had taken the lead in bringing its own domains under firm control and in bringing pressure on neighboring han. By clearing the way for the expedition to the east, it had played a role of the greatest importance in the process of the restoration of antiquity.

This is not by any means to say that Owari completely escaped internal dissension. Since the previous winter, most of the powerful supporters of the imperial cause had gone up to Kyoto with the retired lord, Tokugawa Yoshikatsu. While in Kyoto, Yoshikatsu had been busy day and night with national affairs and he had had no time to look back at his home province. The han officials who favored the shogunate took advantage of his absence to strengthen their influence over the young lord, Motochiyo, and there were frequent rumors that they were going off to Edo to try to encourage an uprising. At last the old lord, realizing that he could wait no longer, conferred with Naruse Higo and Tamiya Jo'un and, after hearing Iwakura's advice on the matter, returned to Nagoya. On the very same day he called the han elder Watanabe Shinzaemon, the acting steward Sakakibara Kageyu, and Ishikawa Kuranosuke, commander of the palace guards, to his residence in the castle grounds and informed them that they were under imperial orders to disembowel themselves. He also ordered the beheading of Yasui Chojuro and ten others known to be supporters of the shogunate. It was early in the first month of the year that the young lord Motochiyo brought the heads of all these men up to court to make clear Owari's attitude.

Now that there was agreement in Owari about the position the han was to take, the positions being taken by other han from Mino into Hida gave no comfort to supporters of the shogunate. Officials from Kiso-Fukushima would come rushing out to try to sound out the situation around Ogaki. The coming and going of these people through Magome in itself signified the approach of the army. On the twenty-second day of the second month, a party arrived in Magome bringing with it a horse as a gift for the young Iwakura princes. The party was led by the retired head of the Yamamura. He was the man whom Hanzo and his father had been in the habit of referring to as "the master of Fukushima," to distinguish him from the lord of Owari, whose deputy he was.

Hanzo rushed to his father's side. He quickly reported that the retired head of the house of Yamamura was presently in the honjin's chamber of honor and would be taking his noon meal there before proceeding on to Nakatsugawa to meet with the commander of the Tosando army. He was also bringing a horse as a gift. Then Hanzo left.

In the retirement quarters Kichizaemon called for Oman to bring out his formal clothing and help him in his preparations to go over to the main house.

"My jacket! My jacket!" he shouted.

Kichizaemon seldom went to the main house these days, nor did he meet with the people of the village or even visit the family graves except on the anniversary of the death of his father. Now suddenly Kichizaemon, as he changed into his hempen formal clothing with the Aoyama family crests, once again became the headman he had been before retiring in Hanzo's favor.

"Oman, since I am retired I will not go so far as to speak to the master. I will leave everything up to Hanzo. I just want to have a look at the horse he has brought."

Saying only this, he went down the stairs with Oman and stepped into a pair of straw sandals made by Sakichi. Then, with a stick in his right hand and helped along by Oman, he worked his way up the path to the main house. He walked very slowly. When he climbed up the slight rise in the stepping stones, he rested there a while before setting off again.

He was heading for a corner of the large wood-floored section at the front of the entrance hall of the honjin. The buds on the camellia in the front garden were just coming into bloom. Next to it was tied a splendid grey. Since the horse was to be presented to the commander of the army, two grooms named Hikosuke and Denkichi had been chosen to accompany it from Fukushima. Kichizaemon hesitantly asked the age of the horse and they replied that it was six years old.

"Father!" called Hanzo, coming out to suggest that he make a formal greeting to the visitor.

"No, I'll just go back from here," replied Kichizaemon as he turned his wondering gaze back to the horse's splendid mane, its large eyes, and the vigorous tail lashing at the flies.

Everyone praised the horse. Everyone was also unable to say just what might await Yamamura when he reached Nakatsugawa. Seisuke's voice soon came ringing out to the entrance hall from inside the house as he called for

Yamamura's escort. This was the signal to bring the palanquin to the front of the entrance hall. Kichizaemon, kneeling in the front corner of the entrance hall, was able to catch a brief glimpse of the face of the master whom his family had served for generations.

"Master. It is Kichizaemon. I have come out to see the horse."

"Oh, and are you well?"

Yamamura turned back to return the greeting.

Kichizaemon stayed there for a long time, his eyes full of tears. He watched the palanquin leave, he watched the horse leave, and he watched the departure of the entire party for Nakatsugawa. Hanzo accompanied the party out of the honjin enclosure. When he came back he found his father still sitting at the edge of the floor, gazing out toward the highway.

"Father, I am finding the duties of the honjin difficult to deal with."

"Don't say that. Whatever the other people in Fukushima may think, it looks as though the elder Yamamura has set out for reasons of his own."

The schedule sent out by the chief of staff showed the Tosando army taking its noon meal at the station of Unuma on the twenty-third day of the second month and spending the night at Ota. On that day the advance guard was to have arrived in Nakatsugawa and Yamamura of Fukushima would meet its leading officers that night. The main body would be coming up the highway three days after the advance guard of troops from Satsuma and Ogaki. Everything was in readiness in Magome station. That is to say, all they had to do was to supply noon meals for the entire army as it passed through. Even though some of the soldiers would be unable to find lodging as scheduled at the neighboring station of Tsumago, all that would be necessary at Magome would be to put them up for one night. Hanzo went alone to his room to plan for the celebration of the passage of the commander of the army. He was trying to write a long poem which he hoped to present to the young Iwakura princes.

Evening came. Hanzo called Sota to the hall along the western side of the honjin where he showed him the view of Mino province. From the hall they could see the great slope of Mt. Ena, wrapped in the somber tones of dusk. The town of Nakatsugawa was out of sight behind a small hill, but the lights of other towns and their reflection in the dim, distant skies were clearly visible to Sota's eyes.

"Look," said Hanzo. "The skies are bright above Nakatsugawa. They must have watch fires going there."

Hanzo sat before his desk in the parlor until very late that evening, working by the light of an old-fashioned lamp. He was making a fair copy of the long poem he had written that day. Musing on the fact that Keizo's home was the command station of the advance guard that night, he reflected on the strange coincidence that had made that house the site of the so-called Nakatsugawa conference when the lord of Choshu had come down from his residence in Edo last year. Even after he lay down beside Otami he could not get to sleep. Just as an early spring snow brings on the trees and herbs with an even greater vigor afterward, so Hanzo awaited the coming of the Tosando army with an eagerness all the greater for the incident with Sagara Sozo and his men. The official at Fukushima had said a great deal about the document proclaiming the chastisement of Tokugawa Yoshinobu, but whatever it might mean on its face, was Yoshinobu's action in surrendering his powers to the emperor and withdrawing to Osaka castle an act of deception or was it misunderstood by the Kyoto forces? And had Yoshinobu ordered the Aizu forces to return home and then insulted the emperor? Although it was claimed that there was proof that Yoshinobu's troops had initiated action at Toba and Fushimi, it seemed clear from what had been said by the wounded Aizu men who passed through this highway on their way home that Satsuma had initiated the action. Hanzo did not really care about such quibbles. Last year on the seventeenth of the seventh month, when the Choshu forces had surrounded Kyoto, it was reported that stray bullets were striking the inner wall of the imperial enclosure. Then it was the Aizu forces that had protected the emperor, returning the fire of the troops from Choshu. Now the warriors of Kiso-Fukushima were asking how it was possible that the lord of Choshu, who had accepted full responsibility for that attack and who was indebted to these very same people for the magnanimity with which he had been treated, could be permitted to call Yoshinobu and the forces of Aizu and Kuwana traitors. But to Hanzo, like most of the other honjin, headmen, toiya, or physicians who were watching from below, there was a still more serious issue at stake.

"Now that there has been a restoration of antiquity and of imperial rule, how can there continue to be pro-imperial or pro-shogunal factions?"

The words that Keizo had spoken when they met at the noodle shop in Nezame came back to him. One of the things that had brought a faint glimmer of the dawn of reunification into this utterly disordered society was the innate quality of the nation of Japan. He imagined the rising of a sun that would pour the spirit of life back into this ancient and exhausted highway. He let his imagination run back to antiquity, to the conquest of the east by Jimmu, the first emperor, in a move that paralleled the present campaign.

Hanzo left the house before dawn and walked across the dark garden to the well. He cleansed himself by pouring cold water over his face and arms. As he walked back toward the main building he heard the first cocks crowing.

The passage of the army for the pacification of the east had begun. The dark blue morning sky gradually grew bright but there was still no activity along the highway. The first person to come knocking on the door of the honjin that day was Shosuke.

"Hanzo! You're up early!"

He said that he was just setting out to inform all the local farmers that beginning today there would be no fields cleared, no burning of trash, and no use of firearms from Aonohara to Irinokata. After consulting with Hanzo about various aspects of the day's preparations in the village, Shosuke left him. In the honjin, the tenant farmers and the old women had already arrived. Some were setting up the big rice kettles in front of the storehouse. Others were coming to the kitchen door with dry pine needles for use as cooking fuel. To the right and left of the entry, long curtains closed off the garden as though it were the camp of a military commander.

Hanzo caught sight of Seisuke.

"Seisuke, they say that the commander is calling for all persons more than eighty years of age to have audience with him. Should we spread some sand in the garden for them to sit on?"

"That would be a good thing to do."

"I want to leave things in your charge here, Seisuke, while I go down to Nakatsugawa to meet the Iwakura princes."

Their discussion covered every detail.

The sun gradually mounted higher. A messenger came running up from Shinjaya on the Mino border to report that the advance guard was expected momentarily. Hanzo, as head of the station, Kyurobei, the toiya, and the elders Inosuke of the Fushimiya, Kozaemon of the Masudaya, and Gosuke of the Umeya set out for the western edge of the village to meet the advance guard. From Stonemason slope down to Machida, the road was solidly lined with people.

> Majesty, majesty, before your august horse
> What is it that waves so proudly?
>   Toko ton'yare, ton'yare na!
>
> Don't you see the brocade banners
> Ordering punishment for enemies of the court?
>   Toko ton'yare, ton'yare na!

The voices of the troops advancing up the road from the west could be heard over the sound of a great drum beating out the rhythm of the march. Presently they came into view, marching behind a banner bearing a cross in a circle, the crest of the house of Shimazu of Satsuma. It would be well to imagine the effect of this new march being sung by this band of fierce "hawk men" from Satsuma. The barbarous noise they were raising resounded through the mountain air, mingled with the wild whinnying of horses, sounding as though they had come face to face with the foe. If one compared this with the passage over the same highway a few years before by the Mito ronin, marching quietly with drawn swords, speaking little and only in low voices, moving as men face to face with death, the contrast was overwhelming. This band from the far western extremity of Japan, each member looking like a match for a thousand, was heading not for Kyoto but for Edo, that great city which had been the center of culture, of mores, and of fashions for the past three centuries. Was it Edo's present lack of any prospect other than to remain as a mere corpse left behind by the middle ages that had infused these men with such firm resolve to turn away from the past? Or had the occasion of the restoration of antiquity brought their hearts to flame with a passionate desire to participate in the great undertaking of the creation of a new state?

Hanzo could not tell. The guns that these spirited men were carrying on their shoulders were all the latest imported models, gleaming examples of contemporary ordnance. They moved with the lightness and sureness that mark the veteran. Each man wore a small brocade patch on his sleeve to identify him as a member of the imperial forces. Red and green blanket rolls were slung across their shoulders. The sleeves of their coats were tight fitting in the European style and they carried bags for powder and shot.

CHAPTER FOUR

1

THE TOSANDO ARMY took four days to pass through Magome. In the preparations for the passage of Princess Kazu back in 1861, the roads had all been widened to twelve feet and in some places the stone walls in front of the houses had been moved back as much as two feet, but all that still did not seem to be enough when the road had to deal with traffic like this. Magome was crowded with people cleaning up after the procession. Some were repairing banks that had crumbled under the passage of men and horses. Others were collecting burnt out torches. Still others were gathering up litter such as horse manure and the straw sandals and straw horse shoes that had been discarded as they wore out.

"There's always a heavy rain after a big procession goes through."

The man who said this hurried to sweep the area in front of his home, glancing up continually at the threatening skies above the station. Every house had begun cleaning up and putting away the innumerable serving trays, dishes, and sets of bedding that had been used by the immense party passing through.

Just as with the great processions of the past, the passage of the commander and his army left all kinds of things in its wake. The chamberlain of Takato han, serving in the place of his lord and assuming responsibility for financial affairs, stayed an additional night at Magome to take care of all obligations, but he did not have sufficient funds to cover the cost of the porters and found it difficult to leave the station. After sending off the last stragglers, Hanzo, as master of the station, went out to have a look around. He looked in at the gate of the Tsutaya, a lodging house for porters. All the porters who had accompanied the army from Oi station in Mino were gathered there, as well as various others, and a fierce argument had broken out over the distribution of wages. He looked in at the gate of Onoya Kambei, who made his living as an innkeeper. There he heard how Onoya had lodged the samurai from Inaba serving as the second division in this army and how they had made merciless demands on the people of the inn with their orders for sake and refreshments. He looked in at the gate of a house that provided post horses. A huge tub had been set out on the highway against the stone wall in order to bathe the horses. He could hear the voices of the grooms urging the animals to lift their legs as they scrubbed the horses with bundles of straw dipped in hot water, the sweat washing away in cascades of white foam. He also learned that the body of a porter had been found along the road between Tsumago and Midono.

The young Prince Iwakura with whom Hanzo had been granted audience in Nakatsugawa was a mere fifteen or sixteen years of age. On the road he wore a brocade robe with a white ground and a tall black court hat. Although he was closely guarded from both the front and the rear, he rode boldly out in the open on horseback as though determined not to disgrace his father's name. Yachimaru, the deputy commander, not to be outdone by his older brother, was wearing a brocade gown with a red ground and sat astride his horse with a sword slung at his side, looking like a seasoned campaigner. There were two hundred and six men attached to the commander's headquarters along with fifty-four porters assigned to carry the necessities for the two young princes. Another fifty-two porters served their retainers. A special detachment of sixteen men in red campaign jackets carried the brocade banners and the white banners of the imperial command. After them came banners bearing the commander's family crest of a cluster of bell flowers on a sky blue ground.

Nor was that all. The banner of Hikone with its black well curb crest, the banner of the Aoyama of Hachiman and Gujo in Mino, the array of guidons and pennants displayed in the accompanying divisions, even an immense streamer bearing a bold inscription to the Great Bodhisattva Hachiman— altogether the sound of these banners and streamers flapping in the wind combined with the neighing of the horses created an atmosphere of awe-inspiring martial vigor. The high spirits of the Tosando army were evident just from the sight of the carriage-mounted cannon being drawn by horses with soldiers riding them. With two men pushing each cannon from behind, they came up the steep slope of Jikkyoku pass on the boundary between Mino and Shinano. With the same determination they passed on into the inner reaches of the Kiso road, the gun carriages leaving deep scars on the road over Magome pass.

Accompanying the army as guides were fourteen or fifteen men from the Hirata school, including Hanzo's friends Keizo and Kozo. Hanzo wanted to be sure that the farmers of his village saw the elated expressions on their faces. At least that was what he had been thinking before going out to meet the commander. He believed that once the people of his village had the privilege of meeting the Iwakura party here in this remote place, they would be so delighted that they would pour sake into gourds, heap homemade delicacies on dishes and trays, and rush out to comfort the army in its labors. He believed that this was the very day that the farmers had so long awaited. As he looked back over both the recent and the distant past and considered how they had all undergone the indescribable hardships of serving the military

houses, he asked himself what it had all been for if not to see the coming of
this day.

The commander's party, which had been traveling well behind the main
body, now arrived in Magome. It arrived bearing the imperial charge to learn
the true conditions in all the provinces and to relieve the suffering of the people. Yet, although the people along the way had been assured that they could
carry out their trades and professions in peace and confidence, and those who
had long suffered under cruel government could report their grievances to the
honjin in full without fear of retribution, not a single person from among the
farmers and lower classes had come forth on his own initiative. Although
they had been told that the bereaved and the solitary would be compensated
and all those over eighty years of age would be rewarded, there was now
nothing remotely like the mad fervor that had accompanied the "ain't it all
right" craze of a few years ago when young and old, men and women had all
danced together in the streets to the music of flutes and drums. The people
from the post station and nearby villages who lined up along the road were
there as mere spectators, as though watching a festival. Hanzo, who as headman expected to be able to make a show of support for the new government
that would be in no way inferior to that of his fellows accompanying the
army, was brought up short, stunned by the villagers' indifference.

2

As the confusion following the passage was set straight and then set straight
once more, the post station officials completed their remaining duties and all
the excited voices at the meeting room at last subsided. When evening came
it began to rain. It was the twenty-eighth day of the second month of Keio 4,
1868. Since it was the second half of the month the duties of the toiya were
being assumed by Kyurobei, in accord with the custom that these duties were
exchanged every half month. Late in the day, Hanzo completed his inspection
of the meeting room, no longer accompanied by his neighbor Inosuke and
the other post officials, and then returned to his home through the side
entrance of the honjin gate. The main doors were already closed and barred.

"How far have the Iwakura brothers gotten by now?"

Sakichi, sitting in his usual place by the hearth, was talking about the passage of the army with Seisuke, who had come over to work as he did each
day. They were discussing the question of whether the party would be spending that night in Midono or in Nojiri. Everyone looked very tired, including
Oman and Otami. The children were there. Hanzo felt relieved to be home.

"Sota, where did you see the Iwakura brothers?" asked Sakichi.

"Me? At Stonemason slope," replied Sota, his childish eyes sparkling. "A
man from Yamaguchi came over to see them. You know what he said? He
said they were just like something out of a wood-block print, and this was

surely how Ariwara no Narihira must have looked when he went down to the east back in the ninth century."

"Narihira—that's a good one!" said Seisuke with a laugh.

"By the way, did you hear about the retired head of the Yamamura?" asked Oman.

"Yes, I heard."

"Wasn't that awful? Refusing to meet him after he went all the way down to Nakatsugawa."

"You might say that."

"But now that this has happened, a lot of his men in Fukushima are going to be asking questions. Because the only thing that went the way he planned was that the commander accepted the horse he offered."

"Anyway, it would really be something to see the army going through Fukushima."

"But just think about Ogaki, Seisuke. Even they, powerful as they are, had to open their castle, and now they have sent something like five hundred and seventy men along with the army. The Fukushima people aren't going to be able to do very much."

"That's just why I said it would be something to see. But when you come down to it, our villagers are really an indifferent lot. It doesn't seem to matter to them one bit that the shogunate has fallen or that there has been an imperial restoration."

"You mean the way they acted the other day? But Seisuke, everyone is so worried."

"What do you mean? They all act as though it was happening to somebody else," said Seisuke, casually disposing of the matter.

Hanzo listened to the talk as he took a late supper in the kitchen that adjoined the hearth room on one side. That day the maids who had finished cleaning up after the visitors looked as tired as though they had just finished the annual housecleaning. Later Hanzo went from the hearth room, where the rest of the family was gathered, across the wood-floored area of the entrance hall to the door of the parlor. The epoch-making passage of the army, certain to affect every part of the country, occupied his thoughts. Even a consideration of the reasons why the chief of staff of the Tosando army had issued so many proclamations promising to respect the will of the people, and the reaction of the farmers for whom he was responsible, brought a deep sigh to his lips.

"I expected them to be more pleased."

He kept coming back to that.

The next day it rained heavily, and everyone at the honjin surrendered to fatigue. The rain shutters in the parlor facing to the southeast were half closed to keep the rain from beating in. Hanzo spread a carpet on the floor of his room. He treasured every day that he could spend here, and he would spread this carpet and lie down whenever he could get away from the demands of the highway. The whole station was taking a day of rest. No callers came. He stretched his legs out, then crossed them, listening to the sound of the rain. It was both warm and depressing at the same time. Soon his thoughts turned to the men who made up the Tosando army. They were from Satsuma and Choshu, Tosa and Inaba, and from closer points such as Hikone and Ogaki.

The sound of the marching of vast numbers of men and horses still echoed in Hanzo's ears. On the peak day, more than fifteen hundred fifty men had passed through, and on the lightest day there had still been more than three hundred and thirty.

Earlier, on the day of departure from Ogaki, all the high-ranking officers of the various divisions had been called to headquarters for a conference. After the conference, they were served with sake. One of the Tosa men, Kataoka Kenkichi, who was in command of a special attack group directly under the staff officer Itagaki Taisuke, was so exuberant when he emerged from the headquarters that he promptly fell into the gutter. This immediately became one of the stories that the army carried along with it. Even in such petty matters as this, Satsuma and Choshu tried to make Tosa the butt of every joke. Tosa's was by far the largest single contingent of any of the han in this army, twelve companies totaling eight hundred eighty-six men. But when most of the others were saying that this Tosa force was all form and no substance and were even digging up old folk songs to make fun of them, it was difficult to see how they could all be part of the same army. The inspector of the Tosa contingent was among those eager to disarm these critics by having the Tosa men distinguish themselves in battle as soon as possible. The plan to have the army divide so that part of it could pass through Kai province, a plan whose merits had been argued ever since setting out from Ogaki, was also a product of the contempt in which Satsuma and Choshu held Tosa. Things had gone so far that even when troops from Satsuma were dispatched to investigate the situation in Kai, Tosa sent other men, saying that it was best that Tosa proceed through Kai even if this meant separating from Satsuma and Choshu. It was the footsteps of such people that continued to echo in Hanzo's ears—the sound of the passage of this great army made up of men all ruthlessly pursuing their own selfish ends. The memory of their constant bickering remained behind, a reminder of the rapidly increasing coarseness of everyday life. Some of them had simply forced their way through. Some, fearing a change of heart on the part of Hikone and Ogaki, seemed to threaten anyone who looked back. There was really nothing so revealing as the sound made by men on the march. Some footsteps were hesitant, others were rough and violent. Still others trod the highway in the rhythms of men being moved by forces beyond their control. However much he had welcomed the coming of the new government, Hanzo could not help being shaken by what he had heard in those footsteps.

"Kill him!"

The cry rose from people who were prepared to regard yesterday's shogun as today's outlaw. Hanzo heard that voice too, mingling with the footsteps. No! This restoration must be for the sake of all the people. Troubled by confused thoughts, Hanzo tried to set his own feelings in order. Why was the intent of the new government not apparent to the villagers in the country-side? It could only be because there were still too many in the village who did not look kindly on such rapid change.

As always, it was the children who continued to shout and play, needing no rest. The girl's festival was approaching and Okume was running happily about with the new doll that the neighbors at the Fushimiya had given her. She brought it in to show Hanzo.

When the rain at last ended on the third day after the completion of the cleanup, the station of Magome looked like a place that had just been uncov-ered by the receding waters of a great flood. A bucket of the kind used to transport human heads arrived from Nojiri, accompanied by an Inaba retainer in battle helmet. It contained the head of one of his comrades who had bro-ken military discipline. The man had been condemned to die at Nojiri and to have his head exposed at the edge of the village of Magome for a period of three days. Hanzo rushed out of the honjin to consult with the other post station officials.

The Inaba man entrusted with the unpleasant mission was a well-seasoned veteran who told Hanzo that it had not at all been his wish to leave this kind of memento behind when the army passed through. It was a matter of the deepest regret that such a casualty should have come from his own han. It seems that a Kiso girl of fair complexion had been washing clothes in the nearby stream. When the eyes of the miscreant took in the rustic scene, he had been unable to resist temptation. The unfortunate girl was the daughter of a lowly local watchman. The story was coming out only now.

The Inaba man turned to Hanzo.

"Well, sir, I have been thinking about how to do this while I was on the road. Is there any bamboo to be had around here?"

"Bamboo? There's plenty behind the honjin."

"Farther on there isn't any bamboo. Although our place is in the Kiso, it is still at the very western edge," came the unasked for explanation from a bystander.

"That will do very well. I would like to make the stand out of green bam-boo. I will put the proclamation up in front of it. Could you please call the village carpenter right away?"

All the preparations were made simply and quickly. Masudaya Kozaemon, a post station official, rushed off to find the carpenter while Fushimiya Inosuke ran to the grove behind the honjin to look for suitable bamboo. Word got around quickly in the small village and people came running, wide-eyed, to see for themselves. A large crowd gathered in front of the toiya.

Sota was in the crowd. As the son of the honjin, he was given special per-mission by Kyurobei to heft the bucket and see how heavy it was with its burden.

"How can Sota possibly lift it? They say that the head makes up half the body's weight," said someone in the crowd. This drew Hanzo's attention to what was happening.

"Stop it! Put it down! That's no plaything!"

It was decided that the head would be displayed at the bottom of Stonemason slope at the lower edge of the village, since that marked the western entrance to the eleven Kiso stations. A green bamboo pole was cut from the honjin grove and the samurai's head was impaled on its sharp end. To emphasize the seriousness of the offense and the rigorous correctness with which it was being handled, a wooden notice board inscribed with the particulars of the offense was set up beside it. People crowded around to look and to talk about the incident. Someone said that since they had been called to account for it by Owari, the Inaba forces had been unable to let the matter drop with no action. Another ventured the guess that it must have been this particular samurai who had created such a disturbance on the night of the twenty-sixth after the drinking party at Onoya Kambei's place. Presently the Inaba samurai who had brought the head left to rejoin his unit. When the nighthawks began to fly over the highway, traffic along Stonemason slope at last died down.

"I just can't imagine that someone would get his head cut off just for flirting with a watchman's daughter."

"He must have forced her to go into the woods with him."

"It was Owari that insisted on the severest punishment. After all, it happened in their domain. Besides, a high official from Nagoya is with the commander. And with seven han in the army, it looks like the kind of thing they have to do once in a while just to maintain discipline."

Such remarks arose spontaneously around Hanzo.

Hanzo wanted to conceal this hideous sight from the villagers' eyes as soon as possible. His gaze rested on the Mampukuji. In its grounds was a grave plot for unclaimed bodies. He decided to get that head back in its bucket quickly, consult the temple priest Sho'un, and bury the samurai's head. He could scarcely bear to wait until the end of the third day. He felt that such extreme punishments, far from demonstrating the vigor of the new government, simply served to sow nameless terrors. As headman he had to protect the villagers from the rumors that drifted down the highway.

3

At the beginning of the third month, an unusually heavy snow buried the highway. By the time it melted away, a fellow disciple who had been in Kyoto, one Tatematsu Hosuke of Nanjo village in Ina, came up the road from Mino on his way home.

Hosuke had brought all the surviving manuscripts of Atsutane from Edo to safe-keeping in the Ina valley and had then reported to the Hirata household in Kyoto on the successful completion of his mission. Now, his duties done, he was heading back to Ina, clearly satisfied that he had managed to get the precious documents out of Edo since the latest reports indicated a general attack on that city was imminent. Hanzo greeted him when he arrived at the Magome honjin and received from him the messages relayed from Kanetane, who was always in Hanzo's thoughts, and the senior disciple Kureta Masaka.

"I have just come from the honjin in Nakatsugawa, Hanzo. You know the Isekyu in Kyoto—I was asked by the master of that shop to deliver some dyework to Keizo and I brought it with me at some trouble, but unfortunately Keizo was not at home. They said that he is accompanying the commander of the army. I learned that only when I got to Nakatsugawa."

Then Hosuke described how he could sense that he was traveling in the first spring of the restoration just from the simple fact that he was able to go down the highway from Ogaki in Mino through Oi, Nakatsugawa, and Ochiai in the wake of the Tosando army without having to worry about being picked up by Tokugawa police. Clearly the posthumous disciples of Atsutane, joined together by love of the same master, all burned with the same hope for the restoration. Hanzo was able to say things to Hosuke that he had not been able to say to his fellow officials in the post station, who looked at events from a point of view very different from his these days. While waiting for the arrival of the army, he had thought that the commander would be guarded only by samurai from the western han. It was only after the commander's party had arrived in Magome that he understood the character of the Tosando army. Although the Tosa troops claimed to be the core of the army, it was made up of activists, country samurai, low-ranking soldiers, and headmen who had joined up. There were even some ronin mixed in.

"I suppose it is as you say. Among those who want to give their all for the imperial cause, people in the lower levels of society seem most numerous."

It was early in the third month. Even in the mountain households, it had become possible to live without charcoal braziers. Hanzo was still talking with Hosuke, who had come back from Kyoto with a great many stories. Hosuke was a plainspoken man who seldom gave himself airs. Hanzo could now ask what Kyoto was like and what Kureta Masaka was doing these days.

In contrast to the vague rumors that continually drifted in, Hosuke's account of the Koromonotana district where Masaka lived and of the street where the dyer Isekyu's shop was located conveyed a sense of the reality he had just witnessed. He told of how Masaka had invited him to have a look around Kyoto under the imperial restoration and how he and Masaka had stood on the corner of Maruta street to witness the passage of the three foreign ambassadors on their way to court for an imperial audience, an event totally without precedent in the history of this nation. He said that he had not been able to see the French ambassador, Roches, who was coming from the Sokokuji, but that he had been able to get a good look at the Dutch chargé d'affaires, van Polesbroek, as he came from the Nanzenji accompanied by his secretary, both men riding through the crowds in litters with black woolen sunshades. He said that for him, who had never seen a Westerner, it seemed like a dream to have the narrow bounds of his experience so abruptly shattered.

Hosuke then went on to describe how he and Masaka had waited with the rest of the crowd for the British ambassador, Parkes, who was coming in from the Chion'in. But Parkes had canceled his appearance after his party was attacked en route by two anti-foreign fanatics. By the time that Hosuke had stopped at Hirata Kanetane's residence in Nishikinokoji to take his leave and had said good-bye to Masaka, the streets of Kyoto were full of rumors of a coming second attempt to accord an audience to Sir Harry Parkes. Security along his projected route was extreme—thirty men each from Satsuma, Choshu, Aki, and Kii were assigned to the task, all traffic had been halted for the day along the affected streets, and the gates were closed tightly at each intersection. It was no longer the kind of world in which a nation could stand isolated. The emperor himself had taken the initiative in clearing the way for international relations, and it was necessary to deal with the people of the world through treaty arrangements that covered every last detail. In the future, anyone who broke discipline to kill a foreigner or even to behave improperly toward them would be in rebellion against the imperial will. Such acts would not only compromise the dignity of Japan but would invite national disaster. Times had so changed that anyone of samurai rank perpetrating such offenses would now be subject to the extreme penalty. When one remembered how recently Kyoto had been the center of a national consensus for the expulsion of foreigners, it seemed part of a different world.

"But I was really put out by the way every last person in Kyoto would sooner or later appeal to international law. Whenever anyone started to talk about international problems, it would immediately be 'international law, international law'! It really got to me. I think that impressed me more than anything else."

These were the tales that Hosuke left behind at Hanzo's place.

After he had seen off his guest, who would be reaching home after spending one more night on the road, Hanzo muttered appreciatively to himself.

"It's good to find solid men like that even among the farmers."

4

A party of thirteen men, all Hirata disciples from Mino, came through just three days later. They were on their way back after guiding the commander of the Tosando army as far as Shimo-Suwa. The party had arranged their plans so as to arrive at Magome for their noon meal and all of them of course went into Hanzo's home to untie their straw sandals.

They made an impressive group as they crowded into the wood-floored area of the entrance hall, all wearing long jackets with split tails and with swords at their sides. Some were taking off their helmets, others were untying their walking trousers and brushing off the dust of the road. A few went directly inside as soon as they had washed their feet.

"Welcome! Welcome! Please come right in!"

Seisuke was the first to come out to the entrance hall to conduct the arriving guests inside. Overlooking nothing, he quickly removed the sliding panels between the inner room and the central room to prepare a spacious chamber for the guests. The thirteen Hirata disciples from Mino, now safely back from guiding the army, prepared to enjoy themselves in the home of their fellow disciple and to rest from their journey. Keizo was among them. Hanzo came in to greet his guests. He was moved by the thought of entertaining these people in his own home, but he noticed that Kozo was missing.

"Kozo is coming back from Suwa by way of Ina. He will be along in two or three days."

It was Keizo who replied, but Keizo seemed strangely stiff and formal that day. Among the members of the party were some who were on their way back to Naegi.

"Keizo had a big job this time. We guided the army as far as Suwa, but there were two factions developing in the army. Satsuma and Choshu wanted to continue on the main route while Tosa was advocating a campaign of pacification down toward Kai province. It was a big squabble."

"So, we watched the army divide and march off in two directions and then we came back."

Keizo was not the only one to report his dismay over this development.

After Seisuke finished helping Hanzo get his guests settled, he went back to the kitchen to help Otami with the meal preparations. Meal trays for thirteen were being laid out. Since the guests had appeared so suddenly, the people in the kitchen had to make do with whatever was at hand. They made a simple stew of sliced dried squid, oak mushrooms, burdock root, and frozen beancurd. With that they served an asparagus-like wild vegetable prepared with vinegar and miso. The meal was completed with miso soup prepared with pieces of dried gourd in the style of mountain households. It was the time of year when all the vegetables put up for winter were gone and the new vegetable crop was not yet ready.

"All the guests are disciples of Master Hirata." Okume slipped in to whisper this to her mother. She was now old enough to help out with chores such as wiping the plates and bowls. Oman came in from the retirement quarters to help. She suggested that for such an occasion it would be suitable to put out a container of sake even if the guests had not asked for it. She added that it would also be appropriate for the honjin to entertain the guests in an old-fashioned way and that this would please Hanzo. She placed the old family cups on a tall, footed tray of unfinished wood and gave Okume the small decanter of sake. Then she went to the parlor to pay her own respects.

"You have all worked very hard."

Oman bowed low before the men from Mino and then went over before

Ono Saburobei, a man from Nakatsugawa who was well known as an activist, and also bowed to him. Sitting next to him at the end of the row was Keizo. Oman placed the cup on its footed tray before him and offered him cold sake.

"Please have some sake."

"Why, thank you very much."

Keizo emptied the cup of cold sake with obvious pleasure. Then Hanzo came over to him.

"Anyway, Keizo, I didn't expect them to get past Fukushima so smoothly."

"At least no one got hurt."

"They really laid down the law to me when I was called up about the Sagara Sozo affair."

"Well, this was a pretty large body of troops. A man came to us from the Yamamura residence when we were at our headquarters in Fukushima. He gave us a letter swearing obedience."

"My father was terribly worried. He'll be relieved to hear about this. You know what a long time we have served under the Yamamura."

"By the way, Keizo," Saburobei joined in, "maybe you ought to tell him what happened to Sagara Sozo."

" 'Once the gallant warrior sets forth he never comes back.' Well, that's the way it always is. On the second day of the third month, Sagara and several of his men were called to the headquarters in Suwa and on the next day eight of the most important ones were beheaded and their heads exposed just outside Shimo-Suwa. Thirteen others were banished after having one eyebrow and one side of their beards shaved off. Every one of us begged them to spare Sagara, but they said that since he had passed himself off as the vanguard of the imperial army and had then gone on to behave in a high-handed manner, the matter could not be overlooked. Our pleas were useless."

Presently the trays for the guests were set out in the inner room. Keizo, Saburobei, and the others moved to their new seats. Keizo seemed to take this noon meal at the Magome honjin as a solemn ceremony.

The date for the attack on Edo was set for the fifteenth of the month. The commander-in-chief, who was going by way of the Tokaido, would have arrived in Suruga by now. The Mino men brought with them from Suwa the speculation that the Tosa troops, eager for combat, were rushing to the attack on Edo and would probably be engaging the newly raised shogunal troops in the Tosando army's first battle.

Keizo talked very little that day. Nor did Hanzo find the opportunity to speak privately to his friend. Implicit in Keizo's every act, however, was his resolve, now that he had carried out this mission to guide the Tosando army, to return to Kyoto.

"The imperial cause needs every last man it can get in these times. I have to go up to Kyoto and help Kanetane form the new government."

Although he did not say this in so many words, Keizo's manner conveyed his intent. It was manifest in the way he took up his chopsticks when he sat down to his meal with the others, and it was manifest in the way he tasted the food Otami had prepared with such care.

Most of the Mino men were in a hurry to get home. Some began to rise to their feet almost as soon as the meal was finished. In the confusion Hanzo went up to his friend.

"Keizo, just wait until you get to Nakatsugawa. There's something fine waiting for you there. Hosuke from Ina brought it. He came through here, too, and told me all kinds of things about Kyoto."

Two days later, Kozo arrived in Magome from his detour through Ina. Like the thirteen Mino men who had preceded him, he was still in the full panoply in which he had guided the commander, wearing a flat helmet shaped like a tortoise shell and a swordsman's jacket with split tail. He was even wearing a sword. Hanzo was delighted to be able to entertain him.

"At last. At last."

In the tone of Kozo's voice Hanzo could sense the strain of going over the long road from Ogaki in Mino to Suwa in Shinano.

Before anything else, Hanzo conducted Kozo into the parlor and had him remove his walking trousers while he took his sword. After consulting with Otami, he invited Kozo to stay over for the night and had the bath heated for his very tired friend. The occasion being what it was, Kozo was not hesitant to accept the hospitality. Otami came up to Hanzo while their guest was bathing.

"Kozo must be uncomfortable in his traveling clothes. Why don't we let him have one of your kimono when he gets out of the bath?"

Hanzo was pleased by Otami's womanly thoughtfulness.

Kozo, deeply tanned by the sun, looked very fit. In the evening, after refreshing himself in a hot bath and slipping into the fresh kimono offered him by Otami, he came into Hanzo's room to relax, self-conscious in his borrowed clothing.

"Sagara Sozo really got himself into something," said Kozo, opening the conversation.

"I heard about it from Keizo, too," Hanzo responded.

"Every one of us begged for his life but it was no use. You probably don't know the details of how Sagara Sozo's men were causing trouble in Edo even before the battles of Toba and Fushimi. I learned a lot of things from being around people like the chief of staff of the Tosando army. They say that Sozo's group had secretly set up three categories: 'Those who help the shogunate.' 'Those who harm masterless samurai.' 'Those who deal in foreign goods.' They viewed all three as enemies of the emperor and set about to execute as many of them as possible. At the same time they did not sanction robbing people for private gain. Just think what it must have been like when a band of them, acting under these rules, broke into the foreign goods store in Kanabuki-cho in Edo. They closed off the street gates and stole six revolvers from the store. Then they went to a shop called the Harimaya that was a special trader for the shogunate. They say that they called out the manager, put one of the new revolvers to his head, and told him that they found nothing inside his skull but the shogunate and that if he had any regrets over his previous offenses, he should donate funds to the imperial forces. Two apprentices then led them to the cellar and handed over more than ten thousand ryo. That's the way they acted.

"Anyway, their base was in the Satsuma mansion in Mita. Everyone had gone back to Satsuma and there was only a caretaker's staff of about twenty left behind. These ronin split up into three groups and acted in accord with their three categories throughout the Edo area. But they also seemed to be planning something bigger while the shogunal officials were distracted. There were stories that they were planning to set fire to Edo castle and rescue Princess Kazu in the confusion. From what I heard, they actually were planning to do just that. That's the kind of crowd we had coming around to our part of the country. Well, those who live by the sword do die by the sword, don't they? This time they got just what they had been dishing out to others. They certainly didn't get very far once they started making trouble in the countryside."

Early on in the conversation, Otami brought out a decanter of warm sake and some light food for the comfort and relaxation of her husband's guest.

"We really don't have anything suitable to offer you, Kozo."

"Please make yourself comfortable."

Under the attentions of both husband and wife, Kozo enjoyed his sake in complete informality. Along with the sake were wild greens from the mountains and small clams boiled down with soy sauce and seasonings. These were all festively served on a bright new wooden tray.

"Otami, Keizo was not just on his way to Nakatsugawa. He's going on to Kyoto."

"Isn't that just what you would expect him to be doing?"

Kozo joined in on this interchange between husband and wife.

"Yes, I'll probably be going with Keizo. I think I'll go up to Kyoto and stay with the master again for a while."

"Otami, Kozo will be leaving us again soon. Bring us another bottle of sake. But don't tell mother."

Hanzo pulled absently at his earlobe as he spoke. Even at this age he was still somewhat intimidated by his stepmother.

"I wanted to roast some gohei mochi for you tonight. It's being prepared in the kitchen right now," said Otami. "Please take your time."

"Thank you. I would very much enjoy that. Kiso walnuts are especially good," said Kozo.

Hanzo looked over toward his friend and began to talk about their fellow disciples. He also told the stories about Kyoto that Hosuke of Nanjo village had brought back with him.

"Kozo, you know Kyoto. We're hearing all kinds of things from there nowadays. If you spend a month there this time, it will be like three months or half a year before. I really envy you and Keizo."

"I wonder just how Kyoto has changed."

"Well, according to what Hosuke said, Kyoto is at the center of the restoration now."

"There was a lot of talk about it in Ina. Just look how powerful the armies are that are moving against the shogunate. The world has really taken a big turn. All the same, Hanzo, we are both disciples of Hirata sensei. We really have to take thought in such times."

"I agree."

"Sometimes actors on the stage get too wrapped up in their own roles and lose sight of the play as a whole. The more completely involved the actor is, the greater the danger. I became very much aware of this while I was with the commander. Even though the playwright has fashioned a script in which the power of the daimyo will be broken, it appears that the actors are not reading it very carefully.

"Anyway, Hanzo, I'm going off to Kyoto to see what it's like to be in the capital of the restoration. I'll write you about it. Because no matter how excited the Kanto forces become, Yoshinobu, who is the key man, keeps on making placatory gestures. It's obvious what's going to happen to the powers surrounding the shogunate. I'm more concerned about the newly opened ports like Hyogo and Osaka. Just because the imperial audience for the foreign ambassadors finally went off all right doesn't mean that everything is secure. That's because it's right now when everything is just getting started that we can't make proper preparations. If the foreigners use military force to ensure that we act in accordance with the treaty, this country is going to have to put up even with that. Patience, and more patience—we're going to have to put up with an awful lot for the sake of our children and grandchildren. The question of whether the country is really opened up or not is going to be settled from here on—"

"Here are the gohei mochi!" came the voices of the children as Okume and Sota, accompanied by their mother, came in from the hearth room carrying platters heaped with the walnut dumplings.

"Please help yourself. Eat them while they're hot!" said Otami, looking back toward the children. "There was a great fuss out in the hearth room a little while ago. 'The guest is wearing daddy's kimono,' they were saying—children are really something."

"Daddy's kimono" made her husband laugh too.

Kozo, rubbing his hands in anticipation, said, "Well, shall I have one?"

He bit into a freshly roasted dumpling with pleasure. The local custom was to roast five of the dumplings on a skewer and to eat them by pulling them one by one off the skewer. The appetizing color to which they had been roasted and the scent of the walnuts made both guest and host forget everything else.

Early next morning, Kozo expressed his thanks to Hanzo and his wife and began making hurried preparations to depart. Half his mind seemed already to be in Kyoto.

"These are great times to be alive, Hanzo," were his parting words.

After seeing his friend off, Hanzo stepped into the hall leading from the parlor to the back room. From here he could look out over Mino in the direction of Kozo's home. Most of his fellow disciples were now gathering around the master, and he reflected on how everything seemed to be drawn into the great struggle of the new government against the Tokugawa shogunate. He thought of his fellow disciples in the armies moving eastward along the three great highways, determined to see the feudal age buried, and he paced nervously up and down the quiet hallway.

The dream of a true restoration of antiquity had flared up within him once again. Yamagata and Takeuchi had taken the lead long ago in advocating the imperial cause, and now Maki Izumi's vision of a great movement for the overthrow of the shogunate had come to fruition. It was a time when individual tragedies such as those in Shimo-Suwa were quickly washed away in the great wave of events. Hanzo reflected on how naturally the dreams of the thousands of Hirata disciples throughout the country matched the new government's desire to repudiate all vestiges of the middle ages in order to realize a better society, and he envisioned the return to the straightforwardness and wholesomeness evident in the national character of the Japanese of antiquity.

He looked around him. Suddenly he recalled the time last year when Yamaguchi Suruga, then chief inspector and commissioner of foreign relations for the shogunate, had stayed at the Magome honjin. Hanzo could never forget how Suruga had traveled from Kyoto back to Edo in disguise and how, hidden away in the chamber of honor of the honjin, he had wept tears of dark despair over the condition of the shogunate. Hanzo remembered how he had said that the day was no longer distant when the country would be opened. That day had finally come but the beginning of direct rule by the emperor coincided with a most difficult time in foreign relations.

Tomorrow—the oldest and at the same time the newest sun. What kind of new antiquity would it bring to the waiting people of this nation? Ultimately, it was beyond the powers of the imagination to tell. Hanzo himself, as a Hirata disciple dedicated to learning, wanted to learn still more, but the time had not yet arrived when he could have the comfort of counting even the ten thousandth part of his desires as having been realized. It was his fervent wish to be able to rely on people in a spirit of complete faith and to join hands with his fellow disciples in firmly establishing the new government. In this manner they would follow in the footsteps of the great masters such as Motoori Norinaga who had opened the way for those who came after.

5

At the end of the third month, the news came to the Magome honjin that the Tosando army had reached Itabashi, the eastern terminus of the Kiso road, and that the attack on Edo had been canceled. Tokugawa Yoshinobu, who had already surrendered his powers and given up his vast domains, was show-ing no signs of wanting to hold Edo castle. Even those who most hated and mistrusted the Tokugawa found themselves without any pretext for attacking the master of Edo castle, whose obedience to the new government was by now clear even to every foreign ambassador. By giving up everything that he had to give up, Yoshinobu had spared the people of Edo.

All this became a subject of gossip. It had been Okubo Ichio, Katsu Awa, and Yamaoka Tetsutaro, in charge of negotiations with the imperial army, who had prevented serious disorder by remaining in the masterless Edo castle and maintaining strict control over the officials there. However, what would have happened if Yoshinobu had not had the determination to place Oguri Kozuke, the shogunal official most determined to fight, under house arrest and strip him of his titles? Cries of "Kill him!" were being raised not only in the imperial army but among his own men as well. The imperial soldiers, who did not understand the thinking that lay behind Yoshinobu's moves, saw his submission as a mere tactical yielding to a show of force from Kyoto, and they raged, tearing their hair and weeping as they cried, "Yoshinobu must be killed! The sovereign must be recognized!" In this atmosphere, charged with bloodthirstiness, it was clear that some other high-ranking offi-cials would have taken over if Yoshinobu had not been able to ride out the storm of misunderstanding opposition and rage and make clear his desire for peace between court and shogunate. But those officials would have been less informed about foreign affairs than Yoshinobu. Lacking the experience of having complied with the treaties forced on them by the foreign powers, they would have given no thought to the foreign nations that had loaned such vast amounts of money to Japan and that now had no wish to see the country fall into internal disorder. They would have paid no attention to the damage to future prospects or to the question of the nation's viability, and all the efforts of Katsu Awa, Yamaoka Tetsutaro, and Okubo Ichio would have been in vain.

But those who knew how Yoshinobu had given up the crucial Tokugawa policy of alternate attendance, and how he appeared weak but was in fact strong, and how keenly attuned he was to the trends of the time, how free he was from blind obstinacy—those who knew how twice, once in the early 1860's and again a few years later, he had committed himself to so many far reaching reforms—those who knew this would not have found his present behavior at all surprising. Unfortunately, there were many among the inner circles of the Tokugawa family who did not care for this man. Discontent arose among the shogunal officials who had long-standing grudges against Yoshinobu and among those who felt that the present situation was the result not of genuine reverence for the emperor but of a play by Satsuma and Choshu to seize national power. It arose among the Tokugawa retainers who intensely resented both Yoshinobu's complete lack of resistance to letting them all be labeled as rebels and their being forced to endure the spectacle of foreign barbarians treading the streets of this great city, demeaning the glories accumulated over the past three hundred years. "What would Ieyasu have thought of this?"—there was no telling what form this cry would take or where it was likely to rise. The skies over Edo grew dark and threatening, and the tense, heavy atmosphere drifted down the more than two hundred miles of highway to bring somberness to the region around Magome.

There were reports that the remaining retainers in the Edo mansions of the daimyo were beginning to leave. The time for the surrender of Edo castle drew near while negotiations were under way for turning it over to the imperial troops. It was said that there were only four courses open to these retainers. They could go into hiding, they could take up commerce or agriculture, they could emigrate, or they could become retainers of the imperial court. Circumstances did not permit them to live in the great Edo mansions as they had done for so long.

For those who were members of the Tokugawa family or its direct retainers, the situation was still more difficult. The bannermen were all confronted with the necessity to reform their household managements and reduce expenses in order to get by because the shogunate, plunged into a program of desperate building of naval and land forces, had taken over half the income of their lands during the previous year. In effect, the bannermen were rapidly being deprived of their only source of income. The document given them by Yoshinobu had said that it was his personal fault that things had come to this pass and that he was deeply ashamed and grieved. Therefore, if some were forced to leave his service out of economic necessity, he would not begrudge them the right to do so but would leave such decisions to each individual.

Rumors said that refugees from the great han establishments in Edo were beginning to pour down the Tokaido on their way home. How his old-fashioned father must be suffering in this darkness that had enfolded the highways. The thought depressed Hanzo. It was the one thing that had caused him time after time to give up the idea of leaving home, and to bear up with the duties of a headman without following after his friends Keizo and Kozo. It was what made him turn his attention to his duties to the farmers in his own region.

Hanzo ran out the front gate of the honjin just after noon to have a look at the road before going back to see his parents.

"The villagers!"

He was addressing no one in particular. All the proclamations that had been posted by the old shogunate were now cleared away and replaced by notices from the council of state, showing that the new age had come even to this remote village. As he stood before his gate, he looked up the steep slope toward the notice board and down along the familiar highway with the stone-weighted shingled roofs lined up on both sides.

There was no resisting the new influences that had come to the village. Each year, during the fine days beginning with the blooming of the peach blossoms, the number of travelers would suddenly increase. The officials from Fukushima had always come up the highway in this season. But this

spring there was no trace of officials coming to Magome to inspect the transport facilities and the highway. Since the passage of the Tosando army, the
Yamamura deputies had fallen into an unfathomable silence, a silence as profound as the stillness of the primeval forests of the Kiso valley. Only the forest commissioner from Owari came up the highway from the inner Kiso to
check on possible illegal cutting of timber by the villagers.

Just two days earlier, the sound of the drums of some two hundred Owari
men had been heard in Magome as they moved down the highway from the
west. The villagers had gazed up at the banners carried high before the three
detachments making up the group. After they passed on toward Matsumoto,
on their way to answer a need for security forces in Echizen, the restless
movement along the highway continued. Hanzo stood for a time looking out
at the highway running past his gate, hoping that the news from Nagoya
would be brought by the couriers bearing fast freight. The afternoon sunlight flooded the road, people were coming and going—merchants up from
Nakatsugawa to collect accounts, travelers from various provinces, all of
whom, in the manner of that time, were carrying their account books in the
bosoms of their kimono so that they could note down how much they had
paid for regular horses, for light horses, or for porters.

There was nothing untoward along the highway. Somewhat reassured by
this, Hanzo went back along the narrow path between the main house and
the newer side buildings toward the retirement quarters. The ground floor,
now used for storing miso and pickled vegetables, dated from the time of
Hanzo's grandfather, Hanroku, and there was a separate entrance that led to
the living quarters on the second floor. Arrangements had been made so that
it was not necessary to climb up and down the steep stairs in order to go to
the toilet. From the large, old-fashioned sliding panels that hid the closet, on
which some unknown calligrapher had written in bold strokes, to the two
rooms whose shoji could be opened onto a bright and sunny southern prospect, Kichizaemon had left everything just as his father had designed it.

Kichizaemon was now spending half of each day in bed. There he reflected
upon his seventy years of life and from there he gazed out into the twilight of
his lifetime. When Hanzo reached the head of the stairs, he found his father
at rest.

"Are you asleep?" asked Hanzo as he went over to look at his father's
face.

"Don't wake father up!" came the voice of Oman from the next room.

His father's face with its big nose, its quiet mouth, and its bushy eyebrows
did not seem much changed to Hanzo's eyes. As he looked down from his
father's hands, he noticed the way Kichizaemon had his legs crossed, the
right leg undermost as was his habit when taking a nap. He was snoring
softly. After listening closely to his breathing, Hanzo went to join Oman in
the next room.

"I hear things are really bad in Edo, Hanzo," she said. "Just now I was
telling your father that he should not be worrying about these things the way

you do. That's your job now. But he doesn't say a thing. And there is Kimbei. He always dwells on the most petty details. I can hardly stand to sit here and listen to him. However much an old friend he may be, he still ought to know when it's time to go home. All I can do is just sit here and hope that father won't get as tired this time as he did the last. And what do you think father said after Kimbei left? 'I hope we get through these times quickly. I just hope we get through these times quickly. That's all I ask . . .' "

In the next room Kichizaemon, exhausted after the visit of his old friend, slept on peacefully without stirring. Someone came over to bring Hanzo back to the main house. There were endless small details to be attended to in the management of the village. Hanzo decided to visit with his father another time. He took a document out of the breast of his kimono and showed it to Oman. It was a memorandum that seemed somewhat more reliable than most of the reports that the couriers were bringing through from Kyoto. Never had rumors been so rife along the highway as they were now. There were, for example, groundless rumors that the emperor was going to take personal command of the expedition against the Kanto and that he was about to leave Osaka for this purpose, or that the emperor had been abducted while on the way to Mt. Hiei. So many wild stories were making the rounds that people no longer knew what to believe.

"Mother, please show this to father when he wakes up."

The document that Hanzo showed his stepmother was a copy dated the day before the imperial army was scheduled to enter Edo castle and it was addressed to the people of the entire nation. The emperor said that the urgent business of the present time was to lay the foundations for the future. The Five Article Oath that the emperor had sworn to the people was included. All matters were to be settled by public consensus, high and low were to stand unified, and not only warriors and officials but the common people as well were to make their desires known. The evil practices of the past were to be eliminated, the nation placed on a basis of righteousness and consensus, and the imperial government made sound by knowledge gathered from all over the world. It was indeed a document for everyone.

6

Toward the middle of the fourth month, Hanzo received messages by courier from Edo that made it clear that Edo castle had been surrendered without fighting.

Then he waited until the end of that month. Reports would come in that yesterday the shogun and his family had left the Kan'eiji on Toeizan in Edo and had set out accompanied by some two hundred retainers, or that today some four thousand people fleeing the Edo mansions were now gathering in the vicinity of Shimosa, Kazusa, and Ueno, carrying arms and provisions. As each report came in, no one from the post station officials down to the tenant farmers got much work done. Then a comet suddenly appeared and Hanzo could do no more than to share his worries with the villagers as they tried to guess what this omen might presage.

At last they were able to get news not only of what had happened to the Tosando army, but also of the Owari forces that had joined troops from Choshu, Satsuma, Kii, Todo, Bizen, and Tosa to form the Tokaido army. To Hanzo, who looked upon the retired lord of Owari and his son as the ultimate lords of the Kiso, the movements of that han were a constant preoccupation. By accident he happened to obtain a copy of a memorandum written by a physician who had accompanied a mixed group of Owari men to Edo. It could be called a first-hand report, recounting the experiences of this Nagoya physician.

Eagerly taking up the paper and skimming it, Hanzo saw that the group to which the physician had been attached left Nagoya on the twenty-sixth day of the second month as an escort for the commander-in-chief. At Suruga they joined with a force of some seven hundred eighty men that had left earlier under the command of Tominaga Magodayu. Hanzo began to reread the paper carefully.

On one page he found the name Tokugawa Gendo—there was a rumor that Gendo was rushing to Suruga to rescue Tokugawa Yoshinobu. Gendo was the pen name of the former lord of Owari, a familiar figure to Hanzo and his father. He had been forced to resign as lord of Owari because of disagreements with the retired lord of Owari, Yoshikatsu, and he had then succeeded to the house of Hitotsubashi through the manipulations of the lord of Echizen. Hanzo still remembered the day long ago when the retired lord had passed over the Kiso road, carrying the report of the payment of the indemnity for the Namamugi incident. More than two thousand porters had been called out from the villages of the Kiso to serve him—it was impossible ever to forget how crowded it had been in Magome. It was written in the memorandum that in Owari, this lord had now become aroused, that he had made two high-ranking han officials accompany him, and that by insisting that Yoshinobu's intentions had been misrepresented, he had been able to exert crucial influence on the commander-in-chief.

Now another delicate matter arose. As the Tokaido army was moving from Odawara to Kanagawa, there appeared before it a force recruited from various foreign nations that said that its purpose was to protect the foreigners resident in Yokohama. They made many difficult requests. They said that Yoshinobu was a man with whom the foreign countries had had friendly relations and that an explanation was clearly owed the foreigners for any action that was contemplated against him, yet no such explanation had been forthcoming. Moreover, although an advance warning should be given to resident foreigners if the opening of hostilities was imminent, no such warning had been received. Most of the foreigners who stood there making these demands were looking to the prospect of opening Edo to trade and they wanted only the quickest restoration of order. The hidden fever of xenophobia that had produced the Sannomiya incident in Kobe and the Asahi teahouse incident in Sakai was still not extinguished. Even a foreign ambassador had barely escaped with his life in Kyoto. The foreigners were apprehensive of the effect that a general outbreak of hostilities in Edo might have on their safety, and they were extremely reluctant to permit the Tokaido army to pass Kanagawa. Marines had been landed from the foreign warships standing offshore. This was a source of great concern to the commander-in-chief, and the Satsuma troops were outraged. The physician reported that the opinions of the foreigners had by no means been ignored in planning the movement of the imperial forces into the Kanto. He wrote that the commander-in-chief was deeply concerned about the possibility that an attack on Edo might plunge the entire region into disorder, resulting in the killing and wounding of innocent bystanders and the reduction of the city to ashes. Very grave international repercussions could ensue from any extension of these effects to the foreign community.

Preoccupied with these problems, the Tokaido army was unable to reach Shinagawa. By that time the Tosando army had moved from Itabashi into Yotsuya and Shinjuku. They occupied the Owari residence at Ichigaya and pulled down walls here and there to put up breastworks. Eight or nine cannon were made ready to open fire on Edo castle from within the grounds of the mansion if fighting should break out. Unfortunately, the late arrival of the Tokaido army was misunderstood by the Tosando army, which had come into town flushed with victories on the Kozuke and Koshu roads. They saw the attitude of the Tokaido army, which was inclined to cancel the general attack on Edo, as pusillanimous vacillation. For its part, the Tokaido army viewed the attitude of its allies as mindless bellicosity and the engagements in Kai and elsewhere were spoken of in slighting terms. It was only to be expected that the relationships between the commanders of the two armies should grow cool.

As Hanzo read further, he grew still more discouraged. Wanting to share the news with his father, he went back once again with the copy of the military physician's report.

"Have the wisteria come into bloom yet?"

Kichizaemon addressed this question to Hanzo and to Oman as he sat up in bed. It was already time for the pastures to be opened when the collapse of the shogunate had at last become a fully accepted fact even here in the mountains.

"Did they hand over Edo castle on the eleventh, Hanzo?" asked Kichizaemon.

"Yes, they did," replied Hanzo. "The imperial forces entered Edo after all. They say that they were just in time to see the cherries in full bloom. The soldier poured into all the han residences, dragging their cannon over the fallen petals—it must have been a depressing sight."

"Well, there's nothing an old-timer like me can say about it."

Hanzo then reached into his kimono and took out the report. He read aloud the sections relating to the surrender of Edo castle.

It described how, on the night before the surrender of the castle, a great deal of planning had gone on in the quarters of Saigo Takamori at the Zojoji temple in Shiba. The time for accepting control of the castle was set for the fifth hour on the following morning, eight o'clock. If there should be any resistance to the imperial command at that point, the castle was to be taken by force. All the troops of the various han were to be in readiness before the western ramparts of the castle. The morning came. When Owari troops under the imperial brocade banners advanced to the main gate, they were met by former Tokugawa bannermen in full formal dress. Most of the field artillery pieces had already been removed from the castle and only siege guns and light pieces remained, but the report said that even these came to more than one hundred items. The former bannermen left the castle and the soldiers of the other han returned to their encampments while the Owari troops entered the castle. There they took up defensive positions. The final act in the drama of the great castle of the shoguns that had dominated the eight hundred and eight districts of Edo began on the morning of the eleventh day of the fourth month of Keio 4, 1868.

"Father, it tells about Kamiya Hachiroemon here. He was in charge of the guard of the outer Sakurada gate."

"If that is the Kamiya Hachiroemon from Nagoya, I have met him."

" 'From the main gates on the west to Kanda bridge, the riding grounds, the Wadakura gate, and the guard post at the double bridge, all the strategic points are occupied by Owari men.' "

"That means that Edo castle has been entrusted to Owari."

"Wait, here's something about Jokakuin and Tenshoin. Jokakuin would be Princess Kazu. It says that both of them remained in Edo castle to the end."

"Really?" said Oman. "It must have been a difficult position for both of them. Just think, Princess Kazu traveled all the way from Kyoto to marry the shogun and Tenshoin came from Satsuma."

"But wait! There's this about Tenshoin. It's telling about the time when Princess Kazu first arrived in Edo and Tenshoin, her mother-in-law, was meeting her. They observed that Tenshoin did not immediately take the seat reserved for her. She first sat among her numerous ladies-in-waiting and looked the person from Kyoto over very carefully. Then she abruptly got up and reseated herself in the position of honor. That seems to be characteristic of her. I can't forget that story. Tenshoin seems to be that kind of person. Even now, when the castle is to be handed over to the imperial forces and Princess Kazu is told to move to the Tayasu palace and she to the Hitotsubashi residence, Tenshoin would be in no hurry to move. According to this report, she literally had to be brought out by force."

"This is a sad story," responded Kichizaemon.

"Why, I've been so interested listening to your story that I haven't started the tea!"

Oman got up and went into the next room, where she could be heard bringing out the tea implements from behind a small folding screen.

"Hanzo," Kichizaemon continued, still sitting up in bed, "what's going to become of Edo now?"

"Well, I've heard that people in Kyoto are talking about moving the capital. I got a letter about it from Kozo. He is in Kyoto now."

"Well, this is quite a story. There's no telling just how far this restoration is going to go."

"What they seem to be saying, father, is that if we're going to do it at all, we had best go all the way."

While they were talking, Oman brought in some tea made from the new crop that had been sent over from the Fushimiya. Fresh tea from this time of year was very fragrant but it had a little too much bitterness for an old person. Oman, ever alert to such details, said that she had mixed in a little old tea while brewing it.

"Why don't you lie down again?" said Oman, looking toward her husband. "If you keep sitting up like that you'll get tired."

"That's right. I'll talk lying down."

Kichizaemon and Oman liked drinking tea together. Kichizaemon took up the teabowl that Oman offered him, and enjoying the feel of his hands on the heavy object he had used for so many years, he breathed in the aroma of the tea which he had come to appreciate more and more as he grew older. With Hanzo at his side, his talk turned to family reminiscences. Then he noted that since even he had been stunned to learn of the fall of the Tokugawa, what must it have been like for those who had actually witnessed the fall of the mighty with their own eyes? He expressed his concern about this. Had their forebears, who had served in the three offices of honjin, headman, and toiya, knowing only the full power of the military houses, been happier? Or had Kichizaemon and Hanzo, living in this age of violent change, able to experience two different epochs in one lifetime, indeed to live two different lives, been the happier? He went on talking about such things.

"That reminds me. When Kimbei came over to see me the other day, we got to talking about the finances of the new government. It must be costing an immense amount of money just to move that many soldiers around. Kimbei suddenly said, 'They're all like a bunch of merchants, so just where do you think the money from this campaign is coming from?' When I replied that it had to be coming from the various han, Kimbei lowered his voice and said, 'Of course, it's coming from the han, but have you heard that the Kyoto and Osaka merchants have also made big contributions? They say that several of the big houses have committed themselves to raise more than one million ryo each. Of course, they are expecting to get something back from the new government in return for all that money. And they won't settle for being given surnames and the right to wear swords the way the shogunate did with us. It is a blessing to know of the restoration of imperial rule, but we'll be lucky if some real trouble doesn't come out of all of this.' I thought a lot about what Kimbei said after he went home."

Then Kichizaemon changed the subject.

"Kimbei reminded me," he said, drawing the smoking set over and lighting his pipe. "For me it's pretty late in the day, but that old man from the Fushimiya is really holding up well. He's two years older than I am but for him the sun still seems to be high in the sky."

" 'His sun still seems to be high in the sky'—that's good," said Oman, laughing softly. "But just the same, Kimbei saw his son Tsurumatsu die before he did and he has just buried Otama, his second wife, at the beginning of the year, so he must feel pretty discouraged."

"But he's the kind of person who, even at his age, is all set to go out to the Tanabata festival when he's invited. Besides, I know that Kimbei has planted a hundred and twenty cedar seedlings in the gully behind his old house. He did it while everyone else was all worked up over rebuilding. I just don't have that kind of greed. As you know, I made my way through this world walking as quietly as I could. I've seen everything that was built up by the Tokugawa gradually disappear. I won't be around much longer.

" 'You did a fine job as honjin, toiya, and headman!' I feel that that is what my father, Hanroku, is saying as he calls to me from beneath the grass."

"You mustn't say such depressing things, father."

"No, but a fortune teller once told me that I have lived to my seventieth year only because Hanzo went on that pilgrimage up to Mt. Ontake for me."

"Just look at him, Hanzo. He's always saying that."

There was one thing after another. Now, even the families of the daimyo who had not moved when the alternate attendance system was suspended some years earlier began their departure from the Edo residences where they had lived for so long, and without a backward glance rushed back to the provinces.

"An Edo residence staff is coming through!"

When Hanzo heard the shout of Okume and Sota, he could not remain talking any longer in his father's quarters. He had to go to the meeting room to help Seisuke and Kyurobei with everything from horses and porters to the preparations for lodgings.

These parties who elected to return to their provinces by the Kiso road, apparently to avoid the congestion along the Tokaido, were usually made up of the women or the retired lord and his attendants from this or that han.

"Homeward, homeward!"

This time the cry was not one of liberation as it had been when the families of the allied lords had come through some years back. Most of the residence staffs who now came through were the exact opposite, wanting to stay in Edo as long as possible to learn what had become of their households, wanting to know what lay ahead for them in today's crises, and finding it hard to part from relatives who might need, or who could offer, comfort and assistance in time of sickness or death. They had hesitated, only in the end to find themselves forced to leave their homes by order of the imperial council of state and the commander-in-chief of the imperial armies.

The Edo with the shogun's castle at its center, sixty percent of whose vast area had been occupied by military households, was now coming to an end. Those who found it impossible to leave Edo immediately, such as retainers and officials of han traditionally close to the Tokugawa, were likely to be suspected of disloyalty to the emperor. They were also likely to find themselves under pressure by the military to move. Such was the power of the commander of the imperial armies. Among those who passed through Magome on the way to the home provinces in the west, one left word of the Edo residence of the Tokugawa house of Kii. According to this person, there were, when one included the residence, the secondary residence, and the inferior residence, as well as all the other dwellings, more than six hundred residences large and small belonging to Kii. Counting everyone down to the private maids, there had been a total of more than four thousand men and women in Edo serving the house of Kii. Even though this great crowd of people had been ordered to leave their homes and the graves of their ancestors of the past three hundred years and move to a province more than three hundred miles to the south, how could they be expected to clear the city in only four or five days? Hanzo could see all around him the effects of this dispersal of the Edo residence personnel who shared the fate of the Tokugawa. Throughout the season when people in the Kiso were busy with the picking and roasting of tea, one party after another of displaced men and women passed through in an endless stream.

CHAPTER FIVE

1

BETWEEN THE MIDDLE of the fifth month and the beginning of the sixth month, Hanzo took Heibei, the assistant headman from Toge, along with him on a trip to Nagoya, Ise, and Kyoto. He had recently learned that his old teacher, Miyagawa Kansai, had died a lonely death in wretched circumstances in the village of Uji just outside Ise, and so he planned to visit his grave on this trip. The journey was now near its end and he and Heibei were once again on the Kiso road heading back to Magome.

The two men were in a hurry, worried about what might have happened in their absence. On their way down from Kyoto through Otsu and Kusatsu, they had begun to hear disquieting rumors from home. The road as far as Kano has many steep slopes and it was there, already on the Mino road, that the rumors of happenings in Nakatsugawa first reached Hanzo's ears. But it was still too far away to gain any sense of their accuracy.

They reached Unuma. With the credibility of the new government not yet established in the minds of the people, rumors of no particular substance were constantly drifting along the highways. Hanzo found it impossible to believe that the farmers around Nakatsugawa, farmers on whom he had long relied and who had never once risen up even in the evil old days when the excesses of the Nikko emissary and the military had brought them endless suffering, should have risen now right in the midst of this reconstruction of society. He found it still more unlikely that the farmers around Magome could have joined in the uprising.

The closer he got to home the more uneasy he became. Even on the road it was clear that the countryside was extremely turbulent. For example, when one wished to have the assistance of horses or porters on a journey, the custom had always been that a regular packhorse could carry three hundred pounds, a combination pack and saddle horse could carry from eighty to a hundred fifty pounds in addition to its rider, and a light saddle pony could carry from twenty-five to seventy pounds in addition to its rider. A porter's load was set at forty-two pounds. This was the rule that everyone who traveled on the highways in those times was required to follow. The base rate was the rate paid for a standard packhorse, and that rate multiplied by two and divided by three gave the rate for a light saddle pony. If the standard rate was one hundred mon, the amount for a saddle pony came to sixty-seven mon. The charge for a porter was half the base rate. But when Hanzo and Heibei went to pay their carrying charges, they found that even though they paid in the new gold certificates rather than in the old coinage, a note with the face value of one ryo was only worth two bu, just half the face value.

That year, Keio 4, there was unseasonable weather throughout the intercalary fourth month and the rain continued even into the fifth month. From Nagoya to Ise, they had had rain almost every day. Good weather came only on the day that Hanzo bowed his head before Kansai's grave. This old master, who also bore the name Shunjukaen, now slept beneath the ground of Imakitayama in Uji. In his lonely final years, Kansai had lectured on Chinese and Japanese studies as head of the Hayashizaki library and had practiced medicine on the side. Although he was far from home, Hanzo was reluctant to rely on the local people. He picked out a memorial stone and left orders for the inscription "Contributed in early summer of the fourth year of Keio" to be carved on it. When he went on to Kyoto to tell Kureta Masaka about the stone and to meet his friends Keizo and Kozo, the rain started up again as the unsettled weather continued.

On that day, walking those streets of Kyoto once again, this city never forgotten even in his dreams and for which he had longed ceaselessly, he made his way to the lodgings of his old friends from Nakatsugawa and there he untied his sandals. Once more testing the atmosphere of a Kyoto under the restoration, he set out with Keizo and Kozo for Nishikikoji, where the Hirata family lived. The old master Hirata Kanetane and his son Nobutane were in good health and delighted to see him. Reluctant to let Hanzo return to his lodgings, they shared with him a long talk about the times since the death of Atsutane. When he saw Kureta Masaka, looking far younger and fitter than he had during his long stay in Ina, Hanzo was reminded that in this restoration of imperial rule all things medieval must be denied. Again he was not permitted to leave until he had been treated to an explanation of the necessity of overthrowing the centuries-old power of the military and the Buddhist priesthood. Throughout these happy reunions, the sound of the endlessly falling rain was always in his ears.

Departing from Kyoto on the way home, Hanzo and Heibei began to catch glimpses of the sun but now came the news of floods everywhere. Along the Yodo river there were reports of flood damage and many places were difficult to get through, and from the Tokaido came news that the levees along the Tenryu river had burst. In Hamamatsu more than seventy homes had been washed away. When they reached Kusatsu in Omi province, they saw Lake Biwa, brim full of water.

How were things at home? That one question was constantly before them. They could not forget how last year the crops had been so poor that they had had to distribute plain rice gruel to the villagers.

As it happened, these floods occurred just after the announcement that the punishment of the Tokugawa was to be carried out in consultation with the

daimyo and their chief retainers. Many from Satsuma and Choshu wanted to
see Yoshinobu executed, and this prospect stirred complex feelings among the
people. It was no accident that the men of Aizu who had come to Kyoto by
crossing Lake Inawashiro and traveling hundreds of miles over the highways,
and who for many years had supported Yoshinobu as protectors of Kyoto,
should now find themselves in absolute opposition to the men of the western
han. Defeated at the battles of Toba and Fushimi, their names entered in the
list of rebels along with those of Sendai and others, their protests against the
destruction of their residences proving futile, they were setting out on the
long road to defend their homeland to the death. This was what lay behind
the formation of the powerful alliance of northeastern daimyo.

This faction from the northeast supported the policies of Owari. They not
only sent troops to guard Edo castle and to serve in the Kanto area but also
advanced on Echigo. Hanzo had finally gotten a clear picture of these developments when he reached Nagoya. There he heard that the staff of the Edo
residences, refusing to lay down their arms, had taken up positions at Ueno
in Edo and were fighting the imperial forces, while the priestly Prince Rin-
noji from Nikko had fled to Aizu with one hundred and eighty men. By the
time Hanzo reached Kyoto there were rumors of a punitive expedition
against the northeast.

There was also much talk of the financial difficulties of the new government. It had issued gold certificates in five denominations, from ten yen to
one shu, in order to cover the vast expenses of the Kanto expedition, but the
representatives of the foreign governments, supplying arms in response to the
present emergency, wanted only real gold. The people in the hinterlands, particularly the merchants, were not pleased with the new gold certificates
either, because they had long been accustomed to dealing in silver. Whether
for this reason or not, Hanzo had soon learned from the merchants he met on
the journey of the sudden rise in prices following immediately upon the
issuance of the new currency. A packhorse load of rice that would have
brought two ryo two bu yesterday was today worth three ryo two bu. The
retail price of a quarter bushel of rice had risen four hundred twenty-four
mon. The fighting in Aizu, the abrupt rise in prices, the unseasonable
weather; each had contributed to the hardships of their journey.

2

Hanzo had walked more than a hundred miles from Kyoto to Okute, a backwoods station where the roads to Nagoya and to Ise branched off. To the east
of the station one came immediately into the Mino basin. After passing over
the ten-mile-long Jusan pass, he would be at the station of Oi. It was only
about seven miles from Oi to Nakatsugawa.

This was the road over which the vanguard and the main command of the Tosando army had passed with their brocade banners only a little more than four months earlier. The barley was ripe in the fields and rice transplanting was just ending. The road before them was enveloped in fresh green leaves as trees and grass alike breathed the invigorating air of the sixth month. The end of the long rains had been followed by hot, sunny days and Hanzo and Heibei stopped frequently in the shade of peach or persimmon trees to wipe the perspiration from their faces and bodies.

"Well, Hanzo, we've come a long way. It really feels like I've been away from home a long time."

"I wonder what everyone's doing in Magome."

"I wonder. By now they should have the rice all transplanted and they're probably wondering about us."

They continued to move on down the road as they talked.

There were still occasional showers. The fresh, green leaves would sound as though they were saying they had already had plenty. The roadway that had finally dried out would become wet again. There were all kinds of travelers about, some tipping their broad brimmed hats, some calling after traveling companions, some meeting in the middle of the road. These were no longer the rains that had made the journey to Ise and Kyoto so miserable for Hanzo and Heibei but rather the gentle summer showers that always came to the highway. Their trip had taken longer than expected, and they were concerned about the rumors they had heard from home. They rushed on, not even wanting to stop for rest. They were determined to cross the ten-mile-long pass by mid-afternoon and reach Oi, their scheduled lodging place for the night, even if it meant fighting their way through the rain.

They reached the inn in Oi at dusk. Now they were back in that special territory which, like Nakatsugawa, was in the domains of the lord of Owari but which sent its annual rice tax to the Yamamura in Fukushima. The host of the inn who came to greet them was well acquainted with Hanzo.

"It rained the whole trip. We had a bad time of it. How about you people?" asked Hanzo.

"We got a lot of it, too. There was a big storm on the twenty-third of last month. It washed out the bridge at Nakatsugawa. For a while it stopped traffic there and the ferry boats at Sakashita were not operating either. I hear they had a lot of trouble up the Kiso, too. But it looks as though the weather has settled down now. Once it gets hot like this there should be no more problems, but we were really worried there for a while."

Hanzo learned from his host that the rumors he had been half-doubting and half-believing were not to be brushed aside. On the twenty-ninth of the previous month, there had been an uprising of the farmers which subsided by the following night. It had unfortunately occurred while both Kozo and Keizo were away in Kyoto. Ono Saburobei, an important figure around Nakatsugawa, had had to rush through the day and night by litter to Nagoya.

"So it was true after all."

Hanzo looked at Heibei. Neither of them was easily able to contain his feelings.

Heibei was of no use to Hanzo as an advisor in such situations. He was a hard worker, willing to rush about on business, and he was indispensable in raising subscriptions and the like, but when something like this came up, he would get up, take his seat again, and do nothing but listen.

"The minute our eyes are off them, this happens."

Heibei, taking the posture of the assistant headman from Toge, said only this. He went out into the hall of the inn to look after the baggage. Then he went to the kitchen to have Hanzo's wet cape dried. These were the kind of chores he felt most comfortable doing.

"Well, I'll see when I get to Nakatsugawa," thought Hanzo. Just what did this all mean? Had the uncertainties of the time led the simple farmers so far astray? Were their constricted lives so lacking in ways of making themselves heard? Hanzo could not tell. But even so, they had had a perfectly good opportunity, if only they had been willing to take advantage of it, when the commander of the Tosando army passed through. A way had been opened for them to be heard. There had even been a proclamation that those who had suffered under the long-standing evils of the old system should report without hesitation or constraint to the commander-in-chief. The commander-in-chief had come bearing news of the imperial will to aid the people in their misery. Not a single farmer had come forward then and now they had chosen this way to protest.

Hanzo reflected on the sudden increase in prices. As they had learned from their experiences at the time of the opening of Yokohama, there was no reason not to expect the profit-greedy merchants to begin buying up the old silver. Yet however slight the faith in the new paper currency might be, it had only just been issued and the farmers could not remain ignorant of the new government's intention to sweep away the antiquated fiscal policies of the shogunate. That was what Hanzo regretted. That night, in the quiet of this mountain station, he was kept awake by his memories.

The facts of the farmer's rebellion became clearer once Hanzo and Heibei arrived in Nakatsugawa. A group of some fifteen hundred farmers, mostly from eastern Mino but with many allies from the Kiso, not only from Hanzo's own village but also from Tsumago and Nojiri, and from villages like Araragi, Kakisore, and Yogawa, had taken up a position between the entrance to Nakatsugawa and Komaba. There had been total disorder all the way from the great bridge at Nakatsugawa to Ochiai. The officials of the neighboring post stations and villages had rushed out to try to persuade them to return home. The next day an official from Fukushima came in, but the farmers all remained in Nakatsugawa and showed no signs of dispersing.

The street along which Hanzo and Heibei walked was lined by the shops of Nakatsugawa merchants. The walls were thick, the second floors low, and the windows set deep behind heavy wooden grills, echoing the style of the buildings in Kyoto that Hanzo had so recently seen. Here lived merchants who did not simply work the inner road from Magome to Narai, but were willing to travel hundreds of miles for the raw silk trade. Yorozuya Yasubei, Yamatoya Risuke, and even the concern of Kadoya Jubei, who had once controlled the trade down to the seacoast and who had provoked the drovers' strike, were all to be found here. The uprising had broken out just across the bridge from this town. Whether true or false, it was still being said that the farmers, their matting banners flying from bamboo spears, had been on the point of coming into town to smash up the business establishments. Hanzo and Heibei could sense that the merchants who had gotten rich in the Yokohama trade still seemed to be in terror of some unseen thing.

In Nakatsugawa, Hanzo looked in on the families of his friends Keizo and Kozo. The former was the honjin of Nakatsugawa, the latter was the toiya, and they both had left good men in charge of their affairs. They were completely taken up in imperial politics and had no time to spare for their family offices. Now that there had been an uprising, the people of both households complained of the neglect of their heads and their failure to give proper attention to the local people. The wife whom Kozo had left behind in the country was particularly concerned to know about conditions in Kyoto, and she would not let Hanzo leave.

"I hate for you to hear this, Hanzo, but it seems to me that my husband has forgotten all about coming home."

As he looked at the face of his friend's wife, unable to conceal her longing for her husband as she tried in roundabout ways to scent out what was happening, saying that there must be many attractive women in Kyoto, Hanzo realized that it was going to be impossible to leave her with nothing more than a few formal words of greeting. If Heibei had not been there to urge him on, he would have remained standing before the gate, hat in hand, still in his sandals, unable to tear himself away.

3

When they reached Ochiai they went once again to the house of Hanzo's disciple, Katsushige. Over the years Hanzo had taught many students from towns such as Ochiai, Yubunezawa, and Yamaguchi, but among them he had never found another as promising as Katsushige. Close as he was to his disciple, he also wanted to see Katsushige's father, an old-fashioned village type, still hale and hearty, who understood local conditions very well. Hanzo, wanting a clearer picture of the events of the twenty-ninth of the previous month, knew that a call at this household would be useful.

"Oh, it's the master!"

Katsushige was the first to come running out the back door of the Inabaya. Hanzo and Heibei were soon unfastening their sandals in the earthen-floored entry hall, having accepted an invitation to stop and rest a while.

Hanzo had not seen Katsushige for some time. His disciple had just gotten married that spring and the shaven forehead of the married man looked very good on him. Hanzo explained to Katsushige that he was returning from a visit to the grave of Miyagawa Kansai, who had had such deep connections to Ochiai, and told of how he had met with Hirata Kanetane, now the leader of more than three thousand disciples. This talk of his elders delighted Katsushige.

At the Inabaya a broad area covered with tatami was continuous with the wood-floored hearth room. After a short time, Katsushige's mother came out to greet the guests. Then the old master of the house, Katsushige's father, appeared. The hair at his temples was completely white and there was something of the Nagoya man in his posture and movements even though he seemed on the whole to belong more to the mountains. As an elder of Ochiai station, he was on more familiar terms with Hanzo's father, Kichizaemon, than he was with Hanzo himself.

"So you're just back from Kyoto. That's fine, that's fine," said Gijuro. "Katsushige talks about you all the time. Before he got married he wanted to make sure that you could be there, and you have no idea how happy he was when you performed his coming of age ceremony for him. He is still so pleased."

Then Gijuro called a manservant who had just looked in from the back door and told him to inform Katsushige's wife that they had guests.

"She's just out back, making eggplant pickles. I want you to meet her."

At this point, Katsushige's mother joined the conversation.

"Have them come on in."

"Maybe we should. I know you're in a hurry, Hanzo, but I'd like to serve you some tea," said Gijuro.

Hanzo and Heibei were conducted to a large double room far back in the house. Now that they had gotten as far as Ochiai, they had only to cross one more pass before reaching the western edge of the Kiso. The Mino school of haikai had long flowed out of Ochiai and Nakatsugawa into the Kiso, and prominently displayed in the adjoining room was an illustrated folding screen by the Magome artist Rankei. Katsushige's new bride, still immature at only sixteen or seventeen years of age, was brought out by Katsushige's mother. She carried the tea implements as she came to make her greetings. Although Ochiai was in the next province, Hanzo half felt that he was already home.

Even while he was being so hospitably entertained, Hanzo did not neglect to ask all the questions he had been saving for Gijuro. He wondered just how many Magome farmers had been in the crowd that had rampaged from the great bridge on into Ochiai, and as a headman he found it embarrassing that such unfortunate creatures should have burst forth out of his own village during his absence.

"It's about that time, so why don't you have a little bit to eat with us? It's nothing special, but we'll eat over at Katsushige's," began Gijuro. "While you were away, Hanzo, all kinds of things took place around here. The fighting is getting worse up around Aizu . . . the farmers here have been raising a fuss . . . No, it's really been lively in these parts, I'm telling you."

There was nothing forced about Gijuro's laughter. He had served the highway for decades as an elder of Ochiai station with this same ease. Now he was watching everything that had been built up during the Tokugawa era fade away. Even when he reported on the farmers' uprising, he did not seem greatly perturbed. His son Katsushige, seated beside him at the huge lacquer table facing his guests, was grave as he contemplated the times. It was difficult to believe that father and son shared the same blood.

"All the same, father, wasn't it something to hear that mob of farmers, a thousand or more, all bellowing as they came? I really wondered what was going to happen."

Katsushige seemed to be speaking for Hanzo's benefit.

Katsushige's mother brought in the trays for the noon meal. String beans, butterbur, wild yams, and other country-style foods were served on the kinds of dishes one saw in old households. Katsushige's wife, her movements still girlish, followed carrying a dish of eggplants cooked with hot peppers. There were also cucumbers, thinly sliced and freshly salted.

"This is not the kind of meal we would want to serve when the master is visiting us, but please help yourself," said Katsushige's mother to Hanzo. She turned to his companion. "Heibei, please eat in here with us."

"No, thank you. I'll go eat in the kitchen."

Heibei picked up the tray that had been set before him and withdrew.

Katsushige, his youthful eyes flashing as he looked back and forth from his father to Hanzo, took up his chopsticks.

"I've never heard of a farmer's uprising in these Owari domains before."

"Well, that's because, as Hanzo well knows, Owari took good care of things," said Gijuro.

"Father, have there ever been uprisings directed at the toiya and the landlords before?"

"Yes, there have. Just go look at the other domains. There are all kinds of toiya. There are toiya who won't let the farmers pass before their houses without taking off their sandals. They flaunt their positions, claiming that it offends the eye to see farmers who have not taken off their sandals. But now look! We've got this restoration and as soon as the change takes place, bands of farmers go out and smash things up. One even hears of cases where the farmers most intimate with the toiya take the lead—on a dark night, they wrap their faces in carrying cloths, break into the residence, empty the closets, even uproot the shrubs in the gardens. There's no one in this district who is hated that way by the farmers. That's because most of the people who are post officials around here are members of respected old families."

Gijuro laughed quietly. Turning to Hanzo, he continued his speech.

"Just the same, some of the big old establishments around Nakatsugawa had something to do with this uprising. The farmers may be the ones who actually started it, but they're not the only ones to blame. Some of the big merchants have been secretly buying up rice and people began to hear about it. If you start digging around a little in this affair, all sorts of things come up. They're tearing everything right down to the ground and starting over again, and it's not just because of these wild changes in fiscal policy. When things start changing this fast, people's hearts begin to change too. But anyway, I'm telling you there were more than a thousand farmers here and they were all worked up. If Ono Saburobei had not gone out and talked with them—I don't want to steal Katsushige's line—but there is really no telling what might have happened. I suppose he decided that he couldn't just stand there and watch it happen. The farmers felt that since he was a Hirata disciple he wouldn't lie to them, and so they left everything up to him. Once they heard that Saburobei had gone off to Nagoya, they went right back home. We can really be thankful that nothing more serious came of it.''

Gijuro continued to talk as he ate. He ate far more heartily than one would expect of a person his age.

Gijuro had always been playful. Now he teased Hanzo, reminding him that if this had happened under the old government, Hanzo the headman would not have been able to escape responsibility. He laughed again as he described how Hanzo would probably have been led away on a rope with all the others.

Gijuro's cheerful casualness helped to ease Hanzo's mind a bit. Presently, as they were finishing their meal, Gijuro suddenly got up and went to another room to fetch a memorandum, a copy of the one that Ono Saburobei had displayed to the farmers and a draft of the petition that he later presented to Nagoya. Everything that had been on Hanzo's mind on this trip, from the failure of the new currency to the extreme rise in prices, was all written up there and the requests for emergency aid, a ten percent increase in wages and horse rentals, and the undertaking of the purchase of half the rice needed to establish a local reserve were each taken up in turn. Saburobei had not forgotten to include Owari's conscripting of peasant soldiers as one of the grievances felt by the farmers. Reading this memorandum, Hanzo learned that all the village and post station officials from the immediate vicinity who had then gathered at Nakatsugawa had approved Saburobei's plan and had signed the draft, and that Gijuro, elder of Ochiai, was one of the signers.

"Inosuke from Magome came running right down. One of the elders was with him," said Gijuro.

"Is that right? I'm relieved to hear that. It's not good to have this kind of thing break out while I'm away. What happens now?"

"Just this. Owari is involved, so it's going to have to be reported to Kyoto. We'll probably report that we are terribly ashamed to say that a disturbance has arisen because of our administrative inadequacies. We'll report it all right, but I think we should begin by saying that this outbreak which was reported to have involved more than fifteen hundred men was in fact made up of only four or five hundred, or maybe only two or three hundred. And what will happen to the ringleaders? I suspect that the whole thing may just be permitted to die quietly somewhere in the Owari bureaucracy. Or maybe the ringleaders alone will be called down to Fukushima for questioning. They're not going to be anything like as tough as they were in the old days. Of course, then they would have treated this as a major lapse in responsibility and by now there would have been some people in chains or even having their heads put up on display somewhere."

"But father," interjected Katsushige, "didn't they behead a samurai just for fooling around with a watchman's daughter when the Tosando army came through? Isn't the new government being especially strict about people who get mixed up with rebel factions? They've even put up notices in all the post stations saying that drifters and rebels are strictly forbidden on the premises."

"So they'll have to cut Owari's six hundred nineteen thousand five hundred koku in half or something?" teased Gijuro.

Shortly afterward, when Hanzo withdrew from the room where the meal had been served and rejoined Heibei at the front entrance, they found that their hosts had thoughtfully supplied them with new straw sandals. As if that were not enough, Katsushige's mother and his bride came out to the gate to see them off.

Then Katsushige came running after them, waving his hand and shouting. Everything they had heard or seen in Kyoto—the story of the naval maneuvers being staged for the first time for the new emperor off Mt. Tempo under the Osaka commissioner, and all the untried new things being attempted as part of the restoration, from religious reforms to a complete redistricting of the nation—all this had completely engrossed Katsushige. He walked with them until they reached the outskirts of Ochiai and then, just as he was parting from them, he spoke again.

"That's just it. This is the kind of time when you just don't know what you should do. What do you think, master? Will the farmers' uprising really be settled the way my father says?"

"I wonder."

"Ono Saburobei really did do a lot, and maybe, given the times, Owari will give the farmers a hearing. But what concerns me is those who stand to be charged with complicity. And then, with the fighting going on in Aizu right now, how can such a thing be covered up altogether?"

"Well, we don't want anyone to get hurt."

4

In the fields the rice transplanting was finished and the barley harvest was almost over. Along the sides of the road people were flailing away on the barley, although in some places it was still laid out in the sun to finish drying. Radishes and the like were just being planted.

Thin puffs of mist floated through the air while summer clouds rose like distant hills. The scene was overflowing with light and heat. The fields, recovered from the long rains, were full of promise of rich harvests for the Mino basin. The sweet potato vines were in full growth. Eggplants were in bloom. The cucumber vines were lengthening out.

Passing along the side of a shingle-roofed shed, Heibei broke off a twig from a peach tree at the edge of the road, stripped the leaves from it, and stuffed them under his hat. Then he rejoined Hanzo.

"I enjoy being with you, Hanzo, but it's hard sometimes."

"Why?"

"Well, you're always staring at me when I make these great big yawns. I don't like it."

"But doesn't it seem peaceful now? You couldn't imagine that there had been an uprising here ten days ago, could you?"

Near at hand they spotted the legs of a man from the village who was sprawled out flat on his back on the grass, sound asleep. In the shade of a barley stack farther off, a woman had opened her clothing to nurse a young child.

They came to the little mountain shrine of the healing Buddha, a good place to stop and wipe off the perspiration. All the offerings at the shrine—a bundle of sharp awls offered as a prayer for relief from ear trouble, a painting of a woman squeezing milk from her breast, a woman's long hair tied in a bundle with hemp thread—expressed the simplicity of the farmer's faith. From here they could see the road that ran along the foot of Mt. Ena. Only by climbing that mountain now covered with lush green grass could a place be found where the distant Kiso river could be seen. When late autumn came, thousands of small birds would come in at dawn, flying up out of Mino toward the Kiso forests over this same Jikkyoku pass.

Hanzo and Heibei came at last to the western entrance of their village. Past the great elms on either side of the road, past the zero milestone marking the province border, they came up from Shinjaya toward Aramachi. Here they could see the lush forests around the Suwa shrine and the stalls selling loquat leaf tea, a potion for hot weather.

"Let's stop at the shrine for a moment."

After reporting their safe return before the village shrine, Hanzo sat for a while on a cedar stump near the torii of the shrine to catch his breath. Heibei, also showing the effects of the climb up the hot, steep road, sat near him. From this spot they could look out on a pleasing view of the road, packed hard by the feet of endless passersby, both human and animal.

Some sixty days earlier, the conscription of farmer-soldiers mentioned in the memorandum had taken place within the precincts of this shrine. It had come about as the result of an innovation by Owari. The han, needing troops for the Echigo border, had sent down an order to Yamamura to provide two hundred farmer-soldiers from the Kiso valley. The farmers at Magome had almost no time to prepare. The officials came down from the offices at Fukushima on the fifth of the intercalary fourth month, called everyone to the shrine, and made the announcement. By the ninth the selection had been made by lot and seven farmers were sent to Fukushima, in the charge of a common soldier.

Hanzo had not forgotten that time. One of the young men called up did not even know how to fire a gun, and another had just been married a few days earlier. They knew nothing of the precedents for this sort of thing in Choshu and Mito and besides, it was a busy time for cutting hay and tending silkworms. The young men complained bitterly and there were many old women who saw them off with eyes swollen from weeping. Of course, this did not happen in Magome alone. On the twentieth of the same month, the leaders throughout the Kiso valley consulted together and agreed that if the action on the Echigo frontier should become a prolonged one, great hardship would ensue in the villages. They appealed to Fukushima to return the conscripts.

Hanzo, keenly aware of having been absent from his post, was concerned about this as well. The petition taken to Nagoya by Ono Saburobei had listed this conscription of soldiers from among the farmers as one of the grievances. Before he did anything else, Hanzo wanted to meet with Inosuke, who had been entrusted with things in his absence. With this in mind, he got to his feet and, with Heibei, walked away from the torii.

Aramachi is a section of Magome station, separated from the main settlement by the stony area around the bridge. Here the stream that runs down the gentle valley cuts across the highway. Their road led them on into the village of Magome by way of Stonemason slope. There was no household here that did not double as an inn.

"Heibei! Did you just get back?"

"That's right."

"What have you been doing?"

At the top of Stonemason slope, Heibei met Shosuke of the Sasaya, the sound and honest assistant headman of Magome, coming down from the village. Hanzo had fallen a bit behind.

The highway was not at all wide where it sloped steeply upward through the station. They worked their way past this stretch. Here they met men bringing in great packloads of cedar bark from four or five miles back in the forest. Shosuke called Heibei over to the edge of the road where they would not block the way.

"I'm telling you, Heibei, I had quite a time of it while you were gone," Shosuke began. "It was hard enough to do anything with Hanzo gone, but you had to go and have yourself a little trip too."

Heibei untied the strings of his hat, eyeing Shosuke's face all the while. For all that Shosuke was a fellow assistant headman, he was also the representative of all the farmers in Magome and he would meet with the master of the Fushimiya and the other elders to consult on all matters pertaining to the station. Heibei had always deferred to him.

"No, I mean it," continued Shosuke. "On the twenty-sixth of last month one of the officials came over from Fukushima about the recall of the conscripted farmers. And on the twenty-ninth, if you please, the young lord of Hikone came through on his way home with a party of five hundred. Everybody, samurai to porters, spent the night in Magome. It was so crowded that the Fushimiya had to take fourteen men. I suppose you've already heard about it, but a farmer's uprising broke out right in the middle of all that."

"I really can't find any excuse to offer."

"But you're the head from Tōge hamlet. Shouldn't you be keeping your eye on things just a little better? If you had really been looking after Hanzo's interests, wouldn't you have gotten back just a little bit earlier?"

"Now, just a minute! It takes a certain amount of time to go to Kyoto and back, and then we had all that rain. All the way from Ise to Kyoto it rained, rained, rained. Every day—"

"We had an awful lot of rain here, too."

"And on top of that, Shosuke, once the rain stopped on the way back, it turned terribly hot. How could we have made better time? Oh, was it hot!"

As Shosuke began to soften his tone toward Heibei, Hanzo came up the slope and joined them.

"Well, well. The retired head of the Fushimiya just caught hold of me and gave me a good going over. He was on his way to the village shrine. All I could do was stand there and bow my head. Anyway, let's have a talk later, Shosuke."

Having excused himself, Hanzo hurried homeward.

His wife and children were safe.

After Hanzo had changed out of his travel clothes, he immediately went to look in at the retirement quarters. There Kichizaemon, who was now up, now down but making little progress in his recovery, and Oman, tireless as ever in her care of the invalid, were waiting for him.

"Father, when I come straight back from Kyoto and see this place, it's much more countrified than I realized."

This was the first thing that Hanzo, sunburnt from his journey, said when he found himself once again in his parents' company.

He felt rushed. All the stories he had saved up came tumbling out one after another. The first person he wanted to see was Inosuke. After nightfall, he stepped through the small family door in the great front gate. The nighthawks were calling out above the station. There were no more travelers in sight. All was still—a stillness here in the mountains that was lacking even in the station of Ochiai. As Hanzo reached the doorway of the house next door, the old-fashioned bundle of cedar boughs hung under the eaves caught his eye, reminding him, just back from his journey, that there was good sake to found here.

The retired Kimbei had given way to Inosuke. Instead of Otama, the wife whom Kimbei had seen depart before him at the beginning of the year, there was Inosuke's wife, Otomi. They were both adopted children, born in Mino, taking care of the household that Kimbei had relinquished to them. The young couple had two children. Although they were not blood relatives of the honjin family, they were on as close terms as if they were. Inosuke prepared seats in the parlor, near the grillwork door with its new sunshades, and greeted Hanzo cheerfully.

"How was the trip, Hanzo? I'm afraid I wasn't very successful in looking after things while you were gone."

The further he came into the prime of life, the more retiring and self-effacing Inosuke became. His manner was that of the Mino resident but he had long since been completely at home in the Kiso, and he was Hanzo's most trusted confidant.

"No, I had no intention of staying away that long," said Hanzo. "I should have come straight back from Ise. I thought of it at the time, but I was really concerned about what might be happening in Kyoto, so it turned out to be a long trip."

"Otomi was saying that you would surely want to go to Kyoto while you were away."

"You're the only people who have been so understanding."

Hanzo then took out a simple souvenir that he had brought back from his trip. Inosuke took up the Kyoto fan and opened it, obviously pleased. He examined the ribs, rather more delicately cut than the usual man's fan, and gazed with pleasure at the harmonious blend of gray and pale lavender in the paper glued to the black-speckled bamboo ribs.

"The two most troublesome things that happened while you were away were the question of the return of the conscripted farmers and the uprising. The reason it got so far out of hand is that there was a rumor coming down the road that no one knew where the seven men who were taken from here were going to go."

"But that wasn't true."

"All the same, there were people saying that we had no idea whether the conscripts were to be sent to the east or to the west, that there was no telling how the two hundred farmer-soldiers might be used. So some of the farmers began to lose their heads."

"But they were to go to the Echigo frontier as infantry attached to Owari. Everyone knows that Owari is completely loyal to the emperor."

"Wait a moment, if the Yamamura at Fukushima were going along with Owari, then of course there would be no problem. But it was Fukushima soldiers who took them away and everyone got concerned about where they were to be taken. Then people began to get upset and rumors ran wild . . ."

"And all the time I had assumed that it was just because the farmers were afraid that they were going to be short-handed in the fields."

"Of course, there was that too. Finally there got to be meetings between the farmers of the villages and the post station officials. People like Shosuke were caught in between and they had a bad time of it. On the twenty-sixth of last month—that was the end of the barley harvest—an official finally came down from Fukushima and there was another big to-do. They wanted the conscripts back no matter what and the official returned to Fukushima after agreeing. It was just three days after that the uprising broke out."

"I really went away at the wrong time. I heard about most of it when I stopped in at the Inabaya in Ochiai. They said that you had to run off to Ochiai by yourself."

"Yes. That was quite an affair. The lord of Hikone was stopping over here that day. The whole station was turned upside down trying to handle a party of five hundred men. If the new paper currency wasn't being refused altogether, it was being accepted at only half its face value, and the porters refused to serve at the standard rates. But I decided that it was the kind of situation that you could just let work itself out, so I asked Kyurobei to look after things here. Then I sent a fast courier to Fukushima and rushed off to Ochiai, half beside myself. The next evening, I went to a meeting of the village elders who had gathered in Nakatsugawa and by the time things settled down and I got back home, it was already after daybreak."

Hanzo forgot the fatigue of his journey as the time passed there in the parlor of the Fushimiya. A soft, cool breeze came in through the blinds in front.

"I really have no excuse to offer you," said Hanzo, expressing his gratitude to Inosuke as he got to his feet. "How could Shosuke possibly not have seen this uprising coming?"

"I don't think that even his people knew, Hanzo. After all, they farm their own land."

"I'll call Kenkichi and Sosaku in. There are thirteen tenant families that have always been attached to our household. And then there are some others who came up from Mino with one of the women who married into our family. They're the ones who come on New Year's to make rice cakes and to set up the pines before the gate. I'll just call them in and ask them about this."

"There were all sorts of things I wanted to ask you about Kyoto. The nights are too short."

5

"Oshimo!"

"Yes?"

"They say that the master of the honjin wants to see Ken."

"Yes."

"Tell him that, will you? And by the way, tell him to bring So along with him."

"Yes, yes."

This dialogue occurred at the kitchen door of the Magome honjin. The aged and nearly deaf Oshimo recited her instructions from the maid and went out of the kitchen as she had been doing for decades.

It was the morning that the seven soldiers conscripted for the Echigo border were escorted back home. After serving in the infantry for sixty days, the young men who were being returned to the village, their obligations ful-

filled, all stopped by the honjin to pay their respects. At that moment
Kenkichi and Sosaku arrived.

Hanzo, just returned from the west, had no time to recover from the
fatigue of the journey. He could not rest until he had called in these two tenants of his and learned of the situation in the village.

"Kenkichi! Sosaku! Come up here by the hearth," said Hanzo in his usual
tone of voice.

There was no fire in the hearth. Usually Kenkichi and Sosaku would have
sat on the edge of the floor, dangling their sandaled feet, but today they
removed the sandals, carefully wiped their feet, came in, and sat stiffly before
Hanzo. They were after all before their hereditary master. With them Hanzo
felt no constraint in asking questions. He spoke to the two men before him
out of deep sadness and shame in the knowledge that the misfortune that had
befallen the village in his absence was all due to his derelictions. At the very
least he wanted everyone to understand this and, if they had anything to say,
for them to say it to him.

"Master, I just can't tell you anything," said Kenkichi, bringing his big
farmer's hand to his forehead. "We weren't part of this, but it's all over, like
burnt-out ashes. All the tenant farmers in the village have agreed not to say
anything at all about it to outsiders."

"Well, if that's the case, it's all right. I don't want anyone from the village
to get hurt either. I thought you people would be happy to see this new age
coming. Just think about the way the samurai always used to bully you along
the highway. They used to say that you people counted for nothing and they
used you as if you were machines. Didn't you always have some samurai after
you with his hand on his sword hilt? Then came the restoration. We've
finally got this far. Aren't you happy when you think of that?"

"Of course, we're happy."

"Are you really?"

Kenkichi's reply sounded as though it had been made only because it was
expected of him, and Hanzo found his 'Of course, we're happy' a bit unsatisfactory. Sosaku sat beside Kenkichi, saying nothing. And yet, of all his thirteen tenant farmers, these were the two in whom he felt the most confidence. Hanzo tried once again to get his message across.

"Just let me say this. This is no time for the people in the provinces to
start acting up. What's going to happen to us all if the farmers and the merchants don't really work together? It seems to me that this uprising would
never have occurred if people had just put more faith in the government in
Kyoto. Tell that to your friends."

"We'll be sure to tell all our friends," said Sosaku.

"After all, nobody wants to starve," continued Hanzo. "And then, there
are any number of ways to register complaints. Hasn't the new government
said that it will give attention to them? And Owari is not simply going to
ignore them either. Look here, last year everyone in the village got together
and made up a petition and as a result the taxes for the year were reduced by
half. Now there aren't going to be many crop failures like that one, but the

han was worried about us and they not only cut our taxes in half but also sent up sixty koku of rice in three different installments. And that was at a time when we would have had to pay seventeen ryo for ten bales of rice. Didn't they give you all of that when you were in trouble?"

"But the point is," cut in Kenkichi, "it's still all very well for farmers like the Sasaya who have their own land. They've always got a little to spare, no matter what the times. But we are tenant farmers, water drinkers! Where are we going to get our reserves, I ask you? And merchants are not going to be well liked from now on either. It's really hopeless being a tenant farmer. Hand to mouth, hand to mouth, that's the way we live. But we can only get from hand to mouth when times are good. Just look at us when our winter supplies have run out in the third or fourth month. However much money we may have set aside, we have to spend it all to buy expensive rice and everything else."

"It's as bad as that for you, is it? But if it's bad, isn't it bad for both sides? Just when was it when Prince Iwakura came through? The assistance that was promised you at that time must surely have been delivered by now."

"I hate to tell you this, but how long did you expect that to last? Everybody's drunk it up already."

Rough and crude as he was, tears flowed from the eyes of the simple Kenkichi and fell into his lap.

Sosaku just sat there, hanging his head and listening to his companion, making not a sound. Presently he bowed, and as he started to leave the hearthside with Kenkichi, Sosaku took his leave with a characteristically short speech.

"Were you actually expecting someone to tell you how things really are?"

"Do I really know that little about the farmers?"

The thought brought a sigh from Hanzo. These same farmers who had watched the Iwakura brothers pass through late in the second month, as unconcerned as if they were watching a festival—now some eleven hundred and fifty of them had joined in an uprising. The passionate hopes with which Hanzo had greeted the first year of the new government had been betrayed, not once but twice.

"Do the people still have so little trust in the new government?" That thought brought another sigh.

To Hanzo, this did not seem appropriate behavior for these same farmers who had borne up so long under service to the military. After all, it was no longer the time when the military had run wild, when there was no possibility of protest unless the protester was willing to accept at least a whipping, tattooing, or expulsion, or when serious cases would incur life imprisonment, beheading, even display of the severed head. To Hanzo, this was now a time when even the lowliest laborers should wait for the light of the new age of imperial rule to shine on them.

He could not, however, remain immersed in his thoughts. After he had seen the two tenant farmers out, he faced the great heap of letters and papers that had accumulated on his desk while he was away. There was so much to be done about the villagers that he scarcely knew where to begin. Seisuke had looked after things in his absence, and he had Seisuke come in. Everything that Seisuke told him about the movements of Naruse Masatomo, lord of Inuyama castle, and Mamiya Jo'un, the high Owari official, bespoke the atmosphere of the region, enwrapped in the reek of the fighting in Aizu. He met with his cousin Eikichi, who had taken charge of the family post of toiya in his absence. The new system of dividing the nation into urban administrative districts, prefectures, and han had already been put into effect. Eikichi had held for him the new seals of authority for post officials that had come in from all over the country, and now he brought out several and showed them to Hanzo. One was from the Kyoto administrative district, another from Kashiwazaki prefecture, and yet another from the ministry of justice.

Hanzo next went to the meeting room. There they were talking about Matsushita Chisato, the priest at Aramachi, who was about to leave as a volunteer for the Owari forces on the Echigo frontier. They planned to see him off as far as Toge.

6

The summer festival came to Fukushima, deep in the Kiso valley. The priest of the Suwa shrine in Aramachi hamlet of Magome, Matsushita Chisato, was a man of spirit and on the day he was due to set out for Echigo, he knocked at Hanzo's gate early in the morning.

"Why, good morning, sir!" said Sakichi, as he opened the small side door in the big front gate and let the priest in. Light came early to the open skies over the highway and there was not another soul in sight. The business of the post station had not yet begun. Chisato, however, was completely prepared. With a long old sword, still in its bag, that had been handed down in his family slung over his back, a rough, cheap blanket tightly rolled and slung over one shoulder, and a package in a carrying cloth hung at his waist, he had come striding up the silent morning road from Aramachi.

The priest had come not just to bid Hanzo farewell but to obtain a passport for the checkpoints ahead. Before he could travel freely on his way to the battlefront, he had to have a wooden tablet bearing the signature and the burned-in seal of the Magome station. Hanzo had it all signed and ready for him. He passed it over to Chisato and called his wife to assist him in making preparations to accompany the priest along the first part of his journey. Dressed in his short, full honjin trousers and wearing straw sandals, he left the honjin with Chisato.

All the houses were still closed up, their occupants fast asleep. Hanzo pounded on the gate and got the people up at the home of the elder Umeya Gosuke directly across the street, and he called out before the home of

Kyurobei in the next house up the street, separated from the Umeya by a low stone wall. In the meantime, Inosuke had opened his door and looked out. The assistant headman Sasaya Shosuke was coming up from the lower end of the village. The assistant honjin and elder Masudaya Kozaemon and his colleague and neighbor Horaiya Shinsuke were separated by only one house from the Fushimiya below them. All these men were called together and they set out through the morning mists for Toge village.

"I wonder how the fighting is going. They say that the Tosando army has had quite a time of it heading out of Edo for Shirakawa."

"They're going to have to be careful on the Echigo frontier too. They say that people have been asked for support all the way to Iiyama in the east."

"Well, just the way the supreme command changed commanders for the Tosando army shows that things are not going well."

The voices of the party rose one after another, not addressed to anyone in particular and not seeming to come from anyone in particular.

It was just at the time of this summer festival that rumors came down on the wind about the incident that had occurred in Fukushima. Several retainers of the Yamamura, all of them highly skilled swordsmen and disciples of Endo Goheiji, acting under cover of the evening festivities in Fukushima, had attacked Uematsu Shosuke on his way back from the branch shrine of the Mizunashi shrine and had taken his head. Uematsu Shosuke had been the chief officer of the barrier. He had also been a gunnery instructor. His second wife had come from the Miyatani, a famous Owari house of scholars, and it was said that he had been attacked out of suspicion that he sympathized with Nagoya.

This tragedy on the evening of the festival was kept absolutely secret from Owari. It was said that this was because a major figure of the Yamamura was behind the killing. But that very effort to keep the matter secret soon began to cast a pall of unhealthy silence presaging the inevitable collision between Nagoya and Fukushima. With the power of the lord of Owari now directed against Aizu and the country divided between east and west, in this dark hour when the eventual unification of the nation was still uncertain, not even the Kiso could remain in peace.

At the top of the pass was Toge, another small settlement that was part of the station of Magome. At its eastern edge was a sign advertising Kitsune Ointment. Another sign advertising the local specialty of rice and chestnuts hung on the eaves of a rest station set up for travelers along the Kiso road. Heibei lived in this hamlet near the elm that served as a mile post. That morning Hanzo and the others gathered around Heibei's hearth with Chisato to drink their parting cups. They were in sight of the stable and the horses stared out at them.

"Some of the farmers who were drafted have fled back from Echigo and now here you are, sir, volunteering to serve there. Things really do work out in this world," said Kyurobei.

*   *   *   *   *   *   *

"Inosuke . . . if only we can keep anyone from the village from getting hurt by all this."

"The uprising? That reminds me, I just heard that seven men from Yogawa have been called to Fukushima. But they say that every last one of the seven disappeared on the way."

Hanzo and Inosuke laughed over this story as they sat in Toge.

After they had seen Matsushita Chisato off for Matsumoto and the Echigo frontier, Hanzo and Inosuke headed back home. Hanzo always enjoyed the walk down from the pass along the steep road, through the shallow valleys. Here the sound of the early mountain cicadas was a reminder of the coming summer heat.

A summer of crisis seemed inescapable even here at the outskirts of this remote post station. The aura of the fighting in Aizu soaked into everyone's life. Hanzo could read it in the look of the village children they met along the road. He could see it in the appearance of the farmers going out to their fields, and in the look of the ox drovers from Toge leading their oxen down to the middle of town to pick up freight. Loads of freight headed for the battle zone and marked OFFICIAL BUSINESS—OWARI passed by on the backs of packhorses. The horse bells resounded in the deep valleys as they formed an unending chain along the road.

When they passed Iwata, they were at the approaches to the eastern edge of Magome proper. Hanzo spoke up suddenly.

"Inosuke, you may think this is a strange place to talk about such things but I've got something I want to ask you."

"There you go again, Hanzo. Sometimes you come out with the oddest things."

"Please, just listen. Is it the best thing, in the midst of these great changes, simply to ignore them and think only about your next meal, or should we put the affairs of the nation first and willingly accept any hardship to assist those above in their mission—which do you think is right?"

"Well, they're both all right, aren't they?"

"But, Inosuke, don't you wish the farmers would be just a little bit more cooperative?"

Hanzo sighed and began walking once more. Even though his hopes had now been twice betrayed, he had still not stopped believing in the eventual awakening of the farmers which he had so long anticipated. Unlike Inosuke, who tried to take the middle road, Hanzo felt that the farmers should continue to behave as though there were an established path even when there was none. Just as he had been unable to laugh at the ox drovers' strike when it occurred years ago, and for all that he was himself a honjin, a headman, and a toiya, neither could he laugh now at the nameless people who had risen up, eleven hundred and fifty strong, completely indifferent to the great work of reconstruction that was taking place.

CHAPTER SIX

1

WHEN THE RUMORS that the new emperor would be making a progress to the east proved to have a basis in fact, they gave rise to even stronger feelings than when Princess Kazu had gone down to Edo to become the shogun's bride. These feelings arose not only along the Tokaido, which was to be the official route, but in all the stations and villages of the Kiso as well.

The fourth year of Keio, 1868, had already been renamed the first year of Meiji. In the ninth month of that year the fighting in the northeast was coming to an end. But there were still disturbing rumors of the escape of a Tokugawa warship; it was a time when every day seemed to bring its new incident.

There was no longer an Edo. It had now become Tokyo. The present imperial progress, part of a major move toward Tokyo by the Kyoto people, was something that required the firmest resolve in order to be carried out. On the one hand there was the continuing turbulence in Kyoto and on the other, concern for the safety of the progress from Shizuoka eastward. There were repeated rumors that attempts would be made en route to interfere with its passage. All the officials along the Tosando felt their palms sweat whenever they heard them. The unforgettable experience of Princess Kazu's progress had taught them of the perilous condition of the roads these days.

The mass of travelers diverted from the Tokaido disturbed the peace of even such isolated stations as Magome. As village elder and assistant to the toiya, Inosuke of the Fushimiya called all the responsible people together in the meeting room as always. They discussed the upkeep of the heavily traveled road and consulted with the other three stations of the lower Kiso. The rumors about the imperial progress left by the couriers were such that Kozaemon of the Masudaya compared their present situation with the confusion that had prevailed when Princess Kazu passed through. Gosuke of the Umeya was thinking about the difficulty they would have in calling up supplementary porters and horses. It was Shinsuke of the Horaiya, youngest of them all, who brought the news that Yoshikatsu, the retired lord of Owari, would be going out to Atsuta in full panoply to meet the emperor. Kyurobei came in and as he wedged his huge body in among them, Inosuke was keenly aware of his manliness. Now all of them began to imagine the imperial palanquin being borne along the Tokaido: long solid lines moving forward under banners of deep scarlet bearing the chrysanthemum crest; the strength of the men who gently waved these huge banners as they bore them along; the escort of men in yellow green trousers. They imagined not only the equipment of these escorting warriors, armed with both imported rifles and Japanese swords, but also the headgear that they would wear: military caps, tall black horsehair court hats, the helmets shaped like tortoise shells traditionally worn by low-ranking soldiers, and old-fashioned steel helmets. They pictured the endless variety of the procession in its blending of old and new and the wild excitement of the people along the route as this unprecedented spectacle approached.

At the beginning of the tenth month, the report came in that the new emperor had reached the station of Arai on the Tokaido after stopping his palanquin for a time at the place called Shiomisaka, or "seaview slope," where he had his first glimpse of the ocean. What he viewed there was no longer the limitless sea of the age of seclusion but an ocean which could now be crossed. That was a moving thought even to Inosuke up in the Kiso.

"This is interesting. I wish Hanzo could hear it."

But Hanzo did not make an appearance in the meeting room that day. The illness of his father had taken a turn for the worse just as this confusion along the highway was reaching its height. The family of the honjin was completely preoccupied with bringing a physician up from Nakatsugawa by litter and then with having Shosuke hurry off to Yamaguchi village.

2

There was not a single day without some incident along the highways. They struggled through their duties one day at a time. As he finished his day's work at the meeting room and got up to leave, Inosuke was thinking about what was happening. He had been saddened to hear that Hanzo had not left his ailing father's bedside for two or three days. He went through the graveled inner passage to the toiya quarters, where Eikichi was just finishing his own work, and asked how things were. Eikichi, closing his daily record, came over to the raised section of floor where he leaned with both hands, a worried look on his face. He said to Inosuke that since Kichizaemon had been suffering from the effects of a stroke for years, it was a wonder that he had survived so long.

Inosuke went on over to the main honjin building to pay his respects. It appeared that Hanzo, Otami, and even Okume and Sota were all up in the retirement quarters in back; the vast hearth room was still. There he discovered Seisuke sitting with his arms folded, staring into the red glowing fire of pine boughs, as he looked after the main house.

Seisuke spoke first.

"Inosuke, Hanzo hasn't slept for three or four nights now. He keeps saying that he is possessed of the divine spirit and I needn't worry about him since he is protected, that he is not the least bit sleepy. Of course his father is ill, but he can't go on this way. I'm getting worried about Hanzo himself."

Inosuke decided not to go back to the retirement quarters for fear of tiring the invalid. After hearing Seisuke's explanation that for one suffering from a stroke and so terribly debilitated by age as Kichizaemon, there was little that could be done beyond cooling his head with cold water and warming his feet with hot stones, Inosuke stepped back out of the gate of the honjin.

At thirty-six, just three years younger than Hanzo, Inosuke was in the prime of life. Their closeness in age brought them naturally together. Because he had to deal with Kimbei, a foster father who was very difficult to please, Inosuke could sympathize with Hanzo's problems with his stepmother, Oman. On the day that Kichizaemon and Kimbei's retirements had been accepted, the two of them, he and Hanzo, had received their papers from Fukushima appointing Hanzo honjin, headman, and toiya and Inosuke village elder and assistant toiya. They had continued to serve in the two most important positions in the village.

Yet Inosuke was no longer the Inosuke of the old days. He had gradually become aware of just how different he and his neighbor were. He could only be astonished by Hanzo's extreme concern for his father, by the way in which, at the time of Kichizaemon's original attack, he had set out on a pilgrimage to Mt. Ontake to offer a year of his own life in return for his father's health, and by the way he had been nursing his father for three or four nights without sleep.

"What makes Hanzo that way?"

The austere dwelling of a sake brewer awaited the returning Inosuke. The Fushimiya stood on a stone terrace just above the honjin. To the west were thick white walls. On the southeast a massive wooden grill faced the highway. His home seemed a secure refuge from the storms of a dark age.

Once past the grill, one found a parlor on one side and a large wood-floored room near the entrance on the other. The kegs of sake that the head clerk brought from the warehouse in back were kept here. The brewing of the new sake had already been completed and it was now time to record the brew. The scent of the new sake only just put on sale came to Inosuke as he got out of his station official's broad trousers and into more comfortable clothing.

"How is father?"

Inosuke addressed the question to his wife, Otomi. The retired Kimbei had gone to Nakatsugawa for a visit late in the previous month and after his return early this month his chronic cough had returned. As a result, he had not gone back to his retirement quarters up the street but was staying in bed on the second floor of the main house. Both Inosuke and Otomi were adopted. However vigorous their foster father was at seventy-two, older than the ailing Kichizaemon next door, both husband and wife carefully avoided speaking to each other of the fact that he could not possibly last much longer, or how nice it would be to be able to do, at long last, as they pleased. It had long since become a sore point for both.

Otomi, preparing the evening meal, came from the kitchen to her husband's side with an air of being interrupted in her work. She found him muttering something to himself as he paced back and forth in front of the darkly polished main pillar of the house.

"It would be better to pay more attention to the ordinary things."

"What on earth are you talking about?"

"Oh, I wasn't talking about father. I was talking about the world in general."

Otomi didn't know how to react. She simply couldn't imagine what he meant by "the ordinary things."

Then Otomi took out a hanging scroll that Heibei had left in Inosuke's absence. The Yamamura family of Fukushima, finding itself hard pressed for funds, had selected one of their treasured paintings in hope that someone would buy it. When he was in Fukushima on business, Heibei had been asked by one of the officials to undertake the commission and, unable to refuse, had been scurrying here and there in search of a buyer.

"So this is what Heibei left, is it?"

"He said that he had been asked to sell it and he asked us to keep it here while he went down to Nakatsugawa. He also asked me to explain to you when you got home."

"Heibei likes to do things for people. But all the same, I hadn't realized the Yamamura had reached the point where they were selling this kind of thing. I suppose I had better talk it over with father later."

His foster father, Kimbei, had learned his trade at the side of Soemon of the Masudaya of Magome, one of the richest men in the Kiso valley. In addition to brewing sake, he had operated a pawnshop, kept horses, cultivated rice fields, planted saplings in the forests, and from time to time had engaged in the rice trade. The same Uematsu Shosuke who met an untimely end during the summer festival in Fukushima last year had earlier found himself in financial trouble, and for all his importance as commander of the barrier guards, he had come to Kimbei for help in raising money. So great was Kimbei's power that the Yamamura retainers had come to hold him in a certain amount of fear, but Kimbei remained a true merchant. That is to say, as with so many people of low rank, he had become completely resigned to the fact that forming attachments with those of high rank was the best guarantee of prosperity for his descendants. Whenever they were asked for help in great money-raising schemes, beginning with the six thousand six hundred ryo subscription of the Yamamura family in 1786 and continuing to their subscription for seven thousand ryo in 1862, not to mention the subscription for thirty thousand ryo by the lord of Iwamura han two years later, the Fushimiya would always pledge two hundred or so ryo to be paid in annual installments. But that was not all. All the money that the Yamamura had received over the years from the Fushimiya, whenever they found themselves short of funds or in need for a special occasion, would add up to an immense sum.

Inosuke had grown up watching his foster father compromise and abase himself. In these days when promises of change seemed to be on every tongue, he only became even more cautious than Kimbei had been. The prospect that he might himself be drawn into all the confusion and uncertainty was terrifying to him. He had no place of refuge other than the roof that had been handed down to him by his foster father. There was no teaching open to him other than the merchant's belief that what was called for was loyalty, filial piety, honesty, thrift, and endurance, and to be satisfied with his lot.

Until the beginning of adolescence Inosuke had lived in the neighboring province of Mino, a place advanced in learning, in religion, and in the fine arts and commerce, and he was by no means an unlettered man. He had recently been composing straightforward poems that won the admiration of Hanzo. Among the books that he was in the habit of reading were old and new block-printed books that he had ordered from merchants in Kyoto and Osaka. What he had discovered in them was this world in which people led ordinary lives. If he allowed himself to be disturbed by the things he read and the things he heard, then the tranquility, the peace, and the gentleness that he so desperately needed would be lost to him. He loved the ascetic ideal that led the great merchants of the cities to live hidden away on obscure side streets. He loved the tact and delicacy of taste that such a life expressed. With the circumspection of an adopted son, he had thought about the great excitement that was infecting not only the people around him but also those who, calling themselves men of spirit, rushed up and down the highways. He could not help being shocked. He observed the new Fuji cult, with its "faith of practice," that was arising among the people of the Ina valley, maintaining that in these times it was absolutely necessary that the blessings of heaven be repaid through special abstention and austerities. Entire families would select their particular austerities and, in an extraordinary display of faith, everyone down to the smallest children would get up early, practice obedience, do cleaning, and abstain from the purchase of candy and pastries. He could not help being shocked by this also.

However, unlike his foster father, Kimbei, and like his neighbor Hanzo, he possessed the youthful resilience necessary to make his way through this difficult time. His youthfulness enabled him to sympathize when he heard that the great Kyoto and Osaka merchants were still loyal to the memory of Toyotomi Hideyoshi more than two and a half centuries after his death. They had supported the plans to overthrow the Tokugawa, had underwritten the vast expenses of the military campaigns, and had helped to set up the new government. But no matter what, he was a merchant, accustomed to passivity, and he shrank in terror from the icy winds that were blowing down the highway. His feelings were forever predisposed toward an indescribable terror and uncertainty.

After finishing his evening meal and his bath, Inosuke took up the painting that Heibei had left and climbed to the second floor, using the stairway at the edge of the hearth room.

"Father," he called out as he came near the window facing west on the second floor. Through the window he could hear water being drawn by lantern light from the deep well next door.

"Father," he called out again. "They're drawing water from the well in the honjin. I can hear the well rope running."

Kimbei had his pillow to the southeast and he had drawn the lamp near so that he could write in his diary. He had not missed a single entry in thirty years. He immediately sensed the significance of Inosuke's words.

"It looks as though Kichizaemon has taken a turn for the worse again," said Kimbei, his voice heavy with sadness, and he listened for a time with Inosuke at his side. Kimbei was now afflicted with chronic bronchitis and he was unable to walk. He had little interest in talking with anyone except those with whom he felt completely at ease, and even then he would often give them little more than polite formalities, as though wanting to get rid of them as soon as possible. Still he was not the kind of person who could remain idle for very long, even when bedfast.

"I dropped by the honjin a little while ago. Hanzo is constantly at his father's bedside and they say he hasn't slept for three or four days. He'll probably be up all night again tonight."

While reporting conditions in the Aoyama household, he placed the painting that the Yamamura were trying to sell at the bedside. He then recounted Heibei's story and started to ask what he should do about it.

"You don't have to consult me about things like this, Inosuke."

Kimbei slipped out of his bedding and sat up on the tatami. For a moment he looked like the Kimbei of old who had wrapped paper bags around the pears on the tree in front of the storehouse, later reporting that of the three pears that had fallen in the windstorm the largest had weighed thirteen and one-quarter ounces and the other two, nine and a half ounces each.

"I'm going to take the lamp for a moment, father. Let's hang it up where we can get a good look at it."

Inosuke hung the painting in the alcove of the sick room, where it called to mind the manner of living of the Fukushima deputies. It was a painting of bamboo and orchids with five chickens. Its old-fashioned elegance seemed to tell the tale of a powerful old family at the end of its fortunes. To see this kind of item offered for sale was an indication that the Yamamura of Fukushima, who had been in charge of the crucial Fukushima barrier controlling this Kiso valley for well over two hundred years, had descended into a state of utter helplessness. They were now no less abject than the Tokugawa family of Kii, who had been forced to leave their Edo residences. The Yamamura, it seemed, were about to share the fate of the Tokugawa.

"Well, shall we have a look?"

Kimbei, who had returned to his bed, could not see from where he lay. He got out of bed again, put a cape over his nightclothes, and crawled over to the alcove. His old eyes were still sharp, and he joined Inosuke in inspecting the painting. First, he assumed a posture of abject respect, as though he had come into the presence of Yamamura himself. Then he looked. In the dappled light and shade of the room, some of the colors could not be made out while others had been faded by time.

"It seems cold and mean to take leave of the Yamamura, to whom we have been obligated for so long, with money. Cold and mean, but that's the kind of time we live in. Give it a good looking over."

"Here's a seal, father. It says Tsung Tzu-shan."

"He must be a Chinese painter, but I've never heard of him."

"Me either."

"Anyway, it's old. It's painted on silk . . . Well, it doesn't matter whether we like it or not, we'll take it. After all, we have an obligation."

"What do you think we should pay for it?"

"Let's see. We're going to have to be pretty generous."

Suddenly, Kimbei thrust his wrinkled hand in front of Inosuke's face and spread out his five fingers.

"Five ryo."

Kimbei turned back to the painting hanging in his merchant's alcove and bowed deeply before it as though it were a passing lord. Then he returned to his bed.

3

Through the bullets
Falling like rain.
　　Toko ton'yare, ton'yare na!

For the emperor, no thought
Of our own lives.
　　Toko ton'yare, ton'yare na!

To conquer or to kill,
Though it's not what we want.
　　Toko ton'yare, ton'yare na!

We'll do it since it
Is for our native land.
　　Toko ton'yare, ton'yare na!

Around the notice board at the center of Magome station, the children's voices rose every day with the most popular new tune in the country, singing as though in choral practice.

The first reports came in that the new emperor, whose name was not yet familiar to most people, was now safely lodged in his temporary palace in the western enclosure of the former Edo castle. These reports also said that the Tokugawa themselves had volunteered to mount guard as he passed through Suruga province, a place where there had been much concern for the emperor's safety, particularly in the area around Shizuoka. At about the same time there was also a report that a mixed force of three or four thousand men from several different han had come back to Tokyo from the Aizu front, and had enjoyed a wild welcome from the people of Tokyo. Such news was coming in almost daily to the Magome station. Not only that, but spirits were also refreshed by the fact that Kichizaemon's illness, which had only recently seemed so hopeless, had suddenly taken a turn for the better.

Inosuke was in the parlor of the Fushimiya one day, feeling greatly relieved about matters in general and getting ready to go over to the meeting room. He knew that Hanzo would still not be up to looking after the station and he was determined to let him get as much rest as possible. Through the heavy wooden grill at the front of the parlor he could hear the voices of the children playing in the highway. Donning his station official's trousers, he listened casually to them singing a popular song.

Otomi found him there. She had just been telling him that even their own children were completely taken up in war games.

"But it's strange. Children do exactly the same thing as adults. The children from the Umeya are Choshu, those from the main Masudaya household are Satsuma, and the ones from the Masudaya branch are Tosa. I asked our Jiro what he was going to be. His answer was really good. He said, 'I want to be Owari.' "

"Is that right? Owari, eh?"

"Yes, Owari. But nobody wants to be Aizu."

Inosuke laughed again when he heard that.

"But that's the way children are," Otomi continued. "Jiro asked Momo from the Horaiya if she would be Aizu, but she didn't say a thing. She just refused to go along. Jiro told her, 'Momo, if you'll be Aizu, I'll let you use the nice wooden sword my father bought me. I'll let you use it today, and tomorrow, and the day after!' Momo obviously wanted to use the sword and she finally agreed to be Aizu. Those who play Aizu get a pretty rough time of it because Aizu gets beaten."

"Oh, stop it! That's going too far!"

Inosuke could not let Otomi go on about these children's games. Before going to the meeting room he went around back to have a look at the sake warehouse, but he was still upset by the way events were crowding in on even the innocent children. Unable to forget what Otomi had told him, he took a turn about the brewery, with its high ceilings, and then came back to ask about it again.

"Otomi, what do the children do when they play war?"

"Well, no one has taught them this but they make a great lot of noise in certain spots, like alongside the stone walls, and they chase the ones who are playing Aizu. When they catch them in a corner of the wall, the ones who have been defeated have to say, 'I give up!' Where could they have learned about the Aizu fighting? They're still such tiny children!"

The end of the tenth month was approaching. It was time for the annual Ebisu services. The northeast had been completely pacified and the time came to greet the warriors on their way home. In the intercalary fourth month of that year, Tokugawa Yoshikatsu, the retired lord of Owari, had received an imperial order to set up a command post in Nagoya for the policing of the provinces of Kai and Shinano. He had set out for Ota at the head of fifteen hundred troops while his steward, Chika Yohachiro, led an advance party to the Echigo frontier. Seven months had passed since then. The han that had been placed under the command of Owari included eight from Mikawa, four from Omi, three from Suruga, eight from Mino, and eleven from Shinano. These activities among the han of central Japan made clear just how grave the crisis along the Echigo frontier had been.

The companies from Yamabuki han that had been at the front with the Tosando army were now back in the Ina valley, and those from Takato and Iida, which had been sent to the Echigo frontier, were also coming home one after another. Detachments that had advanced beyond the Echigo frontier, another one hundred fifty miles or more over difficult mountain terrain to reach Aizu, had passed back through Magome, heading west in great numbers. They left behind the story of how the order for dispersal had been sent out on the twenty-second of the ninth month, the day that Aizu castle fell, and of how fierce the fighting had been.

The procession of soldiers returning in triumph lasted until around the tenth of the eleventh month. Sometimes parties as large as five hundred would come in from Midono and the station of Magome would be swamped. When the confusion at last ended, they learned that the Shinto priest Matsushita Chisato, who had gone off to the war from Magome, was returning safely from the distant northern provinces. Shosuke of the Sasaya, acting in his official capacity, went to the top of the pass to meet him.

"That was quick, wasn't it, Otomi? The priest is already coming back to Aramachi."

Inosuke said this as he was going out the door of the Fushimiya. He was eager to greet the returning priest and to get to work at the meeting room.

Everyone at the meeting room was sprawled about in relaxed attitudes, tired after the long run of busy days. They were talking about the victorious soldiers. Noon passed without any sign and some of the post officials, pleading family business, went home to rest. Finally Inosuke was left by himself. The toiya office attached to the honjin had suddenly become quiet, the bustle of arriving freight faded away. Two men came in from Tsumago. They were the honjin, Juheiji, and the assistant honjin, Tokuemon.

"Well, I'm really glad to hear that Kichizaemon's getting better. It feels as though we have gotten through a tough patch."

When he heard the voices of Juheiji and Tokuemon, Inosuke pulled himself together and set out cushions for them. He was impressed that Juheiji, who had had his own honjin duties, did not seem the least tired, and he was pleased that they had come directly over to look in on Kichizaemon without taking any time off to rest up from the long run of unbroken work.

"Please have a cushion. I can't really entertain you properly here in the meeting room, but at least I can offer you a cup of tea," he said, calling for the servant that was assigned to the meeting room. After giving his order, he turned to talk about Kichizaemon.

"Well, anyway, the old man has a tough side to him," said Juheiji.

"Of course, Juheiji. He has worked on the highway for years and years. It has tempered his body so that he is not like the rest of us," said Tokuemon. "But he worries about the station even in bed. He really worries that his illness might affect Hanzo's work. He says that he wouldn't be able to stand it if it were ever said that the Aoyama were neglecting their duties. He's still the same old Kichizaemon."

"Did he talk about that?" said Inosuke. "But it was the nursing that did it. Hanzo scarcely slept for seven or eight days. It's amazing he held up. I took over the work here as much as I could to give Hanzo a chance to rest. Then the troops started coming through. The supernumerary porters and horses weren't coming in. Special orders came down. I was really in over my head for a while."

"All those people going through gave us a bad time at Tsumago, too," said Tokuemon, lowering his voice. "They were really riding high, coming back from winning a war. It was the twenty-eighth of last month. We got a notice in Tsumago from the lord of Kuwano saying that a huge body of his troops would be coming through the next day and that every post station was to treat them to special food and lodging, so Tsumago had better get ready. That's just what it said. As if it wasn't going to be hard enough for us to handle such a big party, we were supposed to prepare a feast for them. We didn't know what to do. Did you get that in Magome, too?"

"Yes, we did," Inosuke replied. "When the first notice came, I thought they were just dissatisfied with their treatment on the highway. We heard that there was a lot of trouble with that party up in the inner stations but we didn't really know what it was all about. Then the second notice came in. This time it came by courier, in the middle of the night. It said that they had taken two heads in the upper four stations; one of a station official and the other of a maid."

"That's the one. I heard that they shook up every lodging around Midono," said Tokuemon.

"Wait a minute," said Inosuke. "As a matter of fact, I thought about that a lot afterward. I learned some of the details. That's not the kind of thing that happens just because somebody has had a few too many victory drinks. Fukushima's all turned upside down now. Surely they must be meeting the government armies in a very different spirit than we are down here in the lower four stations. When I talked with my father about this, he was quiet for a while. I kept expecting him to say something, and then he came out with, 'To kill a post station official while he is serving the highway is going too far. That can't be accepted no matter how much the official army may have the upper hand.' That's just what he said."

"Well, I certainly agree with that," said Juheiji. "Your father may be a hard man with the money, but he really has spirit."

A man who had been with the army for five months came down from Mutsu to Shibata in Echigo, to Muramatsu, to Nagaoka, to Ochiya, then to Iiyama, Zenkoji and Matsumoto. He was wearing a three-pointed army cap and carrying a pack on his back. He had on Western-style trousers with old-fashioned leggings and straw sandals. A cloth patch on his left shoulder marked him as a member of the imperial forces and he came with the confident stride of a man who had seen combat. This was the priest from Aramachi. It was clear that it was Matsushita Chisato just from the way he wore the long sword at his side.

Chisato was escorted into Magome by Shosuke, the assistant headman, and the others who had gone out to meet him. He first went to the honjin to report his safe return and from there he went to the meeting room to pay his respects and to say that he had just learned of Kichizaemon's illness.

"Reverend sir!"

The exclamation rose repeatedly, from Eikichi over in the toiya office, and from the servants going in and out of the meeting room. Chisato took off his army hat, untied his sandals, and relaxed for a time in the meeting room while people gathered around him, eager to hear of the fighting in Aizu. Even Juheiji and Tokuemon, who had been out in the sitting room, came in to join the group.

Chisato's story was careful and thoughtful as befitted one of his calling. A member of the supply troops, he had been attached to the division that had advanced from the Echigo frontier, appearing before Wakamatsu castle on the fourteenth day of the ninth month. Before dawn on the nineteenth, there was a rumor that three emissaries from Aizu had come to the imperial army to negotiate through the good offices of Komazawa han for the surrender of the castle. The emissaries had worn deep, basket-shaped hats, they were swordless, and they were wearing bonds that they had tied on themselves. They were a pitiable sight, Chisato said, as they stood against the eaves of the imperial army headquarters. The commanders of the divisions that had entered Aizu by way of Shirakawa, Komazawa, Honari or through Echigo each had their own opinions and the rumor came out that they could not decide whether or not the surrender offer was genuine. On the next day, the twentieth, Suzuki Tamesuke and Kawamura Sansuke of Aizu came out of the castle carrying documents from the major han officials. Chisato himself had observed these two men approaching the headquarters, disguised as ordinary soldiers, and carrying supplies on their backs as though returning from a foraging expedition. Neither their friends nor their enemies in the front lines knew anything about what they were doing. The besieging forces subjected the castle to an intense bombardment and the return fire from the castle was heavier than usual. The twenty-second came. Finally the ceasefire order went out to the imperial forces. Chisato told of how a great banner, the agreed-upon signal of surrender, had been raised before one of the castle gates at eight o'clock in the morning.

"What I actually saw with my own eyes was very different from what I had imagined. I was amazed by how fierce the competition was within the imperial forces. They were always talking about whose soldiers were half-hearted or whose soldiers had just come along to see the sights. Serious enmities developed and some said that they would no longer be willing to work together. That was on the nineteenth of the ninth month, when the soldiers from Komazawa arrived. Some of those Komazawa soldiers had seven-shot repeaters and others had matchlocks that threw a quarter-pound ball. Still others had what they called something like 'Minbeer guns.' Their colors were a combination of large and small peonies. On top of that, they were wearing Western-style trousers and carrying dog skins on their backs. Everybody laughed and hooted. Their strange appearance became a favorite subject of conversation. And that's just one little example."

The tales that Chisato told to his eager listeners were without artifice or embellishment. He just tried to tell things as they had been. Now, in a still more relaxed mood, he added:

"Well now, I can't say this very loudly, but there's something else I heard at the front. The Tosa people were saying that the purpose of this fighting is to unify the nation, but who is going to control the people in the powerful han when they come home drunk with victory? That's what they were saying. After all, it is unlikely that the court nobles, who have had no experience in military matters in seven hundred years, are going to be able to maintain control for very long. There's sure to be a time of unrest coming, with fighting between Satsuma and Choshu at the very least. The Tosa people were saying that when they got back home from this they were going to build up their strength and try for a true imperial restoration another day. Just think of it—that's the spirit in which the Tosa people were fighting at Aizu. If one han was successful in the fighting, the other han would become jealous and some of them would be sure to make their unhappiness known. There was no way around it. That's the kind of thing I kept hearing over and over. This fighting has given the Tosa people a pretty good opinion of themselves, too."

When Chisato left to go on to Aramachi, Juheiji and Tokuemon glanced at each other but could not seem to get moving. The priest's story had left Inosuke strangely silent as well.

"That's Aizu, fighting to the end," said Tokuemon, half to himself. Then, changing his tone, he went on. "So what do you think of the priest's story? What about it, Inosuke, the story he said he got from the Tosa people?"

Inosuke made no immediate reply.

"Well now," began Tokuemon again, trying to get a response. "What would Hanzo say about this? Wouldn't he say that things are about to fall into chaos? Isn't that what he would say?—I really can't stand it! I want nothing more to do with serving the military houses!"

"Tokuemon," Inosuke said with sudden forcefulness, "if you want to know what Hanzo would say, I can tell you exactly what he would say. He would say that Satsuma and Choshu would not be free to act on their own. Since this restoration has come up from below, there is no possibility of going back to military rule so long as the people do not lose heart."

"How about it, Juheiji? What do you think?"

"Me? Well, I'll just watch and wait."

4

This fighting in the northeast—the expedition of 1868 that was to be the climax of the long-standing anti-shogunal movement—if you go back to its sources, they would be found in the great quarrels that raged on after the purge of Ansei in the late 1850's over the question of opening the country. Not only had they made this war certain, but the new age itself took a different direction as a result of the fighting.

There were all kinds of stories about the people who had so long awaited this day. There was a man, a retainer of the Tokugawa bannerman Ajima, who had become concerned about the state of the nation and who grieved over the condition of the imperial family. Becoming a masterless samurai, he served the Choshu activists in the fighting of 1864. Dressing himself as a fisherman, he would sit on the banks of the Katsura river day after day, ostensibly fishing, but actually observing the movements of the troops of the shogunate, of Aizu, and of Kuwana. He reported to the Choshu garrison in the Tenryuji. When that fighting ended with the defeat of Choshu, he was taken prisoner by shogunal agents and imprisoned in Kyoto along with Sunouchi Shikibu and scores of others. Later he was pardoned but his mental condition soon deteriorated, apparently because of an excess of jubilation upon hearing of the Meiji restoration. That unhappy supporter of the imperial cause was most likely unaware that this day of national unification had come.

Just how thick a pall lay over the times is manifest in the story of a member of the Tengu band of Mito who at last came out into the light of day after hiding in his own attic for five years. This samurai was part of an important family from Otsu that was in the service of Mito. He had not joined Fujita Koshiro and the Tsukuba band, but as a leader of the remaining survivors of the Tengu faction he was under constant pressure from its enemies. His name was posted on every street corner and a price of five hundred ryo had been placed on his head. His position helps to make more clear the ferocity of the internal conflicts in Mito. After the Tsukuba band moved toward the west, he and his friends found themselves in almost total isolation, with no support from any quarter. They were threatened and their entire families had to flee. His son went with an old servant of the household. They hid out in a farmhouse, buried in the straw of the stable, and pulled feed buckets over their heads so that no one could see them. His wife, their two young children, and a woman servant fled to the home of an acquaintance who had saved their lives once before. There she was turned away because there was an order out strictly forbidding the lodging of refugees. She was on the way back when a farm family took pity on her and hid them for three or four days. At last, hearing that the threat was over and that there was no more danger, she returned home. By this time the party of Ichikawa Sazaemon was in complete control over policy matters in Mito and with shogunal assistance was trying to join up with Nakayama han to exterminate its remaining opponents. Aware of this, the man decided to break out and take his stand on Mt. Ten'on, but he had only seven firearms for his men. The local people rose up to form the vanguard of his opponents, fighting with bamboo lances beneath banners of matting. He lost ten of his comrades to them. Others were taken prisoner by the soldiers of Matsudaira Suo no Kami, but he escaped, empty-handed. He hid out in the forests during the day and walked at night. Checkpoints had been set up at the entrance to each village by order of the han authorities. There was simply no place for him to go. In desperation, he retraced his route and managed to slip back into his own house. It was already under strict surveillance but there was no other place. He thought of the attic. Once there he found that a search party was still coming to inspect the house every day. Each time they would thrust lances through the ceilings. He would lie on a heavy beam and watch the keen blades groping toward him. Behind the house stood Mt. Mitsumine. In the daytime, he would hide in the attic where no one would see him, but at night, fearing that the house might be set on fire, he would climb the mountain and hide out in a bamboo grove, keeping watch on the countryside below. Before dawn he would go back to the attic. This became his daily routine.

How did he keep alive? His family made up rice balls, two days' supply at a time, and put them in a basket along with a bottle full of hot water. They would place the basket in a closet. The man would lift the ceiling boards off the closet, come down, and take his food. He would also come down into the closet whenever guests came so that he could listen to the conversation and keep some track of what was happening in the world. One day his second son went to hide in the closet while playing hide-and-seek with the neighborhood children. There he was startled to discover the father he thought had disappeared long ago. His father's face was black from dirt and exposure. His hair and beard were long. His eyes gleamed. When the son recognized his father, he promptly closed the door and hid elsewhere. For all that he was a child, he apparently sensed that it would be wrong to say anything about this. Another time, when the man had come down from the ceiling to relieve himself, he was seen by a manservant. The servant rushed off to report to his mistress that a black creature like a badger had come down out of the ceiling. She could not very well explain what it really was and so she said that it must be a dog or a badger and told him to take a club to it. The manservant came back with a long bamboo pole, but fortunately the room had a deep hearth that was hidden under the matting at this time of year and the fugitive was able to conceal himself there. He spent five years hiding in dark places. Then came the imperial restoration and he crawled down out of his attic a free man, able at last to move around as he wished. More than that, he met with a complete reversal of fortune when Mito received imperial orders to eliminate his old enemies because of their loyalty to the shogunate. He must have felt that his time had finally come. Shortly thereafter, he received orders from the han to lead a small group of men into Mutsu to take his long-hated enemy Ichikawa Sazaemon and his party into custody. When the imperial forces went up into the northeast to smash the combined forces of Mutsu and Dewa, Mito also sent soldiers into Aizu. It was said that this man was seen there fighting at the head of a rifle company.

But not everything was like this. There was no other han that had gone through such prolonged and bitter internal struggles as Mito, nor were there many that suffered such a period of terror after the restoration. Yet even in the Ina valley of Shinano, the number of people who poisoned themselves when their secret missions for the imperial armies were discovered, or who had been locked away in the great prison in Kyoto after sharing the fate of Choshu in 1864, was beyond counting. When the outcome of the war in the northeast at last became clear, the memory of those who had fallen in bitter struggle or who had crawled out of their dark hiding places returned to the hearts of the people along with the frosted and dead leaves of the season.

We cannot get ourselves involved again here in the consequences of the punitive expeditions against Choshu, but it is not possible to quarrel with the proposition that it was this great failure that opened the eyes of the shogunate and made it aware of the need for a reform of the feudal order. These were the reforms of the Keio era, just before the restoration. Much of the red tape and empty ritual established over the previous two hundred years was cut away at one stroke and everyone from top to bottom strove to outdo each other in simplifying things in the European style. This was a direct result of the Choshu fiasco. Plans for the reform of the old post horse system began to be made, and officials were no longer permitted to add to the sufferings of the people by forcing them to provide free post horses. The number of men and horses to be provided for daimyo on the road was decreased, the kickbacks on the toiya receipts were cut, and even the provisions for lodging along the highways were simplified. The recent fighting in the northeast added impetus to these changes and widened their scope. They began with changes in military organization, in weapons, and in uniforms, and went on to a breaking down of the class system, of hereditary rank, of vassalage, and of all the other deeply entrenched and utterly stagnant forms of feudalism. Now they had reached the stage where there was even talk of the abolition of the han.

Everything depends on the foundation. Before the problem of the privileges of the han and the monasteries left over from the previous age was taken up, the transportation system that was the very pulse of the nation began to undergo change.

In place of the transport commission that used to be in Edo, a bureau of post and transport was created in Kyoto, and the various categories of supernumerary transport workers ceased to exist. Formerly there had been the most extreme inconsistencies between travel for officials and for ordinary people, extending even to the weight of baggage permitted. These abuses were all corrected and special treatment was discontinued for everyone but imperial emissaries. All districts, whether in shogunal or private domains, were required to furnish men and porters without distinction. All travelers for the han were required to pay the going rates for porters and horses, and the kickbacks that had imposed such a hardship on the porters were eliminated. Nor was there to be any difference in the pay received by the regular post station workers and the supernumeraries who came in from neighboring districts in time of need. This policy of the bureau of post and transport was directed in all respects to ensuring equitable treatment for everyone who lived along the highways, from merchants and farmers to suppliers of post horses. The resolution of the long-standing problem of supernumerary porters and horses had at least made its first step.

In Magome there were nevertheless mutterings about this reform of the post system. The talk was first heard at the Masudaya and its branch, and it spread to the other influential houses in Magome, such as the Horaiya and the Umeya. Soon it included the twenty-five families who had so long served as suppliers of post horses. These families had originally been landless farmers. But starting with the porters' lodging set up by the Umeya and the hostel established by the Masudaya, they had begun one after another to change to a new trade, well content to be lowly townsmen. After a time they began to set themselves above the farmers. Previously, there had still been many daimyo passing through from their domains in the west to alternate attendance in Edo and whenever it became impossible to handle the traffic with the porters in the immediate area, the villagers from the Ina valley, first from thirty-one villages and eventually from one hundred and nineteen, would cross over the Kazekoshi pass to the Kiso valley to serve as supernumerary porters. It was when these farmers were suffering most at this brutal labor that the merchants in the post stations spat on their hands and began to build themselves up. There were even some among them who had found favor with a currently powerful official in Edo, and by acting as his special agent they managed to rise to the status of merchants in direct service to the lord of Owari. There was no reason to expect these people to be willing indefinitely to be despised as members of the very lowest class, even below the farmers. The more firmly they were held down the more their pride welled up—they began to wear fine cloth in both their inner and outer garments, and even to wear daggers on their hips. By now they looked like leading citizens such as one might see riding by in litters.

Of course, the second Masudaya Soemon was just a little bit different from the rest. The business and the morals of his household remained unchanged from the days when the Tokugawa policy of oppressing merchants still prevailed; even now he never forgot his family's origins as landless farmers. He remembered how human life was granted, that this life was a gift from heaven, and he clearly understood that the wealth and possessions that had come down to the family from their ancestors was all entrusted to them by heaven—it had to be carefully maintained. He taught this to his children. If the money that is one of the treasures of Japan were to be treated as their own, heaven would be sure to hear of it sooner or later. Looking back on his seventy years in this floating world, Soemon would sit at the front of his sake shop writing up his memoirs for his children, who were busy brewing sake. He would tell them stories from the lifetime of the first Soemon, and of how up until then they had all been desperately poor landless farmers for generation after generation. He reminded them that their generation's ability to live without wanting for anything was due to their parents and their ancestors and that all people must return to their origins. Even the head of the house continued to wear wadded cotton jackets in winter and plain cloth jackets in summer. For special occasions he would wear cotton with just a bit of silk in it or at most raw silk. Soemon reminded his children in his memoirs that townsmen should be satisfied with such clothing and that it was most fitting for them to work quietly and inconspicuously.

The second Masudaya Soemon died still worrying that for all their lowly past, his children were turning out to be clever in speech and inclined to put themselves forward. They tended to rank themselves at the bottom of the hierarchy of post officials, forgetting their origins. However, the third-generation and fourth-generation heads of the house knew nothing of the desperate struggles that the two Soemon had carried on in this village of Magome. That the wife of the first Soemon had ever sold beancurd on the side, grinding the beans in a mortar all night long without ever getting a full night's sleep—all this gradually began to seem like distant fantasy.

And then there was the old custom of filling vacancies among the village elders, assistant headmen, and similar offices by sealed bid—those who were designated highest bidders would serve as post officials. Just seeing the way the candidates for these positions would make themselves known to the Yamamura in Fukushima—to the stewards, personal attendants, finance officers, even down to the foot soldiers and clerks—made it clear that under this system, which was carried on until late in the eighteenth century, competition had grown out of hand. At some point, it was completely abandoned. All the offices became hereditary. However unsuitable he might be, if a person was born into a certain house or belonged to a branch of that family, he automatically became an object of respect and would be thought of as a "leading citizen." It worked in much the same way that certain Edo merchants came to acquire special status and privileges.

These were the leading citizens. There were all sorts among them. Before the intentions of the bureau of post and transport services could be made clear, there were those who perceived it as a radical reform and thought only of its effect on them. In this they were joined by the old post horse people who perceived that they could no longer have things their way on the highway. This deepened the unrest.

"This is a matter of the survival of the post station. People like the master of the Fushimiya ought to speak out just a little bit more."

So said some of the members of the old post horse service.

It was not surprising that the more perceptive people in Owari, which had always placed particular emphasis on the popular will, should have been among the first to welcome the policies of the bureau of post and transport. Nor was it surprising that this trend should spread very rapidly toward the Kiso valley. Under these new policies, not even freight bearing the seal of one of the great han would be permitted to pass free of charge through the toiya offices as it had before. It was no longer permitted to have freight underweighed because it belonged to the shogun or the han. Nor were bribes effective any more. All freight, whether official or private, was to be weighed up on the same basis at each toiya.

The post horse service of Magome, linking up the center of the Kiso road between Tokyo and Kyoto, made up of men who had long made their living off the old post system, could not be expected to take pleasure in these reforms. All of them had become accustomed to the long-standing abuse of transporting the freight that they wanted to transport and pushing the rest off on the supernumerary workers. Every time a large retinue accompanying an official or a daimyo came through, at least five or six hundred of these supernumeraries would be called to serve the lower four Kiso stations, divided into morning and evening shifts. Then the post horse service would take the best jobs and turn the rest over to the others. Like the leading citizens who had grown fat on service to the highway, these people too were unable to forget the good old days when the post stations had flourished. To them, the bureau of post and transport's policy of equal treatment was an abomination.

Shoshichi of the Kozasaya, one of the members of the old post horse service, went so far as to knock on the gate of the Fushimiya late one night, trying to get Inosuke's opinion of the matter.

"Go ask at the honjin," came the reply.

"But, Fushimiya, it just won't do! The supernumeraries are different from the post horse service here at the station. The Masudaya and the Horaiya and everybody agrees. A person in your position ought to have more concern for the people of the station."

Even when Shoshichi went this far, Inosuke, taking refuge in the fact that he had come from the neighboring province as an adopted son, made no clear reply. Although he too was one of the "leading citizens," Inosuke always tried to find the middle road. His last defense was always, "Go ask at the honjin."

By the twelfth month there had already been several snowfalls at the station. An unexpected detachment of some seventy or eighty Owari men,

bound for Fukushima, came over the highway from the west. They were to
have their noon meal at Magome. It was getting close to the new year and
not enough men and horses could be found within the station, but supernumeraries could not be brought in on such short notice. Under the provisions
of the reform of the post system, the equitable distribution of such obligations pertained also to the leading citizens. At least until the reorganization
of the transport system was complete, all the people along the highways and
all the people in the neighboring areas were to be liable for service as supernumeraries, and such emergencies were to be met by ordering one person out
from each household. Accordingly, everyone who was asked to perform porter service would have to help in moving the freight, whether he be merchant or farmer.

One of the leading citizens bridled at the order and bellowed his reply.

"What? You're asking our household to supply a porter? Go ask at the
honjin for porters!"

Kichizaemon was now well along in his recovery and Hanzo was sufficiently encouraged to be able to leave the honjin and try to arrange for porters. He had already heard from Inosuke about the attitudes of the leading
citizens and the post horse service.

Hanzo conducted himself as though he were doing the most natural thing
in the world. He changed into porter's clothes and called for Sakichi to bring
him the Kiso-style pack frame from the woodshed. He provided himself with
ropes. He didn't argue with the other leading citizens, preferring to make his
reply by joining the porters and helping them move that day's freight.

"Are you going out too, master?" asked Sakichi, rushing up out of
breath. "I'll go in your place. They only want one person from each household."

But Hanzo had already drawn the matting cover over his pack and was
going out the door. The Owari men were divided into several squads; their
officers were taking a noon break at the honjin. Lances were lying on the
floor inside the entry. Seisuke would look after them, so Hanzo did not have
to be concerned.

"Keep an eye on things, Otami!"

With these words, he stepped out of the front door.

The toiya service, which rotated twice each month, was now operating
out of Kyurobei's place. The grooms of the post station had drawn up their
horses in front of the toiya. The porters were drawn up in order from the top
of the street to the bottom.

"Master Hanzo, all the good horses are already out. No matter where I
look I can only find brood mares and packhorses."

One of the horse masters, rushing here and there to assign men and horses,
found this opportunity to address Hanzo.

"I'm going out with the rest of you today. Give me my share of the
freight."

These words from Hanzo astonished not only the head porters but also

Kyurobei, who was standing nearby. Each porter had to carry nearly sixty pounds of freight. Hanzo tied his load firmly onto his pack frame, laid the matting over the top of it, and trudged off into the falling snow alongside Kenkichi, one of his own tenant farmers.

"Look, it's the master of the honjin!" several of the porters exclaimed, clearly looking on him as an object of curiosity. Some of the farmers would glance over at Hanzo, then pull their necks in so that their faces were hidden under their hats, and snicker.

"From here it's a tough five miles over to Tsumago, sir," said Kenkichi.

The stretch from the top of the pass, past Ichikokutochi and on to Tsumago, is one of the most remote sections of the highway. Over all the preceding years whenever a daimyo or important shogunal official passed over this portion of road, the villagers from the neighboring Ina valley would have to throw down their hoes, leave their fields, and come over ten miles of steep mountain passes to the lower four Kiso post stations to work as porters.

Hanzo was not used to carrying such loads on his back. He began to fall behind. He was soon out of earshot of the horsebells that had provided a rhythm for his steps, and from time to time Kenkichi or one of the other farmers would wait for him. The farmers were used to heavy loads and their bodies were hardened by incessant labor in the mountains. Hanzo's arms and legs began to tremble. The farmers waiting for him to catch up would note his condition, laugh out loud, and start walking again.

Never had Hanzo found himself so bathed in cold sweat as on that day. Whenever he opened his mouth to gasp for air, fine snow came blowing into it. It was the end of the year and the footing was bad on the frozen road. There was a merciless wind whistling through the bamboo grass, and yet he found pleasure in being with his own tenant farmers and doing the same work. He whipped up his courage once more, trudged along the road and came down into the deep valley, leaning on the stout staff that he had picked up at the top of the pass. At last they reached the bridge on the edge of Tsumago. As they were crossing it, the Owari detachment overtook them.

5

By the beginning of the second month of Meiji 2, 1869, Hanzo found himself at the center of a maelstrom of change. Such was its intensity that the return of daimyo domains to imperial control had been proclaimed and the prohibition of the intermingling of Buddhist and Shinto practices, so long an accepted part of life, was being ever more strongly enforced. But before either of these measures could be carried out, all kinds of things began happening along the major highways.

The Kiso barrier was pulled down. The seventy or eighty Owari men who

had come through Magome on their way to Fukushima at the end of the year
were a detachment of lancers under orders from the lord of Owari. He in
turn had his orders from the court to relieve the Yamamura deputies of control of this barrier. Hanzo only learned of this later. It had been on the
twenty-sixth day of the last month of the previous year that the Yamamura
handed over to the Owari men the equipment used to guard this barrier,
including two cannon, two gun carriages, twenty light firearms, ten bows,
twelve lances, and two sets of tools for catching and holding those who
attempted to resist. At the same time, they assigned a squadron of cavalry, a
company of light foot soldiers, and several dozen low-ranking people of miscellaneous functions to the Owari troops. They were all to be placed under
the command of Shirasu Gozaemon and Hara Saheita. Owari, however,
requested that only seven of the cavalrymen should be retained in this service
and on the sixth day of the second month, manning of the barrier was discontinued.

Next came the elimination of the office of Fukushima deputy. Although
the Yamamura family retained nominal control over the Kiso valley, the real
power passed into the hands of Yoshida Sarumatsu, a high-ranking Owari
official who set up his temporary headquarters in the Kozenji in Fukushima.
All those who had served the Yamamura for many years were discharged and
told to wait for further word on the future of their stipends.

Such was the way in which the Kiso valley met its new master. When the
name of the Fukushima deputy's office was changed to that of the management office, notices came down to Hanzo from that office, notifying him of
the elimination of the office of toiya under the policies of the new government. The office of village elder was also eliminated, and the office in charge
of providing relays of men and horses was hereafter to be known as the office
of post horses. The letter ended with an urgent summons for two representatives of the post station officials to appear in Fukushima. There was reform
on top of reform; disruption on top of disruption.

"They're doing away with the toiya, mother."

"That's what they say. I heard it from Otami."

"And they will be putting an end to the village meeting room and there
aren't going to be any more village elders."

Hanzo and his stepmother exchanged anxious glances.

"I was just talking to Otami. If father hears about this he is sure to get terribly upset. I wonder if you would agree to help us see that the word doesn't
get to him," Oman asked suddenly.

Even his keen-witted stepmother was so upset that she was beginning to
talk about hiding things from Kichizaemon. Kichizaemon himself had recovered to the point where on New Year's day he had sent symbolic gifts of
buckwheat noodles to his relatives and acquaintances, combining the celebration of the beginning of his seventieth year with thanks to all who had
wished him well. At the same time, there was no denying the ravages of age.
His feelings had come to be very easily hurt, possibly because of his physical

weakness. To Oman it was unthinkable that Hanzo should simply report the changes to him as he had to her.

"Just look," said Oman, "this last big illness came on because he was upset. That's the kind of person your father is."

"But there's no way that we can keep this kind of thing hidden from him. I think it would be best to just go ahead and tell him."

"What do you mean? Your father never leaves the second floor now. I'll just tell everyone who comes in and keep them all quiet. There's no chance he would ever hear anything about it."

"What should I do, I wonder."

"Never mind. I'll take full responsibility. Because if you do anything that might damage his health again, there'll be no second chance this time."

When Oman made it a question of damaging his father's health, Hanzo had no choice but to accede to her wishes.

After he saw his stepmother back to her quarters, Hanzo looked around him. The news of the reforms that had so worried Oman were now being universally discussed. The more one tried to hide them, the more hopeless it would become. Nor were they confined to the station of Magome. The same kind of thing was happening in Nakatsugawa and Ochiai and in Tsumago. The headmen and toiya of the five stations of Fukushima, Narai, Miyanokoshi, Agematsu, and Midono had all been called up before the management office, severely reprimanded, relieved of their offices, and forbidden to see anyone but their relatives and family. It did not stop with the post stations, either; the headman of the village of Kurokawa was also relieved of his office in the same way.

In these times, Hanzo's principal confidant was the master of the Fushimiya next door. "Hanzo, maybe this would be best," or "Maybe that would be best," were the words of help that would come out of the warmth of Inosuke's heart, for all that he was still held as something of an outsider by the other leading citizens of the village. Even as he worried about his father, Hanzo went around explaining to the leading citizens that their long service up to now had been all for the convenience of the military and that the great task of restoring the virtuous rule of antiquity was under way. Since this was so, they should stifle their cries of discontent.

He had to make them understand that these changes would bring about a brighter world. The members of the old post horse service had to be encouraged to yield to the new pressures. Certainly if one went according to ideals, these reforms were exactly what one would expect. But if one accepted these reforms, it then became necessary to give up the ancient family functions that had been passed down from father to son as family distinctions. This put his own feelings in something of a turmoil.

The two representatives from Magome who had been called up to the management office in Fukushima came back homeward over roads that were wet and sloppy in the thaw of the second month. They brought back a copy of the guidelines from the management office:

Item: A seal is to be made, reading "post horse office," and giving the name of the station. The old toiya seal is to be discarded.

Item: The ledgers kept by the toiya are to be revised according to the new rules, with freight handled under seal, freight handled under special orders, and freight handled for cash to be recorded separately. These categories must not be confused.

Item: The expenditure of writing brushes, ink, paper, candles, and charcoal must be recorded in a separate ledger without fail.

Item: Litters, tung oil, and paper lanterns are to be inventoried and appropriately recorded.

Item: In the new office of post horses, two people are to be appointed to each of the offices of overseer, disbursing officer, secretary, accountant, head porter, and head groom. A third person may also be made disbursing officer. The functions of overseer, disbursement officer, and secretary are to be assigned either by agreement or by lot while the positions from accountant on down will be filled by appointments made by these three, with their names to be announced within a day or two. Of course, the salaries will be determined later.

Item: The post station officials must be polite and considerate in all matters dealing with supernumerary transport workers and refrain from being overbearing with the villages concerned.

Item: Until the restoration is completed, twenty-five men and twenty-five horses will be kept on call at each station as before and freight being moved under seal or under written order will be handled by the men and horses of the station or by supernumeraries from villages who are to be paid at the established rates. All wages due must be paid immediately and in full.

Item: All freight handled for cash is to be given to the freight handlers from the stations and to the supernumeraries as it comes up in their turns. Moreover, all the above will be subject to further consultation.

These were the guidelines written up for the new post horse service. The language was clear and straightforward and, as the words "until the restoration is completed" made clear, it was a temporary arrangement. Such a tone had never been taken by the old district officials. Hanzo was particularly pleased by the way in which the new men sent out by Owari to manage the Kiso emphasized the importance of unity and equality for the station people and the supernumeraries.

However, when it came time to discuss the details, arguments began to arise among the post officials of the eleven Kiso post stations. The guidelines from the management office established four categories of freight for the stations: under seal, under certificate, under fixed rates, and under negotiated rates. According to the surface meaning of the guidelines, the freight handled under seal and under certificate was to be moved by the men and horses of the post stations and if supernumeraries had to be called in, they were to be paid the standard wage. Some argued that this meant that the post station people and the supernumeraries were to be used together without distinction. The eleven stations soon found themselves hard-pressed for funds and some felt that each of the eleven stations should apply to the management office for a special loan, since it was going to be difficult to start hiring men and horses from new places. The new government itself was determined to encourage the circulation of the new gold certificates, and this caused serious problems since the rice merchants in other areas were still refusing to accept them. There was one rumor that the gold certificates were being taken at twenty percent below face value in Matsumoto. What was to be done? The merchants in other han were not accepting the new paper money at any discount, no matter how great, and as a result it was impossible to get it changed for other money. This caused much confusion and unhappiness. Some of the post station officials said that a fixed rate of exchange for the gold certificate ought to be a part of any new agreement. All of this was written up in a formal letter of inquiry from the eleven Kiso stations to the management office in Fukushima.

"Hanzo!"

Shosuke, the assistant headman, had been making frequent, furtive visits, calling out to announce his presence each time. He was greatly troubled over the selection of the new officials, partly because, as the representative of the landed farmers, he had come to feel considerable antagonism toward the leading citizens with their townsmen's ways.

"How about it, Shosuke, there won't be any more big processions going through here the way they have up to now, will there?"

"We can be sure of that."

"In that case, I have an idea."

Hanzo suggested that he was of a mind to close the toiya attached to the honjin, since there was no longer any need for two such organizations in the village. He would yield the new post horse service to the household of Kyurobei. He had already spoken to Inosuke about it.

Shosuke protested immediately.

"But Hanzo, you shouldn't let go of things so easily. You ought to stand up for your rights more than that. After all, it was the ancestors of your family who founded this village. The firmer stand you take, the better it will be for everyone."

In the end, Hanzo let the new post horse service go to Kyurobei as he had planned and the new transportation system for the village was developed there. The seven new post officials were once again being chosen by sealed bids. The long-established custom of hereditary succession was ended and emphasis now shifted from family status to personal qualifications. Hanzo's cousin Eikichi of the Kameya, whose good work in the toiya office attached to the honjin had long been recognized, now advanced to take his place among the new officials.

With that done, it came time to close the meeting room. All the ledgers had to be handed over to the new officials. Hanzo told his manservant, Sakichi, to help the meeting room servant take the equipment of the toiya office to the new post horse service. He shut himself up in his study next to the parlor and began to select from among all the records that his family had kept in carrying out the hereditary offices of honjin, toiya, and headman all those that needed to be handed over to the post horse service. When he untied the cords of a box that had come down from the time when his father, Kichizaemon, was in charge of the toiya, he found receipts for the litters and porters Kichizaemon had used on his trip to Kyoto, along with signed certificates for couriers and for festival expenses. He untied the strings of another box. From it fell seals, large and small, some from the office of post and transport in Kyoto, some from the new administrative districts around Ise and Kofu, which were not to last long, all authorizing use of official transport facilities. These were the new post station seals that the post horse service would be needing, and they traced the development of the new administrative districts. For Hanzo, it was no easy matter to set out the appropriate papers from correspondence with Owari, those that had been sent as part of the joint responsibility of the lower four stations of the Kiso, and so on. It was almost like a moving day in the meeting room and the toiya. Hanzo became choked up as he thought of it and he could not go on sorting out the ledgers.

When Otami came to tell him about Kichizaemon, the windows in the parlor were dark.

"What are you doing sitting there without a light?"

Otami was startled to find Hanzo sitting in the dark room, staring vacantly, but still in formal posture.

"How is father?" he asked.

"That's just it. He keeps asking mother if something isn't happening to the family. She doesn't know what to say," replied Otami as she left the room to fetch a light. The lantern she brought back with her brightened the room.

"I'm so upset I don't know what to do," said Hanzo, gazing around him. "I've just been trying to sit here for a while and think it out."

"I wonder how they are doing in Tsumago," said Otami.

"Well, I'll tell you. It's the same at Juheiji's place as it is here. Right now they will be talking about exactly the same things."

"I suppose so."

"Juheiji is saying the same things to Osato that I am saying to you. Look here, I don't know how—it was a really long time ago—but my grandfather and my father devoted their entire lives to the highway and the post station. I don't think that all that work over all that time is going to just disappear like foam. At the very least, they will have to remember that the honjin and the toiya have been in the Aoyama family for generations. That is even written out in the memorandum that came down from Fukushima. We are an old house that has held the offices of honjin, toiya, and headman ever since our ancestors first cleared the land here, but we have learned that we must not make too much of the antiquity of our claim in these titles. Shosuke keeps coming over here and telling me that I have to take a firm stand, but if we don't look beyond our own selfish interests, we'll never be able to reform the post station."

"Well, I really don't know. But all the same, it's beginning to get me upset too, what with mother so worried and all."

Otami had not, however, forgotten about feeding the children. She broke off the conversation and headed for the hearth room with a businesslike air.

This was the season when the mountain families began to break out of their long winter confinement. The great avalanches that occurred daily in the valleys of Mt. Ena were visible from Hanzo's home, and there was the dismal drip of the melting snow from the eaves day after day. The sound brought unwelcome thoughts to Hanzo's mind. He passed a restless night by Otami's side and then went out first thing in the morning to have a last look at the meeting room. Thinking of Kichizaemon, who was getting no news at all, he was about to open the door of the meeting room when he found himself face to face with Inosuke, who was just coming in.

"Well, it looks as though the meeting room won't be around much longer."

Hanzo and Inosuke walked through as though inspecting a recently surrendered castle and then went over to look at the now vacant toiya office. They came at last to the sitting room. In the yellow walls, in the soot-stained sliding panels, there was nothing that did not speak of the past of this post station that had been forced to comply with the demands of a brutal and arbitrary power. In everything that caught the eye in this deserted room could be felt the indescribable hardships of all those who had worked together on this highway.

Hanzo had not expected to find himself spending his final time in the meeting room with Inosuke. Feeling that he could speak freely, he said that when they sent off to Owari for assistance last year the future of the post station had already been in doubt. A look at the account books at that time had revealed that over the past seven years there had been an average deficit of one hundred seventy-five ryo per year in the operation of the station. On top of that accumulating deficit, the debts of the post station officials who had borrowed to cover it had reached a level sufficient to support sixteen families, and the interest payments alone had come to another two hundred forty-four ryo per year. Even if they did obtain assistance from Owari, they could not go on this way for very long without facing ruin. All of the bad practices that had lurked in the post station system had at last reached their limit. Everyone was talking about this complete revision of the operating rules. He and his colleagues on the highway had thought only of bearing up under their service to the military households, looking upon this reorganization as one more thing that had to be borne. But now that they realized the toiya and the village meeting room were mere remnants of the feudal age, they were beginning to grasp the true implications a little better. They understood that when even the most highly placed person might find himself face to face with violent change, there was no reason for those below to expect to remain tranquil.

Inosuke bit his fingernails as he listened to Hanzo. He noticed that Hanzo's ears were somewhat red.

"Thanks for everything, Inosuke. We've served together a long time," Hanzo added.

All the furnishings had been moved to the post horse office. Hanzo called Sakichi, told him to close the door and lock it, and left the meeting room with Inosuke.

6

Hirata Nobutane's journey over the Kiso road took place during these changes at Magome. On his way back from Tokyo, Nobutane had chosen to pass through Shimo-Suwa and then to visit the Ina valley, where there were so many disciples. From the home of his disciple Hara Mayomi in Seinaiji, he was to pass through Hashiba and arrive in Magome about mid-afternoon. He planned to rest briefly there at the western extremity of the Kiso road and then move on. Nobutane, of course, was not traveling alone. He was accompanied by several disciples, and there were people like Tatematsu Hosuke from Nanjo village who planned to accompany him as far as Magome.

Nobutane was the son of Hanzo's master, Kanetane, and the grandson of Atsutane. The Hirata disciples were now calling Kanetane the old master and Nobutane the young master. That Hanzo was not only to receive this totally unexpected visit from Nobutane but would be able to welcome the party into his own home and have them see the countryside in which he lived seemed like a dream. He guided Nobutane out into the western hallway where he showed him that for all that had been said about the Kiso being nothing but deep valleys, here was a place where the view was open. He pointed out the various peaks of Mino and Omi silhouetted against the hazy sky. From the hallway it was not possible to see the entire range of peaks that extended out from Mt. Ena, but Hanzo was able to please his guest by pointing out the direction in which lay hidden the Misaka that was mentioned in the *Man'yoshu*. He then conducted his guest into the chamber of honor. In that secluded room he heard of Nobutane's experiences on the road back to Kyoto, and of his visit to Yamabuki village, where a group of disciples led by Katagiri Shun'ichi had established the Koedayama shrine under the auspices of the Yamabuki shrine; Nobutane had paid his respects to the four great masters of National Learning who were enshrined there. He had also expressed his gratitude to the disciples in Ina who had made such great sacrifices to print Atsutane's *Commentaries on History*, and he had acted in his father's stead in welcoming new disciples.

Oman and Otami paid their respects as they brought tea in to the guests. Hanzo took his place beside them and was deeply moved at this opportunity to introduce his mother and his wife to the grandson of Hirata Atsutane. Okume and Sota, too, delighted to have a special guest in the house, emerged hand in hand from behind their mother to make their bows, their faces reflecting the knowledge that they had just had a change of clothing for the occasion. Hanzo's daughter was thirteen and his son eleven.

Nobutane was in a hurry to continue his journey. It was Hosuke, deciding to accompany him as far as his night's lodging in Nakatsugawa, who asked Hanzo to come along. Now that he had come as far as Magome Hosuke wanted to accompany Nobutane to Keizo's home. The prospect could not fail to excite Hanzo. He sent Sakichi next door to invite Inosuke to share the pleasure. Inosuke had been at the Upper Fushimiya and it was some little time before he appeared in formal dress, apologizing for the delay.

"This is the young master."

Inosuke responded to the introduction, obviously curious about this person who was the successor to the Master Hirata of whom Hanzo spoke so often.

Everyone was ready for the trip to Nakatsugawa and so they set out. As they walked along the road, Hanzo enjoyed hearing about Kanetane. Just now there was nothing that encouraged him so much as to find out what was happening in the center of things. He tried to miss nothing that Nobutane said. He learned that the new emperor, who had arrived at Edo castle on the thirteenth day of the tenth month of the previous year, had made one trip back to Kyoto. That had been on the eighth of the twelfth month. He would be returning to Tokyo in the coming third month. On that occasion Kanetane planned to move his own household back to Tokyo. This was why Nobutane was in such a hurry. Kanetane, who had always presented himself as an explicator of the old ways, was now a part of the imperial establishment. This year he had advanced to the post of tutor to the new emperor, and as he led the scholars of the Hirata school who were to become the central force in the offices of religious administration, he was said to be playing a direct role in setting the course of the new government. The old master was now the aged pilot insofar as the civil and religious aspects of the new government were concerned. The new national council soon to be established in Tokyo was to draw representatives from every part of the nation in order to establish new systems and organizations, and this council too needed the vigor and experience of a man such as the young master.

Nobutane had important news from behind the scenes in Kyoto concerning the coming return of the emperor to Tokyo. It was not without reason that the people throughout the nation should all try to welcome him when he was on the road. It was no longer possible for the emperor to remain secluded as hitherto deep behind the "jade curtains," unseen by anyone beyond a small number of court nobles. He would have to return to his natural role as father of the people. The customs that had prevailed—in which the dwelling of the emperor was referred to as "above the clouds" and the emperor was neither to be seen by ordinary mortals nor even permitted to set foot on the ground—were all part of the excesses that had for centuries been creating a gulf between high and low. Now there was a new beginning, a restoration of imperial rule, and the first order of business was to do away with these evil practices. If the people of Japan were to take their standards from the sacred antiquity of their own nation and heroically defy even the best qualities of foreign government, then the emperor would have to emerge from behind the jade curtains, travel through the various provinces, and nurture the people in directness and simplicity. Such was the thinking behind the plans for this unprecedented imperial progress.

But there was more. A still larger matter awaited the completion of the progress. That was the proposal to move the imperial residence from Kyoto to Tokyo and to create a new capital there. If the court failed to take full advantage of the opportunity to lay the basis for a sound and permanent order, then it would be difficult to avoid the futile cycle in which the corrupt would be succeeded by the traitorous, just as the Hojo had been succeeded by the Ashikaga back in the middle ages. Now, within the country, there was a medieval feudal system falling apart, and beyond it, the might of Europe advancing steadily toward the East. There was no longer room for the slightest doubt on anyone's part that these great changes in society were far reaching beyond anything that had happened since the founding of the nation. What was needed in these times was deep and careful attention to the affairs of the nation—to take note of the plans of the great world powers, to achieve the unity of the people of the nation, body and soul, and to make them feel that the sun of a bright new day was shining upon them. This required extraordinary determination. If petty, short-run problems were permitted to stand in the way of this opportunity to move the capital, then all would be lost for the nation—the tide of events had risen to a level where such things were being said.

According to what Nobutane said to Hanzo as he walked with him down from Magome pass, proposals to move the capital were already to be found among the writings left by one or two earlier National Scholars. And now they were confronted by the actual move to Tokyo. Inosuke took great interest in this part of the conversation.

They were, of course, making their way to the Nakatsugawa honjin. Both Keizo and Kozo were back from Kyoto at the time, and so the three close friends soon found themselves together in one of their rare reunions. Hanzo's disciple Katsushige came over from Ochiai. Sake was brought out to welcome Nobutane to this east Mino town, and Inosuke drank much more than usual that evening. When he and Hanzo set out for home it was already very late.

Three months later, when Kozo left Nakatsugawa and Mino and headed up Jikkyoku pass on his way to Tokyo, most travelers were heading in that direction. The emperor was now settled in his new home in Tokyo and the Hirata family was also in Tokyo, having closed their Kyoto house.

When Kozo paused briefly to call in from the gate, Hanzo found that he was not able to detain his friend for very long. Kozo kept his sandals on and paced between the front entrance and the garden, finally sitting down on the veranda of the parlor. From here the tree peony could be seen, now long past its season of blossom. He laid his hat there and drank the tea that Hanzo offered him.

But literally before there was time to warm his seat, Kozo rushed off to follow his master, with no concern for such matters as the elimination of the toiya. Hanzo found the parting very painful. After Kozo's departure for his next night's lodging at Nojiri, Hanzo suddenly changed clothes and set out to accompany him as far as the inn in Fukushima.

He did not catch up with Kozo until they were almost in Yabuhara. Five days later, he had taken final leave from his friend and was returning alone down the highway from Yabuhara. The strong sun of the old fifth month shone in his face. He could think of nothing but the activities of the Hirata disciples. By now Morooka Masatane, Miwata Mototsuna, Gonda Naosuke, and all the others were gathered around the master in Tokyo. Kureta Masaka had advanced to the position of inspector in the imperial institute in Kyoto.

"And all the disciples were looking ahead ten years or more," he thought to himself. "No one imagined that the campaign in the north would have been so decisive or that the time to act would have come so soon."

He could scarcely believe that things could have changed so much since that war to unify the nation. He thought of Keizo, who would himself be leaving Nakatsugawa soon to follow Kozo to Tokyo. Keizo had no desire to accept any office no matter how prestigious, and it pleased Hanzo to reflect on this friend who was so modest, so little fond of notoriety.

Now that the Kiso-Fukushima barrier had been eliminated, there was no longer any trace of the guards who used to check the travelers. He passed through Agematsu and came to Midono. That there was a headman and toiya living here under house arrest spoke eloquently of the difficult times. This man, still not fully awakened from the old dreams, was forbidden to step out of his home for any reason. He could not have his forehead shaved, nor, if he should fall ill, could he visit a physician for treatment. If he planned to call a physician in, he would have to report his intention and the blinds would have to remain drawn, the main gate closed, and all entrances and exits made through the side gate. Nor could he have anything to do with trade or business. He was under strict orders from Fukushima to address any further questions to them through the new post station officials.

Juheiji was out when Hanzo reached Tsumago and looked in on the honjin, but there too the meeting room had been closed and the toiya was changing. The reforms, once begun, showed a strange ability to force their way to the very end.

Leaving Tsumago, Hanzo could no longer see the blue waters of the Kiso. The road left the deep valley and headed up through the heavily forested mountains. The farther he climbed the closer he came to the western end of the Kiso country. At last Hanzo found himself back in Magome standing before the new post horse office. The iris festival of the fifth month was already past but iris leaves still remained along the eaves of the mountain houses. The old meeting room was next to the main gate of the honjin, visible just below the Fushimiya. There a person who seemed unable to leave the vicinity of this deserted place was walking up and down, leaning on a stick. It was his father, Kichizaemon, who had been staying in his quarters since his illness. Hanzo became aware of him only as he approached the honjin. He gave an involuntary start.

"Father! Where are you going?"

Kichizaemon had just paid his first visit in a long time to his old friend Kimbei and had returned as far as the gate of his own home.

"Are you all right, father? You shouldn't be out alone this way."

Hanzo looked around for one of his children to escort Kichizaemon back to his quarters, but Sota was nowhere to be seen. Hanzo then assisted him as far as the door to the rear building.

It was no longer possible for Hanzo to conceal the fact that he had relinquished the position of toiya. His father had already seen the new post horse office. It had been futile to try to hide worrisome facts from him as Oman and Otami had wished. He reflected on this as he returned to the main house.

"Otami! I'm back!"

As soon as she heard Hanzo's voice, Otami began telling him how she had prepared a bath of irises for him on the previous night and had waited up until late. She was expecting another child soon and she was already the mother of five children. Of the five, the eldest boy was Sota and the second son was Masaki, who had been adopted by her family in Tsumago. The other three children were all girls. After Okume, the eldest, there was the second daughter, Onatsu, and the third daughter, Omari, but both of them had died in early childhood. They wanted above all to be able to keep the child who was about to be born. Otami spoke of this whenever she was alone with her husband. Her pregnancy was too far advanced to be hidden and she was preoccupied with it.

In the evening, Hanzo went to see his father. Kichizaemon and Oman were together on the second floor of the rear building. Kichizaemon's bedding was spread out in a corner of the room. All that they had been trying to hide from him had not waited for Hanzo's explanations. Kichizaemon had heard everything from Kimbei in the Upper Fushimiya and he could now only hope that the reversals that the Aoyama household was experiencing would soon come to an end.

"I'm tired out today," began Kichizaemon. "I had been feeling a lot better the last few days and since I hadn't even gone to congratulate Kimbei on his seventieth birthday, I decided to go up and see him. I'm not good for very much any more. I was completely out of breath just walking up to the Upper Fushimiya. And then Kimbei wouldn't let me go. He told me all kinds of stories about the post station. It was really a long session."

Hanzo was somewhat relieved to find how well his father had taken all the news, and he went on to explain to him that the necessity for a reform of the post system had not just come up over night. The times would no longer permit great processions to demand hundreds of porters from the Kiso valley and a thousand or more from Ina, and it seemed to be the intention of the Fukushima offices to require only thirteen men and thirteen horses to be available at each post station. Not even the basic staff of twenty-five men and twenty-five horses at each station was needed now.

"Well, things nowadays are just too much for an old-timer like me to comprehend," said Kichizaemon. "Kimbei put it best. He said, 'I just can't stand to watch it.' He would feel that way."

"By the way," said Hanzo, looking closely at his father's face, "I heard that you had a dream. What kind of dream was it?"

"I dreamt that the roof beams fell down. It was such a strange dream that I thought of going to a fortune teller to have it interpreted. The family is in trouble. Otherwise I would never have had such a dream. That's what I was thinking and I got quite upset."

"Well, father, I had thought all along that we should tell you about things just as they happened, but Otami and Oman were worried. 'We mustn't let anything upset him,' they said, and they kept stopping me—so we ended up hiding it all from you."

Oman was going in and out of the room. She seemed concerned about what Hanzo and his father were saying as she brought the tea in from the next room. She said that she would have liked to have served Hanzo some of the special cakes from the previous day's festival but there were none left. She also said that, in keeping with the times, they had observed the festival in a very simple way this year, inviting in only those who were closest, like Eikichi and Seisuke.

Kichizaemon interrupted abruptly.

"I knew it would come to this. I haven't said anything until now, but when they stopped alternate attendance I knew what it meant for us."

"· · ·"

"What's to become of the honjin and headman's office, Hanzo?"

"Yes, that's really it. Well, we've got word that the honjin, toiya, and assistant headman are to stay as they are for the time being. But that's just for the time being, so I suppose the reforms will affect them too."

When he heard that reply, Kichizaemon just looked steadily at Hanzo and said nothing for a while.

"But you must be tired today, father. Please lie down," Hanzo continued.

"Yes, you should. It takes a lot out of you to hear things like this," said Oman.

"Well, I think I will. Recently I've been going to bed as soon as it gets dark. I seem to affect Oman. As soon as I lie down she lies down too."

Kichizaemon laughed. Then he put his arms into the fresh lined silk nightgown that Oman brought him. As Hanzo watched, he tied the thin sash and sat on top of his bedding. There in his quarters in the second floor rear, at age seventy-one, he had already lived a year longer than had been predicted by a fortune teller.

"Look at this, Hanzo," said Oman. "I made this for your father this year. I made the lining of silk, too. Up to now, he has always insisted on cotton nightwear. 'Soft nightwear is too fine for a headman. Cotton is good enough for me.' That's what he always said. I'm telling you, even when he went down to the village shrine he would always insist on carrying his old purse lined with calico. But I told him, when you get to be seventy, it's all right for you to wear something soft to bed. Right? But he just wouldn't hear of it. He finally gave in just this year."

Such concern on the part of Oman helped to soften Kichizaemon's sadness. Sitting on the bed, Kichizaemon pulled the pillow to him and laid it on his knees.

"Well, I'm glad I got out to see Kimbei. Tomorrow or the next day I'd like to take Okume and Sota over to sweep the graves."

As Kichizaemon spoke, it was apparent not only that he was remembering the approaching anniversary of the death of his own father, but that the new graves of his granddaughters Onatsu and Omari were also very much on his mind.

"I'm always thinking about these things, but I never get around to them."

7

At the beginning of the sixth month, Hanzo learned of the impending return of the Owari domains to imperial control. He brought the news from the offices at Fukushima directly to his father to discuss it with him. The proclamation was simple:

> On the matter of the return of lands to the emperor—we have taken current conditions under deep consideration and have consulted widely, and we now announce our intentions to carry out this policy.

This had come out from the executive offices of the new government and that implied that it had the consent of the emperor. It was accompanied by another document from the Fukushima offices ordering that this be made known throughout all the villages. It had come to Hanzo in his capacity as headman.

The reforms that had already put an end to the barrier at Fukushima and eliminated the Fukushima deputy, the category of assisting districts, the transport offices, the village meeting rooms, and toiya fees had now come to this. Although the han of southern Kyushu had accepted in principle the return of their lands to the emperor, Owari had gone ahead of them in putting the principle into actual practice. This was not without good reason. It was by no means strange that Owari, as one of the three cadet branches of the Tokugawa, should be moved to set an example of righteous adherence to the national polity, an example to be taken note of by Mito, Kii, and the ordinary daimyo. Nor was it strange, at the time when Tokugawa Yoshinobu resigned the office of shogun and returned political power to the emperor, that it was Owari who advised him to yield up his vast lands and who stood at the head of the imperial forces asking for the surrender of Edo castle.

"Here's another notice, father. It says that Lord Tokugawa has been named governor of Nagoya han."

"That makes him milord the governor, right?"

"That's right, at least to begin with. They wouldn't be doing away with the toiya and the meeting rooms and then leaving themselves to go on as before."

Kichizaemon listened to Hanzo, nodding as his son spoke, but his eyes were filled with tears.

By the seventh month, Kichizaemon was not getting out of bed any longer. He had had another stroke. Inert in his bed, he heard of Otami's safe delivery in the middle of the month and that his new grandson looked strong and healthy, but he himself was eating less and less. This continued until the beginning of the eighth month. In the end, all the care that Oman and Hanzo could provide had proved unavailing. Surrounded by his wife, his son, and his grandchildren, he ended his life of seventy-one years in that bed. It was the fourth day of the eighth month, in the sixth hour of the evening.

That night, Kichizaemon's body was moved from the retirement quarters to the inner room of the main house. Eikichi and Shosuke, and later, Inosuke, came running directly to the honjin as soon as they heard of the death. Inosuke had just that moment returned from a meeting in Fukushima at a new bureau called the national office of production, which had been founded by the new government to encourage commerce, and he was still out of breath. When Hanzo saw the master of the Fushimiya come running up, he felt the occasion still more deeply and he was moved to reflect on his father, who had sunk into death like a setting sun.

Early the next morning, all the tenants who had been obligated to Kichizaemon when he was alive were at work in the hearth room and at the service entrance. It was the custom of the tenants to come to help on every occasion, happy or sad, talking together and eating together. Now they had to work with Hanzo, Eikichi, and Seisuke and consult with Oman and Otami to see that Kichizaemon had a funeral worthy of a honjin. Hanzo had wanted to give his father a Shinto burial, but the relationship between the Aoyama family and the Mampukuji was old and deep and Oman had her heart set on burying her husband there. He soon agreed to go along with her wishes. Above all he wanted this funeral to memorialize his father's long service on the highway. He told Inosuke and Oman that he wanted the ceremony to be as solemn and memorable as possible. When the coffin was at last prepared, old friends and relatives from the neighboring post stations came to spend the night in mourning. Juheiji and Tokuemon came over from Tsumago and Katsushige came up from Ochiai.

Candles burned quietly throughout the day on the desk in the inner room. It being the Kiso, there was no shortage of wood. The coffin was made of thick, unseasoned lumber. Inside it, all the things needed for a Buddhist funeral were placed. The white hempen shroud that Oman and the other women had sewn for Kichizaemon, the rosary, the little bag containing his personal effects, a traveler's hat, straw sandals, and the staff that he had used in his final years. This latter had been brought in by Okume and included at her insistence. Oman came to the side of the coffin and folded Kichizaemon's hands on his breast. With his heavy eyebrows, his quiet mouth, and his big honjin nose, Kichizaemon looked more at peace than he ever had in life. Despite the crush of people who had gathered around the coffin to take their leave, Hanzo did not forget his children. Sota had just reached the age where he was able to understand. He was sitting in the corner of the room, arms folded, apparently lost in thoughts of his grandfather's death. Okume, who had been particularly loved by her grandfather, had wept until her eyes were rimmed in red and had gone and hidden herself away in the hallway leading to the inner courtyard.

Juheiji's wife, Osato, came with her eight-year-old foster child Masaki, Hanzo's second son, arriving from Tsumago in the evening. After dark Hanzo met the assistant priest who had come to represent the Mampukuji in the inner room and gathered with everyone else before the coffin. They listened to the chanting of a sutra. Among the remembrances of Kichizaemon that came up later, Hanzo spoke of how gentle he had been to the tenant farmers, how he had eaten almost nothing in the last three days before he died, how one morning he had suddenly felt better. Saying that he was ready to eat anything, Kichizaemon had wondered if he would ever get to taste one of the local yellow raspberries again. He had called his grandchildren in and would not let them leave. That had been his last day. Hanzo spoke of how his father had written beautifully and distinctively, of how he himself had never managed to duplicate his father's writing with his own clumsy hand, but that Okume seemed to have inherited her grandfather's talent. He also spoke of how his father had been fond of composing haikai in the Mino style, of how he had been asked to read him a section from one of the anthologies before his death, and of how sad his father had been as he listened. He had finally said, "Hanzo, I'm going."

Inosuke responded.

"Well, our Kimbei said this: 'When Kichizaemon came up to the Upper Fushimiya, he talked for a long time. I didn't realize it at the time, but now that I look back at it, I see that he had come to take his leave of the world.' "

Kichizaemon's remains were brought to the front door of the honjin in the afternoon of the next day. Those who would not be accompanying him to the temple were asked by Seisuke to see the rest off from the main gate. It was mostly the housewives and old women from the neighborhood who were gathered there.

"Oshimo!"

"Yes!"

"Hurry up and come over!"

"Yes!"

The mother of Kenkichi, the tenant farmer, ran over unsteadily when she was called. Even this deaf old woman seemed to be recalling Kichizaemon's life and she had come to pay her respects. Inosuke's wife, Otomi, was also in the group, rosary in hand.

The farmer Sosaku came pushing through the crowd in search of Hanzo. He led in one of the youths who had been tending the watchfire at the main gate.

"Master, this is the grandson of your old nurse, Ofuki. He's been over in Yamaguchi village for a long time and you probably don't remember him, but just look at how big he has gotten! I would like for you to let him join us today. That's why I brought him over."

Soon the funeral procession formed up and began to move along the road to the temple. Kichizaemon's body was preceded by a pair of white paper lanterns borne high. Hanzo came next, then Kameya Eikichi, Fushimiya Inosuke, Umeya Gosuke, Masudaya Kozaemon, Horaiya Shinsuke, Kyurobei and Shosuke and Heibei, and finally Juheiji of the Tsumago honjin and his assistant, Tokuemon. All were wearing pilgrim's hats and straw sandals. Only Otami remained behind with her newborn son, Morio, but Oman, Okisa, and Osato all came out and Okume could be seen among her elders, her rich, heavy hair unornamented and tied up in a simple roll.

The procession turned right from the main highway toward the hill on which the Mampukuji stood. There Katsushige and Seisuke left the ranks and went ahead to the temple to prepare to receive the rest of the procession. A funeral director from a nearby village had already arrived at the temple. The priest Sho'un received Katsushige and Seisuke as though he had been waiting impatiently and put out seats for them between the main hall and the reliquary.

"I'll let you keep charge of the guest book, Katsushige."

But without waiting for Seisuke's instructions, Katsushige had already set up an old desk there and was diligently recording the day's events.

They were seated in a long narrow hallway running from the temple hearth room, in which assistant priests were coming and going, to the dark stained wooden door leading into the main hall of the temple at the other end. They could also see into the inner guest room past an intervening, dimly lighted room. Katsushige took up his position there and as the mourners came in, he wrote their names in the guest book, reflecting on the range of Kichizaemon's acquaintances. After a brief wait, the coffin arrived before the main hall. Around Katsushige people were walking up and down the hallway, waving their fans as they went.

From time to time, Seisuke came to look at the guest book, as though to see who had come from Yamaguchi, or from Yubunezawa, or from Ochiai or Nakatsugawa. Katsushige turned over the pages, pointing out that people from Mino seemed to be in the majority, and telling of a fellow haikai poet who had come all the way from Mino to mourn Kichizaemon. Then he added:

"Don't work so hard, Seisuke. Take a little rest. You know I was really surprised when I came up to Magome this time to see how big my master's children have gotten to be. They're really growing up. That's what I noticed first. When I was living at the master's house, Okume was just a little thing that I used to take up and hold on my knee."

Just then the three children under discussion came out into the hallway of the temple. Masaki, over from Tsumago for the day, was particularly unable to stay still. He seemed curious about the Magome temple, and guided by Okume and Sota, both of whom he had not seen for a long time, he went out to look into the main hall where the great drum hung, then at the room where the name tablets of the deceased were displayed, and at the sliding panels at the side of the main hall which had been illustrated by the Magome artist Rankei. He then went out to the outer hallway to look at the garden so painstakingly maintained by the priest Sho'un. Okume was charming in her white tabi as she led her lively little brother through the hallway again and again.

It was almost time for the ceremony to begin. The aged Kimbei was one of those who had come to the temple early to await the arrival of the coffin, and he came out of the ritual room with Inosuke and bowed before Katsushige. The old man, freshly shaved and with his hair drawn up tightly, looked much younger than his age as he moved down the hallway toward the main hall, assisted by Inosuke. He seemed lost in thought as he moved along with short, mincing steps.

"Ka!"

As the ceremony in the temple drew to an end, the priest Sho'un startled the mourners with a mighty shout that seemed to come from some hitherto unknown part of his body. The parting that he gave before the remains of this traveler who had just left the world expressed the long years of training and preparation that this Zen priest had undergone.

The ceremony ended and everyone finished lighting incense. Hanzo expressed his thanks to those who had come to the funeral and left the main hall together with the others who would be going off to the graveyard. Near the bell tower that stood beside the great gingko tree, Hanzo parted with the mourners from the immediate neighborhood. Beside the stone bearing the inscription "Stone of the Supreme Sutras," he left Kimbei. There were several stone images of Kannon standing in a row at the bottom of the stone stairway leading downward from the temple gates. Here he parted from those who would be returning to Toge and Aramachi.

Preparations for burial had been made in the graveyard on the slope of the hill. Sakichi came out to meet Hanzo at the entrance to the graveyard. He reported that the grave was of a certain depth and width and that it would serve well to hold the coffin of the master. The sharp scent of freshly turned soil struck into Hanzo's nostrils. This was the resting place where seventeen generations of the Aoyama family slept, beginning with the founder of the village. The soil was heaped high and the paving of the surrounding graves was buried by it.

Hanzo waited for the other people to gather. Oman and her party came down the narrow trail, carrying a basin of consecrated water, flowers, and smoking sticks of incense. They gathered in the graveyard. Others were walking down among the cedar trees, looking at the view out over the village to Mt. Ena. Still others walked about among the moss-covered graves.

"Every time I see them, these graves of our ancestors look good to me," Juheiji said to Hanzo. Here was the memorial for Aoyama Dosai, who had founded the Mampukuji. On the ancient gravestone were deeply incised the characters MAMPUKUJI DENSHO-OKU JOKYU ZENJOMON. Every time they visited the grave, this ancestor seemed to be gazing patiently out over the village he had founded.

"This is really how the grave of a person of long ago should be," said Juheiji once more.

At some time, Sho'un had arrived to stand behind Hanzo but if it had not been for the soft voice chanting sutras, Hanzo would never have realized he was there. Soon the new grave marker was borne in under Seisuke's careful direction and it was time for the burial.

The tenant farmers who had left their work in the fields to come and assist in the funeral began to argue about which way the head of the coffin should be pointing. Some said the tradition was that the head should be to the north and so they had no choice but to arrange things that way. Others said that since it was a Buddhist ceremony, the head had to be to the west. The grave was on a slope looking out over the back of the village and in the end there was nothing to do but place the coffin in the position the site demanded.

"Ready with the ropes?"

"Get a good grip!"

The farmers bent to their task. The coffin was quietly lowered into the grave. The dirt that Sakichi pulled in with his mattock came rattling down on the cover. Everyone from Oman down to her grandson Masaki threw in clods of earth and through the efforts of those closest to him, Kichizaemon was buried deep in the ground.

In the evening after the funeral, all those who had been close to Kichizaemon were invited to the honjin. As was the custom in the Aoyama household, not only were the leading men from the neighborhood invited to the traditional meal of buckwheat noodles, but even the tenant farmers whom Kichizaemon had favored in life.

It was not the custom in those days to keep close track of time. Even though Sakichi was sent out from the honjin to urge them on, the guests were late in coming. Juheiji and his wife, Osato, would be spending the night with Hanzo, along with Tokuemon and Katsushige. While they were waiting for the evening guests, Hanzo took Juheiji out to the veranda of the inner room to talk as they looked out into the gathering dusk of the courtyard.

It had become clear to Hanzo that it was not simply his father who had just been buried. Just as the great earthquakes of Ansei had not stopped with one or two shocks, the elimination of alternate attendance had marked the beginning of a vast avalanche of change engulfing the shogunate. As the violent upheavals shook society time after time, everything that the cautious Tokugawa age had created was being buried as Hanzo watched.

After a while, Hanzo was called away from Juheiji by the members of his family. A courier had brought him several messages. They had to do with the fact that the rice which was to be imported into the Kiso and which had had to be bought with contributions levied by the Fukushima offices, since the new currency was not being accepted, had now arrived in the neighboring station of Nakatsugawa. There was word of another farmers' uprising to the west. At a time when there was no telling just when or in what form the resentment of those who opposed the reform of the post system would burst out, it even seemed pitiful that the Fukushima officials who were themselves threatened by these changes would go so far as to put out their own money to buy rice to try to save the situation.

"I've been feeling low ever since the elimination of the toiya," Hanzo thought to himself. "With a world full of hope right before my eyes, I'm wilting away—what a fool I must be."

Hanzo went back to where Juheiji was. They were both honjin and they were both headmen. What caused him concern also caused concern for Juheiji.

"Was it a courier, Hanzo?"

"Yes. It was about post station business. The rice from Oi is starting to come in."

"Isn't Nagoya han about to become Nagoya prefecture? And when that happens, they say the district offices in Fukushima will be called the Fukushima local offices. They say that Tsuchiya Sozo, the person who will come up to take charge, is the finance commissioner of Owari. If that's the kind of man who will be taking over local government here, we can expect some big changes."

"And if you consider how Owari is returning all its lands to the emperor, then our surrender of the toiya and the meeting room is really a small thing."

"I suppose so."

"But anyway, don't you think that as long as you are going to smash something up, you should go ahead and smash it up completely?"

"You're a Hirata man, Hanzo, so you can be expected to say that kind of thing."

"But how can there be any possibility of a real renewal otherwise?"

"Maybe so, but you're going to have to accept the fact that on the day when they really smash things up, as you put it, you're going to go down yourself, right along with the honjin and the toiya. If that happens, you'll find it fortunate that you have your religious beliefs. But we'll just have to wait and see how the new government handles things. I'm not sure of anything yet."

Then Sho'un and the senior benefactors of the temple began to take their seats and the conversation was ended. The sliding panels had been removed from the inner room, the middle room, and the connecting room and the guests were seated in all three rooms. Some of the guests had walked seven or eight miles to attend the funeral and they were staying overnight in the Fushimiya or the Mampukuji. Servants bearing lanterns were sent out for them. The carpenter who did work for the honjin came, as did the tatami maker. Naoji the hairdresser was getting old now, but this same Naoji who had brought his oil-stained work box over to shave Kichizaemon's beard right up to the very end also came, wearing formal dress and with a solemn expression on his face.

Eikichi sat before Sho'un, Tokuemon had Seisuke before him, and Katsushige sat before the guests who had come from Mino. Sake was served.

"Well, let's all drink to each other tonight. I'll drink too."

Hanzo stepped out impulsively and sat before the serving trays of Inosuke and Juheiji, who were sitting side by side.

"I'm amazed that you were able to make such preparations under the circumstances," said Inosuke as he drank. Even on such occasions Inosuke could be counted on to sit quietly looking at his serving tray and to note appreciatively the shape of the sake cup on it. Hanzo spoke again as he offered a second cup of sake to each.

"We've been doing things very simply lately, in keeping with the times, but this once we wanted to do things as they had been done when father was living. That's what we had in mind."

Hanzo offered the cup he had received from Inosuke to Juheiji.

"This sake is from the Fushimiya, Juheiji. Drink as much as you want tonight."

By the light of the huge candles placed here and there throughout the three rooms, the people of the village who had been invited to the memorial dinner began to eat. As he looked out over the guests, Hanzo began to nibble nervously at an appetizer of eggplant seasoned with peppers, bean paste, and miso. Coming in from the kitchen, one course after another, were vegetables in ground sesame and white miso, tofu topped with sweet bean paste, omelettes, and so on, each served in appropriate dishes that had come down from Kichizaemon's time. There was also a stew of small tubers, oak mushrooms, and lotus root.

As Hanzo passed among the guests exchanging cup after cup of sake, the sound of a sudden shower of rain came up. It was a late summer shower that could be heard in the courtyard. By the time it passed, Hanzo had exchanged cups with the carpenter and with Naoji, the hair dresser.

"Exchange cups with me, too," said Otora, who had come in her son's place. She was from a tenant family that had been with the Aoyama house for generations.

"Pardon me for saying so, but your father was fond of having guests in like this. He often had people of the village in for sake. He was really a generous man," said Otora. Kenkichi and Sosaku were sitting there also. Hanzo took the cup from Otora, drained it, and presented it to Kenkichi and then to Sosaku.

"Now then, everybody! My father left a memento to everyone who has ever passed over our threshold. They are all ready."

"That's the kind of person he was," said Otora, now in high spirits, and taking great care to show the glistening black teeth which she had touched up just for the occasion. The old woman, so fond of her sake, put down the cup and, rubbing her face, kept repeating over and over that she would never be able to forget the time of Kichizaemon.

Hanzo's hands and face grew flushed from the sake. He became quite drunk that night, something very unusual for him. The buckwheat noodles were served to each guest and when people began to get up to leave, his eyes were vague and unfocused. Eventually, he slipped out to the edge of the hall-way of the inner room and collapsed. He scarcely remembered Katsushige coming to help him.

CHAPTER SEVEN

1

IN ITS EAGERNESS to greet the new age in accordance with "international law" the new government had even done away with the old calendar and adopted the solar calendar used by the other nations of the world. The date was therefore April of 1873, the sixth year of Meiji. By that time, Kichizaemon of the Magome honjin was no longer in this world and even his hardy contemporary Kimbei, at the age of seventy-three, had entered the ranks of the departed. If those two could have seen how rapidly the Kiso road was changing, they would surely have been startled. It was now an age in which the four social classes were declared to be equal. The old customs requiring subordinates to kneel on the ground when speaking to persons of high rank had been eliminated, and even commoners were permitted to take surnames and to ride horses. Everyone had become proud and haughty. This was particularly true of the packhorse men from Ina, who were no longer content merely to lead their packhorses. They would allow their animals to choke the roads, blocking traffic and causing trouble for everyone else. But the old spirit of discipline in highway matters still remained. Notices would be sent down saying that it had come to the attention of the authorities that some of the packhorse men and ox drovers were walking through the stations with lighted pipes in their mouths. They were ordered to correct their behavior. The difficulty that the new authorities had in dealing with the forces boiling up from below was revealed in such petty details. The time had come when even people who had been treated as subhuman outcasts could walk about boldly. Some were only too happy to be admitted to the ranks of commoners. Others felt that if they were now to be counted among that class, they could ignore the debts they had incurred. The force of such feelings swept over the country like a flood and no one could remain unaffected. The age of the military houses was a thing of the past. Everything from the feudal order was crumbling to dust.

In the villages along the highway there was no longer a honjin or an assistant honjin. Nor was there any social distinction made between landed and landless farmers. The custom of maintaining a distinct class from which village officials were drawn was dropped, and the offices of headman, village elder, and assistant headman were all eliminated, along with the special ration of six koku of unpolished rice that had been granted to the headmen ever since the Kyoho era in the early eighteenth century. The headmen themselves were given the less imposing title of "manager," and it was decided that transportation along the highways would be handled by a commercial land transport company. With this step the problem of moving men and horses that had occasioned so much agony and exhaustion in the past was at last resolved.

These changes followed upon the general breakup of institutions that accompanied the government's proclamation of the abolition of the han. Some of the old han, obsessed with protecting samurai privileges, had encouraged a mass movement of colonists to Hokkaido, hitherto a land populated only by savages. A law of general conscription had been passed in the twelfth month of the previous year, completely destroying the old basis of samurai influence. No longer could the samurai boast of any exclusive privileges, not even in military affairs.

All this had taken place during the past three years, and the force of the disruptions was severe. People who had been dependent on daimyo or bannerman patronage for support in some art or skill now shared the fate of their masters. The effects gradually reached even into the Kiso. It was not at all unusual for a No actor who had once been the head of a major school to appear at the Magome summit as part of a band of wandering entertainers.

In this social chaos it was entirely due to the work of Tsuchiya Sozo that the people of the region were able to understand something of the direction of the new government's policies. In Fukushima, where many were still smarting from the elimination of the barrier, relative calm had been maintained. People like Tsuchiya, who had been transferred from his post as finance commissioner of Owari to head up the office of local administration in the Kiso valley, and who was to be long remembered for his virtuous and capable government, were rare. From the time he took charge as director of the Nagoya prefectural office in Fukushima to the time he turned over supervision of the local office to Chikuma prefecture—that is, from the autumn of 1870 until the second month of 1872—was something less than two years. Those two years were the best time that the people of the Kiso had ever known. The establishment of complaint boxes, the explanation of the new press laws, the reforms of the family register system, and the establishment of a mail system all took place during this period. Sozo also encouraged the planting of Irish potatoes, which would grow well even in the cool mountains or on marginal soil, to help break the cycle of crop failures to which the Kiso had always been subject. He encouraged silkworm culture and brought in silk reeling machinery. He permitted the people who lived by trading in cattle and horses to operate without special licenses, and he took special measures to discourage anyone who robbed or intimidated the poor. He even ordered dubious mountain priests who had not already given up their religious pretensions to return to farming. Altogether the number of useful measures he enacted was beyond counting. But, on the seventeenth day of the second month of 1872, he ordered all the headmen to come to Fukushima to hear an explanation of the transfer of lands to Chikuma prefecture. About the time the local people were beginning to concern themselves with getting all the children into school, Sozo was forced to bid farewell to the people of the Kiso. He had not had time to work with them on education.

In those days everything was an experiment. When the solar calendar was adopted, the old day divided into six hours of daytime and six hours of night was replaced by the twenty-four hour day. The months now came almost a full month earlier than under the old calendar. The beginning of the twelfth month was proclaimed as the end of the lunar calendar and the beginning of the new solar year came immediately afterward.

The renewal of mind and spirit had reached even to the calendar. And yet, to the farmers who had always timed the opening of pasture lands or the sowing of seed according to their own special reckoning, the fact that in the old calendar the first of the month always coincided with the new moon and the fifteenth with the full moon was not without meaning. To the villagers, who could not feel that they were greeting the new year properly unless they went by the old calendar, the new system meant that New Year's was celebrated twice in the same year. Most people put up new and old calendars side by side on their soot-stained walls. Without knowing that April first of the new calendar corresponded to some time in the third month of the old calendar, they were unable to feel that spring had come, and would lose all sense of the seasons.

That year, 1873, the third of April brought the newly established festival of Jimmu Tenno, the first emperor, to the Kiso for the first time. Everyone was to rest from work, drink ceremonial sake, and celebrate. The directive came to the villages under the name of the vice-governor of Chikuma prefecture. The brilliant national flags rising high over the stone-weighted shingled roofs was yet another scene never before witnessed in these mountains.

Otami, no longer the wife of a headman, but the wife of a village manager who was also in charge of the schools, took advantage of the holiday to visit her brother in Tsumago. Of course she did not travel alone. In the second month of the previous year, a fourth son had been born and she took the young child Wasuke and her maid Otoku along with her. Before them lay the road from Magome into the interior. Plum trees were blooming in the hedges. They looked up to see the flags waving over the mountain houses as they walked the five miles of road to Otami's childhood home.

2

Otami had something she wished to discuss with her brother and her grandmother in Tsumago. The plans for Okume's marriage were already well under way. They had made arrangements through the good offices of Oman to marry Okume to a certain Inaba in the village of Minami Tono in Ina, Oman's old home. During the winter the betrothal gifts had come in from Minami Tono and by February of that year they were already discussing the date for the ceremony. Otami was going to Tsumago to tell her brother and grandmother about it and to ask their advice.

Otami was already the mother of five children. Between her second son, Masaki, now living in Tsumago, and her third son, Morio, she had lost two daughters in infancy, so she had borne seven children in all. She was no longer sentimental about her old home. All the same, now that she was back in Tsumago at her grandmother's side, she felt as though she still belonged there. Juheiji had just gone out with Masaki to invite his neighbor Tokuemon along on an outing in the mountains. Her grandmother, aged but still vigorous, was in the front garden of the honjin, drying home-dyed yarns with Osato. They were apparently preparing to weave some yellow Hachijo fabric to be made into men's underclothing, and the rich burnished gold of the yarn drying in the breeze caught Otami's attention. As people in these mountains had long done, the grandmother had gone out and picked wild pears and then had pounded their skins off with a wooden mallet. After drying in the sun, the skins were boiled and the liquid used to dye the thread. The old woman took charge of all sewing, weaving, and dyeing in this house. Otami, on this rare visit home to consult about her daughter, Okume, could not but recall her own girlhood days.

The grandmother, Osato, and Otami retired to the high-ceilinged hearth room. Beside the darkly gleaming main pillar, they began to talk about their children. Osato and Juheiji had had no children of their own for years after their marriage and for that reason Masaki had been adopted from Magome, but eventually a girl was born. She was named Kotoji. Now in her third year, Kotoji could already talk quite well, but Wasuke could neither speak nor walk. He crawled about on the tatami like a cicada just out of the chrysalis.

"Hello!"

When Kotoji spoke to him with her girlish certainty, Wasuke came crawling over to bow to her. It was hard to know how he had learned this but he was always bowing his head on every occasion. He went over to bow to the grandmother and then to Osato. Such actions from a child still wearing a blank, infantile stare made everyone laugh.

"That's enough now!" said Otami, and Wasuke bowed again.

"Are you still nursing him, Otami?" asked the grandmother. "You can feed him rice, too, as soon as he is born. This is the most dangerous time for them. You really can't take your eyes off them for a minute."

Being mothers had changed both Otami and Osato. The sickly, childless, discouraged Osato now showed a matronly solidity of flesh. She was no longer the unchanging, girlish person to whom Otami had long been accustomed. Otami herself was completely taken up with her children and scarcely had time to notice anything else. She was much more concerned that her children should not catch cold than she was with the problem of access to the

forests that was keeping her husband so busy even though it affected the livelihood of all the thirty-three villages of the Kiso.

Juheiji and Masaki came in from outdoors, both of them wearing baggy
mountain-style trousers. When Juheiji, just starting to untie the cord of his
trousers, caught sight of Otami, he simply said, "You're here," his usual
greeting to her.

Like Hanzo, Juheiji was now a village manager. In the near future, Chikuma prefecture was going to consolidate the village administrations into a
new system of large and small subdivisions. That morning, Juheiji had been
called into the planning as the head of the eighth major district and his good
spirits came in part from that. He also had his delightful daughter Kotoji and
the pleasure of being accompanied by Masaki wherever he went. Masaki had
grown. He was twelve years old. Juheiji told Otami that he planned to send
the boy to Fukushima to enter the academy of Owaki Jisho so that he might
become a worthy successor.

The fashion for wearing short hair in the European style had not yet
reached Tsumago. It still looked strange to most people in the mountains,
but on this visit Otami found that her brother had already had his hair cut.

"How do you think it looks on me, Otami?" he asked.

Then Juheiji asked after Hanzo.

"I wish you could just come over and see how busy he is. He's so frantic
running around he scarcely has time to shave. Whenever I ask him what it's
about, he just says it's something to do with the forest problem and I can't
follow it at all."

"Hanzo is really going all out on this. He has talked with me about it and
of course I am completely in favor of it, but it would be better if Tsuchiya
Sozo were still here."

"That's what my husband seems to think too."

"Well, when Nagoya prefecture established a local office in Fukushima and
set out to govern us directly, their tone was one of kindness, instruction, and
leadership. Tsuchiya Sozo came over to assume his duties here and immediately brought a party of six officials along with him to check on the opening
of new fields and the like. They inspected everything from Niekawa to
Magome.

"I'll never forget the time I guided Tsuchiya over to the boundary marker.
Since we breed horses in the Kiso, in each village he asked the age of all the
horses, their bloodlines, their color, and the names of their owners. After
that survey, he sent a circular around to all the villages, and then a second
one. Even though he didn't make any issue of lodging and said he would be
content with whatever was at hand, many of the villages went overboard in
preparations to entertain him. His second notice said that since improprieties
can so easily occur when an official travels, he did not want to be entertained
in this way in the future. That was in the ninth month of Meiji 3, when
Kikuchi, the head of the transport office, was out here on business. No matter what you say, Tsuchiya's time here was a good one for us. The person
who came out from Chikuma prefecture in his place is making a big show of

his authority, as if he wanted to give us a basis for distinguishing good and evil.

"Even if the reform of the land tax does get under way, there won't be much coming out of it with all these excesses. I'm telling you, Otami, no matter how hard Hanzo works on this forest problem, no matter what he goes through for this region, the new commissioner from Chikuma prefecture is not going to change one bit. I think it's hopeless . . .''

3

The same evidence of destruction so noticeable at Magome was also to be found at the Tsumago honjin. With a little time before the evening meal, Otami walked through the rooms of the honjin with her brother. It too had an entrance hall and a chamber of honor, two things that were to be seen only in a honjin until the restoration. Once it had eliminated the office of honjin, the new government went on to permit ordinary inns to construct entrance halls and chambers of honor. The honjin building which up to then had served as a lodging for official or military travelers now looked as though it had removed its armor and fittings and was taking a rest.

Otami went out to the entrance hall with Juheiji. In the wood-floored section that she remembered from childhood, there was no longer any trace of military encampment. There were no longer any daimyo to be brought up to it in shaded palanquins, nor was there any need for the great curtains with the crests of the dignitary lodged within that used to be put up outside. The broad, wood-floored area was now a playroom for the children. And where the ancient lances that had come down from the Aoyama ancestors used to stand, Osato now stored her loom.

They went to the chamber of honor. There was no way of counting up all the men of rank who had slept in that room at one time or another during the confusion and frantic movement that had begun with the arrival of the Black Ships at Uraga. Some of these men had been going to take up new duties. Others had been rushing back home. Now this room too was unused. Even the Korean-style edgings of the mats with their black cloud patterns woven on a white ground were stained with mildew.

"Otami, what do you use the chamber of honor for at your place?"

"My husband has made it into a shrine dedicated to Ubusuna. He makes me take the children in there to worship every morning."

"That sounds like Hanzo's place, all right."

They continued to talk for a while longer.

"Come see this, too," said Juheiji as he led Otami through the wooden door at the service entrance into the garden. All the outbuildings that had belonged to the honjin had been torn down—the meeting room, the toiya, the additional lodgings. Other than the main building, the storehouse, and a shed or two, there was nothing left but the flat stones on which the pillars of the buildings had stood. Beyond the storehouse a mulberry field had been planted, and here and there one could also see young paulownia saplings.

Otami searched her memory.

"When was it that you were over at our place? You leaned your hands over the edge of the brazier and said, 'Otami, there won't be a honjin or an assistant honjin much longer.' I couldn't believe what you were saying then. Even when the hundredth day after father's death came, I still couldn't believe that you really meant it. But within a year, at our place too, there was nothing left but the main house. All the new buildings were torn down. They tied ropes to the main pillars and pulled everything down in a heap. It made a terrible noise. I can still hear them cutting up the pillars with their big saws and axes."

That evening Otami put Wasuke to bed early and joined her grandmother and Osato in Juheiji's room. She informed them that she had come to discuss Okume's wedding plans.

This was the story that Otami began telling them, prefacing it with the remark that they may have heard it already in Tsumago. Originally, there was a family to which Okume had been betrothed since early childhood by agreement of the parents. But now, the elimination of the honjin, headmen, and toiya had changed the status of her daughter, and since the relationships between the two households could no longer be maintained on the same basis as before, the other party had asked to be relieved of their promise to Okume. From that time on, Okume began to say that she did not want to go anywhere in marriage. But Hanzo, with strong backing from Oman, insisted that girls had to get married. They could not go on serving their fathers forever. Nor could they get by on the scholarship that Okume loved. So they had worked out an agreement to marry her to the family in Minami Tono village.

Oman had expended no small effort in making these arrangements. The Inaba family was the one into which she had been born, and she was enthusiastic from the beginning. When the arrangements were completed, she wrote a long letter saying that nothing in her life had ever pleased her as much as concluding this arrangement with her old home. Hanzo of course was the kind of person who would say, "Anyone who will not listen to what her own grandmother says is no daughter of mine." He had never gone against Oman in anything.

Okume could not refuse this marriage that her grandmother wanted so much. The go-between had already come over from Ina twice in February to ask that a date be set, saying that any month would be suitable except for the fifth, sixth, seventh, and eighth. The Aoyama family then chose the coming September as it seemed likely that Hanzo would have a little time then. But Okume had quite unexpectedly fallen into a state of deep depression and Otami was very much aware of it.

"Anyway, my husband can think of nothing else but that other matter. Once he starts thinking about the Kiso forests, he scarcely sleeps at night. I can hardly stand to watch it. He just says that the wedding is already settled and he will leave the details up to us. But how can he not be worried about Okume?"

"But wasn't this marriage agreed upon in the spring of last year? That's more than a year ago. Weren't things already settled then?" asked Juheiji.

"I knew you would say that," responded Otami. "Once the agreement was reached they informed us that they would have the robe of assent woven and send it directly to Kyoto for dyeing. Don't you know that first you weave it, then you dye it, and then you send it to the other party? That's when the agreement becomes final."

"It's just not as simple as you men say. You have to weave it first," added the grandmother.

"If you ask me," Juheiji resumed, "this whole thing has been dragging on a little too long. You ought to have done it and gotten it over with. It doesn't matter whether the girl cries or not—everybody should get together and push it through. That's the way to handle it. The first thing you know there will be a cute little baby."

"How old is Okume now?" asked the grandmother.

"She's seventeen."

"Really? That old?" replied the grandmother, staring at Otami. "But then she'd have to be, because it will soon be three years since Kichizaemon died."

"Well, I guess none of us should be surprised that we are getting older," added Osato.

"It looks as though Okume has something holding her back," said Juheiji.

"That's just it," Otami replied. "If you mean that she can't forget the person she was first engaged to, it doesn't seem to be that at all."

"Then what is it? How is she acting?" asked the grandmother.

"No matter what I ask her, she just keeps her head down and says nothing."

"There's no telling what the problem might be. It's often that way with bright young people."

"We've really produced a strange girl. At that age, paying no attention to anything but the shrine—she's just exactly like her father."

"All the same, Otami, she's a fine looking girl."

Juheiji was trying to end the evening's conversation on a bright note. Otami, too, unable to admit that she had really come to seek the advice of her brother and grandmother, pursued the matter no further.

Magome stood on top of a silent pass, but the roar of the Kiso river is often quite audible in Tsumago. For the first time in a very long time, that sound lulled Otami to sleep beside her child that night.

4

The next morning a new signboard hung out over the highway in front of Juheiji's house:

Shinano Province, Tsumago Station, Mail Service
Aoyama Juheiji

Otami had never seen such a sign before. A villager who had recently become a mail carrier came in with a businesslike air about him. The parlor was set aside as the mail room and a new octagonal clock was hanging on the wall, ticking away very loudly.

Juheiji put the little bit of mail that was still being collected into bags and sent it off to the next station. He noted the precise time that it was handed over to the mail carrier with exactly the same punctiliousness that he had earlier applied to his duties as toiya. After that he put on the formal trousers appropriate to his other role as village manager and made preparations to go off to the manager's office.

"Well, there's really nothing to the mail business yet. Nobody quite believes that a letter will actually be delivered if you just stick a stamp on it and mail it. Most of them would still prefer to hire a courier. They think that mail is just something that goes out to disappear somewhere. It's really a pain."

Juheiji was in high spirits as he got ready to go out. While they were both village managers, Hanzo had been put in charge of schools for his second office and Juheiji had taken over the mail. Each was setting out along the new way in work that suited his character. The mail service had just been initiated in the Kiso and Otami was as yet unable to sense anything of his new calling in her brother's manner.

During this visit home, Otami was able to gain some perspective not only on her daughter Okume but also on her husband, Hanzo. The day after her arrival it began to rain in the afternoon. The sound of the April rains, seeming to issue an invitation to the flower buds, brought her to these thoughts. Hanzo seemed to have become a different person after the death of Kichizaemon. She could not say exactly what the changes within him were, nor just how his thoughts were now different, but at the very least the death of his father had been a crucial turning point in his life. Being with him made that much clear to her. It was perhaps not surprising that Hanzo, growing up under the domination of his stepmother, Oman, should sooner or later have undergone such a change. Thoughts such as these made Otami unusually sensitive to what people were saying, and she was very interested in hearing the impressions of the people in Tsumago.

"Otami! What a rare pleasure!"

Through the open doorway came a familiar voice from her childhood. It was Tokuemon, who had braved the rain to pay a call. Tokuemon was the one who had always sent fresh carp over with orders that they go to Otami.

With his office as assistant honjin eliminated, Tokuemon had retired from his long service to the highway. All the people of the village wanted him to stay on under Juheiji as assistant manager, but he resigned from that position also in favor of his patient and hard-working adopted son, Jitsuzo, to enter into a complete and serene retirement.

"How about it, Otami? Hasn't Tsumago changed?" he asked, sitting down in the hearth room that served in Juheiji's house as both dining room and reception room. Tokuemon liked to be near the fire even though the warm rains had come. He seemed like an uncle to Otami, and there was something about him that reminded her of Kichizaemon. The sight of him made her realize that such people were becoming rarer in the Kiso.

"Well, it ought to have changed," he continued. "We're in a time when the master of the honjin himself is perfectly willing to be the first to have a short haircut. When the manager has short hair like that, it wouldn't look right for his assistant to wear his hair long. That's what Jitsuzo said, and so he got his hair cut too, just a little while ago. The night before, he called in a hairdresser and had his hair put up—he made a big thing of it. He kept saying that this was his farewell to traditional hair style, and then he had it cut. By the way, is Hanzo still wearing his hair long?"

"Yes, he wears his hair long and he ties it up with a purple cord," Otami replied.

"Speaking of Hanzo reminds me now . . . Right! Right! I hear that the court did not accept his memorial on the calendar. He must have been quite disappointed. I heard it from Juheiji, you know."

Hanzo had poured heart and soul into the memorial on the calendar reform, arguing that there was no reason to change something so intimately bound up with the lives of the people as the calendar. He had maintained that this nation ought to have a calendar that suited its customs, and had asked the persons responsible for such decisions to consider this point. He insisted that such a calendar should begin on the first day of spring, and he proposed the name "imperial calendar" for it. Unfortunately, the authorities had not accepted his proposal for a new calendar because it could not easily be related to the calendar used throughout the rest of the world.

"I suppose so," Otami replied. "I can't really tell, but he did seem to be pretty disappointed about it."

At that time it was not unheard of for commoners to address a memorial to the throne. However, with the newly adopted solar calendar seemingly still on trial, Hanzo's memorial came to be the subject of local gossip. In this narrow mountain society, it was the memorial itself rather than its contents that was talked about, and the writing of such a memorial was generally looked upon as outside the normal range of behavior. Some even suggested that the disappointment had left Hanzo not quite right mentally.

When Juheiji came back from the manager's office, he found Tokuemon still talking with Otami. Suddenly becoming aware that her baby was crying, Otami took Wasuke from the maid and carried him into the middle room for a nap.

"From that time on, everyone began to say that Aoyama of Magome was an odd one," came Juheiji's voice.

"At any rate, that memorial was a big setback for him," said Tokuemon.

"It's just not right for everyone to be calling him eccentric. Hanzo himself keeps saying, 'I don't want people to be saying that I am odd,' " came Juheiji's voice again.

Otami leaned on one elbow as she nursed Wasuke. Playing with the tiny fingers that reached inside her clothing, she listened closely to the voices in the next room. The conversation about her husband continued. Juheiji, who appeared to be stubborn and backward, in fact accepted the new times and moved easily with them, while the old-fashioned Tokuemon neither welcomed nor despised the rapid changes of the age. They observed that Hanzo seemed to be a bit more confiding than he had been before but that he was still by no means what one would call a frank and open person. Juheiji, who had observed Hanzo from the time they had visited their distant relatives in Kugo until his present age of forty-two, said that he had not really changed a bit in all that time. They agreed that the more than four thousand Hirata followers throughout the nation had begun to come into their own when the Mito school became influential. Working with the Mito school for a revival of antiquity, they had certainly played an important, although largely hidden, role. Juheiji and Tokuemon further agreed that it remained to be seen just how well this National Learning that Keizo and Kozo of Nakatsugawa and Hanzo of Magome espoused could ride out the storms of this world.

"Stop it!"

Otami suddenly pinched the nose of the infant lying beside her. Wasuke had bitten her nipple. After a while Otami carefully began to get up. She quietly left the sleeping child and was about to go off to join Osato and her grandmother when Wasuke began to gurgle and coo. She did not find him easy to leave.

5

"But there's no need for you to be so worried."

Her grandmother said this on the morning of the fourth day, as Otami was preparing to leave Tsumago. Although she had not received any real advice about Okume on this visit, and in fact had not even been able to initiate any serious consultation on the matter, Otami nevertheless tried to take satisfaction in the pleasure of seeing her grandmother, Osato, and her brother in good health.

Osato came up and said, "Otami, there's still some time before Okume's wedding, so just make her some nice clothes and see how things go."

"That's right," said her grandmother.

"Okume will change her mind," said Osato, showing something of her husband's cold practicality. "No matter how much a girl may like reading and writing, when she is only seventeen or so she doesn't really know her own mind all that well."

"Osato's right," the grandmother added. "Just make her some clothes that she will really like and see what happens. That's the way. When we were girls we all went off and got married and we got more pleasure out of filling our hope chests than anything else."

This old woman who had seen her children born, and then her grand-children, and now her great-grandchildren, remembered her own old-fashioned girlhood. She put special emphasis on the words "hope chest."

With that discussion concluded, Otami went back to her preparations for her return to Magome. Waiting for her there was not only her daughter but her husband as well, and she could not remain away any longer. Still, her grandmother was trying to feed the granddaughter whom she saw so seldom with every delicacy that she could find, saying that although it was too early for most wild greens, the time was just right for gathering the artemisia buds used to flavor rice cakes. Otami was surfeited just by hearing of them. She put a sling with little bells on it under Wasuke's hips and tied him to Otoku's back, just as she had done coming over.

"Why, Otami, are you leaving already? That's terrible. And Wasuke's leaving too! He'll be a big boy the next time I see him. I'll be here waiting for you."

Somehow Otami got through the farewells to her grandmother.

On the highway, it was the season for bands of pilgrims bound for Ise. The Kiso road was no longer the Kiso road of old. Still less was it the road on which Kichizaemon and the other officials had donned their hempen formal clothing to meet each important party at one edge of the village and escort them through to the other side. The scenes along the old post road had changed. The trains of the daimyo with vast numbers of attendants, even personal physicians, and equipment boxes, parasols, guns, chests, and other appurtenances, overwhelming one post station after another as they moved along the roads, were now a thing of the past. Even so, up to the second year of Meiji, 1869, parties of daimyo and court nobles bound for Kyoto had passed through occasionally, greatly simplified but still consisting of twenty to eighty men. Now even those had disappeared.

"Hurry up!" called Otami to Otoku, who was lagging behind. Otami was hastening back to her husband, Hanzo. In her brother's words, Hanzo was struggling on behalf of the local people who were about to lose all access to the Kiso mountains. Having gone out from under the jurisdiction of Owari, they were now forced to deal with the officials of Chikuma prefec-ture. Juheiji had said that the present officials, when you compared them with the time of Tsuchiya Sozo, provided a clear contrast of good and evil.

Now even the castles were being torn down as useless relics. The offices in Agematsu called the Agematsu camps or the Kiso timber office had been eliminated in the first year of Meiji. The buildings of the Kiso-Fukushima barrier, which Otami had heard discussed so much in her time, and the Yama-mura deputies' offices to which her husband had been called so often—they were all gone now. The deputies' residence with its three tall, shingle-roofed buildings dominating the region, from which the Kiso had been governed for more than two hundred years—the great gate, the library, the barbican, the three-story tower, the great main hall, the thirty or forty samurai residences large and small that had stood before it along the Kiso river—all had vanished without a trace.

There was still no way of knowing how far this destruction would go or what would come afterward. There were various opinions on the matter. Her husband, a disciple of Hirata Atsutane, had never doubted that the fall of the shogunate would lead to anything but a restoration of antiquity and a better life. Now he was one of those who had to respond to this question in some way.

CHAPTER EIGHT

1

ON A SMALL folding screen:

> Both high and low may pass easily through this world of dreams.
> Spring flowers and autumn leaves ease us through the years.
> Though we like our parents grow old, spring awaits us now.

The screen was newly made. Okume was there. Sota, the eldest son, was there. Oman was there, praising the screen and Hanzo's calligraphy. The third son, Morio, now at his most mischievous, had come to gaze in wonder.

It was the residence of Hanzo of Magome. As a family residence it was far too large and too expensive to maintain, so, as with the Tsumago honjin, part of it had been torn down and the land planted to mulberries. The retirement quarters where Kichizaemon had spent his last years were left intact. Oman would come down from the second floor and walk along the path beside the mulberry field to reach the main house for her meals. In the spring of 1873, Meiji 6, Oman was already sixty-four years of age. After Kichizaemon's death she had cut her hair short and she passed her lonely days in the isolation of the retirement quarters. Hanzo had written out some of his poems on large sheets of paper and had made them into a folding screen to comfort her. The screen stood about two feet tall.

The harmony between the white paper and the unpainted cedar frame revealed his love of the plain and simple. The screen would be perfect in the corner to block the drafts from the shoji or at Oman's bedside when she caught a cold. It could serve as a companion when there were no callers. Hanzo's suggestions delighted his stepmother.

Otami, off in Tsumago, had not yet returned. Okume, now a young girl at her most sensitive age, had come up to the retirement quarters to join the others at her father's side. She was closer to Hanzo than to her mother, Otami, and some thought her dress seemed terribly subdued for a young girl about to be married. But she did display a bit of girlish crimson at the collar, and her dress was in fact quite becoming to her. Taking special interest in things such as this screen which her father had made, she would come to him and offer to grind the ink, never taking her eyes from his hand as he wrote. The breaking of the engagement that had been made for her when she was a child was an unhappy consequence of this time in which everything seemed to be uprooted. Because the relationship between the two families could no longer be continued on the same basis, all the old promises had been broken. This had come as a terrible shock to Okume. But she did not simply turn in on herself. Coming up to look at Oman's new screen, she seemed to be doing her best to recover and her girlish laughter eased her father's heart.

This was the first occasion in a long while that Hanzo had been able to enjoy with his family in this way. It was rare for him to have found the leisure to make the screen, even though it had long been on his mind. Since the beginning of February, when he had set out for the Chikuma prefectural offices in Fukushima carrying a petition, he had been running in all directions, with scarcely time to return home. It had not been an easy period for Hanzo. The reform of the tax system, for which he was responsible as village manager, involved major undertakings such as the review of all land deeds before it could be carried out. As principal of the village school, he also had to work with Sho'un to do everything possible to educate the children in the temple until the school building going up beside the Mampukuji could be completed. He had always been interested in teaching children but there had never been adequate facilities.

He did not undertake such tasks because he enjoyed them. He was a member of an old family that had served this village as headmen, honjin, and toiya ever since his ancestors had founded it. They had served the village and highway for three hundred years. But now, with the changes sweeping away all the old practices, the headmen of the villages, forced to give up their traditional offices, were struggling to keep afloat. Some had decided to take a firmer stand and to express their dissatisfaction with the reforms. Of these more than a few had been punished by house arrest. Hanzo, on the other hand, had felt that it was not good to remain attached to old ways. It was this attitude and nothing else that caused him so ungrudgingly to put his own interests last in these reforms. The charter oath that the new emperor had sent down when the imperial armies were dispatched to the east was still fresh in his memory. The emperor's words were everything. Yet the people living in these mountains had themselves witnessed cases in which it had been difficult to carry out the intent of the oath due to a shortage of qualified men for the provincial offices. There was a matter of life and death that concerned the people living along the upper Kiso river and it could not be disposed of as a problem affecting only a single province. It was known as the forest problem.

2

As the people along the seashores make their livings by fishing and salt making,
so the people who live in the mountains get by with what they can make out of
the trees and animals of the forest. Nowhere are the people of the seashores
altogether forbidden to fish or to make salt. Of course, some areas of the seashore are restricted, and in the mountains there are closed forests. Yet, in all the
remaining areas of open forests, the authorities still forbid a great number of
trees to be cut, and this, we regret to say, does not seem to be a policy of treating the people like their true children.

This was the general thrust of the first petition that had been sent to the
Fukushima offices of Nagoya prefecture in the twelfth month of Meiji 4,
1871. As this analogy between the mountains and the seashore makes clear,
the forest problem was rather simple in its beginnings. Until recently this
region had been under the administration and protection of Owari, and each
village had received an annual grant from the han in compensation for the
restrictions on its use of the forests. Further relief was provided by allowing
tax credits on the rice that had to be imported from Oi in Mino, and the villages were permitted to take until the end of the following year to pay for it.
When the han were abolished and replaced by prefectures, the institutions
peculiar to each han had to be reorganized. A notice soon came out from
Nagoya prefecture that this assistance would cease after 1871. At the same
time, as everything came to be simplified in the Western style, profound
effects were to be seen throughout the entire system of communications. The
region could no longer draw wealth from the travelers over the Kiso road as
it had before. The reforms had returned it to the conditions prevailing at the
beginning of the eighteenth century. The people of the region, no longer able
to live without free access to the forests, had expressed the need to have the
prohibition of the cutting of reserved trees lifted. That was the first petition.
Hanzo had drafted it. They had presented the petition to Fukushima just as
Nagoya prefecture was relinquishing control of the Kiso. Tsuchiya Sozo was
still in office but happened to be in Nagoya on business that day. The petition
was accepted by Isobe Yagoroku, to be given to Iwata Ichiemon for safekeep-
ing. Hanzo had left the Fukushima offices in the company of the other representatives of the villages, who had come from Otaki, Niekawa, and Yabuhara. They had been assured that the petition would be discussed upon
Tsuchiya's return. All the village heads of the Kiso valley were hoping
against hope that Tsuchiya, who could be counted on to understand the situation, would be left enough time in office to act. Unfortunately, Tsuchiya
almost immediately yielded up all his authority to the officials of Chikuma
prefecture, entrusting the plans for the coming century to them. It was a
disaster for the villagers.

The Kiso came under the control of Chikuma prefecture shortly afterward.
In the second month of Meiji 5, 1872, the establishment of a new prefectural

administration based in Matsumoto was announced in the Kiso. Hanzo and the others immediately drafted a letter of assent in which they noted that, unlike the Matsumoto region, which lay in the midst of rich farmland, the Kiso was mountainous. Since the business of the post stations had fallen off, everyone in the area, the teahouses and the inns most of all but even the small tradesmen and the charcoal burners, had fallen into the most dire poverty; it was imperative that the prohibition of the cutting of certain trees be lifted.

When the old province of Shinano was divided into the two prefectures of Nagano and Chikuma, the lands under the jurisdiction of Chikuma prefecture extended from the Ina valley in the south to the Hida region in the northwest. In addition to the main prefectural offices at Matsumoto, there were branch offices in Iida and in Takayama; nothing had as yet been set up in Fukushima. It was sixty miles or more from the most distant villages to Matsumoto, and every affair required direct dealings with the central office and therefore a walk over the whole distance and back. That was already a source of hardship. The letter of assent that Hanzo and the other headmen submitted touched on this. It had now been four years since the end of the fighting in the northeast and the systems of administration under the han had been made consistent. The new system of prefectures and counties that had been eagerly awaited by even the more astute people of the shogunate had at last arrived. It was an opportunity that the people who lived in the mountains could not afford to miss.

The forest problem had not begun with Meiji. The prohibition of the cutting of certain trees had always been counted as the greatest single hardship of the Kiso, and it was the source of endless friction between the old feudal lords and the local people. It was no mere coincidence that it should have flared up again with the beginning of Meiji. The exacerbation of the problem was of course in part due to the collapse of the old post system, but it was also a consequence of the movement to restore the condition of antiquity in all things.

All the people, down to the very lowest levels, had felt that their time had come and they had awaited the arrival of a new government that would bring with it a better life. The charter oath with its vow to eliminate all the evil practices of the old days had awakened a hope of unimaginable intensity. When Hanzo and his colleagues looked to the mountains, they were astonished at the great wealth of the vast forests in which the five trees flourished—the hinoki, the sawara, the asuhi, the koya maki, and the nezuko. They were further astonished that such trees could have been proscribed since the beginning of the eighteenth century. It was not at all unreasonable that they should now count on these trees to rescue the villages from their misery. To them the possibility of a true restoration of antiquity would be proved by their ability to draw on the words of the charter oath in their first petition. What they wrote had above all been an appeal for true mercy, and it was further proof of their good faith.

Chikuma prefecture soon established local offices in Fukushima. As the villages began to learn about Motoyama Moritomo, the official in charge of the local office, they found that his attitude was completely different from that of his predecessor, Tsuchiya Sozo. He seemed already to have decided before taking office that if the prohibitions were lifted and a return made to the practices prevailing at the beginning of the eighteenth century, the vast forest regions that Owari had so conscientiously preserved would promptly be reduced to bald mountains. Motoyama treated the petition as completely out of order. He announced that not only were the lands in which the villages were located government property, but the forests in which the five trees grew were also government forests by virtue of that very fact. Therefore, all the land on which the five trees grew was government land and it must now be included in the government's closed forests without regard for established practice.

During the past several months, Hanzo had seen unfortunate people from villages all over the area being driven down the highway in bonds. A constant stream of people had entered the forbidden forests and violated the orders against cutting. It seemed that to the officials these people were simply too ignorant to know the rules or too dull to comprehend them, and no mercy must be shown.

To Hanzo, this sight awakened a memory from his youth. Once before, all the people of Magome had been investigated by officials coming out from Fukushima. The interrogation had been conducted on the grounds of the honjin. The official in charge and his attendants had sat on the highest step of the entrance hall, flanked by four foot soldiers. The people of the village were called before them. Sixty-one villagers had been bound hand and foot and turned over to the station officials. Only people over the age of seventy were excused from having their hands bound, and those who were already deceased were let off with a reprimand, sparing their households from having to take their punishment for them.

Hanzo, only seventeen at the time, had been scolded by his father for watching the proceedings from under the cover of the pear tree in the corner of the garden. Kichizaemon later said that never before had so many people been hurt by such an affair. After that, whenever there were rumors that the officials were about to search the village, people were likely to panic and burn up all their spare lumber. The officials of the forestry office had been fond of reminding the people, "In the old days, when a tree fell in the Kiso, a head went with it." But even in such a dark time, only the cutting of the five trees in the open forests was forbidden. So long as that proscription was not violated, the villagers could come and go in the mountains as they pleased, cutting lesser trees, gathering firewood, and making charcoal.

Now, not only had the official in charge failed to lift the prohibition but he even took away the freedoms that Owari had recognized. There were villages where one was in government forest from the moment one stepped out of one's house. Even though ample supplies of charcoal were needed in these places because of the cold climate, and plenty of grass for compost for the poor soil, the surrounding areas had all been declared national forests. The people of the Kiso valley never ceased to appeal this decision. However arrogant Motoyama Moritomo might be, they maintained that he simply could not carry out such a brutal policy. There was little arable land in the Kiso, agriculture was difficult, and everyone had to look to the forests for sustenance. It soon reached the point where in certain mountain villages whose only income came from the manufacture of hats and baskets woven from thin slats of hinoki, almost the entire population was being led away in bonds. When conditions reached this unbearable state, Hanzo and his colleagues decided to draw up another petition and send representatives directly to Matsumoto with it.

Before starting on his rounds again, Hanzo had made exhaustive preparations. He had already drafted a version of the petition in the second month of Meiji 5, but since the Chikuma prefectural government was only just being established at the time, nothing further could be done with it. He waited a full year. In February of 1873, he made further preparations, consulting local traditions and searching out the old records. He found certificates sent up to the commissioners' office by a village headman and his assistant, contracts between the farmers of one village and those of another, and contracts drawn up between the representatives of the joint responsibility groups of neighboring villages.

The more he found, the stronger the case became for opening the forests in the Kiso. In fact, the Kiso had long ago been a region where people known as *somabito* cut wood for a living. Others, the *yamagatsu*, planted millet and buckwheat on fields they cleared by cutting and burning, and still others pastured horses in the high mountains. They had all lived independent lives in their remote valleys. In the middle ages, when population rapidly increased and the region came under the control of Ishikawa Bizen no Kami of Inuyama, taxes in rice were imposed on the villages in the valleys that had residential or crop lands and a tax in wood products was imposed in the mountain areas. Since it was not a good area for grain production, the rice tax was actually paid in soybeans, buckwheat, and millet. Each year the people had to cope with the heavy burden of bringing out the tax timber, and the expenses of doing this were covered by special grants of rice to the people each spring and autumn. When the Tokugawa took over and a new deputy was placed in the Kiso to serve directly under the shogunate, conditions continued just as they had been under Ishikawa Bizen no Kami. The names of the rice and timber taxes were changed but they remained the same in practice.

These old precedents in taxation told the history of the Kiso more clearly than anything else did, and they proved that the common people had not been barred from cutting trees and creating farmlands. Of course, the shogunate had divided up the timber tax, assigning six thousand packhorse loads of timber to the people of the Kiso and five thousand to the Yamamura. They also assigned additional lands to the Yamamura in eastern Mino and entrusted them with control of the Fukushima barrier. Later, when the Kiso passed into the domains of the lord of Owari and the Yamamura were transferred

from direct service to the shogunate to positions under Owari, the final defi-
nitions of forest policy were made by that han. The distinctions between
nesting forests, closed forests, and open forests came into practice then. Nesting forests and closed forests were unconditionally closed to the people. But
the open forests making up the greater part of the area were still accessible
until the beginning of the eighteenth century, and the people of the region
cut their tax timber there. They were forbidden to cut the five trees only
after they were excused from the timber tax.

This was the indisputable history of the matter. After establishing the
facts, Hanzo turned to an investigation of more recent precedents. Here he
discovered the origins of what was called "licensed hinoki freight," a practice
dating from the time of direct Tokugawa rule but given great importance by
Owari. According to its terms, from the hinoki that was to be taken out of
the Kiso each year, six thousand packhorse loads were to be given to the people of the Kiso valley. Of this amount, three thousand packhorse loads were
to be made available for local use while the remaining three thousand loads
were to be sold on the open market and the resulting cash given to the people. In the old records of the Aoyama house that had been left to him by
Kichizaemon, he found clear and detailed accounts of how two hundred
packhorse loads of hinoki and sawara were allocated to the people of Magome
each year. Even under Owari, this practice had been maintained. Recognizing the hardship of life in the mountains, they never forgot to divide the
income from the area with the people who lived there. Hanzo felt that if
reforms were really to be effected by the new prefecture, it should give careful attention to the actual conditions of this valley and follow the wishes of
the local people.

The petition was drafted. From February through April, Hanzo took it
around to the various villages and solicited the opinions of the headmen and
others. They asked for revisions. He made a final draft. He then had to get
the seal impressions of fifteen people to represent the district. On the twelfth
of May, the representatives of the villages of Niekawa, Yabuhara, Otaki, and
Magome, as representatives of the whole, would proceed to the main offices
in Matsumoto.

Hanzo was under terrible pressure. In addition to his other duties, he had
to go out to the village of Otaki at the foot of Mt. Ontake to consult with
the headman there. He was hoping to do this quickly. First, however, he had
to take care of the business of his own village, placing the supervision of the
school in Sho'un's hands while waiting for his wife to return from Tsumago.

It was then that he received a completely unexpected request from his
daughter.

"Please let me go with you, father."

Okume appeared to feel that there was no good reason that a daughter
could not accompany her father on a walk deep into the lonely mountains.

Hanzo was at a loss for an answer. Then he tried to dissuade her. He had
the feeling that she had said something strange, but he soon returned to his
preoccupation with the forest problem and Okume did not insist.

3

Otami now returned with Wasuke and Otoku, bearing news of Tsumago.

"What did Juheiji have to say, Otami?"

"About the forest problem? Well, my brother said that nothing can come of it until the officials are changed in the Fukushima office."

"Did he really say that?"

That was all they said to each other. There was no time for leisurely conversation. The carrying cloth filled with gifts from Tsumago was soon opened and its contents brought out to the delight of Sota and Morio. For a while everyone in the house was talking about Tsumago. Otami took out a paper packet of beautifully dyed silk yarn, telling Okume that it was a present to her from her great-grandmother. Wasuke, now down off Otoku's back, crawled about among everyone.

Hanzo had already called the hairdresser in and had greeted his wife clean shaven. Ever since the time of Atsutane, ancient purple had been popular among Hirata disciples because of its associations, so much so that the master's works were all bound with purple thread. Hanzo himself was fond of the color and he had Naoji tie up his hair with a purple cord. Naoji, who had served Kichizaemon in his time, was the father of the maid Otoku.

"Otami! I'm going up to Otaki village."

Otami looked closely at her husband before saying anything to the others. He looked completely different to her now that she had been to Tsumago for a few days. Hanzo turned to go into the parlor.

"I'm always off for somewhere, even when I'm waiting for you to get back. While you were away, I finished the screen for mother."

Even though Hanzo spoke so casually, it did not mean that he did not share his wife's concerns about Okume's marriage. Nor did he fail to understand the meaning of Otami's expression when she shared with him the concerns of a mother with a marriageable daughter. Those who had not yet met Okume and knew her only by hearsay imagined her as a skinny and angular girl, but when people actually met her they were surprised to find that she was fair skinned and plump. There was within her, however, an easily wounded soul that did not seem to match her robust body. In these recent times not only had she seen the elimination of the toiya that had been in the family for so many generations, followed by the elimination of the offices of honjin and headman, but even her betrothal, the most important thing in a woman's life, had vanished. In the midst of this wholesale destruction, Okume could not sit serenely by as her grandmother did.

But precisely because the present marriage negotiations with the Inaba family in Minami Tono village were being made through Oman, she said nothing about them to her grandmother. To Hanzo and the rest of the family, Okume appeared simply as a girl lost in her own dark thoughts.

Hanzo suddenly stamped on the wooden floor of the hallway leading to the parlor and returned to his study. Surrounded by piles of old books and papers stacked everywhere, he went back to work on the forest problem.

"This should be this way . . . That should be that way," he muttered to himself.

Inosuke, who had been secretly worried about the petition, came calling on Hanzo. He also wanted to hear from Otami about her visit to Tsumago. It did not look as though Hanzo was going to get out of Magome that afternoon. Inosuke said that he simply could not stomach the way the head of the Fukushima office was handling things, and he had a great many questions for Hanzo. What was this about all lands where the five trees grow being included in the government lands even if they had been privately owned up to then? And what about the report that if the people insisted on access to the forests they would have to pay taxes on them, but that if the lands remained in government hands there would be no taxes?

When the han were abolished and the prefectures established in their place, the mountain watchmen and patrols of each village were also eliminated. Inosuke had given up those duties and their accompanying right to wear a sword and draw a stipend and had confined himself to the family business. Unable to watch in silence when the issue concerned the very lifeblood of the thirty-three villages of the Kiso, he freely expressed himself concerning his unhappiness with the new head of the local office. But now he simply said that he himself intended to bear up under it for the time being and returned home. At last, shortly before the evening meal, Hanzo and his wife were able to talk in the privacy of the parlor.

"Okume said something really strange just now," Hanzo began. "Can you imagine, she said that if I was going to Otaki, she wanted to go with me."

"Really?"

"It's because she has heard about the shrine at Ontake. It sounds as though she wants to make a pilgrimage there."

"She hasn't said anything about it to me."

"Maybe she's changed her mind. Anyway, Okume's still young. When I went up there to pray for father when he was ill, I was upset when Katsushige wanted to go along. Seisuke stopped me then and asked me if I intended to take such a young person along with me. But Katsushige wanted to go so much that I had no choice. I learned from that experience. This time, I'm going alone. This is no time to be taking a daughter along. After all, she's only seventeen and a woman besides! How can she make the trip up to the shrine? I told her she must have taken leave of her senses."

"Why should she want to do a thing like that just when she's about to be married?"

Otami was repeatedly on the verge of telling Hanzo about the counsel on Okume's marriage that she had gone all the way to Tsumago to obtain, but she was never able to come out with it. This was because she had in fact failed to obtain any real counsel there. Even though she thought Hanzo would want to hear the opinions of the people in Tsumago on the matter, she began the story of her long-delayed journey home by describing how she had found her grandmother and Osato dyeing yarn in the front courtyard. Then she told of how on the evening of her arrival she had put Wasuke to bed early and then had talked with her brother and his wife. But she had been able only to mention Okume's problem and did not go into it further with her family. Hanzo listened but made no comment beyond an occasional grunt. Then he cut in.

"But what did your grandmother and brother have to say?"

"Well, it was my brother's opinion that things have gone too slowly. He thinks we ought to have pushed it right through."

"No, that's not what I'm asking. I was asking what they think we should do."

"That's just what Osato was saying. That there's still some time before the wedding, that Okume will surely change her mind, and that we ought to just wait and watch for a while. She says that girls Okume's age don't really know their own minds anyway. That's what Osato thinks. Grandmother says that we should make her some nice clothes. She thinks that's what really counts."

Otami then turned to the matter of what kind of clothes they should choose for her. Fortunately they had long been on close terms with the dyer Isekyu in Kyoto, and the adopted son of that concern would soon be coming up to Mino to take orders for dyeing. Otami thought that they should have everything ready for him. She added that she thought the people in Minami Tono would be pleased to see good clothes that were becoming to Okume.

"I'll leave the details to mother and you."

"That's what you always say. I can't consult with you on anything."

"I can't help what you say, but right now—"

"Of course I know you're busy. It's no use scolding somebody who gets wrapped up in things the way you do. Go ahead and do what you have to do. I'll talk with mother about Okume's preparations. Are you listening to what I'm saying . . . ?"

Otami abruptly fell silent and began to stare down at the matting. The two sat in silence for a long time. At last Otami got up and went off to look after Morio, who she could hear quarreling with someone in one of the inner rooms. When mealtime came, everyone gathered as usual in the hearth room, each in his accustomed position, from head of the house down to man-servant, just as the practice had been in the time of the honjin. Even the children took their seats in order of age. When at last everyone from Oman, over from the retirement quarters, to Sakichi, who had been working in the woodshed, was seated before a tray, soup bowls were thrust out from all directions to be filled by Otoku, who was serving. Otami put Wasuke beside her and ate in silence. Hanzo looked over at his stepmother, then at Okume sitting beside her brothers, and finally at Otami, but he too ate in silence.

After dinner Hanzo went to the parlor and made his preparations to leave for Otaki the next morning, but Otami remained silent and unable to do much of anything. People can be wounded by the smallest things.

For his part, his ancestors had served as headmen without any compensation until the beginning of the eighteenth century and they were recognized both as the arbiters of the village and its most distinguished citizens. The only purpose of people born into this family was to try to be of some service at times such as these. Although it had not been his intention to neglect his wife and children, Hanzo tried to console himself for having done so by thinking of the day when he would present his petition to the Chikuma prefectural offices. He ran through in his mind just what he would say if by chance he was asked about the timber tax that had existed before any distinctions were made between closed and open forests. It would not be difficult to answer. Long ago the forests had been required to supply more than two hundred sixty-eight thousand heavy planks and more than four thousand three hundred packhorse loads of beams. Since the costs of moving this lumber out of the mountains was very high, the mountain people were compensated with a sum equal to, and therefore canceling out, the taxes on their lands and buildings. That evening he took out a letter he had received from Kozo, and lying in bed beside his melancholy wife, he read over and over again the news of Tokyo that his friend had sent.

Hanzo got up early the next day and inhaled the fresh air of the April morning as though he had just returned to life. Otami had recovered her spirits and she was helping her husband with his preparations. That also gave Hanzo strength. He put some of his favorite books of poetry in the breast of his kimono. Whenever he was able to steal a bit of time from his duties, he was fond of turning to this refined pursuit and he hoped to carry out his mission and also call on some of his companions in poetry at the same time.

"How about this, Otami? If I meet someone on the way and he asks me what I am doing, I'll just show him these books." He was wearing formal trousers. A portable writing set and a flute were thrust into his sash.

"You look marvelous!" said Otami as she lightheartedly pointed out her husband's costume to her daughter who had just then dashed out. "Look, Okume! Your father's going out with a flute in his sash!"

Hanzo laughed as he accepted his hat.

"Okume! When I get to Otaki, I'll make a pilgrimage for you too!"

The preparations were complete. Hanzo left quickly. A village manager was allowed thirteen sen a day for travel expenses, reflecting a price scale that later generations can scarcely imagine. This time, however, Hanzo was going on a private trip of his own, and would not be presenting a bill on his return. He walked from Magome to Tsumago, where he looked in on Otami's family and explained the purpose of his trip to Otaki to Juheiji. Then he started once more down the familiar highway into the hinterlands. The Kiso valley near Tsumago was an important site for the winter enterprise of forming the logs into rafts that would float down the river in spring. Here the bright blue waters of the Kiso river splashed around the white boulders and broke over them as it came swirling down from the deep forests upstream.

4

"I haven't written to the master for a long time."

Hanzo reflected on this as he walked up the highway toward his night's lodging in Nojiri. It was the second day since leaving Magome and there were quite a few travelers out on the highway, including a wandering entertainer who passed by with a monkey riding on his shoulder. Even on this hurried journey, Hanzo's thoughts had turned to his fellow disciples who were with Hirata Kanetane. From the highway, the density of the forest on the opposite bank was almost palpable.

"It might not be much, but I'm working for the restoration of antiquity too." The thought gave him courage. He had not forgotten his master.

As he approached the hanging bridge, his thoughts were on Okume. Here the valley was much narrower than it was near Tsumago, and the road was closer to the river than on most of the highway. Travelers coming from the west would have to work their way along the banks as they descended the steep, damp slope. Beneath a cliff covered with moss and grass, they would discover a teahouse. Hanzo stopped there to wipe away the perspiration. By coincidence, a traveling foreigner, accompanied by an interpreter, stopped his baggage-laden horse before the teahouse and came in. He sat beside Hanzo.

This sudden appearance of a foreigner drew amazed stares from everyone resting there. Some came up to peer at him from in front or from behind. However, he was no longer in any danger of assassination as he might have been a few years earlier. During the time of Tsuchiya Sozo's tenure, a memorandum had come around to Magome pointing out the mistakes that those not yet accustomed to the presence of Westerners might make and giving instructions to the people who lived in the countryside. Hanzo remembered reading it, but he had never before heard of a Westerner actually traveling along the Kiso road. Out of curiosity, he went up to the interpreter and introduced himself as a local headman. Then he asked about the nationality of the foreigner, his point of departure, and his destination. He learned that the traveler was an Englishman who had come to Yokohama from Hong Kong. He was on his way to Nagoya, where he was to be a teacher in the Aichi Prefectural English School which was scheduled to open in October. For some reason the Englishman suddenly took his passport out of his coat pocket and began to display it, but Hanzo told him that he did not need to see it. When the Englishman heard from his interpreter what Hanzo's office was, he asked if there was a place up ahead where he could stop with their horses. Since Hanzo had to rely on the interpreter, he was not sure exactly what the question meant but he replied that there were eleven post stations in these mountains and that he himself had formerly been the head of one of these stations. The interpreter, an experienced man who was also acting as a guide for the foreigner, explained to Hanzo that it was still very difficult to bring a foreigner through the hinterlands and he complained of the nuisance created by the great crowds of curious people that followed them through every post station.

"Here come our famous bean cakes!" called the old woman of the teahouse as she brought out the freshly made delicacies to distribute to the customers. The foreigner, traveling like a deaf man, heard an explanation from the interpreter but made no move to sample one.

Hanzo soon left the teahouse. But even after he had arrived at his next night's lodging in the excellent inn in Fukushima, he could not readily forget his totally unexpected first meeting with a foreigner there by the hanging bridge. What had first appeared off Kurihama at the station of Uraga in the summer of 1853, the sixth year of Kaei, the aftermath of those Black Ships, had come to Shimoda and to Yokohama with a momentum that could not be denied. Ending three centuries of isolation, like trout swimming upstream, they had now reached this remote mountain land. Yesterday's Black Ships were today's teachers for Aichi prefecture. Hanzo was astonished.

The next day Hanzo set out from Fukushima for Otaki. He crossed the Kojin bridge, entered the Ontake road, and went on toward Tokiwa ford. He waited at Misawa for the raft, crossed the stream, and soon was giving his greetings once again to the family of the priest with whom he had stayed so long ago.

"We have a guest! I think he's from the Magome honjin!"

"It's Aoyama, isn't it? This is a rare treat!"

Toyama Gohei, the headman of Otaki, lived not too far away, and he had been expecting Hanzo's arrival. Gohei had worked with Hanzo from the beginning on the petition concerning the forestry problem. He had not only talked with the headmen of Niekawa and Yabuhara but had gone with them and Hanzo to present the first petition to Fukushima when it was still under Nagoya prefecture. That the second petition was now ready was due in no small measure to Gohei's strenuous efforts along the inner road from Agematsu on. There was good reason for this. His ancestors had lived for generations at the foot of Mt. Ontake and they had looked after the affairs of the people scattered along the mountainside from Otaki village to the other side of the mountain. This old headman was one of those who felt most directly the suffering of the people who were about to lose the greater part of the Kiso forests. Otaki, unlike Magome, was not located on the highway, and Gohei's family had not held the offices of honjin and toiya. Yet as headmen under the Yamamura they had long taken care of the people and land of this region.

Leaving his hat and sandals at the priest's home, Hanzo went on to make his call on Gohei.

"Aoyama, a person like me who deals with the mountains everyday just can't stand to watch this. It is terrible for the people of the Kiso. It's just like taking fish away from water."

This was Gohei's observation, though as far as the aptness of the simile was concerned, the people of the Kiso had little to do with fish. The only water creatures they knew anything about were the carp that were raised in ponds and the river fish that came up as far as the Otaki river. So little did they know about fish that the rare salted mackerel that reached these mountains were relished right down to the bones, which they would also try to eat after thoroughly roasting them in the fire. On the other hand, they could give the names of any of the small birds that flew into the valley as soon as they heard them sing, and they were thoroughly versed in the ways in which wood would become available in the mountains, whether through the dying of trees, windfalls, snow damage, or broken limbs.

Just why was it that the forests in the Kiso where the forest problem had arisen should have been so assiduously protected by Owari, which had established a guard station in Agematsu as well as a timber office, a commissioner of forests, and even mountain watchmen and inspectors of closed forests? Neither Hanzo nor Gohei could answer that question. It was the common opinion that for Owari these forests were a major source of revenue and it therefore watched over these lands in order to protect the vast annual timber crop. But in fact the process of transporting the logs by river required an immense expenditure of labor. They were brought out of the side valleys into the main valleys and then down to the river, where they were made into rafts and floated down the Kiso to the booms downstream in Mino and on to the distant markets. There was no possibility that it could be made into a profitable undertaking.

That Owari nevertheless did not begrudge its efforts was clearly the result of a spirit of responsibility more than anything else. It could be said to be related to the history of great water control projects that Owari had carried out in its effort to prevent floods in the lower Kiso. Of course it was the people who lived along the lower stretches of the river who spoke of this, and those along the upper Kiso were not very much aware of it. But even Hanzo and his acquaintances knew that the deep and heavily forested Kiso valley was a natural strategic point of great importance, and therefore a crucial section of the Tosando. This was why the barrier at Fukushima had been established as a checkpoint for outgoing women and incoming arms and placed under a deputy at first directly responsible to the shogunate and later to the great han of Owari.

"What will the han people in Owari say when they hear of this?" said Gohei. "Will they say that the branch office is correct and the people of the Kiso are being unreasonable? According to what I have heard, this is very different from the return of lands to the throne. I understand perfectly well that when they surrendered their lands, it meant all the lands and all the people living in them. They wanted to bring all the people under imperial rule. Didn't Owari's taking the lead in returning its lands arise out of that desire? Surely they could not have given up their old mountain domains with no concern for the number of people injured in the process."

After saying this, Gohei brought out the documents concerning the forest problem that Hanzo had loaned him. The final draft of the petition had been circulated among the fifteen representatives of the Kiso villages and had been returned to Gohei. It had everyone's signature and seal, beginning with the headman of Yabuhara. As correct form required, the petition had "superior" written at the top and it opened with the formula "That which we implore, with the greatest respect, is . . ." It stated that hitherto, since the beginning of the eighteenth century, the Kiso had been under the exclusive control of Owari, and since they now wished to inform the present prefecture of the way things have been handled elsewhere, this document is being presented. Furthermore, so that the prefectural offices will be well aware of the way things have been handled in this area, the present document is accompanied by true copies of three petitions that were presented to the former lord of Owari.

"It's very important to include the copies of the old petitions."

"Yes, it is. Now they will understand that this problem did not begin today."

As the two continued their conversation they decided that since the new petition would be submitted on the twelfth of May, the four representatives who would actually be presenting it should meet in Niekawa on the day before to go up to Matsumoto together. If the officials at the prefectural offices should ask about the hardships of the people, each of the four would respond in his own words, telling them that the policy announced by the local office would multiply the hardships of the people of the district a hundredfold and could not be accepted.

Gohei then said, "This petition does not in any way take issue with the establishment of government forests. It is absolutely necessary that places be reserved for the production of timber for official use, and once a reasonable policy for defining such lands is determined and made public, we will surely comply with it. In exchange we are asking only that the people be permitted to enter the open forests. Under the new rules there have been many cases where land that was privately owned has been annexed to government lands, and we want to have those lands restored to their original status. That's what it all comes down to. We only want fair treatment. We want the policies for the next century to be established through the cooperation of the officials and the people. We want to go back to the situation as it was in the seventeenth century."

Hanzo had not slept well in the inn at Nojiri on the way out, nor had he slept well in Fukushima. After returning from Gohei's place he spent the night in the priest's house but was still terribly tired the next morning. He stayed in bed while the priest Miyashita went out to the shrine to perform his morning services. The priest beat on the great drum and then returned some quarter of a mile to the house. Hanzo crawled out of bed only when he heard the people of the household pushing back the rain shutters.

"You slept quite late," said Miyashita's wife as she brought him his tea and some small salted plums.

This old house which doubled as a priest's residence and a lodging for pilgrims was a little more than ten miles up in the mountains above Fukushima. Hanzo had come here frequently since starting to work on the forest problem. On each successive visit what caught his attention most were the changes in the pilgrim's lodging. This was no longer a shrine of Dual Shinto.

The walls of the rooms were decorated with sacred straw ropes as before, but the scroll in the alcove that had read "The Great Diamond World Avatar of Ontake" had been taken away and replaced by one that addressed a prayer to the three Ontake shrines.

"Why don't you just relax today, Aoyama? My son is getting ready to take you up to the shrine."

The priest had come up to his room just to tell him this. The scent of plum blossoms brought to mind his trip to this mountain village to pray for his father's health in the fourth month of 1863. At that time, Katsushige, who had accompanied him, had still not shaved his forehead, and how handsome he had looked in the pale yellow collar of his underrobe.

"Is it already eleven years since then? It must be! My son, for whom you wrote something that time, is now seventeen years old."

They continued to reminisce for a while.

Presently, Hanzo performed his ablutions and then, leaving his straw sandals and hat at the priest's house, he started up the pilgrim's road to the mountain temple.

"This is getting to be the time when the pheasants fly up in the spring. It's not so bad in the mountains then."

With the passing of eleven years, the priest's son whom Hanzo remembered as a mere child had become a young man who could address such remarks to him.

Here too the religious reforms had left a deep imprint. The narrow path that Hanzo was climbing passed before the great stone torii, and he could see that the offensive Buddhist statues from the days of Dual Shinto, which had so confounded the gods and the Buddhas, had already been overthrown. Their inscriptions indicated that the shrines and memorials were mostly from the 1850's and 1860's. But no one had touched the statues and tablets dedicated to the Buddhist priests Fugen, Shinsan, and Ittoku, who had brought so many disciples here from throughout the nation. They had made the access easier and had organized pilgrim's groups, pouring their heart's blood into this mountain. For that reason alone, a few Buddhist statues from the old days had escaped destruction.

They passed under the great stone torii and climbed the long stone stairway made of a series of flights of sixteen to twenty steps each. Just to walk up this long stairway through the dappled shade of the cedar and horse-chestnut trees seemed enough to purify the heart of a pilgrim. Passing around the foot of a cliff, they found the ancient shrine standing near a spring that bubbled forth from alpine vegetation. Here was the dwelling of the two gods Onamuchi and Sukunabikona.

Hanzo was amazed by the changes that had been made inside the shrine itself. The memorial plaque presented by Yamamura Somon, the most outstanding of the line of Fukushima deputies, and the two great *tengu* masks, the female of which particularly betrayed its close affinity to Dual Shinto with its great mouth open nearly to the ears and long, sharp, beastlike nose—these now appeared merely as mementoes of the past. All their content had been dissipated. The old *goma* ceremonies had been discontinued and no longer was there any scent of burning sumac bark. The statue of Mahavairocana that had long stood in its own shrine in the corner was gone. The sutra desk no longer stood before the curtain in front of the sanctuary. Here, high on the mountain, what had formerly seemed like a medieval Buddhist hall of discipline, where the most rigorous training had been carried out in order to enable the faithful to bear up under extreme cold and hunger, was now restored to its proper function. The throne of the Great Avatar of Ontake, enjoying for centuries pride of place as king of this mountain, had been overthrown and supremacy returned to the two ancient gods. The mountain air from the surrounding forests of cedar and hinoki, the sound of pure waters trickling among the stones, all made the interior of the temple seem quiet and peaceful. Hanzo stayed there for some time, not forgetting to offer prayers for his daughter.

After returning to the priest's house, Hanzo spent the rest of the day in his room gazing out over the mountains. Miyashita told him that they were heating up the bath and he could forget his fatigue with a good soak in the hot tub that had so long been here to serve the pilgrims who came in during the winter and early spring.

In the afternoon Gohei came over to call on Hanzo and the two of them spent a quiet time composing poems. Then the priest came in carrying a piece of red woolen felt. He laid it out, spread some fine paper on top, and asked Hanzo for a memento of his visit. His son came up to grind the ink. Hanzo took out the books of poetry that he had carried from Magome and laid out the silk-wrapped writing brush that he had brought with him. Then he wrote out an old poem of his own on the paper as he was asked.

> I should like
> This spring day with
> Old friends
> To stretch on and on
> Like green willow boughs.
>
> Hanzo

"That was well written," said Gohei, who had sat by his side observing the motions of the brush.

"But I don't like the last line," replied Hanzo, gazing down at what he had written. "It just doesn't scan properly."

"It's perfectly sound," said Gohei.

At every opportunity, Hanzo would get up and walk out into the hallway to look at the splendid mountain scenery around the base of Mt. Ontake. Gohei came out and joined him in gazing at the far off shimmer of the Otaki river. Here they could sense the vast expanse of the dense virgin forests. There was now scarcely a place where people could go in and cut freely. Conscious of being a guest in the priest's house, Hanzo spoke not a word about the business that had brought him to Otaki. For his part, Gohei simply pointed out the various valleys and mountains of his native district.

The warm rains had already come to the Kiso several times. Spring birds were singing bravely. After Gohei left with a promise to meet him again in Niekawa, Hanzo returned to his books of poetry. In the evening, the valley was enveloped in spring mists that rose up out of the river. Lights were gradually coming on in the farmhouses. Hanzo brought out the flute that he had carried in his sash and gave himself for a time to its solitary but pleasant secrets.

People began to leave the mountain very early the next morning. Pilgrims from the most distant provinces got up while it was still dark to prepare for their journey home. Their robes and sashes were white, their headbands were white. Presently, Hanzo too took leave of his hosts and went out to join the pilgrims descending the mountain. He could hear the bells jingling from their waists as they strode along the mountain road ahead of him carrying the new walking staffs that would serve as their souvenir of this pilgrimage.

In this April of the sixth year of the restoration, Hanzo followed the Otaki river down from the slopes of Mt. Ontake to Fukushima, where the first newspaper to be distributed in the province was starting to come into town. It was the *Nagoya Shimbun,* printed by wood block and running six pages per issue. Little more than a listing of current events, it was published by Tanaka Fujimaro, a samurai of the former han of Owari, who had also set out to create an educational system in the European and American style in his home district.

The main focus of attention for most people was the question of just what was being brought back by the Iwakura mission to America and Europe that had gone out more than a year earlier, in the eleventh month of 1871. That mission had numbered one hundred seven in all, including attendants and students taken along to enter schools overseas. Among them was one Kume Kunitake from Saga. He had been attached to the mission not only to handle the paperwork but also as a National Scholar especially chosen by the new ministry of religion to observe the culture of Europe and America. Knowing this could not but be encouraging to all the Hirata disciples. Yet while Hanzo, trudging down the Kiso road toward Magome, was pursuing his own affairs as headman of an obscure village, the time was approaching for him that sooner or later all the latter day disciples of Motoori Norinaga and Hirata Atsutane had to face.

5

As the twelfth of May approached, a summons came to the village manager's office from Fukushima. It was addressed to Aoyama Hanzo.

Hanzo took the summons to his office to read. It ordered him to appear in the Fukushima office at ten o'clock in the morning on May twelfth. He was not to send a substitute. There were things he had to be told in person. Hanzo carried the summons back to his house and read it over again. If he responded to it, he would not be able to keep his promise to Toyama Gohei and the others. It did not appear that the four district representatives would be able to set out for the main prefectural offices that day, and he could not avoid a certain grim presentiment as he looked at the summons.

He told Inosuke that he had been suddenly called to Fukushima and sent a messenger to Otaki. Then, wearing the formal trousers of the headman, he set out once again down the Kiso road. He was not happy to be going to Fukushima this time.

The Chikuma prefecture local office was located on the grounds of the Kyozenji in Fukushima where its predecessor had been set up by Nagoya prefecture. It was to the right when one came into Fukushima on the highway and crossed the main bridge. Hanzo arrived promptly at these temporary offices. He was kept waiting about thirty minutes and then he was called before the head of the local office and his subordinates. After a brief delay, a clerk took up a paper and read an announcement to Hanzo.

"As of this day, you may consider yourself relieved of all duties as manager of Magome station."

That had been the purpose of the summons. Of course he had been relieved only of the office of village manager and he still remained in charge of the schools as before, but he had to recognize that his confrontation with the local office had ended in total defeat. This was beyond all doubt. He bowed and withdrew.

As he emerged from the gate of the Kyozenji, Hanzo encountered a member of an old samurai family that lived in the nearby residential area. This man was a fellow poet who followed the school of the late Kagawa Kageki. He was just setting out on an errand and he was startled by the look on Hanzo's face. The farther Hanzo walked the more the shock of being relieved of office told on him. The authorities in the Fukushima office had obviously learned that the representatives of the local villages were planning to go over their heads and appeal to Matsumoto, and that Hanzo was the one who had drafted the petition.

Feeling as he had never felt before, Hanzo passed by the site where the Yamamura residence had so recently stood. Grass and weeds were already beginning to cover the grounds. He walked through them, trying to remember where the three great halls had stood, where the main courtyard had been, where the library used to be. Then he walked across the main bridge. The swift current of the Kiso river caught his eye, the sparkle of its riffles, the stones beneath the surface. He picked up his sandals and his hat at the inn and set out for home. He had no heart to call on acquaintances in Fukushima.

One shower followed another along the highway. The rain falling on the late cherry blossoms and on the fresh new foliage moistened his cheeks and ears but he did not notice. He pushed on through the seasonal squalls as far as Agematsu, and then on to Nojiri. He did not sleep well in the inn that night.

The next morning the sun was shining down on the road home. As he set out under blue skies, Hanzo was at last able to bring his feelings under some control. Memories came flooding to the surface.

"Is this what the restoration was supposed to be?" he asked himself. Once he laid his hat down on a stone beside the road and sat in the shade of the tender green foliage of a graceful jujube tree. Lost in his thoughts, he gazed at the Kiso river sparkling in the sun.

From out of his deepest feelings his thoughts ran back to the time when the Tosando army had passed along this Kiso highway under the command of the young Prince Iwakura, appearing to be the vanguard of a new age. Little was as yet known about the new government and it was difficult to fathom the attitudes of the han along its route. It had been important above all else to win the trust of the people, and the staff of that Tosando army had repeatedly issued proclamations assuring the people of their aid and understanding. They had announced that it was their mission under the charter oath to learn of conditions in each province and to help the people in their hardship. They had asked all those who had endured cruel government under the Tokugawa or the han or who had any other problems to come forward without hesitation and report them to the honjin. Hanzo recalled as though it were yesterday how he himself had taken advantage of that offer in his capacity as honjin. Simple, straightforward people like Hanzo could not forget no matter how they tried those passionate protests of the new government that it intended to respect the wishes of the people. He had willingly given up his offices of honjin, headman, and toiya over the protests of many of his fellow post station officials because he had wanted to help the new government carry out its promises.

He got to his feet, gazing downward into the depths of a river pool shaded by a small pine tree, and set out once again toward the home of Juheiji. Juheiji had agreed in principle with the petition but had said that it would be futile without a change in the personnel of the local office.

"Juheiji was right as always," Hanzo said to himself.

Then his thoughts turned to his friend Inosuke.

"Inosuke? He told me just to shut my eyes. That's what he told me . . . 'Don't look at it.' "

Next he thought of the priest Sho'un in the Mampukuji.

"And he, too, would have said that there was no need to do this."

All the same, he knew that Sho'un was also fighting back but in the style of a Zen priest.

The May forests stood all about him. The foliage of the common trees mixed among the hinoki and the zelkova had come to life again and the lavender mountain azaleas of the Kiso road were blooming in profusion. Of the three hundred seventy thousand hectares of the Kiso forests, ninety percent had become government lands. All the lands accessible to the people for croplands, buildings, forests, and grasslands totalled no more than ten percent. It was impossible to say whether this had happened because the new rulers of the Kiso thought the destruction of the old Owari domains was a natural part of their job or whether it simply proved that those in charge of the new prefectures and counties trusted the people no more than the feudal rulers had. Regardless of which it might be, Hanzo could not imagine that the people would accept the new forest regulations and the hardships they entailed no matter how much the officials of the local office might try to insist. If the father's protest was unsuccessful the burden would pass on to the son. He could not believe that this forest problem, already the subject of generations of dispute, could not be brought to a satisfactory solution. As he walked from Suwara to Midono and from Midono toward Tsumago, he continued to brood about the future of the Kiso if the people should remain cut off from the forests. But now, on his way home, he was no longer a headman.

CHAPTER NINE

1

AUGUST CAME and the date for Okume's wedding drew near. In the spring Oman and Otami had said that surely by this time the forest problem would be resolved and Hanzo would have a bit more time for private matters. When the go-between came over from Ina to discuss an auspicious date for the wedding, the Aoyama family had chosen September. But as the date approached, Hanzo betrayed their expectations by becoming more involved than ever in the forest problem. He was now working as the representative of the thirty-three villages of the Kiso and he scarcely had time to eat or sleep.

Of course, the Chikuma local office had intended to inflict a severe punishment by depriving Hanzo of the post of village manager. He had lost his office precisely because of his determination to help the new government follow its proper course. His life as a headman, which is what the manager's position had originally been, had come to an end. The functions of the hereditary head of the village, relaying orders to the farmers and looking after them in every way, were now a thing of the past. Only his duties as principal of the village school remained. This consequence of the forest problem was one that his mother and his wife had not at all expected. As Okume's wedding day approached, the status of the Aoyama family was dwindling away.

"When the go-between arrives, there will be just the one person in the party. There will be no need to provide a special banquet. Of course, festive wine, two soup dishes, three side dishes, and one night's lodging will be required."

The letter concerning the preparations for setting the marriage date had arrived in February. Otami, making arrangements as the other party had asked, had already undertaken to accept the confirmation gifts. But the promised roll of obi fabric was not ready in time, and the Inaba sent instead some twelve yards of plain white cloth and a cask of sake.

Oman, who stood in the place of a mother to Hanzo, had brought Okume's wedding plans to this point. Yet the crucial person, his daughter Okume, was still not willing to go through with the match. To Otami, concerned about how the Inaba household would react to Hanzo's loss of office and title, her daughter seemed more and more like Hanzo. It was not in

Okume's younger brother, already appointed apprentice manager by Nagoya prefecture in 1871, at the age of thirteen, that Hanzo's character was reflected, but in his daughter. Otami was particularly struck by the resemblance whenever she chanced to see Okume from behind.

Hanzo believed passionately in education for women and Okume had come under his influence, holding in reverence the same great masters that her father revered. She had been deeply hurt by the sight of her father returning pale and wan from the trip to Fukushima, and she lay awake at night beside her mother, reflecting on the strange turns of fate, repeating to herself that she just couldn't go on this way.

Otami was encouraging her daughter in the marriage and at the same time trying her best to stand between her strong willed mother-in-law and Hanzo, who had not yet recovered from his loss of position. Visiting the Tsumago honjin earlier in the year, she had seen how her brother's family was trying to become self-sufficient and she wanted this for her family too. She had considered the possibilities. Silkworm racks could be installed in the rooms of the old honjin if she were to try to do more with silkworm culture, and the camellias that bore their fruit every year in the corner of the front garden would also be suited for making her own hair oil. Otami, determined to raise her four children in security, especially the two youngest ones, had set to work in her natural good spirits, her cheeks as lush as a ripe apple.

One day Otami went out to the storehouse in back to get some utensils. She was worrying that the fabric that was to be dyed for Okume's wedding wardrobe was not going to be ready in time. On the top step, she found her husband's slippers; the heavy door with its rusty iron grill was unlocked. A sound of movement came down from the second floor. Otami climbed the stairs with nothing particularly in mind and peered in. There she found Hanzo with a preoccupied expression on his face, sitting among all the old swords, hanging scrolls, and tea implements that Kichizaemon had collected during his lifetime. The old chests that belonged to Oman and the ones that Otami had brought from Tsumago on her wedding day were lined up in the middle of the room. Against the wall were stacked the Chinese and Japanese books that Hanzo had collected over the decades. There had been rumors of other old houses selling off their possessions, and Otami, catching this unexpected glimpse of her husband looking so vulnerable, was suddenly choked with emotion.

2

The storehouse and the retirement quarters were separated by a narrow path leading back toward the well. Otami went directly over to see Oman. She had no one else with whom to consult, even on the matter of sending her daughter to Ina.

"Mother!" she called. But Oman had stepped out for a moment. The white cat of which the old woman was so fond was curled up on a cushion. The sliding panels between the two rooms had been taken down for the summer and everything was being very carefully kept just as it had been when Kichizaemon was still living. Fabric from an underrobe that Oman, fond of sewing, was making for her granddaughter was scattered about, still another reminder that Okume's wedding date was near. Otami smiled at the little jug of sweet sake that had been left out next to the old sewing box. She was well aware that Oman usually kept the jug hidden away in her closet.

At that moment Oman returned.

"Otami? You came at just the right time. I've sent out a reply to Osono of the Inaba. It looks as though she is worrying about us. She says that since it takes a woman three days to walk from Magome to Minami Tono in upper Ina, we shouldn't haul everything over. We should leave Okume's chest of drawers, her clothing chest, her sewing box, and those kinds of things here. Even the wash basins. Well, we had to say something on our part, so I wrote her that we are well aware it is a long trip, that you are not terribly adept, that our preparations will not be complete, but to please bear with us—that's what I wrote."

"What do you think, mother? Will this forest problem affect their attitude? We're no longer headmen . . ." said Otami.

"The Inaba? But we've already exchanged confirmation gifts and promised that we would renew our pledge of kinship. If they were the kind of people who would go back on their word just because of a reversal in our fortunes, I wouldn't have arranged for Okume to go there in the first place. They're all very honorable and straightforward people."

Here it would not be amiss to say a bit more about Hanzo's stepmother so that the reader might know about the women of this mountain country. Although Oman was old now and the hair which she wore short was more than half gray, she had not lost the spirit with which she had stood alone in the entrance hall, completely unafraid of bare lances and drawn swords, when the Mito ronin came through many years ago. The upbringing that made her that way had come from her mother, the daughter of Sakamoto Magoshiro, who had been famous as the founder of the Sakamoto school of gunnery in Takato han under Naito Yamato no Kami. Although a woman, Oman knew the Chinese classics and had taught Okume to read and write. She further directed the education of her granddaughter by having her read aloud from the preface to the *Kokinshu* or *The Tale of Genji* and by showing her how to hold the shuttle and use the kitchen knives. The older Oman got the more she seemed to revert back to the samurai quality of her grandfather, Magoshiro.

For years Oman had watched over her stepson, Hanzo. Before anyone else in the household, Oman had known that Hanzo and his friends Kozo and Keizo had become committed to the imperial cause. She found that she was not so much surprised after all that Hanzo, having done what he had to do, had received such a severe punishment from the office in Fukushima. All the same, Oman remembered how Kichizaemon and Kimbei had so often discussed the question of whether Hanzo could restore the fortunes of the Aoyama, and she too was worried about this.

With Otami sitting before her, Oman took up the underrobe she had been working on and began talking again. The bright red silk dyed in Kyoto was perfect for a girl to wear to her new home.

"By the way, Otami, have you heard that Hanzo is thinking of selling our land and our bamboo grove to the Fushimiya?"

Oman was speaking of a part of the bamboo grove that was behind the honjin and about two acres of building land. They were to get five ryo for the bamboo grove and twenty-five ryo for the land. Eikichi was standing surety as a relative and the guarantor was Heibei of Toge. Oman had heard the details from Seisuke, who still came over to help. Both Oman and Otami assumed that the money would be applied to the preparations for Okume's wedding.

"I thought we might be getting down to that," said Oman. "If a honjin family cannot give a daughter seven formal kimono when she gets married, she will be cutting a very poor figure. There has to be a white one, a red one, a black one, one with an all-over pattern, one with a pattern to the waist, one with a pattern on the skirt, and one with crests. That's the way the old ceremonies require it to be. But this marriage is a special case. It can't be helped. We still have quite a lot of forest and farmland that has come down to us from my husband's time. I have always thought that was one thing that might get us through. If you're born inept then it can't be helped, but when my husband was still in good health, he always used to say that he wished Hanzo had just a little more talent with money."

Oman was clearly longing for the days when Kichizaemon had been in charge. In the heyday of this post station there was not a single daimyo or high public official who had not spent the night or rested in the chamber of honor of the honjin. They had included, to count only the most important people, Ii Naosuke of Hikone, Naruse Hayato Yukimasa from Nagoya, the Nagasaki commissioner Mizuno Chikugo no Kami from Edo, the elder councillor Manabe Shimosa no Kami, the lord rector Hayashi, and the censor Iwase Higo no Kami. More recently, Takeda Ko'unsai of Mito and the censor and commissioner of foreign affairs Yamaguchi Suruga no Kami had also been counted among the historical personages that spent time in the honjin. With memories such as these, the Aoyama household in which she had passed her life with her husband, Kichizaemon, did not seem a lowly one to Oman. She was prepared to fight to the death to see that it did not lose the status it had held then.

"Mother, if you keep worrying like this, there will never be an end to it," said Otami, preparing to return to the main house. "Just watch. I'll do everything I can from now on. By the way, the Inaba have said that the twenty-second or the twenty-third of next month will suit them. I have to get back to work."

3

At the end of the month, Hanzo received word that Kureta Masaka, the senior disciple of the Hirata school to whom he felt closest, would be coming from Tokyo by way of the Kiso. He shared with Otami his pleasure at the prospect of seeing Masaka once again after so many years, and together they awaited his arrival.

Hanzo had of course acceded to the wishes of the entire village by volunteering to assume the teacher's duties at the school which was still temporarily quartered in the Mampukuji. He had given it the name Keigigakko, or School of Respectful Justice, and he took great satisfaction in his new role as village sage. He never tired of teaching. On the day Masaka was due to arrive, he came back from the temple and began hurried preparations to receive the honored guest in his parlor. When Otami came to look in, he was putting the room in order.

Since the elimination of the three primary offices of the old post stations, the Aoyama family was no longer the honjin family it had always been. But all the same, when the first group of young men went up to Fukushima for their physical examinations under the new general conscription law, they first came around, solemn faced and led by a representative of the villagers, to the old honjin gates to pay their respects. By then the August sun was beating down on the highway. To take good care of any traveler who walked down this grass-choked highway from a distant place was a habit inculcated by long practice in people like Hanzo and his wife.

Otami went out to the western veranda to bring in the colorful quilts and mattresses that she had been airing for the guest. This veranda went along the northwest side of the main house, continuing as far back as the inner room, which was now used only as a guest room, and on to the upper room or chamber of honor, now a shrine dedicated to Ubusuna no Mikoto. It was quiet in the northern courtyard. When Otami came to the point on the veranda that looked out on this courtyard, she found that the neighborhood cats had taken advantage of its nearly abandoned state to congregate there. A tortoise-shell cat and a black cat with a voice that sounded like a crying baby had been coming to call on the white cat that was Oman's special pet. But the animals were quiet now and they had made the deep shade under the pear tree in the garden their meeting place. Otami forgot the passage of time as she watched them. The wiles of an unusually beautiful kitten less than half a year old charmed her. There was no hesitancy or calculation in its movements, nor even a spot of dirt on its fur. Otami was captivated by its sheer youthfulness—it was doing nothing but growing up rapidly. The cats in the garden, creating their own buoyant atmosphere, seemed to have forgotten about eating. They ran, they rolled over, and the postures they assumed brought to mind young girls with no thought but of sweet herbs and bright flowers.

Although the clumps of dark green ornamental grass in that corner of the garden normally gave it a rather somber air, the cats had transformed it into a playground. Hidden in the grass were two more cats that Otami did not recognize. When she came to herself again, Otoku had come out from the kitchen to watch. Otoku's attitude when the cats had first begun to gather there was that they were nuisances and she would throw water from a hand basin on them to drive them away. But gradually she had come to realize that good comrades might be found even in the world of animals. Otoku stood motionless beside the column on the veranda. Then Okume came out from the wood-floored section of the entrance hall where she had been weaving. They were standing outside the small sitting room that Otami and Okume used to dress their hair. Before Otami could observe her daughter carefully, Okume looked down as though she had seen something she shouldn't have seen below the window of the storeroom and then ran toward the western end of the veranda and disappeared.

"I think I've found out what's bothering Okume," said Otami as she looked into the parlor. Hanzo was quietly pacing the floor while waiting for the arrival of his guest. According to Otami, Okume had been under great pressure from Oman to marry but she had no understanding of what it was that men and women did together, and this had turned her against the idea of marriage. It had all been due simply to her being so uninformed in such matters. Of course, Otami added, Okume was wise far beyond her years in other ways, so that she was a better guide to her younger brother than her mother was.

"What are you talking about?" said Hanzo with a laugh. He did not pursue the conversation.

Hanzo was awaiting Masaka with great impatience. Since the abolition of the han, he had been unable to keep in close touch with the activities of his fellow Hirata disciples and he was deeply concerned about the problems the restoration of antiquity was facing and the future course of the Hirata school.

Masaka arrived in Magome that evening. He was on horseback and he had one companion. He had chosen a lightly equipped horse instead of riding on quilts above baggage panniers. When he dismounted and untied the strings of his hat, he looked as he always did when traveling.

Masaka and Hanzo, finding themselves together again after so many years, exchanged simultaneous shouts of joy. Even Okume, who came out behind Otami to help carry the tea into the parlor, seemed transformed from the gloomy person she had been lately. Otami, completely devoted to her children, watched Okume closely amidst the kitchen bustle.

"Sota, our guest is a member of the Hirata school," said Okume to her fifteen-year-old brother, and then she called out gaily to her other brother, who was five.

"Come here, Morio! You've got to change your clothes!"

She acted as though her father's guest had come to visit her as well. Otami was startled. She took a new look at this daughter of hers, who had freshly changed into cool, spotless clothing. Then Sakichi came to announce that the bath was ready.

Hanzo turned to Masaka.

"Kureta, the bath is hot. Wouldn't you like to wash up a bit before we do anything else?"

"I think I will. Traveling always feels different when you get to the Kiso. You can really hear the birds singing up here."

4

The guest who presently came from the bath and sat down before Hanzo had been appointed inspector of the imperial academy in the second year of Meiji, member of the committee to investigate the national education system in the third year, and a special member of the university staff in the fourth year. But his extremely rapid rise had aroused the jealousy of his colleagues, causing him to lose his effectiveness, and he had recently been placed on detached service in out of the way places such as Yamaguchi and Wakayama. Now he was proceeding to Kyoto to take up a post as priest of the lower Kamo shrine.

Hanzo began by apologizing for not writing. Then he told Masaka of how overburdened he had been with the affairs of the highway and the village. With the elimination of the barrier in Fukushima and the offices of honjin, assistant honjin, headman, and assistant headman had come the total reorganization of the post system. Then there was the Kiso forest problem. He told Masaka that he had not even written to Kanetane for a long time even though the master was never out of his thoughts.

He related to Masaka the news of his friend Kozo, who had left Nakatsugawa to follow the master to Tokyo and had risen to the position of acting undersecretary in the ministry of religion. This was after the master had been appointed to the posts of councillor and judge in the ministry of religion and the interior ministry while also serving as rector of the imperial university. Kozo was now said to be lying ill in his lodgings. Hanzo spoke of how they had all worked together for the restoration even though they had each taken a different road. Then he mentioned the letter he had received from Kozo which had stated, "When the disciples have advanced the restoration of antiquity to the point where they all practice Shinto burial rites, why aren't you doing so in your family?" Reading that letter by lamplight in a moment stolen from the blind rush of business, he had suddenly burst into tears.

"I've got something to show you, Kureta," said Hanzo as he took a scroll out of the closet. He hung it on the wall for Masaka to see.

It was a portrait of the great seventh-century poet Kakinomoto Hitomaro with a poem, both in the hand of Motoori Norinaga. A second signature showed that it had been presented to Hanzo by Morooka Masatane. It was a memento not just of the activities of the Hirata people but of the time when the senior disciple Morooka, who often traveled between Tokyo and Kyoto as head of the Matsuno temple, had gotten together in Nakatsugawa with four

or five fellow disciples from eastern Mino. Masatane had given the scroll to
Hanzo on that occasion. Masaka could not of course fail to be moved by seeing a portrait of Hitomaro drawn by Motoori Norinaga, but what affected
him even more was the praise of Hitomaro that was written above the picture. There was some special quality in the writing, which was certified to be
that of Norinaga, and it seemed as though that great scholar who had spent
thirty-five years in studying the *Kojiki* was present in this very room, not
only reminding Masaka and Hanzo of the poets of old but exhorting them to
look with the clear eyes of the present upon this complete man who had possessed the two fundamental qualities of fierceness and gentleness, to listen to
his poetry, and to encourage the disciples of his disciples.

At that moment, Hanzo's stepmother came in with her grandchildren to
greet the guest and the conversation broke off. Introduced by Oman as Hanzo's eldest and third sons, Sota and Morio bowed solemnly before Masaka.

"I understand that you originally came from Iwamurata in Shinano," said
Oman. "You always did seem like a mountain person to me." Then, looking
back toward Okume, who was bringing in the serving tray from the kitchen,
she added, "We can't really do things well in this mountain household, but
please make yourself comfortable."

On the tray that Okume placed between her father and his guest were
freshly salted cucumbers, red shiso, green soybeans boiled in the hull in salted
water, all of which were just now in season, and chopped dried squid. There
were chopsticks and large sake cups as well. Oman supervised the service and
then left the room. Masaka moved out of his formal kneeling posture to sit
cross-legged.

"Well, have you seen the fan we wrote up in commemoration of that
day?" asked Hanzo as he spread it out before Masaka. Both sides were covered with verses expressing the feelings of the posthumous disciples of Hirata
Atsutane. Once they were gathered together in this way, eight years of separation were no more than a dream. The verses reflected a world that afforded
not only the bitter and the sweet but countless other flavors as well.
Morooka's poem was about how long ago they used to try not to be left
behind but now they were unworthy successors.

"What? Morooka wrote that kind of poem?" exclaimed Masaka as he
looked at the fan. Masatane had been one of the party that had gone with
Masaka to take the heads of the statues of the Ashikaga shoguns in the Toji'in
and display them in the Sanjo riverbed back in 1864. Later, when Masaka was
in hiding in the Ina valley, Masatane had spent six years under the guard of
Ueda han. In the first year he had not been permitted to wear clothing with
crests. He had been required to dress in pure white as if awaiting execution
and was kept in a northward facing room where the sun was never seen. For
a writing brush he made do with the chewed end of a chopstick, and he kept
a poetic diary by writing on facial tissues with indigo wrung from the sleeve
of his underrobe. This had been his only pastime. There was no telling what
might have happened to Masatane had it not been for the general amnesty
declared at the time of the emperor's death. Masaka knew him well.

Then, offering sake to his guest, Hanzo began to describe his own bitter experiences beginning with the loss of the office of headman. When he came to the forest problem, he maintained that the affair would have come to a happier conclusion if only the Kiso, which had been governed by people who knew something about the area, had remained under Nagoya prefecture a little longer. They would surely have heeded the petitions from the village representatives who had wanted only to work together with the officials to establish the policies for the coming century.

This isolated valley deep in the mountains enjoyed neither the convenience of water transport nor the productivity of rich fields. It was only the income from the forests that had enabled the population to reach its present level, but even then food had to be brought in from the outside. If all these lands were to be taken over by the government and the people barred from them, there would be no way for most of the people of the region to live. Surely Owari han would have appreciated that. Unfortunately, the officials who had come from Chikuma prefecture were uninformed about local conditions. Besides, ever since the abolition of the han it had seemed natural for the central government, which had assumed the immense debts of the han, to expropriate every bit of the wealth of the han. At any rate, the Fukushima office had made no effort to find out what the established customs were in the Kiso area. All that it could say was that the rules for government forests had to be accepted.

If anyone protested the cruelty of the new policy and drafted a petition seeking a little more generosity from the administrators of the area, he would be stripped of his offices.

When the other village representatives failed to be intimidated by this and went ahead with the petition, no attention was paid to it. When their pleas became impassioned they aroused the anger of the officials. Some had been whipped. A stern warning had been issued saying that those who still did not submit would be brought before the appropriate officials in the main prefectural offices and dealt with there. Terrified by this threat, the people had promptly, though with the gravest reservations, accepted the establishment of the government forests.

"When you hear about one of these forest problems, you've heard about them all," said Masaka with a sigh.

"We don't have a single proper thing to offer you, Kureta," said Otami, coming in to serve sake to the guest. She took away the appetizers from the tray and Okume brought in fresh dishes from the kitchen. The only unusual thing they could offer was trout from the Kiso river, which was served coated with miso and roasted on a skewer. It was precisely the rustic quality of the meal that Masaka found most delightful.

"Pardon me for mentioning this before you, madam," said Masaka, taking a sip from his cup and putting it back down on the tray. "Long ago, when you so kindly hid me away in your storehouse, Aoyama brought me a gourd full of sake to drink. I remembered its flavor while I was in Ina and even later when I was in Kyoto and Tokyo. I don't think I'll forget it as long as I live."

"It's been more than ten years now," said Hanzo.

Okume came in carrying bowls of soup on a tray. Otami offered a bowl to the guest.

"It's fiddlehead soup."

"That's unusual in this season."

"Well, it's some that we salted down this spring. I washed the salt out of them and boiled them in miso. I thought that they might go well with the sake. Please try some."

"Madam, I called on you once before with the people from Nakatsugawa, but this is the first time I've ever had the privilege of meeting the whole family. You have a splendid daughter."

Coming from Masaka, the further statement that people are different when they are brought up in places like the Kiso where the water is pure did not seem farfetched. Otami was delighted to hear her daughter praised by the guest.

"Why, thank you. She is soon going to be married to a family in Ina."

Passing through the turbulence of the Meiji restoration had completely changed Masaka from the fugitive hiding out in Ina he had once been. After Otami left the parlor, Hanzo expressed his concern about the future of the Hirata school.

"Well, Aoyama, I can tell you that I wish Master Kanetane were ten years younger," said Masaka as he downed another cup of sake. "He was already sixty-six years old when the restoration came. He was really in charge only through the third year of Meiji."

"I heard that he gave up his post at the university in the third month of that year," said Hanzo.

"But this is it," responded Masaka, his eyes flashing, "we were all looking at a point ten years ahead. None of us ever expected recognition to come so soon to the National Scholars. At first there was only Tamamatsu Misao saying that a restoration of antiquity must go back beyond the restoration of the fourteenth century all the way to the accession of the emperor Jimmu himself. A true restoration of antiquity could not be achieved through halfhearted measures. However, most people did not share that opinion. Still, they were beginning by around 1870 to say that you could not be fully human if you weren't familiar with the works of Motoori and Hirata. Everything from cats to soupstrainers was saying it and everybody was reading Atsutane. But when you look at the results, you see that they only skimmed the books and laid them aside before they really understood what Motoori and Hirata were saying. No matter what anyone says about this being an age when what was new yesterday is old today, this is going too far."

"Kureta," replied Hanzo, gazing at his friend's slightly flushed face, "I think our best time is still ahead of us."

"Well—"

"We're just getting started, aren't we?"

"I suppose you're right. If you really think about it there is no way of knowing how many years or even decades it might take before this restoration is completed. Kanetane's first aim seems to have been to raise the level of political life. Among his disciples were people like Nakane Yukie of Echizen who were a great help to him, but in the end not even Kanetane could conquer old age. He became an old man during the years leading up to the restoration. But even so, things were still all right up to the fourth year of Meiji.

"The han returned their domains to the throne, the former daimyo were reinstated as governors, and the people of the old han still carried out the administration of the domains under them. In many han there was the feeling that this reorganization was simply an expedient to be rescinded when the restoration was actually completed. Then the abolition of the han began in earnest and things got tough. There were han that had no objection to seeing the Tokugawa surrender Edo castle but did have second thoughts when it came to surrendering their own castles. And then the administration by prefectures and counties began. The competition for official posts became ferocious. Some of the new officials who had suddenly come up from nowhere were extremely arrogant and heavy-handed. As you said a while ago, such people just don't work out in local administration.

"If the affairs of the nation get all entangled in the arbitrary acts of the officials, then we'll soon have a situation where the bureaucracy is all-powerful. But even you don't seem to believe that could really happen, Aoyama. You have to realize that a lot of people are beginning to show up from the samurai who are strictly out for power. And what about all this talk of sending an expedition to Korea? Of course, due punishment must not be overlooked—even if we do have peaceful relations with a foreign country, we still must make clear the difference between right and wrong. We also have to correct improprieties within the country. That's a matter of course. But what about these people who are managing to wield such power without any popular backing? It may very well help to placate the samurai who have no other outlet for their frustrations, but what's to become of the farmers and the townsmen? We can't have people setting about to create a new feudalism right in the middle of a restoration that is still by no means firmly established. Didn't Motoori and the others all advise that we should break away from the middle ages as quickly as possible?"

After he had a few more drinks, Masaka said that he would like to read some of the poetry of Tu Fu, of whom he had always been so fond. Hanzo went out and got several books from his study. Masaka wanted to read some of his favorite poems for Hanzo, the one about the hut in the Man-hua valley and the eight odes on autumn. They searched through the books for them.

"Here it is! Here it is!"

Masaka leaned forward toward the lamp and began to read Tu Fu's poem slowly and softly, and with intense feeling.

> The wealthy do not starve;
> The scholars are often in error.
> The hero tries to listen quietly;
> The contemptible display their learning.

Long ago when I was young,
I was honored as a precocious man.
Reading, I covered a myriad volumes;
Writing, I was as though possessed by a god.
I was equal to the hero Yang in the old texts;
I was close to Tsu-chien in versifying.
Li and Yü wanted to meet me;
Wang and Han begged me to live nearby.
I put myself above all others,
To place my lord above Yao and Shun,
To restore customs to virtue,
But that hope was, alas, forlorn—

When he had read that far, Masaka could not go on. As he read the line
"But that hope was, alas, forlorn" over and over to Hanzo, tears began to
flow down his cheeks.

5

Masaka stayed only one night.

"Well, Aoyama, I'll be going down to heave some deep sighs at Kamo,"
he said early the next morning. The light saddle horse he had ordered was
ready. The villager who led it to Hanzo's front gate had Masaka's baggage
tied to the saddle.

"Mother!" called Okume. "Kureta's leaving!"

Otami came running out with Wasuke in her arms.

"Are you leaving already? When you get to Nakatsugawa please give my
best wishes to Keizo's wife."

Everyone in the house came out of the front gate to see Masaka off. They
watched until his hat vanished around the curve of the slope below. Since he
was the former honjin it was rare for Hanzo's family to come out together to
see a guest off in this way. Hanzo spoke to Okume about the Kamo shrines
where Masaka was going to serve, telling her that they had the next highest
rank after Ise itself. He explained how, long ago in the Heian period, one
imperial princess was always consecrated to a period of service at the Kamo
shrines and another at Ise.

Masaka was gone. Hanzo set out as always to take up his duties at the village school at the Mampukuji. He spoke to Sho'un about the previous
night's guest. But when he returned home in the afternoon after finishing his
work he found that Masaka's departure had left a terrible void. Hanzo
wanted to explain his vision of the restoration of antiquity to his absent
friend once again—the vision that his old classmates Keizo and Kozo had
rushed off to pursue, forgetting even to eat or sleep. He, Masaka, and his

two friends had each chosen his own way. Reflecting on how the influences he had received when he was young and impressionable had controlled his life, Hanzo was secretly amazed. He began again to ponder the future of the Hirata school.

By this time, it was obvious that the first year of Meiji, when the posthumous disciples of Hirata Atsutane had numbered four thousand, had marked the zenith of the movement. In the Ina district where the study of Atsutane flourished, one hundred twenty disciples had been initiated in that year, but in the third year of Meiji the number had fallen to nineteen. In the fourth year there were only four initiations. And this was happening in the very same Ina valley that had produced Kurasawa Yoshiyuki, Katagiri Shun'ichi, Kitahara Inao, and Hara Mayomi. Atsutane's *Commentaries on History* had been printed and distributed there, and the Koedayama shrine had been founded in Yamabuki village. It had been a virtual hotbed of Hirata studies. The ideal of "raising the level of political life" that Masaka had mentioned had produced a ministry of Shinto in the new government and had placed this ministry under the direction of Kanetane. It was a position that had almost complete control of civil education in the nation. At the time of the surrender of power by the shogunate, the emperor had even gone to the ministry of Shinto to report the restoration of righteous rule to the spirits of his ancestors. In the fourth year of Meiji, however, the ministry was reorganized, and in the following year it was abolished altogether and replaced by a ministry of religion. Now the master was old, and even such important disciples as Masaka were being rusticated to places like Kamo. Among Hanzo's friends in the movement, Kozo was ill and Keizo had disappeared. And he himself had his hands tied.

6

As the sixth autumn under the new government began, the new age was still slow to come to the remote villages of the Kiso. Finally, a restoration even of the conditions that had prevailed at the beginning of the eighteenth century proved a vain hope. A great many people in the upper Kiso and its hinterlands could no longer rely on the forests for their livelihoods, and there was a steady increase in the number of villagers being punished for defying the new regulations by cutting trees illegally in the government forests. There were rumors that the bribes extorted from those punished in the valley had amounted to no small sum.

For all the talk of reform, the reality that confronted Hanzo was very dark. Moreover, his daughter Okume was still living in the shelter of his home, and the atmosphere surrounding her was heavy.

It is well to remember that up to the time when the fifteenth shogun,

Yoshinobu, carried out the reforms that were to be his parting gift to these highways, women could not pass through the barriers without special papers. It is also well to remember the long feudal history of checking for "departing women and entering firearms." The women had been minutely categorized as "long-hairs" or adult women in normal life, nuns, female ecclesiastics, widows, and young girls, and they could not pass a barrier until they had been examined down to their breasts. Not only were women refused permission to go to the sacred sites in the high mountains, but in most families they were not even permitted to enter places like the storerooms of sake brewers. The heavy, almost unbreakable fetters of countless ages bound the hands and feet of women. And it had transformed the women of this country. The admirable qualities that had characterized the women of ancient Japan, with their happiness and their firm self-confidence, had for the most part disappeared. One must also remember how it was for the girls of that time, who had to live under these restrictions, completely closed away in their houses and cut off from everything that was happening outside. Moreover, this lack of contact with the outside world was to set the tone for their entire lives. These women who groomed themselves by blackening teeth and shaving eyebrows had almost no contact with anyone other than their spouses. And what single quality was most marked in these girls who lived lives of such confinement, as if part of the policy of national isolation itself? In a word, it was precocity.

The daughter of the former honjin was no exception to this rule. The learning that Okume had acquired under the rigorous direction of Oman had extended even to the kind of pillow she had to use. It was a wooden object called a fulling block because that is just what it looked like, and in order not to disturb her hair she had to keep her head on the paper covering of this tiny pillow. Oman would even come in to make sure that Okume had not thwarted the purpose of the pillow by turning over in her sleep, and she would be scolded if she did. It was while she was still only fourteen or so that, as proof of her awareness of things, she came to her mother one day saying "Oh, my ears itch!" and asking if Otami did not know of something good for the condition. This precocity was not peculiar to Okume. All the girls of this region were already adults by the time they were fifteen.

However, the restoration that had brought about an awakening of the entire nation came at last even to the deep windows behind which these girls were hidden. They were filled with burning hopes, overflowing with hot passions, determined to have the doors thrown open for them. In the eleventh month of the fourth year of Meiji, 1872, five girls were sent along with the Iwakura mission to study in distant America. The first Japanese women to study overseas, they included the fifteen-year-old Yoshimasu Akiko, sent by the Hokkaido development office, the eleven-year-old Yamakawa Sasho, and even Tsuda Umeko, destined to become very famous later but then only seven years old. They attracted much attention and, with their orders—to journey to the West and to serve upon their return as a model for all women—clutched to their breasts for encouragement, they set out, their hair still cut in juvenile style. In Yokohama, they were put aboard the finest ship in the harbor, the packet *America* of the Pacific Steamship Company, a great vessel of forty-five hundred tons.

The story of this dreamlike occurrence was relayed down the highway where it told as nothing else could of the way in which Japan was leaping onto the stage of this new world. Great emphasis was then being placed on the education of women. There was even a rumor that Tanaka Fujimaro, formerly of Owari, who had just recently returned from a survey of education in Europe and America, was going to open, in Nagoya, the first women's school in central Japan. On the one hand, the waves of "civilization and enlightenment" kept pounding in while on the other hand strident voices were calling for the dispatch of an expeditionary force against Korea. With old and new scrambled together, there was a foreboding sense that no one could know what might happen next. How could young girls remain quiet through all this turbulence?

As September began, Okume had received several messages from the Inaba family in Minami Tono village about preparations for the wedding. It was going to take her three days to make the trip. Spending the first night en route at the Temmachoya in Iida and the second night at the Ogiya in Iijima, she would arrive in Minami Tono on the third day. The Inaba family had said that if porters and horses from Magome could take her and her possessions as far as Iida, they would take care of transportation from there.

"Okume! This is a fine kimono we've finished! Let's show it to your father!"

Displaying the wedding gown to the admiration of the other women in the house, Otami then went into the parlor carrying the gown in her arms and hung it up over the sliding panels for her husband to see.

The garment was pure white, beautiful even to a man's eyes. Lining the color of red plum blossoms showed from within the hanging sleeves, which were more than two feet deep. The contrast of the red and the white was pleasant enough, but what caught at Hanzo's heart was the sense of his daughter that came to him from the long sweep of the garment. The pattern of tiny swastikas woven into the white damask seemed quiet, subdued, and altogether appropriate for the daughter of a former honjin. The colors were pure and they spoke of youth.

Sad to say, even this splendid wedding gown on which Otami had lavished so much care failed to bring real pleasure to her daughter. There were only twenty days left and the closer the wedding date came the less Okume smiled.

7

In the room near the entrance of the Aoyama household there was no sound of the shuttle. The sash that Okume had been weaving for her brother Sota was nearly finished, but the loom stood silent on the wooden floor. Okume seemed to have tired of weaving and she was nowhere to be seen.

Otami passed by the loom on her way from the hearth room and on down the hall to see her husband in the parlor. Hanzo was not there. He had gone out to sweep the garden around the foot of the tree peony.

"Okume won't be with us much longer, Otami," he said as he continued to ply the bamboo broom.

There was something very lonely about his movements. It was no easy thing for the parents either when a daughter was about to be married. This was particularly true for Hanzo, who could not give himself up completely to the business at hand in these difficult times when even a senior disciple like Masaka seemed about to be swept away. Hanzo came over and sat on the edge of the veranda in front of the parlor, his feet still in garden clogs.

"I just can't get my mind off of it. Ever since Kureta left I've been coming back from school every day and just sitting with my arms folded."

Otami had learned not to rely too much on her husband since the forest problem came up. She was not inclined to say anything about the fact that she had been required to bring her daughter's marriage preparations to this stage without any help from him. Rather, she had come to talk with him about Okume herself, who still showed no sign of pleasure in the beautiful clothing that was being made for her.

"The Inaba really do everything right, don't they?" she began. "Just look, they've even thought about a gift for the woman who presided over Okume's coming-of-age ceremonies when her teeth were first blackened. They say that they would like for her to be given about one yen worth of fabric on the day that Okume leaves. They also said that they would prefer it if Okume were not accompanied by her own maid if at all possible, but that if such a person were to come, she should come alone four days ahead of the bride. They've even thought about that."

"Why four days early?"

"Why, that's so she will be used to the layout of the new house and won't get flustered on the day of the ceremony. Only the most considerate people would have thought of it. We should be grateful to them. You should speak to Okume about it, too."

"Wait a moment! Are you suggesting that if I speak to Okume then she will cease to object to this wedding? But the whole problem is due to the fact that young girls just can't make up their minds. I'm telling you that in our house my mother's wishes are to be regarded as sacred. If she has said that the groom would be suitable for Okume, then there is no possibility that he might not be. Isn't that right?"

"Whether it's right or not, we can't have Okume go on remaining silent as she has been. No matter what we do for her, she shows no pleasure in it. I've told her myself, 'If you think that we are going to be making money out of this, you are greatly mistaken. Everyone is going to so much trouble for you. The least you could do is get into the spirit of things.' Do you know what she said? She said, 'Don't worry about me, mother. I am my father's daughter.' "

". . ."

"And then she comes out with things like 'I won't be lonely if the gods are with me. Please, gods, watch over me.' "

". . ."

"Well, Okume is closer to you. She listens to what you say. Please speak to her."

Hanzo slipped out of his clogs and began to pace the floor of the parlor. The wind that blew in past the tree peony carried a hint of autumn, as if to remind him further that his daughter would soon be leaving this house. But Okume, though she did not talk about it, was not the sort of person to forget her gratitude to those who had brought her up. Of that he felt certain. Everything about her spoke of her love for her family. She was seventeen and Hanzo had no fear that she would betray the hopes of the people who had been so kind to her. He had complete faith in his daughter.

It may seem a bit abrupt to begin talking about girls in Korea but there is a story I have heard from someone who witnessed the wedding of a girl from the class called *yangban.* The girl, dressed like a doll in beautiful brocades of red, blue, and yellow, could scarcely be recognized as a living being. Her face was heavily powdered, making it very pale in the lamplight and the lashes of her tightly closed eyes seemed very long. My friend reported that she went out the door leaning on the shoulders of those around her as though she had lost the power to move on her own, and that she got into the palanquin as though being sent off for sacrifice, leaving her weeping parents behind. From that night she was not permitted to open her eyes. She could not open them even if she had wanted to. Her upper and lower eyelashes were firmly glued together with paste—or, in some districts, pomade. When he asked what that signified, he was told that it meant that she was not to look back. Now the *yangban* of Korea and the old honjin families of the Kiso cannot be placed in the same category, but in the end the Aoyama family too, with the same determination that she should not look back, placed a white silken headdress on their daughter's head and waited for this ceremony that comes once in a lifetime. They had already received very thoughtful gifts for Okume from Inosuke and his wife. Even the young boys were full of curiosity to see what was coming in, now from the Masudaya, then from the Horaiya. But Okume herself would only lie down for a nap or else flee to the old chamber of honor at the north of the house and take refuge in the shrine to Ubusuna there, remaining silent and unmoving for hours. If it's going to happen, let it happen. Hanzo had taught that lesson to his daughter in many ways, and

Otami, even when she said that she would like Okume to take along her old girl's festival dolls from the storehouse, had no thought but to complete Okume's preparations and to find some peace of mind for herself.

Eikichi and Seisuke served as consultants to Hanzo and Otami during this time. They would gather in the room next to the hearth room and discuss who should accompany the bride and which men should serve as her escort. They put it a bit differently than had Juheiji, but Eikichi and Seisuke also said that they should go ahead with the ceremony even if the bride wept and that they should instead concentrate their attention on seeing that nothing was overlooked in the preparations.

"What should I do about Okume's baggage?"

Heibei came down from Toge to ask Hanzo this question. Heibei, who loved to be busy, still functioned as the head of Toge hamlet even after the elimination of his post of assistant headman.

"The baggage?" Hanzo replied. "Well, if the baggage gets there four or five days before the ceremony, that will be fine. Just so everything doesn't get all piled up together on the last day. That's what they said. They said that they would leave it to our judgment. I suppose it would be easiest if we asked the packhorse men to take it as far as Iida."

On the fourth of September, a violent west wind blew through this windswept pass. It was particularly strong around dawn. Several of the chestnut trees by the shrine in back of the Aoyama residence went down. Okume spent the entire day at the loom, expressionless as she sent the shuttle back and forth like a machine. She finished Sota's sash by evening. Otami came to see it. Okume enjoyed weaving and she was skillful at it. Otami praised the newly woven fabric, still fragrant with the indigo dye, and then went on into the kitchen. Okume remained seated at the loom. In that posture, the similarity of her forehead to Hanzo's was especially noticeable. Her large, dark eyes stared unseeing. Her appearance suggested nothing more than the fatigue of a long hard day at the loom. She did not shed a single tear. But her hands gripped the ends of her sleeves so tightly that they quivered. She seemed to be suppressing some unspeakable sorrow.

The moon rose late that evening. Whenever the evening pines were outlined on the shoji of the parlor, Okume would go out and wander under the trees in the moonlight. This had started four or five days earlier and Otami had paid no particular attention to it. Otami saw Okume step out the kitchen door into the moonlight again, and worried that the girl might catch a cold just before her wedding, she slipped into clogs and went out to call her back. Otami could see nothing except the dark blue light from the sky. Crickets were singing bravely outside the kitchen.

"Okume!"

Upon hearing her mother's voice, the girl returned from the darkness under the persimmon tree in front of the storehouse.

The next day was an uneventful one in the Aoyama household. The evening meal was finished. Sakichi said that he had forgotten something in the woodshed and left the hearthside to fetch it. He was away some time and when he did return he reported to Hanzo and Otami that the door to the storehouse which he was sure he had closed was now open again. Oman had come down for dinner and she was talking beside the hearth. But Okume was not there. Everyone immediately became alarmed and Hanzo and Sakichi rushed to the storehouse with lanterns. Oman and Otami followed them. When they reached the second floor they found Okume lying beside the two old chests. She had tried to kill herself.

CHAPTER TEN

1

THERE WAS no way that the tragedy that had befallen the Aoyama family could remain unknown in the tiny village of Magome.

Magome itself had little drinking water, but in the mountains behind the village there was a small spring with the sweet water that one finds only in high country. This water was brought down in a flume to a great basin that served as the village reservoir, overflowing with sweet mountain coolness. Women from houses that did not have their own well would go out with buckets and carrying poles to this reservoir. Below the bank at the southern edge of Magome, along the narrow path in the shade of cedars and elms, the women would gather on their way to get water and in this hidden retreat they would learn about all the happenings in the village.

There were various versions of the story going around. One woman said that she had known about the daughter of the former honjin on the very night it happened. Another reported that she had heard about it only the next morning. Whether coming or going, the conversations of the women fetching water were all devoted to the subject of Okume. Only prompt discovery and skillful treatment by her family had prevented her from dying on the spot, but she was in serious condition and it was still not certain that she would live. Not even the physician who had come rushing up from Nakatsugawa in the middle of the night could tell. Some, who knew the history of the Aoyama family, even brought up the subject of Kichizaemon's grandfather, Shichirobei. He had gone with several friends to fish in the Kiso river and had drowned at the place called Jiryu at Yaejima in neighboring Yamaguchi. It was suggested that the two incidents proved that the family was under some kind of curse.

It was not at all surprising that such rumors about Okume should be so freely spread by outsiders. Not even the members of her own family could understand her attempted suicide. The four or five days immediately following the incident seemed like forty or fifty days to them. During that time Okume hung on the brink of death, unable to eat or drink.

Hanzo aged suddenly. The agonies of a single evening had made him ten years older. All he could say to people who inquired after Okume was that he himself felt completely helpless. He said that he could not think clearly.

The treatments took effect and Okume gradually began to recover. It appeared that her life would be spared. Hanzo, embarrassed that his daughter should have caused concern to so many people, now felt that once this crisis was over, he would turn away from everything in his past life and start anew. He did not hesitate to say this to those who came to inquire about the girl. He would often go directly from his classes at the school to Okume's bedside, not even stopping to change his clothing. Screens had been put up around the inner room in the main house where she was convalescing. Her face was still swollen and the white bandage over the wound on her throat, which she had made with a short sword, caught the eye and took the breath away of all who saw it. Otami was beside herself over this terrifying transformation in her daughter. In her sorrow and with a single-minded desire to help, she undertook a hundred ambulations to the Inari shrine in back of the house.

Just why a girl belonging to the Aoyama family, one of the oldest in the Kiso, who had such a splendid wedding to look forward to should have done such a terrible thing was a subject of futile speculation to all who knew her. Juheiji's wife, Osato, came from Tsumago and Hanzo's disciple Katsushige came from Ochiai, their faces troubled as they made their calls. Katsushige speculated that she might have despaired of this world, and Osato thought that Okume might have wanted to pursue her studies further. The subject even came up when Hanzo met his neighbor Inosuke, who suggested that, a young person like Okume did not really perceive things all that clearly and probably had not intended to go so far. He said that even such a fine, intelligent girl as Okume still needed guidance. Then there were those who saw the incident as a proof of Okume's maidenly purity—she had become obsessed with the importance of the vows between husband and wife and the approach of her wedding day had consequently overwhelmed her. Others noted that there was nothing in Okume's everyday behavior to suggest that in the body of one seemingly so favored in previous lives there could be lodged such a fearful demon. They suggested that she had been overcome by a melancholy such as can be known only by the most sensitive people.

Hanzo could see no other way to save his daughter than to write a letter to the Inaba family in Minami Tono village recounting the incident just as it had happened, and asking that the betrothal be dissolved. But it was not easy for a father to write such a letter, breaking his promise, when the other party had already exchanged betrothal gifts and had shown such consideration in their preparations to receive Okume into their home. He also thought that he should at least inform the go-between, but the agreed upon day of September twenty-second came without his having done so. Nor was he able to write at the end of the month. Although he completed a rough draft by the middle of October, he was unable to proceed further.

DEAR SIR:

I trust that the onset of cooler weather finds you all in the very best of health.

Now our daughter Okume, whom you so kindly arranged last win-

ter to be married into the Inaba family of Minami Tono village, has on
the fifth of last month, through a misunderstanding, stabbed herself
with a sword while on the second floor of our storehouse. She was
promptly discovered by my wife and my mother, who both rendered
aid. Our relatives came and offered counsel and a physician was called.
She was so severely wounded that she could not swallow food or drink
for four or five days. Fortunately the treatment was effective and she is
showing steady improvement. She now has no difficulty in eating and
the wound is healing satisfactorily. However, she must as yet have total
rest. I assure you that no one in the house recognized her condition
ahead of time or suspected in any way that such a thing might happen.
We are at a loss for words to describe our feelings. We can only beg you
to extend our apologies to those in Minami Tono village.

Because of the above, I must ask you to consent to voiding the contract that existed between us, and at the same time I extend the most
humble and heartfelt apologies. Since we have had a long-standing
promise and since preparations had all been completed, I should have
informed everyone of this incident immediately, but various things have
interfered and in spite of my best intentions the matter has dragged on
until today. I had hoped that we might strengthen our ties of friendship
with you, since both you and the Inaba family have been so kind and
considerate to us, but for some reason the girl misinterpreted our intentions. So, however much it may pain her parents, we are left only with
the prayer that you might take our plea in the best spirit. We will soon
be coming to offer our apologies in person, but for now we can only
request this great favor of you.

Please inform the people of Minami Tono village of our profound
regrets and tell them that there is nothing I can say for myself directly at
this time. I beg of you to perform this service for me. That to which we
had once agreed to commit ourselves has now become a source of
regret.

I must once again say that everyone in the family from my aged
mother on down shares in the deep sense of shame and regret that I
have expressed in the body of this letter.

Aoyama Hanzo

The letter which had been so difficult to write was at last finished on the
twenty-third of October. As Hanzo wrote it, he recalled the prodigious
efforts that Oman had made in securing this match. He was concerned about
whether Okume could ever be forgiven by Oman, whose character had been
forged in a feudal world where absolute acceptance of the word of superiors
was viewed more in terms of lord and vassal rather than of parent and child.

"Otami."

Hanzo read out the letter to his wife before putting two of the new one-
sen postage stamps on it and mailing it.

"If only you had given a little more attention to your own daughter, this would never have happened."

As Otami said this, she fell to weeping beside her husband.

There was nothing that Hanzo could say in reply. He had been busy night and day with the forest problem, preoccupied with the welfare of the people who were about to lose their livelihood in the Kiso forests. He had scarcely spared so much as a glance toward his wife and daughter during the whole time. Now he tasted the bitter fruit of his neglect of his unyieldingly righteous stepmother, his weeping wife, and his suffering daughter.

One day he went to the inner room to see Okume. The swelling had finally left her face. In his joy, he touched the forehead and cheeks of the sleeping girl and reassured himself once again of her progress. Suddenly Okume opened her large, dark eyes.

"I have no excuse, father. I acted terribly. I feel—I feel as though I am about to start a new life. Please forgive me for this one."

"Oh, you were awake!" he replied.

Early in November, Heibei came back from a visit to Minami Tono village in Ina. He had gone at Hanzo's request to meet with the Inaba family and to tell them precisely of Okume's condition. He was to ask that the betrothal be dissolved. The letter that Heibei brought back said that the entire Inaba family, from the head of the house on down, was most reluctant to do so. Suggesting that Okume had displayed a most promising strength of character, they asked instead for a renewal of the betrothal.

The kindness of the Inaba family only made things still more difficult. Oman, determined to renew the relationship between her own family and the Aoyama household, remained adamant. It was not easy for Hanzo to go against her.

Oman was not really interested in Hanzo's feelings on the matter. She simply considered him to have failed in carrying out his assigned role. Even in ordinary times he had seemed inadequate to her, forever doing strange things, but now she no longer treated him as a human being, much less as anyone in a position to face her family. Her grandfather had been the illustrious warrior Sakamoto Magoshiro, with the pen name Tensan, and this was the uncompromising tone she took.

She called Okume, still very pale and not wholly recovered from her wound, into her presence and forced her to listen to a lengthy description of just how understanding the Inaba family had been in this entire affair. Oman maintained that their obligations were now too heavy to be ignored. She even had Eikichi and the other relatives come in to speak to Okume. Okume could only kneel there, her palms flat on the floor, begging over and over again to be excused from her obligation. She made no reference to any of the details. In the end, this reduced even Oman to sighs.

Hanzo saw a bitter family struggle growing out of this confrontation. It was clear in Oman's manner that she was concerned about the expenses that her family had incurred, and about what people might say, and that if this had been her real granddaughter, the matter would have been properly resolved regardless of the cost. As for Okume, she had barely returned to life. If she was to be constantly tormented after she had just regained her strength, there was no telling what she might do the next time. Hanzo and Otami had no alternative but to intercede with his stepmother and try to release Okume from her bonds.

"Ever more pure and simple."

With this in mind, Hanzo felt a growing desire to sweep away all the affairs that had been coming to plague him one after another and open a new way for himself. It was no time for hesitation. He was determined to simplify his life, and he wrote another letter to the Inaba family, intending it to be the final letter to Minami Tono village.

DEAR SIR:

I have received your letter. I extend greetings and felicitations to you along with my ever deepening wish that these days of late autumn warmth may find you and your entire family enjoying the best of health and happiness.

Now, since the situation in our wretched household has not changed in any way, I can only ask with the greatest trepidation that you abandon your hopes concerning us. To put it more plainly, when Heibei of Toge village recently called upon you and learned of your still greater generosity and forbearance toward us, our unworthy daughter failed to display the slightest sign of gratitude. On that occasion, not only I and my wife, but my stepmother and other relatives came and attempted to admonish her, but in the end they were moved by feelings of pity for her in her deep shame. It is not that she rejects your family. She is so taken aback by the results of her own actions that, except for close relatives, she is unwilling to meet with other people of the village. She will not even go next door for a bath. To return to my first point, for these reasons she is too ashamed to go to your family and would be unable to bear the pain of facing you and your relatives. Therefore I must say that there is no possibility whatsoever that she will ever be going to your house. This puts us in a position where we are unable to respond with proper gratitude for your generosity and consideration in this matter. It pains us most deeply.

We beg you not to bear anger toward us and we wish to repeat endlessly our sincere regrets to you and your family. I should have replied to your esteemed letter much earlier but repeated attempts to admonish our unworthy daughter have led to unexpected delays, compounding our already numerous offenses against you. My stepmother and my wife join me in expressing our most profound regrets.

Aoyama Hanzo

2

At last Hanzo had made his way through the storms to a great divide in his own life. There are few who reach the age of forty-three without becoming aware that this world is full of unrealistic hopes and deep disappointments. For Hanzo, a Hirata disciple, the experience of seeing how difficult it was to realize a restoration of antiquity, and the disasters that had befallen his colleagues, had been in itself enough to make this clear. However, he had been sustained by a feeling of righteousness such as can be experienced only by those who care deeply about the world, and his unwillingness to exchange that feeling for anything else was what had enabled him to reach the age of forty-three still undeterred from trying to follow in the footsteps of his elders.

When he looked back, it was to 1856, the third year of Ansei, when he had received his father's permission to make his first trip to Edo. There he had knocked at the gate of Hirata Kanetane and had made his vows. He had shared refreshments, been given a fan, and entered on the roll of Hirata disciples. He could not take those vows lightly. Now the day had come when Kanetane himself had said, "I have guided you this far but in the rest of the journey, you must find your own way." That was only natural, for in this year of 1873, Meiji 6, Kanetane had reached seventy-one years of age.

Hanzo's unease had been intensified by the death of the young master Hirata Nobutane in January of the previous year. That the central figure of the school, of whom so much had been hoped by the disciples, should have died at the age of forty-four was a terrible loss to the National Learning movement. Then Okume had so grievously wounded herself. The sorrows of this world could be felt but never expressed in words. The flashes of lightning that seemed so remote actually struck people from time to time. Hanzo passed days of such profound disorientation that he began to wonder if this was not a time granted him for truly appreciating the uncertainty and fearfulness of life. The resolve that grew in him was very simple: to wipe out his past and to create himself anew. That resolve reflected his total commitment to National Learning.

Hanzo began to grow restless. At times he held to the thought of contenting himself in his role of village sage, bringing learning to the untutored children of the farmers. At other times he would realize that this was no time to remain hidden away in the mountains, simply observing the fate of a defunct post station. These impulses were in constant conflict within him, giving him no rest. It is said that an excess of sorrows may lead one to the service of the gods, and Hanzo now became aware that there might still be a way to make antiquity manifest in the present world. That the posthumous disciples of Hirata Atsutane had all gone to serve in Shinto shrines after their disappointments in political life came to seem like a revelation to him. Even without the examples of Morooka Masatane, now priest of the main shrine at

Matsuo, or Kureta Masaka, priest of the lesser Kamo shrine, there were
many disciples from the Ina valley who had adopted similar courses.

> In a mountain chamber
> Awakened in the middle of the night
> Before any trace of dawn
> I listen to the sound
> Of wind-blown rain.

> If our ancestors'
> Ancestors were gods
> Long ago
> Then the people are gods
> And we must serve them.

These were the verses inspired by Hanzo's newfound desire to enter the
service of the gods. He felt at least this course might meet the approval of the
old masters.

As a first step along his new way, Hanzo began to think about his family's
funeral practices. Originally, the emphasis on Shinto burial, one of the thrusts
in the movement to restore antiquity, had been born out of a desire to repudiate the middle ages. Among the samurai, Ogawa Yaemon of Oka han in
Bungo and, among commoners, the headman Kurasawa Yoshiyuki of Ono
village in Ina had been the first to recognize its fundamental importance and
to obtain official sanction for carrying out Shinto services. Kurasawa, in particular, had announced in 1865 that he could not tolerate carrying out the
major sacraments of human life in a Buddhist temple for a single additional
day. Not in the least intimidated by the fact that funeral ceremonies had been
the prerogative of the Buddhist temples of the region ever since the beginning of the middle ages, he broke with the four hundred and three Soto Zen
temples in Shinano province and removed his family from the temple rolls.
As a consequence he was relieved of the office of headman, and thereafter
traveled back and forth between the commission of temples and shrines in
Kyoto and the village offices at Chimura with a passion that led him willingly to exhaust his wealth in a four year struggle to realize his goal.

Men like Kurasawa had taken the lead in doing away with the privilege of
maintaining family records which the Tokugawa shogunate had entrusted to
the Buddhist temples. But the world was different now. In November of
1873, an order came out under the name of the vice-governor of Chikuma
prefecture that henceforth funeral practices would be left to the religious
preferences of the people concerned. This order had been hinted at earlier but
never circulated until now. When the time came for this order to be transmitted through the local offices in Fukushima down to the heads of the three
districts under its supervision, Hanzo saw it as an opportunity not to be
missed. He went to his neighbor and confidant Inosuke to invite him to join
in a reform of their families' funeral practices.

Hanzo proposed that they first retrieve the name tablets of their ancestors from the Mampukuji. They would wipe the dust off them and bring them back to the house. They would no longer leave the cleaning of the family graves to the temple staff but would have members of their own families look after them. Since the land on which the temple stood had originally been donated by the Aoyama household, they would continue to use the temple grounds whenever they had a funeral. But in the house, all the hateful Buddhist statues still confounding Shinto and Buddhist beliefs would be burned immediately. These words startled Inosuke, but abandoning his usual caution, he said that this matter had a bearing on the upbringing of their children and could not simply be let slide. Up to now the funerals for those closest to them had been left too much to strangers. He said that he had been thinking about his family's relationship to the temple ever since the days when he was a post official, and that if the former honjin was going to carry out these measures, the Fushimiya, too, would take advantage of this opportunity to rectify its funeral practices and restore the old ways.

"Inosuke is a true friend."

Hanzo was impelled to act. Accompanied by Inosuke, he set out up the north slope along the path through the rice fields toward the Mampukuji to inform the priest of his decision.

Sho'un's original name was Chigen. After six years of training and pilgrimage, he had received permission from the main temple in Kyoto to adopt the name Sho'un. It had already been twenty years since he had come to Magome to take charge of the Mampukuji.

That was in 1854, the first year of Ansei, and at that time both Hanzo's father, Kichizaemon, and Inosuke's foster-father, Kimbei, were still in charge of service along this section of the highway. On a rainy day in the old second month, Sho'un had come up the Jikkyoku pass from Mino accompanied by the old priest of the Sosenji in Nakatsugawa. The young Hanzo had met him at Shinjaya. Before going to the temple, the priest Sho'un had first called on the honjin, where he had changed into priestly garments. Then he had been borne up to the Mampukuji in a litter, accompanied by a parasol bearer.

In twenty years not only Hanzo and Sho'un but their surroundings as well had changed. The priest was already past fifty. Over the years he had observed the great processions moving along the Kiso road and the people rushing in desperation back and forth over the passes as though they were no more than the changing clouds or the alternation of yin and yang, his only companion the painting of Bodhidharma that hung on the wall in the priest's quarters. Even the act of washing his face each morning was a part of his discipline—each morning's beating of the temple drum and reading of the sutras, each ascent into the bell tower at dawn to sound the great bell, was a part of that day's application to the Way. From a great teacher of long ago, Hakujo Zenshi, he had learned that not to observe the rituals on any day meant that one did not eat that day. Everything Sho'un did was done in that spirit—the offering of rice to the Buddha, the collection of alms, the dedication of candles and flowers, the services in the hall containing the ancestral tablets, the readings from the *Prajna Paramita Sutra,* the training of acolytes, the cleaning of the graves. His long experience had made him alert to the smallest details. When, for example, the women of a certain family of contributors to the temple came to make their annual offerings on the eighth day of the first month, he would always put out enough walnut cookies for ten people, the bath would be fired up from early morning, and afterward boiled beans and winter vegetables would be served with rice and tea. Sho'un had also taken the idea that the temple was consecrated ground further by beginning to improve the hill in back from around 1869 on, bringing in boulders and planting azaleas to improve the view from the main buildings. The sound of the clear water brought down from the mountains tumbling into this garden made the temple grounds seem even more removed from the bustle and confusion of the highway.

However quiet the life of this Zen priest may appear to have been, it could not be said to be free of change. In this age when all positions from that of the shogun and the daimyo down to the honjin, toiya, headmen, and assistant headmen were being eliminated, it would have seemed almost uncanny if priests alone should remain as before. But with the anti-Buddhist movement that had been gathering force since before the restoration, there came a revival of Shinto burial rituals, and the temples lost the exclusive function of maintaining the family records which they had kept since the beginning of the Tokugawa period. The increase in the number of people leaving the congregation was so great that the very survival of the temples became questionable, and this came as a heavy blow not only to the priests of the various sects but also to those millions throughout the country who depended upon the charity of the temples for their sustenance.

All this led Sho'un in his middle age to become interested in the history of the Japanese emperors. He was particularly attracted by the words attributed to Prince Umayado, the son of the thirty-first emperor, Yomei. Now Prince Umayado was none other than the Shotoku Taishi who had first sponsored the dissemination of Buddhist teachings in this country. He said that Shinto is the root of our nation while Confucianism and Buddhism are its branches. When the root is vigorous the branches flourish, and the root must therefore never be damaged. In Sho'un's view, a return to the roots of Shinto was to some degree necessary for the protection of Buddhism itself. But an opposing point of view held that it was an erroneous and perverse doctrine that maintained that Buddhism was based on Shinto. He had heard this attitude expressed by fellow priests in the neighboring villages and in the temples in nearby Mino. Then he began to get letters attacking his one-sided and partial point of view.

Sho'un prepared a statement of his own position and circulated it among his fellow Zen priests. It argued that this return to the roots was a way of assuring that the branches would flourish. Yet even when the roots are firm, the branches can be withered by frost and snow and lose their leaves. Branches may even die. But in the spring fresh sprouts appear, and new branches are put out. This process is completely natural, in no way reflecting any weakness at the roots. So long as the main root does not die, the tree will once again flourish. But, needless to say, if the root should once be severed the branches will surely die. How can a doctrine which recognizes the roots as roots and the branches as branches be considered one-sided and partial?

Buddhism was transmitted to this land in 552, in the thirteenth year of the reign of the emperor Kimmei. Since then great temples have been established in every province and the faith of the imperial family and of the aristocracy has been beyond the power of mere words to describe. It is also beyond the power of words to describe the excesses of the Buddhists during the most recent centuries. All believers are not the same. There are good and bad among them. Wherever there is increase, it gives birth to decrease. Both praise and blame arise from this inescapable fact, but precisely because Buddhists also live in this land of the gods we must devote all our strength to the service of the heavenly grandson, that is to say, the imperial line, and guard the roots of the nation. Who can say that it is one-sided and partial to assist Shinto in its basic mission of guidance in the process of giving that service? In this time of restoration, it is unavoidable that we should be seen as people unable to break away from archaic practices, yet if we fulfill our duties to the founder of Buddhism and follow the Way in righteousness, how can we be said to be one-sided and partial? If we bring calm to our hearts by never opposing the will of the court, by taking the imperial rescript on education as our guide, by always behaving correctly, suppressing evil and maintaining our balance, then there is no possibility that we could ever be in opposition to the way of heaven.

Rather than concerning ourselves with the opinions of others, we must stand firmly on our own feet in establishing the true spirit of Yamato. We must achieve a clear discrimination between good and evil, correct and incorrect, truth and falsehood, gain and loss. While always concerned that the roots do not deteriorate, we must also dedicate ourselves to looking after the vigor of the leaves and branches. The law that teaches us to revere the gods and Buddhas is based on meeting obligations and rewarding virtue. It is what we call true faith. The only thing that might lead one to desire profit for oneself is simple greed, but so long as we possess a true will to recognize obligation and reward virtue, we will have the protection of the gods. Though we call ourselves Buddhists, that is still no reason to lack common sense. We neither crave for ease in this world nor lust after a favorable position in future lives. If we render unto heaven what is heaven's, act with propriety, and never associate ourselves with impropriety, then no one will be able to stand against us in this life or in future lives. Since our only pleasure is in following the way of the gods with complete sincerity, there cannot be in our actions either the greed or the self-importance that could lead to charges of partiality and one-sidedness.

This was Sho'un's position and he made it very clear.

Although Sho'un, as befits a Zen priest, did not appear to change, he was in fact changing in this quiet way. From his point of view, the movement of time and the world's changes were like the passing of the seasons. When the clouds came out, the sun and moon were obscured; when the clouds departed, the sky was bright once again. Similarly, in a time of disorder, sagely wisdom would remain hidden, but when the world was restored to order, the Way would be followed once again. Sho'un's faith was founded on the teachings of Bodhidharma, that great priest who long ago had come out of the west to bring his teachings to the east. Sho'un therefore found nothing the least bit unsettling about the Meiji restoration. Even though others found his attitude irritating in its excessive high-mindedness, Sho'un simply concentrated his thoughts in his daily practice and looked out on the affairs of the world as though from a great distance.

When Hanzo and Inosuke arrived at the Mampukuji, they found that the village hairdresser Naoji was there shaving the priest's head. Sho'un, who always said that long hair was a disgrace to a priest, never neglected to keep his head cleanly shaved. Hanzo and Inosuke went to the hearth room of the temple to wait until Naoji had finished.

The hearth room had seemed empty since the death of the woman who had lived in the temple and had looked after the priest for some twelve or thirteen years. Her name was Oshima and she had come from Midono. Since she was at the temple with the permission of the post officials, there had never been any need for her to feel any constraint, but, possibly because she was aware that she did not really fit in with these surroundings, she never came out into the main hall. She had helped Sho'un from behind the scenes and had been well regarded by the important families in the village. Hanzo could clearly remember Oshima coming in from the kitchen and untying her sleeve cords to serve tea to the guests. Still fresh in his memory, too, was Sho'un's distribution of gifts to the honjin and to the Fushimiya in her memory.

It seemed that even Naoji, for all his long practice, was finding Sho'un's head difficult to shave and they were kept waiting for some time. While they waited, Hanzo and Inosuke left the hearthside and went out to walk in the garden that the priest had created. Presently they were led into the living quarters by an acolyte, who seemed to be twelve or thirteen.

"I'm delighted."

Sho'un greeted them as always. He treated all guests the same, whether familiar to him or not, whether good or evil. With his head freshly shaved, the priest looked even more gentle than usual. He had volunteered to help Hanzo with the education of the village children in a section of the main hall set aside for that purpose and he had never said a word about the additional burden. For a moment, in the quiet presence of the priest, Hanzo found it difficult to bring up the purpose of the day's visit. He was well aware that Sho'un, Buddhist though he might be, did not neglect the village tutelary deity and never failed to go down to Aramachi and pay his respects on the first and fifteenth day of every month. He was still more keenly aware that Sho'un was a thoroughly admirable person whom it was impossible to hate.

Yet Hanzo's mission was not one that he could permit himself to be deflected from simply because of personal feelings and established practices. With Inosuke beside him, he informed Sho'un of the meaning of the announcement that had come down from the Chikuma prefectural offices and explained that the Aoyama and Satake households had decided to change their burial practices. Although the bushel of rice that came from each of their houses on the anniversaries of the deceased ought properly to be discontinued immediately following this change, they would, out of respect for long-standing precedent, still continue to send a half-bushel each beginning next year. The change of ceremonies that Hanzo described, amounting to a total rejection of Buddhism, shook even Sho'un's composure. It was Hanzo's distant ancestor Aoyama Dosai who had founded this temple, and Sho'un had been the beneficiary of the unstinting patronage of the Fushimiya ever since he had begun his training under the name of Chigen. Kimbei had seen to everything from the thatching of the roof of the main hall to the donation of the great drum.

"I understand your intentions. I understand quite well. Since, unlike the other priests, I have always viewed Shinto as the foundation for our lives, I cannot take issue with you. All these things are due to evils in previous lives. They cannot be helped. Well, now that we have had our talk, I would like you to have some tea."

Sho'un rose to his feet. That he performed every action with the most careful attention could be seen in the way he poured a bit of fresh water into the furiously boiling kettle and in the way he got out the teacups and brewed tea from the previous year's crop grown at the temple. For Sho'un, living in the world of men, these priest's quarters were an ephemeral dwelling, and he was by no means one to insist on his own pleasures. At the same time he found these Hirata followers with their cold disdain and their desire to arouse the people of this world much too remote to be sympathetic.

"Let me take you to the hall of the ancestral tablets. I knew that such a day would be coming sooner or later. The question of Shinto burial rites has been at issue ever since the passage of Princess Kazu."

Then he took up his rosary and set out ahead of them, leading them down the hallway to the back of the main building. There, in a dark room, the offertory trays, the tea, the incense and flowers, and the candle holders were carefully laid out.

The ancestral tablets of generations of the Aoyama family were all gathered here. In the center of the room was the tablet of the man who had founded this village at the foot of the mountains and who had founded the Mampukuji itself. With a grandeur befitting his life, it bore the posthumous title MAMPUKUJI DENSHO-OKU JOKYU ZENJOMON. The tablets were of various sizes, some of them bearing the family crest consisting of a circle with three parallel lines drawn through it. Each had a posthumous title inscribed on the front. These names had been assigned by the priests of the Mampukuji and each reflected the character of the deceased individual. Some were intimidating, others were gentle. Among them was one marked "MYOSHIN JITOKU KOJI, age seventy-one years." This was Hanzo's father. "SEISHIN MYOJO TAISHI, age thirty-one years" was his mother. Hanzo and Inosuke spent some time walking back and forth in front of these tablets.

At last Sho'un spoke.

"Aoyama, I have something to ask of you on this occasion. I would very much like to have the tablets of your ancestor who founded this temple and his wife remain here."

Hanzo nodded his assent.

3

In this year of 1874, the seventh year of Meiji, Hanzo decided to travel to Matsumoto and Tokyo. Oman had at last given up her plans to marry Okume into her own family. She consented to the return of the betrothal gifts, gave away the garments that had been specially dyed for the occasion, and broke off negotiations with the Inaba household. Okume was like one restored to life. Hanzo had told her about what Kureta Masaka had said, and explained that she had found the "second life" that so many of the Hirata disciples were seeking these days. She listened to her father's words of encouragement with eyes full of tears, and seemed to recover her spirits day by day. As for Otami, it was in her nature to recover quickly once she had wept. Even this terrible incident had not shocked her, as a mother, as deeply as it had Hanzo as a father. Their eldest son, Sota, was now in his seventeenth spring and no longer a child. It seemed an appropriate time for Hanzo to ask the family to look after things in his absence while he left home for a while to try to find a new way for himself.

When Hanzo was about ready to leave, a fortune teller came to Magome and put up at the inn. Although he usually paid no attention to such people, Hanzo let Inosuke persuade him to consult the travel-worn mendicant. The man took his divining sticks out of an old sack, counted them out as though performing a solemn ritual, and divided the remaining number into even and odd. He then told Inosuke his fortune for the coming year. The portents seemed most favorable. Inosuke's wishes would be granted. If he did business he would find it profitable; what he sought would be found; the people he awaited would come; and marriage negotiations that he undertook would be successful. Then he repeated the process for Hanzo, but he did not find the same favorable portents that he had found for Hanzo's neighbor.

The fortune teller stood before Hanzo, twisting his neck as he spoke.

"One would not think of it just to look at you, but according to the *I Ching* the person who fits that trigram must resign himself to the fact that things are not open to him—he must fear the coming of each new year, be circumspect in all things, and wait for the coming of a better time. It would really be best if you did not attempt anything at all for this whole year."

Hanzo found himself somehow unable to laugh at the fortune teller's words. Even after he had returned to the house to continue his preparations for travel, he felt a vague but persistent disquiet. Although his path seemed to become narrower and narrower the farther he walked, he believed the only way left for the posthumous disciples of Hirata Atsutane led toward the old Shinto shrines, and he was interested in pursuing anything that would move him even one step closer to the goal. In the same way that one must first climb the stairway in order to approach a shrine, he had first to exhaust all the preliminary measures. His path resembled Sho'un's and yet at the same time it was entirely different. His desire was not only to be protected by the gods, but also to go forth and protect the gods. He had not yet mentioned this to his family. Now he regretted having consulted with this fortune teller, who was, after all, a total stranger.

He left home in the middle of May, not letting even his closest friends see him off. He had last seen Edo in the sixth month of Genji 1, 1864. That year, as one of the representatives of the eleven Kiso post stations, he had been summoned to Edo by the commissioners of transport and had traveled in the company of his fellow headmen. Now he was alone. The new system of administration through prefectures and counties was still being implemented, and the Kiso valley was now divided into three principal districts. In addition, smaller school districts had been set up and village administrations were being consolidated in several areas. As Hanzo began to climb Torii pass, his thoughts returned to the ramifications of the forest problem. At the summit of the pass, from the shrine offering a prospect of Mt. Ontake in the distance, he looked back toward the Kiso valley.

When he reached Matsumoto, he found that Chikuma prefecture had convened a series of lectures for the local schoolteachers. A normal school had been set up in the Zuishoji, the old temple in Miyamura-cho, and people had been invited to attend from all over the prefecture.

There Hanzo found a replacement who could take over his teaching duties in the Magome school. He decided to name him to the post immediately. He explained to the candidate that although the school was temporarily located in the Mampukuji, a new building was presently under construction on a site near the temple and would soon be completed. The man's name was Kokura Keisuke and he was from a family of Shinto priests. He was an extremely proper and straightforward person. Having found such a promising teacher for his village, Hanzo could now set out for Tokyo with one burden lifted. He himself had struggled from a very early age to advance his own education; regretting the absence of teachers in his remote village, he had tried not only to make up for his own backwardness but at the same time to teach the village children. His concern with the education of the young went far beyond that of most people.

In Matsumoto Hanzo was able to observe the education system that was being prepared for the new age, and his earlier impressions were all confirmed. There was to be a complete change from the hitherto existing temple school system and a wholesale adoption of European and American methods. The lectures at the normal school were all directed to this end.

Elementary school was to be divided into two sections, the standard schools and the grammar schools. Each would last four years. Students would enter the lower grades at age six and complete them at age nine. Their courses would be divided into eight classes, each lasting six months, and the entering students would be designated members of the eighth class.

The purpose of the teachers would above all else be to impart the knowledge of the entire world to the students—great emphasis was placed in the lectures on the concept of "enlightenment." Even the basic procedures would differ from that of the temple schools. The students would learn vocabulary. First the syllabaries would be taught with the use of the slate; then the students would be given calligraphy primers introducing them to Chinese characters. They would be shown the map of the world, with the idea of the globe explained to them, and they would be taught appropriate responses to standard questions on Japanese and world history. When Hanzo looked at one of the new elementary school readers, he found that it began with an account of the races of the world. The greater part of what was written in it was unassimilated new learning. Moreover, contrary to his wish that both Japanese and European mathematics be taught, the prefectural officials insisted that only European mathematics should be offered.

Hanzo was repelled by most of what he saw. Deciding that nothing was to be gained by staying longer, he prepared to leave Matsumoto immediately, consoling himself with the thought of his good fortune in having found a person of the quality of Kokura Keisuke for his own village school. He was suffering from fatigue of both body and spirit. Telling himself that he needed to rest, and looking forward to seeing the new capital city of Tokyo, he moved on from Shiojiri to Shimo-Suwa, over to Oiwake, and then toward Karuizawa. From there, still on the long road that stretched all the way back to his home in Magome, he descended Usui pass.

This spring of 1874 when Hanzo set out on his journey, hoping to find a new beginning, had been preceded by the greatest disturbance in the central government since the civil war at the beginning of Meiji. Set off by a fierce clash among the members of the upper levels of the administration in the previous October, it had involved Saigo Takamori and his faction on one side, insisting upon a settlement of the dispute with Korea, by force of arms if necessary, and Iwakura Tomomi and Okubo Toshimichi, recently returned from their mission abroad, on the other. Iwakura had ridiculed the proposal to attack little Korea when Japan itself was still at the mercy of the might of Europe and America. The end result was that men who had worked together to overthrow the Tokugawa shogunate, bringing down Tokugawa Yoshinobu and cooperating in the establishment of a new national order, found themselves, just six years later, utterly estranged from each other over the Korean question.

The Meiji restoration—the ideal and the reality. There was no way for such a complex matter to be smoothly resolved. Most of those who saw only the ideal and ignored the reality had already fallen. At the same time, those who looked only at the reality and ignored the ideal had also fallen. Yet there was no doubt that the unequal treaties signed between Japan and the foreign powers from 1866 on constituted, along with the Korean question, one of the major barriers to the further development of the nation. The objective of Iwakura's mission to Europe as the first Japanese minister plenipotentiary to go abroad had simply been the improvement of relations with foreign countries; he had no hope of treaty revision at the time. It was even said that he had left the country promising not to bring the subject up abroad. If that policy had not been altered, the mission would probably have returned home much sooner.

By the fourth month of 1872, Iwakura had been made plenipotentiary for treaty revision and the mission consisting of one hundred and seven diplomats plus a group of students ended up spending nearly a year and a half abroad. The frustrations of their efforts in foreign relations, including disagreements among the members of the mission and language difficulties—compared with the magnificent send-off under fireworks from Shinagawa which had marked the departure of the mission, the end of their journey was melancholy and bitter. The mission to Europe and America was effective in demonstrating that Japan had achieved the outward forms of a modern state; it helped to strengthen the position of the new government vis-à-vis the foreign powers, and it gave great impetus to the movement to send students abroad, which was important to the new government. Yet for such eminent people as Iwakura, Okubo, Kido, and the others to be out of the country for such a long time immediately following the abolition of the han could only invite difficulties. The new system of prefectures and counties had betrayed the hopes of most of the people, and there were uprisings in Takamatsu, Tsuruga, Oita, Myoto, and Hojo as well as in Fukuoka, Tottori, and Shimane prefectures. The number of people who were beheaded, hanged, or sentenced to prison could be counted in the tens of thousands. All of this took place while the mission was abroad. Moreover, prompted by the uncertainties of the time and the absence of the ministers, voices were being raised proposing to resolve the difficulties through force of arms.

The soldiers that the three han of Satsuma, Choshu, and Tosa had turned over to the imperial government were the same soldiers that had been so successful in the campaigns in the northeast. Their position became that of men through whom the foundations of imperial rule had been established and the abolition of the han carried out. In other words, they had come to occupy a position very much like that of the bannermen under the Tokugawa and they were looked upon with the greatest respect by many.

But plainspoken people like Tani Kanjo of Tosa, drawing upon the saying that once the bird is shot the bow is put away, began to point out the shortcomings of this arrangement. The unification of the military forces at this time was proving to be unimaginably hard going and these difficulties poisoned the atmosphere. The repeated clashes in the army ministry grew so heated that even Yamagata Aritomo, then commander of the Konoe guards, the only military force then at the direct disposal of the central government, submitted his resignation on several occasions. Finally the resignation was accepted and Saigo Takamori was put in his place. It was decided that when the term of the Konoe guards ran out, they would be replaced with ordinary conscript troops. The discontent and unrest of the people of the western han who had been the victors in the restoration did not wait for the Korean problem to appear. It had already begun to take shape in the period immediately following the campaigns in the northeast.

Signs of weakness and ineptitude in foreign relations and the unease that radiated throughout East Asia from Korea were added to the internal problems. The heroes of the restoration who espoused military ideals began to feel a growing discontent with the rapid changes taking place in society, and they suspected that all the talk about civilization and enlightenment would only lead to a weakening of national spirit. Some latter-day iconoclasts even called for a revival of the spirit of Kusunoki Masashige, the sixteenth-century warrior who had opposed the machinations of the Ashikaga. They insisted that the trend toward softness and weakness in the nation must be reversed, the decline of the nation stopped, and the insolence of the foreign powers brought to an end. Their scheme for the restoration of society was based on the argument that in the history of our country and of foreign countries, both in modern times and in antiquity, whenever a nation had fallen into a crisis of extreme weakness and lassitude such that it was despised by foreign nations and unable to stand against its own internal enemies, no course of recovery was possible except through martial discipline.

These people did not deny that both martial and civil culture were required for the present reforms. However, they maintained that martial culture should be promoted now and the civil culture could be looked after later. A foreign war was needed to establish once and for all the complete independence of the nation. Having gone this far, some were determined to put such a policy into operation before the return of the Iwakura mission, since then the opinions of its important ministers would have to be reckoned with and they could be expected to oppose the venture.

It was proposed that the national revenues be divided into thirds and that two-thirds should go to the army and the navy. All members of the samurai class now separated from their traditional profession of arms would be called back into it, and the samurai of the nation placed directly under the command of one of six garrisons located at strategic points throughout the country. All males between the ages of twenty and forty-five would be enlisted in either the regular or the reserve corps of the two services, and all commoners who showed military talent would be brought into the samurai class. The training of all males would be martial in character, and one of the two top ministers of the nation under the prime minister should always hold the rank of general or admiral and be directly under imperial command. Thus would the nation be truly unified through military means.

Many came to press Saigo Takamori to underwrite this plan, but he was not easily convinced that he should do so. He brought up the vows made by all the ministers and high-ranking officials at the time of the departure of the

Iwakura mission. He said that it was impossible for them now to turn their backs on this promise and to undertake such a grave course of action on their own. He insisted that action be deferred until the return of the Iwakura mission. Saigo was a man of few words. He did not argue the way that Kirino Toshiaki did.

Yet in 1867, when there had been a sharp difference of opinion among the leaders of the military about what to do with Tokugawa Yoshinobu, it had been Saigo who set a martial example for all by insisting that the final disposition of the Tokugawa could be settled only with the sword. Now, as he surveyed the current state of affairs, he realized that it would not be possible in the end to hold out against the demands of his subordinates. He therefore came to express a desire that he himself might be sent to Korea as an ambassador to resolve the problem.

The collapse of the plans to send an expedition to Korea and a split in the government which led to the resignations of many Satsuma men from Saigo on down, as well as of councillors such as Soejima, Goto, Itagaki, and Eto, ensued. Many made serious threats against the government in their letters of resignation. The plague of resignations among men who made a brave show of following the demands of the hour went on and on. The Konoe guards, the imperial army of the time, was virtually disbanded. Of the three han of Satsuma, Choshu, and Tosa that had contributed troops, only Choshu stayed with the government. In January 1874, Iwakura was attacked and wounded by a group of eight Tosa men led by Takechi Kumakichi while his party was passing through the district of Akasaka near the imperial palace in Tokyo. It did not stop there. In February the uprising of the so-called Patriotic Party broke out in Saga prefecture, lighting the first signal fire of open rebellion. This uprising passed like a flash of lightning in a dark sky. Its leader, Eto Shimpei, was stripped of all ranks and honors, and he and one hundred and thirty-six others were imprisoned. There was no telling just how far its effects might reach.

Now on horseback, now on foot, Hanzo moved on toward Tokyo through the fifth month greenery of the Kiso road. Talk of uprisings had quieted a bit, but the central stage was in turmoil as though in the aftermath of a great storm.

4

Scatter the salt!
Scatter the salt!

From Itabashi, the eastern terminus of the Kiso road, Hanzo turned toward Sugamo and then down the main street through Hongo until he found himself once again passing alongside the Kanda shrine. The first thing that

caught his ear was the voices of children chanting these lines. He was
entering Tokyo while festivals were being held in every neighborhood.

The great drums resounded throughout the city and the festive lanterns
hanging below the eaves of all the houses were unexpectedly lively, perhaps
in an effort to bolster spirits. From time to time a group of children, bells jingling on their sleeve cords, and with round yellow fans stuck into their headbands, would cut across his path pushing an image made of rice bags. Then
his way would be barred by scores of people in matching kimono following
after a group of lion dancers, all waving their fans as they danced through the
streets. He looked to the right and to the left as he crossed a new bridge, the
so-called Meganebashi or "eye-glass bridge." The Sujikai bastion was no
longer there, the area having been converted into a broad secondary street,
but the bright green of the willows along the Yanagihara embankment
reminded him of former days.

This time he was not planning to stay at the Juichiya in Ryogoku, which
no longer existed even though the bustling shopping street in Ryogoku
remained as before. The much younger wife of the innkeeper had given it up
to open a small restaurant in Asakusa following the death of the retired master who had always been such a thoughtful host. Since it was on his way,
Hanzo called at the house of Takichi and his wife in Aioi-cho in Honjo, and
found that they had moved to Saemon-cho in Asakusa. The day was coming
to an end. Hanzo went back to Ryogoku and found an inn displaying the
Naniwa Society legend on its signboard, marking it as a member of an old,
nation-wide association of small, respectable inns. He untied his sandals
there.

Tokyo was still quiet, and Hanzo found this somewhat reassuring. The
next day he promptly paid a call on the retirement quarters of Hirata Kanetane. He had not seen the master since Kyoto and when he expressed his condolences for the death of Kanetane's heir, Nobutane, the master displayed an
alarming weakness. He went on to take care of other business, including a
call on Tanaka Fujimaro of Owari, now at the ministry of religion. Then he
found his way to the new home of Takichi and Osumi near the Saemon
bridge.

They had not seen each other for a very long time. Takichi and Osumi
were both pleased that he had remembered them after all these years. Hanzo
in his turn was happy to accept their invitation to bring his things over from
the inn and stay with them.

"It's been ten years since we last saw Aoyama, Osumi."

Takichi had changed and Osumi, too, had changed. When Hanzo had
come to Edo at the summons of the commissioners of transport, he had lived
with this couple for five months. On his departure they had gone to the trouble of providing him with two pairs of straw sandals interwoven with blue
cotton.

This time, of course, Hanzo was not in Tokyo on a mere sightseeing trip.
He had come on business, concerning which he had already called on Tanaka
Fujimaro. Fujimaro was an acquaintance from the old days when he had been

known as Tanaka Torasaburo of Owari. Hanzo and his father, Kichizaemon, had felt close to the lord of Owari and the people of Nagoya ever since the time of the old lord, Yoshikatsu. To Hanzo it seemed no accident that people like Fujimaro, so passionately committed to education, should be a product of the Meirindo, the han academy in Nagoya. Hanzo had told Fujimaro of his hopes and had asked for his support.

With the recent reorganization of the ministry of religion, Fujimaro now held the rank of undersecretary, placing him on the third level below the minister himself. He was in charge of all the routine administration of the ministry, and he was interested in raising the general level of education. Hanzo was quite encouraged. Since his return from a survey of European and American education, Fujimaro was trying to introduce the free system of public education that he had seen in America. To Fujimaro it was still a time of beginnings and of experiments.

Takichi responded by saying:

"How about it, Aoyama? The town's a lot different than it was when it was called Edo, isn't it? Since last spring there has been a strict prohibition of vendetta—that's right, a prohibition of vendetta! The government is really out to change everything. The duty to kill the person who has slain one's parents or brother is now just another old tale for the storytellers. The world has really changed. But all the same, anyone who has lived in Edo for a long time has to feel sorry for the Tokugawa. Even Osumi says that her eyes grow moist whenever she sees the Tokugawa crest."

When Hanzo went out he noticed that while the old-fashioned Takichi still used Japanese-style lamps, there were places in the neighborhood using the brighter, Western-style oil lamps. In the evenings their brightness would light the entire area around them. Though they were still to be seen only here and there, even the very lights of Tokyo were changing.

Now there was no longer any need to bring up the subject of Black Ships, or to point to the opening of Osaka and Kobe by force in 1866 and 1867, or even to mention the reception by the emperor of foreign ambassadors in direct audience, an event unprecedented in the more than twenty-five hundred years of Japanese history. The effects of the opening of Japan to the world were making themselves felt in the lives of each individual. This was particularly true in a place like Tokyo, where it was evident in the love of current fads among the city people and in the changes in the colors of their clothing. Clothing that had looked fine in the dim light of Japanese lanterns or candles often did not show to advantage in the brilliant light of the lamps that had replaced them. Osumi was very much aware of such things and it was she who pointed out to Hanzo the great changes that had come about in the colors that women now wore to evening occasions, explaining that before fashions could change illumination had first to change.

Both Takichi and Osumi enjoyed telling Hanzo about all the things that had happened in the capital during the many years he had been away. They made him laugh by quoting some of the comic verses from the music halls that were beginning to contain scraps of English. Osumi then showed Hanzo one of the ukiyo-e of Utagawa Yoshifuji. Here the struggle was between native and imported implements, cleverly personified and conveying the tone of the times. Looking at them, one could only wonder whether such feelings had also been aroused when long ago the literary and material culture of China was being adopted in this country. Anything that came from across the seas was being called "civilization and enlightenment"—the world had come to the point where, as a popular song of the day had it, if you rapped a head that wore a short haircut, you would hear the ring of civilization. The old litter bearers of Edo, running off with something between a chant and a rhythmic grunt, stark naked, or with only a loin cloth in summer and perhaps a wadded jacket in the coldest weather, were no longer to be seen. It seemed that in this new city, trades that had traditionally been practiced in a condition of near nudity, such as that of the fishmongers who had worn their kimono tucked up to the waist in front or of the people who came in from Tsukuda to peddle clams, were all thought likely to cast our customs in an embarrassing light in the eyes of foreigners.

Each time Hanzo set out on business or to visit fellow Hirata disciples, he had an opportunity to observe the conditions in the various parts of Tokyo very closely. That the city was so vast as to defy any clear perception of its size was one impression that remained unchanged from his previous visits. He could not begin to say how many people, young and old, men and women, lived here. Some spoke of how much the population had shrunk; others said that there was no telling just how much it would grow in the new age. For one who had known Edo in the 1860's, the absence of the guard posts at each intersection was most noticeable. Only the great wooden gates that closed off the streets at night remained as reminders of the feudal age. Most of the sixteen bastions and ten outer gates of Edo castle had been pulled down. Hanzo remembered that the Choshu mansion in Hibiya had been razed during his stay with Takichi and Osumi in Aioi-cho. Now he found the entire district an open plain. In some places the sites of the former samurai residences, great and small, had been turned into mulberry fields. Wherever he went he saw signs of precipitous decline in this city that once was described as six parts military and four parts townsmen.

Yet Tokyo was also undergoing a boom. Hanzo went to see the Ginza, a district that everyone was talking about. There he found a new roadway many yards wide, lined with two-story brick buildings with round columns, all in the latest style. The Ginza was a new shopping street that had been created as a result of the prohibition of wooden buildings in the area after the great fire of 1872. At first not a single person would enter the brick buildings. There was still talk that those who lived in them would in time go pale and puffy and waste away.

The Ginza of that day was full of street entertainers. There was a wrestling bear at Nichome, dancing dogs at Takegawa-cho, and seashell carvers at Yonchome. There were sand paintings, street chanters, comic dancers, and tumblers, all of which rivaled the attractions of the Rokku district of Asakusa in their ability to draw sightseers. This part of town, for all its great promise of future prosperity, was at present a confused mixture of old and new.

Hanzo was keenly aware of being away from home, and he was moved by everything he saw and heard. The litter was disappearing, to be replaced by one and two passenger rickshas and horse-drawn omnibuses. Western clothes were occasionally to be seen on passersby but they were as yet poorly worn in most cases. There would be Japanese jackets worn over Western trousers, women with their hair dressed in the Western style but wearing Japanese clogs, and young men wearing random bits and pieces of Japanese costume but with Western-style short hair and carrying Western books and Western-style umbrellas. It seemed as though each person he met had invented his own style of dress.

Through a stroke of good fortune, Hanzo found temporary employment in the ministry of religion. The ministry had just been reorganized, moving from Babasaki to a location near Tokiwabashi, and people with a background in National Learning were in demand. This unexpected employment came to him through Tanaka Fujimaro, and although it was not really what Hanzo was looking for—he had come up to Tokyo because he wanted to find a post in some old Shinto shrine where he might establish a new life—Fujimaro asked him to work in the ministry while he was waiting. The expense of living as an idle traveler was already beginning to trouble Hanzo, and the ministry of religion was one place where there was still work for Hirata people. Because of his relationship to Fujimaro, and because he wanted to see at first hand what Kanetane and the disciples had accomplished, he accepted the offer.

He immediately informed his wife and children back home of this development, giving Takichi's place as a temporary address, and reported that he was beginning to find himself in Tokyo. He was still committed to religious service in the long run, but ever since he had crossed Usui pass and come down to the inn in Ryogoku, then moving on to the rich and varied neighborhood near the Kanda river where Takichi lived, he had become like a different person. He was glad once again to enjoy the company of this carefree and cheerful couple. He began to get up while it was still dark, going out to the well behind the kitchen to take deep breaths of pure morning air before washing himself clean. From that time on Hanzo acquired the habit of purifying himself each morning.

He was now far from all his intimates. On the sixteenth of the month, a regular holiday from the office, he sat in his room on the second floor of Takichi's house and looked out over the city. The skies were heavy, telling of the approach of the early summer rainy season. He thought of his home in Magome, and of his wife and children. The punitive expedition against the Taiwan aborigines was taking place at this time, and rumors had come of the creation of some kind of organization in Satsuma by the followers of Saigo Takamori. There was nothing at all peaceful about the times and yet Hanzo found himself with a clear and tranquil sense of the problems that lay ahead.

If they were not careful, the reforms of the restoration were likely to be reversed. The building of the new world for which so many people had hoped and the movement toward equality were still in grave doubt.

Thoughts of Mito, which he had nearly forgotten, came once again to mind. He remembered how Mito's fierce factional struggle had become virtually a religious war, going beyond mere considerations of victory or defeat, gain or loss. He remembered how the remarkable power of the Mito men had been directed at everyone whom they viewed as an enemy, even such great ministers as Ii Naosuke and Ando Tsushima. He looked back over all those happenings that he had witnessed—how the rebel faction in Mito had first raised their banners on Mt. Tsukuba, how they had become an expression of the popular will to revere the emperor and expel the barbarians—now it appeared as if the same thing was about to be repeated in somewhat different form in Saga, in Tosa, and in Satsuma.

"Can one really call this a restoration of antiquity?"

What he saw spreading before him was not a restoration of antiquity but rather a completely unexpected persistence of more recent times.

CHAPTER ELEVEN

1

OCTOBER SOON CAME to the streets of Tokyo. Another working day was ending at the offices of the ministry of religion near Tokiwa bridge. A man wearing white Japanese tabi and leather sandals was stuffing documents into the breast of his kimono as he walked across the bridge.

As he strode through the yellow willow leaves lying along the Kamakura embankment, Hanzo was angry and upset, so much so that he felt he could never enter the office or see any of his colleagues there again. He made his way back to Takichi's house brooding on his experiences since coming up to Tokyo. He had come resigned to a rootless life in the city, but had spent nearly six months at the ministry of religion trying to find satisfaction in continuing the work that his predecessors in the Hirata school had begun there. Suddenly he stopped at a street corner and let out a deep sigh. Walking back and forth over this road for half a year, he had experienced time and again the feeling that it had been a great mistake to take a job at the ministry which seemed so inappropriate to one of his background.

"Perhaps this was not how I should have done it," he thought, and began walking again. He had left the ministry in a state of emotional turmoil, but the closer he got to his room at Takichi's house the more deeply he sank into a taciturn and melancholy state of mind.

Even after returning to his room on the second floor of the house near Saemon bridge and removing his formal trousers, Hanzo felt as though he were still back in the office. He could still see the room as it had looked just before the end of the working day. One man had finished his assignments and was putting his desk in order. Another was sitting with his chin propped on his hands, listening to the chatter of his colleagues. There was much loud laughter. One of his colleagues had begun talking about Motoori Norinaga.

He began with a reference to a passage that he said he had found in the diaries of Motoori's disciple Saito Hikomaro. One day Hikomaro and some other disciples were gathered at the master's house. They were eating and talking among themselves about the master, whom they considered to be a "living god," when suddenly the maidservant who was waiting on them burst into tears. They asked her what was troubling her and she replied that this living god was coming to her room every night and making such a nuisance of himself that last night she had kicked him. Now after hearing what these men had to say, she was afraid that such an august living god might punish her by making her leg crooked or something even worse. Hikomaro reported that he could only sit and listen with his mouth gaping open.

Everyone in the office except Hanzo laughed at the story. The man who had told it, encouraged by the response, went on to say, "Really, only a man of great character would have come crawling into a maidservant's room that way." The line "man of great character" got another good laugh. Hanzo turned pale. He could not argue since he had no idea whether the man was telling the truth or whether Hikomaro's diaries were reliable, but he was deeply offended at the unseemly pleasure the others were taking in the story. If there had not been a Motoori Norinaga before him, even Hirata Atsutane would probably have ended up a mere antiquarian. Without Hirata Atsutane there could not have been a Hirata Kanetane. Without Hirata Kanetane there would probably never have been a ministry of religion. All this came to Hanzo in a flash. He became so incensed that before he could think, he had given his colleague a violent slap on the back and rushed out of the office.

On these late October afternoons the feeling of autumn and of being away from home struck Hanzo more and more deeply with each passing day. A vast, disorderly jumble of roofs stretched far beyond the limits of the view from his window near the Kanda river. The dull skies that hung over them caught his eye through the open shoji. He sat alone for a long time staring out at the damp urban scenery, trying to collect his thoughts.

"However much you may know of a person's shortcomings, what does it amount to?" he thought as he reflected on the story his colleague had told.

An acquaintance of his owned a portrait of Motoori Norinaga. It had been commissioned by the master himself from the artist Yoshikawa Gishin of Nagoya and he had inscribed a poem on it in his own hand before giving it to a disciple. There was no sign of the ravages of age in his clear brow and cool eye and his hair was tied up with a purple cord in the old-fashioned tea whisk style. It was hard to believe that this was the portrait of a man who had been sixty-one years of age at the time. The master had designed his own costume, consisting of black crepe dyed in a key pattern, to be suitable for poetry meetings or the lectern. He called it the Suzunoya robe after his house. A purple lining could be seen through the sleeve openings but the master looked so young that this bold flash of color did not seem inappropriate. In this nation where people tend to age early, it was difficult to imagine how this person could have managed to remain so youthful in appearance.

To Hanzo, that such a man could so easily be misunderstood was a point in his favor, reflecting Norinaga's undiminished youth and vitality in his old age, rather than a shortcoming. The Motoori Norinaga that he saw in his mind's eye was unlike the firm masculine figure that he imagined Hirata Atsutane to have been. Norinaga's character was sensitive, with many feminine qualities. He had created a life for himself of generous scale and ease, but he was, among the men of the eighteenth century, the one who had stood highest and seen farthest. Atsutane, in contrast, had been completely open and absolutely straightforward in expression. That had made him seem familiar and accessible to his followers. There was nothing like this in Norinaga. To the end of his life the richness and complexity of his feelings had been kept locked away in his breast, revealed only in his scholarly works. Even his most intimate disciples seemed to have found him difficult to approach. Yet this Norinaga who was such a source of strength had been transformed into a caricature by these irreverent gossipers. The same people who had been willing to revere Norinaga as a living god also wanted to laugh at him as a clown. Not only did Hanzo find this attitude wanting in sincerity, but he was sickened by the circulation of idle gossip at the office. They had enjoyed hearing of Norinaga being rebuffed by some insignificant woman and had wanted to expose the unbridled sexuality that they fancied was to be found on the hidden side of this "living god." Hanzo simply could not stand it.

2

"Why am I just sitting here with a vacant stare. Something has been wrong with me ever since Okume tried to do away with herself. Have I lost my way . . ."

Although Hanzo had left his home in the country determined to enter into some form of service to the Shinto religion, now that he found himself on the first step of that path he was already beginning to have doubts.

He told Takichi and Osumi that he was considering giving up his position for personal reasons and began to pass lonely days at Saemon-cho. His greatest comfort was to go to the Kanda shrine and kneel in a corner of the main shrine, where he passed many a quiet hour. Occasionally Takichi would invite him out to listen to a famous storyteller in the music hall in Ryogoku. Then one day he received a visit from a physician, one Kanamaru Kyojun, who lived in Shinnorimono-cho. Kyojun was also a Hirata disciple. Out of simple good will as a fellow disciple, this man unselfishly became Hanzo's confidant.

Hanzo told Kyojun about his experiences of the past several days and explained that he had found the incident at the office so unpleasant that he was staying away. He asked Kyojun if he had heard of Motoori Norinaga having had a disciple named Saito Hikomaro. When Kyojun heard the story he laughed until he clutched his stomach. Saito Hikomaro had been an Edo man. He had been taught by Norinaga's heir, Motoori Ohira, and he had served in the Fujinokaki shrine. He had never met Norinaga.

"Then the story must not be about Norinaga."

"It would seem not."

"Thank you very much."

"Well now, even when they say 'Motoori,' that doesn't mean only Norinaga. Ohira was a Motoori and Haruniwa was a Motoori."

According to Kyojun, Ohira, the senior disciple who succeeded Norinaga as head of the Motoori family, had lost his wife at an early age. From that time on this diligent scholar had suffered greatly from loneliness. Even so, it was hard to imagine that an intimate disciple such as Hikomaro could have written such a thing in his diaries. Even if he had been shocked to discover such lustfulness in his master, that would only have exposed Saito himself as a dim scholar. After all, love was not to be rebuked by those who followed the way of National Learning. Wasn't it said in the writings left by Norinaga that the virtuous person accepts love but the person who is not virtuous rejects it?

"Anyway, Norinaga himself was quite a lover," Kyojun added, and then had another good laugh.

After his guest left, Hanzo found himself in somewhat better spirits. "The virtuous person accepts love, but the person who is not virtuous rejects it." Kyojun had left him with some very helpful words. He thought them over. If the master had made a fool of himself, then hadn't those people who later took pleasure in observing that fact made even bigger fools of themselves? The way of man and woman was unpredictable; petty rules could not be applied to it. There was not a single one of his predecessors who could claim to have entirely avoided making some such mistake. No matter how carefully they thought things through, there were many cases in this world of people being led by an irrepressible and intractable power that they found impossible to stand against for all that they knew that what they were doing was wrong.

Hanzo did not for a moment believe that Ohira could have been as abandoned to passion as his colleague claimed to have read in Hikomaro's diary. But even if there had been a time when, after finding it impossible to sleep on the short hot summer nights, he might have sought other beds, still, as a successor to Norinaga, who had never capitulated to others, surely he would not have capitulated to himself. He must have recognized that he was being foolish. All the same, the true message of Norinaga and his successors was different. To Norinaga, love, from the most exalted spiritual love to the simple animal urge, even the lapse of the lady Fujitsubo in *The Tale of Genji*, was in all its manifestations permeated with a sad beauty.

It was Norinaga's conviction that love could never be confined by simple ideas of good or evil. What Hanzo most wanted to know was just how he had managed to bring himself so far in understanding. He tried to imagine Norinaga as he wrote *The Jeweled Comb*, his critical work on *Genji*, and as he achieved such depth in his readings of the many love poems in the old anthologies and the love episodes in the *Tales of Ise* and *The Tale of Genji*. He tried to fathom the depth of Norinaga's quest for antiquity. How in the midst of that feudal age which so rigorously observed the Confucian practice of separating boys and girls from their seventh year on had he come to value love so highly, so boldly? Hanzo even tried to imagine the women hidden in Norinaga's life.

* * * * * * *

But it was not just the attitudes of his colleagues that led Hanzo to consider leaving the ministry of religion. In its earlier days the ministry had been the stage on which National Scholars like Hirata Kanetane, Juge Shigekuni, Mutobe Uta, and Fukuba Yoshikiyo had played founding roles in matters of religion and shrine administration during the restoration. Gathered around Kanetane had been Hirata Nobutane, Morooka Masatane, Gonda Naosuke, Maruyama Saraku, Yano Gendo, and Hanzo's friend Kureta Masaka. They had worked directly and indirectly for the restoration of antiquity. Although Hanzo's old classmate Hachiya Kozo, so long his companion in the Hirata school, had now returned to his home in Nakatsugawa to nurse his illness, even he had held the rank of acting undersecretary in the old ministry while aiding the master in his work.

When Hanzo took up his position in this place with such profound links to his life's dreams, the offices had been moved and the staff had changed but clear traces of the work of Kanetane still remained. Hanzo had arrived at his desk in a corner of the ministry with the feeling that he was entering a field of flowers. Each record he opened would yield its cluster of familiar names until it seemed he could survey in them the struggle against the middle ages, a struggle best represented by the Hirata disciples. The reform in the dress of priests, the elimination of Buddhist images as objects of Shinto worship, the elimination of the Buddhist title Bodhisattva from the names of Shinto deities, the prohibition of the performing of Buddhist funeral rites by Shinto priests—all these actions reflected the ardor with which the National Scholars had worked to achieve the separation of Buddhism and Shinto.

It was often said that only a priest, who had no worries about eating during his lifetime since he would always be sought out and supported by men and women of virtue and could therefore get by with the performance of funerals and other solemn rituals, would neither practice the way of righteousness nor attempt to lead people out of confusion toward enlightenment. Although the priests of the Shin sect of Buddhism were the only ones who married and ate meat, there was no one who did not know that "kitchen god" referred to a priest's concubine, "canopy" to the flesh of the octopus, and "draft of wisdom" to sake. As long ago as the end of the seventeenth century, this observation had already been made: "Now even the most remote and isolated mountain temple can have its status raised if plenty of cash is forwarded to the home temple. The priest who yesterday wore drab grey robes today wears robes of scarlet, thanks to the power of gold. Although subscriptions, contributions, and donations are supposed to be used for the construction of new religious buildings, they are in fact nothing more than extortion—those who spend their nights in these halls are a pack of degenerates."

The excessive number of temples and monasteries throughout the nation, the uselessness of these temples, and the arrogant, lazy, lustful character of the priesthood, not to mention the great number of outright criminals among them or the frequency with which they were the object of litigation for encroaching on neighboring property—none of this needed to wait for outsiders to discover. Those among the Buddhists themselves who were at all perceptive had long since recognized the fact.

Shocking news about the temples continued to add to this immense list of failings. The priests, always alert to any opportunity for gain, had been making unauthorized use of names from the palace and court nobility to loan money at high interest. This practice was quickly stopped. The government next did away with the court titles and perquisites of temples such as the Ninnaji and the Daikakuji, where men of the imperial family resided after taking orders, as well as of the convents for women of the imperial family and the places of retreat for the court nobility. Memorials to the throne from Buddhist institutions, the practice of temple concubinage, public demonstrations of faith, and all offerings were prohibited. From this time on all men and women who wished to serve as priests or nuns would require a license from the prefectural offices. Solicitation of alms by the Zen mendicants called *komuso*, the practices of the Tensha sect of Shinto with its admixtures of Confucianism and yin-yang theories, and the strongly shamanistic Shugen sect of Buddhism were also prohibited. The areas formerly closed to women around Shinto shrines and Buddhist temples were abolished. In all the lands controlled by shrines and temples, these orders were made the law—the priests were freed from their charade of false abstinence and nuns were permitted to let their hair grow, to eat meat, to marry, and to renounce their vows whenever they chose. Almost all the major Shinto shrines had been in fact a part of the Buddhist establishment, but the complete confusion of Buddhism and Shinto that had prevailed since the time of the priest Tenkai at the beginning of the seventeenth century was now being dug out at the root.

When Hanzo came to the ministry of religion, these great reforms had just been carried out and order was beginning to be introduced into the administration of temples and shrines. But ceremonials for high occasions, one of the most serious responsibilities of the ministry in its earlier form, had been transferred to the bureau of protocol. That one fact alone indicated how the work of the ministry had lost the urgency and drive that had propelled it when starting out under the supervision of the Hirata school.

Although this was clearly still a time of experimentation, the first task of the ministry was to achieve harmony between the Shinto and Buddhist priesthoods despite their differences in belief, in values, and in character, so that learning and enlightenment could be disseminated among the people. But the officials of the ministry were gradually coming to realize that this mission could only end in failure. It began to appear that one of the major shortcomings of the new government lay in its assumption that it could harmonize the inherently disharmonious, that it could reconcile the irreconcilable. The scope of the ministry's plan for the instruction and enlightenment of the people had been incredibly vast. At the center was the Great Academy, responsible for both Buddhist and Shinto learning, and in the provinces there were two levels of branch academies as well as innumerable Shinto and Buddhist educational institutions. This plan, called the "three-line education system," called for the establishment of standards of instruction for all the people.

Yet the ministry did not long continue at its task of working through the Shinto and Buddhist priesthoods in order to disseminate learning. Complaints of arbitrariness and one-sidedness soon arose, along with incessant bickering over doctrinal points. The ministry enjoyed little success in either the external mission of instruction or the internal one of establishing harmony. Even the five factions of the Shin sect of Buddhism were soon asking to be separated from the main church so that they could be free to teach their own views. It was at this stage that Hanzo arrived at the offices of the ministry of religion. His duties primarily involved the hunting down of precedents, although he was also responsible for filing the vast quantities of documents that came in from the Great Academy, for examining the textbooks that were being compiled there, and for replying to the various inquiries sent in from teaching institutions in the provinces. None of his previous experience had prepared him for these tasks and he applied himself to them only after some hesitation. By now the atmosphere of innovation at the ministry had given way to one of endless conferences and compromises with the dissatisfied members of the teaching staffs of each school and sect. Hanzo felt total despair whenever he compared what this ministry must have been like in its early days with what he saw in his present colleagues. It was clear that they gave their work nothing more than was absolutely necessary and were content to receive from it merely a living and the realization of their own petty interests. Nor did it end there.

The documents that came in from the provincial institutions buried his desk and he became the target for an endless barrage of ignorant and petty inquiries. "I am a Buddhist priest but I would like to discard my robes and clothe myself in the garments of civilization and enlightenment. Would it be acceptable for me to wear Western dress except when I am actually performing ceremonies?" Or, "The temples and shrines have traditionally been passed down in our families for generations and we have been accustomed to making our own use of the donations contributed by our parishioners. Must we now turn them over to the ministry of religion?"

"Is it permissible for the families of resident priests to go into business while still living in the temple precincts?" "Would it be permissible for a resident priest of a Buddhist temple to make a pilgrimage to Ise if he wore a wig?"

And so on. It was perhaps understandable how Motoori Norinaga himself, the great figure of the National Learning movement, could be reduced to a mere caricature in such an atmosphere. Hanzo realized that the ministry of religion had become completely inconsequential.

He no longer felt any desire at all to return to the ministry or his colleagues. Nor was it really possible. It had become clear to him that he did not want to waste any more of his time there, and he made up his mind to resign.

3

Hanzo's career at the ministry of religion was over. He had spent less than half a year there, but he had learned a great deal. It had become apparent that his seniors in the Hirata school had had their fingers badly burned with the project to unify government and religion. Their plan for the government to institute programs of indoctrination with the cooperation of the Buddhist and Shinto organizations was clearly doomed to failure. Moreover, he had just witnessed how the great Motoori Norinaga, the man who had opened the way for the restoration, was seen by most of the vulgar clerks in the new government.

Exhausted mentally and physically, he began to ruminate on past events in endless detail. In November, the mornings and evenings in his lodging became quite chilly. He passed long nights in his lonely, cheerless quarters on the second floor of Takichi and Osumi's home, wondering what to do next. Strange feelings came to him by the dim light of the night lamp. At some point he had lost his way in his journey through this world. He would seem to be walking through the streets, never getting to where he wanted to go no matter how far he walked. He would encounter Tanaka Fujimaro, now risen to undersecretary of the ministry. The physician and fellow Hirata disciple Kanamura Kyojun would be present as well. At that particular moment he had no idea where he was walking. Suddenly he would become conscious of the stares of passersby which he would not normally have noticed. Each stare was piercing and he sensed that their owners were thinking, "Now what is it that is so odd about that fellow walking over there—oh, I see! His hair is done in the old-fashioned way!"

Hanzo still had not had his hair cut and he wore it hanging down behind, tied with a purple cord. He was not making any particular point of preserving this old custom, but he felt that if he ever did get a post in a Shinto shrine it would be more appropriate if his hair was long. Those sharp, penetrating stares were still being directed his way. They made him cringe. He felt the stares not only along the new streets filled with new bureaucrats in their Western dress, but even in districts that were still more like Edo than Tokyo, streets lined with old shops with old-fashioned dark blue curtains and massive storehouses, heavy with the atmosphere of conservative merchant houses. Terrifying stares would be directed his way even out of rickshas passing over the bridge.

Now the scene resembled the Kiso river back home as well as the Sumida river in Tokyo. Someone was poling a boat downstream. As the boat approached the shore, he could see the person in it. It was Kichizaemon. His father beckoned to him vigorously. There was a woman in the boat. She had her back turned and her head wrapped in a kerchief. He called out an inquiry to his father from the bank. When the reply came back that the woman was Osode, his real mother, he was astonished. He tried to call out to his mother too, but his throat was dry and constricted. No sound came forth. The water rushed blindly past the bridge, swift as an arrow, and the boat drew away from him. He was awakened by his own groans.

It was unusual for Hanzo to dream about his father and mother. He did not know why he should be having such dreams now, having been away from home for more than half a year. It was too early to get up and he lay in the dim light of dawn, still filled with the mood of the dream. Usually when he awoke from a dream all he had to do was turn over and the feeling would go away, but this morning he retained a clear sense of the terror of the dream and the way his father and mother had looked. He could remember having seen his dead father in a dream only once before. That was after the elimination of the Aoyama family's hereditary offices, on the hundredth day after Kichizaemon's death. He recalled the poem he had composed then.

> If only I could
> Ask the departed:
> Is the dream road
> That leads to the hidden world
> A happy one?

The sound of the chilly autumn wind came to his ears, and the gradually fading song of a cricket somewhere in the house took his thoughts back to the Kiso. He thought of the graveyard in the Mampukuji where his parents were buried. He saw the hearth room in his home where his wife and four children were waiting for him. He saw the parlor where he had had one of his rare meetings with Kureta Masaka, to whom he felt closer than to any other senior disciple. Masaka had passed down the Kiso road on his way to the Kamo shrine in Kyoto, inspiring Hanzo to try to find a post in a shrine somewhere. They had drunk sake together and had talked about the future of the Hirata school—he remembered how in the end tears had flowed. Again, he remembered his meeting in Nakatsugawa with another senior disciple, Morooka Masatane, who at that time was traveling regularly between Tokyo and Kyoto in connection with his duties at the Matsuo shrine. He remembered how the participants in that small gathering had each written a poem on a fan, and particularly how one person had written that this meeting made the preceding eight years of separation seem like a dream. Another had written of how this world contains immeasurable quantities of the bitter and the sweet. Remembering the fan on which Morooka Masatane had inscribed a poem for him on that occasion, he felt again its startling intensity and his own determination not to do any less. This thought brought him back sharply to his present inability to find anything effective to do.

At last he got up and opened the rain shutters of his room. He looked out the two small windows facing north and west, but it was still quite dark. Since coming to Tokyo he had been in the habit of going out to the well next to the kitchen and washing himself each morning. When it came time to perform this morning ritual once more, the terrible sense that he had lost his way had still not left him. But he felt clear-headed in spite of that. The rain had ended.

"Takichi came in late last night, didn't he?"

"It must have been a nuisance for you for him not only to come back so late but then to pound on the door as well."

Hanzo was talking with Osumi in his room on the second floor.

"Listen to this. It seems my husband has a good pastime. Whenever there is a haikai gathering, he is usually asked to participate. The meeting last night was in the Yoshiwara. They served box lunches and sake and they were trying to complete a hundred-link verse sequence in one sitting, so he really got tired out. But he said that he didn't feel very manly about how the occasion ended. To go to the Yoshiwara and come back without spending the night— it just doesn't look right. He kept saying things like that. I had to laugh."

In his embarrassment, Hanzo could do no better than to say, "You're too much for me, madam."

"But all the same, isn't it good to hear my husband say something like that? When he comes home late at night, to hear him say that he has been out composing haikai?"

To Takichi, serving as an accountant for a rice wholesaler in Fukagawa and then as secretary to a tea exporting firm, ten years had passed like a single day. For all his townsman background, he was completely free of greed. Wherever he went, he always carried a portable writing set stuck in his sash so that he could note down the verses that came to him. He seemed like one of the odd characters out of the old tales, completely given up to his poetry. With his unselfish and honest nature, and the gallantry and warm hospitality of his wife, theirs was not a household that a traveler like Hanzo would ever wish to leave.

The bookstore that Takichi had told Hanzo about was in the Hanayashiki area of Yagenbori in Ryogoku. Hanzo spent a great deal of time browsing there. The owner was an eccentric old man with a large stock of books on haikai, popular novels, and albums of woodblock prints, all left from the Edo period. Hanzo discovered that most of the books that Takichi owned had been bought from this old man's store. He himself had collected quite a few books since coming to Tokyo and, deciding one day that there were some he no longer had use for and would like to sell, he left Takichi's house with a carrying cloth full of them.

Once out, it seemed that before he could get to the bookstore Hanzo's feet turned of their own accord to the home of Kanamaru Kyojun, the physician who had been so kind to him. When he arrived in Shinnorimono-cho, he found that Kyojun had just come back from making his house calls, and Hanzo was not only warmly received but given completely unexpected news. Kyojun told him that Tanaka Fujimaro had been concerned about him, and that there had been some talk of placing him in charge of the Minashi shrine in Hida. All this had come about through Fujimaro's efforts.

"How about it, Aoyama?" Kyojun continued. "The Hida assignment may be a bit beneath your abilities but why don't you give it a try?"

Hanzo felt that the post in Hida, rather than being beneath him, was the granting of a long-standing wish. Kyojun made it clear that he was merely relaying Fujimaro's message. He had himself been worried about Hanzo and he said that while the Minashi shrine was in a remote and lonely place, the post was by no means intended simply to get Hanzo out of the way. He hoped that there would be no misunderstanding on that account.

"Not at all. I am most grateful to you," said Hanzo, putting his hands on the floor and bowing deeply before Kyojun. "I will think it over carefully and then give Tanaka my reply."

"I am happy to hear you say that. By the way, Aoyama, I've got something I would like to show you."

Kyojun brought out a black lacquer writing box of good quality from the closet in the inner room. He took from it a small, handmade notebook and set it before Hanzo.

"Here it is."

The notebook had been left with Kyojun by Hachiya Kozo. Kyojun told Hanzo that he had kept it shut away for a long time and had even lost track of it, but he had recently found it again in the drawer of a bookcase. Kozo had followed Master Kanetane to Tokyo in 1869, Meiji 2, and then had fallen ill in his lodgings.

"All the same, Aoyama, the world may seem big but it's really quite small. It's really a long shot that I should have been the one to have looked after your friend."

As the conversation continued, Hanzo felt that he owed a debt of gratitude to this physician who had recommended that he go to Hida, to Fujimaro, who had sent the message through Kyojun, and to the people of Hida, who had asked that Hanzo be persuaded to come to the Minashi shrine after hearing that he was both a posthumous disciple of Hirata Atsutane and a longtime advocate of the restoration. Presently, he asked to borrow Kozo's diary and then left Kyojun's home. It seemed like a dream that the day had at last come when he would be going to an ancient shrine.

It was a long way to the mountains of Hida but there he could carry out his desire to serve the gods. His heart was full of the thought as he returned directly to Takichi's house. It seemed that his period of turmoil and uncertainty was about to give way to one where peace of mind might predominate. He immediately told Takichi the import of his news and went straight up the stairway to his room.

The room was filled by the evening sun. With an air of "this first of all," he put the diary he had borrowed from Kyojun on his desk and began to skim quickly through it. On the front cover was written "Tokyo Diary, Fifth Month Hachiya Kozo." It was full of incidents from 1869, when Kanetane had still been vigorous. There was an account of a memorial service for the recently deceased disciple Noshiro Hirosuke that had been arranged by Wakana Motosuke. More than twenty people had attended, including

Morooka Masatane, then a high-ranking police officer, Gonda Naosuke, a doctor in the imperial academy, and Miwata Mototsuna, a middle-ranking functionary in the academy. Also present was Matsuo Taseko, from the village of Tomono in Ina, who, though a woman, had played an important role in the activities of the National Learning movement since the mid-1860's. Kozo did not write in great detail but in his accounts of whom he had met yesterday or whom he had called on today was reflected the vigor of the Hirata school at its height.

Hanzo was touched by everything he read, even by the slight medicinal scent that the notebook gave off from having been shut up so long in a bookcase belonging to a physician. Through the diary, he was able not only to see Tokyo through his friend's eyes but to feel as though he were consulting with him. Of the three disciples of their first master, who now slept at Kitayama village outside Uji in Ise province, and who, in his lifetime, had been fond of calling them the "three Zo's," Kozo, the author of this diary, was lying ill back home in Nakatsugawa, and Keizo had lived the life of a recluse at his home ever since the restoration. Then there was Hanzo, who stood at an important turning point in his life.

4

In the province of Hida, in Ono county, the lesser national shrine of Minashi, popularly known as Ichinomiya or "the first shrine," awaited Hanzo. It was some two hundred thirty miles from Tokyo down the Kiso road to Nakatsugawa in Mino. From Nakatsugawa, another sixty miles of wild and isolated road led northward into mountainous country before one reached the Minashi shrine. Travel was still difficult everywhere, but when one entered the Takayama road beyond the village of Kashimo in Mino, the road became extremely hard. Along the highway that passes from the Kiso valley into Ina, the forests were dark even at midday and mountain leeches would drop from the trees onto travelers, while violent winds howled across the open stretches covered with bamboo grasses. Hanzo was familiar with the trials the traveler faced on this road, but the Takayama road was said to be even worse.

This move to Hida, recommended to Hanzo by Tanaka Fujimaro and endorsed by Kanamura Kyojun with the assurance that it was not simply a move to get him out of the way, did not seem anything of the sort to Hanzo. It would not have bothered him in the least even if his colleagues at the ministry had found him difficult to deal with and had asked that he be sent away. Yet he did have to decide whether he wanted to bury himself in those remote mountains, and that was no easy matter.

By now the National Scholars found themselves in difficult times. Even Hanzo's seniors in the movement appeared on the verge of being washed away by the turbulent flow of events. One of the things that had inspired such great changes in the final years of the shogunate and the opening years of the Meiji government was the restoration of moral order to the government, and the cries for this change had been rooted in the studies of history that had been carried out in Mito, in Owari, and among the Confucian scholars in Kyoto. But it had been the early National Scholars who had taught the newest path to the most ancient truths. Through the time of Kamo Mabuchi in the generation before Norinaga, most of the scholars had still concentrated their attention on the *Man'yoshu*. Norinaga continued Mabuchi's quest, turning to the *Kojiki* for his life work, and it was he who had perceived antiquity in its completeness for the first time. From his writings a certain spirit came into being. That spirit took lodging in the breasts of many idealists, developing into an outlook that became the activism of Hirata Atsutane and his followers. Determined to be faithful to history as it stood in the written record, they soon realized that their purpose was not merely to yearn for antiquity but to restore it. Through their discovery of a vigorous and admirable national character in antiquity, they had come to believe in this possibility. Motoori Norinaga had been the first to attempt to drive all the falsity out of this world. Collectively the National Scholars left behind them, as a lesson for future generations, an affirmation of the national character that did not distort the emotions or reject desire. It did not seem possible that National Learning could so quickly become outdated as a subject of serious study in the modern world.

Now Hirata Atsutane's heir, Kanetane, was not one subject to personal vanity. The clearest proof was that Kanetane, true successor though he was, viewed all the members of the school as posthumous disciples of Atsutane rather than as his own. Nor was there any shortage of disciples who preserved the spirit of Atsutane, although there were many, too, who rushed off blindly in their enthusiasm to realize the dream of antiquity restored, passing beyond the line that the master had drawn. The very simplicity and straightforwardness of the doctrine was the source of the intimacy and solidarity that linked the disciples together. When the actual restoration of imperial rule came about, some of the disciples immediately joined the imperial forces, others acted as guides to those forces, and still others bent their efforts to stripping the priests and temples of the privileges that had been accorded them by the Tokugawa, and to reviving Shinto funeral practices. All these energies arose out of the purest, most unadorned motives. Furthermore, it was the National Scholars who first made clear the distinction between the root and branches of the nation in their efforts to separate Buddhism and Shinto. With these efforts began an age of religious revival.

To cast out the spurious and return to the innate qualities of the Japanese nation—it was the teachings of the Hirata school that prepared the way for the liberation of the priests and nuns shut away in their dark monasteries, forbidden to eat meat or to marry. At the very least, the National Learning movement stimulated the true Buddhists and encouraged them to awaken and to face up to the challenges of the new age. Unfortunately, as people joined together to carry out these laudable aims, the movement acquired a life of its own. In the end there were even pressures for the outright abolition of Buddhism. Shinto priests, unfrocked Buddhist priests, and all sorts of ordinary people joined in. Abandoned temples were razed, their outer walls were torn down, and graves were moved. By the time the ruins began to take on the appearance of old battlefields, the original purpose of the National Scholars had been forgotten. It could be said that the anti-Buddhist campaign marked the high point of the National Learning movement. But at the same time, as soon as the abolition of Buddhism came to be mistakenly perceived as constituting the whole of the National Learning movement's program, it led directly to the downfall of the movement.

Despite Hanzo's concern, there was nothing he could do about this decline. Everything was taking place in the midst of a natural world where nothing flourishes without fading and even the learning that had hitherto dominated the age could not escape from that law. This realization saddened him. He felt that he could not leave the city with his mind in such turmoil.

It was still not definite that Hanzo would be going to Hida. He went around the city to ask his acquaintances for their opinions. No one had any work to offer him as an alternative, nor did anyone suggest that the time was not right for going to Hida. When he went to the home of the retired master, a call he had long delayed, he apologized for his neglect and asked for Kanetane's counsel. Not only did Kanetane fail to detain him as he had half-hoped, but he said that everyone, once in his life, should go on such a journey.

Even then, Hanzo still vacillated. He turned his inquiries inward. A new way was opening for him and the dwelling of the gods was in sight—all he had to do was move straight ahead. What was causing his hesitation? The answer seemed obvious, but it was not. When he had held the offices of honjin, headman, and toiya, he had at least been situated on the Kiso road which bound Tokyo and Kyoto together. Isolated though it was, Magome was on an important highway between eastern and western Japan. All the currents of the age had passed before his eyes, and as head of the Magome post station he had been forced to observe them whether he wanted to or not. But now, in this time of confused struggle between old and new, he was reluctant to turn his back on everything and devote himself solely to the service of the gods. Moreover, once he retreated into the back country of Hida, it did not appear that he could easily get out again.

Hanzo longed to consult with his neighbor Inosuke back in Magome. It was most unfortunate that he had no way of knowing his friend's opinion. He wondered what Takichi and Osumi thought of his going to Hida. Although the strong-willed Osumi was an obscure townswoman with little education, Hanzo had come to recognize her extraordinary ability to grasp the essential point in a complicated problem. She was always saying that it was important for people to judge things, and to discard what should be discarded without a second thought. People who could not learn to do this never got ahead. Hanzo returned from his walk about the city deciding to rely on the counsel of nearby acquaintances since his intimates were so far away.

Takichi had just returned home from his job at Kayaba-cho. When Hanzo came in, Takichi invited him into the parlor downstairs.

"Well, Aoyama, have you decided to go to Takayama?"

"No," Hanzo replied, "I haven't accepted the post yet, but if I do go, it will probably be soon. Still, at my age, I just can't bring myself to head off into the mountains. Not at all."

Takichi looked toward Osumi. "Osumi, the place where Aoyama is thinking of going is unbelievably far away. It's still another fifty miles beyond his home. That's right, another fifty miles! And it's a terrible mountain road. They say that horses can't even get over it. Aoyama is really determined to serve!"

The moment he heard Takichi say that, Hanzo resigned himself to going. Osumi, for her part, did not seem to be inclined to make any great effort to stop him. They said exactly the kind of thing that Kanetane had said to him and then began to concern themselves with helping him prepare for the long, difficult journey.

"I was sure that Takichi and Osumi would ask me not to go," Hanzo said to himself as soon as he reached his room on the second floor.

He had in fact been hoping against hope that someone would ask him not to go. He had thought that if even a single person did so, he would refuse the post. Not only was it distant, isolated, and difficult of access, but the current fad for "civilization and enlightenment" that was engulfing the nation had already reached even to Hida. Motoori Norinaga had been the first to attempt to break out of the shell created in the middle ages. To Hanzo, who believed in the true modern world, it was doubtful whether this civilization and enlightenment that everyone was talking about was really civilization and enlightenment at all. Those who had set their minds on the path of learning so that they could serve the gods and guide the people had to know themselves first of all. Then they had to take a critical stance toward the things that were coming in from Europe. Hanzo wondered whether he would be able to do any of this in the mountains of Hida.

5

The nation of Japan had been closed for two hundred and twenty years, beginning in the 1630's when contact with the outer world was cut off. Notices had been posted in Nagasaki forbidding the construction of ships with a cargo capacity of more than five hundred koku and forbidding any but ships with the imperial charter from crossing the seas. The policies of the Tokugawa shogunate ensured that all the doors were closed to foreign countries, yet one window did remain open.

Chinese ships came to Nagasaki for the first time during the third quarter of the sixteenth century, and European ships appeared just a few years later. From that time on, they came every year, perhaps thirty or forty Chinese ships and four or five Dutch ships, until they reached a peak in the late seventeenth century. In 1688, Genroku 1, there were one hundred and seven Chinese ships, thirty-three Korean ships, and three Dutch ships. The largest numbers of Chinese came to Nagasaki in the 1680's and 1690's. After the collapse of the Ming dynasty and the establishment of the Ch'ing in 1644, a considerable number of Ming loyalists and scholars took refuge in this country. A steady stream of priests of sufficient importance to be well known in China came to Japan from that time on. Around 1750 the Tokugawa limited to fifteen the number of Chinese ships that could enter Nagasaki harbor in a single year, and in 1791 this quota was further reduced to ten ships a year. The effect of this traffic was that foreign things continued to flow into the nation in various forms, and it was this stimulus that led to the creation of the National Learning movement by Kada no Azumamaro in the late seventeenth century.

This pattern of reaction to foreign stimulus was clearly true even of Motoori Norinaga, who was able to hone such a purely Japanese edge by beginning with Confucianism, Buddhism, and Taoism as his rough stones. Now, with the change in national policy following the restoration, foreign books that had been proscribed until recently were being translated and foreign scholars who had been kept at a distance were being welcomed into our midst. It was not surprising that Western studies should flourish as Confucian and Buddhist learning had flourished in earlier days. The subjects studied were astronomy and geography, mathematics, medicine, agronomy, chemistry, and military science. Foreign history and languages were of course included as well. The people of this nation, fond of novelty, were at first astonished by the profundity of European scientific inquiry, by the new European theories, by the European skill with machinery. They were particularly impressed by the European grasp of medicine.

In the society of that time, still not fully conversant with foreign learning, it was easy to find people who were filled with unreserved admiration for the West. One of them in fact was very close to Takichi. This person, so eager to take the lead in accepting new customs, was Takichi's employer, who had stores in both Tokyo and Yokohama. From these establishments he was operating a trading business exporting tea, dried mushrooms, and raw silk. Yet Takichi himself showed no interest in Western things. He did not see the point of the Western thermometer which his employer was so proud to have obtained, and he ignored the passionate curiosity with which his employer recorded the high and low readings of the thermometer in his diary each day. Any spare time that Takichi had went to his beloved haikai. Then there were those among the most enthusiastic who claimed that Japanese would soon be abandoned and everyone would be speaking English. Others advocated intermarriage with the Westerners, with their fair skins and prominent noses, saying that it would produce a better race of people. Even actors on the stage would shout to their audiences, "Anyone who doesn't understand civilization and enlightenment is a fool." Such was the temper of the times that when the Kabuki actor Otowa V took up the study of English, he was written up in the newspapers as a model of progressive spirit for all that he was an actor.

Since the beginning of Meiji, everyone in the country had been confronted with an overwhelming pressure to change everything, from the direction of scholarly inquiry to the least detail of customary behavior. Hanzo was acutely aware of this. Yet there was one thing that seemed incontrovertible to him out of his experience as head of the Magome post station. This was that of all the coming changes, the ones in transportation and communication would result in the most deep-rooted and substantial transformations of society. Their effects would be like those of water, the weakest and most subtle but in the end the most powerful of all the agents of change. Such changes affected all, high and low, rich and poor. They determined the success or failure of human society. They wove the fabric of history, and changed the maps. And they led to the exchange of all kinds of goods. Hanzo had been honjin at Magome at the time the ports were being opened and he could clearly remember how many people had come all the way to the Kiso to buy up undervalued coins, and how quickly the old coins had vanished from circulation. The gold coins poured out of the country, and foreign coins of inferior quality were imported to replace them. He felt keenly the threat of the disaster that would ensue if something similar were now to happen in the cultural exchange taking place between East and West. Here too all the equivalents of fine old gold might leave the country, to be replaced by debased Western coinage.

By the middle of the month, Hanzo's appointment to the Minashi shrine became official. Now there was nothing to do but spend his few remaining days in Tokyo as well as possible.

Morning came. As always, Hanzo went out in the dim light to wash himself beside the well. The maid was not up yet and the kitchen door by the well was still firmly shut. The sound of roosters crowing came to him through the mists.

Hanzo had heard that there would be an imperial progress through the city today. Knowing that he would be able to see it from Kanda bridge, he decided that he should at least have a glimpse of the imperial carriage before he left the capital. After finishing his breakfast, he told Takichi and Osumi where he was going, changed into formal clothing, and left even before Takichi went out to his job in Kayaba-cho. As he walked along the Kanda river over the dew-damp road, the skies gradually cleared over the city. He was filled with a sense of solemn dedication. Not only was he the priest of the Minashi shrine but he was to be its lecturer as well.

Knots of spectators were beginning to gather on the site of the old bastion by Kanda bridge. There were still two hours to wait. During that time the entire space from the edge of the bridge clear back to the windows of the tenement houses became crammed with people. Many of the latecomers were trying to crowd in before those like Hanzo who had come early to get a good spot. Policemen began to restrain the people pushing up in the front row.

It was November 17, 1874, the seventh year of Meiji. The collapse earlier that year of the plan to invade Korea shared a place, along with the falling leaves of autumn, in the thoughts of many. The vast crowd that had come out to witness the imperial progress was proof to Hanzo of the great number of people who shared a common devotion for the emperor, representing the unity of the nation in these difficult times of governmental crisis within and contempt for foreign countries without. He recalled when the emperor had opened the Kenshun gate of the imperial enclosure in Kyoto to foreign emissaries, breaking a precedent going back two thousand five hundred years. He then had vowed to enable everyone from the nobility and the military down to the common people to realize their goals. This new emperor was still only twenty-three years of age. Following his move to Tokyo, Hirata Kanetane had served as his personal tutor. Hanzo's eyes suddenly filled with tears.

In his sash was a new fan that he had picked up before leaving his lodgings. He had written one of his own poems on it, not with the intention of showing it to anyone, but out of the conviction that even an obscure person from the hinterlands could have a concern for the future of the country equal to anyone else's. The poem pleaded that for the sake of our posterity the flood of European influence pouring into the East should not be permitted to continue unchecked.

> Is it not time
> To stop up
> The crab's burrow
> If the great dike
> Is not to crumble away?
>
> Hanzo

With fan in hand, he awaited the passage of the emperor's carriage. Thirty minutes passed. They began to hear hoofbeats. People on both sides of Hanzo strained forward for their first glimpse of the red and white banners fluttering from the lance tips of the mounted guards.

The moment he saw the first carriage approaching, Hanzo was suddenly gripped by a powerful impulse to present his valueless fan to the emperor. When he saw what he assumed to be the first carriage of the escort, he leaped out of the crowd and tossed the fan into the carriage. Then he quickly drew back, kneeled down in his formal trousers, and pressed his forehead against the ground.

"I saw him! I saw him!"

Cries of astonishment rose out of the crowd. Voices called out to each other asking what kind of person it was who had perpetrated this act of disrespect. Hanzo was firmly seized by the first policeman to reach him. The crowd swept over him like a vast wave.

CHAPTER TWELVE

1

HANZO HAD LEFT Takichi's house on the seventeenth of November, saying that he was going to Kanda bridge to watch the imperial procession. It was five days before he returned.

His friends at Saemon-cho waited for news of Hanzo with the greatest anxiety. People all over town were talking about how he had attempted to present his fan to the emperor and there were all kinds of rumors about the incident. Takichi would come home from work each day with a new collection of stories to add to their worries. Neither he nor Osumi was able to believe that Hanzo could be involved in such a bizarre incident.

Then a policeman came to the house. Takichi happened to be out at the time and Osumi met him at the door. He said that he was from the ward headquarters and he was presenting her with a report from the Tokyo court, but first he had to confirm that Aoyama Hanzo was in fact a lodger in this household. The report that he delivered, standing outside in the street, was that Aoyama Hanzo had been granted permission to leave jail and return to his lodgings. It was, however, necessary for someone to go to police headquarters to receive him.

Osumi's voice was a bit unsteady as she replied.

"Well, I don't know what he's been charged with, but I know Aoyama has never done anything bad. A long time ago when we were still living in Aioi-cho, he came to Tokyo at the summons of the transport commission and he stayed with us then. That was why he came back this time. Until just a little while ago he was working as a researcher in the ministry of religion. We are very well acquainted with him. He is a good and honest man."

Upset by this sudden visit from a policeman, Osumi launched into a full-scale defense of their lodger. The policeman cut her off, saying that he was merely carrying out his duty to report this matter to her and that as soon as Takichi came with his registered seal, Hanzo would be handed over to him. Then he left.

Now that she knew Hanzo was to be released, Osumi had another worry. Her husband, unlike people actually born into townsman families, was completely unworldly. He was not at all the kind of person who could be relied

643

upon to carry out the task which the policeman had assigned to him. He was completely taken up with his poetry, so much so that just the other day, when he had left the house to call at the furniture shop of Gembei in Muko-jima to press him for speedy completion of a piece that had been ordered some time ago, he happened to take the same ferry that Gembei had boarded at Imado. Yet when Gembei spoke to him, he did not realize who it was. He simply recited his errand by way of conversation, and only when asked, "But am I not the very Gembei you are talking about?" did he notice who he was talking to. Osumi was fully aware of her spouse's character. She decided that she had better go in his place to secure Hanzo's release from jail. She put her clothing in order and waited for Takichi to come home. When he learned what was happening, he became far more upset than Osumi had been.

"Look here! There had to be some reason for it! It was Aoyama who did it after all! He must have had something in mind!"

Osumi explained to Takichi why she was worried about having him go to police headquarters, a place he so little understood. Takichi, tall and solidly built, shook his head and said that he would go. Fortunately at that moment the physician Kanamaru Kyojun dropped by. A fellow Hirata disciple, he too had been worrying about Hanzo and had come to ask about him. He immediately volunteered to accompany Takichi.

"Wait a moment, please!" said Osumi. She went to get some of her husband's clothing for Hanzo to change into when he was released. She found a spare jacket of the fine, lustrous cotton that her husband was so fond of, but that would not do at all for Hanzo. She picked out a plain jacket, a blue-flecked wadded cotton robe, an underrobe, and even white muslin underwear, packing them quickly and efficiently into a carrying cloth. She did not forget to include a new pair of blue tabi.

"They will surely have a waiting room there, so have him change into this at the headquarters. Put everything he is wearing now into this carrying cloth and bring it back."

With this send-off from Osumi, Takichi and Kyojun left Saemon-cho. Osumi watched her husband walk away, his robe casually tucked up behind so that he could walk more freely. She could not be at ease until Hanzo, who before the incident had been on the point of leaving for Hida, was safely back in her home.

It was four o'clock in the afternoon when Hanzo, accompanied by Takichi and Kyojun, returned to the house in Saemon-cho. Osumi stopped them at the door and made them wait outside until she could send the maid to the kitchen to fetch flint and steel to strike sparks over them. Only then did she permit them into the house.

After this unexpected purification by fire, a greatly relieved Hanzo at last found himself back under a friendly roof. He was pale and dirty. A stubble of beard and a tangle of hair that had not felt a comb for five days told of what a dismal place he had come from. His obvious self-consciousness in wearing Takichi's clothing and his look of utter dejection were painful for Osumi to see. He put his forehead to the floor before Osumi as though to say that mere words could not express his gratitude to her for so concerning herself about an outsider. Then he thrust forward the bundle of dirty clothing. It was clear that he was concerned about them because they had become louse infested during his stay in jail.

"Well, that's really a relief," said Takichi, pacing around the parlor. "Osumi, I'm going to take Aoyama over to the bath. Please wait for us, Kanamaru."

"That's a good idea. You go get him all cleaned up. He'll feel a lot better then. I'll just sit here and have a cup of tea."

Hanzo, still in his borrowed clothing, started to go upstairs to get some of his own things, but Osumi stopped him, telling him that she wanted to see him all cleaned up first, and he did as he was told.

"Well, let's go over and have a good soak. We can talk about it later."

Takichi got up and draped the towel Osumi gave him over his shoulder. Then he started out the door.

"Osumi! We need umbrellas! It's starting to rain."

Hanzo accepted one and together they set out for the neighborhood bath-house that had become so familiar to him.

The neighborhood where Takichi lived had long been known for its stone-mason's shops. The riverbank in front of the house was locally known as the stonecutter's bank, and it was a continuation of the saddlemaker's embank-ment that began one block beyond the main street at the Saemon bridge, fac-ing the embankment of Yanagiwara across the river. A narrow alley past shops dealing in sand, gravel, and pumice stone led directly to the Kanda river. This was a crowded and confused area of warehouses and wharves, but it was not far from the old main street in Ryogoku. It was relatively quiet, yet within earshot of the bustle of the streets. It fitted Takichi's tastes per-fectly.

The bath was not far away. The entrance was marked by a vermillion door topped by paneling figured in gold and silver leaf. They passed through the entrance and up onto a narrow step. It was one of the old-fashioned Edo baths. An interior partition open at the bottom stood before the bathing area to block drafts; bathers had to crawl under it. It was dark inside. When they entered the steamy room, Hanzo felt that he was returning to life. After cleansing themselves thoroughly and then soaking in the hot water, they headed back home along the same road. Night had fallen and lamps were being lighted. They returned to find Kyojun waiting for them by the light of an old-fashioned floor lamp.

"Kanamaru sensei. Osumi says that she would like to give us some home-made buckwheat noodles tonight. Please join Aoyama and me."

"Buckwheat noodles? Perfect!"

Takichi went on talking with his guests. Osumi soon came in from the kitchen, untying her sleeves and leaving the serving trays to the maid. She brought them a small bottle of warm sake, saying that it was to celebrate Hanzo's return.

"A time like this really calls for sake. Nothing else will do," said Kyojun.

Hanzo, now dressed in his own clothes, sat stiffly upright before his congratulatory meal. For appetizers to go with the sake, they had toasted seaweed, bean paste seasoned with bitter orange, and oysters in vinegar and soy sauce, all simply served. To the sound of a dreary late autumn rain, Hanzo, restored by the sake, began to tell them what had happened to him. He had been certain that the first carriage would be part of the escort, and horrified when he learned that he had actually thrown his fan into the imperial carriage. It was not so rare in those days for commoners to memorialize the throne, but it was entirely unprecedented for anyone to do what he had done. After being taken into custody, he was led around to the police barracks in each of the four major wards and to all twelve lesser wards and then finally to the metropolitan headquarters, where he was thoroughly interrogated. He was ordered to jail that night. The next day he was brought before a physician, who first asked his family, his age, and his occupation. While questioning him the physician watched his reactions very closely as if trying to ascertain his mental condition. Then he gave him a general physical examination and asked him a great many more questions. What time had it been when he left his lodgings to wait at Kanda bridge? What did he have for breakfast that morning? And so on. When the examination was completed, he was sent to the Tokyo court building and that same night returned to jail. On the nineteenth he was again taken to the court building, where the statement written up at the police headquarters was read to him. He was asked if that account was correct and he replied that it was. He remained in jail until the morning of the twenty-second. Then he was informed that his landlord was to be called in and he would be released into his custody.

"But haven't I been a real fool? When they were questioning me in court and I was asked why I had chosen this course of action when there were any number of other ways to make my feelings known, I couldn't begin to answer."

Hanzo sighed. The expression on Takichi's face as he listened showed clearly that as far as he was concerned he was simply glad to have Hanzo safely back.

"Aoyama," he replied, "you did what you did because you felt it was good for the country. Drink up!"

Hanzo had been released pending a further summons from the court. In spite of his obligation to serve in the traditional family offices of honjin, headman, and toiya of Magome station, he had always felt so passionately involved with the affairs of the nation that he had been constantly on the verge of rushing off to assist in the still greater task of restoring imperial rule. But he had been required to sit still the whole time, watching his friends neglect home and family to race up and down the country while he stayed with the demanding service of the highway. All the emotions that he had kept dammed up from that time suddenly burst forth when he saw the procession of the emperor whom he revered so deeply. His action was not premeditated nor had there been any thought of possible consequences. There had only been an explosion of feelings.

2

The festive sake that Takichi and Osumi offered him brought out the fatigue of his imprisonment. For the first time since coming to Tokyo, Hanzo failed to observe his early morning ritual and he was not aware when Takichi left for work. The rain of the previous evening had ended, the streets were washed clean. When the shutterboxes of the houses across the way were beginning to dry and the maid came up to open the shutters in his room, he was still snoring loudly. When he finally crawled out of the bedding and looked around the room he had been away from for five days, the sun was high in the sky.

"What is wrong with you?"

Someone was bound to ask him. Imprisonment, court appearances, house arrest—all from that impulsive tossing of the fan. It was particularly appalling that by mistake the fan had actually landed in the imperial carriage. He would have to accept his punishment for having interfered with the imperial procession.

"What a stupid thing to do!"

That was all he could say. Now that he had done it, he could no longer reprove his daughter Okume. It was still a complete riddle to the entire village why on the night of September fifth of the previous year, she should have attempted suicide. When Hanzo tried to understand what he himself had just done, he could not explain his actions either.

In the afternoon, after telling Osumi, he went out to a barbershop in Yanagiwara to get a shave. The shop was one favored by Takichi and he had told Hanzo of the long experience of the people who worked there. All the members of Takichi's poetry circle patronized this shop. There were even priests who would come all the way from the Zojoji over in Shiba to get their heads shaved at the Yana-toko, so widespread was the fame of the master of the shop.

"Well! Come on in!"

Greeted by the owner, Hanzo sat down beside two or three other customers who were already waiting. Some of the people in the shop had long hair, tied high on the back of the head, and shaved foreheads. Others had their hair cut short in the Western style while still others wore their hair long and tied back with a string as he did. One customer had found a new book by the satirist Kanagaki Robun and was reading it intently; another had laid out a chess board and was playing with one of the apprentices of the shop. It was a spot that still seemed to belong to a leisurely world. When Hanzo's turn came, even the sound of the master sharpening his razor on the whetstone seemed indescribably pleasing to him. His unkempt beard was wet down and shaved away, the stubble now falling on the master's hand, now on a little board that Hanzo was given to hold.

After a time he became aware of what one of the later arrivals was saying. This customer was talking about how he had waited the other day at Kanda bridge to see the imperial procession. He told of how someone had run out into the road and had immediately been arrested. He had not actually witnessed the incident himself, but alarmed by the rumors that it was a madman, he had fled from the scene. Hanzo froze. But an extraordinary calm quickly took the place of the tension and he listened to the story as though it were about a stranger as the barber continued to shave him. Every trace of hair was removed, even from his ears and from the thick "honjin" nose that he had inherited from his father.

Hanzo stepped casually out of the barber shop. He had been shaved closely without any unpleasant burning and the breeze felt cool on his cheeks. He returned directly to his room in Saemon-cho. There the window with the quiet view to the west awaited him. He had often let in cooling breezes through that window while suffering in the unaccustomed heat of a Tokyo summer. Outside the room was a balcony with a good view of the street. The diligent Osumi had repapered the shoji while he was in jail. He had spent more than half a year in Tokyo and by now even the plaque that Takichi had put up on the wall for him was a familiar object.

How dark those five days had been! As he was putting things in order in his room, he recalled his feelings in the lonely jail cell. When he was called before the court, the officials seemed determined to make a crime of his action and all he could say was that he had long been concerned over the relentless incursions of Christianity, that he had wished to memorialize the throne on the subject, and that when he had actually seen the emperor's party passing, he had been overwhelmed with his concern for the national well-being. It just happened that he was carrying with him a fan inscribed with one of his own poems, and when he threw that fan into the first carriage, which he had been certain was the carriage of an escort, it had been with the thought that it would naturally come to the emperor's attention and that it might be of some assistance in establishing future standards for the enlightenment of the people.

At the very least, he had acted out of the deepest concern for the future of the nation, but he made no effort to hide his chagrin that his behavior had seemed so uncouth and eccentric. Even before the opening of the nation, those who had in one way or another accepted the West had in another sense been struggling against it. Unfortunately the people of Japan had repeatedly lost opportunities to take a calm and careful look at European culture. If internal disorder should now rob them of the leisure to observe what lay outside, and they were to slide into a mere imitation of the surface texture of this Western culture so different from our own in history, in customs, and in language without at the same time continuing the struggle against that culture, what would come of it in the end? Is it not imperative that we maintain an attitude of well-informed skepticism toward the West? He could not bear to think of the possible consequences of such a failure. Nor was this simply a mindless resistance to the spread of a foreign religion. The nation had been agonizing over the problems presented by Christianity ever since the days of Oda Nobunaga. Two and a half centuries had already passed since the introduction of the requirement that each family maintain its permanent records of births, deaths, marriages, and adoptions in a Buddhist temple. This had been a direct response to those problems. It was impossible to think about the meaning and purpose of the long closing of the nation without at the same time thinking about the problem of religion.

Now that the nation was opened to the world, those who recalled the words spoken by Shotoku Taishi in the eighth century saw that they were once again applicable in this new age. He had said that Shinto was in fact the root of the nation and Confucianism and Buddhism the branches. Under the Meiji government the primary purpose of the ministry of religion had been to graft Christianity onto that same tree. But the foreign missionaries could not even agree with each other and they would not follow the government's policies in any case. Then the Shin Buddhist priests took heart from the defiance of the Christians and began to assert their own arbitrary opinions. People began disseminating their faiths without concern for governmental aims or policies. A painful awareness of these difficulties grew on Hanzo as he worked in the ministry of religion. If they were to continue to pile compromise upon compromise, giving in to the foreign missionaries on each issue, it was going to be impossible to restrain the discontent of the other sects and schools. The effort to enlighten and advance the nation would become chaotic and without direction. In the end the great goal of a thorough renewal of society would surely be lost. The office of religion under the Meiji government had become the ministry of religion and then the ministry of doctrine. Now it seemed likely to be eliminated altogether. The prospect was deeply disturbing to Hanzo.

No doubt the foreign countries were very different from what they had been when the Portuguese and the Spanish had been expelled more than two hundred years earlier. They might be less concerned with religion now than they had been then. Townsend Harris, the first American consul to this country, had said as much, and furthermore that people choose their religion according to their own feelings in present-day America. Such freedom might very well exist. That people should be free to follow the dictates of their own consciences was part of the very foundation of modern Europe. Hanzo had not failed to take this into consideration, but he had come to the conclusion that he did not want this chaos masquerading as freedom for his own children and grandchildren. There was nothing whose sources were so pure but whose consequences were so subject to pollution as was religion. The history of the confounding of the Buddhist and Shinto faiths in our own country testified to that fact as clearly as anything could. It was not at all unlikely that a similar confounding of Shinto and Christianity might take place in the future. Nor was it in the least likely that determined, capable, and personable Christian missionaries might be able to play on the Japanese love of the novel and exotic, causing them to forget altogether about the distinction between the roots and the branches of this nation. It was imperative that the religious basis of the nation be made explicit in these times when the restoration was not yet firmly established. This was what concerned Hanzo.

Now that he had time to think these things over in tranquility, his thoughts stretched out in all directions like invisible threads. He thought often of his stepmother, his wife, and his children back home. He wondered what kind of gossip this incident had produced in Magome and how it might affect his going to Hida.

3

Hanzo was called before the court. His statement was read to him once more and he once again said that it was correct. Then he was required to listen to the transcript of his previous appearance before the court and was asked if it was also correct. When he replied that it was, he was asked to affix his seal to both documents. He was then informed that a judgment would soon be handed down and he was dismissed.

Hanzo told Takichi and Osumi about this as soon as he returned to his lodgings and then wrote up an account of the whole affair, exactly as it had happened, to send home. He apologized to Oman for the worry his impulsiveness must have been causing her. He also informed her that these events had led to a delay in his plan to return to Magome before going on to take up the post in Hida. This was a great inconvenience to everyone and he deeply regretted it, but since for now he was not permitted to leave Tokyo, there was nothing he could do but wait until the judgment came down. They would have to get along without him for a while longer. He also informed the Kanamura residence in Shinnorimono-cho of the way things had gone at court.

Early in December, Kyojun came over to look in on him.

"You don't have to stay all shut in like this, Aoyama, even if you are under restriction. At least come over to Ryogoku with me. The soldiers are starting to come back from Taiwan."

But Hanzo kept wretchedly to his room, leaving it to his imagination to picture just how lively the town might become as the soldiers returned in triumph from the punitive expedition against Taiwan. When he saw Kyojun again, Hanzo told him how impatiently he had been awaiting the decision of the court and how concerned he was about possible repercussions in Hida, where the people had so kindly invited him to the shrine. Kyojun merely shook his head and reassured him that since his action had been the result of an excess of patriotic fervor, he need have no concern about the way it would be received in Hida. Kyojun added that he would at any rate ask Tanaka Fujimaro to send a letter of explanation to Hida.

"How about it, Aoyama? Why don't you move over to Shinnori-mono-cho?"

This question was the main purpose of Kyojun's visit. He explained further.

"If you do that, I will have somebody to talk to. It won't trouble me to feed one more person, and you can have a room to yourself."

Kyojun's sincerity was written plainly on his face and there was great warmth and sensitivity hidden beneath his half-joking manner of speech. Hanzo could only feel the deepest gratitude for the consideration this fellow disciple had shown him. Yet he replied that he did not feel free to change his residence while under restriction, and grateful as he was for Kyojun's offer, he would have to stay put for the time being. Hanzo was painfully concerned about his expenses now that he had no income, but if the stay became a prolonged one, he could ask his friend and neighbor Inosuke for help. For now he simply did not want to leave Saemon-cho.

When the middle of December came, Hanzo was still waiting for word from the court. He had been certain that he would hear by then, but perhaps because of the press of other business, the final week of the month came with still no decision from the court.

The first snow had come to Tokyo. Of course, it was thin and soft, and even a single night's rain would wash it all away. The snowfalls here in the capital, so different from those in the Kiso, turned Hanzo's thoughts homeward for that very reason. He was also concerned about the delay in his journey to Hida. The later in the season it became, the deeper the snows on that forbidding mountain pass would be.

> Alone I
> Am awakened by
> The sound
> Of snow spilling
> From overloaded pine boughs.
>
> Chill night rains:
> Soon I shall cross
> Distant mountains;
> The eaves still drip
> In broken rhythms.
>
> In the mountain
> Village snow piles up
> Day after day;
> No visitor fights his way
> Through it all to see me.
>
> White snow:
> Only the smoke is
> Left unburied
> To mark the site of
> The remote mountain village.

Hanzo had written these winter poems in Magome. Now he recalled them in his room in Saemon-cho, imagining the snow-covered Kiso road and the travelers on it, the leather breast straps, the hempen fly-whisks, the cloth aprons with crests dyed on them, and the packhorses themselves wet from their manes to their tails. He imagined the garden at home—a few red berries would still be on the branches of the evergreens; the bamboo grove would still be behind the woodshed. He went on to imagine the valleys high on the Ena range that each year were buried so deeply in snow.

Hanzo greeted the new year in Tokyo. Together with Takichi and Osumi, he welcomed 1875, Meiji 8, with New Year's rice cakes, pickled plums, boiled rice dumplings, herring roe, and all the other special seasonal dishes.

A letter from home that had been mailed before the first of the year reached Hanzo soon afterward. It was from Oman and Okume. Okume said that she was constantly concerned about her father's welfare but that everyone at home was well, and they were all waiting, from Otami to little Wasuke, for his return. The writing was still that of a young girl. The message from his stepmother was not so gentle. It was concerned with the gossip that had started once news of Hanzo's fan-tossing incident reached Magome. It described Okume's progress, saying that she seemed to be completely recovered and the scar was becoming less conspicuous day by day, and then reporting that there had been new marriage inquiries from the Uematsu family in Fukushima. Oman even took up Hanzo's drinking; she had heard that he was drinking very heavily. She worried about him constantly and reminded him of how Kichizaemon had often spoken of the need for great caution when one reached the critical age for men. If he was going to show the proper respect for his father, he would think about that each time he drank and exercise restraint.

After the New Year's holidays were over, Osumi brought a package of tea up to Hanzo's room, telling him that the tea was a gift from Takichi, who was fond of this variety.

"Haven't you heard anything from the court yet, Aoyama?"

There was something strong and a bit forbidding about Osumi, and she was much more the head of this household than was Takichi, who left everything to her. Away from home though he was, Hanzo counted his good fortune in being among warm and considerate people and having friends in Tokyo who knew him.

"Did you get a letter from home?"

"Yes, everyone is all right. They all expressed their gratitude to you for taking such good care of me."

"Your wife must be quite worried . . ."

"I wouldn't tell anyone but you about this, Osumi, but it's always my daughter who writes the letters. She writes very well. My wife has never written."

Such conversation is reassuring to a traveler. Osumi was completely straightforward and free of ambiguity, and it was as though Hanzo were talking with a man. He even told her about the content of Oman's letter, and of how she was scolding him about his drinking. Of course, he had had the greatest respect for his keen-witted stepmother ever since his childhood, so much so that he confessed there was nothing he feared so much as Oman. He said that even after he grew up, became head of the house in his turn, and took up the business of the post station and the highway, he had still not let her know about his drinking.

"But how would you be able to get by without drinking a little sake?"

Osumi's response was, as always, completely in character.

They were still officially in the holiday season and Osumi was somewhat formal in her manner, but she began to talk with Hanzo about her women friends, something she almost never did. Otora was the disciple of the Kiyomoto performer Oyo. She had an exceptionally fine voice and she was giving lessons to the geisha over in Yanagibashi. She was a bit wild but an interesting woman. For all that she was the exact opposite of Osumi in temperament, they were the closest of friends. Otora was so completely the artist that she always wore fine clothing, even when she had to go short on food. On the other hand, she was quite capable of pawning her precious samisen so she could lie on the tatami all day long reading cheap novels from the rental library. It was the subject of women writing letters that brought up the name of Otora. Osumi told Hanzo that this friend was another one of those women who seemed to find letter writing impossible. She described how delighted Otora had been to learn that she did not have to use the complicated, old-fashioned language of the formal epistolary style but that she could write just as if she were speaking. She immediately went home and sent a letter back to Saemon-cho. Osumi said that she and Takichi still talked about it. The letter had read in full:

> Oh, Osumi. Good evening. Hot, isn't it? Since then I've been thinking. If only I had a husband—but I don't have a husband—right?"

Osumi left Hanzo to ponder this story.

The pleasant, bustling sound of the streets mixed with that of the wind blowing through a clump of bamboo outside came through the shoji. He could hear Omiwa, Takichi and Osumi's daughter, playing the New Year's game of battledore and shuttlecock with the maid. Omiwa was of an age to remind Hanzo of Okume. She had been a little girl when he had known her in Aioi-cho, but now she was living at the residence of the famous Urasenke tea master Sho'u'an as a favored disciple. Since she did not often come to Saemon-cho, just having her home transformed the atmosphere of the household. Takichi and Osumi had three children. Omiwa's elder brother, Kazuichiro, was apprenticed to a trading company in Yokohama and her younger brother, Risuke, was an apprentice in a wholesale grain dealer's establishment near Nihombashi. The family was eagerly awaiting their New Year's visit home.

Hanzo remained in his room observing the strictures against his movement even while the boisterous Mikawa clowns made their way through the streets, leaving a sense of promise for the new year in their wake. Omiwa, her hair freshly put up in the shimada style, came up to visit Hanzo, leaving him a confection presented on crisp red and white paper.

When the stew of seven spring vegetables had been served on the seventh of the month to mark the end of the New Year festivities, there was still no word from the Tokyo court. Hanzo went on waiting day after day. Takichi, a man of taste, had a great many interesting books and pictures which he brought out for Hanzo to see. Even the yellowish walls of the room, papered along their lower edges, became a comfort to Hanzo.

One day, Hanzo suddenly became aware of the voice of a street peddler selling newly printed popular songs. He was reading them out with a sharp, harsh voice like a mountain bird as he went along, and it cut through the street noise with startling clarity. As Hanzo listened, one verse of a song about the way new things and old things were mixing together caught his ear.

> In Western dress,
> Wearing trousers,
> But at a loss
> Without sleeve pouches.

It was not only the popular songs that spoke of headlong change. The past seven years had altered everything. Many of the brave warriors that had come up from the furthest extremity of Kyushu, eager for the conquest of Edo, now found themselves captives of women of the capital. Authors such as Kanagaki Robun, then very popular, skillfully depicted these situations in humorous satires. Takichi brought up a copy of Robun's *The Beefeater* for Hanzo to read. In this story about the newly opened restaurants specializing in beef, the epitome of "enlightenment," was the line "Nowadays the sun wouldn't even come up if it weren't for Western learning."

If you wondered what sort of creature might emit such a statement, you were given a man with a brand new Western-style haircut, a French-style cape, and an English vest—a set of Western clothing assembled from the flea market in Yanagiwara. He wore a watch-chain, prominently displayed, but owned no watch. Everything about him expressed a desperate effort to appear cosmopolitan. With an air of the utmost self-satisfaction, this civilized man was exceedingly generous with the scraps of knowledge he had picked up from the popular works of the day. He was ready to speak his mind about anything concerning the West. After all, these were times when such an outwardly splendid, inwardly pitiful civilized man could take his seat in a beef restaurant, a pot of beef stew and a bottle of cold sake before him, and bask in his own glory.

Even the songs in the music halls had changed. Now they had to have a few scraps of English in them to be accepted. *Matsu yo no nagaki,* or "how long the nights I wait," was rejected as a backward and old-fashioned line. One had to say, "*Matsu yo no* long." An expression such as *neko-nade koe,* which meant the "cat-petting voice" used for currying favor, was seen as passé. It was now "cat-*nade koe.*"

Hanzo, sitting with his arms folded in the strong sun coming through the open shoji, reflected on the incredibly chaotic state of the world. Even gentle young girls believed that Japan was soon to become a country where it would be impossible to get by without learning English, and they were rushing off to their language lessons with foreign books and umbrellas under their arms. Just to think about such people as he sat in his room in Saemon-cho filled Hanzo's breast with outrage.

He began to read all day long.

The specter that had haunted Hanzo from his youth appeared to him once again. It was difficult to describe exactly. It had to do with the Black Ships but in his mind that term held three distinct meanings. The first was Christianity. Western science was a second meaning, and the third was the unification of the world through trade. He realized that those who studied Western subjects were not all of a kind. At the very least, there had been a difference in the attitudes of the scholars of Western learning before and after the opening of the country. Even before Sakuma Shozan formulated his maxim "Eastern morality, Western technology," those scholars had all believed that Japan had a special mission. Hashimoto Sanai and Habu Genseki in earlier times and Watanabe Kazan and Takano Choei later were all of the same mind. Even a person like Sato Nobuhiro of Akita, a Western scholar with a specialized knowledge of agriculture and economics, was at the same time deeply committed to the teachings of Motoori Norinaga. It was not at all unusual then for a man to retire at the age of sixty, turning the family affairs over to a younger brother or son, and to devote the remainder of his life to Western studies. Of course, the permission of the han authorities was required to undertake such studies. The scholars also had to accept the penalties that came with their studies—that is, the social and political pressures they entailed. But the more difficulties they encountered in their surroundings, the more determined they became, and their scholarship was of high quality. They left behind works establishing the basis for later progress in the fields of astronomy, geography, history, languages, mathematics, agriculture, chemistry, and military science.

In contrast, the new scholars of Western learning who appeared after the opening of the nation were working in totally different conditions. It had become relatively easy to carry on Western studies. In the present world, those who might earlier have gone all the way to Nagasaki would know that there were better English teachers to be found in and around Nagoya. What Hanzo was witnessing was a shallow but all-encompassing flood of Western learning.

Naturally, there were still a few Western scholars who continued to pursue the goals of old. But they were a group of very well read and articulate people who had formerly been associated with the shogunate, and their attitude toward the West was more sophisticated. They had already worked in an environment that made them familiar with Western things, having for the most part been associated with the shogunate's Institute for the Study of Foreign Books, or else with the trading port facilities in Yokohama. These people came from different backgrounds and they had held various ranks in the shogunal government. Some had been well paid, some had not, but they had all shared the experience of witnessing the collapse of the institutions in which they functioned. When one wondered what had become of former shogunal officials like Yamaguchi Suruga and Mukoyama Eigoro, the name of Kitamura Zuiken came naturally to mind. Zuiken had been sent to France before the collapse of the shogunate, and had returned with a greatly expanded breadth of learning and experience. Soon he reappeared from his old home in Honjo Kita Futaba-cho to emerge on the stage of public debate as the founder of a very influential newspaper.

Now Zuiken, of course, had started out as a physician to the shogunal court, and he was also learned as a herbalist. Western learning was not the only string to his bow. But those who began writing after him were by no means all of the same quality. Some of them so completely lost hope in their own country that they became totally committed to a Europe they could never really know. Others concealed their obsession with things foreign in the writing of light fiction. Completely lacking any rational outlet for their discontent, they would say, "Of course the world is changing. But it's changing for the better. No doubt about it." And they raised a powerful storm of criticism that could be heard throughout the country. In Hanzo's eyes this present time was important in the same way that the period many centuries ago when Japan first began to adopt Chinese culture was important. What was to become of this nation which had not yet completely broken out of the shell of the middle ages, but was now enamored of all things Western? The attitude was the same as that with which it had once uncritically admired China; the underlying pattern was the same. Yet it was crucial that while the West was being accepted on the one hand, it also had to be resisted on the other. For that reason, the posthumous disciples of Hirata Atsutane had to protect the spirit that was within them from the vicissitudes of the times. It was unthinkable to Hanzo that the path that had been opened by so many masters from Kada no Azumamaro on could now be completely overwhelmed by imported learning.

4

FAIR COPY OF A COURT DECISION

Aoyama Hanzo, commoner, Misaka village, Chikuma county, Shinano province. Presently priest and lecturer, Minashi shrine.

Now, out of an excess of patriotic fervor and wishing to have his fan inscribed with a poem of his own composition seen by the emperor, who was then in progress through the city, he threw the aforementioned fan directly into the imperial carriage, mistaking that carriage for a part of the escort.

This comes under the category of direct affront to the emperor, but, in consideration of the feelings that accompanied the act, we have seen fit to reduce the charge by five degrees. Therefore, instead of the normal punishment of fifty days imprisonment, we impose a fine of three yen, seventy-five sen.

January 13, Meiji 8

The Court of Tokyo

Hanzo's home was given as Misaka village because Magome and the neighboring village of Yubunezawa had been combined to make a new village. It was now officially Magome hamlet, Misaka village, Chikuma county, Chikuma prefecture. The ancient Kiso route known as Misaka was buried deep in the mountains of the Ena range, but the name of the new village was taken from it. The consolidation of villages that was one of the policies of the new government had finally reached as far as his home village.

The court had at last handed down its decision. In the evening, Hanzo joined Takichi and Osumi in the downstairs parlor, where they all breathed sighs of relief and began to discuss his new freedom. A visitor for Takichi came to the door. He was the head of a major vegetable wholesale house whom Takichi had known from Kawagoe, and he was also a fellow lover of haikai. When this guest happened by, giving a hearty greeting to Takichi, who went out into the entrance to meet him, it seemed that this visit was somehow part of the happy occasion.

"Well now! If it isn't Takichi!"

Takichi was delighted to hear this. This particular guest tended to begin every sentence with "Well now," and Osumi, with the relaxed familiarity she reserved for close friends, had made it his nickname, so that even the maid called him "Well Now." It therefore sounded to everyone within as though the guest had unwittingly announced himself by name as he came in. When Osumi heard it, she could not contain herself and she had to leave the parlor while the maid fled out the back door.

After five days in prison and nearly fifty days of restriction, Hanzo's action had finally been judged. Although he had avoided the possible fifty days of hard labor and had gotten away with a fine, it was still no laughing matter for him. In trying to breast the great waves of the new age, he had been knocked off his feet and badly pummelled by them. Now the only way open for him was the one that led into the mountains of Hida.

Night came. As he slept by the dim nightlight in the room in Saemon-cho, Kureta Masaka made a rare appearance in his dreams. Masaka, to whom he felt closest among all the senior disciples, had been transferred from his post as priest of the Kamo shrine to take up a similar post in the Atsuta shrine in Nagoya. Recently he had been promoted to high priest. In his dream that night, Hanzo saw Masaka, dressed in formal clothing, strike him with the wand he was carrying. He awoke weeping, the tears streaming down his face.

*   *   *   *   *   *   *

Hanzo stayed in Tokyo through the end of January, completing his preparations for the trip to Hida. However long, lonely, and hard the road of service to the gods might be, Hanzo reassured himself that he could endure it.
Now he only wanted to leave Tokyo as quickly as possible and head back
down the Kiso road, stop in at home on the way, then continue on to Nakatsugawa and finally to Hida. Yet things kept delaying his departure.

He was terribly ashamed of the fan-tossing incident, and feeling that he
should have to bear the full consequences of it, he had sent a letter to the
appropriate person in the ministry of religion reporting the entire incident
and its outcome and requesting permission to resign his post. Although Hida
was presently under the jurisdiction of Chikuma prefecture, Minashi shrine
was not a prefectural shrine; it was a minor national shrine and everything
concerning it was at the disposal of the ministry. Furthermore, having
incurred a considerable indebtedness during his long stay in Tokyo, Hanzo
had asked Inosuke of the Fushimiya for assistance in meeting his obligations
and he was waiting for a reply to that letter. Fortunately, the ministry replied
that there was no need for him to resign and he received word that Inosuke
had asked Heibei from Toge to take money to Tokyo for him. He was filled
with a sense of anticipation. What changes would there be in Tokyo by the
time he saw it again? With this on his mind, he went around to take leave of
his acquaintances.

On a cold, clear day at the beginning of February, Heibei, who was still
acting as head of the hamlet of Toge even though all such offices had been
abolished, arrived at the house in Saemon-cho. The relationship between
Hanzo and Heibei had been formed in the days of the post stations, and it
was almost that of master and retainer. No matter what changes of time and
place might occur, Heibei still addressed him as "honjin." He also shared
with Hanzo the memories of the long journey to Ise and Kyoto that they had
made in the sixth and seventh months of Keio 4, 1868. Heibei had brought
not only money but also news from home. He told Hanzo about how the
forest problem had been going, how Kokura Keisuke, whom Hanzo had
chosen as the new schoolmaster, was being received, and various other developments in Magome. He reported that there was no one in the village who
had not been startled by the news about Hanzo that had been coming up
from Tokyo—particularly about the incident at Kanda bridge and his subsequent imprisonment. It was Inosuke of the Fushimiya who had suffered most
on his account.

"I'm telling you, when some know-nothing starts asking questions about
it, you just don't know what to say," Heibei continued.

". . ."

"Really, what ever comes of gossip? They were even saying that you had
gone crazy. When Otami heard that she started crying. Everybody has been
saying that the master of the honjin had gotten too much wrapped up in his
studies and that there was surely some basis in fact for all the gossip. That's

what they were saying—right there in the village. And the only one who took your side and said that it was all a lot of stupid, irresponsible nonsense was the master of the Fushimiya. I have to admit that even I am relieved now that I've gotten here and had a look at you."

". . ."

Hanzo had no first-hand knowledge of Hida. Whenever he thought of the snows of the rugged Kashimo pass and the remoteness of those mountains there on the border between Mino and Hida, he was overcome by dread of its fearful cold. He found it difficult to believe that anyone could actually travel over it in the winter. He was somewhat relieved after Heibei arrived in Tokyo. Inosuke, hearing that there was a person who regularly came from Hida to Nakatsugawa on business, had talked with him and had written down everything he had learned. He sent the report along with Heibei.

According to the report, the Minashi shrine was not actually in Takayama but about four miles away. The Minashi river flowed before the shrine. It was a tributary of the Jinzu river. The settlement that had grown up around the shrine was called Miyamura and pilgrims from throughout Hida were constantly gathering there. The major festival at the shrine came on the twenty-fifth of September. One custom that seemed unique to the area was the New Year's eve pilgrimage, an ancient custom in which groups of men and women in costume would dance before the shrine to welcome in the new year. To reach the shrine from Mino in the winter, it was necessary to acquire straw snow boots and put on special snow shoes with crampons; only then could one cross the Kashimo pass, famous as the most difficult of passes. Even so there was never a day when some travelers did not make the trip; the snow was not so terribly deep as rumor would have it. It was about thirty miles from Nakatsugawa to Gero. The road was in fact difficult and horses could not get over the pass. If one rode, it had to be on an ox. In Gero, where there was a good hot spring, travelers could get warmed up. From Gero the walking was not too difficult. After Hagiwara and Kosaka, one came to the top of the Miya pass, from which one could see the Minashi shrine at the foot of the mountain. An added note said that the Takayama region was one which had early on produced outstanding National Scholars, such as Motoori Norinaga's favored disciple Tanaka Ohide. Hanzo would find no shortage of sympathetic people to talk with.

On the day before his departure, as Heibei put the baggage together beside him, Hanzo exchanged commemorative poems with Takichi. Takichi wrote one of the seventeen syllable hokku of which he was so fond, and Hanzo responded with a thirty-one syllable classic verse. Takichi and Osumi were both sad to see Hanzo leaving, and their parting gifts had been carefully and considerately chosen both to express their feelings and not to add to the traveler's burden. Takichi gave him a stick of fine Chinese ink wrapped in yellow paper. Osumi, saying that it was for his wife, gave him some of the famous cherry-scented hair oil that one would never be able to obtain in the Kiso and some fine paper cords for tying up the hair.

"Our lives seem to be linked together in surprising ways."

The next morning, Hanzo heard these parting words from Takichi and Osumi and then took his leave. The horse he had ordered was waiting in the street. Like the previous time he had left Tokyo, his baggage was wrapped in a piece of Ryukyu matting and loaded on the horse. He and Heibei left the gate of the house in Saemon-cho.

"I'll go with you a little way!"

Takichi suddenly slipped into his sandals and accompanied them as far as the Saemon bridge. During his time in Tokyo, Hanzo had so often crossed this bridge on his way to work at the ministry or on business in town. He could not but be intensely aware that this time he was saying good-bye to his room on the second floor at Saemon-cho. Everything this morning seemed to stand out with a sharp clarity—the boats being towed along close to the riverbank, the dark, stagnant waters of the Kanda river, the birdcages drying in the sun behind the warehouses standing on stone foundations.

It was now the eighth year since the restoration. All kinds of measures were being taken by the government to keep in touch with the lower levels of society, yet whenever any major displacement at the foundations of society occurred, aftershock after aftershock would be felt in the life of every citizen. Throughout these years, foreigners taking advantage of the importation of Western culture were coming into Japan both from the home countries and from the colonies. Among these Europeans were many who were obsessed, like their predecessors, with the idea that Japan must be made to adopt Western culture either by force or by admonition. There were also others who came with a considerable amount of sympathy and good will, noting that although many backward countries had been destroyed by the intervention of the advanced nations, trade with Japan was highly developed. Profit and humanism had joined hands and Japan could be guided to take its place as the mentor of the backward Oriental nations. Could the standards of European civilization be applied not only in government but throughout the nation without the danger of destroying the national character? It was the Japanese who had to furnish the answer to that question. Proposals were already being heard for a popularly elected national assembly, while at the same time other voices were advocating the reestablishment of the old samurai class. Unheeded catastrophes still occurred, and desperate cries were rising from unemployed samurai and from townsmen whose businesses had failed. It seemed to be a time when no one could get by unaided. Hanzo was very thoughtful as he left Tokyo, passed through Itabashi, and entered the Kiso road.

5

"It's the teacher!"

The cry rose from the children who were out sliding on the ice along the road. Some of them were hurtling down the steep slope with great skill. Others fell and got up again amid much childish laughter.

These mountain children, carrying pikes to deal with the ice, oblivious to the frost that nipped at their fingers, were completely lost in their play on the frozen road. All of them were pupils from the village school, attending the new school building which was now known as the Misaka elementary school. In the second week of February, Hanzo and Heibei arrived back in Magome and as they passed in front of the Fushimiya, Hanzo heard the familiar voices of the children he had taught.

"Father!"

The child who left the others with a shout was his third son, Morio. Even Wasuke, his fourth son, had grown big enough to join the older children and he delighted in walking around on the snow in his mountain breeches, his cheeks a bright scarlet.

The village was still locked in winter stillness. In Hanzo's house everyone from Oman, Otami, and Okume down to the manservant Sakichi was awaiting his return. He had already traveled more than two hundred miles since leaving Tokyo and he was tired and chilled, but he would not be able to rest in his own home for long. In three days he would be going on to Hida. Given his situation, he simply could not delay his arrival in Hida any longer. The baggage was unloaded from the horse and the gifts for the children were taken out. As the people in the house began to talk about everything that had happened during his long absence, the villagers, who soon knew Hanzo was home, began to crowd in to see him. The school principal, Kokura Keisuke, whom Hanzo had not seen since Matsumoto, came to report on the elementary school. The assistant manager for Magome, Sasaya Shosuke, brought word of the progress of the forest dispute and described how silk culture was being further encouraged in the village. The priest Matsushita Chisato from Aramachi told Hanzo about the restoration of religious services at the village shrine.

The three short days that Hanzo spent at home were hectic. Otami, bringing a heap of live coals from the hearth to the footwarmer in the next room for her husband, told him about the marriage proposal for Okume that had come from the Uematsu family in Fukushima. Then Oman brought in her old-fashioned smoking set and sat down to tell him of the family's misgivings about his continued absence. She pointed out that Sota was now a youth of seventeen, respected in the village for his filial conduct, and with Hanzo's cousin Eikichi looking after them and Seisuke still their chief clerk as in the days of the honjin, the family ought to be able to get along. Still, since Hanzo was going away again, to serve no one knew how long at Minashi shrine, he really ought to consider passing on the position of head of the household to Sota, so that he would be completely free. Oman's hair had grown whiter, but she still disposed of matters in her own way. Hanzo kneeled before her, hands on the floor, unable to raise his head. Listening to an account of the miserable condition of the family finances from this stepmother who was prepared to fight to the death to prevent the old honjin family from losing its status in the world, he had nothing to say in his own defense.

These brief days at home were among the most difficult of Hanzo's entire life. At forty-three he reconciled himself to retiring as head of the house. This would be twenty years earlier than his father, Kichizaemon, and twenty-two years earlier than his grandfather, Hanroku.

Overwhelmed by stress and loneliness, Hanzo went over to the Fushimiya whenever he had the chance. There he looked at Inosuke's reassuring face, thanked him for his assistance, and especially for sending money all the way to Hanzo's lodgings in Saemon-cho. He said that while Oman would very likely take him to task for it, he wanted to repay Inosuke by turning over to him a portion of the woods belonging to the honjin. He told Inosuke of his doubts that Sota could assume such responsibilities at his age. But then Otami would be there to keep an eye on things. Since he himself was no longer of any use to the ancient Aoyama family, he had decided to comply with Oman's request. When he returned home after this conversation, Sakichi, who had always been a bachelor, came up to Hanzo wringing his great, chapped hands. He too was asking to take his leave, saying that he wanted to return to the neighboring village of Yamaguchi, where he planned to get married and set up housekeeping.

"Master, there is something else I would like to ask of you at this time."

"What is it, Sakichi? Speak up!"

"As you know, I don't have a family name."

"You mean you still haven't taken one?"

"No, but I want to have a family name just like everyone else. If you were the one to give me a name, I would really feel that all the years here had been well spent."

Sakichi explained that he did not have any strong feelings about what his name should be. He would be happy with anything that Hanzo thought proper. As with so many uneducated people, his father had passed his life in hard labor in the fields, without leaving a single written document behind him, not even a household account book. No record of the family lineage had been passed down. They had all worked in silence and died in silence, generation after generation. Sakichi did not aspire to a grand name, but since the line would be starting with his generation, he wanted something appropriate. He suggested that, since he had worked so long in the pine forest to the north of the honjin, Kitabayashi might be a possibility. Hanzo agreed and gave him the name of Kitabayashi Sakichi. He also urged Sakichi to report his new name to the village office in Yamaguchi as soon as he arrived.

In lieu of salary and settlement Hanzo gave Sakichi some of the farmlands that had belonged to the honjin to cultivate as his own. Sakichi had never paid any attention to women. He never asked leave to go out at night. In the daytime he worked in the woodshed and at night he worked beside the hearth in the main house. All the vegetables served at his master's table had been grown by Sakichi.

The Aoyama genealogy, the account books, the tax records, the official seal for Magome station, the register of land holdings and the other old documents that remained in the family, the two lances that had been passed down from distant ancestors and the hanging scroll given to Hanzo by the Yamagami family in Sagami that had become a family treasure—the time had come to pass them all on. Hanzo scarcely had time to sit still for a minute. As soon as he sat down at his paulownia desk in the parlor, he would get up again and begin putting documents in order for Sota. When Okume came to look in on him, she could read in his expression that he was desperately concerned about this family that had lost its three offices of honjin, headman, and toiya. Among the women of the family it was this precocious girl who most clearly perceived the extent of their reverses.

"Oh, Okume!" Hanzo called out as he paced the document-littered floor of the parlor.

Okume was nineteen years old. A new proposal of marriage had come to this girl who had once been determined to fight to the death against her fate. This proposal, from the Uematsu family in Fukushima, had been altogether unexpected. An extraordinary connection between the two families was being forged through the workings of mere chance.

"I've finally made up my mind, father."

As Okume spoke, she pulled the scarlet silk crepe collar of her underrobe together as if to cover the scar that she had worn on her throat since the year before last. Then she went off to the dimly lighted wood-floored room that adjoined the entrance hall to the west of the parlor.

After three days, Hanzo went on to Nakatsugawa. He had wanted Otami to go with him on this trip to Hida or at least to come over later after he was settled in, but without her to keep an eye on Sota there was no chance that the Magome household could be kept afloat. Sakichi, too, sad about leaving him at this juncture, had offered to accompany him at least to Miyamura in Hida, but he was not making the trip either. Hanzo loaded his baggage on a packhorse to be led by his tenant farmer Kenkichi. The two left Magome by way of the hamlet of Shinjaya and headed on across the boundary between Shinano and Mino and down the snowy Jikkyoku pass.

At Nakatsugawa, he visited the two friends who lived there, bringing them word from the master Hirata Kanetane and from their colleague Kanamaru Kyojun in Tokyo. Keizo had been keeping very much to himself but when they met he was still the same Keizo.

Hanzo was oppressed by thoughts of the road ahead. He told Kenkichi, who was to accompany him all the way to Miyamura, that they would go as far as they could with a horse and then transfer the baggage to an ox. Before he set out to penetrate the mountains of Hida, Hanzo retired to a room in

Keizo's house, the former Nakatsugawa honjin, and wrote a letter to the
Fushimiya.

SATAKE INOSUKE:

I am writing this because I will not be seeing you again for some
time. I have put Magome behind me and have come to Nakatsugawa
thinking of this trip to Hida as a command from heaven, and in the
hope that I can lead the people who live in that high country along a
way that will bring them fulfillment. I am very much aware of the
impatience with which the people of Hida are awaiting my arrival. It
may be that I will return in failure after two or three years. Or it may
be that in the end only my bones will be coming back home. I will be
satisfied either way so long as I can carry out heaven's command. Ever
since I went to Tokyo you have been most helpful and I thank you from
the bottom of my heart. I must ask you to lend me your strength still
further in the matter of Okume. If her marriage is made definite, I plan
to come back for a visit at that time. This is the only request I leave
behind. I am in the best of health and my mind is more at peace than
usual. Please take care of yourself.

Hanzo

CHAPTER THIRTEEN

1

MORE THAN four years passed. An Englishman on his way over the Kiso road from Tokyo stopped his horse before the Miuraya in Magome. He was accompanied by his wife. They had brought their own food, simple bedding, and cooking utensils with them, and they were traveling with an interpreter and a cook, who was busy unloading a great trunk from the packhorse.

The Englishman's name was Gregory Holsom. As a railway engineer in the employ of the Japanese government, he had succeeded chief engineer England in charge of the Tokyo-Yokohama railway. Much had happened between 1871 and 1877. There had been an uprising in Saga, a punitive expedition against Taiwan, and the Satsuma rebellion. These events had preoccupied the government and the development of railways had not proceeded as rapidly as had been hoped. As yet the government had not even decided whether the rail line between Tokyo and Kyoto should follow the Tokaido or the Tosando. Under the pressure of events, the project of surveying the routes had been temporarily halted. The only railways in the country other than the Tokyo-Yokohama line, which had been the first to be built, were the Kobe-Kyoto line and the Kyoto-Otsu line, on which construction had at last begun during the previous year. Holsom had taken advantage of this slack period to ask for a temporary leave. Leaving the management of the Tokyo-Yokohama line to his subordinates, he was taking the inland route on his way to visit a fellow countryman who was in charge of the Kobe-Kyoto line.

It was the beginning of the summer of 1879 on the Kiso road and a pleasant season even for one such as Holsom, who was unaccustomed to travel in the hinterlands. Since Westerners were still extremely rare along this highway, they were likely to attract the liveliest interest among the people of the mountains. This had been the direct cause of most of the difficulties of the journey. Even in this time of intercourse there were still those in the Kiso who had never before seen a Western couple, and they would be met in each village by great crowds of children. When the man got off his horse in front of the inn in Magome and was told that this was the western end of the Kiso road, near the border between Shinano and Mino, he took out his binoculars and studied the plateau that extended from the foot of Mt. Ena. He was immediately surrounded by children and adults who came up to steal a look at his face and to marvel over foreign styles in clothing and manners, eagerly discussing all of this with each other. Holsom fled in exasperation into the entrance of the inn.

This journey through the hinterlands was not a mere sightseeing journey for Holsom. When he arrived in Japan, his fellow countryman Richard Vicars Boyle had already received a request from the Japanese government to prepare a plan for railway development in this country. Boyle had made two trips over the Tosando, first in May 1874 and again in September 1875. Holsom needed to inspect the route Boyle had surveyed and this was the reason for their leisurely schedule. They had spent the night in Midono, had stopped for lunch in Tsumago, and were stopping for the night in Magome.

The Europeans were the first to advocate the construction of railroads in this country, and they had been involved in the effort since before the overthrow of the shogunate. In recommending that a railroad be built between Edo and Yokohama, and then in obtaining the permission to begin construction and selling the surveying services and equipment for the project, they had demonstrated how fiercely they could compete among themselves. They of course protested vociferously when the permission granted by the shogunate seemed likely to be withdrawn by the new government. Into this controversy came Sir Harry Parkes, who took the 1869 famines in Kyushu and northern Honshu as examples to point out how urgently railroads were needed. The government accepted his arguments and decided to begin laying tracks. Soon other influential Englishmen appeared, offering to supply the needed capital, and the projects began to move. It was not surprising that experienced British railroad men soon began to pour into the country.

The first two modern ships, the *Seiki* and the *Tsukuba,* were built during this time. Their maiden voyages in the spring of 1879 were the occasion of much excitement. With less than twenty years of experience in modern ocean navigation, Japan had built its own ships, using its own labor, and was sailing them with its own navigators. Their calls at places that had never before known Japanese to demonstrate such a capability, and before eyes that had never before seen Japanese, could not fail to attract a great deal of attention at home. But for the beginnings of the railway system, it was necessary to import all the technology from Europe. Fortunately, among the first railroad men to come to this country was Edmond Morrell. He had a genius for organization as well as for timely and far-sighted advice. He suggested that Japan should prepare for the day when it could take charge of affairs without European help by establishing a training office for the production of technicians and engineers.

Boyle came after Morrell. He expanded Morrell's efforts several times over. He maintained that the planning of a railway network for Japan was an essential undertaking and that, although extremely interesting, it would be far from easy. He issued a memorandum stating that if Japan was to have a truly effective railway system, it must first decide where the main lines were to be established and then lay out a network of branch lines. As this had been the experience of all other countries, it would hold true for Japan as well. Boyle advocated routing the national trunk line over the Tosando, reasoning that the Tokaido, being very close to the sea and already containing the most highly developed and valuable land in the nation, could be well served by ocean transportation. The Tosando, in contrast, passed through mountainous territory where transport was difficult; a rail line, in helping to move goods, would not only develop the mountain regions but also improve communications between Tokyo and Kyoto and between the Pacific and the Japan sea. Boyle led two survey parties through the Tosando and produced a plan for the rail line between Tokyo and Kyoto, reporting his results to the government. The plan included a survey of the route through the Tosando and Owari and an analysis of the recommended methods of construction, materials needed, transportation requirements, geological reports, labor, and freight charge schedules, all in great detail.

Holsom's present journey through the interior was for the most part along the route marked by Boyle's surveyors. The line that Boyle proposed ran from Tokyo to Takazaki, then over to Matsumoto, and finally to Kano near Gifu before going on to Otsu. It was calculated that it was one hundred twenty-five miles from Matsumoto to Kano. On the way from Matsumoto it would pass through Seba and Narai, then cut a tunnel through the southern side of the Torii pass, with the mouth of the tunnel emerging from the foot of the mountain behind Yabuhara. From there it would draw near the Kiso river, actually running along its banks between Yabuhara and Miyanokoshi, go on to Tokuonji, and again follow the banks of the river to Fukushima, Agematsu, Suwara, Nojiri, and Midono. It would finally pass through Tadachi and cross over the river at the provincial border to enter Mino.

Holsom, astonished as he was by the inexhaustible beauty of the Kiso valley, could not but be aware of the cool courage and organizational skill with which Boyle had surveyed this vast region of mountains and forests. According to the documents left behind by Boyle, the mountains penetrated by the Torii pass between Narai and Yabuhara form the divide between waters flowing to the northwest and to the southeast. There is an abrupt change in the geological character of the region here. The northern regions drained by the Sai river were for the most part made up of fragmented olivine while the Kiso basin to the south was made up of coarse-grained igneous stone along both sides of the stream. The river bottom itself was covered with large round stones.

At Yabuhara the Kiso is still a small stream but by the time it reaches Fukushima and is joined by the waters flowing down from Mt. Ontake and other tributaries, it is a great river. Somewhere in the nine miles between Ota station on the Tosando and Nishikori village upstream, transportation by ocean-going vessels becomes possible for the rest of the way to the seacoast. Many logs are cut along the Otaki river each winter, mostly hinoki, cedar, hemlock, and pine. These logs are thrown into the river, where they are carried down over the sharp-edged boulders of the riverbed by the force of the spring flood, to be gathered up at Nishikori, formed into rafts, and sent down to Ise bay. Boyle's observations went even further. He noted that there was a great deal of zelkova produced along the upper reaches of the river. This timber was too heavy to be floated downstream, and for the same reason it was prohibitively expensive to send it out by ordinary land transport, with the result that it had never been exported from the region. But if the rail line were completed along the Tosando, these mountains could be expected to show an extraordinary development.

In Magome Holsom began once again to reflect on Boyle's observations. The stretch between Tsumago and Magome had not been included in Boyle's report. Since it was far too mountainous, he had proposed running the rail line along the opposite bank of the Kiso river from Midono onward. The plan was immense. Its primary purpose of developing the interior of the country by giving it easy access to the cities and to the seacoast was for the overall profit of the entire nation. But, as is likely to be the case when one is opening a rail line, this proposal had to face the stubborn opposition of special groups that had formed to work against its realization. In his room at the Miuraya, Holsom tried to imagine the profits and losses the coming revolution in transportation would bring to this lovely valley.

2

The next morning Holsom's party left the Miuraya and continued on down the road to Mino. The people whose fates were bound up with the fate of this ancient highway still knew nothing about having been bypassed by the plans for the railway. They had no idea what the government was thinking or even that the changes in the nation had reached this far. Least of all were they aware that the old post stations with their complement of twenty-five post horses, five mountain litters, twenty-five litter tarpaulins, twenty horse tarpaulins, and fifty small litter quilts, twenty medium-sized ones, and ten lanterns were all things of the past, or that the transport companies that had just moved in to replace the post stations were themselves no more than transitional phenomena. The changes coming to the Tosando were to affect the lives of everyone.

Among these people, the beginning of Meiji was no longer thought of as a time of "renewal." Everyone now called it the Meiji "restoration." Whenever Inosuke reflected on this, he could only feel amazement, not only for himself, all alone up on Magome pass, but for everyone who had worked on this highway. In fact, the mentality of these people of the highway, combining as it did the characteristics of farmer and townsman, was by no means as uncomplicated as outsiders were likely to imagine. People who had borne up under centuries of machine-like service to the military were not likely to take great pleasure in the restoration. With the elimination of the post stations and all the hereditary offices associated with them, what was happening to these people? Some were in a state of nervous exhaustion. Some were completely demoralized. Some fell ill. Some died suddenly. There was no peace of mind anywhere. Was this to be the final payment for their long service to the highway? The old feudal order from which they had drawn their sustenance was falling apart under a combination of internal and external pressures as the Europeans continued their relentless advance to the East. Were the endless personal disasters suffered by these people simply further proof that society was now undergoing the most violent change since the creation of heaven and earth, or was it all simply due to nervous tension and physical exhaustion? Inosuke could not be sure. One of his colleagues at the post station had told him that when he looked back at the past it all seemed like a dream. At the time Inosuke had found it impossible to shrug off this devastating admission.

There was no one Inosuke could really discuss all these matters with except Hanzo, with whom he had worked on this highway since early youth. They had remained very close despite the fact that Hanzo was suffering such instability of spirit while Inosuke, his exact opposite in temperament, wanted only to find a straight and level way through these difficult times. Hanzo had appeared twice in Magome since taking over the Minashi shrine; once when his daughter Okume was married into the Uematsu family in Fukushima and again when a bride for his heir Sota, a girl named Omaki, was welcomed to the old honjin. He had served in Hida more than four years but it was still not certain when he would be returning home. There was of course nothing to be gained by dwelling on suffering and illness, and for that reason Inosuke was not eager to see Hanzo in such a mood. But if his friend were to come over from Hida in good spirits, he would enjoy the visit. They could hang up on the walls the old scrolls signed by the Mino haikai poets two generations earlier and look at the illustrated verses on the theme of the eight views from around Magome. They could talk about the changes that had taken place along the highway, and he would reminisce about Kimbei, his foster father, who had lived until his seventy-third year, leaving thirty-one volumes of diaries behind him. He could quote the final entry: "Meiji 3, ninth month, fourth day. Rain. It being the first anniversary of the death of the late honjin Kichizaemon, Buddhist services were held." He would perhaps be able to tell Hanzo about how Kimbei had incessantly tried to manage his affairs for him until the very end. Yet now as he recalled the old man, he realized that Kimbei had been no ordinary person.

Inosuke had been ill for many months. His bedding was laid out in the same second floor room where Kimbei had been during his lingering final illness. It was the season in the mountains for cutting brushwood and transplanting rice, and for Inosuke, always sensitive to the change of seasons, a time when he especially missed his friend. He had taken scrupulous care of the letters Hanzo had sent him. He took out a collection of poems that Hanzo had also sent, in the hope that they might comfort Inosuke in his illness. They were written into a small booklet that Hanzo had made in his

usual way by folding sheets of paper in half and sewing them together. The
paper was warm in tone, and Inosuke took pleasure in tracing in it the faint,
greenish threads of paper mulberry fiber.

> Back home—
> The living and the dead
> Night after night,
> I see them in my dreams
> This time of year.

> "Autumn has come,"
> The insects cry out.
> The bush clover
> In the garden back home
> Must be in bloom now.

> Pity me
> In my traveler's lodging
> Sleeping alone.
> How heavy is the dew on
> My sleeve in the morning.

> How sad it is
> You may ask of the moon:
> My traveler's bed
> In the desolate autumn,
> Dew heavy on my sleeve.

> Alone
> On my traveler's bed;
> Even the singing
> Of the insects is
> Blended with my sadness.

> Through long nights
> I remain alone,
> Grass for my pillow
> Full of grief and loneliness
> Autumn has truly come.

> The days that were:
> When you think about them
> They are like dreams.
> The autumns of my forties too
> Will not continue all that long.

These autumn poems had been written by Hanzo in Takayama in Hida. As
Inosuke read them, his thoughts turned to the river that is called the
Minashi, or sometimes the Minase, and to the village deep in the mountains
at the foot of the Miya pass, where, he understood, one could look up to
mountains all around. Hanzo was renting an out-building belonging to a

farmhouse a couple of hundred yards away from the Minashi shrine. The family next door supplied his food and looked after his laundry and other needs. He would leave for work each day from a room that sounded rather elegant from his description of it. There was a pond out in front, and in the room a formal alcove with shelves for ornaments.

"All the same," Inosuke observed, "these poems sound terribly lonely."

Spring, Summer, Autumn, Winter, Love, Miscellaneous. Reading through the sections of Hanzo's collection, Inosuke was particularly attracted by the love poems. These did not seem to have been written in Hida.

> This hateful
> World in which we cannot
> Even dream together;
> What an old and painful
> World it is indeed.

> Foolish
> Is my love for you:
> I know no
> World where we can pledge
> Our dreams to each other.

> Not even the moon
> Can break through these clouds
> That cover us over:
> I shall remain alone
> Throughout the long night.

> Now at last
> I know how hateful
> This world is:
> These days and months
> Without seeing each other.

> If only there were
> A road along which our
> Loving hearts might meet—
> The depth of its ruts
> Would be the measure of our love.

> Months and years
> Without seeing each other
> Have cut us off;
> While still loving
> We have grown far apart.

> If we count up
> The number of those misty
> Spring days—
> Did the flowers have time
> To show off their colors?

If we had
Crowned each other with
Blossoms of plum,
Would I have met you again
Before they faded away?

Months and years
Of dust has settled deep
Since we two
Last laid out our pillows
To dream together.

In the meeting
Shallows of a moment's dream
We shall love
Forever as the rough-cut
Months and years go by.

Months and years
Have passed since our
Path of love broke off.
Now nothing but the grasses
Of forgetfulness grow there.

These days
Is there anyone who
Does not hear
The dismal sound of the wind
Blowing through the summer grasses?

As I gather
The rare grasses of words
Without a wife
All that I retain
Is the dew on my sleeve.

Is my love
To remain forever hidden
Like the waters
That flow through the lush greenery
Of the mountains of summer?

"Should you be working that hard on anything?" asked Otomi, who had
come up the stairway to the back room where her husband lay.

"Me?" replied Inosuke. "I just got completely engrossed in Hanzo's
poems. Whenever I read them I can't help thinking what a gentle person
he is."

"Who's the better poet, Hanzo or his friend in Nakatsugawa?"

"You always ask that kind of question. I can't say right off which one is
better."

"I was only making conversation."

"But they are completely different from each other and so their poetry is different, too."

"I should imagine they would be."

"Well, I am fond of poetry too, so I can say this. Hanzo has written some good poems and some that are not so good. But no matter which, they are always genuine in feeling. He doesn't just line up pretty words. His lack of artifice is his best point. There's something about his verses that's like taking a bite out of a crisp, fresh pear."

To Inosuke, this said everything about Hanzo. All the feelings expressed in his verses could be summed up as a deep, unrequited love. In the long years that they had been together, everything Hanzo had thought, said, or done had been tinged with that sense of unrequited love. Because people simply had not understood that about Hanzo, the fan-tossing incident had been blown out of proportion. When they heard about it, some of the villagers had even said that Hanzo must be crazy.

"That's Hanzo. No matter how much he concerns himself about others, they don't concern themselves very much about him. Just look at how he has always worried about the farmers and how little they think of him in return."

"I guess that's just the kind of person Hanzo is."

"Here's a love poem about waiting for a letter. It ends, 'Here in this hidden shrine/ I shall go on loving you still.' "

"Oh my!"

"Everything he writes is like that."

The conversation turned to the people next door, the family that Hanzo had left behind in Magome. In September of last year Otami, accompanied by Heibei, had visited Hanzo in Hida. She had gone over the Kashimo pass, where not even horses could get through, covering fifty miles of rugged mountain road to see her husband. It appeared that the trip had been very hard on her and she often talked about it when she came over to have a bath at the Fushimiya. Kutsu-Hachiman was a place about twenty miles from Miyamura. When Otami reached it, she met a young man coming from the opposite direction. As he drew near, he asked her if she was not the wife of the priest of the Minashi shrine. Otami replied that she was. Then she learned that it was not so very far to her husband's residence and that this young man had come all the way to meet her. Otami thanked him for his efforts, and he responded by saying that he was a neighbor whom the priest of the shrine had asked to make this trip. He added that since his hands were empty he would help them with their baggage. Otami declined his offer, saying that her husband must surely be worrying about them, and asked the young man to head back immediately with word that they were safe and coming along not far behind. Otami then walked on another twenty miles until, deep in the mountains, at the foot of Miya pass with Mt. Ontake visible in the distance off to the northeast, she finally saw the bed of the Minashi river. She was not able to remain with her husband long but she often spoke of how the fact that it was the season for the Hida festival had made her trip all the more unforgettable.

"Well, Otomi," said Inosuke from his bed, "four years is really too long, isn't it?"

"You mean for Hanzo to be away in Hida?"

"That's right."

"Well, as far as I am concerned, I just couldn't believe it when I heard that he wasn't planning to take Otami along."

"I suppose so. Well, he's been there long enough now. He ought to be coming back to Magome soon. I'll never forget it—when he came over to say good-bye, he said that since he was no longer of any use to the Aoyama family, he was going to do as Oman asked. That was before Okume went off to the Uematsu family. She's such a thoughtful and sensitive girl. Her head was down and her eyes were all red and swollen from crying when she saw her father leaving for Hida. She knew just what he was feeling.

"And then Hanzo sent me a letter from Nakatsugawa. He said that he was thinking of his journey to Hida as a command from heaven. That's so like Hanzo. I remember he also said that he might be coming back in two or three years as a failure, or perhaps only his bones would be coming back, but so long as he carried out heaven's command he would be satisfied. But what I hear from the people coming over from Hida is that the priest of the Minashi shrine is always preaching long-winded sermons. He tells the people of the village about the gods and the history of this country, and he always ends up in tears. Even when he is delivering up prayers in the shrine itself, they say he often starts weeping. The young people of the village even burst out laughing like little children whenever they see his face. Yet everyone agrees that Hanzo is a person who truly reveres the gods. Just think of it—serving as a priest for four years with such intensity! I wonder how he can keep going. I think it's time for him to come home. It's time to come home! The Hirata people have already done everything possible they could do, with all their worrying and rushing about before the restoration. No matter what anyone says, all that effort is not going to be lost."

For Inosuke and his wife, this topic of conversation was never exhausted.

In the mountains the time for the magnolias and the horse chestnuts to bloom had already passed, and although it was still a bit early for mountain lilies, the deutzia filled the valley with their scent. It was just the season for seeing swamp lily in the shade of the bamboo groves. The green plums and apricots had already ripened. But what made Inosuke most aware of the season was the raspberries that the children were bringing in from the edges of the rice paddies.

Whenever he thought about Otomi and the children, Inosuke would find himself bathed in a cold sweat. It came from his determination to battle against his illness but since his physician, Kyoanro, who came carrying his medicine chest up from the neighboring village of Yamaguchi, never said very much, he knew nothing about the progress of his disease. Yet there was not the slightest change in his clear awareness of things, nor did he ever deviate from the townsman's code of uncomplaining acceptance. He was looking forward to seeing his good friend Hanzo. As the days lengthened and the nights grew shorter, he was determined to last through the summer. Still, as he looked at the fans by his bedside, he resented the heat of the June nights.

3

In the latter part of October, Hanzo resigned the post he had held for more than four years at the Minashi shrine and came hurrying home from Hida. Accompanied by Rokusaburo, the son of the shrine porter, he left the mountains of Hida behind him and crossed the border into Mino.

His companion was a vigorous youth of twenty-two or twenty-three who was carrying a Hida-style pack frame on his back. It was loaded with a great wicker basket and a huge, cloth-wrapped bundle. Since Hanzo's baggage consisted almost entirely of books, it was very heavy and he struggled under the load across the steep mountains. Like the Kiso, the Kashimo pass is famous for small birds. It happened to be the season for taking thrushes and Hanzo bought a large number of them at the place called Kashimo. He and Rokusaburo roasted them for their noon meal and Rokusaburo was slowed down still more by the heavy repast. By the time they started up the Jikkyoku pass between Mino and Shinano, Hanzo had spent three nights on the road. From here on he could walk along the Kiso road lined with pine trees. He could see off in the distance the clear waters of the Kiso river flowing through the Mino basin. The brilliant sun shone on the leaves, tinting the shade beneath them as Hanzo moved on. Rokusaburo found a boulder jutting out beside the road and, pack still on his back, sat down to wipe away the perspiration and rest his legs. Then he got up and followed along behind Hanzo.

"Hanzo is back!"

Hanzo heard Heibei's familiar voice as he arrived at Shinjaya. Heibei had been waiting for him at this old rest station with its ancient sign and pilgrim's plaques. The Basho memorial stone that Kimbei of the Fushimiya had set up in a conspicuous place at this western entrance to the Kiso road seemed to be greeting Hanzo.

The thought of the Fushimiya reminded him that Inosuke was by then no longer in this world. News of Inosuke's death had reached Hanzo's lodging in the Hida mountains at the height of the summer's heat. The letter from the Fushimiya told him that in spite of the best care that could be provided, Inosuke's illness had taken a sudden turn for the worse and he was soon gone. He had lived into his forty-fifth year. The remains were to be interred in the graveyard at the Mampukuji, following a Shinto ritual in accordance with the wishes of the deceased. That same letter contained the information that the eldest son, Ichiro, had taken the name Inosuke II. Hanzo regretted that he had not gotten back in time to see Inosuke alive. When they reached the Suwa shrine in Aramachi, Hanzo went in to report his safe return and while there also dropped in to see the shrine's resident priest, Matsushita Chisato. But he still could not accept the reality that Inosuke, his old companion on the highway, was gone.

By the time he reached the center of town, he had already encountered several of his former students, now grown up.

"Master!"

As soon as they saw him, Masuho, the third son of the Umeya, and Saburo, the third son of the Fushimiya, came running to him. Hanzo was standing near the temporary manager's office, where even the names of the prefecture and county had been changed in his absence. The old Shinano province was no longer divided between Nagano and Chikuma prefectures. Rokusaburo looked about him as he climbed the steep street, pack still on his back, gathering in his first impressions of Magome. Hanzo waited for him to catch up. Then they went over to examine the new signpost that stood beside the road in front of the manager's office.

It was about nine feet tall. The new names of the prefecture and county were written in bold characters on the front, and the same legend was repeated in slightly smaller characters on either side of the post to inform travelers coming from east and west:

NAGANO PREFECTURE
NISHI CHIKUMA COUNTY   MISAKA VILLAGE

The old post station of Magome was in the process of a complete reorganization. Formerly required to have twenty-five porters and twenty-five post horses always in readiness, it no longer needed to provide such services. The post horses had been sold for eighteen ryo each and the porters had been given seven ryo two bu in severance pay. Such people had to change their livelihoods completely. While pilgrims still formed their bands and moved along the highway to Ise, to Tsushima, to Kompira, and to Ontake or Zenkoji, and while the road still served as a commercial route for merchants from Nakatsugawa and horses laden with salt going over to Iida, the people in this old post station who had relied on the demand for transport services for their livelihood could no longer be solely dependent on such work.

The professional informers had already left the countryside and the *kumosuke* had quietly vanished. Those who had not taken jobs with the new horse and oxen transport companies were clearing new farmland, planting forests, and busy with farming, silkworm culture, or some other enterprise. The people who were growing millet by slash-and-burn farming and who were carrying off for sale the grass and brushwood from newly opened fields were flourishing. Magome, of course, was in the midst of dense forests and the fields were strewn with great boulders. The land was steep and there was little available water. It was such difficult country that even cutting bamboo grass for compost meant that one had to fasten a smoldering cord at one's waist to ward off the fierce flies and walk four or five miles to the valleys at the foot of Mt. Ena, but few complained. The end of the post station system was creating a new pattern of life. The changes brought hardship mostly to those who had been senior post station officials and to their branch houses and dependents. The former leading citizens who had not had to live like everyone else and who had been free to follow their inclinations found it difficult to break away from old habits. Among them were some houses like the Umeya, which made a determined effort to go into the dyeing business. Only the Fushimiya under the second Inosuke remained the same as always, the ball of cedar boughs hanging under its eaves to signify that it sold sake.

Such was the village to which Hanzo returned. It was around three o'clock in the afternoon when he and Rokusaburo untied their sandals under the roof of the Aoyama house. Six years had passed since he set out from home to make a new way for himself, going first to Tokyo to work at the ministry of religion and then to Hida. Now at last he was rejoining his wife and children. Sota, his heir, was twenty-one years old and his bride, Omaki, was still more girl than woman. Otami, who had remained behind to look after the young couple, had aged a bit but was still as cheerful as ever. When Hanzo learned that she had prepared noodles with her own hands in anticipation of his return, he became choked with emotion. Soon Oman came down from her quarters, leaning on her stick. He bowed before his stepmother's now completely white hair. His third son, Morio, ten years old, and his youngest, Wasuke, seven, came to his side. He found this reunion overwhelming.

Once back home, Hanzo had an almost endless stream of callers and visitors. The manservant Sakichi, who had left the service of the Aoyama family when Hanzo went to Hida, had returned from Yamaguchi after his wife had left him. Seisuke, who had served in the household during the old days of the honjin, was working next door at the Fushimiya, where he managed the brewing business. In his spare time he still acted as a consultant for Otami and Sota. Otoku, the daughter of Naoji, the village hairdresser, who had cared for the infant Wasuke, came in from the kitchen, drying her hands as she came, to bow to Hanzo.

Rokusaburo could at last relieve himself of the heavy pack he had carried all the way from Hida, wash his feet, and go up into the house. This young man from Hida, dragging his tired feet, was taken around the house to see the spacious entry hall that told of the past of the Aoyama family, then into the entry with its ancient lances hanging overhead, and through the inner rooms to the chamber of honor in the rear where traveling daimyo and high officials had lodged in the past. He was so impressed that he forgot his fatigue. He finally found the courage to speak to Otami.

"You have no doubt forgotten me, madam, but I am Rokusaburo, the one who went out to Kutsu-Hachiman to meet you when you came over to Hida."

As dusk came, old acquaintances and relatives came by to see Hanzo. The fire blazed red in the hearth and the room was filled with the scent of small birds roasting on skewers. Among them were thrushes from Kashimo pass that Hanzo had brought with him. Of those invited that evening to share a meal of noodles with Hanzo, there was not a one who referred to him by his old title of "master of the honjin." All called him simply "master" or "teacher."

"I heard that the master was back so I dug some of the mountain yams that he likes and brought them over."

Even the old farm women of the neighborhood talked that way when they came over. Presently all the guests were assembled in the banquet room, where they began to ask Hanzo all kinds of questions. How old is the Minashi shrine? Are the gate and buildings on the same scale as those of the great shrine over in Suwa? Who had carved the image of the divine horse? Does the shrine have a hall for ritual dances and another for votive plaques and are they connected by covered hallways? How many centuries old is the sacred tree? About how many believers turn out to perform the ritual dance peculiar to this shrine, what kind of clothing do they wear, and what kind of drum and gong rhythms do they use?

Rokusaburo listened absently to all the talk about his home country, and after eating his noodles with family and guests, he went to sleep in the room next to the entry. The next morning the young man from Hida took his leave.

Hanzo was home but he was no longer head of the Aoyama family. All the same, he took the keenest pleasure in a leisurely walk around the grounds, his first in many years. He went out to the mulberry patch that occupied the site of the old meeting room, so full of memories, and then to the persimmon tree in the courtyard in front of the storehouse. There he found his wife, her hair covered with a cloth.

"The house has really changed, Otami. I see you've decided to rent the lower house where Okisa used to live. The people down there are new. And I hear that the stylish old woman there has opened a small restaurant for the gentlemen of the village."

"You mean Oyuki? She came up from Nakatsugawa."

"Who brought her up here? They say that she has girls with her who aren't from around here. I don't mind if the gentlemen of the village quietly amuse themselves there, but of course I wouldn't be able to object even if Sota were invited. I'm retired now. I shouldn't give my opinion on anything. But doesn't it bother you to have those girls coming and going next door?"

"You're getting old! You would never have brought the subject up otherwise!"

Otami laughed heartily and then changed the subject to the things that she had tried to build up during her husband's absence. During those years she had struggled ceaselessly to place this old house that her husband had entrusted to her on a firm footing. She made everything by hand. They raised their own tea and silk, and she dyed her own yarn and even pressed her own hair oil from the fruit of the camellias in the garden. They bought almost nothing but salt, sugar, and indigo dye. Even Morio and Wasuke's sandals were being made in the evenings by Sakichi. This policy of self-sufficiency, first instituted at the old Tsumago honjin, had been put into practice here after one of Otami's visits home.

Otami took her husband to see the miso shed. It was directly below Oman's room, the room where Hanzo could remember first his grandfather, Hanroku, and then his father, Kichizaemon, spending their final years. In the miso shed vegetables were being put up for the coming winter. Omaki, the young bride, had come from the main house, the maid Otoku from the well, and Sakichi from the woodshed. Hanzo's eye was caught first by a huge heap of sweet potato vines that they were preparing. Fifteen-gallon tubs in which the vines were to be pickled with plum vinegar and peppers had been brought out. Otami worked with unselfconscious skill as she laid the reddish vines neatly in the tub and sprinkled salt over each layer.

When Hanzo had made the rounds of the house and grounds and was starting back for the parlor that was to serve as his study and sleeping room, he spoke once again to his wife.

"Otami, I can't let you go on working this way."

He told her that he had come home intending to dedicate the rest of his life to the education of the village children. He had strong feelings on the matter.

4

The more than four years Hanzo had spent in Hida were the most difficult time of his entire life. In his second year there, he along with the local people became caught up in the upheavals of the Satsuma rebellion. Although deep in the mountains and far from the scene of combat, they did not escape the wartime atmosphere. Ever since the restoration was proclaimed, everyone had been hanging on, waiting for the completion of this great undertaking. Former headmen like Hanzo had borne everything in that spirit. Over the objections of many of his former post station colleagues, he had given up the honjin, the toiya, and the position of headman. He had accepted the position of manager with its limited remuneration. Being stripped of that position by the new prefectural government because of his activities in the forest dispute had still not shaken that deep faith, shared widely among the people of the country, in the coming radiance of a new sun. Even the news of the fierce conflict that had broken out among the leaders of the new government over the Korean question did not dislodge that faith from his heart. But when the internal struggles broke out into the open, when Prince Iwakura was assaulted, when uprisings flared in Saga and Kumamoto, and when he heard that even Kirino Toshiaki had gone into opposition to the very restoration he had worked so hard to help bring about and was raising the banner of yet another new government, proclaiming that nothing but military force could save the day, Hanzo could no longer escape the fact that the day was yet distant when the restoration would be complete.

Just what kind of person was this Kirino Toshiaki who was the central figure in the outbreak of the Satsuma rebellion? According to what Hanzo had heard, until May 1873, Kirino had been the commander of the Kumamoto garrison with the rank of brigadier general. The Kumamoto garrison was composed of troops from throughout Kyushu, and supposedly under uniform regulations, but the majority of them were an unruly lot from the various han of the island who could only be held together with extreme difficulty. Kirino, who was of the old-fashioned hero type, was not one to control soldiers by enforcing petty rules, so that most of them did as they liked and paid no attention to the regulations of the ministry of the army. Nor were the orders of that ministry carried out by the soldiers of the garrison. Displeased with Kirino's performance, the ministry placed Tani Kanjo in charge of the Kumamoto garrison and ordered Kirino to take up a position as head of the military courts. Kirino was greatly angered by this and he began to ridicule Yamagata Aritomo, the army minister, in Tani's presence. Yamagata, he said, had simply gathered together a mob of dirty peasants and made them into imitation soldiers. What good purpose could they possibly serve? Now to insult Yamagata was to insult Tani, but Kirino had always despised conscript soldiers, thinking that only samurai should bear arms. A permanent parting of the ways for Kirino and Tani was the result. Tani, who completely accepted the new system of universal conscription and placed such weight on drill and following rules that he moved a part of the Osaka garrison to Kumamoto to provide a disciplined nucleus for the local troops, and Kirino, his complete opposite in every respect, found themselves enemies in the rebellion of 1877.

This war was even more unfortunate than the earlier war in the northeast. It was one of those wars among allies of the kind that is so likely to occur, and it became a brutal factional struggle of total perversity. It demonstrated before the nations of the world that for all the unity with which the imperial forces had faced the Tokugawa shogunate and brought down Yoshinobu, the common enemy, they were still unable to avoid such bitter factional strife. In the end, even Saigo Takamori, who had sworn that he would never rebel, did in fact cast his fate with that of his fifteen thousand hot-blooded followers. When Kido Takayoshi of Choshu heard the news, he was appalled, saying in effect that it had only been because of Saigo that he had joined forces with Satsuma and they had been together through the best days of the restoration. It appeared to be Kido who felt the deepest regret over Saigo's decision. He noted that men fail because of their strengths rather than because of their weaknesses and it was most regrettable that Saigo, because of his very strength, should have gone fatally astray out of a passing fit of anger. Fighting began on the last day of February, 1877, the tenth year of Meiji. The Satsuma forces were far stronger than expected and the government troops had a very bad time of it. They were able to advance only nine or ten miles in the first forty days of fighting. Kido now realized that the issue was one of life and death for the Meiji restoration. Fortunately, the uprising under Saigo remained isolated, failing to bring the nation along with it. But since the Meiji restoration had from the beginning been looked upon by many of its supporters as a mere sleight-of-hand trick, the administrators simply continued to carry on as though all that was required was still more sleight-of-hand. They ignored human suffering and destroyed centuries-old institutions with the stroke of a pen, paying heed only to the advancement of their own personal careers. The people of the nation were not at all happy. As he observed these events, Kido found himself falling into the wrathful, warlike mood of the time and he wept bitterly.

It was perhaps inevitable that such a catastrophe should have befallen the restoration. Even deep in the mountains of Hida, Hanzo was unable to remain tranquil as he received reports from the war zone. The longer the fighting went on, the more people around him began to talk. It was not only the retainers of Tosa and Inaba but the common people as well who seemed inclined to rejoice at each report of Satsuma victories. Some even compared the campaign against Satsuma to the punitive expeditions that the shogunate had sent against Choshu before the restoration. As the news from the front came in, that Saigo's fortunes were in the ascendancy and then that communication with the government garrison of Kumamoto castle had been cut off, Hanzo could only join in the worry that everyone was feeling over the situation.

One should remember that the government army consisted of more than fifty thousand soldiers, some six hundred self-supporting troops from the region, a police force of over eleven thousand, and fourteen warships with some twenty-one hundred marines. If such a conflict had taken place at the end of the Tokugawa period, with all the repercussions limited to the internal affairs of the nation, perhaps the outcome of this struggle might indeed have resembled that of the punitive expedition against Choshu. The fact that after this great catastrophe had passed there were those who saw it as no more than a ripple in the course of the restoration showed clearly just how great was the wave of external influence in which the nation was caught up. When the war ended, Saigo and his lieutenants were all dead and the aftereffects reached even to Okubo Toshimichi, the most prominent member of the government. He was a Satsuma man himself and a childhood acquaintance of Saigo Takamori.

The Satsuma rebellion drew the country more closely together, a fortunate by-product of a great misfortune. Of course, the people had suffered, and of course it had been the most lowly who suffered most. Some remarked on the fact that nothing in the history of Meiji had ever been so foolish or looked so bad to outsiders. Others noted how embarrassing it had become to face Yoshinobu, a man who had not hesitated to give up the title of shogun and his control of Edo castle in order to prevent further bloodshed. Now these others had proved unable to understand, even at the cost of their lives, that although Saigo may have been yesterday's national hero, he was certainly today's rebel. The fierce Satsuma men had proclaimed that they had serious questions to put to those in power. As they raised armies and prepared for a march up to the capital under the banners of Saigo Takamori, their first action was to bottle up their old enemy Tani Kanjo in Kumamoto castle. They wanted above all else to put an end to the superficial Europeanization exemplified by the commander of the opposing side and by that to bring about a renewal of true martial spirit. Flatly rejecting the egalitarian thrust of the new conscription system, they fought to restore the old privileges of the samurai class, pledging that they would not be diverted from their purpose though a hundred great leaders might set out to alter the course of national affairs.

This war taught many lessons. It showed us that trouble had been unavoidable when the troops who had triumphed in the civil war of 1868 received so little payment and recognition for their services and when most of the government's efforts to assist the samurai, many of whom were pauperized by the restoration, proved to be unsuccessful. It showed us that although Saigo and his supporters, the last of the old warriors, had vanished, the way of the warrior still could not be ignored. It showed us finally that if the government had continued in its preoccupation with power and personal advantage, forgetting that it was a government of the people, there would have been no telling what might have happened. In fact the issue had hung in the balance for some time. The sense of fear and repression it engendered made it impossible for Hanzo to carry out his duties at the shrine.

Yet there was more to Hanzo's experience in Hida than the suffering and uncertainty caused by the Satsuma rebellion.

Mt. Kurai in Hida has long been celebrated in Japanese literature. In the tenth century the court lady Sei Shonagon wrote, "Among mountains there is Mt. Kurai." It is situated near the village of Ono in Kuguno county. The Mino border is about twenty-five miles to the south, the Etchu border is thirty-three miles to the north, the Shinano border twenty-five miles to the east, and the Mino border twenty-two miles to the west. The mountain stands at the very center of Hida province. From long ago it has been famous for producing the yew wood which was sent to court to be made into tablets of office. Here in Hida, as he sat at the foot of the mountain, Hanzo found someone worthy of his meditations. This was, of course, not a living person but a predecessor who had left a deep impression as he lived out his long life in Hida.

Hanzo found it inspiring to sit before the portrait of this man that Kano Eigaku had painted. The wooden statue preserved in the shrine he had founded was a refuge. With his long white beard and massive features, his broad forehead and fleshy nose, his piercing eyes and gentle mouth, the old man of Hida was the very image of a mountain man. He was massive and immovable as a great rice mortar. His name was Tanaka Ohide.

Tanaka Ohide was also known as master of the Chigusa-en, and in his later years he was called Jin'ya-o and Jin'ya Rojin. He was a senior disciple of Motoori Norinaga and a close friend of Norinaga's heir, Motoori Ohira, as well as the teacher of the poet Tachibana Akemi. During his youth he had studied classical poetry with Kurita Tomochika, the warden of the Atsuta shrine in Owari, and he participated in poetry sessions at the Reizei palace in Kyoto. A little later he became the teacher of Ban Kokei. Hanzo became attracted to him because he was a contemporary of Hirata Atsutane and because, though he was deeply versed in the ways of antiquity, he had nevertheless hidden himself away in these mountains of Hida. Tanaka was the author of an outstanding work, *The Key to the Language of the Taketori Monogatari,* which might be called a model for the explication of the old poetic tales. To Hanzo, he was important not only as a guide to many of the classics of our literature but also as one of the rare National Scholars with the gift of laughter.

Ohide's accomplishments were many. He restored old shrines in Hida that had fallen into disrepair and himself had built the Eno shrine where he served as priest, calling on the people of the region to revere the gods. In Mino he set up a memorial tablet making clear the traditions and associations of the Yoro falls, and he verified the site in Tarui-Shimizu associated with the legendary hero Yamato Takeru no Mikoto and put up a commemorative tablet there. He established the site of the residence of the early emperor Keitai, selecting the stone that was to serve as its monument, and put up a memorial in the Asuwa shrine in Echizen. Although this reverent adherent of Shinto knew very well the inadequacies of Buddhism, he carefully traced out the histories not only of his own ancestral temple but of all the others in the area, treating Buddhism with the greatest respect. He revived abandoned temples, aided those in decline, and reminded all the parishioners that they ought to revere the spirits of their forebears. He was well aware that Dual Shinto was an ancient faith among the people of this region, and he perhaps felt that it too could serve to lead the hearts of men. He was fond of mischievous remarks. On the night of the Bon dances in the countryside, he would go out to watch all of the dancing groups and rate each one. His playful style remains in a letter that he sent to a villager.

Dance, dance! That's what Bon's about! Don't give up! Don't give up! There won't be any tomorrow night! Dance, dance!

That was the voice that caught Hanzo's ear. The smile in the midst of sorrow, the laughter behind tears. Long before the coming of the new age, he had fought against the conditions he found around him and there had been few like him. In all his writings he had kept his eye on the future and what he wrote was far beyond the capacity of the still small children of his home province to comprehend.

Even in the life of such a joyous early National Scholar as Tanaka Ohide there was much sadness to be found. There was all the more for a latter day disciple like Hanzo. He had arrived at Minashi shrine just after the separation of Buddhism and Shinto. As is well known, Takayama in Hida is the home of many temples in the style of Kyoto, and the long-established custom of mixing Buddhist and Shinto practices together was not easily abandoned. Most Shinto shrines still had the appearance of being mere annexes to Buddhist temples, and there was a strong inclination for good families in the region to avoid marriage with the families of Shinto priests. Up to fifty or sixty years ago people were still saying that anyone who married a Shinto priest was sure to go to hell.

The national shrine of Minashi, formerly known as Ichinomiya Hachiman or Ichinomiya Daimyojin, highly prestigious titles for a Shinto shrine, still held traces of the earlier practice of offering services to the Great Bodhisattva of Minashi. When Hanzo first took charge of the shrine he found Buddhist texts wherever he turned, in the reliquaries, behind the sunshades, everywhere. What a strange faith this was which had for so long engaged the belief of the people of this country! In it the most extreme mortifications of the flesh were astonishingly accompanied by the most extreme worship of the joys of the flesh, together reflecting the innumerable changes Buddhism had undergone during its long history. The esoteric Buddhism that had come into Japan under the Nara court in the eighth century was, according to some people, proof of direct Indian influence on the Buddhism of this nation. All the images, the mysteries, and the superstitions had only multiplied as time went on. There were many priests of the Pure Land sect, moreover, who preached an easy way to salvation but were entirely lacking in the passion of the founders of their sect. With their deep worldly involvements, and their shallow accomplishments, they taught people only to call ceaselessly upon the name of Amitabha and to lose themselves in the chanting of Amitabha's name. They were a far cry from the purity and virility of the early believers in Buddhism. In a world where such people were in the ascendant, just how many ears could Hanzo hope to reach? How successful could he be in clarifying for the people the nature of the gods? He had come to Hida following a command from heaven, and his folly was to think that he had been called by the gods to show the people who lived in these mountains a way that would fulfill them. He had believed that there was still a path in this world that would reveal the true antiquity. Yet he was unable to realize even a tenth part of his wishes. The total reconstruction that was to have followed the imperial restoration still existed in name only. Morning and evening, as he passed over the covered walkway of the shrine, he looked out on the barren courtyard with its stone lanterns. There were weeds standing by the gate, and it seemed to him that the dark past still lived in this place, breathing before his very eyes.

During his four years away from home, the policies of the ministry of religion changed. It seemed that the government, realizing that the unification of religion and government would be impossible to carry out, had after studying various examples from abroad now embarked on the separation of church and state. Shinto priests who found this difficult to accept were asked to submit their resignations and the greater part of the Shinto priesthood throughout the country left and was replaced. The Takayama district, originally placed under Chikuma prefecture for religious as well as civil administration, had been transferred to Gifu prefecture and most of the Shinto priests were no longer members of the local priestly families that had carried out this function generation after generation; they were ill at ease in their posts. Even the monthly salaries sent out to the Minashi shrine from the Shinto branch offices in Takayama had become erratic. Hanzo wanted to propagate the faith but he lacked the wherewithal to do so; as priest of the shrine he had all the responsibilities of his office and no means to discharge them. In the end a deep sense of loneliness and futility overtook him.

> Yesterday, today
> Cold autumn rains and
> Autumn leaves
> Compete in falling in this
> Village at the mountain's foot.

He had written this poem in his lodgings in Miyamura in the winter of the previous year, and in the summer of that same year he wrote this:

> My verses
> May comfort their grief
> As through the
> Dismal days of summer rains
> They transplant rice seedlings.

His pity for the farmers laboring in the summer rains presently turned to self-pity. As a posthumous disciple of Hirata Atsutane, determined never to lose sight of his great predecessors, he had followed his calling and had realized his long-standing wish to reside in a shrine. But like the broom tree of Sonohara in the old *Guide to Famous Scenes of the Kiso*, the goal he sought seemed only to recede further the longer he pursued it. In the mountains of Hida, the tears that had been dammed up in him over a lifetime overflowed from the depths of his being. They were the kind of tears that shatter a man. He hid himself away in his lodgings next door to Rokusaburo's family. He pressed his face to the matting on the floor. His pride in being a disciple of Hirata Atsutane was completely undermined and he could not seem to get enough of weeping.

Hanzo felt as though he were still far from home, but he was suddenly brought to himself by the sound of a gust of wind blowing down from the mountain. A late October snow had already touched Mt. Ena and frost had come to the village. He looked out from the west veranda of the main house, feasting his eyes on the mountains of the Kiso. Tanaka Ohide in Hida, feeling an inexhaustible impulse to praise Mt. Kurai, had said that it embodied power without ferocity. To Hanzo, who had gazed at that mountain for more than four years, the observation fit this mountain too. Yet Mt. Ena was a different kind of mountain. The vast slope that ran down to the distant

Mino plains, the semi-circular marking on the side of the mountain that the local people called the pothook, the plateaus of Shidehira and Kasumigahara, the layers of hills gathered about its base—the entire mountain system, viewed from just the right distance at Magome, was something whose like was not to be found elsewhere. Densely forested though this slope was, there was nothing intimidating about it. And autumn was the best time to view it, unlike the summer when the mountain was usually in cloud while the village was clear or would itself be clear when it was raining in the village.

"Father!"

Morio and Wasuke, who both seemed to feel that their father still smelled a bit of Hida, came hurtling in. Hanzo patted his sons on the head.

"Look! Isn't that a fine mountain!"

The children had no way of knowing the feelings of their father who had returned from such a long absence. When they were not busy with school-work, the elder brother would hike in the mountains and climb trees while the younger would play on the paths through the bamboo grove behind the house or look for brightly colored feathers dropped by birds. They were both of an age to be fully caught up in the passion for rolling hoops that was just then going through the village.

Hanzo had left home with a determination to serve the gods and he had returned crushed by those whom he had most counted on. As he sat with his children by his side, he reflected on the events that had overtaken him.

"The way to a restoration of antiquity has been lost and the Hirata school is finished."

A deep sadness welled up inside him. Was it possible that the simple honesty of the people of antiquity no longer had any place in this world? It had been the fervent hope of all the Hirata disciples that they might somehow return to their starting point, the point of departure for the entire National Learning movement—to look at the world anew. But the bitter experiences of recent years had by now amounted to a failure that was not theirs alone. They themselves could not tell whether going to extremes was an inevitable concomitant of the restoration, making it impossible for it to be fully realized in practice, or whether the restoration itself had simply been the stuff of fantasies. By the end of the Satsuma rebellion, the great majority of those among the rebels who had earlier rendered outstanding service to the nation had departed from the stage—wounded, ill, dead in battle or by their own swords. Hanzo's deep sigh brought him a lungful of the chill mountain air.

It was the hundredth day after Inosuke's death. The death of an old friend was in itself cause for sorrow; it was hardly necessary to recall the words of the men of old to notice the speed with which the days passed. The thirtieth and fortieth days had been counted while Hanzo was still in Hida. Now all the intervening days were gone and he was suddenly confronted with the hundredth day.

"Only the people who are needed die early, Otami. Worthless ones like me keep on going."

"I feel so sorry for Otomi. She says that she came early as a bride and now she has finished early with the world. To think of her as a widow—she's still in the prime of life."

After this exchange with Otami, moving as if in a dream, Hanzo trudged up the steep street to his neighbor's house, where the old-fashioned Shinto ceremony was to be held.

At the Fushimiya, the guests from Nakatsugawa and Ochiai in Mino were beginning to gather. Beside the hearth, where the scent of sake came drifting in from the commercial part of the house, Hanzo sat for a while with the surviving family members. Otomi, in deep mourning, seemed to recall her husband when she saw Hanzo's face. She wiped away her tears with the sleeve of her underrobe. It was heartbreaking to see Otomi, so vivid and said to have a good head for sake, now wrapped in mourning clothes. Hanzo was introduced to Osuka, the young woman who had come as a bride for the second Inosuke. Inosuke had left four children, and while each of them strongly resembled their departed father, it was the second Inosuke, fair of complexion and long of face, who most favored him. Even his movements reminded one of the warm, generous, wealthy man who had been his father. Hanzo learned that before his death, Inosuke had called his children to his bedside and told them that, while Jiro had bad eyes and nothing could be done for him, Saburo and Osue should ask Hanzo's permission to become his disciples and they should learn all they could from him. This was now a world where one could not get by without learning. One day, near the end, reminded that no one who went to that other world had ever returned, Inosuke had said that he was desperately unhappy to be leaving this one.

"And then the late master kept saying, 'If only Hanzo would come back! If only Hanzo would come back!' You have no idea how much he wanted to see you."

Even the old woman who had come in to help for the day had this story to tell Hanzo.

Now all the gentlemen of the village came in and they were joined by Matsushita Chisato, the priest from the Suwa shrine in Aramachi, who was to officiate at the ceremony. There was Juheiji and Jitsuzo, the adopted son of Tokuemon, Katsushige from Ochiai, and Kyoanro from Yamaguchi, none of whom Hanzo had seen for a long time. The second floor of the Fushimiya had been opened up to form a double room for the gathering, the sliding panels having been removed from the middle. A hanging scroll that Inosuke had particularly liked was on one wall. The priest Sho'un from the Mampukuji was among the assembled guests. He had said that even though they belonged to different religions, he could not forget the favors that this household had shown him in the past. It was typical of him to have come wearing his brown surplice in the Zen style to perform a solitary service. Conspicuous at the side of the new master of the house, dressed in formal jacket and trousers and with a serious, responsible expression on his face, was Seisuke, who had long served at the old honjin but was now the manager of the Fushimiya's sake business. He had been everywhere at once tending to the guests.

Presently the simple ceremony began with symbolic offerings of spiced sake, white rice, and vegetables to the deceased. Hanzo found his spirits lifted by the sound of the priest's ritual handclaps. But as he listened to the priest reading the services, he became aware that he had lost the best companion of his life, and heedless of the company, he burst into tears.

5

Rest. Rest. Once back home, Hanzo wanted rest before anything else. He watched as Otami inspected his plain black robes and put away the formal headgear that he had brought back as a memento of the life in Hida, but the endless talk that went on as they caught up on everything after their long separation only seemed to bring out his fatigue. There were many people he wanted to see again after all these years. He wanted to visit the homes of the tenant farmers and to see the village school he had helped to found. He thought of offering his assistance to Kokura Keisuke, the present schoolmaster, but he found himself putting everything off until later, so that he could have a good rest first. He did go to the Mampukuji to call at the graves of his ancestors, from Aoyama Dosai down to his father, Kichizaemon, and he sought out the graves of Kimbei and Inosuke of the Fushimiya as well. Deeply moved on these occasions, he would return home exhausted and fall senseless on the tatami of his room.

In the parlor the paulownia desk beside the shoji was old. The room had closets, an alcove, and six mats of floor space. It looked out into the front garden where the branches of the ancient pine, one of the survivors from the old honjin, stretched out over the highway. Since giving up his old study to Sota and his young wife, he had virtually retreated into this room, receiving his guests there and keeping only Wasuke between himself and Otami at night.

Hanzo had already told his wife that he intended to spend the rest of his life in teaching the young, and he was going to start with his own children. On nights when his shoulders ached, he enjoyed calling Morio and Wasuke to his room to pound on his sore, cramped muscles, but he did not let it go at that. He had them recite in order the names of the more than two hundred eras of Japanese history at the same time.

"Let's hear it! Let's hear it!" he would say, and the children would circle behind him, each taking a shoulder and beginning to recite, "Jokyo, Genroku, Hoei, Shotoku . . ." as though they were chanting sutras.

Even though he passed his days in rest, Hanzo did not forget about the people of the Kiso, forced to eke out a living without free access to the mountains. Now that the old post stations were finished and they could no longer use the forests, many had given up on the Kiso valley. Kiso residents were leaving their villages, turning their backs on the land where their ancestors were buried as they set out for the cities to try to carve out a new life for themselves. Others who did not go that far, but who lived in the interior where not even bamboo grows well, where agriculture has always been a bitter struggle because there is so little arable land, turned to illegal cutting of timber since they simply could not support themselves without the forests. In the most unfortunate villages one person was taken from each household and sent off to Matsumoto because of infractions of the rigid forest regulations.

Just what kind of person was this Motoyama Morinori who had so darkened the life of this region, paying no attention at all to the needs of the people who lived there as long as Chikuma prefecture lasted? One need only know that he was later tried for corruption in Shimo-Ina county and sentenced to life imprisonment, failing to serve his full sentence only because of the general amnesty after the Saga rebellion. The government was not a government of the people and little could be done so long as such officials were permitted to serve. The fact that the name of Tsuchiya Sozo was still to be heard on the lips of people everywhere showed how well the people of the Kiso remembered the blessing of able administrators and how obedient they could be to responsive government.

The representatives of the sixteen Kiso villages formed from the consolidation of the former thirty-three villages appeared one day before Hanzo saying that they were no longer able to tolerate the conditions in the district. They were going to send another petition to the new administration of Nagano prefecture requesting a reopening of the inquiry into the division of government and public lands. They needed to consult the petition and supporting documents that Hanzo and his colleagues had prepared in the twelfth month of 1871 and again in the second month of 1872. Hanzo had worked day and night on this matter with Toyama Gohei, the former headman of Otaki, going from village to village to consult the other village heads. He had aroused the ire of Motoyama as a result and had been summarily relieved of his post as village manager. He was of course quite sympathetic to the present undertaking.

A draft of the petition was completed. By February of the following year, 1880, all the village heads concerned had been consulted and a copy of the resultant draft had come to Hanzo. It was a long petition of some sixteen or seventeen pages recounting everything from the early history of the Kiso to developments since the beginning of Meiji, ending with the occasion of the present petition. The presentation was convincing, clearly stating that the petitioners wished to share in the blessings of the Meiji restoration by securing free entry once again into those lands that had been open to all in the old days. The former administration of Chikuma prefecture under Motoyama had closed almost all the forests to the public, leaving no more than ten percent accessible. In consequence the number of people since 1873 and 1874 who had in desperation gone into government land to cut timber illegally and had been punished for so doing was beyond counting; the fines that had been levied against them had reached a shocking total. Since the people of the mountains simply could not live under the present arrangements, they asked that the old records of the villages in the region be once more examined and more closely this time. Hanzo was delighted with the wording of the petition. He felt it was exactly suited to the situation.

The petition, however, had to be revised before it could be presented to the prefectural government because of differences of opinion among the petitioners. Hanzo asked Sota to send for a copy of the revised document.

"Father, this petition has pieces of paper stuck all over it."

Sota was already a well-established young man deeply concerned about the future of the Kiso, and he joined Hanzo in examining the document. The part that dealt with the period since the early eighteenth century was particularly marred by deletions and by wordings that had not been in the original version.

"What? It says here that the public rights have been continuous," said Hanzo. "Let me take this for a while and give it a good going over."

Hanzo read and reread the petition. Although the people living here deep in the mountains of the Kiso tended to be a bit behind the times, they nevertheless had some awareness of current thinking and in addressing this forest problem they had tried, however inadequately, to address the idea of public rights. This was a marked advance over the old traditions of reverence for officials and contempt for the people. When Hanzo had first begun to talk about this forest problem with Toyama Gohei, they had taken the position that the officials and the people ought to work together to establish the policies for the future. The Kiso forests had been under the management of Owari ever since the Kyoho era. It was the wish of the local people to have the new prefecture apply the same kind of regulations here as prevailed in other forested regions—that is, to return to the practices that had prevailed before the eighteenth century.

The development of the Kiso could be divided into three periods. Until the Kyoho era in the early eighteenth century, the local people had been free to cut and sell timber as they saw fit so long as they paid their tax in timber. In the second period, from the early eighteenth century to the Meiji restoration, the distinctions between nesting forests, closed forests, and open forests were established and the cutting of the five trees was prohibited. In compensation the timber tax was abolished. It was a time of constant controversy between the people, cut off from the most important forest lands, and their lord. Yet even then, they were free to cut grass for compost and hay and in the open forests they could cut any trees other than the five prohibited trees. As proof that they had been able to practice slash-and-burn farming in those days, there were formal written agreements that had come out of mediations of forest disputes among the various villages, old documents from Owari itself, and formal permits, some for single villages and some for several villages. Moreover, the shogunate's annual allowance to the Kiso of six thousand packhorse loads of timber had been altered to a cash settlement that resulted in more than two thousand three hundred ryo in silver flowing into the valley each year until the restoration.

The third period was the present one, beginning with the Meiji restoration. The greater part of the forest lands were closed to the people, cutting them off from the compost and timber of the open mountains. When Hanzo and Gohei drew up their first petition, asking that conditions be returned to those prevailing at the beginning of the eighteenth century, they said that they had no objection to having some areas of closed forest so long as the open mountains could be made available again and the people's rights and obligations in forest matters more clearly defined. But it was still unclear what Owari's purpose had been in prohibiting the cutting of the five trees. When it had caused so much suffering for such a long time, what reason could there have been for so rigorously controlling the Kiso forests? If not for the profit of the han or to maintain an asset, was it then for the preservation of the forests against some future need? Or was it merely to serve the purposes of the feudal powers that guarded this strategic section of the Kiso road? Or perhaps for flood control in the lower Kiso? About these questions Hanzo and his associates could not be sure.

The first ten years of the Meiji restoration, up through the Satsuma rebellion, were a chaotic time. After that the atmosphere changed and the uprisings that had been breaking out all over began to quiet down. A new slogan reached Hanzo's ears. "Enrich the nation and strengthen the military." Yet it was clear that the people of this region were still not happy. Once again he recalled the time when the emperor had embarked on that new age to which Hanzo and his colleagues had looked forward with such hope. In the charter oath of 1868, the emperor had sworn to work toward such a future but between those brave words and the people there now loomed something like a stone wall. The emperor had promised that not only would there be unity between government officials and the military but even the commoners would be allowed to realize their hopes. The obstruction between the emperor's words and the government's actions since then could not be seen with the naked eye, nor could it be described with any precision, but here among the common people its effects were obvious. Because of it the light of the sun did not break through, nor did the land smile, nor was it possible for the ruler and his people to be truly reconciled. These images now came to Hanzo because no such wall had existed at the time the Tosando army was advancing on Edo in the early days of the restoration. The staff had then issued repeated proclamations promising wholehearted respect for the people and calling attention to the fact that no great social change had ever been carried out without the support of the people. The new government had first of all to win the complete trust of the people. There were some, of course, who attempted to break through this wall, just as there were those who attempted to force Amaterasu out of her cave when she had hidden her light. The virtue and the power of those people in the *Kojiki* had excelled that of the common run, but they had not succeeded in eliminating the darkness before the cave of heaven. That barrier could not be pierced by strength alone.

These imaginings were no more substantial than the dreams that came to Hanzo along with memories of his sojourn in Hida. But they revealed how dark the world had become around him. Precisely because they found themselves in a society so full of inadequacies, people had become attracted to the new idea of natural human rights. The principle of liberty that had emerged in Europe was being proclaimed here and even the concept of the social contract had been introduced. Men like Fukuzawa Yukichi, Itagaki Taisuke, Ueki Emori, Baba Tatsui, and Nakae Chomin had urged that the level of civilization be raised. They had passionately advocated the concept of civil rights and had argued the necessity of establishing a national parliament. Without more complete knowledge it would be impossible to judge the claims of such rights or to perceive distinctions between the thinking of the West and that of the East. But those who blindly followed the crowd were to be found even in times of enlightenment and now they were making themselves heard in the forest dispute. Hanzo felt deep misgivings. Whenever the number of people who offered to teach multiplied, it became more difficult than ever to learn. For men of conscience there was nothing to do but to hear as many arguments as possible while trying to find the proper way for themselves.

What they all seemed to be saying was, "The Hirata people promised a renewal of antiquity, but where is it now to be seen?"

Hanzo had no reply. He recalled the words of Kureta Masaka, who had said that the restoration of antiquity was precisely what it sounded like and there was no way that it could be brought about. The new petition, at any rate, had already been sent off to the prefectural government although its prospects did not seem bright. But however it might be disposed of, it was unthinkable to Hanzo that such a long-standing source of discord could be permitted to remain unchanged. A satisfactory solution had to be found, if not in his time then in his children's time.

That year turned out to be a memorable one for the people of the Kiso. The emperor announced that he would be making a progress over the Tosando, passing through the Kiso in late June when the new foliage would be at its best.

This was not the first progress that the emperor had made through the provinces but he had not yet had occasion to view the mountains of Shinano. It occurred to Hanzo that if the emperor was once able to view the swift, pure waters of the Kiso river, his mind would be relieved of the anguish of the Satsuma rebellion and all the other difficulties. He was grateful that the emperor, who had moved his capital from Kyoto in Yamashiro to Edo in Musashi, had not altered his intent to break with the ancient precedent of complete seclusion and had continued to move through the provinces, the simplicity of his retinue furnishing inspiration and nurture to the people.

In this Hanzo was aware of the difference between the quiet and subtle elegance of the emperor's conduct and the feudalistic splendor of the European kings. The need for the coming progress was transmitted to the provincial authorities as arising out of the emperor's desire to become more intimately acquainted with the feelings of the people. Thus any ornamenting of daily life would run completely counter to the august intent, which was first of all to cause as little dislocation as possible to the people along the route. Such things as repairs to the bridges along the route that absolutely had to be done would be done at government expense and would impose no hardship on the local residents. No special provisions were to be made in lodgings for the ministers and lower-ranking members of the retinue. They were to be entertained with what was at hand.

In May a party of officials came out from Nagano to inspect the highway. The people from the manager's office in Magome conducted the party to the edge of the village and rendered assistance in their depiction of the route. When the schedule was announced, it turned out that the emperor would be having his noon meal in Magome on one day of the progress. Then the commissioner of Nishi Chikuma county and his secretary inspected the village and determined that the imperial entourage would stop at the old honjin. Hanzo was terrified by this—he was most pleased that the emperor would be stopping at the Aoyama residence, but the prospect of entertaining the emperor in such a rustic dwelling was alarming and he had Sota petition for the right to refuse the honor. He noted that the former assistant honjin, the Masudaya, built by a merchant like the second Soemon, who had been known as far away as Nagoya, was still a much more imposing establishment even though the original building had been lost in a fire. However, it was the Aoyama family that had the older history and the honjin had a view open to the west, a rarity in the Kiso, so that a view of the mountains from the chamber of honor could be enjoyed by the emperor. For Hanzo, that the emperor whom he so revered was coming to the Kiso and that they would be entertaining him in their own home was scarcely to be believed.

"The people in Tsumago must really be busy with this one too, Otami. What are they going to do at Juheiji's?"

"That's what I was just going to tell you. The rest stop at Tsumago will be made at Jitsuzo's place."

"Is that right? It looks as though Juheiji asked to be let off too."

An advance party led by Yamaoka Tesshu arrived. Repairs to the road were begun and the region's first telegraph line was strung up. When he heard that water for the emperor's use was to be taken from the well next door, Hanzo felt bitter regret that his best friend, Inosuke, was not still alive and he himself in office to work together once again on this occasion. Hanzo and his father, Kichizaemon, had seen the retinue of Princess Kazu pass through Magome and while this procession would not place as heavy a burden on the highway, a large number of people would still be coming through. He worried that they would not have enough porters and horses on hand.

On the twenty-fourth of June they received a telegram informing them that the imperial party had left Kami-Suwa. By this time, the petition concerning the forest problem that had been submitted to Nagano prefecture had been completely eclipsed by the events along the highway. No one talked about anything but the coming imperial visit.

The preparations for this progress were being supervised by people sent out from the prefectural offices. Stable grooms, craftsmen, and the like were arriving one after another while police charged with guarding the highway became more numerous day by day. In Magome the people who would be attending directly on the emperor were named. This person and that were responsible for supplies, this person for the lodging, this person for horses and porters, this person for the stable facilities, and this person for lumber and building material. When Hanzo looked at the list of assignments that had been given to Sota, he found that almost all the old post station officials were included. Kameya Eikichi, who had been made a station official during the civil war, the former toiya Kyurobei, the former village elders Masudaya Kozaemon, Horaiya Shinsuke, and Umeya Gosuke, the former assistant headman Sasaya Shosuke, the heads of all the old mutual responsibility groups, the second Inosuke of the Fushimiya, who for all his youth was head of an old family, and even his business manager, Seisuke. Only Hanzo's name was missing. Since he was retired and no longer involved in village affairs, his only consolation would be to see his son Sota, the successor to the old honjin family, serving as host.

Before the arrival of the emperor and his retinue, it was announced that poems appropriate to the occasion in both Chinese and Japanese would be accepted from everyone high and low. Great numbers of people, from old men of eighty years of age and more to girls and boys of ten or so, submitted verses. Hanzo joined in, submitting a single long poem in the style and diction of the *Man'yoshu,* the great eighth-century anthology so revered by the National Scholars.

> Most tranquil
> Our great lord,
> Appearing before us
> In godly guise,
> Sets out to view
> Each in its proper order
> The eighty provinces
> Of our eight great islands.
> In the shrines
> Of the awesome gods,
> Wielding the sacred tassel
> He prays,
> At the graves
> Of his august ancestors
> Most purely
> He prays.
> The seas to the west
> The mountain roads to the east
> Here and there
> He makes his august way,
> In this age of
> Enlightened rule
> Just this year
> Is its thirteenth.

In the summer
Of jewel-like young foliage,
You who dwell
In the hundredfold palace
Served by
Attendants innumerable
You set out from
The eastern capital
To the province of Kai
Called "Namayomi."
Then, passing through
The land called Yamanashi,
Now you have come
To the Shinano road
Gazing across the
Vast waters of Suwa.
You have brought
Your great palanquin
To the village of remoteness
In Matsumoto.
Over the pine-grown
Road through the Kiso mountains
Where the boulders
Are so deeply rooted
You have so augustly
Made your way.
In all the past
There has never been the like.

The boulders
Along the river bed
The groves
Of noble trees
Must be new
To your august eyes,
Must be singular and pleasing
To your august eyes.

My village
Outside the Kiso valley
Bears the name
"God-slope"
And though it is
A hillside village
It has a splendid view.
The mountains of Mino
The mountains of Omi
Can be seen
Off in the distance.
From this village
Mt. Ena rises

Near at hand and
Mt. Ibuki
Can be dimly seen.

When you go
To hundredfold Mino
The mountains end
The country is low
And you will not be able
To see so far.
Therefore let
Your brief rest here
Be a little longer
Than it might otherwise be.

In spring
The flowers bloom
In autumn
The leaves glow red.
Though now
You will see few flowers or leaves
The evergreens
The winter trees
Are all in green
At this time of year.
The layered mountains
Near and far
The fresh foliage
Of the burgeoning trees
You may very well
Deign to find moving.

Awesome is
My great lord:
Though this be the
Mountain-deep Kiso,
May we be favored by
Your presence a second time.

Worthy of reverence
Is my great lord
Stay in peace for a while
And enjoy our view!

Envoys

May my
Great lord's reign
Be eternal,
Piling up the ages
Like the mountains in the south.

> May the bush-warbler
> Hidden among the
> Leaves of summer
> Announce itself to
> Your august party.

> How blessed
> That even the families
> Of the people
> Living among the mountains
> May see this imperial progress.

The imperial party was scheduled to proceed over Torii pass on June twenty-sixth. There would be open-air rest stops on the pass and at Yabuhara and Miyanokoshi before the party would stop in Fukushima for the night. On the twenty-seventh, they would make their first open-air rest stop at the hanging bridge, another at Nezame, and would stop for the night in Midono. On the twenty-eighth, they would have a rest stop at Tsumago, another in the open air at the top of the pass, and would take their noon meal in Magome. The emperor and his ministers found that their enjoyment of the cool scenery of these remote mountain districts began from the very edge of the highway itself. But since the roads were difficult, a lighter palanquin than usual was being used. The imperial guards rode before and behind, and in the accompanying party were Prince Fushimi, the chamberlain Tokudaiji, Prime Minister Sanjo, several councillors of state including Soejima and Yamada, Major-General Chujo, the physicians Ito and Iwasa, and the literary attaché, Ikehara. It was announced that at the Fukushima stop the emperor viewed the local horses. Masuho of the Umeya and Saburo of the Fushimiya brought this report to Hanzo. The boys had begun to study Chinese with Hanzo after his return, and since they were old enough to understand what was happening, they brought Hanzo every scrap of information they could get hold of. As the late Kimbei of the Fushimiya would have said, this progress was "absolutely unprecedented." Just the report that the old requirement that people prostrate themselves on the ground had been rescinded and a simple deep bow was now sufficient even for the passing of the emperor was a source of great excitement.

When the day for the emperor's arrival in Magome came, some four or five hundred porters gathered early in the morning. Hanzo purified himself at the well in back of the house and after reporting the events of the day to the gods, began making his rounds of the house. He found a sign some ten feet tall before the gate, marking it as the site of the emperor's stop. An enclosure of fresh green bamboo had been set up around it.

By the time the family had finished breakfast, the officials were already arriving at the house. Otami called Morio and Wasuke in and had them change into formal clothes. The plate of fresh fish that had been sent in from the west for the occasion was brought out to be shown to the children before it was turned over to the detachment of palace chefs that was already on hand. Among the seasonal foods that might have been served were rockfish, trout, catalpa beans, bamboo shoots, bean curd with chrysanthemums, and the like, but Otami had felt that rather than serving the river fish and fresh vegetables that were hardly a novelty in a mountain household, it would be more appropriate if she brought in rare foods from the sea and had them served in metropolitan style.

"Just look! This fish is called *sayori*. It is going to be served to the emperor!"

The young Wasuke heard his mother's words as though in a dream—his attention was really on the banners and lanterns that had made the old post station suddenly appear so lively. He was aware, too, that the children of the village school had gone out to the edge of the village to welcome the imperial procession.

At last the time came for the Aoyama family to turn the entire main building over to the emperor's party. When a daimyo had gone through in the old days, it had been the duty of the honjin to prepare his home for the party and to make all the rooms available. Not only did they have to supply food for dozens of men, but the people of the household were expected for the most part to wait on their guests directly. This involved great nervous strain. There would invariably be many in each party who would be difficult to deal with, and damage and unpleasantness would be the inevitable result. This time, however, because of the emperor's desire to cause as little trouble as possible, they could get by with merely making the space available. There were even members of the official party present for the sole purpose of looking after the water and the rice for the emperor's meal.

Hanzo, dressed in formal clothes, went around to look at the rooms. All was in readiness. The chamber of honor, where the emperor would be resting, had been repapered in pure white, and the Korin scroll that their relatives in Sagami had given them was hanging in the alcove. The next room was for the attendants, and the middle room was to be occupied by the ministers and councillors. Carpets had been laid over the tatami in the entrance hall, in the western hallway with its fine view, and in the chamber of honor by the advance party so that footwear would not have to be removed. As he thought about the uses to which these rooms would soon be put, Hanzo was once again moved to the point of terror. Otami came in just then, a serious expression on her face, and grasped his sleeve to inform him that the time had come for them to withdraw to the retirement quarters.

Oman, Omaki, Sakichi, and the maid Otoku, all in their best clothes, were gathered by the storehouse in the rear courtyard. Their position faced obliquely across the path to the well, toward the second floor rear apartments. The persimmon tree in front of the storehouse was in full foliage. Throughout Magome all the households were busy preparing tea for the official guests who would soon be arriving, but even so most of the residents had gone off to the eastern edge of the village to await the arrival of the emperor's entourage. But for the Aoyama household, who might be called on for any-thing up to the time that the noon meal was completed, it was necessary to remain in the vicinity of the retirement quarters. Policemen were standing before the two wooden doors at the rear, quietly and unobtrusively guarding the building.

The fan-tossing incident at the Kanda bridge some years ago now came back to haunt Hanzo in an unexpected way. It seemed that the people of the village were all quite concerned that he might mar this important occasion with some impulsive act. Since the earlier incident had been inspired by an excess of concern about the fate of the nation, some feared that he might do something of the sort again here in Magome. With Inosuke gone, there was no one left who really understood him, even though there was hardly anyone in the village who had become literate without his training and everyone rec-ognized his deep and continuing commitment to the education of the village children. He was not treated without consideration, but it was clear that the entire village hoped that he would remain quietly with his family during the emperor's visit. He had not been given a single assignment such as might have enabled him, as a member of an old family, to explain the region to those in attendance upon the emperor. No one had consulted with him and no one had told him anything. He found himself going over to stand among the fallen persimmon leaves in front of the storehouse where he could strug-gle to stifle his sobs.

There at the foot of Mt. Ena came the unaccustomed sound of bugles echo-ing through the valley to announce the arrival of the imperial party. Servings of rice and chestnuts, the local specialty, enough for a thousand men, had been prepared for the attendants who would be stopping for a brief rest at Toge. From the sound of the bugles, it would seem that the rest stop was now completed. Hanzo imagined the vanguard coming down the tree-lined road. He imagined the sounds of the horses of the imperial guards and the brilliant imperial banners, and he stood motionless for a moment, hoping for the safe completion of the imperial passage.

6

It was 1881, Meiji 14. Hanzo was already past fifty. In April Morio and Wasuke were sent off to Tokyo and the house suddenly became lonely.

It was Hanzo's wish that his two youngest sons should be sent to Tokyo to study. He was concerned that as children of one of the oldest families in the Kiso they would be watched a bit too closely and respected a bit too much as "the children of the honjin," and therefore they should not remain at home any longer. Some of the forest and crop lands that Kichizaemon had left were sold off to meet the cost of their education. Fortunately their sister was now in Tokyo. Okume and her husband, Uematsu Yumio, had left Fukushima to take up residence in Yariya-cho in Kyobashi, and she had said she would certainly be willing to take responsibility for her two brothers. Otami, who put the children before all else, had no objection to this plan, and she began to make clothing for them to wear on their journey to Tokyo. Oman was Oman, and on the day of their departure she came down from her apartment in the rear, lined the two children up before her breakfast tray in the hearth room, and gave them a detailed lecture on the history of the Aoyama family, heedless of whether they understood any of it or not. Very much aware that this might be the last time she would see these grandchildren, the seventy-two-year-old Oman paused frequently to wipe her eyes on the sleeve of her underrobe, but she managed to see them off on their first trip to Tokyo without breaking down altogether.

Travel was still far from easy at that time. Four mountain passes had to be crossed on the way from the Kiso to Tokyo. Sota was excited. He had volunteered to accompany the children to Tokyo and had also proposed to the Fushimiya that they send Jiro along with him so that he could have his eyes cared for.

The children left many memories behind after they were gone. Morio, insisting that he would be laughed at if he went to Tokyo still wearing his hair in juvenile style at the age of twelve, had Sota cut his hair short with a pair of shears. He was unconcerned that his new haircut was more than a bit on the uneven side. Little Wasuke, delighted to learn that he was to go to Tokyo to study, set out eagerly, his hair still in bangs. The youngest of the brothers, he was still very small. His mother bought a toy suitcase from a traveling peddler and filled it with candy for him to take on the road. He was just the age to be immensely pleased with this arrangement. He was wearing tiny laced tabi and tiny straw sandals. Hanzo and his wife could still clearly picture the two children outfitted for travel. They later learned that Morio and Wasuke had left some of their most prized playthings with Oyuki in the house below.

Otomi, the widow of the first Inosuke, was now the retired mistress of the Fushimiya, but since she had entrusted her second son to Sota to take to Tokyo for treatment and often came over to share the Aoyama household's bath, they saw her quite frequently. She always said the same thing.

"How could you have sent such adorable children away? I can't imagine how Otami could have let them go. It hurts to think of it."

In the hearth room such talk never ceased. Although Morio and Wasuke were no longer playing around the house, every time the subject came up Otami would say:

"But it's the strangest thing. I still have the feeling that the children are here, playing about somewhere. It seems they should be coming in for a snack at any moment. I always used to wrap hot, salted rice in the leaf of a *ho* tree for them."

"Are you still talking about that?"

This was always Hanzo's response but in truth he could not laugh at his wife. As much as Otami, he still felt the presence of his children everywhere. When evening came and bats began to swarm, fires could often be seen on the lower slopes of Mt. Ena. The villagers said they were will-o-the-wisps, but in the evening skies Hanzo could see his children. They were still playing by the old pond where snowdrops bloomed every spring in the stone walls. The trail that went from the woodshed to the Inari shrine led past the quiet waters of this pond, so deep that not even an adult could touch bottom in it. He could feel his children everywhere. In his study, sitting on the cushions. In the breast of his kimono, in his sleeves.

"You dunce! You dunce!"

It was Morio before his eyes. Morio, who hated books no matter how much he was taught, who would grab his text and flee whenever he was about to receive a box on the ear.

"The candle! Watch the candle!"

Wasuke was beside him, holding a candle as Hanzo wrote out verses late at night, needing this reminder when he became so sleepy he would nearly drop it.

Hanzo had great hopes for his children who had set out with as yet no knowledge of the world. For Wasuke, who was fond of learning, he had selected several of his maxims and had copied them carefully on separate sheets of paper, wrapping them up as a parting gift.

> Here now, Wasuke!
> Reading, writing, and arithmetic:
> Diligently
> And with a quiet mind
> Learn them all well.

Hanzo had begun writing these verses in Hida for his children.

Sota returned from Tokyo with stories of his brothers' journey. There had been four in the party, and when they reached Misayama pass it had looked as though even these children, so used to mountain roads, would not be able to go on. It was getting late in the day. Finally, Sota tied a towel into Wasuke's sash and pulled the little boy along behind him. When they reached Oiwake, they boarded the stagecoach for Tokyo. It was everyone's first ride in one of the stagecoaches, newly imported from America. Among the other passengers was a woman of forty or so. She had sympathized with Sota's concern for the children and had taken over the care of Wasuke, giving him candy and other treats. At night, Wasuke had slept on the lap of that unknown woman. Rocked in the stagecoach, they began to hear cocks crowing by the time they reached Matsuida and the still drowsy boys were delighted to see firemen going through their ladder drills in the riverbed. They went on through the old province of Kozuke and crossed the Karasu river. The April sun bathed the plains as far as the eye could see. The stagecoach reached the main thoroughfare at Mansei bridge in Tokyo and the driver stopped under the shade of the willow trees that lined the street.

There the children had their first view of the great city. They had walked as far as Oiwake and then ridden the stagecoach into Tokyo. The journey had taken seven days. Uematsu Yumio, Okume, and his mother from Nagoya, a woman with a high, finely modeled nose, and their son, who had been born in Tokyo, were waiting to meet them in their home in Yariya-cho.

Oman, Hanzo, Otami, and Omaki were gathered around Sota, wide-eyed with curiosity as he told them of his stagecoach ride back to Oiwake. They clung to every detail of the trip. Even Oyuki came up from the house below to hear about it. Nor could Otoku and Sakichi miss this opportunity to hear about the trip. Otoku had had complete responsibility for Wasuke from the time he was an infant, singing him lullabies while washing up in the kitchen. Now she came carrying out the evening meal trays with the same chapped hands that Wasuke had found so repulsive. Beside the hearth sat Sakichi, spitting on his rough farmer's hands as he worked at his evening chores making items from straw. He had been fond of the children, telling them how tanuki could take human form and how to see the badgers that appeared in the fields, or the fearful wild dogs. He had delighted them with mountain children's stories and riddles such as "What is it that sticks out its red tongue in the middle of the field?"

"What really surprised me when I got to Tokyo was how much weight Okume has put on. She has become a splendid matron."

When they heard this, Omaki, who had been raised in Iida, turned to Otami.

"A little extra weight doesn't look bad on a person with a fair complexion, does it, mother?"

Hanzo was glad to have news of the children so far away and he talked until late with Otami in the parlor. He recalled how just the year before Wasuke had stopped sleeping with them in that room, going instead to his grandmother's apartment in the rear. As he thought of how this last child of his was now in Tokyo to study, he recalled how Kichizaemon, when he was the age that Hanzo was now, would often keep his old-fashioned smoking set beside the bed. The conversation ended with another turn toward the children in Tokyo.

"How many years is it since Okume got married, Otami? I remember Yumio's mother. Her husband, Uematsu Shosuke, the commander of the guard at the Kiso-Fukushima barrier, was seen as a Nagoya sympathizer by some of the other families right after the restoration. He was cut down on the night of the festival. Those were really dark times. His wife came from the Miyatani family who were distinguished teachers in Owari. She was a second wife, but they say that she went out in the middle of the night to recover her husband's head, washed it in the Kiso river, wrapped it in a carrying cloth, and brought it home. That's the kind of woman she is. She plays the koto and she knows classical verse. It's quite a challenge to Okume to have someone like that for a mother-in-law."

It was already very late by the time the conversation reached this stage.

"Oh, oh, I'm not getting any more answers. Otami must be all tired out."

Hanzo went on talking to himself as he looked over at his wife's sleeping face by the night lamp. This gentle, hard-working person, his life's companion, had reached the age of forty-three. She had given herself up to sleep with the same intensity that she did everything else. Quiet, gentle snores could soon be heard. The sound brought him wide awake again.

"Sake!"

There was no one to answer him. Unable to sleep, he crawled out of the bedding, lit a candle, and crept out to the kitchen.

In the cupboards Hanzo found half a pint of sake and some cold vegetables cooked in miso. He brought all of it back to the parlor. As he walked softly around his wife's bedside to prepare the hibachi, adding more charcoal and putting the teakettle on to boil, his movements were amplified by the shadows on the late night walls.

Sending the children off to Tokyo had aroused complex feelings in Hanzo. While Otami continued to sleep, he stoked up the fire and attended to the kettle, thinking of the children all the while. He had done it because he himself had so much wanted the opportunity to learn. He had written a booklet called "The Diligent Scholar" and had made Wasuke memorize it when he was about six years old. Scholarly pursuits were second nature to Hanzo. One could say that it was something he had inherited from his father. When as a young man he had asked permission to join the Hirata school, his father had been sympathetic despite his misgivings about the heir to the honjin being able to think of little but study. He had only said, "So your love of scholarship has come to this," and had let Hanzo have his wish. Kichizaemon would not have done this had he not had strong inclinations in this same direction. But it was extremely difficult in this present age to keep up with advances in learning. So much had come under Western influence that many people were even claiming that without the West the sun would not rise. Hanzo no longer knew what he should teach his children or what he himself ought to study. It was not a time when those who had staked everything on National Learning could sleep easily.

The passage in Atsutane's *The Tranquil Cave* that Hanzo had read so long ago in Otaki village came once more to mind. It had been in 1863 that he had made a pilgrimage to Mt. Ontake to pray for his father's recovery. Katsushige had gone along with him, and in that mountain village among mountain villages he had sat listening to the lonely sound of the Otaki river. Although most people remembered Atsutane as one who had despised everything coming in from foreign countries as a source of error, he had in fact written this:

> Therefore, we must think carefully about the august will of the emperor, who, being open and generous in all things, would be inclined to accept everything that comes from the foreign countries to our august land without discriminat-

ing between those that are good and those that are evil. And, though it is
frightening to say it, we must think of the rule handed down by our many
great gods that we must select carefully those things which we are to adopt
from among all that comes from the foreign countries.

Hanzo had been startled to read this passage in *The Tranquil Cave,* though
he was well aware of the breadth of the master's sympathies. As revealed in
his posthumous publications, Atsutane had, back in the 1830's, predicted
what was now happening. That all these things should come in from Europe
and arouse the people of this country from their long sleep was perhaps a part
of the unknowable will of the gods.

In this world of close international contact, there was much that needed to
be learned from the West in scholarship, industry, politics, education, and
military organization. Since words are an important instrument of communication, if one hoped to be truly of service to the nation in this transitional
period, it was surely urgent to learn foreign languages first and to be able to
communicate freely with Westerners. The present time was called a restoration, and it was said that every day and every month brought its new
advances. It was inevitable in such a time that people like the Hirata disciples
should be cast aside as unable to break away from the old and outdated. But
however long this transitional period might continue, Hanzo could not
believe that the struggle on behalf of the Japanese language that his predecessors had so long carried on would ever come to naught. Without a belief that
at some time in the future National Learning would once again have a role to
play, he would not have been able to go on.

In the words of Motoori Norinaga that Atsutane so often quoted:

> Those who would follow after me in learning must never cling to my views in
> the face of sound ideas that appear after I am gone. Point out where I am
> wrong and encourage correct thought. Since everything that I have to teach
> attempts to make the Way clear, it is precisely in making the Way clear, wher-
> ever it might lead, that making proper use of my work lies. It is contrary to my
> wishes that I should be mindlessly revered without regard for the Way.

Here was presented a means whereby National Learning could be renewed
by those who came later. Norinaga had taught that those who strove for
learning were not to be hindered by the master's own teachings. He had
taught that when one made the Way clear, one was using the master's teachings. Day after day, the Way must be clarified anew. The new antiquity discovered by Hanzo's predecessors had to go on being discovered. For Hanzo,
to make antiquity new was to make history new.

The iron teakettle came to a boil. Hanzo put the sake bottle in it and
reheated the miso dish to accompany his midnight sake. Presently, he was
drinking the sake without stint, enjoying himself, and thinking about the
path that the Hirata disciples should take in the future. If Motoori Norinaga
were to find himself in this age of Meiji, he would surely use the new knowl-

edge as a whetstone just as he had used the thought of China and India as a whetstone to bring a still finer edge to that which was Japanese.

Since Norinaga's outstanding characteristic as a scholar was his easy acceptance of the new, the profound, the gentle, he would surely not have been discomfited by the introduction of Western learning. After all, what the Western scholars were now advocating was nothing more than complying with the principles of reason. If it had been Norinaga who had said such things he would surely have known the principle, then gone beyond that to forgetting the principle, and would finally have made still more clear the Way to antiquity which cannot and need not be explained because it is of itself.

But when he tried to go on from there, Hanzo's thoughts ran up against a barrier immovable as a huge boulder. Even Hirata Atsutane had not fully recognized how brilliant Western scholarship could be in thinking principles through to the end. Though his learning was broad and generous, he had been ultimately unable to accept Western learning. Nor had he ventured so deeply into pure scholarship. That was something only a true scholar like Motoori Norinaga could do. The question was unavoidable—was Atsutane really a scholar? That question applied still more keenly to posthumous disciples like Hanzo himself. Though he had passed through a half century of life loving scholarship and never ceasing to struggle for the opportunity to learn, he could do nothing against this barrier. To go past it was beyond his strength.

One of the reasons he had decided to devote the remainder of his life to teaching the young was that he had come to sense his lack of talent and lifelong ineffectuality. He wanted desperately to abandon the futility of his own life and direct his ardent, solitary thoughts toward those who would follow after him. Nevertheless, he still wondered if there might not be at least some among the four thousand posthumous disciples of Hirata Atsutane who could ride out the turbulence of the age. But for all that, it was painful for him to hear that the restoration of antiquity was merely an empty slogan, unable to influence affairs in any way. The longer he sat there drinking the more wide awake he felt.

CHAPTER FOURTEEN

1

IT HAD GRADUALLY come to be known even in Ochiai that the foundations of the house of Aoyama in Magome were crumbling. In that town directly below Magome on the highway, it was no longer possible to conceal the fact that this family, with traditions and distinguished lineage going back to the late sixteenth century, was being rocked by storms beyond its ability to weather. Magome was the western terminus of the Kiso road; Ochiai was the eastern gate to the Mino road. Magome and Ochiai were so close together that packhorses setting out from one for the other in the morning would be back in time for the noon meal.

Katsushige of the Inabaya in Ochiai had known of the difficulty since March 1884, and he was aware that Hanzo was now living apart from his heir, Sota, in a small retreat. Katsushige himself could never forget the three years he had spent as Hanzo's disciple in the old honjin at Magome. As the spring of 1886 approached, he was nearly forty years of age and in the prime of life. He had become head of his own family and a full-fledged brewer of soy sauce and sake. His predecessors had all served as post station officials through the time of his father, Gijuro, and Katsushige too was very active in village affairs. It was impossible for him to be unmoved by the fact that the ancient house of Aoyama was tottering and seemed likely to be destroyed completely. After consulting with the other residents of Ochiai, he had called together everyone who owed Hanzo a debt of gratitude for discussions about how they might comfort him. Out of all the students whom Hanzo had taught, it was Katsushige who proved most steadfast.

One day, concerned about the plight of his old mentor, he made a sudden trip to Magome. He had heard that Hanzo was drinking heavily, and although concerned about Hanzo's health, when it came time to pay him a call Katsushige could think of nothing better than good sake to bring along as a present. He set out with a long slender container of sake that was as large as he could conveniently carry. He wanted to see Hanzo's delighted face when he told him that this sake was from Ochiai and that he would like him to compare it with the sake brewed by the Fushimiya. From Katsushige's point of view, it was quite understandable how the old families that had served the highways for generations as honjin, toiya, and headmen, and had borne the major responsibilities for local administration at the same time, might have failed to give proper attention to their own household finances. Provisions had somehow been made to provide pensions for the sustenance of former samurai of the han, but nothing at all was being done for the former honjin, toiya, or headmen. The Meiji restoration had overlooked them.

Now that the duties of the headman had been transferred to the manager's office and those of the toiya to the transportation committees, it was only natural that families like the Aoyama that had also been honjin should find it difficult to keep up the big houses that had been built to accommodate high-ranking travelers in the old days. Katsushige could do nothing at this point about the precarious position of the Aoyama family, but he wanted at the very least to ensure for his old master a quiet and secure end to a painful life. He knew that everyone was saying there was something wrong with Hanzo both in body and in spirit ever since his return from those lonely years in Hida.

As Katsushige walked up the recently thawed road on an early April afternoon, it was evident that the springtime which already prevailed in Mino had not yet reached the top of Magome pass. This was not his first visit to Hanzo's retirement quarters, a small, two-story building located in back of the village at some distance from the main Aoyama house. It was called Shizunoya, or "house of tranquility." A traveler coming up from Ochiai would turn off to the right before reaching the gate of the old honjin and would find the Shizunoya near a little stream that ran down from the community reservoir. When Katsushige arrived, he could hear Hanzo reading aloud on the second floor. A board for stretching fabric flat as it dried was leaning against the wall outside, but Otami was nowhere to be seen. Katsushige sat on the edge of the entry and waited until Hanzo finished his reading. This gave him time to examine the construction of the house in which his master would be spending the rest of his life. The Shizunoya was so small that there was only one room and a kitchen downstairs, but it was solidly built of materials from the nearby mountains and it seemed well settled on its site, a reflection of the simple life being led in it. The grass raincapes hanging on the side wall of the entry were a reminder that this was a mountain home.

Presently Hanzo came down from the second floor. He seemed to be amazed that he had a visitor and he invited Katsushige into the downstairs parlor. He was no longer wearing his hair long in the old style and he was freshly and closely barbered. Each of Katsushige's recent visits had found him looking different. One time he would be terribly pale but on the next visit his face would be flushed bright red. His large frame was reminiscent of his father, Kichizaemon, and Katsushige was always touched by the way Hanzo folded his big hands in his lap. That day, explaining that Otami was helping out over at the main house, Hanzo set about preparing tea and refreshments for his old disciple. When Katsushige gave him the gift he had brought up from Ochiai, Hanzo's eyes grew round.

"Oh, did you bring me some sake, Katsushige?"

He was happy as a child. At that time everyone around him was saying that he ought to be more circumspect in his drinking, as befits a retired person. This came not only from Oman and Sota and his wife but from the relatives as well. No one but this steadfast disciple would have come bringing him sake this way, inviting him to forget his miseries. Hanzo accepted Katsushige's gift with delight and went off to the kitchen with it. He soon came back wearing a broad smile on his face.

"I don't like to talk about this, Katsushige, but everyone in my family is giving up on me. They're trying to find ways to make me get old fast."

"Surely that is because your family is concerned about you."

"But, Katsushige, if I just sit here and stare at the mountains all day long every day, I start going over and over my whole life. I can't stand this idleness!"

The aged Hirata Kanetane had passed away in Tokyo at the beginning of Hanzo's second spring in the Shizunoya. Moreover, his friend Kozo in Nakatsugawa had also died. Hanzo detained Katsushige, whom he had not seen for some time, with talk about how sad it was that all his old acquaintances were dying off one after another. Katsushige, however, had come up on other business and he would have been satisfied simply to drop in to see Hanzo and to apologize for his neglect. When he tried to make a casual departure, Hanzo, starved for human companionship, pursued him outside.

"Come to think of it, Katsushige, that pilgrimage we made to Mt. Ontake in 1863. Wasn't that just about this time of year? But the weather has really turned fine now. The nightingales are already here."

Katsushige took his leave. When he was alone again, he said to himself, "The master's just not ready yet to be an old man."

2

The Shizunoya also bore the name of Kanzanro, or "mountain viewing pavilion." With the Ena range equally beautiful in rainy or fair weather and the Misaka pass crossed by travelers of long ago towering off to the southeast, anyone who loved mountains could not help coming to prize the view from this house. Directly in front was a gently sloping but deep valley and Hanzo never missed an opportunity to walk there. Nearby he could rest his eyes on freshwater plants growing in pure water, while before him the dikes of the paddy fields stretched out wherever there was good sunlight. At the bottom of the valley, known only to the local people, the Orisaka river tumbled down in its steep course from Mt. Otaru. On days when he felt like going a bit farther, he could enter the dense forest on the far side of the valley or pass the time by walking up to the isolated farmhouse inhabited by the friendly, sympathetic people who farmed the mountainside. These were the scenes which Hanzo found around him at this stage of life when it was permissible for him to let things go. On one side the Shizunoya looked out onto the small stream that ran behind Magome where the women of the village came to wash their cooking pans. Roosters could be heard crowing here and there in the distance.

If Hanzo had only been capable of spending his remaining years as Katsushige suggested, how delightful he would have found this quiet dwelling. But he could not endure the thought of what was happening to the main house of the Aoyama family, and even worse, now that he was retired he had no say in the matter. Of the four traditional pursuits of retirement—fishing, gathering firewood, gardening, or tending animals—none appealed to him. He did not see how he could simply hide himself peacefully away, even when he became extremely old. Yet he had no choice but to watch the declining fortunes of his family in silence. Alone, unhappy, he was prey to sudden surges of strong emotion. When he gazed around him at what was to be his final dwelling, he could not contain his fury. It did not matter that Otami was still at his side to spend the remaining years with him. But more than anything else, his memories dwelt in the old Magome station that he had known in his youth. When evening came, he often had the impulse to go out onto the highway and mingle with the travelers.

One afternoon he had a sudden fit. Running wildly along the back road in Magome to the place called Iwata on the eastern edge of the village, he burst into the home of some distant relatives who operated a mill there. He made them get out an inkstone and grind some ink. He spread out a sheet of paper and wrote out one of his verses in a bold hand. Then he broke into a fit of laughter. His behavior seemed absurd even to him. He returned along the same road and without a single glance at the women who had come out on their way to the reservoir for water, he rushed back to his quarters.

"What is wrong with you today?" asked Otami, who was very upset.

Hanzo replied that he was not yet altogether useless. And precisely because he was not yet useless, it was permissible for him to behave wildly from time to time.

"It just shows that I'm still alive."

The brief Kiso spring rushed on, from plum blossoms to wild cherries and from wild cherries to lavender azaleas. As the trees around the Shizunoya began to open their buds in concert with the trees and grasses of the distant valleys, the new freshness that they lent to the sun's brilliance only deepened Hanzo's despair. He put his old paulownia desk in the six-mat room on the second floor, intending to work on the two volumes of his poetry that he was compiling. They were called *Pine Boughs* and *Evergreens* and the poems going into them had been composed from his early youth into middle age. But while he was editing the drafts, he was overcome with the realization of how little in his life had borne fruit. From the outset of the family's collapse, his concern had turned inescapably to his five children, who were just beginning to make their own ways. His thoughts were never far from them.

In the summer of 1883, Meiji 16, his daughter, Okume, and her husband had come to Magome for a visit. At that time Hanzo was still living in the main house. They had just closed up their house in Yariya-cho in Kyobashi to move back to Fukushima, leaving the two young brothers that Hanzo had entrusted to them in Tokyo. They came to Magome on foot with their second child, a daughter, carried on the back of a manservant. Okume and her husband were the same age, and perhaps because of a certain closeness that couples who are of different ages cannot experience, she looked younger than her actual age of twenty-seven. At the same time, she preserved that neatness in her person that had always been characteristic of her. As she passed out the gifts for Oman and for Sota and his wife that she had brought on this rare visit home, her speech combined both standard and dialect forms. Her husband was tall, with a long face and a refined bearing that reminded everyone of his father, Shosuke. Relaxed, expansive in movement and gesture, he was immediately at his ease before Hanzo. This was Uematsu Yumio. During his youth his fellow students had recognized him as the most promising young man in the Kiso.

Yumio always called Hanzo "father" and addressed his brother-in-law Sota with a mixture of intimacy and respect. When the conversation turned to personal matters, he told of how he had gone all the way to Nagasaki while still very young in order to learn English, and of how he had studied at the normal school in Nagoya shortly after its founding. Following the assassination of his father, who had been commander of the guards at the Fukushima barrier and a prominent retainer of the Yamamura, Yumio had been one of those who had decided very early to leave home and to seek his fortune in the city. He had always been one step ahead in everything, breathing the atmosphere of civilization and enlightenment before anyone else in Fukushima. He had taught in a Tokyo elementary school and he had experienced life as a bureaucrat, serving as a tax collector in the ministry of finance. During this period he developed an interest in politics and he had joined the newly formed political party called the Kaishinto. After giving up his government post he had taken up the family's patent medicine business, setting out to expand its sales and even attempting to compete directly with the Morita Hotan line of medicines manufactured at Ikenohata in Tokyo. This venture, however, had ended in failure as most samurai businesses did in those days, and in the end Yumio also proved to be the first to give up and return home.

The large house that had belonged to his father, Shosuke, and the family patent medicine business awaited him. Naturally the family's business manager, who had taken charge of things during his long absence, did not welcome Yumio's sudden return. The manager and his staff not only made certain that there was plenty of stock on hand for the annual Fukushima horse fair but they had gone out over scores of miles of road from Owari and Mino in the west to Echigo in the east to sell the Uematsu medicines. Yumio, who had once questioned the value of this old family sideline, leaving to pursue a more promising career elsewhere, now came home to doff his battle gear before the manager and his clerks, all of whom were taken aback by his sudden reappearance. At present he was renting a house in Tsumago until his return to the old family home could be settled and he was supporting his family by teaching at the elementary school in Azuma village.

"I guess it was my ancestors who laid down the solid foundations after all," Yumio would say with a loud laugh.

Okume, once again in this old house that she had not seen for so long, found pleasure in the simplest things, whether reclining in the well-ventilated middle room to nurse her little girl or going with her mother to look at the former chamber of honor that had been reserved for high-ranking guests in the days of the honjin. There was nothing here that did not set Okume's heart at ease. Of course, both Hanzo and Otami were eager to hear of the two young brothers whom she had left back in Tokyo. Yumio and Okume told them that the two boys had been entered in the elementary school at Sukiyabashi, not far from Yariya-cho, but since Morio, the elder, did not seem to like school, they had suggested to him that he try to make his way in the business world. Morio had agreed and they felt that in the long run their decision to apprentice him to a paper wholesaler in Hommachi in Nihombashi would prove to be in his best interest.

Wasuke was continuing to attend school, and Yumio had been teaching him to recite the Chinese *Classic of Filial Piety*. Fortunately a former retainer of Iwamura han in Mino and a distant relative of Yumio's, a man of broad interests by the name of Hyuga Terunoshin, had taken over their house in Yariya-cho to establish a chess club, and Wasuke was now in his care.

"Wasuke likes studying. He's really my child," Hanzo confided to Yumio.

Yumio stayed only one night in Magome. The next day he returned to Tsumago, leaving his wife and daughter behind. Okume, who felt even closer to Otami and Hanzo now that she was alone with them, was still careful always to keep her inner collar closed high even when wearing a cool summer kimono, as if unwilling to have her sister-in-law see the scar there. Still, she had changed considerably. More disciplined and coordinated of body, she was now able to laugh in a loud happy voice. She was interested in everything. She even put up her sister-in-law's hair during her brief visit and when Otami called the household together to enjoy one of the melons that were in season, Okume would not let her mother so much as touch a kitchen knife.

She began to tell them stories about Wasuke, whom she had looked after for a year in Tokyo. When she first gave him fresh, raw fish straight from the market, explaining that it was called *osashimi*, his eyes had turned round and he looked as though he would have much preferred the salt mackerel and sardines that he used to eat beside the hearth in Magome. All the same, Wasuke had been quick to become accustomed to Tokyo ways and to use standard city speech. Hanzo and Otami never tired of hearing about these children whom they had sent so far away to study. They always wanted to hear still more.

But Okume did not spend all her time laughing at her mother's side. Whenever she took up her infant daughter and walked along the veranda or looked out into the garden, she seemed like a different person. She would sit by herself for long periods, gazing out at the familiar plants in the courtyard as though remembering her girlhood. If they had not occasionally heard a quiet sound from her they would have forgotten that there was anyone else around.

One evening she said that she wanted to lie down and talk with her parents, so the three of them put their beds together in the small parlor. It seemed as though she would never run out of things to talk about with her mother. Hanzo dozed off repeatedly, waking up each time to hear the women still talking by his side.

During that short summer night, as Okume related what she called "things that can only be discussed in bed," Hanzo learned about the life his daughter was leading. It seemed that she had often reproached herself for being unable to drink with her husband or join him in song. She had not expected anyone brought up in a family like the Uematsu to know very much about lovemaking, and she was surprised that he spurned the body she offered him, especially since his rejection could not be explained by any lack of virility on his part.

Yet she did not place the blame on her husband. His friends were all fashionable young men in sealskin caps from government or the business world. Always ready to outdo each other, they seemed to regard the keeping of a mistress as a point of honor. While they were living in Tokyo, her husband usually had a political novel or a collection of tales from the demi-monde in classical Chinese near at hand when he was not actually heading off toward the geisha quarter in Yanagibashi. In the end it came to seem to Okume as a kind of sickness. He pursued pleasure like a moth after a flame and she was powerless to stop him. She could not even stop him from pawning her clothing when he was short of cash. She had kept all this a secret from her mother-in-law, and she had even arranged for the adoption of a child that he had fathered with a geisha he had been seeing regularly.

Still, even now she believed in her husband, in his essential sincerity, and at the first gentle word from him she would forget all past wrongs. She went on speaking of her husband's inability to resist temptation, saying that it seemed to be the result not so much of a poverty of affection as of the sad childhood that he had experienced after losing his mother so early. Her mother-in-law was a product of the highest traditions of samurai households. She could play the koto, chant pieces from the No theatre, and talk intelligently about classical verse, but she was also arrogant and unbending. She had come from the Miyatani family in Owari as a second wife to Shosuke. As a stepmother to Yumio, she had imposed on him an extreme discipline that seemed to have had the perverse effect of driving him into the world of self-indulgence.

Okume speculated that what she lacked as a wife was the quality of Yumio's real mother. But how could he possibly find beautiful recollections of his mother, unique in all the world, among those who sold their favors in the demi-monde? The very idea was preposterous. Yet it seemed that Yumio was captivated by every woman who so much as handled a cigarette well in his presence. Even after leaving Tokyo, Yumio remained the same, unable to forget the taste of sake drunk in houses of assignation.

Okume had been moved by the fact that the family's business manager had selected such an unsuitable person as herself to be the bride of the young master, even going so far as to insist that he would accept no other. Aware of the concern that she had caused her father and grandmother, she had been determined to make a success of her marriage but this unknown new world into which she had been thrust was not at all as she had imagined it during her sheltered girlhood. Rather than being limited to herself and her husband, it was instead carved out of that vast world in which tens of millions of people lived and died. There had been times when she wept bitter tears as she looked back over the way she had come. Then her heart would turn to her child. She said that she now had no purpose in life other than to give her daughter the possibility of a life that would not repeat the cycle of weakness that constituted her husband's existence. There was no question but that her husband was a good man. He was gentle to her and presented an appearance that she did not have to be ashamed of anywhere. When prevailed upon to sing the "Kisobushi," he had a very pleasing voice. If only he did not have that one affliction—she regretted only that in her husband.

After they had seen Okume off to Tsumago, Hanzo said to Otami, "Okume's still only twenty-seven, isn't she? What's going to happen to her from now on?"

Otami was wondering the same thing.

"Really, that girl's exactly like her father," she replied. "Everything she does is like you."

In March of the following year, 1884, Sota began to say that the Aoyama family affairs would have to be put in order. Hanzo had turned over the family to Sota when he went to Hida, and in the ensuing ten years the family indebtedness had reached a total of thirty-six hundred yen in principle and interest. Sota now proposed to sell off most of the croplands, forests, buildings, and household possessions to settle that debt.

From that moment the ancient Aoyama family began a precipitous decline. A proposal to rent the main house and the storehouse for two and a half yen a month had come from a physician named Kojima Sessai. Oman, Sota, and his wife began preparations to live together in the second floor rear. They would keep Sakichi to tend the vegetable garden but they let the maid Otoku go. The proposal that Hanzo and Otami should build their own retirement quarters was made at this time, and plans to sell all the remaining lands and buildings belonging to the Aoyama family were set in motion. The dry fields in Inohira would go to the Masudaya, the ones above the temple to the Fushimiya, the site of the old encampment to the manager's office, and so on. Honjin lands that were being rented at a rate far lower than that asked for other lands, a custom begun in the time of Kichizaemon, would be sold very cheaply to the people who farmed them. Nor did it stop there. Both within the family and outside, it began to be said that Hanzo was responsible for letting the old honjin family fall to this state by giving all his attention in past years to national affairs and paying no attention to family matters.

Sota, with the backing of several relatives and acquaintances, including Masaki from Tsumago, presented Hanzo with a contract listing the conditions of his separate residence. He had done this after consulting with Eikichi and Seisuke. Under the terms of this contract, whenever Hanzo might hereafter have anything to say about the conduct of the family's affairs, the relatives would listen to it first and the matter would be disposed of in a manner mutually satisfactory to him and his son. There would be no remissness in performing Shinto burial rites or in maintaining the family grave sites. The old pine and other plants and trees that were remembrances of former generations would not be cut down needlessly. Hanzo would be supplied with food, clothing, and shelter appropriate to the season and he would be provided with one yen each month for pocket money.

This had not come about solely at Sota's instigation. It was also a result of pressures from relatives and neighbors. Still, once confronted with a draft of this contract, Hanzo could not help feeling that it was terribly cold blooded. He went directly to Sota's room in the main house. Sota and Omaki were both there. The old alcove was ornamented with peacock plumes. To Hanzo they seemed completely inappropriate for a young man who proposed to reform the family finances through strict budgeting. He wondered how a debt of thirty-six hundred yen could possibly have been run up during a time when the family was making everything for itself and buying almost nothing but salt, sugar, and indigo. What would happen to this great house that had been left him by Kichizaemon? Countless concerns and regrets filled Hanzo's breast. He was aware of how difficult it would be for the two children they had sent to Tokyo to continue their studies if this household reform was not successful. It had been Oman's wish to turn the family over to Sota and now it had come to this. Oman, who was fonder of her grandson than of her stepson, still said nothing.

"What kind of respect does this show to our ancestors?"

This was what Hanzo intended to say, but he could not get the words out. Without a moment's hesitation, his face deathly pale, he took the fan from his sash and began to strike Sota, who was prostrate before him. Otami came rushing in from the hearth room to protect her child. Hanzo had to be stopped from striking his son with this fan, a whip wielded by the ancestors of the family.

"What do you people mean by saying that I have wasted money? Even though you deny it now, there were seventeen bales of rice in the storehouse. Who used them up? You fool!"

Hanzo, who had never struck Sota before, let his anger boil over that one time. Golden lights like brilliant sparks flashed before his eyes.

No one knew just what had happened afterward, but Otami, trying to intercede, was cut below the left eyebrow by a silver pin she was wearing in her hair. From that time on she had a small dark spot there like an indelible blot. Even after he left Sota's room, Hanzo could not calm himself. He was shocked by what he had just heard himself say. Once the fury and distress of the moment had passed he would never be able to speak that way to his son again. It was understandable that the old Aoyama house should punish a useless person like himself who had forced his son to succeed him as a child of seventeen. Now he would have to prostrate himself before his wife and beg her forgiveness for having injured her by accident.

With the plans for a separate residence under way despite his feelings, Hanzo felt all the more keenly the desolation of the retired. The contract drawn up for him by Sota, in consultation with relatives and acquaintances, had been drafted by Eikichi and Seisuke.

CONTRACT

Item: In view of the family's present indebtedness, the following items must be observed in order that household management may be reformed, and as a means for permanent maintenance.

Item: I agree as part of the reform of household management to live in separate quarters.

Item: I shall expect to receive, in addition to food, clothing, and shelter, an allowance of one yen per month for pocket money.

Item: Being resident in retirement quarters, I shall offer no opinions of any kind on the affairs of the main house. I will not object in any way to the terms of this contract.

Item: Being resident in retirement quarters, I will not inconvenience the household by contracting debts on my own.

Item: For the sake of the family, I will not make use of the admonitions of relatives to put forth my own opinions.

Item: I will drink no more than two ounces of sake at any one time.

As determined by the relatives, I will observe the above conditions and I will never seek to appeal them.

March 3, Meiji 17	Principal	Hanzo
	Witnesses	Masaki
		Shozo
		Eikichi
		Matasaburo
		Seisuke
		Kozaemon
		Shinsuke
		Shosuke

For: Master Sota

"Just look at this, Otami! I can't move hand or foot, can I? I can't drink more than two ounces of sake, I can't give advice to the main house, and I can't borrow money. They've made an old man out of me."

That was all that Hanzo could say to Otami.

*   *   *   *   *   *   *

Hanzo's second son, Masaki, came over from Tsumago to have a long talk with Hanzo about the forest problem. Masaki's political passions ran exactly counter to those of Okume's husband, Yumio. If Yumio belonged to the Kaishinto, then Masaki followed the Jiyuto. At the age of twenty-three, he had talked with Kawai Sadayoshi of Hiyoshi and their ardent political convictions had led them to take up the forest problem. Of course this affair had been a major turning point in Hanzo's life, and he could not help being pleased to find that his son was carrying on the struggle. But Masaki did not have the manager's position that would have made him the natural representative of the local people, and his effort to present himself as the representative of the sixteen villages of the Kiso had aroused considerable resentment.

Both Sota and Masaki were in the first flush of manhood, alike in their fierce pride and their determination to be of public service. Sota, apart from a certain weakness of character, was warm and diligent in his nature, while Masaki, forceful and impatient to settle problems, tended to see his older brother's way of doing things as halfhearted. Masaki had first become involved in the forest problem in July 1881, when the second petition from the people in the Kiso had come back from the Kiso forest office with the notation "The requests made in this document are unacceptable." Thereupon, Masaki and Kawai Sadayoshi decided to address an appeal directly to Saigo Tsugumichi, then minister of agriculture. In September of 1882, they went up to Tokyo for the first time, carrying with them a document entitled "A Petition Concerning the Division of Public and Government Lands in the Kiso Valley."

This third petition prepared by Masaki and his associates was the same in its essential points as the earlier ones, stating that with most of the land in the Kiso now classified as government land, the people could not survive. It asked that the lands formerly classified as open forests be returned to free use by the people. The second petition had been drawn up and signed by the heads of the sixteen Kiso villages at a time when the popular rights movement was at its height throughout the country, and the Kiso representatives had placed particular emphasis on the "rights of the people." The present petition not only did not bring up this point but went out of its way to say that "it was not a question of popular rights." Instead, they cited the history of the various areas that had been incorporated with government lands and brought up other instances where the needs of the people had been considered and land returned to them. As examples they cited lands held in common by the three counties of Ono, Yoshiki, and Masuda in Hida, and Ena county and the three villages of Tsukechi, Kawakami, and Kashimo in Mino. This petition, presented directly to the ministry of agriculture, was also unsuccessful. Masaki and his companions received the report of the officials in charge and returned home empty-handed.

The reason given by the officials was that while they were not overlooking the mismanagement of the affair by Motoyama Morinori under the former Chikuma prefecture, this was after all the Kiso, where forest disputes had a very long history. The government was therefore not prepared to make a final ruling on the management of the vast and rich Kiso forests.

It was then that Masaki told Hanzo his thinking had changed. He said that he had come to realize the futility of continuing to draw up and present petitions. Although the officials seemed determined to establish a sound policy for the future and were well aware of the cruelty and incompetence of Motoyama Morinori and the suffering imposed upon the people as a result, they nevertheless held Masaki and his associates in contempt as mere commoners and malcontents. Since the matter could not be resolved when there was a lack of confidence in the petitioners, they now had to cultivate people at the right level before doing anything else. Masaki had come this far in his thinking on the forest problem. He also told Hanzo that since important developments were taking place in Korea, he had agreed to go to that country in the company of other activists. He would be leaving soon. Although Masaki had no idea how long he would be in Korea, he pledged that once back home, he would again take up the forest problem and he would see it through to a proper conclusion.

Hanzo was disturbed by what Masaki had told him.

"It is very easy to get drawn off on a false trail. Whatever you do in the future, just don't forget how the forest problem started. That's all I have to tell you."

With that, Hanzo spoke no more about the forest problem. The naive idea that he and Toyama Gohei of Otaki had taken as their starting point was that it was simply unthinkable for the people of the Kiso to be barred from the forests in which they lived. It was like taking fish out of water. Following the inauguration of the prefectural system, Motoyama Morinori had, with a stroke of his pen, destroyed the practice of centuries. Without knowledge of local history or concern for the development of the region, thinking only of the honor that might accrue to him for placing all the old Owari domains under government control, he had eliminated the forests as a source of the people's livelihoods. From Hanzo's point of view, since it was precisely in linking these two together that proper forest management lay, it could not be said that the Meiji restoration had kept its promise of making a better world. The road ahead was still very dark.

Photographs had twice come from Morio and Wasuke in Tokyo. There would be a great stir in the household whenever anything came from these two children off studying in the distant city. The first photograph was brought back by Masaki after his trip to Tokyo concerning the forest problem. Masaki's foster father, Juheiji, had gone along on that trip to be fitted for false teeth and he could be seen in the center of the photograph, his hair long and sparse, looking every inch the postmaster of Tsumago. He too was growing older. Behind him stood Masaki, eyes shining, the inner collar of his kimono drawn up high around his neck as was then the fashion. Beside them was Morio, his hair cut short and wearing an apprentice's apron, and

Wasuke, his head slightly tilted and looking as though something had just startled him—everyone was clearly recognizable. The widowed Otomi and old Oyuki, who was renting a room in the house below, both came to see the picture and they commented on how completely Morio looked the part of an employee of a Nihombashi store and how childish Wasuke's face still remained. The next photograph was brought back by the grandson of Ogiya Tokuemon of Tsumago following a trip to Tokyo with his father, Jitsuzo. This one had been taken by a street photographer in Asakusa and it showed only Jitsuzo's son and Wasuke. The image was on a glass plate that came with its own carrying case.

"What? Can this be Wasuke? Can he have grown up so much already?"

Again it was the widowed Otomi who made the comment.

Hanzo could not forget the feelings with which he had patted the heads of his two youngest children when he returned from Hida. It was the sight of these two photographs showing how both were growing up in the city that brought him his greatest pleasure. According to Okume, Wasuke had been left in the care of Hyuga Terunoshin, a former retainer of Iwamura han who was establishing a chess club, but according to Masaki's report after visiting the Hyuga household in Tokyo, it did not seem to be the kind of home where they would want to leave Wasuke very long. Terunoshin himself was an accomplished chess player who could serve as a worthy partner for holders of the second or third rank, but Wasuke was being cared for by an unmarried woman who was so impatient that she was often unable to wait for meals to finish cooking. She would rush off to cook, hurry through the meal, hurry to put things away, and then be eating a snack a short time later. This woman was supposed to be Hyuga Terunoshin's "elder sister." Wasuke looked pale in the photograph. Masaki had made arrangements to take Wasuke out of that household and to place him with a member of an old samurai family from Fukushima, one Noguchi Hiroshi. Hearing of the children made Hanzo long to go to Tokyo once more. Even old Oyuki from the house below was telling everyone about having seen Wasuke on her trip to Tokyo. Little Wasuke from the mountains was now the doorkeeper at the Noguchi residence, and when it was time for Oyuki to leave, he had brought her sandals out and set them neatly on the stepping stones in the garden just as he did for all the other callers. The thought of that mischievous little child doing such things brought tears to Oyuki's eyes.

In April of 1884, Hanzo decided to go to Tokyo to see the children. Although it was a time when the family had to be careful about expenses, Hanzo's feelings would not permit him to continue simply to presume on the generosity of the Noguchi family. On this trip to Tokyo, he did not go over the Kiso road but instead went down the Mino road and up the Tokaido. When he reached Nagoya he had his hair cut in a barbershop in that castle town. From that time on he stopped wearing his hair long and tied back with an old-fashioned purple ribbon. As was the custom with rustic travelers then, he hung a black velvet bag from his neck and wrapped his body in a red blanket which he wore in place of a cape. He presented a strange appearance, but his new short haircut had revived his spirits and his feet were light. At that time the railway coming from Kobe and Kyoto reached only as far as Sekigahara, well to the west of Nagoya. Since it was the government's plan to make the Tosando the main route between Tokyo and Kyoto, there were not as yet even any plans to begin construction on the Tokaido branch lines. Sometimes walking, sometimes riding in a ricksha, sometimes taking a horse-drawn omnibus, he made the long journey and presently found himself once again in Tokyo. It was now a city so flourishing that it seemed altogether different from the Tokyo he had known. His inquiries about the location of Tenkin lane soon brought him to a back street in Ginza Yonchome. Around him were clock and watch repair shops, stores selling matting, and others dealing in tortoise-shell; their signboards were lined up along both sides of the street. Among them he saw a residence made of rammed earth, with narrow windows and a grilled door, and before it a child was industriously sprinkling water from a bucket to settle the dust on the dry street. The child was Wasuke.

Hanzo had set out on this trip to Tokyo with high hopes. He wanted not only to see Wasuke and meet the Noguchi family, but also to find out how Wasuke was doing in school and make arrangements for his continued care. His son had been away from home for nearly four years. He himself had not been to Tokyo since 1875, and he was eager to see it again. In the inner room of the Noguchi house, he met Hiroshi, who was apparently fond of taking in promising boys from the countryside and helping them to get their education. His aged foster mother and her daughter, Hiroshi's wife, were also there. All of them were warm and frank in their greetings. Hiroshi was from Fukushima, the same place as Uematsu Yumio. He was a former samurai trying to establish himself as a lawyer, and he was being aided in this by the efforts of his wife and her mother, both strong-willed women.

By turns, and in a light and cheerful tone, the members of the Noguchi household told Hanzo of everything that had happened since Wasuke had come to live with them. It appeared that when they had first taken over the care of this child, who only a short time before had been accustomed to climbing trees and mountains in the Kiso, he had behaved very badly in the cramped and confining city. In those early days they got many complaints about him from the neighbors. He was still such a child then that he would weep from the pain of his frostbitten feet. The old woman who slept next to him would get up in the middle of the night to massage his swollen and inflamed extremities. But he was growing up with amazing speed, and everyone expected a great deal of him. Hanzo was reassured on that account.

The Noguchi house ran back from the street somewhat farther than most dwellings. There was a hallway down the center. Tall windows let light and air into the earthen-walled building. A small pug dog scampered up and down the hallway, announcing with all its tiny body and absurd face that it found this guest from the country an object of the greatest curiosity. Hanzo accepted it as another of Wasuke's friends. He was conducted to a room on the second floor at the rear, away from the street noise, where he would stay for the next several days as a guest of the Noguchi family.

When Wasuke had approached him the first time, he appeared to have been taken aback by the changes in his father's face. He asked where Hanzo had gotten his hair cut so short, and only just refrained from saying that his father too was moving with the times. Children are strange creatures. When he saw Hanzo taking a small hand mirror out of its wooden case and looking into it each time before he went out, he asked his father if men also look at mirrors. Hanzo replied that men too had to make sure that they looked right, particularly when they were on a trip. Hanzo wanted to see the school that Wasuke was attending and he wanted to meet his friends there. With his own passionate concern for education, Hanzo wanted to learn everything he could about this famous new city school, but without making a nuisance of himself.

The next day he found himself being guided by Wasuke to the school near Sukiyabashi that he heretofore had only heard about. It was a holiday and the school flags that usually flew from the top of each building were not in sight, nor could he meet any of the teachers or watch the children playing in the schoolyard. He did however learn that Wasuke, who was now close to graduation, belonged to a class that met in a corner room on the second floor of a red brick building.

The water of the moat at his feet flowed off toward Tokiwa bridge, a place that had disturbing associations for him. He noticed that there were some stones along the banks that students coming to school might stumble on, and he picked them up and threw them into the moat. For a long while he was unable to tear himself away from the vicinity of the school.

Then Wasuke told him that one of his closest friends lived at Sanjukenbori, not far from the school, and he had Wasuke show him the way. There he found a snug little house facing the moat in the bright spring sun. A lonely woman lived there with her son, her only remembrance of her late husband. Wasuke's friend did not happen to be home at the time, but his mother was delighted that Wasuke and Hanzo had called. As Wasuke watched in an agony of embarrassment, Hanzo took out a mandarin orange that he had bought along the way in lieu of a formal present and borrowing a tray from the lady of the house, got up and set it before the household Buddhist altar as an offering. For Wasuke, his behavior on that occasion was the most painful part of the entire visit. It seemed more eccentric than straightforward, more exaggerated and extravagant than spontaneous or open. It simply made him appear odd. Yet to Hanzo, who had served as priest of a Shinto shrine in Hida, it seemed the most natural thing in the world to make this gesture of respect to an unfortunate family, and it was rather Wasuke's childish embarrassment that seemed unaccountable.

Concerned about Wasuke's lack of connections in the city, Hanzo decided to introduce his son to his old acquaintances. One day he asked Wasuke to accompany him to Ryogoku. Facing the Sumida river at Honjo Yokozuna

was a Western-style building that looked like a villa. It was the residence in
which the old lord of Owari, to whom both Kichizaemon and Hanzo had
felt so close, was spending his final years. The relationship between them
now was that of a former lord of Owari to the former honjin, headman, and
toiya of Magome. Wanting this old man who had played a role no less important than that of the lords of Satsuma and Choshu to meet his son, Hanzo
called upon him. Apologizing for his neglect, he introduced his son, explaining that Wasuke was now in an elementary school in Tokyo.

The old lord asked Wasuke's age. Hanzo replied that he was twelve, handing over some drawings of scenes around Tsukiji that Wasuke had done in
pencil for his own amusement. Wasuke stood by his father's side, rigid with
embarrassment during what seemed to be a series of completely gratuitous
acts. After they left the house at Honjo Yokozuna, Hanzo took Wasuke
along the old main street in Ryogoku and across the Saemon bridge to the
home of Takichi and Osumi at Saemon-cho.

Wasuke could not understand how his father had come to be so closely
acquainted with such typical Tokyo people as these. Hanzo told them of
everything he had done since leaving their home, and of his stay in Hida. It
all seemed very strange and mysterious to Wasuke. Takichi and Osumi openly
showed their delight that Hanzo had not only come calling after all these
years but was accompanied by his son. Their daughter Omiwa happened to
be visiting at the time and she too shared in the excitement. Omiwa was now
a young adult of great dignity who looked very fine in her elegant, high-
standing coiffure.

"I didn't realize that you had a child like this!" she exclaimed as she sat
down before Wasuke. She asked her mother if they didn't have something a
child would like. Osumi brought in a stick of candy on a piece of paper and
Omiwa set this beside Wasuke, explaining that it was an especially good kind
of candy that her parents were very fond of.

After these visits, Hanzo at last sensed that Wasuke was extremely uncomfortable in his company. He had come to Tokyo expecting Wasuke to be
delighted to see him after nearly four years of separation, but once they were
finally together, Wasuke had little to say. There was nothing that they could
talk about easily. It seemed that to the child his father was only someone to
be respected, and to be feared. He was most appallingly stiff-necked and
obstinate besides. To Wasuke the mere presence in this city of a person like
Hanzo constituted an uncomfortable dissonance. He could only think of his
father as someone back in the Kiso mountains, as if he wanted his father to
remain there forever, passing his days quietly at the hearthside with grandmother, mother, and Sakichi. Wasuke seemed to have no need of his father—
he certainly was not one to throw himself on his father's neck. He was the
kind of child who grew more distant the more he was pursued. In the end
Hanzo gave up with a sigh. Was this the child he had come all the way to
Tokyo to see?

The confusion of a city undergoing profound change was also far worse
than he had been able to imagine. He had time to go out from the Noguchi

house by himself to visit old friends or to pay his respects at the paper whole-salers' where Morio was apprenticed, but mostly to experience the vastness of the city. One and two passenger rickshas decorated with bright pictures had increased beyond belief since his last visit, and on the streets he would see peddlers selling one of the more popular patent medicines walking along in groups of four or five under white, Western-style umbrellas.

The transition from old to new had impinged with great force on every-one's life. One day Hanzo set out along the great embankment at Yanagihara toward the former home of the late Hirata Kanetane. Along the way he saw a master of the koto, his former livelihood lost, sitting out on the street and playing his instrument heedless of shame or gossip. He spent an entire night talking with his friend and fellow Hirata disciple the physician Kanamaru Kyojun. On the next day he set out once again to Saemon-cho for another visit with Takichi and Osumi. He found that a master swordsman of the Maniwa school had taken lodging there for a while and Hanzo listened to his sad story, so typical of the times. Swordsmanship had gone out of fashion. Since there was no longer any use for swords, one of the greatest of sword makers, ashamed that he had no way of making a living other than by coun-terfeiting famous pieces, had turned to making mattocks and sickles for farmers.

It was no longer strange to hear that the head of a great school of No actors had left the capital to join a band of wandering entertainers. What all this meant was quite clear to anyone who took the trouble to think about it. The irony was that while everything that had accumulated in Japan over the centuries was being treated as though it had no value, foreigners were teach-ing us at the same time that there were indeed things of the greatest value in this country. Hanzo could not overlook just what it was that was giving such impetus to these trends.

Immense pressure was coming from abroad. It came to be known that the foreign ambassadors were dubious about the adequacy of the Japanese legal system and were unwilling to assent to the revision of the treaties even to the degree necessary to eliminate the shameful provisions of extraterritoriality. Not a single person, high or low, viewed the matter of the unequal treaties as anything but the greatest obstacle to the nation's effort to establish itself as the sole modern nation in the Orient. It was a legacy of policies that had failed to respond not only to Europe and America but even to the most recent developments in the Far East itself. The politicians and statesmen of the time were struggling to break through this barrier even though such major figures as Iwakura, Okubo, and Kido had been unable to overcome it in the mission that had taken them overseas for three years. Legal and court reforms, the nurturing of specialists in the law, the creation of commissions of inquiry, the hiring of foreign legal experts, the sending of law students abroad for study, the translation of foreign legal books—all these developments arose out of this concern.

As success or failure in obtaining treaty revision was a matter of life and death for each successive cabinet, every powerful political figure threw himself into the undertaking, heedless of the cost. The office responsible for the compilation of the legal code, which had formerly been under the ministry of justice, was moved to the foreign ministry. Foreigners were brought in, and for a time the people of this country had to endure overlooking even the most flagrant misbehavior by foreigners.

The key to the plan to achieve revision of the unequal treaties was to yield to the foreigners on every point. First, thirty to forty foreign judges were brought into the Japanese judicial system, and eleven foreign prosecutors were also hired. Second, the legal system was reformed, allowing the use of both English and Japanese in the courtroom. Third, foreigners were given the right to vote. Beyond these incredible concessions, the passion to obtain the consent of the foreign ambassadors even led to formal balls being held in the European style under the pretense that there was little difference in the conventions between the sexes in Japan and the West. Masquerades and parties were held for the sake of the nation, dancing was for the sake of the nation, and every other display of culture and enlightenment was said to be for the sake of the nation. If the bold plan of the foreigners was to unify the world through trade, then the people of this country had no choice but to accept those ideas. Formerly we had despised money, now it was worshiped and it was all the same thing. In this spirit, some of the most impatient began to advocate a concentrated effort to overtake Europe.

To Hanzo it seemed that things had reached a very sorry state. What had this country managed to create in the last fifteen or sixteen years? He could not believe that the people long ago had been so shameless when Chinese culture was first being brought to this country. In such times as these it was hardly possible to recall the example of Motoori Norinaga, even though he seemed to have been born expressly for the purpose of opening the way to a true modern age; of the two great painters Hashimoto Gaho and Kano Hogai, Hanzo heard that one was now drawing maps in the navy ministry while the other was hidden away in a notions store.

Dispirited by what he had seen, Hanzo left Tokyo with the feeling that he would not be likely to come again. At least he had seen his two sons, he had expressed his gratitude to the people who were caring for them, and he had seen old friends and renewed old acquaintances. He tried to take satisfaction in that. He chose to return along the familiar Kiso road, passing through Itabashi on his way out. For a traveler like Hanzo, the visible changes in every one of the old post stations told of the passage of time. His heart dwelt on his four sons during the entire journey. The feelings that Kichizaemon, fond of learning despite his heavy responsibilities, had projected toward Hanzo he now in turn directed toward Sota, Masaki, Morio, and Wasuke. He was determined that they should become aware of the passion and loneliness with which one views the passing of generations. Out of all his sons, he had special hopes for the youngest, Wasuke, of whom he had said, "Wasuke is fond of learning. He's really my child." He was resolved that at least this last son should be well educated. His determination remained unshaken even though he knew that that child was unable to understand his feelings. Children after all were attached only to their mothers. He as a father felt that he was a mere stranger passing among his children.

"I've had my fill of going to Tokyo to see the children," he said to the people at home when he returned. It was precisely because he was so concerned about his children's welfare that he returned from his visit to Wasuke in such low spirits.

In the summer of that year Hanzo began living apart from Sota and Omaki. Even after he had moved with Otami into their new retirement quarters, he did not neglect to write letters filled with news of home to his children. He wrote to Wasuke of how he would like to show him this little house—how, from the second floor, he could watch the ever-changing mountains in morning mist and evening cloud and how the apricot tree that had come from Oman's home in Minami Tono in Ina had bloomed that spring. Surely Wasuke must remember that tree. He told him of how Saburo from the Fushimiya and Masuho of the Umeya still talked about him whenever they came for lessons, and how Sota had gone to Kiso-Fukushima as a secretary in the county government and how his ten yen salary did not cover the added expenses, but that in spite of this the household finances seemed to be on the mend. He wrote that although there were difficulties at home, everyone wanted Wasuke to get a good education and that he should remember this and be a success. He even added that Sota's wife was expecting a child and Wasuke should be pleased. This made Otami, who was sitting beside him, laugh.

"Why on earth do you have to tell Wasuke way off in Tokyo that Omaki is pregnant?"

He was taken aback by the question. For Hanzo, so concerned with the lineage of his ancient household, it was impossible not to share his joy even with Wasuke when another member of the house of Aoyama was about to be born. It never occurred to him that such glimpses into the adult world might not be the best thing for his child. Nor did Wasuke seem to be averse to writing him. His letters to his father came in one after another. Hanzo read these letters, written out on the same paper that Wasuke used for writing compositions at school, over and over. He read them aloud to Otami. He took the greatest comfort in them. Far away he might be, but he did not fail to teach Wasuke all kinds of things. How letters should be written, what kinds of books he should read, and on and on.

Presently the time came when his rapidly growing child in Tokyo was finished with elementary school. Hanzo received a long letter from Wasuke asking his father's permission to study English with a teacher who lived in Tsukiji. Hanzo had known that such a day was coming and he had been agonizing over it. Now it was here. To Hanzo, who had been such an ardent proponent of National Learning, this was not an easy matter to decide. He wanted very much for his son to have the Western learning that he himself lacked. Yet this child was still very young and immature. He had no real idea of what true scholarship was. As he thought of the astonishing changes that he had seen on his last trip and of the intoxication with things Western that had overtaken everyone, high and low, it seemed to him a terrible risk to permit the young and impressionable Wasuke to begin studying a Western language. Was this child too to be swept away by the wild fashions of the time? He spent several evenings wrestling with the question. In the end he acceded to Wasuke's request, but only with the deepest misgivings.

On the second floor of the storehouse at the old honjin, in addition to the old chests that Oman and Otami had brought with them as brides, was everything that belonged to the Aoyama library. All the Chinese and Japanese books that had been accumulated during Kichizaemon's and Hanzo's lifetimes were stored there. There also were a great many records concerning the highway mixed in with the books on haikai and the like that Kichizaemon had owned. As for Hanzo, it seemed as though he had spent decades of the most strenuous effort in collecting books. He was especially fond of the *Man'yoshu* and he had bought every book about it that he could find. His heart never felt so much at ease as when he was walking back and forth before the bookcases stacked up against the wall of the storehouse. Nor was he ever so keenly aware of the coming generation as when he was with these old books that his children would never be able to read—books that would be no more useful to them than a hearth in summer or a fan in winter. But after the entire first floor of the storehouse had to be vacated for the renters, he came to feel his passing through constituted an intrusion and he virtually stopped going up to the library.

3

"Come here!"

It was Hanzo calling a village child. Late June had come to the old highway.

"I'll give you something nice! Come over here!"

Although Hanzo called repeatedly, the child was of an age to be completely engrossed in rolling his hoop and he showed no interest in coming over. Among the children of Magome, most of whose toys were homemade, there was still a great passion for rolling the hoops from barrels and buckets, and this child had his bamboo hoop with him.

"When you still don't come after all this calling, it makes me think that you must not be very bright."

This "not very bright" finally caught the child's attention. He came running to Hanzo, who took a plum out of his sleeve and put it in the boy's hand. Then he led the child to his retirement quarters.

This was the technique that Hanzo had developed to inveigle the children of the village in to read the *Analects* or *The Child's Gateway to Learning*. Even now he had not tired of teaching the children of the unlettered farmers. However, the ages for which formal education was required had not yet been fixed and most of the children of the village were not interested in learning. There was still much superstition around. In those days, if a child suddenly were to turn pale and begin to froth at the mouth, this would be seen not as a childhood disorder but as proof that the child had been possessed by a fox.

The children whom Hanzo taught in the Shizunoya were not only from Magome. Some came tramping four or five miles up from the neighboring villages in their straw sandals, and there were always two or three girls from Yamaguchi or Yubunezawa or Tsumago among them. Saburo of the Fushi-miya and Masuho of the Umeya were outstanding. Already, before reaching adolescence, they were reading the great historical work *Tzu Chih T'ung Chien* in the original Chinese. After these two, there was Chiharu, the son of Matsushita Chisato at the village shrine in Aramachi. Chiharu was fifteen, the same age as Wasuke. Whenever Hanzo noticed how much the writing of this faithful student resembled his own, he would always recall Wasuke in Tokyo.

"It's a strange thing," he said to Otami one day. "I have always believed that you can't go on waiting for tomorrow. If you wait for tomorrow, you only find that it never comes. And today vanishes immediately. Only the past is real—that's what I learned from Master Atsutane. As I pass through this world, experiencing all kinds of things, I've begun to feel that I've come a long way. But when I keep thinking about the children like this, I find that I'm just another fool waiting for tomorrow."

Otami seldom listened to this kind of talk very closely, but she gave Hanzo all her attention when the talk turned to his resolution to stop drinking.

"Otami! Sake is no good any more. If I drink too much, I can't sleep. Recently I broke the contract without Sota or the relatives finding out about it. I just couldn't stand it any longer. But then I couldn't sleep! I didn't sleep for five or six nights, and it got so bad I thought I was finished. I'm not jok-ing. I tried reciting the syllabary and I tried counting to four over and over. I wanted to sleep so badly. And then I finally did. Eh, I don't want any more of that. Maybe it had to get that bad before I could stop drinking."

"It would be best for you if you just stopped drinking altogether. Right now. That's what I was thinking when I put the sake away."

"You're right. Having those two ounces every night did no good at all. There's no such thing as cutting down on sake. If you're drinking you're drinking and if you stop, you stop altogether. Those are the only alterna-tives."

Hanzo's abstinence continued until September. Throughout that summer the cool pure sound of a flute could often be heard coming down from the second floor of the Shizunoya. It was Hanzo playing for his own enjoyment. As the oppressive late summer heat peculiar to the Kiso region began to weigh on him, he was moved to write down the following in Chinese:

> Concerned about the nation, concerned about the emperor, concerned about
> my family, concerned about the village, concerned about my parents, con-
> cerned about my friends, my wife, my children, my relatives. A hundred con-

cerns, a thousand cares fill my breast and I cannot master my sighs. I rise and look out at the peaks to the southeast. The mountains are deep blue. The valleys are lost in gloom. Each has its own quality. I rely on that view to give me comfort. These hundred griefs are surely the gift of the lord of heaven.

This was followed by a poem in the classical Japanese manner:

Grasses of love
Growing wild on summer fields
Covered with dew:
My heart is torn into thousands
Of shreds these days.

Hanzo was fifty-five. It is unusual for a person to reach that age without marked changes in the shape of his face. It is also unusual for at least two people not to be living within each individual by then, manifesting themselves in alternation. This was certainly the case with Hanzo. Before Morio went to Tokyo, Otami had one day been completely at a loss in dealing with the child's extreme waywardness and she had thrown him down on the floor of the entrance, saying that she was going to burn moxa on him to quiet him down. She called on Omaki for help and asked her to hold the child's legs. It was Hanzo who was unable to bear the sight of the child's anguished writhing and he had begged Otami not to resort to the moxa. But it was also Hanzo who took out his fan and struck Sota in the face with it, even though he had never before raised his voice to his son. At times he would hide himself away in the Shizunoya, holding to the words of the ancients that if one looked on in tranquility things would resolve themselves. Yet at other times this same Hanzo would wonder if such detachment was really enough for a posthumous disciple of Hirata Atsutane, and he would decide that sufficient reforms had not yet been achieved, nor sufficient destruction of old evils.

Presently the lingering heat was tempered by the first breath of autumn. The crickets could be heard morning and night along the stone walls and grassy banks. Near dawn one night, lying beside Otami in the downstairs parlor, Hanzo was seized by a sense of extraordinary lucidity. He slipped out of the house unseen by his wife and walked into the village to buy sake. He came to a great doorway. There was a smaller door let into it. A great bundle of cedar boughs was suspended from the eaves over the doorway. He knocked on the door and found that someone inside was already up. The small door was opened for him. There in the storefront of the Fushimiya the second Inosuke went over to his barrels, pulled out a bung, caught the flowing sake in a square measure, and transferred it to one of his own small bottles. He sold it to Hanzo. Things had gone well thus far, but as Hanzo crept home with the forbidden sake, he was overwhelmed by a host of terrifying thoughts. Then, just before he reached his house, he woke up.

The dream, a consequence of his prolonged abstinence, was but the herald of turbulent thoughts that now began to boil up inside him. When he was in this state, things such as the arabesque designs on the sliding panels in his room seemed to move with life. Pots and pans that had nothing of gender about them would appear to him as male or female. The day wore on. It was nearly evening when he looked around him once more. Otami had come back from helping out at the main house and she was preparing the evening meal. He told Otami about his strange dream and how it seemed impossible to continue any longer the abstinence from sake that he had maintained throughout the summer. Otami, her sleeves tied up, told him about the sake that Katsushige had brought up for him on a recent visit, confessing that she had hidden it.

"I've got some sake from Ochiai? I remember that Katsushige brought some up in April."

"He didn't realize that you had stopped drinking. He apologized and asked me not to tell you about it and to use it for cooking instead."

Shortly afterward, Otami brought the serving tray in from the kitchen and set it before Hanzo. On the tray was a small bottle of sake that she had heated for her wan husband.

"I can hardly believe it. You're really going to let me have a drink, Otami?"

Hanzo gazed in amazement at this beloved fluid, breathing deeply of the aroma that rose from the cup. His spirits revived. Otami watched his face closely.

"To tell the truth, you really startled me the other day. I still can't believe it happened."

"Oh, that? I never saw anything like it before. I'm telling you. There was a strange creature who came and hid himself in the corner of the garden. He was a horrible sight. He seemed to be after me. It was too much, so I lit a bunch of dry cedar leaves and threw them at him. That's not going to happen again, so please don't worry about it."

"You're really going to have to be more careful," Otami replied, but such things were in fact beginning to happen to Hanzo.

The day ended while they were eating their austere but pleasant mountain meal. Unlike the days when he had lived on the highway, it was utterly still at the beginning of evening around the Shizunoya. Then they heard the bark of a fox that had come near the village. There were innumerable things to remind one of the dark recesses of the valley. After dinner, Hanzo did not go up to the second floor but stayed beside Otami, reading while she did her evening chores. Suddenly he heard a human voice calling to him from out of the night. He put both hands to his ears.

"Listen! Do you hear someone calling me?" he said to Otami, but she could not hear anything. He went on straining his ears to hear the voice in the night.

Not long afterward, Hanzo was invited to join a moon-viewing party being held by Sho'un at the Mampukuji on the night of the full moon. There was no reason for him to refuse the invitation since the Aoyama family had been associated with the Mampukuji ever since its inception. But there was no denying that the family had become alienated from the temple since Hanzo had adopted Shinto burial practices, bringing home all the ancestral tablets except those of the founder and the restorer of the temple. Yet Sho'un was not one to lose sight of tradition and he even sent a youth to Hanzo's house to fetch him.

It was time to go. Hanzo stepped outside. There was still a bit of light in the sky and there was not a cloud to be seen. It promised to be a good night for moon viewing, but Hanzo could not bring himself to start out. His heart was not in it. At last he moved slowly along the path to the temple, almost turning back several times. He climbed the stone stairs leading to the gate for the first time in a long while. He walked up the slope with its stone wall and its statues of Kannon and entered the grounds of the Mampukuji. The broad front court of the temple brought back memories of the time he had arranged to open temporary quarters for the school here. The old stone monument standing beside the ancient holly tree, the bell tower, everything reminded him of when the school children had frolicked in this courtyard.

"Oh, the master has come!"

Hanzo heard this exclamation from one of the familiar temple servants as he went around and entered the hearth room of the priest's quarters. There he met Sho'un, who had come out in his priest's robes to greet him. Presently he was led into the parlor. On the wall hung a portrait of Bodhidharma. A few guests were already there, including the former assistant headman Sasaya Shosuke and Shonosuke, the successor of Kozasaya Shoshichi. These were the men whom Hanzo liked best among all the villagers. Sho'un presided over the gathering with his usual warmth, never showing whether he felt close or distant, never reflecting on good or bad.

Nothing seemed to have changed in the temple. Hanzo found this reassuring. Persimmons, chestnuts, green soybeans, and the like were arranged on plain wooden ceremonial stands alongside large dumplings. There were arrangements of wildflowers. The prospect of spending an evening with these others in such refined surroundings placed Hanzo in the grip of an absurd but genuine terror. Ridiculous thoughts about how he had to be on the alert for someone coming to this temple to harm him could not be kept out of his mind. It seemed quite ludicrous even to him. Sho'un had the acolytes pass around tea and refreshments, treating his guests with the greatest warmth and consideration. Suddenly Hanzo became aware that even the cakes being served in the temple were male or female. He could not help smiling.

Since other guests were still expected, some of those already there slid on their knees over to the veranda to appreciate the garden that Sho'un had designed. Others admired the bush clover dimly visible through the autumn dusk in a corner of the garden. Hanzo had borrowed a candle from a temple servant, and lighting it, went off down the corridor to the main hall to pay his respects before the tablets of his two ancestors that had remained here in the temple together with the ancestral tablets of the other villagers.

Soon all the guests made themselves comfortable in the priest's quarters and light conversation began. The lighting was kept low. Each turned to his serving tray. The trays were made of the black lacquered bent wood appropriate to a religious institution and the simple repast of squash and bean curd was characteristic mountain food. It was lightly seasoned and went very well with the sake. The grated radish was seasoned with sugar and vinegar and the exact correct touch of grated citron that had been added reflected the priest's care in everything. Hanzo's tray also had salted, boiled green soybeans and small taros skewered and roasted in miso. Shosuke was sitting beside him.

"I heard that you had given up sake. Have you started drinking again?"

Hanzo did not know quite how to reply. Shosuke, a forthright person with a tendency to make a nuisance of himself when he had been drinking, was simply unable to observe Hanzo in silence.

On this autumn night, as the temple garden filled with the brilliant light that everyone had been waiting for, Hanzo drank cup after cup. As he brought each delicious cupful up past his nose, the sake that he had refrained from drinking seemed like not such an evil thing after all. Delighted by the priest's hospitality, and without deliberately setting out to do so, he found that he had drunk himself into high spirits. In time he and the others left their seats and moved over to the veranda. The air had already turned cool and he found this so refreshing that it made him all the more elated. The guests were scattered about, some kneeling, others leaning against a pillar, all gazing up at a sky as clear as pure water. The veranda extended from the priest's parlor around to the main hall and the hall in back where the ancestral tablets were kept. Hanzo walked off in that direction and stood on the covered walkway that connected the two buildings like a bridge. He looked out on a night that seemed as bright as day. Suddenly he caught sight of a form crouching down in the shadows. Something was lying in wait for him there. He could see it quite clearly. At that moment the exhilaration of the sake left him. He returned to the priest's parlor, his face deathly pale.

"Please excuse me now."

He expressed his regrets to Sho'un and started to leave the temple.

Shosuke, thinking that Hanzo had just had too much to drink, followed him out to the hearth room and spoke to him as he was groping in the dark for his clogs.

"Are you going home, master? Will you be all right alone? The steps in front of the gate are dark. Why don't you borrow a lantern from the temple?"

At the Shizunoya, Saburo of the Fushimiya and Masuho of the Umeya had come to pay a call and they were sitting up with Otami to await Hanzo's return. Otami had brought out a chess set for them and her husband's two disciples were engrossed in the game. This old chessboard was one of the few mementoes of Kichizaemon's time to be found in the Shizunoya.

"Hurry up and move!"

"Wait a minute!"

"You can't go on thinking about it forever!"

"What have you taken from me so far?"

"A rook and six pawns."

The chessboard was set up in the parlor downstairs near the veranda. Otami had gone out onto the veranda to look at the moon. When she returned, Saburo seemed to be out of patience with his partner's deliberations. He spoke again, partly to Otami and partly to himself.

"It's really good that the master can enjoy chess."

"So it would seem," said Otami, laughing as she let herself be drawn into Saburo's line of thought. "He certainly has few enough pleasures. He doesn't practice archery or raise fancy poultry. Whenever he has some time to himself all he does is sit at his desk and read. He has been in very low spirits lately and I keep asking him what makes him feel so downcast. Just sitting there seems to make everything look dark to him. He keeps saying that word 'dark' all the time."

Otami was clearly worried about her husband's health. Masuho still sat staring at the chess board. Then they heard someone running through the moonlight. Otami instantly recognized the sound of the footsteps. When he heard that the master was returning, Masuho at last threw down the knight that he had been holding.

Hanzo greeted his wife and disciples casually but he could not conceal the fact that he was upset. Otami could smell the sake on his breath as she came near him.

"Otami, light a lamp for me on the second floor and put the carpet down. It's not all that late yet and I'd like to write something tonight."

Hanzo went directly up to the second floor. He called Saburo and Masuho and put them to work getting out the inkstone and writing brushes and laying out paper. He had them grind the ink for him.

"Would you like to hear this?"

Hanzo took out a brief essay that he had written years ago which he scarcely ever showed to anyone. It had been composed just after the Mito ronin passed over the Kiso road, at a time when he was in close touch with the Hirata people in eastern Mino and Ina. The brush strokes were young and vigorous and what he had written was also young and vigorous. He read it aloud, translating from the original Chinese for his two disciples:

Of all the things to which heaven and earth have given rise, mankind is the
most wondrous and most holy. It is possible for mankind to be wondrous and
holy because mankind has the wondrous and holy lodged in its heart. There are
innumerable varieties of things in the world. In the fields there are thousands of
grasses and herbs, and in the mountains there are tens of thousands of trees.
One can take in all these grasses and trees at a glance, but among herbs the
chrysanthemums and the orchids have fine scents, and among trees the pine and
the oak possess nobility. So it is with mankind. There are those who can surpass the general run because they are superior in spirit to the general run. The
commonplace, however numerous, are all the same; they are like the grasses
and trees that possess neither scent nor nobility. Those who excel, one if there

be only one, ten if there be ten, are all serviceable and profitable to the nation. Among herbs and trees they have the qualities of the chrysanthemum and the pine.

But with chrysanthemum and pine, one glance tells you of their glory. The brilliance or stupidity of a human mind is not reflected in its physical housing, and for that reason one cannot readily recognize its quality. In the mind it is one's thoughts that comprise the wondrous and holy. He who is most enlightened in his soul thinks the farthest ahead; the fool does not dare do so at all. Now, the human mind cannot refrain from thinking. Our thoughts flourish in our breasts. We enumerate them, we line them up, and by bringing them to maturity, we realize them. Our insignificant bodies merely guard this undertaking, as looking upward we serve our parents, and looking downward we nurture our wives and children. Thus are we enabled to act. Why should we flatter the world or seek to enter into it?

It is by being born as they do and by dying as they do that the souls of all things realize themselves.

The way in which we may observe the ancients is through what they have said in their writings and through what they achieved in their valor. Those who preserved their sense of justice and trustworthiness, those who remained loyal and steadfast throughout, those who admonished the throne though they died for it—it is through their example that we may observe antiquity. It is through those who remained apart in order to discipline themselves; it is through those who persevered in the face of danger even to the point of death; it is through those who made wise plans and succeeded, as well as through those who, when they saw that their heroic designs were untenable, were able to revise them. It is through those who, even after a hundred generations of sound rule, were still wracked with concern for the nation. It is through those who have told us how everything may yet be lost in one disastrous reversal. Our models are taken from those who ended violence and suppressed disorder, gaining the respect and submission of all around them. It is in those who recorded hundreds of generations in their histories in order to transmit them to the future.

Thus it is with all things. Thus it is that nothing can be realized by a single person. But will I then be able to live in accordance with what I love?

As he read this last line, the strangeness of his more than fifty years of life welled up in his breast. The times were past when it seemed that everything he saw and heard brought tears to his eyes. Now he could not weep.

Hanzo wrote industriously that night as his disciples looked on. In the Shizunoya the lamps were old-fashioned and the light was dim. Saburo and Masuho held candles for him while he wrote in large characters on white paper, composing classical verse. He wrote all kinds of things, some in Chinese, some in Japanese. When he finally divided what he had written between Masuho and Saburo so that they could return happily home, it was very late. He was still consumed by the need to write, but precisely because there seemed to be no way of satisfying the impulse, he put out the light on the second floor and went downstairs to bed.

"It's not good for you to be unable to sleep like this," said Otami.

"Didn't you have a little too much to drink? It doesn't show when you've been drinking so those around you would never know."

Hanzo was pacing the floor of the parlor. He turned back to his wife.

"What time is it, Otami? I haven't been able to tell you about it until now, but I was in a terrible state when I came back from the temple. I felt that something horrible was following me. That's why I came running home."

"It's because of your mood. You're always saying how dark life seems here. That's what causes it . . . Doesn't Hirata sensei help you at such times?"

Otami's mention of Hirata sensei brought a smile to his lips. He had never expected to hear that from his wife. She went on.

"You keep saying that you feel such gratitude for being able to know about him."

"But, this is it, I seem to have lost sight of Hirata Atsutane in the midst of all this. And not only him—sometimes I can't even see Motoori Norinaga. It's been an effort just to get this far. Isn't that what Okume used to say? That if you were living with the spirit you would never be alone. I must have lost my way. I've got to get my courage back and serve the gods again. But tonight—you have really come up with a good one."

Acting as though she had just thought of it, Otami took a medicine box out of the cupboard. The physician Kojima Sessai, who rented the main house, had left it with her before leaving for Nagoya, telling Otami that the medicine was to be given to Hanzo in case he could not sleep. She went to the kitchen and came back with a cup of water which she offered to her husband along with the medicine.

The next day, Hanzo found himself in a still stranger state of mind. When he awoke, he had no idea how long he had slept. He glanced around the room, still in a somnolent state, and not only Oman and Omaki, who had come over from the retirement quarters behind the main house, but even Otami, who had been with him all day, seemed somehow to have moved a long way away.

On the shoji, bright with autumn sun, was a swarm of Kiso flies. As he watched these insects hurling themselves at the light, he thought of Kureta Masaka, whom he had not heard from in a long time. He recalled how Masaka had said that a true restoration of antiquity could not be achieved through inadequate measures. He had spoken in scorn of this rapidly changing age when what was new yesterday is old today, when people skimmed and put aside Norinaga's *Commentaries on the Kojiki* or Atsutane's *Commentaries on History* without ever coming to grips with what they had really said. That was abominable. The old enthusiasm, when it was said that you could not be fully human without knowing Motoori and Hirata, had it all been a mirage? Was the current consensus, that all the ideas of the National Scholars were nothing more than delusions rooted in passion, any more correct?

Hanzo's eyes became dazzled whenever he attempted to take in these changes. Once the movement to separate Buddhism and Shinto had run its course, the Hirata disciples who had formed the very vanguard of religious purification in the country were treated as blind and obstinate fanatics. For a person like Hanzo, who could practically hear the cries to "squelch the fool," this meant that everything he had said and done had proved futile. Nothing grieved him so deeply as this feeling of enmity that had arisen in some of those around him.

"I have enemies!"

Because he had fallen into such a way of thinking, he began to hear things that his wife could not hear and see things that she could not see.

On the day of the fan incident, years ago, the crowd had rushed in on him with overwhelming force. He could not forget the feeling of that crush at Kanda bridge in Tokyo. Cries of "Police! Police!" that rose everywhere were still in his ears. He could see the expressions of outrage on the faces of the people bearing down on what they took to be this monstrously irreverent person. But the people in that crowd were not his enemy. It was rather the ghosts rising up out of the medieval cemeteries to conceal themselves in those crowds. People who had come out of the great collapse of the Meiji restoration dressed in random scraps of exotic Western clothing appeared to him as so many apparitions in the night. To Hanzo they lacked plausibility.

Exhausted as he was by the world's struggles, Hanzo's spirit was not yet broken. He fought to bear up under the overwhelming sadness that welled up inside him. Gold sparks began to dance before his eyes once again, interweaving in space as though thrown off by a great conflagration. He trembled as though something terrible was about to happen.

"Come after me then if you're going to!"

The two hundred tenth day of the year passed and with it the annual concern about typhoons. Just before the equinox the sudden afternoon storms ceased, and brilliant days in which Mt. Ena stood out still more sharply came to the valley. The farmers were busy cutting grass and harvesting the millet that grew along the dikes in the rice fields. One afternoon a tenant farmer came to call on Hanzo with a somber expression on his face.

"You and your father were always very good to me," said the farmer by way of preface to his remarks of leavetaking. Two years previously, this man had contracted with Sota to buy the land he lived on. Since he was not able to pay the entire sum of twenty-five yen ninety sen at once, he had made an initial payment of five yen ninety sen and had paid off the remaining twenty yen in installments. In September of this year the land had become completely his and he had received a certificate of sale for it. Although he was not required to obtain the retired Hanzo's permission to leave family service, he said that he could not think of breaking off with his former master without a word.

"If you ever have need of me, just say so, any time. I'll come and help you just like Kenkichi and Sosaku. I have been most obliged to you for a very long time."

With these words, he departed. Kenkichi and Sosaku had also bought their fields from Sota. It was at times like these that the absurdity of the family's plan for household management became most apparent. Even the farmers who came to pay their respects spoke only to Hanzo.

In the evening Hanzo returned from a short walk. When he went up to the second floor after dinner and looked out, the stars were already shining. The moon would be rising a little later, but its cool light was already flowing up into the night sky. Hanzo was deeply moved by the translucent majesty of the heavens and his thoughts turned to the long flow of time. The unforgettable words that Hirata Atsutane had left came to his mind.

"All things are as the gods would have them."

He thought once again about the fate of his family. In the sky beyond the sky, in the heavens beyond the heavens, the stars that now shone, now vanished, in endless cycle, seemed to express the movements of human history.

Umeda Umbin, Hashimoto Sanai, Rai Ogai, Fujita Toko, Maki Izumi were all there. In the firmament were Iwase Higo, Yoshida Shoin, Takashi Saemon, Habu Genseki, Watanabe Kazan, and Takano Choei. Hanzo could point them out, even count them on his fingers. Those stars in heaven that had suffered so terribly over the question of opening the ports or expelling the foreigners—there was not a single one among them who had not believed in the lofty mission of this nation, not a one who had not struggled against the overwhelming influence of the West even while welcoming it into our country. When Hanzo compared his own lot with the vast number of fearful sacrifices that had been made in order to lead the nation to its restoration, he realized that his insignificant life simply did not amount to much. Juheiji had often teased him for being a dreamer when he was young, but now he felt that he had been too little rather than too much the dreamer in those days.

The moon rose. The sound of insects filled the dark valley. He stood before the bright moon, lost in reflection on the fact that even though so many things had pressed in upon him with such force and intensity, in his stupidity and weakness he had not managed to grasp a single one.

4

"Where are you going, master?"

On the road that led from the center of Magome to the Mampukuji, Shosuke of the Sasaya and Shonosuke of the Kozasaya caught sight of Hanzo and called out.

"I'm on my way up to the temple."

"To the temple?"

"That's quite an interesting costume you're wearing."

Hanzo was wearing the same formal trousers that he had worn to the elementary school to teach the children. With his straw sandals, he looked very much the part of the village sage. But on his head he was wearing a huge green butterbur leaf.

"I met some of the village children on the way," Hanzo replied. "They were playing at wearing butterbur leaves on their heads, so I got a leaf from them and put it on too." Hanzo's reply was uttered with perfect seriousness. Was he out of his mind? Or was he trying to emulate Watanabe Hoko, the long-departed teacher of one of the early Yamamura of Fukushima, who went about wearing a lotus leaf on his head, reciting Chinese poems? No, it was different with Hanzo. He was dead serious, as though one really could not go to the temple without wearing some such preposterous costume. Shosuke and Shonosuke, barely able to contain their laughter, asked him what his business at the temple was.

"You people ask too many questions. Well, I'll tell you. I'm going over to burn the temple down. We don't need it anymore."

It never occurred to Shosuke and Shonosuke that Hanzo was not joking with them. It was late in September, the day before the autumn festival in Magome. Matsushita Chisato from the village shrine in Aramachi and Kokura Keisuke were hard at work in preparation. Keisuke himself had originally been a Shinto priest. He had all the children dressed in matching jackets. They and the musicians were practicing their march through the village while he exhorted them to do their very best. So successful was he in transmitting this enthusiasm to others that they were finding the preparations for the festival even greater fun than the festival itself. The young musicians of the village were completely caught up in their rehearsals on the samisen and flute, and the lively beat of drums could be heard all the way along the road to the temple.

Shosuke and Shonosuke, on their way to help out with the festival preparations, had of course been startled by Hanzo's words. While they did not actually believe that he was intending to set fire to the temple that his own ancestors had founded, they nevertheless followed after him. Hanzo, still wearing the leaf on his head, had by now disappeared into the cedar grove by the temple.

When the two men climbed the stone stairs up to the gate and entered the temple grounds, they were astonished by the sight that met their eyes. Hanzo was standing in front of the shoji of the main hall and he had taken a box of matches out of his sleeve.

"He's gone crazy!"

The words were implicit in the looks they exchanged. The fire was already beginning to flare up on the shoji. Shonosuke rushed frantically over to put it out, slipping out of his coat as he ran. In the confusion that immediately broke out, with people shouting, buckets of water being fetched, and temple servants and young priests rushing about, Shosuke had already grasped Hanzo from behind. The fire did not amount to much but the partly-burned shoji was completely ruined, a waterlogged wreck lying in the courtyard. Shosuke continued to hold Hanzo's arms tightly even after the excitement died down, and he showed no inclination to release him.

EPILOGUE

1

SASAYA SHOSUKE and Kozasaya Shonosuke brought Hanzo back to the old honjin. Kojima Sessai, the physician who rented the main house, was still in Nagoya. Sota, the present head of the family, was in Fukushima on business. All the other relatives and acquaintances quickly gathered to decide what to do. They felt that Sota's presence was essential and a night courier was dispatched to Fukushima. In the meantime Hanzo was confined in the parlor of the honjin and watched constantly, even when he went to the toilet.

Sota received the message in the office where he was working as secretary for Nishi Chikuma county. He immediately rushed back along the Kiso road, arriving in Magome on the evening of the festival day. Seisuke and Eikichi gave him more details about what had happened while he tried to calm Hanzo, who was still very excited, and to assure the villagers that he would cause them no more trouble. That Hanzo, the patriarch of the village, should have tried to set fire to the village temple had aroused the most intense horror and revulsion among the residents. They decided to get an immediate opinion from Keian Rojin, the physician from Yamaguchi village. Hanzo's behavior since the fan incident was exhaustively discussed. The consensus was that the master had at last become insane.

The celebration of the autumn festival went on in spite of everything. Seisuke, who was very close to the Aoyama family, spent the entire preceding night in the old honjin, returning to his own house only at first cock's crow, but he also had obligations to the festival. When the children were gathered by the torii at the village shrine, he took his place at the head of the procession to set the rhythm with a pair of wooden clappers. Behind the village officials in their formal clothing came the great drum, and the Shinto priest Matsushita Chisato rode on horseback near the middle of the procession in old-fashioned court headgear and robes. A great number of people had come over from neighboring villages, having heard that Magome was reinstating its autumn festival. Some young girls had walked four or five miles over the mountains, eager to see the festival plays that were performed only once each year. The sound of flute and samisen rose into the skies over the old highway as the children of the village, in handsome black jackets with large white crests on their backs, trooped through Magome. Some carried bright yellow banners warning against the danger of fire. Everyone agreed that there had been nothing like it for years. The young people formed in circles before the Fushimiya and danced to the "Kisobushi," singing in loud voices about the log-rafters of the Kiso. Everyone did his best to enjoy the festival day just as though the shocking behavior of the retired master of the old honjin had never occurred.

Why a person like Hanzo should have tried to burn down the Mampukuji was a complete mystery to most of the villagers. His ancestor Dosai had founded the temple after his conversion to Zen Buddhism, and it had deep associations for his family. Sho'un, the present priest, could not have been the cause since he was if anything too fine a person to be spending his life in service at this remote mountain temple. He was a man of virtue, warm and true in all his relationships. Hanzo himself used to say that everyone ought to be thankful that such a person was living here. He never failed to sound the bell eighteen times each dawn or to strike the gong and perform each morning's sutra readings. He would always bring out tea and refreshments for the old women of the village who came over to pray. At the approach of each equinox Sho'un would go around the village begging and on the day of the equinox he would place the offerings he had collected before the images of the Buddha and offer services for the dead of the village households. Nor did he forget to pass out talismans and miso and bamboo shoots to the sponsoring houses. He had even loaned a part of the temple grounds to some village youths who wanted to worship the Shinto god Inari. In all respects this priest had become as much a part of the villagers' lives as the yearly observances and festivals themselves. It was unthinkable that Hanzo could have decided that this temple under the stewardship of a man never remiss in carrying out any of his duties was something useless that had to be burned down.

While the festivities were still going on, Keian Rojin came rushing up by litter from Yamaguchi village. Even the confused and conflicting reports that he heard from the relatives who had taken turns sitting up in the parlor of the old honjin since the previous day should have made his diagnosis clear. Keian went into the room where Hanzo was, seeming to have believed everything he had heard. He took Hanzo's pulse and looked him over. He reported that no physician could make an accurate diagnosis with just one or two examinations. Still, he was well aware that Hanzo had been drinking too much and this, together with his insomnia and his general appearance, made it clear that at the very least there was some mental abnormality. He recommended careful attention. He also said that he would prepare a sleeping potion and send it over. He advised them to put it in Hanzo's tea so that he would not know.

It soon became known that Hanzo himself did not feel that there was anything wrong with him and had tolerated the examination in a spirit of humoring the physician. People became even more upset. Some were saying that if Hanzo should slip away from his attendants and get out again, there would be no telling what he might get into. If no one had been at the temple when he had tried to set fire to it, the shoji would have blazed up very quickly. Once igniting the thatched roof, the fire would have spread through the main hall and the hall of ancestral tablets and even the great drum that Kimbei had donated and the illustrated panels the late Rankei had labored so hard to produce would have been lost. Not only that, the priest's residence and the other buildings would have been endangered and even the temple storehouse might have gone.

Some said that this outrage had been perpetrated in broad daylight and if it was not certified to be the act of a madman not responsible for his actions, they themselves would strangle him for it. Others observed that although the fire had not caused any serious damage, there would certainly be a great deal of trouble if it came to the attention of the district police office. If the Aoyama intended to dispose of the matter within the family, then they had better move the master to a safe place quickly, place a strict guard over him, and take appropriate measures to ensure that the people of the village could once again sleep soundly.

Hanzo's cousin Eikichi carried the greatest weight in the family council. When talk in the village reached this pitch, he felt that they had no choice but to place Hanzo in confinement. The next morning he ordered Sakichi to clean up part of the woodshed and make preparations for Hanzo to be kept there. Then he called the village carpenter over to install windows high up on the wall, put in a floor to ward off the damp, and build a room next to this one where an attendant could sleep, all to be done soundly and in good order. Eikichi invited the leading citizens of the village to consult with him on the construction. He explained that a solid cell was being built in the part of the woodshed that faced to the west and that it could be locked when necessary. Since the place was to be used to confine Hanzo, who was tall and wore the largest size stocking that could be found, and who was quite strong, it was decided that heavy bars should be placed outside all the shoji.

2

The cell was completed. Eikichi called all the relatives and acquaintances to the honjin to announce that the new section of the woodshed was ready for the tatami to be installed, and he put before the meeting the question of just how Hanzo was to be persuaded to enter it. Shosuke was selected as spokesman. It was felt that he would be able to reassure Hanzo just as he had been able to bring him back peaceably from the Mampukuji.

For all his experience, Shosuke was at a loss how to carry out his assignment. When he went into the parlor, he found Hanzo alone. He had taken out a small circular mirror and was repeatedly blowing on it and polishing it. It was an ancient metal mirror that he had acquired long ago, with a cloud pattern in low relief on its reverse side and a cord to attach it to the sash.

Since the main house was being rented to the physician Kojima Sessai, only the chamber of honor had been left in its former state as a shrine and this mirror had been hanging on the pillar of the alcove there. It had not been sent out for a proper polishing for a long time and it had grown clouded.

"We have both changed over the years, Shosuke. Somehow when I look at my face these days, I feel as though it isn't really mine."

Hanzo spoke in the tone of one who was being treated too much as an invalid by everyone around him. He stared into the clouded surface of the mirror, trying to make out his dimly reflected features. Then he spoke again.

"For that matter I've been feeling terrible these last two or three days. I feel that something dreadful is coming to attack me. I can't get any sleep at night."

"You always say that your enemy is coming after you, master, but where is it?" asked Shosuke.

"I can see it even if you can't. It comes wearing all kinds of masks and in different shapes. I can't let my guard down for a moment. It's terrifying, Shosuke. I mustn't say this too loudly, but it is hiding right under the veranda of this house."

Hanzo started to polish the mirror again, shrinking away from Shosuke as he worked.

Shosuke had been trying to find some way to bring up the matter entrusted to him by Eikichi, but he had not been able to get the words out. He was known for being straightforward and he was not the kind of person to resort to stratagems even in this situation. He did not intend to lead Hanzo off under false pretenses. Still he did not go so far as to say that it was a cage that awaited Hanzo in the woodshed. Since it was in one sense a sickroom he suggested to Hanzo that he retire to this sickroom to take care of himself. He explained that everyone in the village was concerned about his health and that the room was already prepared. If Hanzo would consent to go there, in accordance with everyone's wishes, he would receive the best medicines and those whom he had helped would take turns in looking after him. Furthermore he really had no choice. After hesitating several times, Shosuke at last told Hanzo this much.

"Are even you going to treat me as a sick man, Shosuke? It gives me a funny feeling to hear that."

Hanzo's fate began to close in on him very quickly. Eikichi and the others were waiting in another room for Shosuke's report. When he returned alone to tell them that Hanzo was not willing to accept the decision of his relatives, they all looked at each other helplessly, at a loss for the next step. They asked Kyurobei, the former toiya, and other prominent citizens of the village to meet with them in the hearth room. There they reached the same conclusion a second time. In such an isolated place as Magome, the old-fashioned Chinese-style medicine was already being discarded but it was still too early for the new medicine to have become established. It was especially difficult to get the advice of a good physician, and so it was decided to take the extraordinary measure of binding Hanzo with a rope and leading him back to the cell.

This would prevent him from escaping on the one hand, and on the other it would serve the necessary function of allaying the ugly mood that had arisen among the villagers. The assembled group concluded that it could no longer be avoided. But there was no one who was prepared to bind the master.

Then Horaiya Shinsuke, the youngest of the former post officials, spoke out. He said that the binding would have to be done by Sota. Since Sota was the present head of the Aoyama family, the master would surely not resist if he saw that even his own heir believed that he was sick. Sota would be assisted by the former tenant farmers of the honjin, and the toiya Kyurobei, who, at nearly two hundred pounds, was by far the strongest man in the village, would be on hand to watch the proceedings. Shinsuke, who was known in Magome for his wise council, had felt it prudent to include this last suggestion.

Preparations were completed and agreed upon. The autumn day was coming to an end. The Aoyama family was asked to gather in the middle room at Eikichi's request. When she heard their decision, Otami was so shocked that she could scarcely keep her feet and she had to be assisted by Omaki. Hanzo was led into the parlor by Seisuke.

Sota came before him and bowed to the floor.

"Father, I know it is unheard of for a child to put a parent in bonds, but you are ill, so please forgive me."

Those who had come to place fetters on Hanzo were his son, his blood relatives, his fellow villagers whom he had led along the path of learning, and the farmers who had depended on him throughout their whole lives. The breath went out of him.

"So you all think I'm crazy, do you?"

He said this in front of everyone and then he suddenly found himself weeping copiously. At that moment, Sota took the rope from Eikichi's hand and, after bowing very correctly before Hanzo, pulled one unresisting arm behind him. Hanzo permitted his son to bind him.

The late September dusk was falling as he was led from the honjin to the woodshed. Sakichi was waiting for him in front of the storehouse, squatting in the gloom under the persimmon tree, one knee on the ground, unable to raise his head until his once imposing master, now so hideously transfigured, had gone by.

3

Okume soon received the news but it was not until the second week of October that she was able to see her father. She and her husband had by then returned to the family home in Fukushima and were applying themselves to the old family patent medicine business with a complete change of heart. For this visit to Magome, Okume was leaving a house which she seldom so much as stepped out of anymore and she did not take her children along. Her only escort was one of the medicine peddlers who was just then leaving on a business trip to Mino.

"Has my father lost his mind?"

With this question uppermost in her thoughts, she put Mt. Koma looming above Fukushima behind her and rushed down the Kiso road. From the letter that Otami had Omaki write for her and from conversations with Sota, whose duties as county secretary did not permit him to remain away from Fukushima for long, she had some idea of her father's condition. Of the five children, she was the one who had lived longest with her father and had been most strongly under his influence. She could most fully appreciate his feelings. As she walked along the road, tears came to her eyes each time she recalled him.

Okume had spent the night at Midono and was approaching Tsumago. As she reached the rest house on the bank of the Kiso river marking the entrance to the village, she could see the construction work that had just begun on the new prefectural highway that would run through the Shizumo forest, parallel to the river.

Blasting in the distant cliffs reverberated through the mountains. The sound of the shattering boulders that told of the coming changes in the ancient route of this highway was frightful to Okume's ears. Suddenly she caught sight of two prosperous-looking men rushing down the river bank toward her. They were dressed in Kiso-style work trousers and both were barefoot. They were waving their arms and shouting. One was her uncle, Juheiji, running along the river bank in wild abandon. Juheiji, elated by his recovery from a severe attack of hemorrhoids, was exchanging congratulations with another former sufferer.

Catching sight of Okume and the peddler accompanying her, Juheiji spread his arms out wide and laughed until his false teeth seemed ready to fall out. His long illness was completely forgotten. He invited them into the nearby teahouse.

"Are you on your way to Magome, Okume? It's a hard trip. Why don't you rest the night at our place and then go on over tomorrow?"

"Sota has already come back to Fukushima, uncle. I have heard all about father from him."

"Have you? Sota stopped in here too. And Masaki's way over in Korea now. He's going to be in for a shock when he gets my letter. I was over to see your father just three days ago . . . Well, I really wouldn't be able to say anything without being around him a little longer. But here I stand in this strange condition. I haven't even washed my feet yet! Please sit down over there, Okume!"

Juheiji, who was well known at this teahouse, went out to the back to wash his feet. Presently he came back wearing clogs.

"I feel as though I've come back from the grave. Today I'm a real Kiso mountain monkey for the first time in a long while. Your mother has also been suffering from hemorrhoids and I wish there was some way I could share this feeling with her. As long as I had them I was impossible to live with and Masaki couldn't stand to be around me.''

But by the time he and Okume left the teahouse even Juheiji had fallen out of his playful mood. From here it was still a few hundred yards to the main part of Tsumago, where Juheiji and his family lived. They left the banks of the mighty Kiso river, rolling down from the hinterlands, and began a gradual climb into the mountainous country that prevailed from Tsumago onward.

"Who would ever have thought that such a thing could happen to Hanzo? He doesn't understand a thing. The physician says that when a person loses his mind, he can no longer respond to things around him. Cut off from the world—that's what the physician says it feels like. It must be. He doesn't seem to have any connection with the world at all anymore. The physician says that when he diagnoses such a condition he feels as though he has just consigned the patient to his grave. It certainly seems so.''

Okume was too concerned about her father to stay long in Tsumago. For the first time in nearly four years, she set out over the road from Tsumago to Magome. It was still the same ancient highway that passed through places like the deep forest around the old Shiragi guard station, where robbers were rumored to lurk, before reaching Magome pass. It still retained the feeling of the old Kiso. The dense stands of chestnut rising before Okume brought back all kinds of memories. She and her husband, when they were first making plans to return permanently to Fukushima, had once received Hanzo as a guest in the old Uematsu residence. She remembered how her father had arrived for the visit with the breast of his kimono stuffed full of books. From that time on, besides helping her husband to put the family affairs in order, she had been constantly busy with the care of her two children. Her son was now twelve. Morning and night she had said that her one wish was to receive her father again in this house once it was restored to sound condition. Now that could never be. Whenever she thought of how her father's more than fifty years of painful existence had brought him finally to that cell, she felt as though she were being brought into contact with something in herself that she had inherited from him and that she did not want to touch. She was gripped by an inexpressible terror.

Her old home in Magome was no longer the same. Going to the second floor apartment over the miso shed, she found herself once again in the company of her grandmother Oman and her sister-in-law Omaki. Otami, completely taken up with caring for Hanzo, came hurrying up from the woodshed as soon as she learned of Okume's arrival. She reported that Hanzo was sleeping peacefully at the moment and that she had asked Sakichi to keep an eye on things. She told Okume about the unbelievable confusion that had attended the construction of the cell, and how all the people had been eager to take turns looking after Hanzo. They seemed to remember that he had been their teacher. Okume's visit raised her mother's spirits more than anything else could have. Oman was now seventy-eight. She had never been very communicative and there was no way of knowing just what she thought of

Hanzo's madness. Omaki was far advanced in pregnancy, having difficulty just breathing and unable to do any work. Otami was hard-pressed to take proper care of Hanzo.

"Anyway, Okume, your father is not violent. At first the people in the village were frightened and they arranged for two people at a time to keep watch over him day and night. Someone was coming over every day to help, but it's not that way anymore. Your father asks to have books brought in and when they are given to him, he just sits there reading for half a day at a time without saying a word."

"Uncle Juheiji was saying that no one ever thought that father would end up this way. It must have been his drinking," replied Okume, matching sighs with her mother.

Seisuke, who was manager of the sake business at the Fushimiya, joined them. Even though it was the time for selling the new brew, he never forgot the old days and he would regularly make a bit of time in his busy schedule to come around the back way to the woodshed at the Aoyama house. Sakichi had told him of Okume's arrival.

"I'm completely wrung out. I don't suppose you know about this, Okume, but Eikichi and I had to play the ugly roles. Your father had his retirement quarters and if it had just been a matter of depression or something like that, no one would ever have put him in that cell. But he tried to set fire to the temple and that simply couldn't be covered up. It came right in the middle of the Magome festival when everyone was very excited already."

Seisuke was his usual self. Okume remained in the second floor apartment while Hanzo slept soundly under sedation, but after a time she accompanied her mother and Seisuke down the steps beside the storehouse and along the path past the well to the woodshed.

There were wooden gates on the north and west sides of the old honjin grounds, and a bamboo grove covered the area behind the woodshed. To the southeast the roof of the main house soared up above a high stone retaining wall. Directly below the retaining wall was a deep artificial pond. In the days when daimyo and shogunal officials had spent the night here, provisions had been made to enable them to flee out the back way in case of sudden attack. These features were a reminder that the honjin had first of all been a military encampment.

There were three buildings out in back. Two were rice granaries and the third was the woodshed. For all that it was called a shed it was an old two-story building with an impressive entry. The earthen-floored rooms within were of a good size. This was the world of the manservant Sakichi, who had worked here for many years. The firewood and the pine needle kindling that he brought down from the mountains were all stacked here and straw was also stored in the shed. Hanzo's cell was hidden away, looking out at the bamboo grove in back.

Having come this far with Okume and her mother, Seisuke, who had to return to the Fushimiya, left them. They called out to Sakichi, who was sitting in the doorway sharpening a sickle, and he took them to the attendant's room to wait for Hanzo to wake up. Otami took this opportunity to tell Okume that she was still not certain whether Hanzo's innate emotionalism had brought on his illness or whether it was his illness that made him so emotional. He longed constantly to see his children who were so far away and scarcely a day passed without his mentioning Wasuke in Tokyo. She also said that since entering this cell Hanzo had fallen into the habit of pacing and it was very painful to watch him going back and forth, back and forth. Okume wondered if this was not because of a lack of exercise. Suddenly Hanzo called out. Perhaps it was the sound of the wind in the bamboo grove that had awakened him. Okume entered and there in his cell, father and daughter were reunited.

Okume tried as much as possible not to treat Hanzo as a sick person. This pleased him immensely. Forgetting completely his pitiful condition, he said that he would like to write something for Otami and Okume. He asked for writing materials.

"That would be nice," said Okume. "I'd like to have you write something for me. I'll bring brush and paper. Nothing could make me happier than to see you in good spirits."

Okume, not wanting to call on anyone else, left the woodshed to fetch the writing materials herself. When she reached the second floor apartment, Oman told her that all of Hanzo's things were stored over in the Shizunoya. Okume then went next door to the Fushimiya, where she was given some paper of a quality that would meet her father's approval. Inosuke's widow, Otomi, was still living in the Fushimiya and she hunted up a writing brush that had been a special favorite of her late husband's. Okume returned to the woodshed with these articles under her arm. She made do with ink and inkstone that she had found in Oman's apartment. As she ground the ink for her father she caught the scent of the gradually darkening fluid. It reminded her of the many happy days she had spent with her mother and father.

By that time Hanzo had begun to console himself in his loneliness by writing out old poems, finding comfort in sharing the emotions of the people of old. Among the sheets of paper that Okume brought back from the Fushimiya was some valuable stock called Otakadanshi. It was made in Echizen and it was not the kind of thing one usually encountered in mountain households. It had apparently been left by the previous Inosuke. Now well aged, it had a particularly fine feeling under the brush. Hanzo chose this paper to write out his feelings in classical Chinese:

> Unable to overcome his grief for the nation, sunk into bitter tears of rage, he
> has now become deranged. How can one not grieve for him? How fierce are
> the eyes of those without knowledge.
>
> Kansai

Kansai was a pen name that he had taken up in these last years. It came from Kanzanro, the alternate name for the Shizunoya, and it was written in

Chinese with different characters than those used for the name of his old teacher Miyagawa Kansai. Okume's watchful eyes found no trace of disorder in his calligraphy. Its strength and regularity touched her far more deeply than the opposite could have done.

Okume was not able to stay long in Magome. She had planned to visit her father for only two or three days, and she was already uneasy about being away from home. With one night spent on the road each way between Fukushima and Magome, the round trip alone required four days. She intended to take her leave on the afternoon of her third day in Magome, wanting to get at least as far as Tsumago that night, but it was difficult to bring up the subject of leaving. Now that the people who had looked in on Hanzo no longer came by, his terrible loneliness made it very painful for her to speak of her departure.

In the end there was nothing to do but creep away from her father without saying anything. She paused for a time outside the woodshed in lieu of a leave-taking. It was already deep autumn in the Kiso. Her mother was occupied with performing a hundred ambulations to the Inari shrine to pray for her husband's recovery. From the clearing in front of the woodshed, she could see the grape arbor that partly covered the pond and the mossy stone wall with its wildflowers. The path that led beyond the wooden gate to the Inari shrine was covered with fallen chestnuts. Everything here recalled the days when Morio and Wasuke had played out by the stone wall. Now she supposed that for Hanzo, completely cut off from the world in his cell in the woodshed, there was nothing to hear but the sound of raindrops in the old pond. She passed through the workroom in the middle of the woodshed and looked out toward the back. From there the bamboo grove seemed to engulf the place where her father was confined, enfolding the windows in its gloomy shade. The green bamboo crowded up to the very walls, so close that it occasionally knocked shingles off the roof in heavy wind storms. She looked at the deeply accumulated layers of fallen bamboo leaves and turned back toward her father's cell at the southern end of the building. Then it happened.

Hanzo took out a sheet of paper with one huge character written on it and held it up to Okume through the rough wooden bars.

BEAR

Suddenly caught up in the ridiculousness of his present situation, he burst into laughter. It was impossible to tell whether it was at himself or at the absurdity of the world. He laughed and laughed. Before his daughter, he clutched his stomach and laughed. Then the laughter suddenly died away to be replaced by a deep sorrow.

> The crickets
> Cry out; on the chill
> Straw mat

> I spread out my robe
> To sleep all alone.

As he recited this old poem, tears flowed in streams down his pale cheeks. He grasped the bars of his cell and wept aloud. Okume could only pace distractedly before the cell, unable to tear herself away.

4

In November Hanzo's disciple Katsushige came up Jikkyoku pass from Ochiai to visit him. He strode up over the ancient paving stones of the old highway and reached the western end of the Kiso road on the Mino-Shinano border. An elm stood on either side of the road to mark the spot and the place had so many associations that Katsushige could not pass by without looking around him.

Katsushige had been the first to rush up from Mino when word of Hanzo's madness reached Ochiai and now, concerned about the most recent reports of his master's condition, he was coming up again. By the time he reached Shinjaya at the top of the pass, it was nearly noon. He went into the teahouse, intending to ask the owner to prepare whatever he had on hand for a noon meal. He had just ordered a certain local mushroom that had come into season when he spotted Hanzo's old friend Asami Keizo coming down the road from Magome. Keizo, also deeply concerned about Hanzo's illness, was coming back from his first visit in a long time.

Katsushige called Keizo into the teahouse and invited him to take a facing seat. Keizo was now at an age where he laid his staff down very carefully before beginning to talk about Magome. He said that Hanzo had refused to see him in that wretched woodshed, and he was able to form an impression of his condition only from a visit with the Aoyama family in the apartment above the miso shed. Although Keizo and Katsushige were going in opposite directions at the moment, they often met in Mino and when they did they never failed to talk about Hanzo. They could accept the fact that he had had to be put away as a madman, but it remained a riddle to both of them why Hanzo should have tried to burn down the Mampukuji, an institution so important in the histories of both the village and his family.

Katsushige was about to express his shock and dismay over the whole affair one more time when the owner of the teahouse brought him a plate of freshly broiled mushrooms. He recommended to Keizo that he order the same thing and began to eat his meal. It still seemed beyond belief to Katsushige that his master in Magome should have suffered such a terrible reversal. He could never forget the three years between childhood and adolescence that he had spent at the Magome honjin. The shocking circumstances that had led Hanzo's family to confine him in that dark cell must have come as a severe blow for the master's wife. He too, busy with his own affairs, had seldom visited the Shizunoya. But every time he saw Hanzo's face, he had had the feeling that his old master was only improving with age. He had never imagined that Hanzo's life could end like this.

"Asami, I must say that we failed to follow Hanzo the way you people followed Hirata Atsutane. We just didn't have that kind of ardor. If only we had remained closer to the master, all this might not have happened."

Of Hanzo's old companions who had been with him when he had first been introduced to National Learning by Iwasaki Nagayo and Miyagawa Kansai, Kozo was already dead and only Keizo, some ten years older than Hanzo, remained. Asami Keizo, the hereditary honjin of Nakatsugawa, had served as the anchor post for the western end of the Tosando, overseeing the movement of men and freight. Until the restoration he had been extremely active in national affairs and he had been drawn into the wild confusion of Kyoto politics, as had his neighbor Kozo. The famous Nakatsugawa conference had taken place in his house, and shelter had been given there to people hiding out from the shogunate. Once the restoration took place, however, Keizo had hidden himself away, putting all his diaries, memorials to the throne, and other writings into storage, never showing them to anyone. In 1868, the first year of Meiji, he was ordered to a post in Kasamatsu prefecture by the governor, Hayashi Samon, but he refused the post, pleading illness. The refusal was not accepted, so he served for three days and then returned to Kyoto. He never went back. In the next year, he was appointed by the council of state to a position on the board of censors, but again he stated that this was contrary to his wishes and resigned the post after a few months.

In 1876 he was appointed assistant district manager by Gifu prefecture. This post alone he did not refuse and he served diligently until 1879, saying that it was for the sake of his own people. That was the way he always was. Keizo recalled how the late Miyagawa Kansai had said of Hanzo that he was so honest and single-minded and that once he set his course he was completely incapable of altering it. Since the restoration Keizo and Hanzo had taken different paths, but even this old comrade in the Hirata school found it impossible to understand what it was that Hanzo, who so respected his ancestors, thought he was going to destroy by burning the temple that constituted a memorial to those ancestors.

Still, it was Keizo who was able to retrace Hanzo's thinking up to the time when he found himself locked in his cell. Keizo was not one to hide anything from a younger person like Katsushige. According to him, the entire National Learning movement, with its dreams of a restoration of antiquity and its followers from Hirata Kanetane down to all the posthumous disciples of Atsutane, everything that they had said and done, had ended in one colossal failure. How could a purist like Hanzo fail to go mad?

Katsushige was amazed by Keizo's sudden willingness to talk. He was accustomed to a Keizo who seldom spoke of the past and who observed the world in melancholy and silence. Keizo was getting older but his memory was still sound. Katsushige had many questions to ask. How, for example, did a person like Keizo, who had confronted the restoration as a private citizen, really view the vast changes that were occurring? Keizo's response was that views of the restoration varied according to points of view, but that the model that most of his contemporaries had taken was that of the Taika reforms of the mid-seventh century. They had greeted the restoration of imperial rule by establishing a council of state and creating a ministry of religion in an attempt to restore the system established by the Taika reforms. Some had said that once the restoration was achieved the first order of business should be the surrender to the throne of all the lands held by the military houses, but others demanded that the power of the priests must also be broken. The two ideas had become current at about the same time. The priests had been accustomed to the protection of the court ever since it had come under the control of the Fujiwara family in the ninth century, and as a result they had acquired ownership of an indefensibly large amount of land. The abolition of the han and the overthrow of the priesthood—both involved the disposition of land and people.

Keizo felt that those who had worked together to achieve the restoration and to create the state anew had at least been pure of heart. The Hirata school was full of obscure people like himself who had joined and served for many years. But the pure phase of the restoration did not last for long—in the strictest sense, less than three years. By the time the military and the priesthood were beginning to lose their hold, the fresh new spirit that had prevailed at the outset was already dissipating. What took its place was a mere struggle for personal advantage.

With that, Keizo lapsed into his usual silence with little more to say about the Hirata school.

Katsushige tried to revive the conversation.

"Now that you mention it, Asami, I knew about the Meiji restoration one day earlier than the master. I think a lot about it now, but then I was still a child. I was such a child that all I could say was that I had gone to bed one night and when I got up the next morning it was the restoration. Hachiya Kozo laughed at me. He had received your letter. He said that they didn't know about it yet in Magome and he wanted Hanzo to see this letter right away. He took me along. I'll never forget it. It was in the twelfth month of Keio 3. The road was white with snow that crunched under our feet as Hachiya and I came up the pass.

"Yes. I was in Kyoto at the time. I remember that I had the people at Ise-kyu send the letter off by courier," Keizo replied.

"But the master seemed to sense that something was up and he came down from Aramachi to meet us. When we met, he said that he was just setting out for Nakatsugawa to try to learn something about the situation in Kyoto. It worked out perfectly. The master did not have to go all the way down to Nakatsugawa and we did not have to go on up to Magome. We talked about it here at the top of the pass. The three of us had a great talk here in this teahouse."

"Nearly twenty years have passed since that day."

The two men from Mino continued to talk as they sat in the teahouse in Shinjaya with its old signboard and wooden plaques, green with moss, commemorating past pilgrimages. A pleasant autumn wind was blowing down the old highway.

Keizo set out back down Jikkyoku pass for Nakatsugawa and Katsushige left Shinjaya in the opposite direction. On a low stone in front of the Basho memorial across the road, an itinerant entertainer had taken his monkey from his shoulder and was sitting down to rest. By now few travelers took the Kiso road between Kyoto and Tokyo, but it was still the only highway through the deep mountains and forests of central Honshu. As Katsushige climbed up from Nakanokaya to the outskirts of Aramachi, he overtook a string of packhorses carrying bales of salt for Iida.

On the brow of the hill off to the left Katsushige caught sight of the grove of cedar trees in which the Mampukuji lay hidden. Even the roof of the main hall was concealed in the grove, invisible from here, but as he reflected on its size compared with the poverty of the village shrine in Aramachi, he could easily imagine how the old temple with its hillside graveyard had served so long as one of the centers of village life. It was as if the distant middle ages still lingered on, announcing its presence with the morning and evening bells.

The hills rose up one after another like a stairway from the top of Jikkyoku pass, so that coming up from Mino, Katsushige surmounted one only to find another awaiting him immediately beyond. There was a shallow watercourse and a culvert. A small stream ran through it. When he reached the point where the stony fields began to run along either side of the road, he recalled his conversation with Keizo in Shinjaya and breathed a deep sigh. Continuing up the steep, stone-paved road to the edge of Magome, he thought about the future of the master he was going to visit and sighed again.

Since Katsushige planned to spend the night at the Fushimiya, he went first to the family of the second Inosuke, putting off until later the call at the old honjin. There he found the new master and his wife, both of whom were unselfishly helping Otami with everything just as their predecessor would have wished, Osue and Saburo, who had been getting their lessons from Hanzo until his illness, and Otomi, who said that it seemed to her to have been for the best that her husband had died first, because he would have suffered so to see things as they were now. Seisuke, who never failed to make his daily call at the woodshed next door, was there too. This family was not one to forget. When the season came to make the Kiso parched rice, they did not fail to take Hanzo a bit of this snack of which he had always been so fond.

Katsushige then went over to announce himself at the old honjin. Before going to the woodshed, he met Otami and asked about the master. Otami said that Hanzo had been having irrational spells for the past two or three days. She spoke of the difficulty of caring for him, making clear her sympathy for the other villagers.

"Madam," said Katsushige, "I know sake is forbidden to the master, but is it really good for him to be completely without it? Even if he is confined to his room, he should be able to have a drink now and then. I've been thinking about this a great deal and today I brought a bit of sake up from Ochiai. I'll leave it with you. Please take it and give him a little now and then when no one is looking."

Katsushige brought out a gourd from under his cloak and started to walk toward the woodshed. Otami caught at his sleeve.

"You can't just walk in on him anymore, Katsushige. You have to be careful around him. Just the other day he was calling out for me and I went over in front of the bars, thinking nothing of it. He kept saying, 'Come here! Come here!' and beckoning to me. Then he grabbed my arm and began pulling on it with all his strength. I thought it was going to come off. Be careful, Katsushige!"

Loneliness consumed Hanzo day and night as he sat in his cell. Katsushige listened gravely to Otami and then, seeing that there was no one around the woodshed, he went in and walked over to the bars.

"My enemy has come!"

It was Hanzo's voice, but it was also the voice of a person completely cut off from the outer world. Katsushige could not help but be alarmed.

"Master! It's me! Katsushige!"

The unexpected call seemed to bring Hanzo back to himself. His hair and nails were grotesquely long and his beard had grown out even further since the last time Katsushige had seen him. His face was startlingly pale in the midst of the wild tangle of his hair. But he had not yet completely lost his identity. After a considerable silence he spoke again.

"Look at this place I've ended up in, Katsushige! I'm going to die without ever seeing the sun again."

Hanzo grasped the bars of his cell and peered intently into the face of his beloved disciple.

"You mustn't say such things. As soon as you get better you'll be able to go back to the Shizunoya. I'll be there to meet you when you do. And right now, according to the old ways, it is the season to celebrate the chrysanthemums with sake. I have a gourd with a little of the Ochiai sake that you like so much. You haven't had a drink in a long time."

Katsushige took the plug out of the gourd at his hip and began to pour the sake into a little wooden cup. Hanzo listened closely to the sound of the liquid pouring from the narrow opening. He seemed transformed by joy, his mouth watering at the sound of the gurgle. Hanzo accepted the cup through the bars. Katsushige served him only one more tiny cup but he drank even this small amount of sake with the greatest relish. He drank as though of the sweetest dew, as though he had never in his life tasted such delicious sake before.

There was a sound like that of someone coming into the attendant's room and Katsushige quickly went out to see. He could only talk with the master this way if the two of them were alone. He waited in the next room for a while, but no one came in. He turned to go back to Hanzo, but just then he heard Hanzo talking to himself.

"What happened to Katsushige? Isn't Katsushige here? No, no, he isn't here anymore. He's gone back to Ochiai and left me here. He only says nice things. He doesn't really care how I feel. He must be another demon."

When he heard this, Katsushige could not bear to remain in the woodshed any longer. He went out to the bamboo grove in back and wept all alone.

5

The snow comes early to Mt. Ena. In the third week in October it is already showing white at the summit. By the beginning of November some of the children of the mountain families will have put on their heavy wadded jackets. The farmers take the frost up in their fingers as they work the soil, and heavy red chapping and cracking begin to appear on the hands of those who do a lot of washing. Everything reminds the observer of the approach of the long winter.

After Katsushige's return to Ochiai the woodshed became still more lonely and desolate. The mountains rose unseen to the north of the woodshed and the little sunlight that came in filtered through the bamboo grove as through deep water. It was dark and eerie at night. As the days wore on, it became apparent that it would not be feasible to put a brazier in the dank, cheerless cell for the inhabitant to warm himself, because of his proven unreliability with fire. It was not only Otami in her solitary watch over her husband who was appalled by this problem.

Still, no one was ready to propose that Hanzo could be released from his cell any time soon. Everyone said that the master should remain in the cell as long as possible. The woodshed was locked up more carefully than ever, someone was always on watch in the adjoining room, and the village fire watch would come through, sounding his wooden clappers, on his rounds past the Fushimiya and out to the Inari shrine in back.

One afternoon there was a violent sleet and snow storm such as was seldom seen on Magome pass. The late autumn sky suddenly clouded over with dark, heavy clouds and huge hailstones began to fall on the shingled roof of the woodshed. As the storm passed on and the sky grew bright again, Sasaya Shosuke and Kozasaya Shonosuke went together to see how things were in Hanzo's cell. On the way they met several badly shaken farmers. One told them how he had been pulling burdock roots when the storm set in, another said that he had been forced to halt work on his mulberry bed, and a third said that he had barely been able to grab his horse's lead rope and flee, leaving behind the giant radishes he had just pulled up. It was a long-standing village belief that unusual weather was an evil portent.

The two men then ran into Seisuke, who reported that the master did not look at all well. Hearing this, they became more strongly convinced that however agitated Hanzo might become, it would not do to let him out of his cell. They came up to him planning to talk about the unusual violence and coldness of the weather in recent years, but they were met by Hanzo's strangely altered voice, grotesquely rough from behind the bars.

"Come on! If you want to fight, come right ahead! Bring on your arrow or your shot!"

Hanzo was utterly transformed in a way far more unsettling than any hailstorm. He seemed unable to distinguish between friends and foe. Like one who had shot his last arrow in the battles of this world, exhausted but still unready to capitulate, he picked up his own excrement and hurled it between the bars of his cell. He threw it at Shosuke, at Shonosuke, and at Seisuke.

"Master! What are you doing?"

Shosuke was more astonished than revolted. He struggled to gain control of his voice and to calm Hanzo.

"Here comes the enemy again! But I've studied the lore of Kusunoki Masashige! We'll have us a real shit fight!"

He paid no attention to anything that Shosuke said. Looking as if he had come through so much grief and misery that mere weeping was futile, he gathered up another handful of excrement and threatened to throw it through the bars. The three men dodged desperately trying to get out of the room. They stepped into the filth and nearly fell. The stench filled their nostrils.

"Let's get out of here!" cried Seisuke. They spotted some matting in a corner of the earthen-floored room, and hastily covering themselves they fled.

6

It was all over. Just a few days after this incident, Hanzo, still in his miserable cell in the woodshed, fell gravely ill. He passed away at the end of the month. The physician Kojima Sessai was back from Nagoya by then and he attended Hanzo at the end. The cause of death was diagnosed as heart failure due to beri-beri. At daybreak, just before he stopped breathing, Hanzo opened his eyes wide, but by that time he could no longer see. He did not respond to Otami's calls. He was fifty-six years of age. Of his five children, only the eldest son, Sota, was with him at the end. Even Okume had not been able to get there in time.

It had been raining since dawn and there was no sign of any letup. The sound of the rain dripping down through the bamboo grove reminded the villagers of the approach of winter. By the time Otami and the others at the bedside heard the first cock crowing, Hanzo was no longer of this world.

When they came back to look in on him a little later, the rain-darkened skies had lightened and a pale beam of light fell into the room from the high window on the southeast wall. It was full morning by the time they had gathered together to begin cleansing the body. Hanzo lay on a fresh, green mat, and the change in the position of the pillow made it clear that the sickbed had now become a deathbed, but to Otami's eyes he still looked as though he were merely asleep.

Eikichi, Seisuke, Shosuke, Shonosuke and the others all came into the woodshed one by one. The second Inosuke came over from the Fushimiya. Hanzo's two young disciples, Saburo of the Fushimiya and Masuho of the Umeya, were a touching sight as they moved about in the gathering, trying to be of some use. Everyone agreed that the body should be moved as quickly as possible out of these wretched surroundings, but when the question arose whether it should go to the main house or to the Shizunoya, there was no agreement. Most of them wanted very much for it to go to the main house but they also felt that it would not have been Hanzo's wish to force the physician to give up his quarters even for two or three days. The matter was settled when Sessai himself asked them to use the main house. He said that he would feel very bad if they did not use this building that held so much of the history of Magome in it to send off the last person who had served as its honjin, headman, and toiya.

It was a day of scattered showers and they chose a time when the rain had slackened to wrap Hanzo's body in a sheet of matting and carry it out of the woodshed. It was a heart-rending scene. All that remained of this Hanzo, who had been told over and over that he was of no further use to the Aoyama family while he was still living, was now returning once more under the roof of the old honjin.

It was mainly the strength of Sakichi that moved the bundle of matting and quilts that contained the body of his old master from the woodshed to the main house. He was assisted by Kenkichi and Sosaku, two of the family's former tenant farmers. Sota, Saburo, Masuho, and the others accompanied the body, each holding an umbrella over it.

When Hanzo's death became known outside of Magome, many former disciples came to mourn him, but it was Katsushige who rushed up from Ochiai before anyone else arrived.

By the time he reached the old honjin, the master's body was already laid out in the room adjoining the chamber of honor in the rear. He first met the members of the Aoyama family and expressed his condolences to Otami, who looked exhausted after her long siege of nursing, to Oman, who at the advanced age of seventy-eight had now lost her stepson, and to Sota and his wife. He went into the inner room and kneeled before the altar of fresh, unpainted wood that had been set up in the ancient style of Shinto funerals. He pressed his face to the floor and made obeisance before the still imposing face of his dead master. It looked as though it had passed beyond all the sorrow and suffering of this world. The coffin had not yet been delivered nor had the Shinto priest from Aramachi arrived, but most of the important people in Magome were already assembled there. When Katsushige asked where the burial would be, Sota replied that since the family was still in very poor financial condition, they had chosen a corner of the old family plot in the graveyard at the Mampukuji and the temple had already been so informed. Katsushige's spirits sank even lower when he heard this and he said that he would like to see the master buried in a more suitable place. He proposed that if the temple field adjoining the graveyard should be available, he would see to it that the cost would be defrayed by himself and the other disciples, irregular though the offer might be. Katsushige was well aware that the Aoyama family plot was already filled with graves and that there was no space for another.

"This disciple is really taking a lot upon himself."

Sota did not say this in so many words, but the expression in his eyes made his meaning clear. Yet in spite of his initial reaction he was moved that there should be people so grieved by his father's death, and in the end he accepted Katsushige's offer. Eikichi and Seisuke also agreed and the two set out into the rain to look for a place to bury Hanzo.

A night of gloom and sadness fell. Friends and relatives gathered before the body, but neither Juheiji and Jitsuzo from Tsumago nor Okume and her husband from Fukushima had yet arrived. Because it was the old honjin that was concerned, the thirteen former tenant farmers and their families, the carpenter, the tatami maker, and even the hairdresser were all there, reminiscing about incidents in Hanzo's life. Someone told of how he had slipped into the back garden of the honjin to steal a plum one day, only to be suddenly struck from behind by the master. Another spoke of how Hanzo had always been a friend of the village youth, often filling his sleeves with tangerines to pass out among them, and how he himself, tempted by the tangerines, had begun to go to the master's house and from that time on had started to learn to read and write.

It was the night of November 29, 1886, the nineteenth year of Meiji. Heavy rains had returned once again to the mountains. Katsushige listened to the falling rain and to the memories of the villagers around him, reflecting on the qualities in the master that were symbolized by those plums and tangerines.

Katsushige and the second Inosuke approached the gate of the Mampukuji the next afternoon. The temple had agreed to provide another grave site and Katsushige wanted both to pay a call on the priest and to look for a suitable site. The master's funeral was to be held on the first of December, and Sota had asked him to make arrangements for using the temple grounds for the ceremony. This was in accordance with the agreement that had been made between Sho'un and Hanzo and the first Inosuke when the Aoyama and Satake families had reinstated Shinto funeral practices. Katsushige had passed the entire previous night at the master's wake, getting only a two-hour nap at the Fushimiya, and he could expect to pass the coming night once more before the coffin, talking with the people from Tsumago and with Okume and her husband. Then he would be in charge of the funeral ceremony on the following day. But Katsushige was young and strong and he was determined to master his fatigue in return for the many kindnesses he had received from Hanzo during his lifetime.

The priest Sho'un, conscious of the service that the Aoyama family had rendered to the temple for generation after generation, and who felt a special gratitude for Hanzo's assistance with the village school, had just returned from a call on the old honjin. He invited Katsushige and Inosuke into his parlor and informed them that preparations to hold the ceremony on the temple grounds had been made and that the temple would do everything necessary to expedite the transfer of the grave plot to the Aoyama family. He brought out refreshments for his guests. Then, in the calm tones of a Zen priest, he said that he had something to ask Katsushige and Inosuke. He wanted to know if they thought that Hanzo's attempt to burn down the temple was simply an act of madness. The reason he was curious was that Hanzo, as a Hirata disciple, had begun long before to say that the temple was no longer needed. From around the time the title of daimyo at the upper level of society as well as those of the honjin, toiya, and headmen at the lower levels were being eliminated, he had already begun to voice this opinion. Sho'un suspected that he felt that the priesthood itself ought also to have been eliminated at the same time. When Sho'un worked with Hanzo on arrangements for the village school, deciding upon the main hall of the temple as the temporary school building, he had already sensed that feeling in Hanzo. It was not only a complete rejection of Buddhism; it also implied a complete rejection of all previously established customs and relationships. To try to burn down this remote and insignificant temple at a time when freedom of religion had been proclaimed could be thought of as childish, but its moral implications could hardly be said to be slight. Hadn't that been Hanzo's purpose?

That the best elements among the nation's Buddhists had recently become awakened was due to the stimulus of the Hirata school's struggle to restore antiquity. Without that severe shock, most of the followers of Buddhism would no doubt have continued to tolerate the corruption and degradation that had characterized the final years of the Tokugawa shogunate. Hanzo's upright character and his sensitivity had made it impossible for him to accept the policies of the ministry of religion, and he saw freedom of religion as an evasion rather than as a solution. Could that have led to the consequences they had witnessed? That was what Sho'un suspected. He said that precisely because he was the one who had nearly had his temple burned down around him, he could not pass Hanzo's incredible behavior off as a mere riddle. Of course, Sho'un had not mentioned this to anyone. He said that he was speaking to them of it now only because Hanzo was already dead. Katsushige looked sharply at the priest.

"But, your reverence, if that was what you thought, why didn't you speak up earlier and rescue the master?"

The priest replied that public opinion had gone beyond the control of a single priest. If Hanzo had not offended public opinion, he would never have been overpowered by the people of the village that way. He sighed as he said that although he had not intended to leave Hanzo to his fate, this was in fact what he had done.

"I have to tell you two that never have I been so much aware of the impermanence of all things as I am right now."

Then he brought out a small, cloth-wrapped package, as though his real meaning was somehow concealed within it. And so it was, for they were astonished to learn that this priest, now approaching his seventieth year, was preparing to undertake a long journey.

Sho'un had long since recognized that there were four things against which it was useless to struggle. He would not fight against the course of events, against the mind's reason, against the Buddhist teachings, or against fate. Sho'un intended to make clear that he had no attachment to this temple which Hanzo had tried to burn down. He would make it available to compensate for the religious service which he could not perform for Hanzo. But at the same time he could not forget his obligations to his office and to the business of the temple. He confessed to Katsushige and Inosuke that he wanted to prepare someone to take his place as resident priest, to have the leaky roof of the main hall repaired, and once he had everything in perfect order, to set out in his seventieth year for a pilgrimage around the entire country. He would leave this temple where he had lived for so long as one leaves for the battlefield, putting his body at the mercy of the elements, drawing strength only from his priest's staff, and taking the sages of old as his model.

He had drafted papers concerning the annual festivals of Magome for his successor's guidance and instruction on various Zen teachings for the village children: the difficulty of attaining faith, the difficulty of coming to the teachings; the difficulty of arousing the will to do good; the difficulty of attaining human form; the difficulty of acquiring full control of one's faculties, and the consequent blessings of all these things. In his competent way, Sho'un had already prepared his amulet bag for the journey and he took it out and showed it to them. It was a small bag made of brocade with a green ground, containing a neatly folded palm leaf fragment from India that was inscribed with a phrase from a Sanskrit sutra and an amulet from the Suitengu, the great Shinto shrine in Kyushu. As Basho had noted, many men of old had died while traveling. Since it was impossible to know when this dew-like existence might end, Sho'un had prepared a death verse which he intended to leave behind at the temple. It was a Zen-style verse of praise around which he had drawn a thick circle in black ink. He asked them to remember him once he had set out on this journey. Even if he went all the way to Nagasaki in the west, he would still be a wandering priest gazing back toward the skies of his homeland.

Presently the two were ready to leave. When they had once again emerged from the temple gate, Katsushige turned to his companion.

"No one is going to sleep well after seeing the master come to that kind of end. We have to give him the best funeral we possibly can."

The second Inosuke nodded.

*   *   *   *   *   *   *

Fortunately, the rain ended and the weather began to look more promising for the funeral the next day. Katsushige and Inosuke walked among the rows of ancient gravestones in the cedar grove on the hillside below the Mampukuji. Hanzo's grandfather Hanroku, his father, Kichizaemon, and the present Inosuke's grandfather Kimbei, as well as his son the first Inosuke were all sleeping their long sleep there. Some of the stones were still damp from the night's rain. As they passed by them out to the end of the grove they caught sight of the smoke of a bonfire rising from the new section that had been added to the graveyard. Sakichi, Kenkichi, and Sosaku were digging the grave.

When they reached the grave site they found that Seisuke had come ahead of them. The bit of cropland bought from the temple was already cleaned and leveled, and the bamboo around it had been cleared away. From the gentle slope they could look across the narrow valley to the village of Magome nestled at the foot of the Ena range. It was an appropriate site for the master, and it was not Katsushige alone who felt that they had done well. From time to time Kenkichi and Sosaku would put down their mattocks and come over to the fire for a rest. They were discussing their plans to care for the master's grave in the future. Those who were present found themselves contemplating the dirt heaped high from the new grave and the plain wooden marker with Hanzo's name written on it in accordance with the practice of the Hirata school. They thought about the green grass that would soon be growing on that grave.

"Seisuke! Have you sent word to all the people far away?"

"To the Hirata household in Tokyo?"

"Yes, let's not forget them, and we should send word to Kureta Masaka in Atsuta as well."

"But what about Morio and Wasuke? Won't they be coming home for their father's funeral?"

"Well, this is what I did. I went down to Nakatsugawa and sent them a telegram notifying them of their father's death, but I didn't say anything about their coming home. I had no instructions from Sota. But I don't think they will be coming."

Seisuke continued talking with Katsushige and Inosuke for a while. Then Saburo and Masuho came walking along the narrow path carpeted with cedar needles. They told Katsushige and Inosuke that Okume and her husband and the people from Tsumago had just arrived at the old honjin.

There was a great sense of relief now that everyone had come, but even after learning of Okume's arrival, they did not immediately leave the grave site. Someone noted that although during his final years the deceased had been that same Aoyama Hanzo who was the object of so much gossip, now that he was gone no one called him anything but "the master." Another observed that the planets had moved in their courses, the highway had changed, and there would never again be anyone like the master in this mountain village. Seisuke gave a great sigh.

"The master certainly gave us a rough time of it at the end. Talking about Kusunoki Masashige's shit fight—even though we wanted to clean him up, there was no way we could get at him. I've never felt so helpless. It's a wonder he didn't hurt himself. When I think about it now, it never seemed to have any adverse effect on him when he got violent. But then just as he seemed to be calming down a bit, he suddenly broke down physically."

After Seisuke had spoken in his characteristic vein, young Saburo took up the thought.

"All the same, it's really too bad the way things turned out. If he had stayed that way just a little longer they would have let him out of the woodshed. No matter what anyone says, you will hardly ever find a man as pure as the master. I've never seen another."

"That's right. It's just the way Saburo says. If only the master could have lived another ten years."

Katsushige sighed.

It had been decided that they would spend that night with Hanzo's body again, talking with the people from Fukushima and Tsumago. Presently they began to leave the gravesite. The second Inosuke and Seisuke and the young disciples all went back down the narrow path. But Katsushige remained behind, quite still, watching as Sakichi and the others continued to deepen the grave.

Hanzo's life as the former headman and as the former honjin and toiya of Magome was now part of the past. Everything it stood for was in the past. The Meiji era itself, at the end of its nineteenth year, was embarking on a period of new perspectives. Everyone was tired of yesterday's conservatism pregnant with progress and of today's progress pregnant with conservatism. A generation of young people seeking a new Japan had come into being, but a dark gloom still covered the land. While the only certainty was that the feudal age was dead and buried, there was still no sign of the dawning of a day when a true restoration might be realized. At this juncture, the government's plan to build the main railway link between Tokyo and Kyoto through the Tosando was abandoned in favor of the Tokaido route. Schemes for building private railways sprang up everywhere, and the changes in communications that would shrink time and distance began to sweep away the old life like a great flood.

Katsushige recalled in sadness the master's words: "I am going to die without ever seeing the sun again."

"Well, come on, just a little more!"

After this from one of the grave diggers, there were only the grunts of men doing heavy labor. The grave had to be deep but also long, so that Hanzo's coffin could be buried horizontally. The strong scent of newly turned earth filled the air as the dirt from the grave was piled higher and higher. Katsushige watched in pain; it was as though the mattocks were striking him in the pit of the stomach. Each blow was followed relentlessly by another.

GLOSSARY

THE NAMES of the foreground characters were changed by Tōson in recognition of the liberties taken in the course of making fictional characters of them, although they remain for the most part very close to their models. In such cases the names of the models have been given in parentheses after the heading. This glossary is intended as a convenience for the general reader. Those who wish to explore further may be interested in some of the titles in the Bibliographical Note.

Aizawa Seishisai (1782–1863). A leading Confucian scholar of Mito and a student of Fujita Yūkoku, the distinguished father of Fujita Tōko. His *New Treatise (Shinron)*, a work of 1825, argued the uniqueness and centrality of Japan in human history, an obvious transference of the sinocentric world view of Confucianism. He advocated the strengthening of Japanese armaments and the unification of the nation and maintained that the shōgun's responsibility was to make it clear that Japan would fight if attacked. His social policies for building the newer and more resolute Japan that he envisioned came out of the Confucian tradition; he had little use for European civilization aside from its weaponry. The *Treatise* circulated in manuscript for more than thirty years before being printed in 1857, when the coming of Perry made it seem prescient to those who advocated the prompt expulsion of the foreigners.

Aizu. Vassal *han* in the northeast of Japan with a revenue of 230,000 *koku*. The daimyō were the Matsudaira, a cadet branch of irregular descent from the Tokugawa, who in the 1860's were responsible for guarding the imperial palace in Kyoto. Sympathetic to the imperial cause but trapped by their ties to the Tokugawa, they suffered heavily after the restoration. This was in part a result of Chōshū's desire for revenge for the mauling Aizu had earlier inflicted on its forces when Chōshū was attacking the imperial enclosure and Aizu was defending it.

Ajima Tatewaki (1812–1859). A Mito activist and younger brother of Toda Hōken, Ajima had been adopted into another family in infancy. He supported Tokugawa Nariaki in the *han* succession disputes, becoming a bitter enemy of his brother while holding various high *han* offices and advising the shogunate on shipbuilding. After the deaths of Fujita Tōko and Toda, he returned to the service of Nariaki and when the latter was placed under house arrest, Ajima's strenuous protests brought his hitherto close relationship with high shogunal officials to an end. He was imprisoned and later ordered to perform *seppuku*.

Alternate attendance. Daimyō were required to spend alternating periods of residence in their domains and in Edo while their families were required to remain

761

permanently in Edo as hostages. A daimyō normally saw his *han* for the first time only after inheriting his title. These measures assserted Tokugawa power while the costs of maintaining official residences both at home and in Edo, and of the elaborate retinues by which they were accompanied when traveling, dissipated daimyō wealth and rendered them less likely to indulge in adventures.

Andō Tsushima no Kami Nobumasa (1819–1871). Tenth lord of the vassal *han* of Iwaki-Taira in Mutsu province in the north of Japan and a member of the *rōjū*. Andō was the de facto successor to Ii Naosuke although he never held the title of *tairō*. He played a major role in the marriage of Princess Kazu to Iemochi, the fourteenth shōgun. In his earlier years, Nobumasa went by the name of Nobuyuki.

Anenokōji Kintomo (1839–1863). A politically active court noble from one of the many branches of the northern house of the Fujiwara family.

Aoyama Hanzō (Shimazaki Masaki, 1831–1886). *Honjin,* headman, and *toiya* of Magome and its dependent hamlets. He is closely modeled after the author's father and all the writings, both official and unofficial, attributed to Hanzō in the novel were actually written by Shimazaki Masaki.

Aoyama Juheiji (Shimazaki Yojiemon Shigeyoshi, 1837–1900). Head of the Tsumago branch of the Aoyama family, where he held the offices of *honjin,* headman, and *toiya;* elder brother of Hanzō's wife, Otami, and foster father of their son Masaki. Tōson has made the fictional character much closer to Masaki in age; in real life he was the younger brother of Shimazaki Masaki's wife, Nui. He was modestly successful under the new government as an official of the short-lived Chikuma prefecture and later as postmaster in Tsumago.

Aoyama Kichizaemon (Shimazaki Shigetsugu, 1800–1869). Father of Hanzō, Kichizaemon also takes on some of the attributes of Shigetsugu's foster father, Shigeyoshi. The family came from warrior stock and continued in private to use their surnames, a privilege denied to commoners. When Kichizaemon is granted official permission to use a surname, it means that the family name would once again be recognized in official functions. He and his predecessors had previously been addressed by officials in the pattern "Kichizaemon of Magome."

Aoyama Masaki (Shimazaki Hirosuke, 1861–1928). Third child and second son of Hanzō and Otami; adopted when he was two by Juheiji and Osato, who were then childless. He later married their daughter, Kotoji, who was born after his adoption. Hirosuke spent most of his adult life struggling with the forest problem and its further ramifications for the people of the Kiso.

Aoyama Morio (Shimazaki Tomoya, 1869–1920). Fourth child and third son of Hanzō and Otami.

Aoyama Okume (Shimazaki Sono, 1856–1920). The eldest surviving child and only daughter of Hanzō and Otami. She inherited Hanzō's character and interests and was closest to him of all his children. Her later life is treated in two earlier works by Tōson: *The Family* and "The Life of a Certain Woman."

Aoyama Oman (Shimazaki Kei, 1811–1901). Kichizaemon's second wife and Hanzō's stepmother. Kei was the granddaughter of Sakamoto Tenzan, a master of gunnery for Takatō *han,* and was born into the family of Aruga Jirōbei Moriyoshi, landowners in Minami Tono village and the models for the Inaba family of Book Two. She was educated in part by the master of the temple school in Ono, who arranged a marriage for her with Ichinose Tamejiro, the headman of Ichinose village. This marriage lasted only a year because of the interference of an uncle. She was next married into a family in Agematsu but this marriage too soon failed, and she brought the daughter of that marriage (the Okisa of the novel) with her to

Magome. At the time of her marriage to Shigetsugu, the Shimazaki family was already in financial difficulty and it was hoped that Kei's strong and capable management and her connection with the wealthy Aruga family might help to bring them through.

Aoyama Otami (Shimazaki Nui, 1837–1896). Sister of Juheiji, wife of Hanzō, and mother of his children.

Aoyama Sōta (Shimazaki Hideo, 1858–1924). Second child and eldest son of Hanzō and Otami. Married to Omaki, he succeeded Hanzō as head of the house in 1875 when only seventeen years of age.

Aoyama Wasuke (Shimazaki Haruki, pen name Tōson, 1872–1943). Fifth surviving child and fourth son of Hanzō and Otami.

Asami Keizō (Ichioka Shōzō, 1813–1886). One of Hanzō's closest friends and a fellow student of Miyagawa Kansai. Keizō became head of his family at age fourteen and served as *honjin* and headman in Nakatsugawa.

Ashikaga Takauji (1305–1358). Founder of the Ashikaga or Muromachi shogunate (1338–1573). Represented by the Mito school as the archetype of the cynical and treacherous opportunist who prospers through foul means, he was often contrasted with his famous antagonist, the revered popular hero Kusunoki Masashige. Since all writing and discussion of current affairs were rigorously constrained under the Tokugawa, political comments were frequently made through allusions to Muromachi politics.

Baba Tatsui (1850–1888). Born in Kōchi, Baba was a major figure in the popular rights movement. He was a student of Fukuzawa Yukichi before going to London in 1870 to study law on a scholarship from Tosa *han*. Except for one brief visit home in 1874, he stayed in England until 1878, publishing several works on Japan in English, including a translation of the *Kojiki*. His outspoken positions quickly got him into trouble with the authorities after his return, but he continued to write and speak, dying in Philadelphia while on a speaking tour of the United States. Tōson was a schoolmate and close friend of Baba's younger brother, the translator and essayist Baba Kochō.

Bannermen *(hatamoto).* Personal retainers of the shōgun who enjoyed stipends of less than ten thousand *koku* but more than one hundred. They had the privilege of direct audience.

Barrier. Internal customs barriers were located at the borders of provinces or at strategic points along the highways and were systematically organized under the restructurings of the seventh and eighth centuries. Under the Tokugawa, the most important functions of the barriers along the main highways were to control local movement, to prevent the escape of members of the families of daimyō held hostage in Edo under the alternate attendance system, and to keep disruptive elements from approaching Edo. The barrier at Fukushima was one of the most important in the entire country.

Beef eating. In medieval and early modern times, meat in the Japanese diet was restricted to wild game and this was in turn the nearly exclusive prerogative of the upper classes, although there were markets in Edo that sold venison and wild boar meat. The domesticated pig was not raised in Japan and cattle were used only as draft animals. Local dietary habits were so strongly reinforced by Buddhist teachings that beef eating seemed to many to be a barbarous aberration not too far removed from cannibalism.

Bon. The name of the festival of the dead which was generally observed around the fifteenth of the seventh lunar month. It is a contraction of *urabon,* which in turn is a Japanese reading of the Chinese transliteration of the Sanskrit *ullambana*, meaning "extreme suffering." *Bon* is characterized by offerings of food and festivities to provide sustenance and cheer to the souls of the departed.

Book of Odes. The *Shih Ching*, the oldest anthology of Chinese poetry and one of the books of the Confucian canon. The *Hsiao ya*, where Hanzō's first instruction broke off, is the second of four sections.

Bu. *See* Coinage and money.

Cachon, Mermet de (1828–1871?). A French priest, ordained in 1854, who, after service in the south of China, arrived in Naha, in 1855, in the company of two other French priests. Refused permission to carry out missionary activities and kept under house arrest, they made use of the time to begin learning Okinawan as well as Japanese. Following the signing of the Franco-Japanese commercial treaty of 1858, de Cachon went to Nagasaki to serve as interpreter for the French plenipotentiary. In the following year, after a visit to France, he returned to Japan as interpreter for Consul-general Vercours. This mission resided first in Edo but was transferred to Hakodate later in the year. In Hakodate, de Cachon exchanged language lessons with the shogunal official Kurimoto Jō'un (the Kitamura Zuiken of the novel). He stayed in Japan until 1866. After his return home he served as interpreter in the meeting between Tokugawa Naritake, head of the Japanese delegation to the Paris Exposition of 1867, and Napoleon III. He then left his religious order and sank into obscurity, apparently dying in Nice in 1871.

Calendar. Two calendars are used in *Before the Dawn*. The first was the traditional lunar-solar calendar, used up to 1872, at which time the international calendar was introduced. This new means of reckoning time was particularly dislocating to a people who had regulated their lives by the old calendar.

The traditional lunar calendar started the numbering of the years anew with the beginning of the current era. An era, which might last from a few months to twenty years or more, might begin at any time of the year so that a calendar year often began in one era and ended in another. The year was divided into twelve lunar months of either twenty-nine or thirty days. The first day of the month always coincided with the new moon and the fifteenth with the full moon. The beginning of the year was in constant movement in relation to the solar year and intercalary months would be added from time to time to prevent the lunar calendar from falling more than about one month out of phase with the solar year. Both days and years were also reckoned by a sexagesimal cycle in which the ten calendar signs were paired in rotation with the twelve signs of the zodiac. The eras with which this story is most concerned are: Tempō: 1830–1843, Kōka: 1844–1847, Kaei: 1848–1853, Ansei: 1854–1859, Man'en: 1860, Bunkyū: 1861–1863, Genji: 1864, and Keiō: 1865–1867. After the restoration the era names coincide with the reign names: Meiji is 1868–1911.

Censor. The usual rendering for the title of the office of *kansatsu*, although in its current usage the term does not fully suggest the power of the office. It was the duty of the censors to watch for moral, procedural, or political irregularities at all levels of government. In theory, not even the highest officials were immune from the oversight of the censor.

Charter oath. The first major statement of direction by the new Meiji government. It was promulgated on April 6, 1868 in an attempt to reassure the nation at large and the *han* in particular that:

1. An assembly widely convoked shall be established and all matters of state shall be decided by public discussion.

2. All classes high and low shall unite in vigorously promoting the economy and welfare of the nation.

3. All civil and military officials and the common people as well shall be allowed to fulfill their aspirations, so that there may be no discontent among them.

4. Base customs of former times shall be abandoned and all actions shall conform to the principles of international justice.

5. Knowledge shall be sought throughout the world, and thus shall be strengthened the foundation of the imperial polity.

Chinese-mindedness. In the parlance of the National Learning movement, the term stood for a dry and excessive rationalism combined with an uncritical admiration of all things Chinese and a matching denigration of all things Japanese. Since such a stance rules out pure and spontaneous feeling, hypocrisy was also argued to be an integral part of Chinese-mindedness. It must be remembered that none of the National Scholars had any direct experience with Chinese culture. The object of their ire was the bookish and sinophile culture that had grown up in Japan.

Chōshū. An allied *han* of 369,000 *koku* of nominal revenues at the western extremity of Honshu. Ruled by the Mōri, who had never reconciled themselves to Tokugawa hegemony, Chōshū was the earliest center of serious anti-shogunal activity. In the last years of the shogunate the daimyō was Mōri Yoshichika and his heir apparent was Sadahiro.

Class system. The Tokugawa adaptation of the Chinese Neo-Confucian system of Chu Hsi of the Sung dynasty divided society into four classes: samurai, farmers, artisans, and merchants. The actual class structure was far more subtle and complex. Everyday life was subject to a blending of the strictures imposed and privileges conferred by both the official and the actual structures. The official system excluded from its reckoning the imperial family at the top and a wide range of outcasts, artists, and entertainers, including many of the most creative members of society, at the bottom. In most respects the sharpest vertical break in the class structure was between the upper samurai and all others, including the lower samurai. There was considerable opportunity for vertical mobility within some of the other classes, most notably in the officially despised merchant class, but very little for the samurai, many of whom experienced growing privation under the progressive failure of the Tokugawa economic order.

Clocks. As with the calendar, both traditional and modern international usages appear in the novel, and, as with the two calendars, they reflect fundamentally different approaches to the measurement of time. In the traditional scheme the day was divided into two six-unit periods, one starting at midnight and the other at noon.

Each unit was therefore roughly equivalent to two international hours, but the lengths of the units were often adjusted seasonally so that there would always be six units of darkness and six of daylight, giving rise to some highly ingenious clocks. The time units commenced their numbering with nine, equivalent to noon or midnight, and proceeded in descending order. Thus 8:00 A.M. international time would be five o'clock traditional time and 4:00 P.M. would be seven by the local clocks. Each of the twelve periods of the day was assigned one of the zodiacal signs so that one may also hear of the hour of the ox or the hour of the monkey. Both traditional and international readings are given in the few cases where there are references to clock time before the adoption of international time in 1872.

Coinage and money. It is difficult to make meaningful comparisons of monetary values between societies separated both by time and by fundamentally different social organizations and technological levels. The following figures should not be taken as more than a very rough set of average equivalences; they provide some sense of the subjective impression that a given sum of money might make by 1980's standards but no really reliable sense of its actual purchasing power.

1 *ryō*	=	4 *bu*	=	$100.00
1 *bu*	=	4 *shu*	=	$ 25.00
1 *shu*	=	250 *mon*	=	$ 6.25
		1000 *mon*		
		(1 *kammon*)	=	$ 25.00
		1 *mon*	=	$ .025

In 1871 a decimal system of coinage was adopted in which ten *rin* made one *sen* and one hundred *sen* made one *yen*. Once the new currency stabilized it generally traded at about three *yen* to the dollar until the inflation after World War II.

In Edo the coinage tended to be based on gold and in Osaka on silver. Silver was comparatively scarce in Japan and was therefore rated more highly against gold than was the case in international exchange. A rapid buying up of gold by foreign speculators, who often paid in inferior silver coinages, was one of the first consequences of the opening of Japan to foreign trade.

Commentaries on Ancient History *(Koshiden).* A work by Hirata Atsutane, completed in 1821 as an annotation of his less well known historical study *A Complete Ancient History (Koshiseibun),* which Atsutane considered his most representative work. The *Commentaries* were inspired by Motoori Norinaga's *Commentaries on the Kojiki* and were intended to make the accounts of the age of the gods more available to the general public. It is this commentary that presents the essence of Atsutane's reading of ancient Japanese history.

Commentaries on the Kojiki *(Kojikiden). See* Motoori Norinaga.

Commentaries on the Man'yōshū *(Man'yōshūdaishōki).* The major accomplishment of the scholar priest Keichū. The extreme difficulty of deciphering the mixture of logograpic and phonetic usages of Chinese characters with which the *Man'yōshū* was written had caused it, like the *Kojiki,* to be nearly inaccessible for centuries after its writing. Keichū's work was one of the first of the great philological achievements of the seventeenth and eighteenth centuries that restored access to the masterpieces of classical Japanese literature and made possible the rise of a school of National Learning.

Dai Kagura. An entertainment that grew up around the lion dance, itself a blend of entertainment and ritual. In certain parts of Japan the lion dance began to develop into a more varied general entertainment which was called Dai Kagura. There were two schools of the tradition, one based in Edo and one in Nagoya.

Daimyō. The literal meaning is "great name" and under the Tokugawa system it applied to a feudal lord who held independent domains with an annual revenue rating of 10,000 *koku* or more. These domains were known as *han,* a term which also applied to the daimyō and his resources as a unit in Japanese political life. Several daimyō had arrière vassals with revenues greater than 10,000 *koku* but since these men were not directly subject to the Tokugawa, they had neither the title nor the status of daimyō. The Tokugawa divided the daimyō into three categories: the collateral houses, or *shimpan;* the vassals, or *fudai* (literally, "throughout the generations"), who were expected to serve directly in the Tokugawa administrative structure; and the allies, or *tozama* (literally, "outsiders"), the less trusted ones who had for the most part acknowledged Tokugawa hegemony only after the battle of Sekigahara in 1600. Economic development during the Tokugawa period resulted in the appearance of considerable discrepancies between real and nominal revenues in many *han* by the middle of the nineteenth century.

Dazaifu. The viceregal center in northwestern Kyushu, near the site of modern Fukuoka, established in 664 by the emperor Tenchi. Until these functions were taken over by shogunal officials in the thirteenth century, it was responsible for the administration of Kyushu, coastal defense, the outfitting and dispatching of embassies appointed by the central government, and the reception of foreign embassies or trading missions, exercising extensive discretionary powers in carrying out these duties. Aristocrats who lost out in court politics were often sent to Dazaifu, sometimes with nominal promotions, as a kind of exile.

Dengyō Daishi (767–822). Posthumous title of Saichō, the priest who introduced Tendai Buddhism to Japan upon his return from China in 804. He was the founder of what eventually grew into the great complex of temples and monasteries on Mt. Hiei outside Kyoto that was the cradle of most subsequent develoments in Japanese Buddhism.

Deputy. The *daikan,* a hereditary post held by the Yamamura family, administered all the noncontiguous Owari holdings in the Kiso. Major responsibilities were the collection of taxes and special levies, maintenance and operation of the Fukushima barrier, and the general maintenance of order in the region. Although in service under the Tokugawa house of Owari for generations, the Yamamura had first held this office as direct vassals of the shōgun himself, a fact that many of their retainers still remembered at the time of the restoration.

Dual Shintō. One of the more important versions of Shintō, based on the Buddhist doctrine of assimilation that presented the local divinities as manifestations of figures in the Buddhist pantheon. In practice it tended to present Shintō as a mere aspect of Buddhism, a view that was an abomination to the members of the National Learning movement.

Dutch Learning. After the Tokugawa policy of exclusion was imposed in 1639, the Dutch were the only Europeans permitted to maintain contact with Japan through their trading station in Nagasaki, Japan's only port for foreign trade, where a handful of Dutch ships and much larger numbers of Chinese and Korean ships were permitted to land each year. For nearly two centuries the tiny Dutch trading post was Japan's main source of knowledge about the world beyond East Asia. Until the late eighteenth century, only a hereditary guild of interpreters was permitted to learn Dutch under strict Tokugawa supervision. At that time, thanks largely to the achievements of Sugita Gempaku and his circle, it became permissible to learn the language in order to study European medicine. Dutch studies soon expanded to include military science, engineering, and most of the natural sciences. In the Tokugawa period, "Dutch Learning" became the generic term for European studies of any sort, but most particularly of science and technology. Once the trading ports were opened in 1858, Dutch was quickly eclipsed by English, French, and German.

Ebisu rites. Observances carried out at different times in different parts of the country. The festival seems to be of fairly recent origin, appearing in records only after the early eighteenth century. In merchant families the Ebisu rites consisted of a miming of buying and selling before the statue of Ebisu, one of the seven gods of good fortune. There was also a custom of distributing mandarin oranges and small coins in the streets in front of mercantile establishments. Drygoods stores held clearance sales during the festivals.

Egawa Tarōzaemon (1801–1855). A military expert from Izu who wrote extensively on artillery, musketry, and coastal defense. Unlike his aristocratic friend Shimosone Kensaburō, Egawa was close to the people and played a key role in bringing commoners into the artillery service. His effectiveness was in large part due to the influence of such friends as Watanabe Kazan and his circle, men who were comparatively well informed about Europe. He advocated the manufacture of more advanced types of firearms and his greatest accomplishment was the designing and building of the coastal defense batteries off Shinagawa in Edo Bay after Perry's first visit.

Emperor (*Tennō;* nineteenth-century European usage preferred the less usual "mikado"). The highest rank in Japanese society and the traditional source of all legitimacy. The imperial family claimed descent from Amaterasu O-mikami, the sun goddess who is the principal figure in the Shintō pantheon. During most of Japanese history real political power came less from being emperor than from being in a position to speak in the emperor's name. Under the Muromachi shogunate founded by Ashikaga Takauji, the court experienced real privation. Although its living conditions markedly improved under the Tokugawa, the majority of Japanese seem to have been only dimly, if at all, aware of the imperial institution until the mid-nineteenth century. This obscurity was profoundly and bitterly resented by the supporters of the imperial institution, whether followers of the Mito school or of the National Learning movement. The relationship between emperor and shōgun was in some ways analogous in operation to the European separation of the spiritual and temporal powers.

Era. *See* Calendar.

The Essence of the Way of Antiquity (*Kodō Tai-I*). A work by Hirata Atsutane published in 1809 as a prologue to the body of his collected works. It addressed itself to a refinement and clarification of Atsutane's perception of the Way of Antiquity, a concept that stood at the center of his teachings. It discusses the standard disciplines of National Learning: Shintō, poetry, study of the ancient laws and orders and of the tales, the histories, folklore, and ritual. Atsutane here once more advanced his observation that, to the extent that they served the needs of the nation, not only Buddhism and Confucianism but even Dutch Learning had a place in National Learning. National Learning itself he called "the study of antiquity," noting that its purpose was the recovery of the pristine state of Japanese civilization.

Five trees. The five prime trees of the Kiso district, one of Japan's richest forest areas, were protected with the greatest rigor by the authorities. Such policies enabled Japan to come into modern times with far more of her forest resources intact than was the case with most old temperate-zone civilizations, but they also led to conflict and tensions. The trees were *hinoki (chamaecyparis obtusa)* and *sawara (chamaecyparis pisifera)*, two closely related varieties of Japanese false cypress; *asuhi (thujopsis dolabrata)*, an unrelated species whose Japanese name reflects its close resemblance to the false cypresses; *nezuko (thuja Standishii)*, the Japanese arbor vitae, and *kōya maki (sciadoptis verticillata)*, the umbrella pine.

Fujita Tōko (1806–1855). A scholar-official of Mito and son of a director of the Shōkōkan, the *han* academy. He combined military interests with the scholarly and was reputed to be an exceptionally capable administrator. Under the vigorous direction of Tokugawa Nariaki, Mito was a leader in the reforms of the 1830's. In the course of those reforms a schism developed between progressive and conservative factions and the *han* came close to insurrection. Tōko remained loyal to Nariaki and led the progressive faction in the successful implementation of the reforms. It was during this period that Nariaki founded the Kōdōkan, or *han* research institute, but soon afterward he became embroiled in the bitter dispute between the progressive and conservative factions in the shogunal offices in Edo. This time the progressives lost out and Nariaki was placed under house arrest in his city residence in the Koishikawa district of Edo. Tōko shared his confinement and wrote his autobiographical *Poems That Moved the World (Kaiten Shishi)*. Later the place of confinement was moved to the Ko'ume residence and there Tōko composed his *Song of Righteousness (Seiki no Uta)* and his *Hitachi Sash (Hitachi Obi)*, two more works of great influence.

In the *han*, the conservative faction took advantage of the prolonged absence of Nariaki to dominate the young heir apparent, Narinori, whom they unsuccessfully attempted to seat in Nariaki's place. When Tōko was released from house arrest in 1852 he promptly began expanding the private academy that he had founded while under confinement. In the next year Nariaki attempted to force the adoption of a policy of total exclusion of foreigners. His move seems to have amounted to an attempted coup within the shogunate and in this too he had Tōko's loyal support. Tōko began to rally like-minded activists from all over the country and he was the recognized leader of the anti-foreign movement when his career and his life were cut short by the great earthquake of 1855.

Fukan (1731–1801). The priest who initiated regular pilgrimages to the summit of Mt. Ontake.

Fukuzawa Yukichi (1835–1901). One of the leading figures of the "Japanese enlightenment." His highly didactic popularizations in late Tokugawa and early Meiji times introduced the general public to such things as European history, parliamentary democracy, modern science, medicine, and military science. He sailed as an interpreter with the first Japanese ship to cross the Pacific Ocean, founded Keiō University, the first modern Japanese university, and organized the first Tokyo metropolitan police force.

Goban Taiheiki. A one-act historical play, whose title involves a complex play on historical allusions, by the great Chikamatsu Monzaemon (1653–1724). It is his first treatment, one of the more simple and straightforward, of the theme of the forty-seven *rōnin*.

Gohei mochi. A traditional food of the Kiso region consisting of pounded cooked glutenous rice formed into small balls and strung on skewers to be roasted over a fire and served with a sauce made of soy and walnuts.

Goma (from the Sanskrit *homa*). A ritual of the Shingon sect of Buddhism in which an altar is set up before an image of Fudō or Aizen. Strips of wood, usually sumac, are stacked on it to form a hollow square and then burned as an act of purification.

Habu Genseki (1768–1854). A physician from Aki province who specialized in disorders of the eye. He studied with various masters and consulted with Siebold when the latter visited Edo in 1829. Genseki developed many surgical techniques including cataract surgery and became a personal physician to the shōgun. He later fell under suspicion because of his association with Siebold and spent the final years of his life under house arrest.

Hachiya Kōzō (Hazama Hidenori, 1822–1876). The son and heir of a family of sake brewers in Nakatsugawa and a student of Miyagawa Kansai. He served as village elder and in the national government before withdrawing from public life.

Haikai. *See* Poetry.

Haiku. *See* Poetry.

Han. Areas controlled by the daimyō and held at the pleasure, the assignment, or the acquiescence of the shōgun. The money economy of the Muromachi shogunate was abandoned under the Tokugawa so the revenues of the *han* were calculated in *koku* of rice, even though the money economy had by then come into full maturity. There were some three hundred *han*, the areas of which in some cases coincided with an ancient province but in most cases did not, and they often included noncontiguous areas. They were classified as collateral, vassal, or allied according to the status of their daimyō and were ranked according to their relationship to the Tokugawa and total revenues.

Headman *(shōya)*. The senior resident of a village, responsible for transmitting the orders of higher authority to the villagers, for day-to-day administration of the village, and for sending taxes, laborers, and special levies up to the higher authorities. From antiquity through the middle ages, the *shōya* was the resident manager of the estate of an absentee aristocrat or temple. Under the Tokugawa, the lord of a domain would appoint a *shōya* from among the senior families of a village and place him and his heirs in charge of a village or a township, but the title still carried overtones of its original dignity. The title of *shōya* had been held by the Aoyama family since the early seventeenth century. After the restoration the title of the Aoyama family was changed to *kochō,* here translated as "manager," a word of similar operational import but with humiliating resonances of subordinate status.

High antiquity *(kami tsu yo)*. That part of Japanese tradition from the origin myths down to the coming of the heavenly grandson to the Japanese islands. From this point on the accounts in both the *Kojiki* and the *Nihongi* begin gradually to shade into an earthly record that in turn shades into actual history. The literal sense of a "higher" or "superior" age was accepted at face value by the National Learning movement, forming the cornerstone of their beliefs.

Hikone. A vassal *han* with nominal revenues of 350,000 *koku* located on the south shore of Lake Biwa, where it commanded the eastern approaches to Kyoto. The daimyō were the Ii, descendants of one of Tokugawa Ieyasu's most valued retainers and hereditary holders of high shogunal office. Ii Naosuke was daimyō of Hikone.

Hirata Atsutane (1776–1843). The last of the four great leaders of the National Learning movement. Born in Akita *han* as the fourth son of a middle-ranking samurai, he began the study of Chinese classics in the *han* Confucian academy and also took up the study of medicine with his uncle. He later went to Edo, where he was adopted as the heir of an instructor in the martial arts, one Hirata Tōbei Atsuyasu of Matsuyama *han* in Kyushu. At the age of twenty-seven Atsutane began to make himself known as an exponent of the teachings of Motoori Norinaga, acquiring a following among the less-favored members of Edo society and gradually attracting the attention of nonmilitary rural people of influence. Hirata became a formal disciple of Norinaga's school shortly after the master's death and claimed thereafter to be Norinaga's intellectual heir, a claim that was vigorously disputed by Norinaga's descendants.

Like Norinaga, Atsutane proclaimed the supremacy of the emotions and decried the dead, procedure-and-precedent-bound legalism he saw as characterizing the Confucianism practiced in Japan. He maintained that this doctrine was not simply un-Japanese but so completely contrary to human nature that it could lead only to corruption and hypocrisy. Chief among the perversions of Japanese life and society that he attributed to this "Chinese-mindedness" was the dominance of the military leadership and its arrogation to itself of the powers and prerogatives which properly belonged to the emperor. The Hirata school of National Learning which he founded was, along with the Mito school, responsible for setting the intellectual tone of the late Tokugawa and early Meiji periods, and it was the major single source of the ideology of the restoration movement.

Hirata Kanetane (1799–1880). The adopted son and heir of Atsutane, Kanetane built the Hirata school into a potent ideological and political force during the closing years of the Tokugawa shogunate. He claimed no disciples for himself but enrolled all new members as posthumous disciples of Atsutane. Kanetane played a key role in the definition of the institutional framework and the ideological stance of the new Meiji government, but his health was already failing by the time of the restoration and he relinquished control of the school to his son Nobutane, who died shortly thereafter. The influence of the Hirata school subsequently went into rapid decline.

Hirata Nobutane. *See* Hirata Kanetane.

The History of Great Japan *(Dai Nihonshi).* A work begun at the order of Tokugawa Mitsukuni of Mito in 1657 and completed in three hundred fascicles in 1907. It was written in classical Chinese and the first project director was a Chinese scholar who had fled the fall of the Ming dynasty. Its purpose was to create a monument of Tokugawa family piety in the form of a history of Japan, rigorously Confucian in its reading of history, that could stand alongside the great series of Chinese dynastic histories. However, it soon became inescapably clear that a strict Confucian reading of history afforded no place for the Tokugawa family office of shōgun. Arguments about how to deal with this problem soon left the theoretical field to produce fierce factional strife in Mito as Mitsukuni's project of family glorification initiated a chain of ironies that eventually made this Tokugawa bastion one of the most important centers of anti-shogunal activity.

Hitotsubashi. A branch of the senior line of the Tokugawa family that was founded in 1740 by Munetada, the fourth son of the shōgun Yoshimune. It was a potent force in shogunal politics in the final years of Tokugawa rule.

Hitotsubashi Yoshinobu (1837–1913). The fifteenth and last Tokugawa shōgun. A son of Tokugawa Nariaki of Mito, he inherited much of the controversy that surrounded his father in spite of being adopted into the Hitotsubashi family. Yoshinobu was one of the most capable men that the Tokugawa line had produced in a long time. He was also extremely popular, which ensured him many bitter enemies in the crumbling shogunate. He is due much of the credit for minimizing the disorder and bloodshed that accompanied the restoration of 1868, a fact that earned him further resentment among firebrands on both sides. Yoshinobu, whose name is sometimes read "Keiki" in Western sources, lived out the latter part of his life in relative obscurity.

Hokurikudō. One of the eight administrative circuits established under the administrative reforms of the seventh and eighth centuries. The highway that served this circuit branched off to the north just east of Lake Biwa and passed through the seven provinces of Wakasa, Echizen, Kaga, Noto, Etchū, Echigo, and Sado along the coast of the Japan Sea.

Honjin. "Keeper of the posthouse" would closely approximate some of the usages of this term. It applied first to the building which lodged important and high-ranking official travelers, then to the office responsible for that stretch of road, and finally to the official responsible for these charges. The literal meaning is "field headquarters," a reflection of the military origins of the function. The *honjin* building was distinguished from the common inns in villages along the great highways by its impressive gate, its spacious entry, its special rooms and facilities for entertaining high-ranking guests, and its grand scale.

Household titles. It was customary for each commoner household with any claim to dignity and influence to adopt a household title which would always end in "-ya," meaning "household." This title is distinct from the surname which a family might or might not also possess. Families in trade or business would customarily use the household title in their public dealings, e.g. the Fushimiya and the Masudaya, but a household title might also be applied to a purely private and ephemeral establishment such as the Shizunoya in which Hanzō spends his final years.

Ii Kamon no Kami. *See* Ii Naosuke.

Ii Naosuke (1815–1860). Lord of the vassal *han* of Hikone and one of the most powerful and ambiguous figures of the late Tokugawa period. At the end of his life he held the post of *tairō*. His policies led to the checkmating of Tokugawa Nariaki and he was assassinated by samurai from Mito and Satsuma who resented his treatment of Nariaki and his negotiations with foreigners. His way of dealing with the Perry expedition remains controversial down to the present, some charging that he betrayed the nation and others that he saved it. The difficulty of the political situation was exacerbated by his ruthlessness toward his political opponents. He had been brought up in seclusion and in his youth he was judged to be too mild and timid for a public career, but an unsuspected turn in the family succession made him daimyō and subject to all the attendant responsibilities. His rigidity is sometimes explained as overcompensation for a retiring personality and a lack of self-confidence.

Ikedaya incident. On July 28, 1884, a group of Chōshū and Tosa activists were surprised in a Kyoto inn by the Shinsengumi. Seven were killed, four wounded, and twenty captured.

Imperial Academy. The Gakushūin, established in the 1860's for the education of members of the court aristocracy and the imperial family. In 1877 the academy followed the imperial court to Tokyo, where it evolved into the present Gakushūin University and its attached institutions.

Inari. A *kami*, son of Susa no O no Mikoto, who in his initial form is the god of foodstuffs and productivity. His cult goes back to the early ninth century and he is one of the most ubiquitous of deities, seen as a protector of harvests by farmers, of commerce by merchants, and of family well-being by all classes. He was often correlated with the Buddhist figure Dakiniten, who is represented in the iconography mounted on a fox, introducing another note into the Inari cult among the general populace where the fox was believed to possess extraordinary supernatural powers.

Inosuke. *See* Satake Inosuke.

Inoue Kaoru (1835–1915). A low-ranking samurai from Chōshū, where he early came under the influence of Yoshida Shōin. He later held various high offices in the Meiji government.

Institute for the Study of Foreign Books. The Bansho Shirabesho, an institution founded by the shogunate in 1855 for the purpose of collecting, studying, and translating important European materials, particularly in the fields of medicine and military science. At that time Dutch was still the only European language at all known in Japan and the founding of this institute marked the granting of official approval to the once-suppressed Dutch Learning. The institute was taken over by

the Meiji government and was eventually merged with several other institutions
to create Tokyo University.

Institute for Military Studies. The Kōbusho, established by the shogunate in 1855
to instruct direct retainers of the Tokugawa in the use of modern firearms and the
lance as well as in swordsmanship and archery. It was first located at the Tsukiji
coastal battery, later moved to Ogawamachi in Kanda, and ultimately absorbed
into the new, French-style military academy in 1866.

Itagaki Taisuke (1837–1919). A forward-looking and highly influential statesman
from Tosa *han* and one of the foremost advocates of popular rights and parliamentary government. Itagaki left the Meiji government in 1873 over the Korean issue.
He later founded the Jiyūtō and spent the rest of his active career working for popular government and attempting to loosen the grip on national life held by
Satsuma and Chōshū after the restoration.

Itō Hirobumi (1841–1909). One of the leading figures of the restoration, Itō came
from a lower samurai family in Chōshū. He opposed the opening of the ports as a
young man, even leading an attack on the British embassy at one point. Among
the many who underwent a radical change of outlook after Chōshū's unsuccessful
attempt to close the Straits of Shimonoseki to foreign vessels, he was one of a small
and select group of future leaders who slipped out of Japan before the restoration
to study in England. Itō rose to be prime minister and was assassinated in the railway station in Harbin, Manchuria in 1909 by a Korean protesting the recent
annexation of Korea by Japan.

Iwakura Tomomi (1825–1883). A court noble who supported the union of court
and military, Iwakura later held high office in the early Meiji government. From
1871 to 1873 he headed the Japanese mission that traveled in Europe and America
to learn as much as possible about world affairs and to attempt to win revisions of
the unequal treaties that the Western powers had forced on Japan.

Iwasaki Nagayo (1807–1879). A native of Kōfu in what is now Yamanashi prefecture, Iwasaki became a disciple of the school of Hirata Atsutane in 1838 while
residing in Edo. His professional specialty was the music of the Nō theatre, particularly flute and drum, but his intense imperialist sympathies drew the wrath of the
shogunate and he was forced to leave Edo. He went first to Suwa and later to Iida,
supporting himself by teaching Nō and classical verse while also giving public lectures on National Learning. In Iida he was associated with Kitahara Inao, Matsuo
Taseko, Hara Mayomi, and other local leaders of the Hirata school, many of
whom he personally recruited. In 1863 he went to Kyoto, where he was
appointed resident scholar by the court noble house of Shirakawa. Later he moved
from Kyoto to Osaka to serve, under the sponsorship of the wealthy merchant
Hirase Kamenosuke, at the Hōkoku and Sumiyoshi shrines and at the end of his
life he was a priest of the Naniwa shrine.

Iwase Higo (1818–1861). Iwase Tadanari, who often went by the titles of Iga no
Kami or Higo no Kami, was one of the outstanding diplomats under the Tokugawa. Of relatively humble origins, his abilities caught the eye of Abe Masahiro,
who took the virtually unprecedented step of elevating Iwase to an office higher
than his father had ever held. His training was grounded in the Chinese classics
but he was said to be the one best informed on foreign matters in the shogunate.
Iwase argued strongly against the irrationality of continuing to enforce the policy
of exclusion in the face of the new conditions that were emerging. He built coastal
defense batteries and warships and gained official support for the study of English.

He is mentioned in the reports of Lord Elgin and in the diaries of Townsend Harris. In 1858 he was stripped of all his offices and transferred to a minor post by Ii Naosuke, whom he had opposed on the question of the shogunal succession, and in the next year he was placed under house arrest. He then passed his time in isolated scholarship until his death two years later.

The Jeweled Basket *(Tamakatsuma)*. A collection of essays by Motoori Norinaga published between 1791 and 1794. A *katsuma* is a tightly woven basket and the conceit is that Norinaga's words have fallen into the basket at random and are likewise to be picked out at random.

The Jeweled Comb *(Tama no Ogushi)*. Commonly referred to by its abbreviated title, but properly the *Genji Monogatari Tama no Ogushi* or *The Jeweled Comb of the Tale of Genji*, a work by Motoori Norinaga published in 1796. An extremely important and influential work of literary criticism, it rescued *Genji* from the esoteric medieval commentaries, bringing it back to life as a work of literature and to recognition as one of the great triumphs of the human spirit.

The Jeweled Sleevecords *(Tamadasuki)*. A work completed by Hirata Atsutane in 1829, after nearly twenty years in the writing, and published three years later. It consists for the most part of a list of the *kami* to be prayed to on each day of the year along with instructions in the way prayers and offerings are to be made in each instance, and also lists the prayers appropriate to all the major shrines and divinities throughout the nation. Here Hirata argues once again that Japan is the land of the *kami,* that the Japanese alone are descended from the *kami,* and that disorder has been sown in the nation through the introduction of Buddhism and Confucianism. He notes, however, that since the time of Oda Nobunaga the leaders of the nation had begun to pay greater respect to the emperor and that under the Tokugawa he was greatly and properly revered. This reading of history was not shared by most of his later disciples.

Atsutane taught that under the Tokugawa system the shōgun was the deputy of the emperor and that the daimyō were deputies of the shōgun. It therefore behooved the people to follow all orders. In the ninth fascicle the work lists the great patrons of National Learning, beginning with Tokugawa Ieyasu, Tokugawa Mitsukuni, and Tokugawa Nariaki, and the line of great scholars in the tradition beginning with Keichū and continuing with Kamo Mabuchi and Motoori Norinaga. Although quite informal, this work was the first to attempt to create an orderly history of National Learning. The first draft of the work consisted of notes taken down from Atsutane's lectures by his disciples and it was the consequent mixture of elegant and colloquial language that caused Atsutane to delay publication until revisions were completed.

Jiyūtō. A political party founded by Itagaki Taisuke in 1881 for the purpose of pursuing a program advocating popular rights and a constitutional, parliamentary government. The party was broken up in 1884 under government pressure but was reconstituted in 1890, after the promulgation of the Meiji constitution, with Itagaki once again at its head. It is the forerunner of the present Liberal Democratic Party.

Jōruri. The music and libretti of the Osaka puppet theatre.

Kada no Azumamaro (1669–1736). One of the major figures in the development of National Learning, Azumamaro was born into a priestly family of the Inari shrine in Fushimi. Coming of age in the late seventeenth century when competing scholarly schools were burgeoning, he turned away from the Inari cult and became convinced that the essence of the Shintō religion lay in the character of the imperial institution. His works were a major influence in the Shintō revival.

Kaempfer, Engelbert (1651–1716). A scholar and physician born in Lemgo, Westphalia. Studies in Germany and Poland led to a degree in medicine but he continued to pursue a broad range of other interests as well. He joined the party of a Dutchman in charge of a Swedish trade mission to Persia which traveled overland by way of Moscow and completed its assignment in Isfahan in 1684. Kaempfer remained in Persia for a time before joining the Dutch East India Company, which sent him first to India, then to Java, and finally to Nagasaki, where he arrived in 1690 to spend slightly more than two years as surgeon to the Dutch factor. His most ambitious work, written in German, was first published in 1717 in English translation as *A History of Japan*. It remains one of the most important reports on Japan by an outsider during the Tokugawa period. Little practical use was made of the information it contained for more than a century, although it had considerable influence on *Gulliver's Travels*.

Kaga. A vassal *han* corresponding to present-day Ishikawa prefecture on the Japan Sea coast of Honshu. With nominal revenues of one million *koku*, it was the wealthiest of all the *han*, but it played little part in the Meiji restoration. The daimyō were the Maeda, who had originally been sent to Kaga by Oda Nobunaga to put an end to nearly half a century of self-rule under the local Buddhist authorities.

Kagami Shikō (1665–1731). The founder of the still-active Mino school of *haikai*, Shikō was born into the Murase family in the village of Kitano in Mino but later took the name of Kagami. As a child he studied for the Buddhist priesthood for a short time. Around 1690 he met Matsuo Bashō, became a late disciple, and was among the small circle of disciples in attendance during the master's final illness. His career after Bashō's death was marked by unrestrained self-promotion and exploitation of his brief association with the master and he was resented by the disciples of longer standing.

Shikō maintained that *haikai* are concerned with the commonplace and that everyday diction is therefore most appropriate in writing them. Although he was a man of learning, his erudition is seldom reflected openly in his verse and its resultant accessibility helped to make his school popular. He left a large amount of verse of his own, extensive writings on the theory and practice of *haikai*, and a school of poetry that enriched the life of people in the countryside for more than two centuries.

Kaishintō. The "Reform Party" founded in 1882 by Ōkuma Shigenobu. In 1896 it changed its name to the Shimpotō, or Progressive Party. Like its rival, the Jiyūtō, it favored parliamentarianism under a constitution but its program was more paternalistic and bureaucratic.

Kakumyō. A colorful and famous Buddhist priest who flourished in the late twelfth and early thirteenth centuries. He was first associated with Taira Kiyomori but after breaking with him he joined Kiso Yoshinaka until the latter's death, after which he retired to the Kiso region. He appears in Japan's great military epic *The Tale of the Heike*.

Kami. Several homonyms, distinguished from each other in Japanese by the use of different Chinese characters:
   1. Divinity in the Shintō religion. Motoori Norinaga said that the *kami* included distant ancestors, tutelary deities, and all persons or phenomena, whether good

or evil, that inspire awe and respect, including, of course, the emperor. Often translated as "god," a rendering that is at least somewhat misleading in most contexts.

2. The governor of a province under the old imperial court system. The rank was already purely honorific by the end of the tenth century. This term is left untranslated and separated from the province name by a space, e.g. "Iwase Higo no Kami."

3. A second honorary court title identifying its holder as the head of a minor court office or bureau. This title is left untranslated and unseparated from the name of the officer in question, e.g. "Tanuma Gembanokami."

Kamo Mabuchi (1697–1769). The son of a Shintō priest from Okabe shrine near Hamamatsu. On the death of his wife he wanted to enter the Buddhist priesthood but his father would not consent. He was then adopted as son-in-law to the *honjin* in Hamamatsu (his first marriage had also been adoptive). At the age of thirty-seven he went to Kyoto to study with Kada no Azumamaro, returned to Hamamatsu briefly following Azumamaro's death and then went on to Edo, where he spent the rest of his life. His studies were focused on the *Man'yōshū* and his commentary, the *Reflections on the Man'yōshū (Man'yōkō)*, was the second most important of the early studies, surpassed only by Keichū's *Commentaries on the Man'yōshū*. Motoori Norinaga was the most distinguished of his many students.

Kansai. Japan west of the barrier of Hakone on the Tōkaidō near Mt. Fuji but commonly referring to the Kyoto-Osaka area and by extension to the imperial court and its supporters.

Kantō. Japan east of the Hakone barrier but commonly referring specifically to Edo and the surrounding area and by extension to the shogunate and its allies.

Katsu Rintarō (Kaishū) (1823–1899). A distinguished shogunal official and student of Dutch writings on naval warfare, Katsu was one of the few former shogunal officials to find an important place in the Meiji government. He was instrumental in saving Edo from destruction in the civil strife of 1868.

Keichū (1640–1701). The son of a substantial Osaka samurai family who is remembered by his priestly name. He entered a Shingon temple in Osaka at the age of eleven and went on to study at the great center on Mt. Koya two years later. After completing his training he served as resident priest in a succession of important temples but became engrossed in study of the *Man'yōshū* and wrote his *Commentaries on the Man'yōshū (Man'yōshūdaishōki)* while living in Edo. He attracted the attention of Tokugawa Mitsukuni but rejected Mitsukuni's offer of official patronage and returned to Osaka to carry out a complete revision of his great work.

Keizō. *See* Asami Keizō.

Keusukii. The model for this British trader may be William Keswick (1835–1912), a pioneer in the Japan trade who came to Yokohama in 1859 as director of the new Jardine Matheson branch.

Kido Takayoshi (Kōin) (1833–1877). A leader of the Meiji restoration from lower samurai background in Chōshū. The direction of his life was set by his studies under Yoshida Shōin.

Kii. A *han* of 555,000 *koku* of nominal revenues corresponding to modern Wakayama prefecture. Kii, Mito, and Owari were the three senior cadet branches of the Tokugawa family, each founded by a son of Ieyasu. When there was a failure of succession in the main Tokugawa line, a new shōgun was to be chosen from one of these three houses. The fourteenth shōgun, Iemochi, was from Kii.

Kimbei. *See* Satake Kimbei.

Kisobushi. One of the most popular of Japanese folk songs, its central reference is to the rafting of logs down the Kiso River. Like most activities of long standing, this practice had taken on a numinous quality and the song is a tissue of allusions to local folk traditions that do not lend themselves to effective translation. The song is sung at Hanzō's wedding.

Kiso no na	The Kiso *na*
Nakanori-san	Log-rafters
Kiso no Ontake-san	Kiso's Mt. Ontake
Nanchara hoi!	*Nanchara hoi!*
Natsu de mo samui	Cold even in summer
Yoi, yoi, yoi!	*Yoi, yoi, yoi!*
Awase na	Lined robes *na*
Nakanori-san	Log-rafters
Awase yaritaya	Lined robes are what you want
Nanchara hoi!	*Nanchara hoi!*
Tabi soete.	And tabi too.
Yoi, yoi, yoi!	*Yoi, yoi, yoi!*

Kiso Road. Properly, the name given to that portion of the Tōsandō, also known as the Nakasendō, which follows the Kiso River. It is often used to refer to the entire highway of which it is the most scenic and famous section. Mentions of the Kiso Road in historical texts go back to A.D. 702.

Kitahara Inao (1825–1881). Eldest son of the headman of Zakōji village in lower Ina county, Shinano province. His father was fond of learning and followed not only Chinese studies, classical Japanese verse, and *haikai*, but also Dutch Learning, where his interest was in European astronomy and geography. He was an accomplished surveyor. Kitahara first studied with his father, later taking an outside tutor in classical Japanese verse. After becoming head of the house he ran a temple school for village children during the agricultural slack season. He became one of Iwasaki Nagayo's first Iida converts to National Learning and in 1859 he was initiated into the Hirata school under Iwasaki's sponsorship, soon becoming the central figure in Hirata activities in his district. It was through him that such people as Matsuo Taseko and Tatematsu Hōsuke were brought into the movement. He organized and oversaw the building of the Koedayama shrine near his home. Unlike his friend and associate Shimazaki Masaki (Aoyama Hanzō), he was successful after the restoration, holding various offices in the governments of the short-lived Ina and Chikuma prefectures.

Kitamura Zuiken (Kurimoto Jō'un, 1822–1897). A shogunal official and diplomat born in Mino province of a family of hereditary physicians to the shogunate. His studies included work at the Shōheikō. He was appointed to the Tokugawa household medical staff but in 1855 was accused of violating a current prohibition of the study of Western medicine. His superior brought the charge against him because he had gone on board the *Kanko Maru*, a ship presented to the shogunate by the Dutch, and the fact that he had done so at the official invitation of the shogunate was no defense. In 1859 he was sent to Hakodate, where he remained for several years, playing a key role in the development of that city and port. In 1863 he returned to Edo to become rector of the Shōheikō. He later rose to hold, in succession, the positions of censor, of commissioner for foreign relations, Hakodate commissioner, and, finally, commissioner of naval affairs. He was sent by the shogunate on a mission to France in 1867, having prepared for such service by exchanging language lessons with Mermette de Cachon when they were both in Hakodate. The restoration took place during his absence and in spite of his success in carrying out his mission in France at a time when the nation was short of qualified people, he was forced to go into retirement and support himself by farming. He later became active in the development of journalism in Japan. As a young man Shimazaki Tōson was for a time tutored in Chinese literature by Kurimoto.

Kiyomoto. A school of singing to samisen accompaniment that arose in the early nineteenth century. It is distinguished by its constant revisions of repertoire in order to stay in the forefront of popular taste and for its high-pitched, ornate, and strongly nasalized vocal line.

Koga Dōan (1788–1857). An influential Confucian scholar attached to the shogunate.

Kojiki. The oldest surviving book in Japanese. Presented to the empress Gemmyō in A.D. 710, the *Kojiki* is a mixture of mythology, folklore, history, and political theory. Because of the extreme difficulty of reading its archaic language transcribed by means of a complex and irregular use of Chinese characters, it had little impact during the first thousand years of its existence, becoming at last an active part of the Japanese intellectual heritage through the work of Motoori Norinaga.

Koku. A dry measure equivalent to 4.99 bushels.

Korean issue. Korea refused to recognize the new Meiji government and a Japanese mission sent to Pusan in 1872 to restore relations was harshly rebuffed, bringing calls in Japan for a punitive action in the style then so popular among the European powers. Saigō Takamori shared this feeling and also saw that a campaign in Korea would provide a safety valve for one of the new government's most pressing problems: growing samurai discontent. He asked to be sent to Korea as minister plenipotentiary, arguing that his almost certain assassination would provide Japan with a *causus belli*. The plan was frustrated by the return of the Iwakura mission from Europe bearing sober news of the true extent of Japan's weakness in the world. The supporters of the scheme, which included many of the leading figures of the Meiji restoration, then left the government.

Kōshin. An observance reflecting a mixture of Taoist, Buddhist, and Shintō beliefs that varied from place to place and even from household to household. It took place on nights when the sexagesimal pairing (*see* Calendar) combined *kō*, the first calendar sign, and *shin*, the dragon, the fifth zodiacal sign. The divinity feted throughout the night was Taishakuten (Shadevanan Indra) in Buddhist households, and Saruta-hiko in Shintō households. The traditional belief was that if one slept during this night the three worms in the body (a Taoist concept) would leave and report one's sins to the king of heaven and one's life would be shortened in consequence.

Kōzō. *See* Hachiya Kōzō.

Kūkai (774–835). Also known by his posthumous title, Kōbō Daishi, Kūkai went to China on the same embassy as Dengyō Daishi and brought back Shingon Buddhism to Japan, founding the major religious center of Mt. Kōya. A man of great intellect and charisma who was among other things the first Japanese priest to know Sanskrit, he is popularly credited with almost every cultural advance that occurred in Japan in his lifetime.

Kume Kunitake (1839–1931). Born in Saga *han* and educated at the Shōheikō, Kume served in the new Meiji government. He was responsible for the report of the Iwakura mission, one of the monuments of official Japan's intellectual exploration of the new world in which it found itself. Later, as a trail-blazing professor of Japanese history at Tokyo Imperial University, he undertook an objective study of the history and function of the imperial institution and was forced to resign as a result.

Kumo no Hyōshi. A dance piece from the *nagauta* tradition of Kabuki music, the formal title of which is *Wagaseko ga koi ga aizuchi.* It was composed by Kineya Sakichi I and first performed in 1781.

Kumosuke. Casual laborers and drifters who performed odd jobs along the great highways and who not infrequently augmented their incomes through robbery and extortion.

Kuni. *See* Province.

Kureta Masaka (Tsunoda Tadayuki, 1834–1918). A Hirata disciple whose father had also been a follower of National Learning, he first studied under Fujita Tōko of Mito and then turned to the Hirata school, which he joined in 1855. At the recommendation of Matsuo Taseko he took refuge in the Ina valley after fleeing Kyoto and associated with influential Hirata people there. At the time of the restoration he joined Hirata Kanetane in appealing to Atsutane's natal *han* of Akita to come to the imperial cause. He rose rapidly in the early Meiji government but was brought down by jealous rivals and was placed under the control of first Yamaguchi and then Wakayama *han*. In 1872 he was freed to become a priest of the Kamo shrines and later of Atsuta shrine. Tsunoda contributed the text of the inscription when a monument to Shimazaki Masaki was placed beside the torii of the Suwa shrine in Magome in 1912. It was in commemoration of the dedication of this monument that Tōson published some of his father's posthumous manuscripts under the title *Matsugae* (Pine Boughs).

Kusunoki Masashige (1294–1336). When the emperor Godaigo rose against the crumbling Kamakura shogunate in an ill-fated attempt to restore political power to the imperial court, Kusunoki was one of his most effective generals. He was a major factor in bringing down the shogunate and was thus a particularly attractive figure to the imperialist party of the nineteenth century. He died at the battle of Minatogawa in a foredoomed attempt to deny entry into Kyoto to Ashikaga Takauji, who was soon to break Godaigo's forces and found a new shogunate. Idealized by the Mito school, Kusunoki remains one of the most admired of all martial heroes.

Maki Izumi (1813–1864). A passionate supporter of the imperial cause from Kurume in Kyushu, he was the son of a Shintō official. An exponent of the doctrine of "revere the emperor, expel the barbarians," he was an activist leader in Kyoto in 1862–1863 and died by his own hand after the defeat of the Chōshū forces in Kyoto in 1864.

Man'yōshū. The earliest surviving anthology of Japanese verse. In it, Japanese first found its voice as a literary language and the finest of its approximately 4,500 poems remain among the best in the entire tradition. Most of the poems date from the first half of the eighth century but some go back considerably earlier.

Matsudaira Shungaku (1828–1890). Also known as Yoshinaga; lord of Fukui *han* in Echizen, commanding nominal revenues of 320,000 *koku*. As the surname Matsudaira shows, he was one of the kindred houses *(shimpan)* of the Tokugawa, just below the three cadet houses of Mito, Kii, and Owari. A powerful figure in politics, he was appointed supreme councillor *(seiji sōsai)* in 1862, promptly instituting a number of reforms, including the suspension of alternate attendance, in an attempt to meet growing criticism of the shogunate but in the end his measures amounted only to a public confession of Tokugawa weakness.

Matsuo Taseko (1825–1894). A leading activist of the Hirata school, the daughter of Takemura Tsunemitsu, who was the paternal uncle of Kitahara Inao, and the aunt of Ichioka Shōzō (the Asami Keizō of the novel). She grew up in the Kitahara home and there she studied with Inao's father. At the age of nineteen she married Matsuo Sajiemon of Tomono village. Taseko studied the composition of classical verse under several masters and was introduced to National Learning by Iwasaki Nagayo, becoming a registered disciple in 1861. She went to Kyoto the next year to take a direct part in the activities of the school, working in close contact with Hirata Kanetane and others. At her death she left a large body of letters documenting her extraordinary life as wife, mother, political activist, and public personality. In 1903 she was posthumously awarded the fifth court rank and was officially recognized as one of the three outstanding women of the Meiji restoration, an honor she shared with Otagaki Rangetsu and the nun Nomura Bōkō.

Matsuzaki Kōdō (1771–1844). A Confucian scholar from the province of Higo in Kyushu who first studied for the Buddhist priesthood in accord with his father's wishes but later entered the Shōheikō. As a peripatetic advisor to various daimyō, his teachings focused on the eminently Confucian "return to antiquity" that was also the rallying cry for anti-shogunal and anti-Confucian activists in the National Learning movement.

Middle councillor *(chūnagon)*. In the imperial governmental structure as set up in the eighth century, this was the second rank in the council of state, an advisory body directly below the ministers of state. By Tokugawa times it was an honorary office reflecting court favor as in the case of Hitotsubashi Yoshinobu. The eighth-century administrative structure was briefly revived in early Meiji.

Mito. A *han* of 350,000 *koku* of nominal revenues corresponding to modern Ibaraki prefecture. It was, along with Owari and Kii, one of the three senior cadet branches of the Tokugawa line. Tokugawa Nariaki was the last important daimyō.

Mito school. A political and intellectual movement that developed in Mito during the Tokugawa period. Its roots lie in the programs of Tokugawa Mitsukuni and its doctrine combined elements of National Learning, Confucianism, and Shintō in developing arguments for Japanese uniqueness and the intensification of national consciousness. An already turbulent situation in Mito was aggravated by the issues raised by Perry. The faction which remained loyal to the then daimyō, Tokugawa Nariaki, advocated fundamental changes in the shogunate and in its relation to the imperial court as well as a policy of total exclusion of foreigners. The opposing faction advocated the outright abolition of the shogunate. This faction rose in rebellion and made an unsuccessful attempt to march overland to Kyoto. The Hirata school was an uneasy ally of the Mito school in the early stages of the restoration movement but the essentially military outlook of the Mito people and their unbending allegiance to Confucian orthodoxy put the partnership under constant strain. With the annihilation of the Mito *rōnin* the school ceased to be a major factor in the intellectual and ideological life of the Meiji restoration although some elements of Mito thought surfaced again later.

Mitsukuri Gempo (1799–1863). Born into a family of old-style physicians in the hereditary service of Tsuyama shrine, Gempo went to Kyoto at the age of seventeen to learn Chinese medicine. He also studied Confucianism under Kōga Dōan and Dutch medicine under Utagawa Hōsai. Upon his return home he became chief physician for Tsuyama *han*. At the age of forty-one he was made a member of the shogunal board of astronomy and later traveled to Nagasaki, where he met with a Russian emissary. He played a role in the negotiations leading up to the 1858 Treaty of Friendship with the United States and in 1862 he became a direct vassal of the Tokugawa, the first time that a Dutch-style physician had been so honored.

Miyagawa Kansai (Majima Seian, 1811–1868). A learned Nakatsugawa physician with a fine classical education who specialized in disorders of the eye. He tutored Hanzō and his friends and introduced them to the Hirata school of National Learning.

Modorikago (The Return Litter). A dance piece with a long and complex performing tradition that was composed by Tobaya Richō and first performed in 1788.

Mon. *See* Coinage and money.

Mono no aware. Beauty perceived, experienced, and celebrated as the highest value in a context of impermanence that assures that even the greatest joys are always tinged with sadness. It is one of the guiding perceptions of classical Japanese culture. Motoori Norinaga pointed out that it is the central theme of *The Tale of Genji,* the great eleventh-century novel that is the finest product of that culture and the greatest masterpiece of Japanese literature. Such insights had not been possible under the burden of esoteric medieval commentary and exegesis from which Norinaga and his colleagues rescued the classics of Japanese literature.

Motoori Norinaga (1730–1801). The preeminent figure of the National Learning movement. Norinaga was born into a commoner family in the town of Matsuzaka in Ise province and as a young man studied in Kyoto with Hori Keizan, a specialist in the official, Chu Hsi school of Confucianism. Keizan was also a student of the *Man'yōshū* and it seems to have been this side of his teacher's interests that made the strongest impression on Norinaga. In accord with the wishes of his mother, he next turned to the study of pediatrics under the physician, Takegawa Kōjun. At the age of twenty-seven, he discovered the works of Keichū and from that time on his interests focused on the Japanese classics. Upon returning to Matsuzaka he briefly went into medical practice while pursuing his literary and philological interests through study of the works of Kamo Mabuchi. Norinaga left behind an immense body of works in the fields of philology, literary criticism, philosophy, and religion. He was the individual most responsible for the Shintō revival of the eighteenth century and for the application of new advances in philology recently imported from China to the study of classical Japanese literature. Through his work this literature once again became a fully functional part of the furnishings of every educated mind. Norinaga taught his contemporaries to read literature as literature rather than the body of esoterica that the medieval commentators had made of it. It is difficult to single out any one of his major works as most important, but his *Commentaries on the Kojiki (Kojikiden),* which occupied him for thirty-five years, was his most monumental achievement and the foundation on which all subsequent studies of this text stand.

Nakae Chōmin (1847–1901). One of the foremost libertarian thinkers of the Meiji period, Chōmin was born in Kochi, the capital of Tosa. While studying Dutch in Nagasaki, he also studied French on the side and at only twenty years of age served as interpreter to the French ambassador Léon Roches during the opening of the port of Hyōgo. Later he was closely associated with Itagaki Taisuke and the Jiyū-tō. Among his many translations from European languages was the extremely influential 1882 rendering of Rousseau's *Du Contrat Social.*

Nakagawa no Miya (1824–1891). Also known as Asahiko Shinnō; the fourth son of the imperial prince Fushimi no Miya Kuniie and founder of the Kuni no Miya line. In his youth he was deeply involved in Buddhist studies. Later, after being adopted by the emperor Ninkō (r. 1818–1848), he took up residence in the Shoren'in academy as a high ecclesiastic and later became an abbot in the Tendai sect. Upon the death of Ninkō and the accession of Kōmyō, he became involved in court and national affairs. His opposition to all foreign contacts was influential in establishing the negative stance of the court toward the Treaty of Kanagawa.

Naniwa bushi. A popular entertainment, originating in the Osaka region, in which a solo chanter accompanies himself on the samisen while reciting military, popular, or religious tales that have been recast as light entertainment.

National Learning *(kokugaku).* An intellectual movement that arose in the Tokugawa period, the major figures of which were Keichū, Kada no Azumamaro, Kamo Mabuchi, Motoori Norinaga, and Hirata Atsutane. It strove to recover through philogical study and religious speculation the presumably pristine character of early Japan. Studies by its members of the basic texts of classical Japanese civilization laid the foundations for much of modern scholarship. It was the goal of the movement to purge Japan of "Chinese-mindedness," which they perceived as an aberration in the national character that was to be replaced by the spontaneity, sincerity, and natural goodness believed to be characteristic of Japanese life at its beginnings. The movement originated and had its main strength among townsmen and nonmilitary provincial elites, and it regarded the dominance of the military under the successive shogunates as one of the most deplorable legacies of "Chinese-mindedness."

Its total rejection of the Japanese middle ages shaped much of Japanese social, political, and diplomatic thought during the middle years of the nineteenth century. In spite of its effort to revive the Shintō religion as an entity independent of Buddhism and its intense hostility toward "Chinese-mindedness," the movement derived in large part from the transplanting of certain Chinese scholarly techniques and habits of mind into a Japanese context. It was the National Scholars and, to a certain extent, the Mito school who alone advocated the typically Chinese, and notably un-Japanese, response to foreign pressures: that of looking more deeply into the national past and its classical texts. Even though it failed to find the kind of Japanese past it was looking for, both Japan and the world stand deeply in its debt for its recovery of the masterpieces of early Japanese civilization.

For all their disavowal of Confucianism the National Scholars were among the most exemplary of Confucians in many of their family and social postures and in their view of the nature of history. In the end National Learning was a political failure, perhaps as much because of the failure of the succession of the Hirata line as for its seemingly limited relevance to the most urgent problems of the time, but the benefits, and some of the more ambiguous qualities, of its legacy remain. Tōson emphasizes those qualities of National Learning that are most likely to be appealing both to modern Japanese audiences and to the world beyond. He wrote of them at a time when a revisionist view of National Learning that emphasized its darkest and most obscurantist qualities was being officially promulgated. He makes his point quietly, with the "headman's tact" that in the 1930's had once again become necessary when saying anything that reflected upon national policy, but he makes it powerfully nevertheless.

Nihongi *(Nihonshoki).* A history completed and presented to the emperor Genshō in A.D. 720. Among its compilers were many who had worked on the *Kojiki* and who were dissatisfied with the diffuse and elliptical qualities of its style and the near impossibility of reading the work that manifested itself almost as soon as it had been written. The *Nihongi* is in classical Chinese and it attempted to be systematic, scholarly, and critical in its use of sources. For the next millenium it was not only the standard source on early Japanese history but almost the only one available. The point of departure for both the *Nihongi* and the *Kojiki* was the rationalization of the existing social and political order but it was the *Nihongi* that was most effective in spite of its even heavier admixture of Chinese references and borrowings.

Nikkō. The site of the mausolea of Tokugawa Ieyasu and his successors, located in present day Gumma prefecture. In Nikkō, Ieyasu was enshrined as a Shintō *kami* and each year a service was held in his honor. A special emissary known as the *reiheishi* was sent from the imperial court in Kyoto to present a consecrated paper tassel, ostensibly as a religious gesture, but in fact as a recognition of Tokugawa hegemony. Along their established route the Nikkō emissaries built up a reputation for corruption, extortion, and lawlessness as impoverished court nobles and their hangers-on used the occasion to become temporarily wealthy.

Ōgimachi Kintada (died 1879). A court noble adopted from a branch house of the Saionji, itself one of the major branches of the Northern Fujiwara. Kintada served the shogunate in the punitive expedition against Chōshū and later attained the rank of brigadier general in the new army under the Meiji government.

Ōkubo Ichiō (1817–1888). A member of a family of hereditary direct vassals to the Tokugawa, Ōkubo held various posts including the directorship of the Institute for the Study of Foreign Books. He served under five shoguns and was an early advocate of fundamental reforms in the shogunate, including some form of parliamentary body. He later held office in the Meiji government.

Ōkubo Toshimichi (1830–1878). A statesman from Satsuma of lower samurai origin and a childhood acquaintance of Saigō Takamori. He was primarily responsible for the formal return of power to the emperor by the shōgun and for the later elimination of the *han,* the two key moves in the dismantling of the feudal order. After the restoration he soon emerged as the most powerful man in the government, serving as prime minister during the Satsuma rebellion led by Saigō. Shortly after its suppression he was assassinated by surviving partisans who accused him of treason to his old friends and to his old domain. Often called, with some justice, "the Bismarck of Japan."

Onamuchi no Kami. Another name of Ōkuninushi no Mikoto, the primary divinity of Izumo shrine. According to some accounts he is the son of Susa no O no Mikoto and according to others a descendant in the seventh generation. He was aided by Sukunabiko no Kami in bringing the nation into order and he taught the ways of divining and medicine. Later he retired, leaving the nation to Ninigi no Mikoto.

Owari. A *han* possessing 616,000 *koku* of nominal revenues corresponding roughly to modern Aichi prefecture. Along with Mito and Kii, it was one of the three senior cadet branches of the Tokugawa. The largest, wealthiest, and most stable of the three cadet houses, Owari controlled the Kiso district as a noncontiguous portion of its domains. The Aoyama family and the station of Magome served under Owari for control of the forests, under the Yamamura of Fukushima in all matters of routine administration, and under the transport commisioners of the shogunate in Edo for all matters pertaining to the maintenance and facilitation of traffic along the highway.

Pickle market *(bettara-ichi).* A fair held in Temma-chō, Edo, on the nineteenth day of the tenth month. It seems originally to have been held for the purpose of selling the items used in the Ebisu rites, but it evolved into a fair that specialized in selling various vegetables that had been processed in fermented rice bran. The name comes from the mucky *(bettara)* bran mixture with which the pickles were covered. The vendors would cry out, "Oh, mucky, mucky! If you pass without buying, you'll get it all over your clothes!" Those in festive attire were favored targets of this approach.

The Pillar of the Soul *(Tama no Mihashira)*. A work by Hirata Atsutane published in 1805. In it Atsutane attempts to systematize the methodology of National Learning and clarify its purposes as well as to reconcile the cosmological traditions of the ancient texts with contemporary scientific knowledge, including that of Europe.

Poetry. Four poetic traditions are represented in *Before the Dawn:*

1. The classical *waka* or *tanka,* a thirty-one syllable verse in the form 5-7-5,7-7. This most widely practiced of Japanese forms was regularized in the eighth century and is still being written today, often using tenth-century diction.

2. The *chōka* or long poem, the most important examples of which come from the *Man'yōshū.* The form is of indeterminate length; the meter is 5-7, 5-7, . . . 5-7-7. Hanzō's poem on the occasion of the imperial progress through Magome is a *chōka.* His impassioned but awkward poem on the subject of the buying up of Japanese gold is a departure from strict classical form and diction reflecting the style of the Mito school.

3. *Haikai* or light linked verse; light in the sense that it did not observe the strictures of classical diction and decorum. These verses were an important part of popular culture from the late seventeenth century through the early twentieth centuries. The Mino school of *haikai* practiced in Magome was in the tradition of Kagami Shikō.

4. Chinese verse or *kanshi,* a category which includes all verse written in Chinese whether in China or Japan. Up to the Meiji period Chinese was the learned language and the language in which all basic literacy training was given, much as the equivalent training in Europe of that time was in Latin or Greek. Chinese verse was not read aloud in Chinese, a language that few Japanese of the time had ever heard, but in a standardized system of parsing into Japanese in which the original rhyme schemes and tonal harmonies were lost. Hanzō writes no verse in Chinese but his Chinese prose is quite competent.

Province *(kuni)*. One of the thirty-six administrative areas into which the nation was divided under the eighth-century reforms. A *han* was usually smaller than a province, occasionally larger, often including parts of more than one province as well as noncontiguous areas. The post-restoration system of prefectures does not consistently follow the boundaries of the ancient provinces but Shinano province, of which the Kiso district forms the southwestern corner, has remained intact as present day Nagano prefecture.

Rai San'yō (1780–1832). One of the most popular and influential Confucian scholars of the early nineteenth century, Rai was born in Edo and published his first work at the age of eleven. He was a passionate student of history but he also left a considerable body of Chinese poetry on historical themes. His highly influential *Unofficial History of Japan (Nihongaishi)* was one of the most powerful statements of the imperial cause.

Rinnōji. The name of two sister temples of the Tendai sect, one in Edo and the other at Nikkō. They were the Buddhist temples associated with the Shintō institutions constituting the Tokugawa mausolea at Nikkō and throughout the Tokugawa period they were headed by an imperial prince who carried the title of Prince Rinnōji.

Rōjū. The literal significance is "council of elders," but since this English expression is regularly used to translate the names of analagous bodies in earlier shogunates and at other administrative levels under the Tokugawa, the term is often left untranslated. It consisted of a council of four or five senior vassal daimyō who decided most issues of policy concerning the court, the daimyō, and other matters of national import. In normal times the *rōjū* served one at a time in monthly rotation, the *rōjū* on duty at any given time being in effect the highest authority in all but the most extraordinary matters. Appointments were for life. In times of crisis a *tairō* or "great elder" would be appointed to serve as a kind of shogunal prime minister.

Rōnin. Masterless samurai. A samurai might become masterless in one of three ways: (1) the extinction of his lord's family, (2) being released from service by his lord, and (3) renunciation of his vows of loyalty. This latter was very frequent among the anti-shogunal activists, who were thereby able to put aside the constraints imposed by service to their lords or by old *han* rivalries while acting in what they perceived as the national interest. The daimyō were often quite amenable to this because it isolated them from any short-term trouble their former retainers might get into while still in many cases giving them at least a source of knowledge and sometimes an indirect voice in the activities of anti-shogunal groups. In Mito the entire imperialist party became *rōnin* when they rebelled against the policies of those who were acting in the name of the daimyō. There was thus no one to whom they could appeal when Tanuma Gembanokami, commander of the shogunal forces, chose to turn on them without mercy once they were disarmed and helpless.

Ryō. *See* Coinage and money.

Saigō Takamori (1827–1877). A man of lower samurai origins from Satsuma who caught the eye of his daimyō, Shimazu Nariakira, and became influential first in *han* politics and later in the national movement against the shogunate. He played an important role in bringing Satsuma and Chōshū into alliance in spite of a long tradition of mutual suspicion and hostility. He and Ōkubo Toshimichi were also in large part responsible for persuading Shimazu Hisamitsu to come out into open opposition to the shogunate. Saigō was the major figure in the military phase of the restoration and one of its most popular heroes. A big, bulky man of imposing presence, he inspired deep respect even among those who opposed him politically. He left the government over the Korean issue and returned to Kagoshima, where he formed a number of private schools to train local samurai. When his followers opened hostilities against the central government, Saigō first scolded them but then reluctantly took command of the rebel forces in the Satsuma rebellion of 1877. He died at Shiroyama near the city of Kagoshima as the last of his forces were being overrun. He is rivaled in popularity among military heroes only by Kusunoki Masashige.

Sakuma Shōzan (1811–1864). A supporter of the imperial cause who hailed from Matsushiro in Shinano province. As one of the teachers of Yoshida Shōin, he was jailed when Shōin was caught trying to stow away on one of Perry's ships. After many years of confinement he was ordered by the shogunate to go to Kyoto, where he was promptly assassinated by an anti-foreign extremist. While his abrasive personal qualities helped to put him in danger, he had originally aroused the ire of the shogunate by his passionate arguments for the urgency of strengthening coastal defenses against foreign threats at a time when officials were not willing to hear of such things.

Satake Inosuke (Ōwaki Nobutsune, 1834–1879). The adopted heir of Satake Kimbei and the closest friend of Aoyama Hanzō in his later years.

Satake Kimbei (Ōwaki Nobuoki, died 1870). A village elder, sake brewer, and moneylender, Kimbei was the wealthiest man in Magome and one of the wealthiest in the immediate area. The right to wear swords and bear a surname was conferred on the Ōwaki, masters of the Daikokuya and models for the Satake family, as early as 1786.

Satake Senjūrō. The first adopted heir of Satake Kimbei.

Satake Tsurumatsu (Ōwaki Nobumichi, 1843–1859). Son of Satake Kimbei.

Satō Nobuhiro (1765–1850). An important thinker in the field of agrarian economics. Satō came from a family of physicians and both his father and grandfather had been interested in agriculture and mining. He studied at an academy of Dutch Learning in Edo and there he acquired the awareness of the world beyond Japan that characterized his later works and set them apart from those of most of his contemporaries in his chosen field. In his mature years, he was among the most distinguished of the many traveling consultants who served both the shogunate and the *han* administrations. His writings cover a broad field, ranging from mining and agrarian economics to philosophy, administrative reform, national defence, and military science.

Satsuma. An allied *han* of 770,000 *koku* nominal revenues located at the southern tip of Kyushu. The daimyō were the Shimazu, longest in control of their domains of any of the feudal lords, tracing their lineage back to the thirteenth century. Satsuma had a long record of standing up against central authority and a reputation for a particularly fierce strain of the warrior tradition. It enjoyed shogunal favor in spite of its outside status; the eleventh shōgun, Ienari, was married to a daughter of Shimazu Shigehide, predecessor and father of Shimazu Nariakira. Internal politics and national developments gradually brought Satsuma into sharing with Chōshū the leadership of the opposition to the shogunate, and the two domains largely controlled national politics during the early years of Meiji. Until the end of World War II, people with Satsuma connections dominated the navy while people from Chōshū were predominant in the army.

Satsuma rebellion. The last and greatest of the samurai rebellions against the Meiji government. After Saigō Takamori returned to Kagoshima following his resignation from the government over the Korean issue, the government became concerned about its arsenals in Kagoshima. Kirino Toshiaki, one of Saigō's followers, learned of plans to move the arsenals and decided on his own to take them over with the help of fellow members of Saigō's "private schools" while Saigō was away on a hunting vacation. The rebellion went on for ten months in 1877 and the Meiji government was able to put it down only by committing all its resources; it even sent members of the new Tokyo police force to fight alongside the untested conscript army.

Sekigahara. A site along the Tōsandō at the extreme western edge of Mino province where, in the ninth month of 1600, Tokugawa Ieyasu won the battle that established the hegemony of his family. This victory led directly to the establishment of the Tokugawa shogunate in 1603.

Sensei. Literally, "(one who was) born before (me)": a term of respect used to address a teacher or a professional colleague. Two other titles of respect, *shishō sama,* which is used in a slightly more restricted set of contexts and implies a greater degree of deference, and *ushi,* an archaic term used to refer to the great leaders of the National Learning movement, are both rendered as "master" in this translation.

Seppuku. Self-disembowelment, an act generally referred to outside Japan by the vulgarism "hara kiri." A samurai would perform *seppuku* to register a protest, to make a point of honor, to atone for an error or a humiliation, to avoid being taken alive by the enemy, or when ordered to do so as punishment for an offense; samurai were not subject to execution unless the offense was deemed so extreme as to render the culprit already *declassé.* Young men were instructed in the technique and, when conditions permitted, the act was the climax of a solemn ceremony. The man to die would dress himself in white, write a death verse, and then perform the act before witnesses. In most cases there would be a second in attendance who would strike off the principal's head as soon as he had cut himself open. Women did not normally perform *seppuku.* When circumstances required them to kill themselves they would usually cut their throats with a dagger, typically an heirloom kept at hand against this eventuality.

Shiki Sambasō. A dance piece adapted from the *sambasō,* or "third old man" section of the Nō play *Ōkina.* It comes from the repertoire of the Tokiwazu musicians, a school of samisen music, song, and dance with strong roots in Nagoya. The piece now known by this name is a later reworking of one composed in the 1840's. It is difficult to say whether the piece performed in Magome in 1854 was the older or newer version since the changes seem to have been made around that time.

Shimazu Hisamitsu (1817–1887). The younger brother of Shimazu Nariakira. His son, Tadayoshi, was made daimyō upon Nariakira's death and since Tadayoshi was a minor, his first year in office was under the regency of Nariakira's retired predecessor, Narioki. When Narioki died in 1860, Hisamitsu took over the regency and continued to act as de facto daimyō until the abolition of the *han* after the restoration.

Shimazu Nariakira (1809–1858). Daimyō of Satsuma and one of the most vigorous and forward-looking of the outside lords, he was beginning to play an important role in national politics before his untimely death. His lively intellect and wide-ranging interests are hinted at by the fact that he took one of the earliest known Japanese photographs. Nariakira was succeeded by Tadayoshi, the son of Hisamitsu, his younger brother. He is now perhaps most remembered as the man under whose patronage the rise of Saigō Takamori began.

Shimosone Kinzaburō (dates unknown). An artillery specialist active in the middle third of the nineteenth century. He commanded a detachment of guards at the time of Perry's first visit and in 1867 became a professor in the new military academy that replaced the Institute for Military Studies.

Shinsengumi. The "Newly Selected Band," a group led by Kondō Isamu that was sent to Kyoto by the shogunate to combat terrorist actions being carried out by supporters of the imperial court in Kyoto. The character of the band and of the problems it both faced and created has been an inexhaustible source of novels, plays, and motion pictures.

Shintō. A set of religious beliefs of Japanese origin. After the introduction of Buddhism in the mid-sixth century, the name was coined from Chinese elements to distinguish native beliefs from the imported religion. Shintō reflects long-standing official and unofficial efforts to regularize and systematize local folk beliefs so that they could compete effectively with Buddhism. Its roots are in Japanese folk reli-

gion and it overlaps with folk religion but much of folk religion does not readily
fit into the framework of the Shintō religion as defined by scholars and officials.
For centuries Shintō was dominated by syncretic sects such as Dual Shintō that
borrowed from or even subordinated Shintō to Buddhist, Taoist, Confucian, or
Yin-yang beliefs. Since the early nineteenth century many nonofficial sects of
Shintō have arisen, some of which suffered persecution.

Shintō burial ceremonies. As part of the Tokugawa suppression of Christianity, all
funerals except those of Shintō officials had to be conducted according to Buddhist
practice. This accorded with, and reinforced, a tendency to assign questions of origin and local tradition to Shintō, problems connected with living in society to
Confucianism, and those connected with death and the hereafter to Buddhism. In
the mid-ninteenth century those connected with the Shintō revival began to advocate a restoration of Shintō burial ceremonies. The leading figure in this movement was Kurasawa Yoshiyuki (or, as some authorities maintain, Yoshitaka) of
Ono village in Upper Ina county, Shinano province.

Shionoya Toin (1809–1867). A native of Edo and an outstanding Confucian scholar
who entered the Shōheikō at the age of fifteen, became an advisor to the daimyō of
Echizen, and later to the shogunate. He was often called "the Japanese Ou-yang
Hsiu" because of his rejection of the Sung Confucianism officially advocated by
the Tokugawa in favor of a concentration on Han and T'ang texts.

Shiraishi Banashi (The Shiraishi Story). A play on the theme of vendetta written by
the team of Ki no Jōtarō, Yōyō Tai, and Utei Emba, and first performed in 1780
under its full title, *Go Taiheiki Shiraishi Banashi.* It is said to be based on events that
actually took place in the village of Shiraishi, north of Edo. In 1716 a farmer was
killed by a master swordsman and, since he had no sons to avenge him, the vendetta was taken up by his daughters. They avenged their father's death by killing
his murderer in 1718 after stalking him through two years of the greatest hardships and difficulties. In the play the two girls are seven and nine years of age when
they complete their mission.

Shirakawa. A court noble family descended from Prince Naganobu, son of Prince
Kiyohito, grandson of the emperor Kazan. They were in hereditary charge of
Shintō functions at court and of liaison between the court and Shintō institutions
throughout the country.

Shiso *(perilla nankinensis).* A pungent herb somewhat resembling basil but much more
assertive. It has no English name although it is sometimes listed on food packages
as "beefsteak plant." A red-leaved variety is used primarily for seasoning pickled
vegetables and plums and a green-leaved variety is most often used with seafoods.

Shōgun. A title originally belonging to the highest-ranking military office under the
old imperial court system that was bestowed upon Minamoto Yoritomo when the
military achieved dominance in the twelfth century. Since Yoritomo, the new
leader of the military government, was then the most powerful man in the nation,
the shogunate became the most powerful office. Yoritomo established the Kamakura shogunate, giving the nation what was in effect its first uniform national
government. The Kamakura shogunate fell in 1333, to be succeeded by the Muromachi shogunate founded by Ashikaga Takauji. During this period the power,
influence, and physical well-being of the imperial court reached its nadir.

Following the long decline of the Muromachi shogunate, the nation was gradually reunited under Ōda Nobunaga and his successor, Toyotomi Hideyoshi, neither
of whom succeeded in founding a shogunal line. Both Nobunaga and Hideyoshi
accorded the court new deference and military support, hoping to gain court

acquiescence, if not actual support, for their ambitions in order to compensate for the liability of their obscure origins. This policy was continued by the new Tokugawa shogunate, but, as the mid-nineteenth century followers of National Learning pointed out, with growing outrage, the court still had no real power under the Tokugawa, who for all their outward deference routinely employed pressure and intimidation in their dealings with the court. The coming of Perry and subsequent events demonstrated uncertainty and confusion on the part of the outside world about the institutions and responsibilities of emperor and shōgun and only added to the growing difficulty of glossing over the inherent conflicts of interest between the two.

Shōheikō. The Confucian academy created and supported by the shogunate. Its beginnings were in an institution founded in 1630 by Hayashi Razan, Ieyasu's Confucian advisor. In 1690 Tsunayoshi, the fifth shōgun, moved the establishment to its permanent site, changed its name, and placed it under the rectorship of a descendant of Razan. The Hayashi family continued to hold the rectorship down to the restoration. The Shōheikō fulfilled some of the functions of a national university, and it was one of the most important of the forerunners of Tokyo University.

Shōkōkan (Hall of Clear Thought). The research institution founded by Tokugawa Mitsukuni of Mito for the purpose of compiling *The History of Great Japan.*

Shō'un (Torin, dates unknown). The Zen priest of the Mampukuji (Eishōji), the village temple of Magome, founded at the end of the sixteenth century.

Shu. *See* Coinage and money.

Siebold, Phillip Franz von (1796–1866). A Dutch physician who became interested in Oriental studies at an early age, Siebold joined the Dutch East India Company in 1822. He was assigned to the study of Dutch-Japanese relations and reached Nagasaki in the next year. There he obtained the permission of the Nagasaki commissioner to treat townspeople and to open an academy of science and medicine at Narutaki, just outside the city. In 1826 he accompanied the Dutch factor on an obligatory visit to Edo and attracted much attention among daimyō and scholars interested in Dutch Learning. Later that same year he was on the verge of sailing home from Nagasaki when he was placed under house arrest and charged with possession of unauthorized maps and other materials. He was expelled the next year and many of those who had associated with him were arrested and subjected to punishment. He spent the next thirty years in Leiden, where he published several books on Japan. In 1859 he went back to Edo to serve as special advisor to the shogunate for three years. After his final return to Europe in 1862 he met once with shogunal officials who had been dispatched to Paris.

Spring and Autumn Annals *(Ch'ün Ch'iu).* One of the Four Books of the Confucian canon, dealing with the history of China from 770 to 403 B.C.

Sugita Gempaku (1733–1817). A student of Dutch Learning and son of a Dutch-style physician and surgeon, Gempaku was trained in Edo and Kyoto. At that time only official interpreters charged with dealing with the Dutch in Nagasaki were permitted to learn Dutch. Other interested parties, including physicians, had to piece together their often third-hand information as best they could. Gempaku gained possesion of a Dutch anatomy text, Johann Adam Kulmus's *Tafel Anatomia* (1731). Gempaku was startled by the extreme variation between what was illustrated in the plates and what he had been taught by his old-fashioned teachers. Gempaku's circle is often credited with performing the first scientific dissection of a cadaver to be carried out in Japan, but in fact several dissections had been carried out earlier although they failed to attract widespread attention. None of the group knew Dutch but, working from the plates, they succeeded in translating the book, which appeared in 1774 as *Kaitai Shinsho*. Concurrently they produced the first generally available Dutch-Japanese lexicon. Gempaku presented copies of these works to the shogunate and to the imperial court, where their value was quickly recognized. Gempaku was the individual most responsible for the early acceptance of the more scientific and adventurous European medicine among the Japanese aristocracy. Permission was soon granted for medical students to learn Dutch in order to further their studies and this gave the first great impetus to the dissemination of Dutch Learning. He gives a detailed description of the process in his famous *Rangaku Kotohajime* (The Beginnings of Dutch Studies), the manuscript of which, emended by his friend Ōtsuki Gentaku, was found by Fukuzawa Yukichi and published in 1869.

Sugita Gentan. Standard biographical references do not list a Sugita Gentan. They do, however, list a Sugita Genzui (1818–1889) who, from the context, seems to be the person Tōson is referring to. Genzui was the heir of Sugita Gempaku and an important official in the Institute for the Study of Foreign Books.

Sugita Seikei (1817–1859). A grandson of Gempaku and a student of Dutch Learning. Seikei was born in Edo, where, like most young intellectuals of his time, he was first trained in the Confucian classics. At the age of nineteen he took up the study of medicine and in the course of those studies established a reputation as a Dutch scholar. In 1854 he resigned his position as translator of official documents for the shogunate and moved to one of the coastal batteries in Edo Bay, where he concentrated on the study of European books dealing with artillery. After losing all his possessions in the earthquake of 1855, he was given a professorship in the Institute for the Study of Foreign Books.

Sukunabiko no Kami. One of the Shintō divinities, son of Takamimusubi no Kami. He assists his father in watching over the nation and is credited with extraordinary powers of healing.

A Survey of Western Learning *(Seiseki Gairon)*. A work by Hirata Atsutane published in 1811. At that time "the West" in Japan still meant China and this work is an exposé of the evils of Confucianism, with special emphasis on the lamentable tendency of Confucian scholars in Japan to extoll all things Chinese and denigrate all things Japanese.

Tachibana Akemi (1812–1868). A major poet in the late *waka* tradition (*see* Poetry). Tachibana was born in Fukui, the son of a sword polisher of distinguished lineage. He first studied to become a priest of the Nichiren sect but his master in training was also a poet and it was this influence that set the course of Tachibana's life. He brought originality and fresh life into a tradition that seemed nearly moribund at the time.

Tairō. *See* Rōjū.

Takahashi Sakuzaemon (1785–1829). An astronomer who used the Latin "Globius" as one of his pen names and who sometimes is known as Kageyasu but whose real given name was Yoshitoki. He learned traditional calendar lore from his father, studied Dutch, and through that language acquired all that he could of European astronomy. He later served the shogunate as astronomer and surveyor. He was also interested in geography and published a treatise about the island of Karafuto (Sakhalin), a region which was little known at the time. In 1810 he established an office of translation that was one of the forerunners of the Institute for the Study of Foreign Books.

Takano Chōei (1804–1850). A physician who was greatly interested in the world beyond Japan, an interest that led in 1838 to his writing a pamphlet attacking the shogunate's exclusion policy just as that policy was about to be applied against the *Morrison,* an American vessel attempting to repatriate Japanese castaways. He and his friend Watanabe Kazan were arrested the next year and sentenced to prison. Chōei escaped in 1844 and lived as a fugitive until 1850 when, hardpressed by the authorities, he performed *seppuku.*

Takasugi Shinsaku (1839–1867). An activist and supporter of the imperial cause from Chōshū, where he studied with Yoshida Shōin before going on to the Shō-heikō in Edo. He was involved in a wide range of activities directed toward modernizing and strengthening Chōshū's military posture. One of the most brilliant and energetic among the many outstanding young men Chōshū produced around this time, his creation of the Kiheitai, a force of commoner soldiers that easily handled the Tokugawa forces during the second punitive expedition against Chōshū, greatly influenced subsequent military development in Japan. He died of illness in his twenty-ninth year.

Takeda Kō'unsai (1803–1865). A high-ranking Mito retainer who served Nariaki as steward. He later joined Fujita Koshirō, the son of Fujita Tōko, in the uprising around Mt. Tsukuba and became one of the leaders of the Mito *rōnin* who marched through the center of Honshu in an attempt to reach Kyoto.

Tanaka Fujimaro (1845–1909). A politician and educator of the Meiji period who was born into a family of retainers of the Tokugawa of Owari. Tanaka was active from a very early age in attempting to unite the *han* in support of the restoration of imperial power. He held various offices in the Meiji government, including that of minister plenipotentiary to France in 1886. He was active in establishing modern schools in Nagoya and in starting one of the earliest newspapers in Japan in the same city.

Tani Kanjō (1837–1911). One of the leading military figures of the Meiji era, Tani was born in Tosa of a family of Shintō officials. He took up the study of artillery from an early age in addition to the standard classical subjects in which he was a student of Yasui Sokken. In *han* councils he advocated progressive social and political policies, but under the new Meiji government he concentrated on military matters. Tani was commander of the Kumamoto garrison when the Satsuma rebellion broke out and his successful defense gave the central government the time it needed to gather its forces. He went on to a distinguished career in both the civil and military fields during middle and late Meiji times.

Tanuki. A tree-climbing, omnivorous animal native to East Asia, of the dog family but vaguely reminiscent of the raccoon. Its stocky build and black-and-white coloring often cause it to be confused with the badger but it lacks the badger's fierce temperament and formidable claws and it tends to respond to fright by feigning sleep. In Japanese folklore it is credited with supernatural powers similar to those of the fox but whose exercise more usually falls into the realm of farce than that of dangerous enchantment.

Tekomai. Female dancers in male dress who precede the bearers of a portable shrine in festival parades.

Tengū. Mythical creatures of Chinese origin that originally stood for the influence of comets and of mountain creatures; they represent the heavens and the deep mountains and are conceived of as embodiments of the powers of the mountain divinities. They became important in *shūgendō,* the Buddhist-shamanistic cult of the mountain mystics or *yamabushi,* and are often represented in the costume of that cult, with red faces, long noses, claws on the hands and feet, winged, and carrying the eight-sided staff of the *yamabushi,* a palm-leaf fan, and a sword, but there are many varieties. The *tengū* resemble the goblins of European folklore but are more specifically and colorfully conceived. The militant loyalist faction in Mito was known as the Tengū party, a reference to the traditional association of the *tengū* with the martial arts.

Teradaya incident. On March 8, 1866, a group of *rōnin* headed by Sakamoto Ryōma, a Tosa man who was instrumental in bringing about the Satsuma-Chōshū alliance that brought down the shogunate, was attacked by men from the shogunate in an inn in the Kyoto suburb of Fushimi. Sakamoto escaped during the carnage but was later killed in a similar ambush in Kyoto.

Testament of Righteous Service *(Seiken Igen).* A book of philosophical writings by Asami Keisai (1652–1711). It begins with short biographies of eight Chinese paragons of loyalty, beginning with Ch'ü Yüan of Ch'u, and then describes the careers of comparable model subjects in Japan. The work was influential in developing popular support for the imperial cause.

Tobacco dish style *(o-tabako-bon).* A hair style originating in the Edo *demi monde* and favored by girls and young women of fashion. The hair is neatly gathered up into a narrow horizontal roll high on the back of the head and secured by a tie at either end.

Toda Hōken (1804–1855). An activist from Mito who took part in the succession dispute that ensued when Tokugawa Nariaki's predecessor fell ill without having named an official heir. Toda helped to gain the succession for Nariaki and subsequently rose in his service. His meritorious rebuilding of the western enclosure of Edo castle after the fire of 1838 won him an award from the shogunate, the money from which he used to buy cannon for coastal defense. Toda was active in all aspects of *han* government and in the founding of the Kōdōkan, the *han* academy. When Nariaki was placed under house arrest, Toda and Fujita Tōko shared his confinement. Upon the arrival of Perry, Nariaki was called upon for advice in coastal defense and he passed much of the responsibility on to Toda until the career of this valued subordinate was cut short by his death in the earthquake of 1855.

Toiya. The official in charge of moving freight along a given stretch of one of the great highways, his family, the head of which held the office by inheritance, and the buildings in which the business of the office was carried out.

Tōkaidō. One of the eight administrative circuits established under the administrative reforms of the seventh and eighth centuries. The famous highway that served this circuit passed along the seacoast from Kyoto to Edo and during the Tokugawa period it was the mainstreet of Japan. It has become familiar throughout the world in Hiroshige's woodblock print series.

Tokugawa. The family of the shogunal dynasty founded by Ieyasu at the beginning of the seventeenth century. The family arose from an obscure corner of Mikawa, an area that later constituted the southern part of the domains of Owari. Succession in the main family was backed up by the three cadet branches of Kii, Owari, and Mito.

Tokugawa Ieyasu (1542–1616). The founder of the Tokugawa shogunal dynasty and the designer of most of the institutional and ideological supporting structure that enabled it to survive for more than two and a half centuries. He instituted an elaborate set of measures to preserve Tokugawa hegemony and renewed the proscription of Christianity first instituted under Hideyoshi, paving the way for the final persecutions of the 1630's. He also encouraged an aggressive pursuit of foreign trade which was ended by the policy of exclusion promulgated under Iemitsu, the third shōgun, and given definitive form in 1639. Under his sponsorship the Chu Hsi school of Sung Confucianism provided a rationalization for the structure of society as it stood once Tokugawa power and hegemony were firmly established.

Tokugawa Mitsukuni (1628–1700). Son of Tokugawa Yoshifusa, eleventh child of Ieyasu. The second daimyō of Mito, Mitsukuni was a key figure in the launching of the National Learning movement and the initiator of the *History of Great Japan* project. He was remembered with reverence by both the Mito and the Hirata schools.

Tokugawa Mochinori (1831–1884). The fifteenth daimyō of Owari. He took up a policy of direct opposition to the shogunate in a reversal of that of his predecessor, Yoshikatsu, who was still alive and a force to be reckoned with. His heavy-handed measures within the *han* added to the opposition to his policies and the shogunate forced him to resign in 1863, at the same time arranging for him to be adopted into the house of Hitotsubashi. He was succeeded by Yoshikatsu's five-year-old son, Motochiyo, who was also known as Yoshinori.

Tokugawa Nariaki (1800–1860). The eighth daimyō of Mito and a member of the "progressive" but anti-foreign faction in both Mito and the shogunate itself. Although he was a personality of great force and ability, his career came to little. He was viewed with suspicion and resentment by many powerful figures in the shogunate. *See also* Fujita Tōko and Toda Hōken.

Tokugawa Yoshikatsu (1825–1883). The fourteenth daimyō of Owari and one of the most influential of the daimyō during the final years of the shogunate. He resigned in 1858 by order of Ii Naosuke, with whom he had clashed on the question of opening the country and over the shogunal succession. He was succeeded by his younger brother, Mochinori, who opposed the shogunate. A major schism in *han* affairs soon forced people to take sides and Mochinori was forced to resign in favor of Yoshikatsu's son Motochiyo, who was then only five years of age, making this in fact a recovery of power by Yoshikatsu. In 1870 he was appointed governor of Nagoya *han* after the abolition of the traditional feudal structure but the title was withdrawn the next year. He was also known by his court title as the Owari Middle Councillor.

Tokugawa Yoshinobu. *See* Hitotsubashi Yoshinobu.

Tosa. An allied *han* with nominal revenues of 242,000 *koku* located on the southern coast of Shikoku. During the final years of the shogunate the daimyō was Yamauchi Yōdō. Tosa was one of the leading centers of opposition to the shogunate and was particularly distinguished by the relatively advanced and well-thought-out ideas that emanated from there about the institutions that might succeed it.

Tōsandō. One of the eight administrative circuits established under the administrative reforms of the seventh and eighth centuries. Long after these administrative institutions had lapsed, the highways created to serve them remained important. The Tōsandō was also known as the Nakasendō or the Kiso Road, a term that sometimes applied to the entire road and sometimes only to that part of the road that lay in the Kiso valley. It is the latter usage that is followed in this novel. The Tōsandō branched off from the more famous Tōkaidō at Kusatsu near Lake Biwa in the west and passed through the mountains of central Honshu, the only alternative to the Tōkaidō for the overland traveler between Kyoto and Edo. Tokugawa policy kept these roads unsuitable for wheeled traffic as a hindrance to possible rebel armies.

The Tranquil Cave *(Shizu no Iwaya).* A short work by Atsutane published in 1811. It is subtitled "The Essentials of Healing" and presents a syncretic theory of medicine, placing major emphasis on the Japanese medical tradition but accepting all things of proven efficacy regardless of origin.

Treaty of Kanagawa. The first modern treaty between Japan and a foreign nation, signed with the United States in 1854 in Kanagawa. It opened the ports of Shimoda and Hakodate to American ships for provisioning, guaranteed good treatment of American sailors, and provided for an American consul to reside at Shimoda.

True Jewels of Ancient Writing *(Kobun Shimpō).* An anthology of Chinese prose and poetry of obscure provenance. It seems to have been compiled during the Ming dynasty and was not well received in China, but in Japan it was widely used until the eighteenth century by Zen monks in the study and teaching of Chinese. It then came under attack as a corrupt text by several leading intellectuals of the day, most notably Ogyū Sōrai, and was superseded by another anthology of approximately the same date. Nothing more typifies Hanzō's struggles to become educated in his isolated village than that he should have spent an important part of his youth studying a textbook that had been discredited more than a century earlier.

Tsurumatsu. *See* Satake Tsurumatsu.

Tzu Chih T'ung Chien (The General Mirror for the Aid of Government). A vast historical work compiled by Ssu-ma Kuang of the Sung dynasty emphasizing political history: the rise and fall of states, and the successes and failures of rule over a stretch of more than 1,300 years, ending around A.D. 954 with the reign of Shih-tsung of the Later Chou dynasty. It draws primarily on the official dynastic histories for its materials and was important in both China and Japan as a more compact and convenient source for the student of Chinese history than the massive dynastic histories.

Ubusuna. Also known as Ubusunagami or Ubusuna no Mikoto, he was the *kami* of "the region of one's birth," the meaning of the word *ubusuna.* In later years he came to be confused with the tutelary deity of the kinship group but the two are properly quite distinct.

Ueki Emori (1857–1892). Ranked with Nakae Chōmin as a leading libertarian thinker of the early and mid-Meiji periods, Ueki was active in attempting to introduce personal liberty and parliamentary democracy to Japan. Like Chōmin, he was born in Tosa and was closely associated with Itagaki Taisuke.

Uematsu Shōsuke (Takase Kanenobu, 1818–1869). Finance officer under the Yamamura at Fukushima. The Uematsu line had for generations been instructors in firearms and commanders of the guards at the Fukushima barrier. Shōsuke was the father of Uematsu Yumio.

Uematsu Yumio (Takase Kaoru, 1856–1914). Son of Shōsuke, and husband of Aoyama Okume. After their marriage, he and Okume moved to Tokyo, where he engaged in various lines of government and private work. It was to his home that Aoyama Morio and Wasuke went when they first arrived in Tokyo as small boys.

Umeda Umbin (1815–1859). An activist from Ohama *han* who, after completing a traditional education in the Chinese classics, went to Kumamoto and became acquainted with a circle of activists, foremost among whom was Yokoi Shōnan. He deepened his involvement after the coming of Perry, establishing contact with Yoshida Shōin and Takeda Kō'unsai, whose advocacy of "revering the emperor and expelling the barbarians" he shared. When a Russian ship made an unannounced appearance in Osaka harbor he made preparations to attack it, but the ship left before he could carry out his plan. He tried to influence Chōshū to take an active stance in relation to the rights and prerogatives of the imperial court, and in 1858 he was among the more active agitators in Kyoto when Hotta Masayoshi came to implore the court to accept the Treaty of Kanagawa. He was arrested and remained true to his convictions under severe interrogation, but his health was broken and he died in prison.

Union of court and military *(kōbugattai)*. A policy of reconciliation between the military administration of the shogunate and the civil administration of the imperial court. The shogunate was to place itself in a more clearly subordinate posture and thenceforth to formulate policy only in close consultation and cooperation with the court. In return the court would actively discourage anti-shogunal activities and would continue to leave the shōgun primary responsibility for the day-to-day conduct of national affairs. In the end the idea proved unacceptable to both sides. Matsudaira Shungaku was the leading advocate of this policy and Shimazu Hisamitsu was a strong supporter before he was brought around to an anti-shogunal stance by Saigō Takamori.

Watanabe Kazan (1793–1841). An important painter and student of things European, Kazan was closely associated with Takano Chōei. As the son of a top-ranking retainer of Tahara *han,* he was originally inclined toward Confucian studies but turned to painting because it offered greater promise as a way of making a living. He headed an informal group that discussed ways of improving Japan by making use of European learning and through his high social rank he was able to help his friends make connections and gain access to important people. When Chōei wrote his pamphlet critical of shogunal policy in the *Morrison* affair, Kazan was among those who were both sufficiently notable and sufficiently vulnerable to serve as exemplary victims of shogunal wrath. After spending some time in prison he was released and returned home, but there enemies spread false rumors that he was about to be arrested again and he performed *sepppuku* rather than cause further difficulties for his lord.

Yamauchi Yōdō (1827–1872). The vigorous and creative daimyō of Tosa in Shikoku. He directed a policy of reform and rationalization within his domain and was influential in shogunal politics, supporting the initial candidacy of Hitotsubashi Yoshinobu to become the fourteenth shōgun and later advocating the union of court and military. Some authorities give his surname the more common reading of Yamanouchi.

Yasui Sokken (1799–1876). A Confucian scholar from the remote province of Hyuga in Kyushu who was small in stature and hideously scarred by smallpox. He managed only after the greatest difficulty to get to Edo and enter the Shōheikō, where he had a successful career in spite of his opposition to the established policies and practices of the Hayashi family, founders of the academy.

Yatabori Keizō (1829–1887). A commissioner of warships during the late years of the shogunate who worked closely with Katsu Rintarō during the early years of the latter's career.

Yokoi Shōnan (1809–1869). A Confucian scholar and thinker born into a family of retainers of Kumamoto *han* in southwestern Kyushu, Shōnan went to Edo for further studies in 1839 at the order of his *han.* While there he met various members of the Mito school, most notably Fujita Tōko. He then went back to Kumamoto, where he continued his own studies while opening a school specializing in the books of the Confucian canon. A period of extensive travel followed, in the course of which he discussed national affairs with leading intellectuals in each place he visited. His wandering ended when he found a permanent post as advisor to Matsudaira Shungaku of Echizen. Shōnan's thought is reflected in much of what Shungaku did from then on. He was later forced to flee Edo because of his advocacy of European learning, the product of wide-ranging thought and study that had moved him far from the fiercely obscurantist anti-foreignism of his youth. By 1866 he was fully in favor of the complete opening of the country to world influence and this position cost him his life at the hands of assassins.

Yoshida Shōin (1830–1859). A scholar of Dutch Learning, patriot, and charismatic teacher whose influence was immense in spite of his short and outwardly anticlimactic life. He studied under Sakuma Shōzan and was particularly interested in military science and the defense of Japan. Convinced that he had to study abroad if he was to serve Japan to the best of his ability, he tried to stow away aboard one of Perry's ships in 1854, but the Americans promptly turned him over to the shogunal authorities. He was sent back to his native Chōshū a marked man. When the Treaty of Kanagawa was signed in 1858 he planned an attack on the *rōjū* Abe Masahiro, but when his plans were discovered he was once again arrested and in the following year he was executed.

Yoshiwara. The most important licensed quarter of Edo, formed when the fiercely puritanical Tokugawa government found it impossible to outlaw all frivolity and immorality. Licensed brothels were first gathered together into a single location in Fukiya-chō in the Nihombashi district. It was moved to the more remote San'ya district of Asakusa after the great fire of 1657 and remained there until prostitution became illegal in 1958. The Yoshiwara and its counterparts in other cities became centers of the more elegant and refined aspects of the townsmen's culture, not only in dress and deportment but in literature and the arts. As Takichi's poetry circle demonstrates, the licensed quarters were often the preferred scene of completely innocent enjoyments.

BIBLIOGRAPHICAL NOTE

BEFORE THE DAWN first appeared in quarterly installments in the monthly journal *Chūō Kōron* between April 1929 and October 1935. Tōson made extensive revisions in the text before the publication in book form of Book One in 1932 and Book Two in 1935. Another revision was begun in 1936 but soon abandoned and the many subsequent editions are all based on the first revision. Three uniform editions of Shimazaki Tōson's complete works have been published since his death in 1943. The most recent is the definitive, eighteen-volume *Tōson Zenshū* by Chikuma Shobō between 1966 and 1971. The text on which this translation is based comprises volumes eleven and twelve of that edition.

The following is a selective listing of references and studies which were particularly helpful in preparing this translation.

Beasley, W. G. *The Meiji Restoration.* Stanford: Stanford University Press, 1972.
Chiba Noburō. *Kisoji Yo-ake Mae Oboegaki* (The Kiso Road, A *Before the Dawn* Memorandum). Tokyo: Sanichi Shobō, 1972.
Haga Noboru. Yo-ake Mae *no Jitsuzō to Kyozō* (Fact and Fiction in *Before the Dawn*). Tokyo: Kyōiku Shuppan Center, 1984.
Hayasaka Raigo. Yo-ake Mae *no Sekai* (The World of *Before the Dawn*). Tokyo: Kokusho Kankōkai, 1973.
Hayashiya Tatsusaburō. *Bakumatsu Bunka no Kenkyū* (A Study of Culture in Late Tokugawa Times). Tokyo: Iwanami Shoten, 1978.
Hiroshige and Eisen. *Kiso Kaidō Rokujūkū Tsugi* (The Sixty-nine Stations of the Kiso Highway). Edited by Kikuchi Sadao. Tokyo: Shūeisha, 1966.
Ichimura Minato. *Ina Sonnō Shisōshi* (A History of Imperialist Thought in Ina). Tokyo: Kokusho Kankōkai, 1973.
Ikoma Kanshichi. *Kiso no Shōmin Seikatsu* (How the Common People Lived in the Kiso). Tokyo: Kokusho Kankōkai, 1975.
Irokawa Daikichi. *The Culture of the Meiji Period.* Edited by Marius Jansen. Princeton: Princeton University Press, 1985.
Itō Kazuo, ed. *Shimazaki Tōson—Kadai to Tembō* (Shimazaki Tōson—Topics and Perspectives). Tokyo: Meiji Shoin, 1979.
————. *Shimazaki Tōson Jiten* (A Shimazaki Tōson Handbook). Tokyo: Meiji Shoin, 1972.
————. *Tōson Shoshi* (A Tōson Bibliography). Tokyo: Kokusho Kankōkai, 1973.
Jansen, Marius. *Changing Japanese Attitudes Toward Modernization.* Princeton: Princeton University Press, 1965.

————. *Japan and Its World: Two Centuries of Change.* Princeton: Princeton University Press, 1980.

Kaempfer, Engelbert. *The History of Japan, together with a Description of the Kingdom of Siam, 1690–92.* 3 vols. Glasgow: Maclehose, 1906. (A reprinting of the translation from the Dutch manuscript by J. G. Scheuzer, originally published in 1727.)

Kawazoe Kunimoto. *Shimazaki Tōson.* Tokyo: Meiji Shoin, 1965.

Keene, Donald. *The Japanese Discovery of Europe.* Stanford: Stanford University Press, 1969.

Kikuchi Saburō. *Kiso Magome.* Tokyo: Oyama Shoten Shinsha, 1958.

Kiso Kyōikukai, ed. *Kiso Fukushima Sekisho* (The Kiso-Fukushima Barrier). Fukushima: Shinano Kyōikukai Kisobukai, 1934.

Kitaōji Ken. *Kisoji: Bunken no Tabi,* Yo-ake Mae *Tankyū* (The Kiso Road: A Bibliographical Journey, Research into *Before the Dawn*). Tokyo: Unsōdō, 1970.

————. *Zoku Kisoji: Bunken no Tabi,* Yo-ake Mae *Tankyū* (The Kiso Road: A Bibliographical Journey, Research into *Before the Dawn* Continued). Tokyo: Unsōdō, 1971.

Kitaōji Ken, Itō Kazuo, and Hayasaka Raigo. *Tōson ni okeru Tabi* (Tōson and Travel). Tokyo: Mokujisha, 1973.

Kubo Tasaburō, ed. *Ō-Shinano* (Great Shinano). Tokyo: Naganokenjin Tōkyōrengōkai, 1940.

McClellan, Edwin. *Two Japanese Novelists: Sōseki and Tōson.* Chicago: University of Chicago Press, 1969.

Nagano Prefecture, Nishi-Chikuma County Offices, ed. *Nishi Chikumagunshi* (A Gazetteer of Nishi-Chikuma County). Nagano: Shinano Mainichi Shimbun Kabushiki Kaisha, 1915.

Najita, Tetsuo, and J. Victor Koschmann. *Conflict in Modern Japanese History.* Princeton: Princeton University Press, 1982.

Reischauer, Edwin O., and Albert M. Craig. *Japan, Tradition and Transformation.* Boston: Houghton Mifflin, 1978.

Saimaru Yomo. *Shimazaki Tōson no Himitsu* (The Secrets of Shimazaki Tōson). Tokyo: Yūshindō, 1966.

Senuma Shigeki. *Hyōden Shimazaki Tōson* (Shimazaki Tōson, A Critical Biography). Tokyo: Jitsugyō no Nihonsha, 1959.

————. *Kisoji to Shimazaki Tōson* (The Kiso Road and Shimazaki Tōson). Tokyo: Heibonsha, 1982.

Shibukawa Gyō. *Shimazaki Tōson.* Tokyo: Chikuma Shobō, 1974.

Shimazaki Osuke. *Tōsonshiki* (Tōson, a Personal Account). Tokyo: Kawade Shobō, 1967.

Shimazaki Tōson. *The Broken Commandment.* Translated by Kenneth Strong. Tokyo: University of Tokyo Press, 1974.

————. *The Family.* Translated by Cecilia Segawa Seigle. Tokyo: University of Tokyo Press, 1976.

Shimonaka Yasaburō, ed. *Dai Jimmei Jiten* (The Great Biographical Dictionary). 10 vols. Compact ed. Tokyo: Heibonsha, 1957–1958.

Tanaka Mitsuaki, supervisor. *Mito Bakumatsu Fū'unoku* (A Record of the Troubles in Mito in Late Tokugawa Times). Edited by Sawamoto Taketora. Mito: Ibaraki Kenchōnai, Jōyō Meiji Kinenkai, 1933.

Totman, Conrad. *The Collapse of the Tokugawa Bakufu, 1862–1868.* Honolulu: University Press of Hawaii, 1980.

Yūseidō, ed. *Shimazaki Tōson.* Tokyo: Yūseidō, 1973.

DOMAINS (HAN)

(hatched)	Collateral
(horizontal lines)	Vassal
(gray)	Allied
○	Han capitals
●	Other towns

1 TSUGARU

2 SATAKE

3 NAMBU

4 SAKAI

5 DATE

6 UESUGI

7 MATSUDAIRA (AIZU)

8 TOKUGAWA (MITO)

9 MAEDA (KAGA)

10 TOKUGAWA (OWARI)

11 MATSUDAIRA (ECHIZEN)

12 II (HIKONE)

13 TŌDŌ

14 TOKUGAWA (KII)

15 SAKAKIBARA

16 HACHISUKA

17 YAMANOUCHI (TOSA)

18 IKEDA

19 IKEDA

20 ASANO

21 MŌRI (CHŌSHŪ)

22 KURODA

23 ARIMA

24 HOSOKAWA

25 NABESHIMA (HIZEN)

26 SHIMAZU (SATSUMA)

27 SŌ

OKI

TSUSHIMA
27

IKI

Shimonoseki

HIRADO

22

Hagi

HONSHŪ

18

Tottori

21

20

Hiroshima

19

Okayama

15

Himeji

GOTŌ

25

Saga

Fukuoka

Kurume

23

INLAND

SEA

Kōbe

Nagasaki

AWAJI

Osaka

SHIMABARA PN

24

Kumamoto

KYŪSHŪ

SHIKOKU

Uwajima

17

Kōchi

Tokushima

16

16

Wakayama

14

26

Kagoshima

26

TANEGASHIMA

PACIFIC

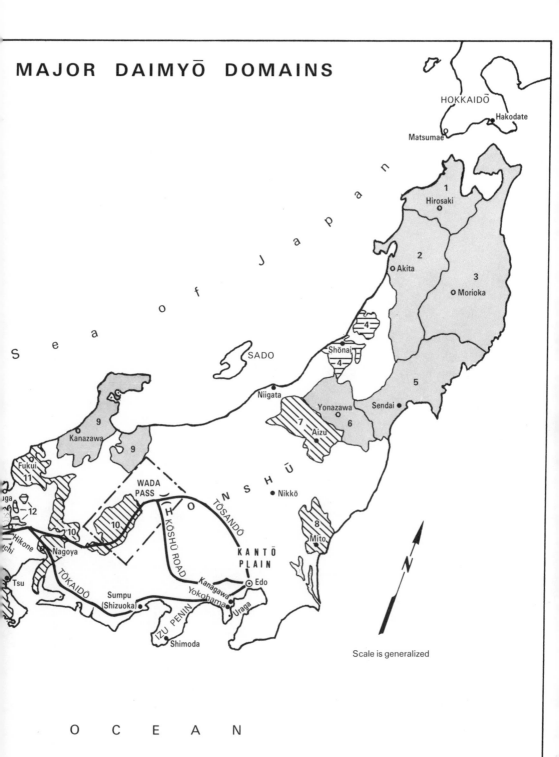

MAJOR DAIMYŌ DOMAINS

HOKKAIDŌ

Hakodate

Matsumae

1

Hirosaki

2

Akita

3

Morioka

4

Shōnai

4

5

Niigata

Yonazawa

Sendai

7

Aizu

6

9

Kanazawa

9

Fukui

11

uga

12

Hikone

chi

10

Nagoya

Tsu

SADO

S e a   o f   J a p a n

H O N S H Ū

WADA
PASS

TŌSANDŌ

KŌSHŪ ROAD

Nikkō

8

Mito

KANTŌ
PLAIN

Kanagawa

Edo

TŌKAIDŌ

Sumpu
(Shizuoka)

Yokohama

Uraga

IZU PENIN.

Shimoda

N

Scale is generalized

O C E A N

DOMAINS (HAN)

1 TSUGARU
2 SATAKE
3 NAMBU
4 SAKAI
5 DATE
6 UESUGI
7 MATSUDAIRA (AIZU)
8 TOKUGAWA (MITO)
9 MAEDA (KAGA)
10 TOKUGAWA (OWARI)
11 MATSUDAIRA (ECHIZEN)
12 II (HIKONE)
13 TŌDŌ
14 TOKUGAWA (KII)
15 SAKAKIBARA

16 HACHISUKA
17 YAMANOUCHI (TOSA)
18 IKEDA
19 IKEDA
20 ASANO
21 MŌRI (CHŌSHŪ)
22 KURODA
23 ARIMA
24 HOSOKAWA
25 NABESHIMA (HIZEN)
26 SHIMAZU (SATSUMA)
27 SŌ

Collateral
Vassal
Allied
○ Han capitals
● Other towns

OKI

TSUSHIMA
27

IKI
Shimonoseki
HIRADO
22
Fukuoka
GOTŌ
Saga
25
Kurume
23
Nagasaki
SHIMABARA PN
24
Kumamoto
KYŪSHŪ

26
Kagoshima

26
TANEGASHIMA

H O N S H Ū

○Hagi
21
20
○Hiroshima
18
Tottori

19
○Okayama
15
Himeji
Kōbe
K

INLAND
SEA
AWAJI
Osaka

S H I K O K U
Uwajima
17
Tokushima
16
●Kōchi
16
Wakayama

14

PACIFIC